Twelve Short Novels

Thomas Mann
Thornton Wilder
Joseph Conrad
Edith Wharton
Leo Tolstoy
Henry James
James Hilton
Antoine de Saint Exupéry
Robert Nathan
Jan de Hartog
Edward Streeter
John Steinbeck

TWELVE
SHORT
NOVELS

SELECTED BY

Thomas B. Costain

 1961

Doubleday & Company, Inc.

Garden City, New York

COPYRIGHT ACKNOWLEDGMENTS

YOUNG JOSEPH by Thomas Mann. Reprinted with the permission of the publisher from YOUNG JOSEPH, the second part of the tetralogy, JOSEPH AND HIS BROTHERS by Thomas Mann, translated by H. T. Lowe-Porter. Copyright 1935 by Alfred A. Knopf, Inc.

THE BRIDGE OF SAN LUIS REY by Thornton Wilder. Copyright, 1927, by Albert and Charles Boni, Inc. Renewal copyright 1955 by Thornton Wilder.

THE DUEL by Joseph Conrad. Copyright 1907, 1908 by Joseph Conrad. Copyright 1908 by Doubleday & Company, Inc.

THE OLD MAID by Edith Wharton. Copyright, 1924, D. Appleton & Company. Copyright, 1952, Frederic R. King. Reprinted by permission of the publisher Appleton-Century-Crofts, Inc.

FATHER SERGIUS by Leo Tolstoy. Copyright 1912 by The Page Company. Used by permission of the publishers, Farrar, Straus and Cudahy, Inc.

THE TURN OF THE SCREW by Henry James. Copyright by The Macmillan Company. All rights reserved.

GOOD-BYE, MR. CHIPS by James Hilton. Copyright, 1934, by James Hilton. Reprinted by arrangement with Little, Brown and Company by whom the work is published in association with the Atlantic Monthly Press.

PRISONER OF THE SAND by Antoine de Saint Exupéry. From WIND, SAND AND STARS, copyright, 1939, by Antoine de Saint Exupéry. Translated by Lewis Galantière. Reprinted by permission of Harcourt, Brace & World, Inc.

PORTRAIT OF JENNIE by Robert Nathan. Reprinted with the permission of the publisher, Alfred A. Knopf, Inc. Copyright, 1939, by Robert Nathan.

THE LOST SEA by Jan de Hartog. Copyright 1951 by Jan de Hartog. Reprinted by permission of Harper & Brothers.

FATHER OF THE BRIDE by Edward Streeter. Copyright 1948, 1949 by Edward Streeter and Gluyas Williams. Reprinted by permission of Simon and Schuster, Inc.

THE SHORT REIGN OF PIPPIN IV by John Steinbeck. Copyright © 1957 by Jon Steinbeck. Reprinted by permission of The Viking Press, Inc.

JUST A FEW WORDS...

BEFORE INDULGING in a perhaps rather extravagant expression of liking for the short novel, which I share with so many, it seems proper to say just a few words about the general field of fiction.

The novel has been tending of recent years to ever greater lengths, in what is sometimes called the Grand Tradition. This is not strange, for the reading public, finding less satisfaction in periodical fiction, which has veered to ever shorter lengths, has been turning to books. Finding so much pleasure in them, people have developed a willingness to follow the lives and adventures of characters, for whom they conceive a liking, to almost any length that the author cares to carry them. This has made favorites of the long autobiographical novel, the multiple generation story, and the historical novel.

The short novel, sometimes called a novelette or *novella,* which comes next in the rather arbitrary divisions set by usage, ranges in length from the neighborhood of twenty thousand words to something slightly in excess of fifty thousand. Since many magazine editors have lost faith in continuity of interest as a prime factor in holding circulation, they have turned from serials to short novels which they run complete in single issues, calling them by the decidedly undignified designation of "one shots." This has resulted in a tendency on the part of writers to turn their pens to fiction within this range. The "one shot" has proven a popular feature, but not enough of them, sad to relate, achieve the distinction of swift-paced narrative or the compact delineation of character which convey so great a delight in the really fine short novel.

Between the short novel and the next great division, the short story, there is an indeterminate class, stories too long to be called accurately short stories and yet lacking the length and substance to qualify as novelettes. We have been curiously slapdash in finding terms to convey the distinctions of length and too prone to accept the first phrase offered. Tales which run from ten thousand words, or even a little less, to the neighborhood of twenty thousand are called long short stories. This term has been in use so long that it has ceased to convey the impression that it is as exact as speaking of a fat, thin man or a clear, foggy day.

I confess to an enthusiasm for many of the fine samples which fall within this awkward length. It is impossible to compute how often I have turned, for instance, to *Enoch Soames* by Max Beerbohm, *"They"* by

Rudyard Kipling, *The Man Who Conquered Death* by Franz Werfel, several of Ernest Hemingway's, *The Alien Corn* by Somerset Maugham, *Will-o'-the-Will* by Robert Louis Stevenson, and *A Dream of John Ball* by William Morris. For some of my friendly stories I have not always succeeded in winning entire agreement on the part of other readers. But they are old friends and I go on loving them.

The largest division of all, at least in America where the popularity of magazines has provided an unquenchable demand, is the short story. There was a period when a tale of ten thousand words could be considered as within this classification. During the last quarter century, however, the pendulum has swung the other way and it is unusual to encounter today any exceeding six or seven thousand words. This may not have been due to a change in popular demand. It can be accounted for, in part at least, by the mammoth proportions of modern magazine advertising.

There have always been very short stories, Guy de Maupassant and O. Henry having been pioneers in the field. Of recent years they have become a regular magazine feature, running in length from one thousand to fifteen hundred words. Someone coined for them the name "short shorts," and, unfortunately, it is solidly embedded now in editorial patter. This far from euphonious term was not lifted from the narrow sphere of haberdashery, but it is very much out of place certainly as a means of labeling the often crisp and surprising tales which fall into this class.

To complete this brief discussion of lengths in fiction, we finally come down to a rather amusing exercise in writing technique. How short can a story be? When H. L. Mencken and George Jean Nathan were joint editors of *Smart Set,* they succeeded in getting one into the limits of a single sentence. It went as follows, if my memory is not at fault:

> *Late the next morning, as they breakfasted together in his apartment, a tear stole down her cheek.*

And now back to the classification which, in the esteem of many, offers readers the most pleasure—the short novel. It results from the decision of an author to deal with a single idea or situation without resorting to the leisurely methods or the deliberate padding in what is sometimes called the "blockbuster" type of long novel (an expression of recent invention in the publishing world), and without the teeming lists of minor characters which the Grand Tradition seems to demand. If the theme is sufficiently gripping or beguiling in conception, and if the author's treatment has been deft and skillful, it becomes a story of fine precision and even jewel-like perfection of form. It must be built around the kind of situation, moreover, which can be explored without the introduction of many characters to clutter the scene with ill-defined relationships. It can be enjoyed at one long sitting or at least without undue prolongation of attention.

Just a Few Words . . .

It is probably true that it takes maturity in a writer to produce a good short novel. It is seldom purely episodic; in fact it will often cover a developing tension over periods of time. The author must be capable of leading readers into the story at the moments which count most but without neglecting the factors of past and future. This is something beyond the skill of so many who shamble through the leisurely narration of the less exacting long novel.

There would be more great short novels if it were not true that they are better suited to satisfy discerning readers than to reward authors. It is unusual for them to sell as well as the longer varieties, and for this the publisher is as much to blame as the public. Book readers in general are very happy to settle down with books which will hold their interest for days at a time, and publishers strive to supply the demand. The word "blame" is probably unfair in any discussion of this point. It is true also that the shorter book, even though it may be a gem of purest ray serene, does not enjoy as much share in the subsidiary rewards, such as book-club selection, paperback use, or sales to motion-picture companies. Nor, except in rare cases, does it have the same comfortable longevity. From the lists of an author's complete works, which publishers place at the beginning of all new volumes, the short novel will sometimes make a silent appeal. "Don't you remember me?" it seems to ask. "I too was well thought of when I first came out." It is sadly true that there is a tendency to let novelettes fall more quickly into the dreadful limbo of the publishing world which is known as Out of Print.

To prepare an anthology of short novels is to immerse oneself in a long spell of pleasant reading on a wide and varied plane where the standards are high, higher certainly than will be found in the vast storehouses of the short story. Only great stories may be admitted among the ten, twelve, or fifteen (whichever the number may be) to make up the final list, but there are other considerations. If literary standards were so well defined and understood that the best could be discerned without any question, there would be a sameness about the final choice. To prevent the monotony of perfection from manifesting itself, a formula must be found to provide variety in theme and scene and treatment. Often there will be two books of equal claim but which offer a degree of similarity, particularly in theme; one only may be chosen, obviously. The best books are timeless, but some, even among the authentic great, have a tendency to become dated. The author's absorption in affairs of the day in which the story is laid may tend to lessen the interest of the modern reader. Occasionally the reason why one book will seem dated and another will remain fresh and absorbing is hard to identify and impossible to define. Practical difficulties also are likely to enter the problem. There are always highly desirable selections which, alas, are unavailable.

I found all the books on this list as engrossing as when I first dis-

covered them. Some of them I have read many times and always with the keenest appreciation. They offer wide variety in theme and treatment. It does not seem too much to hope that readers will find in them the same pleasure I have experienced.

The works are presented in an order imposed by the time in which the action is laid.

CONTENTS

CONTENTS

I

YOUNG JOSEPH

by Thomas Mann

A Story from the Bible

Thomas Mann conceived the idea of his magnificent series of novels on *Joseph and His Brothers* in the year 1926. He prepared for the great task by extensive travel in Palestine and Egypt and in an exhaustive study of the history of the two races. He had completed the first volume only when his dissent from the purposes of a fascist state, and his spiritual shrinking from the conditions created in his native Germany, drove him into voluntary exile. *Young Joseph*, the second volume, was completed, therefore, in Zurich. The Egyptian books were written during his long stay in California.

We have no apologies to offer for using *Young Joseph* by itself, divorced from the scholarly exposition of the life, the beliefs, the customs, and the mysteries of the Israelites which preceded it as well as the later volumes dealing with Joseph in Egypt. As it stands, it is the core of the Biblical story, told with remarkable insight and poetic imagination, and it is complete in itself.

The stories in the Bible reach us from that long dead and sadly unexplored past as legends of an articulate and passionate race. They are brief, sometimes obscure in the telling, and always shadowy. Writers who have attempted to retell them have seldom been successful. Only the massive scholarship on which he had to draw and the almost incandescent quality of his imagination, made it possible for Thomas Mann to succeed where others had failed. His inspired pen turns Joseph and his brothers into life-and-blood figures. It becomes easy to understand the strange happenings which began when Joseph wheedled the Coat of Many Colors from his doting father. The jealousy of the less fortunate brothers now seems natural. Joseph's rescue from the well is explained, his sale to the traders into Egypt is made clear and rational.

For once a great story from the Scriptures has been told again with added dimensions and a radiance of narration which makes it unnecessary to offer any excuses to the board of forty-seven learned men who collaborated on the King James version.

The Dreamer

THE COAT OF MANY COLOURS

Not for the harvesting, as had been expected, but as early as the night of the spring full moon, the sons of Leah came tumbling heels over head back to Hebron from the plains of Shechem. They came, ostensibly, to eat the Passover lamb with their father and with him to observe the moon; but actually because they had heard an exciting piece of news, affecting all of them. They came to convince themselves, on the spot, of its truth, with their very own eyes, and to see if anything about it could be changed. The thing was so startling and portentous that the sons of the maids had found it of the first importance to select one of their number to make the four-day journey from Hebron to Shechem to fetch news. Of course it was the nimble Naphtali who had been chosen. At bottom, actually, it did not matter who went, or how fast. For Naphtali rode on an ass, as another would have done; whether a longer or shorter pair of legs hung down on either side the beast was of no importance. In any case the journey took four days. But it was with Naphtali, son of Bilhah, that the idea of celerity was bound up. The rôle of messenger was his traditionally; and as his tongue was as nimble as his legs, there was perhaps some sense in the idea that he would, at least in the last moment, give the brothers the benefit of what he had learned a little quicker than anyone else.

What was it had happened? Jacob had made a present to Joseph.

That was nothing new. The father in wilful indulgence of his feeling toward his son, his lamb, his scion, his heavenly youth and son of a virgin—or whatever other appellations might occur to him—had always made him gifts and tender remembrances: sweetmeats, pretty bits of pottery and stones, purple laces, scarabs, and what not. Seeing them in his careless possession, the brethren would scowl. They would feel their rights curtailed and be aggrieved. To such fundamental and almost intentionally emphasized injustice they had had plenty of opportunity to accustom themselves. But this particular gift was so startling in its nature, one could not but fear that the act was decisive. It appeared to mean a slap in the face for them all.

Here is what happened. It was tenting weather, the latter rains had come on. Jacob had withdrawn himself in the afternoon into his house of hair, that secure and complete protection against the blessing-bringing

3

downpour: a woven felt of black goats' hair, stretched over nine stout poles and fastened by strong ropes to pegs driven into the ground. It was the largest tent in the rather scattered settlement. Jacob lived in it alone, being a rich man and setting store by being able to give the women their separate dwelling. It was divided from front to back by a curtain hanging to the middle posts. One of the rooms served as private storeroom and supply chamber: camel saddles and pockets, unused carpets rolled or folded, hand-mills, and other gear lay about and there were skins hung up, full of grain, butter, drinking-water, and palm wine made of soaked dates.

The other half was the dwelling of the bearer of the blessing; the conveniences it displayed were in strong contrast to the half-Bedouin kind of life to which he clung. Jacob needed ease. He disliked the effeminacy of city life, but that did not prevent him from wanting certain comforts when he withdrew from the world into himself for meditation and laboured upon his thoughts of God. Open in front to the height of a man, the chamber was warmly carpeted with felt and over that with gaily coloured rugs; some of these also hung upon the walls. A cedar-wood bedstead with covers and cushions and bronze feet stood in the background. Several earthen lamps with ornamental bases and shallow bowls with short snouts for the wick were always burning here, for it would have been unfitting and poverty-stricken for the bearer of the blessing to sleep in the dark; they were even lighted in the daytime, that they might lend no sinister meaning to the phrase: "Jacob's lamp is out." Painted jugs with handles stood on the flat top of a sycamore coffer, the sides of which were decorated with intaglio in blue glaze. Another tall-legged coffer, carved and written over with texts, had a vaulted lid. There did not lack a glowing brazier in the corner, for Jacob was inclined to chilliness. Low stools were everywhere, less as seats than as places whereon to lay things: on one stood a small incense-burner, shaped like a tower, out of whose little window-openings came clouds of smoke scented with cinnamon, styrax, and galbanum. On another was a valuable specimen of Phoenician art, which only a well-to-do person could possess: a flat gold basin on a dainty stand. When you pressed the bottom with your hand, it showed a female figure playing on a lute.

Jacob and Joseph were sitting on cushions by a low tabouret at the entrance to the tent, playing a game with pieces spread out on the engraved bronze surface. He had summoned his son to play the game at which Rachel once had been his companion. Outside the rain plashed down on stones and shrubbery and olive trees, the blessing of God's moisture upon the corn of the valley, that it might bear up under the summer's heat until the harvest time. The wind lightly rattled the wooden rings on the roof, to which the tent ropes were fastened.

Joseph let his father win the game. He had purposely got into the field of the "evil eye" and put himself at a disadvantage; thus Jacob,

though playing with his attention greatly distraught, had to his pleasurable surprise finally won the game. He admitted his absence of mind and said the victory was his more by good luck than good management.

"Hadst thou not been defeated in time, my child," he said, "I must have been so; for my thoughts wandered and I made many blunders, whereas thou hast drawn cleverly and never failed to make good thy mischances. Thy way of playing reminds me of Mami's, she used so often to put me in the corner. Even her way of biting her little finger as she considered, and certain little stratagems she loved, thou hast and I am moved by them as I play."

"All that is as nothing," Joseph answered, stretching himself, putting his head back, one arm out sideways and the other bent to his shoulder. "The issue speaketh against me. If my dear father won even with his thoughts distracted, how would it have gone with the child if he had had his full attention upon the game? The end would have come quickly."

Jacob smiled. "My experience," he said, "is longer and my school the best, for as a boy I played with Yitzchak, thy grandfather upon my side, and after that often with Laban, thy grandfather on the side of my beloved, in the land of Naharain, beyond the water; he too played with great deliberation."

Jacob too, more than once, had let Laban and Yitzchak win, when he was wanting to put them in a good mood; but it never occurred to him that Joseph might have done the same.

"It is true," he went on, "that I played badly today. More than once a thought came over me that made me forget the position of the pieces. What I was thinking had to do with the approaching feast and the night of sacrifice, when after sunset we slaughter the sheep and dip the sprig of hyssop into the blood to strike it upon the two side posts, that the Avenger may pass over. For it is the night of the Passover, and the substitution of the sacrifice, in token that the firstling is slain in expiation for man and beast whom it lusteth him to slay. Upon all this I fell a-musing, for lo, a man will do much and know not what he doth. Yet were he to know and think about it, it might be that his entrails would turn over within him and he would be sick to his very bottom, as it hath happened to me many a time in my life, and the first time was when I heard that Laban, at Shinar beyond the river Prath, had slain his first-born little son as a sacrifice and buried it in a jar in the foundations to bring good fortune to his house. But dost thou think it brought him blessing? No, but harm, hindrance, and adversity; and had I not come and given a little life to house and business, it would all have foundered in misery. Never again would he have been fruitful with his wife Adina. And yet Laban would not have walled up his little son had such a deed not brought his forbears blessing in earlier times."

"Thou sayest it," Joseph responded. He had folded his hands at the back of his neck. "And it is clear to me, from thy words, how this came

to pass. Laban behaved according to outworn custom, and thereby committed serious blunders. For the outworn is repulsive to the Lord; He is already beyond it and wisheth us to be so too, and He rejecteth and curseth it. Therefore, if Laban had understood himself and the times, he would have slaughtered instead of his son a goat or a kid and struck the blood upon the posts and threshold; then would he have been glad and his incense would have mounted up to heaven."

"Again," said Jacob, "thou sayest it and takest the thoughts and the words out of my mouth. For the Avenger lusteth not alone after the beast, but also after the blood of man; and we appease his desire not only in respect to the flocks through the blood on the doorposts, but also by the sacrificial meal, which we eat and devour in haste by night that nothing of the roast meat may remain over by the morning. But when we think of it, what sort of roast meat is that, and doth the lamb atone only for the flock when we slay it? What should we slay and eat, if we were mad like Laban, and what was slain and eaten in more indecent times? Do we know what we do in the feast, when we slay and eat, and would not our very inwards come uppermost if we thought of it, so that we vomited?"

"Let us slay and let us eat," said Joseph, lightly, in a high-pitched voice, rocking himself in his hands at the back of his neck. "The feast and the feasting are both good, and if they are also salvation, then let us joyfully save ourselves from being obscene, by dint of understanding the Lord and the times in which we are. Lo, there is a tree," he cried, and pointed with outstretched arm into the tent, as though a tree actually stood there, "splendid in trunk and crown, planted by the fathers for the delight of those coming after. Its tips move and sparkle in the wind, its roots cleave to the kingdom of the earth, in darkness, in the dust, and among the stones. But doth the blithe tip know overmuch of the dirt-encrusted root? No, for it hath come out beyond it with the Lord, swayeth in the air, and thinketh not thereupon. So, in my view, is it with the tradition and the indecency. But if we want to have the pious tradition taste well in our mouths, by all means let us leave the underneath things quietly underneath."

"Thy parable is charming," Jacob said, nodding. He stroked his beard, holding it at one side and letting it glide through the hollow of his hand. "Thy words are witty and well invented. But even so, we must still meditate, still stoop under the cares and the unrest which were Abraham's portion and must be ours for ever and ever, that we may free ourselves according to the Lord's will; and it may be are already free of that from which He would release us: namely, care. But say, who is the Avenger and what is his passing over? Doth not the moon, on the night of the feast, go full and beauteous through the pass which is the northernmost point and zenith of his way, where he himself turneth in his fullness? But the northernmost point is Nergal's, the murderer; the night is his,

Sin ruleth for him, Sin is Nergal at the time of this feast, and the Avenger, who passeth over and whom we appease, he is the Red One."

"That is clear," Joseph said. "We hardly think of it, but so he is."

"Such was the unrest," went on Jacob, "that was distracting me as we played. For it is the stars that determine this feast for us, the moon and the Red One; and on that night they change places. But shall we then throw kisses to the stars and celebrate their histories? Must we not rather distress ourselves over the Lord and the time, whether we do truly and in fact understand them and not transgress against both, considering that we continue out of sheer idle habit in the ritual indecency from which He would win us? Sometimes I seriously ask myself if I ought not to call the people together under the tree of wisdom, that they might hear my misgivings and hearken to my cares in the matter of the feast Pesach."

"My dear father," said Joseph, as he bent over and laid his hand on the old man's beside the board which registered his defeat, "is much too precise in his interpretations; I must pray him not to let himself be moved to undue haste and so to destruction. If thy child may regard himself as having been asked, then he would advise that the feast be spared and not too hotly attacked on account of its legends, instead of which perchance another might come up, which then thou wouldst relate at the roast meal: for instance the saving of Isaac, which would be very suitable. Or else we wait on time, whether God might not for once glorify Himself in us by a great redemption and deliverance; which then we would make the basis of the feast and its legend, and sing songs of rejoicing. Have I, in my folly, spoken consolingly?"

"Thy words," responded Jacob, "are like balsam: very sage and comforting, which is what I mean by balsamic. For thou spokest for the custom and yet at the same time for the future, and that shall be reckoned to thy honour. And spokest at the same time for an abiding, which is at the same time a station on the way; and thereover my soul smileth at thine, Joseph-el, thou shoot of the tenderest tree. Let me kiss thee!"

And across the board he took Joseph's lovely head between his hands and kissed him, rejoicing in his son from the depths of his heart.

"If only I knew," Joseph said, "whence wisdom cometh to me at this hour, or the small sagacity I have to meet the shrewdness of my lord in his speech! Thou saidst that thy thoughts wandered during our game; then, to be frank, so did mine. They kept slipping aside from the pieces, and the Elohim alone know how I managed to keep going on so long."

"Whither then, my child, went thy thoughts?"

"Ah," answered the youth, "thou canst easily guess. A word of thine tcheth in mine ear day and night; a word which my father spoke of late o me by the fountain, and which hath robbed me of peace, so that curiosity plagueth me wherever I go, for it was a word of promise."

"What said I, then, and what promise gave I to thee?"

"Oh, thou knowest—I can tell by thy face thou knowest! Thou had-

dest in mind, so saidst thou—well, canst thou guess now?—'I purpose to give thee somewhat to make thy heart rejoice, and which will be fitting unto thee.' Thus word for word didst thou speak. I remember it only too well, it keepeth on tickling me in my ear. What then did my little father mean with this promise of his?"

Jacob reddened, and Joseph saw it. It was a slight rosy flush, which ran up into the grey hair on his cheeks, and his eyes clouded over in mild confusion.

"It was nothing, nothing at all," he said defensively. "My child is indulging in vain imaginings. What I said was mere chance, uttered without purpose or significance. Have I not given thee various things, as my heart prompteth me? Thus, then, was the meaning of what I said, that I might give thee something some day, at a fitting hour. . . ."

"Nay and indeed," Joseph cried, sprang up and embraced his father. "This wise and good man who sitteth here cannot speak without meaning—that would be unheard of. As though I had not seen plain and clear as he spoke, that he spoke not emptily, but had a plain thing in his mind's eye, beautiful and definite, not just anything at all, but some particular and splendid thing which he thought of for me. But not only hast thou thought of, thou hast spoken and promised. May I not know what is mine and what awaiteth me? Dost thou think I could find rest or give thee any peace until I knew?"

"How thou teasest me," said Jacob, hard-pressed. "Shake me not so, and take away thy hands from the lobes of mine ears, that I may not look like a child in thy hands. Thou wouldst know—well, why shouldst thou not know? I will tell thee, I will admit that I did have one clear thing in my mind, and not anything indefinite. Hearken then, and stand down upon the ground. Hast thou heard of Rachel's *ketonet passim?*"

"A garment of Mami's? Something she wore? Oh, I understand: thou wilt make me from her robe . . ."

"Hearken, Jehosiph! Thou dost not understand. Let me tell thee. When I had served seven years for Rachel and the time approached when I should receive her in the Lord, Laban spoke to me: 'I will give thee a veil, wherein the bride may veil herself and dedicate herself to Nana and be a consecrated one. Long ago,' he said, 'I bought the *haik* from a pilgrim and preserved it in the chest, for it is precious. It is supposed to have belonged to a king's daughter in times past and been the maiden garment of a princess, a thing easy to believe, so skilfully is it embroidered everywhere with all sorts of emblems of idols. But she shall veil her head in it and be as one of the *enitu* and like to the bride of heaven in the tower Etemenanki.' In some such words spoke the devil Laban to me. And lied not in these words which he spake, for Rachel received the garment and was a splendour incomparable in it as we sat at the wedding feast and I kissed the image of Ishtar. But when I handed the bride the flower and lifted her veil that I might see her with my see-

ing hands, lo, it was Leah, whom the devil had craftily brought into the bedchamber, so that I was happy only in my imagination, but not in the fact. All which maketh one to lose one's reason to think upon, so I pass it over. But at the time I was glowing in the sun of my fancied bliss, and I folded the sacred weave and laid it upon a chair and to the bride I said: 'We shall hand it down through the generations, and countless blissful brides shall wear it.'"

"And did Mami too wear the wrap at her time?"

"It is no wrap, it is a sumptuousness, a piece of material to be used as one will, ankle-length, with sleeves, and one can put it on as suiteth one's taste and one's looks. Mami? Yea, she wore it and kept it; when she went away, when we broke the dusty bolts and swindled that devil Laban, she faithfully packed it up and took it with her. Always it went where we went, and as Laban preserved it for years in his chest, so have we done."

Joseph's eyes darted about through the tent and rested on the coffers. He asked:

"Is it close to us?"

"Not far off."

"And my lord will give it me?"

"I have designed it for the child."

"Designed and promised."

"But for later, not this very minute," cried Jacob in his distress. "Be reasonable, child, and let it stop for the moment at the promise. Lo, things are in the balance, and the Lord hath not yet pronounced upon them in my heart. Thy brother Reuben fell away and I was driven to take from him his right as first-born. Is it then thy turn next, that I should give thee the right to array thee in the *ketonet?* One might say no, for after Reuben came Judah and then Simeon and Levi. One might answer yes, for after Leah's first-born fell and was cursed, then came the turn of Rachel's first-born. But all that is doubtful and unclear. We must wait and let the signs make it plain to our understanding. But if I garb thee in the *ketonet,* then might the brethren falsely interpret it in the sense of the blessing and the choice and rise up in jealousy against thee and against me."

"Against thee?" asked Joseph, in great astonishment. "I almost think that my ears deceive me. Art thou not our father and our lord? If they murmur, canst thou not rise up and overwhelm them with thy words and say unto them: 'I choose whom I choose and show favour to whom I show favour? Who are ye that ye oppose me? Sooner than any of you will I clothe him in the garment and with his mother's *ketonet passim.'* But I think not that mine ears deceive me, they are young and keen. And especially when my dear father speaketh I prick them up. Saidest thou once to the bride: 'Countless ones among beloveds shall wear it?' Or saidest thou not? Tell me, then! Who, saidest thou, shouldst wear it?"

"Be quiet, tempter. Leave me, and coax me not, that thy folly may not overflow and fall upon mine own head."

"Dear father—let me see it!"

"See it? Well, seeing is not having. But seeing is wanting to have. Be reasonable."

"Shall I not see what is mine and promised unto me? Shall we make a bargain? I will sit here and not stir from the spot. Then thou goest and showest me the festal garment, holding it up before thee as the merchants in the bazaar at Hebron display their wares and drape the cloth upon themselves before the eyes of him who coveteth it. But he is poor and cannot buy. So then the merchant putteth it away again."

"So be it, in the name of the Lord," said Jacob. "Although an on-looker would think thou tookest liberties with me. Stop where thou art. Squat upon thy heels, put thy hands behind thee. Then shalt thou see that which perhaps, under certain circumstances, might be thine."

"What is mine already," Joseph cried, "only that I may not yet enjoy it."

He rubbed his eyes with his knuckles, to see the better. Jacob went over to the round-topped coffer, slipped the bolt, and flung back the lid. On top were woollen things, mantles, covers, skirts, headcloths, smocks, which he dropped, folded, on the floor in a pile. He found the veil where he knew that it lay, took it, turned round, and spread out the folds.

The lad stared in amaze. He drew a long breath through his open, laughing mouth. The metal embroideries glittered in the lamplight. The flashing silver and gold blotted out at times the quieter colours as the old man held it up in his unsteady arms: the purple, white, olive-green, rose-colour, and black of the emblems and images, the stars, doves, trees, gods, angels, men, and beasts, lustrous against the bluish mist of the background.

"Ye heavenly lights!" Joseph burst out. "How beautiful! O dearest father merchant, what showest thou to thy customer, there under thy arch? There is Gilgamesh, with the lion in the bend of his arm. I recognize him from here. And there is a man fighting with a griffin and swinging a club. Wait, wait! Ye heavenly hosts, what animals are here! I see the paramours of the goddess—bat, steed, wolf, and bright-coloured bird. Let me look—ah, let me look! I cannot make out, I cannot distinguish. And my eyes burn from staring across such a distance. Is that the scorpion-human pair, with the prickly tails? It seemeth so, but I cannot be certain, though mine eyes water with staring. One moment, merchant, while I hitch a little nearer, still with my hands behind my back. But oh, ye Elohim, how it groweth in beauty as I come nearer it! And all becometh clear. What are the bearded spirits doing at the tree? They are fructifying it. . . . And what is it that is written here? 'I have put off my coat; how shall I put it on?' Wonderful! Always Nana, with sun, moon, and dove. Ah, I *must* stand up! Merchant, I *must* get up, else I cannot

see the top: the date palm, out of which a goddess stretcheth her arms with food and drink. I may touch it, may I not? There is no charge, I hope, if I lift it up, ever so carefully, in my hand, to feel its weight and its mixture of lightness and heaviness. . . . Merchant, I am poor, I cannot buy. Merchant, give it to me! Thou hast so many wares—give me the veil! Or be so kind to lend it me, that I show myself to the people to the honour of thy shop. No, thou wilt not—thou art adamant? Or waverest thou, perhaps, a tiny bit, and despite all thy severity wouldst like to see me in it? No, I am wrong, thou swayest a little only from the holding up and spreading out. Thou hast strained thyself much too long already. Give it to me. How doth one wear it, how put it on? Like this—or like this? Or this way? How do I please thee? Am I the gay shepherd-bird in the many-coloured coat? Mami's raiment—how doth it become her son?"

He looked, of course, like a young god. The effect he produced was only to be expected, and his eagerness to bring it about did anything but strengthen Jacob's resistance. We shall do well to recognize at once the irresistible guile by which he had finessed the garment out of Jacob's hands into his own. And this was scarcely done when the thing was on his back—put there by two or three deft and assured motions which themselves evinced great skill in the art of dressing. How well it set him off! It covered his head and wrapped his shoulders, the silver doves glittered and the gay embroideries glowed, it fell in folds about his youthful form and made him look taller than he really was. But not only so. For the festal garment became his face to such an extent that nobody who saw him could have disputed the popular verdict upon his charms. It made him so lovely and so well-favoured that the phenomenon was actually no longer quite earthly; in fact it bordered on the supernatural. Worst of all, the likeness to his mother—her look, her forehead and brows, the shape of her mouth—had never stood out so clearly as in this dress; poor Jacob was so smitten by it that his eyes overflowed, and he thought nothing else than that he was beholding Rachel in Laban's house, on the day of the fulfilment.

It was the mother-goddess who stood there before him smiling, in the boy's lovely guise, and asked:

"I have put on my coat—shall I take it off?"

"No, no, keep it, keep it!" the father said. The young god rushed away. Jacob lifted his brow and his hands, and his lips moved in prayer.

THE NIMBLE RUNNER

The excitement was tremendous. The first to see Joseph in his coat of many colours was Benjamin; but Benjamin was not alone. Joseph found him in the women's tent, with the concubines. He entered their quarters in his new finery and said: "Greeting to you all. I have just

come by chance to look in on my little brother. Lo, thou art here, my Beni; I only wanted to ask how you all are. So you are combing flax? And Turturra is helping? Do any of you know the whereabouts of old Eliezer?"

"Turturra" meant "little one"—Joseph often called his brother by this Babylonian pet name. And Turturra was already giving vent to long-drawn-out cries of admiration. Bilhah and Zilpah chimed in. He wore his robe with a careless air, drawn up and thrust through the girdle of his smock.

"What are you all chirping about and making eyes like cartwheels? Oh, you mean my garment, Mami's veil *ketonet?* I am wearing it for a while, Israel having made me a present of it a few minutes ago."

"Joseph-el, thou sweetest lord, son of the favourite," cried Zilpah. "Hath Jacob then given thee the coat of many colours, in which he first received Leah my mistress? He hath done wisely and justly indeed, for the heart melteth within one at the sight so that one could not imagine another wearing it. One of those now on a journey perhaps, the offspring of Leah, from whom Jacob lifted it for the first time? Or my Gad or Asher, born on Leah's lap? The very idea maketh one to smile, albeit ruefully."

"Joseph-ja, loveliest one!" Bilhah cried. "Nothing more beautiful can be conceived than thy looks in this robe! One is tempted to prostrate oneself at the sight; and especially I, who am only a handmaid, though sister and favourite to Rachel thy mother, to whom by the power of Jacob I bore thy elder brothers Dan and Naphtali. They too will fall down before thee or be like to it, when they see the youth in their mother's wedding garment. Go then swiftly and show thyself to them unawares, while they are yet all innocence and dream not that our lord hath chosen thee. Likewise thou shouldst go across country and show thyself to Leah's six red-eyed sons, that thou mayest hear their exulting shouts and their hosannas may strike upon thine ear."

It is almost incredible, but Joseph did not notice the thick layer of bitterness and spite which coated the women's words. His self-absorption, his blissful though none the less reprehensible self-confidence made him deaf and unresponsive to any warning. He sucked up the honey of their words, quite convinced that he deserved it all. It never occurred to him to look beneath the surface. But precisely therein lay the blame. Indifference to the inner life of other human beings, ignorance of their feelings, display an entirely warped attitude toward real life, they give rise to a certain blindness. Since the days of Adam and Eve, since the time when one became two, nobody has been able to live without wanting to put himself in his neighbour's place and explore his situation, even while trying to see it objectively. Imagination, the art of divining the emotional life of others—in other words, sympathy—is not only commendable inasmuch as it breaks down the limitations of the ego; it is

always an indispensable means of self-preservation. But of these rules Joseph knew nothing. His blissful self-confidence was like that of a spoilt child; it persuaded him, despite all evidence to the contrary, that everyone loved him, even more than themselves, and that therefore he needed to take no thought of them. To pardon such conduct as his on the score of his beautiful eyes would be weakness indeed.

But with Benjamin the thing was different. Here for once complete whole-heartedness was in place. He cried out:

"Jehosiph, thou heavenly one! Not as in our waking life but as in a dream it seemeth; and the Lord hath wrapped thee in a garment of splendour, woven full of coloured lights and hath put upon thee a mantle full of pride and glory. It must ravish the soul of a little urchin like me. Go not, I pray thee, to the sons of Bilhah, and leave the sons of Zilpah yet in ignorance a little. Stay by thy little brother, that I may admire thee the more and look my fill!"

All that Joseph might take at its face value; it rang true. Even so, he might draw a warning from his little brother's simple words. For we cannot help feeling that Benjamin was afraid of the meeting of the brothers and wanted at least to delay it. Joseph himself possessed enough instinct, if not enough insight, not to appear straightway before the children of the maids in his new garment. With the exception of a few underlings, who saw him in passing and outdid themselves in adulation, hand-kissings, and obvious envy, the only person who beheld him that day was Eliezer. The old man fell into a prolonged nodding, which might be taken for approval, but equally for a sort of general contemplation of mankind and his destiny. He then, with an abstracted and godlike mien, began to enlarge upon his so-called recollections, those which the sight of the garment called up in him. How, that is, he, Eliezer, had once as wooer in Isaac's stead brought Rebecca up out of Harran's underworld, and when they had reached the upper regions and the bridegroom was approaching, had shrouded her in the veil. And for what reason? That Isaac might know her. For how should he have known her and lifted her veil unless she had veiled herself beforehand? Eliezer's countenance, as he talked, was so unmoved that it looked like a false face, which you could perhaps take off and show another one beneath it. "A marvellous thing, my child," said he, "hath Israel given thee; for in the veil is life and death. But death is in life, and life in death, and he who hath learned this truth hath penetrated the mysteries. The sister-mother-bride had to unveil herself and stand naked at the seventh gate of hell and in the face of death. But when she returned again to the light she veiled herself, in token of life. Lo, the seed-corn, how it sinketh to earth and dieth, that it may arise again for the harvest time. For the sickle lieth already close to the blade—the sickle which waxeth in the darkness of the moon as young life, yet is it death and taketh the manhood of the father that it

may assume new lordship over the world; and from the harvest of the sickle rolleth the fruit of life and death. Thus the veil signifieth life after the unveiling in death, and therewith already possesseth knowledge and death, since after all in knowledge is procreation and life. A great thing hath the father given thee, he hath given light and life when he veiled thee with the veil which thy mother had to leave behind her in death. Therefore cherish it, my child, that no one rend it from thee and that death may not know thee."

"Thanks, Eliezer," answered Joseph. "Many thanks, wise old servant, who in Abram's train struck down the kings and toward whom the earth did spring! How weightily thou speakest of all these mingled things, of veil and sickle and seed-corn; rightly too, since these things are related and are one in God, though to our eyes they are embroidered many-fold upon the veil. But now, as for me, I will take off my coat and cover me with it upon my couch, that I may sleep beneath it as sleepeth the earth beneath the world-mantle of the stars."

Thus he did. And thus they found him sleeping, the children of the maids, when, instructed by their mothers, they entered the tent which he shared with them. The four brothers, Dan, Asher, Gad, and Naphtali, stood at his bedside, and the youngest, Asher the sweet-tooth, barely twenty-two, held the lamp to lighten his sleeping face and the gay robe that covered him.

"Behold," he said, "there hast thou it! It is precisely and no other than what the women said, when they told us that the coxcomb had shown himself to them in his mother's *ketonet passim*. He hath spread it out and sleepeth beneath it the sleep of the just, with a sanctimonious expression on his face. Is there any more doubt? Our father, poor man, hath given it him, beguiled thereto with honeyed words. Oh, for shame! For we feel equally angered over this abomination that hath come to pass; and it is Asher who taketh our combined anger into his mouth and spitteth it out over the head of this offence that here sleepeth—may it give him at the very least bad dreams!"

He greatly loved, this Asher, to be of one mind and heart with his fellows and to strengthen his sense of unity by expressing it in words which should do full justice to the common opinion; this gave him a feeling of warmth and comfort even in the midst of his rage, and the characteristic harmonized with his humid lips and eyes and his love of eating. He went on:

"So I have cut pieces out of live rams and sheep and eaten them, have I? He told that to our dear, good, credulous father, who then gave him the *ketonet* as a reward for his lying. And so with each of us: he hath charged each one of us with some fault, and now lieth there under the garment gained by his falsity and the evil reputation he hath given to us. So then, brethren, let us stick together and be of one mind in our

wrath, and let me name him by some name that shall ease all our hearts—such as 'thou—puppy'!"

He had wanted to call him, quite simply, "thou dog"; but at the last minute a fear of Jacob made him soften the epithet.

It was Dan who spoke next. He was seven-and-twenty, the same age as Leah's Simeon. He wore a tight-fitting embroidered smock; had no moustaches, but a pointed beard, and his prominent eyes lay close together at the root of a crooked nose. "It may be," said he, "that I am called snake and adder, forsooth, because I am said to be somewhat malicious. But what is that compared with him who lieth here? He is a monster in the guise of a lovely youth. Cursed be that lying shape, which maketh the folk to ogle and gape and bewitcheth our father utterly! I would I knew the charm which could force him to reveal his true form!"

Then Gaddiel took his turn, a sturdy fellow, a year older than Asher, with an expression of rude honesty. He wore a sugar-loaf cap and had a military air, due to the baldric round his short coat, and the breast-plates he had sewn upon it. His red and sinewy arms, with their stubby and equally sinewy hands, stuck out from the short sleeves of his coat. "Let me advise thee, Asher," he said, "to take heed to thy lamp, that thou lettest no oil drip down, to awaken the sleeper with its smart. For if he awake, he shall feel my fist straightway in his jaw, and it will swell till he seem to have a lump of flour in it, and so remain till nine days from tomorrow, as sure as my name is Gad. For I am hot with rage and sick to death at sight of him and of the coat beneath which he sleepeth, the price of his shameless betrayal of our father. I am no coward; but something, I know not what, rumbleth in my belly and admonisheth me out of my entrails. Here we stand, we brethren, and there lieth he—the rascal, the coxcomb, the puppy, the turner of heads—and he hath the coat. Are we to bow down before him? I keep hearing those words 'bow down' as though some cursed insect kept buzzing them in mine ear. Therefore it is that my hand itcheth to be at his ear; that would be the right treatment for him and would satisfy the hatred in my belly."

The straightforward Gad had uttered much profounder things than any that Asher—despite all the latter's need to consolidate opinion and achieve unity through the spoken word—had even tried to reach. For Asher's one thought was to call out affection and produce solidarity by expressing only what was simple and easy to grasp. Gad took more trouble. He struggled to get at the things that tormented and frightened them all, things which lay far beneath the simple emotions of envy and rage. He wrestled to find words for obscure memories, anxieties, apprehensions; for some shadowy train of associations which should combine the essence of manifold conceptions—such as first-born, deception, exchange, world-dominion, brother-vassalage—and which, while not properly recognizable as either past or future, as legend or as prediction, yet

perversely evoked the words "bow down," "they shall bow before thee."
The others felt greatly, even inexplicably challenged by the power of
Gad's words. Especially the long, lean, stoop-shouldered Naphtali, who
was already shifting from one foot to the other, so greatly had Gad's
words made him tingle in all his limbs with eagerness to be off. He had
the instinct of a carrier-pigeon, and his calves had for long been fairly
twitching and his body shaken. His imagination was completely con-
trolled by the conceptions of space and separation. He regarded space
as his most familiar enemy, and himself as the appointed means of its
conquest. In other words, he felt it his mission to even out those differ-
ences in men's knowledge which were effected by distance. When any-
thing happened in the place where he was, he immediately connected
it in his mind with some distant spot where nothing of it was yet known.
And to be in such a state of so to say vegetable unconsciousness was
intolerable in Naphtali's eyes; it made him quiver with the urgency of
striding out with his legs and of loosening his tongue to set things right;
in order wherever possible to equalize the sum of man's information by
spreading it from where it existed to regions still disgracefully ignorant.
The place in point at present was that where the rest of the brethren
were; straightway, and before any of the others, he thought of it. They
were in ignorance, they knew naught, thanks to the deplorable working
of space and distance, but they must learn speedily. In his mind Naphtali
was already running.

"Listen and hearken, brethren, children and friends," he began, in
his quick, soft voice. "We are standing here and see with our eyes what
has happened, we are on the spot. But at this very moment in the vale of
Shechem the red-eyed brothers are sitting about the fire, chatting of this
and that and the other, of anything save the fact that Jacob hath exalted
Joseph's head, to their own undoing. For they know it not, and however
loud their shame crieth aloud, theirs and ours, they hear it not. But
shall we then content ourselves with the advantage we have, saying:
'They are distant and thus foolish, for to be distant is to be foolish,' and
let it go at that? No, for we must tell them, that it may be there as it is
here and that they may not go on living as though it were not. Send me,
send me! I will speed to them across country and give them word that
shall lighten their darkness and make them to shriek aloud. But to thee,
hastening back again, will I announce how they shrieked."

The others were of the same mind. The red-eyed brethren must
hear the truth. Indeed it almost touched them more closely than it did
the present four. Naphtali knew the road. They would tell their father
that he had gone on pressing business. He scarcely slept for impatience
and saddled his ass before dawn; when Joseph awaked under his world-
mantle he was already far off, and knowledge well on its way to the
distant brethren. Nine days later, exactly on the day of the full moon,

they all returned to Hebron, together with the messenger—Reuben, Simeon, Levi, Judah, Issachar, and Zebulun—and peered dourly about them. Naphtali said that the twins—Simeon and Levi, so called because they were only a year apart—had roared like bulls on hearing the news.

OF REUBEN'S ALARM

Joseph did have enough sense and understanding not to appear at once before his brothers in the coat, though he had the greatest desire to do so. A faint doubt whether they really did love him so much more than themselves that they would have no other feeling than pure joy at his elevation made him lay aside the garment for the time and greet them in his everyday clothes.

"Greetings, dear sons of Leah, brothers and strong men," he addressed them. "Welcome to our father's house. A few of you at least I will kiss."

And he went among them and kissed three or four on the shoulder, they standing like images and not touching him at all, save Reuben, now a man of twenty-nine years. Without any particular change of feature he lifted one heavy hand when he felt Joseph's kiss on his shoulder, and stroked the lad's hair lightly, almost furtively. He was tall and heavy and wore a skin apron, with leather straps wound round his powerful legs. His face was red, clean-shaven, fleshy, and muscular; it had a pugnacious expression, yet the rather blunt profile suggested both dignity and self-consciousness. His low brow was darkened by a mop of curly black hair. Jehudah, the next elder son, but three years younger than Reuben, was quite as tall, but walked with a stoop and showed traces of suffering about his nostrils and lips. He wore a cloak, in which he wrapped his hands, and a close-fitting cap from which a shock of red-brown hair streamed out like a mane. Red-brown too was the heavy, pointed beard and the narrow, drooping moustaches that covered the thick red lips. These last spoke of sensuality, but the nose, finely shaped and delicately arched, which drooped over them, suggested some gift of the spirit; while the eyes, large and prominent and heavy-lidded, like a stag's, had a melancholy cast. Like several of his brothers and half-brothers, Judah was already a married man. Reuben, for instance, had wooed a daughter of the soil and with her raised up several children to Abram's god, among them the lads Hanoch and Pallu, whom Jacob sometimes trotted on his knees. Simeon had married a maid of Shechem, named Bunah, carried off as booty when they had sacked the town; Levi a worshipper of Yahu, who passed for a grandchild of Eber; Naphtali a young female whose origin Jacob somewhat arbitrarily derived from Nahor, brother of the Chaldaean; and Dan quite simply a Moabite woman. It would not have been possible to compass marriages entirely irreproachable from

the religious point of view; and in Judah's case Jacob had perforce to be satisfied with any which might bring the youth some tranquillizing and steadying influence, for his sex life had from the first been marked by disorder and suffering. His relations with the love-goddess kept him strained and unsatisfied, he writhed beneath her lash and was her unsubmissive slave—hence the deep conflict in his soul and the lack of unity in his character. His intercourse with the consecrate and the whores in the temples of Ishtar brought him into contact with the follies and abominations of the worship of Baal and the shamelessness of Canaan; and nobody, not even Jacob himself, could find that more repugnant than did Judah, he being of a religious temperament, seeking a pure and reasoned worship and from the bottom of his heart abominating Sheol and the follies and mysteries with which the folk defiled themselves. Moreover he felt he had good reason to think well of himself; for since the stumbling of Reuben and the night when the twins had plundered Shechem, there was something to be said for the view that Judah, the fourth son, was next in line for the blessing and the bearer of the promise. Of course, these things were not said among the brethren, no claims being put forward save in the form of their common ill-will against Rachel's son.

Through one of his shepherds, named Hirah, from the village of Adullam, Judah had got to know a Canaanite man called Shuah, and Shuah's daughter found favor in his eyes. He married her, with Jacob's consent. Up to now she had borne him two sons, whom he brought up in the fear of God. But just as Ishmael had resembled Hagar, so these sons were like their mother and not like their father. At least Judah thought and said so, saying that they were an evil generation, children of Canaan, of the bad breed of Baal, Sheol, and Melech, though it was possible that the trouble was not all of Shuah's daughter's making. She was now pregnant with a third child, and Judah already looked forward with misgivings to its appearance. In short, the shadow of melancholy lay in Judah's eyes, but that did not make him better-natured nor lead him to stroke Joseph's hair, as Reuben had done. He said:

"Well, writing-man, is it seemly of thee to come thus before thy elders, in an ordinary smock full of ink-spots, they having been long away and now are returned home? Carest thou so little to please us, when thou art so ready to curry favour among common folk with fine garments? We hear thou hast fine and dazzling raiment in thy chest, worthy of a prince's son. Wouldst thou insult us by being so niggardly with it at our homecoming?"

Next spoke Simeon and Levi, the twins, leaning upon their heavy cudgels; their eyes were hot, their tattooed breasts glistened with oil, their whole bodies were marked with scars. They burst out together into a short bellowing laugh. Said one: "Since when do wantons walk about unveiled?" And the other: "How long since have the temple

whores ceased to cover their eyes?" He spoke unmindful of Judah, who started at the words.

"Oh, thou meanest my picture robe?" questioned Joseph. "Hath our brother Naphtali told thee on the way how your father Jacob hath had his heart moved toward me? But in thy goodness forgive my lack"— and he made the most charming obeisance before them all, with his arms crossed. "It is hard," said he, "to hit upon the right thing in doing and in leaving undone, and whatever he doth a man falleth into sin. I thought, in my folly: shall I spread myself before my elders? No, for I should come before them in humility, so that they take no umbrage at my arrogance, but love me instead. And lo, I have done foolishly, for I hear that I should have made myself fine in your honour. But believe me, on the evening of the roast meal, when you have washen yourselves and put on feast-day garments, I will sit on Jacob's right hand in my *ketonet,* and you shall see our father's son in all his glory. Shall it be a promise?"

Again the savage twins gave a roar of laughter. And the others bored deep into his eyes trying to distinguish between simplicity and impudence in what he had said, and not succeeding.

"A golden promise!" said Zebulun. He was the youngest, and tried to look like a Phoenician. His beard was trimmed to a round shape and he had a mop of short curls. His upper garment was patterned in gay colours and ran over one shoulder and under the other, showing the undershirt. His mind was set on the sea, so that he had liefer not been a shepherd. "A delicious promise, like a sacrificial cake of fine meal made with honey—a promise which I should like to thrust back down thy throat that thou mightst choke upon it!"

"Come, come, Zebulun, these are but coarse jests," Joseph replied, casting down his eyes and smiling as though embarrassed. "Hast thou heard them from the galley-slaves at Gaza and Ascalon?"

"He hath called my brother Zebulun a drunken galley-slave," said Issachar, twenty-one years old, tall and heavy-limbed, nicknamed "the bony ass." "Reuben, thou hast heard, and thou must take it up, if not with thy fist, as I could wish, yet with such words as shall make him remember."

"Thy words are inexact, Issachar," Reuben replied, in the high, effeminate voice which men of his powerful build may sometimes have. "He hath not called him that, but merely asked if he heard the words from such a one. It was pert enough as it was."

"I understood him to say that he would like to choke me with the sacrificial cake," put in Joseph, "which would have been blasphemous to boot, as well as very unfriendly. But if he did not say that or mean it, then of course I will take back what I said too."

"And now," concluded Reuben, "let us go our ways, that our coming together may not end in tauntings and misunderstanding."

They separated, the ten and the one. But Reuben followed Joseph and called him by name. He stood before him, just they two alone, Reuben on his leather-bound legs like heavy columns, and Joseph gazing up with polite attention into the hard-fleshed face, which expressed both embarrassment and dignity, since he was conscious both of his strength and of his proneness to err. His eyes, with their inflamed lids, were close to Joseph's; they lost themselves in Joseph's face or rather they stopped at it and returned into themselves. He kept kneading his brother's shoulder with his powerful right hand, as he was wont to do when he talked with anyone.

"Thou keepest the robe, young one?" asked he, moving his lips, but scarcely opening his mouth.

"Yes, Reuben, my lord, I will keep it," answered Joseph, "for Israel hath given it me, when he was merry from play."

"Did he defeat thy men?" Reuben asked. "Thou playest shrewdly and discreetly, for thou art practised by Eliezer in all sorts of mental exercise, which can stand thee in good stead in a game. Doth he often win?"

"Now and again," Joseph said, showing his teeth.

"When thou wilt?"

"It doth not depend on me alone," replied the other evasively.

"Yes, yes, so is it," thought Reuben to himself, and his gaze grew even more brooding. "That is the deceitfulness of the blessing-bearer, and his way of deceiving. He must hide his light under a bushel, that it light him not to his harm, and the others must boast of more light than they have in order to keep up with him." He looked at his half-brother. "Rachel's child," he thought, "what charm he hath! The people are right to smile upon him. He is precisely tall enough and casteth up his lovely eyes at me and mocketh within himself, of that I am certain, as I stand here before him like a tower, disproportioned, tall and unwieldy, with this loutish body of mine, the veins of it fairly bursting with strength, so that I forgot myself like a young bull with Bilhah, not even looking to see if we were alone. Then with innocent malice Joseph goeth and telleth Jacob and I am undone. For he is wise as the serpent and gentle as the dove, and thus one should be. Malicious in his innocence and innocent in his malice, so that innocence becometh a danger and malice a sign of grace, and these are the unmistakable marks of the blessing, and one could do naught against it, even if one would, and one would not at all, for there is God. With a single blow I could stretch him out upon the earth so that he rose not again. The strength that overcame Bilhah were enough for that, and the thief of my first-born right should feel it as a man, even as Bilhah felt it as a woman. But what would that avail me? Abel would lie slain, and I should be he whom I understand not, that is Cain. For how can one act against his conviction and open-eyed strike

down the pleasing one, because one is oneself unpleasing? I will deal not against mine own conviction, I will be fair and just, as is more conformable to my soul. I shall betray it in nothing. I am Reuben, my veins full of strength, Leah's first-born, Jacob's eldest son, and head of the twelve. I will make no lovesick faces at him, nor humble myself before his charms. It was silly of me even to have stroked his hair, silly and weak. I will lay no hand upon him, one way or the other. I stand before him like a tower, clumsy if you like, but in dignity."

The muscles of Reuben's face were drawn as he asked: "Thou hast wheedled the coat out of him, hast thou not?"

"He promised it me of late," answered Joseph, "and when I reminded him of the promise, he gave it to me out of the coffer and said: 'Keep it, keep it.'"

"Ah, so thou hast reminded him and begged him for it. He gave it thee against his will, tempted by thine. Knowest thou that it is against God to misuse the power that is given thee so that he willeth unjustly and doth what he regretteth?"

"What power have I over Jacob?"

"Thou liest in asking. For thou hast over him Rachel's power."

"Then have I not stolen it."

"Nor earned it."

"The Lord saith: 'I favour whom I favour.'"

"Thou'rt impudent," Reuben said, with drawn brows, shaking him slowly to and fro as he held him by the shoulder. "It is said of me that I am unstable as water and that sin is not far from me. But what is far from me is impenitent frivolity like unto thine. Thou boasteth of thy God and fleerest at the heart that lieth in thine hand. Dost thou know that thou hast brought the old man into anguish and stress by beguiling him of the coat?"

"Into what sort of stress, big Reuben mine?"

"I know already thou liest, since thou askest. Hast thou then such joy in being able to do this? In stress over thee, who art his dearest without desert, according to the wish of his heart that is so proud and yet so soft. He was blessed before Esau, his twin; yet hath he not suffered enough, in that Rachel died a furlong from Ephron, and in the matter of Dinah his child, and even through me—which I mention myself, seeing that thou wast about to remind me?"

"Not so, big Reuben. For I had not in mind that day when thou didst sport with Bilhah so that thou wast to the father in his wrath like to a hippopotamus."

"Hold thy tongue! How canst thou mention it, when I took it out of thy mouth and said it before thee? Always thou thinkest of new sorts of lies, saying thou thinkest not thereupon when thou expressly spakest of it. Is it that which thou learnest from the tablets of stone and connest

when thou and Eliezer study the wisdom of the temple? Thy lips move, I know not how, having been carved in this wise by the Creator, and thy teeth glisten between them. But the words that come forth are naught but insolence. Have a care, have a care, my young one," he said, and held him so that Joseph rocked to and fro on heels and toes. "Have I not saved thee ten times out of the hands of the brethren and from the wrath of those who trod Shechem under their feet for the sake of the ravished one—ten times and more, when they would have given thee a good pummelling for telling tales to the father about 'cutting pieces from the living flesh' and more of the same sort? And for that thou wouldst go and beguile our father of the coat, while we are pasturing far away, and wouldst in thy folly defy the wrath of nine brothers if not ten? Tell me who thou art, and how much is thine arrogance, that thou makest thyself different from us all and walkest as one set apart? Fearest thou not that thy conceit will draw down about thee the dark clouds out of which the lightning striketh? Hast thou no gratitude at all for those who mean kindly by thee, that thou causest them anguish? Thou'rt as one who climbeth high in rotting branches and laugheth at those who stand beneath and call to him in fear lest the branch break and he fall and his bowels gush out."

"Put me down upon the ground, Reuben, and hearken to what I say. For I am grateful that thou speakest a word for me against the brethren's ill-will. And I am grateful too that thou holdest me thus and shakest me about, both together. But now set me upon my feet that I may speak. I cannot collect my thoughts being so shaken about. But now, standing here upon my feet, I will collect them, and sure am I that thou wilt in thy justice grant me right. I have not got the coat by stealth or stealing. For he promised it to me by the well, and ever since I have known of his purpose to give it to me, to keep. But as I saw him, our gentle-hearted father, somewhat at odds with his own will, I held to what he had said and easily got him to give it to me—give, I say, and not present, for mine it was before he gave it me."

"How so thine?"

"Thou askest? I will answer. For who was it from whom Jacob first lifted the veil and made a promise concerning it at that hour?"

"It was Leah."

"Yes, actually, it was. But in deeper truth it was Rachel. Leah was only arrayed in it, but Rachel was the owner of the robe, and she kept it to her death, a furlong from Ephron. But since she died, where is she now?"

"Where the earth is her portion."

"Yes, actually again. But in very truth it is otherwise. Knowest thou not that it is in the power of death to change the sex, and that Rachel still liveth for Jacob though in another form?"

Reuben started back.

"I and my mother are one," Joseph said. "Knowest thou not that Mami's garment is likewise her son's and that they wear it by turns, one in the other's place? Name her and thou namest me. Name what belonged to her and thou namest what is mine. Well then, whose is the veil?"

He had stood there quite simply and modestly as he spoke, his eyes cast down. But when he had done he suddenly directed his wide-open gaze upwards upon his brother's face. Not as though he wanted to force his view aggressively upon the other, but rather as though he were silently offering his soul to be looked into; as though he were receiving the astonished and blinking stare of Leah's red-eyed son deep into the unfathomableness of his own gaze.

The tower shook. Big Reuben shuddered. What did the lad mean, what was he trying to express, what was the origin of it all? Reuben had taunted him with his arrogance—and now he was sorry, for he had had his answer. He had asked in his wrath who the lad thought that he was— ah, would that he had not done so! For now he had heard, heard so riddlingly that it made him shiver all the way down his back, long as it was. Was it chance that had shaped the words in the boy's mouth? Had he meant to play upon the divine and make use of it to justify his own duplicity, or . . . or—and this *or* gave rise in the very marrow of Reuben's being to the same horror of which Brother Gaddiel had complained as they stood at Joseph's bedside. Only it was stronger in Reuben, a profounder shock, and it was accompanied by a sort of admiration, a gentle, even tender amazement and terror.

We must try to understand Reuben. He was not the man to be unique in misconstruing the significance of the question as to who one was, in whose footsteps one walked, to what past one's present had reference, in order to give it reality. Joseph had given evidence—in so monstrously presumptuous a way as to make Reuben shudder. But the magic of the word, whereby the uppermost was turned undermost, an unforced and flexible and perfectly genuine use of language to work enchantment, brought before Reuben's eyes in brilliant clarity the footsteps in which his younger brother walked. He did not go so far at this moment to think of Joseph as a veiled god-goddess; that we must not suppose. But yet his love was not very far from becoming belief.

"Child, child," said he, in that piping voice out of his powerful body, "spare thine own soul, spare thy father, spare the light thou walkest in! Put it under a bushel, that it may not light thee unto thine undoing." He took three backward steps, with drooping head, then turned and walked away.

But at the evening meal Joseph wore the coat. The brothers sat there like graven images. Jacob was full of fears.

THE SHEAVES

When these things had happened, and after many days, it came about that they were cutting the wheat in the vale of Shechem; it was the time of the harvest and of joyous and sweating labour up till the day of the first fruits, when they made offering of leavened bread of the new wheaten flour, seven weeks after the spring full moon. For the late rains had been plenteous, but the hatches of the sky were early closed, the waters ran off, and the land dried. Marduk-Bel, the sun, the triumphant, drunk with his victory over the dripping leviathan, ruled flaming in the heavens and sent up golden spears into the blue. Even at the turn between the second and the third months so great was the ardour of his sovereignty that there might have been fears for the sowing but that a wind sprang up, the welcome approach of which was first scented by Zebulun, sixth son of Leah, who said:

"My nose is pleasantly assailed by this wind, for it bringeth moisture from afar and beareth on its wings the refreshing dew. Lo, now, as I always say, what great good cometh from the sea! Better it were to dwell by the edge of the green vast and close to Sidon, rather than to tend the sheep, which pleaseth me but little. For upon the wave and on the shapen plank one can reach folk who wear tails, and a lighted horn upon their foreheads. Or to such as have ears so great as to cover the whole body, and others whose forms are covered with grass. A man from the port of Khadati told me of all this."

Naphtali agreed with him. It would be good to exchange news with those grass-grown folk; for most likely neither they nor the ear-lapped nor the tailed creatures had the least notion what went on in the world. But the others dissented and would hear nothing of the sea, even though it brought the moisture-bearing wind. Those were subterranean regions, full of monsters of the prime; Zebulun might just as well express admiration for the desert. Simeon and Levi expressed themselves with peculiar force, in this sense; they were crude but religious, and at bottom they did not much care for the shepherd's life, preferring something more exciting, though they stuck to this one for the sake of the succession.

The harvesting, beginning with the reaping of the barley, was a welcome change for them all; they sweated blithely in their hopes of profit, as one does at this season; even their relations with Joseph sensibly improved, as he worked by their side cutting and binding—until by his irresponsible chatter he ruined everything again and reduced them to extremes. All which I shall relate in due course. As for Jacob, these seasonal joys touched him but little, though all the district yielded to them with gusto, his own sons swinking in the midst of the sweating peasantry. Rather he had a dampening effect upon the gaiety, even without

appearing on the field, which he seldom did. This time he came once, by way of exception and at the request of Joseph, who had his own reasons for making it. But on the whole Jacob troubled little about the sowing and mowing, carrying on his bit of farming as it were without looking at it and only out of prudence, not inclination. Nay, he felt not only indifference but even disinclination to the whole sphere, the religious hostility of the moon shepherd toward the duty which the sunburnt farmer paid the earth. The harvest time was even, in a certain sense, an embarrassment to him, in the sense that it made him draw profit from the cult of fertility which the children of the country paid from spring to spring to the sun-gods and love-women of their temples—a cult abhorrent to his soul. He was rather ashamed of drawing profit from it, and closed his lips tightly when he heard the thanksgiving hymns of the workers bringing home their sheaves.

After the barley harvest he ordered the wheat to be cut for the provisioning of his own people; and as every pair of arms was needed, Eliezer having also taken on a few hired hands for the harvest weeks, Joseph's studies with the latter were interrupted, and he too, in his own exalted person laboured from early morn to dewy eve in the fields. He attacked the bearded grain with the sickle, gathering the stalks together with his right hand; he bound the sheaves with straw and helped the brethren and the hands to load them on carts or hang them on asses to be brought to the threshing-floor. We must recognize that he did all this gladly and willingly, not looking upon it as an imposition, and in simple modesty; but it is also true that his attitude toward the work was in flat contradiction to certain revelations of his inward life, which he permitted himself precisely at this very time. In any case it would have been easy for him to get Jacob's permission not to appear on the field, yet he never thought of doing so. Partly because he liked the work, but even more because it brought him into contact with the brethren, and he felt pride and pleasure in working among them, helping them, hearing them call him by name; all that was literally true. Labour upon a common task improved relations between him and them, it .uplifted his heart, it made him happy. However inconsistent all this may seem, it was the truth; the seeming contradictions cannot do away with the fact that he loved his brothers; that, however senseless and even deluded it may seem, he counted on their love and expected some advantage from it—for the unhappy lad little imagined how much he asked.

The field work tired him very much, and he often took short naps; was asleep, indeed, at the midday hour which found all the sons of Jacob, save Benjamin, gathered to rest and eat, beneath a brown awning stretched over crooked poles. They had broken bread and talked, squatting on their heels. Each of them wore for all clothing a leather apron; their bodies were burnt by the ardour of the sun, which blazed down

between fleecy clouds upon the half-harvested field. Here and there, the sickle had made breaches in the golden host, leaving patches of stubble dotted with leaning sheaves and bounded by low walls of rubble which served to divide Jacob's land from that of the peasants. At a little distance stood the hill which served his people for a threshing-floor; laden asses were on their way thither and men were on top, using pitchforks to separate the stalks and toss them down before the oxen.

Joseph then, likewise in his working apron, his skin glowing from the sun, was asleep in a squatting posture, with his head on his arm. When he lay down, he had in all simplicity begged Issachar, the bony ass, who sat next to him, to lend him one of his knees to prop up his head. But Issachar had inquired whether he would not also like him to scratch his head and to keep off the flies; and then curtly bade him to be his own pillow. Joseph had laughed and taken it in good part, resigning himself to sleep without the desired prop. He found it elsewhere, as we shall see. But for the moment nobody was paying him any attention, only Reuben glanced now and again at the sleeper's face, as it lay turned toward him. It was not in repose; the forehead was drawn, the lips twitched, and the partly open mouth moved as though to speak.

Meanwhile the brethren had been discussing the pros and cons of a new sort of implement which had come into use of late, the threshing-table. It was drawn by oxen and had pointed stones on the under side, which tore the ears. It was undeniable that it saved time. But some of them said that the winnowing afterwards was harder work than if the grain had been thoroughly trodden out by means of oxen. Also they spoke of a threshing-cart used by many of the peasants; it ran on rollers and was fitted with sharp iron plates. At that point Joseph roused and sat up.

"I have had a dream," he said, looking round upon the brethren and smiling as though in surprise.

They turned away their heads and went on talking.

"I have had a dream," he repeated, and rubbed his hands across his brows as though still dazed, smiling pleasantly as he gazed into space; "such a vivid and wonderful dream!"

"What is that to us?" retorted Dan, suddenly turning his prominent eyes upon Joseph. "Better is it to sleep without dreams, if thou needs must sleep, for dreams, so they say, are not refreshing."

"Would you like to hear my dream?" asked Joseph.

Nobody answered. One of them—it was Jehudah—went on with their discussion in a tone which was itself a proper reply to such a question.

"It is needful," he said, in a clear, detached voice, "to keep the iron blades very sharp, as otherwise they do not cut but crush and the grain cometh not fully out of the ear. But consider if we can rely upon the

labourers, especially the hired hands, to sharpen them regularly. And then, if the little wheels, on the other hand, are very sharp, they cut the grain and so cometh it that the meal . . ."

Joseph listened awhile to the talk passing over his head. But finally he interrupted and said:

"Forgive me, brothers, but I feel drawn to tell you this dream which I have had. It was not a long dream, but so real and marvellous that I desire not to keep it to myself, but from my heart I yearn to put it before each of your eyes, that ye may laugh for joy and slap your thighs."

"Hearken," said Judah, and shook his head. "What aileth thee that thou troublest us with matters that concern us not? For what do we care about thine inward workings or the ferment of thy dreams or what riseth from thy belly to thy head after eating? It is not seemly to speak of it, and it concerneth us not at all; therefore be quiet!"

"But it doth concern you," Joseph eagerly cried. "It concerneth you all, for you all come into it and so do I; and my dream is so full of meaning and marvel that you might well sit with your heads in your hands and think of naught else for three days long."

"Shall he tell us it then, in few words, without more ado, so that we may know it?" Asher asked. People with a sweet tooth are often very inquisitive—and indeed they were all curious and liked well to hear stories told, and the fact and fable, the legend, dream, song, and story of primitive time.

"Very good, then," Joseph said with satisfaction, "if you like, I will tell you my vision, which is worth hearing on account of its meaning alone. For the dreamer shall not interpret his dream, but another shall do it for him. If any of you dream and ask me, I will tell him the meaning; it costeth me naught, for the Lord giveth it to me for the asking. But with mine own it is different."

"Dost thou call that a few words?" asked Gad.

"Listen, then," Joseph began. But at the last moment Reuben would have prevented him. He had been watching the owner of the veil all this time, and his mind misgave him.

"Joseph," said he, "I know not thy dream, for I lay not with thee in thy sleep, there thou wast alone. But meseemeth it were better each one should be alone with his own dreams and thou shouldst keep thy dream to thyself, that we may all go to work."

"We were at work," Joseph snatched up his words, "for upon the field saw I us all together, us sons of Jacob, and we were harvesting the grain."

"Marvellous," cried Naphtali. "That is a dream like to an unreal vision, forsooth, and thy dreams are remote from us, and very fantastic and high-coloured indeed!"

"But it was not our own field," went on Joseph, "it was the field of

another, very strange to us. But we spoke not of it. We laboured together without speech and bound the sheaves after cutting the stalks."

"That is a great dream before the Lord," said Zebulun. "A vision incomparable. For of course, thou dolt, we should have bound first and cut afterwards. Must we hear it all, even to the end?"

Some of the brethren had already got up, shrugging their shoulders and making ready to leave.

"Yea, hear it up till the end," cried Joseph, lifting his hands. "For now cometh the marvel: each of us was binding a sheaf and we were twelve, for Benjamin too was with us in the field and bound his little sheaf with you in a circle."

"Do not talk rubbish," ordered Gad. "Why 'with you' in a circle, when thou meanest 'with us'?"

"Not so, Gaddiel, for my meaning is far otherwise. For ye made up the circle, the eleven of you, and were binding, but I stood in the centre of the circle and bound my sheaf."

He paused and looked into their faces. They had all lifted their brows and tipped back their necks so that the Adam's apple stood out as their heads swayed slightly. Misgiving, amazement, mockery, and warning were expressed in all their attitudes. They were waiting.

"Hearken now how it fell out and how wonderful was my dream," said Joseph again. "When we had bound our sheaves, each one his own, we left them and went away, not speaking and as though we had nothing more to do there. But we had gone only twenty paces or so together when lo, Reuben turned round to look and motioned backward with his hand to the place where we had been. Yea, Reuben, it was thou. We all stood and looked, shading our eyes. And behold, my sheaf arose there in the middle and also stood upright, and your sheaves stood round about and made obeisance to my sheaf. And mine stood upright."

There was a long silence.

"Is that all?" asked Gad, breaking the silence, in a low, curt voice.

"Yea, for after that I awaked," replied Joseph, rather crestfallen. His dream had disappointed him in the telling, though in the dreaming it had been strange and gratifying and even a little frightening, especially the part about Reuben pointing silently behind them. However, the narration had sounded meagre, even foolish; in Joseph's opinion it could not have impressed any of his hearers, and his view was confirmed by Gad's words: "Is that all?" He was ashamed of himself.

Silence had fallen again, broken by Gad with an oath, so suppressed that only the first syllables were anything but a whisper.

Joseph lifted his head, he took heart. It would seem that his dream, even as he had told it, was not without any effect upon his hearers. "Is that all?" had been crushing, but the oath was full of encouragement. It meant all sorts of things, it meant no little, it meant: "What the devil!"

and that sort of thing. He looked into their faces. They were all pale, and vertical folds stood between their brows—altogether they made a singular impression indeed, as when one gnaws his under lip, or his nostrils go in and out like gills, as many of theirs did. Their breath came fast and uneven, so that it sounded like an irregular, tenfold snorting. And all this went on under the awning where they sat, and if regarded as the effect of his narrative might well have made young Joseph feel disturbed.

And so it did, to a certain extent, but in a way that made the scene seem to him like a continuation of his dream, having, for all its actuality, the same extraordinary character of uncanny joy and joyful uncanniness. True, the effect upon the brethren was not very happy, but it was obviously much stronger than Joseph had dared to hope; so that he was evenly balanced between the sinking feeling he had at sight of them and gratification that his tale had after all not missed fire.

He felt no different when—after the lip-biting and the snorting had gone on for some while—Jehudah burst out in a hoarse, throaty voice: "A more disgusting piece of nonsense have I never heard in all the days of my life!" For such words could only be an expression, not very happy indeed, of Jehudah's amaze.

Then came another pause, filled with pallid silence and gnawing of lips.

Then: "Thou brat! Thou jackanapes! Thou poison toad! Thou stinking fart," roared Simeon and Levi both at once. They could not even speak in turn and make a sort of couplet as they usually did, but all mixed up together, with crimson faces and veins standing out on their foreheads. Actually they displayed the phenomenon reported of them at the time of the plundering of Shechem; for the hair on their chests rose up and bristled like porcupine quills as they roared with one voice: "Thou peacock, thou swaggering puppy, thou blackguardly fool! What care we what thou hast dreamed and what seen behind thine eyelids, thou shameless, thou thorn in our flesh and stone of stumbling to our feet, thou stench in our nostrils—that we should interpret it unto thee? 'Bow down, bow down'—ah, the falsehood and vanity of what thou dreamest and forcest us honest men to hear! So our sheaves stand in a circle and flop down before thee, but thine standeth upright? It turneth the stomach as nothing I have before heard in this world. Thou foul, thou filthy sink of abominations, so thou wouldst play the master and lord with us by filching the *ketonet* behind the backs of thy elders! Thou trickster and thief of the birthright! But we will teach thee all about standing and bowing down, and will show thee thy masters, and thou wilt name to us thy name and wilt perceive thine own shameless lies!"

Thus bellowed the twins. And when they had done roaring, all the ten left the shadow of the awning and went out on the field, still red and

pale, still gnawing their lips. But Reuben, as he went out, said to Joseph: "There hast thou it, my lad." Joseph still sat awhile, pondering, upset and cast down because the brethren did not believe in his dream. For this was the thing he had grasped of all they had said, that they did not believe him—had not the twins several times used word like "lies" and "vanity"? He asked himself, sadly, what he could do to prove to them that he had not said a word too much, but only quite honestly related what he had dreamed in their very presence. If they only believed him, he thought, their violent humour would abate; for surely he had shown brotherly good feeling in telling them what God had revealed to him in a dream, that they might likewise rejoice and with him discuss the significance of the matter? It was impossible that they should take umbrage at his confidence in them and the bond between them, which had been the whole ground of his revealing God's mind concerning him. True, the dream displayed him exalted over them; but that they, to whom he had always, in one sense, looked up, could find that fact intolerable would have been such a disappointment to him that he simply could not have thought of it. At all events, he perceived that the harmony between them was destroyed for the day; he did not go back to the field, but went home and found his little brother. To him he confided that he had told the brethren an altogether modest dream, comparatively speaking, the content being such and such. But that the brethren had not believed it and the twins had been furious—although by comparison with the eagle dream, of which he had not mentioned a single syllable, this one was modesty itself.

Turturra was glad that nothing had been said of that monstrous dream, and for his part displayed such delight over the dream of the sheaves that it entirely made up to Joseph for the fact that it had missed fire with the elder brethren. The little one jumped and laughed at the thought of his own small sheaf bowing down with the rest—it so precisely corresponded to his feelings.

THE COUNCIL

Meanwhile the ten stood on the meadow in the light of the setting sun and took council together in anger and in fear, leaning on their tools. At first they had silently acquiesced in the interpretation given by Simeon and Levi to the dream—namely, that the little liar had made up the whole thing himself. Indeed, they preferred this interpretation, for it fortified their own inward position. It had been Judah who had wanted to explore all the possibilities; and he it was who pointed out that Joseph might actually have so dreamed as he reported himself to have done and not drawn a long bow at all. After that they all explicitly reckoned

with the possibility and thereupon subdivided it into two: namely, that the dream, if actually so dreamed, had indeed come from God—this they naturally regarded as the greatest conceivable catastrophe; or, contrariwise, that it had nothing to do with God, but had originated entirely in the insufferable vanity of Joseph, which, overweeningly nourished by the gift of the *ketonet,* had given rise to these visions. Reuben's contribution to the discussion was that if the dream came from God, then there was nothing for it but to pray—to God, of course, not to Joseph. But if, on the other hand, it had been born of conceit, then they could afford to shrug their shoulders over it and leave the dreamer to his folly. In the end he reverted to the probability that the lad had childishly made up the dream and deserved a beating for the same.

Big Reuben, in short, proposed that Joseph be beaten for telling lies. At the same time, he recommended that they all shrug their shoulders—which proves that he was not very serious about the thrashing, for you cannot thrash with any conviction while shoulder-shrugging. And from this one might deduce that Reuben wished to believe in the second interpretation in order to discount the first and distract the minds of the brethren from thinking of it. Reuben, in short, was afraid that belief in the theory that God had sent the dream would not at all incline the brethren to humility and self-restraint, but rather to conduct infinitely more drastic than mere thrashing. They were not at all prepared, he felt, to view the matter objectively and let their attitude be governed according as Joseph had dreamed out of sheer conceit or had really had a revelation of God's plans for him. For their words seemed to show that in the latter case they did not find his conduct one whit the less worthy of vituperation. If the dream really came from God and was a token of great preferment, then of course there was nothing to say against God— as little as there was to say against Jacob for his honourable weakness. With them the whole point was Joseph. If God had actually preferred him over them and made their sheaves flop down before his, it was because God too had been made a fool of, even as Jacob, and by the same means: namely, the double-dealing by which he supplanted them in the father's affections. God was great, He was holy and irresponsible—but Joseph was a viper. It is clear—and Reuben saw it too—that their notion of Joseph's relation to God perfectly agreed with his own view; they considered it the same as his relation to their father. Indeed, it had to be so, for proper hate is only generated on a basis of some common belief.

Reuben was afraid of this train of thought. Therefore he did not dream. Rather he wanted to convince them that the lad had humbugged them and ought to suffer for it—while shrugging their shoulders. But he was, in reality, as little capable as the others of shrugging his shoulders. For even more, perhaps, than they, Reuben knew in the pit of his stomach the sinking sensation to which the downright Gad had first referred

and of which now not only the four sons of the maids but all the ten were painfully aware. It was a horror springing from mythical and prophetic associations wrapped about such ideas as bartered birthrights, world-domination, and fraternal submission; Reuben suffered in his soul more even than the others on the score of them; except that they did not put him in a fury of rage against the lad who was the source of his oppression, but only gave rise to unnamable emotions toward the innocent babble of the chosen one, as well as an overpowering sense of surrender in the face of destiny.

"It would have been the last straw if he had said: 'bow down,'" Gaddiel said through his clenched teeth.

"He said 'made obeisance,'" remarked the bony Issachar, who loved a quiet life and for its sake was willing to make sacrifices. If he dissociated himself at all for the brethren on this occasion it was because of this pacific leaning of his.

"I know," answered Gad. "But he may only have said that to play a trick, and anyhow, it is just as disgusting either way."

"Not quite," Dan answered; he was a stickler by nature and never failed to stickle conformably to his nature. "To make obeisance is not quite so much as to bow down. We have to admit that it is really less."

"Why do we?" yelled Simeon and Levi, determined to bear witness to their savage stupidity, let the occasion be foul or fair.

Dan and some of the others, including Reuben, insisted that to make obeisance was rather less than to bow down. The former might happen not out of inner conviction but as an empty and formal gesture. One made obeisance only on occasion, whereas bowing down was a constant attitude of the heart which honestly took cognizance of facts as they were; and thus, as Reuben explained, one might make obeisance out of caution and shrewdness, without really bowing down, or, on the other hand, might actually bow down and yet be too proud to make the gesture of obeisance. Jehudah disagreed. He did not think that the position could be sustained, for that they were dealing with a dream, in which making obeisance was only the picture representation of the attitude for which Reuben would reserve the words "bow down." At this point young Zebulun interpolated that they were now doing the very thing to which Joseph had shamelessly invited them and which all of them had refused to consider: namely, they were blithely engaged in interpreting his shameful dream. The comment was so exasperating that it broke up the meeting, amid shouts from Simeon and Levi that it was all stuff and nonsense and that one neither bowed down nor made obeisance before such insults, but only took steps to get rid of the author of them, as had been their course at Shechem. Thus the council came to an end without other result than unappeased bitterness.

SUN, MOON, AND STARS

And Joseph? He had no notion, of course, of the torment which his dream was causing to the brethren, but thought of nothing else than that they had not believed him and of how he could carry conviction— conviction in two directions, both as to the actuality and the truth of his dream. How should he best bring this about? Insistently he asked himself the question, and later was surprised that he had not known the answer, but had to be given it or rather that it had given itself to him. That is to say, he had another dream, or rather he had the same dream, only in a form so much more splendid that the confirmation was more impressive than if he had dreamed exactly the same dream the second time. He was sleeping under the open starry sky, on the threshing-floor, where he and some of the brothers and hands often spent the night at harvest time, to guard the grain which had not yet been threshed and put into the pits. Very likely—though this is in no sense an explanation of the source of dreams—the character of his had been influenced by the starry heavens spanned above him, also by the companionship in sleep of those whom he wished to convince. Still another element was introduced by the content of his day, the fact that he had spent hours receiving instruction upon the last things from old Eliezer under the tree of wisdom: upon world-judgment and blessing-time, the final triumph of God over all the powers to which the peoples had so long sent up the smoke of incense; upon the triumph of the Saviour over the pagan kings, the planetary powers and gods of the zodiac, whom He was to subdue and cast down, shut up in the underworld, and mount above them to a universal and glorious world-dominion. Of all this Joseph dreamed; but in such confusion that he childishly substituted his own person for that of the eschatological god-hero, and beheld or rather perceived himself, the boy Joseph, as the actual sovereign and ruler of the whole world as it revolved through the zodiac. He perceived, I say, rather than beheld this, for it would be impossible to reduce such a dream to an ordered narrative, and in repeating it he had to put it into the simplest and shortest words in order to express the feelings it gave him rather than to narrate it as a series of events. All which did not help to make it more acceptable to the hearer.

He began to be concerned over the form and manner of his communication, directly he roused from his dream and sat up in joyful possession of such striking confirmation of the earlier vision. His concern had to do with the question whether the brethren would give him a chance to tell them another dream—it seemed unlikely. Even the first time it had been a toss-up whether they would not refuse their attention or simply get up and leave the tent before he was done. A second oppor-

33

tunity appeared to him the more unlikely in that they had not seemed to derive unmixed pleasure from the first.

It behoved him to find some means to enforce them; and even as he lay upon the threshing-floor Joseph conceived how this might be done. In the morning he went to his father, as he usually did, since Jacob desired to see him at the beginning of each day, to look into his son's eyes, assure himself of his well-being, and give him his blessing for the day.

Joseph said: "A right good morning to thee, my father and lord! Lo, here is a new day born of the night and methinketh it will be a hot one. One followeth another like to a string of pearls, and life is joyous to this child of thine, especially at this season, when we bring in the harvest. It is lovely upon the meadow, whether we toil or whether we rest; and men grow to understanding of each other in common tasks."

"What thou sayest is pleasant unto mine ears," Jacob replied. "So it goeth well with you all on the field and the threshing-floor and you come together in the Lord, the brethren and thou?"

"Excellently well," answered the lad. "Aside from small differences of opinion such as each day of necessity bringeth forth, and the division of the world displayeth them, everything is in the best of order. For honest words, even though they may be rude, help to clear up error, and then harmony ruleth once more. I wish that our father might but witness it. For thou art never there, and often do we regret it together."

"I do not love the field work."

"It is natural. And yet what a pity that the workers get no sight of the master and no feeling that his eye is upon them, especially the hired hands, upon whom is no reliance. My brother Jehudah complained to me only lately that they do not sharpen the little wheels on the threshing-cart, so that they crush the grain instead of cutting it. But thus it is when the master's eye lacketh."

"I must admit the justice of thy reproach."

"Reproach! May God preserve my tongue from such! It is but a request, proffered by thy offspring in the name of the eleven. And nobody suggesteth that thou shouldst share our labours, the service of the soil, the work of Baal. But only our midday rest, when the sun is high in the heaven and we break bread in the shade and talk among ourselves, we sons of the one and the four, and one or another may relate some jest or dream that he hath had. Often we nudge each other with our elbows and say how fine it would be to see our father's head in the midst of the circle."

"Ah, well, I will come, for once in a way."

"Hurrah! Come then today and rejoice the hearts of thy sons. The work neareth its end, there is no time to lose. So it shall be today, then? I will say naught to the red-eyed ones, nor blab it out to the sons of the maids, for it shall come to them as a surprise. But thy child will hug to

himself in secret the knowledge to whom they owe it and who hath so cunningly and loyally schemed to bring it about."

Such, then, was Joseph's device. It so came about that midday of that very day found Jacob sitting under the awning on the field, after he had inspected the grain-pits and the threshing-floor and tested with his thumb the sharpness of the little wheels. The ten were amazed. For the last few days the dreamer had not shared their noontide rest; now he was here again, with his head in his father's lap. Naturally, he ought to be here, if the father was; but what was it that had brought the old man, so suddenly? They sat stiff and silent, all decently covered out of respect to Jacob's views. The latter was surprised to find none of the hearty good feeling which according to Joseph's account reigned at the harvesting. Perhaps its absence was due to respect for the father and master. Even Joseph had not much to say. He was afraid, even though he lay in his father's lap and had the protection and the hearing for his tale which that implied. He was, indeed, troubled by his dream and the results which might flow from it. He could say in a sentence all there was to say, there would be nothing left. If Gad were to ask: "Is that all?" he would be a beaten man. Of course, the briefness of his tale had the advantage that it would all be out at once, before anyone could stop him. But the large lines and scant ornament might be the very things which would defeat his purpose.

He almost let slip his chance, in the end, for they were all so bored that they were tempted to break up early. Even the signs of departure were not enough to conquer his misgivings, and perhaps nothing at all would have happened if Jacob had not helped him out by saying genially:

"I hear you tell each other stories at the rest hour—recite and so on—did I not?" They stared in bewilderment.

"Yes, yes," Joseph cried, starting up, "funny stories and dreams. Sometimes we are full of them. Do we know anything new?" he asked brazenly, looking round the circle.

They kept on staring at him and saying nothing.

"But I do," said he, and sat up on Jacob's lap with an absorbed look. "There is a dream, which I dreamed last night on the threshing-floor; father and brethren, ye should hear and be amazed. I dreamed," he went on—and then stopped. There was a curious writhing of the limbs, a spasmodic lifting of the neck and shoulders, a twisting of the arms. His head drooped, the smile upon his lips seemed to deprecate and extenuate the sudden whiteness of his eyes. "I dreamed," he repeated, in a sort of gasp, "and I saw in my dream, this I saw: I saw the sun, the moon, and the eleven *kokabim* waiting upon me. They came and bowed down before me."

Nobody stirred. Jacob, the father, kept his eyes severely cast down. It was very still; but in the stillness came an evil, mysterious, and yet

35

distinct sound. It was the gnashing of the brethren's teeth. Most of them kept their lips closed, but Simeon and Levi showed their teeth as they gnashed. Jacob heard the gnashing. It is hard to say whether Joseph grasped its significance. He was smiling quietly and dreamily to himself, with his head on one side. It was out, let them do what they chose about it. Sun, moon, and stars, eleven in number, had attended him. Let them look to it. Jacob looked timidly round the circle. It was as he expected: ten pairs of eyes were fixed wildly and importunately upon him. He summoned up his powers. And sitting at the boy's back he addressed him, as harshly as he could:

"Jehosiph! What sort of dream is this thou hast dreamed, and how couldst thou dream so unsavoury a thing and tell it unto us? Shall I and thy mother and thy brethren come and worship thee? Thy mother is dead and therewith beginneth the crackbrainedness, but is far from ending it. Shame upon thee! By all human reckoning, this stuff thou hast served up to us is so preposterous that it might just as well have been nothing but *aulas-aulalakaula* and done just as much good. I am grieved in my soul that thou, with full seventeen years, and despite all the enlightenment of the written word and reason which thou hast enjoyed by my permission through instruction from my servant Eliezer, hast made no greater progress in the understanding of the divine than to allow thyself to dream that which dishonoureth thee and to play the buffoon before thy father and brethren. Let this be the punishment meted out to thee. I would punish thee more severely and perhaps pull thy hair till thou didst cry out for pain, were not thy prattle too childish for riper minds to take note of it or the man settled in years be tempted to repay thee with great harshness. Fare thee well, sons of Leah! And greetings after the meal, sons of Zilpah and Bilhah!"

Saying which he stood up, behind Joseph, and went hence. The reproof had cost him much to utter; he only hoped that it had satisfied the brethren. If any real anger had spoken in it, that could be only on the score that the lad had not told the dream to him alone, instead of being so mad as to make the brethren witness of the telling. Had he done it of set purpose to cause the father embarrassment, Jacob thought, he could not have found a better device. That he would certainly tell him when they were alone, since he could not have done it now; probably he understood how shrewdly the lad had used the brothers as protection against himself, and himself as protection against the brothers. For he even suppressed a smile in his beard, as he went homewards, over the cleverness of this double-dealing. He certainly felt the irritation he had expressed on the score of the boy's soul, as well as the anxiety over his tendency to dreams and prophetic spasms; but both anger and anxiety were swallowed up in the yearning, half-credulous satisfaction which filled him when he thought of Joseph's presumptuous dreams. Quite absurdly, he prayed God that the dream might have come from Him—which was

utter nonsense, seeing how highly unlikely it was that He had had anything to do with it. And tears of sheer tenderness came into his eyes at the thought that his son's innocent prattle might represent, though vaguely and uncomprehendingly, actual premonitions of future greatness. Ah, poor weak father-heart! He might well have been angry to hear that he and the brethren would come to bow down before the good-for-nothing—that was perplexing for him to hear, for did he not adore him?

As for the brethren, hardly was Jacob gone than they flung as one man into the open, but after a few paces out into the meadow stood still together and took stormy council. Big Reuben spoke, he told them what was to be done. Away! That was the thing. Unanimous departure from the paternal hearth, voluntary banishment. That, Reuben said, would be dignified and impressive behaviour and the only possible answer to such detestable treatment. Away from Joseph, was what he had in mind, in order that no disaster might befall the lad. Of course he did not express his feelings, but put his advice entirely in the light of a reproach and a protest.

That very evening they came before Jacob and told him they were going. A place where such dreams were told, without other risk than at worst of getting one's hair pulled, was no place for them; they had nothing to lose by leaving it. They had helped mightily with the harvesting, now they would go to Shechem: not only the six, but also the four, in fact all ten. For the meadows of Shechem were fat and fertile, and there, in unchanged if also in unrewarded loyalty, they would pasture their father's flocks, and the camp at Hebron should know them no more, now that it was become a place of such high dreaming. They made obeisance and bowed down, they said (suiting the action to the words), in taking reverent leave of their father and lord. They needed not to fear that their going would give him pain, since it was well known that Jacob would give ten for one.

Jacob bowed his head. Did he begin to fear lest the ascendancy of the emotions which, basing on an exalted model, he permitted himself, was being taken amiss in the high place of its origin?

The Journey to the Brothers

THE CHALLENGE

We have been told how Jacob bowed his head when he heard the embittered brethren announce their departure from his hearth. From then on he lifted it but seldom. It was now the season of parching heat; at no other time in the year did the sun's rays so cruelly scorch the land, for the moment of its waning was at hand. This was the solstice, the season in which the true wife had presented Joseph to Jacob, in the month of Tammuz. Yet even so Jacob's spirit was wont to suffer beneath the blackened desolation of this quarter of the circle; that he suffered now might be explained in the same way. But no. The true ground of his depression was the unanimous departure of his sons. I should be saying too much if I asserted that this had given Jacob great pain. In his heart he truly did "give ten for one"; yet it was quite another matter to reckon with the objective fact, to realize that the brothers' notice to quit was decisive; and that he, Jacob, would be left with two sons instead of twelve, a tree lopped of its branches. It was a blow to his dignity, first of all; but also it put him in an embarrassing position before his God, and he inquired of himself how much these actions of his went counter to the plans of the Lord of the Promise, and how great was the accounting he had invited upon his own head. For He that ruled future things, had He not taken care that not all matters should go after Jacob's heart and he be fruitful in Rachel alone? Yes, He had made him fruitful against his own will, and even those unwanted sons from the unloved wife were themselves the fruit of the blessing and bearers of destinies unknown. Jacob was well aware that his elevation of Joseph was a piece of arbitrary self-indulgence, which might easily come to clash with the vast designs of God and so reveal itself as culpable presumption. Indeed, it seemed already to have done so; for though Joseph's folly may have been the immediate occasion of the catastrophe, and though Jacob had suffered in chiding him, yet the father well knew who it was who must pay for this folly, before God and man. In contending with Joseph he contended with himself. The boy had been only the medium of whatever mischief had been done; the real culprit was Jacob's own loving heart. It had not availed to hide it from himself; for God knew it, and one hid not himself before God. For the truth was, therein lay the inheritance of Abram, it meant no more than that one did not give false evidence in matters known to God.

Young Joseph

Such were the mental struggles, in the time after the grain harvest, which slowly shaped Jacob's decisions. He had conceived evil in his heart; now that heart must conquer its weakness by seeing to it that the spoilt darling who had been the medium of the harm should also be the medium of the healing. He would treat the lad with a little severity, would lay a responsibility upon him by way of doing penance himself.

Seeing him at a distance he summoned him rather peremptorily: "Joseph!"

"Here am I," answered the boy, and was beside him at once. He was glad to be called, for since the departure of the brothers his father had spoken to him but little. Besides, that last meeting with the brethren had left him, even in his folly, with a feeling of discomfortable anxiety.

"Hearken," said Jacob. Some obscure motive made him feign absent-mindedness; he blinked repeatedly and drew his beard through his hand. "Tell me if I am right in thinking that thy elder brothers are grazing the sheep together in the vale of Shechem?"

"Yes, of a surety," responded Joseph; "for it seemeth to me too, if my memory erreth not, they desired to go together to Shechem to tend thy flocks, on account of the fat meadows there and because this valley will not hold all of thine."

"So it is," confirmed Jacob, "and it is for this reason that I called thee. For I hear naught of the sons of Leah, and of the sons of the maids all knowledge is hidden from me. It is not known to me how it standeth in the meadows of Shechem; whether Yitzchak's blessing was upon the summer lambing or whether my herds are afflicted with swelling and with liver fluke. For my children thy brothers, I know naught of them nor hear whether they exercise our pasture rights in peace, in that district where, as I mind me, serious things once came to pass. It giveth me to think; and in such thoughts I resolved to send thee to them to greet them from me."

"Here am I," cried Joseph again. He flashed his white teeth at his father, hopped up and down, and stamped with his heels, on fire to be off.

"When I consider," went on Jacob, "that thou enterest into the eighteenth year of thy age, methinks it is time to put thy manhood to some sterner test than thou hast known. And therefore I am resolved to stir thee up to this mission; that thou leavest me for thy brothers, for some short space; to inquire of them concerning all that of which I am ignorant, and to return to me, with God's help, after ten or nine days and tell me what thou hast learned."

"Verily, here am I," cried Joseph again, enraptured with the idea. "My father's words are golden and silver. I will make a journey across the land, I will visit the brethren and look after things in the vale of Shechem, and all that will be the greatest pleasure. Could I have wished for my heart's desire, it would not have been other than this."

39

Jacob said: "Thou dost not go to look after things. Thy brethren are men enough to do that themselves and need not a child. Moreover, that is not the sense in which I send thee. Rather shalt thou bow before them with all seemliness and the forms of courtesy and speak thus: 'I am come some days' journey to greet you and ask after your well-being, from my own desire as well as at my father's bidding, for our wishes in this matter are one.'"

"Give me Parosh to ride; he is long-legged and hard, very strong-boned, and like to my brother Issachar."

"It speaketh for thy manliness," answered Jacob after a pause, "that thou rejoicest over thy mission and regardest it not as strange to go away from me for a number of days, so that the moon shall change from a sickle to a half-round before I see thee again. But say to thy brethren: 'The father willed it.'"

"Shall I have Parosh?"

"I am indeed minded not to deal with thee softly, but according to thy age. Yet the ass Parosh I will not give thee, for he is balky, and his intelligence doth not keep pace with his fire. A much better choice is white Hulda, a friendly and careful beast, also smart to look at; when thou journeyest abroad thou shalt ride her. But that thou mayst know that I expect somewhat of thee, and that the brothers may know it too, it is my command that thou makest the journey alone, from here to the meadows of Shechem. For I will give thee no servant along with thee nor let Eliezer ride at thy side. Thou shalt travel independently and shalt tell the brethren: 'Alone I come, upon a white ass, to visit you, according to our father's will.' Then may it be that thou needest not ride back alone, but that the brethren may journey with thee, some or all. At least such is my second purpose in this order."

"That I will contrive," promised Joseph; "I make myself bail to bring them back to thee; indeed, I will be guarantee therefor and say to thee I come not again unless to bring them to thee."

Thus Joseph pranced about his father, prattling away heedlessly and giving praise to Yah that he was to travel by himself and see the world. He ran off to Benjamin and to Eliezer the old man to tell them all. Jacob, looking after him, nodded his head. For he perceived that if one could speak of a challenge, it was directed toward himself and nobody else. But was he not doing rightly and acting as his inward responsibility for Joseph bade him act? He would not see the lad for several days; it seemed to him sufficient penance; and he refused to speculate as to what the upper spheres would have considered due severity. He reckoned with a failure of Joseph's mission; that is, he realized that the latter might return without the brethren. That they might return without him was so frightful a thought that his conscious mind did not even deal with the possibility. But since things always turn out otherwise than as one had

thought, we might forestall destiny by our fears and apprehensions as with an exorcism; and therefore fate paralyses our imagination, that it may deal its crushing blows unhampered by our preventive spells.

The needful preparations for Joseph's journey put Jacob in mind of his own past and of that fateful day when Rebecca got him ready and he left, after the transfer of the blessing which she had conceived and carried through. And his soul was full of the solemn emotions of recurrence. Certainly the comparison was far-fetched enough. For his was by no means the heroic part which Rebecca had played when she deliberately sacrificed her own heart, assumed responsibility for the rectifying deceit, and then, fully conscious that she would probably never see him again, sent away the beloved son into a strange land. The theme admitted of some variations. True, Joseph too was leaving home on account of his outraged brethren's wrath; yet he was not flying from the wrath; Jacob was sending him as it were into Esau's arms. It was the scene by Jabbok ford which Jacob had in mind and whose recurrence he was so eager to bring about: the outward humiliation, the outward reconciliation which was inwardly so full of reservations; the smoothing over of obvious discords, the achievement of apparent harmony. How different from all that was Rebecca's resolute assumption of the guilt! Jacob's aim in sending Joseph was the impossible one of putting things back where they were; but since it was already plain that that could not be done, the result would simply be a resumption of the game, in which the pieces were Jacob's weakness, Joseph's blind conceit, and the brothers' deadly grudge, and which would have led, in all probability, to the same result.

But it held so far good, that the favourite was being sent a journey on account of fraternal discord; and Jacob conformed to the pattern by fixing the time of Joseph's departure for the earliest dawn, before sunrise, it having been so in his own case. But when the parting took place, Jacob—or rather Rebecca, for he was playing the mother's rôle—held the traveller in long embrace, murmuring blessings against his cheek; took an amulet from his own neck and hung it round the boy's, pressed him to his heart again and again, and all in all behaved as though Joseph were to be gone for years or for ever, seventeen days or more distant Naharain-wards, into the unknown, whereas instead, amply supplied with provisions, he was setting out, to his own great joy, on safe roads and to travel no farther than to Shechem. Which shows that a man can behave out of all proportion, as measured by his own knowledge; while from the point of view of the still unknown destiny his conduct may turn out to have been only too suitable. There may even lie some consolation therein, when we learn the real state of the case. Thus men should never take leave of each other lightly; for then, should the worst happen, they can say to themselves: "At least I did press him to my heart!"

Father and son took leave in the dawning, standing at the stirrup of white Hulda, who was laden down with good things and adorned with glass beads and bright worsted flowers. The leave-taking, of course, was only the last of the many counsels, admonitions, warnings which had gone before. Jacob had instructed the boy in his route and the well-known stages on it, just in his mother's way; had warned him of the dangers of overheating and sudden cold; given him the names of folk and brethren in the faith in the various villages at which the traveller might spend the night; and sternly forbade him, when he touched at the city of Urusalim and saw at Baal's temple the dwellings of those consecrate to Ashera, who lived and moved and had their being in her, to permit himself the smallest speech with them. Above all he enjoined him to behave with particular courtesy toward the brethren. It could do no harm, he remarked, were Joseph to fling himself down seven times before them, addressing them frequently as lords, when they would in all likelihood resolve to dip their hand at once in the bowl with him and not to go from his side for the rest of their lives.

Much of all this Rebecca-Jacob repeated afresh in the grey morning, before he allowed the youth to fling his leg over his ass, chirrup to it, and ride off northwards. Jacob even went a piece alongside the lively Hulda, as she curvetted in the high spirits of the dawn. But he could not keep it up long, and stopped with an absurdly heavy heart. One last gleam of Joseph's teeth as the lad looked laughing back and waved his hand; then his son's figure was hidden by a turn in the road. Joseph had ridden away, he saw him no more.

JOSEPH JOURNEYS TOWARD SHECHEM

The boy, no longer under the father's eye, but pleasantly absorbed in his own well-being, sitting far back on the crupper of his beast, with his slim brown legs stretched out and his body leaning gallantly backwards, trotted in the tender light of the morning sun through hilly country, on the road to Bethlahma. He felt entirely in harmony with the whole situation as he saw it, viewed with amused and indulgent forbearance the long-drawn-out character of Jacob's farewell, and felt not a whit weighed down by the consciousness that at this first separation he had snapped his fingers at the parental concern.

Jacob, certainly, had expended himself in instruction and advice, forgetting neither precept nor warning. One thing only had he neglected; by reason of a singular and not quite innocent lapse of memory he had refrained from cautioning the boy on a certain matter, upon a certain subject, or object; nor did it again occur to his mind's eye until so horribly made present to his material sight. It was the *ketonet;* he had not

told Joseph to leave it at home and Joseph had slyly and silently taken advantage of the lapse. He had it with him. He was so on fire to show himself to the great world in the garment that he had literally trembled lest the father at the last minute might think to forbid it. It is quite possible that he would in this case have lied to the old man, saying that the sacred embroidery lay in the chest, whereas in reality it was packed among his luggage. The milkwhite Hulda was a charming beast, a three-year-old, wise and sweet-tempered, if also inclined to the harmless and engaging tricks which will sometimes betray the individuality of the dumb brute. She had eloquent velvet ears and a droll fuzzy forelock hanging down to the great soft, playful eyes, the corners of which were too prone to gather flies. From Hulda's back various supplies and requisites for the journey were hung on both sides: the goatskin full of sour thin milk to slake the thirst; and many-coloured baskets and earthen pots with oatmeal and fruit cakes, parched corn, salt olives, cucumbers, roast onions, and fresh cheeses. All this and more, designed for the refreshment of the traveller himself and for presents to his brothers, the father carefully inspected; only one thing he failed to examine, an object which since time immemorial had formed the most indispensable luggage on a journey: a circular piece of leather, sewn round the edge with metal rings, which served the traveller as table-cloth and as table too. It was a Bedouin invention, particularly in use by desert folk; they ran a string through the rings and hung it up as a bag for the journey. Joseph had done this too; and with thievish joy he had thrust the *ketonet* into this leather bag.

Since he had inherited it, he reasoned, since it was his own, why not show himself in it on his travels? The neighbourhood folk on road and field recognized him and joyfully called him by name. But after some hours' travel no one would know him; it would be well to show them, and not alone by the wealth of his provisioning, that a fine gentleman was riding by. And thus, the more so that the sun was rising too, he soon drew out the splendid garment and put it on in his own way, to protect his head; so that the myrtle garland which he wore rested not upon his hair, but upon the veil that framed his face.

On this first day he did not reach the shrine, to honour which had been another reason for wearing the *ketonet*. Jacob had admonished him with tears, also his own desire urged him, to stop there for sacrifice and prayer. It was only a furlong from Bethlahma, where he spent the night with a man of Jacob's acquaintance, a carpenter, who believed in God. Early on the second morning, after parting from his host, his wife, and their friends, he reached the spot. Hulda waited under the crutched mulberry tree while Joseph, arrayed in the bridal finery, performed his prayers and poured his libations at the stone which had been erected by the way—the memorial for God, who, seeing it, might be reminded of what He had once done at this place.

The stillness of the morning lay upon the vineyards and the rocky plots of ground; there was as yet no movement upon the Urusalim road. A little wind played carelessly in the shining foliage of the tree. The landscape was still; and silently the shrine where Jacob once had laid the child of Laban to rest received the oblations and prayers of her son. He put water by the stone, and raisin bread; kissed the ground, beneath which a life so ready and willing had gone down; and stood up again, to murmur formulas of veneration with lifted hands, and the eyes and lips which he had from the departed. Nothing answered from the depths. The past kept silence, folded in forgetfulness, unable to feel. Such of it as had survived and was here present was himself, who wore her bridal gown and turned her very eyes toward heaven. Why could the maternal spirit, residing still in his own flesh and blood, not have warned him against his fate? Alas, it could not speak, being held in bonds by childish folly and self-indulgence.

Joseph went on his way in great good cheer, upon made roads and along mountain paths. It was the smoothest journey in the world, its pleasantness unmarred by any mishap or unforeseen incident. Not that the earth exactly sprang to meet him. Rather it spread itself charmingly before his eyes and bade him welcome through the eyes and mouths of people whithersoever he came. He was strange to all, but his type is extraordinarily popular in these regions, and not alone by virtue of the veil did his appearance meet with favour and applause from all who saw him, especially the women. They sat suckling their babes, by the garish sunlit village walls, made of loose baked loam and dung; and the comfort afforded them by the suckling was heightened by the sight of the charming and well-favoured youth who rode past.

"Health to thee, thou sight for sore eyne!" they called to him. "Blessed be she who bore thee, heart's darling!"

"And to you all health," responded Joseph, flashing his teeth. "May your sons have dominion over many!"

"Thousand thanks," they called after him. "May Ashtar favour thee. Thou art like to one of her gazelles." For they all swore by Ashera and thought of naught but her service.

Many, again thanks to the veil, but also on the ground of his lavish provisioning, actually took him for a god and were inclined to worship him. Still this was only in the countryside, not in the walled towns such as Beth Shemesh, Kirjath Ajin, Kerem Baalat, or the like, by whose ponds and city gates he chatted with the people, a crowd of whom often gathered round him. He astonished and delighted them by his urban culture, speaking of the magic numbers of God, of the wonders of the pendulum, and of the peoples of the globe. He told them too, in order to flatter them, of the harlot of Uruk, who civilized the man of the forest; and in all that he said he displayed such a charming sense of form and

langauage that they thought amongst themselves: he might well be the *mazkir* of a city prince and a great king's admonisher!

He dazzled them by the knowledge of tongues which he had gleaned with old Eliezer's help; speaking Hittite at the city gate with a man from Hatti, Mittannian with one from the north, and a few words of Egyptian with a cattle-dealer from the delta. It was not much that he knew; but a clever man speaks better with ten words than a fool with a hundred, and he knew how to create, if not in his interlocutor, at least in the crowd, the impression of wonderful polyglot facility. For a woman who had had a horrible dream he interpreted her dream for her at the fountain. She dreamed that her little son, a three-year-old boy, had suddenly grown larger than herself and wore a beard. That meant, he told her, rolling the whites of his eyes into view, that her son would soon leave her and she would indeed see him again, but only after many years, as a grown man, with a beard. . . . As the woman was very poor and would quite possibly be forced to sell her son into slavery, the interpretation had a certain probability in itself, and all the folk marvelled at so much beauty and wisdom embodied in the young traveller.

He always had many invitations and might have been a guest for days at a time. But he did not pause longer than human courtesy required, following as well as might be his father's directions for the journey. Of the three nights which separated his four days of travel, he spent the second in a house as the guest of a silversmith, named Abisai, who had once visited Jacob and who, while not exclusively adhering to the God of Abraham, yet paid Him homage and excused the fact that he made idols of the moon metal by saying that after all he had to live. That Joseph granted him as a man of the world, and slept under his roof. The third of the brief spans of darkness he passed in the open, in a fig grove where he made his bed; for he had rested in the heat of the day and thus reached his third station so late that he hesitated to enter the town. The same thing happened the last night, as he neared his goal. For he had slept again under trees in the daytime, overcome by the power of the sun, and taken the road again only toward evening. Thus the second night watch had come on as he reached the narrow valley of Shechem. And from this moment on, in the measure that his journey had been easy and pleasant, by so much did it now seem altogether bewitched and bedevilled. He entered the valley and by the light of the moon that swam, a slender bark in the skies, beheld the walled town with citadel and temple lying on the slope of Garizim; and thereafter nothing went right, but everything wrong and wry to the extreme; Joseph, indeed, was tempted to connect the change in his fortunes with the person of the man who met him in the night before Shechem and made himself his companion for the last stage of his journey, leading up to the greatest change of all.

THE MAN ON THE FIELD

We are told that "he was wandering in the field." But what is the meaning of that? Had his father expected too much of him, and did young Joseph order his affairs so badly that he went astray and wandered lost? By no means. Wandering is not necessarily going astray, and if one seeks what is not there, he does not need to stray in order not to find it. Joseph had as a boy spent several years in the vale of Shechem; the neighbourhood was not strange to him, even though his familiarity with it had the quality of dreams, and likewise it was night, with an ineffectual moon. He did not stray, he sought; and since he did not find, his seeking became a straying in space. In the darkness and stillness, leading his beast by the bridle, he wandered about among rolling stretches of meadow and plough-land, above which the mountain brooded darkly in the starlight, and he thought: "Where may the brothers be?" He came upon sheepfolds, of course, where the sheep slept standing; but whether these were Jacob's sheep was unknown, and there were no human creatures, the stillness being intense.

Then he heard a voice and perceived that he was addressed by a man whose approaching step he had not heard, but who nevertheless had overtaken him and was now by his side. If he had come toward Joseph the lad would have spoken; as it was, the stranger got in first, and said:

"Whom seekest thou?"

He did not ask: "What seekest thou here?" but simply: "Whom seekest thou?" and it may be that just this way of asking conditioned Joseph's rather childish and thoughtless answer. The lad was tired and confused, and his joy at meeting a human being in this accursed night walk was so great that he made the man, just because he was a man, the object of a simple and uncalled-for confidence. He said:

"I am seeking for my brethren. Tell me, dear man, I pray thee, where they graze."

The dear man took no offence at the simplicity of this request. He seemed to be in a position to disregard it and forbore to say to Joseph that his request was somewhat vague. He answered:

"They are not here, nor yet even in this neighbourhood."

Joseph looked at him in bewilderment as they went. He saw him quite clearly. This was not yet a man in the full meaning of the word, being only a few years older than Joseph; but taller, really tall; wearing a sleeveless linen tunic drawn loosely through a girdle, thus freeing the knees, and a little mantle flung back over the shoulder. His head, resting upon a somewhat thick neck, seemed small by comparison; his brown hair made an oblique wave that partly covered the forehead down to the

46

eyebrows. His nose was large, straight, and firmly modelled, the space between it and the small red mouth very narrow, but the depression beneath so soft yet so pronounced that the chin jutted out like a full round fruit. He turned his head rather affectedly on his shoulder and looked across it at Joseph. His eyes were not unlovely, but half-shut, with weary, half-dazed expression, as of one politely forbearing to yawn. His arms were round, but white and rather weak. He wore sandals and carried a stick which he had obviously cut for a staff.

"Not here, then," repeated the boy. "How can that be? They said so definitely that they were all going together to Shechem when they left home. Dost thou know them, then?"

"A little," answered his companion. "As much as is needful. Oh no, very familiar with them I am not, indeed no. Why dost thou seek them?"

"Because my father sent me to them, to greet them and to see whether things go well with them."

"Indeed! Then thou art a messenger. Even as I. I often make journeys on foot with my staff. But also I am a guide."

"A guide?"

"Yes, truly. I guide travellers and open the ways for them; that is my business and therefore I spoke to thee as I saw that thou wast seeking as thou wentest."

"Thou seemest to know that my brethren are not here. But dost thou know where they are?"

"I think so."

"Then tell me."

"Art thou then so eager to see them?"

"Certainly I am eager for my goal, and that is my brethren, to whom my father hath sent me."

"Well, then, I will name it to thee, thy goal. When I came by this place the last time on my ways, a few days ago, I heard thy brethren say: 'Up, we will go to Dothan with a part of the sheep, for a change.'"

"To Dothan?"

"Why not to Dothan? It occurred to them and they did it. There is sweet pasturage in the valley of Dothan, and the people of the settlement on their hill are good for trade, they buy sinews, milk, and wool. Why art thou surprised?"

"Surprised I am not, for there is no matter for it. But it is an evil star. I was so certain I should find the brethren here."

"Thou art not much used to having things go against thy will? Thou seemest a mother's boy to me."

"I have no mother," replied Joseph in some annoyance.

"Nor I," said the stranger. "Perhaps a father's boy?"

"No matter for that," responded Joseph. "Rather advise me, what shall I do now?"

"Very simple. Thou goest to Dothan."

"But it is night and we are tired, Hulda and I. To Dothan, for so much I know already, is more than a furlong from here. With easy going it is a day's journey."

"Or a night's. Since thou sleepest under the trees by day, thou must take the night to reach thy goal."

"How dost thou know that I slept under the trees?"

"Asking thy pardon, I saw. I came past on my staff where thou layest, and left thee behind. Then found I thee here."

"I do not know the way to Dothan, especially by night," Joseph complained. "The father hath not described it to me."

"Rejoice then," said the other, "that I found thee. I am a guide and will lead thee, if thou wilt. I will open to thee the road to Dothan without price, since I must go thither myself; I will take thee the shortest way if thou wilt. We can take turns riding on thy ass. A pretty beast," said he, and looked at Hulda with his half-open eyes, whose gaze expressed a negligence and contempt out of harmony with his words. "Pretty as thyself. But its pasterns are too weak."

"Hulda," Joseph said, "is next to Parosh the best ass in Israel's stables. No one thinketh that her pasterns are weak."

The stranger made a wry face. "Thou wouldst do better," he said, "not to contradict me. It is foolish in more than one way, first because thou art in my care that thou mayest find thy brothers, and second because I am older than thou. These two reasons will be clear to thee. When I say thy ass hath frail pasterns, then they are frail; there is no occasion for thee to defend them as though thou hadst made the ass, when thou canst only step before him and name him. And while we are talking about names, I should also like to beg thee not to call the good Jacob Israel in my hearing. It is unfitting and annoyeth me. Give him his proper name and leave these high-flown titles alone."

Pleasant the man was not. He continued to speak across his own shoulder with a weary politeness which seemed every minute about to pass into an incomprehensible irritation. This inclination to ill temper seemed to contradict his ready offer to help a complete stranger; indeed, it took away half the effect, since he appeared to be helpful against his own will. Perhaps he only wanted to lift to Dothan. For he mounted the ass as they set out, and Joseph walked alongside, chafing under the man's ill-will over the name of Israel. He said:

"It is his title of honour which he got at Jabbok ford after his victory."

"I find it absurd," the other retorted, "that thou talkest of victory, where there can be no talk of anything of the sort! A proper victory, from which one cometh off halting all the rest of one's life, carrying off, indeed, a name, but not that of him with whom he wrestled! Moreover," he said suddenly, making his eyeballs roll round in a circle in the most

extraordinary way, "pay no heed to me, but call thy father Israel if it please thee. It hath its justification, and my opposition was mere caprice. Likewise I note that I am sitting upon thy ass," he added, making his eyeballs perform the circuit once again. "If thou preferrest I will get off so that thou canst mount."

A singular man. He appeared to regret his former unfriendliness; yet even the repentance seemed no deeper or more spontaneous than his readiness to help. Joseph on the other hand was friendly by nature, and held with the principle that one best meets strangeness with increase of friendliness. He answered:

"Since thou guidest me and openest out of kindness the way to my brethren, thou hast a right to my animal. Sit still, I pray thee, and we shall change anon. Thou hast walked the whole day, whereas I could ride."

"Many thanks," said the youth. "Thy words are indeed no more than becoming, but still I thank thee kindly. I have been temporarily robbed of certain facilities for travel," he added, and shrugged his shoulders. "Do missions and messages make thee pleasure?" he next inquired.

"I rejoiced when the father called me," answered Joseph. "Who then sendeth thee?"

"Thou mayest understand that many messengers go to and fro between the great lords east and south through this land," responded the other. "Who actually sendeth thee, that thou dost not know at all; the commission goes through many mouths and it helps thee little to follow it to its source; in any case thou must take to the road. At present I have a letter to deliver in Dothan," said he, "which I carry in my girdle. But I can see in the future that I must also play the guard."

"The guard?"

"Yes, I am liable, for instance, to be commanded to watch over a well or some shrine or other, of which there is question. Messenger, guide, guard—all these I must play as they come, according to the taskmaster's will. Whether it give one pleasure and whether one actually feel made for the task is another matter, which I put aside. Likewise will I not inquire whether one has understanding for the ideas which give rise to these missions. No, I prefer to leave such questions open; only saying, as between ourselves, that there is much incomprehensible urgency about the matter. Dost thou love mankind?"

He put the question abruptly; yet it did not come to Joseph as a surprise, since the stranger's whole bearing displayed an arrogant displeasure with the human species, and a disinclination to go about his business among men. Joseph answered:

"We usually smile at each other, mankind and I."

"Yes, because thou art known to be beautiful and well-favoured," said his guide. "Wherefore they smile at thee and thou smilest back, in order to strengthen them in their folly. Thou wouldst do better to show

them a gloomy mien and say: 'What would you with your smiling? These hairs will fall out, alas, and these now white teeth as well; these eyes are only a jelly of blood and water; they will dissolve away and this whole hollow charm of the flesh will shrivel and shamefully decay.' It would be decent for thee to sober them, by the remembrance of what they know already, though they let themselves be beguiled by the servile smile of the present moment. Such creatures as thou are naught but a fleeting and dissembling gloss upon the horror of all flesh beneath the surface. I do not say that even this skin and husk is the most appetizing in the world, with its steaming pores and sweat-glands; but scratch it ever so little and the salt scarlet brew comes out, while the deeper one goes, the worse it gets; it is sheer guts and stink. The beautiful and well-favoured should be beautiful and well-favoured through and through, solid and fine-grained and not filled up with dirt and jelly."

"Then," said Joseph, "you must stick to graven and carven images, for instance to the beautiful god which the women hide in the shrubbery and seek lamenting that they may bury him in the pit. He is beautiful through and through, of solid olive-wood, not gory and steaming. But they wish him to look as though he were not solid, but bleeding from the tusk of the boar; they paint upon him red wounds and deceive themselves so that they may weep over his dear life lost. So it is: either life is deception, or beauty. Thou canst not find both united in truth."

"Fie," said the guide, puckering his round chin and looking down over his shoulder with half-closed eyes at his companion.

"No," he added after a pause, "say what thou wilt, it is an ugly breed, that drinketh unrighteousness like water and has long since merited another flood, this time without an ark."

"Thou art most likely just, in the matter of the unrighteousness," Joseph responded. "But consider that everything cometh in pairs in the world, part and counterpart, to the end that one may distinguish between them; and if the one were not next the other, then they both were not. Without life were no death, without riches no poverty, and if we made an end of stupidity, who could speak of cleverness? But thus is it with purity and impurity, so much is clear. The unclean beast speakest to the clean one: 'Give thanks to me, for if I were not, then how shouldst thou know that thou art pure, and who would call thee so?' And the evil man to the just: 'Fall at my feet, for without me where were thine advantage?'"

"Thou hast said it," answered the stranger. "For it is just that which I mistrust from my soul, this dual world; I do not understand the necessity for a breed whose purity can be spoken of only comparatively and in retrospect. Yet one hath always to be mindful of him, there are always plans regarding him, goodness knows how far-reaching, and this and that to be brought about respecting his puny little future—just as now, for instance, I must see that thou comest to thy right goal, thou bag of wind! It maketh me to weep with boredom."

"The vexatious creature, why then does he show me the way, if it is such a burden to him?" Joseph thought. "It is stupid to play the agreeable and then to sulk. It is clear he has only been thinking of the ride. He might get off too; we were going to take turns. He talks just like a man," he thought, and smiled to himself over the way people have of criticizing their own kind and excepting themselves, so that the man sits in judgement over mankind as though he were not one of them. Then he said:

"Yea, thou talkest of humanity and sittest in judgement, saying of what bad stuff it is composed. But there was a time when even to the children of God themselves man seemed not so evil, since they went in unto his daughters, and giants and mighty men were conceived."

The guide turned his head in his affected way toward the shoulder farther from Joseph.

"Thou knowest all the little stories, I see," he answered with titter. "For thy years thou'rt informed in events, that I must say. For my part, be it said, I consider the tale to be idle gossip. But if it be true, then let me tell thee why it was that the children of light so behaved to the daughters of Cain. They did so from excess of contempt, yes, verily. Knowest thou why destruction came upon the daughters of Cain? They went with uncovered shame and mated like cattle. Their whoredom so mocked all bounds that man as it were could not look at it without being tempted—I know not if thou understandest that. They went to all extremes, they threw their garments on the ground and went forth without them. If they had not known shame, it might have answered and the sight of them would not have got into the bones of the children of light. But they well knew shame, they were, on religious grounds, very chaste indeed, and their lust consisted precisely therein, that they would tread shame underfoot—can such a thing be borne? The man had intercourse with mother and daughter and brother's wife openly and on the streets, and they had altogether one thought in mind: the frightful enjoyment of wounded shame. Must that not seize upon the members of the children of light? They were tempted by their scorn—canst thou not understand that? The last shred of respect was gone from them for this breed, who were set under their noses, as though there were not enough already in the world, and whom they should have respected on grounds of higher necessity. They found that man simply existed for unchastity, and their contempt took the form of lasciviousness. If thou canst not understand all that, thou art but a calf."

"I can understand it if I try," replied Joseph. "But how dost thou come to know it?"

"Ask thy old Eliezer, too, whence cometh what he teacheth thee. I know as much of the events too, perhaps even more, moving to and fro in the world as I do, as messenger, guide, and guard; I come to hear the most various things. I can assure thee that the flood only came at

last because it appeared that the contempt of the children of light for mankind had taken the form of desire. That turned the scale; otherwise it would perhaps never have happened. I need only add that the children of light were of fixed purpose to bring on the flood. But unfortunately there was the ark, and man came in again by the back door."

"Let us be glad of that," said Joseph. "Otherwise we should not be here chatting on the way to Dothan and *taking turns* to ride according to our agreement."

"Thou art right," replied the other, and again rolled his eyes round. "I forget everything chattering. Of course I must lead thee and guard thee that thou comest to thy brethren. But who is more important, the watcher or the watched? Not without some bitterness must I answer: the watched is more important, for for him is the watcher there, and not the other way about. Therefore I will now dismount and thou shalt ride, and I walk beside thee in the dust."

"I can stand that too," said Joseph, as he mounted. "It is after all pure chance that thou canst ride even a part of the time and not go all the way in the dust."

So they went on under the stars by the pale moonlight, northwards from Shechem toward Dothan through broad and narrow valleys, over steep hills, clothed in forests of cedar and acacia, past sleeping villages. Joseph too slept by the hour as he sat on the ass, and the guide walked in the dust. But awaking out of such slumber—it was already dawn—he missed a little basket of pressed fruit and another of roast onions from the ass's load and noted reluctantly that the folds of his guide's girdle were correspondingly fuller. The man stole! It was a painful discovery and showed how little ground he had had to except himself when he criticized the race of mankind. Joseph said never a word; indeed, he himself in their conversation had defended the evil for the sake of its opposite. Moreover, the man was a guide and thus dedicate to Nabu, the lord of the westernmost point in the cycle, leading down into the underworldly half of the world—a servant, that is, of the god of thieves. One might assume that he had performed a pious and symbolic act when he stole from his sleeping charge. For all these reasons Joseph said naught of his discovery, but reverenced the dishonesty of the man, in the guise of religious duty. Yet it was painful to learn that the guide had stolen, out and out. The fact might be a fresh explanation of his willingness to play the guide; in my case it impressed Joseph unfavourably and cast him down.

But something much worse than the theft happened soon enough. The sun had come up behind field and wood and Dothan's green hill was already in sight; it lay diagonally on their right in the morning sunshine, with the village on its top. Joseph, sitting on the ass while the thief held the bridle, was looking thither; there was a jerk and a fall, and it

had happened. Hulda had gone into a hole with her forefoot, had fallen, and could not get up again. She had broken her pastern. They both examined it.

"Broken," said the guide, shortly. "What a fix! Have I not said to thee the pasterns were weak?"

"Thou shouldst not rejoice even if thou art right; the words should not come in thy mouth. Thou wast leading her and wast not careful, so that she stepped into the hole."

"I was not careful and thou complainest of me? But so it is with human beings; they must have someone to blame when things go wrong, even though it was prophesied beforehand."

"It is also the way of mankind to have wilfully foreseen misfortune and to make a petty triumph of it. Be glad that I complain of thee only for heedlessness, I might have accused thee of other things as well. If thou hadst not advised me to ride by night, then we should not have overtired Hulda and a wise beast like her would never have stumbled."

"Dost thou think the pastern will be made good again by thy lamentings?"

"No," Joseph said. "That I do not. But that brings me back to the question: what shall I do? I cannot after all leave my beast lying here with all the load of provisions which I was to present to the brethren in Jacob's name. There remaineth much though I have eaten some and more has been got rid of in other ways. Shall Hulda die helpless here and the beasts of the fields eat my goods? I am near to weep from vexation."

"And who knows again what to do but I?" responded the stranger. "Did I not say that I can play the watchman, when need is? Go then, for I will sit here and watch thy beast, and the provisions, and frighten off birds and other thieves. Whether I am born for such a task is another matter which we need not talk of here. Enough, I will sit and guard thy ass until thou hast gone to the brethren and come back with them or a couple of servants to fetch the goods and look after the beast to see if it is to be cured or killed."

"Thanks," said Joseph, "so let us do. I can see thou art just like a man; thou hast thy good sides and of the others we will not speak. I will make all haste and return again with help."

"I will await thee. Thou canst not go wrong: round the hill and then back into the valley behind it five hundred paces through scrub and clover—there wilt thou find thy brethren, near a well where there is no water. If thou needest aught from thy ass bethink thee now. Not a head-cloth to shield thee from the sun?"

"Thou'rt right," cried Joseph. "The mischance hath robbed me of my head. That will I not leave here," said he, and drew the *ketonet* out of the beringed leather bag, "nor in thy care either, whatever good side

53

thou showest. For I will take it with me afoot into the vale of Dothan, that I may arrive in splendour even if not on white Hulda as Jacob would have wished. I will put it on at once and before thine eyes—so—and so—and thus, and thus. How dost thou like it? Am I not a gay shepherd-bird in my coat of many colours? Mami's veil, how doth it become her son?"

OF LAMECH AND HIS HURT

Meanwhile Leah's sons and those of the maids sat, all ten, behind the hill at the bottom of the valley round a burnt-out fire where they had cooked their morning mess; they stared into the ashes. They had all risen betimes from their striped tents set up at some distance in the shrubbery; had risen singly, but all very early, some even before dawn; for their sleep had relished them little. They had got, in fact, but little refreshment from it since they had left Hebron; indeed, they had exchanged the pastures of Sechem for the vale of Dothan out of no other than the desolate hope that it might refresh them better elsewhere.

They had gone grumbling to the well, stumbling with stiff joints over the matted and twisted roots of gorse. It was a well of fresh water near the place where the flocks were scattered over the field; for the well close at hand was dry at this time of year. They had drunk, washed themselves, and prayed, looked after the lambs, and then assembled at the eating-place in the shade of a group of red-trunked, branching pines. The view from here took in the level country dotted with single trees and shrubbery, the hill with the village of Dothan on top, the distant flocks of sheep, and the low mountains in the background. The sun was already well up. The air was full of scents of sun-warmed grass, of fennel, thyme, and other field odours beloved of sheep.

The sons of Jacob sat in a circle upon their haunches, in their midst the dying brushwood fire with the pot atop. They had long since finished eating and sat there idle and red-eyed, their bodies sated, but their souls gnawed by a hunger and dry thirst to which they could not have given a name, but which spoiled their sleep and made their food like ashes to them. A thorn was in their flesh, in the flesh of each one. It could not be pulled out, it festered, tortured, and consumed. They felt slack, and most of them had headache. When they tried to clench their fists they could not. These men who once, to do vengeance for Dinah, had bathed Shechem in blood, asked themselves if they were the men for like deeds today; and they answered no, they were no longer those men. The gnawing worm of their grievance, the festering thorn, the hunger in their inwards unnerved and unmanned them. Simeon and Levi, that savage pair, suffered especially from their shameful state. One of them poked dully

54

with his crook in the dying embers. The other, Simeon, swaying his body
to and fro, began a half-muttered singsong, in which some of the rest
joined one after another. It was an ancient ditty, a fragment of some
half-forgotten ballad or epic, from times far remote:

> And Lamech the hero took unto him two wives,
> The name of the one was Adah and the name of the other was Zillah.
> Adah and Zillah, hear my voice;
> Ye wives of Lamech, hearken unto my speech!
> For I have slain a man to my wounding
> And a young man to my hurt.
> If Cain shall be avenged sevenfold,
> Truly Lamech seven and seventyfold.

That was all they knew, it was without beginning or ending. So they
stopped there; yet hung on the sound, as it died away, seeing in their
mind's eye Lamech the hero, how he came up armed and glowing with
pride from his deed and told his women, as they bowed before him, how
that he had washen his heart clean. They saw the young man laid low
and lying in the blood-stained grass, the almost guiltless sin-offering for
Lamech's frantically sensitive honour. The plain word "man" was sof-
tened to the tenderer "young man" in the next line, and in the sacredness
of his suffering and death might well have roused emotions of pity at
least in the hearts of Adah and Zillah, being women. Even so, they could
only have enhanced their adoration of Lamech's implacable and incor-
ruptible virility and unquenchable thirst for revenge, these being the
ringing theme of the ancient saga.

"Lamech he was called," said Leah's Levi, thrusting his charred
stick into the fire till it broke. "Does it please you all? I ask that because
it pleaseth me well and even very well. That was a man, a blade, a lion-
heart, a fellow of the ancient mould; there are no more of his like. He
lives only in a song, which we sing to refresh ourselves with thoughts of
the past. With his heart washed clean he might come before his wives;
and if he visited his strength upon them, one after the other, then they
knew what manner of man they received, and trembled with desire.
Dost thou come so before Shuah's daughter, Judah, or thou, Dan, before
the Moabitess? Tell me what has become of the breed since then, that it
begets only the prudent and pious, but no true men?"

Reuben answered him:—

"I will tell thee what takest man's revenge out of his hand and
bringeth it about that we are grown unlike to Lamech, the hero. It is two-
fold: Babel's law and the jealousy of God, both of which say: 'Venge-
ance is mine.' For revenge must be taken from the man, otherwise it
breeds furiously on, rank as the swamp, and the world is full of blood.
For what was Lamech's end? Thou dost not know, for the song telleth

it not. But the youth whom he slew had a son or a brother, who struck Lamech down, that the earth received his blood likewise. Then one out of Lamech's loins slew Lamech's murderer out of revenge, and thus it went on, until neither of Lamech's seed nor of the seed of the slain youth was there any left, but the earth might close its maw, for it was sated. But it is not good so, it is a weedy growth of revenge and groweth by no rule. Hence it was, when Cain slew Abel, God set His mark upon him, that he belonged to Him and spoke: 'Whosoever slayeth Cain, vengeance shall be taken on him sevenfold.' But Babel decreed that man should humble himself to judgement for blood-guilt and not revel in revenge."

Thereto Gad, son of Zilpah, in all his directness:

"Yea, so speakest thou, Reuben, with thy thin voice which cometh out of thy mighty body, and however often one heareth it one is surprised. Had I thy limbs I would not speak like thee and defend the revolution of time and its changes, which unman heroes and breed no more lion-hearts in the world. Where is the pride of thy body, that thou speakest with thin voice and wilt put thy vengeance into God's hands for submit it to judgement? Shamest not thou thyself before Lamech, who spoke: 'This is a thing between three, between me, and him who offended me, and the earth?' Cain said to Abel: 'Will God console me when Noemah our sweet sister taketh thy gifts and smileth upon thee; or will the judgement decide to whom she belongeth, thee or me? I am the first-born, and so is she mine. Thou art her twin, so is she thine. That God decideth not, nor the judgement of Nimrod. Let us go out upon the field that we may decide it!' And they decided it together; and as I sit here, named Gaddiel, whom Zilpah bore upon Leah's lap, I am for Cain."

"And I, for my part," said Jehudah, "would no more be the young lion as I am called of the people if I were not for Cain and still more for Lamech. He thought well of himself, on my word, and thought not meanly of his pride. 'Seven times?' quoth he. 'Bah! I am Lamech. Seven and seventy times will I be avenged, and there lieth he, the lout, for the sake of my hurt!'"

"What sort of hurt may that have been?" asked Issachar, the bony ass, "and wherein may the pitiful youth have fallen under the mighty Lamech's displeasure, that he left it neither to God nor to Nimrod to avenge, but took vengeance abundantly with his own hand?"

"That no man now knoweth," responded his half-brother Naphtali Bilhah's son. "The nature of the youth's insolence is unknown and what it was which Lamech washed off in his blood, that is lost to the world's memory. Still I have it from hearsay that men in our time swallow shame much more loathsome than that which Lamech suffered. They swallow it, the craven creatures, so we hear, and go away elsewhither, and si them down; and in their belly the shame fermenteth and consumeth that they care neither to eat nor to sleep; and if Lamech whom they ad

mire should see them he would give them a kick behind, for they are worth no more."

He spoke with glib and spitefully fluent tongue, and his face was distorted. The twins groaned and tried to clench their fists but could not. Zebulun said:

"There were Adah and Zillah the wives of Lamech; and Adah is to blame, as I shall show you. For she bore Jabal, the father of such as dwell in tents and of such as have cattle, the ancestor of Abram, of Yitzchak and Jacob our gentle father. Therefrom have we our trouble and our destruction, and are no more men, as thou sayst, brother Levi, but cautious and pious, and as though castrate with the sickle, which may God forbid. Yes, were we huntsmen or even seafarers, all would be changed. But with Jabal, Adah's son, came love of tents into the world, the shepherd nature and Abram's dreams of God, and all that hath weakened us so that we tremble to do our worthy father a hurt, and big Reuben sayeth: 'Vengeance belongeth unto God.' But can one rely by means of abominable dreams upon God and upon His justice when He is a party in the strife and Himself instils arrogance into the good-for-nothing youth? For what can we do against the dreams?" he cried out, his voice cracking in his anguish, "if they are from God and it is ordained that we should bow?"

"But something we might do against the dreamer of the dreams!" shrieked Gad, likewise with heaving chest; and Asher added: "So that the dreams were without a master and no longer knew how to come true!"

"That," replied Reuben, "would likewise have meant setting oneself against God. For it were all one, to set oneself against the dreamer or against God, provided the dreams were from Him." He spoke in the past tense, saying not "would mean" but "would have meant," in token that the question was solved.

It was Dan who spoke after him. He said:

"Hearken, brethren, and give heed to my words, for Dan is called snake and adder, and on account of a certain subtlety he availeth as judge. It is surely true and Reuben is right. If we punish the dreamer, so that the dreams become masterless and powerless, we thereby expose ourselves to the wrath of the self-willed and invoke upon us the vengeance of the unjust. There is no gainsaying it. But so," saith Dan, "we must run the risk, for there is naught imaginable that could be worse or even as bad as the fulfilling of the dream. For in any case self-will will have lost, let it rage and storm as it will, and the dreams shall seek their dreamer in vain. We must act, for only the accomplished deed instructeth. Hath not Jacob too suffered this and that for his deceitfulness and found Laban's service no matter for laughter on account of Esau's bitter tears? Yet he hath endured, for he carried off the main advantage, that

57

is the blessing; it was put aside and in safety, and no God, whoever he was, could have done aught against him however much he would. One must endure tears and revenge for the sake of the good, for what is put aside and in safety, that cometh not again. . . ."

Here his speech, which had begun so subtly, began to wander. But Reuben answered; and it was strange to see that man, strong like a tree in strength, turn pale and white:

"Thou has spoken, Dan, and mayst now be silent. For we have gone thence and departed from the father's hearth. And our annoyance is afar from us and in safety, and in safety we sit at Dothan, five days distant, and all that is an accomplished deed."

And then, after all these speeches, they let their heads droop low, almost between their knees, which stood up high as they squatted on their haunches; and there they crouched round the ashes of their fire, like ten sheaves of misery.

JOSEPH IS THROWN INTO THE PIT

Now it happened that Asher, Zilpah's son, with curiosity unquenched even by affliction, peered out over his knees so that his eyes roved across the plain. And afar off in the morning light he saw something glitter like a flash of silver, which disappeared and came again, sometimes in a single flash, sometimes two or more close together.

Asher jogged his brother Gad as they sat next each other, pointed out the will-o'-the-wisp, and asked him what it meant. They shaded their eyes to look and gestured their surprise; the others saw and heard, and those who sat with their backs to the plain turned round to gaze, following the direction of Asher's eyes; until at last all the brothers had lifted their heads and peered out together at a shimmering figure which was moving toward them.

"One cometh, all shining," Judah spoke. But after they had waited awhile for the figure to come nearer, Dan answered:

"It is not a man, it is a boy."

And with one accord their sunburnt faces all went ashen as Reuben's had done a little time before, and their hearts beat with a wild and rapid rhythm, like drums, so that a hollow concerted drumming noise arose in the breathless stillness.

Joseph came on across the plain, directly toward them, in his coat of many colours, and his garland resting on his veiled head.

They did not believe it. They sat with their thumbs in their cheeks, fingers before their mouths, elbows on their knees, and stared out over their fists with starting eyes at the approaching illusion. They hoped they were dreaming, yet feared to find it so. Some of them, even, in a con-

fusion of fear and hope, refused to believe their eyes when the oncoming figure smiled and spoke, and there was no more doubt.

"Yea, verily, and greetings to you all," he said in his very voice, and came close up to them. "It is indeed I. I am come for our father's sake on Hulda, the she-ass, to look after things with you and to—" he stopped, disconcerted. They sat without word or stir and stared, a sinister group, like men bewitched. But as they so sat—although there was no sunrise and no sunset which might have painted their faces, yet these grew red as the twisted trunks of the trees at their backs, red as the desert, dark red as the star in the sky, and their eyes looked as though blood would spurt out. He stepped back. There arose and swelled a thunderous roar, that bull's roar of the twins, which made one's inwards to quake; and with a long-drawn shriek as from tortured gullets, a furiously exultant yell of rage and hate and sudden release, they all ten sprang up as one man and flung themselves savagely upon him.

They fell upon him as the pack of hungry wolves falls upon the prey; their blood-blinded lust knew no pause or consideration, it was as though they would tear him into fourteen pieces at least. Rending, tearing apart, tearing off—upon that they were bent, to their very marrow. "Down, down, down!" they panted with one voice; it was the *ketonet* they meant, the picture-robe, the veil. It must come off, and that was not so easy, for it was wound about him and fastened at head and shoulder; and they were too many for the deed. They got in each other's way; one thrust another away from the victim as he flew and fell and bounded among them. The blows meant for him showered upon themselves— though he indeed received a plenty as well. His nose bled almost at once, and one eye was closed with a great blue weal.

But the confusion served Reuben's ends, as he towered among them shrieking: "Down, down," with the rest. He used the immemorial tactics of those who wish to control a savage mob and keep a grip upon the course of events: he took part with apparent zeal in the fray, in order to prevent the worst from coming to pass. He dealt out blows while feigning to receive them, all the while cuffing and pushing those nearest Joseph, protecting him as best he might when they were about to strike him and tear off his robe. He aimed particularly at Levi, on account of the crook in his hands, blundering against it as often as he could. But despite all Reuben's manoeuvres, Joseph was served worse than the petted youth could ever have dreamed possible. He reeled half-dazed, with his head drawn down between his shoulders, and his elbows spread against the hail-storm of brutality, descending out of a blue sky, which horribly seemed not to care where it struck, but beat down upon him, cutting into very little pieces his trust, his whole notion of the world, his conviction that everybody must love him more than themselves, as though it were a law of nature.

"Brothers," he stammered, with the blood streaming down his chin from his nose and his bruised lips, "what are you—" A rude blow, which Reuben failed to fend off, knocked the words from his mouth. Another, landing in the pit of the stomach, between the ribs, made him collapse and disappear beneath the pack. I cannot deny, rather I must emphatically say, that this uprising of the sons of Jacob, however much justice they had on their side, was a most shameful relapse into savagery. They sank below the level of the human and availed themselves of their teeth, being otherwise busy with their hands, to tear his mother's garment from the body of the bleeding, reeling lad. They were not dumb at the work, they said other things besides "Down, down, down!" They were like labourers pulling and heaving and with monotonous cries subduing themselves to the common task; bringing up broken words out of the depths of their hate to feed their rage and stave off thought. "Bow down, bow down, thou sayest?" "Look after things, wilt thou, thou thorn in the flesh, thou lingering sickness! There for thy dreams!" And their unhappy victim?

To him the most horrible and incredible thing of all was what happened to the *ketonet.* That was worse, crueller, even, than all this howling horror about him. Desperately he tried to protect the garment and keep the remnants and ruins of it still upon him. Several times he cried out: "My coat! My coat!" and even after he stood naked, still begged them like a girl to spare it. Yes, he was naked, for the violence of the brothers' onslaught not only carried off the veil, but shift, loincloth, and myrtle wreath lay in tatters beside it on the moss; while blows rained down upon his naked flesh and he sought as best he could to ward them off with his arms. "Bow down, bow down! Take that for thy dreams!" Big Reuben did what he could to keep them off by behaving as though the others prevented him from coming at the victim and dealing his blows. "Thou thorn in the flesh, thou lingering sickness!" he cried out with the rest. But also he cried out something else, which occurred to him on the spur of the moment; cried it loud and repeatedly, in order that they might all hear it and be guided in their blind rage: "Bind him, bind him! Tie his hands and feet!" It was a new suggestion, invented in haste to a good end: namely, to set a definite goal to this otherwise incalculable business and introduce a breathing-space, in the which big Reuben, as he feverishly prayed, might avert the worst. They would not strike Joseph while they were busy binding him; and when he lay bound, that would be a temporary gratification, a stage at which they might stand off and consider what next. Such was Reuben's hasty calculation. And thus with desperate zeal he proposed his expedient, as though he were indicating the one and only useful and reasonable plan and as though anyone was a fool who did not hearken to it. "There—that for thy dreams!" he shrieked. "Bind him—bind him! You fools! What a sense-

less revenge! Instead of hitting me, bind him. Is there no rope?" he cried once more with all his strength.

Yes, Gaddiel for one wore a length round his waist; and he took it off. As their heads were empty, there was room in them for Reuben's words. They bound the naked lad, bound his arms and legs with one long piece of cord, trussed him up properly while he moaned and groaned; and Reuben assisted zealously at the work. When it was done, he stepped back and wiped off his sweat with a gasp, as if he had worked harder than any.

The others stood there, their lust for battle slaked for the present; panting, inactive, dazed. Before them lay Rachel's son, in grievous state. He lay on his bound arms, with the back of his head buried in the grass, his knees drawn up stiffly, his ribs going in and out, all bludgeoned. Moss and dirt clung to his body, it was slobbered with the foam of his brothers' fury, and across it ran in winding streams the red juice which gushes out of beauty when its surface is marred. His undamaged eye now gazed terror-struck at his murderers, now closed spasmodically in a reflex action against fresh violence.

The evil-doers stood getting their wind; they exaggerated their breathlessness in order to cover the lack of counsel, of which, as reason returned, they were slowly aware. They, like Reuben, wiped off their sweat with the backs of their hands; they puffed out their lips and made faces expressive of justified revenge, as who should say: "Whatever we have done, can any reproach us for it?" They said the same in words. They panted out words justifying themselves in each other's eyes or before any court in the world: "Cuckoo! Thorn in the flesh! But we have shown him, we have cast him out!" "Could one credit it? Cometh here— here before us, in his coat—before our eyes—to look after things—but we've looked after them—so he'll not forget it!"—and all the while there was stirring within them a horror and shuddering, which all their words were meant to quiet. And if the horror and shuddering were looked at nearly, it would turn out to be—the thought of Jacob.

Great God, what had they done with the father's lamb—to what state had they brought the youthful heir of the departed Rachel? How would the master of words behave when he knew or learned it, how would they stand before him and what would happen to them? Reuben thought of Bilhah. Simeon and Levi thought of Shechem and of Jacob's wrath and now he had come down upon them when they returned from their heroic deeds. Naphtali, Naphtali especially, found it a present consolation that Jacob was five days away and entirely unsuspecting. Yes, for the first time Naphtali realized as a blessing the power of space, which separates and spares. But they all realized that the blessing could not be preserved. Jacob must presently hear all. When Joseph came again before his eyes, the storm of emotion, the rolling thunder of

his words, the flashing lightning of his curses—the brethren could not escape nor yet endure them. Grown men as they were, they were frightened like children, possessed with the fear of the curse in itself, and in all its meaning and consequence. Cursed they would be, one and all, because they had raised their hand against the lamb; and now the young hypocrite would definitely be exalted above them as the chosen heir. They would actually have themselves to thank for the fulfilment of those shameful dreams; precisely that which God willed would have been brought about by this accomplished fact. They perceived that big Reuben had made fools of them with his advice. Here they stood, and there lay the thief of the blessing; pretty well punished indeed, and bound—but was that really an accomplished fact? It would be different if Joseph never did come before his father's eyes again; if something final and conclusive happened to him. The calamity and the lamentation would be even greater, of course—too great to think on. But—somehow or other —it would pass. Stopping half-way, even so they were guilty. If they went on, they needed not to be. All this went through their heads as they stood—through Reuben's too. He could not help recognizing the situation. He had brought the brawl to a halt with a shrewdness which came from his heart. But his reason told him that too much had happened for it to stop there. That more had to happen, and yet on no account and at no price must happen—this it was which made him giddy. Big Reuben's sinewy features had never before worn that baffled, sullen look.

Each moment he feared they would voice the inevitable—and he had no answer. Then they voiced it, and he heard. One of them said it—no matter who, since they must all be thinking the same thing: "He must away."

"Away," nodded Reuben with grim confirmation. "Thou sayest it. But thou sayest not where."

"Away altogether," answered the voice. "He must go down to the pit and be no more. Long time he ought not to have been; now certainly he must be no more."

"I agree," responded Reuben with bitter scorn. "And then come we before Jacob, his father, without him. 'Where is the boy?' he will ask. 'He is no more,' we answer. But if he ask: 'Why is he no more,' then we answer: 'We have killed him.'"

They were silent.

"No," said Dan, "not so. Brothers, hear me, I am called serpent and adder, and a certain subtlety is not to be denied me. Thus will we do. We will put him in the pit, down in the dry well here, half choked, in which is no water. There lieth he in safety and put away, and will see what his dreams bring him to. But before Jacob we must lie and speak with assurance: 'We have not seen him and know not whether he still is or is not. If not, then in any case a ravening beast hath devoured him, oh woe, alas!' We must add 'Oh woe' for the sake of the lie."

"Be quiet," said Naphtali, "he lieth close at hand and heareth us."

"No matter," answered Dan. "He will tell no one. That he heareth it is one reason more that he may not go from here; even before that he could not, but now everything goeth together. We can speak as we like before him, for he is already as good as dead."

A cry came from Joseph, he wailed out of his breast stretched taut under his bonds on which the tender red nipples stood out. He wept.

"Can you hear it and not pity?" Reuben asked.

"Of what avail is that, Reuben?" answered him Judah, "and what talkest thou of pity, though the rest of us may feel it as well as thou? Doth his weeping in this hour blot it out that he hath been a shameless toad all his days and stank to heaven and hath supplanted us with the father with most shameless guile? Doth pity avail against necessity and is it a good reason why he should go from hence and tell all? What good to talk of pity, even if it be felt? Hath he not already heard how we shall lie before Jacob? That is enough to end his life, that he hath heard it; and whether with or without pity Dan spoke the truth: he is as good as dead."

"Thou art right," said Reuben then. "Let us throw him in the pit."

Again Joseph wailed piteously.

"But he still weepeth," one of them reminded them.

"Must he then not even weep?" cried Reuben. "Let him go weeping into the pit; what more can you ask?"

I would fain pass over what was said next, for it would shock our modern taste and however delicately put would place the brothers or some of them in an exceedingly bad light. The truth is that Simeon and Levi, as well as the downright Gad, offered to make an end of the lad with more ado. The twins wanted to do it with their staves, hitting out with the full strength of their arms, as Cain had done, until he was no more. But Gad asked to be given the job of cutting his throat quickly with the knife, as Jacob had once done with the kid whose skin he needed for the forged blessing. That these suggestions were made is undeniable; but I am not anxious that the reader be finally disgusted with the sons of Jacob, therefore I will not put their thoughts into precise words. They uttered them because those things had to be said; because, so to speak, they lay in the nature of the business. Besides, it was only natural that those best suited to the rôle were they who expressed their readiness and so conformed to their myth on earth: namely, the savage twins and the stout Gad.

But Reuben opposed. It is known that he opposed, and would not have it happen to Joseph as it had to Abel or to the kid. "To that I will not agree," he said, protesting in his character as Leah's eldest, which despite fall and curse entitled him to a voice. The boy was as good as dead, they had said so themselves. He was only sobbing a little still, it

would suffice to throw him into the pit. Let them look at him and say whether that was still Joseph the dreamer. He was already unrecognizable from the punishment, in which he, Reuben, had taken part, and would have done more had he not been struck from all sides. But what had happened had been just a happening, it was not an act, not a deed, you could not call it so. It had come about, indeed, through them, but they had not done it, it had simply happened to them. Now, however, they were deliberately proposing, of set purpose, to commit a crime and raise their hands against the boy; they were about to spill their father's blood, whereas up to now it had only flowed. And that was a world-wide difference, it was all the difference between an act and an occurrence; and if they did not see that, then they were short in their understanding. Were they, he asked, appointed judges of life and death, to judge in their own matter and then carry out the blood-decree as well? No, there should be no shedding of blood, he would not stand for it. What remained to them to do, after what had occurred, was to put the boy into the pit and leave the rest to happen.

Thus big Reuben, but nobody believed that he was deceiving himself or that he was so stoutly convinced of the hard and fast difference between happening and doing. Or that he did not see that putting Joseph in the pit would be the same as killing him. After a while Jehudah asked him what it would avail to kill the boy and conceal his blood; the question told Reuben nothing new. For all along we have looked into Reuben's heart and seen that his great desire was to gain time. He could not have said for what; simply time to feed the hope that he might save Joseph out of the brethren's hands and somehow bring him back to his father. It was his fear of Jacob which actuated him, as well as his crabbed and shamefaced love of the culprit; they drove him to conceal his thoughts and meditate treason against the clan—for it can be called nothing else. Moreover, Reuben the unstable had manifold sins to atone for in Jacob's eyes, on account of Bilhah. What if he brought Joseph safe home? Would not then the ancient wrong be more than made good, the curse lifted and his first-born-ship be restored? I do not assume to understand all Reuben's thoughts and actions, nor would I minimize the motives of his deeds. But need it belittle them to guess that in his secret heart he hoped both to save and to vanquish Rachel's son?

In any case his words met with scarcely any opposition from the brothers. They were willing to refrain and to let events decide. Probably they would have preferred that the "happenings" should have continued and led in one blind thrust to the goal they sought. But to continue deliberately and to shed blood, to "act" now that a pause for reflection had intervened—nobody wanted to do that, not even the twins, however savage, nor yet Gaddiel, no matter how stoutly he spoke. They were all glad, indeed, that their offer about bludgeons and knives had not been

taken up, but that Reuben's authority should prevail again: first the tying-up, now the pit.

"Into the pit," was the word. They seized the cord which bound Joseph, caught hold here and there, and dragged the poor wretch across the field toward the pit at the edge of the pasture-land. Some dragged in front, some tugged at the sides, the rest ran behind. Reuben did not run, but moved with a long stride at the tail of the convoy; when a stone lay in the way, a gnarled root or stump or a prickly shrub, he lifted the poor soul that he might not suffer needless pain.

So it was off with Joseph to the pit, with a heigh and a ho, for as they went, a fury of merriment seized upon the brethren, the animal spirits of men working in unison. They laughed and joked and shouted nonsense to each other; as that this was a sheaf which had been well bound and now should bow itself into the pit, into the well, into the depths. In all this they were venting the relief they felt at not being impelled to follow the pattern represented by Abel and the kid. Besides, it drowned the sound of Joseph's prayers and lamentations: "Brothers! Have pity!" he mumbled with his bruised mouth. "What is it you do? Stop, stop! Woe, alas, what will befall me?"

His moans helped him not at all; on they went at a trot, through bush and grass, a long way across country to a mossy slope. Here some steep, broken steps led down to a walled-in bottom, paved with cracked flags. The air was cool, and oak scrub and fig trees grew out of the ruined walls. They dragged Joseph down the steps, he struggling desperately in their arms and against his bonds, for he shuddered at the thought of the well that was there and of the hole of the well, but even more at the broken, mossy well-stone that lay on the flags and was meant to lie over the top. But let him struggle and weep as he might, his unclosed eye directed in horror into the blackness of the well, they hoisted him to the brink with a heave and a ho and tipped him in, to fall who knew how far!

It was far enough, though not an abyss, not a bottomless pit. Such wells often reach a hundred feet and more down, but this one had been long out of use and choked with earth and broken stone—perhaps on account of old quarrels about the place. It was no more than five or six fathoms deep if that. Certainly too much to climb out of with bound limbs. But he fell with as much care for life and limb as he could, braking here and there with feet and elbows round the wall, and moderating his fall to a slipping which landed him fairly sound among the rubbish at the bottom, to the discomfiture of all sorts of beetles, wood-lice, and other crawling things. While he was collecting himself, the brethren did the rest, shouting as they lifted the stone at the top and heaved it into place. It was heavy—not one man's work to roll it on top of the pit; so they all laid hold and shared in the task. For the ancient stone, all green with moss and full five foot round, was sprung into two halves; and

when they had rolled each into place the two did not meet, but yawned; and through the uneven gap some light fell into the hole. Joseph looked up at it with his one eye as he lay huddled anyhow, naked and exposed, in the depths.

JOSEPH CRIES OUT OF THE PIT

Their task being done, the brothers sat down on the steps of the well-chamber to rest; some drew bread and cheese out of their girdles and ate. Levi, religious in all his savagery, gave them to remember indeed that one should not eat at the shedding of blood, but they answered him that what they had done was to avoid bloodshed. Upon which, Levi ate too.

They ruminated as they chewed. For the moment their thoughts were occupied with sensations which, though of little importance, yet altogether possessed them: their hands and arms, that is, bore the memory of the contact with Joseph's bare skin, as they dragged him to his doom. No matter how ungentle the contact had been, now that it was all over, it gave them a retrospective feeling of tenderness which was very strong, however little they understood what it meant. Nobody gave expression to it by so much as a syllable; and what they said concerned only the fact that Joseph was now safely out of the way, together with his dreams, and that they were greatly lightened thereby.

"Now he is no more," said they. That was that; now they could sleep; they could sleep in peace, they repeated, the more emphatically the more uncertain they felt about it. It might be true with regard to the dreamer who was gone and could tell the father nothing. But the thought failed to soothe, for it reminded them of the father waiting in vain for Joseph's home-coming—eternally in vain. Such a picture, however much security it contained, noways invited to slumber. For all the ten, including the savage twins, it was a picture full of horror. Their childish fear of Jacob and of the tenderness and power of his soul was clear and lively. True, Joseph would never be able to accuse them. But they had bought their security by means of an offence against their father's emotions, which it terrified them to realize. What they had done to Joseph had its cause in jealousy; but we all know what feeling it is that suffers this distortion. It seems little convincing, looking at the slick brutality of the twins, to ascribe any such feeling to them; and precisely on this ground it is that I do not make any positive statements. There are cases where only half-words will serve.

So they mused and blinked as they chewed, feeling on hands and arms the memory of the softness of Joseph's flesh. Their reflections were not light, and they were further weighted by the weeping and begging that rose faintly out of the pit. After the fall he had so far gathered him-

self together as to realize the need of crying out, and he implored them
from below:

"Brothers, where are you? Ah, go not away, leave me not alone in
the pit. It is so earthy and so horrible. Brothers, have pity and save me
still out of the night of this pit where I perish. I am your brother Joseph.
Brothers, hide not your ears from my sighs and cryings, for you do falsely
to me. Reuben, where art thou? Reuben, I cry thy name from below in
the pit. You have all misunderstood, you have misunderstood, dear
brothers, so help me still and save my life. I came to you on our father's
account five days' journey on Hulda the white ass, to bring you presents,
ears of corn and fruit cakes. Ah, how it hath all gone wrong! The man is
to blame that it went wrong, the man who led me. Brothers in Jacob,
hearken and understand me, I came not to you to see how things were,
for I am but a child. I came to bow before you with decorum and the
forms of courtesy and to ask after your welfare, that you should return
home to our father. Brothers! the dreams . . . was I so unmannerly as
to relate my dreams? Believe me, I have only told quite modest dreams
by comparison with what I could have, but not this was it I wanted to
say. Oh, oh, my bones, my sinews right and left, and all my limbs! I
thirst, brothers, the child thirsteth, for he hath lost much blood, and all
through a mistake. Are ye yet there? Am I already quite forsaken? Reu-
ben, let me hear thy voice. Tell them that I will say nothing if they will
but spare my life. Brothers, I know you think you must leave me in the
pit; otherwise I would tell. But by the God of Abraham, God of Isaac,
God of Jacob, by the heads of your mothers and by Rachel's head, my
little mother's, I swear that I will not tell for ever and ever, if you let me
out of the pit but this one time."

"He would tell, of a certainty, if not today, then tomorrow," mut-
tered Judah between his teeth; and there was none who did not share
this view, Reuben not excepted, however much it might conflict with his
wavering hopes and plans. But so much the more must he keep these
secret and assert the contrary; therefore he hollowed his hands about his
mouth and called:

"If thou art not quiet we will throw down stones upon thee that
shall kill thee entirely, for we will hear no more of thee, thou art sped."

When Joseph heard this and recognized Reuben's voice, he was
terrified and ceased to speak and they might sit undisturbed and taste
their fear of Jacob. Of course, if they had meant to prolong their self-
imposed exile and live in lasting discord with their father, then they need
not have troubled themselves over the agony of waiting and long despair
which was hovering over Jacob's head. But the truth was exactly the op-
posite. The casting away of Joseph could serve one only purpose: that of
removing the obstacle between them and the father's heart. Upon that
they were childishly bent. The trouble was that they had been driven to

extremes in order to win this soft but mighty heart for their own. This was the point of view under which they at all times saw the affair. Not punishment of Joseph's presumption, they were of one mind in thinking, nor yet revenge, nor even, in the first instance, the obliteration of the dreams, was their main concern. What they thought of was how to smooth their path to their father's heart. This now was done, and they would return—without Joseph, as they had set out. Where was he? He had been sent after them. And thus sent, to those who by their departure had demonstrated that they could not stand him, their return without him would look very suspicious. Certainly Jacob would have an awful right to question them. They might shrug their shoulders in reply. Were they their brother's keepers? Of course not; but the answer would not satisfy Jacob's piercing, mistrustful gaze which he would direct upon them relentlessly, while they continued to be witnesses of his tortured expectancy and of the prolonged despair which in the nature of things must be its only issue. It was a penance before which they quailed. On the other hand, were they to stop away until all hope had died and waiting had given way to the knowledge that Joseph would never return? That would last long, for the stout-hearted can bear long suspense, and besides in the meantime the question might easily answer itself and become a curse for them all. No, it was clear that they must once and for all establish the fact that Joseph would not come back; that alone could clear their skirts. Their minds were all busy with these thoughts, but snake-and-adder Dan brought to them speech. He combined his own earlier idea of telling the old man that a wild beast had killed Joseph with Gad's reminder of the kid which Jacob had killed to obtain the blessing; and he said:

"Hear me, brothers, for I have power to judge and I know what we should do. For we shall take a beast of the flock and cut its throat and let the blood run out. But in the blood of the beast we shall dip the accursed thing, the coat of many colours, Rachel's bridal garment that lieth all in rags. Bring we it before Jacob and say to him: 'This have we found on the ground, torn and covered with blood. Is it not thy son's garment?'' Then may he draw his conclusion from the state of the garment, and it will be as when a shepherd showeth to the master the remains of the sheep that a lion hath slain; thus is he cleansed and needeth not to swear himself free from guilt."

"Hush," muttered Judah, shuddering. "For he can hear what you say under the stone and can understand what we shall do."

"What harm in that?" Dan retorted. "Shall I whisper and mutter for his sake? It hath naught to do with his life; it is our affair, but no longer his. Thou forgettest that he is as good as dead and done for. When he hath understood that and also this that I now say with my natural voice, then everything is settled. Never have we been able to

speak freely and without caution when he was amongst us, for we well knew that he would tell the father and then we had to pay. But now at last we have him amongst us as our brother, whom we trust and he may hear everything we say—it maketh me to feel that I should like to throw a kiss to him there in the pit. But what think you all of my idea?"

They were about to speak; but Joseph lifted up his voice once more, imploring them from the pit not to do it.

"Brothers," he cried, "do not that with the beast and the robe, treat not the father so, for he will not survive it. Ah, I beg you not for myself, for body and soul are broken in me and I lie in the grave. But spare our father and bring him not the bloody garment—it would kill him. Ah, hadst thou heard how he warned me in anxiousness about the lion, when he found me alone by night, and now it will be that a lion hath eaten me. Had you seen the care with which he prepared me for the journey and I indifferently endured his concern! Woe is me, it is most likely unwise that I speak to you of his love of me, but what shall I do, dear brothers, and how counsel myself that I do not vex you? Why after all is my life involved with his, that I cannot adjure you to spare his without begging for my own? Ah, dear brothers, hear my weeping and do no violence to his suffering by showing him the bloody robe, for his gentle soul will bear it not and he will be stricken to the earth."

"Nay," Reuben said, "that is more than I can stand, it is unbearable." He stood up. "Let us move farther away, if you like; one cannot talk with him wailing, nor think for his crying out of the depths. Come to the huts." He said it angrily, they might think he had gone pale with rage. But actually his pallor was due to his having agreed in his heart with what the boy had said. He, too, realized that Jacob, at sight of the robe, would literally be struck to the earth. But more than that, Joseph's words had impressed it upon Reuben that the lad, in his hour of need, was mindful of their father and pleaded with the brethren on his behalf and for himself only for the father's sake. But was he perhaps pretending as of old? No, no, this time it was different. This was another Joseph who cried out from beneath the stone from the one whom he once had shaken by the shoulder to awaken him from vanity and folly. What the shaking had not achieved the fall into the pit had done: Joseph was aroused, he pleaded for the father-heart, he mocked no more, but felt distress and remorse. The discovery strengthened big Reuben's vacillating purpose, while at the same time it made him more acutely sensitive of its helpless and hopeless character.

Thence his pallor, as he got up and suggested to them all to go with him away from the place where Joseph was buried. They followed him, they went from thence, to gather up the rags of the veil on the spot of the beating, to bring them to the tents and there to take counsel over Dan's idea. So Joseph was left alone.

IN THE PIT

His soul was anguished to remain alone in the grave; for some time he wailed after the brothers and implored them not to leave him. Yet he scarcely knew what he cried out; his actual thoughts were not with these mechanical and superficial prayers and lamentations but far below them, while lower down again were others yet more real, like their undertones and ground-basses, so that the whole was like a moving music, perpendicularly composed, which his spirit was occupied in conducting on all three levels. This preoccupation was what caused him to commit the blunder of telling the brethren that he had only told them comparatively modest dreams, considering those others which he had also dreamed. No one in his right senses could even for a moment think that the remark was calculated to soften their hearts; but an absent and preoccupied mind might have done so, and thus was it with Joseph.

Much had gone on within him, even since that astonishing and horrible moment when the brethren fell upon him like wolves and he had looked into their faces distorted by fury and hate, out of the eye which they had not closed at once with their fists. Their faces had been very near to him while they with nails and teeth tore the picture-robe from his body—frightfully near; and the hatred which he had read therein had been the greatest torture and the main cause of the horror he felt at the onslaught. Certainly he had quaked with fear and wept for pain under their blows; but fear and pain were quite permeated with the pity he felt for the torturing hatred which he read in the mask-like faces, dripping with sweat, that rose and fell and were thrust into his own. But pity for a pain the source of which we must recognize to be ourselves comes close to being remorse. Reuben's intuition had been quite right: this time Joseph had been so rudely shaken that his eyes were opened and he saw what he had done—and that he had done it. While he was flung hither and thither among their raging fists, while his robe was torn off, while he lay bound, and during his penitential journey to the well-house, amid all his daze of horror his thoughts had never once stood still. They had not paused upon the frightful present, but sped back over a past in which all this, hidden to his blissful self-conceit though partly and presumptuously known to it, had been preparing itself the while.

My God, the brothers! To what had he brought them? For he did understand that he had brought them to this: through manifold and great mistakes which he had committed in the assumption that everybody loved him more than themselves—this assumption which he believed and yet did not actually quite believe, but according to which he had always acted and which had brought him—as he now clearly and distinctly recognized—to the pit. In the brothers' distorted and sweating

masks he had read clearly with his one eye that the premise had gone beyond human power and over a long period had strained their souls and given them great suffering, until now at last the final issue had been reached in this end, so frightful for him and doubtless for them too.

Alas, poor brothers! What must they have borne before in desperation they laid hold on the father's lamb and actually threw it into the pit! Into what a state had they thereby brought themselves—to say nothing of his own, which was hopeless, as he shudderingly confessed himself. It was not credible that he would hold his tongue if he were restored to his father. He could never make them believe it, he could not believe it. And so they must leave him in the grave, to perish there; there was nothing else for it. This he saw; yet wonderful to say, horror at his own impending fate left him room in his soul for pity for his murderers. We know this to be true. Joseph was quite aware, he admitted it to himself openly and honourably as he sat at the bottom of the well, that the unashamed presumption which had been the guiding principle of his life had been a game in which he himself had not seriously believed nor could have done; that, for one thing, he ought never to have told his brothers his dreams. It had been impossibly and incredibly tactless. He even realized that he had actually known this all the time—and yet he had done it. Why? That he did not know. Apparently, that he might be destroyed. But at the bottom of his heart Joseph did not believe it. Privately he was convinced that God looked further than the pit, that He had far-reaching things in mind as usual and had His eye upon some distant purpose, in the service of which he, Joseph, had been made to drive the brethren to the uttermost. They were being sacrificed to the future, and he suffered for them, however badly things went with himself. They would send their father the robe, unhappy men, after they had dipped it in the blood of the kid in lieu of his own; and Jacob would be struck to the earth. At the thought Joseph was moved to start up, to protect his father from the sight—with the only result of course that he felt shooting pains through and through him, sank back in his bonds against the stones of the well, and began once more to weep.

He had an agony of leisure in which to weep, to feel anguish, remorse, and pity; and despairing of his life, yet in his inmost being to believe in the wise and healing future purposes of God. For, frightful as it is to think of it, he was to remain three days in the pit, three days and nights in his bonds, naked and exposed, in dirt and earth mould, among crawling worms, without bite or sup, without consolation or any reasonable hope of ever reaching the light again. I, who tell it, must take care that I paint it as it was, that I make clear what it meant for Jacob's little son, who had never imagined that fate could be so harsh: how dismally the hours passed, till his scrap of daylight died in the crack between the stones and a pitying star sent down its diamond ray into the grave; how the pale dawn twice came, abode, and went again; how he constantly

peered up in the twilight at the round walls of his house to see whether there were footholds in the broken wall, or crevices made by pushing roots—but his bonds, and the stone well-cover, each by itself and certainly together, quenched every hope in the bud; how he twisted himself about in the cords to find an easier posture, which quickly became even worse than the other; how thirst and hunger tortured him and the emptiness of his stomach gave him burning sensations in his back; how like the sheep he soiled himself with his own filth and therein nestled and shivered till his teeth chattered. I am greatly concerned to give a lively and exact picture of this all-embracing unpleasantness; at the same time I must be careful to cling to reality and not let my imagination get the upper hand and lose itself in empty emotion. Reality is sober—precisely in its character as reality. At grips with the actual and undeniable, driven to an understanding with it, reality insists upon our suiting ourselves to the circumstances and adapting us without loss of time. We are easily persuaded to call a situation unbearable. Our easily aroused humanity protests indignantly, and that probably does the sufferer good; but it becomes a little absurd in the face of the *really* intolerable. The sympathetic friend's relation to this reality, which is of course not his own, is an unreal and sentimental one. He commits an error of the imagination, for the sufferer, thanks to his suffering, is in a different category. What do we really mean by the unbearable, when there is nothing to be done but bear it so long as we are in our senses?

But young Joseph had not been entirely and clearly in his senses for a long time; not since the moment when the brethren had turned into wolves before his eyes. The storm which then broke over him had numbed him very much, effecting those palliations which the unbearable needs in order to be borne. The beatings he had received had dulled his feeling, as had that unbelievable conveyance into the well. His situation was certainly desperate, but at least it had put a period to those frightful shocks and produced a sort of equilibrium. However objectionable his present state, it had the advantage of security. Buried in the womb of the earth he needed not to fear further violence and had time to pursue his labouring thoughts—for these at times almost made him forget his physical sufferings and dangers. And his security (if we may use the word with reference to almost certain death—but why not, since death is at all times certain and yet we feel secure), his feeling of security then, inclined him to sleep. His exhaustion was so great that it outweighed all else. He fell asleep and through long stretches of time knew little or nothing of himself. When he roused, his astonishment at the refreshment which the sleep had brought (for food and sleep can for a while replace each other) mingled with a fresh sense of horror that he was still in the pit and still in misery. Even in sleep he did not entirely lose the sense of misery; but its worst rigours did, as it were, manage to relax a little. The bonds were hard, the cramped position still endured;

but even they began to relax, on the second and third days the cords had given way a little and yielded to the needs of the poor tortured limbs. I say all this, once more, to confront our sympathy with the solid reality of facts. But on the other hand, if I add that Joseph was of course growing weaker all the time, it will serve to keep our pity from quite dying out, even though I must add that his very weakness was an amelioration to his sufferings. From this point of view one might almost say that the longer his stay in the pit lasted, the more tolerable it was; so that by the end he was scarcely aware of his own misery.

But his thoughts worked on and on, the body almost forgotten. It was as though, in the piece of music which we have imagined them to represent, those undertones and basses at the bottom came out stronger and stronger, thanks to that dreamy weakness of his, until at last they almost drowned out the overtones. So long as the brethren were near, the fear of death had been apparent, as expressed in his urgent entreaties and wailings. But now they were gone and the cries had died away, why was it that Joseph did not shout in hopes of a chance rescue? Because he quite forgot to, absorbed as he was in far other trains of thought, having to do with his abrupt downfall, with the past and its errors, perhaps ordained by God, but not on that account less heavy and grievous.

The garment which the brothers had torn off his body—partly with their teeth, shocking to say—played a prominent rôle in his reflections. That he ought not to have spread himself in it before them, nor made his ownership visible to their eyes; above all things that he ought not to have appeared before them in it here and now came over him so forcibly that he could have beat himself on the head but for his bonds. He did so in spirit; but even so he had to confess to himself the futility and curious hypocrisy of the gesture; for now he saw that he had always understood the whole thing and yet had so behaved. With amazement he contemplated the riddle of self-destructive arrogance presented to him by his own extraordinary behaviour. His wits could not cope with the riddle successfully—nor can anyone's. Perhaps because so much of the incalculable is implicit therein, so much that is contrary to reason and even perhaps holy. How he had trembled lest Jacob discover the *ketonet* in the bag—trembled, that is, before his own salvation! He had deceived his father, taken advantage of the old man's failing memory, and packed the *ketonet;* but not because he had disagreed with the father as to the effect which the sight of the veil would have upon the brothers. He had understood perfectly and had packed it none the less. How could he have done so? Again, since he had not forgotten to take care for his own destruction, why had Jacob forgotten to prevent it? Another puzzle. Joseph's desire to smuggle the coat could not have been stronger than the father's loving concern that he should leave it at home. Why had not love and anxiety been strong enough to remind the old man and so to foil Joseph's plan? Joseph had succeeded in beguiling away the rich garment

from Jacob's tent; it was partly the effect of the game, partly because Jacob wanted the child to have the robe, quite as much as the latter desired it. The consequences followed promptly. Together they had brought the lamb to the pit, and now Jacob would be struck to earth.

But after that he might well bethink him of the mistakes of the past, common to them all—just as Joseph was now doing. The boy was honest with himself: he admitted that he had forsworn himself when he said he would say nothing to Jacob if the brothers released him. The promise had been born of fear; Joseph knew that if the old state of things were restored—which with some part of his being he ardently desired—he must unavoidably tell all, and the brethren would suffer the consequences. Restoration was out of the question; but even if it were not, he was in a way at one with the brethren in not wishing for it. He could almost have returned the kiss which Dan had wanted to throw to him in the pit, so much did he feel that for the first time he was really among them as their brother and might hear all that they said; might even hear that about the blood of the kid which should pass for his blood; it did not matter, since he was as good as dead and buried already.

A strong impression had been made upon Joseph by what Dan had said: that they might say what they liked before Joseph, since every word they uttered only heightened the impossibility of his return home, and that it was good to utter them, since each one bound him more firmly to the lower world and made of him more and more a ghost before whom one shudders. Joseph saw in such words the counterpart and inversion of the rôle which he had played so far in life, that of needing to heed nobody because all the world loved him more than they did themselves. For it was come to this, that no one heeded him at all! The thought conditioned those undertones and basses of his composition, and the weaker he became, the more did they sonorously predominate over the overtones.

But they had begun to play even earlier; at the moment when the undreamed-of became reality; when his provocative conduct had called down punishment and he was tossed to and fro like a toy amongst the brethren and they had torn the picture-robe with their nails and teeth. From that moment on, then, they had been vocal; in the midst of that hail of horrifying blows his ear had in good part hearkened to them. It would be wrong to suppose that under such deadly serious circumstances Joseph had stopped playing and dreaming—if one may still speak of his activity as playing and dreaming, in this connection. He was a true son of Jacob, the man of thoughts and dreams and mystical lore, who always understood what happened to him, who in all earthly events looked up to the stars and always linked his life to God's. Granted that Joseph's way of dignifying his life by attaching it to the higher law and reality was not the same as Jacob's, less spiritual, more shrewdly calculating; yet he seriously held that a life and activity without the hall-mark of higher

reality, which does not base upon the traditionally sacred and support itself thereupon, nor is able to mirror itself in anything heavenly and recognize itself therein, is no life or activity at all. He was convinced that nothing in the lower world would know how to happen or be thought of without its starry prototype and counterpart; and the great certainty guiding his life was belief in the unity of the dual, in the fact of the revolving sphere, the exchangeability of above and below, one turning into the other, and gods becoming men and men gods. Not for nothing was he the pupil of old Eliezer, who knew how to say "I" in such an ample way that Joseph's eyes grew dim with musing as he beheld him. The transparency of being, the characteristic recurrence of the prototype—this fundamental creed was in his flesh and blood too, and all spiritual dignity and significance seemed to him bound up with awareness of it. That was as it should be. What was after all not quite as it should be, but seemed more like a degenerate deviation from the significant and admirable type, was Joseph's inclination to draw advantage from the general prepossession in his favour and consciously to impose himself upon those about him.

From the first moment on he was aware of all this. Incredible as it may seem, in the thick of the turmoil, in the acutest moment of fear and danger of death, he had kept his mental eye open to realities. Not that fear and danger grew less thereby; but he actually experienced a sort of joy as well; the pleasure of enlightenment, almost like the relief which laughter brings, had illuminated the dark terror in his soul.

"My coat!" he had cried out in the anguish of his concern; "tear it not, I pray you." Yes, they had rent it in pieces and torn it off him, that was his mother's robe and that belonged also to her son, so that they wore it by turns and became one, and god and goddess by its means. Mercilessly had the brethren unveiled him. As love unveils the bride in the bedchamber, thus had their fury done to him, and they had known him naked, so that his frame quivered with the deathly shame. In his mind thoughts of unveiling and of death dwelt close together—how could he then have helped holding the rags of the garment round him in his fright, begging them to tear it not? Yet no more could he have helped being filled with the joy of understanding, coming to him through association of thought, through the conviction of repetition and realization. No danger of the flesh and the soul could prevent the concentration of his spirit upon the wealth of allusion by which the event proclaimed itself as higher reality, as a transparency of the ancient pattern, as the uppermost turning undermost; in short, as written in the stars. And his concentration was very natural, as the allusions all had to do with being and selfhood, with the vista of his ego which he had opened to Reuben a little time ago to the latter's amaze and which now was growing brighter and brighter. He had wept and wailed when big Reuben had given his voice that they should throw him into the pit; yet at the same time his reason had laughed as at

75

a joke, the word used was so laden with allusions: *"Bor"* the brothers had said. And the monosyllable was capable of various interpretations. It meant not only well, but prison; not only prison, but the underworld, the kingdom of the dead; so that prison and the underworld were one and the same thought, one being only a word for the other. Again, the well, in its property as entrance to the underworld, likewise the round stone which covered it, signified death; for the stone covered the round opening as the shadow covers the dark moon. In Joseph's mind the primeval prototype of the death of the planet peeped through the present event: the dead moon, which is invisible for three days until its new birth, means the death of the gods of light, who must for a time descend to the underworld. When the horror happened and the brothers hoisted him onto the edge of the well and on the margin of the pit, so that he must descend below the daylight with all the caution he could muster—then his quick mind had clearly understood the allegory of the star which one evening is a woman and in the morning a man and which sinks into the well of the abyss as evening star.

It was the abyss into which the true son descends, he who is one with the mother and wears the robe by turns with her. It was the nether-earthly sheepfold, Etura, the kingdom of the dead, where the son becomes the lord, the shepherd, the sacrifice, the mangled god. Mangled? They had torn only his lips and his skin here and there, but the robe they had torn off and rent with nails and teeth, those red murderers and conspirators, his brothers, and they would dip it in the blood of a kid, which should pass for his blood, and they would bring it before the father. God demanded from the father the sacrifice of the son, for the soft-hearted one, who shuddering had confessed that he "could not do it." Poor man, he would have to do it, and it was like God that He paid little heed to what man thinks he can do.

Here Joseph wept in his transparent misery, presided over by his understanding. He wept over poor Jacob, who would have to summon his endurance, and over the brethren's confidence in his death. He wept for weakness and giddiness from the exhalations of the well; but the more lamentable his situation became in the course of the seventy-two hours which he spent here below, the more clearly the undertones of his thoughts came out, the more deceptively his present mirrored itself in its heavenly prototype; so that by the end he no longer distinguished the heavenly from the earthly at all and in the dreamy self-satisfaction of death saw only the unity of the double. We may with justice regard that as a device of nature to tide him over the unbearable. For the natural hope, to which life clings up to the last, needs a reasonable justification; and Joseph found it in this identification. Indeed it extended beyond his life, his hope that he would not finally perish but somehow be saved out of the pit. For, literally speaking, he gave himself up for dead. There was the brethren's confidence, there was the bloody robe, which Jacob should

receive. The pit was deep; and return to his former life was inconceivable—a thought as monstrous as that the evening star might return out of the abyss wherein it was sunk, and the shadow be withdrawn from the dark moon, that it should again be full. But the conception of the death of the planet, the darkening and setting of the sun, whose habitation becomes the lower world, included likewise the idea of reappearance, new light, resurrection. And therein Joseph's natural hope that he might live justified itself by faith. It was not a hope that he might return out of the grave into his former life; yet by its means the grave was defeated. Joseph cherished it not only for itself and for its own sake but for the poor old man at home, whom he had brought down into the pit together with himself and who would be stricken to the earth. It would probably be after the son's death that Jacob would receive the bloody robe. But if only the father could have faith beyond death according to the ancient hope, then, thought Joseph in the grave, the blood of the beast would be taken as once it had been, for the blood of the son.

The Stone Before the Grave

THE ISHMAELITES

Men came from Gilead, from the East and beyond the river; rocking along on their camels, four or five, with a few extra pack-animals laden with wares; and with slaves and camel-boys bringing their number up to eight or ten. They were travelling merchants, at home neither here nor in the place whence they came; strange men, very brown of face and hands, with felt circlets round their head-cloths, each wrapped in a burnous with diagonal stripes; they had sharp eyes, showing the whites as they rolled them observantly round. One of their number, who rode at the head of the train, was of dignified age; a thick-lipped boy in a white cotton garment led his animal on a long rein, while the master sat in the high saddle, his head consideringly on one side, with his hands, wrapped in his mantle, resting on the saddle-bow. It was clear that he was the head of the party. The others were his nephew, son-in-law, and sons.

What manner of men were these? That can be told in general, and also with some precision. They lived in the south of the Edom-Seir country, at the edge of the Arabian desert, on the Egyptian side. Their domain, which was a passage and crossing into the land of mud, was called Mizraim, another name for Egypt. But it was also called Muzri; in another dialect Mosar, or even Midian, after the son of Abram and Ketu-

rah. It was a colony of the people of Ma'in, farther south, near the land of incense, who traded between Arabia and the kingdom of beasts and of the dead; they had fixed market in western Canaan and the land of the two rivers and at Muzri, went to and fro with wares between the peoples, and convoyed all the state and royal caravans between one country and another.

In other words, our travellers were Ma'onites from Ma'in, or Minaeans, called Midianites. But since one scarcely distinguished between Medan and Midian, Abraham's sons by his desert concubine Keturah, they might be called Medanim as well as Midianites—it made no difference to them. Even if you gave them the generic name of all desert folk, taking not Keturah but Hagar the Egyptian as their foremother and simply called them Ishmaelites, they had no objection either. It was of no importance to them what people called them and who they were; the main point for them was that they existed and could trade to and fro on the trade routes. Indeed there was some reason to call the old man and his companions Ishmaelites; for as men of Muzri they were half Egyptian, as had been the fiery and beautiful youth named Ishmael. You might, loosely speaking, say that they were descended from him.

This was no royal or state caravan coming on from the East—by no means. They were private travellers, bound on their own business, and without ostentation. They had been marketing their wares on the hither side of the Jordan, at the fairs which were held on feastdays. They sold Egyptian linens, coarse and fine, also pretty glass trifles of various kinds, taking in exchange, with a good profit to themselves, all sorts of sweetmeats, balsams, incense, and gums. And if on this side of the river they managed to acquire some of the native products, such as honey and mustard, a camel-load of pistachios and almonds, they would be well content. As for their route, they were as yet undecided: whether to follow the road running north and south which ran along the crest of the mountain and would take them by way of Urusalim and Hebron to Gaza by the sea, or whether they would do better first to keep to the north and east and then by way of the Megiddo plain reach the coast and follow along it to their country, which was a passage and a crossing into the land of Egypt.

It was past midday when they entered the valley, the old man in the lead, the others behind him in a row. They intended to see whether the people of Dothan were holding a fair where they could do business. They let their animals pace along on low ground which fell away into a mossy slop. And their quick eyes spied below them the ruined steps and the masonry among the thickets. The old man, crooking his neck, saw it first; he pointed it out to the others, made them stop, and sent down the youth in the cap to spy out the place; for travellers such as these are explorers and inquisitive by nature and must see all there is to see.

The boy was not gone long; he simply jumped down and sprang

up again and announced with his thick lips that a covered well was below.

"If it be covered and hidden," said the old man shrewdly, "then it will be worth looking into. The people of the land hereabouts are jealous and stingy; I think it is possible that the well hath water of unusual coolness and freshness—we can use it and take our vessels full; I see nobody who could hinder us; moreover, why are we called Ishmaelites if we may not take what we can in defiance of their jealousy? Take a skin and some bottles and let us go down."

They did as he bade them, for he was their leader. They made their animals lie down, untied the vessels, and climbed down into the well-chamber: uncle, nephew, son-in-law, and sons, with some of the slaves. They soon saw that the well had no bucket and no windlass. But that was no matter, they would let down a leather bottle and fill it with the jealously guarded water. The old man sat down on a fallen quarrystone, settled his clothing, and motioned with his dark-skinned hand that they should roll away the stone from the hole. The stone was broken in two.

"This well," the old man said, "is covered indeed, and hidden, but also it is in a very bad state. The children of the land seem jealous, but likewise heedless. Meanwhile I will cherish no doubts of the goodness of the water; that would be premature. Good, one-half of the stone is rolled aside. Seize me now the other with your young arms and lay it down beside its moss-grown sister on the flags. So! Doth now the round of the water within laugh in its purity and is the mirror clear?"

They stood close to the well, on the low ledge that ran round it, and bent over the depths.

"The well is dry," said the son-in-law, still looking without turning his head toward the old man. As he said it they all pricked up their ears. A wailing rose out of the depths.

"It cannot be that the wailing cometh out of this hole," said the old man. "I trust not my ears. Let us be still and silent and hearken if perchance we may hear it again."

It wailed once more.

"Now am I forced to trust my ears," the elder said; he stood up and mounted the step, shoving those aside with his arms who were in his way, and in his turn looked into the depths.

The others waited courteously for his verdict; but his sight was already dim and he saw naught.

"Dost thou see anything, Mibsam, my son-in-law?" he asked.

The son-in-law permitted himself to answer: "I see a white thing on the ground, that moveth and seemeth like a being, and a living thing."

Kedar and Kedma, the sons, confirmed his words.

"It is amazing," said the old man. "I confide in your sharp eyes and will call to see if it will answer. Halloo!" he called down the well in

his ancient high-pitched voice. "Who or what is it moaneth in this well? Is thy place native to thee or wouldst thou be elsewhere?"

They listened. There was a little pause. Then they heard faint and far away:

"Mother! Save thy son!"

At once they were all excitement.

"Up! No delay!" the elder cried. "Bring a rope, that we may throw it down and draw the creature up to daylight, for plainly that abode is not native to him. Here is no mother," he shouted down, "but we are pious people up here who desire to save thee if it is thy wish. See now," he turned to his men, "what one may come upon on a journey! But this is more extraordinary than aught I have met between the two rivers. Was it not shrewdly done, to spy out this hidden and covered well? And was it not I who proposed it? Men of small courage might falter or take to their heels; I can see in your faces that the thought has entered your minds; for it is uncanny to be spoken to thus, out of the depths; and it is very possible that that which speaketh is the genius of the abandoned well or some spirit of the abyss. But we must look at the matter on its practical side and meet the situation with all our energy; for the wailing from below indicateth extreme need. Where is the rope?" He bent and called into the pit: "Canst thou seize a rope which we will throw and tie it round thee that we may draw thee up?"

Again there was a pause before answer came. Faintly it sounded: "I lie in bonds."

The old man had put his hands to his ears, but the others had to repeat to him what the voice had said.

"You hear," he said then. "In bonds it lieth. It both heighteneth his need and maketh harder our task. One of you must go down into the hole to loose the creature's bonds. Where is the rope? We have it. Mibsam, my son-in-law, I appoint thee to go down. Thou shalt be well attached to the rope and it shall be like an arm which we stretch down into the depths and draw it up again with the bundle in it. So soon as thou hast it fast, thou must call out and with our united powers we shall draw thee and our booty up to us again."

Mibsam declared himself ready, for good or for ill. He was a young man with a short face, a rather long, flat nose, and prominent eyes whose whites gleamed in the darkness of his face. He took the head-cloth from his curly hair, laid off his burnous, and lifted his arms to let himself be wound round with the rope. It was no hempen rope, but a cord of Egyptian papyrus, wonderfully softened, pounded, and smoothed, practically unbreakable. He knew its quality well, for the men carried several bales of it, to sell.

Soon son-in-law was tied and harnessed, ready to swing down. They all took part in winding him up; Epher, the old man's nephew, the sons, and the slaves. Then Mibsam sat down on the edge of the well, let go

his hold, and dropped into the empty depths, while those at the rope braced their legs and passed it in little jerks through their hands. It soon slackened; Mibsam was on the ground. They could relax their legs and go to peer into the well. They could just hear his voice speaking to the creature down there, panting as he lifted him to attach the rope. "Haul up," he cried then. They hauled away on the double burden, shouting in unison, while the old man stood by directing them with gestures. Up came the son-in-law above the ruin, bearing in his arms the inhabitant of the well.

Great was the amazement of the merchants when they saw the fettered boy. They lifted eyes and hands to heaven, shook their heads, and clacked with their tongues. They rested their hands on their knees to look at their prize as he sat on the step leaning against the well, with hanging head, in his bonds, spreading abroad a mouldy air. He wore an amulet on a bronze cord round his neck and a ring with a lucky stone on his finger, but nothing else at all. His wounds were closed over and nearly healed by this time and the bump on his eye so far reduced that he could open it. Now and then he did, though mostly he had kept both eyes shut. Now, however, he feebly lifted the long-lashed lids and looked upwards pathetically but with interest at his rescuers. He even smiled over their astonishment.

"Merciful mother of God!" the old man said. "What have we fished up out of the depths? Is he not like the spirit of the abandoned well, miserable, wretched, and half dead, when the water receded and left him stranded? But let us abide by the common-sense side of the affair and the needs of this creature we have found. For from the practical point of view he seems to me to be a boy of good quality, if not of the best, and fallen into bad luck I know not how. Look well at these eyelashes and the delicate growth of the limbs, however befouled they are and stinking from the pit. Kedar and Kedma, shame upon you for holding your noses, for sometimes he openeth his eyes. Loose him first from his fetters, cut them through. Now bring milk to refresh him. Wilt thy tongue obey thee, my son, to make us know who thou art?"

Joseph might have found words, despite his feebleness. But he had no wish to speak, nor any thought of uncovering the family quarrel to these Ishmaelites—it was no affair of theirs. Therefore he only looked dyingly at the old man and smiled piteously as with his freed hand he made a gesture of negation before his lips. He received milk and drank it out of a pot which a slave held for him, for his arms were lame from the bonds. He drank so greedily that a good part of the milk dribbled out of his mouth again directly he had done, as though he were a suckling. When the old man, upon this, asked him how long he had been in the pit, he stretched out three fingers in sign that it had been three days, which the Minaeans found very significant and thrilling in view of the

81

three dark days of the moon. When they asked how he got into the pit—in other words, who had thrown him in—he confined his answer to a gesture and motioned with his forehead upwards, so that one could not tell whether men had done so to him or heavenly powers been in play. But when they asked him again who he was, he whispered: "Your servant," and collapsed; so that they were none the wiser.

"Our servant," repeated the elder. "Well, in so far as he is a foundling and without us would not have had breath for his nostrils. I know not what you think, but so much I see, there is a mystery here, for many such there are in the world, as sometimes on journeys one discovereth to one's great amaze. Naught remaineth to us to do but to take this creature with us, for here can we not leave him, nor yet here build huts until he get his strength. I find," he added, "that this lad from the well toucheth my heart in some way, I know not how. For it is not pity alone nor the mystery about him. But about every human being there is an encircling ring, which is not his own flesh, but yet of his flesh, and light or dark as the case may be. Old experienced eyes perceive it better than young heedless ones, who look indeed, but do not see. Now as I look fixedly at this foundling his aura seemeth to me strikingly light and I conceive that he is the sort of find which one doth not throw away."

"I can read tablets and write cuneiform," said Joseph, lifting himself a little. Then he fell back again.

"You hear?" asked the elder, after he had had Joseph's words repeated to him. "He can write and is well brought up. Then is he worth finding, as I said, and not made to be left lying. We will take him with us, for, thanks to my inspiration which led me to look into the well, nobody can say us nay or call us robbers because we exercise a finder's right and do not trouble overmuch to ask after those who threw away or heedlessly lost what we have found. If the owners turn up we have a right to a reward and ransom, and it looketh as though we shall make something either way. Come, put this mantle upon him, for he came naked and foul out of the depth as from the body of his mother and is as it were twice born."

The old man pointed to the mantle which son-in-law Mibsam had thrown down; its owner grumbled against handing it over to the boy from the well, that he might pollute it. But grumbling was of no avail; he yielded to the old man's will, and two slaves bore the child in the mantle to the camels, where he was mounted with Kedma, one of the sons, a youth with severe and regular features and a lofty carriage of the head, so that he looked down upon all things underneath drooping lids. Round his head, atop the white head-cloth, he wore a black felt ring. At the old man's bidding Kedma took Joseph before him on the saddle, and the train got under way, taking the road to Dothan, for it might be market day there.

OF REUBEN'S PLAN

All this time the sons of Jacob were very ill at ease. They were in no wise happier than when the thorn had sat in their flesh and they had stumbled about in the broom hot with their shame. Now the thorn had been pulled out, but the wound was unhealed. It kept on rankling, as though the thorn had been a poisoned one. They had washed out their shame, but it would be too much to say that their sleep tasted better than before. They did not say so, they kept quiet about it.

In fact, in these days they were silent altogether; spoke only when necessary and then grudgingly and between their teeth. They did not meet each other's eyes, but looked anywhere and everywhere, only not in one another's faces when they had to speak. The result was that nobody felt settled about any arrangement, since bargains struck only by word of mouth and not also with the eyes always seem to lack validity. But they did not even care, apparently, whether they were valid or not. Sometimes one or other let fall comments like "All very well—" or "So far, so good," or even "If that were all," which were but gloomy allusions to the thing which stood in the background of all their thoughts and which, not being settled, but very far from it, made worthless every word they uttered.

However, this would have to come to an end some time and somehow, however long, lingering, and disgusting the process: that slow perishing and dying down in the depths, though nobody could prophesy how long it would take. On the one hand they would have liked to hasten the process, on the other they would gladly have slowed it down, on the chance of some less ugly termination—though they could not imagine what that should be. I have repeatedly warned my readers against taking these sons of Jacob for particularly hardened ruffians and withdrawing all sympathy from them. Even the most partisan weakness for Joseph (a centuries-old weakness from which I strive to be free) should remember that such a judgement would be very one-sided, and that Joseph himself would not concur in it. For the truth is that they had all of them stumbled unawares into the mess they were in, and would much rather be quit of it. More than once in these dreadful days they wished that they had finished with the business at once, and grumbled at Reuben, who had prevented them. But these dismal regrets were only a consequence of the tight place they were in. They felt put in a corner and checkmated; in a situation such as life will often confront us with, and for which a game of chess furnishes a good analogy.

Big Reuben was by no means alone in the wish to save Rachel's child alive out of the grave. Indeed, hardly one among the brethren but would start up every few hours under the spur of such a wish. But then

would come the question: was it possible? Alas, no, it was not; the hasty resolve died down, being defeated by the relentless claims of reason. Suppose they were to rescue the dreamer just in time to save him—what could they do with him? It was a blank wall, there was no way out; he must stop where he was. They had not only thrown him in; in every other way as well they had consigned him to the tomb and taken every precaution against his rising from it. He was logically dead; their part was to do nothing but wait until he was actually so: an unnerving programme and without a time limit. For these poor souls knew nothing of three days. On the contrary; they knew of people who got lost in the desert and spent seven, yes, twice seven days without food or drink before they were found. It was good to know this, for it gave some room for hope. And it was dreadful to know it, since the hope was a mad and impossible one. Not often have men been in such a tight place; to think only of Joseph's sufferings in these three days would be to give way to prejudice in his favour.

These tormented souls were sitting one afternoon beneath the red-trunked trees, on the spot where they had beaten Joseph and where, a little earlier, they had talked of Lamech, that primitive hero, and blushed in their shame that they were not as he. Only eight of them were there; Naphtali the runner was about somewhere in the neighbourhood seeking to hear new things and report them from place to place; and Reuben had been missing since early morning. He had mumbled something about going up to Dothan to buy spiced wine and breadfruit in exchange for some of their own wares. The others had approved of Reuben's going, on account of what he would bring back; they were unwontedly eager to comfort themselves and blur their understandings with some of the myrrh wine which was made at Dothan.

But the real truth was that Reuben had left them being bent on quite other activity and had only told them about the wine to make them approve his going. Tossing sleepless the night before, big Reuben's resolve had come to maturity: he would deceive the brethren and save the boy. Three days he had held out and left Jacob's lamb to perish in the well. He could endure no more—God grant it was not too late. He would steal away and with his own hand free him whom they had consigned to the grave. He would take him by the hand and lead him back to their father and speak to him: "I am unstable as water, and sin is not far from me. But lo, here I have flowed to good purpose, for I bring thee thy lamb, which they would have rent. Is my sin thereby blotted out, and am I again the first-born?"

Reuben tossed no longer, but lay open-eyed and motionless the rest of the night and made detailed plans for the rescue and the flight. It would not be too easy: the boy was bound hand and foot and would be very weak. He would not be able to grasp the rope which Reuben would throw to him; a cord would not do, there must be a strong hook on it, to

catch the knotted rope, in order to haul up the prize. Perhaps a web of cords would be better, a net to take his fish in. Or even a board among the cords, on which the boy, clumsy in his bonds as he was, could sit and be drawn up over the edge. Reuben went over all the necessary preparations and equipment, including his own clothes, which he would have ready for the naked lad; he chose in his mind the stout ass which he would drive to Dothan with wool and cheeses, and then ride, with the boy before him and in the shelter of darkness, the five days' journey to Hebron, to the father. Big Reuben's heart was full of eager joy, only dampened somewhat by the fear least Joseph might not survive until dark of the third day. When he took leave of his brethren that morning, he had ado to speak and act with the dour ill-temper which had become their settled mood.

THE SALE

Eight of them, then, sat beneath the spreading branches of the pines and gazed gloomily into space in the direction whence the shining had come and that wandering will-o'-the-wisp that had so dazed their senses and lured them to their present pass. As they looked they saw their brother Naphtali, Bilhah's son, come running among the shrubbery on their right. He came on with great leaps of his long sinewy legs, and they could tell even at this distance that he was bringing them news. They cared but little for it, however.

"Brothers, children, friends," he unfolded, "I bring you news: a train of Ishmaelites is riding from Gilead, their noses directed hitherwards, and must soon be here and pass by three stones' cast from where you sit. They seem friendly heathen, with bales of goods, and trade with them would be possible if we were to call to them."

They hearkened, then turned their heads listlessly away.

"It is so far good," said one. "Good, Naphtali, we thank thee for thy news."

"If that were all," another added, sighing. Then they were quiet, tortured with irritation and feeling no desire for trade.

Yet after a while they became restless, fidgeted to and fro, and stared about them. And when Jehudah—for it was he—lifted up his voice and addressed them, they all started and turned toward him: "Speak, Judah, for we hearken." And Judah spoke:

"Sons of Jacob, I have somewhat to ask you, and it is this: of what profit is it to us that we slay our brother and hide his blood? I answer for you all: no profit whatever. It was utterly weak and contemptible that we threw him in the pit and persuaded ourselves that his blood was spared thereby, that we might eat by the well; for to shed it we were all afraid. But do I blame our fear? Nay, yet I blame that we lied to our-

85

selves over it and made distinctions like doing and happening, hiding ourselves behind them, yet standing naked and bare, for that they are but wind. We lusted to be like Lamech in the song and slay the young man for our hurt. But our customs are not those of the ancient time and of heroic mould. Somewhat we must yield to the present; and lo, instead of killing the youth we could only let him die. Fie upon us, for it was but a bastard thought, begot of the ancient saga and the modern customs! Therefore I say to you, since we did not know how to do like unto Lamech and had to yield somewhat to the conditions as they exist, let us then be honest to conform to them altogether and let us sell our brother to these Ishmaelites."

A stone fell from all their hearts, for Judah had spoken after their thoughts. Now were their eyes entirely open, which indeed had already begun to blink at the light as they considered the news brought by Naphtali. Here was the way, simple and clear, out of their impasse. It was the way of Naphtali's Ishmaelites, coming God knew whence and passing into the immensity, the misty distance whence there was as little return as from the grave. They could not have lifted up the boy, however much they had wished—and suddenly now they could; for he should be delivered to these oncoming ones of the desert, and with them should depart out of sight and knowledge as the falling star and its trail quench in nothingness together. Even Simeon and Levi, seeing that heroic methods were out of fashion, found nothing to object to in the plan.

They all broke out together in eager, low-toned haste, saying: "Yea, yea, yea, yea! Thou sayest it, Judah, thou hast spoken most excellently. To the Ishmaelites; sell him, sell him, for that is the way out; thus are we freed and our troubles at an end. Bring Joseph here; up, and raise him out of the well, for they are coming, and it is still conceivable that he liveth. A man may live twelve or fourteen days, so experience teacheth. Some to the well straightway, while the others . . ."

But lo, even as they spoke, here came the Ishmaelites. The foremost appeared three stones' throw away, an old man with his hands wrapped in his mantle, and his camel led by a boy. Behind him in single file came the others, riders, pack-camels, and drovers—no very stately train; these traders seemed not to be very rich, two even sat on one camel. They moved like shadows tranquilly across the scene, their eye directed upon Dothan's hill.

It was too late to fetch Joseph. Too late for the moment. But Jehudah was firmly resolved, and the others as well, not to lose the opportunity, but to clutch it by the forelock and attach the boy to these Ishmaelites that they should take him out of sight and sound and so set the brethren free, for the situation was no longer endurable. The ancestor of these travellers—had he not been sent by Abraham, with Hagar into the desert, because he had "sported" in an underworldly manner with Isaac, the son of the true wife? With Ishmael's sons should Joseph be put off

into the desert—the situation had roots; it had been once, and it recurred. New, if you like, a really original contribution, was the idea of the sale. But even so it has for thousands of years been booked too high on the debit side of the brethren's account. To sell a man, to sell one's own brother! But after all it is sentimental to judge without soberly taking into account the customs of the time and the country, which deprive the sale of almost all its unique and dubious character. A needy man sold his sons—and surely the brethren were in sore need! Fathers sold their daughters in marriage—the eight now sitting here would never have drawn breath or been sitting there at all if Jacob had not bought their mothers from Laban with fourteen years' toil.

It was a bit awkward, after all, that the merchandise was not at hand, but stored, so to speak, in a pit in the field. But it could be fetched at the right moment, and the first thing was to accost the strangers and try if they had desire to buy.

Therefore the eight set their hands to their lips and cried out abroad:

"Halloo, men and strangers, whence come ye and whither go? Stay a little. For here are shade-trees and folk with whom to talk."

The sound travelled across and found hearing from the merchants. They turned their eyes from the hill of Dothan and their heads toward those who called. The leader nodded, gestured, and turned aside to visit these natives, who had got up and greeted the travellers, putting their fingers under their eyes in token that they were glad to see the guests. The brethren touched brow and breast to indicate that here as there all was in readiness to receive them. The boys ran, flourishing their switches, among the camels and making clucking sounds to induce them to kneel and lie down. The riders dismounted, went through the formalities of greeting, and sat down together. The brothers remained where they were, with the strangers opposite. The old man held the middle place, right and left of him the row of his companions, sons, nephew, and son-in-law. The retinue kept farther back. But between it and the heads of the party, behind the strangers, and in a space directly between the master and one of his sons, sat a figure with a cloak drawn over his head and before his face so that only a gap of forehead showed.

Why were the brothers impelled, during the preliminary exchange of courtesies, to keep looking at the shrouded figure in the second row? The question answers itself. The silence of the isolated figure involuntarily drew all eyes upon it—everyone would have done as the brethren did, for who wraps himself up to the eyes in fine weather as though a dust-spirit were approaching? The brothers were not at their ease, they were distracted. Not on account of that solitary figure—it best knew why it shunned the light, and might keep the knowledge to itself. No, it was because the merchandise they had to sell ought to be fetched, and it would have been well if some of them, two or three, had got up and gone to take it from where it was kept and somewhat freshen it up before offer-

ing it for sale, as they had arranged in whispers to do, while the company was approaching. Why did they not go? Probably because it had not been decided who should go. But they might have decided among themselves. Perhaps they feared to seem rude. But they could have made some excuse. Dan, Zebulun, Issachar, for instance—what held them glued to their places, staring distracted at the figure in the space behind the merchant and his son?

Each side gave account of itself, with phrases in which boasting and self-depreciation were equally balanced. Jehudah stated that he and his were simple shepherd folk, scum of the earth, compared with the lords sitting before them, and sons of an exceeding rich man in the south, a real king of the flocks, and prince of God. Some of his countless possessions were pastured in this valley, a small part only, though more than the eye could take in. The rest were at Hebron, and there too the country was too small to hold them. With whom, then, had they, in their unworthiness, to do?

The old man answered to all this that if one were to turn away his eyes from so much splendour and cast them upon himself and his troupe, one would see scarcely anything, first because their eyes had been dazzled, but secondly because there was not much to see. They were, indeed, sons of the great kingdom of Ma'on in the continent of Arabia, and dwelt in the land of Mozar or Midian. Thus they were Midianites, or, if you liked, Medanites, or, more simply still, Ishmaelites. It mattered not how they were called, since they were too worthless to merit a name. They had equipped caravans which more than once had gone to the ends of the earth; they traded to and fro amongst kingdoms, convoying treasures worth a king's ransom: the gold of Ophir and the balsams of Punt. From the kings they asked royal prices, but amongst friends they were cheap. Their camels were laden with sheets of milk-white tragacanth, of exquisite fracture, such as had never been seen in this valley, and frankincense which would tempt the noses of the gods, so that no one once smelling it would smell any other. So much for the insignificance of the guests.

The brothers kissed their finger-tips and sketched a contact between the earth and their foreheads.

"This land of Mosar, or Ma'inland," Jehudah inquired, "is it very far away indeed, in dim and misty distance?"

"Very far in space and thus also in time, certainly," the old man agreed.

"Seventeen days distant?" asked Jehudah.

"Seven times seventeen," responded the elder. Even at that its remoteness was only approximately indicated. In motion as in rest—for rest, too, belongs to travel—one must patiently leave it to time to overcome space. Some time or other, in the end unexpectedly time would bring that about.

Then one might say, Judah ventured to think, that these regions of their destination lay beyond our ken, God knew how far in immeasurable space?

One might so express oneself, assented the old man, if one had never traversed the distance in question and was not used to league himself with time against space, but rather to take no advantage of time for that end. If one was at home in that distance, one naturally thought about it in less fantastic terms.

He and his, Judah said, were shepherds and not travelling merchants. But if he might say so, the latter were not unique in their understanding of the patient pact with time against space. Shepherds too were travellers, they had to seek new pastures and wells and to rove and wander even as the lord of the road, in this respect being unlike the peasant of the fields, the settled sons of Baal. Their father, the king of the flocks, dwelt, as he had said, five days' journey southwards, and this distance, however insignificant compared with a stretch of seven times seventeen days, they had often traversed to and fro, so that they knew by heart every boundary stone, well, and tree that was in it, and nothing on the way surprised them. As for travel and the conquest of space: of course they could not compete with merchants from the dim and remote distance; yet even as boys they had come from the land of the rivers in the far East, where once their father had laid the foundation of his riches, and come into this land, and dwelt in the vale of Shechem, where indeed their father had built a well fourteen ells deep and very broad because the children of the city had been jealous over the existing water-supply.

"May they be punished unto the fourth generation!" said the old man. It was lucky that the children of the land had not also seized on the well of the speaker's father and zealously filled it up so that it would have become dry, he added.

Two could play at that game, responded the nine. They had in the end been able to leave the Shechemites with a bitter taste in their mouths!

Were they then, the old man asked, such mighty heroes, so cruel and implacable in their wrath?

Shepherds they were, was the answer; accustomed to bear arms, to battle with bandits and beasts of prey, and not to give ground in disputes over pasture and well. But as for distance, and stout-heartedness on the way, Judah went on, after the old man had paid homage to their virility, their ancestor seemed to have had wandering in the blood. He came from Ur, in the land of the Chaldees and had migrated into these valleys, which he had measured across and across, unable to settle down. If one reckoned up all his wanderings, the sum would probably come to seven times seventeen days. But once he had sent his oldest servant on a journey with ten camels toward Naharaim, that was Shinar, to woo a bride for his miraculous late-born and rescued son, and the servant had

fared so briskly that it was scarce exaggeration to say that the earth had sprung to meet him. And at a well in the field he had found the bride and recognized her because that she gave him water with her own hand and had also given his ten camels to drink. All this travelling and conquest of space had been in their family—not to speak of its father and lord, who already as a doughty youth had left home and gone into Chaldaea, some seventeen days and more. There he had come on a well . . .

"Pardon," said the old man, as he stretched his hand out of his cloak and stopped the speech. "Pardon, my good friend and shepherd, if thy elder servant make some comment on thy words. When I list to thee and hear thee tell of thy tribe and its history, it seemeth to me that in it the well hath played a rôle as important as all your experience in moving and wandering."

"How so?" asked Judah, and stiffened his back. All the brothers did the same.

"Thus," replied the elder. "Thou speakest and every second the word 'well' striketh on mine ear. You change well and pasture. You have the wells of the country by heart. Your father hath built a well very deep and broad. Your grandfather's oldest slave wooed at the well. Your father too as it seems. Mine ears are buzzing with all these wells."

"My lord merchant," answered Judah, standing very stiff and erect, "meaneth to say that my words are monotonous and droning. That is grievous to hear. We brothers are herdsmen, not spinners of tales by the we—not lie-mongers of the market-place, who have learned it and do it after their art, for hire. We speak and tell as we think, without artifice or skill. But indeed I would ask how one could tell of the life of man, for instance the life of shepherds, and not talk of travel and therewith of wells, without which there cannot be any coming and going. . . ."

"Very true," the old man interrupted. "My friend, the son of the king of the flocks, answereth me most aptly. What a part doth not the well play in the life of man, and how many tales and sayings are bound up with them, even in the mind of your ancient servant; whether they hold standing or living water, or are dry and choked with refuse! But indeed mine hearing, which is somewhat dull from age, had not been so receptive for the word were it not for a strange matter we have encountered on our travels, which I reckon amongst the most astonishing within my memory. I trust that of your goodness you will give me advice and enlighten me concerning it."

The brothers started bolt upright once more; their backs were quite hollow, their eyes stared unwinkingly.

"Is there not perchance," asked the old man, "in the country hereabouts where you pasture, a child missing, so that it cannot be found at its home, but hath been stolen or carried away or indeed devoured by a

lion or other beast of prey, because it hath not come home for three days?"

"No," answered the brethren. Not that they knew of.

"Then who is this?" said the old man. He reached behind him and jerked Joseph's mantle from off his head. There he sat, behind and between the men, in a nest of falling folds, his eyes modestly cast down. His face looked rather as it had on the day in the field when he sat in his father's lap and related his shameless dream of the stars. At least it reminded the brethren of that.

Several of them had leaped to their feet on recognizing the figure, but they all sat down again at once.

"Oh, thou meantest him," said Dan, seeing that it was time for him to display his snake- and adder-like gifts, "when thou spakest of the well and of lost people? Nobody else? Well, thou hast made a great find. That is a slave, a nobody's son, a villein of the lowest sort, a dog whom we have had to punish for continual theft, for lying, blasphemy, brawling, impenitence, whoredom, and all heaped-up sins against virtue. For young as he is, he is a standing sink of iniquity. Thou hast found him and taken him out of the pit where we put him for his instruction, the gallows-bird? Lo, thou hast been before us, for his punishment was out at this hour and we were about to grant him his life, if perchance he might have profited from the chastisement."

Thus Bilhah's son in all his subtlety. What he said had the boldness of desperation, for there sat Joseph and could open his mouth if he would. But it seemed that his brothers might still have confidence in him, thanks to his thoughts while in the pit, for in fact Joseph said no word, but sat with mild eyes cast down and behaved like a lamb that before the shearers is dumb.

The old Midianite said "Oh" and "Ah," wagging his head, as his eyes roved to and fro between the culprit and his judges. The wagging gradually became a shaking, for something about the tale rang false, and the old man would gladly have asked his foundling the rights of the matter; but tact forbade. Therefore he said:

"What do I hear, what do I hear? Such a rogue is he, on whom we had pity and helped him out of the pit in his extremity? For this I must say, you carried your discipline to the last notch. When we found him, he was already so weak that he could not swallow the milk we gave him. If you set any store by him, you have delayed full long with your rescue; though of course he may not be worth saving, being, as you say, uncommonly full of misdemeanours, as is shown, indeed, by the harshness of the punishment."

Then Dan bit his lip, for he saw that he had said too much. He had spoken incautiously, even if Joseph's silence could be depended upon; a poke in the ribs from Judah apprised him of the fact. Dan had only thought of explaining to the Ishmaelites why they had treated the boy so

cruelly. Judah, however, was thinking of the sale, and the two points of view were hard to reconcile. They were being forced to cry down their merchandise in the ears of the purchaser—it went against all sense, it had never happened to the sons of Jacob, and they were exceedingly ashamed. Apparently in this business of Joseph they got out of one tight place only to fall into another.

Judah undertook to rescue their business honour out of this pass. He said: Well, well, all honour to the truth: the measure of the punishment may have gone beyond the offence and perhaps is misleading as to the worth of the chattel—but let that pass. We sons of the king of the flocks are somewhat harsh and hasty masters; stern, mayhap over-stern in anger against moral lapses, a little hard-handed and ruthless in our decisions. The misdeeds of this young scapegrace here, if taken singly, were not too considerable; only the sum and the repetition of them gave us to think and decided us on the sharpness of the punishment. Its very excess showeth how highly we valued the slave and what care we took to preserve his worth. For his skill and understanding are remarkable; and as he now sits there with his sins purged by our severity, he is a valuable possession. All this I say and set down in the interest of truth," Judah concluded.

Dan blushed not a little for his misplaced subtlety, yet rejoiced that Leah's son had been so clever in getting out of the trap.

"H'm, h'm," croaked the old man, looking to and fro between Joseph and his brothers, shaking his head the while. "A clever rogue, indeed, as you say. What is the young dog's name?"

"He hath no name," replied Dan. "What should his name be? He has had no name at all up to now, for we said already that he is a nobody's son, a bastard and wild shoot begot in the swamps; he hath no tribe. We simply whistle or shout to call him, or say 'Come hither.'"

"H'm, h'm," went the old man again. "So, a bad stock and wild is this culprit of yours. Strange, strange! How surprising is the truth at times! It is against reason and politeness, and yet one wondereth. When we took him out of his prison, this rush-born rascal told us he could read written, and write himself. Was he lying?"

"Not quite that," answered Judah. "We said already that he hath an understanding worthy of mention and is of no common dexterity. He can keep a list and books about jugs of oil and bales of wool. If he said no more, he kept his tongue clear of false witness."

"May it be at all times avoided," responded the elder. "For truth is god and king, and Neb-ma-rê is its name. One must bow before it, no matter what its sound. Can my lords and the lords of the swamp boy read and write?" asked he, with narrowed eyes.

"We consider that a slave's business," answered Judah shortly.

"That it sometimes is," granted the old man. "But also gods write

the name of kings on trees, and great is Thoth. Possibly he hath himself sharpened the rushes and instructed him; may the ibis-headed one not set down the jest against me! But true it is: all ranks of men are governed. Only the scribe is not, for he governeth himself and needeth not to drudge. There are countries where this child of the calamus would be set over you and the sweat of your brows. For lo, I can imagine—and my imagination doth not entirely desert me, if I choose to put the case, in jest—that he were the lord and you his slaves. See," he went on, "I am a merchant, and a skilled one, believe me; for I have grown old in appraising things and the value of them; so that it is not easy to fool me when I have stuff between thumb and forefinger, as to whether it be of worth, and whether the weave is coarse or fine or of medium quality. All that I can tell between my fingers; and my old head too is bent askew with the old habit of testing, so that no one can sell me poor for good. See now, the youth is fine in grain and fibre, if also worn from hard usage. I put my head on one side and rub my fingers and I can tell. I speak not of his skill, his understanding and dexterity in writing, but of the stuff and the texture—and there I am a judge. Therefore I make bold to jest and say: My reason would not stand still were I to hear that the 'Come hither' was the master and you his servants. But ye tell me truly it is the other way round."

"Of a certainty," replied the brethren, and stiffened their backs again.

The old man was silent.

"Well," he said after a while, and again he narrowed his eyes, "since he is your slave, sell me the boy!"

In this way he put them to the test. Something in the affair was dark to him, and he made the offer suddenly and at random, slyly curious as to its effect.

"Take him as a gift," murmured Judah mechanically. And when the Midianite had shown that his head and heart were receptive to the flourish of speech, the other went on:

"Though it is against fairness that we should have had trouble with the boy and, having purged him from moral offence, should give you to inherit the fruit of our discipline! But since you have a mind to him, then make your offer."

"Do you, on the contrary, make your own price," said the old man. "For not otherwise will I consider it."

And now began the bargaining and the haggling over Joseph, and persisted unabated five hours long, until sunset and late in the day. Thirty silver pieces Judah demanded in the name of the brethren. The Minaean replied that he must be jesting. One might smile at the joke, but naught else would come of it. Was he to pay in moon metal for a mere son of the swamps and nameless "Come hither," who, on their own

evidence, suffered from great moral weakness? (This was the retort upon Dan's over-zealous crying down of the merchandise by justifying the severity of the penance.) The old man made full use of the blunder to cheapen the price. But he too had made a mistake, in rubbing his fingers and boasting of his knowledge of quality, for thus he committed himself to his high valuation of the goods by texture and weave—and that was to the advantage of the sellers. Judah took him at his word and on his honour as a judge of quality, crying up the lad's superior fineness as though he and his had never cherished the smallest ill-will against it, nor on account of it had thrown the object of their competition into the well. In the heat of the bargaining they forgot all shame; yes, Judah did not hesitate to say that a youth so fine that he could be master of them all and they his slaves should not be flung away under thirty pieces of silver! He behaved as though he were quite infatuated with the article of sale, saying that five-and-twenty silver pieces was the very lowest sum, with which he went over and kissed the mute and blinking Joseph on the cheek and exclaimed that not even for fifty shekels could he or would he part with such a treasure of cleverness and charm!

But the old man did not let himself be led away in suchwise; and his position was the stronger, seeing that he was fairly sure that the brothers were bent on being rid of the boy at any price. It was easy to find this out, by feigning to break off the chaffering. Fifteen silver shekels, namely according to the lighter Babylonian weight, were what he had offered; but when the brethren, by urging upon him his own words, had made him go up to twenty Phoenician shekels, he stopped there and would not be screwed up any further. It was in his power to say that he had found the boy in utter danger of death and to assert a finder's right to ransom money. So that he was showing very high business standards in not subtracting anything from the purchase price but rather in being prepared to pay the good round sum of twenty shekels Phoenician. If that were not worth their while, then he would withdraw the offer and would hear no more talk about this lad of the swamps who could wield the reed.

So the bargain was struck: twenty silver pieces, weighed out according to custom. The brethren slew a lamb of the flock beneath the trees in honour of the guests, let the blood run out, and fanned their fire to roast the flesh, that they might lift their hands and eat together in confirmation, and to celebrate the bargain. Joseph too received a piece from his new master, the Minaean. And as he ate, he saw how the brethren took occasion privily to take the tattered festal garment and stain it all over in the blood of the sacrifice. Before his eyes and unashamed they had done this, confiding in his silence. And he ate of the lamb whose blood was to stand for his own.

The meal and the strengthening were in place, for the chaffering was very far from being finished. The large lines had been laid down when

the price was fixed. But now began, so to speak, the retail trading; namely, the laying out of the sum in goods. For we need not think, no matter how often we have heard it, that the brothers, when they sold Joseph, received this price from the Ishmaelites in ringing coin paid out of the bag into their hands. The old man never dreamed of paying in silver, to say nothing of currency. He had his own reasons. For who carries such a weight of metal about with him on journeys? Moreover, what buyer would not prefer to liquidate his debt in articles of value, since thereby he assumes the part of the seller, and every article thus sold becomes itself an opportunity for profit? One and a half shekels of silver, in silver pieces, the Minaean weighed out to the shepherds on the delicate scale he carried at his girdle. The rest of the sum would be made up by the merchandise in his packs. They unloaded the camels and spread out their wares in the grass: incense and fine-fractured gums from beyond the river and all sorts of other delightful and useful objects: razors and knives of copper and flint, lamps, ointment-spoons, canes with inlaid work, blue glass beads, oil of resin, and sandals—a whole bazaar of notions that lay before the buyers' covetous eyes. Up to the sum of eighteen and a half silver pieces they might pocket what they chose for their own. Each object now began to be haggled over, as though it were an end in itself. The evening came on, long before they got to the end and Joseph had been sold for a little silver, a great many knives, bits of scented gum, lamps, and walking-sticks.

Then the Ishmaelites packed up again and made their adieux. They had taken time for the deal, sparing not the hours. So now they must make time spatially fruitful again and had in mind to travel another stretch in the night before they encamped. The brothers did not urge them to stop. But they advised them concerning their journey and the roads to take.

"Above all," they said, "avoid going inland or along the watershed to Hebron—it is inadvisable, let our friends be warned. The roads are rough, the animals will stumble, and vagabonds are lurking everywhere. Go farther along the plain and turn into the road that leads down through the hills along the foot of the orchards to the borders of the country. Thus you will be safe and can ride always on the pleasant sea-sand seven times seventeen days or as far as you like; it is a pleasure to travel by the sea, one never tires of it, and it is on all accounts most sensible."

The merchants promised, as they took their leave. The camels got up beneath them, and Joseph, the bartered slave, was mounted with Kedma, the old man's son. His eyelids drooped as they had done the whole time, even when he ate of the lamb. And the brothers, too, stood with downcast eyes as the train disappeared in the quickly falling twilight. Then they took a long breath and breathed it out again:

"Now is he gone and is no more!"

REUBEN COMES TO THE PIT

But in the falling dusk and in the whispering evening that drew on, lighted by great stars, Reuben, Leah's son, was driving his laden ass from Dothan along sequestered paths toward the grave of Joseph, that he might fulfil the plans he had made the night before in anguish and in love.

In his broad, powerful breast his heart throbbed strongly; for though he was big, he was soft and excitable, and he feared the brethren, that they might seek him and prevent the work of rescue, which was to be likewise the instrument of his atonement and reinstatement. His muscular face was pale in the darkness, and his great legs like columns in their bands trod the ground noiselessly. He spoke no word to his ass, but grimly prodded the phlegmatic beast in the flesh of its rump to make it get on. One thing Reuben feared above all: that the stillness of death might prevail in the well when he came up and softly called his brother's name. That Joseph might not have kept soul and body together, but be gone beyond reach, and all preparations be vain, including the ladder which the ropemakers of Dothan had made under his eye.

For Reuben had, after much thought, decided on the ladder. It would do for various contingencies: Joseph could climb up on it if his strength held out; or, if it did not, he might seat himself between the treads and be drawn up to the daylight by Reuben's muscular arms, which had once enfolded Bilhah and would surely be strong enough to draw up Jacob's lamb out of the depths. He had a coat to cover Joseph's nakedness, and food for five days hung from the animal's flanks—for five days' time would be needed for the flight from his brothers, whom Reuben would thus betray and bring to grief. He bowed his head and owned as much to himself as he stole by night to the grave. This much evil big Reuben would do in order to do good. For that it was good and necessary to save Joseph, of that he had no doubts at all, and if the good and the evil mingled in his deed, it could not be helped. Life was like that. But Reuben also had faith that he could turn evil into good. Once he had put himself right with the father and was again the first-born son, he could hope to rescue the brethren too and hack a way for them out of their impasse. His word would avail much, and he would give it on their side, in asking all to share the guilt, including even the father himself, that there might come a great insight and mutual pardon, and righteousness might prevail for ever.

Thus Reuben sought to still his throbbing heart and to console himself for his mixed motives, which were turbid and involved like everything in life. But now he had come to the slope and the wall, where he stopped to see that he was not being watched. Then he took rope and

coat and descended on tiptoe to the broken steps and penetrated through the fig-tree scrub into the well-chamber.

The stars shone down on the broken flags, but there was no moon, and Reuben walked warily, drawing a deep breath as he went down, for his excitement had winded him and he needed breath for the call he was to cry down into the depths. "Joseph, art thou alive?" With what a passionate joy would he hear the answer, with what heart-sinking the lack of it! And then the call died unuttered, or changed into a hoarse cry of fear. For he was not alone down here. Someone was sitting there in the starlight.

How could that be? Someone sat there beside the well, and it was uncovered. The two halves of the lid lay one on top of the other on the flags, and the figure sat on them in a short mantle, leaning on his staff, and looked at Reuben sleepily, saying not a word.

Big Reuben's legs felt shaky from his stumbling. He was so dazed that for a moment he thought he saw Joseph before him, Joseph who had died and now, a spirit, sat beside his tomb. But this unlovable presence was not at all like Rachel's son: even Joseph's ghost would surely not have been so uncommon tall; nor would he have had such a thick neck and little head on top. But then why was the stone rolled away from the well? Reuben was utterly puzzled. He stammered:

"Who art thou?"

"One of many," coolly answered the seated figure. He raised his chin and well-shaped mouth so that they looked particularly plastic. "I am nothing startling, be not afraid. But whom seekest thou?"

"Whom I seek?" repeated Reuben, put out by the unexpected encounter. "First of all I will hear what thou dost in this place."

"Oh, so thou wouldst know that? I am the last to imagine that there is anything here to seek. I am set to guard this well, therefore I sit here and watch. If thou imaginest that I have particular pleasure or sit here for the fun of the thing, then thou mistakest. I act according to duty and to carry out orders—it easeth many a vexed question to do so."

Curiously enough Reuben's anger at the presence of the stranger was somewhat appeased by these words. It was so unwelcome and annoying to find anyone on the spot that he was glad to hear that the man was not here by his own wish. It made a sort of bond between them.

"But who hath placed thee here?" he asked, somewhat mollified. "Was it the people of the place?"

"Of the place, yes. Whence such an order cometh, we shall let that pass. It is commonly transmitted through many mouths and there is small use in following it back to its source, for one must stand guard in any case."

"Stand guard by an empty well!" cried Reuben, his voice choking.

"Empty, certainly," the watcher replied.

"An uncovered one," Reuben amended, and pointed with trembling

finger at the well-hole. "Who hath rolled away the stone from the well? Was it thou, perchance?"

The man smiled and looked down at his arms in the sleeveless linen garment; they were round, but weak. He was right, these were no arms to roll the lid either on or off.

"Neither on nor off have I rolled the stone," said the stranger, smiling again and shaking his head. "The one thou knowest, the other thou seest. Others have toiled and moiled, and I should not be needing to sit here and watch, were the stone still in its place. But who can say where is the true place of such a stone? Sometimes it is on the hole, but must not the lid be rolled away if refreshment is to come out of the well?"

"What sayest thou?" cried Reuben, tortured by his impatience. "I think thou prattlest, stealing my costly time with thy nonsense. How shall a dry well give refreshment, wherein is naught but dust and mould?"

"That dependeth," the seated one replied, pursing his lips, his little head laid on one side, "what one had previously confided to the dust and what one sank into its womb. If it were life, then will life and refreshment come out again a hundredfold. A kernel of wheat for instance. . . ."

"Thou fellow," Reuben interrupted him in a trembling voice, and the ladder and the mantle for Joseph shook in his hands, "it is intolerable that thou sittest there speaking of the rudiments of things as one knoweth them by heart and as the child is taught in its mother's lap. I charge thee—"

"Thou art right impatient," said the stranger. "Permit me to say that thou remindest me of a rushing stream. Thou shouldst learn patience and to await; for these are the rudiments of things and must be understood by all, for he who cannot abide nor have patience findeth nothing, either here or anywhere. For all fulfilment is a slow matter. It may begin and may cast this way and that and appear as the temporary present both in heaven and on earth, when as yet it is but a trial and a promise. Thus will fulfilment roll along but slowly, like the stone when it is heavy and hard to roll from the tomb. Yet must one roll and push until it be really rolled away, though meanwhile I myself sit here only as a trial and a promise."

"Sit here then no longer," Reuben cried out. "Dost thou understand? I would pack thee off and have thee vanish that I may be alone with this well, which is my affair more than thine; up, this minute, or I will help thee find thy legs. Canst thou not see, spindle-arms, thou who canst not roll but only sit there and gape, that God hath made me strong as a bear and I am provided with a knotted rope to serve various ends? Up and away, or I will fly at thy throat."

"Touch me not," said the stranger, and stretched out his long round arm toward the angry man. "Bethink thee that I am of this place and thou wilt have them about thine ears if thou layest hand on me. Have I not told thee that I am set here? Vanish of course I could and with ease, but

not at thy behest and in neglect of my duty, which telleth me to sit here for practice and watch. Comest thou with thy fine coat and thy trumpery cords and markst not at all how absurd thou art in coming thus to an empty well—as thou sayest thyself!"

"Empty as a well," explained Reuben impetuously, "empty of water!"

"Empty altogether," answered the watchman. "The grave is empty, now that you are here."

But Reuben held in no longer; he rushed to the well, leaned over, and cried, low but urgently, into the depths:

"Joseph, Joseph, art alive and hast yet strength?"

The man on the stone shook his head and smiled pityingly. He even copied Reuben's voice, calling and clucking with his tongue. Then he said: "Comest here to talk into an empty hole? What unreason! Here is no boy, far and wide. If one was once there, then the place did not hold him. Cease thou to make a fool of thyself with thy gear and thy crying into the void!"

Reuben stood there still bent over the gulf out of which no word answered him.

"Horrible!" he cried. "He is dead or gone. What shall I do? Reuben, what wilt thou do now?"

And all his pain, his disappointment, his despair burst out of him.

"Joseph!" he cried out. "I would save thee and help thee out of the pit with my arms. Here is the ladder, here is the coat for thy body. Where art thou? Thy door is open. Thou art lost. I am lost. Where shall I go, since thou art gone, stolen and dead?— Thou fellow, thou man of the place," he cried, in an abandonment of suffering, "sit not there dumb, on these stones which the thieves have rolled away, but advise and help me. A boy was here; Joseph, my brother, Rachel's child. His brethren and I, we put him here three days ago in punishment for his arrogance. But his father waiteth for him—with what infinite waiting cannot be told; and if they say to him that a lion hath torn the lamb, he will be struck to earth. Therefore I am come with cord and coat, to draw up the boy out of the well and bring him to the father, for he must have him back! I am the oldest. How shall I come before the father's face if the boy returneth not, and where shall I go? Tell me, help me, who hath rolled away the stone and where has Joseph gone?"

"Seest thou?" said the stranger. "Thou camest to the well-house, thou wast incensed at my presence and vexed because I sat upon the stone; but now thou comest to me for comfort and advice. And thou dost quite rightly; perhaps it is thou on whose account I am set here near the grave, that I should sink one or other seed-corn in thy understanding and it might germinate there. The boy is no longer here, that thou seest. His dwelling standeth open, it has not held him, thou wilt see him no more. But someone there must be to cherish the seed of expectation, and since it was thou who camest to save the brother, thou shalt be the one."

"What shall I await, if Joseph is gone, stolen and dead?"

"I know not what thou understandest by dead and what by living. Thou hast laughed at the childish elements of things, but yet I may remind thee of the grain of corn when it lieth in the grave, and ask thee how thou thinkest of it in reference to life and death. For these are after all only words. For it is so that the corn falling into the earth and dying bringeth forth much fruit."

"Words, only words," cried Reuben, and wrung his hands. "They are only words thou givest me. Is Joseph dead or living? That it is which I must know."

"Manifestly he is dead," responded the watchman. "Thou and the others laid him to rest, as I hear, and since then he hath been stolen or perhaps torn by wild beasts; there is naught for it but to tell the father and make it manifest to him that he may accustom his heart to the truth. And yet, after all, it remaineth always equivocal; for it is not made to get used to, but rather hides always the seed of expectation. Men do much to penetrate the secret by ritual ways. I saw a youth descend into the grave in garland and festal garment, and above him they slaughtered a beast of the flock, whose blood they let run down, that it ran all over him and he received it with all his limbs and senses. So when he ascended again he was divine and had won life—at least for some time to come; for he had to go again into the grave, for the life of mankind cometh to an end several times, and each time cometh the grave and the rebirth, and many times must he be, until at length he finally is."

"Ah, the wreath and the festal garment," moaned Reuben and buried his face in his hands, "they lie torn and the boy is gone naked into the grave."

"Yes, and therefore thou comest hither with thy coat," responded the watchman, "and will clothe him anew. That can God do too. He can clothe anew the naked, and better than thou. Therefore I counsel thee: go home and take thy coat with thee. God can even throw a cloak over him who is clothed; after all, perhaps it was not so serious with the uncovering of this boy of thine. I would, if thou permittest, sink a seed-corn of thought into thy understanding: I would tell thee that all this is but a play and a feast, like that of the youth sprinkled with blood, a beginning only and attempt toward fulfilment; a present which is not to be taken quite seriously, but is only a jest and an allusion, a symbol, so that we might nudge each other and wink while we behold it. For perhaps this pit was only a grave created by the lesser cycle, and your brother still very much in becoming and by no means already become, as this whole story is in becoming and not already become. Receive this, I pray thee, into the womb of thy understanding and let it quietly die therein and germinate. But if it bear fruit, then give of it to thy father for his comforting."

"My father, my father!" Reuben cried. "Speak not to me of him. How shall I come before the father without the child?"

"Look up," said the watchman. For it had become clearer in the well-house, and the bark of the moon had just swum up above their heads, its darker part faintly visible in the depths of the sky. "Look at it, how it goeth and shineth and maketh the way plain for its brethren. Such allegories happen in heaven and on earth without end. He whose mind is open, and he knoweth how to read them, he abideth in expectation. But the night advanceth apace, and who need not sit and play watchman, he would do well to lie down, wrapped in his coat, with knees comfortably drawn up, that he may rise again in the morning. Go, my friend! Here, at least, thou hast nothing to seek, and as for me I shall not disappear at thy bidding."

Then Reuben turned away shaking his head, and with heavy heart and lagging feet climbed the steps and the slope up to where he had left his animal. Almost the whole way thence to the brethren's huts he did not cease to shake his bewildered head, in desperation half, and half in dumbfounded reflection. He hardly distinguished the one from the other, but he shook his head.

THE OATH

So he came to the huts and roused the nine, snatched the early sleep from their eyes, and spoke with trembling lips:

"The boy is gone. Where shall I go?"

"Thou?" they asked. "Thou speakest as though he had been only thy brother, when after all he was as much ours. Where shall we all go? That is the question. And what meanest thou by 'gone'?"

"Gone—that is, stolen, disappeared, torn in pieces, dead," Reuben shrieked. "Lost to the father, in any case. The pit is empty."

"Wast thou at the pit?" they asked. "To what end?"

"To the end of finding out," he said wrathfully. "That is still allowed, I should think, to the first-born. Shall what we have done give us peace and not harass us? Yea, I desired to see after the boy, and now I tell you that he is gone and that we must ask ourselves whither we shall go."

"To call thyself the first-born," they answered, "is somewhat bold, as we may remind thee simply by uttering the name of Bilhah. There was danger that the rights of the first-born would fall to the dreamer; but now it is the twins who come next; and Dan too could put in his claim, for he was born in the same year as Levi."

But they had seen the ass with ladder and coat— Reuben had not even tried to hide them—and easily put this and that together. So then big Reuben had meant to steal a march on them and rescue Joseph; he had intended to exalt his own head and to put them in a hole. Very fine. They exchanged meaningful glances. But if that was the way of it, their glances said, then they owed Reuben no explanation of what they had

done in the meantime. Unfaith for unfaith. Reuben needed to hear nothing, of the Ishmaelites nor how at that moment they were bearing Joseph out of sight and hearing. If he knew, he might follow after them. Therefore the brethren were silent, shrugged their shoulders at his news, and feigned indifference.

"Gone is gone," they said, "no matter whether it signifieth stolen, vanished, torn to pieces, betrayed, or sold; we would snap our fingers at it, were it worth a snap. Was it not our longing and our just desire that he might cease to be? And now it has been vouchsafed us, the pit is empty."

But he wondered that they took this surprising and monstrous news so coldly; peered into their eyes and shook his head.

"And the father!" he cried, in sudden passion, flinging up his arms.

"That hath been settled and arranged," they said, "by the cleverness of Dan. For the father shall not be let to wait and doubt, but it shall be clean and clear to him and graspable with his hands, that Dumuzi is no more and his pampered darling no longer remaineth. But we shall be united before him by means of the sign. See what we have got ready while thou wentest thine own ways."

And they fetched out the remnants of the garment, which was stiff with half-dried blood.

"Is it his blood?" Reuben cried with his high voice out of his mighty body, and shuddered frightfully. . . . For a moment he thought not otherwise than that they had been beforehand with him at the pit and killed Joseph.

They smiled at one another.

"What all dost thou not dream and spin!" they said. "But it hath been done according to our agreement, and a beast of the flock hath given his blood in sign that Joseph is gone. The garment bring we now before the father and let it be his affair to explain it as he must, for there is nothing left than that a lion surprised him in the field and tore him to pieces."

Reuben sat, his huge knees in front of him, and rubbed his fists in his eye-sockets.

"Unhappy!" he groaned. "Unhappy wretches that we are! You prattle light-heartedly of the future, yet see it not and know it not. For unclear and pale it lieth in the distance and you lack the power in your heads to bring it near, and for even the twinkling of an eyelid to live in the hour when it hath become real. Otherwise you would shudder and would wish rather that lightning would strike you down in time or that you were sunk in water with a millstone round your necks where it is deepest than that you should bring in the dish and serve up the soup that you have brewed. But I have lain before him when I did evilly and he cursed me and I know the fire of his soul when it is angry. And I can see, as though it were happening, the frightful wrestlings of his soul in its affliction. *That* shall we bring before the father and let it speak to him! Ye praters and babblers! Yea, he will interpret it! But who will

dare to look at him when he interpreteth it, and who will bear it when he uttereth his soul? For God created it large and tender and taught it how to reveal itself with overwhelming power. Ye see nothing and imagine nothing with clearness that hath not yet happened; therefore you prattle cheerfully of the future and know no fears. But I am afraid," he cried out, and stood up before them strong like a bear, like a tower, with arms outstretched. "Where shall I go when he interpreteth it?"

The nine sat there each one quite intimidated, looking down at his lap.

"Very good," responded Judah softly. "Here is nobody who spiteth thee on account of thy fear, Reuben, son of thy mother; for likewise it is brave to confess thy fear. And if thou thinkest we are blithe and gay round heart and kidneys and know naught of the fear of Jacob, then thou mistaketh. But what good is it to regret what has happened and what avail to boggle at the inevitable? Joseph is out of the world, and this coat witnesseth the truth. A sign is milder than words. Therefore we shall bring the sign before Jacob and are dispensed of words."

"Must we then," asked Asher, Zilpah's son, and licked his lips after his habit, "must we then, since we speak of carrying the robe, all of us at once bring the sign to Jacob and all of us be there when he interpreteth it? Rather let one go delicately ahead with the garment and bring it to him; but we others come afterwards and get there only when he hath already interpreted it to himself. It seemeth to me milder so. I propose Naphtali, the runner, for bearer and messenger. Or let us draw lots to see who shall bear it."

"Draw lots," cried Naphtali in haste. "I am for drawing lots, for I too imagine the future when I speak of it and I freely confess my fear."

"Listen, men," said Dan. "Now I will be the judge and free you all. For from me cometh the plan and I can shape it in my mind like wet earth and potter's clay. I will improve it; for we shall not bring Jacob the robe, neither one nor all of us. To strangers will we give it, somebody whom we shall hire, people of the place and the neighbourhood, receptive to good words and a little wool and a few curds. We will impress on him what he shall say to Jacob: thus and thus; and 'This found we in the field near Dothan and came upon it in the desert by chance. Look at it closer, father and lord, whether it is not indeed the garment of thy son.' Thus shall they speak, and when they have said, let them go away. But we will tarry a few days before we follow, until he has fully interpreted to himself the sign and knows that he has lost one and gained ten. Are ye satisfied?"

"It is well," they said, "or at least is worth talking about. Therefore let us accept it, for anything that is a practical plan, in a case like this, must be considered good."

They all accepted it, even Reuben, although he had laughed bitterly when Dan spoke of ten whom Jacob was winning for one. But they kept

on sitting before the huts under the stars and continued to take counsel, for they were somewhat uncertain of each other. The nine looked at Reuben, who had obviously intended to steal the lad and cheat them; and they were afraid before him. But he looked at the nine who had remained so strangely unmoved at the news that the pit was empty, and did not know what he should think.

"A frightful oath," said Levi, rude but pious, who liked to arrange religious ceremonies and had knowledge of them; "we must swear a frightful oath, that none of us ever tell Jacob or anyone a single little word of what hath happened here and what we did with the dreamer; not by a sign or a flicker of an eyelash, so long as he shall live."

"Thou sayest it, that we must," agreed Asher. "And this oath must bind us ten together and make us into a league so that we are like one body and one silence, as though we were not single persons, one here and one there, but one man who presseth his lips together and openeth them not, even in death, but dieth, his mouth shut together over his secret. One can stifle and slay an event by silence, which one rolleth over it like a stone. Then the breath goeth out of it for lack of air and light, and the event ceaseth to have happened. Believe me, so dieth much that has happened, if the silence over it is unbroken; for without the breath of words can naught exist. We must keep silence as one man; then will this story be as it had not been; and thereto Levi's frightful oath may help us—for it shall make us a bond."

They agreed to this, no one of them being willing to rely upon himself for his silence, but preferring to share in a mighty common bond, which should shelter him from his weakness. Therefore Levi, Leah's son, devised frightful formulas for the oath; they drew so close together that their noses rubbed and their breath mingled, put their hands in a pile, and with one voice called on the Highest, El Elyon, God of Abraham, Yitzchak, and Jacob. Neither did they forget the several Baals of the land, known unto them: Anu of Uruk, Ellil of Nippur, and Bel Harran, Sin, the moon; but named them as compurgators and swore with one voice, mouth almost on mouth, that he who did not keep silence about "it" or who did even with nod, wink, or sign betray it or glance at it, such a one should turn whore, and the daughter of Sin, mistress of womenkind, should take from him the bow, that is his manhood, that he should be like a mule, but more rightly said a whore, who took her hire upon the street. One land should drive him into the other, so that he should not know where to lay his whorish head and should neither live nor die, but life and death should spit him to one another in disgust his life long.

Thus the oath. When they had sworn it they were easier and steadier, for this was a mighty insurance. But when they broke up the counsel and went each one to his sleep, one said to another (it was Issachar said it to Zebulun):

"I have an envy, and my envy is of Turturra, the little one, Benjamin, our youngest at home, for that he knoweth nothing of all this and remaineth outside this matter and this oath. He is fortunate and I envy him. Thou too?"

"I too, indeed," answered Zebulun.

But Reuben for his part was trying to remember the words of the irritating youth of the place, who had sat on the well-stone. It was not easy to remember them, for they had been vague and full of twilight, more idle than real words and hard to reproduce. Yet in Reuben's deepest understanding a seed did remain behind, which knew naught of itself, as the seed of life knoweth naught of itself in the body of the mother, but the mother knoweth of it. It was the seed of expectation which Reuben cherished, and nourished it secretly, sleeping and waking, till he was a greyhaired man, through as many years as Jacob had served for the devil Laban.

II

THE BRIDGE
OF SAN LUIS REY

by Thornton Wilder

A Classic Story of Latin America

"Then his glance fell upon the bridge, and at that moment a twanging noise filled the air, as when the string of some musical instrument snaps in a disused room, and he saw the bridge divide and fling five gesticulating ants into the valley below."

The bridge of San Luis Rey had been built by the Incas to span a great gorge over a tumultuous stream and it was on July 20, 1714 that the supports broke. Thornton Wilder's justly famous short novel of that title, which was first published in 1927, tells of the accident and traces the lives of the five unfortunates who were crossing it at the time.

The book broke all records. Although a quite short novel, it so delighted the reading public that it went rapidly to the top of the best-seller list of the day, and it has continued in popularity, as well as in critical praise, ever since. Thornton Niven Wilder, a man of thirty who had written one novel before while teaching at Lawrenceville School, was firmly established by its success. In addition to achieving a wide distribution, it won the Pulitzer Prize and has twice been made into motion pictures.

It is in no sense an exaggeration to say that the author creates a picture of Peru with a sureness and an acquaintance with the people and the times which could hardly have been improved upon if he had lived himself in Lima in those days, a full century before the country's war of liberation. Moreover, the figures on his canvas, the old Marquesa Doña María, the Viceroy, Uncle Pio, the Abbess, and that beguiling creature, Micaela Villegas, the toast of the national theatre, become so alive and so fascinating that the reader seems to have undergone a transplanting on wings stronger than the osier supports of the bridge.

The Bridge of San Luis Rey is a familiar story to a very wide audience. But a list of short novels would be sadly incomplete without it. A flawless story, it must not be taken for granted. It is impossible to offer it too often to an audience which changes and grows and perpetuates itself with the passing years.

Part I

PERHAPS AN ACCIDENT

On Friday noon, July the twentieth, 1714, the finest bridge in all Peru broke and precipitated five travellers into the gulf below. This bridge was on the highroad between Lima and Cuzco and hundreds of persons passed over it every day. It had been woven of osier by the Incas more than a century before and visitors to the city were always led out to see it. It was a mere ladder of thin slats swung out over the gorge, with handrails of dried vine. Horses and coaches and chairs had to go down hundreds of feet below and pass over the narrow torrent on rafts, but no one, not even the Viceroy, not even the Archbishop of Lima, had descended with the baggage rather than cross by the famous bridge of San Luis Rey. St. Louis of France himself protected it, by his name and by the little mud church on the further side. The bridge seemed to be among the things that last forever; it was unthinkable that it should break. The moment a Peruvian heard of the accident he signed himself and made a mental calculation as to how recently he had crossed by it and how soon he had intended crossing by it again. People wandered about in a trance-like state, muttering; they had the hallucination of seeing themselves falling into a gulf.

There was a great service in the Cathedral. The bodies of the victims were approximately collected and approximately separated from one another, and there was great searching of hearts in the beautiful city of Lima. Servant girls returned bracelets which they had stolen from their mistresses, and usurers harangued their wives angrily, in defense of usury. Yet it was rather strange that this event should have so impressed the Limeans, for in that country those catastrophes which lawyers shockingly call the "acts of God" were more than usually frequent. Tidal waves were continually washing away cities; earthquakes arrived every week and towers fell upon good men and women all the time. Diseases were forever flitting in and out of the provinces and old age carried away some of the most admirable citizens. That is why it was so surprising that the Peruvians should have been especially touched by the rent in the bridge of San Luis Rey.

Everyone was very deeply impressed, but only one person did anything about it, and that was Brother Juniper. By a series of coincidences

so extraordinary that one almost suspects the presence of some Intention, this little red-haired Franciscan from Northern Italy happened to be in Peru converting the Indians and happened to witness the accident.

It was a very hot noon, that fatal noon, and coming around the shoulder of a hill Brother Juniper stopped to wipe his forehead and to gaze upon the screen of snowy peaks in the distance, then into the gorge below him filled with the dark plumage of green trees and green birds and traversed by its ladder of osier. Joy was in him; things were not going badly. He had opened several little abandoned churches and the Indians were crawling in to early Mass and groaning at the moment of miracle as though their hearts would break. Perhaps it was the pure air from the snows before him; perhaps it was the memory that brushed him for a moment of the poem that bade him raise his eyes to the helpful hills. At all events he felt at peace. Then his glance fell upon the bridge, and at that moment a twanging noise filled the air, as when the string of some musical instrument snaps in a disused room, and he saw the bridge divide and fling five gesticulating ants into the valley below.

Anyone else would have said to himself with secret joy: "Within ten minutes myself . . . !" But it was another thought that visited Brother Juniper: "Why did this happen to *those* five?" If there were any plan in the universe at all, if there were any pattern in a human life, surely it could be discovered mysteriously latent in those lives so suddenly cut off. Either we live by accident and die by accident, or we live by plan and die by plan. And on that instant Brother Juniper made the resolve to inquire into the secret lives of those five persons, that moment falling through the air, and to surprise the reason of their taking off.

.

It seemed to Brother Juniper that it was high time for theology to take its place among the exact sciences and he had long intended putting it there. What he had lacked hitherto was a laboratory. Oh, there had never been any lack of specimens; any number of his charges had met calamity—spiders had stung them; their lungs had been touched; their houses had burned down and things had happened to their children from which one averts the mind. But these occasions of human woe had never been quite fit for scientific examination. They had lacked what our good savants were later to call *proper control*. The accident had been dependent upon human error, for example, or had contained elements of probability. But this collapse of the bridge of San Luis Rey was a sheer Act of God. It afforded a perfect laboratory. Here at last one could surprise His intentions in a pure state.

You and I can see that coming from anyone but Brother Juniper this plan would be the flower of a perfect skepticism. It resembled the effort of those presumptuous souls who wanted to walk on the pavements

of Heaven and built the Tower of Babel to get there. But to our Franciscan there was no element of doubt in the experiment. He knew the answer. He merely wanted to prove it, historically, mathematically, to his converts—poor obstinate converts, so slow to believe that their pains were inserted into their lives for their own good. People were always asking for good sound proofs; doubt springs eternal in the human breast, even in countries where the Inquisition can read your very thoughts in your eyes.

This was not the first time that Brother Juniper had tried to resort to such methods. Often on the long trips he had to make (scurrying from parish to parish, his robe tucked up about his knees, for haste) he would fall to dreaming of experiments that justify the ways of God to man. For instance, a complete record of the Prayers for Rain and their results. Often he had stood on the steps of one of his little churches, his flock kneeling before him on the baked street. Often he had stretched his arms to the sky and declaimed the splendid ritual. Not often, but several times, he had felt the virtue enter him and seen the little cloud forming on the horizon. But there were many times when weeks went by . . . but why think of them? It was not himself he was trying to convince that rain and drought were wisely apportioned.

Thus it was that the determination rose within him at the moment of the accident. It prompted him to busy himself for six years, knocking at all the doors in Lima, asking thousands of questions, filling scores of notebooks, in his effort at establishing the fact that each of the five lost lives was a perfect whole. Everyone knew that he was working on some sort of memorial of the accident and everyone was very helpful and misleading. A few even knew the principal aim of his activity and there were patrons in high places.

The result of all this diligence was an enormous book, which as we shall see later, was publicly burned on a beautiful Spring morning in the great square. But there was a secret copy and after a great many years and without much notice it found its way to the library of the University of San Marco. There it lies between two great wooden covers collecting dust in a cupboard. It deals with one after another of the victims of the accident, cataloguing thousands of little facts and anecdotes and testimonies, and concluding with a dignified passage describing why God had settled upon that person and upon that day for His demonstration of wisdom. Yet for all his diligence Brother Juniper never knew the central passion of Doña María's life; nor of Uncle Pio's, not even of Esteban's. And I, who claim to know so much more, isn't it possible that even I have missed the very spring within the spring?

Some say that we shall never know and that to the gods we are like the flies that the boys kill on a summer day, and some say, on the contrary, that the very sparrows do not lose a feather that has not been brushed away by the finger of God.

Part 2

THE MARQUESA DE MONTEMAYOR

Any Spanish schoolboy is required to know today more about Doña
María, Marquesa de Montemayor, than Brother Juniper was to discover
in years of research. Within a century of her death her letters had become
one of the monuments of Spanish literature and her life and times have
ever since been the object of long studies. But her biographers have
erred in one direction as greatly as the Franciscan did in another; they
have tried to invest her with a host of graces, to read back into her life
and person some of the beauties that abound in her letters, whereas all
real knowledge of this wonderful woman must proceed from the act of
humiliating her and of divesting her of all beauties save one.

She was the daughter of a cloth-merchant who had acquired the
money and the hatred of the Limeans within a stone's-throw of the
Plaza. Her childhood was unhappy: she was ugly; she stuttered; her
mother persecuted her with sarcasms in an effort to arouse some social
charms and forced her to go about the town in a veritable harness of
jewels. She lived alone and she thought alone. Many suitors presented
themselves, but as long as she could she fought against the convention of
her time and was determined to remain single. There were hysterical
scenes with her mother, recriminations, screams and slamming of doors.
At last at twenty-six she found herself penned into marriage with a
supercilious and ruined nobleman and the Cathedral of Lima fairly
buzzed with the sneers of her guests. Still she lived alone and thought
alone, and when an exquisite daughter was born to her she fastened upon
her an idolatrous love. But little Clara took after her father; she was cold
and intellectual. At the age of eight she was calmly correcting her moth-
er's speech and presently regarding her with astonishment and repulsion.
The frightened mother became meek and obsequious but she could not
prevent herself from persecuting Doña Clara with nervous attention and
a fatiguing love. Again there were hysterical recriminations, screams and
slamming of doors. From the offers of marriage that fell to her, Doña
Clara deliberately chose the one that required her removal to Spain. So
to Spain she went, to that land from which it takes six months to receive
an answer to one's letter. The leave-taking before so long a voyage be-
came in Peru one of the formal services of the Church. The ship was
blessed and as the space widened between the vessel and the beach
both companies knelt and sang a hymn that never failed to sound weak

and timid in all that open air. Doña Clara sailed with most admirable composure, leaving her mother to gaze after the bright ship, her hand pressing now her heart and now her mouth. Blurred and streaked became her view of the serene Pacific and the enormous clouds of pearl that hang forever motionless above it.

Left alone in Lima the Marquesa's life grew more and more inward. She became increasingly negligent in her dress and like all lonely people she talked to herself audibly. All her existence lay in the burning center of her mind. On that stage were performed endless dialogues with her daughter, impossible reconciliations, scenes eternally recommenced of remorse and forgiveness. On the street you beheld an old woman her red wig fallen a little over one ear, her left cheek angry with a leprous affection, her right with a complementary adjustment of rouge. Her chin was never dry; her lips were never still. Lima was a city of eccentrics, but even there she became its jest as she drove through the streets or shuffled up the steps of its churches. She was thought to be continuously drunk. Worse things were said of her and petitions were afloat that she be locked up. She had been denounced three times before the Inquisition. It is not impossible that she might have been burned had her son-in-law been less influential in Spain and had she not somehow collected a few friends about the viceregal court who suffered her for her oddity and her wide reading.

The distressing character of the relations between mother and daughter were further embittered by misunderstandings over money. The Condesa received a handsome allowance from her mother and frequent gifts. Doña Clara soon became the outstanding woman of intelligence at the Spanish court. All the wealth of Peru would have been insufficient to maintain her in the grandiose style she fancied for herself. Strangely enough her extravagance proceeded from one of the best traits in her nature: she regarded her friends, her servants and all the interesting people in the capital, as her children. In fact there seemed only one person in the world towards whom she did not expend herself in kind offices. Among her *protégés* was the cartographer De Blasiis (whose *Maps of the New World* was dedicated to the Marquesa de Montemayor amid the roars of the courtiers at Lima who read that she was the *"admiration of her city and a rising sun in the West"*); another was the scientist Azuarius whose treatise on the laws of hydraulics was suppressed by the Inquisition as being too exciting. For a decade the Condesa literally sustained all the arts and sciences of Spain; it was not her fault that nothing memorable was produced in that time.

About four years after Doña Clara's departure Doña María received her permission to visit Europe. On both sides the visit was anticipated with resolutions well nourished on self-reproach: the one to be patient, the other to be undemonstrative. Both failed. Each tortured the

other and was on the point of losing her mind under the alternations of self-rebuke and the outbursts of passion. At length one day Doña María rose before dawn, daring no more than to kiss the door behind which her daughter was sleeping, took ship and returned to America. Henceforth letter-writing had to take the place of all the affection that could not be lived.

Hers were the letters that in an astonishing world have become the text-book of schoolboys and the ant-hill of the grammarians. Doña María would have invented her genius had she not been born with it, so necessary was it to her love that she attract the attention, perhaps the admiration, of her distant child. She forced herself to go out into society in order to cull its ridicules; she taught her eye to observe; she read the masterpieces of her language to discover its effects; she insinuated herself into the company of those who were celebrated for their conversation. Night after night in her baroque palace she wrote and rewrote the incredible pages, forcing from her despairing mind those miracles of wit and grace, those distilled chronicles of the viceregal court. We know now that her daughter barely glanced at the letters and that it is to the son-in-law that we owe their preservation.

The Marquesa would have been astonished to learn that her letters were immortal. Yet many critics have accused her of keeping one eye on posterity and point to a number of letters that have all the air of being bravura pieces. To them it seems impossible that Dona María should have put herself to the same pains to dazzle her daughter that most artists expend on dazzling the public. Like her son-in-law they misunderstood her; the Conde delighted in her letters, but he thought that when he had enjoyed the style he had extracted all their richness and intention, missing (as most readers do) the whole purport of literature, which is the notation of the heart. Style is but the faintly contemptible vessel in which the bitter liquid is recommended to the world. The Marquesa would even have been astonished to learn that her letters were very good, for such authors live always in the noble weather of their own minds and those productions which seem remarkable to us are little better than a day's routine to them.

This was the old woman who hour by hour would sit upon her balcony, her odd straw hat casting a purple shadow across her lined and yellow face. How often as she turned her pages with her gemmed hands, she would ask herself, almost with amusement, whether the constant pain at her heart had an organic seat. She wondered whether a subtle doctor cutting through to that battered throne could at last discover a sign and lifting his face to the amphitheatre cry out to his students: "This woman has suffered, and her suffering has left its mark upon the structure of her heart." This idea had so often visited her that one day she wrote it into a letter and her daughter scolded her for an introspective and for making a cult of sorrow.

The Bridge of San Luis Rey

The knowledge that she would never be loved in return acted upon her ideas as a tide acts upon cliffs. Her religious beliefs went first, for all she could ask of a god, or of immortality, was the gift of a place where daughters love their mothers; the other attributes of Heaven you could have for a song. Next she lost her belief in the sincerity of those about her. She secretly refused to believe that anyone (herself excepted) loved anyone. All families lived in a wasteful atmosphere of custom and kissed one another with secret indifference. She saw that the people of this world moved about in an armour of egotism, drunk with self-gazing, athirst for compliments, hearing little of what was said to them, unmoved by the accidents that befell their closest friends, in dread of all appeals that might interrupt their long communion with their own desires. These were the sons and daughters of Adam from Cathay to Peru. And when on the balcony her thoughts reached this turn, her mouth would contract with shame for she knew that she too sinned and that though her love for her daughter was vast enough to include all the colours of love, it was not without a shade of tyranny: she loved her daughter not for her daughter's sake, but for her own. She longed to free herself from this ignoble bond; but the passion was too fierce to cope with. And then on that green balcony a strange warfare would shake the hideous old lady, a singularly futile struggle against a temptation to which she would never have the opportunity of succumbing. How could she rule her daughter when her daughter saw to it that four thousand miles lay between them? Nevertheless Doña María wrestled with the ghost of her temptation and was worsted on every occasion. She wanted her daughter for herself; she wanted to hear her say: "You are the best of all possible mothers"; she longed to hear her whisper: "Forgive me."

About two years after her return from Spain there took place a series of inconspicuous events that had a great deal to tell about the inner life of the Marquesa. Only the faintest allusion to them occurs in the Correspondence, but as that is found in Letter XXII which contains other signs I shall do my best to give a translation and commentary of the first part of the letter:

"*Are there no doctors in Spain? Where are those good men from Flanders that used to help you so? Oh, my treasure, how can we punish you enough for letting your cold endure so many weeks? Don Vicente, I implore you to make my child see reason. Angels of Heaven, I implore you to make my child see reason. Now that you are better, I beg of you, resolve that when the first warning of a cold comes you will steam yourself well and go to bed. Here in Peru I am helpless; I can do nothing. Do not be self-willed, my beloved. God bless you. I am enclosing in today's packet the gum of some tree which the sisters of San Tomás peddle from door to door. Whether it be of much use I know not. It can do no harm. I am told that in the convent the silly sisters inhale it so diligently that*

one cannot smell the incense at Mass. Whether it be worth anything I know not; try it.

"Rest easy, my love, I am sending His Most Catholic Majesty the perfect gold chain." (Her daughter had written her: *"The chain arrived in good condition and I wore it at the christening of the Infante. His Most Catholic Majesty was gracious enough to admire it and when I told Him that you had given it me He sent you His compliments upon your taste. Do not fail to send Him one as like it as possible; send it at once, by way of the Chamberlain."*) *"He need never know that in order to obtain it I had to walk into a picture. Do you remember that in the sacristy of San Martín there is a portrait by Velasquez of the Viceroy who founded the monastery and of his wife and brat? and that his wife is wearing a gold chain? I resolved that only that chain would do. So one midnight I slipped into the sacristy, climbed upon the robing-table like a girl of twelve and walked in. The canvas resisted for a moment, but the painter himself came forward to lift me through the pigment. I told him that the most beautiful girl in Spain wished to present the finest gold chain that could be found to the most gracious king in the world. It was as simple as that, and there we stood talking, we four, in the gray and silvery air that makes a Velasquez. Now I keep thinking about a more golden light; I keep looking at the Palace: I must pass the evening in a Titian. Would the Viceroy let me?*

"But His Excellency has the gout again. I say 'again' because the flattery of the court insists that there are times when he is free of it. This being Saint Mark's day His Excellency started out to visit the University where twenty-two new doctors were being brought into the world. He had hardly been carried from his divan to his coach when he screamed and refused to go any farther. He was carried back to his bed where he broke a most delicious cigar and sent for the Perichole. And while we listened to long doctrinal addresses, more or less in Latin, he heard all about us, more or less in Spanish, from the reddest and cruellest lips in town." (Doña María permitted herself this passage, although she had just read in her daughter's last letter: *"How many times must I tell you to be more cautious in the things you say in your letters? They often show signs of having been opened on the journey. Nothing could be more ill-judged than your remarks on the you-know-what-I-mean at Cuzco. Such remarks are not funny, even though Vicente did compliment you upon them in his postscript, and they might get us into a great deal of trouble with Certain Persons here in Spain. I continue to be astonished that your indiscretions have not long since led to your being ordered to retire to your farm."*)

"There was a great press at the Exercises and two women fell from the balcony, but God in His goodness saw that they fell on Doña Merced. All three are badly hurt, but will be thinking of other things within a

year. The President was speaking at the moment of the accident and being short-sighted could not imagine what the disturbance of cries and talk and falling bodies could be about. It was very pleasant to see him bowing, under the impression that he was being applauded.

"*Speaking of the Perichole, and of applause, you should know that Pepita and I decided to go to the Comedia this evening. The public still idolizes its Perichole; it even forgives her her years. We are told that she saves what she can, every morning, by passing alternate pencils of ice and fire across her cheeks.*" (Translation falls especially short of this conceit which carries the whole flamboyance of the Spanish language. It was intended as an obsequious flattery of the Condesa, and was untrue. The great actress was twenty-eight at this time; her cheeks had the smoothness and polish of dark yellow marble and would certainly have retained that quality for many years. Apart from the cosmetics required by her performances the only treatment Camila Perichole afforded her face was to throw cold water at it twice a day, like a peasant woman at a horse trough.) "*That curious man they call Uncle Pio is by her all the time. Don Rubío says that he cannot make out whether Uncle Pio is her father, her lover, or her son. The Perichole gave a wonderful perform-ance. Scold me all you like for a provincial ninny, you have no such actresses in Spain.*" And so on.

It is on this visit to the theatre that further matter hangs. She decided to go to the Comedia where the Perichole was playing Doña Leonor in Moreto's *Trampa Adelante;* perhaps some material could be derived from the visit for her daughter's next letter. She took with her Pepita, a little girl about whom later we shall learn much. Doña María had borrowed her from the orphanage connected with the Convent of Santa María Rosa de las Rosas to be her companion. The Marquesa sat in her box gazing with flagging attention at the brilliant stage. Be-tween the acts it was the Perichole's custom to lay aside the courtly rôle and appear before the curtain to sing a few topical songs. The malicious actress had seen the Marquesa arrive and presently began improvising couplets alluding to her appearance, her avarice, her drunkenness, and even to her daughter's flight from her. The attention of the house was subtly directed to the old woman and a rising murmur of contempt ac-companied the laughter of the audience. But the Marquesa, deeply moved by the first two acts of the comedy, scarcely saw the singer and sat staring before her, thinking about Spain. Camila Perichole became bolder and the air was electric with the hatred and glee of the crowd. At last Pepita plucked the Marquesa's sleeve and whispered to her that they should go. As they left the box the house arose and burst into a roar of triumph; the Perichole flung herself into a frenzied dance, for she saw the manager at the back of the hall and knew that her salary had been increased. But the Marquesa remained unaware of what had taken place; in fact she was quite pleased, for during the visit she had contrived a few

felicitous phrases, phrases (who knows) that might bring a smile to her daughter's face and might make her murmur: "Really, my mother is charming."

In due time the report reached the Viceroy's ears that one of his aristocrats had been openly baited in the theatre. He summoned the Perichole to the Palace and ordered her to call upon the Marquesa and to apologize. The trip was to be made barefoot and in a black dress. Camila argued and fought, but all she gained was a pair of shoes.

The Viceroy had three reasons for insisting. In the first place the singer had taken liberties with his court. Don Andrés had contrived to make exile endurable by building up a ceremonial so complicated that it could be remembered only by a society that had nothing else to think about. He nursed his little aristocracy and its minute distinctions and any insult paid to a Marquesa was an insult to His Person. In the second place, Doña María's son-in-law was an increasingly important personage in Spain, laden with possibilities of injury to the Viceroy, nay with the possibility of supplanting him. The Conde Vicente d'Abuirre must not be vexed, even through his half-wit mother-in-law. Finally, the Viceroy was delighted to humble the actress. He suspected that she was deceiving him with a matador, perhaps with an actor—between the flattery of the court and the inertia of gout he could not quite make out who it was; at all events, it was clear that the singer was beginning to forget that he was one of the first men in the world.

The Marquesa, beside not having heard the scurrilous songs, was in other ways unprepared for the actress's visit. You should know that after the departure of her daughter, Doña María had lighted upon a certain consolation: she had taken to drinking. Everyone drank *chicha* in Peru and there was no particular disgrace in being found unconscious on a feast day. Doña María had begun to discover that her feverish monologues had a way of keeping her awake all night. Once she took a delicate fluted glassful of *chicha* on retiring. Oblivion was so sweet that presently she stole larger amounts and tried dissimulating their effects from Pepita; she hinted that she was not well, and represented herself as going into a decline. At last she resigned all pretense. The boats that carried her letter to Spain did not leave oftener than once a month. During the week that preceded the making of the packet she observed a strict regimen and cultivated the city assiduously for material. At last on the eve of the post she wrote the letter, making up the bundle towards dawn and leaving it for Pepita to deliver to the agent. Then as the sun rose she would shut herself up in her room with some flagons and drift through the next few weeks without the burden of consciousness. Finally she would emerge from her happiness and prepare to go into a state of "training" in preparation for the writing of another letter.

Thus on the night following the scandal in the theatre she wrote

Letter XXII and retired to bed with a carafe. All next day Pepita moved about the room, glancing anxiously at the figure on the bed. The next afternoon Pepita brought her needlework into the room. The Marquesa lay staring at the ceiling with wide-open eyes, talking to herself. Towards dusk Pepita was called to the door and informed that the Perichole had come to see the mistress. Pepita remembered the theatre very well and sent back word angrily that the mistress refused to see her. The man carried the message to the street door, but returned awestruck with the news that the Señora Perichole was armed with a letter from the Viceroy presenting her to the lady. Pepita tiptoed to the bed and started talking to the Marquesa. The glazed eyes moved to the girl's face. Pepita shook her gently. With great effort Doña María tried to fix her mind on what was being said to her. Twice she lay back, refusing to seize the meaning, but at last, like a general calling together in a rain and by night the dispersed division of his army she assembled memory and attention and a few other faculties and painfully pressing her hand to her forehead she asked for a bowl of snow. When it was brought her, she long and drowsily pressed handfuls of it against her temples and cheeks; then rising she stood for a long time leaning against the bed and looking at her shoes. At last she raised her head with decision, she called for her fur-trimmed cloak and a veil. She put them on and tottered into her handsomest reception room where the actress stood waiting for her.

Camila had intended to be perfunctory and if possible impudent, but now she was struck for the first time with the dignity of the old woman. The mercer's daughter could carry herself at times with all the distinction of the Montemayors and when she was drunk she wore the grandeur of Hecuba. For Camila the half-closed eyes had the air of weary authority and she began almost timidly:

"I come, señora, to make sure that you could not have misunderstood anything I said on the evening that Your Grace did me the honour to visit my theatre."

"Misunderstood? Misunderstood?" said the Marquesa.

"Your Grace might have misunderstood and thought that my words were intended to be disrespectful to Your Grace."

"To me?"

"Your Grace is not offended at her humble servant? Your Grace is aware that a poor actress in my position may be carried beyond her intentions . . . that it is very difficult . . . that everything. . . ."

"How can I be offended, señora? All that I can remember is that you gave a beautiful performance. You are a great artist. You should be happy, happy. My handkerchief, Pepita. . . ."

The Marquesa brought out these words very rapidly and vaguely, but the Perichole was confounded. A piercing sense of shame filled her. She turned crimson. At last she was able to murmur:

"It was in the songs between the acts of the comedy. I was afraid Your Grace . . ."

"Yes, yes. I remember now. I left early. Pepita, we left early, did we not? But, señora, you are good enough to forgive my leaving early, yes, even in the middle of your admirable performance. I forget why we left. Pepita . . . oh, some indisposition. . . ."

It was impossible that anyone in the theatre could have missed the intention of the songs. Camila could only assume that the Marquesa, out of a sort of fantastic magnanimity, was playing the farce of not having noticed it. She was almost in tears: "But you are so good to overlook my childishness, señora—I mean Your Grace. I do not know. I did not know your goodness. Señora, permit me to kiss your hand."

Doña María held out her hand astonished. She had not for a long time been addressed with such consideration. Her neighbors, her trades-people, her servants—for even Pepita lived in awe of her—her very daughter had never approached her thus. It induced a new mood in her; one that must very likely be called maudlin. She became loquacious:

"Offended, offended at you, my beautiful . . . my gifted child? Who am I, a . . . an unwise and unloved old woman, to be offended at you? I felt, my daughter, as though I were—what says the poet?— *surprising through a cloud the conversation of the angels.* Your voice kept finding new wonders in our Moreto. When you said:

> *'Don Juna, si mi amor estimas,*
> *Y la fe segura es necia,*
> *Enojarte mis temores*
> *Es no quererme discreta.*
> *¿Tan seguros. . . .'*

and so on—that was true! And what a gesture you made at the close of the First Day. There, with your hand *so.* Such a gesture as the Virgin made, saying to Gabriel: *How is it possible that I shall have a child?* No, no, you will begin to have resentment at me, for I am going to tell you about a gesture that you may remember to use some day. Yes, it would fit well into that scene where you forgive your Don Juan de Lara. Perhaps I should tell you that I saw it made one day by my daughter. My daughter is a very beautiful woman . . . everyone thinks. Did . . . did you know my Doña Clara, Señora?"

"Her Grace often did me the honour of visiting my theatre. I knew the Condesa well by sight."

"Do not remain so, on one knee, my child.—Pepita, tell Jenarito to bring this lady some sweetcakes at once. Think, one day we fell out, I forget over what. Oh, there is nothing strange in that; all we mothers from time to time. . . . Look, can you come a little closer? You must not believe the town that says she was unkind to me. You are a great

woman with a beautiful nature and you can see further than the crowd sees in these matters.—It is a pleasure to talk to you. What beautiful hair you have! What beautiful hair!—She had not a warm impulsive nature, I know that. But, oh, my child, she has such a store of intelligence and graciousness. Any misunderstandings between us are so plainly my fault; is it not wonderful that she is so quick to forgive me? This day there fell one of those little moments. We both said hasty things and went off to our rooms. Then each turned back to be forgiven. Finally only a door separated us and there we were pulling it in contrary ways. But at last she . . . took my . . . face . . . thus, in her two white hands. So! Look!"

The Marquesa almost fell out of her chair as she leaned forward, her face streaming with happy tears, and made the beatific gesture. I should say the mythical gesture, for the incident was but a recurring dream.

"I am glad you are here," she continued, "for now you have heard from my own lips that she is not unkind to me, as some people say. Listen, señora, the fault was mine. Look at me. Look at me. There was some mistake that made me the mother of so beautiful a girl. I am difficult. I am trying. You and she are great women. No, do not stop me: you are rare women, and I am only a nervous . . . a foolish . . . a stupid woman. Let me kiss your feet. I am impossible. I am impossible. I am impossible."

Here indeed the old woman did fall out of her chair and was gathered up by Pepita and led back to her bed. The Perichole walked home in consternation and sat for a long time gazing into her eyes in the mirror, her palms pressed against her cheeks.

But the person who saw most of the difficult hours of the Marquesa was her little companion, Pepita. Pepita was an orphan and had been brought up by that strange genius of Lima, the Abbess Madre María del Pilar. The only occasion upon which the two great women of Peru (as the perspective of history was to reveal them) met face to face was on the day when Doña María called upon the directress of the Convent of Santa María Rosa de las Rosas and asked if she might borrow some bright girl from the orphanage to be her companion. The Abbess gazed hard at the grotesque old woman. Even the wisest people in the world are not perfectly wise and Madre María del Pilar who was able to divine the poor human heart behind all the masks of folly and defiance, had always refused to concede one to the Marquesa de Montemayor. She asked her a great many questions and then paused to think. She wanted to give Pepita the worldly experience of living in the palace. She also wanted to bend the old woman to her own interests. And she was filled with a sombre indignation, for she knew she was gazing at one of the richest women in Peru, and the blindest.

She was one of those persons who have allowed their lives to be gnawed away because they have fallen in love with an idea several centuries before its appointed appearance in the history of civilization. She hurled herself against the obstinacy of her time in her desire to attach

a little dignity to women. At midnight when she had finished adding up the accounts of the House she would fall into insane vision of an age when women could be organized to protect women, women travelling, women as servants, women when they are old or ill, the women she had discovered in the mines of Potosi, or in the workrooms of the cloth-merchants, the girls she had collected out of doorways on rainy nights. But always the next morning she had to face the fact that the women in Peru, even her nuns, went through life with two notions: one, that all the misfortunes that might befall them were merely due to the fact that they were not sufficiently attractive to bind some man to their maintenance and, two, that all the misery in the world was worth his caress. She had never known any country but the environs of Lima and she assumed that all its corruption was the normal state of mankind. Looking back from our century we can see the whole folly of her hope. Twenty such women would have failed to make any impression on that age. Yet she continued diligently in her task. She resembled the swallow in the fable who once every thousand years transferred a grain of wheat, in the hope of rearing a mountain to reach the moon. Such persons are raised up in every age; they obstinately insist on transporting their grains of wheat and they derive a certain exhilaration from the sneers of the bystanders. "How queerly they dress!" we cry. "How queerly they dress!"

Her plain red face had great kindliness, and more idealism than kindliness, and more generalship than idealism. All her work, her hospitals, her orphanage, her convent, her sudden journeys of rescue, depended upon money. No one harbored a fairer admiration for mere goodness, but she had been obliged to watch herself sacrificing her kindliness, almost her idealism, to generalship, so dreadful were the struggles to obtain her subsidies from her superiors in the church. The Archbishop of Lima, whom we shall know later in a more graceful connection, hated her with what he called a Vatinian hate and counted the cessation of her visits among the compensations for dying.

Lately she had felt not only the breath of old age against her cheek, but a graver warning. A chill of terror went through her, not for herself, but for her work. Who was there in Peru to value the things she had valued? And rising one day at dawn she had made a rapid journey through her hospital and convent and orphanage, looking for a soul she might train to be her successor. She hurried from empty face to empty face, occasionally pausing more from hope than conviction. In the court-yard she came upon a company of girls at work over the linen and her eyes fell at once upon a girl of twelve who was directing the others at the trough and at the same time recounting to them with great dramatic fire the less probable miracles in the life of Saint Rose of Lima. So it was that the search ended with Pepita. The education for greatness is difficult enough at any time, but amid the sensibilities and jealousies of a convent it must be conducted with fantastic indirection. Pepita was assigned to

the most disliked tasks in the House, but she came to understand all the aspects of its administration. She accompanied the Abbess on her journeys, even though it was in the capacity of custodian of the eggs and vegetables. And everywhere, by surprise, hours would open up in which the Directress suddenly appeared and talked to her at great length, not only on religious experience, but on how to manage women and how to plan contagious wards and how to beg for money. It was a step in this education for greatness that led to Pepita's arriving one day and entering upon the crazy duties of being Doña María's companion. For the first two years she merely came for occasional afternoons, but finally she came to the palace to live. She never had been taught to expect happiness, and the inconveniences, not to say terrors, of her new position did not seem to her excessive for a girl of fourteen. She did not suspect that the Abbess, even there, was hovering above the house, herself estimating the stresses and watching for the moment when a burden harms and not strengthens.

A few of Pepita's trials were physical: for example, the servants in the house took advantage of Doña María's indisposition; they opened up the bedrooms of the palace to their relatives; they stole freely. Alone Pepita stood out against them and suffered a persecution of small discomforts and practical jokes. Her mind, similarly, had its distresses: when she accompanied Doña María on her errands in the city, the older woman would be seized with the desire to dash into a church, for what she had lost of religion as faith she had replaced with religion as magic. "Stay here in the sunlight, my dear child; I shall not be long," she would say. Doña María would then forget herself in a reverie before the altar and leave the church by another door. Pepita had been brought up by Madre María del Pilar to an almost morbid obedience and when after many hours she ventured into the church and made sure that her mistress was no longer there, still she returned to the street-corner and waited while the shadows fell gradually across the square. Thus waiting in public she suffered all the torture of a little girl's self-consciousness. She still wore the uniform of the orphanage (which a minute's thoughtfulness on the part of Doña María could have altered) and she suffered hallucinations wherein men seemed to be staring at her and whispering—nor were these always hallucinations. No less her heart suffered, for on some days Doña María would suddenly become aware of her and would talk to her cordially and humorously, would let appear for a few hours all the exquisite sensibility of the Letters; then, on the morrow she would withdraw into herself again and, while never harsh, would become impersonal and unseeing. The beginnings of hope and affection that Pepita had such need to expend would be wounded. She tiptoed about the palace, silent, bewildered, clinging only to her sense of duty and her loyalty to her "mother in the Lord," Madre María del Pilar, who had sent her there.

Finally a new fact appeared that was to have considerable effect on the lives of both the Marquesa and her companion: *"My dear mother,"* wrote the Condesa, *"the weather has been most exhausting and the fact that the orchards and gardens are in bloom only makes it the more trying. I could endure flowers if only they had no perfume. I shall therefore ask your permission to write you at less length than usual. If Vicente returns before the post leaves he will be delighted to finish out the leaf and supply you with those tiresome details about myself which you seem to enjoy so. I shall not go to Grignan in Provence as I expected this Fall, as my child will be born in early October."*

What child? The Marquesa leaned against the wall. Doña Clara had foreseen the exhausting importunities that this news would waken in her mother and had sought to mitigate them by the casualness of her announcement. The ruse did not succeed. The famous Letter XLII was the answer.

Now at length the Marquesa had something to be anxious about: her daughter was to become a mother. This event, which merely bored Doña Clara, discovered a whole new scale of emotions in the Marquesa. She became a mine of medical knowledge and suggestion. She combed the city for wise old women and poured into her letters the whole folk-wisdom of the New World. She fell into the most abominable superstition. She practiced a degrading system of taboos for her child's protection. She refused to allow a knot in the house. The maids were forbidden to tie up their hair and she concealed upon her person ridiculous symbols of a happy delivery. On the stairs the even steps were marked with red chalk and a maid who accidentally stepped upon an even step was driven from the house with tears and screams. Doña Clara was in the hands of malignant Nature who reserves the right to inflict upon her children the most terrifying jests. There was an etiquette of propitiation which generations of peasant women had found comforting. So vast an army of witnesses surely implied that there was some truth in it. At least it could do no harm, and Perhaps it did good. But the Marquesa did not only satisfy the rites of paganism; she studied the prescriptions of Christianity as well. She arose in the dark and stumbled through the streets to the earliest Masses. She hysterically hugged the altar-rails trying to rend from the gaudy statuettes a sign, only a sign, the ghost of a smile, the furtive nod of a waxen head. Would all be well? Sweet, sweet Mother, would all be well?

At times, after a day's frantic resort to such invocations, a revulsion would sweep over her. Nature is deaf. God is indifferent. Nothing in man's power can alter the course of law. Then on some street-corner she

would stop, dizzy with despair, and leaning against a wall would long to be taken from a world that had no plan in it. But soon a belief in the great Perhaps would surge up from the depths of her nature and she would fairly run home to renew the candles above her daughter's bed.

At last the time came to satisfy the supreme rite of Peruvian households looking forward to this event: she made the pilgrimage to the shrine of Santa María de Cluxambuqua. If there resided any efficacy in devotion at all, surely it lay in a visit to this great shrine. The ground had been holy through three religions; even before the Incan civilization distraught human beings had hugged the rocks and lashed themselves with whips to wring their will from the skies. Thither the Marquesa was carried in her chair, crossing the bridge of San Luis Rey and ascending up into the hills toward that city of large-girdled women, a tranquil town, slow-moving and slow-smiling; a city of crystal air, cold as the springs that fed its many fountains; a city of bells, soft and musical, and tuned to carry on with one another the happiest quarrels. If anything turned out for disappointment in the town of Cluxambuqua the grief was somehow assimilated by the overwhelming immanence of the Andes and by the weather of quiet joy that flowed in and about the side-streets. No sooner did the Marquesa see from a distance the white walls of this town perched on the knees of the highest peaks than her fingers ceased turning the beads and the busy prayers of her fright were cut short on her lips.

She did not even alight at the inn, but leaving Pepita to arrange for their stay she went on to the church and knelt for a long time patting her hands softly together. She was listening to the new tide of resignation that was rising within her. Perhaps she would learn in time to permit both her daughter and her gods to govern their own affairs. She was not annoyed by the whispering of the old women in padded garments who sold candles and medals and talked about money from dawn to dark. She was not even distracted by an officious sacristan who tried to collect a fee for something or other and who, from spite, made her change her place under the pretext of repairing a tile on the floor. Presently she went out into the sunshine and sat on the steps of the fountain. She watched the little processions of invalids slowly revolving about the gardens. She watched three hawks plunging about the sky. The children who had been playing by the fountain stared at her for a moment, and went away alarmed, but a llama (a lady with a long neck and sweet shallow eyes, burdened down by a fur cape too heavy for her and picking her way delicately down an interminable staircase) came over and offered her a velvet cleft nose to stroke. The llama is deeply interested in the men about her, is even fond of pretending that she too is one of them and of inserting her head into their conversations as though in a moment she would lift her voice and contribute a wan and helpful comment. Soon Doña María was surrounded by a number of these sisters who seemed

on the point of asking her why she clapped her hands so and how much her veiling cost a yard.

Doña María had arranged that any letters arriving from Spain should be brought to her at once by a special messenger. She had travelled slowly from Lima and even now as she sat in the square a boy from her farm ran up and put into her hand a large packet wrapped in parchment and dangling some nuggets of sealing-wax. Slowly she undid the wrappings. With measured stoic gestures she read first an affectionate and jocose note from her son-in-law; then her daughter's letter. It was full of wounding remarks rather brilliantly said, perhaps said for the sheer virtuosity of giving pain neatly. Each of its phrases found its way through the eyes of the Marquesa, then, carefully wrapped in understanding and forgiveness it sank into her heart. At last she arose, gently dispersed the sympathetic llamas, and with a grave face returned to the shrine.

While Doña María was passing the late afternoon in the Church and in the Square, Pepita was left to prepare their lodging. She showed the porters where to lay down the great wicker hampers and set about unpacking the altar, the brazier, the tapestries and the portraits of Doña Clara. She descended into the kitchen and gave the cook exact instructions as to the preparations of a certain porridge upon which the Marquesa principally subsisted. Then she returned to the rooms and waited. She resolved to write a letter to the Abbess. She hung for a long time over the quill, staring into the distance with trembling lip. She saw the face of Madre María del Pilar, so red and scrubbed, and the wonderful black eyes. She heard her voice as at the close of supper (the orphans sitting with lowered eyes and folded hands) she commented on the events of the day, or as, by candlelight, she stood among the beds of the hospital and announced the theme for meditation during the night. But most clearly of all Pepita remembered the sudden interviews when the Abbess (not daring to wait until the girl was older) had discussed with her the duties of her office. She had talked to Pepita as to an equal. Such speech is troubling and wonderful to an intelligent child and Madre María del Pilar had abused it. She had expanded Pepita's vision of how she should feel and act beyond the measure of her years. And she had unthinkingly turned upon Pepita the full blaze of her personality, as Jupiter had turned his upon Semele. Pepita was frightened by her sense of insufficiency; she hid it and wept. And then the Abbess had cast the child into the discipline of this long solitude, where Pepita struggled, refusing to let herself believe that she had been abandoned. And now from this strange inn in these strange mountains, where the altitude was making her lightheaded, Pepita longed for the dear presence, the only real thing in her life.

She wrote a letter, all inkstains and incoherence. Then she went downstairs to see about fresh charcoal and to taste the porridge.

The Marquesa came in and sat down at the table. "I can do no more.

What will be, will be," she whispered. She unbound from her neck the amulets of her superstition and dropped them into the glowing brazier. She had a strange sense of having antagonized God by too much prayer and so addressed Him now obliquely. "After all it is in the hands of another. I no longer claim the least influence. What will be, will be." She sat for a long time, her palms against her cheeks, making a blank of her mind. Her eyes fell on Pepita's letter. She opened it mechanically and started to read. She had read a full half of it before her attention was aware of the meaning of the words: ". . . *but all this is nothing if you like me and wish me to stay with her. I oughtn't to tell you but every now and then the bad chambermaids lock me up in rooms and steal things and perhaps My Lady will think that I steal them. I hope not. I hope you are well and not having any trouble in the hospital or anywhere. Though I never see you I think of you all the time and I remember what you told me, my dear mother in God. I want to do only what you want, but if you could let me come back for a few days to the convent, but not if you do not wish it. But I am so much alone and not talking to anyone, and everything. Sometimes I do not know whether you have forgotten me and if you could find a minute to write me a little letter or something, I could keep it, but I know how busy you are. . . .*"

Doña María read no further. She folded the letter and put it aside. For a moment she was filled with envy: she longed to command another's soul as completely as this nun was able to do. Most of all she longed to be back in this simplicity of love, to throw off the burden of pride and vanity that hers had always carried. To quiet the tumult in her mind she picked up a book of devotion and tried to fix her attention upon the words. But after a moment she suddenly felt the need to reread the whole letter, to surprise, if possible, the secret of so much felicity.

Pepita returned bringing the supper in her hands, followed by a maid. Doña María watched her over the top of her book as she would have watched a visitor from Heaven. Pepita tiptoed about the room laying the table and whispering directions to her assistant.

"Your supper is ready, My Lady," she said at last.

"But, my child, you are going to eat with me?" In Lima Pepita generally sat down at the table with her mistress.

"I thought you would be tired, My Lady. I had my supper downstairs."

"She does not wish to eat with me," thought the Marquesa. "She knows me and has rejected me."

"Would you like me to read aloud to you while you are eating, My Lady?" asked Pepita, who felt that she had made a mistake.

"No. You may go to bed, if you choose."

"Thank you, My Lady."

Doña María had risen and approached the table. With one hand on the back of the chair she said haltingly: "My dear child, I am sending

off a letter to Lima in the morning. If you have one you can enclose it with mine."

"No, I have none," said Pepita. She added hastily: "I must go downstairs and get you the new charcoal."

"But, my dear, you have one for . . . Madre María del Pilar. Wouldn't you . . . ?"

Pepita pretended to be busy over the brazier. "No, I'm not going to send it," she said. She was aware during the long pause that followed that the Marquesa was staring at her in stupefaction. "I've changed my mind."

"I know she would like a letter from you, Pepita. It would make her very happy. I know."

Pepita was reddening. She said loudly: "The innkeeper said that there would be some new charcoal ready for you at dark. I'll tell them to bring it up now." She glanced hastily at the old woman and saw that she had not ceased from staring at her with great sad inquiring eyes. Pepita felt that these were not things one talked about, but the strange woman seemed to be feeling the matter so strongly that Pepita was willing to concede one more answer: "No, it was a bad letter. It wasn't a good letter."

Doña María fairly gasped. "Why, my dear Pepita, I think it was very beautiful. Believe me, I know. No, no; what could have made it a bad letter?"

Pepita frowned, hunting for a word that would close the matter. "It wasn't . . . it wasn't . . . brave," she said. And then she would say no more. She carried the letter off into her own room and could be heard tearing it up. Then she got into bed and lay staring into the darkness, still uncomfortable at having talked in such a fashion. And Doña María sat down to her dish amazed.

She had never brought courage to either life or love. Her eyes ransacked her heart. She thought of the amulets and of her beads, her drunkenness . . . she thought of her daughter. She remembered the long relationship, crowded with the wreckage of exhumed conversations, of fancied slights, of inopportune confidences, of charges of neglect and exclusion (but she must have been mad that day; she remembered beating upon the table). "But it's not my fault," she cried. "It's not my fault that I was so. It was circumstance. It was the way I was brought up. Tomorrow I begin a new life. Wait and see, oh my child." At last she cleared away the table and sitting down wrote what she called her first letter, her first stumbling misspelled letter in courage. She remembered with shame that in the previous one she had piteously asked her daughter how much she loved her, and had greedily quoted the few and hesitant endearments that Doña Clara had lately ventured to her. Doña María could not recall those pages, but she could write some new ones, free and generous. No one else has regarded them as stumbling. It is the famous letter LVI, known to the Encyclopedists as her Second Corinthians because of its immortal para-

graph about love: "Of the thousands of persons we meet in a lifetime, my child . . ." and so on. It was almost dawn when she finished the letter. She opened the door upon her balcony and looked at the great tiers of stars that glittered above the Andes. Throughout the hours of the night, though there had been few to hear it, the whole sky had been loud with the singing of these constellations. Then she took a candle into the next room and looked at Pepita as she slept, and pushed back the damp hair from the girl's face. "Let me live now," she whispered. "Let me begin again."

Two days later they started back to Lima, and while crossing the bridge of San Luis Rey the accident which we know befell them.

Part 3

ESTEBAN

One morning twin boys were discovered in the foundlings' basket before the door of the Convent of Santa María Rosa de las Rosas. Names were found for them almost before the arrival of the wet-nurse, but the names were not as useful to them as our names are to most of us, for no one ever succeeded in telling the boys apart. There was no way of knowing who their parents were, but Limean gossips, noticing as the boys grew older how straight they held themselves and how silent and sombre they were, declared them to be Castilian and laid them in turn at all sorts of crested doorways. The person in the world who came nearest to being their guardian was the Abbess of the Convent. Madre María del Pilar had come to hate all men, but she grew fond of Manuel and Esteban. In the late afternoon she would call them into her office, send for some cakes from the kitchen, and tell them stories about the Cid and Judas Maccabeus and the thirty-six misfortunes of Harlequin. She grew to love them so, that she would catch herself gazing deep into their black and frowning eyes, looking for those traits that would appear when they grew to be men, all that ugliness, all that soullessness that made hideous the world she worked in. They grew up about the convent until they were a little past the age when their presence began to be a slight distraction to the dedicated sisters. From thence they became vaguely attached to all the sacristies in town: they trimmed all the cloister hedges; they polished every possible crucifix; they passed a damp cloth once a year over most of the ecclesiastical ceilings. All Lima knew them well. When the priest rushed through the streets carrying his precious burden into a sickroom either

Esteban or Manuel was to be seen striding behind him, swinging a censer. As they grew older, however, they showed no desire for the clerical life. They gradually assumed the profession of the scribe. There were few printing presses in the New World and the boys soon made a fair living transcribing comedies for the theatre, ballads for the crowds, and advertisements for the merchants. Above all they were the copyists of the choirmasters and made endless parts of the motets of Morales and Vittoria.

Because they had no family, because they were twins, and because they were brought up by women, they were silent. There was in them a curious shame in regard to their resemblance. They had to live in a world where it was the subject of continual comment and joking. It was never funny to them and they suffered the eternal pleasantries with stolid patience. From the years when they first learned to speak they invented a secret language for themselves, one that was scarcely dependent on the Spanish for its vocabulary, or even for its syntax. They resorted to it only when they were alone, or at great intervals in moments of stress whispered it in the presence of others. The Archbishop of Lima was something of a philologist; he dabbled in dialects; he had even evolved quite a brilliant table for the vowel and consonant changes from Latin into Spanish and from Spanish into Indian-Spanish. He was storing up notebooks of quaint lore against an amusing old age he planned to offer himself back on his estates outside Segovia. So when he heard one day about the secret language of the twin brothers, he trimmed some quills and sent for them. The boys stood humiliated upon the rich carpets of his study while he tried to extract from them their *bread* and *tree* and their *I see* and *I saw*. They did not know why the experience was so horrible to them. They bled. Long shocked silences followed each of the Archbishop's questions, until finally one or the other mumbled an answer. The priest thought for a while that they were merely in awe before his rank and before the luxury of his apartment, but at last, much perplexed, he divined the presence of some deeper reluctance and sadly let them go.

This language was the symbol of their profound identity with one another, for just as resignation was a word insufficient to describe the spiritual change that came over the Marquesa de Montemayor on that night in the inn at Cluxambuqua, so *love* is inadequate to describe the tacit almost ashamed oneness of these brothers. What relationship is it in which few words are exchanged, and those only about the details of food, clothing and occupation; in which the two persons have a curious reluctance even to glance at one another; and in which there is a tacit arrangement not to appear together in the city and to go on the same errand by different streets? And yet side by side with this there existed a need of one another so terrible that it produced miracles as naturally as the charged air of a sultry day produces lightning. The brothers were scarcely aware of it themselves, but telepathy was a common occurrence in their lives,

and when one returned home the other was always aware of it when his brother was still several streets away.

Suddenly they discovered that they were tired of writing. They went down to the sea and found an occupation in loading and unloading vessels, not ashamed of working side by side with Indians. They drove teams across the provinces. They picked fruit. They were ferrymen. And always they were silent. Their sombre faces took on from these labors a male and gypsy cast. Their hair was seldom cut and under the dark mat their eyes looked up suddenly surprised and a little sullen. All the world was remote and strange and hostile except one's brother.

But at last the first shadow fell across this unity and the shadow was cast by the love of women. They had returned to the city and resumed the copying of parts for the theatre. One night the manager, foreseeing a thinning house, gave them a free admission. The boys did not like what they found there. Even speech was for them a debased form of silence; how much more futile is poetry which is a debased form of speech. All those allusions to honour, reputation, and the flame of love, all the metaphors about birds, Achilles and the jewels of Ceylon were fatiguing. In the presence of literature they had the same darkling intelligence that stirs for a time behind the eyes of a dog, but they sat on patiently, gazing at the bright candles and the rich clothes. Between the acts of the comedy the Perichole stepped out of her rôle, put on twelve petticoats and danced before the curtain. Esteban had some copying still to do, or pretended so, and went home early; but Manuel stayed on. The red stockings and shoes of the Perichole had made their impression.

Both brothers had fetched and carried their manuscripts up and down the dusty stairs behind the stage. There they had seen an irritable girl in a soiled bodice mending her stockings before a mirror while her stage director read aloud her lines for memorization. She had let fall upon the boys for a moment the detonation of her amazing eyes, immediately dissipated in her amused recognition that they were twins. Forthwith she had dragged them into the room and placed them side by side. Carefully, amusedly and remorselessly she had peered into every square inch of their faces, until finally laying one hand on Esteban's shoulder she had cried out: "This one is the younger!" That had been several years before and neither brother had thought of the episode again.

Henceforth all Manuel's errands seemed to lead him past the theatre. Late at night he would drift about among the trees beneath her dressing-room window. It was not the first time that Manuel had been fascinated by a woman (both brothers had possessed women, and often, especially during their years at the waterfront; but simply, latinly), but it was the first time that his will and imagination had been thus overwhelmed. He had lost that privilege of simple nature, the dissociation of love and pleasure. Pleasure was no longer as simple as eating; it was being complicated by love. Now was beginning that crazy loss of one's self, that

neglect of everything but one's dramatic thoughts about the beloved, that feverish inner life all turning upon the Perichole and which would so have astonished and disgusted her had she been permitted to divine it. This Manuel had not fallen in love through any imitation of literature. It was not of him, at all events, that the bitterest tongue in France had remarked only fifty years before: that many people would never have fallen in love if they had not heard about it. Manuel read little; he had only been once to the theatre (where above all there reigns the legend that love is a devotion) and the Peruvian tavern-songs that he might have heard, unlike those of Spain, reflected very little of the romantic cult of an idealized woman. When he said over to himself that she was beautiful and rich and fatiguingly witty and the Viceroy's mistress, none of these attributes that made her less obtainable had the power to quench his curious and tender excitement. So he leaned against the trees in the dark, his knuckles between his teeth, and listened to his loud heart-beats.

But the life that Esteban was leading had been full enough for him. There was no room in his imagination for a new loyalty, not because his heart was less large than Manuel's, but because it was of a simpler texture. Now he discovered that secret from which one never quite recovers, that even in the most perfect love one person loves less profoundly than the other. There may be two equally good, equally gifted, equally beautiful, but there may never be two that love one another equally well. So Esteban sat up in their room by a guttering candle, his knuckles between his teeth, and wondered why Manuel was so changed and why the whole meaning had gone out of their life.

One evening Manuel was stopped on the street by a small boy who announced to him that the Perichole wished him to call upon her at once. Manuel turned in his path and went to the theatre. Straight, sombre and impersonal, he entered the actress's room and stood waiting. Camila had a service to ask of Manuel and she thought a few preliminary blandishments were necessary, but she scarcely paused in combing a blond wig that was dressed upon the table before her.

"You write letters for people, don't you? I want you to write a letter for me, please. Please come in."

He came forward two steps.

"You never pay me the least visit either of you. That's not Spanish of you."—meaning 'courteous.'—"Which are you, Manuel or Esteban?"

"Manuel."

"It doesn't matter. You are both unfriendly. Neither of you ever comes to see me. Here I sit learning stupid lines all day and no one ever comes to see me but a lot of peddlers. It is because I am an actress, no?"

This was not very artful, but for Manuel it was unspeakably complicated. He merely stared at her from the shadows of his long hair and left her to improvise.

"I am going to engage you to write a letter for me, a very secret

letter. But now I can see that you don't like me and that to ask you to write a letter would be as good as reading it aloud in all the wine-shops. What does that look mean, Manuel? Are you my friend?"

"Yes, señora."

"Go away. Send me Esteban. You do not even say *Yes, señora* as a friend would say it."

Long pause. Presently she raised her head: "Are you still there, Unfriendly?"

"Yes, señora . . . you can trust me to do anything for you . . . you can trust . . ."

"If I ask you to write one letter for me, or two letters, you promise never to mention to a human being what is in them, or even that you wrote them?"

"Yes, señora."

"What do you promise by?—by the Virgin Mary?"

"Yes, señora."

"And by the heart of Saint Rose of Lima?"

"Yes, señora."

"Name of the Name, Manuel, anyone would think you were as stupid as an ox. Manuel, I am very angry with you. You are not stupid. You don't look stupid. Please don't say just *Yes, senora* again. Don't be stupid or I'll send for Esteban. Is anything the matter with you?"

Here Manuel cast himself upon the Spanish language and exclaimed with unnecessary vigor: "I swear by the Virgin Mary and the heart of St. Rose of Lima that all that has to do with the letter will be secret."

"Even from Esteban," prompted the Perichole.

"Even from Esteban."

"Well, that's better." She motioned him to sit down at a table where writing materials were already laid out. As she dictated she strode about the room, frowning, swinging her hips. With her arms akimbo, she hugged her shawl about her shoulders defiantly.

"*Camila Perichole kisses the hands of Your Excellency and says*— No, take another piece of paper and begin again. *The señora Micaela Villegas, artist, kisses the hands of Your Excellency and says that, being the victim of the envious and lying friends that Y.E.'s goodness permits about Him, she can no longer endure Y.E.'s suspicions and jealousy. Y.E.'s servant has always valued Y.E.'s friendship and has never committed, nor even thought, an offense against it, but she can no longer fight against the calumnies that Y.E. believes so readily. Señora Villegas, artist, called the Perichole, therefore returns herewith such of Y.E.'s gifts as have not been placed beyond recall, since without Y.E.'s confidence, Y.E.'s servant can take no pleasure in them.*"

Camila continued walking about the room for several minutes, consumed by her thoughts. Presently without so much as glancing at her secretary, she commanded: "Take another leaf. *Have you gone mad? Do not*

ever think of dedicating another bull to me again. It has caused a frightful war. Heaven protect you, my colt. Friday night, the same place, the same time. I may be a little late, for the fox is wide-awake. That will be all."

Manuel rose.

"You swear that you have made no errors?"

"Yes, I swear."

"There is your money."

Manuel took the money.

"I shall want you to write me more letters from time to time. My uncle Pio generally writes my letters; these I do not wish him to know about. Good night. Go with God."

"Go with God."

Manuel descended the stairs and stood for a long time among the trees, not thinking, not moving.

Esteban knew that his brother was continually brooding over the Perichole, but he never suspected that he saw her. From time to time during the next two months a small boy would approach him in great haste and ask whether he were Manuel or Esteban, and being informed that he was only Esteban, the boy would add that Manuel was wanted at the theatre. Esteban assumed that the call was for copyist's work and was therefore utterly unprepared for a visit that they received one night in their room.

It was almost midnight. Esteban had gone to bed, and lay gazing out from under the blanket at the candle beside which his brother was working. There was a light tap at the door and Manuel opened to admit a lady heavily veiled, out of breath and nervous. She threw back the scarf from her face and said hurriedly:

"Quick, ink and paper. You are Manuel, yes? You must do a letter for me at once."

For a moment her glance fell on the two bright eyes that glared at her from the edge of the cot. She murmured: "Eu . . . you must excuse me. I know it is late. It was necessary . . . I must come." Then turning to Manuel, she whispered into his ear: "Write this: *I, the Perichole, am not accustomed to wait at a rendez-vous.* Have you finished that? *You are only a cholo, and there are better matadors than you, even in Lima. I am half Castilian and there are no better actresses in the world. You shall not have the opportunity*—Have you got that?—*to keep me waiting again, cholo, and I shall laugh the last, for even an actress does not grow old as fast as a bull-fighter.*"

To Esteban in the shadows the picture of Camila leaning over his brother's hand and whispering into his ear was complete evidence that a new congeniality had formed such as he would never know. He seemed to shrink away into space, infinitely tiny, infinitely unwanted. He took one more glance at the tableau of love, all the paradise from which he was shut out, and turned his face to the wall.

Camila seized the note the moment it was done, pushed a coin along the table and in a last flurry of black lace, scarlet beads and excited whispers left the room. Manuel turned from the door with his candle. He sat down, put his hand over his ears, his elbows on his knees. He worshipped her. He murmured to himself over and over again that he worshipped her, making of the sound a sort of incantation and an obstacle to thought.

He emptied his mind of everything but a singsong, and it was this vacancy that permitted him to become aware of Esteban's mood. He seemed to hear a voice that proceeded from the shadows saying: "Go and follow her, Manuel. Don't stay here. You'll be happy. There's room for us all in the world." Then the realization became even more intense and he received a mental image of Esteban going a long way off and saying good-bye many times as he went. He was filled with terror; by the light of it he saw that all the other attachments in the world were shadows, or the illusions of fever, even Madre María del Pilar, even the Perichole. He could not understand why Esteban's misery should present itself as demanding a choice between him and the Perichole, but he could understand Esteban's misery, as misery. And at once he sacrificed everything to it, if it can be said we ever sacrifice anything save what we know we can never attain, or what some secret wisdom tells us it would be uncomfortable or saddening to possess. To be sure there was nothing on which Esteban could base a complaint. It was not jealousy, for in their earlier affairs it had never occurred to either of them that their loyalty to one another had been diminished. It was merely that in the heart of one of them there was left room for an elaborate imaginative attachment and in the heart of the other there was not. Manuel could not quite understand this and, as we shall see, he nourished a dim sense of being accused unjustly. But he did understand that Esteban was suffering. In his excitement he groped for a means of holding this brother who seemed to be receding into the distance. And at once, in one unhesitating stroke of the will, he removed the Perichole from his heart.

He blew out the candle and lay down on his bed. He was trembling. He said aloud with exaggerated casualness: "Well, that's the last letter I write for that woman. She can go and find a pander somewhere else. If ever she calls here or sends for me when I'm out, tell her so. Make it plain. That's the last I have to do with her," and with that he began reciting his evening psalm aloud. But he had hardly reached *A sagitta volante in die* when he became aware that Esteban had risen and was lighting the candle.

"What's the matter?" he asked.

"I'm going out for a walk," replied Esteban sombrely, fastening his belt. After a moment, he broke out with an assumption of anger: "You don't have to say . . . what you just said, for me. I don't care whether you write her letters or not. You don't have to change for me. I haven't anything to do with that."

"Go to bed, you fool. God, you're a fool, Esteban. What made you think I said that, for you? Don't you believe I mean it when I say I'm through with her? Do you think I want to write any more of her dirty letters and get paid for them like that?"

"It's all right. You love her. You don't have to change because of me."

"'*Love* her?' *Love* her? You're crazy, Esteban. How could I love her? What chance would there be for me? Do you suppose she'd give me those letters to write if there were any chance? Do you suppose she'd push a piece of money across the table every time. . . . You're crazy, Esteban, that's all."

There was a long pause. Esteban would not go to bed. He sat by the candle in the middle of the room, tapping with his hand on the edge of the table.

"Go to bed, you fool," shouted Manuel, rising on one elbow under the blanket. He was talking in their secret language and the new pain at his heart, gave a greater ring of reality to his assumption of rage. "I'm all right."

"I won't. I'm going out for a walk," replied Esteban picking up his coat.

"You can't go out for a walk. It's two o'clock. It's raining. You can't go and walk about for hours like that. Look, Esteban, I swear to you there's nothing left to all that. I don't love her. I only did for a time."

By now Esteban stood in the dark of the open door. In the unnatural voice with which we make the greatest declarations of our lives, he muttered: "I'm in your way," and turned to go.

Manuel leapt out of his bed. His head seemed to be full of a great din, a voice crying out that Esteban was going away forever, was leaving him alone forever. "In the name of God, in the name of God, Esteban, come back here."

Esteban came back and went to bed and the matter was not mentioned again for many weeks. The very next evening Manuel had an opportunity of declaring his position. A messenger arrived from the Perichole and was told harshly to inform the actress that Manuel would write no more letters for her.

One evening Manuel tore open the flesh on his knee against a piece of metal.

Neither brother had ever been ill for as much as a day in his life, and now Manuel, utterly bewildered, watched his leg swell and felt the waves of pain rise and fall in his body. Esteban sat by and stared at his face trying to imagine what great pain was. At last one midnight Manuel remembered that the signboard of a certain hairdresser in the city described the proprietor as an experienced barber and surgeon. Esteban ran through the streets to fetch him. He pounded on the door. Presently

a woman leaned out of a window and announced that her husband would be back in the morning. During the fearful hours that followed, they told one another that when the doctor had seen the leg all would be well. He would do something about it, and Manuel would be out around the town in a day or two, even in a day perhaps, even less than a day.

The barber arrived and prescribed various draughts and ointments. Esteban was instructed to lay cold cloths on his brother's leg every hour. The barber withdrew and the brothers sat down to wait for the pain to subside. But while they continued staring into one another's face waiting for the miracle of science the pain grew worse. Hour after hour Esteban approached with his dripping towel and they discovered that the moment of its application was the worst of all. With all the fortitude in the world Manuel could not prevent himself from shouting and from flinging himself about upon the bed. Night came on and still Esteban stolidly waited and watched and worked. Nine, ten, eleven. Now when the time drew near to apply the cloths (the hour struck so musically from all those towers) Manuel would plead with Esteban not to do his work. He would resort to guile and declare that he scarcely felt it. But Esteban, his heart bursting with pain and his lips a line of iron, would roll back the blanket and bind the towel fiercely in its place. Manuel gradually became delirious and under this application all the thoughts he did not permit himself in his right mind would burst magnified from his mouth.

Finally at two o'clock, out of his mind with rage and pain, and flinging himself half out of the bed until his head struck the floor, Manuel cried: "God condemn your soul to the hottest hell there is. A thousand devils torture you forever, Esteban. God condemn your soul, do you hear?" At first, the air gone out of his body, Esteban went out into the hall and leaned against the door, his mouth and eyes wide open. Still he heard from within: "Yes, Esteban, may God damn your beastly soul forever, do you hear that? For coming between me and what was mine by right. She was mine, do you hear, and what right had you. . . ." and he would go off into an elaborate description of the Perichole.

These outbursts recurred hourly. It was some time before Esteban was able to realize that his brother's mind was not then clear. After some moments of horror, in which his being a devout believer had its part, he would return to the room and go about his duties with bent head.

Towards dawn his brother became serener. (For what human ill does not dawn seem to be an alleviation?) It was in one of these intervals that Manuel said quite calmly:

"God's son! I feel better, Esteban. Those cloths must be good after all. You'll see. I'll be up and around tomorrow. You haven't slept for days. You'll see I won't cause you any more trouble, Esteban."

"It's no trouble, you fool."

"You mustn't take me seriously when I try and stop you putting on the old cloths, Esteban."

A long pause. At last Esteban brought out, barely audible:

"I think . . . don't you think it would be fine if I sent for the Perichole? She could just come and see you for a few minutes, I mean. . . ."

"Her? You still thinking about her? I wouldn't have her here for anything. No."

But Esteban was not content yet. He dragged up a few more phrases from the very centre of his being:

"Manuel, you still feel, don't you, that I came between you and the Perichole and you don't remember that I told you it was all right with me. I swear to you I'd have been glad if you'd gone away with her, or anything."

"What are you bringing that up for, Esteban? I tell you, in God's own name, I never think of that. She's nothing to me. When are you going to forget that, Esteban? I tell you I'm glad things are as they are. Look, I got to get angry when you keep going back to that."

"Manuel, I wouldn't speak of it again, only when you get angry at me about the cloths . . . you, you get angry at me about that, too. And you talk about it and you . . ."

"Look, I'm not responsible what I say. My old leg hurts then, see."

"Then you don't damn me to hell because . . . it looks like I came between you and the Perichole?"

"Damn you to . . . ? What makes you say that? You're going crazy, Esteban; you're imagining things. You haven't had any sleep, Esteban. I've been a curse to you and you're losing your health because of me. But you'll see, I won't trouble you much more. How could I damn you to hell, Esteban, when you're all I've got? Understand, see, that when the cold cloths go on, I just lose myself, see. You know. Don't think about it twice. It's time to put them on now. I won't say a word."

"No, Manuel, I'll skip this time. It won't do you any harm, I'll just skip this time."

"I've got to get well, Esteban. I've got to get up soon, you know. Put them on. But one minute—give me the crucifix. I swear by the blood and body of Christ that if I say anything against Esteban, I don't mean it and it's just the foolish words when I'm dreaming because of the pain in my leg. God make me well again soon, amen. Put it back. There. Now I'm ready."

"Look, Manuel, it won't hurt if I skip just this once, see. It'll be good for you, sure, to not get it all stirred up just this once."

"No, I've got to get well. The doctor said it had to be done. I won't say a word, Esteban."

And it would begin all over again.

During the second night a prostitute in the next room started beating on the wall, outraged at such language. A priest in the room on the other side would come out into the hall and beat on the door. The whole floor would gather before the room in exasperation. The innkeeper came

up the stairs, loudly promising his guests that the brothers would be dumped into the street the very next morning. Esteban, holding his candle, would go into the hall and permit them to rage at him for as long as they pleased; but after that he took to pressing his hand firmly over his brother's mouth during the moments of greatest stress. This increased Manuel's personal rage at him and he would babble all through the night.

On the third night, Esteban sent for the priest and amidst the enormous shadows Manuel received the sacrament, and died.

Thereafter Esteban refused to come near the building. He would start off upon long walks, but presently drifting back, would hang about, staring at passers-by, within two streets of where his brother lay. The innkeeper failing to make any impression upon him and remembering that the boys were brought up at the Convent of Santa María Rosa de las Rosas, sent for the Abbess. Simply and soundly she directed all that was to be done. At last she went down to the street corner and spoke to Esteban. He watched her approach him, a glance mixed of longing and distrust. But when she stood near him he turned sideways and looked away.

"I want you to help me. Won't you come in and see your brother? Won't you come in and help me?"

"No."

"You won't help me!" A long pause. Suddenly as she stood there full of her helplessness there flashed through her mind an incident of many years before: the twin brothers about fifteen years old were sitting at her knee and she was telling them the story of the crucifixion. Their large grave eyes were fixed upon her lips. Suddenly Manuel had cried out loudly: "If Esteban and I had been there we would have prevented it."

"Well, then, if you won't help me, will you tell me which you are?"

"Manuel," said Esteban.

"Manuel, won't you come and sit with me up there for just a short time?"

After a long pause: "No."

"But Manuel, dear Manuel, can't you remember as children how you did so many things for me? You were willing to go across the town on some little errand. When I was ill you made the cook let you bring me my soup?" Another woman would have said: "Do you remember how much I did for you?"

"Yes."

"I, too, Manuel have lost. I too . . . once. We know that God has taken them into His hands. . . ." But this did not do at all. Esteban turned vaguely and walked away from her. When he had gone about twenty paces he stopped and stared down a side-street, like a dog who wants to go away, but is reluctant to offend the master who calls him back.

That was all they could get out of him. When the fearful procession passed through the city, with its black hoods and masks, its candles in

broad daylight, its display of heaped-up skulls, its terrifying psalms, Esteban followed it in the parallel streets, catching glimpses of it from a distance, like a savage.

All Lima was interested in this separation of the brothers. House-wives whispered together sympathetically about it as they unfurled their carpets from the balconies. The men in the wineshops, alluding to it, shook their heads and smoked in silence for a while. Travellers from the interior told of seeing Esteban as he strayed with eyes like coals along the dried-up beds of rivers or through the great ruins of the old race. A herder of llamas had come upon him standing upon a hilltop, asleep or dazed, wet with dew under the stars. Some fishermen surprised him swimming far out from shore. From time to time he would find work to do, he would become a shepherd or a carter, but after a few months he would disappear and stride from province to province. But he always returned to Lima. One day he appeared at the door of the Perichole's dressing-room; he made as though to speak, gazed earnestly at her and vanished. One day a sister came running into the office of Madre María del Pilar with the news that Esteban (whom the world called Manuel) was lingering about the door of the convent. The Abbess hurried out into the street. For months she had been asking herself what strategy could reconcile this half-demented boy to living among them again. She assembled as grave and calm a manner as she was able and appearing at the street door murmured "My friend" and looked at him. He gazed back at her with the same glance of longing and distrust that he had shown her before, and stood trembling. Again she whispered "My friend" and moved a step forward. Suddenly Esteban turned and breaking into a run disappeared. Madre María del Pilar rushed stumbling back to her desk and fell upon her knees, exclaiming angrily: "I have prayed for wisdom and You have given me none. You have not chosen to give me the least grace. I am a mere scrubber of floors. . . ." But during the penance she set herself for this impudence the thought came to her to send for Captain Alvarado. Three weeks later she had a ten-minute conversation with him. And the next day he started for Cuzco where, it was said, Esteban was doing some copying for the University.

There was this strange and noble figure in Peru during these years, the Captain Alvarado, the traveller. He was blackened and cured by all weathers. He stood in the Square with feet apart as though they were planted on a shifting deck. His eyes were strange, unaccustomed to the shorter range, too used to seizing the appearances of a constellation between a cloud and a cloud, and the outline of a cape in rain. His reticence was sufficiently explained for most of us by his voyages, but the Marquesa de Montemayor had other light on the matter. *"Captain Alvarado is bringing you this letter in person,"* she wrote to her daughter. *"Introduce him to some of your geographers, my treasure, though it may make them a little uncomfortable, for he is the diamond of sincerity.*

They will never see anyone who has travelled so far. Last night he described to me some of his voyages. Imagine him pushing his prow through a sea of weeds, stirring up a cloud of fish like grasshoppers in June; or sailing between islands of ice. Oh, he has been to China and up the rivers of Africa. But he is not merely an adventurer and he seems to take no pride in discovering new places; nor is he a mere merchant. One day I asked him narrowly why he lived so, and he avoided my question. I found out from my laundress what I think is the reason of his wandering: My child, he had a child; my daughter, he had a daughter. She was just old enough to cook a holiday meal, and do a little sewing for him. In those days he merely sailed between Mexico and Peru and hundreds of times she waved him farewell or welcome. We have no way of knowing whether she was more beautiful or intelligent than the thousands of other girls that lived about him, but she was his. I suppose it seems ignoble to you that a great oak of a man should go about the world like a blind man about an empty house merely because a chit of a girl has been withdrawn from it. No, no, you cannot understand this, my adored one, but I understand and grow pale. Last night he sat with me and talked of her. He laid his cheek against his hand and looking into the fire, he said: 'It sometimes seems to me that she is away upon a voyage and that I shall see her again. It seems to me that she is in England.' You will laugh at me, but I think he goes about the hemispheres to pass the time between now and his old age."

The brothers had always entertained a great respect for Captain Alvarado. They had worked for him a short time and the silence of the three of them had made a little kernel of sense in a world of boasting, self-excuse and rhetoric. So now when the great traveller came into the dark kitchen where Esteban was eating the boy drew his chair farther into the shadow, but at a distance, he was glad. The Captain gave no sign of recognizing or even of seeing him until he had finished his meal. Esteban had finished long before, but not wishing to be spoken to, waited until the Captain should have left the cave. At last the Captain walked over to him and said:

"You are Esteban or Manuel. You helped me once with some unloading. I am Captain Alvarado."

"Yes," said Esteban.

"How are you?"

Esteban muttered something.

"I am looking for some strong fellows to go on my next trip with me." Pause. "Would you like to come?" Longer pause. "England. And Russia. . . . Hard work. Good wages. . . . A long way from Peru. —Well?"

Apparently Esteban had not been listening. He sat with his eyes on the table. At last the Captain raised his voice, as to a deaf person:

"I said: Do you want to go on my next trip with me. . . ."

"Yes, I'll go," answered Esteban suddenly.

"Fine. That's fine. I want your brother, too, of course."

"No."

"What's the matter? Wouldn't he want to come?"

Esteban mumbled something, looking away. Then half rising, he said: "I got to go now. I've got to see somebody about something."

"Let me see your brother myself. Where is he?"

". . . 'dead," said Esteban.

"Oh, I didn't know. I didn't know. I'm sorry."

"Yes," said Esteban. "I got to go."

"Hmm.—Which are you? What's your name?"

"Esteban."

"When did Manuel die?"

"Oh, just a . . . just a few weeks. He hit his knee against something and . . . just a few weeks ago."

They both kept their eyes on the floor.

"How old are you, Esteban?"

"Twenty-two."

"Well, that's settled then, you're coming with me?"

"Yes."

"You may not be used to the cold."

"Yes, I'm used to it.—I've got to go now. I got to go in the city and see somebody about something."

"Well, Esteban. Come back here for supper and we'll talk about the trip. Come back and have some wine with me, see. Will you?"

"Yes, I will."

"Go with God."

"Go with God."

They had supper together and it was arranged that they were to start for Lima the next morning. The Captain got him very drunk. At first they poured and drank and poured and drank in silence. Then the Captain began to talk about ships and their courses. He asked Esteban questions about tackle and about the guide-stars. Then Esteban began to talk about other things, and to talk very loudly:

"On the ship you must give me something to do all the time. I'll do anything, anything. I'll climb up high and fix ropes; and I'll watch all night—because, you know, I don't sleep well anyway. And, Captain Alvarado, on the ship you must pretend that you don't know me. Pretend that you hate me the most. So that you'll always give me things to do. I can't sit still and write at a table any more.—And don't tell the other men about me . . . that is, about . . ."

"I hear you went into a burning house, Esteban, and pulled someone out."

"Yes. I didn't get burned or anything. You know," cried Esteban, leaning across the table, "you're not allowed to kill yourself; you know

you're not allowed. Everybody knows that. But if you jump into a burning house to save somebody, that wouldn't be killing yourself. And if you became a matador and the bull caught you that wouldn't be killing yourself. Only you mustn't put yourself in the bull's way on purpose. Did you ever notice that animals never kill themselves, even when they're sure to lose? They never jump into a river or anything, even when they're sure to lose. Some people say that horses run into bonfires. Is that true?"

"No, I don't think that's true."

"I don't think it's true. We had a dog once. Well, I mustn't think of that.—Captain Alvardo, do you know Madre María del Pilar?"

"Yes."

"I want to give her a present before I go away. Captain Alvarado, I want you to give me all my wages before I start—I won't need any money anywhere—and I want to buy her a present now. The present isn't from me only. She was . . . was . . ." Here Esteban wished to say his brother's name, but was unable to. Instead he continued in a lower voice: "She had a kind of a . . . she had a serious loss, once. She said so. I don't know who it was, and I want to give her a present. Women can't bear that kind of a thing like we can."

The Captain promised him that they would choose something in the morning. Esteban talked about it at great length. At last the Captain saw him slip under the table, and himself, rising up, went out into the square before the inn. He looked at the line of the Andes and at the streams of stars crowding forever across the sky. And there was that wraith hanging in mid-air and smiling at him, the wraith with the silvery voice that said for the thousandth time: "Don't be gone long. But I'll be a big girl when you get back." Then he went within and carried Esteban to his room and sat looking at him for a long while.

The next morning he was waiting at the bottom of the stairs when Esteban appeared:

"We're starting when you're ready," said the Captain.

The strange glitter had returned to the boy's eyes. He blurted out: "No, I'm not coming. I'm not coming after all."

"Aïe! Esteban! But you have promised me that you would come."

"It's impossible. I can't come with you," and he turned back up the stairs.

"Come here a moment, Esteban, just a moment."

"I can't come with you. I can't leave Peru."

"I want to tell you something."

Esteban came down to the foot of the stairs.

"How about that present for Madre María del Pilar?" asked the Captain in a low voice. Esteban was silent, looking over the mountains. "You aren't going to take that present away from her? It might mean a lot to her . . . you know."

"All right," murmured Esteban, as though much impressed.

"Yes. Besides the ocean's better than Peru. You know Lima and Cuzco and the road. You have nothing more to know about them. You see it's the ocean you want. Besides on the boat you'll have something to do every minute. I'll see to that. Go and get your things and we'll start."

Esteban was trying to make a decision. It had always been Manuel who had made the decisions and even Manuel had never been forced to make as great a one as this. Esteban went slowly upstairs. The Captain waited for him and waited so long that presently he ventured half the way up the stairs and listened. At first there was silence; then a series of noises that his imagination was able to identify at once. Esteban had scraped away the plaster about a beam and was adjusting a rope about it. The Captain stood on the stairs trembling: "Perhaps it's best," he said to himself. "Perhaps I should leave him alone. Perhaps it's the only thing possible for him." Then on hearing another sound he flung himself against the door, fell into the room and caught the boy. "Go away," cried Esteban. "Let me be. Don't come in now."

Esteban fell face downward upon the floor. "I am alone, alone, alone," he cried. The Captain stood above him, his great plain face ridged and gray with pain; it was his own old hours he was reliving. He was the awkwardest speaker in the world apart from the lore of the sea, but there are times when it requires a high courage to speak the banal. He could not be sure the figure on the floor was listening, but he said, "We do what we can. We push on, Esteban, as best we can. It isn't for long, you know. Time keeps going by. You'll be surprised at the way time passes."

They started for Lima. When they reached the bridge of San Luis Rey, the Captain descended to the stream below in order to supervise the passage of some merchandise, but Esteban crossed by the bridge and fell with it.

Part 4

UNCLE PIO

In one of her letters (the xxixth) the Marquesa de Montemayor tries to describe the impression that Uncle Pio *"our aged Harlequin"* made upon her: *"I have been sitting all morning on the green balcony making you a pair of slippers, my soul,"* she tells her daughter. *"As the golden wire did not take up my whole attention I was able to follow the activity of a coterie of ants in the wall beside me. Somewhere behind the partition they were patiently destroying my house. Every three minutes a little*

workman would appear between two boards and drop a grain of wood upon the floor below. Then he would wave his antennae at me and back busily into his mysterious corridor. In the meantime various brothers and sisters of his were trotting back and forth on a certain highway, stopping to massage one another's heads, or if the messages they bore were of first importance, refusing angrily to massage or to be massaged. And at once I thought of Uncle Pio. Why? Where else but with him had I seen that very gesture with which he arrests a passing abbé or a courtier's valet, and whispers, his lips laid against his victim's ear? And surely enough, before noon I saw him hurry by on one of those mysterious errands of his. As I am the idlest and silliest of women I sent Pepita to get me a piece of nougat which I placed on the ant's highway. Similarly I sent word to the Café Pizarro asking them to send Uncle Pio to see me if he dropped in before sunset. I shall give him that old bent salad fork with the turquoise in it, and he will bring me a copy of the new ballad that everyone is singing about the d—q—a of Ol—v—s. My child, you shall have the best of everything, and you shall have it first."

And in the next letter: *"My dear, Uncle Pio is the most delightful man in the world, your husband excepted. He is the second most delightful man in the world. His conversation is enchanting. If he weren't so disreputable I should make him my secretary. He could write all my letters for me and generations would rise up and call me witty. Alas, however, he is so moth-eaten by disease and bad company, that I shall have to leave him to his underworld. He is not only like an ant, he is like a soiled pack of cards. And I doubt whether the whole Pacific could wash him sweet and fragrant again. But what divine Spanish he speaks and what exquisite things he says in it! That's what one gets by hanging around a theatre and hearing nothing but the conversation of Calderón. Alas, what is the matter with this world, my soul, that it should treat such a being so ill! His eyes are as sad as those of a cow that has been separated from its tenth calf."*

You should know first that this Uncle Pio was Camila Perichole's maid. He was also her singing-master, her coiffeur, her masseur, her reader, her errand-boy, her banker; rumor added: her father. For example, he taught her her parts. There was a whisper around town that Camila could read and write. The compliment was unfounded; Uncle Pio did her reading and writing for her. At the height of the season the company put on two or three new plays a week, and as each one contained a long and flowery part for the Perichole the mere task of memorization was not a trifle.

Peru had passed within fifty years from a frontier state to a state in renaissance. Its interest in music and the theatre was intense. Lima celebrated its feast days by hearing a Mass of Tomás Luis da Victoria in the

morning and the glittering poetry of Calderón in the evening. It is true that the Limeans were given to interpolating trivial songs into the most exquisite comedies and some lachrymose effects into the austerest music; but at least they never submitted to the boredom of a misplaced veneration. If they had disliked heroic comedy the Limeans would not have hesitated to remain at home; and if they had been deaf to polyphony nothing would have prevented their going to an earlier service. When the Archbishop returned from a short trip to Spain, all Lima kept asking: "What has he brought?" The news finally spread abroad that he had returned with tomes of masses and motets by Palestrina, Morales and Vittoria, as well as thirty-five plays by Tirso de Molina and Ruiz de Alarçon and Moreto. There was a civic fête in his honor. The choirboys' school and the green room of the Comedia were swamped with the gifts of vegetables and wheat. All the world was eager to nourish the interpreters of so much beauty.

This was the theatre in which Camila Perichole gradually made her reputation. So rich was the repertory and so dependable the prompter's box that few plays were given more than four times a season. The manager had the whole flowering of the 17th Century Spanish drama to draw upon, including many that are now lost to us. The Perichole had appeared in a hundred plays of Lope de Vega alone. There were many admirable actresses in Lima during these years, but none better. The citizens were too far away from the theatres of Spain to realize that she was the best in the Spanish world. They kept sighing for a glimpse of the stars of Madrid whom they had never seen and to whom they assigned vague new excellences. Only one person knew for certain that the Perichole was a great performer and that was her tutor Uncle Pio.

Uncle Pio came of a good Castilian house, illegitimately. At the age of ten he ran away to Madrid from his father's hacienda and was pursued without diligence. He lived ever after by his wits. He possessed the six attributes of the adventurer—a memory for names and faces, with the aptitude for altering his own; the gift of tongues; inexhaustible invention; secrecy; the talent for falling into conversation with strangers; and that freedom from conscience that springs from a contempt for the dozing rich he preyed upon. From ten to fifteen he distributed handbills for merchants, held horses, and ran confidential errands. From fifteen to twenty he trained bears and snakes for travelling circuses; he cooked, and mixed punches; he hung about the entries of the more expensive taverns and whispered informations into the travellers' ears—sometimes nothing more dubious than that a certain noble house was reduced to selling its plate and could thus dispense with the commission of a silversmith. He was attached to all the theatres in town and could applaud like ten. He spread slanders at so much a slander. He sold rumors about crops and about the value of land. From twenty to thirty his services came to be recognized in very high circles—he was sent out by the

government to inspirit some half-hearted rebellions in the mountains, so that the government could presently arrive and whole-heartedly crush them. His discretion was so profound that the French party used him even when they knew that the Austrian party used him also. He had long interviews with the Princesse des Ursins, but he came and went by the back stairs. During this phase he was no longer obliged to arrange gentlemen's pleasures, nor to plant little harvests of calumny.

He never did one thing for more than two weeks at a time even when enormous gains seemed likely to follow upon it. He could have become a circus manager, a theatrical director, a dealer in antiquities, an importer of Italian silks, a secretary in the Palace or the Cathedral, a dealer in provisions for the army, a speculator in houses and farms, a merchant in dissipations and pleasures. But there seemed to have been written into his personality, through some accident or early admiration of his childhood, a reluctance to own anything, to be tied down, to be held to a long engagement. It was this that prevented his thieving, for example. He had stolen several times, but the gains had not been sufficient to offset his dread of being locked up; he had sufficient ingenuity to escape on the field itself all the police in the world, but nothing could protect him against the talebearing of his enemies. Similarly he had been reduced for a time to making investigations for the Inquisition, but when he had seen several of his victims led off in hoods he felt that he might be involving himself in an institution whose movements were not evenly predictable.

As he approached twenty, Uncle Pio came to see quite clearly that his life had three aims. There was first this need of independence, cast into a curious pattern, namely: the desire to be varied, secret and omniscient. He was willing to renounce the dignities of public life, if in secret he might feel that he looked down upon men from a great distance, knowing more about them than they knew themselves; and with a knowledge which occasionally passed into action and rendered him an agent in the affairs of states and persons. In the second place he wanted to be always near beautiful women, of whom he was always in the best and worst sense the worshipper. To be near them was as necessary to him as breathing. His reverence for beauty and charm was there for anyone to see and to laugh at, and the ladies of the theatre and the court and the houses of pleasure loved his connoisseurship. They tormented him and insulted him and asked his advice and were singularly comforted by his absurd devotion. He suffered greatly their rages and their meannesses and their confiding tears; all he asked was to be accepted casually, to be trusted, to be allowed like a friendly and slightly foolish dog to come and go in their rooms and to write their letters for them. He was insatiably curious about their minds and their hearts. He never expected to be loved by them (borrowing for a moment another sense of that word); for that, he carried his money to the obscurer parts of

the city; he was always desperately unprepossessing, with his whisp of a moustache and his whisp of a beard and his big ridiculous sad eyes. They constituted his parish; it was from them that he acquired the name of Uncle Pio and it was when they were in trouble that he most revealed himself; when they fell from favour he lent them money, when they were ill he outlasted the flagging devotion of their lovers and the exasperation of their maids; when time or disease robbed them of their beauty, he served them still for their beauty's memory; and when they died his was the honest grief that saw them as far as possible on their journey.

In the third place he wanted to be near those that loved Spanish literature and its masterpieces, especially in the theatre. He had discovered all that treasure for himself, borrowing or stealing from the libraries of his patrons, feeding himself upon it in secrecy—behind the scenes, as it were, of his mad life. He was contemptuous of the great persons who for all their education and usage, exhibited no care nor astonishment before the miracles of word order in Calderón and Cervantes. He longed himself to make verses. He never realized that many of the satirical songs he had written for the vaudevilles passed into folk-music and have been borne everywhere along the highroads.

As the result of one of those quarrels that arise so naturally in brothels his life became too complicated and he removed to Peru. Uncle Pio in Peru was even more versatile than Uncle Pio in Europe. Here too he touched upon real-estate, circuses, pleasures, insurrections and antiques. A Chinese junk had been blown from Canton to America; he dragged up the beach the bales of deep-red porcelain and sold the bowls to the collectors of virtú. He traced down the sovereign remedies of the Incas and started a smart trade in pills. Within four months he knew practically everyone in Lima. He presently added to this acquaintance the inhabitants of scores of seacoast towns, mining camps and settlements in the interior. His pretensions to omniscience became more and more plausible. The Viceroy discovered Uncle Pio and all this richness of reference; he engaged his services in many affairs. In the decay of his judgment Don Andrés had retained one talent, he was a master of the technique of handling confidential servants. He treated Uncle Pio with great tact and some deference; he understood which errands the other should not be asked to undertake and he understood his need for variety and intermission. Uncle Pio in turn was perpetually astonished that a prince should make so little use of his position, for power, or for fantasy, or for sheer delight in the manipulation of other men's destinies; but the servant loved the master because he could quote from any of Cervantes' prefaces and because his tongue had a little Castilian salt about it still. Many a morning Uncle Pio entered the Palace through corridors where there was no one to cross but a confessor or a confidential bully and sat with the Viceroy over his morning chocolate.

148

But for all his activity nothing made Uncle Pio rich. One would have said that he abandoned a venture when it threatened to prosper. Although no one knew it, he owned a house. It was full of dogs that could add and multiply and the top floor was reserved for birds. But even in this kingdom he was lonely, and proud in his loneliness, as though there resided a certain superiority in such a solitude. Finally he stumbled upon an adventure that came like some strange gift from the skies and that combined the three great aims of his life: his passion for overseeing the lives of others, his worship of beautiful women, and his admiration for the treasures of Spanish literature. He discovered Camila Perichole. Her real name was Micaela Villegas. She was singing in cafés at the age of twelve and Uncle Pio had always been the very soul of cafés. Now as he sat among the guitarists and watched this awkward girl singing ballads, imitating every inflection of the more experienced singers who had preceded her, the determination entered his mind to play Pygmalion. He bought her. Instead of sleeping locked up in the wine bin, she inherited a cot in his house. He wrote songs for her, he taught her how to listen to the quality of her tone, and bought her a new dress. At first all she noticed was that it was wonderful not to be whipped, to be offered hot soups, and to be taught something. But it was Uncle Pio who was really dazzled. His rash experiment flourished beyond all prophecy. The little twelve-year-old, silent and always a little sullen, devoured work. He set her endless exercises in acting and mimicry; he set her problems in conveying the atmosphere of a song; he took her to the theatres and made her notice all the details of a performance. But it was from Camila as a woman that he was to receive his greatest shock. The long arms and legs were finally harmonized into a body of perfect grace. The almost grotesque and hungry face became beautiful. Her whole nature became gentle and mysterious and oddly wise; and it all turned to him. She could find no fault in him and she was sturdily loyal. They loved one another deeply but without passion. He respected the slight nervous shadow that crossed her face when he came too near her. But there arose out of this denial itself the perfume of a tenderness, that ghost of passion which, in the most unexpected relationship, can make even a whole lifetime devoted to irksome duty pass like a gracious dream.

They travelled a great deal, seeking new taverns, for the highest attribute of a café singer will always be her novelty. They went to Mexico, their odd clothes wrapped up in the self-same shawl. They slept on beaches, they were whipped at Panama and shipwrecked on some tiny Pacific islands plastered with the droppings of birds. They tramped through jungles delicately picking their way among snakes and beetles. They sold themselves out as harvesters in a hard season. Nothing in the world was very surprising to them.

Then began an even harder course of training for the girl, a regimen that resembled more the preparation for an acrobat. The instruc-

tion was a little complicated by the fact that her rise to favor was very rapid; and there was some danger that the applause she received would make her content with her work too soon. Uncle Pio never exactly beat her, but he resorted to a sarcasm that had terrors of its own.

At the close of a performance Camila would return to her dressing room to find Uncle Pio whistling nonchalantly in one corner. She would divine his attitude at once and cry angrily:

"Now what is it? Mother of God, Mother of God, what is it now?"

"Nothing, little pearl. My little Camila of Camilas, nothing."

"There was something you didn't like. Ugly fault-finding thing that you are. Come on now, what was it? Look, I'm ready."

"No, little fish. Adorable morning star, I suppose you did as well as you could."

The suggestion that she was a limited artist and that certain felicities would be forever closed to her never failed to make Camila frantic. She would burst into tears: "I wish I had never known you. You poison my whole life. You just think I did badly. It pleases you to pretend that I was bad. All right then, be quiet."

Uncle Pio went on whistling.

"The fact is I know I was weak to-night, and don't need you to tell me so. So there. Now go away. I don't want to see you around. It's hard enough to play that part without coming back and finding you this way."

Suddenly Uncle Pio would lean forward and ask with angry intensity: "Why did you take that speech to the prisoner so fast?"

More tears from the Perichole: "Oh God, let me die in peace! One day you tell me to go faster and another to go slower. Anyway I shall be crazy in a year or two and then it won't matter."

More whistling.

"Besides the audience applauded as never before. Do you hear me? *As never before.* There! Too fast or too slow is nothing to them. They wept. I was divine. That's all I care for. Now be silent. Be silent."

He was absolutely silent.

"You may comb my hair, but if you say another word I shall never play again. You can find some other girl, that's all."

Thereupon he would comb her hair soothingly for ten minutes, pretending not to notice the sobs that were shaking her exhausted body. At last she would turn quickly and catching one of his hands would kiss it frantically: "Uncle Pio, was I so bad? Was I a disgrace to you? Was it so awful *that you left the theatre?*"

After a long pause Uncle Pio would admit judiciously: "You were good in the scene on the ship."

"But I've been better, Uncle Pio. You remember the night you came back from Cuzco——?"

"You were pretty good at the close."

"Was I?"

"But my flower, my pearl, *what was the matter in the speech to the prisoner?*"

Here the Perichole would fling her face and arms upon the table amid the pomades, caught up into a tremendous fit of weeping. Only perfection would do, only perfection. And that had never come.

Then beginning in a low voice Uncle Pio would talk for an hour, analyzing the play, entering into a world of finesse in matters of voice and gesture and tempo, and often until dawn they would remain there declaiming to one another the lordly conversation of Calderón.

Whom were these two seeking to please? Not the audiences of Lima. They had long since been satisfied. We come from a world where we have known incredible standards of excellence, and we dimly remember beauties which we have not seized again; and we go back to that world. Uncle Pio and Camila Perichole were tormenting themselves in an effort to establish in Peru the standards of the theatres in some Heaven whither Calderón had preceded them. The public for which masterpieces are intended is not on this earth.

With the passing of time Camila lost some of this absorption in her art. A certain intermittent contempt for acting made her negligent. It was due to the poverty of interest in women's rôles throughout Spanish classical drama. At a time when the playwrights grouped about the courts of England and France (a little later, of Venice) were enriching the parts of women with studies in wit, charm, passion and hysteria, the dramatists of Spain kept their eyes on their heroes, on gentlemen torn between the conflicting claims of honour, or, as sinners, returning at the last moment to the cross. For a number of years Uncle Pio spent himself in discovering ways to interest the Perichole in the rôles that fell to her. Upon one occasion he was able to announce to Camila that a granddaughter of Vico de Barrera had arrived in Peru. Uncle Pio had long since communicated to Camila his veneration for great poets and Camila never questioned the view that they were a little above the kings and not below the saints. So it was in great excitement that the two of them chose one of the master's plays to perform before his granddaughter. They rehearsed the poem a hundred times, now in the great joy of invention, now in dejection. On the night of the performance Camila peering out between the folds of the curtain had Uncle Pio point out to her the little middle-aged woman worn with the cares of penury and a large family; but it seemed to Camila that she was looking at all the beauty and dignity in the world. As she waited for the lines that preceded her entrance she clung to Uncle Pio in reverent silence, her heart beating loudly. Between the acts she retired to the dusty corner of the warehouse where no one would find her and sat staring into the corners. At the close of the performance Uncle Pio brought the granddaughter of Vico de Barrera into Camila's room. Camila stood among the clothes that hung upon the wall, weeping with happiness and shame. Finally she flung herself

on her knees and kissed the older woman's hands, and the older woman kissed hers, and while the audience went home and went to bed the visitor remained telling Camila the little stories that had remained in the family, of Vico's work and of his habits.

Uncle Pio was at his happiest when a new actress entered the company, for the discovery of a new talent at her side never failed to bestir the Perichole. To Uncle Pio (standing at the back of the auditorium, bent double with joy and malice) it seemed that the body of the Perichole had become an alabaster lamp in which a strong light had been placed. Without any resort to tricks or to false emphasis, she set herself to efface the newcomer. If the play were a comedy she became the very abstraction of wit, and (as was more likely) it was a drama of wronged ladies and implacable hates, the stage fairly smouldered with her emotion. Her personality became so electric that if she so much as laid her hand upon that of a fellow actor a sympathetic shudder ran through the audience. But such occasions of excellence became less and less frequent. As her technique became sounder, Camila's sincerity became less necessary. Even when she was absent-minded the audience did not notice the difference and only Uncle Pio grieved.

Camila had a very beautiful face, or rather a face beautiful save in repose. In repose one was startled to discover that the nose was long and thin, the mouth tired and a little childish, the eyes unsatisfied—a rather pinched peasant girl, dragged from the cafés-chantants and quite incapable of establishing any harmony between the claims of her art, of her appetites, of her dreams, and of her crowded daily routine. Each of these was a world in itself, and the warfare between them would soon have reduced to idiocy (or triviality) a less tenacious physique. We have seen that in spite of her discontent with her parts, the Perichole knew very well the joy that might reside in acting and warmed herself from time to time at that flame. But that of love attracted her more often, though with no greater assurance of happiness, until Jupiter himself sent her some pearls.

Don Andrés de Ribera, the Viceroy of Peru, was the remnant of a delightful man, broken by the table, the alcove, a grandeeship and ten years of exile. As a youth he had accompanied embassies to Versailles and Rome; he had fought in the wars in Austria; he had been in Jerusalem. He was a widower and childless of an enormous and wealthy woman; he had collected coins a little, wines, actresses, orders and maps. From the table he had received the gout; from the alcove a tendency to convulsions; from the grandeeship a pride so vast and puerile that he seldom heard anything that was said to him and talked to the ceiling in a perpetual monologue; from the exile, oceans of boredom, a boredom so persuasive that it was like pain—he woke up with it and spent the day with it, and it sat by his bed all night watching his sleep. Camila was passing the years in the hard-working routine of the theatre, savoured by

a few untidy love-affairs, when this Olympian personage (for he had a face and port fit to play gods and heroes on the scene) suddenly transported her to the most delicious midnight suppers at the Palace. Contrary to all the traditions of the stage and state she adored her elderly admirer; she thought she was going to be happy forever. Don Andrés taught the Perichole a great many things and to her bright eager mind that was one of the sweetest ingredients of love. He taught her a little French; to be neat and clean; the modes of address. Uncle Pio had taught her how great ladies carry themselves on great occasions; he taught her how they relax. Uncle Pio and Calderón had trained her in beautiful Spanish; Don Andrés furnished her with the smart slang of *El Buen Retiro.*

Uncle Pio was made anxious by Camila's invitation from the Palace. He would have much preferred that she continue with her little vulgarian love-affairs in the theatrical ware-house. But when he saw that her art was gaining a new finish he was well content. He would sit in the back of the theatre, rolling about in his seat for sheer joy and amusement, watching the Perichole intimate to the audience that she frequented the great world about whom the dramatists wrote. She had a new way of fingering a wine-glass, of exchanging an adieu, a new way of entering a door that told everything. To Uncle Pio nothing else mattered. What was there in the world more lovely than a beautiful woman doing justice to a Spanish masterpiece?—a performance (he asks you), packed with observation, in which the very spacing of the words revealed a comment on life and on the text—delivered by a beautiful voice—illustrated by a faultless carriage, considerable personal beauty and irresistible charm. "We are almost ready to take this marvel to Spain," he would murmur to himself. After the performance he would go around to her dressing-room and say "Very good!" But before taking his leave he would manage to ask her where, in the the name of the eleven thousand virgins of Cologne, she had acquired that affected way of saying *Excelencia.*

After a time the Viceroy asked the Perichole whether it would amuse her to invite a few discreet guests to their midnight suppers, and he asked her whether she would like to meet the Archbishop. Camila was delighted. The Archbishop was delighted. On the eve of their first meeting he sent the actress an emerald pendant as big as a playing-card.

There was something in Lima that was wrapped up in yards of violet satin from which protruded a great dropsical head and two fat pearly hands; and that was its archbishop. Between the rolls of flesh that surrounded them looked out two black eyes speaking discomfort, kindliness and wit. A curious and eager soul was imprisoned in all this lard, but by dint of never refusing himself a pheasant or a goose or his daily procession of Roman wines, he was his own bitter jailer. He loved his cathedral; he loved his duties; he was very devout. Some days he regarded his bulk ruefully; but the distress of remorse was less poignant

than the distress of fasting and he was presently found deliberating over the secret messages that a certain roast sends to the certain salad that will follow it. And to punish himself he led an exemplary life in every other respect.

He had read all the literature of antiquity and forgotten all about it except a general aroma of charm and disillusion. He had been learned in the Fathers and the Councils and forgotten all about them save a floating impression of dissensions that had no application to Peru. He had read all the libertine masterpieces of Italy and France and reread them annually; even in the torments of the stone (happily dissolved by drinking the water from the springs of Santa María de Cluxambuqua), he could find nothing more nourishing than the anecdotes of Brantôme and the divine Aretino.

The Archbishop knew that most of the priests of Peru were scoundrels. It required all his delicate Epicurean education to prevent his doing something about it; he had to repeat over to himself his favourite notions: that the injustice and unhappiness in the world is a constant; that the theory of progress is a delusion; that the poor, never having known happiness, are insensible to misfortune. Like all the rich he could not bring himself to believe that the poor (look at their houses, look at their clothes) could really suffer. Like all the cultivated he believed that only the widely-read could be said to *know* that they were unhappy. On one occasion, the iniquities in his see having been called to his notice, he almost did something about it. He had just heard that it was becoming a rule in Peru for priests to exact two measures of meal for a fairly good absolution, and five measures, for a really effective one. He trembled with indignation; he roared to his secretary and bidding him bring up his writing materials, announced that he was going to dictate an overwhelming message to his shepherds. But there was no ink left in the inkwell; there was no ink left in the next room; there was no ink to be found in the whole palace. This state of things in his household so upset the good man that he fell ill of the combined rages and learned to guard himself against indignations.

The addition of the Archbishop to the suppers was so successful that Don Andrés began to think of new names. He had grown increasingly dependent upon Uncle Pio, but waited until Camila should propose his inclusion of her own accord. And in due time Uncle Pio brought with him that courser of the seas, the Captain Alvarado. Generally the reunion had been several hours under way before Camila was able to join them after her performance at the theatre. She would arrive towards one o'clock, radiant and bejewelled and very tired. The four men received her as they would a great queen. For an hour or so she would carry the conversation, but gradually reclining more and more against Don Andrés' shoulder she would follow the talk as it flitted from one humorous lined face to the other. All night they talked, secretly comfort-

ing their hearts that longed always for Spain and telling themselves that such a symposium was after the manner of the high Spanish soul. They talked about ghosts and second-sight, and about the earth before man appeared upon it and about the possibility of the planets striking against one another; about whether the soul can be seen, like a dove, fluttering away at the moment of death; they wondered whether at the second coming of Christ to Jerusalem, Peru would be long in receiving the news. They talked until the sun rose, about wars and kings, about poets and scholars, and about strange countries. Each one poured into the conversation his store of wise sad anecdotes and his dry regret about the race of men. The flood of golden light struck across the Andes and entering the great window fell upon the piles of fruit, the stained brocade upon the table, and the sweet thoughtful forehead of the Perichole as she lay sleeping against the sleeve of her protector. There would ensue a long pause, no one wishing to make the first move to go, and the glances of them all would rest upon this strange beautiful bird who lived among them. But Uncle Pio's glance had been upon her all night, a quick glance from his black eyes, full of tenderness and anxiety, resting on the great secret and reason of his life.

But Uncle Pio never ceased watching Camila. He divided the inhabitants of this world into two groups, into those who had loved and those who had not. It was a horrible aristocracy, apparently, for those who had no capacity for love (or rather for suffering in love) could not be said to be alive and certainly would not live again after their death. They were a kind of straw population, filling the world with their meaningless laughter and tears and chatter and disappearing still lovable and vain into thin air. For this distinction he cultivated his own definition of love that was like no other and that had gathered all its bitterness and pride from his odd life. He regarded love as a sort of cruel malady through which the elect are required to pass in their late youth and from which they emerge, pale and wrung, but ready for the business of living. There was (he believed) a great repertory of errors mercifully impossible to human beings who had recovered from this illness. Unfortunately there remained to them a host of failings, but at least (from among many illustrations) they never mistook a protracted amiability for the whole conduct of life, they never again regarded any human being, from a prince to a servant, as a mechanical object. Uncle Pio never ceased watching Camila because it seemed to him that she had never undergone this initiation. In the months that followed her introduction to the Viceroy he held his breath and waited. He held his breath for years. Camila bore the Viceroy three children, yet remained the same. He knew that the first sign of her entrance into the true possession of the world would be the mastery of certain effects in her acting. There were certain passages in the plays that she would compass some day, simply, easily, and with secret joy, because they alluded to the new rich wisdom of her heart; but

her treatment of such passages became more and more cursory, not to say embarrassed. He presently saw that she had tired of Don Andrés and had returned to a series of furtive love-affairs with the actors and matadors and merchants of the town.

She became more and more impatient of acting and another parasite found its way into her mind. She wanted to be a lady. She slowly contracted a greed for respectability and began to refer to her acting as a pastime. She acquired a duenna and some footmen and went to church at the fashionable hours. She attended the prize days at the University and appeared among the donors of the great charities. She even learned to read and write a little. Any faint discrimination against her as a bohemian she challenged with fury. She led the Viceroy a horrible life with her passion for concessions and her gradual usurpation of privileges. The new vice displaced the old and she became noisily virtuous. She invented some parents and produced some cousins. She obtained an undocumented legitimatization of her children. In society she cultivated a delicate and languid magdelinism, as a great lady might, and she carried a candle in the penitential parades, side by side with ladies who had nothing to regret but an outburst of temper and a furtive glance into Descartes. Her sin had been acting and everyone knows that there were even saints who had been actors—there was Saint Gelasius and Saint Genesius and Saint Margaret of Antioch and Saint Pelagia.

There was a fashionable watering place in the hills not far from Santa María de Cluxambuqua. Don Andrés had travelled in France and had thought to build himself a little mock Vichy; there was a pagoda, some drawing-rooms, a theatre, a little arena for bull-fights and some French gardens. Camila's health had never known a shadow, but she built herself a villa in the vicinity and sipped the hateful waters at eleven o'clock. The Marquesa de Montemayor has left a brilliant picture of this *opéra bouffe* paradise with the reigning divinity parading her fierce sensitiveness along the avenues of powdered shell and receiving the homage of all those who could not afford to offend the Viceroy. Doña María draws a portrait of this ruler, stately and weary, gambling all through the night in sums that would have raised another Escurial. And beside him she sets the portrait of his son, Camila's little Don Jaime. Don Jaime, at seven years, was a rachitic little body who seemed to have inherited not only his mother's forehead and eyes, but his father's liability to convulsions. He bore his pain with the silent bewilderment of an animal, and like an animal he was mortally ashamed when any evidences of it occurred in public. He was so beautiful that the more trivial forms of pity were hushed in his presence and his long thoughts about his difficulties had given his face a patient and startling dignity. His mother dressed him in garnet velvet, and when he was able he followed her about at a distance of several yards, extricating himself gravely from the ladies who tried to detain him in conversation. Camila was never

cross to Don Jaime and she was never demonstrative. When the sun was shining the two could be seen walking along those artificial terraces in silence, Camila wondering when the felicity would begin that she had always associated with social position, Don Jaime rejoicing merely in the sunlight and anxiously estimating the approach of a cloud. They looked like figures that had strayed there from some remote country, or out of an old ballad, that had not yet learned the new language and had not yet found any friends.

Camila was about thirty when she left the stage and it required five years for her to achieve her place in society. She gradually became almost stout, though her head seemed to grow more beautiful every year. She took to overdressing and the floors of the drawing-rooms reflected a veritable tower of jewels and scarves and plumes. Her face and hands were covered with a bluish powder against which she drew an irritable mouth in scarlet and orange. The almost distraught fury of her temper was varied by the unnatural sweetness of her address in the company of the dowagers. In the earliest stages of her progress upward she had intimated to Uncle Pio that he was not to be seen with her in public, but finally she became impatient even of his discreeter visits. She conducted the interviews with formality and evasion. Her eyes never crossed his and she angled for pretexts to quarrel with him. Still he ventured out once a month to try her patience and when the call had become impossible he would climb the stairs and finish the hour among her children.

One day he arrived at her villa in the hills and, through her maid, begged for an opportunity to talk with her. He was told that she would see him in the French gardens a little before sunset. He had come up from Lima on a strange sentimental impulse. Like all solitary persons he had invested friendship with a divine glamour: he imagined that the people he passed on the street, laughing together and embracing when they parted, the people who dined together with so many smiles—you will scarcely believe me, but he imagined that they were extracting from all that congeniality great store of satisfaction. So that suddenly he was filled with the excitement of seeing her again, of being called "Uncle Pio," and of reviving for a moment the trust and humour of their long vagabondage.

The French Gardens were at the southern end of the town. Behind them rose the higher Andes and before them there was a parapet overlooking a deep valley and overlooking wave after wave of hills that stretched toward the Pacific. It was the hour when bats fly low and the smaller animals play recklessly underfoot. A few solitaries lingered about the gardens, gazing dreamily into the sky that was being gradually emptied of its colour, or leaned upon the balustrade and looked down into the valley, noting in which village a dog was barking. It was the hour when the father returns home from the fields and plays for a moment in the yard with the dog that jumps upon him, holding his muzzle closed

or throwing him upon his back. The young girls look about for the first star to fix a wish upon it, and the boys grow restless for supper. Even the busiest mother stands for a moment idle-handed, smiling at her dear and exasperating family.

Uncle Pio stood against one of the chipped marble benches and watched Camila coming towards him:

"I am late," she said. "I am sorry. What is it you wish to say to me?"

"Camila—" he began.

"My name is Doña Micaela."

"I do not wish to offend you, Doña Micaela, but when you let me call you Camila for twenty years, I should think——"

"Oh, do as you like. Do as you like."

"Camila, promise me that you will listen to me. Promise me that you will not run away at my first sentence."

At once she burst out with unexpected passion: "Uncle Pio, listen to me. You are mad if you think you can make me return to the theatre. I look back at the theatre with horror. Understand that. The theatre! The theatre, indeed! The daily payment of insults in that filthy place. Understand that you are wasting your time."

He answered gently: "I would not have you come back if you are happy with these new friends."

"You don't like my new friends, then?" she answered quickly. "Whom do you offer me in their stead?"

"Camila, I only remember . . ."

"I will not be criticized. I don't want any advice. It will be cold in a moment, I must go back to my house. Just give me up, that's all. Just put me out of your mind."

"Dear Camila, don't be angry. Let me talk to you. Just suffer me for ten minutes."

He did not understand why she was weeping. He did not know what to say. He talked at random: "You never even come to see the theatre, and they all notice it. The audiences are falling away now, too. They only put on the Old Comedy twice a week; all the other nights there are these new farces in prose. All is dull and childish and indecent. No one can speak Spanish any more. No one can even walk correctly any more. On Corpus Christi Day they gave *Belshazzar's Feast* where you were so wonderful. Now it was shameful."

There was a pause. A beautiful procession of clouds, like a flock of sheep, was straying up from the sea, slipping up the valleys between the hills. Camila suddenly touched his knee, and her face was like her face twenty years before: "Forgive me, Uncle Pio, for being so bad. Jaime was ill this afternoon. There's nothing one can do. He lies there, so white and . . . so surprised. One must just think of other things. Uncle Pio, it would be no good if I went back to the theatre. The audiences come for the prose farces. We were foolish to try and keep alive the Old Comedy.

Let people read the old plays in books if they choose to. It is not worth while fighting with the crowd."

"Wonderful Camila, I was not just to you when you were on the stage. It was some foolish pride in me. I grudged you the praise that you deserved. Forgive me. You have always been a very great artist. If you come to see that you are not happy among these people you might think about going to Madrid. You would have a great triumph there. You are still young and beautiful. There will be time later to be called Doña Micaela. We shall be old soon. We shall be dead soon."

"No, I shall never see Spain. All the world is alike, Madrid or Lima."

"Oh, if we could go away to some island where the people would know you for yourself. And love you."

"You are fifty years old and you are still dreaming of such islands, Uncle Pio."

He bent his head and mumbled: "Of course I love you, Camila, as I always must and more than I can say. To have known you is enough for my whole life. You are a great lady now. And you are rich. There is no longer any way that I can help you. But I am always ready."

"How absurd you are," she said smiling. "You said that as boys say it. You don't seem to learn as you grow older, Uncle Pio. There is so such thing as that kind of love and that kind of island. It's in the theatre you find such things."

He looked shamefaced, but unconvinced.

At last she rose and said sadly: "What are we talking about! It is growing cold. I must be going in. You must be resigned. I have no heart for the theatre." There was a pause. "And for the rest? . . . Oh, I do not understand. It is just circumstance. I must be what I must. Do not try to understand either. Don't think about me, Uncle Pio. Just forgive, that's all. Just try to forgive."

She stood still a moment, searching for something deeply felt to say to him. The first cloud reached the terrace; it was dark; the last stragglers were leaving the gardens. She was thinking of Don Jaime, and of Don Andrés and of himself. She could not find the words. Suddenly she bent down and kissed his fingers and went quickly away. But he sat for a long time in the gathering clouds trembling with happiness and trying to penetrate into the meaning of these things.

Suddenly the news was all over Lima. Doña Micaela Villegas, the lady that used to be Camila the Perichole, had the small-pox. Several hundred other persons had the small-pox also, but popular interest and malignity were concentrated upon the actress. A wild hope ran about the town that the beauty would be impaired that had enabled her to despise the class from which she sprang. The news escaped from the sick-room that Camila had become ludicrous in homeliness and the cup of the envious overflowed. As soon as she was able she had herself carried

from the city to her villa in the hills; she ordered the sale of her elegant little palace. She returned her jewels to their givers and she sold her fine clothes. The Viceroy, the Archbishop, and the few men at court who had been her sincerest admirers besieged her door still with messages and gifts; the messages were ignored and the gifts were returned without comment. No one but her nurse and maids had been permitted to see her since the commencement of her illness. As an answer to his repeated attempts Don Andrés received a large sum of money from her with a letter compounded of all that is possible in bitterness and pride.

Like all beautiful women who have been brought up amid continual tributes to her beauty she assumed without cynicism that it must necessarily be the basis of anyone's attachment to herself; henceforth any attention paid to her must spring from a pity full of condescension and faintly perfumed with satisfaction at so complete a reversal. This assumption that she need look for no more devotion now that her beauty had passed proceeded from the fact that she had never realized any love save love as passion. Such love, though it expends itself in generosity and thoughtfulness, though it give birth to visions and to great poetry, remains among the sharpest expressions of self-interest. Not until it has passed through a long servitude, through its own self-hatred, through mockery, through great doubts, can it take its place among the loyalties. Many who have spent a lifetime in it can tell us less of love than the child that lost a dog yesterday. As her friends continued in their efforts to draw her again into society she grew more and more angry and dispatched insulting messages to the city. It was said for a time that she was retiring into religion. But new rumours that all was fury and despair on the little farm, contradicted the old. For those near to her the despair was fearful to behold. She was convinced that her life was over, her life and children's. In her hysterical pride she had given back more than she owed and the approach of poverty was added to the loneliness and the gloom of her future. There was nothing left for her to do but to draw out her days in jealous solitude in the center of the little farm that was falling into decay. She brooded for hours upon the joy of her enemies and could be heard striding about her room with strange cries.

Uncle Pio did not allow himself to be discouraged. By dint of making himself useful to the children, by taking a hand in the management of the farm and by discreetly lending her some money he obtained his entrance into the house and even into the presence of its veiled mistress. But even then Camila, convinced in her pride that he *pitied* her, lashed him with the blade of her tongue and derived some strange comfort from heaping him with sneers. He loved her the more, understanding better than she did herself all the stages in the convalescence of her humiliated spirit. But one day an accident befell that lost him his share in her progress. He pushed open a door.

She thought she had locked it. For just one hour a foolish secret

hope had come to her; she wondered whether she could make a paste of chalk and cream to spread upon her face. She who had sneered so often at the befloured grandmothers of the court wondered for a few moments whether she had learned anything on the stage that would aid her now. She thought she had locked the door and with hurried hands and beating heart she laid on the coat, the grotesque pallor, and as she gazed into the mirror and recognized the futility of her attempt she caught the image of Uncle Pio standing in the door amazed. She rose from the chair with a cry and covered her face with her hands.

"Go away. Go away out of my house forever," she screamed. "I never want to see you again." In her shame she drove him out with blasphemy and hatred, she pursued him down the corridor and hurled objects down the stairs. She gave her farmer orders that Uncle Pio was forbidden to come into the grounds. But he continued for a week trying to see her again. At last he went back to Lima; he filled in the time as best he could, but he longed to be by her as a boy of eighteen would long. At last he devised a stratagem and returned up into the hills to put it into effect.

One morning before dawn he arose and lay on the ground below her window. He imitated in the darkness the sound of weeping, and, as nearly as he could, of a young girl's weeping. He continued in this for the whole quarter of an hour. He did not let his voice rise above that degree of loudness which Italian musicians would represent by the direction *piano,* but he frequently intermitted the sound trusting that if she were asleep it would insinuate itself into her mind as well by duration as by degree. The air was cool and agreeable. The first faint streak of sapphire was appearing behind the peaks and in the east the star of morning was pulsating every moment with a more tender intention. A profound silence wrapped all the farm buildings, only an occasional breeze set all the grasses sighing. Suddenly a lamp was lit in her room and a moment later the shutter was thrown back and a head wrapped in veils leaned far out.

"Who is there?" asked the beautiful voice.

Uncle Pio remained silent.

Camila said again in a tone edged with impatience:

"Who is there? Who is there weeping?"

"Doña Micaela, my lady, I beg of you to come here to me."

"Who are you and what do you want?"

"I am a poor girl. I am Estrella. I beg of you to come and help me. Do not call your maid. I pray you, Doña Micaela, to come yourself."

Camila was silent a moment, then said abruptly: "Very well," and closed the shutter. Presently she appeared around the corner of the house. She wore a thick cloak that dragged in the dew. She stood at a distance and said: "Come over here to where I am standing— Who are you?"

Uncle Pio rose up. "Camila, it is I—Uncle Pio. Forgive me, but I must speak to you."

"Mother of God, when shall I be free of this dreadful person! Under-

stand: I want to see no one. I don't want to speak to a soul. My life is over. That is all."

"Camila, by our long life together, I beg of you to grant me one thing. I shall go away and never trouble you again."

"I grant you nothing, nothing. Stay away from me."

"I promise you I shall never trouble you again if you listen to me this once." She was hurrying around to the door on the other side of the house and Uncle Pio was obliged to run beside her to make sure that she heard what he was saying. She stopped:

"What is it then? Hurry. It is cold. I am not well. I must go back to my room."

"Camila, let me take Don Jaime for a year to live with me in Lima. Let me be his teacher. Let me teach him the Castilian. Here he is left among the servants. He is learning nothing."

"No."

"Camila, what will become of him? He has a good mind and he wants to learn."

"He is sick. He is delicate. Your house is a sty. Only the country is good for him."

"But he has been much better these last few months. I promise you I shall clean out my house. I shall apply to Madre María del Pilar for a housekeeper. Here he is in your stables all day. I shall teach him all that a gentleman should know—fencing and Latin and music. We shall read all. . . ."

"A mother cannot be separated from her child like that. It is impossible. You are crazy to have thought of it. Give up thinking of me and of everything about me. I no longer exist. I and my children will get on as best we can. Do not try to disturb me again. I do not want to see any human being."

Now it was that Uncle Pio felt obliged to use a hard measure. "Then pay me the money that you owe me," he said.

Camila stood still, confounded. To herself she said: "Life is too fearful to bear. When may I die?" After a moment she answered him, in a hoarse voice: "I have very little money. I will pay you what I can. I will pay you now. I have a few jewels here. Then we need never see one another again." She was ashamed of her poverty. She took a few steps, then turned and said: "Now I see that you are a very hard man. But it is right that I pay you what I owe you."

"No, Camila, I only said that to enforce my request. I shall take no money from you. But lend me Don Jaime for one year. I shall love him and take every care of him. Did I harm you? Was I a bad teacher to you in those other years?"

"It is cruel of you to keep urging gratitude, gratitude, gratitude. I was grateful—good, good! but now that I am no longer the same woman there remains nothing to be grateful for." There was a silence. Her eyes were

resting on the star that seemed to be leading forth the whole sky in its wonder. A great pain lay at her heart, the pain of a world that was meaningless. Then she said: "If Jaime wishes to go with you, very well. I shall talk to him in the morning. If he wishes to go with you, you will find him at the Inn about noon. Good night. Go with God."

"Go with God."

She returned to the house. The next day the grave little boy appeared at the Inn. His fine clothes were torn and stained now and he carried a small bundle for change. His mother had given him a gold piece for spending-money and a little stone that shone in the dark to look at in his sleepless nights. They set off together in a cart, but soon Uncle Pio became aware that the jolting was not good for the boy. He carried him on his shoulder. As they drew near to the bridge of San Luis Rey, Jaime tried to conceal his shame for he knew that one of those moments was coming that separated him from other people. He was especially ashamed because Uncle Pio had just overtaken a friend of his, a sea-captain. And just as they got to the bridge he spoke to an old lady who was travelling with a little girl. Uncle Pio said that when they had crossed the bridge they would sit down and rest, but it turned out not to be necessary.

Part 5

PERHAPS AN INTENTION

A new bridge of stone has been built in the place of the old, but the event has not been forgotten. It has passed into proverbial expressions. "I may see you Tuesday," says a Limean, "unless the bridge falls." "My cousin lives by the bridge of San Luis Rey," says another, and a smile goes around the company, for that also means: under the sword of Damocles. There are some poems about the accident, classics to be found in every Peruvian anthology, but the real literary monument is Brother Juniper's book.

There are a hundred ways of wondering at circumstance. Brother Juniper would never have arrived at his method had it not been for his friendship with a certain master in the University of San Martín. This student's wife had stolen away one morning on a boat for Spain, following a soldier, and had left him the care of two daughters in their cradle. He was possessed of all the bitterness that Brother Juniper lacked and derived a sort of joy from the conviction that all was wrong in the world. He whispered into the Franciscan's ear such thoughts and anec-

dotes as belied the notion of a guided world. For a moment a look of distress, almost of defeat, would come into the Brother's eyes; then he would begin patiently explaining why such stories held no difficulty for a believer. "There was a queen of Naples and Sicily," the student would say, "who discovered that she was carrying an angry tumor in her side. In great dismay she commanded her subjects to fall to their prayers and ordered that all the garments in Sicily and Naples be sewn with votive crosses. She was well loved by her people and all their prayers and embroideries were sincere, but ineffectual. Now she lies in the splendor of Monreale, and a few inches above her heart may be read the words: *I shall fear no evil.*"

It was by dint of hearing a great many such sneers at faith that Brother Juniper became convinced that the world's time had come for proof, tabulated proof, of the conviction that was so bright and exciting within him. When the pestilence visited his dear village of Puerto and carried off a large number of peasants, he secretly drew up a diagram of the characteristics of fifteen victims and fifteen survivors, the statistics of their value *sub specie aeternitatis*. Each soul was rated upon a basis of ten as regards its goodness, its diligence in religious observance, and its importance to its family group. Here is a fragment of this ambitious chart:

	Goodness	Piety	Usefulness
Alfonso G.	4	4	10
Nina	2	5	10
Manuel B.	10	10	0
Alfonso V.	–8	–10	10
Vera N.	0	10	10

The thing was more difficult than he had foreseen. Almost every soul in a difficult frontier community turned out to be indispensable economically, and the third column was all but useless. The examiner was driven to the use of minus terms when he confronted the personal character of Alfonso V., who was not, like Vera N., merely bad: he was a propagandist for badness and not merely avoided church but led others to avoid it. Vera N. was indeed bad, but she was a model worshipper and the mainstay of a full hut. From all this saddening data Brother Juniper contrived an index for each peasant. He added up the total for victims and compared it with the total for survivors, to discover that the dead were five times more worth saving. It almost looked as though the pestilence had been directed against the really valuable people in the village of Puerto. And on that afternoon Brother Juniper took a walk along the edge of the Pacific. He tore up his findings and cast them into the waves; he gazed for an hour upon the great clouds of pearl that hang forever upon the horizon of that sea, and extracted from their beauty a resignation that he did not permit his reason to examine. The discrepancy between faith and the facts is greater than is generally assumed.

But there was another story of the master of San Martín (not so subversive, this one) that probably gave to Brother Juniper the hint for his procedure after the fall of the bridge of San Luis Rey.

This master was one day walking through the Cathedral of Lima and stopped to read the epitaph of a lady. He read with an increasingly prominent lower lip that she had been for twenty years the centre and joy of her home, that she had been the delight of her friends, that all who met her went away in astonishment at her goodness and beauty, and that there she lay awaiting the return of her Lord. Now on the day that he read these words, the master of San Martín had had much to fret him, and raising his eyes from the tablet he spoke aloud in his rage: "The shame of it, the persecution of it! Everyone knows that in the world we do nothing but feed our wills. Why perpetuate this legend of selflessness? Why keep this thing alive, this rumour of disinterestedness?"

And so saying he resolved to expose this conspiracy of the stone-cutters. The lady had been dead only twelve years. He sought out her servants, her children and her friends. And everywhere he went, like a perfume, her dear traits had survived her and wherever she was mentioned there arose a suffering smile and the protest that words could not describe the gracious ways of her. Even the eager youth of her grandchildren, who had never seen her, was made more difficult by the news that it was possible to be as good as that. And the man stood amazed; only at last he muttered: "Nevertheless, what I said was true. This woman was an exception, perhaps an exception."

In compiling his book about these people Brother Juniper seemed to be pursued by the fear that in omitting the slightest detail he might lose some guiding hint. The longer he worked the more he felt that he was stumbling about among great dim intimations. He was forever being cheated by details that looked as though they were significant if only he could find their setting. So he put everything down on the notion perhaps that if he (or a keener head) reread the book twenty times, the countless facts would suddenly start to move, to assemble, and to betray their secret. The Marquesa de Montemayor's cook told him that she lived almost entirely on rice, fish and a little fruit and Brother Juniper put it down on the chance that it would some day reveal a spiritual trait. Don Rubío said of her that she used to appear at his receptions without invitation in order to steal the spoons. A midwife on the edge of the town declared that Doña María called upon her with morbid questions until she had been obliged to order her away from the door like a beggar. The bookseller of the town reported that she was one of the three most cultivated persons in Lima. Her farmer's wife declared that she was absent-minded, but compact of goodness. The art of biography is more difficult than is generally supposed.

Brother Juniper found that there was least to be learned from those who had been most closely associated with the subjects of his inquiry.

Madre María del Pilar talked to him at length about Pepita, but she did not tell him of her own ambitions for her. The Perichole was at first difficult of approach, but presently even like the Franciscan. Her characterization of Uncle Pio flatly contradicted the stores of unsavory testimonies that he had acquired elsewhere. Her allusions to her son were few and conceded with pain. They closed the interview abruptly. The Captain Alvarado told what he could of Esteban and of Uncle Pio. Those who know most in this realm, venture least.

I shall spare you Brother Juniper's generalizations. They are always with us. He thought he saw in the same accident, the wicked visited by destruction and the good called early to Heaven. He thought he saw pride and wealth confounded as an object lesson to the world, and he thought he saw humility crowned and rewarded for the edification of the city. But Brother Juniper was not satisfied with his reasons. It was just possible that the Marquesa de Montemayor was not a monster of avarice, and Uncle Pio of self-indulgence.

The book being done fell under the eyes of some judges and was suddenly pronounced heretical. It was ordered to be burned in the Square with its author. Brother Juniper submitted to the decision that the devil had made use of him to effect a brilliant campaign in Peru. He sat in his cell that last night trying to seek in his own life the pattern that had escaped him in five others. He was not rebellious. He was willing to lay down his life for the purity of the church, but he longed for one voice somewhere to testify for him that his intention, at least, had been for faith; he thought there was no one in the world who believed him. But the next morning in all that crowd and sunlight there were many who believed, for he was much loved.

There was a little delegation from the village of Puerto, and Nina (Goodness 2, Piety 5, Usefulness 10) and others stood with drawn puzzled faces while their little friar was given to the congenial flames. Even then, even then, there remained in his heart an obstinate nerve insisting that at least St. Francis would not utterly have condemned him, and (not daring to call upon a greater name, since he seemed so open to error in these matters) he called twice upon St. Francis and leaning upon a flame he smiled and died.

.

The day of the service was clear and warm. The Limeans, their black eyes wide with awe, poured through the streets into their Cathedral and stood gazing at the mound of black velvet and silver. The Archbishop enclosed in his wonderful and almost wooden vestments perspired upon his throne, lending from time to time a connoisseur's ear to the felicities of Vittoria's counterpoint. The choir had restudied the pages that, as his farewell to music, Tomás Luis had composed for his friend and patron,

the Empress of Austria, and all that grief and sweetness, all that Spanish realism filtering through an Italian mode, rose and fell above the sea of mantillas. Don Andrés, under the colours and feathered hangings of his office, knelt, ill and troubled. He knew that the crowd was furtively glancing at him, expecting him to play the father who has lost his only son. He wondered whether the Perichole was present. He had never been obliged to go so long without smoking. The Captain Alvarado pushed in from the sunny square for a moment. He looked across the fields of black hair and lace at the trooping of the candles and the ropes of incense. "How false, how unreal," he said and pushed his way out. He descended to the sea and sat on the edge of his boat, gazing down into the clear water. "Happy are the drowned, Esteban," he said.

Behind the screen the Abbess sat among her girls. The night before she had torn an idol from her heart and the experience had left her pale but firm. She had accepted the fact that it was of no importance whether her work went on or not; it was enough to work. She was the nurse who tends the sick who never recover; she was the priest who perpetually renews the office before an altar to which no worshippers come. There would be no Pepita to enlarge her work; it would relapse into the indolence and the indifference of her colleagues. It seemed to be sufficient for Heaven that for a while in Peru a disinterested love had flowered and faded. She leaned her forehead upon her hand, following the long tender curve that the soprano lifts in the Kyrie. "My affection should have had more of that colour, Pepita. My whole life should have had more of that quality. I have been too busy," she added ruefully and her mind drifted into prayer.

Camila had started from the farm to attend the service. Her heart was filled with consternation and amazement. Here was another comment from the skies; that was the third time she had been spoken to. Her small-pox, Jaime's illness, and now the fall of the bridge—oh, these were not accidents. She was as ashamed as though letters had appeared on her forehead. An order from the Palace announced that the Viceroy was sending her two daughters to a convent-school in Spain. That was right. She was alone. She gathered a few things together mechanically and started to the city for the Service. But she fell to thinking of the crowds gaping over her Uncle Pio and over her son; she thought of the vast ritual of the church, like a chasm into which the beloved falls, and of the storm of the *dies irae* where the individual is lost among the millions of the dead, features grow dim and traits fade. At a little more than half the journey, at the mud church of San Luis Rey she slipped in and knelt against a pillar to rest. She wandered through her memory, searching for the faces of her two. She waited for some emotion to appear. "But I feel nothing," she whispered to herself. "I have no heart. I am a poor meaningless woman, that's all. I am shut out. I have no heart. Look, I won't try and think of anything; let me just rest here." And scarcely had she

paused when again that terrible incommunicable pain swept through her, the pain that could not speak once to Uncle Pio and tell him of her love and just once offer her courage to Jaime in his sufferings. She started up wildly: "I fail everybody," she cried. "They love me and I fail them." She returned to the farm and carried for a year the mood of her self-despair. One day she heard by accident that the wonderful Abbess had lost two persons whom she loved in the same accident. Her sewing fell from her hand: then *she* would know, she would explain. "But no, what would she say to me! She would not even believe that such a person as I could love or could lose." Camila decided to go to Lima and look at the Abbess from a distance. "If her face tells me that she would not despise me, I will speak to her," she said.

Camila lurked about the convent church and fell humbly in love with the homely old face, though it frightened her a little. At last she called upon her.

"Mother," she said, "I . . . I"

"Do I know you, my daughter?"

"I was the actress, I was the Perichole."

"Oh, yes. Oh, I have wished to know you for a long while, but they told me you did not wish to be seen. You too, I know, lost in the fall of the bridge of San. . . ."

Camila rose and swayed. There! again that access of pain, the hands of the dead she could not reach. Her lips were white. Her head brushed the Abbess's knee: "Mother, what shall I do? I am all alone. I have nothing in the world. I love them. What shall I do?"

The Abbess looked at her closely. "My daughter, it is warm here. Let us go into the garden. You can rest there." She made a sign to a girl in the cloister to bring some water. She continued talking mechanically to Camila. "I have wished to know you for a long while, señora. Even before the accident I had wished much to know you. They told me that in the *autos sacramentales* you were a very great and beautiful actress, in *Belshazzar's Feast*."

"Oh, Mother, you must not say that. I am a sinner. You must not say that."

"Here, drink this, my child. We have a beautiful garden, do you not think so? You will come and see us often and some day you will meet Sister Juana who is our gardener-in-chief. Before she entered religion she had almost never seen a garden, for she worked in the mines high up in the mountains. Now everything grows under her hand.—A year has gone by, señora, since our accident. I lost two who had been children in my orphanage, but you lost a real child of your own?"

"Yes, Mother."

"And a great friend?"

"Yes, Mother."

"Tell me. . . ."

And then the whole tide of Camila's long despair, her lonely obstinate despair since her girlhood, found its rest on that dusty friendly lap among Sister Juana's fountains and roses.

.

But where are sufficient books to contain the events that would not have been the same without the fall of the bridge? From such a number I choose one more.

"The Condesa d'Abuirre wishes to see you," said a lay-sister at the door of the Abbess's office.

"Well," said the Abbess, laying down her pen, "who is she?"

"She has just come from Spain. I don't know."

"Oh, it is some money, Inez, some money for my house for the blind. Quick, bid her come in."

The tall, rather langorous beauty entered the room. Doña Clara, who was generally so adequate, seemed constrained for once. "Are you busy, dear Mother, may I talk to you for a while?"

"I am quite free, my daughter. You will excuse an old woman's memory; have I known you before?"

"My mother was the Marquesa de Montemayor. . . ." Doña Clara suspected that the Abbess had not admired her mother and would not let the older woman speak until she herself had made a long passionate defense of Doña María. The languor fell away in her self-reproach. At last the Abbess told her of Pepita and Esteban, and of Camila's visit. "All, all of us have failed. One wishes to be punished. One is willing to assume all kinds of penance, but do you know, my daughter, that in love— I scarcely dare say it—but in love our very mistakes don't seem to be able to last long?"

The Condesa showed the Abbess Dona María's last letter. Madre María dared not say aloud how great her astonishment was that such words (words that since then the whole world has murmured over with joy) could spring in the heart of Pepita's mistress. "Now learn," she commanded herself, "learn at last that anywhere you may expect grace." And she was filled with happiness like a girl at this new proof that the traits she lived for were everywhere, that the world was ready. "Will you do me a kindness, my daughter? Will you let me show you my work?"

The sun had gone down, but the Abbess led the way with a lantern down corridor after corridor. Doña Clara saw the old and the young, the sick and the blind, but most of all she saw the tired, bright old woman who was leading her. The Abbess would stop in a passageway and say suddenly: "I can't help thinking that something could be done for the deaf-and-dumb. It seems to me that some patient person could, . . . could study out a language for them. You know there are hundreds and

hundreds in Peru. Do you remember whether anyone in Spain has found a way for them? Well, some day they will." Or a little later: "Do you know, I keep thinking that something can be done for the insane. I am old, you know, and I cannot go where these things are talked about, but I watch them sometimes and it seems to me . . . In Spain, now, they are gentle with them? It seems to me that there is a secret about it, just hidden from us, just around the corner. Some day back in Spain, if you hear of anything that would help us, you will write me a letter . . . if you are not too busy?"

At last after Doña Clara had seen even the kitchens, the Abbess said: "Now will you excuse me, for I must go into the room of the very sick and say a few words for them to think about when they cannot sleep. I will not ask you to come with me there, for you are not accustomed to such . . . such sounds and things. And besides I only talk to them as one talks to children." She looked up at her with her modest rueful smile. Suddenly she disappeared a moment to return with one of her helpers, one who had likewise been involved in the affair of the bridge and who had formerly been an actress. "She is leaving me," said the Abbess, "for some work across the city and when I have spoken here I must leave you both, for the flour-broker will not wait for me any longer, and our argument will take a long time."

But Doña Clara stood in the door as the Abbess talked to them, the lamp placed on the floor beside her. Madre María stood with her back against a post; the sick lay in rows gazing at the ceiling and trying to hold their breaths. She talked that night of all those out in the dark (she was thinking of Esteban alone, she was thinking of Pepita alone) who had no one to turn to, for whom the world perhaps was more than difficult, without meaning. And those who lay in their beds there felt that they were within a wall that the Abbess had built for them; within all was light and warmth, and without was the darkness they would not exchange even for a relief from pain and from dying. But even while she was talking, other thoughts were passing in the back of her mind. "Even now," she thought, "almost no one remembers Esteban and Pepita, but myself. Camila alone remembers her Uncle Pio and her son; this woman, her mother. But soon we shall die and all memory of those five will have left the earth, and we ourselves shall be loved for a while and forgotten. But the love will have been enough; all those impulses of love return to the love that made them. Even memory is not necessary for love. There is a land of the living and a land of the dead and the bridge is love, the only survival, the only meaning."

III

THE DUEL

by Joseph Conrad

A Story of Napoleonic Days

Joseph Conrad, born Teodor Jozef Korzeniowski in Kiev on December 3, 1857, established two records with his short novel *The Duel*. Although he remains today the acknowledged master of the sea story (writing always in English, the language he encountered when he ran away to sea), he has here created a story which establishes the universality of his genius. None of his characters gets nearer the sea than the port of Lübeck and none ever sets foot on the deck of anything larger than an army transport. Moreover, he deals with a period entirely new to him (Napoleon's eagles were flying over Europe) with a fidelity to the French scene that is astonishingly sure.

Readers who gained their first love for the swash-buckling type of story from the pages of *The Three Musketeers* (and who did not?) will find a recurrence of the old thrill when they read the amazing story of Lieut. D'Hubert and Lieut. Feraud (both of whom became generals later), but with a difference. Conrad's two officers are involved in a situation more intense and real than the trumped-up excitements of D'Artagnan and Company. This is adult fare. But a thrill is to be found in the international conflicts that Napoleon created and the curious antagonism which made it necessary for two cavalry officers to fight a war of their own, a war within a war.

This man who lived most of his active life at sea proves in *The Duel* that he needs no more than his immeasurable gifts to make any group of characters in any conceivable situation come fully to life.

Ladies and gentlemen, we have great pleasure in introducing Lieut. D'Hubert and Lieut. Feraud. They do not seem to have had other names but they have everything to stir your interest, to give you a picture of war in its most brilliant phases, to surprise you, to entertain you, and to leave you with the feeling that you have been taught a great deal about the heart which beats under a gaudy and be-frogged military tunic.

Chapter I

NAPOLEON I., WHOSE CAREER had the quality of a duel against the whole of Europe, disliked duelling between the officers of his army. The great military emperor was not a swashbuckler, and had little respect for tradition.

Nevertheless, a story of duelling, which became a legend in the army, runs through the epic of imperial wars. To the surprise and admiration of their fellows, two officers, like insane artists trying to gild refined gold or paint the lily, pursued a private contest through the years of universal carnage. They were officers of cavalry, and their connection with the high-spirited but fanciful animal which carries men into battle seems particularly appropriate. It would be difficult to imagine for heroes of this legend two officers of infantry of the line, for example, whose fantasy is tamed by much walking exercise, and whose valour necessarily must be of a more plodding kind. As to gunners or engineers, whose heads are kept cool on a diet of mathematics, it is simply unthinkable.

The names of the two officers were Feraud and D'Hubert, and they were both lieutenants in a regiment of hussars, but not in the same regiment.

Feraud was doing regimental work, but Lieut. D'Hubert had the good fortune to be attached to the person of the general commanding the division, as *officier d'ordonnance*. It was in Strasbourg, and in this agreeable and important garrison they were enjoying greatly a short interval of peace. They were enjoying it, though both intensely warlike, because it was a sword-sharpening, firelock-cleaning peace, dear to a military heart and undamaging to military prestige, inasmuch that no one believed in its sincerity or duration.

Under those historical circumstances, so favourable to the proper appreciation of military leisure, Lieut. D'Hubert, one fine afternoon, made his way along a quiet street of a cheerful suburb towards Lieut. Feraud's quarters, which were in a private house with a garden at the back, belonging to an old maiden lady.

His knock at the door was answered instantly by a young maid in Alsatian costume. Her fresh complexion and her long eyelashes, lowered demurely at the sight of the tall officer, caused Lieut. D'Hubert, who was accessible to esthetic impressions, to relax the cold, severe gravity of his

face. At the same time he observed that the girl had over her arm a pair of hussar's breeches, blue with a red stripe.

"Lieut. Feraud in?" he inquired, benevolently.

"Oh, no, sir! He went out at six this morning."

The pretty maid tried to close the door. Lieut. D'Hubert, opposing this move with gentle firmness, stepped into the ante-room, jingling his spurs.

"Come, my dear! You don't mean to say he has not been home since six o'clock this morning?"

Saying these words, Lieut. D'Hubert opened without ceremony the door of a room so comfortably and neatly ordered that only from internal evidence in the shape of boots, uniforms, and military accoutrements did he acquire the conviction that it was Lieut. Feraud's room. And he saw also that Lieut. Feraud was not at home. The truthful maid had followed him, and raised her candid eyes to his face.

"H'm!" said Lieut. D'Hubert, greatly disappointed, for he had already visited all the haunts where a lieutenant of hussars could be found of a fine afternoon. "So he's out? And do you happen to know, my dear, why he went out at six this morning?"

"No," she answered, readily. "He came home late last night, and snored. I heard him when I got up at five. Then he dressed himself in his oldest uniform and went out. Service, I suppose."

"Service? Not a bit of it!" cried Lieut. D'Hubert. "Learn, my angel, that he went out thus early to fight a duel with a civilian."

She heard this news without a quiver of her dark eyelashes. It was very obvious that the actions of Lieut. Feraud were generally above criticism. She only looked up for a moment in mute surprise, and Lieut. D'Hubert concluded from this absence of emotion that she must have seen Lieut. Feraud since the morning. He looked around the room.

"Come!" he insisted, with confidential familiarity. "He's perhaps somewhere in the house now?"

She shook her head.

"So much the worse for him!" continued Lieut. D'Hubert, in a tone of anxious conviction. "But he has been home this morning."

This time the pretty maid nodded slightly.

"He has!" cried Lieut. D'Hubert. "And went out again? What for? Couldn't he keep quietly indoors! What a lunatic! My dear girl——"

Lieut. D'Hubert's natural kindness of disposition and strong sense of comradeship helped his powers of observation. He changed his tone to a most insinuating softness, and, gazing at the hussar's breeches hanging over the arm of the girl, he appealed to the interest she took in Lieut. Feraud's comfort and happiness. He was pressing and persuasive. He used his eyes, which were kind and fine, with excellent effect. His anxiety to get hold at once of Lieut. Feraud, for Lieut. Feraud's own good, seemed so genuine that at last it overcame the girl's unwillingness to

speak. Unluckily she had not much to tell. Lieut. Feraud had returned home shortly before ten, had walked straight into his room, and had thrown himself on his bed to resume his slumbers. She had heard him snore rather louder than before far into the afternoon. Then he got up, put on his best uniform, and went out. That was all she knew.

She raised her eyes, and Lieut. D'Hubert stared into them incredulously.

"It's incredible. Gone parading the town in his best uniform! My dear child, don't you know he ran that civilian through this morning? Clean through, as you spit a hare."

The pretty maid heard the gruesome intelligence without any signs of distress. But she pressed her lips together thoughtfully.

"He isn't parading the town," she remarked in a low tone. "Far from it."

"The civilian's family is making an awful row," continued Lieut. D'Hubert, pursuing his train of thought. "And the general is very angry. It's one of the best families in the town. Feraud ought to have kept close at least——"

"What will the general do to him?" inquired the girl, anxiously.

"He won't have his head cut off, to be sure," grumbled Lieut. D'Hubert. "His conduct is positively indecent. He's making no end of trouble for himself by this sort of bravado."

"But he isn't parading the town," the maid insisted in a shy murmur.

"Why, yes! Now I think of it, I haven't seen him anywhere about. What on earth has he done with himself?"

"He's gone to pay a call," suggested the maid, after a moment of silence.

Lieut. D'Hubert started.

"A call! Do you mean a call on a lady? The cheek of the man! And how do you know this, my dear?"

Without concealing her woman's scorn for the denseness of the masculine mind, the pretty maid reminded him that Lieut. Feraud had arrayed himself in his best uniform before going out. He had also put on his newest dolman, she added, in a tone as if this conversation were getting on her nerves, and turned away brusquely.

Lieut. D'Hubert, without questioning the accuracy of the deduction, did not see that it advanced him much on his official quest. For his quest after Lieut. Feraud had an official character. He did not know any of the women this fellow, who had run a man through in the morning, was likely to visit in the afternoon. The two young men knew each other but slightly. He bit his gloved finger in perplexity.

"Call!" he exclaimed. "Call on the devil!"

The girl, with her back to him, and folding the hussar's breeches on a chair, protested with a vexed little laugh:

"Oh, dear, no! On Madame de Lionne."

Lieut. D'Hubert whistled softly. Madame de Lionne was the wife of a high official who had a well-known *salon* and some pretensions to sensibility and elegance. The husband was a civilian, and old; but the society of the *salon* was young and military. Lieut. D'Hubert had whistled, not because the idea of pursuing Lieut. Feraud into that very *salon* was disagreeable to him, but because, having arrived in Strasbourg only lately, he had not had the time as yet to get an introduction to Madame de Lionne. And what was that swashbuckler Feraud doing there, he wondered. He did not seem the sort of man who——

"Are you certain of what you say?" asked Lieut. D'Hubert.

The girl was perfectly certain. Without turning round to look at him, she explained that the coachman of their next door neighbours knew the *maître-d'hôtel* of Madame de Lionne. In this way she had her information. And she was perfectly certain. In giving this assurance she sighed. Lieut. Feraud called there nearly every afternoon, she added.

"Ah, bah!" exclaimed D'Hubert, ironically. His opinion of Madame de Lionne went down several degrees. Lieut. Feraud did not seem to him specially worthy of attention on the part of a woman with a reputation for sensibility and elegance. But there was no saying. At bottom they were all alike—very practical rather than idealistic. Lieut. D'Hubert, however, did not allow his mind to dwell on these considerations.

"By thunder!" he reflected aloud. "The general goes there sometimes. If he happens to find the fellow making eyes at the lady there will be the devil to pay! Our general is not a very accommodating person, I can tell you."

"Go quickly, then! Don't stand here now I've told you where he is!" cried the girl, colouring to the eyes.

"Thanks, my dear! I don't know what I would have done without you."

After manifesting his gratitude in an aggressive way, which at first was repulsed violently, and then submitted to with a sudden and still more repellent indifference, Lieut. D'Hubert took his departure.

He clanked and jingled along the streets with a martial swagger. To run a comrade to earth in a drawing-room where he was not known did not trouble him in the least. A uniform is a passport. His position as *officier d'ordonnance* of the general added to his assurance. Moreover, now that he knew where to find Lieut. Feraud, he had no option. It was a service matter.

Madame de Lionne's house had an excellent appearance. A man in livery, opening the door of a large drawing-room with a waxed floor, shouted his name and stood aside to let him pass. It was a reception day. The ladies wore big hats surcharged with a profusion of feathers; their bodies sheathed in clinging white gowns, from the armpits to the tips of the low satin shoes, looked sylph-like and cool in a great display of bare necks and arms. The men who talked with them, on the contrary,

were arrayed heavily in multi-coloured garments with collars up to their ears and thick sashes round their waists. Lieut. D'Hubert made his unabashed way across the room and, bowing low before a sylph-like form reclining on a couch, offered his apologies for this intrusion, which nothing could excuse but the extreme urgency of the service order he had to communicate to his comrade Feraud. He proposed to himself to return presently in a more regular manner and beg forgiveness for interrupting the interesting conversation . . .

A bare arm was extended towards him with gracious nonchalance even before he had finished speaking. He pressed the hand respectfully to his lips, and made the mental remark that it was bony. Madame de Lionne was a blonde, with too fine a skin and a long face.

"*C'est ça!*" she said, with an ethereal smile, disclosing a set of large teeth. "Come this evening to plead for your forgiveness."

"I will not fail, madame."

Meantime, Lieut. Feraud, splendid in his new dolman and the extremely polished boots of his calling, sat on a chair within a foot of the couch, one hand resting on his thigh, the other twirling his moustache to a point. At a significant glance from D'Hubert he rose without alacrity, and followed him into the recess of a window.

"What is it you want with me?" he asked, with astonishing indifference. Lieut. D'Hubert could not imagine that in the innocence of his heart and simplicity of his conscience Lieut. Feraud took a view of his duel in which neither remorse nor yet a rational apprehension of consequences had any place. Though he had no clear recollection how the quarrel had originated (it was begun in an establishment where beer and wine are drunk late at night), he had not the slightest doubt of being himself the outraged party. He had had two experienced friends for his seconds. Everything had been done according to the rules governing that sort of adventures. And a duel is obviously fought for the purpose of someone being at least hurt, if not killed outright. The civilian got hurt. That also was in order. Lieut. Feraud was perfectly tranquil; but Lieut. D'Hubert took it for affectation, and spoke with a certain vivacity.

"I am directed by the general to give you the order to go at once to your quarters, and remain there under close arrest."

It was now the turn of Lieut. Feraud to be astonished. "What the devil are you telling me there?" he murmured, faintly, and fell into such profound wonder that he could only follow mechanically the motions of Lieut. D'Hubert. The two officers, one tall, with an interesting face and a moustache the colour of ripe corn, the other, short and sturdy, with a hooked nose and a thick crop of black curly hair, approached the mistress of the house to take their leave. Madame de Lionne, a woman of eclectic taste, smiled upon these armed young men with impartial sensibility and an equal share of interest. Madame de Lionne took her delight in the infinite variety of the human species. All the other eyes in the

drawing-room followed the departing officers; and when they had gone out one or two men, who had already heard of the duel, imparted the information to the sylph-like ladies, who received it with faint shrieks of humane concern.

Meantime, the two hussars walked side by side, Lieut. Feraud trying to master the hidden reason of things which in this instance eluded the grasp of his intellect; Lieut. D'Hubert feeling annoyed at the part he had to play, because the general's instructions were that he should see personally that Lieut. Feraud carried out his orders to the letter, and at once.

"The chief seems to know this animal," he thought, eyeing his companion, whose round face, the round eyes, and even the twisted-up jet black little moustache seemed animated by a mental exasperation against the incomprehensible. And aloud he observed rather reproachfully, "The general is in a devilish fury with you!"

Lieut. Feraud stopped short on the edge of the pavement, and cried in accents of unmistakable sincerity, "What on earth for?" The innocence of the fiery Gascon soul was depicted in the manner in which he seized his head in both hands as if to prevent it bursting with perplexity.

"For the duel," said Lieut. D'Hubert, curtly. He was annoyed greatly by this sort of perverse fooling.

"The duel! The . . ."

Lieut. Feraud passed from one paroxysm of astonishment into another. He dropped his hands and walked on slowly, trying to reconcile this information with the state of his own feelings. It was impossible. He burst out indignantly, "Was I to let that sauerkraut-eating civilian wipe his boots on the uniform of the 7th Hussars?"

Lieut. D'Hubert could not remain altogether unmoved by that simple sentiment. This little fellow was a lunatic, he thought to himself, but there was something in what he said.

"Of course, I don't know how far you were justified," he began, soothingly. "And the general himself may not be exactly informed. Those people have been deafening him with their lamentations."

"Ah! the general is not exactly informed," mumbled Lieut. Feraud, walking faster and faster as his choler at the injustice of his fate began to rise. "He is not exactly . . . And he orders me under close arrest, with God knows what afterwards!"

"Don't excite yourself like this," remonstrated the other. "Your adversary's people are very influential, you know, and it looks bad enough on the face of it. The general had to take notice of their complaint at once. I don't think he means to be over-severe with you. It's the best thing for you to be kept out of sight for a while."

"I am very much obliged to the general," muttered Lieut. Feraud through his teeth. "And perhaps you would say I ought to be grateful to

you, too, for the trouble you have taken to hunt me up in the drawing-room of a lady who——"

"Frankly," interrupted Lieut. D'Hubert, with an innocent laugh, "I think you ought to be. I had no end of trouble to find out where you were. It wasn't exactly the place for you to disport yourself in under the circumstances. If the general had caught you there making eyes at the goddess of the temple . . . oh, my word! . . . He hates to be bothered with complaints against his officers, you know. And it looked uncommonly like sheer bravado."

The two officers had arrived now at the street door of Lieut. Feraud's lodgings. The latter turned towards his companion. "Lieut. D'Hubert," he said, "I have something to say to you, which can't be said very well in the street. You can't refuse to come up."

The pretty maid had opened the door. Lieut. Feraud brushed past her brusquely, and she raised her scared and questioning eyes to Lieut. D'Hubert, who could do nothing but shrug his shoulders slightly as he followed with marked reluctance.

In his room Lieut. Feraud unhooked the clasp, flung his new dolman on the bed, and, folding his arms across his chest, turned to the other hussar.

"Do you imagine I am a man to submit tamely to injustice?" he inquired, in a boisterous voice.

"Oh, do be reasonable!" remonstrated Lieut. D'Hubert.

"I am reasonable! I am perfectly reasonable!" retorted the other with ominous restraint. "I can't call the general to account for his behaviour, but you are going to answer me for yours."

"I can't listen to this nonsense," murmured Lieut. D'Hubert, making a slightly contemptuous grimace.

"You call this nonsense? It seems to me a perfectly plain statement. Unless you don't understand French."

"What on earth do you mean?"

"I mean," screamed suddenly Lieut. Feraud, "to cut off your ears to teach you to disturb me with the general's orders when I am talking to a lady!"

A profound silence followed this mad declaration; and through the open window Lieut. D'Hubert heard the little birds singing sanely in the garden. He said, preserving his calm, "Why! If you take that tone, of course I shall hold myself at your disposition whenever you are at liberty to attend to this affair; but I don't think you will cut my ears off."

"I am going to attend to it at once," declared Lieut. Feraud, with extreme truculence. "If you are thinking of displaying your airs and graces to-night in Madame de Lionne's *salon* you are very much mistaken."

"Really!" said Lieut. D'Hubert, who was beginning to feel irritated, "you are an impracticable sort of fellow. The general's orders to me were

to put you under arrest, not to carve you into small pieces. Good-morning!" And turning his back on the little Gascon, who, always sober in his potations, was as though born intoxicated with the sunshine of his vine-ripening country, the Northman, who could drink hard on occasion, but was born sober under the watery skies of Picardy, made for the door. Hearing, however, the unmistakable sound behind his back of a sword drawn from the scabbard, he had no option but to stop.

"Devil take this mad Southerner!" he thought, spinning round and surveying with composure the warlike posture of Lieut. Feraud, with a bare sword in his hand.

"At once!—at once!" stuttered Feraud, beside himself.

"You had my answer," said the other, keeping his temper very well.

At first he had been only vexed, and somewhat amused; but now his face got clouded. He was asking himself seriously how he could manage to get away. It was impossible to run from a man with a sword, and as to fighting him, it seemed completely out of the question. He waited awhile then said exactly what was in his heart.

"Drop this! I won't fight with you. I won't be made ridiculous."

"Ah, you won't?" hissed the Gascon. "I suppose you prefer to be made infamous. Do you hear what I say? . . . Infamous! Infamous! Infamous!" he shrieked, rising and falling on his toes and getting very red in the face.

Lieut. D'Hubert, on the contrary, became very pale at the sound of the unsavoury word for a moment, then flushed pink to the roots of his fair hair. "But you can't go out to fight; you are under arrest, you lunatic!" he objected, with angry scorn.

"There's the garden: it's big enough to lay out your long carcass in," spluttered the other with such ardour that somehow the anger of the cooler man subsided.

"This is perfectly absurd," he said, glad enough to think he had found a way out of it for the moment. "We shall never get any of our comrades to serve as seconds. It's preposterous."

"Seconds! Damn the seconds! We don't want any seconds. Don't you worry about any seconds. I shall send word to your friends to come and bury you when I am done. And if you want any witnesses, I'll send word to the old girl to put her head out of a window at the back. Stay! There's the gardener. He'll do. He's as deaf as a post, but he has two eyes in his head. Come along! I will teach you, my staff officer, that the carrying about of a general's orders is not always child's play."

While thus discoursing he had unbuckled his empty scabbard. He sent it flying under the bed, and, lowering the point of the sword, brushed past the perplexed Lieut. D'Hubert, exclaiming, "Follow me!" Directly he had flung open the door a faint shriek was heard and the pretty maid, who had been listening at the keyhole, staggered away, putting the backs of her hands over her eyes. Feraud did not seem to see her, but she ran

after him and seized his left arm. He shook her off, and then she rushed towards Lieut. D'Hubert and clawed at the sleeve of his uniform.

"Wretched man!" she sobbed. "Is this what you wanted to find him for?"

"Let me go," entreated Lieut. D'Hubert, trying to disengage himself gently. "It's like being in a madhouse," he protested, with exasperation. "Do let me go! I won't do him any harm."

A fiendish laugh from Lieut. Feraud commented that assurance. "Come along!" he shouted, with a stamp of his foot.

And Lieut. D'Hubert did follow. He could do nothing else. Yet in vindication of his sanity it must be recorded that as he passed through the ante-room the notion of opening the street door and bolting out presented itself to this brave youth, only of course to be instantly dismissed, for he felt sure that the other would pursue him without shame or compunction. And the prospect of an officer of hussars being chased along the street by another officer of hussars with a naked sword could not be for a moment entertained. Therefore he followed into the garden. Behind them the girl tottered out, too. With ashy lips and wild, scared eyes, she surrendered herself to a dreadful curiosity. She had also the notion of rushing if need be between Lieut. Feraud and death.

The deaf gardener, utterly unconscious of approaching footsteps, went on watering his flowers till Lieut. Feraud thumped him on the back. Beholding suddenly an enraged man flourishing a big sabre, the old chap trembling in all his limbs dropped the watering-pot. At once Lieut. Feraud kicked it away with great animosity, and, seizing the gardener by the throat, backed him against a tree. He held him there, shouting in his ear, "Stay here, and look on! You understand? You've got to look on! Don't dare budge from the spot!"

Lieut. D'Hubert came slowly down the walk, unclasping his dolman with unconcealed disgust. Even then, with his hand already on the hilt of his sword, he hesitated to draw till a roar, *"En garde, fichtre!* What do you think you came here for?" and the rush of his adversary forced him to put himself as quickly as possible in a posture of defence.

The clash of arms filled that prim garden, which hitherto had known no more warlike sound than the click of clipping shears; and presently the upper part of an old lady's body was projected out of a window upstairs. She tossed her arms above her white cap, scolding in a cracked voice. The gardener remained glued to the tree, his toothless mouth open in idiotic astonishment, and a little farther up the path the pretty girl, as if spellbound to a small grass plot, ran a few steps this way and that, wringing her hands and muttering crazily. She did not rush between the combatants: the onslaughts of Lieut. Feraud were so fierce that her heart failed her. Lieut. D'Hubert, his faculties concentrated upon defence, needed all his skill and science of the sword to stop the rushes of his adversary. Twice already he had to break ground. It bothered him to feel

his foothold made insecure by the round, dry gravel of the path rolling under the hard soles of his boots. This was most unsuitable ground, he thought, keeping a watchful, narrowed gaze, shaded by long eyelashes, upon the fiery stare of his thick-set adversary. This absurd affair would ruin his reputation of a sensible, well-behaved, promising young officer. It would damage, at any rate, his immediate prospects, and lose him the good-will of his general. These worldly preoccupations were no doubt misplaced in view of the solemnity of the moment. A duel, whether regarded as a ceremony in the cult of honour, or even when reduced in its moral essence to a form of manly sport, demands a perfect singleness of intention, a homicidal austerity of mood. On the other hand, this vivid concern for his future had not a bad effect inasmuch as it began to rouse the anger of Lieut. D'Hubert. Some seventy seconds had elapsed since they had crossed blades, and Lieut. D'Hubert had to break ground again in order to avoid impaling his reckless adversary like a beetle for a cabinet of specimens. The result was that misapprehending the motive, Lieut. Feraud with a triumphant sort of snarl pressed his attack.

"This enraged animal will have me against the wall directly," thought Lieut. D'Hubert. He imagined himself much closer to the house than he was, and he dared not turn his head; it seemed to him that he was keeping his adversary off with his eyes rather more than with his point. Lieut. Feraud crouched and bounded with a fierce tigerish agility fit to trouble the stoutest heart. But what was more appalling than the fury of a wild beast, accomplishing in all innocence of heart a natural function, was the fixity of savage purpose man alone is capable of displaying. Lieut. D'Hubert in the midst of his worldly preoccupations perceived it at last. It was an absurd and damaging affair to be drawn into, but whatever silly intention the fellow had started with, it was clear enough that by this time he meant to kill—nothing less. He meant it with an intensity of will utterly beyond the inferior faculties of a tiger.

As is the case with constitutionally brave men, the full view of the danger interested Lieut. D'Hubert. And directly he got properly interested, the length of his arm and the coolness of his head told in his favour. It was the turn of Lieut. Feraud to recoil, with a blood-curdling grunt of baffled rage. He made a swift feint, and then rushed straight forward.

"Ah! you would, would you?" Lieut. D'Hubert exclaimed, mentally. The combat had lasted nearly two minutes, time enough for any man to get embittered, apart from the merits of the quarrel. And all at once it was over. Trying to close breast to breast under his adversary's guard Lieut. Feraud received a slash on his shortened arm. He did not feel it in the least, but it checked his rush, and his feet slipping on the gravel he fell backwards with great violence. The shock jarred his boiling brain into the perfect quietude of insensibility. Simultaneously with his fall the

pretty servant-girl shrieked; but the old maiden lady at the window ceased her scolding, and began to cross herself piously.

Beholding his adversary stretched out perfectly still, his face to the sky, Lieut. D'Hubert thought he had killed him outright. The impression of having slashed hard enough to cut his man clean in two abode with him for a while in an exaggerated memory of the right good-will he had put into the blow. He dropped on his knees hastily by the side of the prostrate body. Discovering that not even the arm was severed, a slight sense of disappointment mingled with the feeling of relief. The fellow deserved the worst. But truly he did not want the death of that sinner. The affair was ugly enough as it stood, and Lieut. D'Hubert addressed himself at once to the task of stopping the bleeding. In this task it was his fate to be ridiculously impeded by the pretty maid. Rending the air with screams of horror, she attacked him from behind and, twining her fingers in his hair, tugged back at his head. Why she should choose to hinder him at this precise moment he could not in the least understand. He did not try. It was all like a very wicked and harassing dream. Twice to save himself from being pulled over he had to rise and fling her off. He did this stoically, without a word, kneeling down again at once to go on with his work. But the third time, his work being done, he seized her and held her arms pinned to her body. Her cap was half off, her face was red, her eyes blazed with crazy boldness. He looked mildly into them while she called him a wretch, a traitor, and a murderer many times in succession. This did not annoy him so much as the conviction that she had managed to scratch his face abundantly. Ridicule would be added to the scandal of the story. He imagined the adorned tale making its way through the garrison of the town, through the whole army on the frontier, with every possible distortion of motive and sentiment and circumstance, spreading a doubt upon the sanity of his conduct and the distinction of his taste even to the very ears of his honourable family. It was all very well for that fellow Feraud, who had no connections, no family to speak of, and no quality but courage, which, anyhow, was a matter of course, and possessed by every single trooper in the whole mass of French cavalry. Still holding down the arms of the girl in a strong grip, Lieut. D'Hubert glanced over his shoulder. Lieut. Feraud had opened his eyes. He did not move. Like a man just waking from a deep sleep he stared without any expression at the evening sky.

Lieut. D'Hubert's urgent shouts to the old gardener produced no effect—not so much as to make him shut his toothless mouth. Then he remembered that the man was stone deaf. All that time the girl struggled, not with maidenly coyness, but like a pretty, dumb fury, kicking his shins now and then. He continued to hold her as if in a vice, his instinct telling him that were he to let her go she would fly at his eyes. But he was greatly humiliated by his position. At last she gave up. She was more

exhausted than appeased, he feared. Nevertheless, he attempted to get out of this wicked dream by way of negotiation.

"Listen to me," he said, as calmly as he could. "Will you promise to run for a surgeon if I let you go?"

With real affliction he heard her declare that she would do nothing of the kind. On the contrary, her sobbed out intention was to remain in the garden, and fight tooth and nail for the protection of the vanquished man. This was shocking.

"My dear child!" he cried in despair, "is it possible that you think me capable of murdering a wounded adversary? Is it. . . . Be quiet, you little wild cat, you!"

They struggled. A thick, drowsy voice said behind him, "What are you after with that girl?"

Lieut. Feraud had raised himself on his good arm. He was looking sleepily at his other arm, at the mess of blood on his uniform, at a small red pool on the ground, at his sabre lying a foot away on the path. Then he laid himself down gently again to think it all out, as far as a thundering headache would permit of mental operations.

Lieut. D'Hubert released the girl who crouched at once by the side of the other lieutenant. The shades of night were falling on the little trim garden with this touching group, whence proceeded low murmurs of sorrow and compassion, with other feeble sounds of a different character, as if an imperfectly awake invalid were trying to swear. Lieut. D'Hubert went away.

He passed through the silent house, and congratulated himself upon the dusk concealing his gory hands and scratched face from the passers-by. But this story could by no means be concealed. He dreaded the discredit and ridicule above everything, and was painfully aware of sneaking through the back streets in the manner of a murderer. Presently the sounds of a flute coming out of the open window of a lighted upstairs room in a modest house interrupted his dismal reflections. It was being played with a persevering virtuosity, and through the *fioritures* of the tune one could hear the regular thumping of the foot beating time on the floors.

Lieut. D'Hubert shouted a name, which was that of an army surgeon whom he knew fairly well. The sounds of the flute ceased, and the musician appeared at the window, his instrument still in his hand, peering into the street.

"Who calls? You, D'Hubert? What brings you this way?"

He did not like to be disturbed at the hour when he was playing the flute. He was a man whose hair had turned grey already in the thankless task of tying up wounds on battlefields where others reaped advancement and glory.

"I want you to go at once and see Feraud. You know Lieut. Feraud? He lives down the second street. It's but a step from here."

"What's the matter with him?"

"Wounded."

"Are you sure?"

"Sure!" cried D'Hubert. "I come from there."

"That's amusing," said the elderly surgeon. Amusing was his favourite word; but the expression of his face when he pronounced it never corresponded. He was a stolid man. "Come in," he added. "I'll get ready in a moment."

"Thanks! I will. I want to wash my hands in your room."

Lieut. D'Hubert found the surgeon occupied in unscrewing his flute, and packing the pieces methodically in a case. He turned his head.

"Water there—in the corner. Your hands do want washing."

"I've stopped the bleeding," said Lieut. D'Hubert. "But you had better make haste. It's rather more than ten minutes ago, you know."

The surgeon did not hurry his movements.

"What's the matter? Dressing came off? That's amusing. I've been at work in the hospital all day but I've been told this morning by somebody that he had come off without a scratch."

"Not the same duel probably," growled moodily Lieut. D'Hubert, wiping his hands on a coarse towel.

"Not the same. . . . What? Another. It would take the very devil to make me go out twice in one day." The surgeon looked narrowly at Lieut. D'Hubert. "How did you come by that scratched face? Both sides, too—and symmetrical. It's amusing."

"Very!" snarled Lieut. D'Hubert. "And you will find his slashed arm amusing, too. It will keep both of you amused for quite a long time."

The doctor was mystified and impressed by the brusque bitterness of Lieut. D'Hubert's tone. They left the house together, and in the street he was still more mystified by his conduct.

"Aren't you coming with me?" he asked.

"No," said Lieut. D'Hubert. "You can find the house by yourself. The front door will be standing open very likely."

"All right. Where's his room?"

"Ground floor. But you had better go right through and look in the garden first."

This astonishing piece of information made the surgeon go off without further parley. Lieut. D'Hubert regained his quarters nursing a hot and uneasy indignation. He dreaded the chaff of his comrades almost as much as the anger of his superiors. The truth was confoundedly grotesque and embarrassing, even putting aside the irregularity of the combat itself, which made it come abominably near a criminal offence. Like all men without much imagination, a faculty which helps the process of reflective thought, Lieut. D'Hubert became frightfully harassed by the obvious aspects of his predicament. He was certainly glad that he had

not killed Lieut. Feraud outside all rules, and without the regular witnesses proper to such a transaction. Uncommonly glad. At the same time he felt as though he would have liked to wring his neck for him without ceremony.

He was still under the sway of these contradictory sentiments when the surgeon amateur of the flute came to see him. More than three days had elapsed. Lieut. D'Hubert was no longer *officier d'ordonnance* to the general commanding the division. He had been sent back to his regiment. And he was resuming his connection with the soldiers' military family by being shut up in close confinement, not at his own quarters in town, but in a room in the barracks. Owing to the gravity of the incident, he was forbidden to see any one. He did not know what had happened, what was being said, or what was being thought. The arrival of the surgeon was a most unexpected thing to the worried captive. The amateur of the flute began by explaining that he was there only by a special favour of the colonel.

"I represented to him that it would be only fair to let you have some authentic news of your adversary," he continued. "You'll be glad to hear he's getting better fast."

Lieut. D'Hubert's face exhibited no conventional signs of gladness. He continued to walk the floor of the dusty bare room.

"Take this chair, doctor," he mumbled.

The doctor sat down.

"This affair is variously appreciated—in town and in the army. In fact, the diversity of opinions is amusing."

"Is it!" mumbled Lieut. D'Hubert, tramping steadily from wall to wall. But within himself he marvelled that there could be two opinions on the matter. The surgeon continued.

"Of course, as the real facts are not known——"

"I should have thought," interrupted D'Hubert, "that the fellow would have put you in possession of facts."

"He said something," admitted the other, "the first time I saw him. And, by the by, I did find him in the garden. The thump on the back of his head had made him a little incoherent then. Afterwards he was rather reticent than otherwise."

"Didn't think he would have the grace to be ashamed!" mumbled D'Hubert, resuming his pacing while the doctor murmured, "It's very amusing. Ashamed! Shame was not exactly his frame of mind. However, you may look at the matter otherwise."

"What are you talking about? What matter?" asked D'Hubert, with a sidelong look at the heavy-faced, grey-haired figure seated on a wooden chair.

"Whatever it is," said the surgeon a little impatiently, "I don't want to pronounce any opinion on your conduct——"

"By heavens, you had better not!" burst out D'Hubert.

"There!—there! Don't be so quick in flourishing the sword. It doesn't pay in the long run. Understand once for all that I would not carve any of you youngsters except with the tools of my trade. But my advice is good. If you go on like this you will make for yourself an ugly reputation."

"Go on like what?" demanded Lieut. D'Hubert, stopping short, quite startled. "I!—I!—make for myself a reputation. . . . What do you imagine?"

"I told you I don't wish to judge of the rights and wrongs of this incident. It's not my business. Nevertheless——"

"What on earth has he been telling you?" interrupted Lieut. D'Hubert, in a sort of awed scare.

"I told you already, that at first, when I picked him up in the garden, he was incoherent. Afterwards he was naturally reticent. But I gather at least that he could not help himself."

"He couldn't?" shouted Lieut. D'Hubert in a great voice. Then, lowering his tone impressively, "And what about me? Could I help myself?"

The surgeon stood up. His thoughts were running upon the flute, his constant companion with a consoling voice. In the vicinity of field ambulances, after twenty-four hours' hard work, he had been known to trouble with its sweet sounds the horrible stillness of battlefields, given over to silence and the dead. The solacing hour of his daily life was approaching, and in peace time he held on to the minutes as a miser to his hoard.

"Of course!—of course!" he said, perfunctorily. "You would think so. It's amusing. However, being perfectly neutral and friendly to you both, I have consented to deliver his message to you. Say that I am humouring an invalid if you like. He wants you to know that this affair is by no means at an end. He intends to send you his seconds directly he has regained his strength—providing, of course, the army is not in the field at that time."

"He intends, does he? Why, certainly," spluttered Lieut. D'Hubert in a passion.

The secret of his exasperation was not apparent to the visitor; but this passion confirmed the surgeon in the belief which was gaining ground outside that some very serious difference had arisen between these two young men, something serious enough to wear an air of mystery, some fact of the utmost gravity. To settle their urgent difference about that fact, those two young men had risked being broken and disgraced at the outset almost of their career. The surgeon feared that the forthcoming inquiry would fail to satisfy the public curiosity. They would not take the public into their confidence as to that something which had

passed beween them of a nature so outrageous as to make them face a charge of murder—neither more nor less. But what could it be?

The surgeon was not very curious by temperament; but that question haunting his mind caused him twice that evening to hold the instrument off his lips and sit silent for a whole minute—right in the middle of a tune—trying to form a plausible conjecture.

Chapter 2

HE SUCCEEDED IN THIS OBJECT no better than the rest of the garrison and the whole of society. The two young officers, of no especial consequence till then, became distinguished by the universal curiosity as to the origin of their quarrel. Madame de Lionne's *salon* was the centre of ingenious surmises; that lady herself was for a time assailed by inquiries as being the last person known to have spoken to these unhappy and reckless young men before they went out together from her house to a savage encounter with swords, at dusk, in a private garden. She protested she had not observed anything unusual in their demeanour. Lieut. Feraud had been visibly annoyed at being called away. That was natural enough; no man likes to be disturbed in a conversation with a lady famed for her elegance and sensibility. But in truth the subject bored Madame de Lionne, since her personality could by no stretch of reckless gossip be connected with this affair. And it irritated her to hear it advanced that there might have been some woman in the case. This irritation arose, not from her elegance or sensibility, but from a more instinctive side of her nature. It became so great at last that she peremptorily forbade the subject to be mentioned under her roof. Near her couch the prohibition was obeyed, but farther off in the *salon* the pall of the imposed silence continued to be lifted more or less. A personage with a long, pale face, resembling the countenance of a sheep, opined, shaking his head, that it was a quarrel of long standing envenomed by time. It was objected to him that the men themselves were too young for such a theory. They belonged also to different and distant parts of France. There were other physical impossibilities, too. A sub-commissary of the Intendence, an agreeable and cultivated bachelor in kerseymere breeches, Hessian boots, and a blue coat embroidered with silver lace, who affected to believe in the transmigration of souls, suggested that the two had met perhaps in some previous existence. The feud was in the forgotten past. It might have been something quite inconceivable in the present state of their being; but their souls remembered the animosity, and manifested

an instinctive antagonism. He developed this theme jocularly. Yet the affair was so absurd from the worldly, the military, the honourable, or the prudential point of view, that this weird explanation seemed rather more reasonable than any other.

The two officers had confided nothing definite to any one. Humiliation at having been worsted arms in hand, and an uneasy feeling of having been involved in a scrape by the injustice of fate, kept Lieut. Feraud savagely dumb. He mistrusted the sympathy of mankind. That would, of course, go to that dandified staff officer. Lying in bed, he raved aloud to the pretty maid who administered to his needs with devotion, and listened to his horrible imprecations with alarm. That Lieut. D'Hubert should be made to "pay for it," seemed to her just and natural. Her principal care was that Lieut. Feraud should not excite himself. He appeared so wholly admirable and fascinating to the humility of her heart that her only concern was to see him get well quickly, even if it were only to resume his visits to Madame de Lionne's *salon*.

Lieut. D'Hubert kept silent for the immediate reason that there was no one, except a stupid young soldier servant, to speak to. Further, he was aware that the episode, so grave professionally, had its comic side. When reflecting upon it, he still felt that he would like to wring Lieut. Feraud's neck for him. But this formula was figurative rather than precise, and expressed more a state of mind than an actual physical impulse. At the same time, there was in that young man a feeling of comradeship and kindness which made him unwilling to make the position of Lieut. Feraud worse than it was. He did not want to talk at large about this wretched affair. At the inquiry he would have, of course, to speak the truth in self-defence. This prospect vexed him.

But no inquiry took place. The army took the field instead. Lieut. D'Hubert, liberated without remark, took up his regimental duties; and Lieut. Feraud, his arm just out of the sling, rode unquestioned with his squadron to complete his convalescence in the smoke of battlefields and the fresh air of night bivouacs. This bracing treatment suited him so well, that at the first rumour of an armistice being signed he could turn without misgivings to the thoughts of his private warfare.

This time it was to be regular warfare. He sent two friends to Lieut. D'Hubert, whose regiment was stationed only a few miles away. Those friends had asked no questions of their principal. "I owe him one, that pretty staff officer," he had said, grimly, and they went away quite contentedly on their mission. Lieut. D'Hubert had no difficulty in finding two friends equally discreet and devoted to their principal. "There's a crazy fellow to whom I must give a lesson," he had declared curtly; and they asked for no better reasons.

On these grounds an encounter with duelling-swords was arranged one early morning in a convenient field. At the third set-to Lieut. D'Hubert found himself lying on his back on the dewy grass with a hole in

his side. A serene sun rising over a landscape of meadows and woods hung on his left. A surgeon—not the flute player, but another—was bending over him, feeling around the wound.

"Narrow squeak. But it will be nothing," he pronounced.

Lieut. D'Hubert heard these words with pleasure. One of his seconds, sitting on the wet grass, and sustaining his head on his lap, said, "The fortune of war, *mon pauvre vieux*. What will you have? You had better make it up like two good fellows. Do!"

"You don't know what you ask," murmured Lieut. D'Hubert, in a feeble voice. "However, if he . . ."

In another part of the meadow the seconds of Lieut. Feraud were urging him to go over and shake hands with his adversary.

"You have paid him off now—*que diable*. It's the proper thing to do. This D'Hubert is a decent fellow."

"I know the decency of these generals' pets," muttered Lieut. Feraud through his teeth, and the sombre expression of his face discouraged further efforts at reconciliation. The seconds, bowing from a distance, took their men off the field. In the afternoon Lieut. D'Hubert, very popular as a good comrade uniting great bravery with a frank and equable temper, had many visitors. It was remarked that Lieut. Feraud did not, as is customary, show himself much abroad to receive the felicitations of his friends. They would not have failed him, because he, too, was liked for the exuberance of his southern nature and the simplicity of his character. In all the places where officers were in the habit of assembling at the end of the day the duel of the morning was talked over from every point of view. Though Lieut. D'Hubert had got worsted this time, his sword play was commended. No one could deny that it was very close, very scientific. It was even whispered that if he got touched it was because he wished to spare his adversary. But by many the vigour and dash of Lieut. Feraud's attack were pronounced irresistible.

The merits of the two officers as combatants were frankly discussed; but their attitude to each other after the duel was criticised lightly and with caution. It was irreconcilable, and that was to be regretted. But after all they knew best what the care of their honour dictated. It was not a matter for their comrades to pry into over-much. As to the origin of the quarrel, the general impression was that it dated from the time they were holding garrison in Strasbourg. The musical surgeon shook his head at that. It went much farther back, he thought.

"Why, of course! You must know the whole story," cried several voices, eager with curiosity. "What was it?"

He raised his eyes from his glass deliberately. "Even if I knew ever so well, you can't expect me to tell you, since both the principals choose to say nothing."

He got up and went out, leaving the sense of mystery behind him.

He could not stay any longer, because the witching hour of flute-playing was drawing near.

After he had gone a very young officer observed solemnly, "Obviously, his lips are sealed!"

Nobody questioned the high correctness of that remark. Somehow it added to the impressiveness of the affair. Several older officers of both regiments, prompted by nothing but sheer kindness and love of harmony, proposed to form a Court of Honour, to which the two young men would leave the task of their reconciliation. Unfortunately they began by approaching Lieut. Feraud, on the assumption that, having just scored heavily, he would be found placable and disposed to moderation.

The reasoning was sound enough. Nevertheless, the move turned out unfortunate. In that relaxation of moral fibre, which is brought about by the ease of soothed vanity, Lieut. Feraud had condescended in the secret of his heart to review the case, and even had come to doubt not the justice of his cause, but the absolute sagacity of his conduct. This being so, he was disinclined to talk about it. The suggestion of the regimental wise men put him in a difficult position. He was disgusted at it, and this disgust, by a paradoxical logic, reawakened his animosity against Lieut. D'Hubert. Was he to be pestered with this fellow for ever—the fellow who had an infernal knack of getting round people somehow? And yet it was difficult to refuse point blank that mediation sanctioned by the code of honour.

He met the difficulty by an attitude of grim reserve. He twisted his moustache and used vague words. His case was perfectly clear. He was not ashamed to state it before a proper Court of Honour, neither was he afraid to defend it on the ground. He did not see any reason to jump at the suggestion before ascertaining how his adversary was likely to take it.

Later in the day, his exasperation growing upon him, he was heard in a public place saying sardonically, "that it would be the very luckiest thing for Lieut. D'Hubert, because the next time of meeting he need not hope to get off with the mere trifle of three weeks in bed."

This boastful phrase might have been prompted by the most profound Machiavellism. Southern natures often hide, under the outward impulsiveness of action and speech, a certain amount of astuteness.

Lieut. Feraud, mistrusting the justice of men, by no means desired a Court of Honour; and the above words, according so well with his temperament, had also the merit of serving his turn. Whether meant so or not, they found their way in less than four-and-twenty hours into Lieut. D'Hubert, sitting propped up with pillows, received the overtures made to him next day by the statement that the affair was of a nature which could not bear discussion.

The pale face of the wounded officer, his weak voice which he had yet to use cautiously, and the courteous dignity of his tone had a great effect on his hearers. Reported outside all this did more for deepening the

mystery than the vapourings of Lieut. Feraud. This last was greatly relieved at the issue. He began to enjoy the state of general wonder, and was pleased to add to it by assuming an attitude of fierce discretion.

The colonel of Lieut. D'Hubert's regiment was a grey-haired, weather-beaten warrior, who took a simple view of his responsibilities. "I can't," he said to himself, "let the best of my subalterns get damaged like this for nothing. I must get to the bottom of this affair privately. He must speak out if the devil were in it. The colonel should be more than a father to these youngsters." And indeed he loved all his men with as much affection as a father of a large family can feel for every individual member of it. If human beings by an oversight of Providence came into the world as mere civilians, they were born again into a regiment as infants are born into a family, and it was that military birth alone which counted.

At the sight of Lieut. D'Hubert standing before him very bleached and hollow-eyed the heart of the old warrior felt a pang of genuine compassion. All his affection for the regiment—that body of men which he held in his hand to launch forward and draw back, who ministered to his pride and commanded all his thoughts—seemed centred for a moment on the person of the most promising subaltern. He cleared his throat in a threatening manner, and frowned terribly. "You must understand," he began, "that I don't care a rap for the life of a single man in the regiment. I would send the eight hundred and forty-three of you men and horses galloping into the pit of perdition with no more compunction than I would kill a fly!"

"Yes, Colonel. You would be riding at our head," said Lieut. D'Hubert with a wan smile.

The colonel, who felt the need of being very diplomatic, fairly roared at this. "I want you to know, Lieut. D'Hubert, that I could stand aside and see you all riding to Hades if need be. I am a man to do even that if the good of the service and my duty to my country required it from me. But that's unthinkable, so don't you even hint at such a thing." He glared awfully, but his tone softened. "There's some milk yet about that moustache of yours, my boy. You don't know what a man like me is capable of. I would hide behind a haystack if . . . Don't grin at me, sir! How dare you? If this were not a private conversation I would . . . Look here! I am responsible for the proper expenditure of lives under my command for the glory of our country and the honour of the regiment. Do you understand that? Well, then, what the devil do you mean by letting yourself be spitted like this by that fellow of the 7th Hussars? It's simply disgraceful!"

Lieut. D'Hubert felt vexed beyond measure. His shoulders moved slightly. He made no other answer. He could not ignore his responsibility.

The colonel veiled his glance and lowered his voice still more. "It's deplorable!" he murmured. And again he changed his tone. "Come!" he

went on, persuasively, but with that note of authority which dwells in the throat of a good leader of men, "this affair must be settled. I desire to be told plainly what it is all about. I demand, as your best friend, to know."

The compelling power of authority, the persuasive influence of kindness, affected powerfully a man just risen from a bed of sickness. Lieut. D'Hubert's hand, which grasped the knob of a stick, trembled slightly. But this northern temperament, sentimental yet cautious and clear-sighted, too, in its idealistic way, checked his impulse to make a clean breast of the whole deadly absurdity. According to the precept of transcendental wisdom, he turned his tongue seven times in his mouth before he spoke. He made then only a speech of thanks.

The colonel listened, interested at first, then looked mystified. At last he frowned. "You hesitate?—*mille tonnerres!* Haven't I told you that I will condescend to argue with you—as a friend?"

"Yes, Colonel!" answered Lieut. D'Hubert, gently. "But I am afraid that after you have heard me out as a friend you will take action as my superior officer."

The attentive colonel snapped his jaws. "Well, what of that?" he said, frankly. "Is it so damnably disgraceful?"

"It is not," negatived Lieut. D'Hubert, in a faint but firm voice.

"Of course, I shall act for the good of the service. Nothing can prevent me doing that. What do you think I want to be told for?"

"I know it is not from idle curiosity," protested Lieut. D'Hubert. "I know you will act wisely. But what about the good fame of the regiment?"

"It cannot be affected by any youthful folly of a lieutenant," said the colonel, severely.

"No. It cannot be. But it can be by evil tongues. It will be said that a lieutenant of the 4th Hussars, afraid of meeting his adversary, is hiding behind his colonel. And that would be worse than hiding behind a haystack—for the good of the service. I cannot afford to do that, Colonel."

"Nobody would dare to say anything of the kind," began the colonel very fiercely, but ended the phrase on an uncertain note. The bravery of Lieut. D'Hubert was well known. But the colonel was well aware that the duelling courage, the single combat courage, is rightly or wrongly supposed to be courage of a special sort. And it was eminently necessary that an officer of his regiment should possess every kind of courage—and prove it, too. The colonel stuck out his lower lip, and looked far away with a peculiar glazed stare. This was the expression of his perplexity—an expression practically unknown to his regiment; for perplexity is a sentiment which is incompatible with the rank of colonel of cavalry. The colonel himself was overcome by the unpleasant novelty of the sensation. As he was not accustomed to think except on professional matters connected with the welfare of men and horses, and the proper use thereof

on the field of glory, his intellectual efforts degenerated into mere mental repetitions of profane language. *"Mille tonnerres! . . . Sacrénom de nom . . ."* he thought.

Lieut. D'Hubert coughed painfully, and added in a weary voice: "There will be plenty of evil tongues to say that I've been cowed. And I am sure you will not expect me to pass that over. I may find myself suddenly with a dozen duels on my hands instead of this one affair."

The direct simplicity of this argument came home to the colonel's understanding. He looked at his subordinate fixedly. "Sit down, Lieutenant!" he said, gruffly. "This is the very devil of a . . . Sit down!"

"Mon Colonel," D'Hubert began again, "I am not afraid of evil tongues. There's a way of silencing them. But there's my peace of mind, too. I wouldn't be able to shake off the notion that I've ruined a brother officer. Whatever action you take, it is bound to go farther. The inquiry has been dropped—let it rest now. It would have been absolutely fatal to Feraud."

"Hey! What! Did he behave so badly?"

"Yes. It was pretty bad," muttered Lieut. D'Hubert. Being still very weak, he felt a disposition to cry.

As the other man did not belong to his own regiment the colonel had no difficulty in believing this. He began to pace up and down the room. He was a good chief, a man capable of discreet sympathy. But he was human in other ways, too, and this became apparent because he was not capable of artifice.

"The very devil, Lieutenant," he blurted out, in the innocence of his heart, "is that I have declared my intention to get to the bottom of this affair. And when a colonel says something . . . you see . . ."

Lieut. D'Hubert broke in earnestly: "Let me entreat you, Colonel, to be satisfied with taking my word of honour that I was put into a damnable position where I had no option; I had no choice whatever, consistent with my dignity as a man and an officer. . . . After all, Colonel, this fact is the very bottom of this affair. Here you've got it. The rest is mere detail. . . ."

The colonel stopped short. The reputation of Lieut. D'Hubert for good sense and good temper weighed in the balance. A cool head, a warm heart, open as the day. Always correct in his behaviour. One had to trust him. The colonel repressed manfully an immense curiosity. "H'm! You affirm that as a man and an officer. . . . No option? Eh?"

"As an officer—an officer of the 4th Hussars, too," insisted Lieut. D'Hubert, "I had not. And that is the bottom of the affair, Colonel."

"Yes. But still I don't see why, to one's colonel. . . . A colonel is a father—*que diable!*"

Lieut. D'Hubert ought not to have been allowed out as yet. He was becoming aware of his physical insufficiency with humiliation and despair. But the morbid obstinacy of an invalid possessed him, and at the

same time he felt with dismay his eyes filling with water. This trouble seemed too big too handle. A tear fell down the thin, pale cheek of Lieut. D'Hubert.

The colonel turned his back on him hastily. You could have heard a pin drop. "This is some silly woman story—is it not?"

Saying these words the chief spun round to seize the truth, which is not a beautiful shape living in a well, but a shy bird best caught by stratagem. This was the last move of the colonel's diplomacy. He saw the truth shining unmistakably in the gesture of Lieut. D'Hubert raising his weak arms and his eyes to heaven in supreme protest.

"Not a woman affair—eh?" growled the colonel, staring hard. "I don't ask you who or where. All I want to know is whether there is a woman in it?"

Lieut. D'Hubert's arms dropped, and his weak voice was pathetically broken.

"Nothing of the kind, *mon Colonel.*"

"On your honour?" insisted the old warrior.

"On my honour."

"Very well," said the colonel, thoughtfully, and bit his lip. The arguments of Lieut. D'Hubert, helped by his liking for the man, had convinced him. On the other hand, it was highly improper that his intervention, of which he had made no secret, should produce no visible effect. He kept Lieut. D'Hubert a few minutes longer, and dismissed him kindly.

"Take a few days more in bed, Lieutenant. What the devil does the surgeon mean by reporting you fit for duty?"

On coming out of the colonel's quarters, Lieut. D'Hubert said nothing to the friend who was waiting outside to take him home. He said nothing to anybody. Lieut. D'Hubert made no confidences. But on the evening of that day the colonel, strolling under the elms growing near his quarters, in the company of his second in command, opened his lips.

"I've got to the bottom of this affair," he remarked.

The lieut.-colonel, a dry, brown chip of a man with short side-whiskers, pricked up his ears at that without letting a sign of curiosity escape him.

"It's no trifle," added the colonel, oracularly. The other waited for a long while before he murmured:

"Indeed, sir!"

"No trifle," repeated the colonel, looking straight before him. "I've, however, forbidden D'Hubert either to send to or receive a challenge from Feraud for the next twelve months."

He had imagined this prohibition to save the prestige a colonel should have. The result of it was to give an official seal to the mystery surrounding this deadly quarrel. Lieut. D'Hubert repelled by an impassive silence all attempts to worm the truth out of him. Lieut. Feraud, secretly

uneasy at first, regained his assurance as time went on. He disguised his ignorance of the meaning of the imposed truce by slight sardonic laughs, as though he were amused by what he intended to keep to himself. "But what will you do?" his chums used to ask him. He contented himself by replying *"Qui vivra verra"* with a little truculent air. And everybody admired his discretion.

Before the end of the truce Lieut. D'Hubert got his troop. The promotion was well earned, but somehow no one seemed to expect the event. When Lieut. Feraud heard of it at a gathering of officers, he muttered through his teeth, "Is that so?" At once he unhooked his sabre from a peg near the door, buckled it on carefully, and left the company without another word. He walked home with measured steps, struck a light with his flint and steel, and lit his tallow candle. Then snatching an unlucky glass tumbler off the mantelpiece he dashed it violently on the floor.

Now that D'Hubert was an officer of superior rank there could be no question of a duel. Neither of them could send or receive a challenge without rendering himself amenable to a court-martial. It was not to be thought of Lieut. Feraud, who for many days now had experienced no real desire to meet Lieut. D'Hubert arms in hand, chafed again at the systematic injustice of fate. "Does he think he will escape me in that way?" he thought, indignantly. He saw in this promotion an intrigue, a conspiracy, a cowardly manoeuvre. That colonel knew what he was doing. He had hastened to recommend his favourite for a step. It was outrageous that a man should be able to avoid the consequences of his acts in such a dark and tortuous manner.

Of a happy-go-lucky disposition, of a temperament more pugnacious than military, Lieut. Feraud had been content to give and receive blows for sheer love of armed strife, and without much thought of advancement; but now an urgent desire to get on sprang up in his breast. This fighter by vocation resolved in his mind to seize showy occasions and to court the favourable opinion of his chiefs like a mere worldling. He knew he was as brave as any one, and never doubted his personal charm. Nevertheless, neither the bravery nor the charm seemed to work very swiftly. Lieut. Feraud's engaging, careless truculence of a *beau sabreur* underwent a change. He began to make bitter allusions to "clever fellows who stick at nothing to get on." The army was full of them, he would say; you had only to look round. But all the time he had in view one person only, his adversary, D'Hubert. Once he confided to an appreciative friend: "You see, I don't know how to fawn on the right sort of people. It isn't in my character."

He did not get his step till a week after Austerlitz. The Light Cavalry of the Grand Army had its hands very full of interesting work for a little while. Directly the pressure of professional occupation had been eased Captain Feraud took measures to arrange a meeting without loss of time.

"I know my bird," he observed, grimly. "If I don't look sharp he will take care to get himself promoted over the heads of a dozen better men than himself. He's got the knack for that sort of thing."

This duel was fought in Silesia. If not fought to a finish, it was, at any rate, fought to a standstill. The weapon was the cavalry sabre, and the skill, the science, the vigour, and the determination displayed by the adversaries compelled the admiration of the beholders. It became the subject of talk on both shores of the Danube, and as far as the garrisons of Gratz and Laybach. They crossed blades seven times. Both had many cuts which bled profusely. Both refused to have the combat stopped, time after time, with what appeared the most deadly animosity. This appearance was caused on the part of Captain D'Hubert by a rational desire to be done once for all with this worry; on the part of Captain Feraud by a tremendous exaltation of his pugnacious instincts and the incitement of wounded vanity. At last, dishevelled, their shirts in rags, covered with gore and hardly able to stand, they were led away forcibly by their marvelling and horrified seconds. Later on, besieged by comrades avid of details, these gentlemen declared that they could not have allowed that sort of hacking to go on indefinitely. Asked whether the quarrel was settled this time, they gave it out as their conviction that it was a difference which could only be settled by one of the parties remaining lifeless on the ground. The sensation spread from army corps to army corps, and penetrated at last to the smallest detachments of the troops cantoned between the Rhine and the Save. In the cafés in Vienna it was generally estimated, from details to hand, that the adversaries would be able to meet again in three weeks' time on the outside. Something really transcendent in the way of duelling was expected.

These expectations were brought to naught by the necessities of the service which separated the two officers. No official notice had been taken of their quarrel. It was now the property of the army, and not to be meddled with lightly. But the story of the duel, or rather their duelling propensities, must have stood somewhat in the way of their advancement, because they were still captains when they came together again during the war with Prussia. Detached north after Jena, with the army commanded by Marshal Bernadotte, Prince of Ponte Corvo, they entered Lübeck together.

It was only after the occupation of that town that Captain Feraud found leisure to consider his future conduct in view of the fact that Captain D'Hubert had been given the position of third aide-de-camp to the marshal. He considered it a great part of a night, and in the morning summoned two sympathetic friends.

"I've been thinking it over calmly," he said, gazing at them with blood-shot, tired eyes. "I see that I must get rid of that intriguing personage. Here he's managed to sneak on to the personal staff of the marshal.

It's a direct provocation to me. I can't tolerate a situation in which I am exposed any day to receive an order through him. And God knows what order, too! That sort of thing has happened once before—and that's once too often. He understands this perfectly, never fear. I can't tell you any more. Now you know what it is you have to do."

This encounter took place outside the town of Lübeck, on very open ground, selected with special care in deference to the general sentiment of the cavalry division belonging to the army corps, that this time the two officers should meet on horseback. After all, this duel was a cavalry affair, and to persist in fighting on foot would look like a slight on one's own arm of the service. The seconds, startled by the unusual nature of the suggestion, hastened to refer to their principals. Captain Feraud jumped at it with alacrity. For some obscure reason, depending, no doubt, on his psychology, he imagined himself invincible on horseback. All alone within the four walls of his room he rubbed his hands and muttered triumphantly, "Aha! my pretty staff officer, I've got you now."

Captain D'Hubert on his side, after staring hard for a considerable time at his friends, shrugged his shoulders slightly. This affair had hopelessly and unreasonably complicated his existence for him. One absurdity more or less in the development did not matter—all absurdity was distasteful to him; but, urbane as ever, he produced a faintly ironical smile, and said in his calm voice, "It certainly will do away to some extent with the monotony of the thing."

When left alone, he sat down at a table and took his head into his hands. He had not spared himself of late and the marshal had been working all his aides-de-camp particularly hard. The last three weeks of campaigning in horrible weather had affected his health. When over-tired he suffered from a stitch in his wounded side, and that uncomfortable sensation always depressed him. "It's that brute's doing, too," he thought bitterly.

The day before he had received a letter from home, announcing that his only sister was going to be married. He reflected that from the time she was nineteen and he twenty-six, when he went away to garrison life in Strasbourg, he had had but two short glimpses of her. They had been great friends and confidants; and now she was going to be given away to a man whom he did not know—a very worthy fellow no doubt, but not half good enough for her. He would never see his old Léonie again. She had a capable little head, and plenty of tact; she would know how to manage the fellow, to be sure. He was easy in his mind about her happiness but he felt ousted from the first place in her thoughts which had been his ever since the girl could speak. A melancholy regret of the days of his childhood settled upon Captain D'Hubert, third aide-de-camp to the Prince of Ponte Corvo.

He threw aside the letter of congratulation he had begun to write as

in duty bound, but without enthusiasm. He took a fresh piece of paper, and traced on it the words: "This is my last will and testament." Looking at these words he gave himself up to unpleasant reflection; a presentiment that he would never see the scenes of his childhood weighed down the equable spirits of Captain D'Hubert. He jumped up, pushing his chair back, yawned elaborately in sign that he didn't care anything for presentiments, and throwing himself on the bed went to sleep. During the night he shivered from time to time without waking up. In the morning he rode out of town between his two seconds, talking of indifferent things, and looking right and left with apparent detachment into the heavy morning mists shrouding the flat green fields bordered by hedges. He leaped a ditch, and saw the forms of many mounted men moving in the fog. "We are to fight before a gallery, it seems," he muttered to himself, bitterly.

His seconds were rather concerned at the state of the atmosphere, but presently a pale, sickly sun struggled out of the low vapours, and Captain D'Hubert made out, in the distance, three horsemen riding a little apart from the others. It was Captain Feraud and his seconds. He drew his sabre, and assured himself that it was properly fastened to his wrist. And now the seconds, who had been standing in close group with the heads of their horses together, separated at an easy canter, leaving a large, clear field between him and his adversary. Captain D'Hubert looked at the pale sun, at the dismal fields, and the imbecility of the impending fight filled him with desolation. From a distant part of the field a stentorian voice shouted commands at proper intervals: *Au pas— Au trot— Charrrgez!* . . . Presentiments of death don't come to a man for nothing, he thought at the very moment he put spurs to his horse.

And therefore he was more than surprised when, at the very first set-to, Captain Feraud laid himself open to a cut over the forehead, which blinding him with blood, ended the combat almost before it had fairly begun. It was impossible to go on. Captain D'Hubert, leaving his enemy swearing horribly and reeling in the saddle between his two appalled friends, leaped the ditch again into the road and trotted home with his two seconds, who seemed rather awestruck at the speedy issue of that encounter. In the evening Captain D'Hubert finished the congratulatory letter on his sister's marriage.

He finished it late. It was a long letter. Captain D'Hubert gave reins to his fancy. He told his sister that he would feel rather lonely after this great change in her life; but then the day would come for him, too, to get married. In fact, he was thinking already of the time when there would be no one left to fight with in Europe and the epoch of wars would be over. "I expect then," he wrote, "to be within measurable distance of a marshal's baton, and you will be an experienced married woman. You shall look out a wife for me. I will be, probably, bald by then, and a little *blasé*. I shall require a young girl, pretty of course, and with a large fortune, which should help me to close my glorious career in the

splendour befitting my exalted rank." He ended with the information that he had just given a lesson to a worrying, quarrelsome fellow who imagined he had a grievance against him. "But if you, in the depths of your province," he continued, "ever hear it said that your brother is of a quarrelsome disposition, don't you believe it on any account. There is no saying what gossip from the army may reach your innocent ears. Whatever you hear you may rest assured that your ever-loving brother is not a duellist." Then Captain D'Hubert crumpled up the blank sheet of paper headed with the words "This is my last will and testament," and threw it in the fire with a great laugh at himself. He didn't care a snap for what that lunatic could do. He had suddenly acquired the conviction that his adversary was utterly powerless to affect his life in any sort of way; except, perhaps, in the way of putting a special excitement into the delightful, gay intervals between the campaigns.

From this on there were, however, to be no peaceful intervals in the career of Captain D'Hubert. He saw the fields of Eylau and Friedland, marched and counter-marched in the snow, in the mud, in the dust of Polish plains, picking up distinction and advancement on all the roads of North-eastern Europe. Meantime, Captain Feraud, despatched southwards with his regiment, made unsatisfactory war in Spain. It was only when the preparations for the Russian campaign began that he was ordered north again. He left the country of mantillas and oranges without regret.

The first signs of a not unbecoming baldness added to the lofty aspect of Colonel D'Hubert's forehead. This feature was no longer white and smooth as in the days of his youth; the kindly open glance of his blue eyes had grown a little hard as if from much peering through the smoke of battles. The ebony crop on Colonel Feraud's head, coarse and crinkly like a cap of horsehair, showed many silver threads about the temples. A detestable warfare of ambushes and inglorious surprises had not improved his temper. The beak-like curve of his nose was unpleasantly set off by a deep fold on each side of his mouth. The round orbits of his eyes radiated wrinkles. More than ever he recalled an irritable and staring bird—something like a cross between a parrot and an owl. He was still extremely outspoken in his dislike of "intriguing fellows." He seized every opportunity to state that he did not pick up his rank in the ante-rooms of marshals. The unlucky persons, civil or military, who, with an intention of being pleasant, begged Colonel Feraud to tell them how he came by that very apparent scar on the forehead, were astonished to find themselves snubbed in various ways, some of which were simply rude and others mysteriously sardonic. Young officers were warned kindly by their more experienced comrades not to stare openly at the colonel's scar. But indeed an officer need have been very young in his profession not to have heard the legendary tale of that duel originating in a mysterious, unforgivable offence.

Chapter 3

THE RETREAT FROM MOSCOW submerged all private feelings in a sea of disaster and misery. Colonels without regiments, D'Hubert and Feraud carried the musket in the ranks of the so-called sacred battalion—a battalion recruited from officers of all arms who had no longer any troops to lead.

In that battalion promoted colonels did duty as sergeants; the generals captained the companies; a marshal of France, Prince of the Empire, commanded the whole. All had provided themselves with muskets picked up on the road, and with cartridges taken from the dead. In the general destruction of the bonds of discipline and duty holding together the companies, the battalions, the regiments, the brigades, and divisions of an armed host, this body of men put its pride in preserving some semblance of order and formation. The only stragglers were those who fell out to give up to the frost their exhausted souls. They plodded on, and their passage did not disturb the mortal silence of the plains, shining with the livid light of snows under a sky the colour of ashes. Whirlwinds ran along the fields, broke against the dark column, enveloped it in a turmoil of flying icicles, and subsided, disclosing it creeping on its tragic way without the swing and rhythm of the military pace. It struggled onwards, the men exchanging neither words nor looks; whole ranks marched touching elbow, day after day and never raising their eyes from the ground, as if lost in despairing reflections. In the dumb, black forests of pines the cracking of over-loaded branches was the only sound they heard. Often from daybreak to dusk no one spoke in the whole column. It was like a *macabre* march of struggling corpses towards a distant grave. Only an alarm of Cossacks could restore to their eyes a semblance of martial resolution. The battalion faced about and deployed, or formed square under the endless fluttering of snowflakes. A cloud of horsemen with fur caps on their heads, levelled long lances, and yelled "Hurrah! Hurrah!" around their menacing immobility whence, with muffled detonations, hundreds of dark red flames darted through the air thick with falling snow. In a very few moments the horsemen would disappear, as if carried off yelling in the gale, and the sacred battalion standing still, alone in the blizzard, heard only the howling of the wind, whose blasts searched their very hearts. Then, with a cry or two of *"Vive l'Empereur!"* it would resume its march, leaving behind a few lifeless bodies lying huddled up, tiny black specks on the white immensity of the snows.

Though often marching in the ranks, or skirmishing in the woods

side by side, the two officers ignored each other; this not so much from inimical intention as from a very real indifference. All their store of moral energy was expended in resisting the terrific enmity of nature and the crushing sense of irretrievable disaster. To the last they counted among the most active, the least demoralized of the battalion; their vigorous vitality invested them both with the appearance of an heroic pair in the eyes of their comrades. And they never exchanged more than a casual word or two, except one day, when skirmishing in front of the battalion against a worrying attack of cavalry, they found themselves cut off in the woods by a small party of Cossacks. A score of fur-capped, hairy horsemen rode to and fro, brandishing their lances in ominous silence; but the two officers had no mind to lay down their arms, and Colonel Feraud suddenly spoke up in a hoarse, growling voice, bringing his firelock to the shoulder. "You take the nearest brute, Colonel D'Hubert; I'll settle the next one. I am a better shot than you are."

Colonel D'Hubert nodded over his levelled musket. Their shoulders were pressed against the trunk of a large tree; on their front enormous snowdrifts protected them from a direct charge. Two carefully aimed shots rang out in the frosty air, two Cossacks reeled in their saddles. The rest, not thinking the game good enough, closed round their wounded comrades and galloped away out of range. The two officers managed to rejoin their battalion halted for the night. During that afternoon they had leaned upon each other more than once, and towards the end, Colonel D'Hubert, whose long legs gave him an advantage in walking through soft snow, peremptorily took the musket of Colonel Feraud from him and carried it on his shoulder, using his own as a staff.

On the outskirts of a village half buried in the snow an old wooden barn burned with a clear and an immense flame. The sacred battalion of skeletons, muffled in rags, crowded greedily to the windward side, stretching hundreds of numbed, bony hands to the blaze. Nobody had noted their approach. Before entering the circle of light playing on the sunken, glassy-eyed, starved faces, Colonel D'Hubert spoke in his turn:

"Here's your musket, Colonel Feraud. I can walk better than you."

Colonel Feraud nodded, and pushed on towards the warmth of the fierce flames. Colonel D'Hubert was more deliberate, but not the less bent on getting a place in the front rank. Those they shouldered aside tried to greet with a faint cheer the reappearance of the two indomitable companions in activity and endurance. Those manly qualities had never perhaps received a higher tribute than this feeble acclamation.

This is the faithful record of speeches exchanged during the retreat from Moscow by Colonels Feraud and D'Hubert. Colonel Feraud's taciturnity was the outcome of concentrated rage. Short, hairy, black faced, with layers of grime and the thick sprouting of a wiry beard, a frost-bitten hand wrapped up in filthy rags carried in a sling, he accused fate of unparalleled perfidy towards the sublime Man of Destiny. Colonel

D'Hubert, his long moustaches pendent in icicles on each side of his cracked blue lips, his eyelids inflamed with the glare of snows, the principal part of his costume consisting of a sheepskin coat looted with difficulty from the frozen corpse of a camp follower found in an abandoned cart, took a more thoughtful view of events. His regularly handsome features, now reduced to mere bony lines and fleshless hollows, looked out of a woman's black velvet hood, over which was rammed forcibly a cocked hat picked up under the wheels of an empty army fourgon, which must have contained at one time some general officer's luggage. The sheepskin coat being short for a man of his inches ended very high up, and the skin of his legs, blue with the cold, showed through the tatters of his nether garments. This under the circumstances provoked neither jeers nor pity. No one cared how the next man felt or looked. Colonel D'Hubert himself, hardened to exposure, suffered mainly in his self-respect from the lamentable indecency of his costume. A thoughtless person may think that with a whole host of inanimate bodies bestrewing the path of retreat there could not have been much difficulty in supplying the deficiency. But to loot a pair of breeches from a frozen corpse is not so easy as it may appear to a mere theorist. It requires time and labour. You must remain behind while your companions march on. Colonel D'Hubert had his scruples as to falling out. Once he had stepped aside he could not be sure of ever rejoining his battalion; and the ghastly intimacy of a wrestling match with the frozen dead opposing the unyielding rigidity of iron to your violence was repugnant to the delicacy of his feelings. Luckily, one day, grubbing in a mound of snow between the huts of a village in the hope of finding there a frozen potato or some vegetable garbage he could put between his long and shaky teeth, Colonel D'Hubert uncovered a couple of mats of the sort Russian peasants use to line the sides of their carts with. These, beaten free of frozen snow, bent about his elegant person and fastened solidly round his waist, made a bell-shaped nether garment, a sort of stiff petticoat, which rendered Colonel D'Hubert a perfectly decent, but a much more noticeable figure than before.

Thus accoutred, he continued to retreat, never doubting of his personal escape, but full of other misgivings. The early buoyancy of his belief in the future was destroyed. If the road of glory led through such unforeseen passages, he asked himself—for he was reflective—whether the guide was altogether trustworthy. It was a patriotic sadness, not unmingled with some personal concern, and quite unlike the unreasoning indignation against men and things nursed by Colonel Feraud. Recruiting his strength in a little German town for three weeks, Colonel D'Hubert was surprised to discover within himself a love of repose. His returning vigour was strangely pacific in its aspirations. He meditated silently upon this bizarre change of mood. No doubt many of his brother officers of field rank went through the same moral experience. But these were

not the times to talk of it. In one of his letters home Colonel D'Hubert wrote, "All your plans, my dear Léonie, for marrying me to the charming girl you have discovered in your neighbourhood, seem farther off than ever. Peace is not yet. Europe wants another lesson. It will be a hard task for us, but it shall be done, because the Emperor is invincible."

Thus wrote Colonel D'Hubert from Pomerania to his married sister Léonie, settled in the south of France. And so far the sentiments expressed would not have been disowned by Colonel Feraud, who wrote no letters to anybody, whose father had been in life an illiterate blacksmith, who had no sister or brother, and whom no one desired ardently to pair off for a life of peace with a charming young girl. But Colonel D'Hubert's letter contained also some philosophical generalities upon the uncertainty of all personal hopes, when bound up entirely with the prestigious fortune of one incomparably great it is true, yet still remaining but a man in his greatness. This view would have appeared rank heresy to Colonel Feraud. Some melancholy forebodings of a military kind, expressed cautiously, would have been pronounced as nothing short of high treason by Colonel Feraud. But Léonie, the sister of Colonel D'Hubert, read them with profound satisfaction, and, folding the letter thoughtfully, remarked to herself that "Armand was likely to prove eventually a sensible fellow." Since her marriage into a Southern family she had become a convinced believer in the return of the legitimate king. Hopeful and anxious she offered prayers night and morning, and burnt candles in churches for the safety and prosperity of her brother.

She had every reason to suppose that her prayers were heard. Colonel D'Hubert passed through Lutzen, Bautzen, and Leipsic losing no limb, and acquiring additional reputation. Adapting his conduct to the needs of that desperate time, he had never voiced his misgivings. He concealed them under a cheerful courtesy of such pleasant character that people were inclined to ask themselves with wonder whether Colonel D'Hubert was aware of any disasters. Not only his manners, but even his glances remained untroubled. The steady amenity of his blue eyes disconcerted all grumblers, and made despair itself pause.

This bearing was remarked favourably by the Emperor himself; for Colonel D'Hubert, attached now to the Major-General's staff, came on several occasions under the imperial eye. But it exasperated the higher strung nature of Colonel Feraud. Passing through Magdeburg on service, this last allowed himself, while seated gloomily at dinner with the *Commandant de Place,* to say of his life-long adversary: "This man does not love the Emperor," and his words were received by the other guests in profound silence. Colonel Feraud, troubled in his conscience at the atrocity of the aspersion, felt the need to back it up by a good argument. "I ought to know him," he cried, adding some oaths. "One studies one's adversary. I have met him on the ground half a dozen times, as all the army knows. What more do you want? If that isn't opportunity enough

for any fool to size up his man, may the devil take me if I can tell what is." And he looked around the table, obstinate and sombre.

Later on in Paris, while extremely busy reorganizing his regiment, Colonel Feraud learned that Colonel D'Hubert had been made a general. He glared at his informant incredulously, then folded his arms and turned away muttering, "Nothing surprises me on the part of that man."

And aloud he added, speaking over his shoulder, "You would oblige me greatly by telling General D'Hubert at the first opportunity that his advancement saves him for a time from a pretty hot encounter. I was only waiting for him to turn up here."

The other officer remonstrated.

"Could you think of it, Colonel Feraud, at this time, when every life should be consecrated to the glory and safety of France?"

But the strain of unhappiness caused by military reverses had spoiled Colonel Feraud's character. Like many other men, he was rendered wicked by misfortune.

"I cannot consider General D'Hubert's existence of any account either for the glory or safety of France," he snapped viciously. "You don't pretend, perhaps, to know him better than I do—I who have met him half a dozen times on the ground—do you?"

His interlocutor, a young man, was silenced. Colonel Feraud walked up and down the room.

"This is not the time to mince matters," he said. "I can't believe that that man ever loved the Emperor. He picked up his general's stars under the boots of Marshal Berthier. Very well. I'll get mine in another fashion, and then we shall settle this business which has been dragging on too long."

General D'Hubert, informed indirectly of Colonel Feraud's attitude, made a gesture as if to put aside an importunate person. His thoughts were solicited by graver cares. He had had no time to go and see his family. His sister, whose royalist hopes were rising higher every day, though proud of her brother, regretted his recent advancement in a measure, because it put on him a prominent mark of the usurper's favour, which later on could have an adverse influence upon his career. He wrote to her that no one but an inveterate enemy could say he had got his promotion by favour. As to his career, he assured her that he looked no farther forward into the future than the next battlefield.

Beginning the campaign of France in this dogged spirit, General D'Hubert was wounded on the second day of the battle under Laon. While being carried off the field he heard that Colonel Feraud, promoted this moment to general, had been sent to replace him at the head of his brigade. He cursed his luck impulsively, not being able at the first glance to discern all the advantages of a nasty wound. And yet it was by this heroic method that Providence was shaping his future. Travelling slowly south to his sister's country home under the care of a trusty old servant,

General D'Hubert was spared the humiliating contacts and the perplexities of conduct which assailed the men of Napoleonic empire at the moment of its downfall. Lying in his bed, with the windows of his room open wide to the sunshine of Provence, he perceived the undisguised aspect of the blessing conveyed by that jagged fragment of a Prussian shell, which, killing his horse and ripping open his thigh, saved him from an active conflict with his conscience. After the last fourteen years spent sword in hand in the saddle, and with the sense of his duty done to the very end, General D'Hubert found resignation an easy virtue. His sister was delighted with his reasonableness. "I leave myself altogether in your hands, my dear Léonie," he had said to her.

He was still laid up when, the credit of his brother-in-law's family being exerted on his behalf, he received from the royal government not only the confirmation of his rank, but the assurance of being retained on the active list. To this was added an unlimited convalescent leave. The unfavourable opinion entertained of him in Bonapartist circles, though it rested on nothing more solid than the unsupported pronouncement of General Feraud, was directly responsible for General D'Hubert's retention on the active list. As to General Feraud, his rank was confirmed, too. It was more than he dared to expect; but Marshal Soult, then Minister of War to the restored king, was partial to officers who had served in Spain. Only not even the marshal's protection could secure for him active employment. He remained irreconcilable, idle, and sinister. He sought in obscure restaurants the company of other half-pay officers who cherished dingy but glorious old tricolour cockades in their breast-pockets, and buttoned with the forbidden eagle buttons their shabby uniforms, declaring themselves too poor to afford the expense of the prescribed change.

The triumphant return from Elba, an historical fact as marvellous and incredible as the exploits of some mythological demi-god, found General D'Hubert still quite unable to sit a horse. Neither could he walk very well. These disabilities, which Madame Léonie accounted most lucky, helped to keep her brother out of all possible mischief. His frame of mind at that time, she noted with dismay, became very far from reasonable. This general officer, still menaced by the loss of a limb, was discovered one night in the stables of the château by a groom, who, seeing a light, raised an alarm of thieves. His crutch was lying half-buried in the straw of the litter, and the general was hopping on one leg in a loose box around a snorting horse he was trying to saddle. Such were the effects of imperial magic upon a calm temperament and a pondered mind. Beset in the light of stable lanterns, by the tears, entreaties, indignation, remonstrances and reproaches of his family, he got out of the difficult situation by fainting away there and then in the arms of his nearest relatives, and was carried off to bed. Before he got out of it again, the second reign of Napoleon, the Hundred Days of feverish agitation and supreme effort, passed away like a terrifying dream. The tragic year 1815, begun in the

trouble and unrest of consciences, was ending in vengeful proscriptions.

How General Feraud escaped the clutches of the Special Commission and the last officers of a firing squad he never knew himself. It was partly due to the subordinate position he was assigned during the Hundred Days. The Emperor had never given him active command, but had kept him busy at the cavalry depôt in Paris, mounting and despatching hastily drilled troopers into the field. Considering this task as unworthy of his abilities, he had discharged it with no offensively noticeable zeal; but for the greater part he was saved from the excesses of Royalist reaction by the interference of General D'Hubert.

This last, still on convalescent leave, but able now to travel, had been despatched by his sister to Paris to present himself to his legitimate sovereign. As no one in the capital could possibly know anything of the episode in the stable he was received there with distinction. Military to the very bottom of his soul, the prospect of rising in his profession consoled him from finding himself the butt of Bonapartist malevolence, which pursued him with a persistence he could not account for. All the rancour of that embittered and persecuted party pointed to him as the man who had *never* loved the Emperor—a sort of monster essentially worse than a mere betrayer.

General D'Hubert shrugged his shoulders without anger at this ferocious prejudice. Rejected by his old friends, and mistrusting profoundly the advances of Royalist society, the young and handsome general (he was barely forty) adopted a manner of cold, punctilious courtesy, which at the merest shadow of an intended slight passed easily into harsh haughtiness. Thus prepared, General D'Hubert went about his affairs in Paris feeling inwardly very happy with the peculiar uplifting happiness of a man very much in love. The charming girl looked out by his sister had come upon the scene, and had conquered him in the thorough manner in which a young girl by merely existing in his sight can make a man of forty her own. They were going to be married as soon as General D'Hubert had obtained his official nomination to a promised command.

One afternoon, sitting on the *terrasse* of the *Café Tortoni,* General D'Hubert learned from the conversation of two strangers occupying a table near his own, that General Feraud, included in the batch of superior officers arrested after the second return of the king, was in danger of passing before the Special Commission. Living all his spare moments, as is frequently the case with expectant lovers, a day in advance of reality, and in a state of bestarred hallucination, it required nothing less than the name of his perpetual antagonist pronounced in a loud voice to call the youngest of Napoleon's generals away from the mental contemplation of his betrothed. He looked round. The strangers wore civilian clothes. Lean and weather-beaten, lolling back in their chairs, they scowled at people with moody and defiant abstraction from under their hats pulled low over their eyes. It was not difficult to recognize them for two of the

compulsorily retired officers of the Old Guard. As from bravado or care-lessness they chose to speak in loud tones, General D'Hubert, who saw no reason why he should change his seat, heard every word. They did not seem to be the personal friends of General Feraud. His name came up amongst others. Hearing it repeated, General D'Hubert's tender anticipations of a domestic future adorned with a woman's grace were traversed by the harsh regret of his warlike past, of that one long, intoxicating clash of arms, unique in the magnitude of its glory and disaster—the marvellous work and the special possession of his own generation. He felt an irrational tenderness towards his old adversary and appreciated emotionally the murderous absurdity their encounter had introduced into his life. It was like an additional pinch of spice in a hot dish. He remembered the flavour with sudden melancholy. He would never taste it again. It was all over. "I fancy it was being left lying in the garden that had exasperated him so against me from the first," he thought, indulgently.

The two strangers at the next table had fallen silent after the third mention of General Feraud's name. Presently the elder of the two, speaking again in a bitter tone, affirmed that General Feraud's account was settled. And why? Simply because he was not like some bigwigs who loved only themselves. The Royalists knew they could never make anything of him. He loved *The Other* too well.

The Other was the Man of St. Helena. The two officers nodded and touched glasses before they drank to an impossible return. Then the same who had spoken before, remarked with a sardonic laugh, "His adversary showed more cleverness."

"What adversary?" asked the younger, as if puzzled.

"Don't you know? They were two hussars. At each promotion they fought a duel. Haven't you heard of the duel going on ever since 1801?"

The other had heard of the duel, of course. Now he understood the allusion. General Baron D'Hubert would be able now to enjoy his fat king's favour in peace.

"Much good may it do to him," mumbled the elder. "They were both brave men. I never saw this D'Hubert—a sort of intriguing dandy, I am told. But I can well believe what I've heard Feraud say of him—that he *never* loved the Emperor."

They rose and went away.

General D'Hubert experienced the horror of a somnambulist who wakes up from a complacent dream of activity to find himself walking on a quagmire. A profound disgust of the ground on which he was making his way overcame him. Even the image of the charming girl was swept from his view in the flood of moral distress. Everything he had ever been or hoped to be would taste of bitter ignomiry unless he could manage to save General Feraud from the fate which threatened so many braves. Under the impulse of this almost morbid need to attend to the safety of his adversary, General D'Hubert worked so well with hands and feet (as

the French saying is), that in less than twenty-four hours he found means of obtaining an extraordinary private audience from the Minister of Police.

General Baron D'Hubert was shown in suddenly without preliminaries. In the dusk of the Minister's cabinet, behind the forms of writing-desk, chairs, and tables, between two bunches of wax candles blazing in sconces, he beheld a figure in a gorgeous coat posturing before a tall mirror. The old *conventionnel* Fouché, Senator of the Empire, traitor to every man, to every principle and motive of human conduct, Duke of Otranto, and the wily artizan of the Second Restoration, was trying the fit of a court suit in which his young and accomplished *fiancée* had declared her intention to have his portrait painted on porcelain. It was a caprice, a charming fancy which the first Minister of Police of the Second Restoration was anxious to gratify. For that man, often compared in wiliness of conduct to a fox, but whose ethical side could be worthily symbolized by nothing less emphatic than a skunk, was as much possessed by his love as General D'Hubert himself.

Startled to be discovered thus by the blunder of a servant, he met this little vexation with the characteristic impudence which had served his turn so well in the endless intrigues of his self-seeking career. Without altering his attitude a hair's-breadth, one leg in a silk stocking advanced, his head twisted over his left shoulder, he called out calmly, "This way, General. Pray approach. Well? I am all attention."

While General D'Hubert, ill at ease as if one of his own little weaknesses had been exposed, presented his request as shortly as possible, the Duke of Otranto went on feeling the fit of his collar, settling the lapels before the glass, and buckling his back in an effort to behold the set of the gold embroidered coat-skirts behind. His still face, his attentive eyes, could not have expressed a more complete interest in those matters if he had been alone.

"Exclude from the operations of the Special Court a certain Feraud, Gabriel Florian, General of brigade of the promotion of 1814?" he repeated, in a slightly wondering tone, and then turned away from the glass. "Why exclude *him* precisely?"

"I am surprised that your Excellency, so competent in the evaluation of men of his time, should have thought worth while to have that name put down on the list."

"A rabid Bonapartist!"

"So is every grenadier and every trooper of the army, as your Excellency well knows. And the individuality of General Feraud can have no more weight than that of any casual grenadier. He is a man of no mental grasp, of no capacity whatever. It is inconceivable that he should ever have any influence."

"He has a well-hung tongue, though," interjected Fouché.

"Noisy, I admit, but not dangerous."

"I will not dispute with you. I know next to nothing of him. Hardly his name, in fact."

"And yet your Excellency has the presidency of the Commission charged by the king to point out those who were to be tried," said General D'Hubert, with an emphasis which did not miss the minister's ear.

"Yes, General," he said, walking away into the dark part of the vast room, and throwing himself into a deep armchair that swallowed him up, all but the soft gleam of gold embroideries and the pallid patch of the face—"yes, General. Take this chair there."

General D'Hubert sat down.

"Yes, General," continued the arch-master in the arts of intrigue and betrayals, whose duplicity, as if at times intolerable to his self-knowledge, found relief in bursts of cynical openness. "I did hurry on the formation of the proscribing Commission, and I took its presidency. And do you know why? Simply from fear that if I did not take it quickly into my hands my own name would head the list of the proscribed. Such are the times in which we live. But I am minister of the king yet, and I ask you plainly why I should take the name of this obscure Feraud off the list? You wonder how his name got there! Is it possible that you should know men so little? My dear General, at the very first sitting of the Commission names poured on us like rain off the roof of the Tuileries. Names! We had our choice of thousands. How do you know that the name of this Feraud, whose life or death don't matter to France, does not keep out some other name?"

The voice out of the armchair stopped. Opposite General D'Hubert sat still, shadowy and silent. Only his sabre clinked slightly. The voice in the armchair began again. "And we must try to satisfy the exigencies of the Allied Sovereigns, too. The Prince de Talleyrand told me only yesterday that Nesselrode had informed him officially of His Majesty the Emperor Alexander's dissatisfaction at the small number of examples the Government of the king intends to make—especially amongst military men. I tell you this confidentially."

"Upon my word!" broke out General D'Hubert, speaking through his teeth, "if your Excellency deigns to favour me with any more confidential information I don't know what I will do. It's enough to break one's sword over one's knee, and fling the pieces. . . ."

"What government you imagined yourself to be serving?" interrupted the minister, sharply.

After a short pause the crestfallen voice of General D'Hubert answered, "The Government of France."

"That's paying your conscience off with mere words, General. The truth is that you are serving a government of returned exiles, of men who have been without country for twenty years. Of men also who have just

got over a very bad and humiliating fright. . . . Have no illusions on that score."

The Duke of Otranto ceased. He had relieved himself, and had attained his object of stripping some self-respect off that man who had inconveniently discovered him posturing in a gold-embroidered court costume before a mirror. But they were a hot-headed lot in the army; it occurred to him that it would be inconvenient if a well-disposed general officer, received in audience on the recommendation of one of the Princes, were to do something rashly scandalous directly after a private interview with the minister. In a changed tone he put a question to the point: "Your relation—this Feraud?"

"No. No relation at all."

"Intimate friend?"

"Intimate . . . yes. There is between us an intimate connection of a nature which makes it a point of honour with me to try . . ."

The minister rang a bell without waiting for the end of the phrase. When the servant had gone out, after bringing in a pair of heavy silver candelabra for the writing-desk, the Duke of Otranto rose, his breast glistening all over with gold in the strong light, and taking a piece of paper out of a drawer, held it in his hand ostentatiously while he said with persuasive gentleness: "You must not speak of breaking your sword across your knee, General. Perhaps you would never get another. The Emperor will not return this time. . . . *Diable d'homme!* There was just a moment, here in Paris, soon after Waterloo, when he frightened me. It looked as though he were ready to begin all over again. Luckily one never does begin all over again, really. You must not think of breaking your sword, General."

General D'Hubert, looking on the ground, moved slightly his hand in a hopeless gesture of renunciation. The Minister of Police turned his eyes away from him, and scanned deliberately the paper he had been holding up all the time.

"There are only twenty general officers selected to be made an example of. Twenty. A round number. And let's see, Feraud. . . . Ah, he's there. Gabriel Florian. *Parfaitement.* That's your man. Well, there will be only nineteen examples made now."

General D'Hubert stood up feeling as though he had gone through an infectious illness. "I must beg your Excellency to keep my interference a profound secret. I attach the greatest importance to his never learning . . ."

"Who is going to inform him, I should like to know?" said Fouché, raising his eyes curiously to General D'Hubert's tense, set face. "Take one of these pens, and run it through the name yourself. This is the only list in existence. If you are careful to take up enough ink no one will be able to tell what was the name struck out. But, *par exemple,* I am not

responsible for what Clarke will do with him afterwards. If he persists in being rabid he will be ordered by the Minister of War to reside in some provincial town under the supervision of the police."

A few days later General D'Hubert was saying to his sister, after the first greetings had been got over: "Ah, my dear Léonie! it seemed to me I couldn't get away from Paris quick enough."

"Effect of love," she suggested, with a malicious smile.

"And horror," added General D'Hubert, with profound seriousness. "I have nearly died there of . . . of nausea."

His face was contracted with disgust. And as his sister looked at him attentively he continued, "I have had to see Fouché. I have had an audience. I have been in his cabinet. There remains with one, who had the misfortune to breathe the air of the same room with that man, a sense of diminished dignity, an uneasy feeling of being not so clean, after all, as one hoped one was. . . . But you can't understand."

She nodded quickly several times. She understood very well, on the contrary. She knew her brother thoroughly, and liked him as he was. Moreover, the scorn and loathing of mankind were the lot of the *Jacobin* Fouché, who, exploiting for his own advantage every weakness, every virtue, every generous illusion of mankind, made dupes of his whole generation, and died obscurely as Duke of Otranto.

"My dear Armand," she said, compassionately, "what could you want from that man?"

"Nothing less than a life," answered General D'Hubert. "And I've got it. It had to be done. But I feel yet as if I could never forgive the necessity to the man I had to save."

General Feraud, totally unable (as is the case with most of us) to comprehend what was happening to him, received the Minister of War's order to proceed at once to a small town of Central France with feelings whose natural expression consisted in a fierce rolling of the eye and savage grinding of the teeth. The passing away of the state of war, the only condition of society he had ever known, the horrible view of a world at peace, frightened him. He went away to his little town firmly convinced that this could not last. There he was informed of his retirement from the army, and that his pension (calculated on the scale of a colonel's rank) was made dependent on the correctness of his conduct, and on the good reports of the police. No longer in the army! He felt suddenly strange to the earth, like a disembodied spirit. It was impossible to exist. But at first he reacted from sheer incredulity. This could not be. He waited for thunder, earthquakes, natural cataclysms; but nothing happened. The leaden weight of an irremediable idleness descended upon General Feraud, who having no resources within himself sank into a state of awe-inspiring hebetude. He haunted the streets of the little town, gazing before him with lacklustre eyes, disregarding the hats raised on his passage;

and people, nudging each other as he went by, whispered, "That's poor General Feraud. His heart is broken. Behold how he loved the Emperor."

The other living wreckage of Napoleonic tempest clustered round General Feraud with infinite respect. He, himself, imagined his soul to be crushed by grief. He suffered from quickly succeeding impulses to weep, to howl, to bite his fists till blood came, to spend days on his bed with his head thrust under the pillow; but these arose from sheer ennui, from the anguish of an immense, indescribable, inconceivable boredom. His mental inability to grasp the hopeless nature of his case as a whole saved him from suicide. He never even thought of it once. He thought of nothing. But his appetite abandoned him, and the difficulty he experienced to express the overwhelming nature of his feelings (the most furious swearing could do no justice to it) induced gradually a habit of silence—a sort of death to a southern temperament.

Great, therefore, was the sensation amongst the *anciens militaires* frequenting a certain little café full of flies when one stuffy afternoon "that poor General Feraud" let out suddenly a volley of formidable curses.

He had been sitting quietly in his own privileged corner looking through the Paris gazettes with just as much interest as a condemned man on the eve of execution could be expected to show in the news of the day. A cluster of martial, bronzed faces, amongst which there was one lacking an eye, and another the tip of a nose, frost-bitten in Russia, surrounded him anxiously.

"What's the matter, General?"

General Feraud sat erect, holding the folded newspaper at arm's length in order to make out the small print better. He read to himself, over again, fragments of the intelligence which had caused, what may be called his resurrection.

"We are informed that General d'Hubert, till now on sick leave in the south, is to be called to the command of the 5th Cavalry brigade in . . ."

He dropped the paper stonily. . . . "Called to the command" . . . and suddenly gave his forehead a mighty slap. "I had almost forgotten him," he muttered, in a conscience-stricken tone.

A deep-chested veteran shouted across the café: "Some new villainy of the Government, General?"

"The villainies of these scoundrels," thundered General Feraud, "are innumerable. One more, one less!" . . . He lowered his tone. "But I will set good order to one of them at least."

He looked all round the faces. "There's a pomaded, curled staff officer, the darling of some of the marshals who sold their father for a handful of English gold. He will find out presently that I am alive yet," he declared, in a dogmatic tone. "However, this is a private affair. An

old affair of honour. Bah! Our honour does not matter. Here we are driven off with a split ear like a lot of cast troop horses—good only for a knacker's yard. But it would be like striking a blow for the Emperor. . . . Messieurs, I shall require the assistance of two of you."

Every man moved forward. General Feraud, deeply touched by this demonstration, called with visible emotion upon the one-eyed veteran cuirassier and the officer of the Chasseurs à Cheval who had left the tip of his nose in Russia. He excused his choice to the others.

"A cavalry affair this—you know."

He was answered with a varied chorus of *"Parfaitement, mon Général. . . . C'est juste. . . . Parbleu, c'est connu. . . ."* Everybody was satisfied. The three left the café together, followed by cries of *"Bonne chance."*

Outside they linked arms, the general in the middle. The three rusty cocked hats worn *en bataille* with a sinister forward slant barred the narrow street nearly right across. The over-heated little town of grey stones and red tiles was drowsing away its provincial afternoon under a blue sky. The loud blows of a cooper hooping a cask reverberated regularly between the houses. The general dragged his left foot a little in the shade of the walls.

"This damned winter of 1813 has got into my bones for good. Never mind. We must take pistols, that's all. A little lumbago. We must have pistols. He's game for my bag. My eyes are as keen as ever. You should have seen me in Russia picking off the dodging Cossacks with a beastly old infantry musket. I have a natural gift for firearms."

In this strain General Feraud ran on, holding up his head, with owlish eyes and rapacious beak. A mere fighter all his life, a cavalry man, a *sabreur,* he conceived war with the utmost simplicity, as, in the main, a massed lot of personal contests, a sort of gregarious duelling. And here he had in hand a war of his own. He revived. The shadow of peace passed away from him like the shadow of death. It was the marvellous resurrection of the named Feraud, Gabriel Florian, *engagé volontaire* of 1793, General of 1814, buried without ceremony by means of a service order signed by the War Minister of the Second Restoration.

Chapter 4

NO MAN SUCCEEDS IN EVERYTHING he undertakes. In that sense we are all failures. The great point is not to fail in ordering and sustaining the effort of our life. In this matter vanity is what leads us astray. It hurries us into situations from which we must come out damaged; whereas pride is our safeguard, by the reserve it imposes on the choice of our endeavour as much as by the virtue of its sustaining power.

General D'Hubert was proud and reserved. He had not been damaged by his casual love affairs, successful or otherwise. In his war-scarred body his heart at forty remained unscratched. Entering with reserve into his sister's matrimonial plans, he had felt himself falling irremediably in love as one falls off a roof. He was too proud to be frightened. Indeed, the sensation was too delightful to be alarming.

The inexperience of a man of forty is a much more serious thing than the inexperience of a youth of twenty, for it is not helped out by the rashness of hot blood. The girl was mysterious, as young girls are by the mere effect of their guarded ingenuity; and to him the mysteriousness of that young girl appeared exceptional and fascinating. But there was nothing mysterious about the arrangements of the match which Madame Léonie had promoted. There was nothing peculiar, either. It was a very appropriate match, commending itself extremely to the young lady's mother (the father was dead) and tolerable to the young lady's uncle—an old *émigré* lately returned from Germany, and pervading, cane in hand, a lean ghost of the *ancien régime,* the garden walks of the young lady's ancestral home.

General D'Hubert was not the man to be satisfied merely with the woman and the fortune—when it came to the point. His pride (and pride aims always at true success) would be satisfied with nothing short of love. But as true pride excludes vanity, he could not imagine any reason why this mysterious creature with deep and brilliant eyes of a violet colour should have any feeling for him warmer than indifference. The young lady (her name was Adèle) baffled every attempt at a clear understanding on that point. It is true that the attempts were clumsy and made timidly, because by then General D'Hubert had become acutely aware of the number of his years, of his wounds, of his many moral imperfections, of his secret unworthiness—and had incidentally learned by experience the meaning of the word funk. As far as he could make out she seemed to imply that, with an unbounded confidence in her mother's affection and sagacity, she felt no unsurmountable dislike for the person of

General D'Hubert; and that this was quite sufficient for a well-brought-up young lady to begin married life upon. This view hurt and tormented the pride of General D'Hubert. And yet he asked himself, with a sort of sweet despair, what more could he expect? She had a quiet and luminous forehead. Her violet eyes laughed while the lines of her lips and chin remained composed in admirable gravity. All this was set off by such a glorious mass of fair hair, by a complexion so marvellous, by such a grace of expression, that General D'Hubert really never found the opportunity to examine with sufficient detachment the lofty exigencies of his pride. In fact, he became shy of that line of inquiry since it had led once or twice to a crisis of solitary passion in which it was borne upon him that he loved her enough to kill her rather than lose her. From such passages, not unknown to men of forty, he would come out broken, exhausted, remorseful, a little dismayed. He derived, however, considerable comfort from the quietist practice of sitting now and then half the night by an open window and meditating upon the wonder of her existence, like a believer lost in the mystic contemplation of his faith.

It must not be supposed that all these variations of his inward state were made manifest to the world. General D'Hubert found no difficulty in appearing wreathed in smiles. Because, in fact, he was very happy. He followed the established rules of his condition, sending over flowers (from his sister's garden and hot-houses) early every morning, and a little later following himself to lunch with his intended, her mother, and her *émigré* uncle. The middle of the day was spent in strolling or sitting in the shade. A watchful deference, trembling on the verge of tenderness was the note of their intercourse on his side—with a playful turn of the phrase concealing the profound trouble of his whole being caused by her inaccessible nearness. Late in the afternoon General D'Hubert walked home between the fields of vines, sometimes intensely miserable, sometimes supremely happy, sometimes pensively sad; but always feeling a special intensity of existence, that elation common to artists, poets, and lovers—to men haunted by a great passion, a noble thought, or a new vision of plastic beauty.

The outward world at that time did not exist with any special distinctness for General D'Hubert. One evening, however, crossing a ridge from which he could see both houses, General D'Hubert became aware of two figures far down the road. The day had been divine. The festal decoration of the inflamed sky lent a gentle glow to the sober tints of the southern land. The grey rocks, the brown fields, the purple, undulating distances harmonized in luminous accord, exhaled already the scents of the evening. The two figures down the road presented themselves like two rigid and wooden silhouettes all black on the ribbon of white dust. General D'Hubert made out the long, straight, military *capotes* buttoned closely right up to the black stocks, the cocked hats, the lean, carven, brown countenances—old soldiers—*vieilles moustaches!* The taller of the

two had a black patch over one eye; the other's hard, dry countenance presented some bizarre, disquieting peculiarity, which on nearer approach proved to be the absence of the tip of the nose. Lifting their hands with one movement to salute the slightly lame civilian walking with a thick stick, they inquired for the house where the General Baron D'Hubert lived, and what was the best way to get speech with him quietly.

"If you think this quiet enough," said General D'Hubert, looking round at the vine-fields, framed in purple lines, and dominated by the nest of grey and drab walls of a village clustering around the top of a conical hill, so that the blunt church tower seemed but the shape of a crowning rock—"if you think this spot quiet enough, you can speak to him at once. And I beg you, comrades, to speak openly, with perfect confidence."

They stepped back at this, and raised again their hands to their hats with marked ceremoniousness. Then the one with the chipped nose, speaking for both, remarked that the matter was confidential enough, and to be arranged discreetly. Their general quarters were established in that village over there, where the infernal clodhoppers—damn their false, Royalist hearts!—looked remarkably cross-eyed at three unassuming military men. For the present he should only ask for the name of General D'Hubert's friends.

"What friends?" said the astonished General D'Hubert, completely off the track. "I am staying with my brother-in-law over there."

"Well, he will do for one," said the chipped veteran.

"We're the friends of General Feraud," interjected the other, who had kept silent till then, only glowering with his one eye at the man who had *never* loved the Emperor. That was something to look at. For even the gold-laced Judases who had sold him to the English, the marshals and princes, had loved him at some time or other. But this man had *never* loved the Emperor. General Feraud had said so distinctly.

General D'Hubert felt an inward blow in his chest. For an infinitesimal fraction of a second it was as if the spinning of the earth had become perceptible with an awful, slight rustle in the eternal stillness of space. But this noise of blood in his ears passed off at once. Involuntarily he murmured, "Feraud! I had forgotten his existence."

"He's existing at present, very uncomfortably, it is true, in the infamous inn of that nest of savages up there," said the one-eyed cuirassier, drily. "We arrived in your parts an hour ago on post horses. He's awaiting our return with impatience. There is hurry, you know. The General has broken the ministerial order to obtain from you the satisfaction he's entitled to by the laws of honour, and naturally he's anxious to have it all over before the *gendarmerie* gets on his scent."

The other elucidated the idea a little further. "Get back on the quiet —you understand? Phitt! No one the wiser. We have broken out, too.

Your friend the king would be glad to cut off our scurvy pittances at the first chance. It's a risk. But honour before everything."

General D'Hubert had recovered his powers of speech. "So you come here like this along the road to invite me to a throat-cutting match with that—that . . ." A laughing sort of rage took possession of him. "Ha! ha! ha! ha!"

His fists on his hips, he roared without restraint, while they stood before him lank and straight, as though they had been shot up with a snap through a trap door in the ground. Only four-and-twenty months ago the masters of Europe, they had already the air of antique ghosts, they seemed less substantial in their faded coats than their own narrow shadows falling so black across the white road: the military and grotesque shadows of twenty years of war and conquests. They had an outlandish appearance of two imperturbable bonzes of the religion of the sword. And General D'Hubert, also one of the ex-masters of Europe, laughed at these serious phantoms standing in his way.

Said one, indicating the laughing General with a jerk of the head: "A merry companion, that."

"There are some of us that haven't smiled from the day *The Other* went away," remarked his comrade.

A violent impulse to set upon and beat those unsubstantial wraiths to the ground frightened General D'Hubert. He ceased laughing suddenly. His desire now was to get rid of them, to get them away from his sight quickly before he lost control of himself. He wondered at the fury he felt rising in his breast. But he had no time to look into that peculiarity just then.

"I understand your wish to be done with me as quickly as possible. Don't let us waste time in empty ceremonies. Do you see that wood there at the foot of that slope? Yes, the wood of pines. Let us meet there tomorrow at sunrise. I will bring with me my sword or my pistols, or both if you like."

The seconds of General Feraud looked at each other.

"Pistols, General," said the cuirassier.

"So be it. Au revoir—to-morrow morning. Till then let me advise you to keep close if you don't want the *gendarmerie* making inquiries about you before it gets dark. Strangers are rare in this part of the country."

They saluted in silence. General D'Hubert, turning his back on their retreating forms, stood still in the middle of the road for a long time, biting his lower lip and looking on the ground. Then he began to walk straight before him, thus retracing his steps till he found himself before the park gate of his intended's house. Dusk had fallen. Motionless he stared through the bars at the front of the house, gleaming clear beyond the thickets and trees. Footsteps scrunched on the gravel, and presently

a tall stooping shape emerged from the lateral alley following the inner side of the park wall.

Le Chevalier de Valmassigue, uncle of the adorable Adèle, ex-brigadier in the army of the Princes, bookbinder in Altona, afterwards shoemaker (with a great reputation for elegance in the fit of ladies' shoes) in another small German town, wore silk stockings on his lean shanks, low shoes with silver buckles, a brocaded waistcoat. A long-skirted coat, *à la française,* covered loosely his thin, bowed back. A small three-cornered hat rested on a lot of powdered hair, tied in a queue.

"Monsieur le Chevalier," called General D'Hubert, softly.

"What? You here again, *mon ami?* Have you forgotten something?"

"By heavens! that's just it. I have forgotten something. I am come to tell you of it. No—outside. Behind this wall. It's too ghastly a thing to be let in at all where she lives."

The Chevalier came out at once with that benevolent resignation some old people display towards the fugue of youth. Older by a quarter of a century than General D'Hubert, he looked upon him in the secret of his heart as a rather troublesome youngster in love. He had heard his enigmatical words very well, but attached no undue importance to what a mere man of forty so hard hit was likely to do or say. The turn of mind of the generation of Frenchmen grown up during the years of his exile was almost unintelligible to him. Their sentiments appeared to him unduly violent, lacking fineness and measure, their language needlessly exaggerated. He joined calmly the General on the road, and they made a few steps in silence, the General trying to master his agitation, and get proper control of his voice.

"It is perfectly true; I forgot something. I forgot till half an hour ago that I had an urgent affair of honour on my hands. It's incredible, but it is so!"

All was still for a moment. Then in the profound evening silence of the countryside the clear, aged voice of the Chevalier was heard trembling slightly: "Monsieur! That's an indignity."

It was his first thought. The girl born during his exile, the posthumous daughter of his poor brother murdered by a band of Jacobins, had grown since his return very dear to his old heart, which had been starving on mere memories of affection for so many years. "It is an inconceivable thing, I say! A man settles such affairs before he thinks of asking for a young girl's hand. Why! If you had forgotten for ten days longer, you would have been married before your memory returned to you. In my time men did not forget such things—nor yet what is due to the feelings of an innocent young woman. If I did not respect them myself, I would qualify your conduct in a way which you would not like."

General D'Hubert relieved himself frankly by a groan. "Don't let that consideration prevent you. You run no risk of offending her mortally."

But the old man paid no attention to this lover's nonsense. It's doubtful whether he even heard. "What is it?" he asked. "What's the nature of . . . ?"

"Call it a youthful folly, *Monsieur le Chevalier*. An inconceivable, incredible result of . . ." He stopped short. "He will never believe the story," he thought. "He will only think I am taking him for a fool, and get offended." General D'Hubert spoke up again: "Yes, originating in youthful folly, it has become . . ."

The Chevalier interrupted: "Well, then it must be arranged."

"Arranged?"

"Yes, no matter at what cost to your *amour propre*. You should have remembered you were engaged. You forgot that, too, I suppose. And then you go and forget your quarrel. It's the most hopeless exhibition of levity I ever heard of."

"Good heavens, Monsieur! You don't imagine I have been picking up this quarrel last time I was in Paris, or anything of the sort, do you?"

"Eh! What matters the precise date of your insane conduct," exclaimed the Chevalier, testily. "The principal thing is to arrange it."

Noticing General D'Hubert getting restive and trying to place a word, the old *émigré* raised his hand, and added with dignity, "I've been a soldier, too. I would never dare suggest a doubtful step to the man whose name my niece is to bear. I tell you that *entre galants hommes* an affair can always be arranged."

"But *saperlotte, Monsieur le Chevalier*, it's fifteen or sixteen years ago. I was a lieutenant of hussars then."

The old Chevalier seemed confounded by the vehemently despairing tone of this information. "You were a lieutenant of hussars sixteen years ago," he mumbled in a dazed manner.

"Why, yes! You did not suppose I was made a general in my cradle like a royal prince."

In the deepening purple twilight of the fields spread with vine leaves, backed by a low band of sombre crimson in the west, the voice of the old ex-officer in the army of the Princes sounded collected, punctiliously civil.

"Do I dream? Is this a pleasantry? Or am I to understand that you have been hatching an affair of honour for sixteen years?"

"It has clung to me for that length of time. That is my precise meaning. The quarrel itself is not to be explained easily. We met on the ground several times during that time, of course."

"What manners! What horrible perversion of manliness! Nothing can account for such inhumanity but the sanguinary madness of the Revolution which has tainted a whole generation," mused the returned *émigré* in a low tone. "Who's your adversary?" he asked a little louder.

"My adversary? His name is Feraud."

Shadowy in his *tricorne* and old-fashioned clothes, like a bowed,

thin ghost of the *ancien régime,* the Chevalier voiced a ghostly memory. "I can remember the feud about little Sophie Derval, between Monsieur de Brissac, Captain in the Bodyguards, and d'Anjorrant (not the pock-marked one, the other—the Beau d'Anjorrant, as they called him). They met three times in eighteen months in a most gallant manner. It was the fault of that little Sophie, too, who *would* keep on playing . . ."

"This is nothing of the kind," interrupted General D'Hubert. He laughed a little sardonically. "Not at all so simple," he added. "Nor yet half so reasonable," he finished, inaudibly, between his teeth, and ground them with rage.

After this sound nothing troubled the silence for a long time, till the Chevalier asked, without animation: "What is he—this Feraud?"

"Lieutenant of hussars, too—I mean, he's a general. A Gascon. Son of a blacksmith, I believe."

"There! I thought so. That Bonaparte had a special predilection for the *canaille.* I don't mean this for you, D'Hubert. You are one of us, though you have served this usurper, who . . ."

"Let's leave him out of this," broke in General D'Hubert.

The Chevalier shrugged his peaked shoulders. "Feraud of sorts. Off-spring of a blacksmith and some village troll. See what comes of mixing yourself up with that sort of people."

"You have made shoes yourself, Chevalier."

"Yes. But I am not the son of a shoemaker. Neither are you, Monsieur D'Hubert. You and I have something that your Bonaparte's princes, dukes, and marshals have not, because there's no power on earth that could give it to them," retorted the *émigré,* with the rising animation of a man who has got hold of a hopeful argument. "Those people don't exist —all these Ferauds. Feraud! What is Feraud? A *va-nu-pieds* disguised into a general by a Corsican adventurer masquerading as an emperor. There is no earthly reason for a D'Hubert to *s'encanailler* by a duel with a person of that sort. You can make your excuses to him perfectly well. And if the *manant* takes into his head to decline them, you may simply refuse to meet him."

"You say I may do that?"

"I do. With the clearest conscience."

"Monsieur le Chevalier! To what do you think you have returned from your emigration?"

This was said in such a startling tone that the old man raised sharply his bowed head, glimmering silvery white under the points of the little *tricorne.* For a time he made no sound.

"God knows!" he said at last, pointing with a slow and grave gesture at a tall roadside cross mounted on a block of stone, and stretching its arms of forged iron all black against the darkening red band in the sky— "God knows! If it were not for this emblem, which I remember seeing on this spot as a child, I would wonder to what we who remained faithful

to God and our king have returned. The very voices of the people have changed."

"Yes, it is a changed France," said General D'Hubert. He seemed to have regained his calm. His tone was slightly ironic. "Therefore I cannot take your advice. Besides, how is one to refuse to be bitten by a dog that means to bite? It's impracticable. Take my word for it—Feraud isn't a man to be stayed by apologies or refusals. But there are other ways. I could, for instance, send a messenger with a word to the brigadier of the *gendarmerie* in Senlac. He and his two friends are liable to arrest on my simple order. It would make some talk in the army, both the organized and the disbanded—especially the disbanded. All *canaille!* All once upon a time the companions in arms of Armand D'Hubert. But what need a D'Hubert care what people that don't exist may think? Or, better still, I might get my brother-in-law to send for the mayor of the village and give him a hint. No more would be needed to get the three 'brigands' set upon with flails and pitchforks and hunted into some nice, deep, wet ditch—and nobody the wiser! It has been done only ten miles from here to three poor devils of the disbanded Red Lancers of the Guard going to their homes. What says your conscience, *Chevalier?* Can a D'Hubert do that thing to three men who do not exist?"

A few stars had come out on the blue obscurity, clear as crystal, of the sky. The dry, thin voice of the Chevalier spoke harshly: "Why are you telling me all this?"

The General seized the withered old hand with a strong grip. "Because I owe you my fullest confidence. Who could tell Adèle but you? You understand why I dare not trust my brother-in-law nor yet my own sister. *Chevalier!* I have been so near doing these things that I tremble yet. You don't know how terrible this duel appears to me. And there's no escape from it."

He murmured after a pause, "it's a fatality," dropped the Chevalier's passive hand, and said in his ordinary conversational voice, "I shall have to go without seconds. If it is my lot to remain on the ground, you at least will know all that can be made known of this affair."

The shadowy ghost of the *ancien régime* seemed to have become more bowed during the conversation. "How am I to keep an indifferent face this evening before these two women?" he groaned. "General! I find it very difficult to forgive you."

General D'Hubert made no answer.

"Is your cause good, at least?"

"I am innocent."

This time he seized the Chevalier's ghostly arm above the elbow, and gave it a mighty squeeze. "I must kill him!" he hissed, and opening his hand strode away down the road.

The delicate attentions of his adoring sister had secured for the General perfect liberty of movement in the house where he was a guest.

He had even his own entrance through a small door in one corner of the orangery. Thus he was not exposed that evening to the necessity of dissembling his agitation before the calm ignorance of the other inmates. He was glad of it. It seemed to him that if he had to open his lips he would break out into horrible and aimless imprecations, start breaking furniture, smashing china and glass. From the moment he opened the private door and while ascending the twenty-eight steps of a winding staircase, giving access to the corridor on which his room opened, he went through a horrible and humiliating scene in which an infuriated madman with blood-shot eyes and a foaming mouth played inconceivable havoc with everything inanimate that may be found in a well-appointed dining-room. When he opened the door of his apartment the fit was over, and his bodily fatigue was so great that he had to catch at the backs of the chairs while crossing the room to reach a low and broad divan on which he let himself fall heavily. His moral prostration was still greater. That brutality of feeling which he had known only when charging the enemy, sabre in hand, amazed this man of forty, who did not recognize in it the instinctive fury of his menaced passion. But in his mental and bodily exhaustion this passion got cleared, distilled, refined into a sentiment of melancholy despair at having, perhaps, to die before he had taught this beautiful girl to love him.

That night, General D'Hubert stretched out on his back with his hands over his eyes, or lying on his breast with his face buried in a cushion, made the full pilgrimage of emotions. Nauseating disgust at the absurdity of the situation, doubt of his own fitness to conduct his existence, and mistrust of his best sentiments (for what the devil did he want to go to Fouché for?)—he knew them all in turn. "I am an idiot, neither more nor less," he thought—"A sensitive idiot. Because I overheard two men talking in a café. . . . I am an idiot afraid of lies—whereas in life it is only truth that matters."

Several times he got up and, walking in his socks in order not to be heard by anybody downstairs, drank all the water he could find in the dark. And he tasted the torments of jealousy, too. She would marry somebody else. His very soul writhed. The tenacity of that Feraud, the awful persistence of that imbecile brute, came to him with the tremendous force of a relentless destiny. General D'Hubert trembled as he put down the empty water ewer. "He will have me," he thought. General D'Hubert was tasting every emotion that life has to give. He had in his dry mouth the faint sickly flavour of fear, not the excusable fear before a young girl's candid and amused glance, but the fear of death and the honourable man's fear of cowardice.

But if true courage consists in going out to meet an odious danger from which our body, soul, and heart recoil together, General D'Hubert had the opportunity to practise it for the first time in his life. He had charged exultingly at batteries and at infantry squares, and ridden with

messages through a hail of bullets without thinking anything about it. His business now was to sneak out unheard, at break of day, to an obscure and revolting death. General D'Hubert never hesitated. He carried two pistols in a leather bag which he slung over his shoulder. Before he had crossed the garden his mouth was dry again. He picked two oranges. It was only after shutting the gate after him that he felt a slight faintness.

He staggered on, disregarding it, and after going a few yards regained the command of his legs. In the colourless and pellucid dawn the wood of pines detached its columns of trunks and its dark green canopy very clearly against the rocks of the grey hillside. He kept his eyes fixed on it steadily, and sucked at an orange as he walked. That temperamental good-humoured coolness in the face of danger which had made him an officer liked by his men and appreciated by his superiors was gradually asserting itself. It was like going into battle. Arriving at the edge of the wood he sat down on a boulder, holding the other orange in his hand, and reproached himself for coming so ridiculously early on the ground. Before very long, however, he heard the swishing of bushes, footsteps on the hard ground, and the sounds of a disjointed, loud conversation. A voice somewhere behind him said boastfully, "He's game for my bag."

He thought to himself, "Here they are. What's this about game? Are they talking of me?" And becoming aware of the other orange in his hand, he thought further, "These are very good oranges. Léonie's own tree. I may just as well eat this orange now instead of flinging it away."

Emerging from a wilderness of rocks and bushes, General Feraud and his seconds discovered General D'Hubert engaged in peeling the orange. They stood still, waiting till he looked up. Then the seconds raised their hats, while General Feraud, putting his hands behind his back, walked aside a little way.

"I am compelled to ask one of you, messieurs, to act for me. I have brought no friends. Will you?"

The one-eyed cuirassier said judicially, "That cannot be refused."

The other veteran remarked, "It's awkward all the same."

"Owing to the state of the people's minds in this part of the country there was no one I could trust safely with the object of your presence here," explained General D'Hubert, urbanely.

They saluted, looked round, and remarked both together:

"Poor ground."

"It's unfit."

"Why bother about ground, measurements, and so on? Let us simplify matters. Load the two pairs of pistols. I will take those of General Feraud, and let him take mine. Or, better still, let us take a mixed pair. One of each pair. Then let us go into the wood and shoot at sight, while you remain outside. We did not come here for ceremonies, but for war— war to the death. Any ground is good enough for that. If I fall, you must

leave me where I lie and clear out. It wouldn't be healthy for you to be found hanging about here after that."

It appeared after a short parley that General Feraud was willing to accept these conditions. While the seconds were loading the pistols, he could be heard whistling, and was seen to rub his hands with perfect contentment. He flung off his coat briskly, and General D'Hubert took off his own and folded it carefully on a stone.

"Suppose you take your principal to the other side of the wood and let him enter exactly in ten minutes from now," suggested General D'Hubert, calmly, but feeling as if he were giving directions for his own execution. This, however, was his last moment of weakness. "Wait. Let us compare watches first."

He pulled out his own. The officer with the chipped nose went over to borrow the watch of General Feraud. They bent their heads over them for a time.

"That's it. At four minutes to six by yours. Seven to by mine."

It was the cuirassier who remained by the side of General D'Hubert, keeping his one eye fixed immovably on the white face of the watch he held in the palm of his hand. He opened his mouth, waiting for the beat of the last second long before he snapped out the word, "*Avancez.*"

General D'Hubert moved on, passing from the glaring sunshine of the Provençal morning into the cool and aromatic shade of the pines. The ground was clear between the reddish trunks, whose multitude, leaning at slightly different angles, confused his eye at first. It was like going into battle. The commanding quality of confidence in himself woke up in his breast. He was all to his affair. The problem was how to kill the adversary. Nothing short of that would free him from this imbecile nightmare. "It's no use wounding that brute," thought General D'Hubert. He was known as a resourceful officer. His comrades years ago used to call him The Strategist. And it was a fact that he could think in the presence of the enemy. Whereas Feraud had been always a mere fighter—but a dead shot, unluckily.

"I must draw his fire at the greatest possible range," said General D'Hubert to himself.

At that moment he saw something white moving far off between the trees—the shirt of his adversary. He stepped out at once between the trunks, exposing himself freely; then, quick as lightning, leaped back. It had been a risky but it succeeded in its object. Almost simultaneously with the pop of a shot a small piece of bark chipped off by the bullet stung his ear painfully.

General Feraud, with one shot expended, was getting cautious. Peeping round the tree, General D'Hubert could not see him at all. This ignorance of the foe's whereabouts carried with it a sense of insecurity. General D'Hubert felt himself abominably exposed on his flank and rear. Again something white fluttered in his sight. Ha! The enemy was still

on his front, then. He had feared a turning movement. But apparently
General Feraud was not thinking of it. General D'Hubert saw him pass
without special haste from one tree to another in the straight line of ap-
proach. With great firmness of mind General D'Hubert stayed his hand.
Too far yet. He knew he was no marksman. His must be a waiting game
—to kill.

Wishing to take advantage of the greater thickness of the trunk, he
sank down to the ground. Extended at full length, head on to his enemy,
he had his person completely protected. Exposing himself would not do
now, because the other was too near by this time. A conviction that
Feraud would presently do something rash was like balm to General
D'Hubert's soul. But to keep his chin raised off the ground was irksome,
and not much use either. He peeped round, exposing a fraction of his
head with dread, but really with little risk. His enemy, as a matter of fact,
did not expect to see anything of him so far down as that. General D'Hu-
bert caught a fleeting view of General Feraud shifting trees again with
deliberate caution. "He despises my shooting," he thought, displaying
that insight into the mind of his antagonist which is of such great help in
winning battles. He was confirmed in his tactics of immobility. "If I could
only watch my rear as well as my front!" he thought anxiously, longing
for the impossible.

It required some force of character to lay his pistols down; but, on
a sudden impulse, General D'Hubert did this very gently—one on each
side of him. In the army he had been looked upon as a bit of a dandy
because he used to shave and put on a clean shirt on the days of battle.
As a matter of fact, he had always been very careful of his personal ap-
pearance. In a man of nearly forty, in love with a young and charming
girl, this praiseworthy self-respect may run to such little weaknesses as,
for instance, being provided with an elegant little leather folding-case
containing a small ivory comb, and fitted with a piece of looking-glass on
the outside. General D'Hubert, his hands being free, felt in his breeches'
pockets for that implement of innocent vanity excusable in the possessor
of long, silky moustaches. He drew it out, and then with the utmost cool-
ness and promptitude turned himself over on his back. In this new atti-
tude, his head a little raised, holding the little looking-glass just clear of
his tree, he squinted into it with his left eye, while the right kept a direct
watch on the rear of his position. Thus was proved Napoleon's saying,
that "for a French soldier, the word impossible does not exist." He had
the right tree nearly filling the field of his little mirror.

"If he moves from behind it," he reflected with satisfaction, "I am
bound to see his legs. But in any case he can't come upon me unawares."

And sure enough he saw the boots of General Feraud flash in and
out, eclipsing for an instant everything else reflected in the little mirror.
He shifted its position accordingly. But having to form his judgment of

the change from that indirect view he did not realize that now his feet and a portion of his legs were in plain sight of General Feraud.

General Feraud had been getting gradually impressed by the amazing cleverness with which his enemy was keeping cover. He had spotted the right tree with bloodthirsty precision. He was absolutely certain of it. And yet he had not been able to glimpse as much as the tip of an ear. As he had been looking for it at the height of about five feet ten inches from the ground it was no great wonder—but it seemed very wonderful to General Feraud.

The first view of these feet and legs determined a rush of blood to his head. He literally staggered behind his tree, and had to steady himself against it with his hand. The other was lying on the ground, then! On the ground! Perfectly still, too! Exposed! What could it mean? . . . The notion that he had knocked over his adversary at the first shot entered then General Feraud's head. Once there it grew with every second of attentive gazing, overshadowing every other supposition—irresistible, triumphant, ferocious.

"What an ass I was to think I could have missed him," he muttered to himself. "He was exposed *en plein*—the fool!—for quite a couple of seconds."

General Feraud gazed at the motionless limbs, the last vestiges of surprise fading before an unbounded admiration of his own deadly skill with the pistol.

"Turned up his toes! By the god of war, that was a shot!" he exulted mentally. "Got it through the head, no doubt, just where I aimed, staggered behind that tree, rolled over on his back, and died."

And he stared! He stared, forgetting to move, almost awed, almost sorry. But for nothing in the world would he have had it undone. Such a shot!—such a shot! Rolled over on his back and died!

For it was this helpless position, lying on the back, that shouted its direct evidence at General Feraud! It never occurred to him that it might have been deliberately assumed by a living man. It was inconceivable. It was beyond the range of sane supposition. There was no possibility to guess the reason for it. And it must be said, too, that General D'Hubert's turned-up feet looked thoroughly dead. General Feraud expanded his lungs for a stentorian shout to his seconds, but, from what he felt to be an excessive scrupulousness, refrained for a while.

"I will just go and see first whether he breathes yet," he mumbled to himself, leaving carelessly the shelter of his tree. This move was immediately perceived by the resourceful General D'Hubert. He concluded it to be another shift, but when he lost the boots out of the field of the mirror he became uneasy. General Feraud had only stepped a little out of the line, but his adversary could not possibly have supposed him walking up with perfect unconcern. General D'Hubert, beginning to wonder at what had become of the other, was taken unawares so com-

pletely that the first warning of danger consisted in the long, early-morning shadow of his enemy falling aslant on his outstretched legs. He had not even heard a footfall on the soft ground between the trees!

It was too much even for his coolness. He jumped up thoughtlessly, leaving the pistols on the ground. The irresistible instinct of an average man (unless totally paralyzed by discomfiture) would have been to stoop for his weapons, exposing himself to the risk of being shot down in that position. Instinct, of course, is irreflective. It is its very definition. But it may be an inquiry worth pursuing whether in reflective mankind the mechanical promptings of instinct are not affected by the customary mode of thought. In his young days, Armand D'Hubert, the reflective, promising officer, had emitted the opinion that in warfare one should "never cast back on the lines of a mistake." This idea, defended and developed in many discussions, had settled into one of the stock notions of his brain, had become a part of his mental individuality. Whether it had gone so inconceivably deep as to affect the dictates of his instinct, or simply because, as he himself declared afterwards, he was "too scared to remember the confounded pistols," the fact is that General D'Hubert never attempted to stoop for them. Instead of going back on his mistake, he seized the rough trunk with both hands, and swung himself behind it with such impetuosity that, going right round in the very flash and report of the pistol-shot, he reappeared on the other side of the tree face to face with General Feraud. This last, completely unstrung by such a show of agility on the part of a dead man, was trembling yet. A very faint mist of smoke hung before his face which had an extraordinary aspect, as if the lower jaw had come unhinged.

"Not missed!" he croaked, hoarsely, from the depths of a dry throat.

This sinister sound loosened the spell that had fallen on General D'Hubert's senses. "Yes, missed—*à bout portant,*" he heard himself saying, almost before he had recovered the full command of his faculties. The revulsion of feeling was accompanied by a gust of homicidal fury, resuming in its violence the accumulated resentment of a lifetime. For years General D'Hubert had been exasperated and humiliated by an atrocious absurdity imposed upon him by this man's savage caprice. Besides, General D'Hubert had been in this last instance too unwilling to confront death for the reaction of his anguish not to take the shape of a desire to kill. "And I have my two shots to fire yet," he added, pitilessly.

General Feraud snapped-to his teeth, and his face assumed an irate, undaunted expression. "Go on!" he said, grimly.

These would have been his last words if General D'Hubert had been holding the pistols in his hands. But the pistols were lying on the ground at the foot of a pine. General D'Hubert had the second of leisure necessary to remember that he had dreaded death not as a man, but as a lover; not as a danger, but as a rival; not as a foe to life, but as an obstacle to

marriage. And behold! there was the rival defeated!—utterly defeated, crushed, done for!

He picked up the weapons mechanically, and, instead of firing them into General Feraud's breast, he gave expression to the thoughts uppermost in his mind, "You will fight no more duels now."

His tone of leisurely, ineffable satisfaction was too much for General Feraud's stoicism. "Don't dawdle, then, damn you for a cold-blooded staff-coxcomb!" he roared out, suddenly, out of an impassive face held erect on a rigidly still body.

General D'Hubert uncocked the pistols carefully. This proceeding was observed with mixed feelings by the other general. "You missed me twice," the victor said, coolly, shifting both pistols to one hand; "the last time within a foot or so. By every rule of single combat your life belongs to me. That does not mean that I want to take it now."

"I have no use for your forbearance," muttered General Feraud, gloomily.

"Allow me to point out that this is no concern of mine," said General D'Hubert, whose every word was dictated by a consummate delicacy of feeling. In anger he could have killed that man, but in cold blood he recoiled from humiliating by a show of generosity this unreasonable being—a fellow-soldier of the *Grande Armée,* a companion in the wonders and terrors of the great military epic. "You don't set up the pretension of dictating to me what I am to do with what's my own."

General Feraud looked startled, and the other continued, "You've forced me on a point of honour to keep my life at your disposal, as it were, for fifteen years. Very well. Now that the matter is decided to my advantage, I am going to do what I like with your life on the same principle. You shall keep it at my disposal as long as I choose. Neither more nor less. You are on your honour till I say the word."

"I am! But, *sacrebleu!* This is an absurd position for a General of the Empire to be placed in!" cried General Feraud, in accents of profound and dismayed conviction. "It amounts to sitting all the rest of my life with a loaded pistol in a drawer waiting for your word. It's—it's idiotic; I shall be an object of—of—derision."

"Absurd?—idiotic? Do you think so?" queried General D'Hubert with sly gravity. "Perhaps. But I don't see how that can be helped. However, I am not likely to talk at large of this adventure. Nobody need ever know anything about it. Just as no one to this day, I believe, knows the origin of our quarrel. . . . Not a word more," he added, hastily. "I can't really discuss this question with a man who, as far as I am concerned, does not exist."

When the two duellists came out into the open, General Feraud walking a little behind, and rather with the air of walking in a trance, the two seconds hurried towards them, each from his station at the edge of the wood. General D'Hubert addressed them, speaking loud and dis-

tinctly, "Messieurs, I make it a point of declaring to you solemnly, in the presence of General Feraud, that our difference is at last settled for good. You may inform all the world of that fact."

"A reconciliation, after all!" they exclaimed together.

"Reconciliation? Not that exactly. It is something much more binding. Is it not so, General?"

General Feraud only lowered his head in sign of assent. The two veterans looked at each other. Later in the day, when they found themselves alone out of their moody friend's earshot, the cuirassier remarked suddenly, "Generally speaking, I can see with my one eye as far as most people; but this beats me. He won't say anything."

"In this affair of honour I understand there has been from first to last always something that no one in the army could quite make out," declared the chasseur with the imperfect nose. "In mystery it began, in mystery it went on, in mystery it is to end, apparently."

General D'Hubert walked home with long, hasty strides, by no means uplifted by a sense of triumph. He had conquered, yet it did not seem to him that he had gained very much by his conquest. The night before he had grudged the risk of his life which appeared to him magnificent, worthy of preservation as an opportunity to win a girl's love. He had known moments when, by a marvellous illusion, this love seemed to be already his, and his threatened life a still more magnificent opportunity of devotion. Now that his life was safe it had suddenly lost its special magnificence. It had acquired instead a specially alarming aspect as a snare for the exposure of unworthiness. As to the marvellous illusion of conquered love that had visited him for a moment in the agitated watches of the night, which might have been his last on earth, he comprehended now its true nature. It had been merely a paroxysm of delirious conceit. Thus to this man, sobered by the victorious issue of a duel, life appeared robbed of its charm, simply because it was no longer menaced.

Approaching the house from the back, through the orchard and the kitchen garden, he could not notice the agitation which reigned in front. He never met a single soul. Only while walking softly along the corridor, he became aware that the house was awake and more noisy than usual. Names of servants were being called out down below in a confused noise of coming and going. With some concern he noticed that the door of his own room stood ajar, though the shutters had not been opened yet. He had hoped that his early excursion would have passed unperceived. He expected to find some servant just gone in; but the sunshine filtering through the usual cracks enabled him to see lying on the low divan something bulky, which had the appearance of two women clasped in each other's arms. Tearful and desolate murmurs issued mysteriously from that appearance. General D'Hubert pulled open the nearest pair of shutters violently. One of the women then jumped up. It was his sister. She

stood for a moment with her hair hanging down and her arms raised straight up above her head, and then flung herself with a stifled cry into his arms. He returned her embrace, trying at the same time to disengage himself from it. The other woman had not risen. She seemed, on the contrary, to cling closer to the divan, hiding her face in the cushions. Her hair was also loose; it was admirably fair. General D'Hubert recognized it with staggering emotion. Mademoiselle de Valmassigue! Adèle! In distress!

He became greatly alarmed, and got rid of his sister's hug definitely. Madame Léonie then extended her shapely bare arm out of her *peignoir*, pointing dramatically at the divan. "This poor, terrified child has rushed here from home, on foot, two miles—running all the way."

"What on earth has happened?" asked General D'Hubert in a low, agitated voice.

But Madame Léonie was speaking loudly. "She rang the great bell at the gate and roused all the household—we were all asleep yet. You may imagine what a terrible shock. . . . Adèle, my dear child, sit up."

General D'Hubert's expression was not that of a man who "imagines" with facility. He did, however, fish out of the chaos of surmises the notion that his prospective mother-in-law had died suddenly, but only to dismiss it at once. He could not conceive the nature of the event or the catastrophe which would induce Mademoiselle de Valmassigue, living in a house full of servants, to bring the news over the fields herself, two miles, running all the way.

"But why are you in this room?" he whispered, full of awe.

"Of course, I ran up to see, and this child . . . I did not notice it . . . she followed me. It's that absurd Chevalier," went on Madame Léonie, looking towards the divan. . . . "Her hair is all come down. You may imagine she did not stop to call her maid to dress it before she started. . . . Adèle, my dear, sit up. . . . He blurted it all out to her at half-past five in the morning. She woke up early and opened her shutters to breathe the fresh air, and saw him sitting collapsed on a garden bench at the end of the great alley. At that hour—you may imagine! And the evening before he had declared himself indisposed. She hurried on some clothes and flew down to him. One would be anxious for less. He loves her, but not very intelligently. He had been up all night, fully dressed, the poor old man, perfectly exhausted. He wasn't in a state to invent a plausible story. . . . What a confidant you chose there! My husband was furious. He said, 'We can't interfere now.' So we sat down to wait. It was awful. And this poor child running with her hair loose over here publicly! She has been seen by some people in the fields. She has roused the whole household, too. It's awkward for her. Luckily you are to be married next week. . . . Adèle, sit up. He has come home on his own legs. . . . We expected to see you coming on a stretcher, perhaps—what do I know?

Go and see if the carriage is ready. I must take this child home at once. It isn't proper for her to stay here a minute longer."

General D'Hubert did not move. It was as though he had heard nothing. Madame Léonie changed her mind. "I will go and see myself," she cried. "I want also my cloak.—Adèle——" she began, but did not add "sit up." She went out saying, in a very loud and cheerful tone: "I leave the door open."

General D'Hubert made a movement towards the divan, but then Adèle sat up, and that checked him dead. He thought, "I haven't washed this morning. I must look like an old tramp. There's earth on the back of my coat and pine-needles in my hair." It occurred to him that the situation required a good deal of circumspection on his part.

"I am greatly concerned, mademoiselle," he began, vaguely, and abandoned that line. She was sitting up on the divan with her cheeks unusually pink and her hair, brilliantly fair, falling all over her shoulders—which was a very novel sight to the general. He walked away up the room, and looking out of the window for safety said, "I fear you must think I behaved like a madman," in accents of sincere despair. Then he spun round, and noticed that she had followed him with her eyes. They were not cast down on meeting his glance. And the expression of her face was novel to him also. It was, one might have said, reversed. Those eyes looked at him with grave thoughtfulness, while the exquisite lines of her mouth seemed to suggest a restrained smile. This change made her transcendental beauty much less mysterious, much more accessible to a man's comprehension. An amazing ease of mind came to the general—and even some ease of manner. He walked down the room with as much pleasurable excitement as he would have found in walking up to a battery vomiting death, fire, and smoke; then stood looking down with smiling eyes at the girl whose marriage with him (next week) had been so carefully arranged by the wise, the good, the admirable Léonie.

"Ah! mademoiselle," he said, in a tone of courtly regret, "if only I could be certain that you did not come here this morning, two miles, running all the way, merely from affection for your mother!"

He waited for an answer imperturbable but inwardly elated. It came in a demure murmur, eyelashes lowered with fascinating effect. "You must not be *méchant* as well as mad."

And then General D'Hubert made an aggressive movement towards the divan which nothing could check. That piece of furniture was not exactly in the line of the open door. But Madame Léonie, coming back wrapped up in a light cloak and carrying a lace shawl on her arm for Adèle to hide her incriminating hair under, had a swift impression of her brother getting up from his knees.

"Come along, my dear child," she cried from the doorway.

The general, now himself again in the fullest sense, showed the readiness of a resourceful cavalry officer and the peremptoriness of a

leader of men. "You don't expect her to walk to the carriage," he said, indignantly. "She isn't fit. I shall carry her downstairs."

This he did slowly, followed by his awed and respectful sister; but he rushed back like a whirlwind to wash off all the signs of the night of anguish and the morning of war, and to put on the festive garments of a conqueror before hurrying over to the other house. Had it not been for that, General D'Hubert felt capable of mounting a horse and pursuing his late adversary in order simply to embrace him from excess of happiness. "I owe it all to this stupid brute," he thought. "He has made plain in a morning what might have taken me years to find out—for I am a timid fool. No self-confidence whatever. Perfect coward. And the Chevalier! Delightful old man!" General D'Hubert longed to embrace him also.

The Chevalier was in bed. For several days he was very unwell. The men of the Empire and the post-revolution young ladies were too much for him. He got up the day before the wedding, and, being curious by nature, took his niece aside for a quiet talk. He advised her to find out from her husband the true story of the affair of honour, whose claim, so imperative and so persistent, had led her to within an ace of tragedy. "It is right that his wife should be told. And next month or so will be your time to learn from him anything you want to know, my dear child."

Later on, when the married couple came on a visit to the mother of the bride, Madame la Générale D'Hubert communicated to her beloved old uncle the true story she had obtained without any difficulty from her husband.

The Chevalier listened with deep attention to the end, took a pinch of snuff, flicked the grains of tobacco from the frilled front of his shirt, and asked, calmly, "And that's all it was?"

"Yes, uncle," replied Madame la Générale, opening her pretty eyes very wide. "Isn't it funny? *C'est insensé*—to think what men are capable of!"

"H'm!" commented the old *émigré*. "It depends what sort of men. That Bonaparte's soldiers were savages. It is *insensé*. As a wife, my dear, you must believe implicitly what your husband says."

But to Léonie's husband the Chevalier confided his true opinion. "If that's the tale the fellow made up for his wife, and during the honeymoon, too, you may depend on it that no one will ever know now the secret of this affair."

Considerably later still, General D'Hubert judged the time come, and the opportunity propitious to write a letter to General Feraud. This letter began by disclaiming all animosity. "I've never," wrote the General Baron D'Hubert, "wished for your death during all the time of our deplorable quarrel. Allow me," he continued, "to give you back in all form your forfeited life. It is proper that we two, who have been partners in so much military glory, should be friendly to each other publicly."

The same letter contained also an item of domestic information. It

was in reference to this last that General Feraud answered from a little village on the banks of the Garonne, in the following words:

"If one of your boy's names had been Napoleon—or Joseph—or even Joachim, I could congratulate you on the event with a better heart. As you have thought proper to give him the names of Charles Henri Armand, I am confirmed in my conviction that you *never* loved the Emperor. The thought of that sublime hero chained to a rock in the middle of a savage ocean makes life of so little value that I would receive with positive joy your instructions to blow my brains out. From suicide I consider myself in honour debarred. But I keep a loaded pistol in my drawer."

Madame la Générale D'Hubert lifted up her hands in despair after perusing that answer.

"You see? He *won't* be reconciled," said her husband. "He must never, by any chance, be allowed to guess where the money comes from. It wouldn't do. He couldn't bear it."

"You are a *brave homme,* Armand," said Madame la Générale, appreciatively.

"My dear, I had the right to blow his brains out; but as I didn't, we can't let him starve. He has lost his pension and he is utterly incapable of doing anything in the world for himself. We must take care of him, secretly, to the end of his days. Don't I owe him the most ecstatic moment of my life? . . . Ha! ha! ha! Over the fields, two miles, running all the way! I couldn't believe my ears! . . . But for his stupid ferocity, it would have taken me years to find you out. It's extraordinary how in one way or another this man has managed to fasten himself on my deeper feelings."

IV

THE OLD MAID

by Edith Wharton

A Story of High Society

Edith Wharton has been called "the *grande dame*" of American letters. A handsome woman, with a hint of haughtiness on the surface, she belonged by birth and preference in an aristocratic setting. Although most of her life was lived abroad, her best work was a reflection of social life in America as she had seen it in her own early years.

In 1924 she published four novelettes in one volume under the title of *Old New York,* and it was the consensus among the critics of the day that the most significant of these was *The Old Maid,* which dealt with the eighteen fifties. I saw the manuscript during my first years in magazine work. I can still recall how convincing it seemed to me after the far from successful efforts of so many writers to tell, from outside observation, of wealth and social exclusiveness. This story of two women at war over the affections of a very pretty and engaging girl, the adopted daughter of one and the unacknowledged illegitimate child of the other, was told with ease and simplicity but with complete conviction.

The Old Maid is a picture of high society in America before the multimillionaire era had developed extravagant entertainment and bizarre competition. But despite the comparative quiet of the background, the story is one of great dramatic power. This was manifested in the triumph scored in 1935 when a dramatization by Zoë Akins was brought to the stage.

Part I

I

IN THE OLD NEW YORK of the 'fifties a few families ruled, in simplicity and affluence. Of these were the Ralstons.

The sturdy English and the rubicund and heavier Dutch had mingled to produce a prosperous, prudent and yet lavish society. To "do things handsomely" had always been a fundamental principle in this cautious world, built up on the fortunes of bankers, India merchants, ship-builders and ship-chandlers. Those well-fed slow-moving people, who seemed irritable and dyspeptic to European eyes only because the caprices of the climate had stripped them of superfluous flesh, and strung their nerves a little tighter, lived in a genteel monotony of which the surface was never stirred by the dumb dramas now and then enacted underground. Sensitive souls in those days were like muted key-boards, on which Fate played without a sound.

In this compact society, built of solidly welded blocks, one of the largest areas was filled by the Ralstons and their ramifications. The Ralstons were of middle class English stock. They had not come to the colonies to die for a creed but to live for a bank-account. The result had been beyond their hopes, and their religion was tinged by their success. An edulcorated Church of England which, under the conciliatory name of the "Episcopal Church of the United States of America," left out the coarser allusions in the Marriage Service, slid over the comminatory passages in the Athanasian Creed, and thought it more respectful to say "Our Father *who*" than "*which*" in the Lord's Prayer, was exactly suited to the spirit of compromise whereon the Ralstons had built themselves up. There was in all the tribe the same instinctive recoil from new religions as from unaccounted-for people. Institutional to the core, they represented the conservative element that holds new societies together as seaplants bind the seashore.

Compared with the Ralstons, even such traditionalists as the Lovells, the Halseys or the Vandergraves appeared careless, indifferent to money, almost reckless in their impulses and indecisions. Old John Frederick Ralston, the stout founder of the race, had perceived the difference, and emphasized it to his son, Frederick John, in whom he had scented a faint leaning toward the untried and unprofitable.

"You let the Lannings and the Dagonets and the Spenders take risks and fly kites. It's the county-family blood in 'em: we've nothing to do with that. Look how they're petering out already—the men, I mean. Let your boys marry their girls, if you like (they're wholesome and handsome); though I'd sooner see my grandsons take a Lovell or a Vandergrave, or any of our own kind. But don't let your sons go mooning around after their young fellows, horse-racing, and running down south to those d——d Springs, and gambling at New Orleans, and all the rest of it. That's how you'll build up the family, and keep the weather out. The way we've always done it."

Frederick John listened, obeyed, married a Halsey, and passively followed in his father's steps. He belonged to the cautious generation of New York gentlemen who revered Hamilton and served Jefferson, who longed to lay out New York like Washington, and who laid it out instead like a gridiron, lest they should be thought "undemocratic" by people they secretly looked down upon. Shopkeepers to the marrow, they put in their windows the wares there was most demand for, keeping their private opinions for the back-shop, where through lack of use, they gradually lost substance and colour.

The fourth generation of Ralstons had nothing left in the way of convictions save an acute sense of honour in private and business matters; on the life of the community and the state they took their daily views from the newspapers, and the newspapers they already despised. The Ralstons had done little to shape the destiny of their country, except to finance the Cause when it had become safe to do so. They were related to many of the great men who had built the Republic; but no Ralston had so far committed himself as to be great. As old John Frederick said, it was safer to be satisfied with three per cent: they regarded heroism as a form of gambling. Yet by merely being so numerous and so similar they had come to have a weight in the community. People said: "The Ralstons" when they wished to invoke a precedent. This attribution of authority had gradually convinced the third generation of its collective importance, and the fourth, to which Delia Ralston's husband belonged, had the ease and simplicity of a ruling class.

Within the limits of their universal caution, the Ralstons fulfilled their obligations as rich and respected citizens. They figured on the boards of all the old-established charities, gave handsomely to thriving institutions, had the best cooks in New York, and when they travelled abroad ordered statuary of the American sculptors in Rome whose reputation was already established. The first Ralston who had brought home a statue had been regarded as a wild fellow; but when it became known that the sculptor had executed several orders for the British aristocracy it was felt in the family that this too was a three per cent investment.

Two marriages with the Dutch Vandergraves had consolidated these qualities of thrift and handsome living, and the carefully built-up Ralston

character was now so congenital that Delia Ralston sometimes asked herself whether, were she to turn her own little boy loose in a wilderness, he would not create a small New York there, and be on all its boards of directors.

Delia Lovell had married James Ralston at twenty. The marriage, which had taken place in the month of September, 1840, had been solemnized, as was then the custom, in the drawing-room of the bride's country home, at what is now the corner of Avenue A and Ninety-first Street, overlooking the Sound. Thence her husband had driven her (in Grandmamma Lovell's canary-coloured coach with a fringed hammer-cloth) through spreading suburbs and untidy elm-shaded streets to one of the new houses in Gramercy Park, which the pioneers of the younger set were just beginning to affect; and there, at five-and-twenty, she was established, the mother of two children, the possessor of a generous allowance of pin-money, and, by common consent, one of the handsomest and most popular "young matrons" (as they were called) of her day.

She was thinking placidly and gratefully of these things as she sat one afternoon in her handsome bedroom in Gramercy Park. She was too near to the primitive Ralstons to have as clear a view of them as, for instance, the son in question might one day command: she lived under them as unthinkingly as one lives under the laws of one's country. Yet that tremor of the muted key-board, that secret questioning which sometimes beat in her like wings, would now and then so divide her from them that for a fleeting moment she could survey them in their relation to other things. The moment was always fleeting; she dropped back from it quickly, breathless and a little pale, to her children, her house-keeping, her new dresses and her kindly Jim.

She thought of him today with a smile of tenderness, remembering how he had told her to spare no expense on her new bonnet. Though she was twenty-five, and twice a mother, her image was still surprisingly fresh. The plumpness then thought seemly in a young wife stretched the grey silk across her bosom, and caused her heavy gold watch-chain—after it left the anchorage of the brooch of St. Peter's in mosaic that fastened her low-cut Cluny collar—to dangle perilously in the void above a tiny waist buckled into a velvet waist-band. But the shoulders above sloped youthfully under her Cashmere scarf, and every movement was as quick as a girl's.

Mrs. Jim Ralston approvingly examined the rosy-cheeked oval set in the blonde ruffles of the bonnet on which, in compliance with her husband's instructions, she had spared no expense. It was a cabriolet of white velvet tied with wide satin ribbons and plumed with a crystal-spangled marabout—a wedding bonnet ordered for the marriage of her cousin, Charlotte Lovell, which was to take place that week at St. Mark's-in-the-Bouwerie. Charlotte was making a match exactly like Delia's own: marrying a Ralston, of the Waverly Place branch, than which nothing

could be safer, sounder or more—well, usual. Delia did not know why the word had occurred to her, for it could hardly be postulated, even of the young women of her own narrow clan, that they "usually" married Ralstons; but the soundness, safeness, suitability of the arrangement, did make it typical of the kind of alliance which a nice girl in the nicest set would serenely and blushingly forecast for herself.

Yes—and afterward?

Well—what? And what did this new question mean? Afterward: why, of course, there was the startled puzzled surrender to the incomprehensible exigencies of the young man to whom one had at most yielded a rosy cheek in return for an engagement ring; there was the large double-bed; the terror of seeing him shaving calmly the next morning, in his shirtsleeves, through the dressing-room door; the evasions, insinuations, resigned smiles and Bible texts of one's Mamma; the reminder of the phrase "to obey" in the glittering blur of the Marriage Service; a week or a month of flushed distress, confusion, embarrassed pleasure; then the growth of habit, the insidious lulling of the matter-of-course, the dreamless double slumbers in the big white bed, the early morning discussions and consultations through that dressing-room door which had once seemed to open into a fiery pit scorching the brow of innocence.

And then, the babies; the babies who were supposed to "make up for everything," and didn't—though they were such darlings, and one had no definite notion as to what it was that one had missed, and that they were to make up for.

Yes: Charlotte's fate would be just like hers. Joe Ralston was so like his second cousin Jim (Delia's James), that Delia could see no reason why life in the squat brick house in Waverly Place should not exactly resemble life in the tall brownstone house in Gramercy Park. Only Charlotte's bedroom would certainly not be as pretty as hers.

She glanced complacently at the French wall-paper that reproduced a watered silk, with a "valanced" border, and tassels between the loops. The mahogany bedstead, covered with a white embroidered counterpane, was symmetrically reflected in the mirror of a wardrobe which matched it. Coloured lithographs of the "Four Seasons" by Léopold Robert surmounted groups of family daguerreotypes in deeply-recessed gilt frames. The ormolu clock represented a shepherdess sitting on a fallen trunk, a basket of flowers at her feet. A shepherd, stealing up, surprised her with a kiss, while her little dog barked at him from a clump of roses. One knew the profession of the lovers by their crooks and the shape of their hats. This frivolous time-piece had been a wedding-gift from Delia's aunt, Mrs. Manson Mingott, a dashing widow who lived in Paris and was received at the Tuileries. It had been entrusted by Mrs. Mingott to young Clement Spender, who had come back from Italy for a short holiday just after Delia's marriage; the marriage which might never have been, if

The Old Maid

Clem Spender could have supported a wife, or if he had consented to give up painting and Rome for New York and the law. The young man (who looked, already, so odd and foreign and sarcastic) had laughingly assured the bride that her aunt's gift was "the newest thing in the Palais Royal"; and the family, who admired Mrs. Manson Mingott's taste though they disapproved of her "foreignness," had criticized Delia's putting the clock in her bedroom instead of displaying it on the drawing-room mantel. But she liked, when she woke in the morning, to see the bold shepherd stealing his kiss.

Charlotte would certainly not have such a pretty clock in her bedroom; but then she had not been used to pretty things. Her father, who had died at thirty of lung-fever, was one of the "poor Lovells." His widow, burdened with a young family, and living all the year round "up the River," could not do much for her eldest girl; and Charlotte had entered society in her mother's turned garments, and shod with satin sandals handed down from a defunct aunt who had "opened a ball" with General Washington. The old-fashioned Ralston furniture, which Delia already saw herself banishing, would seem sumptuous to Chatty; very likely she would think Delia's gay French timepiece somewhat frivolous, or even not "quite nice." Poor Charlotte had become so serious, so prudish almost, since she had given up balls and taken to visiting the poor! Delia remembered, with ever-recurring wonder, the abrupt change in her: the precise moment at which it had been privately agreed in the family that, after all, Charlotte Lovell was going to be an old maid.

They had not thought so when she came out. Though her mother could not afford to give her more than one new tarlatan dress, and though nearly everything in her appearance was regrettable, from the too bright red of her hair to the too pale brown of her eyes—not to mention the rounds of brick-rose on her cheek-bones, which almost (preposterous thought!) made her look as if she painted—yet these defects were redeemed by a slim waist, a light foot and a gay laugh; and when her hair was well oiled and brushed for an evening party, so that it looked almost brown, and lay smoothly along her delicate cheeks under a wreath of red and white camellias, several eligible young men (Joe Ralston among them) were known to have called her pretty.

Then came her illness. She caught cold on a moonlight sleighing-party, the brick-rose circles deepened, and she began to cough. There was a report that she was "going like her father," and she was hurried off to a remote village in Georgia, where she lived alone for a year with an old family governess. When she came back everyone felt at once that there was a change in her. She was pale, and thinner than ever, but with an exquisitely transparent cheek, darker eyes and redder hair; and the oddness of her appearance was increased by plain dresses of Quakerish cut. She had left off trinkets and watchchains, always wore the same

grey cloak and small close bonnet, and displayed a sudden zeal for visiting the indigent. The family explained that during her year in the south she had been shocked by the hopeless degradation of the "poor whites" and their children, and that this revelation of misery had made it impossible for her to return to the light-hearted life of her young friends. Everyone agreed, with significant glances, that this unnatural state of mind would "pass off in time"; and meanwhile old Mrs. Lovell, Chatty's grandmother, who understood her perhaps better than the others, gave her a little money for her paupers, and lent her a room in the Lovell stables (at the back of the old lady's Mercer Street house) where she gathered about her, in what would afterward have been called a "day-nursery," some of the destitute children of the neighbourhood. There was even, among them, the baby girl whose origin had excited such intense curiosity two or three years earlier, when a veiled lady in a handsome cloak had brought it to the hovel of Cyrus Washington, the negro handy-man whose wife Jessamine took in Dr. Lanskell's washing. Dr. Lanskell, the chief medical practitioner of the day, was presumably versed in the secret history of every household from the Battery to Union Square; but, though beset by inquisitive patients, he had invariably declared himself unable to identify Jessamine's "veiled lady," or to hazard a guess as to the origin of the hundred dollar bill pinned to the baby's bib.

The hundred dollars were never renewed, the lady never reappeared, but the baby lived healthily and happily with Jessamine's piccaninnies, and as soon as it could toddle was brought to Chatty Lovell's day-nursery, where it appeared (like its fellow paupers) in little garments cut down from her old dresses, and socks knitted by her untiring hands. Delia, absorbed in her own babies, had nevertheless dropped in once or twice at the nursery, and had come away wishing that Chatty's maternal instinct might find its normal outlet in marriage. The married cousin confusedly felt that her own affection for her handsome children was a mild and measured sentiment compared with Chatty's fierce passion for the waifs in Grandmamma Lovell's stable.

And then, to the general surprise, Charlotte Lovell engaged herself to Joe Ralston. It was known that Joe had "admired her" the year she came out. She was a graceful dancer, and Joe, who was tall and nimble, had footed it with her through many a reel and *schottische*. By the end of the winter all the match-makers were predicting that something would come of it; but when Delia sounded her cousin, the girl's evasive answer and burning brow seemed to imply that her suitor had changed his mind, and no further questions could be asked. Now it was clear that there had, in fact, been an old romance between them, probably followed by that exciting incident, a "misunderstanding"; but at last all was well, and the bells of St. Mark's were preparing to ring in happier days for Charlotte. "Ah, when she has her first baby," the Ralston mothers chorused . . .

"Chatty!" Delia exclaimed, pushing back her chair as she saw her cousin's image reflected in the glass over her shoulder.

Charlotte Lovell had paused in the doorway. "They told me you were here—so I ran up."

"Of course, darling. How handsome you do look in your poplin! I always said you needed rich materials. I'm so thankful to see you out of grey cashmere." Delia, lifting her hands, removed the white bonnet from her dark polished head, and shook it gently to make the crystals glitter.

"I hope you like it? It's for your wedding," she laughed.

Charlotte Lovell stood motionless. In her mother's old dove-coloured poplin, freshly banded with narrow rows of crimson velvet ribbon, an ermine tippet crossed on her bosom, and a new beaver bonnet with a falling feather, she had already something of the assurance and majesty of a married woman.

"And you know your hair certainly *is* darker, darling," Delia added, still hopefully surveying her.

"Darker? It's grey," Charlotte suddenly broke out in her deep voice. She pushed back one of the pommaded bands that framed her face, and showed a white lock on her temple. "You needn't save up your bonnet; I'm not going to be married," she added, with a smile that showed her small white teeth in a fleeting glare.

Delia had just enough presence of mind to lay down the bonnet, marabout-up, before she flung herself on her cousin.

"Not going to be married? Charlotte, are you perfectly crazy?"

"Why is it crazy to do what I think right?"

"But people said you were going to marry him the year you came out. And no one understood what happened then. And now—how can it possibly be right? You simply *can't!*" Delia incoherently cried.

"Oh—people!" said Charlotte Lovell wearily.

Her married cousin looked at her with a start. Something thrilled in her voice that Delia had never heard in it, or in any other human voice, before. Its echo seemed to set their familiar world rocking, and the Axminster carpet actually heaved under Delia's shrinking slippers.

Charlotte Lovell stood staring ahead of her with strained lids. In the pale brown of her eyes Delia noticed the green specks that floated there when she was angry or excited.

"Charlotte—where on earth have you come from?" she questioned, drawing the girl down to the sofa.

"Come from?"

"Yes. You look as if you had seen a ghost—an army of ghosts."

The same snarling smile drew up Charlotte's lip. "I've seen Joe," she said.

"Well?—Oh, Chatty," Delia exclaimed, abruptly illuminated, "you don't mean to say that you're going to let any little thing in Joe's past—?

Not that I've ever heard the least hint; never. But even if there were . . ."
She drew a deep breath, and bravely proceeded to extremities. "Even
if you've heard that he's been . . . that he's had a child—of course he
would have provided for it before . . ."

The girl shook her head. "I know: you needn't go on. 'Men will be
men'; but it's not that."

"Tell me what it is."

Charlotte Lovell looked about the sunny prosperous room as if it
were the image of her world, and that world were a prison she must
break out of. She lowered her head. "I want—to get away," she panted.

"Get away? From Joe?"

"From his ideas—the Ralston ideas."

Delia bridled—after all, she was a Ralston! "The Ralston ideas?
I haven't found them—so unbearably unpleasant to live with," she smiled
a little tartly.

"No. But it was different with you: they didn't ask you to give up
things."

"What things?" What in the world (Delia wondered) had poor
Charlotte that any one could want her to give up? She had always been
in the position of taking rather than of having to surrender. "Can't you
explain to me, dear?" Delia urged.

"My poor children—he says I'm to give them up," cried the girl
in a stricken whisper.

"Give them up? Give up helping them?"

"Seeing them—looking after them. Give them up altogether. He got
his mother to explain to me. After—after we have children . . . he's
afraid . . . afraid our children might catch things. . . . He'll give me
money, of course, to pay some one . . . a hired person, to look after them.
He thought that handsome," Charlotte broke out with a sob. She flung
off her bonnet and smothered her prostrate weeping in the cushions.

Delia sat perplexed. Of all unforeseen complications this was surely
the least imaginable. And with all the acquired Ralston that was in her
she could not help seeing the force of Joe's objection, could almost find
herself agreeing with him. No one in New York had forgotten the death
of the poor Henry van der Luydens' only child, who had caught small-
pox at the circus to which an unprincipled nurse had surreptitiously taken
him. After such a warning as that, parents felt justified in every precau-
tion against contagion. And poor people were so ignorant and careless,
and their children, of course, so perpetually exposed to everything catch-
ing. No, Joe Ralston was certainly right, and Charlotte almost insanely
unreasonable. But it would be useless to tell her so now. Instinctively,
Delia temporized.

"After all," she whispered to the prone ear, "if it's only after you
have children—you may not have any—for some time."

244

"Oh, yes, I shall!" came back in anguish from the cushions.

Delia smiled with matronly superiority. "Really, Chatty, I don't quite see how you can know. You don't understand."

Charlotte Lovell lifted herself up. Her collar of Brussels lace had come undone and hung in a wisp on her crumpled bodice, and through the disorder of her hair the white lock glimmered haggardly. In her pale brown eyes the little green specks floated like leaves in a trout-pool.

"Poor girl," Delia thought, "how old and ugly she looks! More than ever like an old maid; and she doesn't seem to realize in the least that she'll never have another chance."

"You must try to be sensible, Chatty dear. After all, one's own babies have the first claim."

"That's just it." The girl seized her fiercely by the wrists. "How can I give up my own baby?"

"Your—your—?" Delia's world again began to waver under her. "Which of the poor little waifs, dearest, do you call your own baby?" she questioned patiently.

Charlotte looked her straight in the eyes. "I call my own baby my own baby."

"Your own—? Take care—you're hurting my wrists, Chatty!" Delia freed herself, forcing a smile. "Your own—?"

"My own little girl. The one that Jessamine and Cyrus—"

"Oh—" Delia Ralston gasped.

The two cousins sat silent, facing each other; but Delia looked away. It came over her with a shudder of repugnance that such things, even if they had to be said, should not have been spoken in her bedroom, so near the spotless nursery across the passage. Mechanically she smoothed the organ-like folds of her silk skirt, which her cousin's embrace had tumbled. Then she looked again at Charlotte's eyes, and her own melted.

"Oh, poor Chatty—my poor Chatty!" She held out her arms to her cousin.

II

THE SHEPHERD CONTINUED to steal his kiss from the shepherdess, and the clock in the fallen trunk continued to tick out the minutes.

Delia, petrified, sat unconscious of their passing, her cousin clasped to her. She was dumb with the horror and amazement of learning that her own blood ran in the veins of the anonymous foundling, the "hundred dollar baby" about whom New York had so long furtively jested and conjectured. It was her first contact with the nether side of the smooth social surface, and she sickened at the thought that such things were, and that she, Delia Ralston, should be hearing of them in her own house, and from

the lips of the victim! For Chatty of course was a victim—but whose? She had spoken no name, and Delia could put no question: the horror of it sealed her lips. Her mind had instantly raced back over Chatty's past; but she saw no masculine figure in it but Joe Ralston's. And to connect Joe with the episode was obviously unthinkable. Some one in the south, then—? But no: Charlotte had been ill when she left—and in a flash Delia understood the real nature of that illness, and of the girl's disappearance. But from such speculations too her mind recoiled, and instinctively she fastened on something she could still grasp: Joe Ralston's attitude about Chatty's paupers. Of course Joe could not let his wife risk bringing contagion into their home—that was safe ground to dwell on. Her own Jim would have felt in the same way; and she would certainly have agreed with him.

Her eyes travelled back to the clock. She always thought of Clem Spender when she looked at the clock, and suddenly she wondered—if things had been different—what *he* would have said if she had made such an appeal to him as Charlotte had made to Joe. The thing was hard to imagine; yet in a flash of mental readjustment Delia saw herself as Clem's wife, she saw her children as his, she pictured herself asking him to let her go on caring for the poor waifs in the Mercer Street stable, and she distinctly heard his laugh and his light answer: "Why on earth did you ask, you little goose? Do you take me for such a Pharisee as that?"

Yes, that was Clem Spender all over—tolerant, reckless, indifferent to consequences, always doing the kind thing at the moment, and too often leaving others to pay the score. "There's something cheap about Clem," Jim had once said in his heavy way. Delia Ralston roused herself and pressed her cousin closer. "Chatty, tell me," she whispered.

"There's nothing more."

"I mean, about yourself . . . this thing . . . this . . ." Clem Spender's voice was still in her ears. "You loved some one," she breathed.

"Yes. That's over—. Now it's only the child . . . And I could love Joe—in another way." Chatty Lovell straightened herself, wan and frowning.

"I need the money—I must have it for my baby. Or else they'll send it to an Institution." She paused. "But that's not all. I want to marry—to be a wife, like all of you. I should have loved Joe's children—our children. Life doesn't stop . . ."

"No; I suppose not. But you speak as if . . . as if . . . the person who took advantage of you . . ."

"No one took advantage of me. I was lonely and unhappy. I met some one who was lonely and unhappy. People don't all have your luck. We were both too poor to marry each other . . . and mother would never have consented. And so one day . . . one day before he said goodbye . . ."

"He said goodbye?"

"Yes. He was going to leave the country."

"He left the country—knowing?"

"How was he to know? He doesn't live here. He'd just come back—come back to see his family—for a few weeks . . ." She broke off, her thin lips pressed together upon her secret.

There was a silence. Blindly Delia stared at the bold shepherd.

"Come back from where?" she asked at length in a low tone.

"Oh, what does it matter? You wouldn't understand," Charlotte broke off, in the very words her married cousin had compassionately addressed to her virginity.

A slow blush rose to Delia's cheek: she felt oddly humiliated by the rebuke conveyed in that contemptuous retort. She seemed to herself shy, ineffectual, as incapable as an ignorant girl of dealing with the abominations that Charlotte was thrusting on her. But suddenly some fierce feminine intuition struggled and woke in her. She forced her eyes upon her cousin's.

"You won't tell me who it was?"

"What's the use? I haven't told anybody."

"Then why have you come to me?"

Charlotte's stony face broke up in weeping. "It's for my baby . . . my baby . . ."

Delia did not heed her. "How can I help you if I don't know?" she insisted in a harsh dry voice: her heart-beats were so violent that they seemed to send up throttling hands to her throat.

Charlotte made no answer.

"Come back from where?" Delia doggedly repeated; and at that, with a long wail, the girl flung her hands up, screening her eyes. "He always thought you'd wait for him," she sobbed out, "and then, when he found you hadn't . . . and that you were marrying Jim . . . He heard it just as he was sailing . . . He didn't know it till Mrs. Mingott asked him to bring the clock back for your wedding . . ."

"Stop—stop," Delia cried, springing to her feet. She had provoked the avowal, and now that it had come she felt that it had been gratuitously and indecently thrust upon her. Was this New York, *her* New York, her safe friendly hypocritical New York, was this James Ralston's house, and this his wife listening to such revelations of dishonour?

Charlotte Lovell stood up in her turn. "I knew it—I knew it! You think worse of my baby now, instead of better . . . Oh, why did you make me tell you? I knew you'd never understand. I'd always cared for him, ever since I came out; that was why I wouldn't marry any one else. But I knew there was no hope for me . . . he never looked at anybody but you. And then, when he came back four years ago, and there was no *you* for him any more, he began to notice me, to be kind, to talk to me about his life and his painting . . ." She drew a deep breath, and her voice cleared. "That's over—all over. It's as if I couldn't either hate him

247

or love him. There's only the child now—my child. He doesn't even know of it—why should he? It's none of his business; it's nobody's business but mine. But surely you must see that I can't give up my baby."

Delia Ralston stood speechless, looking away from her cousin in a growing horror. She had lost all sense of reality, all feeling of safety and self-reliance. Her impulse was to close her ears to the other's appeal as a child buries its head from midnight terrors. At last she drew herself up, and spoke with dry lips.

"But what do you mean to do? Why have you come to me? Why have you told me all this?"

"Because he loved you!" Charlotte Lovell stammered out; and the two women stood and faced each other.

Slowly the tears rose to Delia's eyes and rolled down her cheeks, moistening her parched lips. Through the tears she saw her cousin's haggard countenance waver and droop like a drowning face under water. Things half-guessed, obscurely felt, surged up from unsuspected depths in her. It was almost as if, for a moment, this other woman were telling her of her own secret past, putting into crude words all the trembling silences of her own heart.

The worst of it was, as Charlotte said, that they must act now; there was not a day to lose. Chatty was right—it was impossible that she should marry Joe if to do so meant giving up the child. But, in any case, how could she marry him without telling him the truth? And was it conceivable that, after hearing it, he should not repudiate her? All these questions spun agonizingly through Delia's brain, and through them glimmered the persistent vision of the child—Clem Spender's child—growing up on charity in a negro hovel, or herded in one of the plague-houses they called Asylums. No: the child came first—she felt it in every fibre of her body. But what should she do, of whom take counsel, how advise the wretched creature who had come to her in Clement's name? Delia glanced about her desperately, and then turned back to her cousin.

"You must give me time. I must think. You ought not to marry him— and yet all the arrangements are made; and the wedding-presents . . . There would be a scandal . . . it would kill Granny Lovell . . ."

Charlotte answered in a low voice: "There *is* no time. I must decide now."

Delia pressed her hands against her breast. "I tell you I must think. I wish you would go home.—Or, no: stay here: your mother mustn't see your eyes. Jim's not coming home till late; you can wait in this room till I come back." She had opened the wardrobe and was reaching up for a plain bonnet and heavy veil.

"Stay here? But where are you going?"

"I don't know. I want to walk—to get the air. I think I want to be alone." Feverishly, Delia unfolded her Paisley shawl, tied on bonnet and

veil, thrust her mittened hands into her muff. Charlotte, without moving, stared at her dumbly from the sofa.

"You'll wait," Delia insisted, on the threshold.

"Yes: I'll wait."

Delia shut the door and hurried down the stairs.

III

SHE HAD SPOKEN THE TRUTH in saying that she did not know where she was going. She simply wanted to get away from Charlotte's unbearable face, and from the immediate atmosphere of her tragedy. Outside, in the open, perhaps it would be easier to think.

As she skirted the park-rails she saw her rosy children playing, under their nurse's eye, with the pampered progeny of other square-dwellers. The little girl had on her new plaid velvet bonnet and white tippet, and the boy his Highland cap and broad-cloth spencer. How happy and jolly they looked! The nurse spied her, but she shook her head, waved at the group and hurried on.

She walked and walked through the familiar streets decked with bright winter sunshine. It was early afternoon, an hour when the gentlemen had just returned to their offices, and there were few pedestrians in Irving Place and Union Square. Delia crossed the Square to Broadway.

The Lovell house in Mercer Street was a sturdy old-fashioned brick dwelling. A large stable adjoined it, opening on an alley such as Delia, on her honey-moon trip to England, had heard called a "mews." She turned into the alley, entered the stable court, and pushed open a door. In a shabby white-washed room a dozen children, gathered about a stove, were playing with broken toys. The Irishwoman who had charge of them was cutting out small garments on a broken-legged deal table. She raised a friendly face, recognizing Delia as the lady who had once or twice been to see the children with Miss Charlotte.

Delia paused, embarrassed.

"I—I came to ask if you need any new toys," she stammered.

"That we do, ma'am. And many another thing too, though Miss Charlotte tells me I'm not to beg of the ladies that comes to see our poor darlin's."

"Oh, you may beg of me, Bridget," Mrs. Ralston answered, smiling. "Let me see your babies—it's so long since I've been here."

The children had stopped playing and, huddled against their nurse, gazed up open-mouthed at the rich rustling lady. One little girl with pale brown eyes and scarlet cheeks was dressed in a plaid alpaca frock trimmed with imitation coral buttons that Delia remembered. Those buttons had been on Charlotte's "best dress" the year she came out. Delia stopped and took up the child. Its curly hair was brown, the exact colour

of the eyes—thank heaven! But the eyes had the same little green spangles floating in their transparency. Delia sat down, and the little girl, standing on her knee, gravely fingered her watch-chain.

"Oh, ma'am—maybe her shoes'll soil your skirt. The floor here ain't none too clean."

Delia shook her head, and pressed the child against her. She had forgotten the other gazing babies and their wardress. The little creature on her knee was made of different stuff—it had not needed the plaid alpaca and coral buttons to single her out. Her brown curls grew in points on her high forehead, exactly as Clement Spender's did. Delia laid a burning cheek against the forehead.

"Baby want my lovely yellow chain?"

Baby did.

Delia unfastened the gold chain and hung it about the child's neck. The other babies clapped and crowed, but the little girl, gravely dimpling, continued to finger the links in silence.

"Oh, ma'am, you can't leave that fine chain on little Teeny. When she has to go back to those blacks . . ."

"What is her name?"

"Teena they call her, I believe. It don't seem a Christian name, har'ly."

Delia was silent.

"What I say is, her cheeks is too red. And she coughs too easy. Always one cold and another. Here, Teeny, leave the lady go."

Delia stood up, loosening the tender arms.

"She doesn't want to leave go of you, ma'am. Miss Chatty ain't been in today, and the little thing's kinder lonesome without her. She don't play like the other children, somehow . . . Teeny, you look at that lovely chain you've got . . . there, there now . . ."

"Goodbye, Clementina," Delia whispered below her breath. She kissed the pale brown eyes, the curly crown, and dropped her veil on rushing tears. In the stable-yard she dried them on her large embroidered handkerchief, and stood hesitating. Then with a decided step she turned toward home.

The house was as she had left it, except that the children had come in; she heard them romping in the nursery as she went down the passage to her bedroom. Charlotte Lovell was seated on the sofa, upright and rigid, as Delia had left her.

"Chatty—Chatty, I've thought it out. Listen. Whatever happens, the baby shan't stay with those people. I mean to keep her."

Charlotte stood up, tall and white. The eyes in her thin face had grown so dark that they seemed like spectral hollows in a skull. She opened her lips to speak, and then, snatching at her handkerchief, pressed it to her mouth, and sank down again. A red trickle dripped through the handkerchief onto her poplin skirt.

"Charlotte—Charlotte," Delia screamed, on her knees beside her cousin. Charlotte's head slid back against the cushions and the trickle ceased. She closed her eyes, and Delia, seizing a vinaigrette from the dressing-table, held it to her pinched nostrils. The room was filled with an acrid aromatic scent.

Charlotte's lids lifted. "Don't be frightened. I still spit blood some-times—not often. My lung is nearly healed. But it's the terror—"

"No, no: there's to be no more terror. I tell you I've thought it all out. Jim is going to let me take the baby."

The girl raised herself haggardly. "Jim? Have you told him? Is that where you've been?"

"No, darling. I've only been to see the baby."

"Oh," Charlotte moaned, leaning back again. Delia took her own handkerchief, and wiped away the tears that were raining down her cousin's cheeks.

"You mustn't cry, Chatty; you must be brave. Your little girl and his—how could you think? But you must give me time: I must manage it in my own way . . . Only trust me . . ."

Charlotte's lips stirred faintly.

"The tears . . . don't dry them, Delia. . . . I like to feel them . . ."

The two cousins continued to lean against each other without speak-ing. The ormolu clock ticked out the measure of their mute communion in minutes, quarters, a half-hour, then an hour: the day declined and darkened, the shadows lengthened across the garlands of the Axminster and the broad white bed. There was a knock.

"The children's waiting to say their grace before supper, ma'am."

"Yes, Eliza. Let them say it to you. I'll come later." As the nurse's steps receded Charlotte Lovell disengaged herself from Delia's embrace.

"Now I can go," she said.

"You're not too weak, dear? I can send for a coach to take you home."

"No, no; it would frighten mother. And I shall like walking now, in the darkness. Sometimes the world used to seem all one awful glare to me. There were days when I thought the sun would never set. And then there was the moon at night." She laid her hands on her cousin's shoulders. "Now it's different. By and by I shan't hate the light."

The two women kissed each other, and Delia whispered: "Tomorrow."

IV

THE RALSTONS GAVE UP old customs reluctantly, but once they had adopted a new one they found it impossible to understand why every-one else did not immediately do likewise.

When Delia, who came of the laxer Lovells, and was naturally in-

clined to novelty, had first proposed to her husband to dine at six o'clock instead of two, his malleable young face had become as relentless as that of the old original Ralston in his grim Colonial portrait. But after a two days' resistance he had come round to his wife's view, and now smiled contemptuously at the obstinacy of those who clung to a heavy mid-day meal and high tea.

"There's nothing I hate like narrow-mindedness. Let people eat when they like, for all I care: it's their narrow-mindedness that I can't stand."

Delia was thinking of this as she sat in the drawing-room (her mother would have called it the parlour) waiting for her husband's return. She had just had time to smooth her glossy braids, and slip on the black-and-white striped moire with cherry pipings which was his favourite dress. The drawing-room, with its Nottingham lace curtains looped back under florid gilt cornices, its marble centre-table on a carved rosewood foot, and its old-fashioned mahogany armchairs covered with one of the new French silk damasks in a tart shade of apple-green, was one for any young wife to be proud of. The rosewood what-nots on each side of the folding doors that led into the dining-room were adorned with tropical shells, feld-spar vases, an alabaster model of the Leaning Tower of Pisa, a pair of obelisks made of scraps of porphyry and serpentine picked up by the young couple in the Roman Forum, a bust of Clytie in chalk-white biscuit de Sèvres, and four old-fashioned figures of the Seasons in Chelsea ware, that had to be left among the newer ornaments because they had belonged to great-grandmamma Ralston. On the walls hung large dark steel-engravings of Cole's "Voyage of Life," and between the windows stood the life-size statue of "A Captive Maiden" executed for Jim Ralston's father by the celebrated Harriet Hosmer, immortalized in Hawthorne's novel of the Marble Faun. On the table lay handsomely tooled copies of Turner's Rivers of France, Drake's Culprit Fay, Crabbe's Tales, and the Book of Beauty containing portraits of the British peeresses who had participated in the Earl of Eglinton's tournament.

As Delia sat there, before the hard-coal fire in its arched opening of black marble, her citron-wood work-table at her side, and one of the new French lamps shedding a pleasant light on the centre-table from under a crystal-fringed shade, she asked herself how she could have passed, in such a short time, so completely out of her usual circle of impressions and convictions—so much farther than ever before beyond the Ralston horizon. Here it was, closing in on her again, as if the very plaster ornaments of the ceiling, the forms of the furniture, the cut of her dress, had been built out of Ralston prejudices, and turned to adamant by the touch of Ralston hands.

She must have been mad, she thought, to have committed herself so far to Charlotte; yet, turn about as she would in the ever-tightening

circle of the problem, she could still find no other issue. Somehow, it lay with her to save Clem Spender's baby.

She heard the sound of the latch-key (her heart had never beat so high at it), and the putting down of a tall hat on the hall console—or of two tall hats, was it? The drawing-room door opened, and two high-stocked and ample-coated young men came in: two Jim Ralstons, so to speak. Delia had never before noticed how much her husband and his cousin Joe were alike; it made her feel how justified she was in always thinking of the Ralstons collectively.

She would not have been young and tender, and a happy wife, if she had not thought Joe but an indifferent copy of her Jim; yet, allowing for defects in the reproduction, there remained a striking likeness between the two tall athletic figures, the short sanguine faces with straight noses, straight whiskers, straight brows, candid blue eyes and sweet selfish smiles. Only, at the present moment, Joe looked like Jim with a tooth-ache.

"Look here, my dear: here's a young man who's asked to take pot-luck with us," Jim smiled, with the confidence of a well-nourished husband who knows that he can always bring a friend home.

"How nice of you, Joe!—Do you suppose he can put up with oyster soup and a stuffed goose?" Delia beamed upon her husband.

"I knew it! I told you so, my dear chap! He said you wouldn't like it—that you'd be fussed about the dinner. Wait till you're married, Joseph Ralston—." Jim brought down a genial paw on his cousin's bottle-green shoulder, and Joe grimaced as if the tooth had stabbed him.

"It's excessively kind of you, cousin Delia, to take me in this evening. The fact is—"

"Dinner first, my boy, if you don't mind! A bottle of Burgundy will brush away the blue devils. Your arm to your cousin, please; I'll just go and see that the wine is brought up."

Oyster soup, broiled bass, stuffed goose, apple fritters and green peppers, followed by one of Grandmamma Ralston's famous caramel custards: through all her mental anguish, Delia was faintly aware of a secret pride in her achievement. Certainly it would serve to confirm the rumour that Jim Ralston could always bring a friend home to dine without notice. The Ralston and Lovell wines rounded off the effect, and even Joe's drawn face had mellowed by the time the Lovell Madeira started westward. Delia marked the change when the two young men rejoined her in the drawing-room.

"And now, my dear fellow, you'd better tell her the whole story," Jim counselled, pushing an armchair toward his cousin.

The young woman, bent above her wool-work, listened with lowered lids and flushed cheeks. As a married woman—as a mother—Joe hoped she would think him justified in speaking to her frankly: he had her husband's authority to do so.

"Oh, go ahead, go ahead," chafed the exuberant after-dinner Jim from the hearth-rug.

Delia listened, considered, let the bridegroom flounder on through his embarrassed exposition. Her needle hung like a sword of Damocles above the canvas; she saw at once that Joe depended on her trying to win Charlotte over to his way of thinking. But he was very much in love: at a word from Delia, she understood that he would yield, and Charlotte gain her point, save the child, and marry him . . .

How easy it was, after all! A friendly welcome, a good dinner, a ripe wine, and the memory of Charlotte's eyes—so much the more expressive for all that they had looked upon. A secret envy stabbed the wife who had lacked this last enlightenment.

How easy it was—and yet it must not be! Whatever happened, she could not let Charlotte Lovell marry Joe Ralston. All the traditions of honour and probity in which she had been brought up forbade her to connive at such a plan. She could conceive—had already conceived—of high-handed measures, swift and adroit defiances of precedent, subtle revolts against the heartlessness of the social routine. But a lie she could never connive at. The idea of Charlotte's marrying Joe Ralston—her own Jim's cousin—without revealing her past to him, seemed to Delia as dishonourable as it would have seemed to any Ralston. And to tell him the truth would at once put an end to the marriage; of that even Chatty was aware. Social tolerance was not dealt in the same measure to men and to women, and neither Delia nor Charlotte had ever wondered why: like all the young women of their class they simply bowed to the ineluctable.

No; there was no escape from the dilemma. As clearly as it was Delia's duty to save Clem Spender's child, so clearly, also, she seemed destined to sacrifice his mistress. As the thought pressed on her she remembered Charlotte's wistful cry: "I want to be married, like all of you," and her heart tightened. But yet it must not be.

"I make every allowance" (Joe was droning on) "for my sweet girl's ignorance and inexperience—for her lovely purity. How could a man wish his future wife to be—to be otherwise? You're with me, Jim? and Delia? I've told her, you understand, that she shall always have a special sum set apart for her poor children—in addition to her pin-money; on that she may absolutely count. God! I'm willing to draw up a deed, a settlement, before a lawyer, if she says so. I admire, I appreciate her generosity. But I ask you, Delia, as a mother—mind you, now, I want your frank opinion. If you think I can stretch a point—can let her go on giving her personal care to these children until . . . until . . ." A flush of pride suffused the potential father's brow . . . "till nearer duties claim her, why, I'm more than ready . . . if you'll tell her so. I undertake," Joe proclaimed, suddenly tingling with the memory of his last glass, "to make it right with my mother, whose prejudices, of course,

while I respect them, I can never allow to—to come between me and my own convictions." He sprang to his feet, and beamed on his dauntless double in the chimney-mirror. "My convictions," he flung back at it.

"Hear, hear!" cried Jim emotionally.

Delia's needle gave the canvas a sharp prick, and she pushed her work aside.

"I think I understand you both, Joe. Certainly, in Charlotte's place, I could never give up those children."

"There you are, my dear fellow!" Jim triumphed, as proud of this vicarious courage as of the perfection of the dinner.

"Never," said Delia. "Especially, I mean, the foundlings—there are two, I think. Those children always die if they are sent to asylums. That is what is haunting Chatty."

"Poor innocents! How I love her for loving them! That there should be such scoundrels upon this earth unpunished—. Delia, will you tell her that I'll do whatever—"

"Gently, old man, gently," Jim admonished him, with a flash of Ralston caution.

"Well, that is to say, whatever—in reason—"

Delia lifted an arresting hand. "I'll tell her, Joe: she will be grateful. But it's of no use—"

"No use? What more—?"

"Nothing more: except this. Charlotte has had a return of her old illness. She coughed blood here today. You must not marry her."

There: it was done. She stood up, trembling in every bone, and feeling herself pale to the lips. Had she done right? Had she done wrong? And would she ever know?

Poor Joe turned on her a face as wan as hers: he clutched the back of his armchair, his head drooping forward like an old man's. His lips moved, but made no sound.

"My God!" Jim stammered. "But you know you've got to buck up, old boy."

"I'm—I'm so sorry for you, Joe. She'll tell you herself tomorrow," Delia faltered, while her husband continued to proffer heavy consolations.

"Take it like a man, old chap. Think of yourself—your future. Can't be, you know. Delia's right; she always *is*. Better get it over—better face the music now than later."

"Now than later," Joe echoed with a tortured grin; and it occurred to Delia that never before in the course of his easy good-natured life had he had—any more than her Jim—to give up anything his heart was set on. Even the vocabulary of renunciation, and its conventional gestures, were unfamiliar to him.

"But I don't understand. I can't give her up," he declared, blinking away a boyish tear.

"Think of the children, my dear fellow; it's your duty," Jim in-

sisted, checking a glance of pride at Delia's wholesome comeliness.

In the long conversation that followed between the cousins—argument, counter-argument, sage counsel and hopeless protest—Delia took but an occasional part. She knew well enough what the end would be. The bridegroom who had feared that his bride might bring home contagion from her visits to the poor would not knowingly implant disease in his race. Nor was that all. Too many sad instances of mothers prematurely fading, and leaving their husbands alone with a young flock to rear, must be pressing upon Joe's memory. Ralstons, Lovells, Lannings, Archers, van der Luydens—which one of them had not some grave to care for in a distant cemetery: graves of young relatives "in a decline," sent abroad to be cured by balmy Italy? The Protestant grave-yards of Rome and Pisa were full of New York names; the vision of that familiar pilgrimage with a dying wife was one to turn the most ardent Ralston cold. And all the while, as she listened with bent head, Delia kept repeating to herself: "This is easy; but how am I going to tell Charlotte?"

When poor Joe, late that evening, wrung her hand with a stammered farewell, she called him back abruptly from the threshold.

"You must let me see her first, please; you must wait till she sends for you—" and she winced a little at the alacrity of his acceptance. But no amount of rhetorical bolstering-up could make it easy for a young man to face what lay ahead of Joe; and her final glance at him was one of compassion . . .

The front door closed upon Joe, and she was roused by her husband's touch on her shoulder.

"I never admired you more, darling. My wise Delia!"

Her head bent back, she took his kiss, and then drew apart. The sparkle in his eyes she understood to be as much an invitation to her bloom as a tribute to her sagacity.

She held him at arms' length. "What should you have done, Jim, if I'd had to tell you about myself what I've just told Joe about Chatty?"

A slight frown showed that he thought the question negligible, and hardly in her usual taste. "Come," his strong arm entreated her.

She continued to stand away from him, with grave eyes. "Poor Chatty! Nothing left now—"

His own eyes grew grave, in instant sympathy. At such moments he was still the sentimental boy whom she could manage.

"Ah, poor Chatty, indeed!" He groped for the readiest panacea. "Lucky, now, after all, that she has those paupers, isn't it? I suppose a woman *must* have children to love—somebody else's if not her own." It was evident that the thought of the remedy had already relieved his pain.

"Yes," Delia agreed, "I see no other comfort for her. I'm sure Joe will feel that too. Between us, darling—" and now she let him have her hands—"between us, you and I must see to it that she keeps her babies."

"Her babies?" He smiled at the possessive pronoun. "Of course, poor girl! Unless indeed she's sent to Italy?"

"Oh, she won't be that—where's the money to come from? And, besides, she'd never leave Aunt Lovell. But I thought, dear, if I might tell her tomorrow—you see, I'm not exactly looking forward to my talk with her—if I might tell her that you would let me look after the baby she's most worried about, the poor little foundling girl who has no name and no home—if I might put aside a fixed sum from my pin-money . . ."

Their hands flowed together, she lifted her flushing face to his. Manly tears were in his eyes; ah, how he triumphed in her health, her wisdom, her generosity!

"Not a penny from your pin-money—never!"

She feighed discouragement and wonder. "Think, dear—if I'd had to give you up!"

"Not a penny from your pin-money, I say—but as much more as you need, to help poor Chatty's pauper. There—will that content you?"

"Dearest! When I think of our own, upstairs!" They held each other, awed by that evocation.

V

CHARLOTTE LOVELL, at the sound of her cousin's step, lifted a fevered face from the pillow.

The bedroom, dim and close, smelt of eau de Cologne and fresh linen. Delia, blinking in from the bright winter sun, had to feel her way through a twilight obstructed by dark mahogany.

"I want to see your face, Chatty: unless your head aches too much?"

Charlotte signed "No," and Delia drew back the heavy window curtains and let in a ray of light. In it she saw the girl's head, livid against the bed-linen, the brick-rose circles again visible under darkly shadowed lids. Just so, she remembered, poor cousin So-and-so had looked the week before she sailed for Italy!

"Delia!" Charlotte breathed.

Delia drew near the bed, and stood looking down at her cousin with new eyes. Yes: it had been easy enough, the night before, to dispose of Chatty's future as if it were her own. But now?

"Darling—"

"Oh, begin, please," the girl interrupted, "or I shall know that what's coming is too dreadful!"

"Chatty, dearest, if I promised you too much—"

"Jim won't let you take my child? I knew it! Shall I always go on dreaming things that can never be?"

Delia, her tears running down, knelt by the bed and gave her fresh hand into the other's burning clutch.

257

"Don't think that, dear: think only of what you'd like best . . ."

"Like best?" The girl sat up sharply against her pillows, alive to the hot fingertips.

"You can't marry Joe, dear—can you—and keep little Tina?" Delia continued.

"Not keep her with me, no: but somewhere where I could slip off to see her—oh, I had hoped such follies!"

"Give up follies, Charlotte. Keep her where? See your own child in secret? Always in dread of disgrace? Of wrong to your other children? Have you ever thought of that?"

"Oh, my poor head won't think! You're trying to tell me that I must give her up?"

"No, dear; but that you must not marry Joe."

Charlotte sank back on the pillow, her eyes half-closed. "I tell you I must make my child a home. Delia, you're too blest to understand!"

"Think yourself blest too, Chatty. You shan't give up your baby. She shall live with you: you shall take care of her—for me."

"For you?"

"I promised you I'd take her, didn't I? But not that you should marry Joe. Only that I would make a home for your baby. Well, that's done; you two shall be always together."

Charlotte clung to her and sobbed. "But Joe—I can't tell him, I can't!" She put back Delia suddenly. "You haven't told him of my— of my baby? I couldn't bear to hurt him as much as that."

"I told him that you coughed blood yesterday. He'll see you presently: he's dreadfully unhappy. He has been given to understand that, in view of your bad health, the engagement is broken by your wish— and he accepts your decision; but if he weakens, or if you weaken, I can do nothing for you or for little Tina. For heaven's sake remember that!"

Delia released her hold, and Charlotte leaned back silent, with closed eyes and narrowed lips. Almost like a corpse she lay there. On a chair near the bed hung the poplin with red velvet ribbons which had been made over in honour of her betrothal. A pair of new slippers of bronze kid peeped from beneath it. Poor Chatty! She had hardly had time to be pretty . . .

Delia sat by the bed motionless, her eyes on her cousin's closed face. They followed the course of a tear that forced a way between Charlotte's tight lids, hung on the lashes, glittered slowly down the cheeks. As the tear reached the narrowed lips they spoke.

"Shall I live with her somewhere, do you mean? Just she and I together?"

"Just you and she."

"In a little house?"

"In a little house . . ."

"You're sure, Delia?"

"Sure, my dearest."

Charlotte once more raised herself on her elbow and sent a hand groping under the pillow. She drew out a narrow ribbon on which hung a diamond ring.

"I had taken it off already," she said simply, and handed it to Delia.

Part 2

VI

YOU COULD ALWAYS HAVE TOLD, every one agreed afterward, that Charlotte Lovell was meant to be an old maid. Even before her illness it had been manifest: there was something prim about her in spite of her fiery hair. Lucky enough for her, poor girl, considering her wretched health in her youth: Mrs. James Ralston's contemporaries, for instance, remembered Charlotte as a mere ghost, coughing her lungs out— that, of course, had been the reason for her breaking her engagement with Joe Ralston.

True, she had recovered very rapidly, in spite of the peculiar treatment she was given. The Lovells, as every one knew, couldn't afford to send her to Italy; the previous experiment in Georgia had been unsuccessful; and so she was packed off to a farm-house on the Hudson—a little place on the James Ralstons' property—where she lived for five or six years with an Irish servant-woman and a foundling baby. The story of the foundling was another queer episode in Charlotte's history. From the time of her first illness, when she was only twenty-two or three, she had developed an almost morbid tenderness for children, especially for the children of the poor. It was said—Dr. Lanskell was understood to have said—that the baffled instinct of motherhood was peculiarly intense in cases where lung-disease prevented marriage. And so, when it was decided that Chatty must break her engagement to Joe Ralston and go to live in the country, the doctor had told her family that the only hope of saving her lay in not separating her entirely from her pauper children, but in letting her choose one of them, the youngest and most pitiable, and devote herself to its care. So the James Ralstons had lent her their little farm-house, and Mrs. Jim, with her extraordinary gift of taking things in at a glance, had at once arranged everything, and even pledged herself to look after the baby if Charlotte died.

Charlotte did not die. She lived to grow robust and middle-aged, energetic and even tyrannical. And as the transformation in her char-

acter took place she became more and more like the typical old maid: precise, methodical, absorbed in trifles, and attaching an exaggerated importance to the smallest social and domestic observances. Such was her reputation as a vigilant house-wife that, when poor Jim Ralston was killed by a fall from his horse, and left Delia, still young, with a boy and girl to bring up, it seemed perfectly natural that the heart-broken widow should take her cousin to live with her and share her task. But Delia Ralston never did things quite like other people. When she took Charlotte she took Charlotte's foundling too: a dark-haired child with pale brown eyes, and the odd incisive manner of children who have lived too much with their elders. The little girl was called Tina Lovell: it was vaguely supposed that Charlotte had adopted her. She grew up on terms of affectionate equality with her young Ralston cousins, and almost as much so—it might be said—with the two women who mothered her. But, impelled by an instinct of imitation which no one took the trouble to correct, she always called Delia Ralston "Mamma," and Charlotte Lovell "Aunt Chatty." She was a brilliant and engaging creature, and people marvelled at poor Chatty's luck in having chosen so interesting a specimen among her foundlings (for she was by this time supposed to have had a whole asylum-full to choose from).

The agreeable elderly bachelor, Sillerton Jackson, returning from a prolonged sojourn in Paris (where he was understood to have been made much of by the highest personages) was immensely struck by Tina's charms when he saw her at her coming-out ball, and asked Delia's permission to come some evening and dine alone with her and her young people. He complimented the widow on the rosy beauty of her own young Delia; but the mother's keen eye perceived that all the while he was watching Tina, and after dinner he confided to the older ladies that there was something "very French" in the girl's way of doing her hair, and that in the capital of all the Elegances she would have been pronounced extremely stylish.

"Oh—" Delia deprecated, beamingly, while Charlotte Lovell sat bent over her work with pinched lips; but Tina, who had been laughing with her cousins at the other end of the room, was around upon her elders in a flash.

"I heard what Mr. Sillerton said! Yes, I did, Mamma: he says I do my hair stylishly. Didn't I always tell you so? I *know* it's more becoming to let it curl as it wants to than to plaster it down with bandoline like Aunty's—"

"Tina, Tina—you always think people are admiring you!" Miss Lovell protested.

"Why shouldn't I, when they do?" the girl laughingly challenged; and, turning her mocking eyes on Sillerton Jackson: "Do tell Aunt Charlotte not to be so dreadfully old-maidish!"

The Old Maid

Delia saw the blood rise to Charlotte Lovell's face. It no longer painted two brick-rose circles on her thin cheek-bones, but diffused a harsh flush over her whole countenance, from the collar fastened with an old-fashioned garnet brooch to the pepper-and-salt hair (with no trace of red left in it) flattened down over her hollow temples.

That evening, when they went up to bed, Delia called Tina into her room.

"You ought not to speak to your Aunt Charlotte as you did this evening, dear. It's disrespectful—you must see that it hurts her."

The girl overflowed with compunction. "Oh, I'm so sorry! Because I said she was an old maid? But she *is,* isn't she, Mamma? In her inmost soul, I mean. I don't believe she's ever been young—ever thought of fun or admiration or falling in love—do you? That's why she never understands me, and you always do, you darling dear Mamma." With one of her light movements, Tina was in the widow's arms.

"Child, child," Delia softly scolded, kissing the dark curls planted in five points on the girl's forehead.

There was a soft foot-fall in the passage, and Charlotte Lovell stood in the door. Delia, without moving, sent her a glance of welcome over Tina's shoulder.

"Come in, Charlotte. I'm scolding Tina for behaving like a spoilt baby before Sillerton Jackson. What will he think of her?"

"Just what she deserves, probably," Charlotte returned with a cold smile. Tina went toward her, and her thin lips touched the girl's proffered forehead just where Delia's warm kiss had rested. "Goodnight, child," she said in her dry tone of dismissal.

The door closed on the two women, and Delia signed to Charlotte to take the armchair opposite to her own.

"Not so near the fire," Miss Lovell answered. She chose a straight-backed seat, and sat down with folded hands. Delia's eyes rested absently on the thin ringless fingers: she wondered why Charlotte never wore her mother's jewels.

"I overheard what you were saying to Tina, Delia. You were scolding her because she called me an old maid."

It was Delia's turn to colour. "I scolded her for being disrespectful, dear; if you heard what I said you can't think that I was too severe."

"Not too severe: no. I've never thought you too severe with Tina; on the contrary."

"You think I spoil her?"

"Sometimes."

Delia felt an unreasoning resentment. "What was it I said that you object to?"

Charlotte returned her glance steadily. "I would rather she thought me an old maid than—"

"Oh—" Delia murmured. With one of her quick leaps of intuition

she had entered into the other's soul, and once more measured its shuddering loneliness.

"What else," Charlotte inexorably pursued, "*can* she possibly be allowed to think me—ever?"

"I see . . . I see . . ." the widow faltered.

"A ridiculous narrow-minded old maid—nothing else," Charlotte Lovell insisted, getting to her feet, "or I shall never feel safe with her."

"Goodnight, my dear," Delia said compassionately. There were moments when she almost hated Charlotte for being Tina's mother, and others, such as this, when her heart was wrung by the tragic spectacle of that unavowed bond.

Charlotte seemed to have divined her thought.

"Oh, but don't pity me! She's mine," she murmured, going.

VII

DELIA RALSTON SOMETIMES FELT that the real events of her life did not begin until both her children had contracted—so safely and suitably—their irreproachable New York alliances. The boy had married first, choosing a Vandergrave in whose father's bank at Albany he was to have an immediate junior partnership; and young Delia (as her mother had foreseen she would) had selected John Junius, the safest and soundest of the many young Halseys, and followed him to his parents' house the year after her brother's marriage.

After young Delia had left the house in Gramercy Park it was inevitable that Tina should take the centre front of its narrow stage. Tina had reached the marriageable age, she was admired and sought after; but what hope was there of her finding a husband? The two watchful women did not propound this question to each other; but Delia Ralston, brooding over it day by day, and taking it up with her when she mounted at night to her bedroom, knew that Charlotte Lovell, at the same hour, carried the same problem with her to the floor above.

The two cousins, during their eight years of life together, had seldom openly disagreed. Indeed, it might almost have been said that there was nothing open in their relation. Delia would have had it otherwise: after they had once looked so deeply into each other's souls it seemed unnatural that a veil should fall between them. But she understood that Tina's ignorance of her origin must at all costs be preserved, and that Charlotte Lovell, abrupt, passionate and inarticulate, knew of no other security than to wall herself up in perpetual silence.

So far had she carried this self-imposed reticence that Mrs. Ralston was surprised at her suddenly asking, soon after young Delia's marriage, to be allowed to move down into the small bedroom next to Tina's that had been left vacant by the bride's departure.

"But you'll be so much less comfortable there, Chatty. Have you thought of that? Or is it on account of the stairs?"

"No; it's not the stairs," Charlotte answered with her usual bluntness. How could she avail herself of the pretext Delia offered her, when Delia knew that she still ran up and down the three flights like a girl? "It's because I should be next to Tina," she said, in a low voice that jarred like an untuned string.

"Oh—very well. As you please." Mrs. Ralston could not tell why she felt suddenly irritated by the request, unless it were that she had already amused herself with the idea of fitting up the vacant room as a sitting-room for Tina. She had meant to do it in pink and pale green, like an opening flower.

"Of course, if there is any reason—" Charlotte suggested, as if reading her thought.

"None whatever; except that—well, I'd meant to surprise Tina by doing the room up as a sort of little boudoir where she could have her books and things, and see her girl friends."

"You're too kind, Delia; but Tina mustn't have boudoirs," Miss Lovell answered ironically, the green specks showing in her eyes.

"Very well: as you please," Delia repeated, in the same irritated tone. "I'll have your things brought down tomorrow."

Charlotte paused in the doorway. "You're sure there's no other reason?"

"Other reason? Why should there be?" The two women looked at each other almost with hostility, and Charlotte turned to go.

The talk once over, Delia was annoyed with herself for having yielded to Charlotte's wish. Why must it always be she who gave in, she who, after all, was the mistress of the house, and to whom both Charlotte and Tina might almost be said to owe their very existence, or at least all that made it worth having? Yet whenever any question arose about the girl it was invariably Charlotte who gained her point, Delia who yielded: it seemed as if Charlotte, in her mute obstinate way, were determined to take every advantage of the dependence that made it impossible for a woman of Delia's nature to oppose her.

In truth, Delia had looked forward more than she knew to the quiet talks with Tina to which the little boudoir would have lent itself. While her own daughter inhabited the room, Mrs. Ralston had been in the habit of spending an hour there every evening, chatting with the two girls while they undressed, and listening to their comments on the incidents of the day. She always knew beforehand exactly what her own girl would say; but Tina's views and opinions were a perpetual delicious shock to her. Not that they were strange or unfamiliar; there were moments when they seemed to well straight up from the dumb depths of Delia's own past. Only they expressed feelings she had never uttered, ideas she had hardly avowed to herself: Tina sometimes said things which Delia Ralston, in

far-off self-communions, had imagined herself saying to Clement Spender.

And now there would be an end to these evening talks: if Charlotte had asked to be lodged next to her daughter, might it not conceivably be because she wished them to end? It had never before occurred to Delia that her influence over Tina might be resented; now the discovery flashed a light far down into the abyss which had always divided the two women. But a moment later Delia reproached herself for attributing feelings of jealousy to her cousin. Was it not rather to herself that she should have ascribed them? Charlotte, as Tina's mother, had every right to wish to be near her, near her in all senses of the word; what claim had Delia to oppose to that natural privilege? The next morning she gave the order that Charlotte's things should be taken down to the room next to Tina's.

That evening, when bedtime came, Charlotte and Tina went upstairs together; but Delia lingered in the drawing-room, on the pretext of having letters to write. In truth, she dreaded to pass the threshold where, evening after evening, the fresh laughter of the two girls used to waylay her while Charlotte Lovell already slept her old-maid sleep on the floor above. A pang went through Delia at the thought that henceforth she would be cut off from this means of keeping her hold on Tina.

An hour later, when she mounted the stairs in her turn, she was guiltily conscious of moving as noiselessly as she could along the heavy carpet of the corridor, and of pausing longer than was necessary over the putting out of the gas-jet on the landing. As she lingered she strained her ears for the sound of voices from the adjoining doors behind which Charlotte and Tina slept; she would have been secretly hurt at hearing talk and laughter from within. But none came, nor was there any light beneath the doors. Evidently Charlotte, in her hard methodical way, had said goodnight to her daughter, and gone straight to bed as usual. Perhaps she had never approved of Tina's vigils, of the long undressing punctuated with mirth and confidences; she might have asked for the room next to her daughter's simply because she did not want the girl to miss her "beauty sleep."

Whenever Delia tried to explore the secret of her cousin's actions she returned from the adventure humiliated and abashed by the base motives she found herself attributing to Charlotte. How was it that she, Delia Ralston, whose happiness had been open and avowed to the world, so often found herself envying poor Charlotte the secret of her scanted motherhood? She hated herself for this movement of envy whenever she detected it, and tried to atone for it by a softened manner and a more anxious regard for Charlotte's feelings; but the attempt was not always successful, and Delia sometimes wondered if Charlotte did not resent any show of sympathy as an indirect glance at her misfortune. The worst of suffering such as hers was that it left one sore to the gentlest touch . . .

Delia, slowly undressing before the same lace-draped toilet-glass

which had reflected her bridal image, was turning over these thoughts when she heard a light knock. She opened the door, and there stood Tina, in a dressing-gown, her dark curls falling over her shoulders.

With a happy heart-beat Delia held out her arms.

"I had to say goodnight, Mamma," the girl whispered.

"Of course, dear." Delia pressed a long kiss on her lifted forehead. "Run off now, or you might disturb your aunt. You know she sleeps badly, and you must be as quiet as a mouse now she's next to you."

"Yes, I know," Tina acquiesced, with a grave glance that was almost of complicity.

She asked no further question, she did not linger: lifting Delia's hand she held it a moment against her cheek, and then stole out as noiselessly as she had come.

VIII

"BUT YOU MUST SEE," Charlotte Lovell insisted, laying aside the *Evening Post*, "that Tina has changed. You do see that?"

The two women were sitting alone by the drawing-room fire in Gramercy Park. Tina had gone to dine with her cousin, young Mrs. John Junius Halsey, and was to be taken afterward to a ball at the Vandergraves', from which the John Juniuses had promised to see her home. Mrs. Ralston and Charlotte, their early dinner finished, had the long evening to themselves. Their custom, on such occasions, was for Charlotte to read the news aloud to her cousin, while the latter embroidered; but tonight, all through Charlotte's conscientious progress from column to column, without a slip or an omission, Delia had felt her, for some special reason, alert to take advantage of her daughter's absence.

To gain time before answering, Mrs. Ralston bent over a stitch in her delicate white embroidery.

"Tina changed? Since when?" she questioned.

The answer flashed out instantly. "Since Lanning Halsey has been coming here so much."

"Lanning? I used to think he came for Delia," Mrs. Ralston mused, speaking at random to gain still more time.

"It's natural you should suppose that every one came for Delia," Charlotte rejoined dryly; "but as Lanning continues to seek every chance of being with Tina—"

Mrs. Ralston raised her head and stole a swift glance at her cousin. She had in truth noticed that Tina had changed, as a flower changes at the mysterious moment when the unopened petals flush from within. The girl had grown handsomer, shyer, more silent, at times more irrelevantly gay. But Delia had not associated these variations of mood with the presence of Lanning Halsey, one of the numerous youths who had

haunted the house before young Delia's marriage. There had, indeed, been a moment when Mrs. Ralston's eye had been fixed, with a certain apprehension, on the handsome Lanning. Among all the sturdy and stolid Halsey cousins he was the only one to whom a prudent mother might have hesitated to entrust her daughter; it would have been hard to say why, except that he was handsomer and more conversable than the rest, chronically unpunctual, and totally unperturbed by the fact. Clem Spender had been like that; and what if young Delia—?

But young Delia's mother was speedily reassured. The girl, herself arch and appetizing, took no interest in the corresponding graces except when backed by more solid qualities. A Ralston to the core, she demanded the Ralston virtues, and chose the Halsey most worthy of a Ralston bride.

Mrs. Ralston felt that Charlotte was waiting for her to speak. "It will be hard to get used to the idea of Tina's marrying," she said gently. "I don't know what we two old women shall do, alone in this empty house—for it will be an empty house then. But I suppose we ought to face the idea."

"I *do* face it," said Charlotte Lovell gravely.

"And you dislike Lanning? I mean, as a husband for Tina?"

Miss Lovell folded the evening paper, and stretched out a thin hand for her knitting. She glanced across the citron-wood work-table at her cousin. "Tina must not be too difficult—" she began.

"Oh—" Delia protested, reddening.

"Let us call things by their names," the other evenly pursued. "That's my way, when I speak at all. Usually, as you know, I say nothing."

The widow made a sign of assent, and Charlotte went on: "It's better so. But I've always known a time would come when we should have to talk this thing out."

"Talk this thing out? You and I? What thing?"

"Tina's future."

There was a silence. Delia Ralston, who always responded instantly to the least appeal to her sincerity, breathed a deep sigh of relief. At last the ice in Charlotte's breast was breaking up!

"My dear," Delia murmured, "you know how much Tina's happiness concerns me. If you disapprove of Lanning Halsey as a husband, have you any other candidate in mind?"

Miss Lovell smiled one of her faint hard smiles. "I am not aware that there is a queue at the door. Nor do I disapprove of Lanning Halsey as a husband. Personally, I find him very agreeable; I understand his attraction for Tina."

"Ah—Tina *is* attracted?"

"Yes."

Mrs. Ralston pushed aside her work and thoughtfully considered her cousin's sharply-lined face. Never had Charlotte Lovell more completely

presented the typical image of the old maid than as she sat there, upright on her straight-backed chair, with narrowed elbows and clicking needles, and imperturbably discussed her daughter's marriage.

"I don't understand, Chatty. Whatever Lanning's faults are—and I don't believe they're grave—I share your liking for him. After all—" Mrs. Ralston paused—"what is it that people find so reprehensible in him? Chiefly, as far as I can hear, that he can't decide on the choice of a profession. The New York view about that is rather narrow, as we know. Young men may have other tastes . . . artistic . . . literary . . . they may even have difficulty in deciding . . ."

Both women coloured slightly, and Delia guessed that the same reminiscence which shook her own bosom also throbbed under Charlotte's strait bodice.

Charlotte spoke. "Yes: I understand that. But hesitancy about a profession may cause hesitancy about . . . other decisions . . ."

"What do you mean? Surely not that Lanning—?"

"Lanning has not asked Tina to marry him."

"And you think he's hesitating?"

Charlotte paused. The steady click of her needles punctuated the silence as once, years before, it had been punctuated by the tick of the Parisian clock on Delia's mantel. As Delia's memory fled back to that scene she felt its mysterious tension in the air.

Charlotte spoke. "Lanning is not hesitating any longer: he has decided *not* to marry Tina. But he has also decided—not to give up seeing her."

Delia flushed abruptly; she was irritated and bewildered by Charlotte's oracular phrases, doled out between parsimonious lips.

"You don't mean that he has offered himself and then drawn back? I can't think him capable of such an insult to Tina."

"He has not insulted Tina. He has simply told her that he can't afford to marry. Until he chooses a profession his father will allow him only a few hundred dollars a year; and that may be suppressed if—if he marries against his parents' wishes."

It was Delia's turn to be silent. The past was too overwhelmingly resuscitated in Charlotte's words. Clement Spender stood before her, irresolute, impecunious, persuasive. Ah, if only she had let herself be persuaded!

"I'm very sorry that this should have happened to Tina. But as Lanning appears to have behaved honourably, and withdrawn without raising false expectations, we must hope . . . we must hope . . ." Delia paused, not knowing what they must hope.

Charlotte Lovell laid down her knitting. "You know as well as I do, Delia, that every young man who is inclined to fall in love with Tina will find as good reasons for not marrying her."

"Then you think Lanning's excuses are a pretext?"

"Naturally. The first of many that will be found by his successors—for of course he will have successors. Tina—attracts."

"Ah," Delia murmured.

Here they were at last face to face with the problem which, through all the years of silence and evasiveness, had lain as close to the surface as a corpse too hastily buried! Delia drew another deep breath, which again was almost one of relief. She had always known that it would be difficult, almost impossible, to find a husband for Tina; and much as she desired Tina's happiness, some inmost selfishness whispered how much less lonely and purposeless the close of her own life would be should the girl be forced to share it. But how say this to Tina's mother?

"I hope you exaggerate, Charlotte. There may be disinterested characters . . . But, in any case, surely Tina need not be unhappy here, with us who love her so dearly."

"Tina an old maid? Never!" Charlotte Lovell rose abruptly, her closed hand crashing down on the slender work-table. "My child shall have her life . . . her own life . . . whatever it costs me . . ."

Delia's ready sympathy welled up. "I understand your feeling. I should want also . . . hard as it will be to let her go. But surely there is no hurry—no reason for looking so far ahead. The child is not twenty. Wait."

Charlotte stood before her, motionless, perpendicular. At such moments she made Delia think of lava struggling through granite: there seemed no issue for the fires within.

"Wait? But if *she* doesn't wait?"

"But if he has withdrawn—what do you mean?"

"He has given up marrying her—but not seeing her."

Delia sprang up in her turn, flushed and trembling.

"Charlotte! Do you know what you're insinuating?"

"Yes: I know."

"But it's too outrageous. No decent girl—"

The words died on Delia's lips. Charlotte Lovell held her eyes inexorably. "Girls are not always what you call decent," she declared.

Mrs. Ralston turned slowly back to her seat. Her tambour frame had fallen to the floor; she stooped heavily to pick it up. Charlotte's gaunt figure hung over her, relentless as doom.

"I can't imagine, Charlotte, what is gained by saying such things—even by hinting them. Surely you trust your own child."

Charlotte laughed. "My mother trusted me," she said.

"How dare you—how dare you?" Delia began; but her eyes fell, and she felt a tremor of weakness in her throat.

"Oh, I dare anything for Tina, even to judging her as she is," Tina's mother murmured.

"As she is? She's perfect!"

"Let us say then that she must pay for my imperfections. All I want is that she shouldn't pay too heavily."

Mrs. Ralston sat silent. It seemed to her that Charlotte spoke with the voice of all the dark destinies coiled under the safe surface of life; and that to such a voice there was no answer but an awed acquiescence.

"Poor Tina!" she breathed.

"Oh, I don't intend that she shall suffer! It's not for that that I've waited . . . waited. Only I've made mistakes: mistakes that I understand now, and must remedy. You've been too good to us—and we must go."

"Go?" Delia gasped.

"Yes. Don't think me ungrateful. You saved my child once—do you suppose I can forget? But now it's my turn—it's I who must save her. And it's only by taking her away from everything here—from everything she's known till now—that I can do it. She's lived too long among unrealities: and she's like me. They won't content her."

"Unrealities?" Delia echoed vaguely.

"Unrealities for her. Young men who make love to her and can't marry her. Happy households where she's welcomed till she's suspected of designs on a brother or a husband—or else exposed to their insults. How could we ever have imagined, either of us, that the child could escape disaster? I thought only of her present happiness—of all the advantages, for both of us, of being with you. But this affair with young Halsey has opened my eyes. I must take Tina away. We must go and live somewhere where we're not known, where we shall be among plain people, leading plain lives. Somewhere where she can find a husband, and make herself a home."

Charlotte paused. She had spoken in a rapid monotonous tone, as if by rote; but now her voice broke and she repeated painfully: "I'm not ungrateful."

"Oh, don't let's speak of gratitude! What place has it between you and me?"

Delia had risen and begun to move uneasily about the room. She longed to plead with Charlotte, to implore her not to be in haste, to picture to her the cruelty of severing Tina from all her habits and associations, of carrying her inexplicably away to lead "a plain life among plain people." What chance was there, indeed, that a creature so radiant would tamely submit to such a fate, or find an acceptable husband in such conditions? The change might only precipitate a tragedy. Delia's experience was too limited for her to picture exactly what might happen to a girl like Tina, suddenly cut off from all that sweetened life for her; but vague visions of revolt and flight—of a "fall" deeper and more irretrievable than Charlotte's—flashed through her agonized imagination.

"It's too cruel—it's too cruel," she cried, speaking to herself rather than to Charlotte.

Charlotte, instead of answering, glanced abruptly at the clock.

"Do you know what time it is? Past midnight. I mustn't keep you sitting up for my foolish girl."

Delia's heart contracted. She saw that Charlotte wished to cut the conversation short, and to do so by reminding her that only Tina's mother had a right to decide what Tina's future should be. At that moment, though Delia had just protested that there could be no question of gratitude between them, Charlotte Lovell seemed to her a monster of ingratitude, and it was on the tip of her tongue to cry out: "Have all the years then given me no share in Tina?" But at the same instant she had put herself once more in Charlotte's place, and was feeling the mother's fierce terrors for her child. It was natural enough that Charlotte should resent the faintest attempt to usurp in private the authority she could never assert in public. With a pang of compassion Delia realized that she herself was literally the one being on earth before whom Charlotte could act the mother. "Poor thing—ah, let her!" she murmured inwardly.

"But why should you sit up for Tina? She has the key, and Delia is to bring her home."

Charlotte Lovell did not immediately answer. She rolled up her knitting, looked severely at one of the candelabra on the mantelpiece, and crossed over to straighten it. Then she picked up her work-bag.

"Yes, as you say—why should any one sit up for her?" She moved about the room, putting out the lamps, covering the fire, assuring herself that the windows were bolted, while Delia passively watched her. Then the two cousins lit their bedroom candles and walked upstairs through the darkened house. Charlotte seemed determined to make no further allusion to the subject of their talk. On the landing she paused, bending her head toward Delia's nightly kiss.

"I hope they've kept up your fire," she said, with her capable housekeeping air; and on Delia's hasty reassurance the two murmured a simultaneous "Goodnight," and Charlotte turned down the passage to her room.

IX

DELIA'S FIRE HAD BEEN KEPT UP, and her dressing-gown was warming on an armchair near the hearth. But she neither undressed nor yet seated herself. Her conversation with Charlotte had filled her with a deep unrest.

For a few moments she stood in the middle of the floor, looking slowly about her. Nothing had ever been changed in the room which, even as a bride, she had planned to modernize. All her dreams of renovation had faded long ago. Some deep central indifference had gradually made her regard herself as a third person, living the life meant for another woman, a woman totally unrelated to the vivid Delia Lovell who

had entered that house so full of plans and visions. The fault, she knew, was not her husband's. With a little managing and a little wheedling she would have gained every point as easily as she had gained the capital one of taking the foundling baby under her wing. The difficulty was that, after that victory, nothing else seemed worth trying for. The first sight of little Tina had somehow decentralized Delia Ralston's whole life, making her indifferent to everything else, except indeed the welfare of her own husband and children. Ahead of her she saw only a future full of duties, and these she had gaily and faithfully accomplished. But her own life was over: she felt as detached as a cloistered nun.

The change in her was too deep not to be visible. The Ralstons openly gloried in dear Delia's conformity. Each acquiescence passed for a concession, and the family doctrine was fortified by such fresh proofs of its durability. Now, as Delia glanced about her at the Léopold Robert lithographs, the family daguerreotypes, the rosewood and mahogany, she understood that she was looking at the walls of her own grave.

The change had come on the day when Charlotte Lovell, cowering on that very lounge, had made her terrible avowal. Then for the first time Delia, with a kind of fearful exaltation, had heard the blind forces of life groping and crying underfoot. But on that day also she had known herself excluded from them, doomed to dwell among shadows. Life had passed her by, and left her with the Ralstons.

Very well, then! She would make the best of herself, and of the Ralstons. The vow was immediate and unflinching; and for nearly twenty years she had gone on observing it. Once only had she been not a Ralston but herself; once only had it seemed worth while. And now perhaps the same challenge had sounded again; again, for a moment, it might be worth while to live. Not for the sake of Clement Spender— poor Clement, married years ago to a plain determined cousin, who had hunted him down in Rome, and enclosing him in an unrelenting domesticity, had obliged all New York on the grand tour to buy his pictures with a resigned grimace. No, not for Clement Spender, hardly for Charlotte or even for Tina; but for her own sake, hers, Delia Ralston's, for the sake of her one missed vision, her forfeited reality, she would once more break down the Ralston barriers and reach out into the world.

A faint sound through the silent house disturbed her meditation. Listening, she heard Charlotte Lovell's door open and her stiff petticoats rustle toward the landing. A light glanced under the door and vanished; Charlotte had passed Delia's threshold on her way downstairs.

Without moving, Delia continued to listen. Perhaps the careful Charlotte had gone down to make sure that the front door was not bolted, or that she had really covered up the fire. If that were her object, her step would presently be heard returning. But no step sounded; and it be-

came gradually evident that Charlotte had gone down to wait for her daughter. Why?

Delia's bedroom was at the front of the house. She stole across the heavy carpet, drew aside the curtains and cautiously folded back the inner shutters. Below her lay the empty square, white with moonlight, its tree-trunks patterned on a fresh sprinkling of snow. The houses opposite slept in darkness; not a footfall broke the white surface, not a wheel-track marred the brilliant street. Overhead a heaven full of stars swam in the moonlight.

Of the households around Gramercy Park Delia knew that only two others had gone to the ball: the Petrus Vandergraves and their cousins the young Parmly Ralstons. The Lucius Lannings had just entered on their three years of mourning for Mrs. Lucius's mother (it was hard on their daughter Kate, just eighteen, who would be unable to "come out" till she was twenty-one); young Mrs. Marcy Mingott was "expecting her third," and consequently secluded from the public eye for nearly a year; and the other denizens of the square belonged to the undifferentiated and uninvited.

Delia pressed her forehead against the pane. Before long carriages would turn the corner, the sleeping square ring with hoof-beats, fresh laughter and young farewells mount from the door-steps. But why was Charlotte waiting for her daughter downstairs in the darkness?

The Parisian clock struck one. Delia came back into the room, raked the fire, picked up a shawl, and, wrapped in it, returned to her vigil. Ah, how old she must have grown, that she should feel the cold at such a moment! It reminded her of what the future held for her: neuralgia, rheumatism, stiffness, accumulating infirmities. And never had she kept a moonlight watch with a lover's arms to warm her . . .

The square still lay silent. Yet the ball must surely be ending: the gayest dances did not last long after one in the morning, and the drive from University Place to Gramercy Park was a short one. Delia leaned in the embrasure and listened.

Hoof-beats, muffled by the snow, sounded in Irving Place, and the Petrus Vandergraves' family coach drew up before the opposite house. The Vandergrave girls and their brother sprang out and mounted the steps; then the coach stopped again a few doors farther on, and the Parmly Ralstons, brought home by their cousins, descended at their own door. The next carriage that rounded the corner must therefore be the John Juniuses', bringing Tina.

The gilt clock struck half-past one. Delia wondered, knowing that young Delia, out of regard for John Junius's business hours, never stayed late at evening parties. Doubtless Tina had delayed her; Mrs. Ralston felt a little annoyed with Tina's thoughtlessness in keeping her cousin up. But the feeling was swept away by an immediate wave of sympathy. "We must go away somewhere, and lead plain lives among plain people."

If Charlotte carried out her threat—and Delia knew she would hardly have spoken unless her resolve had been taken—it might be that at that very moment poor Tina was dancing her last *valse*.

Another quarter of an hour passed; then, just as the cold was finding a way through Delia's shawl, she saw two people turn into the deserted square from Irving Place. One was a young man in opera hat and ample cloak. To his arm clung a figure so closely wrapped and muffled that, until the corner light fell on it, Delia hesitated. After that, she wondered that she had not at once recognized Tina's dancing step, and her manner of tilting her head a little sideways to look up at the person she was talking to.

Tina—Tina and Lanning Halsey, walking home alone in the small hours from the Vandergrave ball! Delia's first thought was of an accident: the carriage might have broken down, or else her daughter been taken ill and obliged to return home. But no; in the latter case she would have sent the carriage on with Tina. And if there had been an accident of any sort the young people would have been hastening to apprise Mrs. Ralston; instead of which, through the bitter brilliant night, they sauntered like lovers in a midsummer glade, and Tina's thin slippers might have been falling on daisies instead of snow.

Delia began to tremble like a girl. In a flash she had the answer to a question which had long been the subject of her secret conjectures. How did lovers like Charlotte and Clement Spender contrive to meet? What Latmian solitude hid their clandestine joys? In the exposed compact little society to which they all belonged, how was it possible—literally—for such encounters to take place? Delia would never have dared to put the question to Charlotte; there were moments when she almost preferred not to know, not even to hazard a guess. But now, at a glance, she understood. How often Charlotte Lovell, staying alone in town with her infirm grandmother, must have walked home from evening parties with Clement Spender, how often have let herself and him into the darkened house in Mercer Street, where there was no one to spy upon their coming but a deaf old lady and her aged servants, all securely sleeping overhead! Delia, at the thought, saw the grim drawing-room which had been their moonlit forest, the drawing-room into which old Mrs. Lovell no longer descended, with its swathed chandelier and hard Empire sofas, and the eyeless marble caryatids of the mantel; she pictured the shaft of moonlight falling across the swans and garlands of the faded carpet, and in that icy light two young figures in each other's arms.

Yes: it must have been some such memory that had roused Charlotte's suspicions, excited her fears, sent her down in the darkness to confront the culprits. Delia shivered at the irony of the confrontation. If Tina had but known! But to Tina, of course, Charlotte was still what she had long since resolved to be: the image of prudish spinsterhood.

And Delia could imagine how quietly and decently the scene below stairs would presently be enacted: no astonishment, no reproaches, no insinuations, but a smiling and resolute ignoring of excuses.

"What, Tina? You walked home with Lanning? You imprudent child—in this wet snow! Ah, I see: Delia was worried about the baby, and ran off early, promising to send back the carriage—and it never came? Well, my dear, I congratulate you on finding Lanning to see you home . . . Yes—I sat up because I couldn't for the life of me remember whether you'd taken the latch-key—was there ever such a flighty old aunt? But don't tell your Mamma, dear, or she'd scold me for being so forgetful, and for staying downstairs in the cold . . . You're quite sure you have the key? Ah, Lanning has it? Thank you, Lanning; so kind! Goodnight—or one really ought to say, good morning."

As Delia reached this point in her mute representation of Charlotte's monologue the front door slammed below, and young Lanning Halsey walked slowly away across the square. Delia saw him pause on the opposite pavement, look up at the house-front, and then turn lingeringly away. His dismissal had taken exactly as long as Delia had calculated it would. A moment later she saw a passing light under her door, heard the starched rustle of Charlotte's petticoats, and knew that mother and daughter had reached their rooms.

Slowly, with stiff motions, she began to undress, blew out her candles, and knelt by her bedside, her face hidden.

X

LYING AWAKE TILL MORNING, Delia lived over every detail of the fateful day when she had assumed the charge of Charlotte's child. At the time she had been hardly more than a child herself, and there had been no one for her to turn to, no one to fortify her resolution, or to advise her how to put it into effect. Since then, the accumulated experiences of twenty years ought to have prepared her for emergencies, and taught her to advise others instead of seeking their guidance. But these years of experience weighed on her like chains binding her down to her narrow plot of life; independent action struck her as more dangerous, less conceivable, than when she had first ventured on it. There seemed to be so many more people to "consider" now ("consider" was the Ralston word): her children, their children, the families into which they had married. What would the Halseys say, and what the Ralstons? Had she then become a Ralston through and through?

A few hours later she sat in old Dr. Lanskell's library, her eyes on his sooty Smyrna rug. For some years now Dr. Lanskell had no longer practised: at most, he continued to go to a few old patients, and to give

consultations in "difficult" cases. But he remained a power in his former kingdom, a sort of lay Pope or medical Elder to whom the patients he had once healed of physical ills often returned for moral medicine. People were agreed that Dr. Lanskell's judgment was sound; but what secretly drew them to him was the fact that, in the most totem-ridden of communities, he was known not to be afraid of anything.

Now, as Delia sat and watched his massive silver-headed figure moving ponderously about the room, between rows of medical books in calf bindings and the Dying Gladiators and Young Augustuses of grateful patients, she already felt the reassurance given by his mere bodily presence.

"You see, when I first took Tina I didn't perhaps consider sufficiently—"

The Doctor halted behind his desk and brought his fist down on it with a genial thump. "Thank goodness you didn't! There are considerers enough in this town without you, Delia Lovell."

She looked up quickly. "Why do you call me Delia Lovell?"

"Well, because today I rather suspect you *are*," he rejoined astutely; and she met this with a wistful laugh.

"Perhaps, if I hadn't been, once before—I mean, if I'd always been a prudent deliberate Ralston it would have been kinder to Tina in the end."

Dr. Lanskell sank his gouty bulk into the armchair behind his desk, and beamed at her through ironic spectacles. "I hate in-the-end kindnesses: they're about as nourishing as the third day of cold mutton."

She pondered. "Of course I realize that if I adopt Tina—"

"Yes?"

"Well, people will say . . ." A deep blush rose to her throat, covered her cheeks and brow, and ran like fire under her decently-parted hair.

He nodded: "Yes."

"Or else—" the blush darkened—"that she's Jim's—"

Again Dr. Lanskell nodded. "That's what they're more likely to think; and what's the harm if they do? I know Jim: he asked you no questions when you took the child—but he knew whose she was."

She raised astonished eyes. "He knew—?"

"Yes: he came to me. And—well—in the baby's interest I violated professional secrecy. That's how Tina got a home. You're not going to denounce me, are you?"

"Oh, Dr. Lanskell—" Her eyes filled with painful tears. "Jim knew? And didn't tell me?"

"No. People didn't tell each other things much in those days, did they? But he admired you enormously for what you did. And if you assume—as I suppose you do—that he's now in a world of completer enlightenment, why not take it for granted that he'll admire you still more for what you're going to do? Presumably," the Doctor concluded sar-

donically, "people realize in heaven that it's a devilish sight harder, on earth, to do a brave thing at forty-five than at twenty-five."

"Ah, that's what I was thinking this morning," she confessed.

"Well, you're going to prove the contrary this afternoon." He looked at his watch, stood up and laid a fatherly hand on her shoulder. "Let people think what they choose; and send young Delia to me if she gives you any trouble. Your boy won't, you know, nor John Junius either; it must have been a woman who invented that third-and-fourth generation idea . . ."

An elderly maid-servant looked in, and Delia rose; but on the threshold she halted.

"I have an idea it's Charlotte I may have to send to you."

"Charlotte?"

"She'll hate what I'm going to do, you know."

Dr. Lanskell lifted his silver eyebrows. "Yes: poor Charlotte! I suppose she's jealous? That's where the truth of the third-and-fourth generation business comes in, after all. Somebody always has to foot the bill."

"Ah—if only Tina doesn't!"

"Well—that's just what Charlotte will come to recognize in time. So your course is clear."

He guided her out through the dining-room, where some poor people and one or two old patients were already waiting.

Delia's course, in truth, seemed clear enough till, that afternoon, she summoned Charlotte alone to her bedroom. Tina was lying down with a headache: it was in those days the accepted state of young ladies in sentimental dilemmas, and greatly simplified the communion of their elders.

Delia and Charlotte had exchanged only conventional phrases over their midday meal; but Delia still had the sense that her cousin's decision was final. The events of the previous evening had no doubt confirmed Charlotte's view that the time had come for such a decision.

Miss Lovell, closing the bedroom door with her dry deliberateness, advanced toward the chintz lounge between the windows.

"You wanted to see me, Delia?"

"Yes.—Oh, don't sit there," Mrs. Ralston exclaimed uncontrollably.

Charlotte stared: was it possible that she did not remember the sobs of anguish she had once smothered in those very cushions?

"Not—?"

"No; come nearer to me. Sometimes I think I'm a little deaf," Delia nervously explained, pushing a chair up to her own.

"Ah." Charlotte seated herself. "I hadn't remarked it. But if you are, it may have saved you from hearing at what hour of the morning Tina came back from the Vandergraves' last night. She would never

forgive herself—inconsiderate as she is—if she thought she'd waked you."

"She didn't wake me," Delia answered. Inwardly she thought: "Charlotte's mind is made up; I shan't be able to move her."

"I suppose Tina enjoyed herself very much at the ball?" she continued.

"Well, she's paying for it with a headache. Such excitements are not meant for her, I've already told you—"

"Yes," Mrs. Ralston interrupted. "It's to continue our talk of last night that I've asked you to come up."

"To continue it?" The brick-red circles appeared on Charlotte's dried cheeks. "Is it worth while? I think I ought to tell you at once that my mind's made up. I suppose you'll admit that I know what's best for Tina."

"Yes; of course. But won't you at least allow me a share in your decision?"

"A share?"

Delia leaned forward, laying a warm hand on her cousin's interlocked fingers. "Charlotte, once in this room, years ago, you asked me to help you—you believed I could. Won't you believe it again?"

Charlotte's lips grew rigid. "I believe the time has come for me to help myself."

"At the cost of Tina's happiness?"

"No; but to spare her greater unhappiness."

"But, Charlotte, Tina's happiness is all I want."

"Oh, I know. You've done all you could do for my child."

"No; not all." Delia rose, and stood before her cousin with a kind of solemnity. "But now I'm going to." It was as if she had pronounced a vow.

Charlotte Lovell looked up at her with a glitter of apprehension in her hunted eyes.

"If you mean that you're going to use your influence with the Halseys—I'm very grateful to you; I shall always be grateful. But I don't want a compulsory marriage for my child."

Delia flushed at the other's incomprehension. It seemed to her that her tremendous purpose must be written on her face. "I'm going to adopt Tina—give her my name," she announced.

Charlotte Lovell stared at her stonily. "Adopt her—adopt her?"

"Don't you see, dear, the difference it will make? There's my mother's money—the Lovell money; it's not much, to be sure; but Jim always wanted it to go back to the Lovells. And my Delia and her brother are so handsomely provided for. There's no reason why my little fortune shouldn't go to Tina. And why she shouldn't be known as Tina Ralston." Delia paused. "I believe—I think I know—that Jim would have approved of that too."

"*Approved?*"

"Yes. Can't you see that when he let me take the child he must have foreseen and accepted whatever—whatever might eventually come of it?"

Charlotte stood up also. "Thank you, Delia. But nothing more must come of it, except our leaving you; our leaving you now. I'm sure that's what Jim would have approved."

Mrs. Ralston drew back a step or two. Charlotte's cold resolution benumbed her courage, and she could find no immediate reply.

"Ah, then it's easier for you to sacrifice Tina's happiness than your pride?" she exclaimed.

"My pride? I've no right to any pride, except in my child. And that I'll never sacrifice."

"No one asks you to. You're not reasonable. You're cruel. All I want is to be allowed to help Tina, and you speak as if I were interfering with your rights."

"My rights?" Charlotte echoed the words with a desolate laugh. "What are they? I have no rights, either before the law or in the heart of my own child."

"How can you say such things? You know how Tina loves you."

"Yes; compassionately—as I used to love my old-maid aunts. There were two of them—you remember? Like withered babies! We children used to be warned never to say anything that might shock Aunt Josie or Aunt Nonie; exactly as I heard you telling Tina the other night—"

"Oh—" Delia murmured.

Charlotte Lovell continued to stand before her, haggard, rigid, unrelenting. "No, it's gone on long enough. I mean to tell her everything; and to take her away."

"To tell her about her birth?"

"I was never ashamed of it," Charlotte panted.

"You do sacrifice her, then—sacrifice her to your desire for mastery?"

The two women faced each other, both with weapons spent. Delia, through the tremor of her own indignation, saw her antagonist slowly waver, step backward, sink down with a broken murmur on the lounge. Charlotte hid her face in the cushions, clenching them with violent hands. The same fierce maternal passion that had once flung her down upon those same cushions was now bowing her still lower, in the throes of a bitterer renunciation. Delia seemed to hear the old cry: "But how can I give up my baby?" Her own momentary resentment melted, and she bent over the mother's labouring shoulders.

"Chatty—it won't be like giving her up this time. Can't we just go on loving her together?"

Charlotte did not answer. For a long time she lay silent, immovable, her face hidden: she seemed to fear to turn it to the face bent down to her. But presently Delia was aware of a gradual relaxing of the stretched

muscles, and saw that one of her cousin's arms was faintly stirring and groping. She lowered her hand to the seeking fingers, and it was caught and pressed to Charlotte's lips.

XI

TINA LOVELL—now Miss Clementina Ralston—was to be married in July to Lanning Halsey. The engagement had been announced only in the previous April; and the female elders of the tribe had begun by crying out against the indelicacy of so brief a betrothal. It was unanimously agreed in the New York of those times that "young people should be given the chance to get to know each other"; though the greater number of the couples constituting New York society had played together as children, and been born of parents as long and as familiarly acquainted, yet some mysterious law of decorum required that the newly affianced should always be regarded as being also newly known to each other. In the southern states things were differently conducted: headlong engagements, even runaway marriages, were not uncommon in their annals; but such rashness was less consonant with the sluggish blood of New York, where the pace of life was still set with a Dutch deliberateness.

In a case as unusual as Tina Ralston's, however, it was no great surprise to any one that tradition should have been disregarded. In the first place, everybody knew that she was no more Tina Ralston than you or I; unless, indeed, one were to credit the rumours about poor Jim's unsuspected "past," and his widow's magnanimity. But the opinion of the majority was against this. People were reluctant to charge a dead man with an offense from which he could not clear himself; and the Ralstons unanimously declared that, thoroughly as they disapproved of Mrs. James Ralston's action, they were convinced that she would not have adopted Tina if her doing so could have been construed as "casting a slur" on her late husband.

No: the girl was perhaps a Lovell—though even that idea was not generally held—but she was certainly not a Ralston. Her brown eyes and flighty ways too obviously excluded her from the clan for any formal excommunication to be needful. In fact, most people believed that—as Dr. Lanskell had always affirmed—her origin was really undiscoverable, that she represented one of the unsolved mysteries which occasionally perplex and irritate well-regulated societies, and that her adoption by Delia Ralston was simply one more proof of the Lovell clannishness, since the child had been taken in by Mrs. Ralston only because her cousin Charlotte was so attached to it. To say that Mrs. Ralston's son and daughter were pleased with the idea of Tina's adoption would be an exaggeration; but they abstained from comment, minimizing the effect of

their mother's whim by a dignified silence. It was the old New York way for families thus to screen the eccentricities of an individual member, and where there was "money enough to go round" the heirs would have been thought vulgarly grasping to protest at the alienation of a small sum from the general inheritance.

Nevertheless, Delia Ralston, from the moment of Tina's adoption, was perfectly aware of a different attitude on the part of both her children. They dealt with her patiently, almost parentally, as with a minor in whom one juvenile lapse has been condoned, but who must be subjected, in consequence, to a stricter vigilance; and society treated her in the same indulgent but guarded manner.

She had (it was Sillerton Jackson who first phrased it) an un-doubted way of "carrying things off"; since that dauntless woman, Mrs. Manson Mingott, had broken her husband's will, nothing so like her attitude had been seen in New York. But Mrs. Ralston's method was different, and less easy to analyze. What Mrs. Manson Mingott had accomplished by dint of epigram, invective, insistency and runnings to and fro, the other achieved without raising her voice or seeming to take a step from the beaten path. When she had persuaded Jim Ralston to take in the foundling baby, it had been done in the turn of a hand, one didn't know when or how; and the next day he and she were as un-troubled and beaming as usual. And now, this adoption—! Well, she had pursued the same method; as Sillerton Jackson said, she behaved as if her adopting Tina had always been an understood thing, as if she wondered that people should wonder. And in face of her wonder theirs seemed foolish, and they gradually desisted.

In reality, behind Delia's assurance there was a tumult of doubts and uncertainties. But she had once learned that one can do almost any-thing (perhaps even murder) if one does not attempt to explain it; and the lesson had never been forgotten. She had never explained the taking over of the foundling baby; nor was she now going to explain its adoption. She was just going about her business as if nothing had hap-pened that needed to be accounted for; and a long inheritance of moral modesty helped her to keep her questionings to herself.

These questionings were in fact less concerned with public opinion than with Charlotte Lovell's private thoughts. Charlotte, after her first moment of tragic resistance, had shown herself pathetically, almost pain-fully, grateful. That she had reason to be, Tina's attitude abundantly revealed. Tina, during the first days after her return from the Vandergrave ball, had shown a closed and darkened face that terribly reminded Delia of the ghastliness of Charlotte Lovell's sudden reflection, years before, in Delia's own bedroom mirror. The first chapter of the mother's history was already written in the daughter's eyes; and the Spender blood in Tina might well precipitate the sequence. During those few days of silent observation Delia discovered, with terror and compassion, the

justification of Charlotte's fears. The girl had nearly been lost to them both: at all costs such a risk must not be renewed.

The Halseys, on the whole, had behaved admirably. Lanning wished to marry dear Delia Ralston's protégée—who was shortly, it was understood, to take her adopted mother's name, and inherit her fortune. To what better could a Halsey aspire than one more alliance with a Ralston? The families had always intermarried. The Halsey parents gave their blessing with a precipitation which showed that they too had their anxieties, and that the relief of seeing Lanning "settled" would more than compensate for the conceivable drawbacks of the marriage; though, once it was decided on, they would not admit even to themselves that such drawbacks existed. Old New York always thought away whatever interfered with the perfect propriety of its arrangements.

Charlotte Lovell of course perceived and recognized all this. She accepted the situation—in her private hours with Delia—as one more in the long list of mercies bestowed on an undeserving sinner. And one phrase of hers perhaps gave the clue to her acceptance: "Now at least she'll never suspect the truth." It had come to be the poor creature's ruling purpose that her child should never guess the tie between them . . .

But Delia's chief support was the sight of Tina. The older woman, whose whole life had been shaped and coloured by the faint reflection of a rejected happiness, hung dazzled in the light of bliss accepted. Sometimes, as she watched Tina's changing face, she felt as though her own blood were beating in it, as though she could read every thought and emotion feeding those tumultuous currents. Tina's love was a stormy affair, with continual ups and downs of rapture and depression, arrogance and self-abasement; Delia saw displayed before her, with an artless frankness, all the visions, cravings and imaginings of her own stifled youth.

What the girl really thought of her adoption it was not easy to discover. She had been given, at fourteen, the current version of her origin, and had accepted it as carelessly as a happy child accepts some remote and inconceivable fact which does not alter the familiar order of things. And she accepted her adoption in the same spirit. She knew that the name of Ralston had been given to her to facilitate her marriage with Lanning Halsey; and Delia had the impression that all irrelevant questionings were submerged in an overwhelming gratitude. "I've always thought of you as my Mamma; and now, you dearest, you really are," Tina had whispered, her cheek against Delia's; and Delia had laughed back: "Well, if the lawyers can make me so!" But there the matter dropped, swept away on the current of Tina's bliss. They were all, in those days, Delia, Charlotte, even the gallant Lanning, rather like straws whirling about on a sunlit torrent.

The golden flood bore them onward, nearer and nearer to the en-

chanted date; and Delia, deep in bridal preparations, wondered at the comparative indifference with which she had ordered and inspected her own daughter's twelve-dozen-of-everything. There had been nothing to quicken the pulse in young Delia's placid bridal; but as Tina's wedding day approached imagination burgeoned like the year. The wedding was to be celebrated at Lovell Place, the old house on the Sound where Delia Lovell had herself been married, and where, since her mother's death, she spent her summers. Although the neighbourhood was already over-spread with a net-work of mean streets, the old house, with its thin colonnaded verandah, still looked across an uncurtailed lawn and leafy shrubberies to the narrows of Hell Gate; and the drawing-rooms kept their frail slender settees, their Sheraton consoles and cabinets. It had been thought useless to discard them for more fashionable furniture, since the growth of the city made it certain that the place must eventually be sold.

Tina, like Mrs. Ralston, was to have a "house-wedding," though Episcopalian society was beginning to disapprove of such ceremonies, which were regarded as the despised *pis-aller* of Baptists, Methodists, Unitarians and the other altarless sects. In Tina's case, however, both Delia and Charlotte felt that the greater privacy of a marriage in the house made up for its more secular character; and the Halseys favoured their decision. The ladies accordingly settled themselves at Lovell Place before the end of June, and every morning young Lanning Halsey's cat-boat was seen beating across the bay, and furling its sail at the anchorage below the lawn.

There had never been a fairer June in any one's memory. The damask roses and mignonette below the verandah had never sent such a breath of summer through the tall French windows; the gnarled orange-trees brought out from the old arcaded orange-house had never been so thickly blossomed; the very haycocks on the lawn gave out whiffs of Araby.

The evening before the wedding Delia Ralston sat on the verandah watching the moon rise across the Sound. She was tired with the multitude of last preparations, and sad at the thought of Tina's going. On the following evening the house would be empty: till death came, she and Charlotte would sit alone together beside the evening lamp. Such re-pinings were foolish—they were, she reminded herself, "not like her." But too many memories stirred and murmured in her: her heart was haunted. As she closed the door on the silent drawing-room—already transformed into a chapel, with its lace-hung altar, the tall alabaster vases awaiting their white roses and June lilies, the strip of red carpet dividing the rows of chairs from door to chancel—she felt that it had perhaps been a mistake to come back to Lovell Place for the wedding. She saw herself again, in her high-waisted "India mull" embroidered with

daisies, her flat satin sandals, her Brussels veil—saw again her reflection in the sallow pier-glass as she had left that same room on Jim Ralston's triumphant arm, and the one terrified glance she had exchanged with her own image before she took her stand under the bell of white roses in the hall, and smiled upon the congratulating company. Ah, what a different image the pier-glass would reflect tomorrow!

Charlotte Lovell's brisk step sounded indoors, and she came out and joined Mrs. Ralston.

"I've been to the kitchen to tell Melissa Grimes that she'd better count on at least two hundred plates of ice-cream."

"Two hundred? Yes—I suppose she had, with all the Philadelphia connection coming." Delia pondered. "How about the doylies?" she enquired.

"With your aunt Cecilia Vandergrave's we shall manage beautifully."

"Yes.—Thank you, Charlotte, for taking all this trouble."

"Oh—" Charlotte protested, with her flitting sneer; and Delia perceived the irony of thanking a mother for occupying herself with the details of her own daughter's wedding.

"Do sit down, Chatty," she murmured, feeling herself redden at her blunder.

Charlotte, with a sigh of fatigue, sat down on the nearest chair.

"We shall have a beautiful day tomorrow," she said, pensively surveying the placid heaven.

"Yes. Where is Tina?"

"She was very tired. I've sent her upstairs to lie down."

This seemed so eminently suitable that Delia made no immediate answer. After an interval she said: "We shall miss her."

Charlotte's reply was an inarticulate murmur.

The two cousins remained silent, Charlotte as usual bolt upright, her thin hands clutched on the arms of her old-fashioned rush-bottomed seat, Delia somewhat heavily sunk into the depths of a high-backed armchair. The two had exchanged their last remarks on the preparations for the morrow; nothing more remained to be said as to the number of guests, the brewing of the punch, the arrangements for the robing of the clergy, and the disposal of the presents in the best spare-room.

Only one subject had not yet been touched upon, and Delia, as she watched her cousin's profile grimly cut upon the melting twilight, waited for Charlotte to speak. But Charlotte remained silent.

"I have been thinking," Delia at length began, a slight tremor in her voice, "that I ought presently—"

She fancied she saw Charlotte's hands tighten on the knobs of the chair-arms.

"You ought presently—?"

"Well, before Tina goes to bed, perhaps go up for a few minutes—"

Charlotte remained silent, visibly resolved on making no effort to assist her.

"Tomorrow," Delia continued, "we shall be in such a rush from the earliest moment that I don't see how, in the midst of all the interruptions and excitement, I can possibly—"

"Possibly?" Charlotte monotonously echoed.

Delia felt her blush deepening through the dusk. "Well, I suppose you agree with me, don't you, that a word ought to be said to the child as to the new duties and responsibilities that—well—what is usual, in fact, at such a time?" she falteringly ended.

"Yes, I have thought of that," Charlotte answered. She said no more, but Delia divined in her tone the stirring of that obscure opposition which, at the crucial moments of Tina's life, seemed automatically to declare itself. She could not understand why Charlotte should, at such times, grow so enigmatic and inaccessible, and in the present case she saw no reason why this change of mood should interfere with what she deemed to be her own duty. Tina must long for her guiding hand into the new life as much as she herself yearned for the exchange of half-confidences which would be her real farewell to her adopted daughter. Her heart beating a little more quickly than usual, she rose and walked through the open window into the shadowy drawing-room. The moon, between the columns of the verandah, sent a broad band of light across the rows of chairs, irradiated the lace-decked altar with its empty candlesticks and vases, and outlined with silver Delia's heavy reflection in the pier-glass.

She crossed the room toward the hall.

"Delia!" Charlotte's voice sounded behind her. Delia turned, and the two women scrutinized each other in the revealing light. Charlotte's face looked as it had looked on the dreadful day when Delia had suddenly seen it in the looking-glass above her shoulder.

"You were going up now to speak to Tina?" Charlotte asked.

"I—yes. It's nearly nine. I thought . . ."

"Yes; I understand." Miss Lovell made a visible effort at self-control. "Please understand me too, Delia, if I ask you—not to."

Delia looked at her cousin with a vague sense of apprehension. What new mystery did this strange request conceal? But no—such a doubt as flitted across her mind was inadmissible. She was too sure of her Tina!

"I confess I don't understand, Charlotte. You surely feel that, on the night before her wedding, a girl ought to have a mother's counsel, a mother's . . ."

"Yes; I feel that." Charlotte Lovell took a hurried breath. "But the question is: *which of us is her mother?*"

Delia drew back involuntarily. "Which of us—?" she stammered.

"Yes. Oh, don't imagine it's the first time I've asked myself the

question! There—I mean to be calm; quite calm. I don't intend to go back to the past. I've accepted—accepted everything—gratefully. Only tonight—just tonight . . ."

Delia felt the rush of pity which always prevailed over every other sensation in her rare interchanges of truth with Charlotte Lovell. Her throat filled with tears, and she remained silent.

"Just tonight," Charlotte concluded, *"I'm* her mother."

"Charlotte! You're not going to tell her so—not now?" broke involuntarily from Delia.

Charlotte gave a faint laugh. "If I did, should you hate it as much as all that?"

"Hate it? What a word, between us!"

"Between us? But it's the word that's been between us since the beginning—the very beginning! Since the day when you discovered that Clement Spender hadn't quite broken his heart because he wasn't good enough for you; since you found your revenge and your triumph in keeping me at your mercy, and in taking his child from me!" Charlotte's words flamed up as if from the depth of the infernal fires; then the blaze dropped, her head sank forward, and she stood before Delia dumb and stricken.

Delia's first movement was one of an indignant recoil. Where she had felt only tenderness, compassion, the impulse to help and befriend, these darknesses had been smouldering in the other's breast! It was as if a poisonous smoke had swept over some pure summer landscape . . .

Usually such feelings were quickly followed by a reaction of sympathy. But now she felt none. An utter weariness possessed her.

"Yes," she said slowly, "I sometimes believe you really have hated me from the very first; hated me for everything I've tried to do for you."

Charlotte raised her head sharply. "To do for me? But everything you've done has been done for Clement Spender!"

Delia stared at her with a kind of terror. "You are horrible, Charlotte. Upon my honour, I haven't thought of Clement Spender for years."

"Ah, but you have—you have! You've always thought of him in thinking of Tina—of him and nobody else! A woman never stops thinking of the man she loves. She thinks of him years afterward, in all sorts of unconscious ways, in thinking of all sorts of things—books, pictures, sunsets, a flower or a ribbon—or a clock on the mantelpiece," Charlotte broke off with her sneering laugh. "That was what I gambled on, you see —that's why I came to you that day. I knew I was giving Tina another mother."

Again the poisonous smoke seemed to envelop Delia: that she and Charlotte, two spent old women, should be standing before Tina's bridal altar and talking to each other of hatred, seemed unimaginably hideous and degrading.

"You wicked woman—you *are* wicked!" she exclaimed.

Then the evil mist cleared away, and through it she saw the baffled pitiful figure of the mother who was not a mother, and who, for every benefit accepted, felt herself robbed of a privilege. She moved nearer to Charlotte and laid a hand on her arm.

"Not here! Don't let us talk like this here."

The other drew away from her. "Wherever you please, then. I'm not particular!"

"But tonight, Charlotte—the night before Tina's wedding? Isn't every place in this house full of her? How could we go on saying cruel things to each other anywhere?" Charlotte was silent, and Delia continued in a steadier voice: "Nothing you say can really hurt me—for long; and I don't want to hurt you—I never did."

"You tell me that—and you've left nothing undone to divide me from my daughter! Do you suppose it's been easy, all these years, to hear her call you 'mother'? Oh, I know, I know—it was agreed that she must never guess . . . but if you hadn't perpetually come between us she'd have had no one but me, she'd have felt about me as a child feels about its mother, she'd have *had* to love me better than any one else. With all your forbearances and your generosities you've ended by robbing me of my child. And I've put up with it all for her sake—because I knew I had to. But tonight—tonight she belongs to me. Tonight I can't bear that she should call you 'mother'."

Delia Ralston made no immediate reply. It seemed to her that for the first time she had sounded the deepest depths of maternal passion, and she stood awed at the echoes it gave back.

"How you must love her—to say such things to me," she murmured; then, with a final effort: "Yes, you're right. I won't go up to her. It's you who must go."

Charlotte started toward her impulsively; but with a hand lifted as if in defense, Delia moved across the room and out again to the verandah. As she sank down in her chair she heard the drawing-room door open and close, and the sound of Charlotte's feet on the stairs.

Delia sat alone in the night. The last drop of her magnanimity had been spent, and she tried to avert her shuddering mind from Charlotte. What was happening at this moment upstairs? With what dark revelations were Tina's bridal dreams to be defaced? Well, that was not matter for conjecture either. She, Delia Ralston, had played her part, done her utmost: there remained nothing now but to try to lift her spirit above the embittering sense of failure.

There was a strange element of truth in some of the things that Charlotte had said. With what divination her maternal passion had endowed her! Her jealousy seemed to have a million feelers. Yes; it was true that the sweetness and peace of Tina's bridal eve had been filled, for Delia, with visions of her own unrealized past. Softly, imperceptibly,

it had reconciled her to the memory of what she had missed. All these last days she had been living the girl's life, she had been Tina, and Tina had been her own girlish self, the far-off Delia Lovell. Now for the first time, without shame, without self-reproach, without a pang or a scruple, Delia could yield to that vision of requited love from which her imagination had always turned away. She had made her choice in youth, and she had accepted it in maturity; and here in this bridal joy, so mysteriously her own, was the compensation for all she had missed and yet never renounced.

Delia understood now that Charlotte had guessed all this, and that the knowledge had filled her with a fierce resentment. Charlotte had said long ago that Clement Spender had never really belonged to her; now she had perceived that it was the same with Clement Spender's child. As the truth stole upon Delia her heart melted with the old compassion for Charlotte. She saw that it was a terrible, a sacrilegious thing to interfere with another's destiny, to lay the tenderest touch upon any human being's right to love and suffer after his own fashion. Delia had twice intervened in Charlotte Lovell's life: it was natural that Charlotte should be her enemy. If only she did not revenge herself by wounding Tina!

The adopted mother's thoughts reverted painfully to the little white room upstairs. She had meant her half-hour with Tina to leave the girl with thoughts as fragrant as the flowers she was to find beside her when she woke. And now——.

Delia started up from her musing. There was a step on the stair—Charlotte coming down through the silent house. Delia rose with a vague impulse of escape: she felt that she could not face her cousin's eyes. She turned the corner of the verandah, hoping to find the shutters of the dining-room unlatched, and to slip away unnoticed to her room; but in a moment Charlotte was beside her.

"Delia!"

"Ah, it's you? I was going up to bed." For the life of her Delia could not keep an edge of hardness from her voice.

"Yes: it's late. You must be very tired." Charlotte paused; her own voice was strained and painful.

"I *am* tired," Delia acknowledged.

In the moonlit hush the other went up to her, laying a timid touch on her arm.

"Not till you've seen Tina."

Delia stiffened. "Tina? But it's late! Isn't she sleeping? I thought you'd stay with her until—"

"I don't know if she's sleeping." Charlotte paused. "I haven't been in—but there's a light under her door."

"You haven't been in?"

"No: I just stood in the passage, and tried—"

"Tried—?"

"To think of something . . . something to say to her without . . . without her guessing . . ." A sob stopped her, but she pressed on with a final effort. "It's no use. You were right: there's nothing I can say. You're her real mother. Go to her. It's not your fault—or mine."

"Oh—" Delia cried.

Charlotte clung to her in inarticulate abasement. "You said I was wicked—I'm not wicked. After all, she was mine when she was little!"

Delia put an arm about her shoulder.

"Hush, dear! We'll go to her together."

The other yielded automatically to her touch, and side by side the two women mounted the stairs, Charlotte timing her impetuous step to Delia's stiffened movements. They walked down the passage to Tina's door; but there Charlotte Lovell paused and shook her head.

"No—you," she whispered, and turned away.

Tina lay in bed, her arms folded under her head, her happy eyes reflecting the silver space of sky which filled the window. She smiled at Delia through her dream.

"I knew you'd come."

Delia sat down beside her, and their clasped hands lay upon the coverlet. They did not say much, after all; or else their communion had no need of words. Delia never knew how long she sat by the child's side: she abandoned herself to the spell of the moonlit hour.

But suddenly she thought of Charlotte, alone behind the shut door of her own room, watching, struggling, listening. Delia must not, for her own pleasure, prolong that tragic vigil. She bent down to kiss Tina goodnight; then she paused on the threshold and turned back.

"Darling! Just one thing more."

"Yes?" Tina murmured through her dream.

"I want you to promise me—"

"Everything, everything, you darling mother!"

"Well, then, that when you go away tomorrow—at the very last moment, you understand—"

"Yes?"

"After you've said goodbye to me, and to everybody else—just as Lanning helps you into the carriage—"

"Yes?"

"That you'll give your last kiss to Aunt Charlotte. Don't forget—the very last."

V

FATHER SERGIUS

by Leo Tolstoy

The Story of a Hermit

It was soon after he had renounced all claim to his estates and his wealth and had spent some years working in the fields like a peasant that Leo Tolstoy wrote *Father Sergius*. He had started on his koni novel (as he called it himself), to which he would give the title of *Resurrection*, when he paid a visit to the Shamardin Convent and had long talks with two of the monks. An idea came into his mind which seemed at once to gain complete control of him—the story of a holy hermit who believes in taking out of life only enough to sustain him in his solitude and contemplation but who finally perceives that the real function of man is to *give*. Out of this came his vision of *Father Sergius* and he laid *Resurrection* aside to write it.

Someone has said, "Tolstoy was not a man to whom writing came easily," but his skill in the telling of this short novel of an aristocratic army officer, who goes to live in a cave, demonstrates how deft he was in the construction of a story. His noble recluse does not sit himself down and think it all out; things happen to mark each step of his progress to understanding. In the story an intensity of interest combines with the spiritual uplift which fills all his books of this period.

Father Sergius has been somewhat hidden by the immensity of Tolstoy's better-known novels, and so a limited number have enjoyed the pleasure it offers. Permit us to state our conviction that among short novels it must be ranked very high indeed. There is great satisfaction in offering it to new readers.

Chapter I

THERE HAPPENED IN ST. PETERSBURG during the forties an event which startled society.

A handsome youth, a prince, an officer in the Cuirassiers for whom every one had predicted the rank of aide-de-camp and a brilliant career attached to the person of Emperor Nicholas I., quitted the service. He broke with his beautiful *fiancée*, a lady-in-waiting, and a favourite of the empress, just a fortnight before the wedding-day, and giving his small estate to his sister, retired to a monastery to become a monk.

To those who were ignorant of the hidden motives, this was an extraordinary and unaccountable step; but as regards Prince Stephen Kasatsky himself, it was such a natural move that he could not conceive an alternative.

His father, a retired colonel of the Guards, died when the son was twelve. Although it was hard for his mother to let him go from her, she would not act in defiance of the wishes of her late husband, who had expressed the desire that in the event of his death the boy should be sent away and educated as a cadet. So she secured his admission to the corps.

The widow herself with her daughter Varvara moved to St. Petersburg in order to be in the same town with the boy and to take him home for his holidays. He showed brilliant capacity and extraordinary ambition, and came out first in military drill, in riding, and in his studies—mathematics especially—for which he had a particular liking.

In spite of his abnormal height he was a handsome, graceful lad, and had it not been for his violent temper he would have been an altogether exemplary cadet. He never drank or indulged in any sort of dissipation, and he was particularly truthful. The fits of fury which maddened him from time to time, when he lost all control over himself and raged like a wild animal, were the only faults in his character. Once, when a cadet ragged him because of his collection of minerals, he almost threw the boy out of the window. On another occasion he rushed at an officer and struck him, it was said, for having broken his word and told a direct lie.

For this he would surely have been degraded to the rank of a common soldier, if it had not been for the head of the school, who hushed up the matter and dismissed the officer.

At eighteen Kasatsky left with the rank of lieutenant and entered an aristocratic Guard regiment. The Emperor Nicholas had known him while he was in the cadet corps, and had shown him favour while in the regiment. It was on this account that people prophesied that he would become an aide-de-camp. Kasatsky desired it greatly, although less from ambition than from passionate love for the emperor whom he had cherished since his cadet days. Each time the emperor visited the school —and he visited it very often—as Kasatsky saw the tall figure, the broad chest, the aquiline nose above the moustache, and the close-cropped side whiskers, the military uniform, and the brisk, firm step, and heard him greeting the cadets in his strident voice, he experienced the momentary ecstasy of one who sees his well-beloved. But his passionate adoration of the emperor was even more intense. He desired to give up something, everything, even himself, to show his infinite devotion. The Emperor Nicholas knew that he inspired such admiration, and deliberately provoked it. He played with the cadets, made them surround him, and treated them sometimes with childish simplicity, sometimes as a friend, and then again with an air of solemn grandeur.

After the incident with the officer, the emperor, who did not allude to it, waved Kasatsky theatrically aside when the latter approached him. Then, when he was leaving, he frowned and shook his finger at the boy, saying, "Be assured that everything is known to me; but there are things I do not wish to know. Nevertheless they are *here*," and he pointed to his heart.

When the cadets were formally received by the emperor on leaving the school, he did not remind Kasatsky of his insubordination, but told them all, as was his custom, that they could turn to him in need, that they were to serve him and their country with loyalty, and that he would ever remain their best friend. All were touched—as usual—and Kasatsky, remembering the past, shed tears and made a vow to serve his beloved Tsar with all his might.

When Kasatsky entered the regiment, his mother and sister left St. Petersburg, going first to Moscow and then to their estate in the country. Kasatsky gave half his fortune to his sister. What remained was quite sufficient to support him in the expensive regiment which he had joined.

Viewed from outside, Kasatsky seemed like an ordinary brilliant young officer of the Guards making a career for himself. But within his soul there were intense and complex strivings. Although this striving, which had been going on ever since his childhood, seemed to vary in its nature, it was essentially one and the same, and had for its object that absolute perfection in every undertaking which would give him the applause and admiration of the world. Whatever it might be, accomplishments or learning, he worked to merit praise, and to stand as an example to the rest. Mastering one subject he took up another, and so

obtained first place in his studies. For example, while he was still in the corps, conscious of a lack of fluency in his French, he contrived to master the language so that he knew it like his own. Then again, when he became interested in chess while still in the corps, he worked at the game till he acquired proficiency.

Apart from the chief end of life, which was in his eyes the service of the Tsar and his country, he had always some self-appointed aim, and, however unimportant it might be, he pursued this with his whole soul, and lived for it until it was accomplished. But the moment it was attained another arose in its place. This passion for distinguishing himself and for pursuing one object in order to distinguish himself filled his life. So it was that after entering upon his career he set himself to acquire the utmost perfection in the knowledge of the service, and, except for his uncontrollable temper, which was sometimes the occasion of actions that were inimical to his success, he soon became a model officer.

Once, during a conversation in society, he realised the need of a more general education. So setting himself to work to read books, he soon attained what he desired. Then he wanted to hold a brilliant position in aristocratic society. He learned to dance beautifully, and was presently invited to all the balls and parties in the best circles. But he was not satisfied with this. He was accustomed to being first in everything, and in this instance he was very far from that. Society at that time consisted, as I suppose it has done in every time and place, of four kinds of people—rich people who are received at court; people who are not rich, but are born and brought up in court circles; rich people who ape the court; and people, neither rich nor of the court, who copy both.

Kasatsky did not belong to the first two, but was gladly received in the last two sets. On entering society his first idea was that he must have a *liaison* with a society lady; and quite unexpectedly it soon came about. Presently, however, he realised that the circle in which he moved was not the most exclusive, and that there were higher spheres, and that, notwithstanding he was received there, he was a stranger in their midst. They were polite to him, but their manner made it plain that they had their own intimates, and that he was not one of them. Kasatsky longed to be one of them. To attain this end he must become an aide-de-camp—which he expected to be—or else he must marry into the set. He resolved upon this latter course. His choice fell upon a young girl, a beauty, belonging to the court, and not merely belonging to the circle he wished to move in, whose society was coveted by the most distinguished and the most firmly rooted in this circle. This was the Countess Korotkova. Kasatsky began to pay court to her purely for the sake of his career; she was uncommonly attractive, and he very soon fell in love with her. She was noticeably cool towards him at first, and then suddenly everything changed. She treated him graciously, and her mother continually invited him to the house.

Kasatsky proposed, and was accepted. He was rather astonished at the facility with which he gained his happiness, and he noticed something strange in the behaviour towards him of both mother and daughter. He was deeply in love, and love had made him blind, so he failed to realise what nearly the whole town knew—that the previous year his *fiancée* had been the favourite of the Emperor Nicholas.

Two weeks before the day arranged for the wedding Kasatsky was at Tsarskoye Selo, at the country place of his *fiancée*. It was a hot day in May. The lovers had had a walk in the garden, and were sitting on a bench in the shade of the lindens. Mary looked exceedingly pretty in her white muslin dress. She seemed the personification of love and innocence —now bending her head, now gazing at her handsome young lover, who was talking to her with great tenderness and self-restraint, as though he feared by look or gesture to offend her angelic purity. Kasatsky belonged to those men of the 'forties, who do not exist nowadays, who deliberately, while condoning impurity in themselves, require in their wives the most ideal and seraphic innocence. Being prepared to find this purity in every girl of their set, they behaved accordingly. This theory, in so far as it concerned the laxity which the men permitted themselves, was certainly altogether wrong and harmful; but in its relation to the women I think, compared with the notion of the modern young man who sees in every girl nothing but a mate or a female, there was much to be said for it. The girls, perceiving such adoration, endeavoured with more or less success to be goddesses.

Kasatsky held the views of his time, and looked with such eyes upon his sweetheart. That day he was more in love than ever, but there was nothing sensual in his feelings towards his *fiancée*. On the contrary he regarded her with the tender adoration of something unattainable. He rose and stood at his full height before her, leaning with both hands on his sabre.

"Now for the first time I know what happiness is. And it is you— darling—who have given me that happiness," he said, smiling shyly.

He was still at that stage where endearments are not yet a habit, and it made him gasp to think of using them to such an angel.

"It is you who have made me see myself clearly. You have shown me that I am better than I thought," he added.

"I knew it long ago. That is what made me begin to love you."

The nightingales were beginning their song somewhere near, and the young leaves moved in the sudden gusts of wind. He raised her hand to his lips and there were tears in his eyes.

She understood that he was thanking her for having said that she loved him. He took a few steps backwards and forwards, remaining silent, then approached her again, and sat beside her.

"You know, when I began to make love to you, it was not dis-

interested on my part. I wanted to get into society. And then, when I came to know you better, how little all that mattered, compared to you! Are you angry with me for that?"

She did not answer, but touched his hand. He understood that it meant "I am not angry."

"Well, you said—" he stopped. It seemed too bold to say what he intended. "You said—that you—began to love me—forgive me—I quite believe it—but there is something that troubles you and stands in the way of your feelings. What is it?"

"Yes—now or never," she thought. "He will know it anyhow. But now he will not forsake me because of it. Oh, if he should, how dreadful!" And she gazed with deep affection upon that tall, noble, powerful figure. She loved him now more than the Tsar, and were it not for Nicholas being an emperor, her choice between them would rest on Kasatsky.

"Listen," she said, "I cannot deceive you. I must tell you everything. You asked me what stood in the way. It is that I have loved before."

She again laid her hand on his with an imploring gesture.

He was silent.

"Do you want to know who it was? The emperor."

"We all loved him. I can imagine you, a school-girl in the institute—"

"No. After that. It was only a passing infatuation, but I must tell you—"

"Well—what?"

"No; it was not simply—" She covered her face with her hands.

"What! You gave yourself to him?"

She was silent.

"His mistress?"

Still she did not answer.

He sprang to his feet, and pale as death, with his teeth chattering, stood before her. He now remembered how the emperor, meeting him on the Nevsky, had congratulated him.

"Oh, my God, what have I done! Stephen!"

"Don't touch me—don't touch me! Oh, how terrible!"

He turned and went to the house.

There he met her mother.

"What's the matter with you, prince?" she stopped, seeing his face. The blood rushed suddenly to his head.

"You knew it! And you wanted me to shield them! Oh, if you weren't a woman—" he shouted, raising his large fist. Then he turned and ran away.

Had the lover of his *fiancée* been a private individual he would have killed him. But it was his beloved Tsar.

The next day he asked for furlough, and then for his discharge. Feigning illness, he refused to see any one, and went away to the country.

There he spent the summer putting his affairs in order. When summer was over he did not return to St. Petersburg, but entered a monastery with the intention of becoming a monk.

His mother wrote to dissuade him from his momentous step. He answered that he felt a vocation for God which was above all other considerations. It was only his sister, who was as proud and ambitious as himself, who understood him.

She was quite right in her estimate of his motives. His becoming a monk was only to show his contempt for all that seemed most important to the rest of the world, and had seemed so to himself while he was still an officer. He climbed to a pinnacle from which he could look down on those he had previously envied. However, contrary to his sister's opinion, this was not the only guiding motive. Mingled with his pride and his passion for ascendancy, there was also a genuine religious sentiment which Varvara did not know he possessed. His sense of injury and his disappointment in Mary, whom he had thought such an angel, were so poignant that they led him to despair. His despair led where? To God, to faith, to a childish faith which had never been destroyed.

Chapter 2

ON THE FEAST of the Intercession of the Virgin, Kasatsky entered the monastery to show his superiority over all those who fancied themselves above him.

The abbot was a nobleman by birth, a learned man, and a writer. He belonged to that monastic order which hails from Walachia, the members of which choose, and in their turn are chosen, leaders to be followed unswervingly and implicitly obeyed.

This abbot was the disciple of the famous Ambrosius, disciple of Makardix of the Leonidas, disciple of Païssy Velichkovsky.

To this abbot Kasatsky submitted himself as to the superior of his choice.

Beside the feeling of ascendancy over others, which Kasatsky felt in the monastery as he had felt it in the world, he found here the joy of attaining perfection in the highest degree inwardly as well as outwardly. As in the regiment, he had rejoiced in being more than an irreproachable officer, even exceeding his duties; so as a monk his endeavour was

to be perfect, industrious, abstemious, meek, and humble: and, above all, pure, not only in deed but in thought; and obedient. This last quality made his life there far easier. In that much-frequented monastery there were many conditions objectionable to him, but through obedience he became reconciled to them all.

"It is not for me to reason. I have but to obey, whatever the command." On guard before the sacred relics, singing in the choir, or adding up accounts in the hostelry, all possibility of doubt was silenced by obedience to his superior. Had it not been for that, the monotony and length of the church service, the intrusion of visitors and the inferiority of the other monks, would have been extremely distasteful to him. But as it was he bore it all perfectly and found it even a solace and a support.

"I don't know," he thought, "why I ought to hear the same prayers many times a day, but I know that it is necessary, and knowing this I rejoice." His superior had told him that as food is necessary for the life of the body, so is spiritual food, such as prayers in church, necessary for maintaining the life of the spirit. He believed it, and though he found the service for which he had to rise at a very early hour a difficulty, it brought him indubitable comfort and joy. This was the result of humility and the certainty that anything done in obedience to the superior was right.

The aim of his life was neither the gradual attainment of utter subjugation of his will, nor the attainment of greater and greater humility; but the achievement of all those Christian virtues which seemed in the beginning so easy of possession.

Being not in the least half hearted, he gave what fortune remained to him to the monastery without regret.

Humility before his inferiors, far from being difficult, was a delight to him. Even the victory over the sins of greed and lust were easy for him. The superior had especially warned him against this latter sin, but Kasatsky was glad to feel immunity from it. He was only tortured by the thought of his *fiancée*. It was not only the thought of what had been; but the vivid picture of what might have been. He could not resist recalling to himself the image of the famous mistress of the emperor who afterwards married and became a good wife and mother. Her husband had a high position, influence, and esteem, and a good and penitent wife.

In his better hours Kasatsky was not distressed by this thought. At such times he rejoiced that these temptations were past. But there were moments when all that went to make up his present life grew dark before his mind; moments when, if he did not actually cease to believe in the foundation of his present life, he was at least unable to perceive it; when he could not discover the object of his present life; when he was overcome with recollections of the past, and terrible to say, with regret

at having abandoned the world. His only salvation in that state of mind was obedience and work, and prayers the whole day long. He went through his usual forms at prayers, he even prayed more than was his wont, but it was lip-service, and his soul took no part. This condition would sometimes last a day or two days, and would then pass away. But these days were hideous. Kasatsky felt that he was neither in his own hands nor God's, but subject to some outside will. All he could do at those times was to follow the advice of his superior and undertake nothing, but simply wait.

On the whole, Kasatsky lived then, not according to his own will but in complete obedience to his superior; and in that obedience he found peace.

Such was Kasatsky's life in his first monastery, which lasted seven years. At the end of the third year he was ordained to the priesthood and was given the name of Sergius. The ordination was a momentous event in his inner life. He had previously experienced great comfort and spiritual uplifting at holy communions. At first, when he was himself celebrating mass, at the moment of the oblation, his soul was filled with exaltation. But gradually this sense became dulled; and when on one occasion he had to celebrate mass in an hour of depression as he sometimes had, he felt that this exaltation could not endure. The emotion eventually paled until only the habit was left.

On the whole, in the seven years of his life in the monastery, Sergius began to grow weary. All that he had to learn, all that he had to attain was done, and he had nothing more to do.

But his stupefaction only increased. During that time he heard of his mother's death and of Mary's marriage. Both events were matters of indifference to him, as all his attention and all his interest were concentrated on his inner life.

In the fourth year of his monastic experience, during which the bishop had shown him marked kindness, his superior told him that in the event of high honours being offered to him he should not decline. Just then monastic ambition, precisely that quality which was so disgusting to him in all the other monks, arose within him. He was sent to a monastery close to the capital. He would have been glad to refuse, but his superior ordered him to accept, so he obeyed, and taking leave of his superior, left for the other monastery.

This transfer to the monastery near the metropolis was an important event in Sergius's life. There he encountered many temptations, and his whole will power was concentrated on the struggle they entailed. In the first monastery women were no trial to him, but in the second instance this special temptation assumed grave dimensions and even took definite shape.

There was a lady known for her frivolous behaviour, who began to seek his favour. She talked to him and asked him to call upon her.

Sergius refused with severity, but was horrified at the definiteness of his desire. He was so alarmed that he wrote to his superior. Moreover, for the sake of humiliation, he called a young novice and, conquering his shame, confessed his weakness. He begged him to keep an eye on him and not let him go anywhere but to service and to do penance.

Besides that, Sergius suffered severely on account of his great antipathy to the abbot of this monastery, a worldly man and clever in worldly ways who was making a career for himself within the church. In spite of his most earnest endeavours, Sergius could not overcome his dislike for him. He was submissive to him, but in his heart he criticised him unceasingly. At last, when he had been there nearly two years, his real sentiments burst forth.

On the feast of the Intercession of the Virgin, the vesper service was being celebrated in the church proper. There were many visitors from the neighbourhood, and the service was conducted by the abbot himself. Father Sergius was standing in his usual place, and was praying; that is to say, he was engaged in that inner combat which always occupied him during service, especially in this second monastery.

The conflict was caused by his irritation at the presence of all the fine folk and especially the ladies. He tried not to notice what was going on around him. He could not help, however, seeing a soldier who while conducting the better dressed people pushed the common crowd aside, and noticing the ladies who pointed out the monks, often himself and another monk as well, who was noted for his good looks. He tried to concentrate his mind, to see nothing but the light of the candles on the ikonostasis, the sacred images, and the priests. He tried to hear nothing but the prayers which were spoken and chanted; to feel nothing but self-oblivion in the fulfilment of his duty. This was a feeling he always experienced when he listened to prayers and anticipated the word in the prayers he had so often heard.

So he stood, crossing himself, prostrating himself, struggling with himself, now indulging in quiet condemnation, and now giving himself up to that obliteration of thought and feeling which he voluntarily induced in himself.

When the treasurer, Father Nicodemus (also a great stumbling-block in Father Sergius's way—that Father Nicodemus!), whom he couldn't help censuring for flattering and fawning on the abbot, approached him, and saluting him with a low bow that nearly bent him in two, said that the abbot requested his presence behind the holy gates, Father Sergius straightened his cassock, covered his head, and went circumspectly through the crowd.

"*Lise, regardes à droite—c'est lui,*" he heard a woman's voice say.

"*Où, où? Il n'est pas tellement beau!*"

He knew they were referring to him. As his habit was when he was tempted, he repeated, "Lead us not into temptation." Dropping his

eyes and bowing his head, he walked past the lectern and the canons, who at that moment were passing in front of the ikonostasis; and went behind the holy gates by the north portal. According to custom, he crossed himself, bending double before the ikon. Then he raised his head and looked at the abbot, whom, together with some one standing beside him in brilliant array, he had already seen out of the corner of his eye.

The abbot stood against the wall in his vestments, taking his short fat hands from beneath his chasuble and folding them on his fat stomach. Fingering the braid on his chasuble, he smiled as he talked to a man wearing the uniform of a general in the emperor's suite, with insignia and epaulettes, which Father Sergius at once recognised with his experienced military eye. This general was a former colonel in command of his regiment, who now evidently held a very high position. Father Sergius at once noticed that the abbot was fully aware of this, and was so pleased that his fat red face and his bald head gleamed with satisfaction. Father Sergius was grieved and disgusted, and all the more so when he heard from the abbot that he had only sent for him to satisfy the curiosity of the general, who wanted to see his famous "colleague," as he put it.

"I am so glad to see you in your angelic guise," said the general, holding out his hand. "I hope you have not forgotten your old comrade."

The whole thing—the abbot's red and smiling face above his white beard in evident approval of the general's words; the well-scrubbed face of the general with his self-satisfied smile, the smell of wine from the general's breath, and the smell of cigars from his whiskers—made Sergius boil.

He bowed once more before the abbot, and said, "Your grace deigned to call me—" and he stopped, asking by the very expression of his face and eyes, "What for?"

The abbot said, "Yes, to meet the general."

"Your grace, I left the world to save myself from temptation," he said, pale and with quivering lips; "why, then, do you expose me to it during prayers in the house of God?"

"Go! go!" said the abbot, frowning and growing angry.

Next day Father Sergius asked forgiveness of the abbot and of the brethren for his pride. But at the same time, after a night spent in prayer, he decided that his only possible course was to leave this monastery; so he wrote a letter to his superior imploring him to grant him leave to return to his monastery. He wrote that he felt his weakness and the impossibility of struggling alone against temptation without his help. He did penance for his sin of pride. The next post brought him a letter from the superior, who wrote that the sole cause of all his trouble was pride. The old man explained to him that his fits of anger were due to the fact that in refusing all clerical honour he humiliated himself not for the sake of God, but for the sake of his pride; merely for the sake of

saying to himself: "Now, am I not a splendid fellow not to desire anything?" That was why he could not tolerate the abbot's action. "I have renounced everything for the glory of God, and here I am exhibited like a wild beast!" "If you would just give up vanity for God's glory you would be able to bear it," wrote the old man; "worldly pride is not yet dead in you. I have thought often of you, Sergius, my son. I have prayed also, and this is God's message with regard to you: Go on as you are, and submit."

At that moment tidings came that the recluse Hilary, a man of saintly life, had died in the hermitage. He had lived there for eighteen years. The abbot of that hermitage inquired whether there was not a brother who would take his place.

"Now with regard to that letter of yours," wrote the superior, "go to Father Païssy, of the T—— Monastery. I have written to him about you, and asked him to take you into Hilary's cell. I do not say you could replace Hilary, but you want solitude to stifle your pride. And may God bless you in your undertaking."

Sergius obeyed his superior, showed his letter to the abbot, and, asking his permission, gave up his cell, handed all his belongings over to the monastery, and departed for the hermitage at T——.

The abbot of that hermitage, a former merchant, received Sergius calmly and quietly, and left him alone in his cell. This cell was a cave dug in a mountain, and Hilary was buried there. In a niche at the back was Hilary's grave, and in front was a place to sleep, a small table, and a shelf with ikons and books. At the entrance door, which could be closed, was another shelf. Upon that shelf food was placed once a day by a brother from the monastery.

So Father Sergius became a hermit.

Chapter 3

DURING THE CARNIVAL in Sergius's second year of seclusion a merry company of rich people, ladies and gentlemen from the neighbouring town, made up a troika party after a meal of carnival pancakes and wine. The company was composed of two lawyers, a wealthy landowner, an officer, and four ladies. One of the ladies was the wife of the officer; another was the wife of the landowner; the third was his sister, a young girl; the fourth was a *divorcée,* beautiful, rich, a little

mad, whose ways gave rise to amazement and indignation in the town.

The night was fine; the roads smooth as a floor. They drove ten miles out of town, and then held a consultation as to whether they should turn back or go on.

"But where does this road lead?" asked Madame Makovkin, the beautiful *divorcée*.

"To T——, twelve miles further on," said the lawyer who was having a flirtation with Madame Makovkin.

"And beyond?"

"Then to L——, past the monastery."

"Oh, the one where Father Sergius is?"

"Yes."

"The handsome hermit—Kasatsky."

"Yes."

"Oh—messieurs et mesdames!—let us go in and see Kasatsky. We can rest at T—— and have a bite."

"But we shan't get home to-night?"

"We'll just spend the night at Kasatsky's then."

"Of course. There is a hostelry at the monastery, and a very good one. When I was defending Makine I stopped there."

"No, I shall spend the night at Kasatsky's!"

"Even your great power, dear lady, could not make that possible."

"Not possible? I'll bet you!"

"Good! If you spend the night at Kasatsky's I'll pay you whatever you like."

"*A discrétion!*"

"And you the same, remember."

"Agreed! Let's start."

They gave the driver some wine, and they opened a basket of pies, cakes, and wines for themselves. The ladies drew their white furs round about them. The postillions broke into a dispute as to which should go ahead, and the younger one, turning sharply round, lifted his whip-handle high up and shouted at the horses; the bells tinkled, and the runners creaked beneath the sledge. The sledge swayed and rocked a little; the outer horses trotted smoothly and briskly, with their tightly-bound tails under the gaily decorated breech-bands. The slippery road faded away rapidly. The driver held the reins tightly.

The lawyer and the officer who sat on the back seat talked nonsense to Madame Makovkin's neighbour, and she herself, huddled in her furs, sat motionless and in thought.

"Eternally the same old things! The ugliness of it. Shiny red faces reeking with liquor and with tobacco, the same words, the same thoughts, for ever the same abomination; and they are all content and satisfied that it should be so, and thus they will go on till they die. But I can't—it

bores me. I want something to happen that will upset and shatter the whole thing. We might at least be frozen to death as they were at Saratov. What would these people do? How would they behave? Execrably, I suppose. Everybody would think of nothing but himself, and I no less than the rest. But I have beauty—that's something. They know it. Well—and that monk—I wonder if he really is indifferent to beauty. No, they all care for it, just like that cadet last autumn. And what a fool he was!"

"Ivan Nicolaievich," she said.

He answered, "Yes?"

"How old is he?"

"Who?"

"Why, Kasatsky."

"Over forty, I should think."

"Does he receive visitors? Does he see everybody?"

"Everybody, yes; but not always."

"Cover up my feet. Not that way—how clumsy you are? Yes, like that. But you needn't squeeze them."

Thus they came to the forest where the cell was.

She stepped out of the sledge and bade them drive on. They tried to dissuade her, but she grew irritable, and commanded them to go on.

Father Sergius was now forty-nine years old. His life in solitude was very hard: not because of fasting and prayers. He endured those easily. But it was the inner struggle which he had not anticipated. There were two reasons for this struggle: his religious doubts and the temptations of desire. He thought these were two different fiends. But they were one and the same. When his doubts were gone lust was gone. But thinking these were two different devils, he fought them separately. They, however, always attacked him together.

"O my God, my God," he cried, "why dost Thou not give me faith? There is lust of course, but even St. Anthony and the rest had to fight that; but faith—they had that! There are moments and hours and days when I do not possess it. Why does the world exist with all its charm, if it is sinful and we must renounce it? Why hast Thou created this temptation? Temptation? But isn't this temptation to renounce the joys of the world and to prepare for the life beyond, where there is nothing and where there can be nothing?" Saying this to himself, he became horrified and filled with disgust at himself.

"You vile thing! And you think of being a saint!" he said.

He rose to pray. But when he began praying he saw himself as he appeared at the monastery in his vestments and all his grandeur, and he shook his head.

"No, that is not so. It is a lie. I may deceive all the world, but not myself, and not God. I am insignificant. I am pitiable." And he pushed

back the skirts of his cassock, and gazed at his thin legs in their under-clothing.

Then he dropped his robe again, and began to repeat his prayers, making the sign of the cross and prostrating himself.

"Will that couch be my bier?" he read; and, as if a demon whispered to him, he heard: "The solitary couch is also the coffin."

"It is a lie!" and he saw in imagination the shoulders of a widow who had been his mistress. He shook himself and went on reading. After having read the precepts he took up the Gospels. He opened the book at a passage that he had often repeated and knew by heart.

"Lord, I believe. Help thou my unbelief."

He stifled the doubts that arose. Just as one replaces an object without disturbing its balance, he carefully put his faith back into its position while it trembled at its base, and stepped back cautiously so as neither to touch it nor upset it. He again pulled himself together and regained his peace of mind and repeating his childish prayer: "O Lord, take me, take me!" felt not only at ease, but glad and thrilled. He crossed himself and lay down to sleep on his narrow bench, putting his light summer garment under his head. He dropped off to sleep at once. In his light slumber he heard small tinkling bells. He did not know whether he was dreaming or waking. But a knock at the door aroused him. He sat up on his couch, not trusting his senses. The knock came again. Yes, it was nearer, it was at his own door, and after it came the sound of a woman's voice.

"My God! is it true that the devil takes the form of a woman, as I have read in the lives of the saints? Yes—it is a woman's voice! So timid —so sweet—so tender!" And he spat to exorcise the devil. "No! It was only imagination!" and he went to the corner where the lectern stood and fell on his knees, his regular and habitual motion that of itself gave him comfort and pleasure. He bowed low, his hair falling forward on his face, and pressed his bare forehead to the damp, cold floor. There was a draught from the floor. He read a psalm which, as old Father Piman had told him, would ward off the assaults of the devil. His light, slender frame started up upon its strong limbs, and he meant to go on reading his prayers. But he did not read. He involuntarily inclined his head to listen. He wanted to hear more.

All was silent. From the corner of the roof the same regular drops fell into the tub below. Without was a mist, a fog that swallowed up the snow. It was still, very still. There was a sudden rustle at the window, and a distinct voice, the same tender, timid voice, a voice that could only belong to a charming woman.

"Let me in, for Christ's sake."

All the blood rushed to his heart and settled there. He could not even sigh.

"May the Lord appear and his enemies be confounded."

"But I am not the devil!"

He could not hear that the words were spoken by smiling lips. "I am not the devil. I am just a wicked woman that's lost her way, literally and figuratively." (She laughed.) "I am frozen, and I beg for shelter."

He put his face close to the window. The little ikon lamp was reflected in the glass. He put his hands up to his face and peered between them. Fog, mist, darkness, a tree, and—at the right— She herself, a woman in thick white furs, in a fur cap with a lovely, lovely, gentle, frightened face, two inches away, leaning towards him. Their eyes met and they recognised each other—not because they had ever seen each other before. They had never met. But in the look they exchanged they felt—and he particularly—that they knew each other; that they understood.

After that glance which they exchanged how could he entertain any further doubt that this was the devil instead of just a sweet, timid, frightened woman?

"Who are you? Why have you come?" he asked.

"Open the door, I say," she said with a whimsical authority. "I tell you I've lost my way."

"But I am a monk—a hermit."

"Open that door all the same. Do you want me to freeze while you say your prayers?"

"But how—"

"I won't eat you. Let me in for God's sake. I'm quite frozen."

She began to be really frightened and spoke almost tearfully.

He stepped back into the room, looked at the ikon representing the Saviour with His crown of thorns.

"God help me—help me, O God!" he said, crossing himself and bowing low. Then he went to the door which opened into the little porch, and feeling for the latch tried to unhook it. He heard steps outside. She was going from the window to the door.

"Oh!" he heard her exclaim, and he knew she had stepped into a puddle made by the dripping rain. His hands trembled, and he could not move the hook which stuck a little.

"Well, can't you let me in? I'm quite soaked, and I'm frozen. You are only bent on saving your own soul while I freeze to death."

He jerked the door towards him in order to raise the latch, and then, unable to measure his movements, pushed it open with such violence that it struck her.

"Oh—pardon!" he said suddenly, reverting to his former tone with ladies.

She smiled, hearing that "pardon." "Oh, well, he's not so dreadful," she thought. "Never mind; it is you who must pardon me," she said,

passing by him. "I would never have ventured, but such an extraordinary circumstance—"

"If you please," he said, making way for her.

He was struck by the fragrance of fine perfume that he had not smelt for many a long day.

She went through the porch into the chamber. He shut the outer door without latching it and passed into the room after her. Not only in his heart but involuntarily moving his lips he repeated unceasingly, "O Lord Jesus Christ, Son of God, have mercy on me, a sinner, have mercy on me, a sinner."

"If you please," he said to her again.

She stood in the middle of the room, dripping, and examined him closely. Her eyes smiled.

"Forgive me for disturbing your solitude," she said, "but you must see what a position I am placed in. It all came about by our coming out for a drive from town. I made a wager that I would walk by myself from Vorobievka to town. But I lost my way. That's how I happened to find your cell." Her lies now began.

But his face confused her so that she could not proceed, so she stopped. She expected him to be quite different from the man she saw. He was not as handsome as she had imagined, but he was beautiful to her. His grey hair and beard, slightly curling, his fine, regular features and his eyes like burning coals when he looked straight at her, impressed her profoundly. He saw that she was lying.

"Yes; very well," he said, looking at her and dropping his eyes. "Now I will go in there, and this place is at your disposal."

He took the burning lamp down from before the ikon, lit a candle, and making a low bow went out to the little niche on the other side of the partition, and she heard him begin to move something there.

"He is probably trying to shut himself up away from me," she thought, smiling. Taking off her white fur, she tried to remove her cap, but it caught in her hair and in the knitted shawl she was wearing underneath it. She had not got wet at all standing outside at the window. She said so only as a pretext to be admitted. But she had really stepped into a puddle at the door, and her left foot was wet to the ankle, and one shoe was full of water. She sat down on his bed, a bench only covered with a carpet, and began to take her shoes off. The little cell pleased her. It was about nine feet by twelve, and as clean as glass. There was nothing in it save the bench on which she sat, the book-shelf above it, and the lectern in the corner. On the door were nails where his fur coat and his cassock hung. Beside the lantern was the image of Christ with His crown of thorns, and the lamp. The room smelt strangely of oil and of earth. She liked everything, even that smell. Her wet feet were uncomfortable, the left one especially, and she took off her shoes

and stockings, never ceasing to smile. She was happy not only in having achieved her object, but because she perceived that he was troubled by her presence. He, the charming, striking, strange, attractive man!

"Well, if he wasn't responsive, it doesn't matter," she said to herself. "Father Serigius! Father Sergius!—or what am I to call you!"

"What do you want?" answered a low voice.

"Please forgive me for disturbing your solitude, but really I couldn't help it. I would have fallen ill. And even now I don't know if I shan't. I'm quite wet and my feet are like ice."

"Pardon me," answered the quiet voice. "I cannot be of any assistance to you."

"I would not have come if I could have helped it. I shall only stop till dawn."

He did not answer. She heard him muttering something, probably his prayers.

"I hope you will not come in here," she said, smiling, "for I must undress to get dry."

He did not answer, continuing to read his prayers in a steady voice.

"That is a man," she thought, as she attempted to remove her wet shoe. She tugged at it in vain and felt like laughing. Almost inaudibly, she did laugh; then, knowing that he would hear, and would be moved by it just as she wanted him to be, she laughed louder. The kind, cheerful, natural laughter did indeed affect him just as she had wished.

"I could love a man like that. Such eyes; and his simple, noble face, passionate in spite of all the prayers it mutters. There's no fooling us women in that. The instant he put his face against the window-pane and saw me, he knew me and understood me. The glimmer of it was in his eyes and a seal was set upon it for ever. That instant he began to love me and to want me. Yes—he wants me," she said, finally getting off her shoe and fumbling at her stocking.

To remove those long stockings fastened with elastic, she had to raise her skirts. She felt embarrassed and said, "Don't come in." But there was no answer from the other side and she heard the same monotonous murmurs and movements.

"I suppose he's bowing down to the ground," she thought, "but that won't help him. He's thinking about me just as I'm thinking about him. He's thinking about these very feet of mine," she said, taking off the wet stockings and sitting up on the couch barefooted, with her hands clasped about her knees. She sat awhile like this, gazing pensively before her.

"It's a perfect desert here. Nobody would ever know—"

She got down, took her stockings over to the stove and hung them on the damper. It was such a quaint damper! She turned it, and then slipping quietly over to the couch she sat up there again with her feet upon it. There was absolute silence on the other side of the partition.

She looked at the little watch hanging round her neck. Two o'clock. "My people will return about three." She had more than an hour before her.

"Well! Am I going to sit here by myself the whole time? Nonsense! I don't like that. I'll call him at once. Father Sergius! Father Sergius! Sergei Dimitrievich! Prince Kasatsky!"

No answer.

"I say! That's cruel. I wouldn't call you if I didn't need you. I'm ill. I don't know what's the matter," she said in a tone of suffering. "Oh! oh!" she groaned, falling back on the couch, and, strange to say, she really felt that she was getting faint, that everything ached, that she was trembling as if with fever.

"Here, listen! Help me! I don't know what's the matter with. Oh! oh!"

She opened her dress, uncovering her breast, and raised her arms, bare to the elbows, above her head. "Oh, oh!"

All this time he stood on the other side of the door and prayed.

Having finished all the evening prayers, he stood motionless, fixing his eyes on the end of his nose, and praying in his heart he repeated with all his soul: "Lord Jesus Christ, Son of God, have mercy on me!"

He had heard everything. He had heard how the silk rustled when she took off her dress; how she stepped on the floor with her bare feet. He heard how she rubbed her hands and feet. He felt himself getting weak, and thought he might be lost at any moment. That was why he prayed unceasingly. His feelings must have been somewhat like those of the hero in the fairy tale who had to go on and on without ever turning back. Sergius heard and felt that the danger was there just above his head, around him, and that the only way to escape it was not to look round on it for an instant. Then suddenly the desire to see her came upon him, and at that very instant she exclaimed, "Now this is monstrous! I may die."

"Yes, I will come. But I will go like that saint who laid one hand upon the adulteress but put the other upon burning coals."

But there were no burning coals. He looked round. The lamp! The lamp!

He put a finger over the flame and frowned, ready to endure. In the beginning it seemed to him that there was no sensation. But then of a sudden, before he had decided whether it hurt him or how much it hurt him, his face writhed, and he jerked his hand away, shaking it in the air.

"No, that I can't do."

"For God's sake, come to me. I am dying. Oh!"

"Must I be lost? No! I'll come to you presently," he said, opening the door. And without looking at her he passed through the room to the

porch where he used to chop wood. He felt about to find the block and the axe which were leaning against the wall.

"Presently!" he said, and taking the axe in his right hand, he laid the forefinger of his left hand upon the block. He raised the axe and struck at the finger below the second joint. The finger flew off more lightly than wood, and bounding up, turned over on the edge of the block and then on to the floor. Sergius heard that sound before he realised the pain, but ere he could recover his senses he felt a burning pain and the warmth of the flowing blood. He hastily pressed the end of his cassock to the maimed finger, pressed it to his hip, and going back into her room stood before the woman.

"What do you want?" he asked her in a low voice.

She looked at his pale face with its trembling cheeks and felt ashamed. She jumped up, grasped her fur, and throwing it around her shoulders tucked herself up in it.

"I was in pain—I've taken cold—I—Father Sergius—I—"

He turned his eyes, which were shining with the quiet light of joy upon her, and said—

"Dear sister, why have you desired to lose your immortal soul? Temptation must come into the world, but woe to him by whom temptation cometh. Pray that God may forgive us both."

She listened and looked at him. Suddenly she heard the sound of something dripping. She looked closely and saw that blood was dropping from his hand on to his cassock.

"What have you done to your hand?"

She remembered the sound she had heard, and seizing the little ikon lamp ran out to the porch; there on the floor she saw the bloody finger.

She returned with her face paler than his, and wanted to say something. But he went silently to his little apartment and shut the door.

"Forgive me," she said. "How can I atone for my sin?"

"Go."

"Let me bind your wound."

"Go hence."

She dressed hurriedly and silently and sat in her furs waiting.

The sound of little bells reached her from outside.

"Father Sergius, forgive me."

"Go—God will forgive you."

"Father Sergius, I will change my life. Do not forsake me."

"Go."

"Forgive—and bless me!"

"In the name of the Father and of the Son and of the Holy Ghost," she heard from behind the door. "Go."

She sobbed and went out from the cell.

The lawyer came forward to meet her.

"Well," he said, "I see I have lost. There's no help for it. Where will you sit?"

"I don't care."

She took a seat in the sledge and did not speak a word till they reached home.

A year later she entered a convent as a novice and led a life of severe discipline under the guidance of hermit R—— who wrote her letters at long intervals.

Chapter 4

ANOTHER SEVEN YEARS Father Sergius lived as a hermit. In the beginning he accepted a great part of what people used to bring him—tea, sugar, white bread, milk, clothes, and wood.

But as time went on he led a life of ever greater austerity. Refusing anything that could be thought superfluous, he finally accepted nothing but rye bread once a week. All that was brought to him he gave to the poor who visited him.

His entire time was spent in his cell in prayer or in conversation with visitors whose number continually increased.

Father Sergius appeared in church only three times a year, and when it was necessary he went out to fetch water and wood.

After the episode with Madame Makovkin, the change he effected in her life, and her taking the veil, the fame of Father Sergius increased. Visitors came in greater and greater numbers, and monks came to live in his neighbourhood. A church was built there, and a hostelry. Fame, as usual, exaggerated his feats. People came from a great distance and began bringing invalids to him in the belief that he could heal them.

His first cure happened in the eighth year of his seclusion. He actually healed a boy of fourteen brought to him by his mother who insisted on Father Sergius putting his hand on the child's head. The idea had never occurred to him that he could heal the sick. He would have regarded such a thought as a great sin of pride.

But the mother who brought the boy never ceased imploring him, on her knees.

"Why wouldn't he help her son when he healed other people?" she asked, and again besought him in the name of Christ.

When Father Sergius replied that only God could heal, she said she wanted him only to lay his hands on his head and pray.

Father Sergius refused and went back to his cell. But next morning—for this happened in the autumn and the nights were already cold —coming out of his cell to fetch water, he saw the same mother with her child, the same boy of fourteen, and heard the same petitions.

Father Sergius remembered the parable of the righteous judge, and contrary to his first instinct that he must indubitably refuse, he began to pray, and prayed until a resolve formed itself in his soul. This decision was that he must accede to the woman's request, and that her faith was sufficient to save her child. As for him, Father Sergius, he would be in that case but the worthless instrument chosen by God.

Returning to the mother, Father Sergius yielded to her request, put his hand on the boy's head and prayed.

The mother left with her son. In a month the boy was cured, and the fame of the holy healing power of "old Father Sergius," as he was called then, spread abroad. From that time not a week passed without sick people coming to Father Sergius.

Complying with the requests of some, he could not refuse the rest; he laid his hands on them and prayed. Many were healed and his fame became more and more widespread.

Having thus passed seven years in the monastery and many years in the hermitage, he looked now like an old man. He had a long grey beard, and his hair had grown thin.

Chapter 5

NOW FATHER SERGIUS HAD FOR WEEKS been haunted by one relentless thought, whether it was right for him to have acquiesced in a state of things not so much created by himself as by the archimandrite and the abbot.

This state of things had begun after the healing of the boy of fourteen. Since that time Sergius felt that each passing month, each week and each day, his inner life had somehow been destroyed and a merely external life had been substituted for it. It was as if he had been turned inside out. Sergius saw that he was a means of attracting visitors and patrons to the monastery, and that, therefore, the authorities of the monastery tried to arrange matters in such a way that he might be most profitable to them. For instance, he had no chance of doing any work. Everything was provided that he could require, and the only thing they asked was that he should not refuse his blessing to the visitors who came to seek it. For his convenience days were appointed on which

he should receive them. A reception room was arranged for men; and a place was also enclosed by railings in order that the crowds of women who came to him should not overwhelm him, a place where he could bestow his blessing upon those who came.

When he was told that he was necessary to men, and that if he would follow the rule of Christ's love, he could not refuse them when they desired to see him, and that his holding aloof from them would be cruel, he could not but agree.

But the more he gave himself up to such an existence the more he felt his inner life transformed into an external one. He felt the fount of living water drying up within him; and that everything he did now was performed more and more for man and less for God. Whatever he did, whether admonishing or simply blessing, or praying for the sick, or giving advice on the conduct of life, or listening to expressions of gratitude from those he had helped, or healed (as they say) or instructed or advised, he could not help feeling a certain pleasure when they expressed their gratitude to him. Neither could he be indifferent to the results of his activity, nor to his influence. He now thought himself a shining light. But the more he harboured that idea, the more he was conscious of the fact that the divine light of truth which had previously burned within him was flickering and dying.

"How much of what I do is done for God and how much for man?" That was the question that tormented him. Not that he could not find an answer to it, but he dared not give an answer. He felt deep down in his soul that the devil had somehow changed all his work for God into work for man. Because just as it had formerly been hard for him to be torn from solitude, now solitude itself was hard. He was often wearied with visitors, but in the bottom of his heart he enjoyed their presence and rejoiced in the praise which was heaped on him.

There came a time when he made up his mind to go away, to hide. He even thought out a plan. He got ready a peasant shirt and peasant trousers, a coat and a cap. He explained that he wanted them to give to the poor, and he kept these clothes in his cell, thinking how he would one day put them on and cut his hair, and go away. First he would take a train and travel for about three hundred miles. Then he would get out and walk from village to village. He asked an old soldier how he tramped; if people gave alms, and whether they admitted wayfarers into their houses. The soldier told him where people were most charitable, and where they would take a wanderer in for the night, and Father Sergius decided to act on his advice. One night, he even put on those clothes and was about to go. But he did not know which was best, to remain or to run away. For a time he was undecided. Then the state of indecision passed. He grew accustomed to the devil and yielded to him; and the peasant clothes only served to remind him of thoughts and feelings that were no more.

Father Sergius

Crowds flocked to him increasingly from day to day, and he had less and less time for prayers and for renewing his spiritual strength. Sometimes, in his brighter moments, he thought he was like a place where a brook had once been. There had been a quiet stream of living water which flowed out of him and through him, he thought. That had been real life, the time when she had tempted him. He always thought with ecstasy of that night and of her who was now Mother Agnes. She had tasted of that pure water. Since then the water had hardly been given time to collect before those who were thirsty arrived in crowds, pushing one another aside, and they had trodden down the little brook until nothing but mud was left. So he thought in his clearer moments; but his ordinary state of mind was weariness and a sort of tenderness for himself because of that weariness.

It was spring, the eve of a festal day. Father Sergius celebrated Vespers in the church in the cave. There were as many people as the place could hold—about twenty altogether. They all belonged to the better classes, rich merchants and such like. Father Sergius admitted every one to his church, but a selection was made by the monk appointed to serve him and by a man on duty who was sent to the hermitage every day from the monastery. A crowd of about eighty pilgrims, chiefly women, stood outside, waiting for Father Sergius to come out and bless them. In that part of the service, when he went to the tomb of his predecessor to bless it, he felt faint, and staggered, and would have fallen had it not been for a merchant who served as deacon who caught him.

"What is the matter with you? Father Sergius, dear Father Sergius! O God!" exclaimed a woman's voice. "He is as white as a sheet!"

But Father Sergius pulled himself together and though still very pale, pushed aside the deacon and the merchant and resumed the prayers. Father Serafian, the deacon, and the acolytes and a lady, Sophia Ivanovna, who always lived close by the hermitage to attend on Father Sergius, begged him to bring the service to an end.

"No, there's nothing the matter," said Father Sergius, faintly smiling from beneath his moustache and continuing his prayers. "Ah, that is the way of saints," he thought.

"A holy man—an angel of God," he heard Sophia Ivanovna and the merchant who had supported him a moment before murmur. He did not heed their entreaties, but went on with the service. Crowding one another as before, they all filed through narrow passages back into the little church where Father Sergius completed vespers, merely curtailing the service a little. Directly after this, having pronounced the benediction on those present, he sat down outside on a little bench beneath an elm tree at the entrance to the cave. He wanted to rest; to breathe fresh air. He felt the need of it; but the moment he appeared, a crowd of people rushed to him soliciting his blessing, his advice, and his help. In the crowd was a number of women, pilgrims going from one holy place to

another, from one holy man to another, ever in ecstasy before each sanctuary and before each saint.

Father Sergius knew this common, cold, irreligious, unemotional type. As for the men in the crowd, they were for the most part retired soldiers, long unaccustomed to a settled life, and most of them were poor, drunken old men who tramped from monastery to monastery merely for a living. The dull peasantry also flocked there, men and women, with their selfish requirements seeking healing or advice in their little daily interests; how their daughters should be married, or a shop hired, or land bought, or how a woman could atone for a child she had lain over in sleep and killed, or for a child she had borne out of wedlock.

All this was an old story to Father Sergius and did not interest him. He knew he would hear nothing new from them. The spectacle of their faces could not arouse any religious emotion in him. But he liked to look at them as a crowd which was in need of his benediction and revered his words. This made him like the crowd, although he found them fatiguing and tiresome.

Father Serafian began to disperse the people saying that Father Sergius was weary. But Father Sergius recollected the words of the Gospel, "Suffer the little children to come unto me and forbid them not," and touched at his recollection of the passage he permitted them to approach. He rose, walked to the little railing beyond which the crowd had gathered, and began to bless them, but his answers to their questions were so faint that he was moved at hearing himself.

Despite his wish to receive them all, it was too much for him. Everything grew dark again before his eyes, and he staggered and grasped the railings. He felt the blood rushing to his head, and grew pale and then scarlet.

"I must leave the rest till to-morrow, I can do no more now," he said, and pronouncing a general benediction, returned to the bench.

The merchant supported him again, and taking him by the arm assisted him to be seated. Voices exclaimed in the crowd—

"Father, dear father, don't forsake us. We are lost without you."

The merchant, having helped Father Sergius to the bench under the elm tree, took upon himself the duties of policeman and began energetically to disperse the crowd. It was true he spoke in a low voice so that Father Sergius could not overhear, but he spoke very decidedly and in an angry tone.

"Get away, get away, I say! He has blessed you. What else do you want? Get along! or you'll catch it. Move on there! Get along there, old woman, with your dirty rags. Go on! Where do you think *you're* going; I told you it was finished. To-morrow's coming, but to-day he's done, I tell you!"

"Dear father! I only want to look on his dear face with my own little eyes," said an old woman.

"Little eyes indeed! You don't get in here!"

Father Sergius noticed that the merchant was doing it rather too thoroughly, and spoke to his attendant saying the crowd was not to be turned away. He knew perfectly well that the crowd would be dispersed all the same, and he desired to remain alone and rest, but he sent his attendant with the order merely to make an impression.

"Well—well—I'm not turning them away; I'm only talking to them," answered the merchant. "They'll drive the man to death. They have no mercy. They're only thinking of themselves. No, I say! Get away! To-morrow!" and he drove them all away.

The merchant took all this trouble because he loved order and liked to turn people away and abuse them; but more because he wanted to have Father Sergius to himself. He was a widower and had an only daughter, an invalid and unmarried. He had brought her fourteen hundred miles to Father Sergius to be healed. During the two years of the girl's illness he had taken her to various cures. First to the university clinic in the principal town of the province, but this was not of much use; then to a peasant in the province of Samara, who did her a little good. Afterwards he took her to a doctor in Moscow and paid him a huge fee; but this did not help at all. Then he was told that Father Sergius wrought cures, so he brought her to him. Consequently when he had scattered the crowd he approached Father Sergius, and falling upon his knees without any warning, he said in a loud voice—

"Holy Father! Bless my afflicted child and heal her of her sufferings. I venture to prostrate myself at your holy feet," and put one hand on another, palms up, cup-wise. All this he did as if it were something distinctly and rigidly appointed by law and usage; as if it were the sole and precise method by which a man should request the healing of his daughter. He did it with such conviction that even Sergius felt for the moment that that was just the right way. However he bade him rise from his knees and tell him what the trouble was. The merchant said that his daughter, a girl of twenty-two, had fallen ill two years before, after the sudden death of her mother. She just said "Ah!" as he put it, and went out of her mind. He had brought her fourteen hundred miles, and she was waiting in the hostelry till Father Sergius could receive her. She never went out by day, being afraid of the sunlight, but only after dusk.

"Is she very weak?" asked Father Sergius.

"No, she has no special weakness, but she's rather stout, and the doctor says she's neurasthenic. If you will just let me fetch her, Father Sergius, I'll be back with her in a minute. Revive, O holy father, the heart of a parent, restore his line, and save my afflicted offspring with your prayers!" and the merchant fell down on his knees again and bending sideways with his head over his palms, which appeared to hold little heaps of something, remained like a figure in stone. Father Sergius

315

again told him to get up, and thinking once more how trying his work was, and how patiently he bore it in spite of everything, sighed heavily. After a few moments' silence, he said:

"Well, bring her to-night. I will pray over her. But now I am weary," and he closed his eyes. "I will send for you."

The merchant went away, stepping on tiptoe, which made his boots creak still louder, and Father Sergius remained alone.

Father Sergius's life was filled with church services and with visitors; but this day was particularly difficult. In the morning an important official had come to hold a long conference with him. Then a lady came with her son. The son was a young professor, an unbeliever, and his mother, who was ardently religious and devoted to Father Sergius, brought him to Father Sergius that he might talk to him. The talk was very trying. The young man evidently did not wish to have a discussion with the monk, and just agreed with him in everything, as with an inferior. Father Sergius saw that the youth was an infidel, but that he had never-theless a clear and tranquil conscience. The memory of the conversation was now unpleasant to him.

"Won't you eat something, Father Sergius?" asked the attendant.

"Very well—bring me something."

The attendant went to a little hut built ten paces from the cave, and Father Sergius remained alone.

The time was long past when Father Sergius lived alone, doing everything for himself and having but a holy wafer and bread for nourish-ment. He had been warned long ago that he had no right to be careless of his health and he was given wholesome meals, although of Lenten quality. He did not eat much, but more than he had done; and some-times he even felt a pleasure in eating; the disgust and the sense of sin he had experienced before was gone.

He took some gruel and had a cup of tea with half a roll of white bread. The attendant went away while he remained alone on the bench under the elm-tree. It was a beautiful evening in May. The leaves of the birches, the aspens, the elms, the alder bushes, and the oaks were just beginning to blossom. The alder bushes behind the elms were still in full bloom. A nightingale was singing near at hand, and two or three more in the bushes down by the river trilled and warbled. From the river came the songs of working-men, perhaps on their way home from their labour. The sun was setting behind the forest and was throwing little broken rays of light among the leaves. This side was bright green and the other side was dark. Beetles were flying about and, colliding to-gether, were falling to the ground. After supper Father Sergius began to repeat a prayer mentally:

"O Lord Jesus Christ, Son of God, have mercy on us," and then he read a psalm. Suddenly, in the middle of the psalm a sparrow flew out from a bush on the ground, and hopping along, came to him; then

it flew away frightened. He was reading a prayer that bore upon renunciation of the world and hastened to get to the end of it in order that he might send for the merchant and his daughter. He was interested in the daughter because she offered a sort of diversion, and also because she and her father thought him a saint, a saint whose prayer was efficacious. He repudiated the idea, but in the depths of his soul he nevertheless concurred. He often wondered how he, Sergius Kasatsky, had contrived to become such an extraordinary saint and worker of miracles, but that it was a fact he did not doubt. He could not fail to believe in the miracles he saw with his own eyes, beginning with the sick boy and ending with this last old woman who had recovered her sight through his prayers. Strange as it was, it was a fact. Accordingly the merchant's daughter interested him as a new individual that had faith in him, and besides, as an occasion of bearing witness to his healing power and to his fame.

"People come thousands of miles. Papers talk about it. The emperor knows. All Europe knows—all godless Europe." And then he felt ashamed of his vanity and began to pray:

"God, King of Heaven, Comforter, True Soul, come into—inspire me—and cleanse me from all sin, and save, O All-merciful, my soul. Cleanse me from the sin of worldly vanity that has overtaken me," he said, remembering how often he had made that prayer and how vain it had been. His prayers worked miracles for others, but as for himself God had not granted him strength to conquer this petty passion. He remembered his prayers at the commencement of his seclusion when he asked for the grace of purity, humility, and love, and how it seemed to him at that time that God heard his prayers. He had retained his purity and had hewn off his finger. He raised the stump of the finger with folds of skin on it to his lips, and kissed it. It seemed to him now, that at that time when he had been filled with disgust at his own sinfulness, he had been humble; and that he had also possessed love. He recalled also the tender feelings with which he had received the old drunken soldier who had come to ask alms of him; and how he had received *her*. And now; he asked himself whether he loved anybody; whether he loved Sophia Ivanovna or Father Serafian; whether he had any feeling of love for those who had come to him that day. He asked himself if he had felt any love toward the learned young man with whom he had held that instructive discussion with the object only of showing off his own intelligence and proving that he had not fallen behind in knowledge.

He wanted love from them, and rejoiced in it; but felt no love himself for them. Now he had neither love nor humility. He was pleased to hear that the merchant's daughter was twenty-two, and was anxious to know if she was good-looking. When he inquired if she was weak, he only wanted to know if she had feminine charm. "Is it true that I have fallen so low?" he thought. "God help me! Restore my strength—restore

317

me, O God my Saviour!" and he clasped his hands and began to pray.

The nightingales sang, a beetle flew at him and crept along the back of his neck. He brushed it away.

"But does He exist? What if I am knocking at a house which is locked from without. The bar is on the door, and we can see it. Nightingales, beetles, nature are the bar to our understanding. That young man was perhaps right." He began to pray aloud, and prayed long, till all these thoughts disappeared and he became calm and firm in the faith. He rang the bell, and told the attendant to say that the merchant might now come with his daughter.

The merchant came, leading his daughter by the arm, and brought her to the cell, where he left her.

The daughter was pale, with fair hair. She was very short, and had a frightened, childish face and full figure. Father Sergius remained seated on the bench at the entrance. When the girl passed him and stood near him he blessed her, feeling aghast because of the way in which he looked at her figure. As she passed by him, he felt a sting. He saw by her face that she was sensual and feeble minded. He rose and entered his cell. She was sitting on a stool waiting for him, and when he entered she rose.

"I want to go back to my papa," she said.

"Do not be afraid," he said. "Where do you feel pain?"

"I feel pain all over," she answered, and suddenly her face brightened with a smile.

"You will regain your health," he said. "Pray."

"What's the use? I've prayed. It doesn't help," and she continued smiling. "I wish you would pray and lay your hands on me. I saw you in a dream."

"How so?"

"I saw you put your hand on my chest."

She took his hand and pressed it to her breast.

"Here."

He yielded his right hand to her.

"What is your name?" he asked, his whole body shaking, and feeling that he was overcome and could not control his instinct.

"Marie, why?"

She took his hand and kissed it, and then put her arm around his waist and pressed him.

"Marie, what are you doing?" he said. "You are a devil, Marie!"

"Oh, perhaps. Never mind."

And embracing him, she sat down at his side on the bed.

At dawn he went out of the door. Had all this really happened? Her father would come. She would tell. "She's a devil. But what have *I* done? Oh, there is the axe which I used to chop off my finger."

He took the axe and went back to the cell.

The attendant came toward him. "Do you want some wood cut? Give me the axe."

He gave him the axe, and entered the cell. She lay asleep. He looked on her with horror. Going back into the cell he put on the peasant clothes, seized the scissors, cut his hair, and then, issuing forth, took the path down the hill to the river, where he had not been for four years.

The road ran along the river. He went by it, walking till noon. Then he went into a cornfield and lay among the corn. Toward evening he approached a village, but did not enter it. He went again to the river, to a cliff.

It was early morning, half an hour before sunrise. All was grey and mournful around him, and a cold, early morning wind blew from the west.

"I must end it all. There is no God. How can I do it? Throw myself in! I can swim; I should not drown. Hang myself? Yes; just with this belt, to a branch."

This seemed so feasible and so easy that he wanted to pray, as he always did in moments of distress. But there was nothing to pray to. God was not. He dropped down on his elbow, and such a longing for sleep instantly overcame him that he couldn't hold his head up with his arm any longer. Stretching out his arm, he laid his head upon it and went to sleep. But this sleep lasted only a moment. He woke at once, and what followed was half dream and half recollection.

He saw himself as a child in the house of his mother in the country. A carriage was approaching, and out of it stepped Uncle Nicholas Sergei-vich, with a long black beard like a spade, and with him a slender girl, Pashinka, with large soft eyes and a timid, pathetic little face. This girl was taken to the place where the boys were playing, and they were forced to play with her, which was very tedious indeed. She was a silly little girl, and it ended in their making fun of her, and making her show them how she swam. She lay down on the floor and went through the motions. They laughed and turned her into ridicule; which, when she became aware of it, made her blush in patches. She looked so piteous that his conscience pricked him, and he could never forget her kind, submissive, tremulous smile. Sergius remembered how he had seen her since then. A long time ago, just before he became a monk, she had married a landowner who had squandered all her fortune, and who beat her. She had two children, a son and a daughter; but the son died when he was little, and Sergius remembered seeing her very wretched after that, and then again at the monastery, when she was a widow. She was still just the same, not exactly stupid, but insipid, insignificant, and piteous. She had come with her daughter and her daughter's *fiancé*. They were poor at that time, and later on he heard that she was living in a little provincial town and was almost destitute.

Low effort—straightforward

"Why does she come into my head?" he asked himself, but still he could not help thinking about her. "Where is she? What has become of her? Is she as unhappy as she was when she had to show us how she swam on the floor? But what's the use of my thinking of her now? My business is to put an end to myself."

Again he was afraid, and again, in order to spare himself, he began to think about her. Thus he lay a long time, thinking now of his extraordinary end, now of Pashinka. She seemed somehow the means of his salvation. At last he fell asleep, and in his dream he saw an angel, who came to him and said:—

"Go to Pashinka. Find out what you have to do, and what your sin is, and what is your way of salvation."

He awoke, convinced that this was a vision from on high. He rejoiced, and resolved to do as he was told in the dream. He knew the town where she lived, three hundred miles away, so he walked to that place.

Chapter 6

PASHINKA WAS NO LONGER PASHINKA. She had become Praskovia Mikhailovna, old, wrinkled, and shrivelled, the mother-in-law of a drunken official, Mavrikiev—a failure. She lived in the little provincial town where he had occupied his last position, and had supported the family: a daughter, a nervous, ailing husband, and five grandchildren. Her sole means of supporting them was by giving music lessons to the daughters of merchants for fifty kopeks an hour. She had sometimes four, sometimes five lessons a day, and earned about sixty roubles a month. They all lived for the moment on that in expectation of another situation. She had sent letters to all her friends and relations, asking for a post for her son-in-law, and had also written to Sergius, but the letter had never reached him.

It was Saturday, and Praskovia Mikhailovna was kneading dough for currant bread such as the cook, a serf on her father's estate, used to make, for she wanted to give her grandchildren a treat on Sunday.

Her daughter Masha was looking after her youngest child, and the eldest boy and girl were at school. As for her husband, he had not slept that night, and was now asleep. Praskovia Mikhailovna had not slept well either, trying to appease her daughter's anger against her husband.

She saw that her son-in-law, being a weak character, could not talk or act differently, and she perceived that the reproaches of his wife availed nothing. All her energies were employed in softening these re-

proaches. She did not want harsh feelings and resentment to exist. Physically she could not stand a condition of ill-will. It was clear to her that bitter feelings did not mend matters, but simply made them worse. She did not think about it. Seeing anger made her suffer precisely as a bad odour or a shrill sound or a blow.

She was just showing Lucaria, the servant, how to mix the dough when her grandson, Misha, a boy six years old, with little crooked legs in darned stockings, ran into the kitchen looking frightened.

"Grandmother, a dreadful old man wants to see you!"

Lucaria looked out of the door.

"Oh, ma'am, it's a pilgrim."

Praskovia Mikhailovna wiped her thin elbows with her hands, and then her hands on her apron, and was about to go into the room to get five kopeks out of her purse, when she remembered that she had only a ten kopek piece, so, deciding to give bread instead, she turned to the cupboard. But then she blushed at the thought of having grudged him alms, and ordering Lucaria to cut a slice of bread, went to fetch the ten kopeks. "That serves you right," she said to herself. "Now you must give twice as much."

She gave both bread and money to the pilgrim with apologies, and in doing so she was not at all proud of her generosity. On the contrary, she was ashamed of having given so little. The man had such an imposing appearance.

In spite of having tramped three hundred miles, begging in the name of Christ, and being nearly in rags; in spite of having grown thin and weather-beaten, and having his hair cut, and wearing a peasant cap and boots; in spite, also, of his bowing with great humility, Sergius had the same impressive appearance which had attracted every one to him. Praskovia Mikhailovna did not recognise him. How could she, not having seen him for many years?

"Excuse this humble gift, father. Wouldn't you like something to eat?"

He took the bread and money, and Praskovia Mikhailovna was astonished that he did not go, but stood looking at her.

"Pashinka, I have come to you. Won't you take me in?"

His beautiful black eyes looked at her intently, imploringly, and shone, tears starting; and his lips quivered painfully under the grey moustache.

Praskovia Mikhailovna pressed her hand to her shrivelled breast, opened her mouth, and stared at the pilgrim with dilated eyes.

"It can't be possible! Steph—Sergius—Father Sergius!"

"Yes, it is I," said Sergius in a low voice. "But no longer Sergius or Father Sergius, but a great sinner, Stephen Kasatsky—a great sinner, a lost sinner. Take me in—help me."

"No, it can't be possible! Such great humility! Come?" She stretched out her hand, but he did not take it. He only followed her.

But where could she lead him? They had very little space. She had a tiny little room for herself, hardly more than a closet, but even that she had given up to her daughter, and now Masha was sitting there rocking the baby to sleep.

"Please, be seated here," she said to Sergius, pointing to a bench in the kitchen. He sat down at once, and took off, with an evidently accustomed action, the straps of his wallet first from one shoulder and then from the other.

"Heavens! What humility! What an honour, and now—"

Sergius did not answer, but smiled meekly, laying his wallet on one side.

"Masha, do you know who this is?" And Praskovia Mikhailovna told her daughter in a whisper. They took the bed and the cradle out of the little room, and made it ready for Sergius.

Praskovia Mikhailovna led him in.

"Now have a rest. Excuse this humble room. I must go."

"Where?"

"I have lessons. I'm ashamed to say I teach music."

"Music! That is well. But just one thing, Praskovia Mikhailovna. I came to you with an object. Could I have a talk with you?"

"I shall be happy. Will this evening do?"

"It will. One thing more. Do not say who I am. I have only revealed myself to you. No one knows where I went, and no one need know."

"Oh, but I told my daughter—"

"Well, ask her not to tell any one."

Sergius took off his boots and slept after a sleepless night and a forty-mile tramp.

When Praskovia Mikhailovna returned Sergius was sitting in the little room waiting for her. He had not come out for dinner, but had some soup and gruel which Lucaris brought in to him.

"Why did you return earlier than you said?" asked Father Sergius. "May I speak to you now?"

"What have I done to deserve the happiness of having such a guest! I only missed one lesson. That can wait. I have dreamed for a long time of going to see you. I wrote to you. And now this good fortune!"

"Pashinka, please—listen to what I am going to tell you, as if it were a confession; as if it were something I should say to God in the hour of death. Pashinka, I am not a holy man. I am a vile and loathsome sinner. I have gone astray through pride, and I am the vilest of the vile."

Pashinka stared at him. She believed what he said. Then, when she had quite taken it in, she touched his hand and smiled sadly, and said—

"Stevie, perhaps you exaggerate."

"No, Pashinka, I am an adulterer, a murderer, a blasphemer, a cheat."

"My God, what does he mean?" she muttered.

"But I must go on living. I, who thought I knew everything, who taught others how to live, I know nothing. I ask you to teach me."

"O Stevie! You are laughing at me. Why do you always laugh at me?"

"Very well; have it as you will that I am laughing at you. Still, tell me how you live, and how you have lived your life."

"I? But I've lived a very bad life, the worst life possible. Now God is punishing me, and I deserve it. And I am so miserable now—so miserable!"

"And your marriage—how did you get on?"

"It was all bad. I married because I fell in love from low motives. Father didn't want me to, but I wouldn't listen to anything. I just married. And then, instead of helping my husband, I made him wretched by my jealousy, which I couldn't overcome."

"He drank, I heard."

"Well, but I didn't give him any peace. I reproached him. That's a disease. He couldn't stop it. I remember now how I took his drink away from him. We had such frightful scenes!" She looked at Kasatsky with pain in her beautiful eyes at the recollection.

Kasatsky called to mind that he had been told that her husband beat Pashinka, and looking at her thin withered neck with veins standing out behind her ears, the thin coil of hair, half grey, half auburn, he saw it all just as it happened.

"Then I was left alone with two children, and with no means."

"But you had an estate!"

"Oh, that was sold when Vasily was alive. And the money was—spent. We had to live, and I didn't know how to work—like all the young ladies of that time. I was worse than the rest—quite helpless. So we spent everything we had. I taught the children. Masha had learnt something. Then Misha fell ill when he was in the fourth class in the school, and God took him. Masha fell in love with Vania, my son-in-law. He's a good man but very unfortunate. He's ill."

"Mother," interrupted her daughter, "take Misha. I can't be everywhere."

Praskovia Mikhailovna started, rose, and stepping quickly in her worn shoes, went out of the room and came back with a boy of two in her arms. The child was throwing himself backwards and grabbing at her shawl.

"Where was I? Yes—he had a very good post here, and such a good chief, too. But poor Vania couldn't go on, and he had to give up his position."

"What is the matter with him?"

"Neurasthenia. It's such a horrid illness. We have been to the doctor, but he ought to go away, and we can't afford it. Still, I hope it will pass. He doesn't suffer much pain, but—"

"Lucaria!" said a feeble and angry voice. "She's always sent out when I need her. Mother!"

"I'm coming," said Praskovia Mikhailovna, again interrupting her conversation. "You see, he hasn't had his dinner yet. He can't eat with us."

She went out and arranged something, and came back, wiping her thin, dark hands.

"Well, this is the way I live. I complain, and I'm not satisfied, but, thank God, all my grandchildren are such nice healthy children, and life is quite bearable. But why am I talking about myself?"

"What do you live on?"

"Why, I earn a little. How I used to hate music! and now it's so useful to me!"

Her small hand lay on the chest of drawers that stood beside her where she was sitting, and she drummed exercises with her thin fingers.

"How much are you paid for your lessons?"

"Sometimes a rouble, sometimes fifty kopeks, and sometimes thirty. They are all so kind to me."

"And do your pupils get on well?" asked Kasatsky, smiling faintly with his eyes.

Praskovia Mikhailovna did not believe at first that he was asking her seriously, and looked inquiringly into his eyes.

"Some of them do," she said. "I have one very nice pupil—the butcher's daughter. Such a good, kind girl. If I were a clever woman I could surely use my father's influence and get a position for my son-in-law. But it is my fault they are so badly off. I brought them to it."

"Yes, yes," said Kasatsky, dropping his head. "Well, Pashinka, and what about your attitude to the church?"

"Oh, don't speak of it! I'm so bad that way. I have neglected it so! When the children have to go, I fast and go to communion with them, but as for the rest of the time I often do not go for a month. I just send them."

"And why don't you go?"

"Well, to tell the truth—" she blushed—"I'm ashamed for Masha's sake and the children's to go in my old clothes. And I haven't anything else. Besides, I'm just lazy."

"And do you pray at home?"

"I do, but it's just a mechanical sort of praying. I know it's wrong, but I have no real religious feeling. I only know I'm wicked—that's all."

"Yes, yes. That's right, that's right!" said Kasatsky, as if in approval.

"I'm coming—I'm coming!" she called, in answer to her son-in-law, and, tidying her hair, went to the other room.

This time she was absent a long while. When she returned, Kasatsky was sitting in the same position, his elbow on his knee and his head down. But his wallet was ready strapped on his back.

When she came in with a little tin lamp without a shade, he raised his beautiful, weary eyes, and sighed deeply.

"I didn't tell them who you were," she began shyly. "I just said you were a pilgrim—a nobleman—and that I used to know you. Won't you come into the dining-room and have tea?"

"No."

"Then I'll bring some in to you here."

"No; I don't want anything. God bless you, Pashinka. I am going now. If you have any pity for me, don't tell any one you have seen me. For the love of God, tell no one. I thank you. I would kneel down before you, but I know it would only make you feel awkward. Forgive me, for Christ's sake."

"Give me your blessing."

"God bless you. Forgive me, for Christ's sake."

He rose to go, but she restrained him and brought him some bread and butter, which he took and departed.

It was dark, and he had hardly passed the second house when he was lost to sight, and she only knew he was there because the dog at the priest's house was barking.

"That was the meaning of my vision. Pashinka is what I should have been, and was not. I lived for man, on the pretext of living for God; and she lives for God, imagining she lives for man! Yes; one good deed—a cup of cold water given without expectation of reward—is worth far more than all the benefits I thought I was bestowing on the world. But was there not, after all, one grain of sincere desire to serve God?" he asked himself. And the answer came: "Yes, there was; but it was so soiled, so overgrown with desire for the world's praise. No; there is no God for the man who lives for the praise of the world. I must now seek *Him*."

He walked on, just as he had made his way to Pashinka, from village to village, meeting and parting with other pilgrims, and asking for bread and a night's rest in the name of Christ. Sometimes an angry housekeeper would abuse him, sometimes a drunken peasant would revile him; but for the most part he was given food and drink, and often something to take with him. Many were favourably disposed towards him on account of his noble bearing. Some, on the other hand, seemed to enjoy the sight of a gentleman so reduced to poverty. But his gentleness vanquished all hearts.

He often found a Bible in a house where he was staying. He would read it aloud, and the people always listened to him, touched by what he read them, and wondering, as if it were something new, although so familiar.

If he succeeded in helping people by his advice or by knowing how to read and write, or by settling a dispute, he did not afterwards wait to see their gratitude, for he went away directly. And little by little God began to reveal Himself within him.

One day he was walking along the road with two women and a soldier. They were stopped by a party consisting of a lady and gentleman in a trap drawn by a trotter, and another gentleman and lady riding. The gentleman beside the lady in the trap was evidently a traveller—a Frenchman—while her husband was on horseback with his daughter.

The party stopped to show the Frenchman the pilgrims, who, according to a superstition of the Russian peasantry, show their superiority by tramping instead of working. They spoke French, thinking they would not be understood.

"Demandez-leur," asked the Frenchman, *"s'ils sont bien sûres de ce que leur pèlerinage est agréable à Dieu?"*

The old woman answered—

"Just as God wills it. Our feet have arrived at the holy places, but we can't tell about our hearts."

They asked the soldier. He answered that he was alone in the world, and belonged nowhere.

They asked Kasatsky who he was.

"A servant of God."

"Qu'est-ce-qu'il dit? Il ne répond pas?"

"Il dit qu'il est un serviteur de Dieu."

"Il doit être un fils de prêtre. Il a de la race. Avez-vous de la petite monnaie?"

The Frenchman had some change, and gave each of them twenty kopeks.

*"Mais dites-leur que ce n'est pas pour les cierges que je leur donne, mais pour qu'ils se régalent du thé. Tea—*tea," he said, with a smile. *"Pour vous, mon vieux."* And he patted Kasatsky on the shoulder with his gloved hand.

"Christ save you," said Kasatsky, and without putting on his hat, bent his bald head.

Kasatsky rejoiced particularly in this incident, because he had shown contempt for the world's opinion, and had done something quite trifling and easy. He accepted twenty kopeks, and gave them afterwards to a blind beggar who was a friend of his.

The less he cared for the opinion of the world the more he felt that God was with him.

Father Sergius

For eight months Kasatsky tramped in this fashion, until at last he was arrested in a provincial town in a night-shelter where he passed the night with other pilgrims. Having no passport to show, he was taken to the police-station. When he was asked for documents to prove his identity he said he had none; that he was a servant of God. He was numbered among the tramps and sent to Siberia.

There he settled down on the estate of a rich peasant, where he still lives. He works in the vegetable garden, teaches the children to read and write, and nurses the sick.

VI

THE TURN
OF THE SCREW

by Henry James

A Ghost Story

The Turn of the Screw was written in 1898, more than twenty years after Henry James had decided to live his life abroad, first in France temporarily and later in England permanently. Although some critics are content to call it the most celebrated of James's ghost stories, it may reasonably be called the greatest of all ghost stories. Certainly it was one of the most widely read and discussed pieces of writing that came from his pen.

To allow a ghost story its full chance to mystify and surprise readers and to chill their blood, it is unfair to say much about it in advance. Perhaps this much may be told: that an English governess is sent to a large country house called Bly by its owner who has been given the responsibility of two charming children but does not relish the role of guardian. Bly stands in wooded grounds, old and aloof and silent, a rambling place inside, dark and fit scene for the appearance of restless spirits.

Other writers who have been asked to comment on it have generally reacted to this strange and macabre tale much as the author hoped they would, waking at nights and feeling a sense of dread as they waited for—for what happens in the story.

This is a new age, of course, and most people have become harder and more realistic in their reaction to fiction. The ghost story may have lost the power to excite that it once had. But we must not be too sure. Henry James was at his best in writing of these curious happenings in one of the stately homes of England. Give him a chance to raise the hair on *your* scalp and be ready to pull tightly together the curtains on your window!

THE STORY HAD HELD US, round the fire, sufficiently breathless, but except the obvious remark that it was gruesome, as, on Christmas eve in an old house, a strange tale should essentially be, I remember no comment uttered till somebody happened to say that it was the only case he had met in which such a visitation had fallen on a child. The case, I may mention, was that of an apparition in just such an old house as had gathered us for the occasion—an appearance, of a dreadful kind, to a little boy sleeping in the room with his mother and waking her up in the terror of it; waking her not to dissipate his dread and soothe him to sleep again, but to encounter also, herself, before she had succeeded in doing so, the same sight that had shaken him. It was this observation that drew from Douglas—not immediately, but later in the evening—a reply that had the interesting consequence to which I call attention. Someone else told a story not particularly effective, which I saw he was not following. This I took for a sign that he had himself something to produce and that we should only have to wait. We waited in fact till two nights later; but that same evening, before we scattered, he brought out what was in his mind.

"I quite agree—in regard to Griffin's ghost, or whatever it was—that its appearing first to the little boy, at so tender an age, adds a particular touch. But it's not the first occurrence of its charming kind that I know to have involved a child. If the child gives the effect another turn of the screw, what do you say to *two* children——?"

"We say, of course" somebody exclaimed, "that they give two turns! Also that we want to hear about them."

I can see Douglas there before the fire, to which he had got up to present his back, looking down at his interlocutor with his hands in his pockets. "Nobody but me, till now, has ever heard. It's quite too horrible." This, naturally, was declared by several voices to give the thing the utmost price, and our friend, with quiet art, prepared his triumph by turning his eyes over the rest of us and going on: "It's beyond everything. Nothing at all that I know touches it."

"For sheer terror?" I remember asking.

He seemed to say it was not so simple as that; to be really at a loss how to qualify it. He passed his hand over his eyes, made a little wincing grimace. "For dreadful—dreadfulness!"

331

"Oh, how delicious!" cried one of the women.

He took no notice of her; he looked at me, but as if, instead of me, he saw what he spoke of. "For general uncanny ugliness and horror and pain."

"Well then," I said, "just sit right down and begin."

He turned round to the fire, gave a kick to a log, watched it an instant. Then as he faced us again: "I can't begin. I shall have to send to town." There was a unanimous groan at this, and much reproach; after which, in his preoccupied way, he explained. "The story's written. It's in a locked drawer—it has not been out for years. I could write to my man and enclose the key; he could send down the packet as he finds it." It was to me in particular that he appeared to propound this—appeared almost to appeal for aid not to hesitate. He had broken a thickness of ice, the formation of many a winter; had had his reasons for a long silence. The others resented postponement, but it was just his scruples that charmed me. I adjured him to write by the first post and to agree with us for an early hearing; then I asked him if the experience in question had been his own. To this his answer was prompt. "Oh, thank God, no!"

"And is the record yours? You took the thing down?"

"Nothing but the impression. I took that *here*"—he tapped his heart. "I've never lost it."

"Then your manuscript——?"

"Is in old, faded ink, and in the most beautiful hand." He hung fire again. "A woman's. She has been dead these twenty years. She sent me the pages in question before she died." They were all listening now, and of course there was somebody to be arch, or at any rate to draw the inference. But if he put the inference by without a smile it was also without irritation. "She was a most charming person, but she was ten years older than I. She was my sister's governess," he quietly said. "She was the most agreeable woman I've ever known in her position; she would have been worthy of any whatever. It was long ago, and this episode was long before. I was at Trinity, and I found her at home on my coming down the second summer. I was much there that year—it was a beautiful one; and we had, in her off-hours, some strolls and talks in the garden—talks in which she struck me as awfully clever and nice. Oh yes; don't grin: I liked her extremely and am glad to this day to think she liked me too. If she hadn't she wouldn't have told me. She had never told anyone. It wasn't simply that she said so, but that I knew she hadn't. I was sure; I could see. You'll easily judge why when you hear."

"Because the thing had been such a scare?"

He continued to fix me. "You'll easily judge," he repeated: *"you* will."

I fixed him too. "I see. She was in love."

He laughed for the first time. "You *are* acute. Yes, she was in love. That is, she had been. That came out—she couldn't tell her story without its coming out. I saw it, and she saw I saw it; but neither of us spoke of it. I remember the time and the place—the corner of the lawn, the shade of the great beeches and the long, hot summer afternoon. It wasn't a scene for a shudder; but oh——!" He quitted the fire and dropped back into his chair.

"You'll receive the packet Thursday morning?" I inquired.

"Probably not till the second post."

"Well then; after dinner——"

"You'll all meet me here?" He looked us round again. "Isn't anybody going?" It was almost the tone of hope.

"Everybody will stay!"

"*I* will—and *I* will!" cried the ladies whose departure had been fixed. Mrs. Griffin, however, expressed the need for a little more light. "Who was it she was in love with?"

"The story will tell," I took upon myself to reply.

"Oh, I can't wait for the story!"

"The story *won't* tell," said Douglas; "not in any literal, vulgar way."

"More's the pity, then. That's the only way I ever understand."

"Won't *you* tell, Douglas?" somebody else inquired.

He sprang to his feet again. "Yes—tomorrow. Now I must go to bed. Good-night." And quickly catching up a candlestick, he left us slightly bewildered. From our end of the great brown hall we heard his step on the stair; whereupon Mrs. Griffin spoke. "Well, if I don't know who she was in love with, I know who *he* was."

"She was ten years older," said her husband.

"*Raison de plus*—at that age! But it's rather nice, his long reticence."

"Forty years!" Griffin put in.

"With this outbreak at last."

"The outbreak," I returned, "will make a tremendous occasion of Thursday night"; and everyone so agreed with me that, in the light of it, we lost all attention for everything else. The last story, however incomplete and like the mere opening of a serial, had been told; we handshook and "candlestuck," as somebody said, and went to bed.

I knew the next day that a letter containing the key had, by the first post, gone off to his London apartments; but in spite of—or perhaps just on account of—the eventual diffusion of this knowledge we quite let him alone till after dinner, till such an hour of the evening, in fact, as might best accord with the kind of emotion on which our hopes were fixed. Then he became as communicative as we could desire and indeed gave us his best reason for being so. We had it from him again before the fire in the hall, as we had had our mild wonders of the previous night. It appeared that the narrative he had promised to

read us really required for a proper intelligence a few words of prologue. Let me say here distinctly, to have done with it, that this narrative, from an exact transcript of my own made much later, is what I shall presently give. Poor Douglas, before his death—when it was in sight—committed to me the manuscript that reached him on the third of these days and that, on the same spot, with immense effect, he began to read to our hushed little circle on the night of the fourth. The departing ladies who had said they would stay didn't, of course, thank heaven, stay: they departed, in consequence of arrangements made, in a rage of curiosity, as they professed, produced by the touches with which he had already worked us up. But that only made his little final auditory more compact and select, kept it, round the hearth, subject to a common thrill.

The first of these touches conveyed that the written statement took up the tale at a point after it had, in a manner, begun. The fact to be in possession of was therefore that his old friend, the youngest of several daughters of a poor country parson, had, at the age of twenty, on taking service for the first time in the schoolroom, come up to London, in trepidation, to answer in person an advertisement that had already placed her in brief correspondence with the advertiser. This person proved, on her presenting herself, for judgment, at a house in Harley Street, that impressed her as vast and imposing—this prospective patron proved a gentleman, a bachelor in the prime of life, such a figure as had never risen, save in a dream or an old novel, before a fluttered, anxious girl out of a Hampshire vicarage. One could easily fix his type; it never, happily, dies out. He was handsome and bold and pleasant, off-hand and gay and kind. He struck her, inevitably, as gallant and splendid, but what took her most of all and gave her the courage she afterwards showed was that he put the whole thing to her as a kind of favour, an obligation he should gratefully incur. She conceived him as rich, but as fearfully extravagant—saw him all in a glow of high fashion, of good looks, of expensive habits, of charming ways with women. He had for his own town residence a big house filled with the spoils of travel and the trophies of the chase; but it was to his country home, an old family place in Essex, that he wished her immediately to proceed.

He had been left, by the death of their parents in India, guardian to a small nephew and a small niece, children of a younger, a military brother, whom he had lost two years before. These children were, by the strangest of chances for a man in his position—a lone man without the right sort of experience or a grain of patience—very heavily on his hands. It had all been a great worry and, on his own part doubtless, a series of blunders, but he immensely pitied the poor chicks and had done all he could; had in particular sent them down to his other house, the proper place for them being of course the country, and kept them there, from the first, with the best people he could find to look after them, parting even with his own servants to wait on them and going

334

down himself, whenever he might, to see how they were doing. The awkward thing was that they had practically no other relations and that his own affairs took up all his time. He had put them in possession of Bly, which was healthy and secure, and had placed at the head of their little establishment—but below stairs only—an excellent woman, Mrs. Grose, whom he was sure his visitor would like and who had formerly been maid to his mother. She was now housekeeper and was also acting for the time as superintendent to the little girl, of whom, without children of her own, she was, by good luck, extremely fond. There were plenty of people to help, but of course the young lady who should go down as governess world be in supreme authority. She would also have, in holidays, to look after the small boy, who had been for a term at school—young as he was to be sent, but what else could be done?—and who, as the holidays were about to begin, would be back from one day to the other. There had been for the two children at first a young lady whom they had had the misfortune to lose. She had done for them quite beautifully—she was a most respectable person—till her death, the great awkwardness of which had, precisely, left no alternative but the school for little Miles. Mrs. Grose, since then, in the way of manners and things, had done as she could for Flora; and there were, further, a cook, a housemaid, a dairywoman, an old pony, an old groom, and an old gardener, all likewise thoroughly respectable.

So far had Douglas presented his picture when someone put a question. "And what did the former governess die of?—of so much respectability?"

Our friend's answer was prompt. "That will come out. I don't anticipate."

"Excuse me—I thought that was just what you *are* doing."

"In her successor's place," I suggested, "I should have wished to learn if the office brought with it——"

"Necessary danger to life?" Douglas completed my thought. "She did wish to learn, and she did learn. You shall hear tomorrow what she learnt. Meanwhile, of course, the prospect struck her as slightly grim. She was young, untried, nervous: it was a vision of serious duties and little company, of really great loneliness. She hesitated—took a couple of days to consult and consider. But the salary offered much exceeded her modest measure, and on a second interview she faced the music, she engaged." And Douglas, with this, made a pause that, for the benefit of the company, moved me to throw in—

"The moral of which was of course the seduction exercised by the splendid young man. She succumbed to it."

He got up and, as he had done the night before, went to the fire, gave a stir to a log with his foot, then stood a moment with his back to us. "She saw him only twice."

"Yes, but that's just the beauty of her passion."

A little to my surprise, on this, Douglas turned round to me. "It *was* the beauty of it. There were others," he went on, "who hadn't succumbed. He told her frankly all his difficulty—that for several applicants the conditions had been prohibitive. They were, somehow, simply afraid. It sounded dull—it sounded strange; and all the more so because of his main condition."

"Which was——?"

"That she should never trouble him—but never, never: neither appeal nor complain nor write about anything; only meet all questions herself, receive all moneys from his solicitor, take the whole thing over and let him alone. She promised to do this, and she mentioned to me that when, for a moment, disburdened, delighted, he held her hand, thanking her for the sacrifice, she already felt rewarded."

"But was that all her reward?" one of the ladies asked.

"She never saw him again."

"Oh!" said the lady; which, as our friend immediately left us again, was the only other word of importance contributed to the subject till, the next night, by the corner of the hearth, in the best chair, he opened the faded red cover of a thin old-fashioned gilt-edged album. The whole thing took indeed more nights than one, but on the first occasion the same lady put another question. "What is your title?"

"I haven't one."

"Oh, *I* have!" I said. But Douglas, without heeding me, had begun to read with a fine clearness that was like a rendering to the ear of the beauty of his author's hand.

Chapter I

I REMEMBER THE WHOLE BEGINNING as a succession of flights and drops, a little see-saw of the right throbs and the wrong. After rising, in town, to meet his appeal, I had at all events a couple of very bad days—found myself doubtful again, felt indeed sure I had made a mistake. In this state of mind I spent the long hours of bumping, swinging coach that carried me to the stopping-place at which I was to be met by a vehicle from the house. This convenience, I was told, had been ordered, and I found, toward the close of the June afternoon, a commodious fly in waiting for me. Driving at that hour, on a lovely day, through a country to which the summer sweetness seemed to offer me a friendly welcome, my fortitude mounted afresh and, as we turned into the avenue, encountered a reprieve that was probably but a proof of

the point to which it had sunk. I suppose I had expected, or had dreaded, something so melancholy that what greeted me was a good surprise. I remember as a most pleasant impression the broad, clear front, its open windows and fresh curtains and the pair of maids looking out; I remember the lawn and the bright flowers and the crunch of my wheels on the gravel and the clustered treetops over which the rooks circled and cawed in the golden sky. The scene had a greatness that made it a different affair from my own scant home, and there immediately appeared at the door, with a little girl in her hand, a civil person who dropped me as decent a curtsey as if I had been the mistress or a distinguished visitor. I had received in Harley Street a narrower notion of the place, and that, as I recalled it, made me think the proprietor still more of a gentleman, suggested that what I was to enjoy might be something beyond his promise.

I had no drop again till the next day, for I was carried triumphantly through the following hours by my introduction to the younger of my pupils. The little girl who accompanied Mrs. Grose appeared to me on the spot a creature so charming as to make it a great fortune to have to do with her. She was the most beautiful child I had ever seen, and I afterwards wondered that my employer had not told me more of her. I slept little that night—I was too much excited; and this astonished me too, I recollect, remained with me, adding to my sense of the liberality with which I was treated. The large, impressive room, one of the best in the house, the great state bed, as I almost felt it, the full, figured draperies, the long glasses in which, for the first time, I could see myself from head to foot, all struck me—like the extraordinary charm of my small charge—as so many things thrown in. It was thrown in as well, from the first moment, that I should get on with Mrs. Grose in a relation over which, on my way, in the coach, I fear I had rather brooded. The only thing indeed that in this early outlook might have made me shrink again was the clear circumstance of her being so glad to see me. I perceived within half an hour that she was so glad—stout, simple, plain, clean, wholesome woman—as to be positively on her guard against showing it too much. I wondered even then a little why she should wish not to show it, and that, with reflection, with suspicion, might of course have made me uneasy.

But it was a comfort that there could be no uneasiness in a connection with anything so beatific as the radiant image of my little girl, the vision of whose angelic beauty had probably more than anything else to do with the restlessness that, before morning, made me several times rise and wander about my room to take in the whole picture and prospect; to watch, from my open window, the faint summer dawn, to look at such portions of the rest of the house as I could catch, and to listen, while, in the fading dusk, the first birds began to twitter, for the possible recurrence of a sound or two, less natural and not without, but within,

that I had fancied I heard. There had been a moment when I believed I recognised, faint and far, the cry of a child; there had been another when I found myself just consciously starting as at the passage, before my door, of a light footstep. But these fancies were not marked enough not to be thrown off, and it is only in the light, or the gloom, I should rather say, of other and subsequent matters that they now come back to me. To watch, teach, "form" little Flora would too evidently be the making of a happy and useful life. It had been agreed between us downstairs that after this first occasion I should have her as a matter of course at night, her small white bed being already arranged, to that end, in my room. What I had undertaken was the whole care of her, and she had remained, just this last time, with Mrs. Grose only as an effect of our consideration for my inevitable strangeness and her natural timidity. In spite of this timidity—which the child herself, in the oddest way in the world, had been perfectly frank and brave about, allowing it, without a sign of uncomfortable consciousness, with the deep, sweet serenity indeed of one of Raphael's holy infants, to be discussed, to be imputed to her and to determine us—I felt quite sure she would presently like me. It was part of what I already liked Mrs. Grose herself for, the pleasure I could see her feel in my admiration and wonder as I sat at supper with four tall candles and with my pupil, in a high chair and a bib, brightly facing me, between them, over bread and milk. There were naturally things that in Flora's presence could pass between us only as prodigious and gratified looks, obscure and roundabout allusions.

"And the little boy—does he look like her? Is he too so very remarkable?"

One wouldn't flatter a child. "Oh, Miss, *most* remarkable. If you think well of this one!"—and she stood there with a plate in her hand, beaming at our companion, who looked from one of us to the other with placid heavenly eyes that contained nothing to check us.

"Yes; if I do——?"

"You *will* be carried away by the little gentleman!"

"Well, that, I think, is what I came for—to be carried away. I'm afraid, however," I remember feeling the impulse to add, "I'm rather easily carried away. I was carried away in London!"

I can still see Mrs. Grose's broad face as she took this in. "In Harley Street?"

"In Harley Street."

"Well, Miss, you're not the first—and you won't be the last."

"Oh, I've no pretension," I could laugh, "to being the only one. My other pupil, at any rate, as I understand, comes back tomorrow?"

"Not tomorrow—Friday, Miss. He arrives, as you did, by the coach, under care of the guard, and is to be met by the same carriage."

I forthwith expressed that the proper as well as the pleasant and friendly thing would be therefore that on the arrival of the public con-

veyance I should be in waiting for him with his little sister; an idea in which Mrs. Grose concurred so heartily that I somehow took her manner as a kind of comforting pledge—never falsified, thank heaven!—that we should on every question be quite at one. Oh, she was glad I was there!

What I felt the next day was, I suppose, nothing that could be fairly called a reaction from the cheer of my arrival; it was probably at the most only a slight oppression produced by a fuller measure of the scale, as I walked round them, gazed up at them, took them in, of my new circumstances. They had, as it were, an extent and mass for which I had not been prepared and in the presence of which I found myself, freshly, a little scared as well as a little proud. Lessons, in this agitation, certainly suffered some delay; I reflected that my first duty was, by the gentlest arts I could contrive, to win the child into the sense of knowing me. I spent the day with her out of doors; I arranged with her, to her great satisfaction, that it should be she, she only, who might show me the place. She showed it step by step and room by room and secret by secret, with droll, delightful, childish talk about it and with the result, in half an hour, of our becoming immense friends. Young as she was, I was struck, throughout our little tour, with her confidence and courage with the way, in empty chambers and dull corridors, on crooked staircases that made me pause and even on the summit of an old machicolated square tower that made me dizzy, her morning music, her disposition to tell me so many more things than she asked, rang out and led me on. I have not seen Bly since the day I left it, and I dare say that to my older and more informed eyes it would now appear sufficiently contracted. But as my little conductress, with her hair of gold and her frock of blue, danced before me round corners and pattered down passages, I had the view of a castle of romance inhabited by a rosy sprite, such a place as would somehow, for diversion of the young idea, take all colour out of storybooks and fairy-tales. Wasn't it just a storybook over which I had fallen a-doze and a-dream? No; it was a big, ugly, antique, but convenient house, embodying a few features of a building still older, half replaced and half utilised, in which I had the fancy of our being almost as lost as a handful of passengers in a great drifting ship. Well, I was, strangely, at the helm!

Chapter 2

THIS CAME HOME TO ME when, two days later, I drove over with Flora to meet, as Mrs. Grose said, the little gentleman; and all the more for an incident that, presenting itself the second evening, had deeply disconcerted me. The first day had been, on the whole, as I have expressed, reassuring; but I was to see it wind up in keen apprehension. The postbag, that evening—it came late—contained a letter for me, which, however, in the hand of my employer, I found to be composed but of a few words enclosing another, addressed to himself, with a seal still unbroken. "This, I recognise, is from the head-master, and the head-master's an awful bore. Read him, please; deal with him; but mind you don't report. Not a word. I'm off!" I broke the seal with a great effort— so great a one that I was a long time coming to it; took the unopened missive at last up to my room and only attacked it just before going to bed. I had better have let it wait till morning, for it gave me a second sleepless night. With no counsel to take, the next day, I was full of distress; and it finally got so the better of me that I determined to open myself at least to Mrs. Grose.

"What does it mean? The child's dismissed his school."

She gave me a look that I remarked at the moment; then, visibly, with a quick blankness, seemed to try to take it back. "But aren't they all——?"

"Sent home—yes. But only for the holidays. Miles may never go back at all."

Consciously, under my attention, she reddened. "They won't take him?"

"They absolutely decline."

At this she raised her eyes, which she had turned from me; I saw them fill with good tears. "What has he done?"

I hesitated; then I judged best simply to hand her my letter—which, however, had the effect of making her, without taking it, simply put her hands behind her. She shook her head sadly. "Such things are not for me, Miss."

My counsellor couldn't read! I winced at my mistake, which I attenuated as I could, and opened my letter again to repeat it to her; then, faltering in the act and folding it up once more, I put it back in my pocket. "Is he really *bad?*"

The tears were still in her eyes. "Do the gentlemen say so?"

"They go into no particulars. They simply express their regret that

it should be impossible to keep him. That can have only one meaning." Mrs. Grose listened with dumb emotion; she forbore to ask me what this meaning might be; so that, presently, to put the thing with some coherence and with the mere aid of her presence to my own mind, I went on: "That he's an injury to the others."

At this, with one of the quick turns of simple folk, she suddenly flamed up. "Master Miles! *him* an injury?"

There was such a flood of good faith in it that, though I had not yet seen the child, my very fears made me jump to the absurdity of the idea. I found myself, to meet my friend the better, offering it, on the spot, sarcastically. "To his poor little innocent mates!"

"It's too dreadful," cried Mrs. Grose, "to say such cruel things! Why, he's scarce ten years old."

"Yes, yes; it would be incredible."

She was evidently grateful for such a profession. "See him, Miss, first. *Then* believe it!" I felt forthwith a new impatience to see him; it was the beginning of a curiosity that, for all the next hours, was to deepen almost to pain. Mrs. Grose was aware, I could judge, of what she had produced in me, and she followed it up with assurance. "You might as well believe it of the little lady. Bless her," she added the next moment—"*look* at her!"

I turned and saw that Flora, whom, ten minutes before, I had established in the schoolroom with a sheet of white paper, a pencil, and a copy of nice "round O's," now presented herself to view at the open door. She expressed in her little way an extraordinary detachment from disagreeable duties, looking to me, however, with a great childish light that seemed to offer it as a mere result of the affection she had conceived for my person, which had rendered necessary that she should follow me. I needed nothing more than this to feel the full force of Mrs. Grose's comparison, and, catching my pupil in my arms, covered her with kisses in which there was a sob of atonement.

None the less, the rest of the day, I watched for further occasion to approach my colleague, especially as, toward evening, I began to fancy she rather sought to avoid me. I overtook her, I remember, on the staircase; we went down together, and at the bottom I detained her, holding her there with a hand on her arm. "I take what you said to me at noon as a declaration that *you've* never known him to be bad."

She threw back her head; she had clearly, by this time, and very honestly, adopted an attitude. "Oh, never known him—I don't pretend *that!*"

I was upset again. "Then you *have* known him——?"

"Yes indeed, Miss, thank God!"

On reflection I accepted this. "You mean that a boy who never is——?"

"Is no boy for *me!*"

I held her tighter. "You like them with the spirit to be naughty?" Then, keeping pace with her answer, "So do I!" I eagerly brought out. "But not to the degree to contaminate——"

"To contaminate?"—my big word left her at a loss. I explained it. "To corrupt."

She stared, taking my meaning in; but it produced in her an odd laugh. "Are you afraid he'll corrupt *you?*" She put the question with such a fine bold humour that, with a laugh, a little silly doubtless, to match her own, I gave way for the time to the apprehension of ridicule.

But the next day, as the hour for my drive approached, I cropped up in another place. "What was the lady who was here before?"

"The last governess? She was also young and pretty—almost as young and almost as pretty, Miss, even as you."

"Ah, then, I hope her youth and her beauty helped her!" I recollect throwing off. "He seems to like us young and pretty!"

"Oh, he *did,*" Mrs. Grose assented: "it was the way he liked everyone!" She had no sooner spoken indeed than she caught herself up. "I mean that's *his* way—the master's."

I was struck. "But of whom did you speak first?"

She looked blank, but she coloured. "Why, of *him.*"

"Of the master?"

"Of who else?"

There was so obviously no one else that the next moment I had lost my impression of her having accidentally said more than she meant; and I merely asked what I wanted to know. "Did *she* see anything in the boy——?"

"That wasn't right? She never told me."

I had a scruple, but I overcame it. "Was she careful—particular?"

Mrs. Grose appeared to try to be conscientious. "About some things —yes."

"But not about all?"

Again she considered. "Well, Miss—she's gone. I won't tell tales."

"I quite understand your feeling," I hastened to reply; but I thought it, after an instant, not opposed to this concession to pursue: "Did she die here?"

"No—she went off."

I don't know what there was in this brevity of Mrs. Grose's that struck me as ambiguous. "Went off to die?" Mrs. Grose looked straight out of the window, but I felt that, hypothetically, I had a right to know what young persons engaged for Bly were expected to do. "She was taken ill, you mean, and went home?"

"She was not taken ill, so far as appeared, in this house. She left it, at the end of the year, to go home, as she said, for a short holiday, to which the time she had put in had certainly given her a right. We had

then a young woman—a nursemaid who had stayed on and who was a good girl and clever; and *she* took the children altogether for the interval. But our young lady never came back, and at the very moment I was expecting her I heard from the master that she was dead."

I turned this over. "But of what?"

"He never told me! But please, Miss," said Mrs. Grose, "I must get to my work."

Chapter 3

HER THUS TURNING HER BACK ON ME was fortunately not, for my just preoccupations, a snub that could check the growth of our mutual esteem. We met, after I had brought home little Miles, more intimately than ever on the ground of my stupefaction, my general emotion: so monstrous was I then ready to pronounce it that such a child as had now been revealed to me should be under an interdict. I was a little late on the scene, and I felt, as he stood wistfully looking out for me before the door of the inn at which the coach had put him down, that I had seen him, on the instant, without and within, in the great glow of freshness, the same positive fragrance of purity, in which I had, from the first moment, seen his little sister. He was incredibly beautiful, and Mrs. Grose had put her finger on it: everything but a sort of passion of tenderness for him was swept away by his presence. What I then and there took him to my heart for was something divine that I have never found to the same degree in any child—his indescribable little air of knowing nothing in the world but love. It would have been impossible to carry a bad name with a greater sweetness of innocence, and by the time I had got back to Bly with him I remained merely bewildered—so far, that is, as I was not outraged—by the sense of the horrible letter locked up in my room, in a drawer. As soon as I could compass a private word with Mrs. Grose I declared to her that it was grotesque.

She promptly understood me. "You mean the cruel charge——?"

"It doesn't live an instant. My dear woman, *look* at him!"

She smiled at my pretension to have discovered his charm. "I assure you, Miss, I do nothing else! What will you say, then?" she immediately added.

"In answer to the letter?" I had made up my mind. "Nothing."

"And to his uncle?"

I was incisive. "Nothing."

343

"And to the boy himself?"

I was wonderful. "Nothing."

She gave with her apron a great wipe to her mouth. "Then I'll stand by you. We'll see it out."

"We'll see it out!" I ardently echoed, giving her my hand to make it a vow.

She held me there a moment, then whisked up her apron again with her detached hand. "Would you mind, Miss, if I used the freedom——"

"To kiss me? No!" I took the good creature in my arms and, after we had embraced like sisters, felt still more fortified and indignant.

This, at all events, was for the time: a time so full that, as I recall the way it went, it reminds me of all the art I now need to make it a little distinct. What I look back at with amazement is the situation I accepted. I had undertaken, with my companion, to see it out, and I was under a charm, apparently, that could smooth away the extent and the far and difficult connections of such an effort. I was lifted aloft on a great wave of infatuation and pity. I found it simple, in my ignorance, my confusion, and perhaps my conceit, to assume that I could deal with a boy whose education for the world was all on the point of beginning. I am unable even to remember at this day what proposal I framed for the end of his holidays and the resumption of his studies. Lessons with me, indeed, that charming summer, we all had a theory that he was to have; but I now feel that, for weeks, the lessons must have been rather my own. I learnt something—at first certainly—that had not been one of the teachings of my small, smothered life; learnt to be amused, and even amusing, and not to think for the morrow. It was the first time, in a manner, that I had known space and air and freedom, all the music of summer and all the mystery of nature. And then there was consideration—and consideration was sweet. Oh, it was a trap—not designed, but deep—to my imagination, to my delicacy, perhaps to my vanity; to whatever, in me, was most excitable. The best way to picture it all is to say that I was off my guard. They gave me so little trouble—they were of a gentleness so extraordinary. I used to speculate—but even this with a dim disconnectedness—as to how the rough future (for all futures are rough!) would handle them and might bruise them. They had the bloom of health and happiness; and yet, as if I had been in charge of a pair of little grandees, of princes of the blood, for whom everything, to be right, would have to be enclosed and protected, the only form that, in my fancy, the after-years could take for them was that of a romantic, a really royal extension of the garden and the park. It may be, of course, above all, that what suddenly broke into this gives the previous time a charm of stillness—that hush in which something gathers or crouches. The change was actually like the spring of a beast.

In the first weeks the days were long; they often, at their finest, gave

me what I used to call my own hour, the hour when, for my pupils, tea-time and bed-time having come and gone, I had, before my final retirement, a small interval alone. Much as I liked my companions, this hour was the thing in the day I liked most; and I liked it best of all when, as the light faded—or rather, I should say, the day lingered and the last calls of the last birds sounded, in a flushed sky, from the old trees—I could take a turn into the grounds and enjoy, almost with a sense of property that amused and flattered me, the beauty and dignity of the place. It was a pleasure at these moments to feel myself tranquil and justified; doubtless, perhaps, also to reflect that by my discretion, my quiet good sense and general high propriety, I was giving pleasure—if he ever thought of it!—to the person to whose pressure I had responded. What I was doing was what he had earnestly hoped and directly asked of me, and that I *could,* after all, do it proved even a greater joy than I had expected. I dare say I fancied myself, in short, a remarkable young woman and took comfort in the faith that this would more publicly appear. Well, I needed to be remarkable to offer a front to the remarkable things that presently gave their first sign.

It was plump, one afternoon, in the middle of my very hour: the children were tucked away and I had come out for my stroll. One of the thoughts that, as I don't in the least shrink now from noting, used to be with me in these wanderings was that it would be as charming as a charming story suddenly to meet someone. Someone would appear there at the turn of a path and would stand before me and smile and approve. I didn't ask more than that—I only asked that he should *know;* and the only way to be sure he knew would be to see it, and the kind light of it, in his handsome face. That was exactly present to me—by which I mean the face was—when, on the first of these occasions, at the end of a long June day, I stopped short on emerging from one of the plantations and coming into view of the house. What arrested me on the spot—and with a shock much greater than any vision had allowed for—was the sense that my imagination had, in a flash, turned real. He did stand there!—but high up, beyond the lawn and at the very top of the tower to which, on that first morning, little Flora had conducted me. This tower was one of a pair—square, incongruous, crenelated structures—that were distinguished, for some reason, though I could see little difference, as the new and the old. They flanked opposite ends of the house and were probably architectural absurdities, redeemed in a measure indeed by not being wholly disengaged nor of a height too pretentious, dating, in their gingerbread antiquity, from a romantic revival that was already a respectable past. I admired them, had fancies about them, for we could all profit in a degree, especially when they loomed through the dusk, by the granduer of their actual battlements; yet it was not at such an elevation that the figure I had so often invoked seemed most in place.

It produced in me, this figure, in the clear twilight, I remember, two distinct gasps of emotion, which were, sharply, the shock of my first and that of my second surprise. My second was a violent perception of the mistake of my first: the man who met my eyes was not the person I had precipitately supposed. There came to me thus a bewilderment of vision of which, after these years, there is no living view that I can hope to give. An unknown man in a lonely place is a permitted object of fear to a young woman privately bred; and the figure that faced me was—a few more seconds assured me—as little anyone else I knew as it was the image that had been in my mind. I had not seen it in Harley Street—I had not seen it anywhere. The place, moreover, in the strangest way in the world, had, on the instant, and by the very fact of its appearance, become a solitude. To me at least, making my statement here with a deliberation with which I have never made it, the whole feeling of the moment returns. It was as if, while I took in—what I did take in—all the rest of the scene had been stricken with death. I can hear again, as I write, the intense hush in which the sounds of evening dropped. The rooks stopped cawing in the golden sky and the friendly hour lost, for the minute, all its voice. But there was no other change in nature, unless indeed it were a change that I saw with a stranger sharpness. The gold was still in the sky, the clearness in the air, and the man who looked at me over the battlements was as definite as a picture in a frame. That's how I thought, with extraordinary quickness, of each person that he might have been and that he was not. We were confronted across our distance quite long enough for me to ask myself with intensity who then he was and to feel, as an effect of my inability to say, a wonder that in a few instants more became intense.

The great question, or one of these, is, afterwards, I know, with regard to certain matters, the question of how long they have lasted. Well, this matter of mine, think what you will of it, lasted while I caught at a dozen possibilities, none of which made a difference for the better, that I could see, in there having been in the house—and for how long, above all?—a person of whom I was in ignorance. It lasted while I just bridled a little with the sense that my office demanded that there should be no such ignorance and no such person. It lasted while this visitant, at all events—and there was a touch of the strange freedom, as I remember, in the sign of familiarity of his wearing no hat—seemed to fix me, from his position, with just the question, just the scrutiny through the fading light, that his own presence provoked. We were too far apart to call to each other, but there was a moment at which, at shorter range, some challenge between us, breaking the hush, would have been the right result of our straight mutual stare. He was in one of the angles, the one away from the house, very erect, as it struck me, and with both hands on the ledge. So I saw him as I see the letters I form on this page; then, exactly, after a minute, as if to add to the spectacle, he slowly changed

his place—passed, looking at me hard all the while, to the opposite corner of the platform. Yes, I had the sharpest sense that during this transit he never took his eyes from me, and I can see at this moment the way his hand, as he went, passed from one of the crenelations to the next. He stopped at the other corner, but less long, and even as he turned away still markedly fixed me. He turned away; that was all I knew.

Chapter 4

IT WAS NOT THAT I DIDN'T WAIT, on this occasion, for more, for I was rooted as deeply as I was shaken. Was there a "secret" at Bly— a mystery of Udolpho or an insane, an unmentionable relative kept in unsuspected confinement? I can't say how long I turned it over, or how long, in a confusion of curiosity and dread, I remained where I had had my collision; I only recall that when I re-entered the house darkness had quite closed in. Agitation, in the interval, certainly had held me and driven me, for I must, in circling about the place, have walked three miles; but I was to be, later on, so much more overwhelmed that this mere dawn of alarm was a comparatively human chill. The most singular part of it in fact—singular as the rest had been—was the part I became, in the hall, aware of in meeting Mrs. Grose. This picture comes back to me in the general train—the impression, as I received it on my return, of the wide white panelled space, bright in the lamplight and with its portraits and red carpet, and of the good surprised look of my friend, which immediately told me she had missed me. It came to me straightway, under her contact, that, with plain heartiness, mere relieved anxiety at my appearance, she knew nothing whatever that could bear upon the incident I had there ready for her. I had not suspected in advance that her comfortable face would pull me up, and I somehow measured the importance of what I had seen by my thus finding myself hesitate to mention it. Scarce anything in the whole history seems to me so odd as this fact that my real beginning of fear was one, as I may say, with the instinct of sparing my companion. On the spot, accordingly, in the pleasant hall and with her eyes on me, I, for a reason that I couldn't then have phrased, achieved an inward revolution—offered a vague pretext for my lateness and, with the plea of the beauty of the night and of the heavy dew and wet feet, went as soon as possible to my room.

Here it was another affair; here, for many days after, it was a queer affair enough. There were hours, from day to day—or at least there were

moments, snatched even from clear duties—when I had to shut myself up to think. It was not so much yet that I was more nervous than I could bear to be as that I was remarkably afraid of becoming so; for the truth I had now to turn over was, simply and clearly, the truth that I could arrive at no account whatever of the visitor with whom I had been so inexplicably and yet, as it seemed to me, so intimately concerned. It took little time to see that I could sound without forms of inquiry and without exciting remark any domestic complication. The shock I had suffered must have sharpened all my senses; I felt sure, at the end of three days and as the result of mere closer attention, that I had not been practised upon by the servants nor made the object of any "game." Of whatever it was that I knew nothing was known around me. There was but one sane inference: someone had taken a liberty rather gross. That was what, repeatedly, I dipped into my room and locked the door to say to myself. We had been, collectively, subject to an intrusion; some unscrupulous traveller, curious in old houses, had made his way in unobserved, enjoyed the prospect from the best point of view, and then stolen out as he came. If he had given me such a bold hard stare, that was but a part of his indiscretion. The good thing, after all, was that we should surely see no more of him.

This was not so good a thing, I admit, as not to leave me to judge that what, essentially, made nothing else much signify was simply my charming work. My charming work was just my life with Miles and Flora, and through nothing could I so like it as through feeling that I could throw myself into it in trouble. The attraction of my small charges was a constant joy, leading me to wonder afresh at the vanity of my original fears, the distaste I had begun by entertaining for the probable grey prose of my office. There was to be no grey prose, it appeared, and no long grind; so how could work not be charming that presented itself as daily beauty? It was all the romance of the nursery and the poetry of the schoolroom. I don't mean by this, of course, that we studied only fiction and verse; I mean I can express no otherwise the sort of interest my companions inspired. How can I describe that except by saying that instead of growing used to them—and it's a marvel for a governess: I call the sisterhood to witness!—I made constant fresh discoveries. There was one direction, assuredly, in which these discoveries stopped: deep obscurity continued to cover the region of the boy's conduct at school. It had been promptly given me, I have noted, to face that mystery without a pang. Perhaps even it would be nearer the truth to say that—without a word—he himself had cleared it up. He had made the whole charge absurd. My conclusion bloomed there with the real rose-flush of his innocence: he was only too fine and fair for the little horrid, unclean school-world, and he had paid a price for it. I reflected acutely that the sense of such differences, such superiorities of quality,

always, on the part of the majority—which could include even stupid, sordid head-masters—turns infallibly to the vindictive.

Both the children had a gentleness (it was their only fault, and it never made Miles a muff) that kept them—how shall I express it?— almost impersonal and certainly quite unpunishable. They were like the cherubs of the anecdote, who had—morally, at any rate—nothing to whack! I remember feeling with Miles in especial as if he had had, as it were, no history. We expect of a small child a scant one, but there was in this beautiful little boy something extraordinarily sensitive, yet extraordinarily happy, that, more than in any creature of his age I have seen, struck me as beginning anew each day. He had never for a second suffered. I took this as a direct disproof of his having really been chastised. If he had been wicked he would have "caught" it, and I should have caught it by the rebound—I should have found the trace. I found nothing at all, and he was therefore angel. He never spoke of his school, never mentioned a comrade or a master; and I, for my part, was quite too much disgusted to allude to them. Of course I was under the spell, and the wonderful part is that, even at the time, I perfectly knew I was. But I gave myself up to it; it was an antidote to any pain, and I had more pains than one. I was in receipt in these days of disturbing letters from home, where things were not going well. But with my children, what things in the world mattered? That was the question I used to put to my scrappy retirements. I was dazzled by their loveliness.

There was a Sunday—to get on—when it rained with such force and for so many hours that there could be no procession to church; in consequence of which, as the day declined, I had arranged with Mrs. Grose that, should the evening show improvement, we would attend together the late service. The rain happily stopped, and I prepared for our walk, which, through the park and by the good road to the village, would be a matter of twenty minutes. Coming downstairs to meet my colleague in the hall, I remembered a pair of gloves that had required three stitches and that had received them—with a publicity perhaps not edifying— while I sat with the children at their tea, served on Sundays, by exception, in that cold, clean temple of mahogany and brass, the "grown-up" dining-room. The gloves had been dropped there, and I turned in to recover them. The day was grey enough, but the afternoon light still lingered, and it enabled me, on crossing the threshold, not only to recognise, on a chair near the wide window, then closed, the articles I wanted, but to become aware of a person on the other side of the window and looking straight in. One step into the room had sufficed; my vision was instantaneous; it was all there. The person looking straight in was the person who had already appeared to me. He appeared thus again with I won't say greater distinctness, for that was impossible, but with a nearness that represented a forward stride in our intercourse and made

me, as I met him, catch my breath and turn cold. He was the same—he was the same, and seen, this time, as he had been seen before, from the waist up, the window, though the dining-room was on the ground-floor, not going down to the terrace on which he stood. His face was close to the glass, yet the effect of this better view was, strangely, only to show me how intense the former had been. He remained but a few seconds—long enough to convince me he also saw him recognised; but it was as if I had been looking at him for years and had known him always. Something, however, happened this time that had not happened before; his stare into my face, through the glass and across the room, was as deep and hard as then, but it quitted me for a moment during which I could still watch it, see it fix successively several other things. On the spot there came to me the added shock of a certitude that it was not for me he had come there. He had come for someone else.

The flash of this knowledge—for it was knowledge in the midst of dread—produced in me the most extraordinary effect, started, as I stood there, a sudden vibration of duty and courage. I say courage because I was beyond all doubt already far gone. I bounded straight out of the door again, reached that of the house, got, in an instant, upon the drive, and, passing along the terrace as fast as I could rush, turned a corner and came full in sight. But it was in sight of nothing now—my visitor had vanished. I stopped, I almost dropped, with the real relief of this; but I took in the whole scene—I gave him time to reappear. I call it time, but how long was it? I can't speak to the purpose today of the duration of these things. That kind of measure must have left me: they couldn't have lasted as they actually appeared to me to last. The terrace and the whole place, the lawn and the garden beyond it, all I could see of the park, were empty with a great emptiness. There were shrubberies and big trees, but I remember the clear assurance I felt that none of them concealed him. He was there or was not there: not there if I didn't see him. I got hold of this; then, instinctively, instead of returning as I had come, went to the window. It was confusedly present to me that I ought to place myself where he had stood. I did so; I applied my face to the pane and looked, as he had looked, into the room. As if, at this moment, to show me exactly what his range had been, Mrs. Grose, as I had done for himself just before, came in from the hall. With this I had the full image of a repetition of what had already occurred. She saw me as I had seen my own visitant; she pulled up short as I had done; I gave her something of the shock that I had received. She turned white, and this made me ask myself if I had blanched as much. She stared, in short, and retreated on just *my* lines, and I knew she had then passed out and come round to me and that I should presently meet her. I remained where I was, and while I waited I thought of more things than one. But there's only one I take space to mention. I wondered why *she* should be scared.

Chapter 5

OH, SHE LET ME KNOW as soon as, round the corner of the house, she loomed again into view. "What in the name of goodness is the matter——?" She was now flushed and out of breath.

I said nothing till she came quite near. "With me?" I must have made a wonderful face. "Do I show it?"

"You're as white as a sheet. You look awful."

I considered; I could meet on this, without scruple, any innocence. My need to respect the bloom of Mrs. Grose's had dropped, without a rustle, from my shoulders, and if I wavered for the instant it was not with what I kept back. I put out my hand to her and she took it; I held her hard a little, liking to feel her close to me. There was a kind of support in the shy heave of her surprise. "You came for me for church, of course, but I can't go."

"Has anything happened?"

"Yes. You must know now. Did I look very queer?"

"Through this window? Dreadful!"

"Well," I said, "I've been frightened." Mrs. Grose's eyes expressed plainly that *she* had no wish to be, yet also that she knew too well her place not to be ready to share with me any marked inconvenience. Oh, it was quite settled that she *must* share! "Just what you saw from the dining-room a minute ago was the effect of that. What *I* saw—just before—was much worse."

Her hand tightened. "What was it?"

"An extraordinary man. Looking in."

"What extraordinary man?"

"I haven't the least idea."

Mrs. Grose gazed round us in vain. "Then where is he gone?"

"I know still less."

"Have you seen him before?"

"Yes—once. On the old tower."

She could only look at me harder. "Do you mean he's a stranger?"

"Oh, very much!"

"Yet you didn't tell me?"

"No—for reasons. But now that you've guessed——"

Mrs. Grose's round eyes encountered this charge. "Ah, I haven't guessed!" she said very simply. "How can I if *you* don't imagine?"

"I don't in the very least."

"You've seen him nowhere but on the tower?"

"And on this spot just now."

Mrs. Grose looked round again. "What was he doing on the tower?"

"Only standing there and looking down at me."

She thought a minute. "Was he a gentleman?"

I found I had no need to think. "No." She gazed in deeper wonder. "No."

"Then nobody about the place? Nobody from the village?"

"Nobody—nobody. I didn't tell you, but I made sure."

She breathed a vague relief: this was, oddly, so much to the good. It only went indeed a little way. "But if he isn't a gentleman——"

"What *is* he? He's a horror."

"A horror?"

"He's—God help me if I know *what* he is!"

Mrs. Grose looked round once more; she fixed her eyes on the duskier distance, then, pulling herself together, turned to me with abrupt inconsequence. "It's time we should be at church."

"Oh, I'm not fit for church!"

"Won't it do you good?"

"It won't do *them*——!" I nodded at the house.

"The children?"

"I can't leave them now."

"You're afraid——?"

I spoke boldly. "I'm afraid of *him*."

Mrs. Grose's large face showed me, at this, for the first time, the far-away faint glimmer of a consciousness more acute: I somehow made out in it the delayed dawn of an idea I myself had not given her and that was as yet quite obscure to me. It comes back to me that I thought instantly of this as something I could get from her; and I felt it to be connected with the desire she presently showed to know more. "When was it—on the tower?"

"About the middle of the month. At this same hour."

"Almost at dark?" said Mrs. Grose.

"Oh, no, not nearly. I saw him as I see you."

"Then how did he get in?"

"And how did he get out?" I laughed. "I had no opportunity to ask him! This evening, you see," I pursued, "he has not been able to get in."

"He only peeps?"

"I hope it will be confined to that!" She had now let go my hand; she turned away a little. I waited an instant; then I brought out: "Go to church. Good-bye. I must watch."

Slowly she faced me again. "Do you fear for them?"

We met in another long look. "Don't *you?*" Instead of answering she came nearer to the window and, for a minute, applied her face to the glass. "You see how he could see," I meanwhile went on.

She didn't move. "How long was he here?"

"Till I came out. I came to meet him."

Mrs. Grose at last turned round, and there was still more in her face. "*I* couldn't have come out."

"Neither could I!" I laughed again. "But I did come. I have my duty."

"So have I mine," she replied; after which she added: "What is he like?"

"I've been dying to tell you. But he's like nobody."

"Nobody?" she echoed.

"He has no hat." Then seeing in her face that she already, in this, with a deeper dismay, found a touch of picture, I quickly added stroke to stroke. "He has red hair, very red, close-curling, and a pale face, long in shape, with straight, good features and little, rather queer whiskers that are as red as his hair. His eyebrows are, somehow, darker; they look particularly arched and as if they might move a good deal. His eyes are sharp, strange—awfully; but I only know clearly that they're rather small and very fixed. His mouth's wide, and his lips are thin, and except for his little whiskers he's quite clean-shaven. He gives me a sort of sense of looking like an actor."

"An actor!" It was impossible to resemble one less, at least, than Mrs. Grose at that moment.

"I've never seen one, but so I suppose them. He's tall, active, erect," I continued, "but never—no, never!—a gentleman."

My companion's face had blanched as I went on; her round eyes started and her mild mouth gaped. "A gentleman?" she gasped, confounded, stupefied: "a gentleman *he?*"

"You know him then?"

She visibly tried to hold herself. "But he *is* handsome?"

I saw the way to help her. "Remarkably!"

"And dressed——?"

"In somebody's clothes. They're smart, but they're not his own."

She broke into a breathless affirmative groan. "They're the master's!"

I caught it up. "You *do* know him?"

She faltered but a second. "Quint!" she cried.

"Quint?"

"Peter Quint—his own man, his valet, when he was here!"

"When the master was?"

Gaping still, but meeting me, she pieced it all together. "He never wore his hat, but he did wear—well, there were waistcoats missed! They were both here—last year. Then the master went, and Quint was alone."

I followed, but halting a little. "Alone?"

"Alone with *us*." Then, as from a deeper depth, "In charge," she added.

"And what became of him?"

She hung fire so long that I was still more mystified. "He went too," she brought out at last.

"Went where?"

Her expression, at this, became extraordinary. "God knows where! He died."

"Died?" I almost shrieked.

She seemed fairly to square herself, plant herself more firmly to utter the wonder of it. "Yes. Mr. Quint is dead."

Chapter 6

IT TOOK OF COURSE MORE than that particular passage to place us together in presence of what we had now to live with as we could—my dreadful liability to impressions of the order so vividly exemplified, and my companion's knowledge, henceforth—a knowledge half consternation and half compassion—of that liability. There had been, this evening, after the revelation that left me, for an hour, so prostrate— there had been, for either of us, no attendance on any service but a little service of tears and vows, of prayers and promises, a climax to the series of mutual challenges and pledges that had straightway ensued on our retreating together to the schoolroom and shutting ourselves up there to have everything out. The result of our having everything out was simply to reduce our situation to the last rigour of its elements. She herself had seen nothing, not the shadow of a shadow, and nobody in the house but the governess was in the governess's plight; yet she accepted without directly impugning my sanity the truth as I gave it to her, and ended by showing me, on this ground, an awe-stricken tenderness, an expression of the sense of my more than questionable privilege, of which the very breath has remained with me as that of the sweetest of human charities.

What was settled between us, accordingly, that night, was that we thought we might bear things together; and I was not even sure that, in spite of her exemption, it was she who had the best of the burden. I knew at this hour, I think, as well as I knew later what I was capable of meeting to shelter my pupils; but it took me some time to be wholly sure of what my honest ally was prepared for to keep terms with so compromising a contract. I was queer company enough—quite as queer as the company I received; but as I trace over what we went through I see how much common ground we must have found in the one idea that, by good fortune, *could* steady us. It was the idea, the second movement, that led me straight out, as I may say, of the inner chamber of my dread.

I could take the air in the court, at least, and there Mrs. Grose could join me. Perfectly can I recall now the particular way strength came to me before we separated for the night. We had gone over and over every feature of what I had seen.

"He was looking for someone else, you say—someone who was not you?"

"He was looking for little Miles." A portentous clearness now possessed me. *"That's* whom he was looking for."

"But how do you know?"

"I know, I know, I know!" My exaltation grew. "And *you* know, my dear!"

She didn't deny this, but I required, I felt, not even so much telling as that. She resumed in a moment, at any rate: "What if *he* should see him?"

"Little Miles? That's what he wants!"

She looked immensely scared again. "The child?"

"Heaven forbid! The man. He wants to appear to *them.*" That he might was an awful conception, and yet, somehow, I could keep it at bay; which, moreover, as we lingered there, was what I succeeded in practically proving. I had an absolute certainty that I could see again what I had already seen, but something within me said that by offering myself bravely as the sole subject of such experience, by accepting, by inviting, by surmounting it all, I should serve as an expiatory victim and guard the tranquillity of my companions. The children, in especial, I should thus fence about and absolutely save. I recall one of the last things I said that night to Mrs. Grose.

"It does strike me that my pupils have never mentioned——"

She looked at me hard as I musingly pulled up. "His having been here and the time they were with him?"

"The time they were with him, and his name, his presence, his history, in any way."

"Oh, the little lady doesn't remember. She never heard or knew."

"The circumstances of his death?" I thought with some intensity. "Perhaps not. But Miles would remember—Miles would know."

"Ah, don't try him!" broke from Mrs. Grose.

I returned her the look she had given me. "Don't be afraid." I continued to think. "It *is* rather odd."

"That he has never spoken of him?"

"Never by the least allusion. And you tell me they were 'great friends?' "

"Oh, it wasn't *him!*" Mrs. Grose with emphasis declared. "It was Quint's own fancy. To play with him, I mean—to spoil him." She paused a moment; then she added: "Quint was much too free."

This gave me, straight from my vision of his face—*such* a face!— a sudden sickness of disgust. "Too free with *my* boy?"

"Too free with everyone!"

I forebore, for the moment, to analyse this description further than by the reflection that a part of it applied to several of the members of the household, of the half-dozen maids and men who were still of our small colony. But there was everything, for our apprehension, in the lucky fact that no discomfortable legend, no perturbation of scullions, had ever, within anyone's memory, attached to the kind old place. It had neither bad name nor ill fame, and Mrs. Grose, most apparently, only desired to cling to me and to quake in silence. I even put her, the very last thing of all, to the test. It was when, at midnight, she had her hand on the schoolroom door to take leave. "I have it from you then—for it's of great importance—that he was definitely and admittedly bad?"

"Oh, not admittedly. I knew it—but the master didn't."

"And you never told him?"

"Well, he didn't like tale-bearing—he hated complaints. He was terribly short with anything of that kind, and if people were all right to *him*——"

"He wouldn't be bothered with more?" This squared well enough with my impression of him: he was not a trouble-loving gentleman, nor so very particular perhaps about some of the company *he* kept. All the same, I pressed my interlocutress. "I promise you *I* would have told!"

She felt my discrimination. "I dare say I was wrong. But, really, I was afraid."

"Afraid of what?"

"Of things that man could do. Quint was so clever—he was so deep."

I took this in still more than, probably, I showed. "You weren't afraid of anything else? Not of his effect——?"

"His effect?" she repeated with a face of anguish and waiting while I faltered.

"On innocent little precious lives. They were in your charge."

"No, they were not in mine!" she roundly and distressfully returned. "The master believed in him and placed him here because he was supposed not to be well and the country air so good for him. So he had everything to say. Yes"—she let me have it—"even about *them*."

"Them—that creature?" I had to smother a kind of howl. "And you could bear it!"

"No. I couldn't—and I can't now!" And the poor woman burst into tears.

A rigid control, from the next day, was, as I have said, to follow them; yet how often and how passionately, for a week, we came back together to the subject! Much as we had discussed it that Sunday night, I was, in the immediate later hours in especial—for it may be imagined whether I slept—still haunted with the shadow of something she had not told me. I myself had kept back nothing, but there was a word Mrs. Grose

had kept back. I was sure, moreover, by morning, that this was not from a failure of frankness, but because on every side there were fears. It seems to me indeed, in retrospect, that by the time the morrow's sun was high I had restlessly read into the facts before us almost all the meaning they were to receive from subsequent and more cruel occurrences. What they gave me above all was just the sinister figure of the living man—the dead one would keep awhile!—and of the months he had continuously passed at Bly, which, added up, made a formidable stretch. The limit of this evil time had arrived only when, on the dawn of a winter's morning, Peter Quint was found, by a labourer going to early work, stone dead on the road from the village: a catastrophe explained—superficially at least—by a visible wound to his head; such a wound as might have been produced—and as, on the final evidence, *had* been—by a fatal slip, in the dark and after leaving the public house, on the steepish icy slope, a wrong path altogether, at the bottom of which he lay. The icy slope, the turn mistaken at night and in liquor, accounted for much—practically, in the end and after the inquest and boundless chatter, for everything; but there had been matters in his life—strange passages and perils, secret disorders, vices more than suspected—that would have accounted for a good deal more.

I scarce know how to put my story into words that shall be a credible picture of my state of mind; but I was in these days literally able to find a joy in the extraordinary flight of heroism the occasion demanded of me. I now saw that I had been asked for a service admirable and difficult; and there would be a greatness in letting it be seen—oh, in the right quarter!—that I could succeed where many another girl might have failed. It was an immense help to me—I confess I rather applaud myself as I look back!—that I saw my service so strongly and so simply. I was there to protect and defend the little creatures in the world the most bereaved and the most loveable, the appeal of whose helplessness had suddenly become only too explicit, a deep, constant ache of one's own committed heart. We were cut off, really, together; we were united in our danger. They had nothing but me, and I—well, I had *them*. It was in short a magnificent chance. This chance presented itself to me in an image richly material. I was a screen—I was to stand before them. The more I saw, the less they would. I began to watch them in a stifled suspense, a disguised excitement that might well, had it continued too long, have turned to something like madness. What saved me, as I now see, was that it turned to something else altogether. It didn't last as suspense—it was superseded by horrible proofs. Proofs, I say, yes—from the moment I really took hold.

This moment dated from an afternoon hour that I happened to spend in the grounds with the younger of my pupils alone. We had left Miles indoors, on the red cushion of a deep window-seat; he had wished to finish a book, and I had been glad to encourage a purpose so laudable in a young man whose only defect was an occasional excess of the

357

restless. His sister, on the contrary, had been alert to come out, and I strolled with her half an hour, seeking the shade, for the sun was still high and the day exceptionally warm. I was aware afresh, with her, as we went, of how, like her brother, she contrived—it was the charming thing in both children—to let me alone without appearing to drop me and to accompany me without appearing to surround. They were never importunate and yet never listless. My attention to them all really went to seeing them amuse themselves immensely without me: this was a spectacle they seemed actively to prepare and that engaged me as an active admirer. I walked in a world of their invention—they had no occasion whatever to draw upon mine; so that my time was taken only with being, for them, some remarkable person or thing that the game of the moment required and that was merely, thanks to my superior, my exalted stamp, a happy and highly distinguished sinecure. I forget what I was on the present occasion; I only remember that I was something very important and very quiet and that Flora was playing very hard. We were on the edge of the lake, and, as we had lately begun geography, the lake was the Sea of Azof.

Suddenly, in these circumstances, I became aware that, on the other side of the Sea of Azof, we had an interested spectator. The way this knowledge gathered in me was the strangest thing in the world—the strangest, that is, except the very much stranger in which it quickly merged itself. I had sat down with a piece of work—for I was something or other that could sit—on the old stone bench which overlooked the pond; and in this position I began to take in with certitude, and yet without direct vision, the presence, at a distance, of a third person. The old trees, the thick shrubbery, made a great and pleasant shade, but it was all suffused with the brightness of the hot, still hour. There was no ambiguity in anything; none whatever, at least, in the conviction I from one moment to another found myself forming as to what I should see straight before me and across the lake as a consequence of raising my eyes. They were attached at this juncture to the stitching in which I was engaged, and I can feel once more the spasm of my effort not to move them till I should so have steadied myself as to be able to make up my mind what to do. There was an alien object in view—a figure whose right of presence I instantly, passionately questioned. I recollect counting over perfectly the possibilities, reminding myself that nothing was more natural, for instance, than the appearance of one of the men about the place, or even of a messenger, a postman or a tradesman's boy, from the village. That reminder had as little effect on my practical certitude as I was conscious—still even without looking—of its having upon the character and attitude of our visitor. Nothing was more natural than that these things should be the other things that they absolutely were not.

Of the positive identity of the apparition I would assure myself as soon as the small clock of my courage should have ticked out the right

second; meanwhile, with an effort that was already sharp enough, I transferred my eyes straight to little Flora, who, at the moment, was about ten yards away. My heart had stood still for an instant with the wonder and terror of the question whether she too would see; and I held my breath while I waited for what a cry from her, what some sudden innocent sign either of interest or of alarm, would tell me. I waited, but nothing came; then, in the first place—and there is something more dire in this, I feel, than in anything I have to relate—I was determined by a sense that, within a minute, all sounds from her had previously dropped; and, in the second, by the circumstance that, also within the minute, she had, in her play, turned her back to the water. This was her attitude when I at last looked at her—looked with the confirmed conviction that we were still, together, under direct personal notice. She had picked up a small flat piece of wood, which happened to have in it a little hole that had evidently suggested to her the idea of sticking in another fragment that might figure as a mast and make the thing a boat. This second morsel, as I watched her, she was very markedly and intently attempting to tighten in its place. My apprehension of what she was doing sustained me so that after some seconds I felt I was ready for more. Then I again shifted my eyes—I faced what I had to face.

Chapter 7

I GOT HOLD OF MRS. GROSE as soon after this as I could; and I can give no intelligible account of how I fought out the interval. Yet I still hear myself cry as I fairly threw myself into her arms: "They *know*— it's too monstrous: they know, they know!"

"And what on earth——?" I felt her incredulity as she held me.

"Why, all that *we* know—and heaven knows what else besides!" Then, as she released me, I made it out to her, made it out perhaps only now with full coherency even to myself. "Two hours ago, in the garden"—I could scarce articulate—"Flora *saw!*"

Mrs. Grose took it as she might have taken a blow in the stomach. "She has told you?" she panted.

"Not a word—that's the horror. She kept it to herself! The child of eight, *that* child!" Unutterable still, for me, was the stupefaction of it.

Mrs. Grose, of course, could only gape the wider. "Then how do you know?"

"I was there—I saw with my eyes: saw that she was perfectly aware."

"Do you mean aware of *him?*"

"No—of *her*." I was conscious as I spoke that I looked prodigious things, for I got the slow reflection of them in my companion's face. "Another person—this time; but a figure of quite as unmistakable horror and evil: a woman in black, pale and dreadful—with such an air also, and such a face!—on the other side of the lake. I was there with the child —quiet for the hour; and in the midst of it she came."

"Came how—from where?"

"From where they come from! She just appeared and stood there— but not so near."

"And without coming nearer?"

"Oh, for the effect and the feeling, she might have been as close as you!"

My friend, with an odd impulse, fell back a step. "Was she someone you've never seen?"

"Yes. But someone the child has. Someone *you* have." Then, to show how I had thought it all out: "My predecessor—the one who died."

"Miss Jessel?"

"Miss Jessel. You don't believe me?" I pressed.

She turned right and left in her distress. "How can you be sure?"

This drew from me, in the state of my nerves, a flash of impatience. "Then ask Flora—*she's* sure!" But I had no sooner spoken than I caught myself up. "No, for God's sake, *don't!* She'll say she isn't—she'll lie!"

Mrs. Grose was not too bewildered instinctively to protest. "Ah, how *can* you?"

"Because I'm clear. Flora doesn't want me to know."

"It's only then to spare you."

"No, no—there are depths, depths! The more I go over it, the more I see in it, and the more I see in it the more I fear. I don't know what I *don't* see—what I *don't* fear!"

Mrs. Grose tried to keep up with me. "You mean you're afraid of seeing her again?"

"Oh, no; that's nothing—now!" Then I explained. "It's of *not* seeing her."

But my companion only looked wan. "I don't understand you."

"Why, it's that the child may keep it up—and that the child assuredly *will*—without my knowing it."

At the image of this possibility Mrs. Grose for a moment collapsed, yet presently to pull herself together again, as if from the positive force of the sense of what, should we yield an inch, there would really be to give way to. "Dear, dear—we must keep our heads! And after all, if she doesn't mind it——!" She even tried a grim joke. "Perhaps she likes it!"

"Likes *such* things—a scrap of an infant!"

"Isn't it just a proof of her blessed innocence?" my friend bravely inquired.

She brought me, for the instant, almost round. "Oh, we must clutch at *that*—we must cling to it! If it isn't a proof of what you say, it's a proof of—God knows what! For the woman's a horror of horrors."

Mrs. Grose, at this, fixed her eyes a minute on the ground; then at last raising them, "Tell me how you know," she said.

"Then you admit it's what she was?" I cried.

"Tell me how you know," my friend simply repeated.

"Know? By seeing her! By the way she looked."

"At you, do you mean—so wickedly?"

"Dear me, no—I could have borne that. She gave me never a glance. She only fixed the child."

Mrs. Grose tried to see it. "Fixed her?"

"Ah, with such awful eyes!"

She stared at mine as if they might really have resembled them. "Do you mean of dislike?"

"God help us, no. Of something much worse."

"Worse than dislike?"—this left her indeed at a loss.

"With a determination—indescribable. With a kind of fury of intention."

I made her turn pale. "Intention?"

"To get hold of her." Mrs. Grose—her eyes just lingering on mine—gave a shudder and walked to the window; and while she stood there looking out I completed my statement. *"That's* what Flora knows."

After a little she turned round. "The person was in black, you say?"

"In mourning—rather poor, almost shabby. But—yes—with extraordinary beauty." I now recognised to what I had at last, stroke by stroke, brought the victim of my confidence, for she quite visibly weighed this. "Oh, handsome—very, very," I insisted; "wonderfully handsome. But infamous."

She slowly came back to me. "Miss Jessel—*was* infamous." She once more took my hand in both her own, holding it as tight as if to fortify me against the increase of alarm I might draw from this disclosure. "They were both infamous," she finally said.

So, for a little, we faced it once more together; and I found absolutely a degree of help in seeing it now so straight. "I appreciate," I said, "the great decency of your not having hitherto spoken; but the time has certainly come to give me the whole thing." She appeared to assent to this, but still only in silence; seeing which I went on: "I must have it now. Of what did she die? Come, there was something between them."

"There was everything."

"In spite of the difference——?"

"Oh, of their rank, their condition"—she brought it woefully out. *"She* was a lady."

I turned it over; I again saw. "Yes—she was a lady."

"And he so dreadfully below," said Mrs. Grose.

I felt that I doubtless needn't press too hard, in such company, on the place of a servant in the scale; but there was nothing to prevent an acceptance of my companion's own measure of my predecessor's abasement. There was a way to deal with that, and I dealt; the more readily for my full vision—on the evidence—of our employer's late clever, good-looking "own" man; impudent, assured, spoiled, depraved. "The fellow was a hound."

Mrs. Grose considered as if it were perhaps a little a case for a sense of shades. "I've never seen one like him. He did what he wished."

"With *her?*"

"With them all."

It was as if now in my friend's own eyes Miss Jessel had again appeared. I seemed at any rate, for an instant, to see their evocation of her as distinctly as I had seen her by the pond; and I brought out with decision: "It must have been also what *she* wished!"

Mrs. Grose's face signified that it had been indeed, but she said at the same time: "Poor woman—she paid for it!"

"Then you do know what she died of?" I asked.

"No—I know nothing. I wanted not to know; I was glad enough I didn't; and I thanked heaven she was well out of this!"

"Yet you had, then, your idea——"

"Of her real reason for leaving? Oh, yes—as to that. She couldn't have stayed. Fancy it here—for a governess! And afterwards I imagined —and I still imagine. And what I imagine is dreadful."

"Not so dreadful as what *I* do," I replied; on which I must have shown her—as I was indeed but too conscious—a front of miserable defeat. It brought out again all her compassion for me, and at the renewed touch of her kindness my power to resist broke down. I burst, as I had, the other time, made her burst, into tears; she took me to her motherly breast, and my lamentation overflowed. "I don't do it!" I sobbed in despair; "I don't save or shield them! It's far worse than I dreamed— they're lost!"

Chapter 8

WHAT I HAD SAID TO MRS. GROSE was true enough: there were in the matter I had put before her depths and possibilities that I lacked resolution to sound; so that when we met once more in the wonder of it we were of a common mind about the duty of resistance to extravagant fancies. We were to keep our heads if we should keep nothing else—

difficult indeed as that might be in the face of what, in our prodigious experience, was least to be questioned. Late that night, while the house slept, we had another talk in my room, when she went all the way with me as to its being beyond doubt that I had seen exactly what I had seen. To hold her perfectly in the pinch of that, I found I had only to ask her how, if I had "made it up," I came to be able to give, of each of the persons appearing to me, a picture disclosing, to the last detail, their special marks—a portrait on the exhibition of which she had instantly recognised and named them. She wished, of course—small blame to her! —to sink the whole subject; and I was quick to assure her that my own interest in it had now violently taken the form of a search for the way to escape from it. I encountered her on the ground of a probability that with recurrence—for recurrence we took for granted—I should get used to my danger, distinctly professing that my personal exposure had suddenly become the least of my discomforts. It was my new suspicion that was intolerable; and yet even to this complication the later hours of the day had brought a little ease.

On leaving her, after my first outbreak, I had of course returned to my pupils, associating the right remedy for my dismay with that sense of their charm which I had already found to be a thing I could positively cultivate and which had never failed me yet. I had simply, in other words, plunged afresh into Flora's special society and there become aware—it was almost a luxury!—that she could put her little conscious hand straight upon the spot that ached. She had looked at me in sweet speculation and then had accused me to my face of having "cried." I had supposed I had brushed away the ugly signs: but I could literally—for the time, at all events—rejoice, under this fathomless charity, that they had not entirely disappeared. To gaze into the depths of blue of the child's eyes and pronounce their loveliness a trick of premature cunning was to be guilty of a cynicism in preference to which I naturally preferred to abjure my judgment and, so far as might be, my agitation. I couldn't adjure for merely wanting to, but I could repeat to Mrs. Grose—as I did there, over and over, in the small hours—that with their voices in the air, their pressure on one's heart and their fragrant faces against one's cheek, everything fell to the ground but their incapacity and their beauty. It was a pity that, somehow, to settle this once for all, I had equally to re-enumerate the signs of subtlety that, in the afternoon, by the lake, had made a miracle of my show of self-possession. It was a pity to be obliged to re-investigate the certitude of the moment itself and repeat how it had come to me as a revelation that the inconceivable communion I then surprised was a matter, for either party, of habit. It was a pity that I should have had to quaver out again the reasons for my not having, in my delusion, so much as questioned that the little girl saw our visitant even as I actually saw Mrs. Grose herself, and that she wanted, by just so much as she did thus see, to make me suppose she didn't, and at the same time, without showing

anything, arrive at a guess as to whether I myself did! It was a pity that I needed once more to describe the portentous little activity by which she sought to divert my attention—the perceptible increase of movement, the greater intensity of play, the singing, the gabbling of nonsense, and the invitation to romp.

Yet if I had not indulged, to prove there was nothing in it, in this review, I should have missed the two or three dim elements of comfort that still remained to me. I should not for instance have been able to asseverate to my friend that I was certain—which was so much to the good—that *I* at least had not betrayed myself. I should not have been prompted, by stress of need, by desperation of mind—I scarce know what to call it—to invoke such further aid to intelligence as might spring from pushing my colleague fairly to the wall. She had told me, bit by bit, under pressure, a great deal; but a small shifty spot on the wrong side of it all still sometimes brushed my brow like the wing of a bat; and I remember how on this occasion—for the sleeping house and the concentration alike of our danger and our watch seemed to help—I felt the importance of giving the last jerk to the curtain. "I don't believe anything so horrible," I recollect saying; "no, let us put it definitely, my dear, that I don't. But if I did, you know, there's a thing I should require now, just without sparing you the least bit more—oh, not a scrap, come!—to get out of you. What was it you had in mind when, in our distress, before Miles came back, over the letter from his school, you said, under my insistence, that you didn't pretend for him that he had not literally *ever* been 'bad?' He has *not* literally 'ever,' in these weeks that I myself have lived with him and so closely watched him; he has been an imperturbable little prodigy of delightful, loveable goodness. Therefore you might perfectly have made the claim for him if you had not, as it happened, seen an exception to take. What was your exception, and to what passage in your personal observation of him did you refer?"

It was a dreadfully austere inquiry, but levity was not our note, and, at any rate, before the grey dawn admonished us to separate I had got my answer. What my friend had had in mind proved to be immensely to the purpose. It was neither more nor less than the circumstance that for a period of several months Quint and the boy had been perpetually together. It was in fact the very appropriate truth that she had ventured to criticise the propriety, to hint at the incongruity, of so close an alliance, and even to go so far on the subject as a frank overture to Miss Jessel. Miss Jessel had, with a most strange manner, requested her to mind her business, and the good woman had, on this, directly approached little Miles. What she had said to him, since I pressed, was that *she* liked to see young gentlemen not forget their station.

I pressed again, of course, at this. "You reminded him that Quint was only a base menial?"

"As you might say! And it was his answer, for one thing, that was bad."

"And for another thing?" I waited. "He repeated your words to Quint?"

"No, not that. It's just what he *wouldn't!*" she could still impress upon me. "I was sure, at any rate," she added, "that he didn't. But he denied certain occasions."

"What occasions?"

"When they had been about together quite as if Quint were his tutor—and a very grand one—and Miss Jessel only for the little lady. When he had gone off with the fellow, I mean, and spent hours with him."

"He then prevaricated about it—he said he hadn't?" Her assent was clear enough to cause me to add in a moment: "I see. He lied."

"Oh!" Mrs. Grose mumbled. This was a suggestion that it didn't matter; which indeed she backed up by a further remark. "You see, after all, Miss Jessel didn't mind. She didn't forbid him."

I considered. "Did he put that to you as a justification?"

At this she dropped again. "No, he never spoke of it."

"Never mentioned her in connection with Quint?"

She saw, visibly flushing, where I was coming out. "Well, he didn't show anything. He denied," she repeated; "he denied."

Lord, how I pressed her now! "So that you could see he knew what was between the two wretches?"

"I don't know—I don't know!" the poor woman groaned.

"You do know, you dear thing," I replied; "only you haven't my dreadful boldness of mind, and you keep back, out of timidity and modesty and delicacy, even the impression that, in the past, when you had, without my aid, to flounder about in silence, most of all made you miserable. But I shall get it out of you yet! There was something in the boy that suggested to you," I continued, "that he covered and concealed their relation."

"Oh, he couldn't prevent——"

"Your learning the truth? I dare say! But, heavens," I fell, with vehemence, a-thinking, "what it shows that they must, to that extent, have succeeded in making of him!"

"Ah nothing that's not nice *now!*" Mrs. Grose lugubriously pleaded.

"I don't wonder you looked queer," I persisted, "when I mentioned to you the letter from his school!"

"I doubt if I looked as queer as you!" she retorted with homely force. "And if he was so bad then as that comes to, how is he such an angel now?"

"Yes, indeed—and if he was a fiend at school! How, how, how? Well," I said in my torment, "you must put it to me again, but I shall not be able to tell you for some days. Only, put it to me again!" I cried in a

way that made my friend stare. "There are directions in which I must not for the present let myself go." Meanwhile I returned to her first example— the one to which she had just previously referred—of the boy's happy capacity for an occasional slip. "If Quint—on your remonstrance at the time you speak of—was a base menial, one of the things Miles said to you. I find myself guessing, was that you were another." Again her admission was so adequate that I continued: "And you forgave him that?"

"Wouldn't *you?*"

"Oh, yes!" And we exchanged there, in the stillness, a sound of the oddest amusement. Then I went on: "At all events, while he was with the man——"

"Miss Flora was with the woman. It suited them all!"

It suited me too, I felt, only too well; by which I mean that it suited exactly the particularly deadly view I was in the very act of forbidding myself to entertain. But I so far succeeded in checking the expression of this view that I will throw, just here, no further light on it than may be offered by the mention of my final observation to Mrs. Grose. "His having lied and been impudent are, I confess, less engaging specimens than I had hoped to have from you of the outbreak in him of the little natural man. Still," I mused, "they must do, for they make me feel more than ever that I must watch."

It made me blush, the next minute, to see in my friend's face how much more unreservedly she had forgiven him than her anecdote struck me as presenting to my own tenderness an occasion for doing. This came out when, at the schoolroom door, she quitted me. "Surely you don't accuse *him*——"

"Of carrying on an intercourse that he conceals from me? Ah, remember that, until further evidence, I now accuse nobody." Then, before shutting her out to go, by another passage, to her own place, "I must just wait," I wound up.

Chapter 9

I WAITED AND WAITED, and the days, as they elapsed, took something from my consternation. A very few of them, in fact, passing, in constant sight of my pupils, without a fresh incident, sufficed to give to grievous fancies and even to odious memories a kind of brush of the sponge. I have spoken of the surrender to their extraordinary childish grace as a thing I could actively cultivate, and it may be imagined if I neglected now to address myself to this source for whatever it would

yield. Stranger than I can express, certainly, was the effort to struggle against my new lights; it would doubtless have been, however, a greater tension still had it not been so frequently successful. I used to wonder how my little charges could help guessing that I thought strange things about them; and the circumstance that these things only made them more interesting was not by itself a direct aid to keeping them in the dark. I trembled lest they should see that they *were* so immensely more interesting. Putting things at the worst, at all events, as in meditation I so often did, any clouding of their innocence could only be—blameless and foredoomed as they were—a reason the more for taking risks. There were moments when, by an irresistible impulse, I found myself catching them up and pressing them to my heart. As soon as I had done so I used to say to myself: "What will they think of that? Doesn't it betray too much?" It would have been easy to get into a sad, wild tangle about how much I might betray; but the real account, I feel, of the hours of peace that I could still enjoy was that the immediate charm of my companions was a beguilement still effective even under the shadow of the possibility that it was studied. For if it occurred to me that I might occasionally excite suspicion by the little oubreaks of my sharper passion for them, so too I remember wondering if I mightn't see a queerness in the traceable increase of their own demonstrations.

They were at this period extravagantly and preternaturally fond of me; which, after all, I could reflect, was no more than a graceful response in children perpetually bowed over and hugged. The homage of which they were so lavish succeeded, in truth, for my nerves, quite as well as if I never appeared to myself, as I may say, literally to catch them at a purpose in it. They had never, I think, wanted to do so many things for their poor protectress; I mean—though they got their lessons better and better, which was naturally what would please her most—in the way of diverting, entertaining, surprising her; reading her passages, telling her stories, acting her charades, pouncing out at her, in disguises, as animals and historical characters, and above all astonishing her by the "pieces" they had secretly got by heart and could interminably recite. I should never get to the bottom—were I to let myself go even now—of the prodigious private commentary, all under still more private correction, with which, in these days, I overscored their full hours. They had shown me from the first a facility for everything, a general faculty which, taking a fresh start, achieved remarkable flights. They got their little tasks as if they loved them, and indulged, from the mere exuberance of the gift, in the most unimposed little miracles of memory. They not only popped out at me as tigers and as Romans, but as Shakespeareans, astronomers, and navigators. This was so singularly the case that it had presumably much to do with the fact as to which, at the present day, I am at a loss for a different explanation: I allude to my unnatural composure on the subject of another school for Miles. What I remember is that I

was content not, for the time, to open the question, and that content-
ment must have sprung from the sense of his perpetually striking show
of cleverness. He was too clever for a bad governess, for a parson's
daughter, to spoil; and the strangest if not the brightest thread in the
pensive embroidery I just spoke of was the impression I might have got,
if I had dared to work it out, that he was under some influence operating
in his small intellectual life as a tremendous incitement.

If it was easy to reflect, however, that such a boy could postpone
school, it was at least as marked that for such a boy to have been "kicked
out" by a school-master was a mystification without end. Let me add
that in their company now—and I was careful almost never to be out
of it—I could follow no scent very far. We lived in a cloud of music and
love and success and private theatricals. The musical sense in each of
the children was of the quickest, but the elder in especial had a marvel-
lous knack of catching and repeating. The schoolroom piano broke
into all gruesome fancies; and when that failed there were confabulations
in corners, with a sequel of one of them going out in the highest spirits in
order to "come in" as something new. I had had brothers myself, and it
was no revelation to me that little girls could be slavish idolaters of little
boys. What surpassed everything was that there was a little boy in the
world who could have for the inferior age, sex, and intelligence so fine
a consideration. They were extraordinarily at one, and to say that they
never either quarrelled or complained is to make the note of praise coarse
for their quality of sweetness. Sometimes, indeed, when I dropped into
coarseness, I perhaps came across traces of little understandings between
them by which one of them should keep me occupied while the other
slipped away. There is a *naïf* side, I suppose, in all diplomacy; but if
my pupils practised upon me, it was surely with the minimum of grossness.
It was all in the other quarter that, after a lull, the grossness broke out.

I find that I really hang back; but I must take my plunge. In going
on with the record of what was hideous at Bly, I not only challenge the
most liberal faith—for which I little care; but—and this is another
matter—I renew what I myself suffered, I again push my way through
it to the end. There came suddenly an hour after which, as I look back,
the affair seems to me to have been all pure suffering; but I have at
least reached the heart of it, and the straightest road out is doubtless to
advance. One evening—with nothing to lead up or to prepare it—I felt
the cold touch of the impression that had breathed on me the night of
my arrival and which, much lighter then, as I have mentioned, I should
probably have made little of in memory had my subsequent sojourn
been less agitated. I had not gone to bed; I sat reading by a couple of
candles. There was a roomful of old books at Bly—last-century fiction,
some of it, which, to the extent of a distinctly deprecated renown, but
never to so much as that of a stray specimen, had reached the sequestered
home and appealed to the unavowed curiosity of my youth. I remember

that the book I had in my hand was Fielding's *Amelia;* also that I was wholly awake. I recall further both a general conviction that it was horribly late and a particular objection to looking at my watch. I figure, finally, that the white curtain draping, in the fashion of those days, the head of Flora's little bed, shrouded, as I had assured myself long before, the perfection of childish rest. I recollect in short that, though I was deeply interested in my author, I found myself, at the turn of a page and with his spell all scattered, looking straight up from him and hard at the door of my room. There was a moment during which I listened, reminded of the faint sense I had had, the first night, of there being something undefinably astir in the house, and noted the soft breath of the open casement just move the half-drawn blind. Then, with all the marks of a deliberation that must have seemed magnificent had there been anyone to admire it, I laid down my book, rose to my feet, and, taking a candle, went straight out of the room and, from the passage, on which my light made little impression, noiselessly closed and locked the door.

I can say now neither what determined nor what guided me, but I went straight along the lobby, holding my candle high, till I came within sight of the tall window that presided over the great turn of the staircase. At this point I precipitately found myself aware of three things. They were practically simultaneous, yet they had flashes of succession. My candle, under a bold flourish, went out, and I perceived, by the un-covered window, that the yielding dusk of earliest morning rendered it unnecessary. Without it, the next instant, I saw that there was someone on the stair. I speak of sequences, but I required no lapse of seconds to stiffen myself for a third encounter with Quint. The apparition had reached the landing halfway up and was therefore on the spot nearest the window, where at sight of me, it stopped short and fixed me exactly as it had fixed me from the tower and from the garden. He knew me as well as I knew him; and so, in the cold, faint twilight, with a glimmer in the high glass and another on the polish of the oak stair below, we faced each other in our common intensity. He was absolutely, on this occasion, a living, detestable, dangerous presence. But that was not the wonder of wonders; I reserve this distinction for quite another circumstance: the circumstance that dread had unmistakably quitted me and that there was nothing in me there that didn't meet and measure him.

I had plenty of anguish after that extraordinary moment, but I had, thank God, no terror. And he knew I had not—I found myself at the end of an instant magnificently aware of this. I felt, in a fierce rigour of confidence, that if I stood my ground a minute I should cease—for the time, at least—to have him to reckon with; and during the minute, accordingly, the thing was as human and hideous as a real interview: hideous just because it *was* human, as human as to have met alone, in the small hours, in a sleeping house, some enemy, some

adventurer, some criminal. It was the dead silence of our long gaze at such close quarters that gave the whole horror, huge as it was, its only note of the unnatural. If I had met a murderer in such a place and at such an hour, we still at least would have spoken. Something would have passed, in life, between us; if nothing had passed one of us would have moved. The moment was so prolonged that it would have taken but little more to make me doubt if even *I* were in life. I can't express what followed it save by saying that the silence itself—which was indeed in a manner an attestation of my strength—became the element into which I saw the figure disappear; in which I definitely saw it turn as I might have seen the low wretch to which it had once belonged turn on receipt of an order, and pass, with my eyes on the villainous back that no hunch could have more disfigured, straight down the staircase and into the darkness in which the next bend was lost.

Chapter 10

I REMAINED AWHILE at the top of the stair, but with the effect presently of understanding that when my visitor had gone, he had gone: then I returned to my room. The foremost thing I saw there by the light of the candle I had left burning was that Flora's little bed was empty; and on this I caught my breath with all the terror that, five minutes before, I had been able to resist. I dashed at the place in which I had left her lying and over which (for the small silk counterpane and the sheets were disarranged) the white curtains had been deceivingly pulled forward; then my step, to my unutterable relief, produced an answering sound: I perceived an agitation of the window-blind, and the child, ducking down, emerged rosily from the other side of it. She stood there in so much of her candour and so little of her nightgown, with her pink bare feet and the golden glow of her curls. She looked intensely grave, and I had never had such a sense of losing an advantage acquired (the thrill of which had just been so prodigious) as on my consciousness that she addressed me with a reproach. "You naughty: where *have* you been?"—instead of challenging her own irregularity I found myself arraigned and explaining. She herself explained, for that matter, with the loveliest, eagerest simplicity. She had known suddenly, as she lay there, that I was out of the room, and had jumped up to see what had become of me. I had dropped, with the joy of her reappearance, back into my chair—feeling then, and then only, a little faint; and she had pattered straight over to me, thrown herself upon my knee, given herself to be

held with the flame of the candle full in the wonderful little face that was still flushed with sleep. I remember closing my eyes an instant, yieldingly, consciously, as before the excess of something beautiful that shone out of the blue of her own. "You were looking for me out of the window?" I said. "You thought I might be walking in the grounds?"

"Well, you know, I thought someone was"—she never blanched as she smiled out that at me.

Oh, how I looked at her now! "And did you see anyone?"

"Ah, *no!*" she returned, almost with the full privilege of childish inconsequence, resentfully, though with a long sweetness in her little drawl of the negative.

At that moment, in the state of my nerves, I absolutely believed she lied; and if I once more closed my eyes it was before the dazzle of the three or four possible ways in which I might take this up. One of these, for a moment, tempted me with such singular intensity that, to withstand it, I must have gripped my little girl with a spasm that, wonderfully, she submitted to without a cry or a sign of fright. Why not break out at her on the spot and have it all over?—give it to her straight in her lovely little lighted face? "You see, you see, you *know* that you do and that you already quite suspect I believe it; therefore why not frankly confess it to me, so that we may at least live with it together and learn perhaps, in the strangeness of our fate, where we are and what it means?" This solicitation dropped, alas, as it came: if I could immediately have succumbed to it I might have spared myself——well you'll see what. Instead of succumbing I sprang again to my feet, looked at her bed, and took a helpless middle way. "Why did you pull the curtain over the place to make me think you were still there?"

Flora luminously considered; after which, with her little divine smile: "Because I don't like to frighten you!"

"But if I had, by your idea, gone out——?"

She absolutely declined to be puzzled; she turned her eyes to the flame of the candle as if the question were as irrelevant, or at any rate as impersonal, as Mrs. Marcet or nine-times-nine. "Oh, but you know," she quite adequately answered, "that you might come back, you dear, and that you *have!*" And after a little, when she had got into bed, I had, for a long time, by almost sitting on her to hold her hand, to prove that I recognised the pertinence of my return.

You may imagine the general complexion, from that moment, of my nights. I repeatedly sat up till I didn't know when; I selected moments when my room-mate unmistakably slept, and, stealing out, took noiseless turns in the passage and even pushed as far as to where I had last met Quint. But I never met him there again; and I may as well say at once that I on no other occasion saw him in the house. I just missed, on the staircase, on the other hand, a different adventure. Looking down it from the top I once recognised the presence of a woman seated on

one of the lower steps with her back presented to me, her body half bowed and her head, in an attitude of woe, in her hands. I had been there but an instant, however, when she vanished without looking round at me. I knew, none the less, exactly what dreadful face she had to show; and I wondered whether, if instead of being above I had been below, I should have had, for going up, the same nerve I had lately shown Quint. Well, there continued to be plenty of chance for nerve. On the eleventh night after my latest encounter with that gentleman— they were all numbered now—I had an alarm that perilously skirted it and that indeed, from the particular quality of its unexpectedness, proved quite my sharpest shock. It was precisely the first night during this series that, weary with watching, I had felt that I might again without laxity lay myself down at my old hour. I slept immediately and, as I afterwards know, till about one o'clock; but when I woke it was to sit straight up, as completely roused as if a hand had shook me. I had left a light burning, but it was now out, and I felt an instant certainty that Flora had extinguished it. This brought me to my feet and straight, in the darkness, to her bed, which I found she had left. A glance at the window enlightened me further, and the striking of a match completed the picture.

The child had again got up—this time blowing out the taper, and had again, for some purpose of observation or response, squeezed in behind the blind and was peering out into the night. That she now saw —as she had not, I had satisfied myself, the previous time—was proved to me by the fact that she was disturbed neither by my reillumination nor by the haste I made to get into slippers and into a wrap. Hidden, protected, absorbed, she evidently rested on the sill—the casement opened forward—and gave herself up. There was a great still moon to help her, and this fact had counted in my quick decision. She was face to face with the apparition we had met at the lake, and could not communicate with it as she had not then been able to do. What I, on my side, had to care for was, without disturbing her, to reach, from the corridor, some other window in the same quarter. I got to the door without her hearing me; I got out of it, closed it and listened, from the other side, for some sound from her. While I stood in the passage I had my eyes on her brother's door, which was but ten steps off and which, indescribably, produced in me a renewal of the strange impulse that I lately spoke of as my temptation. What if I should go straight in and march to *his* window? —what if, by risking to his boyish bewilderment a revelation of my motive, I should throw across the rest of the mystery the long halter of my boldness?

This thought held me sufficiently to make me cross to his threshold and pause again. I preternaturally listened; I figured to myself what might portentously be; I wondered if his bed were also empty and he too were secretly at watch. It was a deep, soundless minute, at the end

of which my impulse failed. He was quiet; he might be innocent; the risk was hideous; I turned away. There was a figure in the grounds—a figure prowling for a sight, the visitor with whom Flora was engaged; but it was not the visitor most concerned with my boy. I hesitated afresh, but on other grounds and only a few seconds; then I had made my choice. There were empty rooms at Bly, and it was only a question of choosing the right one. The right one suddenly presented itself to me as the lower one—though high above the gardens—in the solid corner of the house that I have spoken of as the old tower. This was a large, square chamber, arranged with some state as a bedroom, the extravagant size of which made it so inconvenient that it had not for years, though kept by Mrs. Grose in exemplary order, been occupied. I had often admired it and I knew my way about in it; I had only, after just faltering at the first chill gloom of its disuse, to pass across it and unbolt as quietly as I could one of the shutters. Achieving this transit, I uncovered the glass without a sound and, applying my face to the pane, was able, the darkness without being much less than within, to see that I commanded the right direction. Then I saw something more. The moon made the night extraordinarily penetrable and showed me on the lawn a person, diminished by distance, who stood there motionless and as if fascinated, looking up to where I had appeared—looking, that is, not so much straight at me as at something that was apparently above me. There was clearly another person above me—there was a person on the tower; but the presence on the lawn was not in the least what I had conceived and had confidently hurried to meet. The presence on the lawn—I felt sick as I made it out—was poor little Miles himself.

Chapter 11

IT WAS NOT TILL LATE NEXT DAY that I spoke to Mrs. Grose; the rigour with which I kept my pupils in sight making it often difficult to meet her privately, and the more as we each felt the importance of not provoking—on the part of the servants quite as much as on that of the children—any suspicion of a secret flurry or of a discussion of mysteries. I drew a great security in this particular from her mere smooth aspect. There was nothing in her fresh face to pass on to others my horrible confidences. She believed me, I was sure, absolutely: if she hadn't I don't know what would have become of me, for I couldn't have borne the business alone. But she was a magnificent monument to the blessing of a want of imagination, and if she could see in our

little charges nothing but their beauty and amiability, their happiness and cleverness, she had no direct communication with the sources of my trouble. If they had been at all visibly blighted or battered, she would doubtless have grown, on tracing it back, haggard enough to match them; as matters stood, however, I could feel her, when she surveyed them, with her large white arms folded and the habit of serenity in all her look, thank the Lord's mercy that if they were ruined the pieces would still serve. Flights of fancy gave place, in her mind, to a steady fireside glow, and I had already begun to perceive how, with the development of the conviction that—as time went on without a public accident—our young things could, after all, look out for themselves, she addressed her greatest solicitude to the sad case presented by their instructress. That, for myself, was a sound simplification: I could engage that, to the world, my face should tell no tales, but it would have been, in the conditions, an immense added strain to find myself anxious about hers.

At the hour I now speak of she had joined me, under pressure, on the terrace, where, with the lapse of the season, the afternoon sun was now agreeable; and we sat there together while, before us, at a distance, but within call if we wished, the children strolled to and fro in one of their most manageable moods. They moved slowly, in unison, below us, over the lawn, the boy, as they went, reading aloud from a story-book and passing his arm round his sister to keep her quite in touch. Mrs. Grose watched them with positive placidity; then I caught the suppressed intellectual creak with which she conscientiously turned to take from me a view of the back of the tapestry. I had made her a receptacle of lurid things, but there was an odd recognition of my superiority—my accomplishments and my function—in her patience under my pain. She offered her mind to my disclosures as, had I wished to mix a witch's broth and proposed it with assurance, she would have held out a large clean saucepan. This had become thoroughly her attitude by the time that, in my recital of the events of the night, I reached the point of what Miles had said to me when, after seeing him, at such a monstrous hour, almost on the very spot where he happened now to be, I had gone down to bring him in; choosing then, at the window, with a concentrated need of not alarming the house, rather that method than a signal more resonant. I had left her meanwhile in little doubt of my small hope of representing with success even to her actual sympathy my sense of the real splendour of the little inspiration with which, after I had got him into the house, the boy met my final articulate challenge. As soon as I appeared in the moonlight on the terrace, he had come to me as straight as possible; on which I had taken his hand without a word and led him, through the dark spaces, up the staircase where Quint had so hungrily hovered for him, along the lobby where I had listened and trembled, and so to his forsaken room.

Not a sound, on the way, had passed between us, and I had wondered—oh, *how* I had wondered!—if he were groping about in his little mind for something plausible and not too grotesque. It would tax his invention, certainly, and I felt, this time, over his real embarrassment, a curious thrill of triumph. It was a sharp trap for the inscrutable! He couldn't play any longer at innocence; so how the deuce would he get out of it? There beat in me indeed, with the passionate throb of this question, an equal dumb appeal as to how the deuce *I* should. I was confronted at last, as never yet, with all the risk attached even now to sounding my own horrid note. I remember in fact that as we pushed into his little chamber, where the bed had not been slept in at all and the window, uncovered to the moonlight, made the place so clear that there was no need of striking a match—I remember how I suddenly dropped, sank upon the edge of the bed from the force of the idea that he must know how he really, as they say, "had" me. He could do what he liked, with all his cleverness to help him, so long as I should continue to defer to the old tradition of the criminality of those caretakers of the young who minister to superstitions and fears. He "had" me indeed, and in a cleft stick; for who would ever absolve me, who would consent that I should go unhung, if, by the faintest tremor of an overture, I were the first to introduce into our perfect intercourse an element so dire? No, no: it was useless to attempt to convey to Mrs. Grose, just as it is scarcely less so to attempt to suggest here, how, in our short, stiff brush in the dark, he fairly shook me with admiration. I was of course thoroughly kind and merciful; never, never yet had I placed on his little shoulders hands of such tenderness as those with which, while I rested against the bed, I held him there well under fire. I had no alternative but, in form at least, to put it to him.

"You must tell me now—and all the truth. What did you go out for? What were you doing there?"

I can still see his wonderful smile, the whites of his beautiful eyes, and the uncovering of his little teeth shine to me in the dusk. "If I tell you why, will you understand?" My heart, at this, leaped into my mouth. *Would* he tell me why? I found no sound on my lips to press it, and I was aware of replying only with a vague, repeated, grimacing nod. He was gentleness itself, and while I wagged my head at him he stood there more than ever a little fairy prince. It was his brightness indeed that gave me a respite. Would it be so great if he were really going to tell me? "Well," he said at last, "just exactly in order that you should do this."

"Do what?"

"Think me—for a change—*bad!*" I shall never forget the sweetness and gaiety with which he brought out the word, nor how, on top of it, he bent forward and kissed me. It was practically the end of everything. I met his kiss and I had to make, while I folded him for a minute in

my arms, the most stupendous effort not to cry. He had given exactly the account of himself that permitted least of my going behind it, and it was only with the effect of confirming my acceptance of it that, as I presently glanced about the room, I could say—

"Then you didn't undress at all?"

He fairly glittered in the gloom. "Not at all. I sat up and read."

"And when did you go down?"

"At midnight. When I'm bad I *am* bad!"

"I see, I see—it's charming. But how could you be sure I would know it?"

"Oh, I arranged that with Flora." His answers rang out with a readiness! "She was to get up and look out."

"Which is what she did do." It was I who fell into the trap!

"So she disturbed you, and, to see what she was looking at, you also looked—you saw."

"While you," I concurred, "caught your death in the night air!"

He literally bloomed so from this exploit that he could afford radiantly to assent. "How otherwise should I have been bad enough?" he asked. Then, after another embrace, the incident and our interview closed on my recognition of all the reserves of goodness that, for his joke, he had been able to draw upon.

Chapter 12

THE PARTICULAR IMPRESSION I had received proved in the morning light, I repeat, not quite successfully presentable to Mrs. Grose, though I reinforced it with the mention of still another remark that he had made before we separated. "It all lies in half-a-dozen words," I said to her, "words that really settle the matter. 'Think, you know, what I *might* do!' He threw that off to show me how good he is. He knows down to the ground what he 'might' do. That's what he gave them a taste of at school."

"Lord, you do change!" cried my friend.

"I don't change—I simply make it out. The four, depend upon it, perpetually meet. If on either of these last nights you have been with either child, you would clearly have understood. The more I've watched and waited the more I've felt that if there were nothing else to make it sure it would be made so by the systematic silence of each. *Never*, by a slip of the tongue, have they so much as alluded to either of their old friends, any more than Miles has alluded to his expulsion. Oh yes, we

may sit here and look at them, and they may show off to us there to their fill; but even while they pretend to be lost in their fairytale they're steeped in their vision of the dead restored. He's not reading to her," I declared; "they're talking of *them*—they're talking horrors! I go on, I know, as if I were crazy; and it's a wonder I'm not. What I've seen would have made *you* so; but it has only made me more lucid, made me get hold of still other things."

My lucidity must have seemed awful, but the charming creatures who were victims of it, passing and repassing in their interlocked sweetness, gave my colleague something to hold on by; and I felt how tight she held as, without stirring in the breath of my passion, she covered them still with her eyes. "Of what other things have you got hold?"

"Why, of the very things that have delighted, fascinated, and yet, at bottom, as I now so strangely see, mystified and troubled me. Their more than earthly beauty, their absolutely unnatural goodness. It's a game," I went one; "it's a policy and a fraud!"

"On the part of little darlings——?"

"As yet mere lovely babies? Yes, mad as that seems!" The very act of bringing it out really helped me to trace it—follow it all up and piece it all together. "They haven't been good—they've only been absent. It has been easy to live with them, because they're simply leading a life of their own. They're not mine—they're not ours. They're his and they're hers!"

"Quint's and that woman's?"

"Quint's and that woman's. They want to get to them."

Oh, how, at this, poor Mrs. Grose appeared to study them! "But for what?"

"For the love of all the evil that, in those dreadful days, the pair put into them. And to ply them with that evil still, to keep up the work of demons, is what brings the others back."

"Laws!" said my friend under her breath. The exclamation was homely, but it revealed a real acceptance of my further proof of what, in the bad time—for there had been a worse even than this!—must have occurred. There could have been no such justification for me as the plain assent of her experience to whatever depth of depravity I found credible in our brace of scoundrels. It was in obvious submission of memory that she brought out after a moment: "They *were* rascals! But what can they now do?" she pursued.

"Do?" I echoed so loud that Miles and Flora, as they passed at their distance, paused an instant in their walk and looked at us. "Don't they do enough?" I demanded in a lower tone, while the children, having smiled and nodded and kissed hands to us, resumed their exhibition. We were held by it a minute; then I answered: "They can destroy them!" At this my companion did turn, but the inquiry she launched was a silent one, the effect of which was to make me more explicit. "They

don't know, as yet, quite how—but they're trying hard. They're seen only across, as it were, and beyond—in strange places and on high places, the top of towers, the roof of houses, the outside of windows, the further edge of pools; but there's a deep design, on either side, to shorten the distance and overcome the obstacle; and the success of the tempters is only a question of time. They've only to keep to their suggestions of danger."

"For the children to come?"

"And perish in the attempt!" Mrs. Grose slowly got up, and I scrupulously added: "Unless, of course, we can prevent!"

Standing there before me while I kept my seat, she visibly turned things over. "Their uncle must do the preventing. He must take them away."

"And who's to make him?"

She had been scanning the distance, but she now dropped on me a foolish face. "You, Miss."

"By writing to him that his house is poisoned and his little nephew and niece mad?"

"But if they *are,* Miss?"

"And if I am myself, you mean? That's charming news to be sent him by a governess whose prime undertaking was to give him no worry."

Mrs. Grose considered, following the children again. "Yes, he do hate worry. That was the great reason——"

"Why those fiends took him in so long? No doubt, though his indifference must have been awful. As I'm not a fiend, at any rate, I shouldn't take him in."

My companion, after an instant and for all answer, sat down again and grasped my arm. "Make him at any rate come to you."

I stared. "To *me?*" I had a sudden fear of what she might do. " 'Him?' "

"He ought to *be* here—he ought to help."

I quickly rose, and I think I must have shown her a queerer face than ever yet. "You see me asking him for a visit?" No, with her eyes on my face she evidently couldn't. Instead of it even—as a woman reads another—she could see what I myself saw: his derision, his amusement, his contempt for the break-down of my resignation at being left alone and for the fine machinery I had set in motion to attract his attention to my slighted charms. She didn't know—no one knew—how proud I had been to serve him and to stick to our terms; yet she none the less took the measure, I think, of the warning I now gave her. "If you should so lose your head as to appeal to him for me——"

She was really frightened. "Yes, Miss?"

"I would leave, on the spot, both him and you."

Chapter 13

IT WAS ALL VERY WELL TO JOIN THEM, but speaking to them proved quite as much as ever an effort beyond my strength—offered, in close quarters, difficulties as insurmountable as before. This situation continued a month, and with new aggravations and particular notes, the note above all, sharper and sharper, of the small ironic consciousness on the part of my pupils. It was not, I am as sure today as I was sure then, my mere infernal imagination: it was absolutely traceable that they were aware of my predicament and that this strange relation made, in a manner, for a long time, the air in which we moved. I don't mean that they had their tongues in their cheeks or did anything vulgar, for that was not one of their dangers: I do mean, on the other hand, that the element of the unnamed and untouched became, between us, greater than any other, and that so much avoidance could not have been so successfully effected without a great deal of tacit arrangement. It was as if, at moments, we were perpetually coming into sight of subjects before which we must stop short, turning suddenly out of alleys that we perceived to be blind, closing with a little bang that made us look at each other—for, like all bangs, it was something louder than we had intended—the doors we had indiscreetly opened. All roads lead to Rome, and there were times when it might have struck us that almost every branch of study or subject of conversation skirted forbidden ground. Forbidden ground was the question of the return of the dead in general and of whatever, in especial, might survive, in memory, of the friends little children had lost. There were days when I could have sworn that one of them had, with a small invisible nudge, said to the other: "She thinks she'll do it this time—but she *won't!*" To "do it" would have been to indulge for instance—and for once in a way—in some direct reference to the lady who had prepared them for my discipline. They had a delightful endless appetite for passages in my own history, to which I had again and again treated them; they were in possession of everything that had ever happened to me, had had, with every circumstance the story of my smallest adventures and of those of my brothers and sisters and of the cat and the dog at home, as well as many particulars of the eccentric nature of my father, of the furniture and arrangement of our house, and of the conversation of the old women of our village. There were things enough, taking one with another, to chatter about, if one went very fast and knew by instinct when to go round. They pulled with an art of their own the strings of my

379

invention and my memory; and nothing else perhaps, when I thought of such occasions afterwards, gave me so the suspicion of being watched from under cover. It was in any case over *my* life, *my* past, and *my* friends alone that we could take anything like our ease—a state of affairs that led them sometimes without the least pertinence to break out ino sociable reminders. I was invited—with no visible connection—to repeat afresh Goody Gosling's celebrated *mot* or to confirm the details already supplied as to the cleverness of the vicarage pony.

It was partly at such junctures as these and partly at quite different ones that, with the turn my matters had now taken, my predicament, as I have called it, grew most sensible. The fact that the days passed for me without another encounter ought, it would have appeared, to have done something toward soothing my nerves. Since the light brush, that second night on the upper landing, of the presence of a woman at the foot of the stair, I had seen nothing, whether in or out of the house, that one had better not have seen. There was many a corner round which I expected to come upon Quint, and many a situation that, in a merely sinister way, would have favoured the appearance of Miss Jessel. The summer had turned, the summer had gone; the autumn had dropped upon Bly and had blown out half our lights. The place, with its grey sky and withered garlands, its bared spaces and scattered dead leaves, was like a theatre after the performance—all strewn with crumpled playbills. There were exactly states of the air, conditions of sound and of stillness, unspeakable impressions of the *kind* of ministering moment, that brought back to me, long enough to catch it, the feeling of the medium in which, that June evening out-of-doors, I had had my first sight of Quint, and in which, too, at those other instants, I had, after seeing him through the window, looked for him in vain in the circle of shrubbery. I recognised the signs, the portents—I recognised the moment, the spot. But they remained unaccompanied and empty, and I continued unmolested; if unmolested one could call a young woman whose sensibility had, in the most extraordinary fashion, not declined but deepened. I had said in my talk with Mrs. Grose on that horrid scene of Flora's by the lake—and had perplexed her by so saying—that it would from that moment distress me much more to lose my power than to keep it. I had then expressed what was vividly in my mind: the truth that, whether the children really saw or not—since, that is, it was not yet definitely proved—I greatly preferred, as a safeguard, the fulness of my own exposure. I was ready to know the very worst that was to be known. What I had then had an ugly glimpse of was that my eyes might be sealed just while theirs were most opened. Well, my eyes *were* sealed, it appeared, at present—a consummation for which it seemed blasphemous not to thank God. There was, alas, a difficulty about that: I would have thanked him with all my soul had I not had in a proportionate measure this conviction of the secret of my pupils.

How can I retrace today the strange steps of my obsession? There were times of our being together when I would have been ready to swear that, literally, in my presence, but with my direct sense of it closed, they had visitors who were known and were welcome. Then it was that, had I not been deterred by the very chance that such an injury might prove greater than the injury to be averted, my exultation would have broken out. "They're here, they're here, you little wretches," I would have cried, "and you can't deny it now!" The little wretches denied it with all the added volume of their sociability and their tenderness, in just the crystal depths of which—like the flash of a fish in a stream—the mockery of their advantage peeped up. The shock, in truth, had sunk into me still deeper than I knew on the night when, looking out to see either Quint or Miss Jessel under the stars, I had beheld the boy over whose rest I watched and who had immediately brought in with him—had straightway, there, turned it on me—the lovely upward look with which, from the battlements above me, the hideous apparition of Quint had played. If it was a question of a scare, my discovery on this occasion had scared me more than any other, and it was in the condition of nerves produced by it that I made my actual inductions. They harassed me so that sometimes, at add moments, I shut myself up audibly to rehearse—it was at once a fantastic relief and a renewed despair—the manner in which I might come to the point. I approached it from one side and the other while, in my room, I flung myself about, but I always broke down in the monstrous utterance of names. As they died away on my lips, I said to myself that I should indeed help them to represent something infamous if, by pronouncing them, I should violate as rare a little case of instinctive delicacy as any schoolroom, probably, had ever known. When I said to myself: "*They* have the manners to be silent, and you, trusted as you are, the baseness to speak!" I felt myself crimson and I covered my face with my hands. After these secret scenes I chattered more than ever, going on volubly enough 'til one of our prodigious, palpable hushes occurred—I can call them nothing else—the strange, dizzy lift or swim (I try for terms!) into a stillness, a pause of all life, that had nothing to do with the more or less noise that at the moment we might be engaged in making and that I could hear through any deepened exhilaration or quickened recitation or louder strum of the piano. Then it was that the others, the outsiders, were there. Though they were not angels, they "passed," as the French say, causing me, while they stayed, to tremble with the fear of their addressing to their younger victims some yet more infernal message or more vivid image than they had thought good enough for myself.

What it was most impossible to get rid of was the cruel idea that, whatever I had seen, Miles and Flora saw *more*—things terrible and unguessable and that sprang from dreadful passages of intercourse in the

past. Such things naturally left on the surface, for the time, a chill which we vociferously denied that we felt; and we had, all three, with repetition, got into such splendid training that we went, each time, almost automatically, to mark the close of the incident, through the very same movements. It was striking of the children, at all events, to kiss me inveterately with a kind of wild irrelevance and never to fail—one or the other—of the precious question that had helped us through many a peril. "When do you think he *will* come? Don't you think we *ought* to write?"—there was nothing like that inquiry, we found by experience, for carrying off an awkwardness. "He" of course was their uncle in Harley Street; and we lived in much profusion of theory that he might at any moment arrive to mingle in our circle. It was impossible to have given less encouragement than he had done to such a doctrine, but if we had not had the doctrine to fall back upon we should have deprived each other of some of our finest exhibitions. He never wrote to them— that may have been selfish, but it was a part of the flattery of his trust of me; for the way in which a man pays his highest tribute to a woman is apt to be but by the more festal celebration of one of the sacred laws of his comfort; and I held that I carried out the spirit of the pledge given not to appeal to him when I let my charges understand that their own letters were but charming literary exercises. They were too beautiful to be posted; I kept them myself; I have them all to this hour. This was a rule indeed which only added to the satiric effect of my being plied with the supposition that he might at any moment be among us. It was exactly as if my charges knew how almost more awkward than anything else that might be for me. There appears to me, moreover, as I look back, no note in all this more extraordinary than the mere fact that, in spite of my tension and of their triumph, I never lost patience with them. Adorable they must in truth have been, I now reflect, that I didn't in these days hate them! Would exasperation, however, if relief had longer been postponed, finally have betrayed me? It little matters, for relief arrived. I call it relief, though it was only the relief that a snap brings to a strain or the burst of a thunderstorm to a day of suffocation. It was at least change, and it came with a rush.

Chapter 14

WALKING TO CHURCH a certain Sunday morning, I had little Miles at my side and his sister, in advance of us and at Mrs. Grose's, well in sight. It was a crisp, clear day, the first of its order for some time; the night had brought a touch of frost, and the autumn air, bright and sharp, made the church-bells almost gay. It was an odd accident of thought that I should have happened at such a moment to be particularly and very gratefully struck with the obedience of my little charges. Why did they never resent my inexhorable, my perpetual society? Something or other had brought nearer home to me that I had all but pinned the boy to my shawl and that, in the way our companions were marshalled before me, I might have appeared to provide against some danger of rebellion. I was like a gaoler with an eye to possible surprises and escapes. But all this belonged—I mean their magnificent little surrender —just to the special array of the facts that were most abysmal. Turned out for Sunday by his uncle's tailor, who had had a free hand and a notion of pretty waistcoats and of his grand little air, Miles's whole title to independence, the rights of his sex and situation, were so stamped upon him that if he had suddenly struck for freedom I should have had nothing to say. I was by the strangest of chances wondering how I should meet him when the revolution unmistakably occurred. I call it a revolution because I now see how, with the word he spoke, the curtain rose on the last act of my dreadful drama and the catastrophe was precipitated. "Look here, my dear, you know," he charmingly said, "when in the world, please, am I going back to school?"

Transcribed here the speech sounds harmless enough, particularly as uttered in the sweet, high, casual pipe with which, at all interlocutors, but above all at his eternal governess, he threw off intonations as if he were tossing roses. There was something in them that always made one "catch," and I caught, at any rate, now so effectually that I stopped as short as if one of the trees of the park had fallen across the road. There was something new, on the spot, between us, and he was perfectly aware that I recognised it, though, to enable me to do so, he had no need to look a whit less candid and charming than usual. I could feel in him how he already, from my at first finding nothing to reply, perceived the advantage he had gained. I was so slow to find anything that he had plenty of time, after a minute, to continue with his suggestive but inconclusive smile: "You know, my dear, that for a fellow to be with a lady *always*——!" His "my dear" was constantly on his lips for me, and

nothing could have expressed more the exact shade of the sentiment with which I desired to inspire my pupils than its fond familiarity. It was so respectfully easy.

But, oh, how I felt that at present I must pick my own phrases! I remember that, to gain time, I tried to laugh, and I seemed to see in the beautiful face with which he watched me how ugly and queer I looked. "And always with the same lady?" I returned.

He neither blenched nor winked. The whole thing was virtually out between us. "Ah, of course, she's a jolly, 'perfect' lady; but, after all, I'm a fellow, don't you see? that's—well, getting on."

I lingered there with him an instant ever so kindly. "Yes, you're getting on." Oh, but I felt helpless!

I have kept to this day the heartbreaking little idea of how he seemed to know that and to play with it. "And you can't say I've not been awfully good, can you?"

I laid my hand on his shoulder, for, though I felt how much better it would have been to walk on, I was not yet quite able. "No, I can't say that, Miles."

"Except just that one night, you know——!"

"That one night?" I couldn't look as straight as he.

"Why, when I went down—went out of the house."

"Oh, yes. But I forget what you did it for."

"You forget?"—he spoke with the sweet extravagance of childish reproach. "Why, it was to show you I could!"

"Oh, yes, you could."

"And I can again."

I felt that I might, perhaps, after all succeed in keeping my wits about me. "Certainly. But you won't."

"No, not *that* again. It was nothing."

"It was nothing," I said. "But we must go on."

He resumed our walk with me, passing his hand into my arm. "Then when *am* I going back?"

I wore, in turning it over, my most responsible air. "Were you very happy at school?"

He just considered. "Oh, I'm happy enough anywhere!"

"Well, then," I quavered, "if you're just as happy here——!"

"Ah, but that isn't everything! Of course *you* know a lot——"

"But you hint that you know almost as much?" I risked as he paused.

"Not half I want to!" Miles honestly professed. "But it isn't so much that."

"What is it, then?"

"Well—I want to see more life."

"I see; I see." We had arrived within sight of the church and of various persons, including several of the household of Bly, on their way to it and clustered about the door to see us go in. I quickened our step;

I wanted to get there before the question between us opened up much further; I reflected hungrily that, for more than an hour, he would have to be silent; and I thought with envy of the comparative dusk of the pew and of the almost spiritual help of the hassock on which I might bend my knees. I seemed literally to be running a race with some confusion to which he was about to reduce me, but I felt that he had got in first when, before we had even entered the churchyard, he threw out—

"I want my own sort!"

It literally made me bound forward. "There are not many of your own sort, Miles!" I laughed. "Unless perhaps dear little Flora!"

"You really compare me to a baby girl?"

This found me singularly weak. "Don't you, then, *love* our sweet Flora?"

"If I didn't—and you too; if I didn't——!" he repeated as if retreating for a jump, yet leaving his thought so unfinished that, after we had come into the gate, another stop, which he imposed on me by the pressure of his arm, had become inevitable. Mrs. Grose and Flora had passed into the church, the other worshippers had followed, and we were, for the minute, alone among the old, thick graves. We had paused, on the path from the gate, by a low, oblong, table-like tomb.

"Yes, if you didn't——?"

He looked, while I waited, about at the graves. "Well, you know what!" But he didn't move, and he presently produced something that made me drop straight down on the stone slab, as if suddenly to rest. "Does my uncle think what *you* think?"

I markedly rested. "How do you know what I think?"

"Ah, well, of course I don't; for it strikes me you never tell me. But I mean does *he* know?"

"Know what, Miles?"

"Why, the way I'm going on."

I perceived quickly enough that I could make, to this inquiry, no answer that would not involve something of a sacrifice of my employer. Yet it appeared to me that we were all, at Bly, sufficiently sacrificed to make that venial. "I don't think your uncle much cares."

Miles, on this, stood looking at me. "Then don't you think he can be made to?"

"In what way?"

"Why, by his coming down."

"But who'll get him to come down?"

"*I* will!" the boy said with extraordinary brightness and emphasis. He gave me another look charged with that expression and then marched off alone into church.

Chapter 15

THE BUSINESS WAS PRACTICALLY SETTLED from the moment I never followed him. It was a pitiful surrender to agitation, but my being aware of this had somehow no power to restore me. I only sat there on my tomb and read into what my little friend had said to me the fulness of its meaning; by the time I had grasped the whole of which I had also embraced, for absence, the pretext that I was ashamed to offer my pupils and the rest of the congregation such an example of delay. What I said to myself above all was that Miles had got something out of me and that the proof of it, for him, would be just this awkward collapse. He had got out of me that there was something I was much afraid of and that he should probably be able to make use of my fear to gain, for his own purpose, more freedom. My fear was of having to deal with the intolerable question of the grounds of his dismissal from school, for that was really but the question of the horrors gathered behind. That his uncle should arrive to treat with me of these things was a solution that, strictly speaking, I ought now to have desired to bring on; but I could so little face the ugliness and the pain of it that I simply procrastinated and lived from hand to mouth. The boy, to my deep discomposure, was immensely in the right, was in a position to say to me: "Either you clear up with my guardian the mystery of this interruption of my studies, or you cease to expect me to lead with you a life that's so unnatural for a boy." What was so unnatural for the particular boy I was concerned with was this sudden revelation of a consciousness and a plan.

That was what really overcame me, what prevented my going in. I walked round the church, hesitating, hovering; I reflected that I had already, with him, hurt myself beyond repair. Therefore I could patch up nothing, and it was too extreme an effort to squeeze beside him into the pew: he would be so much more sure than ever to pass his arm into mine and make me sit there for an hour in close, silent contact with his commentary on our talk. For the first minute since his arrival I wanted to get away from him. As I paused beneath the high east window and listened to the sounds of worship, I was taken with an impulse that might master me, I felt, completely should I give it the least encouragement. I might easily put an end to my predicament by getting away altogether. Here was my chance; there was no one to stop me; I could give the whole thing up—turn my back and retreat. It was only a question of hurrying again, for a few preparations, to the house which

the attendance at church of so many of the servants would practically have left unoccupied. No one, in short, could blame me if I should just drive desperately off. What was it to get away if I got away only till dinner? That would be in a couple of hours, at the end of which—I had the acute prevision—my little pupils would play at innocent wonder about my non-appearance in their train.

"What *did* you do, you naughty, bad thing? Why in the world, to worry us so—and take our thoughts off too, don't you know?—did you desert us at the very door?" I couldn't meet such questions nor, as they asked them, their false little lovely eyes; yet it was all so exactly what I should have to meet that, as the prospect grew sharp to me, I at last let myself go.

I got, so far as the immediate moment was concerned, away; I came straight out of the churchyard and, thinking hard, retraced my steps through the park. It seemed to me that by the time I reached the house I had made up my mind I would fly. The Sunday stillness both of the approaches and of the interior, in which I met no one, fairly excited me with a sense of opportunity. Were I to get off quickly, this way, I should get off without a scene, without a word. My quickness would have to be remarkable, however, and the question of a conveyance was the great one to settle. Tormented, in the hall, with difficulties and obstacles, I remember sinking down at the foot of the staircase—suddenly collapsing there on the lowest step and then, with a revulsion, recalling that it was exactly where more than a month before, in the darkness of night and just so bowed with evil things, I had seen the spectre of the most horrible of women. At this I was able to straighten myself; I went the rest of the way up; I made, in my bewilderment, for the schoolroom, where there were objects belonging to me that I should have to take. But I opened the door to find again, in a flash, my eyes unsealed. In the presence of what I saw I reeled straight back upon my resistance.

Seated at my own table in clear noonday light I saw a person whom, without my previous experience, I should have taken at the first blush for some housemaid who might have stayed at home to look after the place and who, availing herself of rare relief from observation and of the schoolroom table and my pens, ink, and paper, had applied herself to the considerable effort of a letter to her sweetheart. There was an effort in the way that, while her arms rested on the table, her hands with evident weariness supported her head; but at the moment I took this in I had already become aware that, in spite of my entrance, her attitude strangely persisted. Then it was—with the very act of its announcing itself—that her identity flared up in a change of posture. She rose, not as if she had heard me, but with an indescribable grand melancholy of indifference and detachment, and, within a dozen feet of me, stood there as my vile predecessor. Dishonoured and tragic, she was all before me; but even as I fixed and, for memory, secured it, the awful image passed

away. Dark as midnight in her black dress, her haggard beauty and her unutterable woe, she had looked at me long enough to appear to say that her right to sit at my table was as good as mine to sit at hers. While these instants lasted indeed I had the extraordinary chill of a feeling that it was I who was the intruder. It was as a wild protest against it that, actually addressing her—"You terrible, miserable woman!"—I heard myself break into a sound that, by the open door, rang through the long passage and the empty house. She looked at me as if she heard me, but I had recovered myself and cleared the air. There was nothing in the room the next minute but the sunshine and a sense that I must stay.

Chapter 16

I HAD SO PERFECTLY EXPECTED that the return of my pupils would be marked by a demonstration that I was freshly upset at having to take into account that they were dumb about my absence. Instead of gaily denouncing and caressing me, they made no allusion to my having failed them, and I was left, for the time, on perceiving that she too said nothing, to study Mrs. Grose's odd face. I did this to such purpose that I made sure they had in some way bribed her to silence; a silence that, however, I would engage to break down on the first private opportunity. This opportunity came before tea: I secured five minutes with her in the housekeeper's room, where, in the twilight, amid a smell of lately-baked bread, but with the place all swept and garnished, I found her sitting in pained placidity before the fire. So I see her still, so I see her best: facing the flame from her straight chair in the dusky, shining room, a large clean image of the "put away"—of drawers closed and locked and rest without a remedy.

"Oh, yes, they asked me to say nothing; and to please them—so long as they were there—of course I promised. But what had happened to you?"

"I only went with you for the walk," I said. "I had then to come back to meet a friend."

She showed her surprise. "A friend—*you?*"

"Oh, yes, I have a couple!" I laughed. "But did the children give you a reason?"

"For not alluding to your leaving us? Yes; they said you would like it better. Do you like it better?"

My face had made her rueful. "No, I like it worse!" But after an instant I added: "Did they say why I should like it better?"

"No; Master Miles only said, 'We must do nothing but what she likes!'"

"I wish indeed he would! And what did Flora say?"

"Miss Flora was too sweet. She said, 'Oh, of course, of course!'—and I said the same."

I thought a moment. "You were too sweet too—I can hear you all. But none the less, between Miles and me, it's now all out."

"All out?" My companion stared. "But what, Miss?"

"Everything. It doesn't matter. I've made up my mind. I came home, my dear," I went on, "for a talk with Miss Jessel."

I had by this time formed the habit of having Mrs. Grose literally well in hand in advance of my sounding that note; so that even now, as she bravely blinked under the signal of my word, I could keep her comparatively firm. "A talk! Do you mean she spoke?"

"It came to that. I found her, on my return, in the schoolroom."

"And what did she say?" I can hear the good woman still, and the candour of her stupefaction.

"That she suffers the torments——!"

It was this, of a truth, that made her, as she filled out my picture gape. "Do you mean," she faltered, "—of the lost?"

"Of the lost. Of the damned. And that's why, to share them——" I faltered myself with the horror of it.

But my companion, with less imagination, kept me up. "To share them——?"

"She wants Flora." Mrs. Grose might, as I gave it to her, fairly have fallen away from me had I not been prepared. I still held her there, to show I was. "As I've told you, however, it doesn't matter."

"Because you've made up your mind? But to what?"

"To everything."

"And what do you call 'everything?'"

"Why, sending for their uncle."

"Oh, Miss, in pity do," my friend broke out.

"Ah, but I will, I *will!* I see it's the only way. What's 'out,' as I told you, with Miles is that if he thinks I'm afraid to—and has ideas of what he gains by that—he shall see he's mistaken. Yes, yes; his uncle shall have it here from me on the spot (and before the boy himself if necessary) that if I'm to be reproached with having done nothing again about more school——"

"Yes, Miss——" my companion pressed me.

"Well, there's that awful reason."

There were now clearly so many of these for my poor colleague that she was excusable for being vague. "But—a—which?"

"Why, the letter from his old place."

"You'll show it to the master?"

"I ought to have done so on the instant."

"Oh, no!" said Mrs. Grose with decision.

"I'll put it before him," I went on inexorably, "that I can't undertake to work the question on behalf of a child who has been expelled——"

"For we've never in the least known what!" Mrs. Grose declared.

"For wickedness. For what else—when he's so clever and beautiful and perfect? Is he stupid? Is he untidy? Is he infirm? Is he ill-natured? He's exquisite—so it can be only *that;* and that would open up the whole thing. After all," I said, "it's their uncle's fault. If he left here such people——!"

"He didn't really in the least know them. The fault's mine." She had turned quite pale.

"Well, you shan't suffer," I answered.

"The children shan't!" she emphatically returned.

I was silent awhile; we looked at each other. "Then what am I to tell him?"

"You needn't tell him anything. *I'll* tell him.

I measured this. "Do you mean you'll write——?" Remembering she couldn't, I caught myself up. "How do you communicate?"

"I tell the bailiff. *He* writes."

"And should you like him to write our story?"

My question had a sarcastic force that I had not fully intended, and it made her, after a moment, inconsequently break down. The tears were again in her eyes. "Ah, Miss, *you* write!"

"Well—tonight," I at last answered; and on this we separated.

Chapter 17

I WENT SO FAR, IN THE EVENING, as to make a beginning. The weather had changed back, a great wind was abroad, and beneath the lamp, in my room, with Flora at peace beside me, I sat for a long time before a blank sheet of paper and listened to the lash of the rain and the batter of the gusts. Finally I went out, taking a candle; I crossed the passage and listened a minute at Miles's door. What, under my endless obsession, I had been impelled to listen for was some betrayal of his not being at rest, and I presently caught one, but not in the form I had expected. His voice tinkled out. "I say, you there—come in." It was a gaiety in the gloom!

I went in with my light and found him, in bed, very wide awake, but very much at his ease. "Well, what are *you* up to?" he asked with a grace of sociability in which it occurred to me that Mrs. Grose, had she

been present, might have looked in vain for proof that anything was "out."

I stood over him with my candle. "How did you know I was there?"

"Why, of course I heard you. Did you fancy you made no noise? You're like a troop of cavalry!" he beautifully laughed.

"Then you weren't asleep?"

"Not much! I lie awake and think."

I had put my candle, designedly, a short way off, and then, as he held out his friendly old hand to me, had sat down on the edge of his bed. "What is it," I asked, "that you think of?"

"What in the world, my dear, but *you?*"

"Ah, the pride I take in your appreciation doesn't insist on that! I had so far rather you slept."

"Well, I think also, you know, of this queer business of ours."

I marked the coolness of his firm little hand. "Of what queer business, Miles?"

"Why, the way you bring me up. And all the rest!"

I fairly held my breath a minute, and even from my glimmering taper there was light enough to show how he smiled up at me from his pillow. "What do you mean by all the rest?"

"Oh, you know, you know!"

I could say nothing for a minute, though I felt, as I held his hand and our eyes continued to meet, that my silence had all the air of admitting his charge and that nothing in the whole world of reality was perhaps at that moment so fabulous as our actual relation. "Certainly you shall go back to school," I said, "if it be that that troubles you. But not to the old place—we must find another, a better. How could I know it did trouble you, this question, when you never told me so, never spoke of it at all?" His clear, listening face, framed in its smooth whiteness, made him for the minute as appealing as some wistful patient in a children's hospital; and I would have given, as the resemblance came to me, all I possessed on earth really to be the nurse or the sister of charity who might have helped to cure him. Well, even as it was, I perhaps might help! "Do you know you've never said a word to me about your school— I mean the old one; never mentioned it in any way?"

He seemed to wonder; he smiled with the same loveliness. But he clearly gained time; he waited, he called for guidance. "Haven't I?" It wasn't for *me* to help him—it was for the thing I had met!

Something in his tone and the expression of his face, as I got this from him, set my heart aching with such a pang as it had never yet known; so unutterably touching was it to see his little brain puzzled and his little resources taxed to play, under the spell laid on him, a part of innocence and consistency. "No, never—from the hour you came back. You've never mentioned to me one of your masters, one of your comrades, nor the least little thing that ever happened to you at school. Never, little Miles—no, never—have you given me an inkling of anything that

may have happened there. Therefore you can fancy how much I'm in the dark. Until you came out, that way, this morning, you had, since the first hour I saw you, scarce even made a reference to anything in your previous life. You seemed so perfectly to accept the present." It was extraordinary how my absolute conviction of his secret precocity (or whatever I might call the poison of an influence that I dared but half to phrase) made him, in spite of the faint breath of his inward trouble, appear as accessible as an older person—imposed him almost as an intellectual equal. "I thought you wanted to go on as you are."

It struck me that at this he just faintly coloured. He gave, at any rate, like a convalescent slightly fatigued, a languid shake of his head. "I don't—I don't. I want to get away."

"You're tired of Bly?"

"Oh, no, I like Bly."

"Well, then——?"

"Oh, *you* know what a boy wants!"

I felt that I didn't know so well as Miles, and I took temporary refuge. "You want to go to your uncle?"

Again, at this, with his sweet ironic face, he made a movement on the pillow. "Ah, you can't get off with that!"

I was silent a little, and it was I, now, I think, who changed colour. "My dear, I don't want to get off!"

"You can't, even if you do. You can't, you can't!"—he lay beautifully staring. "My uncle must come down, and you must completely settle things."

"If we do," I returned with some spirit, "you may be sure it will be to take you quite away."

"Well, don't you understand that that's exactly what I'm working for? You'll have to tell him—about the way you've let it all drop: you'll have to tell him a tremendous lot!"

The exultation with which he uttered this helped me somehow, for the instant, to meet him rather more. "And how much will *you*, Miles, have to tell him? There are things he'll ask you!"

He turned it over. "Very likely. But what things?"

"The things you've never told me. To make up his mind what to do with you. He can't send you back——"

"Oh, I don't want to go back!" he broke in. "I want a new field."

He said it with admirable serenity, with positive unimpeachable gaiety; and doubtless it was that very note that most evoked for me the poignancy, the unnatural childish tragedy, of his probable reappearance at the end of three months will all this bravado and still more dishonour. It overwhelmed me now that I should never be able to bear that, and it made me let myself go. I threw myself upon him and in the tenderness of my pity I embraced him. "Dear little Miles, dear little Miles——!"

My face was close to his, and he let me kiss him, simply taking it with indulgent good-humour. "Well, old lady?"

"Is there nothing—nothing at all that you want to tell me?"

He turned off a little, facing round toward the wall and holding up his hand to look at as one had been sick children look. "I've told you— I told you this morning."

Oh, I was sorry for him! "That you just want me not to worry you?"

He looked round at me now, as if in recognition of my understanding him; then ever so gently, "To let me alone," he replied.

There was even a singular little dignity in it, something that made me release him, yet, when I had slowly risen, linger beside him. God knows I never wished to harass him, but I felt that merely, at this, to turn my back on him was to abandon or, to put it more truly, to lose him. "I've just begun a letter to your uncle," I said.

"Well, then, finish it!"

I waited a minute. "What happened before?"

He gazed up at me again. "Before what?"

"Before you came back. And before you went away."

For some time he was silent, but he continued to meet my eyes. "What happened?"

It made me, the sound of the words, in which it seemed to me that I caught for the very first time a small faint quaver of consenting consciousness—it made me drop on my knees beside the bed and seize once more the chance of possessing him. "Dear little Miles, dear little Miles, if you *knew* how I want to help you! It's only that, it's nothing but that, and I'd rather die than give you a pain or do you a wrong—I'd rather die than hurt a hair of you. Dear little Miles"—oh, I brought it out now even if I *should* go too far—"I just want you to help me to save you!" But I knew in a moment after this that I had gone too far. The answer to my appeal was instantaneous, but it came in the form of an extraordinary blast and chill, a gust of frozen air and a shake of the room as great as if, in the wild wind, the casement had crashed in. The boy gave a loud, high shriek, which, lost in the rest of the shock of sound, might have seemed, indistinctly, though I was so close to him, a note either of jubilation or of terror. I jumped to my feet again and was conscious of darkness. So for a moment we remained, while I stared about me and saw that the drawn curtains were unstirred and the window tight. "Why, the candle's out!" I then cried.

"It was I who blew it, dear!" said Miles.

Chapter 18

THE NEXT DAY, AFTER LESSONS, Mrs. Grose found a moment to say to me quietly: "Have you written, Miss?"

"Yes—I've written." But I didn't add—for the hour—that my letter, sealed and directed, was still in my pocket. There would be time enough to send it before the messenger should go to the village. Meanwhile there had been, on the part of my pupils, no more brilliant, more exemplary morning. It was exactly as if they had both had at heart to gloss over any recent little friction. They performed the dizziest feats of arithmetic, soaring quite out of *my* feeble range, and perpetrated, in higher spirits than ever, geographical and historical jokes. It was conspicuous of course in Miles in particular that he appeared to wish to show how easily he could let me down. This child, to my memory, really lives in a setting of beauty and misery that no words can translate; there was a distinction all his own in every impulse he revealed; never was a small natural creature, to the uninitiated eye all frankness and freedom, a more ingenious, a more extraordinary little gentleman. I had perpetually to guard against the wonder of contemplation into which my initiated view betrayed me; to check the irrelevant gaze and discouraged sigh in which I constantly both attacked and renounced the enigma of what such a little gentleman could have done that deserved a penalty. Say that, by the dark prodigy I knew, the imagination of all evil *had* been opened up to him: all the justice within me ached for the proof that it could ever have flowered into an act.

He had never, at any rate, been such a little gentleman as when, after our early dinner on this dreadful day, he came round to me and asked if I shouldn't like him, for half an hour, to play to me. David playing to Saul could never have shown a finer sense of the occasion. It was literally a charming exhibition of tact, of magnanimity, and quite tantamount to his saying outright: "The true knights we love to read about never push an advantage too far. I know what you mean now: you mean that—to be let alone yourself and not followed up—you'll cease to worry and spy upon me, won't keep me so close to you, will let me go and come. Well, I 'come,' you see—but I don't go! There'll be plenty of time for that. I do really delight in your society, and I only want to show you that I contended for a principle." It may be imagined whether I resisted this appeal or failed to accompany him again, hand in hand, to the schoolroom. He sat down at the old piano and played as he had never played, and if there are those who think he had better have been kicking a football I

can only say that I wholly agree with them. For at the end of a time that under his influence I had quite ceased to measure I started up with a strange sense of having literally slept at my post. It was after luncheon, and by the schoolroom fire, and yet I hadn't really, in the least, slept: I had only done something much worse—I had forgotten. Where, all this time, was Flora? When I put the question to Miles he played on a minute before answering, and then could only say: "Why, my dear, how do I know?"—breaking moreover into a happy laugh which, immediately after, as if it were a vocal accompaniment, he prolonged into incoherent, extravagant song.

I went straight to my room, but his sister was not there; then, before going downstairs, I looked into several others. As she was nowhere about she would surely be with Mrs. Grose, whom, in the comfort of that theory, I accordingly proceeded in quest of. I found her where I had found her the evening before, but she met my quick challenge with blank, scared ignorance. She had only supposed that, after the repast, I had carried off both the children; as to which she was quite in her right, for it was the very first time I had allowed the little girl out of my sight without some special provision. Of course now indeed she might be with the maids, so that the immediate thing was to look for her without an air of alarm. This we promptly arranged between us; but when, ten minutes later and in pursuance of our arrangement, we met in the hall, it was only to report on either side that after guarded inquiries we had altogether failed to trace her. For a minute there, apart from observation, we exchanged mute alarms, and I could feel with what high interest my friend returned me all those I had from the first given her.

"She'll be above," she presently said—"in one of the rooms you haven't searched."

"No; she's at a distance." I had made up my mind. "She has gone out."

Mrs. Grose stared. "Without a hat?"

I naturally also looked volumes. "Isn't that woman always without one?"

"She's with *her?*"

"She's with *her!*" I declared. "We must find them."

My hand was on my friend's arm, but she failed for the moment, confronted with such an account of the matter, to respond to my pressure. She communed, on the contrary, on the spot, with her uneasiness. "And where's Master Miles?"

"Oh, *he's* with Quint. They're in the schoolroom."

"Lord, Miss!" My view, I was myself aware—and therefore I suppose my tone—had never yet reached so calm an assurance.

"The trick's played," I went on; "they've successfully worked their plan. He found the most divine little way to keep me quiet while she went off."

"'Divine?'" Mrs. Grose bewilderedly echoed.

"Infernal, then!" I almost cheerfully rejoined. "He has provided for himself as well. But come!"

She had helplessly gloomed at the upper regions. "You leave him——?"

"So long with Quint? Yes—I don't mind that now."

She always ended, at these moments, by getting possession of my hand, and in this manner she could at present still stay me. But after gasping an instant at my sudden resignation, "Because of your letter?" she eagerly brought out.

I quickly, by way of answer, felt for my letter, drew it forth, held it up, and then, freeing myself, went and laid it on the great hall-table. "Luke will take it," I said as I came back. I reached the house-door and opened it; I was already on the steps.

My companion still demurred: the storm of the night and the early morning had dropped, but the afternoon was damp and grey. I came down to the drive while she stood in the doorway. "You go with nothing on?"

"What do I care when the child has nothing? I can't wait to dress," I cried, "and if you must do so, I leave you. Try meanwhile, yourself, upstairs."

"With *them?*" Oh, on this, the poor woman promptly joined me!

Chapter 19

WE WENT STRAIGHT TO THE LAKE, as it was called at Bly, and I dare say rightly called, though I reflect that it may in fact have been a sheet of water less remarkable than it appeared to my untravelled eyes. My acquaintance with sheets of water was small, and the pool of Bly, at all events on the few occasions of my consenting, under the protection of my pupils, to affront its surface in the old flat-bottomed boat moored there for our use, had impressed me both with its extent and its agitation. The usual place of embarkation was half a mile from the house, but I had an intimate conviction that, wherever Flora might be, she was not near home. She had not given me the slip for any small adventure, and, since the day of the very great one that I had shared with her by the pond, I had been aware, in our walks, of the quarter to which she most inclined. This was why I had now given to Mrs. Grose's steps so marked a direction—a direction that made her, when she perceived it, oppose a

resistance that showed me she was freshly mystified. "You're going to the water, Miss?—you think she's *in*——?"

"She may be, though the depth is, I believe, nowhere very great. But what I judge most likely is that she's on the spot from which, the other day, we saw together what I told you."

"When she pretended not to see——?"

"With that astounding self-possession! I've always been sure she wanted to go back alone. And now her brother has managed it for her."

Mrs. Grose still stood where she had stopped. "You suppose they really *talk* of them?"

I could meet this with a confidence! "They say things that, if we heard them, would simply appall us."

"And if she *is* there——?"

"Yes?"

"Then Miss Jessel is?"

"Beyond a doubt. You shall see."

"Oh, thank you!" my friend cried, planted so firm that, taking it in, I went straight on without her. By the time I reached the pool, however, she was close behind me, and I knew that, whatever, to her apprehension, might befall me, the exposure of my society struck her as her least danger. She exhaled a moan of relief as we at last came in sight of the greater part of the water without a sight of the child. There was no trace of Flora on that nearer side of the bank where my observation of her had been most startling, and none on the opposite edge, where, save for a margin of some twenty yards, a thick copse came down to the water. The pond, oblong in shape, had a width so scant compared to its length that, with its ends out of view, it might have been taken for a scant river. We looked at the empty expanse, and then I felt the suggestion of my friend's eyes. I knew what she meant and I replied with a negative headshake.

"No, no; wait! She has taken the boat."

My companion stared at the vacant mooring-place and then again across the lake. "Then where is it?"

"Our not seeing it is the strongest of proofs. She has used it to go over, and then has managed to hide it."

"All alone—that child?"

"She's not alone, and at such times she's not a child: she's an old, old woman." I scanned all the visible shore while Mrs. Grose took again, into the queer element I offered her, one of her plunges of submission; then I pointed out that the boat might perfectly be in a small refuge formed by one of the recesses of the pool, an indentation masked, for the hither side, by a projection of the bank and by a clump of trees growing close to the water.

"But if the boat's there, where on earth's *she?*" my colleague anxiously asked.

"That's exactly what we must learn." And I started to walk further. "By going all the way round?"

"Certainly, far as it is. It will take us but ten minutes, but it's far enough to have made the child prefer not to walk. She went straight over."

"Laws!" cried my friend again; the chain of my logic was ever too much for her. It dragged her at my heels even now, and when we had got half-way round—a devious, tiresome process, on ground much broken and by a path choked with overgrowth—I paused to give her breath. I sustained her with a grateful arm, assuring her that she might hugely help me; and this started us afresh, so that in the course of but few minutes more we reached a point from which we found the boat to be where I had supposed it. It had been intentionally left as much as possible out of sight and was tied to one of the stakes of a fence that came, just there, down to the brink and that had been an assistance to disembarking. I recognised, as I looked at the pair of short, thick oars, quite safely drawn up, the prodigious character of the feat for a little girl; but I had lived, by this time, too long among wonders and had panted to too many livelier measures. There was a gate in the fence, through which we passed, and that brought us, after a trifling interval, more into the open. Then, "There she is!" we both exclaimed at once.

Flora, a short way off, stood before us on the grass and smiled as if her performance was now complete. The next thing she did, however, was to stoop straight down and pluck—quite as if it were all she was there for—a big, ugly spray of withered fern. I instantly became sure she had just come out of the copse. She waited for us, not herself taking a step, and I was conscious of the rare solemnity with which we presently approached her. She smiled and smiled, and we met; but it was all done in a silence by this time flagrantly ominous. Mrs. Grose was the first to break the spell: she threw herself on her knees and, drawing the child to her breast, clasped in a long embrace the little tender, yielding body. While this dumb convulsion lasted I could only watch it—which I did the more intently when I saw Flora's face peep at me over our companion's shoulder. It was serious now—the flicker had left it; but it strengthened the pang with which I at that moment envied Mrs. Grose the simplicity of *her* relation. Still, all this while, nothing more passed between us save that Flora had let her foolish fern again drop to the ground. What she and I had virtually said to each other was that pretexts were useless now. When Mrs. Grose finally got up she kept the child's hand, so that the two were still before me; and the singular reticence of our communion was even more marked in the frank look she launched me. "I'll be hanged," it said, "if *I'll* speak!"

It was Flora who, gazing all over me in candid wonder, was the first. She was struck with our bareheaded aspect. "Why, where are your things?"

"Where yours are, my dear!" I promptly returned.

She had already got back her gaiety, and appeared to take this as an answer quite sufficient. "And where's Miles?" she went on.

There was something in the small valour of it that quite finished me: these three words from her were, in a flash like the glitter of a drawn blade, the jostle of the cup that my hand, for weeks and weeks, had held high and full to the brim and that now, even before speaking, I felt overflow in a deluge. "I'll tell you if you'll tell *me*——" I heard myself say, then heard the tremor in which it broke.

"Well, what?"

Mrs. Grose's suspense blazed at me, but it was too late now, and I brought the thing out handsomely. "Where, my pet, is Miss Jessel?"

Chapter 20

JUST AS IN THE CHURCHYARD WITH MILES, the whole thing was upon us. Much as I had made of the fact that this name had never once, between us, been sounded, the quick, smitten glare with which the child's face now received it fairly likened my breach of the silence to the smash of a pane of glass. It added to the interposing cry, as if to stay the blow, that Mrs. Grose, at the same instant, uttered over my violence —the shriek of a creature scared, or rather wounded, which, in turn, within a few seconds, was completed by a gasp of my own. I seized my colleague's arm. "She's there, she's there!"

Miss Jessel stood before us on the opposite bank exactly as she had stood the other time, and I remember, strangely, as the first feeling now produced in me, my thrill of joy at having brought on a proof. She was there, and I was justified; she was there, and I was neither cruel nor mad. She was there for poor scared Mrs. Grose, but she was there most for Flora; and no moment of my monstrous time was perhaps so extraordinary as that in which I consciously threw out to her—with the sense that, pale and ravenous demon as she was, she would catch and understand it —an inarticulate message of gratitude. She rose erect on the spot my friend and I had lately quitted, and there was not, in all the long reach of her desire, an inch of her evil that fell short. This first vividness of vision and emotion were things of a few seconds, during which Mrs. Grose's dazed blink across to where I pointed struck me as a sovereign sign that she too at last saw, just as it carried my own eyes precipitately to the child. The revelation then of the manner in which Flora was affected startled me, in truth, far more than it would have done to find her also

merely agitated, for direct dismay was of course not what I had expected. Prepared and on her guard as our pursuit had actually made her, she would repress every betrayal; and I was therefore shaken, on the spot, by my first glimpse of the particular one for which I had not allowed. To see her, without a convulsion of her small pink face, not even feign to glance in the direction of the prodigy I announced, but only, instead of that, turn at *me* an expression of hard, still gravity, an expression absolutely new and unprecedented and that appeared to read and accuse and judge me—this was a stroke that somehow converted the little girl herself into the very presence that could make me quail. I quailed even though my certitude that she thoroughly saw was never greater than at that instant, and in the immediate need to defend myself I called it passionately to witness. "She's there, you little unhappy thing—there, there, *there,* and you see her as well as you see me!" I had said shortly before to Mrs. Grose that she was not at these times a child, but an old, old woman, and that description of her could not have been more strikingly confirmed than in the way in which, for all answer to this, she simply showed me, without a concession, an admission, of her eyes, a countenance of deeper and deeper, of indeed suddenly quite fixed, reprobation. I was by this time—if I can put the whole thing at all together—more appalled at what I may properly call her manner than at anything else, though it was simultaneously with this that I became aware of having Mrs. Grose also, and very formidably, to reckon with. My elder companion, the next moment, at any rate, blotted out everything but her own flushed face and her loud, shocked protest, a burst of high disapproval. "What a dreadful turn, to be sure, Miss! Where on earth do you see anything?"

I could only grasp her more quickly yet, for even while she spoke the hideous plain presence stood undimmed and undaunted. It had already lasted a minute, and it lasted while I continued, seizing my colleague, quite thrusting her at it and presenting her to it, to insist with my pointing hand. "You don't see her exactly as *we* see?—you mean to say you don't now—*now?* She's as big as a blazing fire! Only look, dearest woman, *look—*!" She looked, even as I did, and gave me, with her deep groan of negation, repulsion, compassion—the mixture with her pity of her relief at her exemption—a sense, touching to me even then, that she would have backed me up if she could. I might well have needed that, for with this hard blow of the proof that her eyes were hopelessly sealed I felt my own situation horribly crumble, I felt—I saw—my livid predecessor press, from her position, on my defeat, and I was conscious, more than all, of what I should have from this instant to deal with in the astounding little attitude of Flora. Into this attitude Mrs. Grose immediately and violently entered, breaking, even while there pierced through my sense of ruin a prodigious private triumph, into breathless reassurance.

"She isn't there, little lady, and nobody's there—and you never see

nothing, my sweet! How can poor Miss Jessel? when poor Miss Jessel's dead and buried? *We* know, don't we, love?"—and she appealed, blundering in, to the child. "It's all a mere mistake and a worry and a joke—and we'll go home as fast as we can!"

Our companion, on this, had responded with a strange, quick primness of propriety, and they were again, with Mrs. Grose on her feet, united, as it were, in pained opposition to me. Flora continued to fix me with her small mask of reprobation, and even at that minute I prayed God to forgive me for seeming to see that, as she stood there holding tight to our friend's dress, her incomparable childish beauty had suddenly failed, had quite vanished. I've said it already—she was literally, she was hideously, hard; she had turned common and almost ugly. "I don't know what you mean. I see nobody. I see nothing. I never *have*. I think you're cruel. I don't like you!" Then, after this deliverance, which might have been that of a vulgarly pert little girl in the street, she hugged Mrs. Grose more closely and buried in her skirts the dreadful little face. In this position she produced an almost furious wail. "Take me away, take me away—oh, take me away from *her!*"

"From *me?*" I panted.

"From you—from you!" she cried.

Even Mrs. Grose looked across at me dismayed, while I had nothing to do but communicate again with the figure that, on the opposite bank, without a movement, as rigidly still as if catching, beyond the interval, our voices, was as vividly there for my disaster as it was not there for my service. The wretched child had spoken exactly as if she had got from some outside source each of her stabbing little words, and I could therefore, in the full despair of all I had to accept, but sadly shake my head at her. "If I had ever doubted, all my doubt would at present have gone. I've been living with the miserable truth, and now it has only too much closed round me. Of course I've lost you: I've interfered, and you've seen—under *her* dictation"—with which I faced, over the pool again, our infernal witness—"the easy and perfect way to meet it. I've done my best, but I've lost you. Good-bye." For Mrs. Grose I had an imperative, an almost frantic "Go, go!" before which, in infinite distress, but mutely possessed of the little girl and clearly convinced, in spite of her blindness, that something awful had occurred and some collapse engulfed us, she retreated, by the way we had come, as fast as she could move.

Of what first happened when I was left alone I had no subsequent memory. I only knew that at the end of, I suppose, a quarter of an hour, an odorous dampness and roughness, chilling and piercing my trouble, had made me understand that I must have thrown myself, on my face, on the ground and given way to a wildness of grief. I must have lain there long and cried and sobbed, for when I raised my head the day was almost done. I got up and looked a moment, through the twilight, at the grey pool and its blank, haunted edge, and then I took, back to the house, my

dreary and difficult course. When I reached the gate in the fence the boat, to my surprise, was gone, so that I had a fresh reflection to make on Flora's extraordinary command of the situation. She passed that night, by the most tacit, and I should add, were not the word so grotesque a false note, the happiest of arrangements, with Mrs. Grose. I saw neither of them on my return, but, on the other hand as by an ambiguous compensation, I saw a great deal of Miles. I saw—I can use no other phrase —so much of him that it was as if it were more than it had ever been. No evening I had passed at Bly had the portentous quality of this one; in spite of which—and in spite also of the deeper depths of consternation that had opened beneath my feet—there was literally, in the ebbing actual, an extraordinarily sweet sadness. On reaching the house I had never so much as looked for the boy; I had simply gone straight to my room to change what I was wearing and to take in, at a glance, much material testimony to Flora's rupture. Her little belongings had all been removed. When later, by the schoolroom fire, I was served with tea by the usual maid, I indulged, on the article of my other pupil, in no inquiry whatever. He had his freedom now—he might have it to the end! Well, he did have it; and it consisted—in part at least—of his coming in at about eight o'clock and sitting down with me in silence. On the removal of the tea-things I had blown out the candles and drawn my chair closer: I was conscious of a mortal coldness and felt as if I should never again be warm. So, when he appeared, I was sitting in the glow with my thoughts. He paused a moment by the door as if to look at me; then—as if to share them—came to the other side of the hearth and sank into a chair. We sat there in absolute stillness; yet he wanted, I felt, to be with me.

Chapter 21

BEFORE A NEW DAY, in my room, had fully broken, my eyes opened to Mrs. Grose, who had come to my bedside with worse news. Flora was so markedly feverish that an illness was perhaps at hand; she had passed a night of extreme unrest, a night agitated above all by fears that had for their subject not in the least her former, but wholly her present, governess. It was not against the possible re-entrance of Miss Jessel on the scene that she protested—it was conspicuously and passionately against mine. I was promptly on my feet of course, and with an immense deal to ask; the more that my friend had discernibly now girded her loins to meet me once more. This I felt as soon as I had put to her the

question of her sense of the child's sincerity as against my own. "She persists in denying to you that she saw, or has ever seen, anything?"

My visitor's trouble, truly, was great. "Ah, Miss it isn't a matter on which I can push her! Yet it isn't either, I must say, as if I much needed to. It has made her, every inch of her, quite old."

"Oh, I see her perfectly from here. She resents, for all the world like some high little personage, the imputation on her truthfulness and, as it were, her respectability. 'Miss Jessel indeed—*she!*' Ah, she's 'respectable,' the chit! The impression she gave me there yesterday was, I assure you, the very strangest of all; it was quite beyond any of the others. I *did* put my foot in it! She'll never speak to me again."

Hideous and obscure as it all was, it held Mrs. Grose briefly silent; then she granted my point with a frankness which, I made sure, had more behind it. "I think indeed, Miss, she never will. She do have a grand manner about it!"

"And that manner"—I summed it up—"is practically what's the matter with her now!"

Oh, that manner, I could see in my visitor's face, and not a little else besides! "She asks me every three minutes if I think you're coming in."

"I see—I see." I too, on my side, had so much more than worked it out. "Has she said to you since yesterday—except to repudiate her familiarity with anything so dreadful—a single other word about Miss Jessel?"

"Not one, Miss. And of course you know," my friend added, "I took it from her, by the lake, that, just then and there at least, there *was* nobody."

"Rather! And, naturally, you take it from her still."

"I don't contradict her. What else can I do?"

"Nothing in the world! You've the cleverest little person to deal with. They've made them—their two friends, I mean—still cleverer even than nature did; for it was wondrous material to play on! Flora has now her grievance, and she'll work it to the end."

"Yes, Miss; but to *what* end?"

"Why, that of dealing with me to her uncle. She'll make me out to him the lowest creature——!"

I winced at the fair show of the scene in Mrs. Grose's face; she looked for a minute as if she sharply saw them together. "And him who thinks so well of you!"

"He has an odd way—it comes over me now," I laughed, "—of proving it! But that doesn't matter. What Flora wants, of course, is to get rid of me."

My companion bravely concurred. "Never again to so much as look at you."

"So that what you've come to me now for," I asked, "is to speed me on my way?" Before she had time to reply, however, I had her in check. "I've a better idea—the result of my reflections. My going *would* seem the right thing, and on Sunday I was terribly near it. Yet that won't do. It's *you* who must go. You must take Flora."

My visitor, at this, did speculate. "But where in the world——?"

"Away from here. Away from *them*. Away, even most of all, now, from me. Straight to her uncle."

"Only to tell on you——?"

"No, not 'only!' To leave me, in addition, with my remedy."

She was still vague. "And what *is* your remedy?"

"Your loyalty, to begin with. And then Miles's."

She looked at me hard. "Do you think he——?"

"Won't if he has the chance, turn on me? Yes, I venture still to think it. At all events, I want to try. Get off with his sister as soon as possible and leave me with him alone." I was amazed, myself, at the spirit I had still in reserve, and therefore perhaps a trifle the more disconcerted at the way in which, in spite of this fine example of it, she hesitated. "There's one thing, of course," I went on: "they mustn't, before she goes, see each other for three seconds." Then it came over me that, in spite of Flora's presumable sequestration from the instant of her return from the pool, it might already be too late. "Do you mean," I anxiously asked, "that they *have* met?"

At this she quite flushed. "Ah, Miss, I'm not such a fool as that! If I've been obliged to leave her three or four times, it has been each time with one of the maids, and at present, though she's alone, she's locked in safe. And yet—and yet!" There were too many things.

"And yet what?"

"Well, are you so sure of the little gentleman?"

"I'm not sure of anything but *you*. But I have, since last evening, a new hope. I think he wants to give me an opening. I do believe that—poor little exquisite wretch!—he wants to speak. Last evening, in the firelight and the silence, he sat with me for two hours as if it were just coming."

Mrs. Grose looked hard, through the window, at the grey, gathering day. "And did it come?"

"No, though I waited and waited, I confess it didn't, and it was without a breach of the silence or so much as a faint allusion to his sister's condition and absence that we at last kissed for good-night. All the same," I continued, "I can't, if her uncle sees her, consent to his seeing her brother without my having given the boy—and most of all because things have got so bad—a little more time."

My friend appeared on this ground more reluctant than I could quite understand. "What do you mean by more time?"

"Well, a day or two—really to bring it out. He'll then be on *my* side—of which you see the importance. If nothing comes, I shall only fail, and you will, at the worst, have helped me by doing, on your arrival in town, whatever you may have found possible." So I put it before her, but she continued for a little so inscrutably embarrassed that I came again to her aid. "Unless, indeed," I wound up, "you really want *not* to go."

I could see it, in her face, at last clear itself; she put out her hand to me as a pledge. "I'll go—I'll go. I'll go this morning."

I wanted to be very just. "If you *should* wish still to wait, I would engage she shouldn't see me."

"No, no: it's the place itself. She must leave it." She held me a moment with heavy eyes, then brought out the rest. "Your idea's the right one. I myself, Miss——"

"Well?"

"I can't stay."

The look she gave me with it made me jump at possibilities. "You mean that, since yesterday, you *have* seen——?"

She shook her head with dignity. "I've *heard*——!"

"Heard?"

"From that child—horrors! There!" she sighed with tragic relief. "On my honour, Miss, she says things——!" But at this evocation she broke down; she dropped, with a sudden sob, upon my sofa and, as I had seen her do before, gave way to all the grief of it.

It was quite in another manner that I, for my part, let myself go. "Oh, thank God!"

She sprang up again at this, drying her eyes with a groan. " 'Thank God?' "

"It so justifies me!"

"It does that, Miss!"

I couldn't have desired more emphasis, but I just hesitated. "She's so horrible?"

I saw my colleague scarce knew how to put it. "Really shocking."

"And about me?"

"About you, Miss—since you must have it. It's beyond everything, for a young lady; and I can't think wherever she must have picked up——"

"The appalling language she applied to me? I can, then!" I broke in with a laugh that was doubtless significant enough.

It only, in truth, left my friend still more grave. "Well, perhaps I ought to also—since I've heard some of it before! Yet I can't bear it," the poor woman went on while, with the same movement, she glanced, on my dressing-table, at the face of my watch. "But I must go back."

I kept her, however. "Ah, if you can't bear it——!"

"How can I stop with her, you mean? Why, just *for* that: to get her away. Far from this," she pursued, "far from *them*——"

"She may be different? she may be free?" I seized her almost with joy. "Then, in spite of yesterday, you *believe*——"

"In such doings?" Her simple description of them required, in the light of her expression, to be carried no further, and she gave me the whole thing as she had never done. "I believe."

Yes, it was a joy, and we were still shoulder to shoulder: if I might continue sure of that I should care but little what else happened. My support in the presence of disaster would be the same as it had been in my early need of confidence, and if my friend would answer for my honesty, I would answer for all the rest. On the point of taking leave of her, none the less, I was to some extent embarrassed. "There's one thing of course—it occurs to me—to remember. My letter, giving the alarm, will have reached town before you."

I now perceived still more how she had been beating about the bush and how weary at last it had made her. "Your letter won't have got there. Your letter never went."

"What then became of it?"

"Goodness knows! Master Miles——"

"Do you mean *he* took it?" I gasped.

She hung fire, but she overcame her reluctance. "I mean that I saw yesterday, when I came back with Miss Flora, that it wasn't where you had put it. Later in the evening I had the chance to question Luke, and he declared that he had neither noticed nor touched it." We could only exchange, on this, one of our deeper mutual soundings, and it was Mrs. Grose who first brought up the plumb with an almost elate "You see!"

"Yes, I see that if Miles took it instead he probably will have read it and destroyed it."

"And don't you see anything else?"

I faced her a moment with a sad smile. "It strikes me that by this time your eyes are open even wider than mine."

They proved to be so indeed, but she could still blush, almost, to show it. "I make out now what he must have done at school." And she gave, in her simple sharpness, an almost droll disillusioned nod. "He stole!"

I turned it over—I tried to be more judicial. "Well—perhaps."

She looked as if she found me unexpectedly calm. "He stole *letters!*"

She couldn't know my reasons for a calmness after all pretty shallow; so I showed them off as I might. "I hope then it was to more purpose than in this case! The note, at any rate, that I put on the table yesterday," I pursued, "will have given him so scant an advantage—for it contained only the bare demand for an interview—that he is already much ashamed of having gone so far for so little, and that what he had on his mind last evening was precisely the need of confession." I seemed to myself, for

the instant, to have mastered it, to see it all. "Leave us, leave us"—I was already, at the door, hurrying her off. "I'll get it out of him. He'll meet me—he'll confess. If he confesses, he's saved. And if he's saved——"

"Then *you* are?" The dear woman kissed me on this, and I took her farewell. "I'll save you without him!" she cried as she went.

Chapter 22

YET IT WAS WHEN SHE HAD GOT OFF—and I missed her on the spot—that the great pinch really came. If I had counted on what it would give me to find myself alone with Miles, I speedily perceived, at least, that it would give me a measure. No hour of my stay in fact was so assailed with apprehensions as that of my coming down to learn that the carriage containing Mrs. Grose and my younger pupil had already rolled out of the gates. Now I *was,* I said to myself, face to face with the elements, and for much of the rest of the day, while I fought my weakness, I could consider that I had been supremely rash. It was a tighter place still than I had yet turned round in; all the more that, for the first time, I could see in the aspect of others a confused reflection of the crisis. What had happened naturally caused them all to stare; there was too little of the explained, throw out whatever we might, in the suddenness of my colleague's act. The maids and the men looked blank; the effect of which on my nerves was an aggravation until I saw the necessity of making it a positive aid. It was precisely, in short, by just clutching the helm that I avoided total wreck; and I dare say that, to bear up at all, I became, that morning, very grand and very dry. I welcomed the consciousness that I was charged with much to do, and I caused it to be known as well that, left thus to myself, I was quite remarkably firm. I wandered with that manner, for the next hour or two, all over the place and looked, I have no doubt, as if I were ready for any onset. So, for the benefit of whom it might concern, I paraded with a sick heart.

The person it appeared least to concern proved to be, till dinner, little Miles himself. My perambulations had given me meanwhile, no glimpse of him, but they had tended to make more public the change taking place in our relation as a consequence of his having at the piano, the day before, kept me, in Flora's interest, so beguiled and befooled. The stamp of publicity had of course been fully given by her confinement and departure, and the change itself was now ushered in by our non-observance of the regular custom of the schoolroom. He had already disappeared when, on my way down, I pushed open his door, and I

learned below that he had breakfasted—in the presence of a couple of the maids—with Mrs. Grose and his sister. He had then gone out, as he said, for a stroll; than which nothing, I reflected, could better have expressed his frank view of the abrupt transformation of my office. What he would now permit this office to consist of was yet to be settled: there was a queer relief, at all events—I mean for myself in especial—in the renouncement of one pretension. If so much had sprung to the surface, I scarce put it too strongly in saying that what had perhaps sprung highest was the absurdity of our prolonging the fiction that I had anything more to teach him. It sufficiently stuck out that, by tacit little tricks in which even more than myself he carried out the care for my dignity, I had had to appeal to him to let me off straining to meet him on the ground of his true capacity. He had at any rate his freedom now; I was never to touch it again; as I had amply shown, moreover, when, on his joining me in the schoolroom the previous night, I had uttered, on the subject of the interval just concluded, neither challenge nor hint. I had too much, from this moment, my other ideas. Yet when he at last arrived the difficulty of applying them, the accumulations of my problem, were brought straight home to me by the beautiful little presence on which what had occurred had as yet, for the eye, dropped neither stain nor shadow.

To mark, for the house, the high state I cultivated I decreed that my meals with the boy should be served, as we called it, downstairs; so that I had been awaiting him in the ponderous pomp of the room outside of the window of which I had had from Mrs. Grose, that first scared Sunday, my flash of something it would scarce have done to call light. Here at present I felt afresh—for I had felt it again and again—how my equilibrium depended on the success of my rigid will, the will to shut my eyes as tight as possible to the truth that what I had to deal with was, revoltingly, against nature. I could only get on at all by taking "nature" into my confidence and my account, by treating my monstrous ordeal as a push in a direction unusual, of course, and unpleasant, but demanding, after all, for a fair front, only another turn of the screw of ordinary human virtue. No attempt, none the less, could well require more tact than just this attempt to supply, one's self, *all* the nature. How could I put even a little of that article into a suppression of reference to what had occurred? How, on the other hand, could I make a reference without a new plunge into the hideous obscure? Well, a sort of answer, after a time, had come to me, and it was so far confirmed as that I was met, incontestably, by the quickened vision of what was rare in my little companion. It was indeed as if he had found even now—as he had so often found at lessons—still some other delicate way to ease me off. Wasn't there light in the fact which, as we shared our solitude, broke out with a specious glitter it had never yet quite worn?—the fact that (opportunity aiding, precious opportunity which had now come) it would be preposter-

ous, with a child so endowed, to forgo the help one might wrest from absolute intelligence? What had his intelligence been given him for but to save him? Mightn't one, to reach his mind, risk the stretch of an angular arm over his character? It was as if, when we were face to face in the dining-room, he had literally shown me the way. The roast mutton was on the table, and I had dispensed with attendance. Miles, before he sat down, stood a moment with his hands in his pockets and looked at the joint, on which he seemed on the point of passing some humorous judgment. But what he presently produced was: "I say, my dear, is she really very awfully ill?"

"Little Flora? Not so bad but that she'll presently be better. London will set her up. Bly had ceased to agree with her. Come here and take your mutton."

He alertly obeyed me, carried the plate carefully to his seat, and, when he was established, went on. "Did Bly disagree with her so terribly suddenly?"

"Not so suddenly as you might think. One had seen it coming on."

"Then why didn't you get her off before?"

"Before what?"

"Before she became too ill to travel."

I found myself prompt. "She's *not* too ill to travel: she only might have become so if she had stayed. This was just the moment to seize. The journey will dissipate the influence"—oh, I was grand!—"and carry it off."

"I see, I see"—Miles, for that matter, was grand too. He settled to his repast with the charming little "table manner" that, from the day of his arrival, had relieved me of all grossness of admonition. Whatever he had been driven from school for, it was not for ugly feeding. He was irreproachable, as always, today; but he was unmistakably more conscious. He was discernibly trying to take for granted more things than he found, without assistance, quite easy; and he dropped into peaceful silence while he felt his situation. Our meal was of the briefest—mine a vain pretence, and I had the things immediately removed. While this was done Miles stood again with his hands in his little pockets and his back to me—stood and looked out of the wide window through which, that other day, I had seen what pulled me up. We continued silent while the maid was with us—as silent, it whimsically occurred to me, as some young couple who, on their wedding-journey, at the inn, feel shy in the presence of the waiter. He turned round only when the waiter had left us. "Well—so we're alone!"

Chapter 23

"OH, MORE OR LESS." I fancy my smile was pale. "Not absolutely. We shouldn't like that!" I went on.

"No—I suppose we shouldn't. Of course we have the others."

"We have the others—we have indeed the others," I concurred.

"Yet even though we have them," he returned, still with his hands in his pockets and planted there in front of me, "they don't much count, do they?"

I made the best of it, but I felt wan. "It depends on what you call 'much!'"

"Yes"—with all accommodation—"everything depends!" On this, however, he faced to the window again and presently reached it with his vague, restless, cogitating step. He remained there awhile, with his forehead against the glass, in contemplation of the stupid shrubs I knew and the dull things of November. I had always my hypocrisy of "work," behind which, now, I gained the sofa. Steadying myself with it there as I had repeatedly done at those moments of torment that I have described as the moments of my knowing the children to be given to something from which I was barred, I sufficiently obeyed my habit of being prepared for the worst. But an extraordinary impression dropped on me as I extracted a meaning from the boy's embarrassed back—none other than the impression that I was not barred now. This inference grew in a few minutes to sharp intensity and seemed bound up with the direct perception that it was positively *he* who was. The frames and squares of the great window were a kind of image, for him, of a kind of failure. I felt that I saw him, at any rate, shut in or shut out. He was admirable, but not comfortable: I took it in with a throb of hope. Wasn't he looking, through the haunted pane, for something he couldn't see?—and wasn't it the first time in the whole business that he had known such a lapse? The first, the very first: I found it a splendid portent. It made him anxious, though he watched himself; he had been anxious all day and, even while in his usual sweet little manner he sat at table, had needed all his small strange genius to give it a gloss. When he at last turned round to meet me, it was almost as if this genius had succumbed. "Well, I think I'm glad Bly agrees with *me!*"

"You would certainly seem to have seen, these twenty-four hours, a good deal more of it than for some time before. I hope," I went on bravely, "that you've been enjoying yourself."

410

"Oh, yes, I've been ever so far; all round about—miles and miles away. I've never been so free."

He had really a manner of his own, and I could only try to keep up with him. "Well, do you like it?"

He stood there smiling; then at last he put into two words—"Do *you?*"—more discrimination than I had ever heard two words contain. Before I had time to deal with that, however, he continued as if with the sense that this was an impertinence to be softened. "Nothing could be more charming than the way you take it, for of course if we're alone together now it's you that are alone most. But I hope," he threw in, "you don't particularly mind!"

"Having to do with you?" I asked. "My dear child, how can I help minding? Though I've renounced all claim to your company— you're so beyond me—I at least greatly enjoy it. What else should I stay on for?"

He looked at me more directly, and the expression of his face, graver now, struck me as the most beautiful I had ever found in it. "You stay on just for *that?*"

"Certainly. I stay on as your friend and from the tremendous interest I take in you till something can be done for you that may be more worth your while. That needn't surprise you." My voice trembled so that I felt it impossible to suppress the shake. "Don't you remember how I told you, when I came and sat on your bed the night of the storm, that there was nothing in the world I wouldn't do for you?"

"Yes, yes!" He, on his side, more and more visibly nervous, had a tone to master; but he was so much more successful than I that, laughing out through his gravity, he could pretend we were pleasantly jesting. "Only that, I think, was to get me to do something for *you!*"

"It was partly to get you to do something," I conceded. "But, you know, you didn't do it."

"Oh, yes," he said with the brightest superficial eagerness, "you wanted me to tell you something."

"That's it. Out, straight out. What you have on your mind, you know."

"Ah, then, is *that* what you've stayed over for?"

He spoke with a gaiety through which I could still catch the finest little quiver of resentful passion; but I can't begin to express the effect upon me of an implication of surrender even so faint. It was as if what I had yearned for had come at last only to astonish me. "Well, yes— I may as well make a clean breast of it. It was precisely for that."

He waited so long that I supposed it for the purpose of repudiating the assumption on which my action had been founded; but what he finally said was: "Do you mean now—here?"

"There couldn't be a better place or time." He looked round him uneasily, and I had the rare—oh, the queer!—impression of the very first

symptom I had seen in him of the approach of immediate fear. It was as if he were suddenly afraid of me—which struck me indeed as perhaps the best thing to make him. Yet in the very pang of the effort I felt it vain to try sternness, and I heard myself the next instant so gentle as to be almost grotesque. "You want so to go out again?"

"Awfully!" He smiled at me heroically, and the touching little bravery of it was enhanced by his actually flushing with pain. He had picked up his hat, which he had brought in, and stood twirling it in a way that gave me, even as I was just nearly reaching port, a perverse horror of what I was doing. To do it in *any* way was an act of violence, for what did it consist of but the obtrusion of the idea of grossness and guilt on a small helpless creature who had been for me a revelation of the possibilities of beautiful intercourse? Wasn't it base to create for a being so exquisite a mere alien awkwardness? I suppose I now read into our situation a clearness it couldn't have had at the time, for I seem to see our poor eyes already lighted with some spark of a prevision of the anguish that was to come. So we circled about, with terrors and scruples, like fighters not daring to close. But it was for each other we feared! That kept us a little longer suspended and unbruised. "I'll tell you every-thing," Miles said—"I mean I'll tell you anything you like. You'll stay on with me, and we shall both be all right and I *will* tell you—I *will*. But not now."

"Why not now?"

My insistence turned him from me and kept him once more at his window in a silence during which, between us, you might have heard a pin drop. Then he was before me again with the air of a person for whom, outside, someone who had frankly to be reckoned with was waiting. "I have to see Luke."

I had not yet reduced him to quite so vulgar a lie, and I felt proportionately ashamed. But, horrible as it was, his lies made up my truth. I achieved thoughtfully a few loops of my knitting. "Well, then, go to Luke, and I'll wait for what you promise. Only, in return for that, satisfy, before you leave me, one very much smaller request."

He looked as if he felt he had succeeded enough to be able still a little to bargain. "Very much smaller——?"

"Yes, a mere fraction of the whole. Tell me"—oh, my work pre-occupied me, and I was off-hand!—"if, yesterday afternoon, from the table in the hall, you took, you know, my letter."

Chapter 24

MY SENSE OF HOW HE RECEIVED THIS suffered for a minute from something that I can describe only as a fierce split of my attention—a stroke that at first, as I sprang straight up, reduced me to the mere blind movement of getting hold of him, drawing him close, and, while I just fell for support against the nearest piece of furniture, instinctively keeping him with his back to the window. The appearance was full upon us that I had already had to deal with here: Peter Quint had come into view like a sentinel before a prison. The next thing I saw was that, from outside, he had reached the window, and then I knew that, close to the glass and glaring in through it, he offered once more to the room his white face of damnation. It represents but grossly what took place within me at the sight to say that on the second my decision was made; yet I believe that no woman so overwhelmed ever in so short a time recovered her grasp of the *act*. It came to me in the very horror of the immediate presence that the act would be, seeing and facing what I saw and faced, to keep the boy himself unaware. The inspiration—I can call it by no other name—was that I felt how voluntarily, how transcendently, I *might*. It was like fighting with a demon for a human soul, and when I had fairly so appraised it I saw how the human soul—held out, in the tremor of my hands, at arm's length—had a perfect dew of sweat on a lovely childish forehead. The face that was close to mine was as white as the face against the glass, and out of it presently came a sound, not low nor weak, but as if from much further away, that I drank like a waft of fragrance.

"Yes—I took it."

At this, with a moan of joy, I enfolded, I drew him close; and while I held him to my breast, where I could feel in the sudden fever of his little body the tremendous pulse of his little heart, I kept my eyes on the thing at the window and saw it move and shift its posture. I have likened it to a sentinel, but its slow wheel, for a moment, was rather the prowl of a baffled beast. My present quickened courage, however, was such that, not too much to let it through, I had to shade, as it were, my flame. Meanwhile the glare of the face was again at the window, the scoundrel fixed as if to watch and wait. It was the very confidence that I might now defy him, as well as the positive certitude, by this time, of the child's unconsciousness, that made me go on. "What did you take it for?"

"To see what you said about me."

"You opened the letter?"

"I opened it."

My eyes were now, as I held him off a little again, on Miles's own face, in which the collapse of mockery showed me how complete was the ravage of uneasiness. What was prodigious was that at last, by my success, his sense was sealed and his communication stopped: he knew that he was in presence, but knew not of what, and knew still less that I also was and that I did know. And what did this strain of trouble matter when my eyes went back to the window only to see that the air was clear again and—by my personal triumph—the influence quenched? There was nothing there. I felt that the cause was mine and that I should surely get *all*. "And you found nothing!"—I let my elation out.

He gave the most mournful, thoughtful little headshake. "Nothing."

"Nothing, nothing!" I almost shouted in my joy.

"Nothing, nothing," he sadly repeated.

I kissed his forehead; it was drenched. "So what have you done with it?"

"I've burnt it."

"Burnt it?" It was now or never. "Is that what you did at school?"

Oh, what this brought up! "At school?"

"Did you take letters?—or other things?"

"Other things?" He appeared now to be thinking of something far off and that reached him only through the pressure of his anxiety. Yet it did reach him. "Did I *steal?*"

I felt myself redden to the roots of my hair as well as wonder if it were more strange to put to a gentleman such a question or to see him take it with allowances that gave the very distance of his fall in the world. "Was it for that you mightn't go back?"

The only thing he felt was rather a dreary little surprise. "Did you know I mightn't go back?"

"I know everything."

He gave me at this the longest and strangest look. "Everything?"

"Everything. Therefore *did* you——?" But I couldn't say it again. Miles could, very simply. "No. I didn't steal."

My face must have shown him I believed him utterly; yet my hands—but it was for pure tenderness—shook him as if to ask him why, if it was all for nothing, he had condemned me to months of torment. "What then did you do?"

He looked in vague pain all round the top of the room and drew his breath, two or three times over, as if with difficulty. He might have been standing at the bottom of the sea and raising his eyes to some faint green twilight. "Well—I said things."

"Only that?"

"They thought it was enough!"

"To turn you out for?"

Never, truly, had a person "turned out" shown so little to explain it

as this little person! He appeared to weigh my question, but in a manner quite detached and almost helpless. "Well, I suppose I oughtn't."

"But to whom did you say them?"

He evidently tried to remember, but it dropped—he had lost it. "I don't know!"

He almost smiled at me in the desolation of his surrender, which was indeed practically, by this time, so complete that I ought to have left it there. But I was infatuated—I was blind with victory, though even then the very effect that was to have brought him so much nearer was already that of added separation. "Was it to everyone?" I asked.

"No; it was only to——" But he gave a sick little headshake. "I don't remember their names."

"Were they then so many?"

"No—only a few. Those I liked."

Those he liked? I seemed to float not into clearness, but into a darker obscure, and within a minute there had come to me out of my very pity the appalling alarm of his being perhaps innocent. It was for the instant confounding and bottomless, for if he *were* innocent, what then on earth was *I*? Paralysed, while it lasted, by the mere brush of the question, I let him go a little, so that, with a deep-drawn sigh, he turned away from me again; which, as he faced toward the clear window, I suffered, feeling that I had nothing now there to keep him from. "And did they repeat what you said?" I went on after a moment.

He was soon at some distance from me, still breathing hard and again with the air, though now without anger for it, of being confined against his will. Once more, as he had done before, he looked up at the dim day as if, of what had hitherto sustained him, nothing was left but an unspeakable anxiety. "Oh, yes," he nevertheless replied—"they must have repeated them. To those *they* liked," he added.

There was, somehow, less of it than I had expected; but I turned it over. "And these things came round——?"

"To the masters? Oh, yes!" he answered very simply. "But I didn't know they'd tell."

"The masters? They didn't—they've never told. That's why I ask you."

He turned to me again his little beautiful fevered face. "Yes, it was too bad."

"Too bad?"

"What I suppose I sometimes said. To write home."

I can't name the exquisite pathos of the contradiction given to such a speech by such a speaker; I only know that the next instant I heard myself throw off with homely force: "Stuff and nonsense!" But the next after that I must have sounded stern enough. "What were these things?"

My sternness was all for his judge, his executioner; yet it made him

avert himself again, and that movement made *me,* with a single bound and an irrepressible cry, spring straight upon him. For there again, against the glass, as if to blight his confession and stay his answer, was the hideous author of our woe—the white face of damnation. I felt a sick swim at the drop of my victory and all the return of my battle, so that the wildness of my veritable leap only served as a great betrayal. I saw him, from the midst of my act, meet it with a divination, and on the perception that even now he only guessed, and that the window was still to his own eyes free, I let the impulse flame up to convert the climax of his dismay into the very proof of his liberation. "No more, no more, no more!" I shrieked, as I tried to press him against me, to my visitant.

"Is she *here?*" Miles panted as he caught with his sealed eyes the direction of my words. Then as his strange "she" staggered me and, with a gasp, I echoed it, "Miss Jessel, Miss Jessel!" he with a sudden fury gave me back.

I seized, stupefied, his supposition—some sequel to what we had done to Flora, but this made me only want to show him that it was better still than that. "It's not Miss Jessel! But it's at the window—straight before us. It's *there*—the coward horror, there for the last time!"

At this, after a second in which his head made the movement of a baffled dog's on a scent and then gave a frantic little shake for air and light, he was at me in a white rage, bewildered, glaring vainly over the place and missing wholly, though it now, to my sense, filled the room like the taste of poison, the wide, overwhelming presence. "It's *he?*"

I was so determined to have all my proof that I flashed into ice to challenge him. "Whom do you mean by 'he?' "

"Peter Quint—you devil!" His face gave again, round the room, its convulsed supplication. *"Where?"*

There are in my ears still, his supreme surrender of the name and his tribute to my devotion. "What does he matter now, my own?—what will he *ever* matter? I have you," I launched at the beast, "but he has lost you for ever!" Then, for the demonstration of my work, "There, *there!*" I said to Miles.

But he had already jerked straight round, stared, glared again, and seen but the quiet day. With the stroke of the loss I was so proud of he uttered the cry of a creature hurled over an abyss, and the grasp with which I recovered him might have been that of catching him in his fall. I caught him, yes, I held him—it may be imagined with what a passion; but at the end of a minute I began to feel what it truly was that I held. We were alone with the quiet day, and his little heart, dispossessed, had stopped.

VII

GOOD-BYE, MR. CHIPS

by James Hilton

A Story of School Days

James Hilton was born in 1900 in a mining town in Lanca-
shire, England. As an undergraduate at Christ's College,
Cambridge, he had a first novel published and this launched
him on a career which seemed at the first to move slowly.
In fact, *Lost Horizon,* which was to become finally his most
successful novel, was published in 1933 and did not at first
achieve much in the way of immediate sales. It was soon
after this, however, that he suddenly found himself sky-
rocketing into fame. Having an order from the *British
Weekly,* he conceived the idea for *Good-bye, Mr. Chips*
and wrote it in four days. This rather short novelette was an
immediate success, and the copies of the paper were liter-
ally snatched off the counters.

Lost Horizon benefited quickly from the great popu-
larity of *Mr. Chips* and went on to become a belated best
seller in its own right. Both books were made into motion
pictures which combined popular appeal with an inherent
quality of originality and distinction of treatment. Inevitably
James Hilton was drafted to Hollywood in 1937. He was as
successful in adapting the books of other writers to the
screen as he had been with his own. Among other stories,
he had a part in the adaptation of *Mrs. Miniver.* He remained
in this country until his death in 1954.

Perhaps it was just as well that he had such limited time
for the writing of *Mr. Chips.* It seems perfectly right and
satisfying as it stands. If circumstances had allowed him the
opportunity to write this sentimental little masterpiece at
greater length, its fine balance might have been disturbed.

Here, then, is the story of the gentle schoolmaster who
was known to his boys as "Mr. Chips."

Chapter I

WHEN YOU ARE GETTING ON IN YEARS (but not ill, of course), you get very sleepy at times, and the hours seem to pass like lazy cattle moving across a landscape. It was like that for Chips as the autumn term progressed and the days shortened till it was actually dark enough to light the gas before call-over. For Chips, like some old sea captain, still measured time by the signals of the past; and well he might, for he lived at Mrs. Wickett's, just across the road from the School. He had been there more than a decade, ever since he finally gave up his mastership; and it was Brookfield far more than Greenwich time that both he and his landlady kept. "Mrs. Wickett," Chips would sing out, in that jerky, high-pitched voice that had still a good deal of sprightliness in it, "you might bring me a cup of tea before prep, will you?"

When you are getting on in years it is nice to sit by the fire and drink a cup of tea and listen to the school bell sounding dinner, call-over, prep, and lights-out. Chips always wound up the clock after that last bell; then he put the wire guard in front of the fire, turned out the gas, and carried a detective novel to bed. Rarely did he read more than a page of it before sleep came swiftly and peacefully, more like a mystic intensifying of perception than any changeful entrance into another world. For his days and nights were equally full of dreaming.

He was getting on in years (but not ill, of course); indeed, as Doctor Merivale said, there was really nothing the matter with him. "My dear fellow, you're fitter than I am," Merivale would say, sipping a glass of sherry when he called every fortnight or so. "You're past the age when people get these horrible diseases; you're one of the few lucky ones who're going to die a really natural death. That is, of course, if you die at all. You're such a remarkable old boy that one never knows." But when Chips had a cold or when east winds roared over the fenlands, Merivale would sometimes take Mrs. Wickett aside in the lobby and whisper: "Look after him, you know. His chest . . . it puts a strain on his heart. Nothing really wrong with him—only anno domini, but that's the most fatal complaint of all, in the end."

Anno domini . . . by Jove, yes. Born in 1848, and taken to the Great Exhibition as a toddling child—not many people still alive could boast a thing like that. Besides, Chips could even remember Brookfield in Wetherby's time. A phenomenon, that was. Wetherby had been an old

man in those days—1870—easy to remember because of the Franco-Prussian War. Chips had put in for Brookfield after a year at Melbury, which he hadn't liked, because he had been ragged there a good deal. But Brookfield he *had* liked, almost from the beginning. He remembered that day of his preliminary interview—sunny June, with the air full of flower scents and the plick-plock of cricket on the pitch. Brookfield was playing Barnhurst, and one of the Barnhurst boys, a chubby little fellow, made a brilliant century. Queer that a thing like that should stay in the memory so clearly. Wetherby himself was very fatherly and courteous; he must have been ill then, poor chap, for he died during the summer vacation, before Chips began his first term. But the two had seen and spoken to each other, anyway.

Chips often thought, as he sat by the fire at Mrs. Wickett's: I am probably the only man in the world who has a vivid recollection of old Wetherby. . . . Vivid, yes; it was a frequent picture in his mind, that summer day with the sunlight filtering through the dust in Wetherby's study. "You are a young man, Mr. Chipping, and Brookfield is an old foundation. Youth and age often combine well. Give your enthusiasm to Brookfield, and Brookfield will give you something in return. And don't let anyone play tricks with you. I—er—gather that discipline was not always your strong point at Melbury?"

"Well, no, perhaps not, sir."

"Never mind; you're full young; it's largely a matter of experience. You have another chance here. Take up a firm attitude from the beginning—that's the secret of it."

Perhaps it was. He remembered that first tremendous ordeal of taking prep; a September sunset more than half a century ago; Big Hall full of lusty barbarians ready to pounce on him as their legitimate prey. His youth, fresh-complexioned, high-collared, and side-whiskered (odd fashions people followed in those days), at the mercy of five hundred unprincipled ruffians to whom the baiting of new masters was a fine art, an exciting sport, and something of a tradition. Decent little beggars individually, but, as a mob, just pitiless and implacable. The sudden hush as he took his place at the desk on the dais; the scowl he assumed to cover his inward nervousness; the tall clock ticking behind him, and the smells of ink and varnish; the last blood-red rays slanting in slabs through the stained-glass windows. Someone dropped a desk lid. Quickly, he must take everyone by surprise; he must show that there was no nonsense about him. "You there in the fifth row—you with the red hair—what's your name?" "Colley, sir." "Very well, Colley, you have a hundred lines." No trouble at all after that. He had won his first round.

And years later, when Colley was an alderman of the City of London and a baronet and various other things, he sent his son (also red-haired) to Brookfield, and Chips would say: "Colley, your father was the first boy I ever punished when I came here twenty-five years ago. He

deserved it then, and you deserve it now." How they all laughed; and how Sir Richard laughed when his son wrote home the story in next Sunday's letter!

And again, years after that, many years after that, there was an even better joke. For another Colley had just arrived—son of the Colley who was a son of the first Colley. And Chips would say, punctuating his remarks with that little "umph-um" that had by then become a habit with him: "Colley, you are—umph—a splendid example of—umph—inherited traditions. I remember your grandfather—umph—he could never grasp the Ablative Absolute. A stupid fellow, your grandfather. And your father, too—umph—I remember him—he used to sit at that far desk by the wall—he wasn't much better, either. But I do believe—my dear Colley —that you are—umph—the biggest fool of the lot!" Roars of laughter.

A great joke, this growing old—but a sad joke, too, in a way. And as Chips sat by his fire with autumn gales rattling the windows, the waves of humor and sadness swept over him very often until tears fell, so that when Mrs. Wickett came in with his cup of tea she did not know whether he had been laughing or crying. And neither did Chips himself.

Chapter 2

ACROSS THE ROAD BEHIND A RAMPART of ancient elms lay Brookfield, russet under its autumn mantle of creeper. A group of eighteenth-century buildings centred upon a quadrangle, and there were acres of playing fields beyond; then came the small dependent village and the open fen country. Brookfield, as Wetherby had said, was an old foundation; established in the reign of Elizabeth, as a grammar school, it might, with better luck, have become as famous as Harrow. Its luck, however, had been not so good; the School went up and down, dwindling almost to nonexistence at one time, becoming almost illustrious at another. It was during one of these latter periods, in the reign of the first George, that the main structure had been rebuilt and large additions made. Later, after the Napoleonic Wars and until mid-Victorian days, the School declined again, both in numbers and in repute. Wetherby, who came in 1840, restored its fortunes somewhat; but its subsequent history never raised it to front-rank status. It was, nevertheless, a good school of the second rank. Several notable families supported it; it supplied fair samples of the history-making men of the age—judges, members of parliament, colonial administrators, a few peers and bishops. Mostly, however, it turned out merchants, manufacturers, and professional

men, with a good sprinkling of country squires and parsons. It was the sort of school which, when mentioned, would sometimes make snobbish people confess that they rather thought they had heard of it.

But if it had not been this sort of school it would probably not have taken Chips. For Chips, in any social or academic sense, was just as respectable, but no more brilliant, than Brookfield itself.

It had taken him some time to realize this, at the beginning. Not that he was boastful or conceited, but he had been, in his early twenties, as ambitious as most other young men at such an age. His dream had been to get a headship eventually, or at any rate a senior mastership in a really first-class school; it was only gradually, after repeated trials and failures, that he realized the inadequacy of his qualifications. His degree, for instance, was not particularly good, and his discipline, though good enough and improving, was not absolutely reliable under all conditions. He had no private means and no family connections of any importance. About 1880, after he had been at Brookfield a decade, he began to recognize that the odds were heavily against his being able to better himself by moving elsewhere; but about that time, also, the possibility of staying where he was began to fill a comfortable niche in his mind. At forty, he was rooted, settled, and quite happy. At fifty, he was the doyen of the staff. At sixty, under a new and youthful Head, he *was* Brookfield—the guest of honor at Old Brookfeldian dinners, the court of appeal in all matters affecting Brookfield history and traditions. And in 1913, when he turned sixty-five, he retired, was presented with a check and a writing desk and a clock, and went across the road to live at Mrs. Wickett's. A decent career, decently closed; three cheers for old Chips, they all shouted, at that uproarious end-of-term dinner.

Three cheers, indeed; but there was more to come, an unguessed epilogue, an encore played to a tragic audience.

Chapter 3

IT WAS A SMALL BUT VERY COMFORTABLE and sunny room that Mrs. Wickett let to him. The house itself was ugly and pretentious; but that didn't matter. It was convenient—that was the main thing. For he liked, if the weather were mild enough, to stroll across to the playing fields in an afternoon and watch the games. He liked to smile and exchange a few words with the boys when they touched their caps to him. He made a special point of getting to know all the new boys and having them to tea with him during their first term. He always ordered a

walnut cake with pink icing from Reddaway's, in the village, and during the winter term there were crumpets, too—a little pile of them in front of the fire, soaked in butter so that the bottom one lay in a little shallow pool. His guests found it fun to watch him make tea—mixing careful spoonfuls from different caddies. And he would ask the new boys where they lived, and if they had family connections at Brookfield. He kept watch to see that their plates were never empty, and punctually at five, after the session had lasted an hour, he would glance at the clock and say: "Well—umph—it's been very delightful—umph—meeting you like this—I'm sorry—umph—you can't stay. . . ." And he would smile and shake hands with them in the porch, leaving them to race across the road to the School with their comments. "Decent old boy, Chips. Gives you a jolly good tea, anyhow, and you *do* know when he wants you to push off. . . ."

And Chips also would be making his comments—to Mrs. Wickett when she entered his room to clear away the remains of the party. "A most—umph—interesting time, Mrs. Wickett. Young Branksome tells me —umph—that his uncle was Major Collingwood—the Collingwood we had here in—umph—nought-two, I think it was. Dear me, I remember Collingwood very well. I once thrashed him—umph—for climbing on to the gymnasium roof—to get a ball out of the gutter. Might have—umph —broken his neck, the young fool. Do you remember him, Mrs. Wickett? He must have been in your time."

Mrs. Wickett, before she saved money, had been in charge of the linen room at the School.

"Yes, I knew 'im, sir. Cheeky, 'e was to me, gener'ly. But we never 'ad no bad words between us. Just cheeky-like. 'E never meant no harm. That kind never does, sir. Wasn't it 'im that got the medal, sir?"

"Yes, a D.S.O."

"Will you be wanting anything else, sir?"

"Nothing more now—umph—till chapel time. He was killed—in Egypt, I think. . . . Yes—umph—you can bring my supper about then."

"Very good, sir."

A pleasant, placid life, at Mrs. Wickett's. He had no worries; his pension was adequate, and there was a little money saved up besides. He could afford everything and anything he wanted. His room was furnished simply and with school-masterly taste: a few bookshelves and sporting trophies; a mantelpiece crowded with fixture cards and signed photographs of boys and men; a worn Turkey carpet; big easy-chairs; pictures on the wall of the Acropolis and the Forum. Nearly everything had come out of his old housemaster's room in School House. The books were chiefly classical, the classics having been his subject; there was, however, a seasoning of history and belles-lettres. There was also a bottom shelf piled up with cheap editions of detective novels. Chips enjoyed these. Sometimes he took down Vergil or Xenophon and read for a few moments, but he was soon back again with Doctor Thorndyke or Inspector

French. He was not, despite his long years of assiduous teaching, a very profound classical scholar; indeed, he thought of Latin and Greek far more as dead languages from which English gentlemen ought to know a few quotations than as living tongues that had ever been spoken by living people. He liked those short leading articles in the *Times* that introduced a few tags that he recognized. To be among the dwindling number of people who understood such things was to him a kind of secret and valued freemasonry; it represented, he felt, one of the chief benefits to be derived from a classical education.

So there he lived, at Mrs. Wickett's, with his quiet enjoyments of reading and talking and remembering; an old man, white-haired and only a little bald, still fairly active for his years, drinking tea, receiving callers, busying himself with corrections for the next edition of the Brookfeldian Directory, writing his occasional letters in thin, spidery, but very legible script. He had new masters to tea, as well as new boys. There were two of them that autumn term, and as they were leaving after their visit one of them commented: "Quite a character, the old boy, isn't he? All that fuss about mixing the tea—a typical bachelor, if ever there was one."

Which was oddly incorrect; because Chips was not a bachelor at all. He had married; though it was so long ago that none of the staff at Brookfield could remember his wife.

Chapter 4

THERE CAME TO HIM, stirred by the warmth of the fire and the gentle aroma of tea, a thousand tangled recollections of old times. Spring—the spring of 1896. He was forty-eight—an age at which a permanence of habits begins to be predictable. He had just been appointed housemaster; with this and his classical forms, he had made for himself a warm and busy corner of life. During the summer vacation he went up to the Lake District with Rowden, a colleague; they walked and climbed for a week, until Rowden had to leave suddenly on some family business. Chips stayed on alone at Wasdale Head, where he boarded in a small farmhouse.

One day, climbing on Great Gable, he noticed a girl waving excitedly from a dangerous-looking ledge. Thinking she was in difficulties, he hastened toward her, but in doing so slipped himself and wrenched his ankle. As it turned out, she was not in difficulties at all, but was merely signaling to a friend farther down the mountain; she was an expert

climber, better even than Chips, who was pretty good. Thus he found himself the rescued instead of the rescuer; and neither rôle was one for which he had much relish. For he did not, he would have said, care for women; he never felt at home or at ease with them; and that monstrous creature beginning to be talked about, the New Woman of the nineties, filled him with horror. He was a quiet, conventional person, and the world, viewed from the haven of Brookfield, seemed to him full of distasteful innovations; there was a fellow named Bernard Shaw who had the strangest and most reprehensible opinions; there was Ibsen, too, with his disturbing plays; and there was this new craze for bicycling which was being taken up by women equally with men. Chips did not hold with all this modern newness and freedom. He had a vague notion, if he ever formulated it, that nice women were weak, timid, and delicate, and that nice men treated them with a polite but rather distant chivalry. He had not, therefore, expected to find a woman on Great Gable; but, having encountered one who seemed to need masculine help, it was even more terrifying that she should turn the tables by helping him. For she did. She and her friend had to. He could scarcely walk, and it was a hard job getting him down the steep track to Wasdale.

Her name was Katherine Bridges; she was twenty-five—young enough to be Chips's daughter. She had blue, flashing eyes and freckled cheeks and smooth straw-colored hair. She too was staying at a farm, on holiday with a girl friend, and as she considered herself responsible for Chips's accident, she used to bicycle along the side of the lake to the house in which the quiet, middle-aged, serious-looking man lay resting.

That was how she thought of him at first. And he, because she rode a bicycle and was unafraid to visit a man alone in a farmhouse sitting room, wondered vaguely what the world was coming to. His sprain put him at her mercy, and it was soon revealed to him how much he might need that mercy. She was a governess out of a job, with a little money saved up; she read and admired Ibsen; she believed that women ought to be admitted to the universities; she even thought they ought to have a vote. In politics she was a radical, with leanings toward the views of people like Bernard Shaw and William Morris. All her ideas and opinions she poured out to Chips during those summer afternoons at Wasdale Head; and he, because he was not very articulate, did not at first think it worth while to contradict them. Her friend went away, but she stayed; what *could* you do with such a person, Chips thought. He used to hobble with sticks along a footpath leading to the tiny church; there was a stone slab on the wall, and it was comfortable to sit down, facing the sunlight and the green-brown majesty of the Gable and listening to the chatter of —well, yes, Chips had to admit it—a very beautiful girl.

He had never met anyone like her. He had always thought that the modern type, this "new woman" business, would repel him; and here she was, making him positively look forward to the glimpse of her safety

bicycle careering along the lakeside road. And she, too, had never met anyone like *him*. She had always thought that middle-aged men who read the *Times* and disapproved of modernity were terrible bores; yet here he was, claiming her interest and attention far more than youths of her own age. She liked him, initially, because he was so hard to get to know, because he had gentle and quiet manners, because his opinions dated from those utterly impossible seventies and eighties and even earlier —yet were, for all that, so thoroughly honest; and because—because his eyes were brown and he looked charming when he smiled. "Of course, *I* shall call you Chips, too," she said, when she learned that was his nickname at school.

Within a week they were head over heels in love; before Chips could walk without a stick, they considered themselves engaged; and they were married in London a week before the beginning of the autumn term.

Chapter 5

WHEN CHIPS, DREAMING THROUGH THE HOURS at Mrs. Wickett's, recollected those days, he used to look down at his feet and wonder which one it was that had performed so signal a service. That, the trivial cause of so many momentous happenings, was the one thing of which details evaded him. But he resaw the glorious hump of the Gable (he had never visited the Lake District since), and the mouse-gray depths of Wastwater under the Screes; he could resmell the washed air after heavy rain, and refollow the ribbon of the pass across to Sty Head. So clearly it lingered, that time of dizzy happiness, those evening strolls by the waterside, her cool voice and her gay laughter. She had been a very happy person, always.

They had both been so eager, planning a future together; but he had been rather serious about it, even a little awed. It would be all right, of course, her coming to Brookfield; other housemasters were married. And she liked boys, she told him, and would enjoy living among them. "Oh, Chips, I'm so glad you are what you are. I was afraid you were a solicitor or a stockbroker or a dentist or a man with a big cotton business in Manchester. When I first met you, I mean. Schoolmastering's so different, so important, don't you think? To be influencing those who are going to grow up and matter to the world . . ."

Chips said he hadn't thought of it like that—or, at least, not often. He did his best; that was all anyone could do in any job.

426

"Yes, of course, Chips. I do love you for saying simple things like that."

And one morning—another memory gem-clear when he turned to it —he had for some reason been afflicted with an acute desire to depreciate himself and all his attainments. He had told her of his only mediocre degree, of his occasional difficulties of discipline, of the certainty that he would never get a promotion, and of his complete ineligibility to marry a young and ambitious girl. And at the end of it all she had laughed in answer.

She had no parents and was married from the house of an aunt in Ealing. On the night before the wedding, when Chips left the house to return to his hotel, she said, with mock gravity: "This is an occasion, you know—this last farewell of ours. I feel rather like a new boy beginning his first term with you. Not scared, mind you—but just, for once, in a thoroughly respectful mood. Shall I call you 'sir'—or would 'Mr. Chips' be the right thing? 'Mr. Chips,' I think. Good-bye, then—good-bye, Mr. Chips. . . ."

(A hansom clop-clopping in the roadway; green-pale gas lamps flickering on a wet pavement; newsboys shouting something about South Africa; Sherlock Holmes in Baker Street.)

"Good-bye, Mr. Chips. . . ."

Chapter 6

THERE HAD FOLLOWED THEN a time of such happiness that Chips, remembering it long afterward, hardly believed it could ever have happened before or since in the world. For his marriage was a triumphant success. Katherine conquered Brookfield as she had conquered Chips; she was immensely popular with boys and masters alike. Even the wives of the masters, tempted at first to be jealous of one so young and lovely, could not long resist her charms.

But most remarkable of all was the change she made in Chips. Till his marriage he had been a dry and rather neutral sort of person; liked and thought well of by Brookfield in general, but not of the stuff that makes for great popularity or that stirs great affection. He had been at Brookfield for over a quarter of a century, long enough to have established himself as a decent fellow and a hard worker; but just too long for anyone to believe him capable of ever being much more. He had, in fact, already begun to sink into that creeping dry rot of pedagogy which is the worst and ultimate pitfall of the profession; giving the same lessons

year after year had formed a groove into which the other affairs of his life adjusted themselves with insidious ease. He worked well; he was conscientious; he was a fixture that gave service, satisfaction, confidence, everything except inspiration.

And then came this astonishing girl-wife whom nobody had expected —least of all Chips himself. She made him, to all appearances, a new man; though most of the newness was really a warming to life of things that were old, imprisoned, and unguessed. His eyes gained sparkle; his mind, which was adequately if not brilliantly equipped, began to move more adventurously. The one thing he had always had, a sense of humor, blossomed into a sudden richness to which his years lent maturity. He began to feel a greater sureness; his discipline improved to a point at which it could become, in a sense, less rigid; he became more popular. When he had first come to Brookfield he had aimed to be loved, honored, and obeyed—but obeyed, at any rate. Obedience he had secured, and honor had been granted him; but only now came love, the sudden love of boys for a man who was kind without being soft, who understood them well enough, but not too much, and whose private happiness linked them with their own. He began to make little jokes, the sort that schoolboys like—mnemonics and puns that raised laughs and at the same time imprinted something in the mind. There was one that never failed to please, though it was only a sample of many others. Whenever his Roman History forms came to deal with the Lex Canuleia, the law that permitted patricians to marry plebeians, Chips used to add: "So that, you see, if Miss Plebs wanted Mr. Patrician to marry her, and he said he couldn't, she probably replied: 'Oh yes, you can, you liar!' " Roars of laughter.

And Kathie broadened his views and opinions, also, giving him an outlook far beyond the roofs and turrets of Brookfield, so that he saw his country as something deep and gracious to which Brookfield was but one of many feeding streams. She had a cleverer brain than his, and he could not confute her ideas even if and when he disagreed with them; he remained, for instance, a Conservative in politics, despite all her radical-socialist talk. But even where he did not accept, he absorbed; her young idealism worked upon his maturity to produce an amalgam very gentle and wise.

Sometimes she persuaded him completely. Brookfield, for example, ran a mission in East London, to which boys and parents contributed generously with money but rarely with personal contact. It was Katherine who suggested that a team from the mission should come up to Brookfield and play one of the School's elevens at soccer. The idea was so revolutionary that from anyone but Katherine it could not have survived its first frosty reception. To introduce a group of slum boys to the serene pleasances of better-class youngsters seemed at first a wanton stirring of all kinds of things that had better be left untouched. The whole staff

was against it, and the School, if its opinion could have been taken, was probably against it too. Everyone was certain that the East End lads would be hooligans, or else that they would be made to feel uncomfortable; anyhow, there would be "incidents," and everyone would be confused and upset. Yet Katherine persisted.

"Chips," she said, "they're wrong, you know, and I'm right. I'm looking ahead to the future, they and you are looking back to the past. England isn't always going to be divided into officers and 'other ranks.' And those Poplar boys are just as important—to England—as Brookfield is. You've got to have them here, Chips. You can't satisfy your conscience by writing a check for a few guineas and keeping them at arm's length. Besides, they're proud of Brookfield—just as you are. Years hence, maybe, boys of that sort will be coming here—a few of them, at any rate. Why not? Why ever not? Chips, dear, remember this is eighteen-ninety-seven—not sixty-seven, when you were up at Cambridge. You got your ideas well stuck in those days, and good ideas they were too, a lot of them. But a few—just a few, Chips—want unsticking. . . ."

Rather to her surprise, he gave way and suddenly became a keen advocate of the proposal, and the *volte-face* was so complete that the authorities were taken unawares and found themselves consenting to the dangerous experiment. The boys from Poplar arrived at Brookfield one Saturday afternoon, played soccer with the School's second team, were honorably defeated by seven goals to five, and later had high tea with the School team in the Dining Hall. They then met the Head and were shown over the School, and Chips saw them off at the railway station in the evening. Everything had passed without the slightest hitch of any kind, and it was clear that the visitors were taking away with them as fine an impression as they had left behind.

They took back with them also the memory of a charming woman who had met them and talked to them; for once, years later, during the War, a private stationed at a big military camp near Brookfield called on Chips and said he had been one of that first visiting team. Chips gave him tea and chatted with him, till at length, shaking hands, the man said: "And 'ow's the missus, sir? I remember her very well."

"Do you?" Chips answered, eagerly. "Do you remember her?"

"Rather. I should think anyone would."

And Chips replied: "They don't, you know. At least, not here. Boys come and go; new faces all the time; memories don't last. Even masters don't stay forever. Since last year—when old Gribble retired—he's—um —the School butler—there hasn't been anyone here who ever saw my wife. She died, you know, less than a year after your visit. In ninety-eight."

"I'm real sorry to 'ear that, sir. There's two or three o' my pals, any-

how, who remember 'er clear as anything, though we did only see 'er that wunst. Yes, we remember 'er, all right."

"I'm very glad. . . . That was a grand day we all had—and a fine game, too."

"One o' the best days aht I ever 'ad in me life. Wish it was then and not nah—straight, I do. I'm off to Frawnce to-morrer."

A month or so later Chips heard that he had been killed at Passchendaele.

Chapter 7

AND SO IT STOOD, A WARM AND VIVID PATCH in his life, casting a radiance that glowed in a thousand recollections. Twilight at Mrs. Wickett's, when the School bell clanged for call-over, brought them back to him in a cloud—Katherine scampering along the stone corridors, laughing beside him at some "howler" in an essay he was marking, taking the cello part in a Mozart trio for the School concert, her creamy arm sweeping over the brown sheen of the instrument. She had been a good player and a fine musician. And Katherine turned and muffed for the December house matches, Katherine at the Garden Party that followed Speech Day Prize-giving, Katherine tendering her advice in any little problem that arose. Good advice, too—which he did not always take, but which always influenced him.

"Chips, dear, I'd let them off if I were you. After all, it's nothing very serious."

"I know. I'd like to let them off, but if I do I'm afraid they'll do it again."

"Try telling them that, frankly, and give them the chance."

"I might."

And there were other things, occasionally, that *were* serious.

"You know, Chips, having all these hundreds of boys cooped up here is really an unnatural arrangement, when you come to think about it. So that when anything does occur that oughtn't to, don't you think it's a bit unfair to come down on them as if it were their own fault for being here?"

"Don't know about that, Kathie, but I do know that for everybody's sake we have to be pretty strict about this sort of thing. One black sheep can contaminate others."

"After he himself has been contaminated to begin with. After all, that's what probably *did* happen, isn't it?"

"Maybe. We can't help it. Anyhow, I believe Brookfield is better than a lot of other schools. All the more reason to keep it so."

"But this boy, Chips . . . you're going to sack him?"

"The Head probably will, when I tell him."

"And you're going to tell the Head?"

"It's a duty, I'm afraid."

"Couldn't you think about it a bit . . . talk to the boy again . . . find out how it began . . . After all—apart from this business—isn't he rather a nice boy?"

"Oh, he's all right."

"Then, Chips dear, don't you think there *ought* to be some other way . . ."

And so on. About once in ten times he was adamant and wouldn't be persuaded. In about half of these exceptional cases he afterward rather wished he had taken her advice. And years later, whenever he had trouble with a boy, he was always at the mercy of a softening wave of reminiscence; the boy would stand there, waiting to be told his punishment, and would see, if he were observant, the brown eyes twinkle into a shine that told him all was well. But he did not guess that at such a moment Chips was remembering something that had happened long before he was born; that Chips was thinking: Young ruffian, I'm hanged if *I* can think of any reason to let him off, but I'll bet *she* would have done!

But she had not always pleaded for leniency. On rather rare occasions she urged severity where Chips was inclined to be forgiving. "I don't like his type, Chips. He's too cocksure of himself. If he's looking for trouble I should certainly let him have it."

What a host of little incidents, all deep-buried in the past—problems that had once been urgent, arguments that had once been keen, anecdotes that were funny only because one remembered the fun. Did any emotion really matter when the last trace of it had vanished from human memory; and if that were so, what a crowd of emotions clung to him as to their last home before annihilation! He must be kind to them, must treasure them in his mind before their long sleep. That affair of Archer's resignation, for instance—a queer business, that was. And that affair about the rat that Dunster put in the organ loft while old Ogilvie was taking choir practice. Ogilvie was dead and Dunster drowned at Jutland; of others who had witnessed or heard of the incident, probably most had forgotten. And it had been like that, with other incidents, for centuries. He had a sudden vision of thousands and thousands of boys, from the age of Elizabeth onward; dynasty upon dynasty of masters; long epochs of Brookfield history that had left not even a ghostly record. Who knew why the old fifth-form room was called "the Pit?" There was probably a reason, to begin with; but it had since been lost—lost like the lost books of Livy. And what happened at Brookfield when Cromwell fought at Naseby, near by? How did Brookfield react to the great scare of the

"Forty-Five?" Was there a whole holiday when news came of Waterloo? And so on, up to the earliest time that he himself could remember— 1870, and Wetherby saying, by way of small talk after their first and only interview: "Looks as if we shall have to settle with the Prussians ourselves one of these fine days, eh?"

When Chips remembered things like this he often felt that he would write them down and make a book of them; and during his years at Mrs. Wickett's he sometimes went even so far as to make desultory notes in an exercise book. But he was soon brought up against difficulties—the chief one being that writing tired him, both mentally and physically. Somehow, too, his recollections lost much of their flavor when they were written down; that story about Rushton and the sack of potatoes, for instance—it would seem quite tame in print, but Lord, how funny it had been at the time! It was funny, too, to remember it; though perhaps if you didn't remember Rushton . . . and who would, anyway, after all those years? It was such a long time ago . . . Mrs. Wickett, did you ever know a fellow named Rushton? Before your time, I dare say . . . went to Burma in some government job . . . or was it Borneo? . . . Very funny fellow, Rushton. . . .

And there he was, dreaming again before the fire, dreaming of times and incidents in which he alone could take secret interest. Funny and sad, comic and tragic, they all mixed up in his mind, and some day, however hard it proved, he *would* sort them out and make a book of them. . . .

Chapter 8

AND THERE WAS ALWAYS IN HIS MIND that spring day in ninety-eight when he had paced through Brookfield village as in some horrifying nightmare, half struggling to escape into an outside world where the sun still shone and where everything had happened differently. Young Faulkner had met him there in the lane outside the School. "Please, sir, may I have the afternoon off? My people are coming up."

"Eh? What's that? Oh yes, yes. . . ."

"Can I miss Chapel, too, sir?"

"Yes . . . yes . . ."

"And may I go to the station to meet them?"

He nearly answered: "You can go to blazes for all I care. My wife is dead and my child is dead, and I wish I were dead myself."

Actually he nodded and stumbled on. He did not want to talk to

anybody or to receive condolences; he wanted to get used to things, if he could, before facing the kind words of others. He took his fourth form as usual after call-over, setting them grammar to learn by heart while he himself stayed at his desk in a cold, continuing trance. Suddenly someone said: "Please, sir, there are a lot of letters for you."

So there were; he had been leaning his elbows on them; they were all addressed to him by name. He tore them open one after the other, but each contained nothing but a blank sheet of paper. He thought in a distant way that it was rather peculiar, but he made no comment; the incident gave hardly an impact upon his vastly greater preoccupations. Not till days afterward did he realize that it had been a piece of April foolery.

They had died on the same day, the mother and the child just born; on April 1, 1898.

Chapter 9

CHIPS CHANGED his more commodious apartments in School House for his old original bachelor quarters. He thought at first he would give up his housemastership, but the Head persuaded him otherwise; and later he was glad. The work gave him something to do, filled up an emptiness in his mind and heart. He was different; everyone noticed it. Just as marriage had added something, so did bereavement; after the first stupor of grief he became suddenly the kind of man whom boys, at any rate, unhesitatingly classed as "old." It was not that he was less active; he could still knock up a half century on the cricket field; nor was it that he had lost any interest or keenness in his work. Actually, too, his hair had been graying for years; yet now, for the first time, people seemed to notice it. He was fifty. Once, after some energetic fives, during which he had played as well as many a fellow half his age, he overheard a boy saying: "Not half bad for an old chap like him."

Chips, when he was over eighty, used to recount that incident with many chuckles. "Old at fifty, eh? Umph—it was Naylor who said that, and Naylor can't be far short of fifty himself by now! I wonder if he still thinks that fifty's such an age? Last I heard of him, he was lawyering, and lawyers live long—look at Halsbury—umph—Chancellor at eighty-two, and died at ninety-nine. There's an—umph—age for you! Too old at fifty —why, fellows like that are too *young* at fifty. . . . I was myself . . . a mere infant. . . ."

433

And there was a sense in which it was true. For with the new century there settled upon Chips a mellowness that gathered all his developing mannerisms and his oft-repeated jokes into a single harmony. No longer did he have those slight and occasional disciplinary troubles, or feel diffident about his own work and worth. He found that his pride in Brookfield reflected back, giving him cause for pride in himself and his position. It was a service that gave him freedom to be supremely and completely himself. He had won, by seniority and ripeness, an uncharted no-man's-land of privilege; he had acquired the right to those gentle eccentricities that so often attack schoolmasters and parsons. He wore his gown till it was almost too tattered to hold together; and when he stood on the wooden bench by Big Hall steps to take call-over, it was with an air of mystic abandonment to ritual. He held the School List, a long sheet curling over a board; and each boy, as he passed, spoke his own name for Chips to verify and then tick off on the list. That verifying glance was an easy and favorite subject of mimicry throughout the School —steel-rimmed spectacles slipping down the nose, eyebrows lifted, one a little higher than the other, a gaze half rapt, half quizzical. And on windy days, with gown and white hair and School List fluttering in uproarious confusion, the whole thing became a comic turn sandwiched between afternoon games and the return to classes.

Some of those names, in little snatches of a chorus, recurred to him ever afterward without any effort of memory. . . . Ainsworth, Attwood, Avonmore, Babcock, Baggs, Barnard, Bassenthwaite, Battersby, Beccles, Bedford-Marshall, Bentley, Best . . .

Another one:—

. . . Unsley, Vailes, Wadham, Wagstaff, Wallington, Waters Primus, Waters Secundus, Watling, Waveney, Webb . . .

And yet another that comprised, as he used to tell his fourth-form Latinists, an excellent example of a hexameter:—

. . . Lancaster, Latton, Lemare, Lytton-Bosworth, MacGonigall, Mansfield . . .

Where had they all gone to, he often pondered; those threads he had once held together, how far had they scattered, some to break, others to weave into unknown patterns? The strange randomness of the world beguiled him, that randomness which never would, so long as the world lasted, give meaning to those choruses again.

And behind Brookfield, as one may glimpse a mountain behind another mountain when the mist clears, he saw the world of change and conflict; and he saw it, more than he realized, with the remembered eyes of Kathie. She had not been able to bequeath him all her mind, still less the brilliance of it; but she had left him with a calmness and a poise that accorded well with his own inward emotions. It was typical of him that he did not share the general jingo bitterness against the Boers. Not that he was a pro-Boer—he was far too traditional for that, and he disliked the

kind of people who *were* pro-Boers; but still, it did cross his mind at times that the Boers were engaged in a struggle that had a curious similarity to those of certain English history-book heroes—Hereward the Wake, for instance, or Caractacus. He once tried to shock his fifth form by suggesting this, but they only thought it was one of his little jokes.

However heretical he might be about the Boers, he was orthodox about Mr. Lloyd George and the famous Budget. He did not care for either of them. And when, years later, L.G. came as the guest of honor to a Brookfield Speech Day, Chips said, on being presented to him: "Mr. Lloyd George, I am nearly old enough—umph—to remember you as a young man, and—umph—I confess that you seem to me—umph—to have improved—umph—a great deal." The Head, standing with them, was rather aghast; but L.G. laughed heartily and talked to Chips more than to anyone else during the ceremonial that followed.

"Just like Chips," was commented afterward. "He gets away with it. I suppose at that age anything you say to anybody is all right. . . ."

Chapter 10

IN 1900 OLD MELDRUM, who had succeeded Wetherby as Head and had held office for three decades, died suddenly from pneumonia; and in the interval before the appointment of a successor, Chips became Acting Head of Brookfield. There was just the faintest chance that the Governors might make the appointment a permanent one; but Chips was not really disappointed when they brought in a youngster of thirty-seven, glittering with Firsts and Blues and with the kind of personality that could reduce Big Hall to silence by the mere lifting of an eyebrow. Chips was not in the running with that kind of person; he never had been and never would be, and he knew it. He was an altogether milder and less ferocious animal.

Those years before his retirement in 1913 were studded with sharply remembered pictures.

A May morning; the clang of the School bell at an unaccustomed time; everyone summoned to assemble in Big Hall. Ralston, the new Head, very pontifical and aware of himself, fixing the multitude with a cold, presaging severity. "You will all be deeply grieved to hear that His Majesty King Edward the Seventh died this morning. . . . There will be no school this afternoon, but a service will be held in the Chapel at four-thirty."

A summer morning on the railway line near Brookfield. The rail-

waymen were on strike, soldiers were driving the engines, stones had been thrown at trains. Brookfield boys were patrolling the line, thinking the whole business great fun. Chips, who was in charge, stood a little way off, talking to a man at the gate of a cottage. Young Cricklade approached. "Please, sir, what shall we do if we meet any strikers?"

"Would you like to meet one?"

"I—I don't know, sir."

God bless the boy—he talked of them as if they were queer animals out of a zoo! "Well, here you are, then—umph—you can meet Mr. Jones—he's a striker. When he's on duty he has charge of the signal box at the station. You've put your life in his hands many a time."

Afterward the story went round the School: There was Chips, talking to a striker. Talking to a striker. Might have been quite friendly, the way they were talking together.

Chips, thinking it over a good many times, always added to himself that Kathie would have approved, and would also have been amused.

Because always, whatever happened and however the avenues of politics twisted and curved, he had faith in England, in English flesh and blood, and in Brookfield as a place whose ultimate worth depended on whether she fitted herself into the English scene with dignity and without disproportion. He had been left a vision that grew clearer with each year —of an England for which days of ease were nearly over, of a nation steering into channels where a hair's breadth of error might be catastrophic. He remembered the Diamond Jubilee; there had been a whole holiday at Brookfield, and he had taken Kathie to London to see the procession. That old and legendary lady, sitting in her carriage like some crumbling wooden doll, had symbolized impressively so many things that, like herself, were nearing an end. Was it only the century, or was it an epoch?

And then that frenzied Edwardian decade, like an electric lamp that goes brighter and whiter just before it burns itself out.

Strikes and lockouts, champagne suppers and unemployed marchers, Chinese labor, tariff reform, *H.M.S. Dreadnought,* Marconi, Home Rule for Ireland, Doctor Crippen, suffragettes, the lines of Chatalja. . . .

An April evening, windy and rainy; the fourth form construing Vergil, not very intelligently, for there was exciting news in the papers; young Grayson, in particular, was careless and preoccupied. A quiet, nervous boy.

"Grayson, stay behind—umph—after the rest."

Then:—

"Grayson, I don't want to be—umph—severe, because you are generally pretty good—umph —in your work, but to-day—you don't seem— umph—to have been trying at all. Is anything the matter?"

"N-no, sir."

"Well—umph—we'll say no more about it, but—umph—I shall expect better things next time."

Next morning it was noised around the School that Grayson's father had sailed on the *Titanic,* and that no news had yet come through as to his fate.

Grayson was excused lessons; for a whole day the School centred emotionally upon his anxieties. Then came news that his father had been among those rescued.

Chips shook hands with the boy. "Well, umph—I'm delighted, Grayson. A happy ending. You must be feeling pretty pleased with life."

"Y-yes, sir."

A quiet, nervous boy. And it was Grayson Senior, not Junior, with whom Chips was destined later to condole.

Chapter 11

AND THEN THE ROW WITH RALSTON. Funny thing, Chips had never liked him; he was efficient, ruthless, ambitious, but not, somehow, very likable. He had, admittedly, raised the status of Brookfield as a school, and for the first time in memory there was a longish waiting list. Ralston was a live wire; a fine power transmitter, but you had to beware of him.

Chips had never bothered to beware of him; he was not attracted by the man, but he served him willingly enough and quite loyally. Or, rather, he served Brookfield. He knew that Ralston did not like him, either; but that didn't seem to matter. He felt himself sufficiently protected by age and seniority from the fate of other masters whom Ralston had failed to like.

Then suddenly, in 1908, when he had just turned sixty, came Ralston's urbane ultimatum. "Mr. Chipping, have you ever thought you would like to retire?"

Chips stared about him in that book-lined study, startled by the question, wondering why Ralston should have asked it. He said, at length: "No—umph—I can't say that—umph—I have thought much about it—umph—yet."

"Well, Mr. Chipping, the suggestion is there for you to consider. The Governors would, of course, agree to your being adequately pensioned."

Abruptly Chips flamed up. "But—umph—I don't want—to retire. I don't—umph—need to consider it."

"Nevertheless, I suggest that you do."

"But—umph—I don't see—why—I should!"

"In that case, things are going to be a little difficult."

"Difficult? Why—difficult?"

And then they set to, Ralston getting cooler and harder, Chips getting warmer and more passionate, till at last Ralston said, icily: "Since you force me to use plain words, Mr. Chipping, you shall have them. For some time past, you haven't been pulling your weight here. Your methods of teaching are slack and old-fashioned; your personal habits are slovenly; and you ignore my instructions in a way which, in a younger man, I should regard as rank insubordination. It won't do, Mr. Chipping, and you must ascribe it to my forbearance that I have put up with it so long."

"But—" Chips began, in sheer bewilderment; and then he took up isolated words out of that extraordinary indictment. "*Slovenly*—umph—you said—?"

"Yes, look at the gown you're wearing. I happen to know that that gown of yours is a subject of continual amusement throughout the School."

Chips knew it, too, but it had never seemed to him a very regrettable matter.

He went on: "And—you also said—umph—something about—*insubordination*—?"

"No, I didn't. I said that in a younger man I should have regarded it as that. In your case it's probably a mixture of slackness and obstinacy. This question of Latin pronunciation, for instance—I think I told you years ago that I wanted the new style used throughout the School. The other masters obeyed me; you prefer to stick to your old methods, and the result is simply chaos and inefficiency."

At last Chips had something tangible that he could tackle. "Oh, *that!*" he answered scornfully. "Well, I—umph—I admit that I don't agree with the new pronunciation. I never did. Umph—a lot of nonsense, in my opinion. Making boys say 'Kickero' at school when—umph—for the rest of their lives they'll say 'Cicero'—if they ever—umph—say it at all. And instead of 'vicissim'—God bless my soul—you'd make them say, 'We kiss 'im'! Umph—umph!" And he chuckled momentarily, forgetting that he was in Ralston's study and not in his own friendly form room.

"Well, there you are, Mr. Chipping—that's just an example of what I complain of. You hold one opinion and I hold another, and, since you decline to give way, there can't very well be any alternative. I aim to make Brookfield a thoroughly up-to-date school. I'm a science man myself, but for all that I have no objection to the classics—provided that they are taught efficiently. Because they are dead languages is no reason why they should be dealt with in a dead educational technique. I understand,

Mr. Chipping, that your Latin and Greek lessons are exactly the same as they were when I began here ten years ago?"

Chips answered, slowly and with pride: "For that matter—umph—they are the same as when your predecessor—Mr. Meldrum—came here, and that—umph—was thirty-eight years ago. We began here, Mr. Meldrum and I—in—umph—in 1870. And it was—um—Mr. Meldrum's predecessor, Mr. Wetherby—who first approved my syllabus. 'You'll take the Cicero for the fourth,' he said to me. Cicero, too—not Kickero!"

"Very interesting, Mr. Chipping, but once again it proves my point —you live too much in the past, and not enough in the present and future. Times are changing, whether you realize it or not. Modern parents are beginning to demand something more for their three years' school fees than a few scraps of languages that nobody speaks. Besides, your boys don't learn even what they're supposed to learn. None of them last year got through the Lower Certificate."

And suddenly, in a torrent of thoughts too pressing to be put into words, Chips made answer to himself. These examinations and certificates and so on—what did they matter? And all this efficiency and up-to-dateness—what did *that* matter, either? Ralston was trying to run Brookfield like a factory—a factory for turning out a snob culture based on money and machines. The old gentlemanly traditions of family and broad acres were changing, as doubtless they were bound to; but instead of widening them to form a genuine inclusive democracy of duke and dustman, Ralston was narrowing them upon the single issue of a fat banking account. There never had been so many rich men's sons at Brookfield. The Speech Day Garden Party was like Ascot. Ralston met these wealthy fellows in London clubs and persuaded them that Brookfield was *the* coming school, and, since they couldn't buy their way into Eton or Harrow, they greedily swallowed the bait. Awful fellows, some of them—though others were decent enough. Financiers, company promoters, pill manufacturers. One of them gave his son five pounds a week pocket money. Vulgar . . . ostentatious . . . all the hectic rotten-ripeness of the age. . . . And once Chips had got into trouble because of some joke he had made about a boy's name. The boy wrote home about it, and his father sent an angry letter to Ralston. Touchy, no sense of humor, no sense of proportion—that was the matter with them, these new fellows. . . . No sense of proportion. And it was a sense of proportion, above all things, that Brookfield ought to teach—not so much Latin or Greek or Chemistry or Mechanics. And you couldn't expect to test that sense of proportion by setting papers and granting certificates. . . .

All this flashed through his mind in an instant of protest and indignation, but he did not say a word of it. He merely gathered his tattered gown together and with an "umph—umph" walked a few paces away. He had had enough of the argument. At the door he turned and

439

said: "I don't—umph—intend to resign—and you can—umph—do what you like about it!"

Looking back upon that scene in the calm perspective of a quarter of a century, Chips could find it in his heart to feel a little sorry for Ralston. Particularly when, as it happened, Ralston had been in such complete ignorance of the forces he was dealing with. So, for that matter, had Chips himself. Neither had correctly estimated the toughness of Brookfield tradition, and its readiness to defend itself and its defenders. For it had so chanced that a small boy, waiting to see Ralston that morning, had been listening outside the door during the whole of the interview; he had been thrilled by it, naturally, and had told his friends. Some of these, in a surprisingly short time, had told their parents; so that very soon it was common knowledge that Ralston had insulted Chips and had demanded his resignation. The amazing result was a spontaneous outburst of sympathy and partisanship such as Chips, in his wildest dreams, had never envisaged. He found, rather to his astonishment, that Ralston was thoroughly unpopular; he was feared and respected, but not liked; and in this issue of Chips the dislike rose to a point where it conquered fear and demolished even respect. There was talk of having some kind of public riot in the School if Ralston succeeded in banishing Chips. The masters, many of them young men who agreed that Chips was hopelessly old-fashioned, rallied round him nevertheless because they hated Ralston's slave driving and saw in the old veteran a likely champion. And one day the Chairman of the Governors, Sir John Rivers, visited Brookfield, ignored Ralston, and went direct to Chips. "A fine fellow, Rivers," Chips would say, telling the story to Mrs. Wickett for the dozenth time. "Not —umph—a very brilliant boy in class. I remember he could never— umph—master his verbs. And now—umph—I see in the papers—they've made him—umph a baronet. It just shows you—umph—it just shows you."

Sir John had said, on that morning in 1908, taking Chips by the arm as they walked round the deserted cricket pitches: "Chips, old boy, I hear you've been having the deuce of a row with Ralston. Sorry to hear about it, for your sake—but I want you to know that the Governors are with you to a man. We don't like the fellow a great deal. Very clever and all that, but a bit too clever, if you ask me. Claims to have doubled the School's endowment funds by some monkeying on the Stock Exchange. Dare say he has, but a chap like that wants watching. So if he starts chucking his weight about with you, tell him very politely he can go to the devil. The Governors don't want you to resign. Brookfield wouldn't be the same without you, and they know it. We all know it. You can stay here till you're a hundred if you feel like it—indeed, it's our hope that you will."

And at that—both then and often when he recounted it afterward —Chips broke down.

Chapter 12

SO HE STAYED ON AT BROOKFIELD, having as little to do with Ralston as possible. And in 1911 Ralston left, "to better himself"; he was offered the headship of one of the greater public schools. His successor was a man named Chatteris, whom Chips liked; he was even younger than Ralston had been—thirty-four. He was supposed to be very brilliant; at any rate, he was modern (Natural Sciences Tripos), friendly, and sympathetic. Recognizing in Chips a Brookfield institution, he courteously and wisely accepted the situation.

In 1913 Chips had had bronchitis and was off duty for nearly the whole of the winter term. It was that which made him decide to resign that summer, when he was sixty-five. After all, it was a good, ripe age; and Ralston's straight words had, in some ways, had an effect. He felt that it would not be fair to hang on if he could not decently do his job. Besides, he would not sever himself completely. He would take rooms across the road, with the excellent Mrs. Wickett who had once been linen-room maid; he could visit the School whenever he wanted, and could still, in a sense, remain a part of it.

At that final end-of-term dinner, in July 1913, Chips received his farewell presentations and made a speech. It was not a very long speech, but it had a good many jokes in it, and was made twice as long, perhaps, by the laughter that impeded its progress. There were several Latin quotations in it, as well as a reference to the Captain of the School, who, Chips said, had been guilty of exaggeration in speaking of his (Chips's) services to Brookfield. "But then—umph—he comes of an—umph—exaggerating family. I—um—remember—once—having to thrash his father —for it. [Laughter] I gave him one mark—umph—for a Latin translation, and he—umph—exaggerated the one into a seven! Umph—umph!" Roars of laughter and tumultuous cheers! A typical Chips remark, everyone thought.

And then he mentioned that he had been at Brookfield for forty-two years, and that he had been very happy there. "It has been my life," he said, simply. *"O mihi praeteritos referat si Jupiter annos. . . .* Umph —I need not—of course—translate. . . ." Much laughter. "I remember lots of changes at Brookfield. I remember the—um—the first bicycle. I remember when there was no gas or electric light and we used to have a member of the domestic staff called a lamp-boy—he did nothing else but clean and trim and light lamps throughout the School. I remember when there was a hard frost that lasted for seven weeks in the winter term—

there were no games, and the whole School learned to skate on the fens. Eighteen-eighty-something, that was. I remember when two thirds of the School went down with German measles and Big Hall was turned into a hospital ward. I remember the great bonfire we had on Mafeking night. It was lit too near the pavilion and we had to send for the fire brigade to put it out. And the firemen were having their own celebrations and most of them were—um—in a regrettable condition. [Laughter] I remember Mrs. Brool, whose photograph is still in the tuckshop; she served there until an uncle in Australia left her a lot of money. In fact, I remember so much that I often think I ought to write a book. Now what should I call it? 'Memories of Rod and Lines'—eh? [Cheers and laughter. That was a good one, people thought—one of Chips's best.] Well, well, perhaps I shall write it, some day. But I'd rather tell you about it, really. I remember . . . I remember . . . but chiefly I remember all your faces. I never forget them. I have thousands of faces in my mind—the faces of boys. If you come and see me again in years to come—as I hope you all will—I shall try to remember those older faces of yours, but it's just possible I shan't be able to—and then some day you'll see me somewhere and I shan't recognize you and you'll say to yourself, 'The old boy doesn't remember me.' [Laughter] But I *do* remember you—as you are *now*. That's the point. In my mind you never grow up at all. Never. Sometimes, for instance, when people talk to me about our respected Chairman of the Governors, I think to myself, 'Ah yes, a jolly little chap with hair that sticks up on top—and absolutely no idea whatever about the difference between a Gerund and a Gerundive.' [Loud laughter] Well, well, I mustn't go on—umph—all night. Think of me sometimes as I shall certainly think of you. *Haec olim meminisse juvabit* . . . again I need not translate." Much laughter and shouting and prolonged cheers.

August 1913. Chips went for a cure to Wiesbaden, where he lodged at the home of the German master at Brookfield, Herr Staefel, with whom he had become friendly. Staefel was thirty years his junior, but the two men got on excellently. In September, when term began, Chips returned and took up residence at Mrs. Wickett's. He felt a great deal stronger and fitter after his holiday, and almost wished he had not retired. Nevertheless, he found plenty to do. He had all the new boys to tea. He watched all the important matches on the Brookfield ground. Once a term he dined with the Head, and once also with the masters. He took on the preparation and editing of a new Brookfeldian Directory. He accepted presidency of the Old Boys' Club and went to dinners in London. He wrote occasional articles, full of jokes and Latin quotations, for the Brookfield terminal magazine. He read his *Times* every morning—very thoroughly; and he also began to read detective stories—he had been keen on them ever since the first thrills of Sherlock. Yes, he was quite busy, and quite happy, too.

442

A year later, in 1914, he again attended the end-of-term dinner. There was a lot of war talk—civil war in Ulster, and trouble between Austria and Serbia. Herr Staefel, who was leaving for Germany the next day, told Chips he thought the Balkan business wouldn't come to anything.

Chapter 13

THE WAR YEARS.

The first shock, and then the first optimism. The Battle of the Marne, the Russian steam-roller, Kitchener.

"Do you think it will last long, sir?"

Chips, questioned as he watched the first trial game of the season, gave quite a cherry answer. He was, like thousands of others, hopelessly wrong; but, unlike thousands of others, he did not afterward conceal the fact. "We ought to have—um—finished it—um—by Christmas. The Germans are already beaten. But why? Are you thinking of—um—joining up, Forrester?"

Joke—because Forrester was the smallest new boy Brookfield had ever had—about four feet high above his muddy football boots. (But not so much a joke, when you came to think of it afterward; for he was killed in 1918—shot down in flames over Cambrai.) But one didn't guess what lay ahead. It seemed tragically sensational when the first Old Brookfeldian was killed in action—in September. Chips thought, when that news came: A hundred years ago boys from the school were fighting *against* the French. Strange, in a way, that the sacrifices of one generation should so cancel out those of another. He tried to express this to Blades, the Head of School House; but Blades, eighteen years old and already in training for a cadetship, only laughed. What had all that history stuff to do with it, anyhow? Just old Chips with one of his queer ideas, that's all.

1915. Armies clenched in deadlock from the sea to Switzerland. The Dardanelles. Gallipoli. Military camps springing up quite near Brookfield; soldiers using the playing fields for sports and training; swift developments of Brookfield O.T.C. Most of the younger masters gone or in uniform. Every Sunday night, in the Chapel after evening service, Chatteris read out the names of old boys killed, together with short biographies. Very moving; but Chips, in the back pew under the gallery, thought: They are only names to him; he doesn't see their faces as I do. . . .

1916. . . . The Somme Battle. Twenty-three names read out one Sunday evening.

443

Toward the close of that catastrophic July, Chatteris talked to Chips one afternoon at Mrs. Wickett's. He was overworked and overworried and looked very ill. "To tell you the truth, Chipping, I'm not having too easy a time here. I'm thirty-nine, you know, and unmarried, and lots of people seem to think they know what I ought to do. Also, I happen to be diabetic, and couldn't pass the blindest M.O., but I don't see why I should pin a medical certificate on my front door."

Chips hadn't known anything about this; it was a shock to him, for he liked Chatteris.

The latter continued: "You see how it is. Ralston filled the place up with young men—all very good, of course—but now most of them have joined up and the substitutes are pretty dreadful, on the whole. They poured ink down a man's neck in prep one night last week—silly fool—got hysterical. I have to take classes myself, take prep for fools like that, work till midnight every night, and get cold-shouldered as a slacker on top of everything. I can't stand it much longer. If things don't improve next term I shall have a breakdown."

"I do sympathize with you," Chips said.

"I hoped you would. And that brings me to what I came here to ask you. Briefly, my suggestion is that—if you felt equal to it and would care to—how about coming back here for a while? You look pretty fit, and, of course, you know all the ropes. I don't mean a lot of hard work for you—you needn't take anything strenuously—just a few odd jobs here and there, as you choose. What I'd like you for more than anything else is not for the actual work you'd do—though that, naturally, would be very valuable—but for your help in other ways—in just *belonging* here. There's nobody ever been more popular than you were, and are still—you'd help to hold things together if there were any danger of them flying to bits. And perhaps there *is* that danger. . . ."

Chips answered, breathlessly and with a holy joy in his heart: "I'll come. . . ."

Chapter 14

HE STILL KEPT ON HIS ROOMS with Mrs. Wickett; indeed, he still lived there; but every morning, about half-past ten, he put on his coat and muffler and crossed the road to the School. He felt very fit, and the actual work was not taxing. Just a few forms in Latin and Roman History—the old lessons—even the old pronunciation. The same joke about the Lex Canuleia—there was a new generation that had not heard

it, and he was absurdly gratified by the success it achieved. He felt a little like a music-hall favorite returning to the boards after a positively last appearance.

They all said how marvelous it was that he knew every boy's name and face so quickly. They did not guess how closely he had kept in touch from across the road.

He was a grand success altogether. In some strange way he did, and they all knew and felt it, help things. For the first time in his life he felt *necessary*—and necessary to something that was nearest his heart. There is no sublimer feeling in the world, and it was his at last.

He made new jokes, too—about the O.T.C. and the food-rationing system and the anti-air-raid blinds that had to be fitted on all the windows. There was a mysterious kind of rissole that began to appear on the School menu on Mondays, and Chips called it *abhorrendum*—"meat to be abhorred." The story went round—heard Chips's latest?

Chatteris fell ill during the winter of '17, and again, for the second time in his life, Chips became Acting Head of Brookfield. Then in April Chatteris died, and the Governors asked Chips if he would carry on "for the duration." He said he would, if they would refrain from appointing him officially. From that last honor, within his reach at last, he shrank instinctively, feeling himself in so many ways unequal to it. He said to Rivers: "You see, I'm not a young man and I don't want people to—um —expect a lot from me. I'm like all these new colonels and majors you see everywhere—just a war-time fluke. A ranker—that's all I am really."

1917. 1918. Chips lived through it all. He sat in the headmaster's study every morning, handling problems, dealing with plaints and requests. Out of vast experience had emerged a kindly, gentle confidence in himself. To keep a sense of proportion, that was the main thing. So much of the world was losing it; as well keep it where it had, or ought to have, a congenial home.

On Sundays in Chapel it was he who now read out the tragic list, and sometimes it was seen and heard that he was in tears over it. Well, why not, the School said; he was an old man; they might have despised anyone else for the weakness.

One day he got a letter from Switzerland, from friends there; it was heavily censored, but conveyed some news. On the following Sunday, after the names and biographies of old boys, he paused a moment and then added:—

"Those few of you who were here before the War will remember Max Staefel, the German master. He was in Germany, visiting his home, when war broke out. He was popular while he was here, and made many friends. Those who knew him will be sorry to hear that he was killed last week, on the Western Front."

He was a little pale when he sat down afterward, aware that he had done something unusual. He had consulted nobody about it, anyhow; no

445

one else could be blamed. Later, outside the Chapel, he heard an argument:—

"On the Western Front, Chips said. Does that mean he was fighting for the Germans?"

"I suppose it does."

"Seems funny, then, to read his name out with all the others. After all, he was an *enemy.*"

"Oh, just one of Chips's ideas, I expect. The old boy still has 'em."

Chips, in his room again, was not displeased by the comment. Yes, he still had 'em—those ideas of dignity and generosity that were becoming increasingly rare in a frantic world. And he thought: Brookfield will take them, too, from me; but it wouldn't from anyone else.

Once, asked for his opinion of bayonet practice being carried on near the cricket pavilion, he answered, with that lazy, slightly asthmatic intonation that had been so often and so extravagantly imitated: "It seems—to me—umph—a very vulgar way of killing people."

The yarn was passed on and joyously appreciated—how Chips had told some big brass hat from the War Office that bayonet fighting was vulgar. Just like Chips. And they found an adjective for him—an adjective just beginning to be used: he was pre-War.

Chapter 15

AND ONCE, ON A NIGHT OF FULL MOONLIGHT, the air-raid warning was given while Chips was taking his lower fourth in Latin. The guns began almost instantly, and, as there was plenty of shrapnel falling about outside, it seemed to Chips that they might just as well stay where they were, on the ground floor of School House. It was pretty solidly built and made as good a dugout as Brookfield could offer; and as for a direct hit, well, they could not expect to survive that, wherever they were.

So he went on with his Latin, speaking a little louder amid the reverberating crashes of the guns and the shrill whine of anti-aircraft shells. Some of the boys were nervous; few were able to be attentive. He said, gently: "It may possibly seem to you, Robertson—at this particular moment in the world's history—umph—that the affairs of Caesar in Gaul some two thousand years ago—are—umph—of somewhat secondary importance—and that—umph—the irregular conjugation of the verb *tollo* is—umph—even less important still. But believe me—umph—my

dear Robertson—that is not really the case." Just then there came a particularly loud explosion—quite near. "You cannot—umph—judge the importance of things—umph—by the noise they make. Oh dear me, no." A little chuckle. "And these things—umph—that have mattered—for thousands of years—are not going to be—snuffed out—because some stink merchant—in his laboratory—invents a new kind of mischief." Titters of nervous laughter; for Buffles, the pale, lean, and medically unfit science master, was nicknamed the Stink Merchant. Another explosion—nearer still. "Let us—um—resume our work. If it is fate that we are soon to be—umph—interrupted, let us be found employing ourselves in something—umph—really appropriate. Is there anyone who will volunteer to construe?"

Maynard, chubby, dauntless, clever, and impudent, said: "I will, sir."

"Very good. Turn to page forty and begin at the bottom line."

The explosions still continued deafeningly; the whole building shook as if it were being lifted off its foundations. Maynard found the page, which was some way ahead, and began, shrilly:—

"*Genus hoc erat pugnae*—this was the kind of fight—*quo se Germani exercuerant*—in which the Germans busied themselves. Oh, sir, that's good—that's really very funny indeed, sir—one of your very best—"

Laughing began, and Chips added: "Well—umph—you can see—now—that these dead languages—umph—can come to life again—sometimes—eh? Eh?"

Afterward they learned that five bombs had fallen in and around Brookfield, the nearest of them just outside the School grounds. Nine persons had been killed.

The story was told, retold, embellished. "The dear old boy never turned a hair. Even found some old tag to illustrate what was going on. Something in Caesar about the way the Germans fought. You wouldn't think there were things like that in Caesar, would you? And the way Chips laughed . . . you know the way he *does* laugh . . . the tears all running down his face . . . never seen him laugh so much. . . ."

He was a legend.

With his old and tattered gown, his walk that was just beginning to break into a stumble, his mild eyes peering over the steel-rimmed spectacles, and his quaintly humorous sayings, Brookfield would not have had an atom of him different.

November 11, 1918.

News came through in the morning; a whole holiday was decreed for the School, and the kitchen staff were implored to provide as cheerful a spread as war-time rationing permitted. There was much cheering and singing, and a bread fight across the Dining Hall. When Chips entered in

the midst of the uproar there was an instant hush, and then wave upon wave of cheering; everyone gazed on him with eager, shining eyes, as on a symbol of victory. He walked to the dais, seeming as if he wished to speak; they made silence for him, but he shook his head after a moment, smiled, and walked away again.

It had been a damp, foggy day, and the walk across the quadrangle to the Dining Hall had given him a chill. The next day he was in bed with bronchitis, and stayed there till after Christmas. But already, on that night of November 11, after his visit to the Dining Hall, he had sent in his resignation to the Board of Governors.

When school reassembled after the holidays he was back at Mrs. Wickett's. At his own request there were no more farewells or presentations, nothing but a handshake with his successor and the word "acting" crossed out on official stationery. The "duration" was over.

Chapter 16

AND NOW, FIFTEEN YEARS AFTER THAT, he could look back upon it all with a deep and sumptuous tranquillity. He was not ill, of course—only a little tired at times, and bad with his breathing during the winter months. He would not go abroad—he had once tried it, but had chanced to strike the Riviera during one of its carefully unadvertised cold spells. "I prefer—um—to get my chills—umph—in my own country," he used to say, after that. He had to take care of himself when there were east winds, but autumn and winter were not really so bad; there were warm fires, and books, and you could look forward to the summer. It was the summer that he liked best, of course; apart from the weather, which suited him, there were the continual visits of old boys. Every weekend some of them motored up to Brookfield and called at his house. Sometimes they tired him, if too many came at once; but he did not really mind; he could always rest and sleep afterward. And he enjoyed their visits—more than anything else in the world that was still to be enjoyed. "Well, Gregson—umph—I remember you—umph—always late for everything—eh—eh? Perhaps you'll be late in growing old—umph—like me umph—eh?" And later, when he was alone again and Mrs. Wickett came in to clear away the tea things: "Mrs. Wickett, young Gregson called—umph—you remember him, do you? Tall boy with spectacles. Always late. Umph. Got a job with the—umph—League of Nations—where—I suppose—his—um—dilatoriness—won't be noticeable—eh?"

And sometimes, when the bell rang for call-over, he would go to the window and look across the road and over the School fence and see, in the distance, the thin line of boys filing past the bench. New times, new names . . . but the old ones still remained . . . Jefferson, Jennings, Jolyon, Jupp, Kingsley Primus, Kingsley Secundus, Kingsley Tertius, Kingston . . . where are you all, where have you all gone to? . . . Mrs. Wickett, bring me a cup of tea just before prep, will you, please?

The post-War decade swept through with a clatter of change and maladjustments; Chips, as he lived through it, was profoundly disappointed when he looked abroad. The Ruhr, Chanak, Corfu; there was enough to be uneasy about in the world. But near him, at Brookfield, and even, in a wider sense, in England, there was something that charmed his heart because it was old—and had survived. More and more he saw the rest of the world as a vast disarrangement for which England had sacrificed enough—and perhaps too much. But he was satisfied with Brookfield. It was rooted in things that had stood the test of time and change and war. Curious, in this deeper sense, how little it *had* changed. Boys were a politer race; bullying was nonexistent; there was more swearing and cheating. There was a more genuine friendliness between master and boy—less pomposity on the one side, less unctuousness on the other. One of the new masters, fresh from Oxford, even let the Sixth call him by his Christian name. Chips didn't hold with that; indeed, he was just a little bit shocked. "He might as well—umph—sign his terminal reports—umph—'yours affectionately'—eh—eh?" he told somebody.

During the General Strike of 1926, Brookfield boys loaded motor vans with foodstuffs. When it was all over, Chips felt stirred emotionally as he had not been since the War. Something had happened, something whose ultimate significance had yet to be reckoned. But one thing was clear: England had burned her fire in her own grate again. And when, at a Speech Day function that year, an American visitor laid stress on the vast sums that the strike had cost the country, Chips answered: "Yes, but—umph—advertisement—always *is* costly."

"Advertisement?"

"Well, wasn't it—umph—advertisement—and very fine advertisement—too? A whole week of it—umph—and not a life lost—not a shot fired! Your country would have—umph—spilt more blood in—umph—raiding a single liquor saloon!"

Laughter . . . laughter . . . wherever he went and whatever he said, there was laughter. He had earned the reputation of being a great jester, and jests were expected of him. Whenever he rose to speak at a meeting, or even when he talked across a table, people prepared their minds and faces for the joke. They listened in a mood to be amused and it was easy to satisfy them. They laughed sometimes before he came to the point. "Old Chips was in fine form," they would say, afterward. "Marvelous the way he can always see the funny side of things. . . ."

449

After 1929, Chips did not leave Brookfield—even for Old Boys' dinners in London. He was afraid of chills, and late nights began to tire him too much. He came across to the School, however, on fine days; and he still kept up a wide and continual hospitality in his room. His faculties were all unimpaired, and he had no personal worries of any kind. His income was more than he needed to spend, and his small capital, invested in gilt-edged stocks, did not suffer when the slump set in. He gave a lot of money away—to people who called on him with a hard-luck story, to various School funds, and also to the Brookfield mission. In 1930 he made his will. Except for legacies to the mission and to Mrs. Wickett, he left all he had to found an open scholarship to the school.

1931. . . . 1932. . . .

"What do you think of Hoover, sir?"

"Do you think we shall ever go back to gold?"

"How d'you feel about things in general, sir? See any break in the clouds?"

"When's the tide going to turn, Chips, old boy? You ought to know, with all your experience of things."

They all asked him questions, as if he were some kind of prophet and encyclopaedia combined—more even than that, for they liked their answer dished up as a joke. He would say:—

"Well, Henderson, when I was—umph—a much younger man— there used to be someone who—um—promised people ninepence for fourpence. I don't know that anybody—umph—ever got it, but—umph—our present rulers seem—um—to have solved the problem how to give —umph—fourpence for ninepence."

Laughter.

Sometimes, when he was strolling about the School, small boys of the cheekier kind would ask him questions, merely for the fun of getting Chips's "latest" to retail.

"Please, sir, what about the Five-Year Plan?"

"Sir, do you think Germany wants to fight another war?"

"Have you been to the new cinema, sir? I went with my people the other day. Quite a grand affair for a small place like Brookfield. They've got a Wurlitzer."

"And what—umph—on earth—is a Wurlitzer?"

"It's an organ, sir—a cinema organ."

"Dear me. . . . I've seen the name on the hoardings, but I always —umph—imagined—it must be some kind of—umph—sausage."

Laughter. . . . Oh, there's a new Chips joke, you fellows, a perfectly lovely one. I was gassing to the old boy about the new cinema, and . . .

Chapter 17

HE SAT IN HIS FRONT PARLOR at Mrs. Wickett's on a November afternoon in thirty-three. It was cold and foggy, and he dared not go out. He had not felt too well since Armistice Day; he fancied he might have caught a slight chill during the Chapel service. Merivale had been that morning for his usual fortnightly chat. "Everything all right? Feeling hearty? That's the style—keep indoors this weather—there's a lot of flu about. Wish I could have your life for a day or two."

His life . . . and what a life it had been! The whole pageant of it swung before him as he sat by the fire that afternoon. The things he had done and seen: Cambridge in the sixties; Great Gable on an August morning; Brookfield at all times and seasons throughout the years. And, for that matter, the things he had *not* done, and would never do now that he had left them too late—he had never traveled by air, for instance, and he had never been to a talkie-show. So that he was both more and less experienced than the youngest new boy at the School might well be; and that, that paradox of age and youth, was what the world called progress.

Mrs. Wickett had gone out, visiting relatives in a neighboring village; she had left the tea things ready on the table, with bread and butter and extra cups laid out in case anybody called. On such a day, however, visitors were not very likely; with the fog thickening hourly outside, he would probably be alone.

But no. About a quarter to four a ring came, and Chips, answering the front door himself (which he oughtn't to have done), encountered a rather small boy wearing a Brookfield cap and an expression of anxious timidity. "Please, sir," he began, "does Mr. Chips live here?"

"Umph—you'd better come inside," Chips answered. And in his room a moment later he added: "I am—umph—the person you want. Now what can I—umph—do for you?"

"I was told you wanted me, sir."

Chips smiled. An old joke—an old leg-pull, and he, of all people, having made so many old jokes in his time, ought not to complain. And it amused him to cap their joke, as it were, with one of his own; to let them see that he could keep his end up, even yet. So he said, with eyes twinkling: "Quite right, my boy. I wanted you to take tea with me. Will you—umph—sit down by the fire? Umph—I don't think I have seen your face before. How is that?"

"I've only just come out of the sanatorium, sir—I've been there since the beginning of term with measles."

"Ah, that accounts for it."

Chips began his usual ritualistic blending of tea from the different caddies; luckily there was half a walnut cake with pink icing in the cupboard. He found out that the boy's name was Linford, that he lived in Shropshire, and that he was the first of his family at Brookfield.

"You know—umph—Linford—you'll like Brookfield—when you get used to it. It's not half such an awful place—as you imagine. You're a bit afraid of it—um, yes—eh? So was I, my dear boy—at first. But that was—um—a long time ago. Sixty-three years ago—umph—to be precise. When I—um—first went into Big Hall and—um—I saw all those boys —I tell you—I was quite scared. Indeed—umph—I don't think I've ever been so scared in my life. Not even when—umph—the Germans bombed us—during the War. But—umph—it didn't last long—the scared feeling, I mean. I soon made myself—um—at home."

"Were there a lot of other new boys that term, sir?" asked Linford shyly.

"Eh? But—God bless my soul—I wasn't a boy at all—I was a man—a young man of twenty-two! And the next time you see a young man—a new master—taking his first prep in Big Hall—umph—just think—what it feels like!"

"But if you were twenty-two then, sir—"

"Yes? Eh?"

"You must be—very old—now, sir."

Chips laughed quietly and steadily to himself. It was a good joke. "Well—umph—I'm certainly—umph—no chicken."

He laughed quietly to himself for a long time.

Then he talked of other matters, of Shropshire, of schools and school life in general, of the news in that day's papers. "You're growing up into—umph—a very cross sort of world, Linford. Maybe it will have got over some of its—umph—crossness—by the time you're ready for it. Let's hope so—umph—at any rate. . . . Well . . ." And with a glance at the clock he delivered himself of his old familiar formula. "I'm—umph—sorry—you can't stay . . ."

At the front door he shook hands.

"Good-bye, my boy."

And the answer came, in a shrill treble: "Good-bye, Mr. Chips. . . ."

Chips sat by the fire again, with those words echoing along the corridors of his mind. "Good-bye, Mr. Chips. . . ." An old leg-pull, to make new boys think that his name was really Chips; the joke was almost traditional. He did not mind. "Good-bye, Mr. Chips. . . ." He remembered that on the eve of his wedding day Kathie had used that same phrase, mocking him gently for the seriousness he had had in those days. He thought: Nobody would call me serious to-day, that's very certain. . . .

452

Suddenly the tears began to roll down his cheeks—an old man's failing; silly, perhaps, but he couldn't help it. He felt very tired; talking to Linford like that had quite exhausted him. But he was glad he had met Linford. Nice boy. Would do well.

Over the fog-laden air came the bell for call-over, tremulous and muffled. Chips looked at the window, graying into twilight; it was time to light up. But as soon as he began to move he felt that he couldn't; he was too tired; and, anyhow, it didn't matter. He leaned back in his chair. No chicken—eh, well—that was true enough. And it had been amusing about Linford. A neat score off the jokers who had sent the boy over. Good-bye, Mr. Chips . . . odd, though, that he should have said it just like that. . . .

Chapter 18

WHEN HE AWOKE, for he seemed to have been asleep, he found himself in bed; and Merivale was there, stooping over him and smiling. "Well, you old ruffian—feeling all right? That was a fine shock you gave us!"

Chips murmured, after a pause, and in a voice that surprised him by its weakness: "Why—um—what—what has happened?"

"Merely that you threw a faint. Mrs. Wickett came in and found you —lucky she did. You're all right now. Take it easy. Sleep again if you feel inclined."

He was glad someone had suggested such a good idea. He felt so weak that he wasn't even puzzled by the details of the business—how they had got him upstairs, what Mrs. Wickett had said, and so on. But then, suddenly, at the other side of the bed, he saw Mrs. Wickett. She was smiling. He thought: God bless my soul, what's she doing up here? And then, in the shadows behind Merivale, he saw Cartwright, the new Head (he thought of him as "new," even though he had been at Brookfield since 1919), and old Buffles, commonly called "Roddy." Funny, the way they were all here. He felt: Anyhow, I can't be bothered to wonder why about anything. I'm going to go to sleep.

But it wasn't sleep, and it wasn't quite wakefulness, either; it was a sort of in-between state, full of dreams and faces and voices. Old scenes and old scraps of tunes: a Mozart trio that Kathie had once played in— cheers and laughter and the sound of guns—and, over it all, Brookfield bells, Brookfield bells. "So you see, if Miss Plebs wanted Mr. Patrician to

453

marry her . . . yes, you can, you liar. . . ." Joke . . . Meat to be abhorred. . . . Joke . . . That you, Max? Yes, come in. What's the news from the Fatherland? . . . *O mihi praeteritos* . . . Ralston said I was slack and inefficient—but they couldn't manage without me. . . . *Obile heres ago fortibus es in aro* . . . Can you translate that, any of you? . . . It's a joke. . . .

Once he heard them talking about him in the room.

Cartwright was whispering to Merivale. "Poor old chap—must have lived a lonely sort of life, all by himself."

Merivale answered: "Not always by himself. He married, you know."

"Oh, did he? I never knew about that."

"She died. It must have been—oh, quite thirty years ago. More, possibly."

"Pity. Pity he never had any children."

And at that, Chips opened his eyes as wide as he could and sought to attract their attention. It was hard for him to speak out loud, but he managed to murmur something, and they all looked round and came nearer to him.

He struggled, slowly, with his words. "What—was that—um—you were saying—about me—just now?"

Old Buffles smiled and said: "Nothing at all, old chap—nothing at all—we were just wondering when you were going to wake out of your beauty sleep."

"But—umph—I heard you—you *were* talking about me—"

"Absolutely nothing of any consequence, my dear fellow—really, I give you my word. . . ."

"I thought I heard you—one of you—saying it was a pity—umph—a pity I never had—any children . . . eh? . . . But I have, you know . . . I have . . ."

The others smiled without answering, and after a pause Chips began a faint and palpitating chuckle.

"Yes—umph—I have," he added, with quavering merriment. "Thousands of 'em . . . thousands of 'em . . . and all boys."

And then the chorus sang in his ears in final harmony, more grandly and sweetly than he had ever heard it before, and more comfortingly too. . . . Pettifer, Pollett, Porson, Potts, Pullman, Purvis, Pym-Wilson, Radlett, Rapson, Reade, Reaper, Reddy Primus . . . come round me now, all of you, for a last word and a joke. . . . Harper, Haslett, Hatfield, Hatherley . . . my last joke . . . did you hear it? . . . Did it make you laugh? . . . Bone, Boston, Bovey, Bradford, Bradley, Bramhall-Anderson . . . wherever you are, whatever has happened, give me this moment with you . . . this last moment . . . my boys . . .

And soon Chips was asleep.

He seemed so peaceful that they did not disturb him to say goodnight; but in the morning, as the School bell sounded for breakfast,

Brookfield had the news. "Brookfield will never forget his lovableness," said Cartwright, in a speech to the School. Which was absurd, because all things are forgotten in the end. But Linford, at any rate, will remember and tell the tale: "I said good-bye to Chips the night before he died. . . ."

VIII

PRISONER
OF THE SAND

by Antoine de Saint Exupéry

A Flight over the Desert

In 1944, when Antoine de Saint Exupéry went on a reconnaissance flight and did not return, the world lost a remarkable flying man and a writer of rare distinction. He was, in fact, extremely versatile, a poet, a philosopher, a mathematician, and a scientist. His *Wind, Sand, and Stars* has become recognized as the incomparable record of air experience.

Embodied in that volume are stories of his apprenticeship in the days when they "thrust heads out round the windshield in hard weather to take our bearings: the wind whistling in our ears . . ." It contains vignettes of the great gods of the airline, Bury, Guillaumet, Mermoz, Néri (who prayed to the stars); of his days in the South American service, "where the crust of the earth is as dented as an old boiler," and above all else of his trials and excitements over the Sahara.

The most dramatic episode of all is a story complete in itself called *Prisoner of the Sand*. After he had been transferred out of the desert service it seemed that the perils of existence had been reduced by one, that it was only with the sea and the winds that he must reckon. But the great ocean of sand was not prepared to relinquish him as easily as that.

While engaged in a dangerous mission toward the end of the war, he disappeared. The scene and manner of his death have remained mysteries, but it seems almost certain that he was killed in the crash of his plane in crossing the Mediterranean.

Prisoner of the Sand will leave readers convinced that he was one of the irreplaceable victims of the war.

AFTER THREE YEARS of life in the desert, I was transferred out. The fortunes of the air service sent me wandering here and there until one day I decided to attempt a long-distance flight from Paris to Saïgon. When, on December 29, 1935, I took off, I had no notion that the sands were preparing for me their ultimate and culminating ordeal.

This is the story of the Paris-Saïgon flight.

I paid my final visit to the weather bureau, where I found Monsieur Viaud stooped over his maps like a medieval alchemist over an alembic. Lucas had come with me, and we stared together at the curving lines marking the new-sprung winds. With their tiny flying arrows, they put me in mind of curving tendrils studded with thorns. All the atmospheric depressions of the world were charted on this enormous map, ochre-colored, like the earth of Asia.

"Here is a storm that we'll not hear from before Monday," Monsieur Viaud pointed out.

Over Russia and the Scandinavian peninsula the swirling lines took the form of a coiled demon. Out in Iraq, in the neighborhood of Basra, an imp was whirling.

"That fellow worries me a little," said Monsieur Viaud.

"Sand-storm, is it?"

I was not being idly curious. Day would not yet be breaking when I reached Basra and I was fearful of flying at night in one of those desert storms that turn the sky into a yellow furnace and wipe out hills, towns, and river-banks, drowning earth and sky in one great conflagration. It would be bad enough to fly in daylight through a chaos in which the very elements themselves were indistinguishable.

"Sand-storm? No, not exactly."

"So much the better," I said to myself, and I looked round the room. I liked this laboratory atmosphere. Viaud, I felt, was a man escaped from the world. When he came in here and hung up his hat and coat on the peg, he hung up with them all the confusion in which the rest of mankind lived. Family cares, thoughts of income, concerns of the heart—all that vanished on the threshold of this room as at the door of a hermit's cell, or an astronomer's tower, or a radio operator's shack. Here was one of those men who are able to lock themselves up in the secrecy of their retreat and hold discourse with the universe.

459

Gently, for he was reflecting, Monsieur Viaud rubbed the palms of his hands together.

"No, not a sand-storm. See here."

His finger traveled over the map and pointed out why.

At four in the morning Lucas shook me into consciousness.

"Wake up!"

And before I could so much as rub my eyes he was saying, "Look here, at this report. Look at the moon. You won't see much of her to-night. She's new, not very bright, and she'll set at ten o'clock. And here's something else for you: sunrise in Greenwich Meridian Time and in local time as well. And here: here are your maps, with your course all marked out. And here—"

"—is your bag packed for Saïgon," my wife broke in.

A razor and a change of shirt. He who would travel happily must travel light.

We got into a car and motored out to Le Bourget while Fate spying in ambush put the finishing touches to her plans. Those favorable winds that were to wheel in the heavens, that moon that was to sink at ten o'clock, were so many strategic positions at which Fate was assembling her forces.

It was cold at the airport, and dark. The *Simoon* was wheeled out of her hangar. I walked round my ship, stroking her wings with the back of my hand in a caress that I believe was love. Eight thousand miles I had flown in her, and her engines had not skipped a beat; not a bolt in her had loosened. This was the marvel that was to save our lives the next night by refusing to be ground to powder on meeting the upsurging earth.

Friends had turned up. Every long flight starts in the same atmosphere, and nobody who has experienced it once would ever have it otherwise: the wind, the drizzle at daybreak, the engines purring quietly as they are warmed up; this instrument of conquest gleaming in her fresh coat of "dope"—all of it goes straight to the heart.

Already one has a foretaste of the treasures about to be garnered on the way—the green and brown and yellow lands promised by the maps; the rosary of resounding names that make up the pilot's beads; the hours to be picked up one by one on the eastward flight into the sun.

There is a particular flavor about the tiny cabin in which, still only half awake, you stow away your thermos flasks and odd parts and over-night bag; in the fuel tanks heavy with power; and best of all, forward, in the magical instruments set like jewels in their panel and glimmering like a constellation in the dark of night. The mineral glow of the artificial horizon, these stethoscopes designed to take the heart-beat of the heavens, are things a pilot loves. The cabin of a plane is a world unto itself, and to the pilot it is home.

I took off, and though the load of fuel was heavy, I got easily away. I avoided Paris with a jerk and up the Seine, at Melun, I found myself flying very low between showers of rain. I was heading for the valley of the Loire. Nevers lay before me, and then Lyon. Over the Rhône I was shaken up a bit. Mt. Ventoux was capped in snow. There lies Marignane and here comes Marseille.

The towns slipped past as in a dream. I was going so far—or thought I was going so far—that these wretched little distances were covered before I was aware of it. The minutes were flying. So much the better. There are times when, after a quarter-hour of flight, you look at your watch and find that five minutes have gone by; other days when the hands turn a quarter of an hour in the wink of an eye. This was a day when time was flying. A good omen. I started out to sea.

Very odd, that little stream of vapor rising from the fuel gauge on my port wing! It might almost be a plume of smoke.

"Prévot!"

My mechanic leaned towards me.

"Look! Isn't that gas? Seems to me it's leaking pretty fast."

He had a look and shook his head.

"Better check our consumption," I said.

I wasn't turning back yet. My course was still set for Tunis. I looked round and could see Prévot at the gauge on the second fuel tank aft. He came forward and said:

"You've used up about fifty gallons."

Nearly twenty had leaked away in the wind! That was serious. I put back to Marignane where I drank a cup of coffee while the time lost hurt like an open wound. Flyers in the Air France service wanted to know whether I was bound for Saïgon or Madagascar and wished me luck. The tank was patched up and refilled, and I took off once more with a full load, again without mishap despite a bit of rough going over the soggy field.

As soon as I reached the sea I ran into low-hanging clouds that forced me down to sixty feet. The driving rain spattered against the windshield and the sea was churning and foaming. I strained to see ahead and keep from hooking the mast of some ship, while Prévot lit cigarettes for me.

"Coffee!"

He vanished into the stern of the cockpit and came back with the thermos flask. I drank. From time to time I flicked the throttle to keep the engines at exactly 2100 revolutions and ran my eye over the dials like a captain inspecting his troops. My company stood trim and erect: every needle was where it should be.

I glanced down at the sea and saw it bubbling under the steaming rain like a boiling cauldron. In a hydroplane this bumpy sea would

have bothered me; but in this ship of mine, which could not possibly be set down here, I felt differently. It was silly, of course, but the thought gave me a sense of security. The sea was part of a world that I had nothing to do with. Engine trouble here was out of the question: there was not the least danger of such a thing. Why, I was not rigged for the sea!

After an hour and a half of this, the rain died down, and though the clouds still hung low a genial sun began to break through. I was immensely cheered by this promise of good weather. Overhead I could feel a thin layer of cotton-wool and I swerved aside to avoid a downpour. I was past the point where I had to cut through the heart of squalls. Was not that the first rift in the cloud-bank, there ahead of me?

I sensed it before I saw it, for straight ahead on the sea lay a long meadow-colored swath, a sort of oasis of deep and luminous green reminding me of those barley fields in southern Morocco that would make me catch my breath each time I sighted them on coming up from Senegal across two thousand miles of sand. Here as at such times in Morocco I felt we had reached a place a man could live in, and it bucked me up. I flung a glance backward at Prévot and called out:

"We're over the worst of it. This is fine."

"Yes," he said, "fine."

This meant that I would not need to do any stunt flying when Sardinia hove unexpectedly into view. The island would not loom up suddenly like a mass of wreckage a hundred feet ahead of me: I should be able to see it rising on the horizon in the distant play of a thousand sparkling points of light.

I moved into this region bathed by the sun. No doubt about it, I was loafing along. Loafing at the rate of one hundred and seventy miles an hour, but loafing nevertheless. I smoked a few leisurely cigarettes. I lingered over my coffee. I kept a cautious fatherly eye on my brood of instruments. These clouds, this sun, this play of light, lent to my flight the relaxation of a Sunday afternoon stroll. The sea was as variegated as a country landscape broken into fields of green and violet and blue. Off in the distance, just where a squall was blowing, I could see the fermenting spray. Once again I recognized that the sea was of all things in the world the least monotonous, was formed of an ever-changing substance. A gust of wind mantles it with light or strips it bare. I turned back to Prévot.

"Look!" I said.

There in the distance lay the shores of Sardinia that we were about to skirt to the southward.

Prévot came forward and sat down beside me. He squinted with wrinkled forehead at the mountains struggling out of their shroud of mist. The clouds had been blown away and the island was coming into view in great slabs of field and woodland. I climbed to forty-five hundred feet

and drifted along the coast of this island dotted with villages. After the flower-strewn but uninhabitable sea, this was a place where I could take things easily. For a little time I clung to our greathearted mother earth. Then, Sardinia behind me, I headed for Tunis.

I picked up the African continent at Bizerta and there I began to drop earthward. I was at home. Here was a place where I could dispense with altitude which, as every pilot knows, is our particular store of wealth. Not that we squander it when it is no longer needed: we swap it for another kind of treasure. When a flyer is within a quarter of an hour of port, he sets his controls for the down swing, throttling his motor a little—just enough to keep it from racing while the needle on his speedometer swings round from one hundred and seventy to two hundred miles an hour.

At that rate of speed the impalpable eddies of evening air drum softly on the wings and the plane seems to be drilling its way into a quivering crystal so delicate that the wake of a passing swallow would jar it to bits. I was already skirting the undulations of the hills and had given away almost the whole of my few hundred feet of altitude when I reached the airdrome, and there, shaving the roofs of the hangars, I set down my ship on the ground.

While the tanks were being re-filled I signed some papers and shook hands with a few friends. And just as I was coming out of the administration building I heard a horrible grunt, one of those muffled impacts that tell their fatal story in a single sound; one of those echoless thuds complete in themselves, without appeal, in which fatality delivers its message. Instantly there came into my mind the memory of an identical sound—an explosion in a garage. Two men had died of that hoarse bark.

I looked now across to the road that ran alongside the airdrome: there in a puff of dust two high-powered cars had crashed head-on and stood frozen into motionlessness as if imprisoned in ice. Men were running towards the cars while others ran from them to the field office.

"Get a doctor. . . . Skull crushed. . . ."

My heart sank. In the peace of the evening light Fate had taken a trick. A beauty, a mind, a life—something had been destroyed. It was as sudden as a raid in the desert. Marauding tribesmen creep up on silent feet in the night. The camp resounds briefly with the clashing tumult of a razzia. A moment later everything has sunk back into the golden silence. The same peace, the same stillness, followed this crash.

Near by, someone spoke of a fractured skull. I had no mind to be told about that crushed and bloody cranium. Turning my back to the road, I went across to my ship, in my heart a foreboding of danger. I was to recognize that sound when I heard it again very soon. When the

Simoon scraped the black plateau at a speed of one hundred and seventy miles an hour I should recognize that hoarse grunt, that same snarl of destiny keeping its appointment with us.

Off to Benghazi! We still have two hours of daylight. Before we crossed into Tripolitana I took off my glare glasses. The sands were golden under the slanting rays of the sun. How empty of life is this planet of ours! Once again it struck me that its rivers, its woods, its human habitations were the product of chance, of fortuitous conjunctions of circumstance. What a deal of the earth's surface is given over to rock and sand!

But all this was not my affair. My world was the world of flight. Already I could feel the oncoming night within which I should be enclosed as in the precincts of a temple—enclosed in the temple of night for the accomplishment of secret rites and absorption in inviolable contemplation.

Already this profane world was beginning to fade out: soon it would vanish altogether. This landscape was still laved in golden sunlight, but already something was evaporating out of it. I know nothing, nothing in the world, equal to the wonder of nightfall in the air.

Those who have been enthralled by the witchery of flying will know what I mean—and I do not speak of the men who, among other sports, enjoy taking a turn in a plane. I speak of those who fly professionally and have sacrificed much to their craft. Mermoz said once, "It's worth it, it's worth the final smash-up."

No question about it; but the reason is hard to formulate. A novice taking orders could appreciate this ascension towards the essence of things, since his profession too is one of renunciation: he renounces the world; he renounces riches; he renounces the love of woman. And by renunciation he discovers his hidden god.

I, too, in this flight, am renouncing things. I am giving up the broad golden surfaces that would befriend me if my engines were to fail. I am giving up the landmarks by which I might be taking my bearings. I am giving up the profiles of mountains against the sky that would warn me of pitfalls. I am plunging into the night. I am navigating. I have on my side only the stars.

The diurnal death of the world is a slow death. It is only little by little that the divine beacon of daylight recedes from me. Earth and sky begin to merge into each other. The earth rises and seems to spread like a mist. The first stars tremble as if shimmering in green water. Hours must pass before their glimmer hardens into the frozen glitter of diamonds. I shall have a long wait before I witness the soundless frolic of the shooting stars. In the profound darkness of certain nights I have seen the sky streaked with so many trailing sparks that it seemed to me a great gale must be blowing through the outer heavens.

Prévot was testing the lamps in their sockets and the emergency torches. Round the bulbs he was wrapping red paper.

"Another layer."

He added another wrapping of paper and touched a switch. The dim light within the plane was still too bright. As in a photographer's dark-room, it veiled the pale picture of the external world. It hid that glowing phosphorescence which sometimes, at night, clings to the surface of things. Now night has fallen, but it is not yet true night. A crescent moon persists.

Prévot dove aft and came back with a sandwich. I nibbled a bunch of grapes. I was not hungry. I was neither hungry nor thirsty. I felt no weariness. It seemed to me that I could go on like this at the controls for ten years. I was happy.

The moon had set. It was pitch dark when we came in sight of Benghazi. The town lay at the bottom of an obscurity so dense that it was without a halo. I saw the place only when I was over it. As I was hunting for the airdrome the red obstruction lights were switched on. They cut out a black rectangle in the earth.

I banked, and at that moment the rays of a floodlight rose into the sky like a jet from a fire-hose. It pivoted and traced a golden lane over the landing-field. I circled again to get a clear view of what might be in my way. The port was equipped with everything to make a night-landing easy. I throttled down my engine and dropped like a diver into black water.

It was eleven o'clock local time when I landed and taxied across to the beacon. The most helpful ground crew in the world wove in and out of the blinding ray of a searchlight, alternately visible and invisible. They took my papers and began promptly to fill my tanks. Twenty minutes of my time was all they asked for, and I was touched by their great readiness to help. As I was taking off, one of them said:

"Better circle round and fly over us; otherwise we shan't be sure you got off all right."

I rolled down the golden lane towards an unimpeded opening. My *Simoon* lifted her overload clear of the ground well before I reached the end of the runway. The searchlight following me made it hard for me to wheel. Soon it let me go: the men on the ground had guessed that it was dazzling me. I turned right about and banked vertically, and at that moment the searchlight caught me between the eyes again; but scarcely had it touched me when it fled and sent elsewhere its long golden flute. I knew that the ground crew were being most thoughtful and I was grateful. And now I was off to the desert.

All along the line, at Paris, at Tunis, and at Benghazi, I had been told that I should have a following wind of up to twenty-five miles an

hour. I was counting on a speed of 190 m.p.h. as I set my course on the middle of the stretch between Alexandria and Cairo. On this course I should avoid the danger zones along the coast, and despite any drifting I might do without knowing it, I should pick up either to port or to starboard the lights of one of those two cities. Failing them I should certainly not miss the lights of the Nile valley. With a steady wind I should reach the Nile in three hours and twenty minutes; if the wind fell, three hours and three-quarters. Calculating thus I began to eat up the six hundred and fifty miles of desert ahead of me.

There was no moon. The world was a bubble of pitch that had dilated until it reached the very stars in the heavens. I should not see a single gleam of light, should not profit by the faintest landmark. Carrying no wireless, I should receive no message from the earth until I reached the Nile. It was useless to try to look at anything other than the compass and the artificial horizon. I might blot the world out of my mind and concentrate my attention upon the slow pulsation of the narrow thread of radium paint that ran along the dark background of the dials.

Whenever Prévot stirred I brought the plane smoothly back to plumb. I went up to six thousand feet where I had been told the winds would be favorable. At long intervals I switched on a lamp to glance at the engine dials, not all of which were phosphorescent; but most of the time I wrapped myself closely round in darkness among my miniature constellations which gave off the same mineral glow as the stars, the same mysterious and unwearied light, and spoke the same language.

Like the astronomers, I too was reading in the book of celestial mechanics. I too seemed to myself studious and uncorrupted. Everything in the world that might have lured me from my studies had gone out. The external world had ceased to exist.

There was Prévot, who, after a vain resistance, had fallen asleep and left me to the greater enjoyment of my solitude. There was the gentle purr of my beautiful little motor, and before me, on the instrument panel, there were all those tranquil stars. I was most decidedly not sleepy. If this state of quiet well-being persisted until tomorrow night, I intended to push on without a stop to Saïgon.

Now the flight was beginning to seem to me short. Benghazi, the only troublesome night-landing on the route, had banked its fires and settled down behind the horizon in that dark shuttering in which cities take their slumber.

Meanwhile I was turning things over in my mind. We were without the moon's help and we had no wireless. No slightest tenuous tie was to bind us to earth until the Nile showed its thread of light directly ahead of us. We were truly alone in the universe—a thought that caused me not the least worry. If my motor were to cough, that sound would startle me more than if my heart should skip a beat.

Into my mind came the image of Sabathier, the white-haired engineer with the clear eye. I was thinking that, from one point of view, it would he hard to draw a distinction in the matter of human values between a profession like his and that of the painter, the composer, or the poet. I could see in the mind's eye those watchmaker's hands of his that had brought into being this clockwork I was piloting. Men who have given their lives to labors of love go straight to my heart.

"Couldn't I change this?" I had asked him.

"I shouldn't advise it," he had answered.

I was remembering our last conversation. He had thought it inadvisable, and of course that had settled it. A physician, that's it! Exactly the way one puts oneself into the hands of one's doctor—when he has that look in his eye. It was by his motor that we hung suspended in air and were able to go on living with the ticking of time in this penetrable pitch. We were crossing the great dark valley of a fairy-tale, the Valley of Ordeal. Like the prince in the tale, we must meet the test without succor. Failure here would not be forgiven. We were in the lap of the inexorable gods.

A ray of light was filtering through a joint in the lamp shaft. I woke up Prévot and told him to put it out. Prévot stirred in the darkness like a bear, snorted, and came forward. He fumbled for a bit with handkerchiefs and black paper, and the ray of light vanished. That light had bothered me because it was not of my world. It swore at the pale and distant gleam of the phosphorescence and was like a night-club spotlight compared to the gleam of a star. Besides, it had dazzled me and had out-shone all else that gleamed.

We had been flying for three hours. A brightness that seemed to me a glare spurted on the starboard side. I stared. A streamer of light which I had hitherto not noticed was fluttering from a lamp at the tip of the wing. It was an intermittent glow, now brilliant, now dim. It told me that I had flown into a cloud, and it was on the cloud that the lamp was reflected.

I was nearing the landmarks upon which I had counted; a clear sky would have helped a lot. The wing shone bright under the halo. The light steadied itself, became fixed, and then began to radiate in the form of a bouquet of pink blossoms. Great eddies of air were swinging me to and fro. I was navigating somewhere in the belly of a cumulus whose thickness I could not guess. I rose to seventy-five hundred feet and was still in it. Down again to three thousand, and the bouquet of flowers was still with me, motionless and growing brighter.

Well, there it was and there was nothing to do about it. I would think of something else, and wait to get clear of it. Just the same, I did not like this sinister glitter of a one-eyed grog-shop.

"Let me think," I said to myself. "I am bouncing round a bit, but there's nothing abnormal about that. I've been bumped all the way,

despite a clear sky and plenty of ceiling. The wind has not died down, and I must be doing better than the 190 m.p.h. I counted on." This was about as far as I could get. Oh, well, when I got through the cloud-bank I would try to take my bearings.

Out of it we flew. The bouquet suddenly vanished, letting me know I was in the clear again. I stared ahead and saw, if one can speak of "seeing" space, a narrow valley of sky and the wall of the next cumulus. Already the bouquet was coming to life again. I was free of that viscous mess from time to time but only for a few seconds each time. After three and a half hours of flying it began to get on my nerves. If I had made the time I imagined, we were certainly approaching the Nile. With a little luck I might be able to spot the river through the rifts, but they were getting rare. I dared not come down, for if I was actually slower than I thought, I was still over high-lying country.

Thus far I was entirely without anxiety; my only fear was that I might presently be wasting time. I decided that I would take things easy until I had flown four and a quarter hours: after that, even in a dead calm (which was highly unlikely) I should have crossed the Nile. When I reached the fringes of the cloud-bank the bouquet winked on and off more and more swiftly and then suddenly went out. Decidedly, I did not like these dot-and-dash messages from the demons of the night.

A green star appeared ahead of me, flashing like a lighthouse. Was it a lighthouse? or really a star? I took no pleasure from this supernatural gleam, this star the Magi might have seen, this dangerous decoy.

Prévot, meanwhile, had waked up and turned his electric torch on the engine dials. I waved him off, him and his torch. We had just sailed into the clear between two clouds and I was busy staring below. Prévot went back to sleep. The gap in the clouds was no help: there was nothing below.

Four hours and five minutes in the air. Prévot awoke and sat down beside me.

"I'll bet we're near Cairo," he said.

"We must be."

"What's that? A star? or is it a lighthouse?"

I had throttled the engine down a little. This, probably, was what had awakened Prévot. He is sensitive to all the variations of sound in flight.

I began a slow descent, intending to slip under the mass of clouds. Meanwhile I had had a look at my map. One thing was sure—the land below me lay at sea level, and there was no risk of conking against a hill. Down I went, flying due north so that the lights of the cities would strike square into my windows. I must have overflown them, and should therefore see them on my left.

Now I was flying below the cumulus. But alongside was another cloud hanging lower down on the left. I swerved so as not to be caught

in its net, and headed north-northeast. This second cloud-bank certainly went down a long way, for it blocked my view of the horizon. I dared not give up any more altitude. My altimeter registered 1200 feet, but I had no notion of the atmospheric pressure here. Prévot leaned towards me and I shouted to him, "I'm going out to sea. I'd rather come down on it than risk a crash here."

As a matter of fact, there was nothing to prove that we had not drifted over the sea already. Below that cloud-bank visibility was exactly nil. I hugged my window, trying to read below me, to discover flares, signs of life. I was a man raking dead ashes, trying in vain to retrieve the flame of life in a hearth.

"A lighthouse!"

Both of us spied it at the same moment, that winking decoy! What madness! Where was that phantom light, that invention of the night? For at the very second when Prévot and I leaned forward to pick it out of the air where it had glittered nine hundred feet below our wings, suddenly, at that very instant . . .

"Oh!"

I am quite sure that this was all I said. I am quite sure that all I felt was a terrific crash that rocked our world to its foundations. We had crashed against the earth at a hundred and seventy miles an hour. I am quite sure that in the split second that followed, all I expected was the great flash of ruddy light of the explosion in which Prévot and I were to be blown up together. Neither he nor I had felt the least emotion of any kind. All I could observe in myself was an extraordinary tense feeling of expectancy, the expectancy of that resplendent star in which we were to vanish within the second.

But there was no ruddy star. Instead there was a sort of earthquake that splintered our cabin, ripped away the windows, blew sheets of metal hurtling through space a hundred yards away, and filled our very entrails with its roar. The ship quivered like a knife-blade thrown from a distance into a block of oak, and its anger mashed us as if we were so much pulp.

One second, two seconds passed, and the plane still quivered while I waited with a grotesque impatience for the forces within it to burst it like a bomb. But the subterranean quakings went on without a climax of eruption while I marveled uncomprehendingly at its invisible travail. I was baffled by the quaking, the anger, the interminable postponement. Five seconds passed; six seconds. And suddenly we were seized by a spinning motion, a shock that jerked our cigarettes out of the window, pulverized the starboard wing—and then nothing, nothing but a frozen immobility. I shouted to Prévot:

"Jump!"

And in that instant he cried out:

"Fire!"

We dove together through the wrecked window and found ourselves standing side by side, sixty feet from the plane. I said:

"Are you hurt?"

He answered:

"Not a bit."

But he was rubbing his knee.

"Better run your hands over yourself," I said; "move about a bit. Sure no bones are broken?"

He answered:

"I'm all right. It's that emergency pump."

Emergency pump! I was sure he was going to keel over any minute and split open from head to navel there before my eyes. But he kept repeating with a glassy stare:

"That pump, that emergency pump."

He's out of his head, I thought. He'll start dancing in a minute. Finally he stopped staring at the plane—which had not gone up in flames—and stared at me instead. And he said again:

"I'm all right. It's that emergency pump. It got me in the knee."

Why we were not blown up, I do not know. I switched on my electric torch and went back over the furrow in the ground traced by the plane. Two hundred and fifty yards from where we stopped the ship had begun to shed the twisted iron and sheet-metal that spattered the sand the length of her traces. We were to see, when day came, that we had run almost tangentially into a gentle slope at the top of a barren plateau. At the point of impact there was a hole in the sand that looked as if it had been made by a plough. Maintaining an even keel, the plane had run its course with the fury and the tail-lashings of a reptile gliding on its belly at the rate of a hundred and seventy miles an hour. We owed our lives to the fact that this desert was surfaced with round black pebbles which had rolled over and over like ballbearings beneath us. They must have rained upward to the heavens as we shot through them.

Prévot disconnected the batteries for fear of fire by short-circuit. I leaned against the motor and turned the situation over in my mind. I had been flying high for four hours and a quarter, possibly with a thirty-mile following wind. I had been jolted a good deal. If the wind had changed since the weather people forecast it, I was unable to say into what quarter it had veered. All I could make out was that we had crashed in an empty square two hundred and fifty miles on each side.

Prévot came up and sat down beside me.

"I can't believe that we're alive," he said.

I said nothing. Even that thought could not cheer me. A germ of an idea was at work in my mind and was already bothering me. Telling

Prévot to switch on his torch as a landmark, I walked straight out, scrutinizing the ground in the light of my own torch as I went.

I went forward slowly, swung round in a wide arc, and changed direction a number of times. I kept my eyes fixed on the ground like a man hunting a lost ring.

Only a little while before I had been straining just as hard to see a gleam of light from the air. Through the darkness I went, bowed over the traveling disk of white light. "Just as I thought," I said to myself, and I went slowly back to the plane. I sat down beside the cabin and ruminated. I had been looking for a reason to hope and had failed to find it. I had been looking for a sign of life, and no sign of life had appeared.

"Prévot, I couldn't find a single blade of grass."

Prévot said nothing, and I was not sure he had understood. Well, we could talk about it again when the curtain rose at dawn. Meanwhile I was dead tired and all I could think was, "Two hundred and fifty miles more or less in the desert."

Suddenly I jumped to my feet. "Water!" I said.

Gas tanks and oil tanks were smashed in. So was our supply of drinking-water. The sand had drunk everything. We found a pint of coffee in a battered thermos flask and half a pint of white wine in another. We filtered both, and poured them into one flask. There were some grapes, too, and a single orange. Meanwhile I was computing: "All this will last us five hours of tramping in the sun."

We crawled into the cabin and waited for dawn. I stretched out, and as I settled down to sleep I took stock of our situation. We didn't know where we were; we had less than a quart of liquid between us; if we were not too far off the Benghazi-Cairo lane we should be found in a week, and that would be too late. Yet it was the best we could hope for. If, on the other hand, we had drifted off our course, we shouldn't be found in six months. One thing was sure—we could not count on being picked up by a plane; the men who came out for us would have two thousand miles to cover.

"You know, it's a shame," Prévot said suddenly.

"What's a shame?"

"That we didn't crash properly and have it over with."

It seemed pretty early to be throwing in one's hand. Prévot and I pulled ourselves together. There was still a chance, slender as it was, that we might be saved miraculously by a plane. On the other hand, we couldn't stay here and perhaps miss a near-by oasis. We would walk all day and come back to the plane before dark. And before going off we would write our plan in huge letters in the sand.

With this I curled up and settled down to sleep. I was happy to go to sleep. My weariness wrapped me round like a multiple presence. I was not alone in the desert: my drowsiness was peopled with voices and

memories and whispered confidences. I was not yet thirsty; I felt strong; and I surrendered myself to sleep as to an aimless journey. Reality lost ground before the advance of dreams.

Ah, but things were different when I awoke!

In times past I have loved the Sahara. I have spent nights alone in the path of marauding tribes and have waked up with untroubled mind in the golden emptiness of the desert where the wind like a sea had raised sandwaves upon its surface. Asleep under the wing of my plane I have looked forward with confidence to being rescued next day. But this was not the Sahara!

Prévot and I walked along the slopes of rolling mounds. The ground was sand covered over with a single layer of shining black pebbles. They gleamed like metal scales and all the domes about us shone like coats of mail. We had dropped down into a mineral world and were hemmed in by iron hills.

When we reached the top of the first crest we saw in the distance another just like it, black and gleaming. As we walked we scraped the ground with our boots, marking a trail over which to return to the plane. We went forward with the sun in our eyes. It was not logical to go due east like this, for everything—the weather reports, the duration of the flight—had made it plain that we had crossed the Nile. But I had started tentatively towards the west and had felt a vague foreboding I could not explain to myself. So I had put off the west till tomorrow. In the same way, provisionally, I had given up going north, though that led to the sea.

Three days later, when scourged by thirst into abandoning the plane and walking straight on until we dropped in our tracks, it was still eastward that we tramped. More precisely, we walked east-northeast. And this too was in defiance of all reason and even of all hope. Yet after we had been rescued we discovered that if we had gone in any other direction we should have been lost.

Northward, we should never have had the endurance to reach the sea. And absurd as it may appear, it seems to me now, since I had no other motive, that I must have chosen the east simply because it was by going eastward that Guillaumet had been saved in the Andes, after I had hunted for him everywhere. In a confused way the east had become for me the direction of life.

We walked on for five hours and then the landscape changed. A river of sand seemed to be running through a valley, and we followed this river-bed, taking long strides in order to cover as much ground as possible and get back to the plane before night fell, if our march was in vain. Suddenly I stopped.

"Prévot!"

"What's up?"

Prisoner of the Sand

"Our tracks!"

How long was it since we had forgotten to leave a wake behind us? We had to find it or die.

We went back, bearing to the right. When we had gone back far enough we would make a right angle to the left and eventually intersect our tracks where we had still remembered to mark them.

This we did and were off again. The heat rose and with it came the mirages. But these were still the commonplace kind—sheets of water that materialized and then vanished as we neared them. We decided to cross the valley of sand and climb the highest dome in order to look round the horizon. This was after six hours of march in which, striding along, we must have covered twenty miles.

When we had struggled up to the top of the black hump we sat down and looked at each other. At our feet lay our valley of sand, opening into a desert of sand whose dazzling brightness seared our eyes. As far as the eye could see lay empty space. But in that space the play of light created mirages which, this time, were of a disturbing kind, fortresses and minarets, angular geometric hulks. I could see also a black mass that pretended to be vegetation, overhung by the last of those clouds that dissolve during the day only to return at night. This mass of vegetation was the shadow of a cumulus.

It was no good going on. The experiment was a failure. We would have to go back to our plane, to that red and white beacon which, perhaps, would be picked out by a flyer. I was not staking great hopes on a rescue party, but it did seem to me our last chance of salvation. In any case, we had to get back to our few drops of liquid, for our throats were parched. We were imprisoned in this iron circle, captives of the curt dictatorship of thirst.

And yet, how hard it was to turn back when there was a chance that we might be on the road to life! Beyond the mirages the horizon was perhaps rich in veritable treasures, in meadows and runnels of sweet water. I knew I was doing the right thing by returning to the plane, and yet as I swung round and started back I was filled with portents of disaster.

We were resting on the ground beside the plane. Nearly forty miles of wandering this day. The last drop of liquid had been drained. No sign of life had appeared to the east. No plane had soared overhead. How long should we be able to hold out? Already our thirst was terrible.

We had built up a great pyre out of bits of the splintered wing. Our gasoline was ready, and we had flung on the heap sheets of metal whose magnesium coating would burn with a hard white flame. We were waiting now for night to come down before we lighted our conflagration. But where were there men to see it?

Night fell and the flames rose. Prayerfully we watched our mute

473

and radiant fanion mount resplendent into the night. As I looked I said to myself that this message was not only a cry for help, it was fraught also with a great deal of love. We were begging water, but we were also begging the communion of human society. Only man can create fire: let another flame light up the night; let man answer man!

I was haunted by a vision of my wife's eyes under the halo of her hat. Of her face I could see only the eyes, questioning me, looking at me yearningly. I am answering, answering with all my strength! What flame could leap higher than this that darts up into the night from my heart?

What I could do, I have done. What we could do, we have done. Nearly forty miles, almost without a drop to drink. Now there was no water left. Was it our fault that we could wait no longer? Suppose we had sat quietly by the plane, taking suck at the mouths of our water-bottles? But from the moment I breathed in the moist bottom of the tin cup, a clock had started up in me. From the second when I had sucked up the last drop, I had begun to slip downhill. Could I help it if time like a river was carrying me away? Prévot was weeping. I tapped him on the shoulder and said, to console him:

"If we're done for we're done for, and that's all there is to it."

He said:

"Do you think it's me I'm bawling about?"

I might have known it. It was evident enough. Nothing is unbearable. Tomorrow, and the day after, I should learn that nothing was really unbearable. I had never really believed in torture. Reading Poe as a kid, I had already said as much to myself. Once, jammed in the cabin of a plane, I thought I was going to drown; and I had not suffered much. Several times it had seemed to me that the final smash-up was coming, and I don't remember that I thought of it as a cosmic event. And I didn't believe this was going to be agonizing either. There will be time tomorrow to find out stranger things about it. Meanwhile, God knows that despite the bonfire I had decidedly given up hope that our cries would be heard by the world.

"Do you think it's me . . ." There you have what is truly unbearable! Every time I saw those yearning eyes it was as if a flame were searing me. They were like a scream for help, like the flares of a sinking ship. I felt that I should not sit idly by: I should jump up and run—anywhere! straight ahead of me!

What a strange reversal of rôles! But I have always thought it would be like this. Still, I needed Prévot beside me to be quite sure of it. Prévot was a level-headed fellow. He loved life. And yet Prévot no more than I was wringing his hands at the sight of death the way we are told men do. But there did exist something that he could not bear any more than I could. I was perfectly ready to fall asleep, whether for a night or for eternity. If I did fall asleep, I could not even know whether

474

it was for the one or for the other. And the peace of sleep! But that cry that would be sent up at home, that great wail of desolation—that was what I could not bear. I could not stand idly by and look on at that disaster. Each second of silence drove the knife deeper into someone I loved. At the thought, a blind rage surged up in me. Why do these chains bind me and prevent me from rescuing those who are drowning? Why does our conflagration not carry our cry to the ends of the world? Hear me, you out here! Patience. We are coming to save you.

The magnesium had been licked off and the metal was glowing red. There was left only a heap of embers round which we crouched to warm ourselves. Our flaming call had spent itself. Had it set anything in the world in motion? I knew well enough that it hadn't. Here was a prayer that had of necessity gone unheard.

That was that.

I ought to get some sleep.

At daybreak I took a rag and mopped up a little dew on the wings. The mixture of water and paint and oil yielded a spoonful of nauseating liquid which we sipped because it would at least moisten our lips. After this banquet Prévot said:

"Thank God we've got a gun."

Instantly I became furious and turned on him with an aggressiveness which I regretted directly I felt it. There was nothing I should have loathed more at that moment than a gush of sentimentality. I am so made that I have to believe that everything is simple. Birth is simple. Growing up is simple. And dying of thirst is simple. I watched Prévot out of the corner of my eye, ready to wound his feelings, if that was necessary to shut him up.

But Prévot had spoken without emotion. He had been discussing a matter of hygiene, and might have said in the same tone, "We ought to wash our hands." That being so, we were agreed. Indeed already yesterday, my eye falling by chance on the leather holster, the same thought had crossed my mind, and with me too it had been a reasonable reflex, not an emotional one. Pathos resides in social man, not in the individual; what was pathetic was our powerlessness to reassure those for whom we were responsible, not what we might do with the gun.

There was still no sign that we were being sought; or rather they were doubtless hunting for us elsewhere, probably in Arabia. We were to hear no sound of plane until the day after we had abandoned our own. And if ships did pass overhead, what could that mean to us? What could they see in us except two black dots among the thousand shadowy dots in the desert? Absurd to think of being distinguishable from them. None of the reflections that might be attributed to me on the score of this torture would be true. I should not feel in the least tortured. The aerial rescue party would seem to me, each time I sighted one, to be

475

moving through a universe that was not mine. When searchers have to cover two thousand miles of territory, it takes them a good two weeks to spot a plane in the desert from the sky.

They were probably looking for us all along the line from Tripoli to Persia. And still, with all this, I clung to the slim chance that they might pick us out. Was that not our only chance of being saved? I changed my tactics, determining to go reconnoitering by myself. Prévot would get another bonfire together and kindle it in the event that visitors showed up. But we were to have no callers that day.

So off I went without knowing whether or not I should have the stamina to come back. I remembered what I knew about this Libyan desert. When, in the Sahara, humidity is still at forty per cent of saturation, it is only eighteen here in Libya. Life here evaporates like a vapor. Bedouins, explorers, and colonial officers all tell us that a man may go nineteen hours without water. Thereafter his eyes fill with light, and that marks the beginning of the end. The progress made by thirst is swift and terrible. But this northeast wind, this abnormal wind that had blown us out off our course and had marooned us on this plateau, was now prolonging our lives. What was the length of the reprieve it would grant us before our eyes began to fill with light? I went forward with the feeling of a man canoeing in midocean.

I will admit that at daybreak this landscape seemed to me less infernal, and that I began my walk with my hands in my pockets, like a tramp on a highroad. The evening before we had set snares at the mouths of certain mysterious burrows in the ground, and the poacher in me was on the alert. I went first to have a look at our traps. They were empty.

Well, this meant that I should not be drinking blood today; and indeed I hadn't expected to. But though I was not disappointed, my curiosity was aroused. What was there in the desert for these animals to live on? These were certainly the holes of fennecs, a long-eared carnivorous sand-fox the size of a rabbit. I spotted the tracks made by one of them, and gave way to the impulse to follow them. They led to a narrow stream of sand where each footprint was plainly outlined and where I marveled at the pretty palm formed by the three toes spread fanwise on the sand.

I could imagine my little friend trotting blithely along at dawn and licking the dew off the rocks. Here the tracks were wider apart: my fennec had broken into a run. And now I see that a companion has joined him and they have trotted on side by side. These signs of a morning stroll gave me a strange thrill. They were signs of life, and I loved them for that. I almost forgot that I was thirsty.

Finally I came to the pasture-ground of my foxes. Here, every hundred yards or so, I saw sticking up out of the sand a small dry shrub, its twigs heavy with little golden snails. The fennec came here

at dawn to do his marketing. And here I was able to observe another of nature's mysteries.

My fennec did not stop at all the shrubs. There were some weighed down with snails which he disdained. Obviously he avoided them with some wariness. Others he stopped at but did not strip of all they bore. He must have picked out two or three shells and then gone on to another restaurant. What was he up to? Was he nurseryman to the snails, encouraging their reproduction by refraining from exhausting the stock on a given shrub, or a given twig? Or was he amusing himself by delaying repletion, putting off satiety in order to enhance the pleasure he took from his morning stroll?

The tracks led me back to the hole in which he lived. Doubtless my fennec crouched below, listening to me and startled by the crunching of my footsteps. I said to him:

"Fox, my little fox, I'm done for; but somehow that doesn't prevent me from taking an interest in your mood."

And there I stayed a bit, ruminating and telling myself that a man was able to adapt himself to anything. The notion that he is to die in thirty years has probably never spoiled any man's fun. Thirty years . . . or thirty days: it's all a matter of perspective.

Only, you have to be able to put certain visions out of your mind.

I went on, finally, and the time came when, along with my weariness, something in me began to change. If those were not mirages, I was inventing them.

"Hi! Hi, there!"

I shouted and waved my arms, but the man I had seen waving at me turned out to be a black rock. Everything in the desert had grown animate. I stooped to waken a sleeping Bedouin and he turned into the trunk of a black tree. A tree-trunk? Here in the desert? I was amazed and bent over to lift a broken bough. It was solid marble.

Straightening up I looked round and saw more black marble. An antediluvian forest littered the ground with its broken tree-tops. How many thousand years ago, under what hurricane of the time of Genesis, had this cathedral of wood crumbled in this spot? Countless centuries had rolled these fragments of giant pillars at my feet, polished them like steel, petrified and vitrified them and indued them with the color of jet.

I could distinguish the knots in their branches, the twistings of their once living boughs, could count the rings of life in them. This forest had rustled with birds and been filled with music that now was struck by doom and frozen into salt. And all this was hostile to me. Blacker than the chain-mail of the hummocks, these solemn derelicts rejected me. What had I, a living man, to do with this incorruptible stone? Perishable as I was, I whose body was to crumble into dust, what place had I in this eternity?

Since yesterday I had walked nearly fifty miles. This dizziness that I felt came doubtless from my thirst. Or from the sun. It glittered on these hulks until they shone as if smeared with oil. It blazed down on this universal carapace. Sand and fox had no life here. This world was a gigantic anvil upon which the sun beat down. I strode across this anvil and at my temples I could feel the hammer-strokes of the sun.

"Hi! Hi, there!" I called out.

"There is nothing there," I told myself. "Take it easy. You are delirious."

I had to talk to myself aloud, had to bring myself to reason. It was hard for me to reject what I was seeing, hard not to run towards that caravan plodding on the horizon. There! Do you see it?

"Fool! You know very well that you are inventing it."

"You mean that nothing in the world is real?"

Nothing in the world is real if that cross which I see ten miles off on the top of a hill is not real. Or is it a lighthouse? No, the sea does not lie in that direction. Then it must be a cross.

I had spent the night studying my map—but uselessly, since I did not know my position. Still, I had scrutinized all the signs that marked the marvelous presence of man. And somewhere on the map I had seen a little circle surmounted by just such a cross. I had glanced down at the legend to get an explanation of the symbol and had read: "Religious institution."

Close to the cross there had been a black dot. Again I had run my finger down the legend and had read: "Permanent well." My heart had jumped and I had repeated the legend aloud: "Permanent well, permanent well." What were all of Ali Baba's treasures compared with a permanent well? A little farther on were two white circles. "Temporary wells," the legend said. Not quite so exciting. And round about them was nothing . . . unless it was the blankness of despair.

But this must be my "religious institution!" The monks must certainly have planted a great cross on the hill expressly for men in our plight! All I had to do was to walk across to them. I should be taken in by those Dominicans. . . .

"But there are only Coptic monasteries in Libya!" I told myself.

. . . by those learned Dominicans. They have a great cool kitchen with red tiles, and out in the courtyard a marvelous rusted pump. Beneath the rusted pump; beneath the rusted pump . . . you've guessed it! . . . beneath the rusted pump is dug the permanent well! Ah, what rejoicing when I ring at their gate, when I get my hands on the rope of the great bell.

"Madman! You are describing a house in Provence; and what's more, the house has no bell!"

. . . on the rope of the great bell. The porter will raise his arms to

Prisoner of the Sand

Heaven and cry out, "You are the messenger of the Lord!" and he will call aloud to all the monks. They will pour out of the monastery. They will welcome me with a great feast, as if I were the Prodigal Son. They will lead me to the kitchen and will say to me, "One moment, my son, one moment. We'll just be off to the permanent well." And I shall be trembling with happiness.

No, no! I will *not* weep just because there happens to be no cross on the hill.

The treasures of the west turned out to be mere illusion. I have veered due north. At least the north is filled with the sound of the sea.

Over the hilltop. Look there, at the horizon! The most beautiful city in the world!

"You know perfectly well that is a mirage."

Of course I know it is a mirage! Am I the sort of man who can be fooled? But what if I *want* to go after that mirage? Suppose I enjoy indulging my hope? Suppose it suits me to love that crenelated town all beflagged with sunlight? What if I choose to walk straight ahead on light feet—for you must know that I have dropped my weariness behind me, I am happy now. . . . Prévot and his gun! Don't make me laugh! I prefer my drunkenness. I am drunk. I am dying of thirst.

It took the twilight to sober me. Suddenly I stopped, appalled to think how far I was from our base. In the twilight the mirage was dying. The horizon had stripped itself of its pomp, its palaces, its priestly vestments. It was the old desert horizon again.

"A fine day's work you've done! Night will overtake you. You won't be able to go on before daybreak, and by that time your tracks will have been blown away and you'll be properly nowhere."

In that case I may as well walk straight on. Why turn back? Why should I bring my ship round when I may find the sea straight ahead of me?

"When did you catch a glimpse of the sea? What makes you think you could walk that far? Meanwhile there's Prévot watching for you beside the *Simoon*. He may have been picked up by a caravan, for all you know."

Very good. I'll go back. But first I want to call out for help.

"Hi! Hi!"

By God! You can't tell me this planet is not inhabited. Where are its men?

"Hi! Hi!"

I was hoarse. My voice was gone. I knew it was ridiculous to croak like this, but—one more try:

"Hi! Hi!"

And I turned back.

I had been walking two hours when I saw the flames of the bonfire that Prévot, frightened by my long absence, had sent up. They mattered very little to me now.

Another hour of trudging. Five hundred yards away. A hundred yards. Fifty yards.

"Good Lord!"

Amazement stopped me in my tracks. Joy surged up and filled my heart with its violence. In the firelight stood Prévot, talking to two Arabs who were leaning against the motor. He had not noticed me, for he was too full of his own joy. If only I had sat still and waited with him! I should have been saved already. Exultantly I called out:

"Hi! Hi!"

The two Bedouins gave a start and stared at me. Prévot left them standing and came forward to meet me. I opened my arms to him. He caught me by the elbow. Did he think I was keeling over? I said:

"At last, eh?"

"What do you mean?"

"The Arabs!"

"What Arabs?"

"Those Arabs there, with you."

Prévot looked at me queerly, and when he spoke I felt as if he was very reluctantly confiding a great secret to me:

"There are no Arabs here."

This time I know I am going to cry.

A man can go nineteen hours without water, and what have we drunk since last night? A few drops of dew at dawn. But the northeast wind is still blowing, still slowing up the process of our evaporation. To it, also, we owe the continued accumulation of high clouds. If only they would drift straight overhead and break into rain! But it never rains in the desert.

"Look here, Prévot. Let's rip up one of the parachutes and spread the sections out on the ground, weighed down with stones. If the wind stays in the same quarter till morning, they'll catch the dew and we can wring them out into one of the tanks."

We spread six triangular sections of parachute under the stars, and Prévot unhooked a fuel tank. This was as much as we could do for ourselves till dawn. But, miracle of miracles! Prévot had come upon an orange while working over the tank. We shared it, and though it was little enough to men who could have used a few gallons of sweet water, still I was overcome with relief.

Stretched out beside the fire I looked at the glowing fruit and said to myself that men did not know what an orange was. "Here we are, condemned to death," I said to myself, "and still the certainty of dying cannot compare with the pleasure I am feeling. The joy I take from this

half of an orange which I am holding in my hand is one of the greatest joys I have ever known."

I lay flat on my back, sucking my orange and counting the shooting stars. Here I was, for one minute infinitely happy. "Nobody can know anything of the world in which the individual moves and has his being," I reflected. "There is no guessing it. Only the man locked up in it can know what it is."

For the first time I understood the cigarette and glass of rum that are handed to the criminal about to be executed. I used to think that for a man to accept these wretched gifts at the foot of the gallows was beneath human dignity. Now I was learning that he took pleasure from them. People thought him courageous when he smiled as he smoked or drank. I knew now that he smiled because the taste gave him pleasure. People could not see that his perspective had changed, and that for him the last hour of his life was a life in itself.

We collected an enormous quantity of water—perhaps as much as two quarts. Never again would we be thirsty! We were saved; we had a liquid to drink!

I dipped my tin cup into the tank and brought up a beautifully yellow-green liquid the first mouthful of which nauseated me so that despite my thirst I had to catch my breath before swallowing it. I would have swallowed mud, I swear; but this taste of poisonous metal cut keener than thirst.

I glanced at Prévot and saw him going round and round with his eyes fixed to the ground as if looking for something. Suddenly he leaned forward and began to vomit without interrupting his spinning. Half a minute later it was my turn. I was seized by such convulsions that I went down on my knees and dug my fingers into the sand while I puked. Neither of us spoke, and for a quarter of an hour we remained thus shaken, bringing up nothing but a little bile.

After a time it passed and all I felt was a vague, distant nausea. But our last hope had fled. Whether our bad luck was due to a sizing on the parachute or to the magnesium lining of the tank, I never found out. Certain it was that we needed either another set of cloths or another receptacle.

Well, it was broad daylight and time we were on our way. This time we should strike out as fast as we could, leave this cursed plateau, and tramp till we dropped in our tracks. That was what Guillaumet had done in the Andes. I had been thinking of him all the day before and had determined to follow his example. I should do violence to the pilot's unwritten law, which is to stick by the ship; but I was sure no one would be along to look for us here.

Once again we discovered that it was not we who were shipwrecked, not we but those who were waiting for news of us, those who were alarmed by our silence, were already torn with grief by some atrocious

and fantastic report. We could not but strive towards them. Guillaumet had done it, had scrambled towards his lost ones. To do so is a universal impulse.

"If I were alone in the world," Prévot said, "I'd lie down right here. Damned if I wouldn't."

East-northeast we tramped. If we had in fact crossed the Nile, each step was leading us deeper and deeper into the desert.

I don't remember anything about that day. I remember only my haste. I was hurrying desperately towards something—towards some finality. I remember also that I walked with my eyes to the ground, for the mirages were more than I could bear. From time to time we would correct our course by the compass, and now and again we would lie down to catch our breath. I remember having flung away my waterproof, which I had held on to as covering for the night. That is as much as I recall about the day. Of what happened when the chill of evening came, I remember more. But during the day I had simply turned to sand and was a being without mind.

When the sun set we decided to make camp. Oh, I knew as well as anybody that we should push on, that this one waterless night would finish us off. But we had brought along the bits of parachute, and if the poison was not in the sizing, we might get a sip of water next morning. Once again we spread our trap for the dew under the stars.

But the sky in the north was cloudless. The wind no longer had the same taste on the lip. It had moved into another quarter. Something was rustling against us, but this time it seemed to be the desert itself. The wild beast was stalking us, had us in its power. I could feel its breath in my face, could feel it lick my face and hands. Suppose I walked on: at the best I could do five or six miles more. Remember that in three days I had covered one hundred miles, practically without water.

And then, just as we stopped, Prévot said:

"I swear to you I see a lake!"

"You're crazy."

"Have you ever heard of a mirage after sunset?" he challenged.

I didn't seem able to answer him. I had long ago given up believing my own eyes. Perhaps it was not a mirage; but in that case it was a hallucination. How could Prévot go on believing? But he was stubborn about it.

"It's only twenty minutes off. I'll go have a look."

His mulishness got on my nerves.

"Go ahead!" I shouted. "Take your little constitutional. Nothing better for a man. But let me tell you, if your lake exists it is salt. And whether it's salt or not, it's a devil of a way off. And besides, there is no damned lake!"

Prévot was already on his way, his eyes glassy. I knew the strength

of these irresistible obsessions. I was thinking: "There are somnambulists who walk straight into locomotives." And I knew that Prévot would not come back. He would be seized by the vertigo of empty space and would be unable to turn back. And then he would keel over. He somewhere, and I somewhere else. Not that it was important.

Thinking thus, it struck me that this mood of resignation was doing me no good. Once when I was half drowned I had let myself go like this. Lying now flat on my face on the stony ground, I took this occasion to write a letter for posthumous delivery. It gave me a chance, also, to take stock of myself again. I tried to bring up a little saliva: how long was it since I had spit? No saliva. If I kept my mouth closed, a kind of glue sealed my lips together. It dried on the outside of the lips and formed a hard crust. However, I found I was still able to swallow, and I bethought me that I was still not seeing a blinding light in my eyes. Once I was treated to that radiant spectacle I might know that the end was a couple of hours away.

Night fell. The moon had swollen since I last saw it. Prévot was still not back. I stretched out on my back and turned these few data over in my mind. A familiar impression came over me, and I tried to seize it. I was . . . I was . . . I was at sea. I was on a ship going to South America and was stretched out, exactly like this, on the boat deck. The tip of the mast was swaying to and fro, very slowly, among the stars. That mast was missing tonight, but again I was at sea, bound for a port I was to make without raising a finger. Slave-traders had flung me on this ship.

I thought of Prévot who was still not back. Not once had I heard him complain. That was a good thing. To hear him whine would have been unbearable. Prévot was a man.

What was that! Five hundred yards ahead of me I could see the light of his lamp. He had lost his way. I had no lamp with which to signal back. I stood up and shouted, but he could not hear me.

A second lamp, and then a third! God in Heaven! It was a search party and it was me they were hunting!

"Hi! Hi!" I shouted.

But they had not heard me. The three lamps were still signaling me.

"Tonight I am sane," I said to myself. "I am relaxed. I am not out of my head. Those are certainly three lamps and they are about five hundred yards off." I stared at them and shouted again, and again I gathered that they could not hear me.

Then, for the first and only time, I was really seized with panic. I could still run, I thought. "Wait! Wait!" I screamed. They seemed to be turning away from me, going off, hunting me elsewhere! And I stood tottering, tottering on the brink of life when there were arms out there ready to catch me! I shouted and screamed again and again.

They had heard me! An answering shout had come. I was strangling,

suffocating, but I ran on, shouting as I ran, until I saw Prévot and keeled over.

When I could speak again I said: "Whew! When I saw all those lights . . ."

"What lights?"

God in Heaven, it was true! He was alone!

This time I was beyond despair. I was filled with a sort of dumb fury.

"What about your lake?" I rasped.

"As fast as I moved towards it, it moved back. I walked after it for about half an hour. Then it seemed still too far away, so I came back. But I am positive, now, that it is a lake."

"You're crazy. Absolutely crazy. Why did you do it? Tell me. Why?"

What had he done? Why had he done it? I was ready to weep with indignation, yet I scarcely knew why I was so indignant. Prévot mumbled his excuse:

"I felt I had to find some water. You . . . your lips were awfully pale."

Well! My anger died within me. I passed my hand over my forehead as if I were waking out of sleep. I was suddenly sad. I said:

"There was no mistake about it. I saw them as clearly as I see you now. Three lights there were. I tell you, Prévot, I saw them!"

Prévot made no comment.

"Well," he said finally, "I guess we're in a bad way."

In this air devoid of moisture the soil is swift to give off its temperature. It was already very cold. I stood up and stamped about. But soon a violent fit of trembling came over me. My dehydrated blood was moving sluggishly and I was pierced by a freezing chill which was not merely the chill of night. My teeth were chattering and my whole body had begun to twitch. My hand shook so that I could not hold an electric torch. I who had never been sensitive to cold was about to die of cold. What a strange effect thirst can have!

Somewhere, tired of carrying it in the sun, I had let my waterproof drop. Now the wind was growing bitter and I was learning that in the desert there is no place of refuge. The desert is as smooth as marble. By day it throws no shadow; by night it hands you over naked to the wind. Not a tree, not a hedge, not a rock behind which I could seek shelter. The wind was charging me like a troop of cavalry across open country. I turned and twisted to escape it: I lay down, stood up, lay down again, and still I was exposed to its freezing lash. I had no strength to run from the assassin and under the sabre-stroke I tumbled to my knees, my head between my hands.

A little later I pieced these bits together and remembered that I

484

had struggled to my feet and had started to walk on, shivering as I went. I had started forward wondering where I was and then I had heard Prévot. His shouting had jolted me into consciousness.

I went back towards him, still trembling from head to foot—quivering with the attack of hiccups that was convulsing my whole body. To myself I said: "It isn't the cold. It's something else. It's the end." The simple fact was that I hadn't enough water in me. I had tramped too far yesterday and the day before when I was off by myself, and I was dehydrated.

The thought of dying of the cold hurt me. I preferred the phantoms of my mind, the cross, the trees, the lamps. At least they would have killed me by enchantment. But to be whipped to death like a slave! . . .

Confound it! Down on my knees again! We had with us a little store of medicines—a hundred grammes of ninety per cent alcohol, the same of pure ether, and a small bottle of iodine. I tried to swallow a little of the ether: it was like swallowing a knife. Then I tried the alcohol: it contracted my gullet. I dug a pit in the sand, lay down in it, and flung handfuls of sand over me until all but my face was buried in it.

Prévot was able to collect a few twigs, and he lit a fire which soon burnt itself out. He wouldn't bury himself in the sand, but preferred to stamp round and round in a circle. That was foolish.

My throat stayed shut, and though I knew that was a bad sign, I felt better. I felt calm. I felt a peace that was beyond all hope. Once more, despite myself, I was journeying, trussed up on the deck of my slave-ship under the stars. It seemed to me that I was perhaps not in such a bad pass after all.

So long as I lay absolutely motionless, I no longer felt the cold. This allowed me to forget my body buried in the sand. I said to myself that I would not budge an inch, and would therefore never suffer again. As a matter of fact, we really suffer very little. Back of all these torments there is the orchestration of fatigue or of delirium, and we live on in a kind of picture-book, a slightly cruel fairy-tale.

A little while ago the wind had been after me with whip and spur, and I was running in circles like a frightened fox. After that came a time when I couldn't breathe. A great knee was crushing in my chest. A knee. I was writhing in vain to free myself from the weight of the angel who had overthrown me. There had not been a moment when I was alone in this desert. But now I have ceased to believe in my surroundings; I have withdrawn into myself, have shut my eyes, have not so much as batted an eyelid. I have the feeling that this torrent of visions is sweeping me away to a tranquil dream: so rivers cease their turbulence in the embrace of the sea.

Farewell, eyes that I loved! Do not blame me if the human body cannot go three days without water. I should never have believed that man was so truly the prisoner of the springs and freshets. I had no

notion that our self-sufficiency was so circumscribed. We take it for granted that a man is able to stride straight out into the world. We believe that man is free. We never see the cord that binds him to wells and fountains, that umbilical cord by which he is tied to the womb of the world. Let man take but one step too many . . . and the cord snaps.

Apart from your suffering, I have no regrets. All in all, it has been a good life. If I got free of this I should start right in again. A man cannot live a decent life in cities, and I need to feel myself live. I am not thinking of aviation. The airplane is a means, not an end. One doesn't risk one's life for a plane any more than a farmer ploughs for the sake of the plough. But the airplane is a means of getting away from towns and their bookkeeping and coming to grips with reality.

Flying is a man's job and its worries are a man's worries. A pilot's business is with the wind, with the stars, with night, with sand, with the sea. He strives to outwit the forces of nature. He stares in expectancy for the coming of dawn the way a gardener awaits the coming of spring. He looks forward to port as to a promised land, and truth for him is what lives in the stars.

I have nothing to complain of. For three days I have tramped the desert, have known the pangs of thirst, have followed false scents in the sand, have pinned my faith on the dew. I have struggled to rejoin my kind, whose very existence on earth I had forgotten. These are the cares of men alive in every fibre, and I cannot help thinking them more important than the fretful choosing of a night-club in which to spend the evening. Compare the one life with the other, and all things considered this is luxury! I have no regrets. I have gambled and lost. It was all in the day's work. At least I have had the unforgettable taste of the sea on my lips.

I am not talking about living dangerously. Such words are meaningless to me. The toreador does not stir me to enthusiasm. It is not danger I love. I know what I love. It is life.

The sky seemed to me faintly bright. I drew up one arm through the sand. There was a bit of the torn parachute within reach, and I ran my hand over it. It was bone dry. Let's see. Dew falls at dawn. Here was dawn risen and no moisture on the cloth. My mind was befuddled and I heard myself say: "There is a dry heart here, a dry heart that cannot know the relief of tears."

I scrambled to my feet. "We're off, Prévot," I said. "Our throats are still open. Get along, man!"

The wind that shrivels up a man in nineteen hours was now blowing out of the west. My gullet was not yet shut, but it was hard and painful and I could feel that there was a rasp in it. Soon that cough would begin that I had been told about and was now expecting. My tongue was becoming a nuisance. But most serious of all, I was beginning to see

shining spots before my eyes. When those spots changed into flames, I should simply lie down.

The first morning hours were cool and we took advantage of them to get on at a good pace. We knew that once the sun was high there would be no more walking for us. We no longer had the right to sweat. Certainly not to stop and catch our breath. This coolness was merely the coolness of low humidity. The prevailing wind was coming from the desert, and under its soft and treacherous caress the blood was being dried out of us.

Our first day's nourishment had been a few grapes. In the next three days each of us ate half an orange and a bit of cake. If we had had anything left now, we couldn't have eaten it because we had no saliva with which to masticate it. But I had stopped being hungry. Thirsty I was, yes, and it seemed to me that I was suffering less from thirst itself than from the effects of thirst. Gullet hard. Tongue like plaster-of-Paris. A rasping in the throat. A horrible taste in the mouth.

All these sensations were new to me, and though I believed water could rid me of them, nothing in my memory associated them with water. Thirst had become more and more a disease and less and less a craving. I began to realize that the thought of water and fruit was now less agonizing than it had been. I was forgetting the radiance of the orange, just as I was forgetting the eyes under the hat-brim. Perhaps I was forgetting everything.

We had sat down after all, but it could not be for long. Nevertheless, it was impossible to go five hundred yards without our legs giving way. To stretch out on the sand would be marvelous—but it could not be.

The landscape had begun to change. Rocky places grew rarer and the sand was now firm beneath our feet. A mile ahead stood dunes and on those dunes we could see a scrubby vegetation. At least this sand was preferable to the steely surface over which we had been trudging. This was the golden desert. This might have been the Sahara. It was in a sense my country.

Two hundred yards had now become our limit, but we had determined to carry on until we reached the vegetation. Better than that we could not hope to do. A week later, when we went back over our traces in a car to have a look at the *Simoon,* I measured this last lap and found that it was just short of fifty miles. All told we had done one hundred and twenty-four miles.

The previous day I had tramped without hope. Today the word "hope" had grown meaningless. Today we were tramping simply because we were tramping. Probably oxen work for the same reason. Yesterday I had dreamed of a paradise of orange-trees. Today I would not give a button for paradise; I did not believe oranges existed. When I thought about myself I found in me nothing but a heart squeezed dry. I was tottering but emotionless. I felt no distress whatever, and in a way I regretted it: misery would have seemed to me as sweet as water. I might

then have felt sorry for myself and commiserated with myself as with a friend. But I had not a friend left on earth.

Later, when we were rescued, seeing our burnt-out eyes men thought we must have called aloud and wept and suffered. But cries of despair, misery, sobbing grief are a kind of wealth, and we possessed no wealth. When a young girl is disappointed in love she weeps and knows sorrow. Sorrow is one of the vibrations that prove the fact of living. I felt no sorrow. I was the desert. I could no longer bring up a little saliva; neither could I any longer summon those moving visions towards which I should have loved to stretch forth arms. The sun had dried up the springs of tears in me.

And yet, what was that? A ripple of hope went through me like a faint breeze over a lake. What was this sign that had awakened my instinct before knocking on the door of my consciousness? Nothing had changed, and yet everything was changed. This sheet of sand, these low hummocks and sparse tufts of verdure that had been a landscape, were now become a stage setting. Thus far the stage was empty, but the scene was set. I looked at Prévot. The same astonishing thing had happened to him as to me, but he was as far from guessing its significance as I was.

I swear to you that something is about to happen. I swear that life has sprung in this desert. I swear that this emptiness, this stillness, has suddenly become more stirring than a tumult on a public square.

"Prévot! Footprints! We are saved!"

We had wandered from the trail of the human species; we had cast ourselves forth from the tribe; we had found ourselves alone on earth and forgotten by the universal migration; and here, imprinted in the sand, were the divine and naked feet of man!

"Look, Prévot, here two men stood together and then separated."

"Here a camel knelt."

"Here . . ."

But it was not true that we were already saved. It was not enough to squat down and wait. Before long we should be past saving. Once the cough has begun, the progress made by thirst is swift.

Still, I believed in that caravan swaying somewhere in the desert, heavy with its cargo of treasure.

We went on. Suddenly I heard a cock crow. I remembered what Guillaumet had told me: "Towards the end I heard cocks crowing in the Andes. And I heard the railway train." The instant the cock crowed I thought of Guillaumet and I said to myself: "First it was my eyes that played tricks on me. I suppose this is another of the effects of thirst. Probably my ears have merely held out longer than my eyes." But Prévot grabbed my arm:

"Did you hear that?"

"What?"

488

"The cock."

"Why . . . why, yes, I did."

To myself I said: "Fool! Get it through your head! This means life!"

I had one last hallucination—three dogs chasing one another. Prévot looked, but could not see them. However, both of us waved our arms at a Bedouin. Both of us shouted with all the breath in our bodies, and laughed for happiness.

But our voices could not carry thirty yards. The Bedouin on his slow-moving camel had come into view from behind a dune and now he was moving slowly out of sight. The man was probably the only Arab in this desert, sent by a demon to materialize and vanish before the eyes of us who could not run.

We saw in profile on the dune another Arab. We shouted, but our shouts were whispers. We waved our arms and it seemed to us that they must fill the sky with monstrous signals. Still the Bedouin stared with averted face away from us.

At last, slowly, slowly he began a right angle turn in our direction. At the very second when he came face to face with us, I thought, the curtain would come down. At the very second when his eyes met ours, thirst would vanish and by this man would death and the mirages be wiped out. Let this man but make a quarter-turn left and the world is changed. Let him but bring his torso round, but sweep the scene with a glance, and like a god he can create life.

The miracle had come to pass. He was walking towards us over the sand like a god over the waves.

The Arab looked at us without a word. He placed his hands upon our shoulders and we obeyed him: we stretched out upon the sand. Race, language, religion were forgotten. There was only this humble nomad with the hands of an archangel on our shoulders.

Face to the sand, we waited. And when the water came, we drank like calves with our faces in the basin, and with a greediness which alarmed the Bedouin so that from time to time he pulled us back. But as soon as his hand fell away from us we plunged our faces anew into the water.

Water, thou hast no taste, no color, no odor; canst not be defined, art relished while ever mysterious. Not necessary to life, but rather life itself, thou fillest us with a gratification that exceeds the delight of the senses. By thy might, there return into us treasures that we had abandoned. By thy grace, there are released in us all the dried-up runnels of our heart. Of the riches that exist in the world, thou art the rarest and also the most delicate—thou so pure within the bowels of the earth! A man may die of thirst lying beside a magnesian spring. He may die within

reach of a salt lake. He may die though he hold in his hand a jug of dew, if it be inhabited by evil salts. For thou, water, art a proud divinity, allowing no alteration, no foreignness in thy being. And the joy that thou spreadest is an infinitely simple joy.

You, Bedouin of Libya who saved our lives, though you will dwell for ever in my memory yet I shall never be able to recapture your features. You are Humanity and your face comes into my mind simply as man incarnate. You, our beloved fellowman, did not know who we might be, and yet you recognized us without fail. And I, in my turn, shall recognize you in the faces of all mankind. You came towards me in an aureole of charity and magnanimity bearing the gift of water. All my friends and all my enemies marched towards me in your person. It did not seem to me that you were rescuing me: rather did it seem that you were forgiving me. And I felt I had no enemy left in all the world.

This is the end of my story. Lifted on to a camel, we went on for three hours. Then, broken with weariness, we asked to be set down at a camp while the cameleers went on ahead for help. Towards six in the evening a car manned by armed Bedouins came to fetch us. A half-hour later we were set down at the house of a Swiss engineer named Raccaud who was operating a soda factory beside saline deposits in the desert. He was unforgettably kind to us. By midnight we were in Cairo.

I awoke between white sheets. Through the curtains came the rays of a sun that was no longer an enemy. I spread butter and honey on my bread. I smiled. I recaptured the savor of my childhood and all its marvels. And I read and re-read the telegram from those dearest to me in all the world whose three words had shattered me:

"So terribly happy!"

IX

PORTRAIT
OF JENNIE

by Robert Nathan

A Love Story

We had come to the great circle at the end of the Mall, and my path led away to the left, across the Drive again, and out the west gate. The winter evening wrapped us round in mist, in solitude and silence . . . "Well, goodbye," I said; "I have to go now."

I held out my hand to her, and she took it gravely. "Do you know the game I like to play best?" she asked. "No," I said.

"It's a wishing game."

I asked her what she wished for most.

"I wish you'd wait for me to grow up," she said. "But you won't, I guess."

After this a reader has no doubt that it is going to be a love story, but he can have no idea how very strange and touching a love story.

Portrait of Jennie is one of the most haunting of short novels. I read it when it was first published, then for a second time a few years ago. And now I have just completed it for a third time, and I like it more than ever. Someone has written, "The world of Robert Nathan . . . is a world of pity and irony, of tolerant gentle humor and deep intuitive wisdom, peopled by children and deities . . ." To this might be added, a world of curious happenings and of people who are a little curious also, none of them the recognizable types encountered so often in conventional stories. Robert Nathan has been writing books for many years, and his supply of originality and charm never seems to diminish.

In *Portrait of Jennie*, presented herewith, he is in his most original and charming vein.

Chapter I

THERE IS SUCH A THING AS HUNGER for more than food, and that was the hunger I fed on. I was poor, my work unknown; often without meals; cold, too, in winter in my little studio on the West Side. But that was the least of it.

When I talk about trouble, I am not talking about cold and hunger. There is another kind of suffering for the artist which is worse than anything a winter, or poverty, can do; it is more like a winter of the mind, in which the life of his genius, the living sap of his work, seems frozen and motionless, caught—perhaps forever—in a season of death; and who knows if spring will ever come again to set it free?

It was not only that I could not sell my work—that has happened to good men, even to great men, before—but that I couldn't seem to get through, myself, to the things that were bottled up inside me. No matter what I did, figure, landscape, still-life, it all seemed different from what I meant—from what I knew, as surely as my name was Eben Adams, was the thing I really wanted to say in the world; to tell people about, somehow, through my painting.

I cannot tell you what that period was like; because the worst part of it was an anxiety it is very hard to describe. I suppose most artists go through something of the sort; sooner or later it is no longer enough for them just to live—to paint, and have enough, or nearly enough, to eat. Sooner or later God asks His question: are you for me, or against me? And the artist must have some answer, or feel his heart break for what he cannot say.

One evening in the winter of 1938 I was walking home through the Park. I was a good deal younger then; I carried a portfolio of drawings under my arm, and I walked slowly because I was tired. The damp mist of the winter evening drifted around me; it drifted down across the sheep meadow, and through the Mall which was empty and quiet at that hour. The children who usually played there had gone home, leaving the bare, dark trees and the long rows of benches wet and spidery with mist. I kept shifting the portfolio from one arm to the other; it was heavy and clumsy, but I had no money to ride.

I had been trying all day to sell some of my pictures. There is a sort of desperation which takes hold of a man after a while, a dreadful feeling of the world's indifference, not only to his hunger or his pain, but to the

very life which is in him. Each day the courage with which I started out was a little less; by now it had all run out, like sand from a glass.

That night I was at the bottom, without money or friends, cold, hungry, and tired, without hope, not knowing where to turn. I think I was a little lightheaded, from not having had enough to eat. I crossed the Drive, and started down the long, deserted corridor of the Mall.

In front of me, the spaced, even rows of lights shone yellow in the shadowy air; I heard the crisp sound of my own footsteps on the pavement; and behind me the hiss and whisper of traffic turned homeward at the end of day. The city sounds were muted and far away, they seemed to come from another time, from somewhere in the past, like the sound of summer, like bees in a meadow long ago. I walked on, as though through the quiet arches of a dream. My body seemed light, without weight, made up of evening air.

The little girl playing by herself in the middle of the Mall made no sound either. She was playing hopscotch; she went up in the air with her legs apart, and came down again as silent as dandelion seed.

I stopped and watched her, for I was surprised to see her there, all alone. No other little children were in sight, only the mist and the long, even rows of lights stretching away to the terrace and the lake. I looked around for her nurse, but the benches were empty. "It's getting pretty dark," I said. "Oughtn't you to go home?"

I don't believe it sounded unfriendly. The child marked her next jump, and got ready; but first she looked at me sideways over her shoulder. "Is it late?" she asked. "I don't know time very well."

"Yes," I said; "it's late."

"Well," she said, "I don't have to go home yet." And she added in a matter of fact tone,

"Nobody's ready for me."

I turned away; after all, I thought, what business is it of mine? She straightened up, and pushed the dark hair back from her face, under the brim of her bonnet. Her arms were thin, they made the sharp, bird-like motions of a child. "I'll walk a ways with you, if you don't mind," she said. "I guess it's a little lonesome here all by myself."

I said I didn't mind, and we went up the Mall together, between the empty benches. I kept looking around for someone she might belong to, but there was nobody. "Are you all alone?" I asked after a while. "Isn't anybody with you?"

She came to some chalk marks left there by another child, and stopped to jump over them. "No," she said. "Who would there be?

"Anyway," she added a moment later, "you're with me."

And for some reason that seemed to her quite enough. She wanted to know what I had in the portfolio. When I told her, she nodded her head in a satisfied way. "I knew they were pictures," she said. I asked her how she knew.

"Oh, I just knew," she said.

The damp mist drifted along beside us, cold, with the smell of winter in it. It was my not having eaten all day that made everything seem so queer, I thought, walking up the Mall with a little girl no higher than my elbow. I wondered if I could be arrested for what I was doing; I don't even know her name, I thought, in case they ask me.

She said nothing for a while; she seemed to be counting the benches. But she must have known what I was thinking, for as we passed the fifth bench, she told me her name without my asking. "It's Jennie," she said; "just so's you'll know."

"Jennie," I repeated, a little stupidly. "Jennie what?"

"Jennie Appleton," she said. She went on to say that she lived with her parents in a hotel, but that she didn't see them very often. "Father and mother are actors and actresses," she declared. "They're at the Hammerstein Music Hall. They do juggling on a rope."

She gave a sort of skip; and then she came over to me, and put her hand in mine. "They're not home very much," she said; "on account of being in the profession."

But something has begun to worry me. Wait a minute, I said to myself, there's something wrong here. Wait, I thought . . . wait a minute . . . and then I remembered. Of course—that was it: the Hammerstein Music Hall had been torn down years ago, when I was a boy.

"Well," I said; "well . . ."

Her hand in mine was real enough, firm and warm; she wasn't a ghost, and I wasn't dreaming. "I go to school," she said, "but only in the mornings. I'm too little to go all day yet."

I heard her give a child's sigh, full of a child's trouble, light as air. "I don't have very exciting lessons," she remarked. "They're mostly two and two is four, and things like that. When I'm bigger, I'm going to learn geography and history, and about the Kaiser. He's the King of Germany."

"He was," I said gravely. "But that was long ago."

"I think you're wrong," said Jennie. She walked a little away from me, smiling to herself about something. "Cecily Jones is in my class," she said. "I can fight her. I'm stronger than she is, and I can fight her good.

"She's just a little girl."

She gave a skip. "It's fun having somebody to play with," she said.

I looked down at her: a child dressed in old fashioned clothes, a coat and gaiters and a bonnet. Who was it painted children like that? Henri? Brush? One of the old fellows. . . . There was a picture in the Museum, somebody's daughter, it hung over the stairs as you went up. But children always dressed the same. She didn't look to me as though she played with other children very often.

I said yes, I supposed it was fun.

"Don't you have anyone to play with?" she asked.

"No," I said.

I had an idea that she was sorry for me, and at the same time glad that I had nobody else but her to play with. It made me smile; a child's games are so real, I thought, for children believe everything. We came to an interesting crack, and she hopped along on one foot until she got to the end of it. "I know a song," she said. "Would you like to hear it?"

And without waiting for me to answer, looking up at me from under the brim of her bonnet, she sang in a clear, tuneless voice:

> Where I come from
> Nobody knows;
> And where I'm going
> Everything goes.
> The wind blows,
> The sea flows—
> And nobody knows.

The song caught me off my guard, it was so unlike what I had expected. I don't know what I had been waiting for—some nursery rhyme, perhaps, or a popular tune of the day; little girls whose parents were actors and actresses sometimes sang about love. "Who taught you that?" I asked in surprise.

But she only shook her head, and stood there looking at me. "Nobody taught me," she said. "It's just a song."

We had come to the great circle at the end of the Mall, and my path led away to the left, across the Drive again, and out the west gate. The winter evening wrapped us round in mist, in solitude and silence, the wet trees stood up dark and bare around us, and the distant city sounded its notes, falling and fading in the air. "Well, goodbye," I said; "I have to go now."

I held out my hand to her, and she took it gravely. "Do you know the game I like to play best?" she asked. "No," I said.

"It's a wishing game."

I asked her what she wished for most.

"I wish you'd wait for me to grow up," she said. "But you won't, I guess."

A moment later she had turned and was walking quietly back down the Mall. I stood there looking after her; after a while I couldn't see her any more.

When I got home I heated a can of soup on the gas burner, and cut myself a slice of bread, and some cheese. It was heavy in my stomach, but it made me feel better. Then I took my paintings out of the portfolio, and set them up on the floor, against the wall, and looked at them. They were all New England scenes: Cape Cod, churches, boats, old houses . . . water colors, mostly, with a few drawings among them. But none of the city . . . funny that I had never thought of that before . . .

I went over to the window, and looked out. There wasn't much to see, a line of roofs and chimneys, dark and indistinct, a few lighted windows, and in the north some taller buildings dim against the sky. And over all, the damp, cold air of winter, the raw, heavy air of the coast. A tug boat hooted in the bay; the sad, mysterious sound passed over the roofs, and floated above the city's restless grumble like a sea bird over a river. I wondered why I had never wanted to do any pictures of the city . . . I could do some pastels of the river, I thought, if I could get the cold tone of the sky. And that line of buildings south of the park, in the evening—if I could get that dim blue mountain look they have. But all the time, in the back of my mind, I was thinking about the child I had met in the Mall. Where I am going, nobody knows; The wind blows, And nobody knows. It was a strange little song, its very tunelessness made it hard to forget, the tunelessness was so much a part of it.

I thought of the last thing she had said to me, before she turned and walked away. But people couldn't wait for other people to grow up; they grew up together, side by side, and pace by pace, one as much as the other; they were children together, and old folks together; and they went off together into that something that was waiting—sleep, or heaven, I didn't know which.

I shivered; the big gray dusty radiator in front of the window was only luke-warm. I should have to talk to Mrs. Jekes again, I thought. But I felt suddenly sad, as though someone had just told me an old story about grief. There was no use trying to work any more that night; I went to bed, to keep my courage up.

Chapter 2

I WAS BEHIND IN MY RENT AGAIN. I think Mrs. Jekes would have asked me to leave, if she could have found anyone to take my place; but nobody wanted a studio like mine, with the furniture falling to pieces, and the ceiling dusty with age. Just the same, she took what I had to say about the heat in very bad part. "This isn't a hotel," she said. "Not for what you pay, it isn't.

"That is," she added grimly, "when you pay it."

I used to dread my meetings with her. She would stand there in front of me, her mouth tight, her thin hands folded across her stomach, and a look in her eyes as though she were seeing through me into the future, and finding it as hopeless as the past. You may wonder that I didn't leave and go somewhere else; but the truth is, I had nowhere else

497

to go. Cheap studios were hard to find; and besides, I was almost always in arrears, and so much without hope myself, those days, that I stayed on because I didn't believe that anything else would be any better.

It was a time of depression everywhere. Hatreds clashed and fought in the air above our heads, like the heavenly battles of angels and demons in the dawn of creation. What a world for a painter; a world for a Blake, or a Goya. But not for me. I was neither—neither mystic nor revolutionary; there was too much of my mid-western father in me for the one, and too much of my New England grandmother for the other. Yet their heaven had been bright with faith.

I believe that Mrs. Jekes admired my paintings, although she never said so. She used to stand and look at them, with her tight mouth and folded hands; and once she accepted a sketch of the town landing on the Pamet River in Truro, in place of a week's rent. It would fetch a much bigger price today, I suppose, but I doubt if she knows it. Nor do I know what she saw in it—some memory, perhaps, of sunnier days. I had tried to put the stillness of summer into it, the peace of the ever-moving river, the quiet of old boats deserted in the grass. Perhaps she saw it there, too—or only guessed; I don't know.

She didn't care for my pictures of the city. Now that I look back at it, I can see that they were only an old story to her—only the city, in which she was caught like a fly in molasses. What did she care for the cold sky above the river, or the mountain blue of the windy, shadowy streets? She knew them only too well; she had to live her life with them.

But I was full of hope; it lasted for three days. By the end of that time, I had found out that I could not sell my city sketches, either.

It was late in the afternoon of the fourth day that the turn came. I didn't think of it then as a turn; it seemed to me just a piece of luck, and no more.

I was on my way home from tramping about the streets, my drawings under my arm, when I found myself in front of the Mathews Gallery. I had never been there before; it was a small gallery in those days, on one of the side streets off Sixth Avenue. There was a show going on, of some young painter's work—mostly figures and flower pieces; and I went in more or less out of curiosity. I was looking around when Mr. Mathews came up to me, and asked me what I wanted.

I know Henry Mathews very well by now, I know all about him. In fact, it was he who sold my *Girl In A Black Dress* to the Metropolitan six years ago. I know him to be both timid and kind; he must have hated to see me come in, for he knew at once that I wasn't there to buy anything. But it was getting late, and he wanted to close up; and so he had to get rid of me. Miss Spinney ran the office for him in those days, too; she had gone home, otherwise he would have sent her out to talk to me. She knew how to deal with people who wanted to sell him something.

He came out of his little office at the rear of the gallery, and smiled at me uncertainly. "Yes sir," he said; "what can I do for you?"

I looked at him, and I looked down at the portfolio under my arm. Oh well, I thought, what's the difference? "I don't know," I said; "you could buy one of my pictures, perhaps."

Mr. Mathews coughed gently behind his hand. "Landscapes?" he asked.

"Yes," I said; "mostly."

Mr. Mathews coughed again; I know that he wanted to say to me, My dear young man, there's not a chance. But he could not bring himself to say it; for he dreaded the look in people's eyes when he had to say No. If only Miss Spinney had not gone home—she would have sent me about my business in short order.

"Well," he said doubtfully, "I don't know. Of course, we buy very little . . . almost nothing . . . and the times being what they are . . . However, let me see what you have. Landscapes. Hmm . . . yes; too bad."

I undid the strings of my portfolio, and propped it up on a table. I had no hope of anything, but even to be allowed to show my work, was something. It was warm in the gallery, and I was cold and tired. "Those are some studies from down on Cape Cod," I told him. "That one is the fisheries at North Truro. That's Cornhill. That's the church at Mashpee."

"Landscapes," said Mr. Mathews sadly.

All the tiredness, the hunger, the cold, the long waiting and disappointment, caught me by the throat, and for a moment I couldn't speak. I wanted to take my pictures, and go away. Instead, "Here are one or two sketches of the city," I said. "There's the bridge—"

"What bridge?"

"The new one," I said.

Mr. Mathews sighed. "I was afraid of it," he said.

"And here's a view from the Park, looking south . . ."

"That's better," said Mr. Mathews wanly. He was trying not to look too discouraging; but I could see that he was unhappy. He seemed to be wondering what on earth to say to me. Well, go on, I thought to myself, why don't you say it? Tell me to get out. You don't want any of these . . .

"There's the lake, with ducks feeding . . ."

All of a sudden his eyes lighted up, and he reached out for the portfolio. "Here," he cried; "what's that?"

I looked, myself, with curiosity at the drawing he had in his hand. "Why," I said uncertainly, "that's not anything. That's only a sketch— it's just a little girl I met in the Park. I was trying to remember something . . . I didn't know I'd brought it along with me."

"Ah," said Mr. Mathews happily; "but still—this is different. It's good; it's very good. Do you know why I like it? I can see the past in it.

Yes, sir—I've seen that little girl before, somewhere; and yet I couldn't tell you where."

He held it out in front of him; then he put it down, walked away, and came back to it again. He seemed a lot more cheerful; I had an idea that he was glad because he wouldn't have to send me away without buying anything. My heart began to beat, and I felt my hands trembling.

"Yes," he said, "there is something about the child that reminds me of something. Could it be that child of Brush's up at the Museum?"

I drew in my breath sharply; for a moment I felt again the dream-like quality of that misty walk through the Mall with Jennie. "Not that it's a copy," he said hastily, "or even the same child; and the style is very much your own. There's just something in each that reminds me of the other."

He straightened up briskly. "I'll buy it," he said. But all at once his face fell, and I could see that he was wondering what to pay me for it. I knew that it wasn't worth much, just a sketch done with a little wash . . . if he paid me what it was worth, I should hardly have enough for one decent meal. I am sure now, as I look back on it, that he was thinking so too.

"Look here, young man," he said . . . "What's your name?"

I told him.

"Well, then, Mr. Adams, I tell you what I'll do. I'll take the girl—and that park scene—and give you twenty-five dollars for the pair."

My hands were trembling in good earnest now. Twenty-five dollars . . . that was a lot of money to me then. But I didn't want to seem too eager. What trouble we go to, trying to fool people who see right through us anyhow.

"All right," I said; "it's a deal."

Before he went back to his office to get me the money, he took a little pad out of his pocket, and wrote something down on it. I happened to glance at it where he had left it lying open on the table. It must have been the Gallery expense account, for there were two columns of figures, marked Sales and Expenses. Under Sales he had written: 1 small etching, water scene, Marin, 2nd impression, $35; 1 colored print, blue flower piece, Cézanne, $7.50; 1 litho, Le Parc, Sawyer, pear wood frame, $45.

Under Expenses he had written:

lunch, with beer	$.80
cigar	.10
hatcheck	.10
bus (both ways)	.20
stamps	.39
Spinney	5.00
flag from man in veteran's hat	.10
2 water colors, Adams	15.00

For a moment my heart sank, for I had thought he had said twenty-five. But before I had time to feel too badly about it, he came out again with the full amount, two tens and a five. I tried to thank him, but he stopped me. "No," he said, "don't thank me; who knows, in the end I may have to thank you."

He gave me a timid smile. "The trouble is," he said, "that nobody paints our times. Nobody paints the age we live in."

I murmured something about Benton, and John Stuart Curry. "No," he said, "we'll never find out what the age is like, by peering in a landscape."

I must have looked startled, for he coughed in a deprecating way. "Let me tell you something, Mr. Adams," he said. "Let me give you some advice. The world is full of landscapes; they come in every day by the dozens. Do me a portrait of the little girl in the Park. I'll buy it; I'll buy them all. Never mind bridges; the world is full of bridges. Do a great portrait, and I'll make you famous."

Clapping me timidly on the shoulder, he ushered me out into the cold winter air, blue with twilight. But I no longer knew whether it was winter or not. Twenty-five dollars . . .

It was not until long after that I found out the truth about that fifteen dollars in the expense account. It was all he thought they were worth, and he was afraid of what Miss Spinney would say in the morning. He meant to make up the difference out of his own pocket.

Chapter 3

SO SWIFT IS THE HOT HEART OF YOUTH, that I thought I had already made a success, and wanted all the world to share it with me. That night I had supper at Moore's Alhambra, on Amsterdam Avenue; for all my glory, that was the best I could do for myself. As I came in, Gus Meyer, who owned the taxicab that used to stand at the corner of our street, waved to me from a table. "Hi, Mack," he exclaimed; "park yourself." He called everybody Mack; it was his way of telling people that they meant nothing to him personally; or else that he liked them.

"Well," he said, after I was seated, "how are you doing?" He had a big plate of pigsknuckles in front of him, and a glass of beer. "The specialty today," he said; "you'd ought to have some."

Fred, the smaller of the two waiters, came over and I gave him my order. "I'm doing all right," I said to Gus. "I just sold two pictures to an art gallery."

His fork stopped half way to his mouth; and he gaped at me. "You mean you got money?" he asked.

He put his fork down, and shook his head in wonder. "I guess you probably had it coming to you," he said. "But don't lose it, now. Put it in a bank, like you read about in the advertisements."

I told him that most of it would have to go to my landlady, and he looked sorry for me. "An artist don't make so much," he remarked, to comfort me. "It's the same as me. You don't get a chance to lay nothing aside."

For a moment or two he gazed with a peaceful look at his plate. "I had six hundred dollars once," he remarked. "But I spent it."

Almost as an afterthought, he added, "I gave some of it to my mother."

And he returned to his eating, with an air of having finished off the matter.

"This is elegant pigsknuckles," he declared.

For a while we ate in silence. When he was finished, he pushed his empty plate away, and taking a wooden toothpick from a glass on the table, leaned back to remember, and to reflect.

"Some day," he said thoughtfully, "there'll be no more pigsknuckles, and no more beer. When that time comes, I don't want to be here, neither."

"I don't want to be here now," I said; "but I am."

"Well," he said, "you can't do nothing about that. Here you are, and here you stay. So what's it all about? I ask myself."

He gave his toothpick a long, careful look. "But I don't answer," he declared. "You're born poor, and you die poor; and if you got anything, they try to take it off you."

I made the obvious answer, that some men though born poor died rich. "Then they got other troubles," said Gus. "I don't envy them. All I want is a new coil for the cab. She stalls on me."

"I want more than that," I said.

"You got the wrong idea," he said. "I had six hundred dollars once, and I spent it."

I reminded him that he had given some of it away to his mother.

"So what?" he said. "A feller's got a mother, he's got to look after her, don't he?"

"I don't know," I said. "I haven't got one."

"I'm sorry, Mack," said Gus. He remained downcast, and silent. "Maybe you're married," he said presently. I told him no.

"Well, you're young yet," he said. "Some day you'll meet up with the right one, and you'll be all set." He leaned forward, and looked at me earnestly. "You're a nice kid, Mack," he said. "Put your money in a bank, so when you meet up with the right one, you'll be all set."

I didn't want to talk about things like that. "Listen," I said; "I haven't any money. I never have had any. I just go along, and trust to God."

"Sure," he agreed; "sure. But that don't signify. What you want to ask yourself is, what does God think about it?"

It brought me up short, and made me feel a little uncomfortable. "I don't know, Gus," I said. "What do you think He thinks?"

The toothpick was well chewed out by now; he wrapped his legs around the rungs of his chair, and leaned back. "I wish I could tell you, Mack," he said; "I do indeed. Sometimes you'd almost think He don't know we're here at all. And then when it looks worst, you get a break; along comes a fare for Jersey City, or some drunk tips you what's left of a five dollar bill. That don't make you believe in God, but it shows which way the land lies."

"The pillar of fire," I said, "which went before the chosen people."

But Gus shook his head gloomily. "That was the toughest break we ever got," he said. He brought his chair down, and leaned forward across the table. "Listen, Mack," he said, "did you ever ask yourself what for were we chosen? How I see it is, we weren't chosen for no favors. We were chosen because we were tough; and He needed us like that, so we could tell the world about Him. Well, the world don't want to listen; they want it their way. So they kick us around. God don't care; He says, just keep on telling them."

"And Jesus?" I asked.

"He was a Jew, wasn't He?" said Gus. "He told them; and what did it get Him? If you did what Jesus said today, you'd be kicked around so fast you wouldn't know your tail from a hole in the ground."

He sat up and looked at me, a dark look, like one of the old prophets. "That's where we got a tough break," he said; "being chosen."

"Have another beer," I said; "on me."

"Okay," he said. "I don't mind if I do."

Mr. Moore brought over our beer himself. He was a big man, stout and anxious. "How are you, Gus?" he said. "You look fine. Was everything all right?"

"Elegant," said Gus. "Meet my friend. What's your name, Mack?"

Mr. Moore and I shook hands, and he sat down at our table. "Mind if I sit with you for a minute?" he asked. "Not at all," I said.

"Mack here is a artist," said Gus. "A painter. He just made a lot of money."

The proprietor of the Alhambra beamed at me. "Well now," he said, "that's fine. You satisfied with everything?"

I said yes, that everything was fine.

"We got a nice little place here," said Mr. Moore, looking around slowly, as if he were seeing it all for the first time. "We try to have everybody satisfied."

I felt warm and happy; it was good to be with people, to talk about things without thinking all the time, What am I going to do now?

"You're in a good business, Mr. Moore," I said. "But I guess you know it."

He looked at me, suddenly cautious. "Well, now," he declared, "I don't know. We have a lot of trouble in this business, what with the unions and all. And food costs a lot. We don't make out any too good in this business. At night we don't fill half our tables. It's a lunch business mostly."

"You'd ought to brighten up the place," said Gus. "You take my cab; I give the old bus a going over once a week. Make it shine. That attracts the customers; they like things to look good."

"Sure," said Mr. Moore. "Only I can't afford it."

Gus broke his toothpick in half, and reached for another. "Mack here is a painter," he said. "Leave him paint you something."

Mr. Moore looked from Gus to me; he took up a bowl of sugar, and set it down again. "Well, now," he said, "that's an idea." But I could see that he was waiting to hear what I might have to say.

I thought it was a good idea, too, although it surprised me; it wasn't the sort of thing I would have thought of myself. "Of course," said Mr. Moore, "I couldn't pay much."

"All right," said Gus; "you can feed him, can't you?"

"Yes," said Mr. Moore thoughtfully; "I can feed him."

"Well, Mack," said Gus; "there's your meal ticket."

"It's a good idea," I said.

Mr. Moore gave me a sideways look. "Maybe you could paint me a little something over the bar," he said. "Something tasty, like you'd enjoy standing and looking at."

"He means something with dames in it," explained Gus. "You know —sitting in the grass without nothing on."

The restaurant owner moved uncomfortably; and his fat face grew pink. "It ought to be ladies," he said, "on account of people being a little particular."

"A sort of modern Picnic in the Park," I said, nodding my head. "Yes."

He looked more uncomfortable than ever. "It has to be clean," he said. "Something that wouldn't get me into trouble."

I told him that I thought I knew what he wanted, and he looked grateful. "All right," he said; "go ahead. You can eat here while you're doing it, and afterwards, if it's all right, we can come to an agreement."

It was not a very business-like arrangement, but we shook hands, and he beckoned to the waiter. "Your little dinner was on me," he said, taking our bill and scribbling across it.

When we got outside, Gus patted me on the shoulder. "You're in the

money now, Mack," he said. I tried to thank him, but he waved it aside.
"Listen," he said; "I got my own dinner out of it, didn't I?"

And as he climbed into his cab, he added with a chuckle,
"Keep it clean, Mack."

I went home thinking what a good world it was. That night I gave
Mrs. Jekes the money for two weeks' rent I owed her, and a week's rent
in advance. "What's the matter," she inquired; "you been robbing a bank?"

It didn't even spoil things any, to have her say that. "No," I said.
"I'm doing some murals."

Chapter 4

IT WAS ON A SUNDAY MORNING that I saw Jennie again.
There had been two or three weeks of clear, cold weather, and the big
lake in the Park at Seventy-second Street was frozen, and good for skating.
I took out my old pair of Lunns, and went over. The ice was crowded
with skaters; I sat down on a bench by the shore to put on my skates, and
strapped my shoes to my belt. I stepped off the edge in a wide glide, drew
up in a turn that made the snow fly, and set off with the sun in my face.

It was one of those days of beautiful weather such as we get in New
York in winter, with a blue-white sky, and light, high, white-grey clouds
going slowly over from west to east. The city shone in the sun, roof-tops
gleamed, and the buildings looked as though they were made of water
and air. I struck out in a long stride, taking deep breaths, feeling young
and strong, feeling the blood run warm in my veins, and the air cold and
fresh on my face. Couples crossed me, going by with linked hands and
red cheeks; schoolboys fled past, like schools of minnows, bent over, on
racing skates, cutting ice and wind. An old gentleman was doing fancy
figures by himself; dressed in brown, with a red woolen scarf, he swung
forward, turned, jumped, and circled backward, his skates together in a
straight line, knees bent, and arms akimbo, intent and proud. I stopped
and watched him for a moment, and then went on again, into the sun.
All around me was the quiet flow of skaters moving and gliding, the
creaking sound of steel on ice, the cold air, the bright colors.

I found Jennie near the bridge between the two ponds. She was all in
black velvet, with a short, wide skirt, and white boots attached to her
round, old-fashioned skates. She was doing a figure eight; and none too
well, I thought. But she seemed to me to be taller than I had remembered
her—older, too; I wasn't even sure that it was she, until she looked up
and saw me. "Hello, Mr. Adams," she said.

She coasted over to me, and put out her hands to stop herself. "I didn't know it was you," I told her. "You look older than last time." She smiled, and pressed the toe of one skate down into the ice, to hold herself. "Oh well," she said; "maybe you didn't see me very good."

I don't know how long we stood there, smiling at each other. In a little while, Jennie put her arm in mine. "Come along," she said. "Let's skate."

We started off together arm in arm; and once again the world around me grew misty and unreal. Skaters flowing like a river around us, the little flash of steel in the sun, the sound of that river moving, forms seen for a moment and then gone—our own quiet and gentle motion—all served to bring back to me a feeling I had had once before . . . that feeling of being in a dream, and yet awake. How strange, I thought. I looked down at the slender figure at my side; there was no question about it, she was taller than I had remembered.

"It seems to me," I said, "that you've grown a lot since I saw you."

"I know," she answered.

And as I said nothing, but only smiled uncertainly, she added seriously, "I'm hurrying."

She seemed as light as a feather beside me, but I could feel her arm in mine as we skated. I could see the wide black ripple of her skirt flare out as we swung along; and I wondered if we looked like something in an old print. "How are your parents?" I asked her. "Are they having a good season?"

"Yes," she answered. "They're in Boston now."

I thought: and they left you here all alone. But I suppose that's better than taking you everywhere with them . . .

"I did a little sketch of you," I told her, "and I sold it. It brought me luck."

"I'm glad," she said. "I wish I could see it."

"I'll do one some day just for you," I said.

She wanted to know more about the sketch I had made. I told her about Mr. Mathews, and the portrait he had asked me to do; and about Gus, and the picture I was painting over Mr. Moore's bar. She wanted to see that, too; but it was the portrait for Mr. Mathews that interested her most. "Who will it be of?" she asked; I thought that her voice sounded almost too casual. "I don't know," I answered. "I haven't found out yet."

She skated along a moment or two without saying anything. Then, "Perhaps, . . ." she said. And all at once, in a breathless rush—"Will you let it be me?"

Of course, I thought . . . who else? I realized suddenly that there was no one else, that there never could be anyone else for the picture that Mr. Mathews wanted. If only she were a little older . . .

"I don't know," I said. "Perhaps."

She gave my arm another squeeze, and made a wild swoop to the right. "Hooray," she cried; "I'm going to have my picture painted."

"Won't Emily be mad."

"Emily?" I asked.

"Emily is my best friend," she explained. "She had her picture painted by Mr. Fromkes, and I said you were going to do mine, and she said she'd never heard of you, and so I slapped her, and we quarreled."

"Well," I said. "But I thought it was Cecily you always fought with."

She looked away suddenly, and I felt her hand tremble on my arm. "Cecily died," she said in a whisper. "She had scarlet fever. Now my best friend is Emily. I thought you'd know."

"How would I know?" I asked.

She stumbled suddenly. "My shoe is untied," she said. "I've got to stop."

We coasted to the bank, and I knelt down to tie her shoe lace. Kneeling there, I looked up at her, the flushed face of the child, framed in its dark hair, the brown eyes tenderly dreaming, lost in some other time, some other where and when . . . I thought: she is playing at being Cinderella, or perhaps Snow White, so proud to have me kneeling in front of her, tieing her shoe lace.

We had come to shore near the little refreshment booth which they build each year for the skaters, and I asked Jennie if she would care to go in and rest, and if she would like a cup of hot chocolate. She came out of her dream with a long sigh; then her whole body began to quiver, and she clapped her hands gleefully. "Oh yes," she cried. "I love hot chocolate."

Sitting at the counter together, while the hot, watery brew steamed under our noses, we talked about the weather and the world. She wanted to hear, all over again, about how I had sold the sketch of her to Mr. Mathews; and I for my part wanted to know how she was getting along in school. "It's all right," she said, but without much enthusiasm. "I'm having French."

"French?" I asked; startled, because the last time she had been just beginning her sums. "Yes," she said. "I can say colors, and I can count to ten. Un, deux, trois, quatre . . .

"I can say the war, in French. C'est la guerre."

I couldn't make out what she was talking about. "The war?" I asked. "What war?"

But she only shook her head. "I don't know," she said. "It's just the war."

But then her eyes grew wide, and she looked at me in fright. "They won't hurt children like me," she asked; "will they?"

"No," I said. "No."

She took a deep breath. "That's good," she said. "I don't like being hurt."

And she dipped her little nose happily into the chocolate again.

I was happy too, sitting there, with the air smelling of ice and damp wool, peppermint, and wet wood and leather; and Jennie next to me, drinking her chocolate. Perhaps there was something strange about it; but just the same, it felt altogether right, as though we belonged just there, where we were, together. Our eyes met in a glance of understanding; we looked at each other and smiled, as though we had both had the same thought.

"This is lots of fun," she said.

The chocolate was finished at last; we climbed down from our stools, and clumped our way to the door. "Come along," I said; "we've time for one more round." She took my arm, going down the steps to the ice. "I hate it to stop," she said, "because when will we ever have it again?"

We set off together hand in hand, and made a grand tour of the lake; after that it was time for me to be getting back to work at the Alhambra. I said goodbye to her at the bridge between the two ponds, where we had met. But before I left, I wanted to get one thing straight in my mind.

"Jennie," I said, "tell me—when did Cecily die?"

She looked away; it seemed to me that her eyes grew clouded, and that her small face grew dim.

"Two years ago," she said.

Chapter 5

"SHE HAS A LOOK," I said, "of not altogether belonging to today."

I was showing Mr. Mathews some sketches I had made of Jennie in her skating costume, little pictures of the child in motion, doing an inner edge, or poised on her toes as though to run—the same sketches, as a matter of fact, which were shown last year at the Corcoran, as part of the Blumenthal collection. Miss Spinney was there, too, looking over his shoulder; it was my first meeting with her. I liked her dry voice, her sharp, frosty eyes, and her rough way of talking; for her part, she liked my sketches. When it came to painting and painters, there was no getting around Miss Spinney; she judged a man by his work, and nothing else; she wanted it, or she didn't want it.

Mr. Mathews held the sketches out at arm's length, with his head tilted back, looking at them down his nose. "This girl looks older to me than the first one," he said. "But I rather like it, on the whole. She was, perhaps, a little young, before . . .

"Yes," he said; "they aren't bad—are they, Spinney?"

"Is that all you can say?" remarked Miss Spinney. "That they aren't bad?"

Mr. Mathews tilted his head a little to one side, like a bird. "The thing I like about them," he said, "is the way you've managed to catch that look of not belonging—how was it you said?—not altogether belonging to today. There ought to be something timeless about a woman. Not about a man—we've always been more present-minded."

"You can have the present," said Miss Spinney. "And you know what you can do with it."

Mr. Mathews, who was used to Miss Spinney, went right on. "I don't know what the matter is with women today," he said, sighing. "In my opinion, they lack some quality which they used to have—some quality of timelessness which made them seem to belong to all ages at once. Something eternal—you can see it in all the great paintings from Leonardo to Sargent. Did you ever stop to think how much more real and alive those long-dead women seem to us than the men? The men are done for—finished; there's not a one of them, except perhaps some of the Holbeins, that you'd ever expect to see in the world again. But the women—why, you could meet them anywhere. Mona Lisa, or Madame X . . . on the street, anywhere."

He looked at me accusingly. "The portrait of today," he said, as though it were all my fault, "is planted in the present as firmly as a potato."

"Have you seen Tasker's new portrait of Mrs. Potterly?" asked Miss Spinney.

Mr. Mathews coughed grimly behind his hand. "I understand he received three thousand dollars for it," he remarked.

"One thousand five hundred," said Miss Spinney, "and his trip to Florida."

"One cannot make a living at that rate," said Mr. Mathews.

At my hoarse croak, half envy and half derision, Miss Spinney turned to me and laid a warning hand on my arm. "Now, now, Adams," she said; "control yourself.

"You'll be getting that, too, some day."

It seemed fantastic to me then, fifteen hundred dollars for a portrait; I thought that Tasker must be either a genius or a scoundrel. A man changes his mind about such things as he grows older; but it made me feel bold, and—as I look back at it now—probably a little reckless, too.

"All right," I said; "in that case, what do I get for my sketches?"

"Spinney," murmured Mr. Mathews, "you talk too much."

And Miss Spinney replied almost at the same moment,

"They are hardly worth anything at all."

It was a cruel way to take me down, though I dare say I deserved it. I picked up my sketches, and started to put them away.

509

"My dear young man," began Mr. Mathews unhappily . . .

"Look here . . ."

But I meant to carry it off with a high hand. "Goodbye," I said; and to Miss Spinney, "I'm very glad to have met you."

She looked at me for a moment with eyes like black frost. I thought she was going to help me to the door, but all at once, to my surprise, her face grew warm and rosy, and she burst out laughing. "I like you, Adams," she said, and fetched me a terrific clip on the back. "You're proud, aren't you?

"Come along—take them out again, and let's have a look at them."

She went over them a lot more carefully than Mr. Mathews had done; for one thing, she seemed less interested in Jennie, and more interested in my drawing. Mr. Mathews watched her in a timid sort of way; he wanted her to like them, because that would help him to feel right about me. He kept drumming with his fingers on the table, and clearing his throat.

"I suppose it could be the clothes," he said, "that make her look a little older."

I didn't think so, but I didn't know how to say what I thought; I stood there feeling uneasy, feeling my heart beating a little fast, and wondering what Miss Spinney would say. She put the sketches down at last, and gave me a clear, hard look. "All right, Adams," she said; "we'll give you twenty-five dollars for the lot."

I suppose I might have taken it, if I had been able to forget her remark about the sketches not being worth anything. I was still a little angry, and I wanted to stand up to her. I was young; and I didn't know very much about art dealers. "It isn't enough," I said; and I got ready to go.

I thought to myself that I didn't care, that I'd sell them to somebody else. But I did care, and I had no way of hiding it. "Look, Adams," she said; "you're a nice boy, but you don't know the art business. I know you can paint; but we aren't collectors, we don't buy things we like just for the fun of sitting around and looking at them the rest of our lives. If we buy these sketches, we've got to sell them too. We can give you thirty dollars. What do you say?"

"Yes," said Mr. Mathews eagerly; "what do you say, young man?"

I took a deep breath, and said "Fifty dollars."

Miss Spinney turned slowly away; I thought that she was angry, and I thought what a fool I was being. I was stubborn, but I was unhappy; I looked at Mr. Mathews, but he was looking at Miss Spinney, and drumming on the table. I started to say, "All right, take them," but she didn't wait for me. "The hell with it," she said. "Give him the fifty."

Mr. Mathews jumped with relief. "That's right, Spinney," he exclaimed. "That's right; I'm glad you see it my way."

She shrugged her shoulders. "I'm just a potato, Henry," she said, "with nothing eternal about me. You'll have to sell them yourself."

"Yes," he said. He took up the sketches, looked at them, put them down, and then picked them up again. "Yes," he said; "yes, of course. I'll sell them—never fret; I'll find a customer for them. Not right away, perhaps . . ."

They gave me fifty. It doesn't seem important now, but it did then. I was getting my meals at Moore's Alhambra, and so it seemed like a fortune to me, almost as much as Tasker's fifteen hundred. I suppose it seemed like such a lot because it was my own. It was real, and I could spend it.

Before I left, Mr. Mathews spoke to me again about doing a portrait for him, but this time he said in so many words that he wanted it to be of Jennie. "There's something in the girl," he declared, "reminds me of something . . . I haven't placed it yet, but I can tell you what it feels like. It feels like when I was young."

He looked up at me apologetically. "I don't know if I can express it any other way," he said. "I shouldn't think you'd understand."

But I thought I understood. "Do you mean that she's old fashioned?" I asked.

"No," he said, "that isn't what I mean. Not altogether."

"Well, I do," I replied. "I think she's old fashioned."

Miss Spinney saw me to the door. "Goodbye," she said; "come in again. And if you have any nice flower-pieces, about two or two and a half by four . . ." She looked around for Mr. Mathews, and seeing him behind her with his back turned, lowered her voice to a whisper. "I like flower-pieces," she said.

I went over to Fifth Avenue, because that was the avenue I wanted to walk on. For the first time I felt that it was my world, my city, that it belonged to me, to my youth and to my hopes; there was a taste of exultation in my mouth, and my heart, filled with joy, lifted like a sail and carried me along with it. The windy, high walls over my head, the wide and gleaming shop windows strung out before me with their mingled colors, the women's bright, hard faces, and the sun over everything—the sun and the wind—

I thought of Jennie's song. And then I thought to myself that I didn't know where she lived, or even how to find her; and the light went out of everything.

Chapter 6

"SO WHAT YOU WANT," said Gus, "is I should find a girl whose name is Jennie. You don't know where she lives, nor nothing about her. So you've got what I would call a good start."

"Her parents are jugglers," I told him. "On a tight rope."

"That makes it easier," he said. "Are they on the circuit?"

I didn't know. I told him that their name was Appleton.

"Appleton," he grumbled; "Appleton." He set himself to think for a moment. "There used to be an act called by that name," he declared. "Down at the old Hammerstein."

"That's right," I said eagerly. "That's where they were."

Gus looked at me strangely. "Well, then, Mack," he said, "they'd be in the old folks' home by now. This must be some other people.

"You sure you seen this girl?"

"Yes," I said. "I made some sketches of her."

He shook his head uncertainly. "That don't signify," he remarked. "I was thinking maybe you made her up."

"No," I said. "I didn't make her up."

We were standing in front of his cab, on the corner, in the grey, raw, morning air. There was snow coming. I could smell it back of the wind, and I shivered a little. But Gus, in his two tattered sweaters, one over the other, didn't seem to feel it; he was used to cold, as he was to heat; he made me think of some old fisherman at Truro, whipped by years of weather, blackened and toughened by the sea. But there was no clear salt for Gus; his tides and channels were the streets, and his face was a city face, pale, quick to anger, quick to rejoice, alert, sly, and confident. None of the slow brooding of the ocean there, the patient, sea-way thought . . .

"I'll take a look around if you want," he said, "and ask some people I know. But listen, Mack—" his voice sank to a low and urgent level— "don't go getting into any trouble with the police. A girl as young as that—

"I don't want no trouble myself, neither," he added as an after-thought.

"All I want to do," I said, "is to paint her picture."

And I thought that was all; I would have sworn that was all I wanted.

Back in my studio again, I tried to work. I was doing a fair-sized canvas of the lake with the skaters on it, from memory and from some

sketches, but it was hard to get on with. My heart wasn't in it; my mind flew off in a dozen directions at once. I kept wondering whether I oughtn't to start a flower-piece for Miss Spinney, and whether Gus would be able to find out anything about the Appletons; and I kept thinking about the Alhambra, about my picture over the bar; there was still a lot of work to be done on it. I was restless and uneasy, my brush was uncertain, and the light was poor. I was glad when it was lunch time, and I could put my things away, and go out.

Gus wasn't at the restaurant when I got there. I ate by myself, and then put up my step-ladder back of the bar, and went to work. He came in after I had been working about an hour, and sat down at a table where he could watch me. I looked down at him anxiously, but he shook his head.

"No luck, Mack," he said. "I'm sorry."

"Didn't you find out anything at all?" I asked. He looked back at me with a strange expression on his face. "There were some Appletons did a tight wire act, like I thought," he said, "back in 1914. They had a sort of accident; it seems the wire broke on them one day, back in '22."

We stared at each other for a moment, and then the waiter came with his beer. Gus took a long drink, and, leaning back, gazed solemnly up at my picture. "It's coming along fine," he said.

I had painted a picnic by the shore of a lake not unlike the lake in the Park; and there, by the side of the water, under the trees, my women were gathered to tease and gossip on the grass. They were innocent figures, and I knew that Gus thought that they could do with some men. To that extent he was a realist; but he did not go to extremes. What he asked of a picture was simply this: that it should remind him with the clearest force of what he already knew, along with some further suggestion of a better and a happier world.

"Yes, sir," he declared; "when I see things like that, I think I've been wasting my time."

All at once he sat up in his chair, and pointed to the figure of a young woman lying on her side, her face half turned away, at the edge of the water. "What's the matter with that one?" he demanded. "She don't look so good to me."

"Why?" I asked carelessly, without looking up. "What's the matter with her?"

"She looks drowned," said Gus.

I turned quickly back to the picture. "What do you mean?" I said. But even as I spoke, I saw what he meant; there was something about the way I had placed her under the trees which made her face seem dim, and green with leaf-shadow; her dark hair gave the impression of being wet, and her whole body seemed shadowy with water . . . I felt an indefinable anguish as I looked at it, which I attributed to anger at my

own lack of skill; and reached hurriedly for my tube of raw umber.

But even after I had brought her out into the sun again, I felt a depression which I could not account for. It was that figure, half seen, half hidden, which I had imagined secretly in my heart to be Jennie—as she would some day be—and I could not bear to think that brush and heart had so failed each other.

However, Mr. Moore was well satisfied with the picture. "Well, now," he said, coming over and looking up at me where I sat on my stepladder, "that's just about what I wanted. Yes sir, that's what I had in mind. I'd call it entertaining, but it don't offend. I've got a spot over the service door I've been thinking about; we could maybe do a little something there."

"What's the matter," said Gus; "you want a museum?"

"I like to have it nice here," said Mr. Moore. "A picture brightens things up for the customers."

"All right," said Gus; "tell him to do one of me and my cab. That'll be nice for you, and nice for me, too.

"Only make it look good," he added. "Don't drown me."

The first snow was falling as I went home, small flakes coming down slowly, twisting down through the grey levels of air, on the north east wind. The whole city was grey under the heavy sky which seemed to press against me as I walked. I thought of the Cape, of how this storm must be already singing across the dunes, driving its wet snow in from the sea over the little houses huddled in their hollows, the foam breaking below the cliff at High Land, the thunder of surf filling the long nooks and valleys like the sound of trains rolling and rumbling behind the hills—the storm and the snow driving south, out of the black, empty, wrinkled ocean, out of Labrador, out of Greenland waters dark with winter and night. How little we have, I thought, between us and the waiting cold, the mystery, death—a strip of beach, a hill, a few walls of wood or stone, a little fire—and tomorrow's sun, rising and warming us, tomorrow's hope of peace and better weather . . . What if tomorrow vanished in the storm? What if time stood still? And yesterday—if once we lost our way, blundered in the storm—would we find yesterday again ahead of us, where we had thought tomorrow's sun would rise?

I let myself into the house, shaking the snow from my shoulders on the door sill. As I stood there in the hall, which was as cold and somber as myself, Mrs. Jekes came out of her parlor and looked at me with eyes in which there was suspicion, resentment, and a curious excitement. It was apparent that she had been waiting for me. "Well," she said; "there you are. Hah."

And she folded her hands virtuously in front of her.

I looked back at her without speaking. My rent was paid, and I couldn't think of any reason to be anxious. I had an idea that she disliked

me, and that she was glad to have some bad news for me; but what she said next, wasn't what I expected at all.

"You have a visitor," she said. "A young lady."

And as I only stared at her with my mouth open, she added harshly, "Fine doings, I must say."

With a sniff of disdain, she turned to go back into her parlor again. "The young lady is waiting for you upstairs," she said, and closed the door, as though to say "I wash my hands of all of it."

I went up slowly, puzzled and concerned, my heart beating fast. I had no friends, there was no one it could be. It seemed impossible that anyone should be waiting for me.

But I was wrong. I knew it even before I opened my door; some inner sense told me.

It was Jennie. She was sitting in the old chair near the easel, prim and upright, her hands tucked away in a little muff in her lap, her toes just touching the floor, a round fur bonnet like a little cake on the top of her head. I came in slowly, and leaned for a moment against the side of the door, looking at her. I felt almost weak with happiness.

"I thought maybe you wanted me to come, Eben," she said.

Chapter 7

SHE SAT QUIETLY IN THE BIG CHAIR while I put away my brushes and went to look for something with which to make tea. Her gaze, moving slowly about, lingered on everything, the shabby furniture, the dusty walls, the stacked canvases on the floor, the closet bursting with odds and ends of clothing, sketches, paints, cans, and broken boxes, the tumbled cot with its dilapidated blankets—all that I myself had never thought to look at very carefully, or even notice, before she came. But now I saw it all, and for the first time, as she did. Her eyes widened, and she took a long breath.

"I've never been in a studio before," she said. "It's lovely."

The tin kettle still had some water in it left over from the morning, so I lit the gas ring under it, and went to search in the closet for a box of crackers. "It's an awful place, Jennie," I said. "It's pretty dirty."

"Yes," she agreed, "it is. I didn't want to say it . . . but I guess as long as you said it first . . ."

She got up, and took off her bonnet and laid it with her coat and her muff very neatly on the chair. "I don't suppose you have an apron?" she asked. "And something to dust with?"

I looked at her in consternation. "You're not going to try to clean it?" I cried.

"Yes," she said. "While the water's boiling . . ."

All I could find was a towel and a clean handkerchief. She tied the handkerchief over her hair and under her chin, the way they do on the Cape, and took up the towel with an air of determination. Then, with her slender legs planted wide apart, she looked around once more like a general before a battle, and her face fell. "Oh goodness," she cried; "I don't know where to begin."

I found the crackers, and some lumps of sugar for the tea, and I went down the hall to rinse the cups in the basin. I peered over the bannisters as I went by, to see what I could see; sure enough, there was Mrs. Jekes standing very still in the hall below, listening with all her might. I wondered what she expected to hear, and let out a shrill whistle, to show her what I was doing. She looked up, startled, and then scuttled back into her room again.

When I returned to the studio, Jennie was seated on the floor, the dust-rag towel beside her, and my sketches of the city spread out around her. Smiling, she looked up at me as I entered, a dark smudge across her chin, and another along her arm between her wrist and elbow. "I was looking at these," she said. "Do you mind?"

I told her no, of course I didn't mind.

"They're beautiful," she said. "I think you're a very good artist. Only, some of them . . ." she held a small canvas up to the light . . . "I don't know where they are. I've never seen those places."

I glanced over her shoulder as she sat there on the floor. She was looking at a little picture I had done in tempera of the skyscrapers at Radio City. "Yes," I said; "well . . . they're new, I guess. They haven't been built very long."

"I guess that's it," she agreed.

She looked for a long time at the picture, holding it out toward the window, toward the last grey light of afternoon. "It's funny," she said at last, "how sometimes you've never seen things, and still, you know them. As though you were going to see them some time, and because you were going to see them you could remember what they looked like . . . That doesn't sound right, does it?"

"I don't know," I replied. "It sounds pretty mixed up."

"I guess so," she said. "I guess it does. You couldn't remember what you hadn't ever seen."

She sat with the picture on her lap, staring in front of her. It was almost dark by now in the room, the snow outside, falling more heavily, making a grey light in the window, and everything in shadow. She seemed to be gazing through the shadows themselves into some other where, somewhere far off and strange, for her bosom rose and fell, her lips parted,

and a long sigh escaped her. The snow, caught in a sudden rift of wind, made a soft, spitting sound on the window pane, and in the river somewhere a boat sounded its lonely hoot. She stirred uneasily; her hand crept up and touched mine. "No," she said in a whisper; "you couldn't possibly."

I went over and snapped on the lights, and the bare, untidy room sprang out of the gloom at us, harsh and real, its four stained walls holding the present in a cube of unmoving light. Jennie gave a sort of cry, and rose to her feet. "What a silly," she said; "here I haven't dusted hardly at all."

"Never mind," I told her; "the water's boiling. Let's have our tea."

She was all gayety after that, sitting up in the chair again, with her toes barely touching the floor, pouring water out of the rusty kettle, passing the crackers, and talking happily about a thousand things. I had to tell her all about Miss Spinney, who had such a hard heart and liked flower-pieces, and how we had fought over the sketches, and I had won; and she clapped her hands with excitement. "Oh Eben," she cried, "you are a good one." She wanted to hear about Gus and his taxicab; she thought he must be very rich to have a cab of his own. "Do you think some time he'd let me ride in it?" she asked. "I've never ridden in a taxicab.

"But I've been in a hansom, once, with mother in the Park; the driver sat up on top, and had a high hat."

She told me that her friend Emily was going away to boarding school. "I think perhaps I'll go with her," she said. "It's a convent, really, called St. Mary's, but it isn't Catholic. It's on a hill, and you see the river; and Emily says they go out every Easter and bless the pigs. I don't want to go very much, but mother says I have to, and anyway, Emily's going . . . I'll miss you, Eben."

"I'll miss you, too, Jennie," I said. "Will you pose for me, before you go?"

"I was hoping you'd say that," she answered. "Yes, I will."

"Will you come tomorrow, then?"

But she looked away, and her face took on a puzzled expression. "I don't know," she said. "I don't know if I can."

"The day after?"

She shook her head. "I'll come as soon as I can," she answered; and that was all she would say.

I told her about Tasker's portrait of Mrs. Potterly, and the great price—as it seemed to me—he had got for it. Her face lit up, and she gave a little laugh. "Will you be glad to be so rich?" she asked. "You mustn't forget me."

"Forget you?" I cried incredulously.

"Oh well," she said; "when you're rich and famous.

"But I guess you won't," she added contentedly. "Because maybe I'll be rich and famous too, and we can be it together."

I said: "I don't think I care very much about being rich, Jennie. I just want to paint—and to know what I'm painting. That's what's so hard—to know what you're painting; to reach to something beyond these little, bitter times. . . ."

"Are these bitter times, Eben?" she asked in surprise.

I stared at her, thinking: of course, how would she know about bitterness, how would she know about the artist at all? caught in a mystery for which he must find some answer, both for himself and for his fellow men, a mystery of good and evil, of blossom and rot—the mystery of a world which learns too late, always too late, which is the mold, and which the bloom . . .

She had been watching my face, and now she held out the box of crackers to me. "Here," she said, "take one. Then you won't feel so bad." I burst out laughing at myself, at both of us; and she laughed, too.

But presently she grew serious again. "You're not sad any more, are you, Eben?" she asked. "I mean—you were so sad the first time I saw you."

"No," I said, "I'm fine now. I was scared that night I met you. I felt as though I were lost. . . ."

She cowered down in her chair, and put her hands up as though I were about to strike her. "No," she cried out, "Oh no—don't ever say that, not ever again. And besides, you weren't lost—you were here, and here isn't lost. It can't be; it mustn't be. I couldn't bear it."

And turning to me almost piteously, she added,

"We can't both of us be lost."

It lasted only a moment, and then it was gone—and we were back again, in my room, with the yellow-lighted walls, and the grey snow outside, and my pictures spread out on the floor about me, the world I knew, the world I saw every day real and around me. "No," I said, "I'm not lost. Why should I be?

"What a foolish way to talk."

She smiled up at me in a forlorn sort of way. "Yes," she said; "it's foolish. Don't let's talk like that any more."

"Because," I said, "with little girls like you . . ."

"Yes," she agreed gravely; "little girls like me." She got up, and gave me her cup, and the tea pot. "Here," she said. "You go and wash them out, before you forget."

"All right," I said. "Wait for me; I'll be right back."

"Yes," she said. "I'll wait for you."

I went down the hall; it was dark on the stairs; the door of Mrs. Jekes' parlor was tight shut. I could hear the snow pitting down on the skylight in the roof. I rinsed the cups out, and hurried back. "Jennie," I said.

But she was gone; and the room was empty. I hadn't heard her go; I hadn't heard the hall door close. But she was gone.

It wasn't until later that I remembered that I hadn't even asked her where she lived.

Chapter 8

AFTER THE STORM, THE CITY SPARKLED for a little while; then the snow was gone, upgathered in hard white hills and carted off in trucks to the river. For a day the air was full of winter sounds, the sounds a child remembers from his youth—the wooden tock of shovels on the ice, the clink of picks, the whine and whirr of motors, and the little musical note of chains over the snow. I did a sketch of the river, with its swift and leaden current, and a little oil painting of the Park, with children coasting. But mostly I was content to do nothing, to wander in the city, and to let my mind drift where it pleased. I kept thinking about the portrait I wanted to do of Jennie, and wondering when I would see her again. I no longer thought of her as a child. She seemed to me at that time to be of no particular age, or at that age between ages when it is impossible to say that the child is a young lady, or that the young lady is still a child. From the mystery which surrounded her, my mind hung back, my thoughts turned themselves away. It was enough for me to believe that wherever in this world she actually belonged, in some way, for some reason, she belonged with me.

Even if I had known, it could have made no difference; I can see that now. It was not in my hands, nothing was in my hands; I could not bring the spring nearer before its time, I could not keep the winter from vanishing behind me.

Sometimes in late summer or in early fall there is a day lovelier than all the others, a day of such pure weather that the heart is entranced, lost in a sort of dream, caught in an enchantment beyond time and change. Earth, sky, and sea are in their deepest colors, still, windless, and shining; the eye travels like a bird out across the distance, over the motionless air. All is fixed and clear, never to end, never to change. But in the evening the mist rises; and from the sea comes the grey warning.

In Truro they call it a weather breeder. So it was with me; it seemed to me that the entire world was bathed in a pure and peaceful light. Death had been arrested, and evil was far away; man's cries, the madness, the anguish, were stilled, and in the stillness, like far off surf, I heard the sound of yet more distant things. Far beyond the close horizon

of death, there is something else; beyond evil, some spirit untouched, untroubled, and remote.

Once upon a time, not so very long ago, men thought that the earth was flat, and that where earth and heaven met, the world ended. Yet when they finally set sail for that tremendous place, they sailed right through it, and found themselves back again where they had started from. It taught them only that the earth was round.

It might have taught them more.

This short and happy season was made even happier for me, by the visit of my friend Arne Kunstler, from Provincetown. He arrived one morning in his sheepskin jacket, big, red-faced, and bearded like an artist of the 'eighties. But the resemblance stopped with his beard; there was nothing else of the 'eighties about him. He brought a bundle of canvases down with him from the Cape, and set them up on stretchers in my room. The wild and violent pictures flamed at me from the walls and from the floor, like scenes from an inferno. Next to them, my own paintings seemed restrained and mild, colorless and discreet.

He was not pleased with me. "What is this work you are doing, Eben?" he cried. "Portraits—flower-pieces—what has come over you? Not," he added, "that you ever were on the way to being an important painter; but I always thought there was hope for you, at least."

His voice, like that of an old sea-captain, was always pitched at half a gale. Poor Arne, I never took him very seriously, for all his roaring; and as for his painting, I had long ago given up trying to understand it. But I was fond of him, for we had been students together; and I was delighted to see him. His mind was a cave of winds, blowing from all corners at once, a tempest of ideas; he was in love with color, he was like a Viking gone berserk in a rainbow. He lived on next to nothing: I doubt if he sold more than a canvas a year. But he was a happy man, for he never doubted his own genius. His wants were few; and his sorrows were vast, and without pain.

His favorite remark was this: "Art should belong to the masses." But when I declared that the masses would never understand his paintings, he stared at me in astonishment. "Understand?" he thundered; "understand? Who asked them to understand?

"Art can have meaning only to the creative spirit itself.

"Besides," he added, "the masses aren't as stupid as you think. Look how they took to Homer."

"Not to his water colors," I replied. "And anyhow, what in the name of heaven have you and Homer in common?"

He couldn't answer that, of course. "Oh, well," he mumbled, half in his beard, "I was only trying to show you . . . But you'll see," he bellowed, "just the same."

He brought the past back with him, the old, free, careless days in the wind and sun of New England, the winter at the Atelier Dufoix in

the Rue St. Jacques—the great cold shadowy room with its charcoal stove, and the shivering students, the evenings in the little bistro on the Boule Miche'—the early lessons here at the Academy, under Hawthorne and Olinsky—days of work, and nights of argument, when it was enough to settle forever such things as the eternal verities, and never stop to think of what was to become of the artist and his pictures. I took him to the Modern, to see the Modiglianis, and to the Ferargil, to see the single Brockhurst, my own favorite; but he was as contemptuous of the one as of the other, he had no use for any work except his own.

It was the city he admired most, and coming from the flat, windy winter on the Cape, he helped me to see with fresh eyes the soaring stone, the sun-drenched skylines, the brawling shadows all around me. And my heart, in which the old brew of doubt and anxiety had already begun to clear, stirred by hope, by the bright weather, and by something else which I did not know how to name, opened itself in a thrust of joy to the future.

Needless to say, Mrs. Jekes took an instant dislike to him. The very first night, she came hurrying up the stairs, pale and grim, to ask us to make less noise—though she did not so much ask us, as tell us, standing there in the doorway with her hands folded across her stomach, and her eyes steeped in bitterness. "I don't know what sort of a house you think this is," she said, "or what you think you're doing in it; but there's others want to sleep if you don't, and I can always call the police if I have to."

I can hardly blame her, for we were young, and happy, and we must have been making a lot of noise. I was afraid that Arne would throw something at her, but after one long, startled look, he only mumbled, "Yes ma'am," and went off into a corner. After she had left, marching down the stairs with a tread like an army, I saw that he was pale, and actually uneasy. I started to laugh at him, but he stopped me. "No, Eben," he said, "you're wrong to laugh. That's a dreadful woman. She comes in here like black ice, and my pictures freeze over. Oh no, Oh no, I am going to whisper from now on."

But although I laughed at him, I remembered what he said.

For a week or so, I roamed about the city with Arne, delighting in the fine weather, and in the companionship of my friend. I took him to the Alhambra where, I need hardly add, he thundered at my mural like Dufoix himself in the old days in Paris. In his opinion, I had painted a stupid and vulgar scene; nevertheless, with a plate of sauerbraten in front of him, he went so far as to consider the possibility of doing a panel himself, perhaps the one over the service door, in return for a week's good eating. Mr. Moore thought it over for a while, but after he had seen an example of Arne's work, he shook his head regretfully. "It's not that I don't think Mr. Kunstler is a fine artist," he said, "but I've got to think of the customers. I want everybody to be satisfied around here."

"Never mind," said Arne. "Forget it."

"Yes," said Mr. Moore. "Well, thanks for the offer."

It was Gus who did his best to console him. "Never mind, Mack," he said; "some people don't have no eye for anything but their food. Now you take me; I like to look at something pretty when I got the time. But you take most people, they don't feel that way. What they say is, bring in the soup, and get on with it."

"Forget it," said Arne. He waved his arm in a dignified way. "The artist ought not to have to paint for a living," he declared. "Eben, let us all have another glass of beer, and I will repay you some day when I am able."

"Ho," said Gus; "there's a man for you."

His big, red-knuckled hand wrapped around his glass, Arne beamed at us all. "Here's to art," he said.

"And to friends," I added.

"Any friend of Mack's here is a friend of mine," said Gus.

We dipped our noses into the yellow foam. "Just the same," said Arne in a mild bellow, coming up for air, "art can only mean something to the artist who creates it."

Chapter 9

ARNE WENT BACK TO PROVINCETOWN by boat and bus, leaving behind him by way of a gift, or to repay me for his bed and board, a picture of what he said was a sunset, all in such tones of light as had never been seen on earth before, at least not since the age of reptiles—and which, once his back was turned, I lost no time in hiding under the bed.

During the fortnight which followed, I was busy both at home and at the Alhambra. Among other things, I finished a flower-piece for Miss Spinney, and took it down to the gallery to give to her. As I had feared, Mr. Mathews groaned when he saw it. "Look here," he exclaimed; "whatever put that into your head? A flower-piece . . . and gladiolas, of all things. What do you expect me to do with it, young man?"

I replied that Miss Spinney had asked for it, and that gladiolas were all that I could get at the florist. "It's winter now," I reminded him. "There aren't any summer flowers."

"Spinney," said Mr. Mathews, "you will be my death."

And he gave a cry of indignation.

"Never mind," said Miss Spinney calmly; "I like it. Give Adams thirty dollars, and I'll sell it myself before the week is up."

But for once Mr. Mathews refused to be bullied. Faced with a flower-piece, he put his foot down. "Twenty-five," he said, like a mouse at bay, "and not a penny more."

Miss Spinney looked at him carefully; she knew when to insist, and when to give in. "All right," she said; "twenty-five, then. Is that enough, Adams?"

As a matter of fact, I would have let her have it for less than that, or for nothing. "It isn't enough," I said, "but I'll take it."

"You're hard as nails, aren't you?" she said with her wintry smile. "So am I. That's why I like you.

"Just the same," she added grimly, "we've lost money on you so far. So don't go getting ideas."

Mr. Mathews scratched his chin in an unhappy way. "Well now," he said uncomfortably, "that isn't strictly true, Mr. Adams. I mean to say, we've only sold one sketch, but of course we still have the others."

"Forget it," said Miss Spinney. "Adams here is all right. He understands me."

Nevertheless, as I went out, she drew me aside and pressed a five dollar bill into my hand. "When I say thirty," she declared, "I mean thirty." I tried to give it back to her, but she pushed me out of the door. "On your way, Adams," she said; "on your way. Don't irritate me."

The next day I prepared a five foot canvas; I stretched and mounted it, wet one side of it with water, and worked in a light surface of white lead with my palette knife. Then I set it out to dry. It was a trick Jerry Farnsworth had taught me up on the Cape.

After that there was nothing to do but wait.

Jennie came at the end of the week. I heard her light step on the stairs, and ran to open the door. She looked pale, I thought, and she was dressed in some kind of mourning. She stood in the doorway, and looked at me in a pitiable way.

"It's father and mother," she said. "They had an accident." She tried to smile, but her eyes filled, and she had to wink hard to keep the tears back. "They're dead," she said, almost in surprise.

"I know," I answered, without thinking; and then bit my lip. I took her hand, and led her into the room. I thought that I ought to say something, that I ought to explain how I knew . . . "I read about it," I told her. "In the paper."

"Oh," she said vaguely. "Yes." But she wasn't thinking about me.

I made her sit down, and took her hat and coat and laid them on the bed. "I'm sorry, Jennie," I said.

She drew a deep breath. "They were sweet to me," she said in a voice which trembled a little. "I didn't use to see them very much. But . . . the way they died . . ."

"I know," I said.

"Oh Eben," she cried; and hid her face, and wept.

I wanted to comfort her; but I thought it would be better if I let her cry herself out. Turning my back, I walked over to the window, and stared at the deep blue sky. "Look," I said after a while; "you don't want to pose, do you? I mean—after this?"

I wasn't looking at her, but I could hear her sit up, and blow her nose. "I wanted to come," she said unevenly. "I wanted to see you. Just to be here." She gave a little hiccup, after crying; and then a shaky sigh. "I might as well pose," she concluded. "I don't look very pretty, though."

I thought that if anything, she looked prettier than before. The tears had left no mark on her young face, but they had washed her eyes and left them dark and dreaming. I placed her in the chair, and put a piece of old, yellow silk behind her, something I had bought years before in Paris. It took a long while to get the light to fall just as I wanted it, and to set my easel at the right angle; and all that time she just sat there quietly, staring in front of her, without saying anything. When I was satisfied that I had everything the way I wanted it, I set my canvas up, and began to work.

The picture I started that day needs no description, for most of you have seen it in the Metropolitan Museum, in New York. It is the picture of a girl somewhere in her early 'teens, seated in front of a golden screen. The Museum calls it *Girl In A Black Dress,* but to me it has always been simply Jennie.

I worked in silence, almost in a dream, filled with a strange excitement. So lost was I in what I was doing, that I failed to keep track of the time; I must have been painting well over two hours, when I suddenly saw Jennie droop forward in her chair, and start to slip to the floor. I dropped my brush and ran to her, with my heart in my mouth. But when I lifted her in my arms, she opened her eyes, and smiled timidly up at me. "I'm tired, Eben," was all she said.

She seemed to me to weigh almost nothing. I laid her down on the bed, with her coat over her; and put some water on the stove to heat for tea. When it was ready I made her drink it, and a little color came back into her cheeks. "I'm better now," she said. "I'm not so cold. I can sit there again, if you want me to."

But of course I didn't want her to. "No," I declared, "it's time for you to rest. You've been the best kind of model; we've done very well, we've got a good start. There's lots of time."

She gave another little sigh, almost like a whisper. "No," she said, "there isn't. But I'll do as you say; I'll rest, if you say so."

Shivering a little, she lay back beneath her coat, with closed eyes, her night-dark hair spread out on my pillow, her hand cold as earth in mine. I stood looking down at her, the narrow curve of the young brow, the long lashes which rested so gently on the cheek beneath them; and I felt my heart contract with a sort of fear, and yet at the same time with delight. Who are you? I thought; and what has brought you here to

me? . . . child and stranger, lost and lonely, out of some story in the past? . . .

My hands must have trembled a little, for she opened her eyes and looked gravely up at me. "You're all I have now, Eben," she said.

At my start, half surprise, and half dismay, she let go of my hand, and sat up, huddled under her coat, her thin arms wrapped around her knees. "Except for my aunt," she said, to reassure me. "Only I don't know her very well. She's going to take care of me from now on."

"Well," I said uncomfortably, "that's all right, then, isn't it."

She looked at me beseechingly; it was her turn to ask for reassurance. "You do want me to come," she asked uncertainly, "don't you? To pose, I mean?

"You don't want me never to come again?"

I couldn't speak, but she must have seen in my face the answer to her doubts, for she smiled, and brushed the hair back from her face with the same gesture I had seen her use that first evening—how many years ago?—in the Mall. "I'll come as soon as I can," she said.

"Jennie—" I began hoarsely.

"Yes, Eben?"

I looked away; after all, what was there to say? Nothing; I did not even know what I had been thinking. "Where does your aunt live?" I asked. At least, I thought, I shall know where she is, and then if I must, I can find her. But she shook her head. "What does it matter where I live?" she said. "You can't come to me.

"I can only come to you."

She spoke sadly, with exquisite gentleness, but with infinite finality. For a moment we looked at each other across a gulf of more than air—a gulf over which no soul had ever passed before, either to go or to return. . . . She made a little, helpless gesture, as though to reach out to me. And then the moment was gone, and she withdrew once more into herself, a stranger, dreaming of something I could not see.

But I knew then that we both knew.

After a while she got up and put on her hat and coat. "Goodbye, Eben," she said. "I'll come back as soon as I can. I'll hurry—truly."

She looked up at me with eyes wide and dark and earnest. "I didn't want you to know," she said.

She turned once, in the doorway. "Try to wait," she whispered. "Try to wait for me."

Chapter 10

ONE MUST SOMETIMES BELIEVE what one cannot understand. That is the method of the scientist as well as the mystic: faced with a universe which must be endless and infinite, he accepts it, although he cannot really imagine it. For there is no picture in our minds of infinity; somewhere, at the furthermost limits of thought, we never fail to plot its end. Yet—if there is no end? Or if, at the end, we are only back at the beginning again? . . .

When Jennie returned, a fortnight later, I realized how much taller she had grown in the last few meetings. She was dressed in a uniform such as young ladies wear at a convent boarding school—a middy blouse, and a skirt which hung almost to her ankles. She came bounding up the stairs, and threw her hat on the bed. "Eben," she cried, "what fun."

For a moment I was thoroughly taken aback, for if I had expected anything at all, it was certainly not that. There was nothing to remind me of the last time I had seen her; in fact, there was nothing of the child about her at all, as far as I could see. On the contrary, she seemed to stand almost within the shadow of vigorous young womanhood. I thought: I must finish my portrait quickly, before it's too late . . .

I couldn't avoid saying, "You've grown, Jennie. And those clothes . . ."

She looked down at herself, and laughed ruefully. "I know," she said. "Aren't they awful? They make us wear them at the convent."

Breaking off suddenly, she looked at me in a startled way. "Oh," she cried; "of course . . . you didn't know . . .

"I'm at St. Mary's now, with Emily. My aunt sent me."

"I suppose I guessed as much," I answered. "Well—I've been waiting for you. We'd better begin."

She took her place in the chair, and I brought out an old black coat of my own to put over the middy blouse. "I can do the dress some other time," I told her. "I won't need you for that."

She sat up very stiff and straight in the chair. "Well," she said with a pout, "aren't you glad to see me?"

It was a very different sitting from the one before, and harder, too. Jenny was restless, and in high spirits; she wanted to stop every few minutes, to talk or to walk around. She was full of her life at school, enchanted with the friendships, the comings and goings, the daily incidents of the convent society—happy at having friends, at having secrets—at being, for the first time in her life, part of a little community. There was

the plain-song she had to tell me about; the daily walks to the little green-house, where the girls were allowed to buy fruit from one of the sisters; the little bunches of flowers they gave one another, which they called "bunching"; the convent-school itself, high on its hill above the shining river; and Sister Therese, who taught her mathematics and history, and whose calm, untroubled face had already roused in Jennie's breast the first sharp, sweet experience of love. And then there was Emily, of course, whose secrets and whose room she shared, who exchanged stockings and blouses with her, and on whose dresser there was a picture—but only when nobody would be likely to come in—of a young man in a high collar, with dark eyes and wavy hair, and the printed name beneath it, Mr. John Gilbert.

Yes—Jennie had changed; I even noticed that she had filled out a little. On the whole, I thought it a change for the better. I let her talk on and on, barely listening, my fingers racing in tiny spurts over the canvas, trying at their best speed to follow my eyes; and my eyes, in turn, searching for what they could not see—not only what was there, but what had been, and what would some day be. I felt that I was truly working against time, and felt myself carried forward on a wave of exultation as the picture bloomed under the brush, as I saw, each time I stepped away from it, its growing strength, its gathering beauty.

We stopped at noon for a bite of lunch, although I would gladly have gone on without any. But that would never do for Jennie. It turned out that she had been planning all along to cook lunch for me, on my little gas stove; and that she had even taken lessons in cooking in school. Unfortunately, there was nothing in the studio, as far as I could see, for her to cook.

"I have some sardines," I said, "and some cheese, and crackers, and milk. I'm sorry, Jennie. You see, I didn't know you were coming."

She laughed happily. "That's all I can cook, anyhow," she said. "I could cook an egg, but it doesn't matter. I'll cook the cheese."

And she did, actually, get the cheese to melt, though not without some scorching, and a smell of burning that I was afraid would bring up Mrs. Jekes. After it was melted, she dropped it on the crackers, and there it lay, altogether inedible, and more and more like rubber. I ate a few sardines, and after a while, she did, too. "Isn't this fun?" she said.

And of course, to her, it was. For if Emily had Mr. Gilbert, Jennie had me—her own exciting secret, to be shared in whispers if she felt like it, or held close and inviolable to her breast. Everyone has a secret at that age; a special secret, a private secret—for everything between earth and sky is part of the one great, general secret which young hearts whisper to one another. New sights—new sounds—new meanings—new joys and fears—her heart, which through her childhood was all one color, has turned into a kaleidoscope, made up of shining fragments which fall

at each turn of the glass into ever newer, more breath-taking patterns. Emily . . . Sister Therese . . . plain-song and flowers . . . and finally, myself—all her own, her own private secret, which no one else can know, until she tells.

"The girls keep asking me about you," she confessed. "But I won't tell them anything. Except . . ." she considered a moment . . . "that you're very handsome . . ." And she began to count off on her fingers.

"Jennie," I said; "don't be silly."

". . . and that you're a great artist; and that you nearly starved to death . . ."

She smiled at me shyly. "They loved that part of it," she declared. "They thought it was very romantic."

"Good God," I said.

"Well, they did," she insisted. "And they think it's romantic my coming to see you like this, too."

Her voice was still full of laughter, but her cheeks were pink, and she kept her head bent. "Perhaps it is," I replied a little grimly. "But we've got work to do, and if you've finished with that last bit of milk, we might begin."

Her eyes flew to my face in dismay. "You're not angry, are you, Eben?" she faltered. "I was only joking."

"Of course I'm not angry," I said a little too gruffly, and stood up. "Let's get back to work—shall we?"

She took her place again in a somewhat chastened mood; but she couldn't stay quiet for long. "Eben," she said.

"Mmm?"

"I didn't really say you were handsome."

But that didn't comfort me much.

"I wish I had nicer clothes to wear," she said after a while. "We have a blue dress with a guimpe, for Sundays, and we have to wear long white veils in church. Emily's fell off, the last time; she didn't pin it on right, she was in such a hurry, and she got a whole day's silence."

Receiving no reply to this bit of information, she went on to other things. "I like some of my lessons," she said. "I like things like science, and math. But I don't like history. It makes me feel too sad.

"I have a funny mind, I guess."

I was holding one brush in my teeth while I worked with another, and I mumbled something in reply.

"You have a funny mind, too," she said.

"Perhaps I have," I agreed absently. "Perhaps I have. Just turn your head a little to the right—"

"Eben," she began presently in a queer, breathless voice, "do you think sometimes people can know what lies ahead? I mean—what's going to happen to them?"

But I was working, and thinking only of what I was doing. Otherwise I would have stopped—and thought—and perhaps have been too much troubled by the question to make any answer at all. As it was, I only half heard it; and I answered without thinking.

"Nonsense," I said.

Jennie was silent for a moment; then, "I don't know," she said slowly. "I'm not so sure. You know how you feel sad about things sometimes—things that haven't happened. Perhaps they're things that are going to happen. Perhaps we know it, and are just afraid to admit it to ourselves. Why couldn't you, Eben—if you could see ahead—feel sorry for what was coming? Only you wouldn't know it was coming, you'd call it worry, or something."

I heard it, but I wasn't really paying attention. "You sound like the White Queen," I said.

"The White Queen?"

"The one in Alice," I told her. "She hollered first, and stuck herself afterwards."

"Oh," said Jennie in a small voice. Even with the little mind I had to attend to anything but my painting, I could tell that I had hurt her.

"All right," she said. "I won't talk any more."

And for the remainder of the sitting, she sat there silent and unsmiling, drawn back once more into herself, dreaming and distant. But I was too busy to try to explain; and besides, it did the picture good. When the light began to fail, I put down my brush, and took a deep breath.

"I think I've got it, Jennie," I said.

There was no answer; she seemed to be half asleep. I went quietly down the hall to the washroom, to freshen up; I doubt if I was away for more than a minute or so. But when I got back, Jennie was gone.

She left a note for me, on the bed. "Eben dear," it said; "I'll be back again some day. But not soon. In the spring, I think.

Jennie."

Chapter 11

EVEN BEFORE I TELEPHONED out to the school, I knew what the answer would be. "I'm sorry; there is no one here by that name." I didn't ask them to go back over their files; I knew what the answer would be to that, too.

So there it was.

I must try to describe, if I can, my state of mind in the weeks which followed. I knew that what I had been asked to believe, was impossible; yet I believed it. And at the same time, I was afraid. The fact that my fears were formless, that I did not know what I feared, made it all the worse; for waking or sleeping, nothing frightens us more than the unknown.

I do not know which was harder to bear—the feeling of being afraid, or the sudden sense of desolation which swept down upon me after Jennie had left. She was gone beyond the farthest sea; and there was nowhere I could even look for her.

It made the world around me seem curiously empty—silent, and empty, like the wooden belly of a violin on which nothing is being played. One note would bring it all to life; one note would make an instrument of it. But the note is not played; no one touches it. It remains an empty box.

At first, I was absorbed in my own helplessness; and at the same time, baffled by it. Never before had it occurred to me to ask myself why the sun should rise each morning on a new day instead of upon the old day over again; or to wonder how much of what I did was really my own to do. It may be that here on this earth we are not grateful enough for our ignorance, and our innocence. We think that there is only one road, one direction—forward; and we accept it, and press on. We think of God, we think of the mystery of the universe, but we do not think about it very much, and we do not really believe that it is a mystery, or that we could not understand it if it were explained to us. Perhaps that is because when all is said and done, we do not really believe in God. In our hearts, we are convinced that it is our world, not His.

How stupid of us. Yet we are created stupid—innocent and ignorant; and it is this ignorance alone which makes it possible for us to live on this earth, in comfort, among the mysteries. Since we do not know, and cannot guess, we need not bother our heads too much to understand. It is innocence which wakes us each morning to a new day, a fresh day, another day in a long chain of days; it is ignorance which makes each of our acts appear to be a new one, and the result of an exercise of will. Without such ignorance, we should perish of terror, frozen and immobile; or, like the old saints who learned the true name of God, go up in a blaze of unbearable vision.

I went back to work; and there, before my easel again, I got back a little of my peace of mind. I realized that I was still anchored to earth, and that no matter what God was about, if I was to live, it would have to be by my own efforts. Little by little the sense of being helpless, the fog of fear, burned itself out of my heart, and left me clear, and grateful—and lonely.

It was this loneliness, which I had not expected, and to which I was unused, which kept me from taking the finished portrait to Mr. Mathews

at once. It was all I had of Jennie, all I had to remind me that she was really there in the world; and I could not bring myself to part with it. I found that I kept waiting for her to come back; some part of me which had always been whole and satisfied, was suddenly so no longer; something was missing.

Mrs. Jekes found me talking to the portrait one day. I don't know what I was saying—probably something I had said before, to the real Jennie. She came quietly up behind me, with a duster in her hand, and stood looking over my shoulder. "Well," she said; "well."

It startled me; and disturbed me, too. I moved away, trying to look as though I hadn't been talking out loud to myself, as though it were all a mistake, as though it was something quite natural. But Mrs. Jekes wasn't fooled. "That's the girl who's been visiting you," she said, and her voice was full of malice.

"That's your sweetheart."

I whirled on her in a rage. "You're a fool," I shouted. I wanted to strike her, to push her out of the room. But she stood her ground, and gave me back look for look. "It isn't me is the fool," she said bitterly.

She moved to the door with a sort of bleak dignity. "You can always leave this house if you've a mind to," she said. "There's others will be glad to take your place."

And she added, as she went out,

"You're not a gentleman."

I wanted to run after her and tell her that I was leaving, that I was leaving at once . . . but before I had taken two steps, I halted in dismay. For I realized that I couldn't leave. This was Jennie's room: this was where she had sat, where we had had lunch together, this was what she loved to come back to—how could I leave it? It was full of memories of her.

And besides—if I moved—how would she ever find me again?

I closed the door gently, and turned slowly back into the room again. I'd have to stay; I'd have to tell Mrs. Jekes that I was sorry for what I had said. It put a bitter taste in my mouth. I took Jennie's picture, and turned it to the wall. I didn't want to think about her for a while.

Just the same, I thought about very little else. That was early in March; it was early in April before I saw her again. At least, I know now that I saw her; though I wasn't sure at the time. It was only for a moment; and I had no chance to talk to her.

It was at the gallery, at an exhibition of some of Jerry Farnsworth's things, with one or two of Helen Sawyer's landscapes hanging with them—scenes of the Cape, the crossing at North Truro, an old house, and a painting of the Pamet where it flows past the town landing at Truro. There had been a good crowd in to see them, quite a lot of people; and I had gone back into Mr. Mathews' little office in the rear of the gallery, to

talk to Miss Spinney. She had sold the flower-piece at a profit; and she was feeling friendly, and pleased with herself.

"Adams," she said, after she had greeted me, "tell me something: what is it makes a painter? A man will starve all his life, go around with holes in his pants and his toes sticking out of his boots, and still all he wants to do is slap some paint on a yard of canvas. Who's crazy—him or us? What did you do with the twenty-five dollars you got off us the last time?"

"I spent it," I said.

"Sure," she agreed; "I didn't think you'd bought a bond with it. Only, why not a new coat, or a pair of shoes?"

I looked down at my scuffed and broken shoes, and shrugged my shoulders. I didn't see what business it was of hers. "Oh well," I said, "I could get them shined, and they'd look all right. That is, if I ever thought about it."

"Have they got any soles left on them at all?" she asked.

I grinned at her, but I kept my feet planted firmly on the floor, for I knew it would be like her to pick one of them up the way a blacksmith does when he wants to shoe a horse. "I didn't know you cared," I murmured.

"Don't be an ass," she said. But a slow blush ran up her neck, up over the clean, strong lines of her jaw.

"All right," I said, feeling a little silly, "next time throw in a pair of shoes with the price."

She swore at me like a truck driver; and I went out to look for Mr. Mathews.

I didn't see him at first, for he was at the door saying goodbye to one of the customers. The gallery was nearly empty by this time; a few people were still standing in front of Farnsworth's "Rest After Work," but otherwise the big room was deserted. The Sawyers were over in a far corner, near the door; and I started toward them.

Like all galleries, the room itself was only dimly lighted; the pictures on the wall seemed to have their own light, to give out reflections of sun and sea, or morning sky and noonday earth, which made the air of the room itself seem shadowy and vague. I thought I heard Miss Spinney come out of the office behind me, and turned back for a moment. But there was no one there. When I turned around again, it seemed to me that my heart stopped beating.

There was somebody in front of the Sawyers—a young girl, dressed in a middy blouse, and a skirt which hung almost to her ankles. She was standing directly in front of the picture of the Pamet; that much I could see across the room, in the shadowy light; but no more. She had her hands to her face; and I thought that she was weeping.

"Jennie," I said; or perhaps I only thought I said it. I tried to move, to get across to her, but my legs were like lead. It was all I could do to put

one foot before the other. I could feel the slow, heavy surge of my heart, as I kept trying to breathe, catching at my breath, the way you do in a gale.

She lifted her head, and for a moment I had a glimpse of her face, wet and shiny with tears. And then—she was gone. It was just as simple as that. Perhaps she went out through the door—I don't know. Mr. Mathews, coming in at that moment, bent aside as though to let someone pass. Perhaps it was Jennie.

He came across the floor to me, smiling; but when he saw my face, his expression changed. "Good heavens, Mr. Adams," he cried, "is anything the matter? You look sick, man."

I shook my head; I couldn't say anything. I passed him without speaking, and stumbled out of the door. He looked after me in bewilderment. I left him there wondering what had happened to me.

There were only the usual passers-by in the street. I hadn't expected there would be anyone else.

Chapter 12

SPRING WAS EARLY THAT YEAR; the rainy winds blew themselves out before the end of April. One day the grass in the Park smelt sweet and fresh, and a robin sang on the lawn below the Mall. From then on, the sky seemed made of another blue, and the clouds, too, were a different white, with tones of yellow in them. Yellow is the true color of spring, not green; the new grass, the clouds, the misty, sunny air, the sticky buds like little feathers on the trees, all are mixed with yellow tone, with the haze of sun and earth and water. Green is for summer; blue, for fall.

The city comes up dreaming from the winter, its high roofs seem to melt in the air. The wind blows from the south, across Jersey; it smells sweet, it brings the smell of earth with it. People move more slowly, there is a gentleness about them, the cold is not yet out of their bones, they warm themselves in the sun. The days are longer, and the shadows are not as deep; evenings come down almost imperceptibly, there are long twilights, the dusk is peaceful, and the sounds of evening are tranquil and comforting. Summer lies ahead, the summer of the heart; it is coming, it has been caught sight of, it is on the way, bringing flowers and sea-bathing.

Summer is the worst time of all to be alone. Then earth is warm and lovely, free to go about in; and always somewhere in the distance there

is a place where two people might be happy if only they were together. It is in the spring that one dreams of such places; one thinks of the summer which is coming, and the heart dreams of its friend.

Now in the Park I began to see people walking together, slowly, arm in arm, not hurrying as they did in winter, but taking time to talk to each other, stopping a moment to laugh at the children, or to watch the swans on the lake. When summer came, they would be together still; they could enjoy the spring. But for me, it was different. I had no way of knowing when I should see Jennie again. And as the days passed, I missed her more and more.

There is one thing about distance: that no matter how far away it is, it can be reached. It is over there, beyond the Jersey hills—one can drive to it—it is north, among the pines, or eastward to the sea. It is never yesterday, or tomorrow. That is another, and a crueller distance; there is no way to get there.

Yet, though I missed her, though I could not reach her, I was not altogether without her. For I found that my memory had grown sharper; or else it was beginning to play tricks on me. It was not so much that I began to live in the past, as that the past began to take on more and more the clarity, the actual form of the present, and to intrude itself into my daytime thoughts. The present, on the contrary, seemed to grow a little hazy, to begin to slip away from me . . . so many things reminded me of her. And then I would be seized by memory so urgent that what I remembered seemed almost more real to me than what was before me.

Where others dreamed ahead that spring, toward the summer, I dreamed backward into the past. Sights, sounds, and smells, all served that journey well—the smell of scorching, the sound of wood—perhaps a shovel?—scraped along the pavement; the hoot of a tugboat in the river. At nightfall the shrill, sad voices of children, floating in through my window, brought back to me another evening, in the mist, in the Park, and a child walking beside me down the long avenue of empty benches, skipping along on one foot, hopping over the chalk marks . . . *"Do you know the game I like to play best? It's a wishing game."* Or on a sunny morning, beside the lake on which the boats were lazily drifting, I'd suddenly find myself entranced and motionless, seeing in front of me not the blue, dancing water, but the white, shining ice and the skaters, feeling the cold wind on my cheeks again, and Jennie's arm in mine, so firm and light. . . . Or coming home in the afternoon, I'd hurry up the stairs with a beating heart, because she might be there—remembering so clearly the first time she had come to see me, in her little velvet dress with the muff. *"I thought maybe you wanted me to come,"* she had said.

Such was my state of mind those early days of spring—neither happy nor unhappy; dreaming, and waiting. I didn't want very much, or hope for very much—just to see her again, and to be with her once more. I tried not to think about the summer, or, indeed, about the future at all;

—how could I? I left that to her, just as I had left the past to her. Why we had met, or how it had come about, I did not know. I still do not know. I only know that we were meant to be together, that the strands of her life were woven in with mine; and that even time and the world could not part us altogether. Not then. Not ever.

What is it which makes a man and a woman know that they, of all other men and women in the world, belong to each other? Is it no more than chance and meeting? no more than being alive together in the world at the same time? Is it only a curve of the throat, a line of the chin, the way the eyes are set, a way of speaking? Or is it something deeper and stranger, something beyond meeting, something beyond chance and fortune? Are there others, in other times of the world, whom we would have loved, who would have loved us? Is there, perhaps, one soul among all others—among all who have lived, the endless generations, from world's end to world's end—who must love us or die? And whom we must love, in turn—whom we must seek all our lives long—headlong and homesick —until the end?

By May I had no money left at all, and so I took the portrait down to Mr. Mathews. I hated to give it up, but there was no help for it; I needed money for rent, and for more paints, and canvas. I was still getting some of my meals at the Alhambra, although I had finished my work there; the picnic over the bar seemed to please the customers, and Mr. Moore didn't mind my having one free meal a day, as long as I didn't eat too much. As a matter of fact, he was thinking of getting up a fancy menu with an illustrated cover—possibly a picture of the restaurant, with himself standing in the doorway. Gus wanted me to get his cab into it, too. I didn't mind; an artist works for his meals one way or another.

Gus helped me bring the picture downtown in his cab, and went along with me to see that I wasn't cheated. We carried it into the gallery together, and set it up on the table in the office in the rear. Then we stepped aside, and let Mr. Mathews look at it.

He didn't say anything for a long while. At first I thought that he was disappointed, and my heart sank; but then I saw that he was really very much moved. He had grown a little pale; his eyes first widened, and then narrowed; and he kept stroking the palm of one hand with the fingers of the other. "Well," he said. "Well.

"Yes."

I began to feel excited, too. Up till then, I doubt if I had really looked at the picture myself with any sort of critical eye. There, in my room, it had been so much a part of me; I could still feel the brush strokes in my fingers . . . and besides, it was Jennie, it was all I had of her. . . . But here, in the gallery, seeing it as Mr. Mathews was seeing it, I could realize for the first time what I had done. It made me feel proud, and at the same time humble.

After a while Miss Spinney came in and joined us. She didn't say anything for a minute; and then she took a long breath. "Well, Adams," she said in a strangely gentle voice, "that's it, all right."

Mr. Mathews cleared his throat. "Yes," he said, "that's it. That's what I meant. It's . . . it's . . ." He seemed unable to continue. It was Gus who spoke up for him.

"She's a honey, Mack," he said. "I don't noways blame you."

And turning to Miss Spinney, he added in an easy tone,

"Treat him right, ma'am, on account of he's a friend of mine."

"I'll keep it in mind," said Miss Spinney.

She and Mr. Mathews went outside, to talk it over; and Gus edged up to me and gave me a nudge with his elbow. "I think they like it, Mack," he whispered.

"Yes," I said; "I think they do."

"Well, don't be too easy on them," he said. "Ask for fifty, right off."

"It's worth twice that," I said.

Gus' jaw dropped. "No," he croaked. "Go on. I wouldn't of believed it."

Mr. Mathews and Miss Spinney came back again, looking solemn; and Mr. Mathews settled down to business. "Mr. Adams," he began—

"Why so formal?" said Miss Spinney. "He's in the family."

"Well, then—Eben," said Mr. Mathews, swallowing, "I won't try to disguise my feelings from you. You have given me a great surprise. I am powerfully moved. This picture . . . well . . . I don't like to use the word masterpiece, but just the same . . ."

"Get on with it, Henry," said Miss Spinney.

"Yes," said Mr. Mathews hurriedly. "Quite. The point is, that we don't want to buy it. No," he said, holding up his hand as he saw my face fall—"it's not for the reason you think. The reason is, that I honestly don't know what it's worth."

"Well," I said, "what do you think it's worth?"

"That depends," he answered, "on who buys it. The market isn't very good just at the moment, for individual collectors. But if the museum were to take it—"

"Yes?" I said.

"It might bring more than a thousand dollars," he said.

I heard Gus give a gulp beside me. "What I want to do," continued Mr. Mathews—"what we want to do—is to take it on consignment, and then do the very best we can for it. And as an advance—" he cleared his throat nervously—"as an advance, I can let you have two hundred dollars . . ."

"Henry," said Miss Spinney ominously.

"Three hundred," amended Mr. Mathews unhappily.

Then Gus found his voice again. "Take it, Mack," he said hoarsely; and gave me a shove.

I went home in his cab, leaning back on the cushion, and looking out proudly at my city, which seemed to me to return my look with joy. Through the open window in front, I could see the back of Gus' head; I noticed that he had turned the flag down on his meter, and that the meter was ticking. Well, why not? I was a rich man. But just the same, I was surprised; and it surprised me that Gus wasn't saying anything. His silence wasn't natural; it wasn't like him.

He left me at my house, and took my fare without a word. When I tried to thank him for helping me, he looked away. "Forget it," he said. "It don't signify."

He took his hands off the wheel, and stared at them helplessly, as though in some way or other they had disappointed him. Then he let them drop again.

"I couldn't do nothing for you, Mack," he said. "And that's the truth."

Chapter 13

EARLY NEXT MORNING, in the bright spring sunshine, Jennie came back to me. I heard her voice in the hall, and had only time to slip into my coat, before she was up the stairs and in at the door. She had a little suitcase in her hand; she dropped it just inside the doorway, and came flying across the room, and kissed me.

It was the most natural thing in the world. We held each other out at arm's length and looked at each other, smiling, and not saying anything. We couldn't have spoken . . . The whole sunny, sweet-smelling spring morning had come in with her.

She was older—I saw that at once; a young lady now, dressed in a travelling suit; she even had gloves on. She was breathless, but only from running up the stairs, or from happiness; her brown eyes never faltered as they searched my face. I took a deep breath. "Jennie," I said; "I've missed you."

"I know," she answered. "I've missed you, too. And it's been longer for me." She drew her hands away from mine with sudden gravity. "I'm not in school any more," she said.

"I know," I said. "I can see."

She turned slowly on her heel, and looked around the room with simple joy. "How I've dreamed of this, Eben," she said; "I can't tell you. The nights I've lain awake, thinking of this room . . ."

"I know," I said.

"Do you?" she answered gently. "No, I don't think so."

She stood there, looking around her, and slowly taking off her gloves; and I looked around, too, and wished the room were more in order. I went over to smooth the bed a little, but she stopped me. "No," she said; "don't touch it. Do you remember how I wanted to tidy up for you once, when I was little? Let me do it now. And show me where the coffee is . . . Poor Eben—I did get you up so early. Go and dress yourself, and then we'll have breakfast, and I'll tell you all that's happened."

"But Jennie," I said, "if we have so little time . . ."

"We have a whole long day," she answered breathlessly. "And— and a little more."

I went along down the hall to the washroom, and left Jennie to tidy up, as she wanted. I thought I saw Mrs. Jekes on the landing below, but I didn't pay much attention to her; I was too happy, the day was too lovely . . . a whole long day, and a little more. What did that mean— a little more? I cut myself twice, shaving.

Jennie had learned how to make a bed, and how to make coffee. I hardly knew my room when I got back to it: my work-table was laid with a clean towel, and my two cups, one of them with a broken handle, and the coffee pot, stood side by side, along with a pat of butter I'd had out on the window sill, and some bread she had toasted on a fork over the gas burner. There was a good smell in the air. We sat down together, hand in hand, to our breakfast.

I told her about the picture; and her fingers tightened on mine. "Oh, but that's grand," she cried. "That's wonderful, Eben. Aren't you happy?"

She was silent for a moment, thinking about something. "Eben," she said at last, "let's do something special—shall we? To celebrate? Because I haven't really very long to stay with you. You see . . . I'm being sent abroad—to France—to a finishing school—for two years."

"Jennie," I cried.

"I know," she said quickly. "I don't want to go; but I guess I have to. And anyhow—it won't seem very long. And then . . ."

"And then?" I asked.

"I'm going to hurry," she said earnestly. "And then some day I'll be as old as you."

"I'm twenty-eight, Jennie," I said gravely. She nodded her head. "I know it," she replied. "And so will I be . . . then."

"But not when you come back from France," I said.

"No," she agreed. "There'll be a long time still, after that."

She held my hand tight. "I'm going to hurry, though," she said. "I've got to."

For a moment she seemed to be lost in thought, her head bent, her eyes hidden under their long lashes. Then she roused herself, and sat up

538

with a smile. "Let's go on a picnic, Eben," she said. "Somewhere in the country—for the whole day—

"It's something we've never done before."

Something we'd never done before—as though we'd ever done very much of anything. But she didn't have to urge me. A whole day in the country, in the warm spring weather, together . . . "Yes," I said, "yes. That's what we'll do." She could hardly wait for me to finish my coffee; we hurried down the stairs and out into the street, hand in hand; and the bright sunny morning fell on us like an armful of flowers.

Gus was in his cab, at the corner. When he saw me with Jennie, he took his hat off, and looked frightened. I don't believe he had ever thought she was real, or ever expected to see her. I went up to the cab, and opened the door. "Gus," I said, "we're going on a picnic. We're going out into the country for the day . . . somewhere . . . anywhere. I want you to take us. How much will it cost?"

He twisted his hat in his hands, and tried to smile; he seemed to be having some trouble in swallowing. "Now listen, Mack," he said; "now listen . . ."

"It doesn't matter what it costs," I said, and helped Jennie into the cab.

What was the good of being rich, if I couldn't do what I liked?

Gus looked back once or twice, as though to make sure that we were really there. "So it's a fact," he said finally, more to himself than to me; and in a kind of awe. "Well—

"Where do you want to go, Mack?"

I waved him forward. "Wherever it's green," I said. "Wherever it's country."

I don't know where we went, but it was green and lovely. It was somewhere north of the city—perhaps in Westchester. It took us about an hour to get there. We left the cab by the roadside, and climbed a fence, and ran across a field with a cow in it. The cow didn't notice us. We climbed a little hill, among some trees. Jennie was flushed and breathless, and full of laughter; she and I ran ahead, and Gus came after us.

At noon we sat together on a warm stone wall in the sun at the edge of a meadow, and near a little wood. There were yellow dandelions in the grass, and the air was sweet as honey. We had some sandwiches along—lettuce and bread for Jennie, sausage for Gus and me. We ate our sandwiches, and drank some beer out of cans. It was the first beer Jennie had ever tasted; she didn't like it, she said it tasted bitter.

Gus and Jennie did most of the talking. He told her how he had tried to find her once; and how he had helped me sell the picture; and she told him please to take good care of me, and not to let anything happen. I didn't talk very much; I felt drowsy in the sun, I kept wishing Arne were there, too; I kept thinking about what it would be like some day when we were all together.

Jennie sat on the wall beside me, her head against my shoulder. She had twined a yellow dandelion in her hair; it gave out a fresh, weedy fragrance. The sky was robin's egg blue; I heard a bird singing in the woods. I was happy—happier than I had ever been before, happier than I've ever been since.

Gus left us after lunch, and went back to the cab, to take a nap. Then Jennie too grew silent, resting against me, dreamy and content. After a while, I felt her stir, and draw a long, uneven breath. "What are you thinking, Jennie?" I asked.

She answered slowly and gently, "I'm thinking how beautiful the world is, Eben; and how it keeps on being beautiful—no matter what happens to us. The spring comes year after year, for us, or Egypt; the sun goes down in the same green, lovely sky; the birds sing . . . for us, or yesterday . . . or for tomorrow. It was never made for anything but beauty, Eben—whether we lived now, or long ago."

"Tomorrow," I said. "But when is tomorrow, Jennie?"

"Does it matter?" she asked. "It's always. This was tomorrow—once. "Promise me you'll never forget."

I quoted softly:

> "Where I come from
> Nobody knows;
> And where I'm going
> Everything goes."

She took it up with a little cry of surprise:

> "The wind blows,
> The sea flows—
> And God knows.

"I think He knows, Eben," she said.

And she lifted her lips, trusting and innocent, to mine.

Later we walked in the faint green of the woods, through the shadow of branches, over the ferns and the moss. We found a little brook, and violets hidden among their leaves. Jennie stopped to pick them; she made a tiny bunch, to carry home. "It's to remember today," she said.

The sun began to sink in the west; the shadows fell around us. It grew chilly; we turned, and started home.

Chapter 14

I HAD ONE CLEAR DAY OF HAPPINESS, and I shall never forget it. Even the miserable ending to it cannot change its quality in my memory; for everything that Jennie and I did was good, and unhappiness came only from the outside. Not many—lovers or friends—can say as much. For friends and lovers are quick to wound, quicker than strangers, even; the heart that opens itself to the world, opens itself to sorrow.

I don't think that we spoke of the question of where Jennie was to stay that night. She was sailing in the morning (on the Mauretania, I remember she told me—how strange it was to hear the old name again) and we both seemed to take it for granted that we'd stay together until then.

We had supper at the Alhambra, at a little table near the bar, where she could see my mural, and then we walked home together in the quiet evening. It was cool, the air was still, and in the green west the evening star hung like a lantern over the city.

Those are the scenes, the memories, with which I comfort myself. The spring comes year after year, she had said, and tomorrow is always. When at last there was no tomorrow any more, I remembered yesterday. Yesterday is always, too.

She told me that she had been at the gallery that day of the exhibition, when I thought I had seen her; and that she had been crying. "I don't know why," she said. "It was a picture of a river, and some little hills across on the other side—the Pamet, it was called. And all of a sudden I felt that I knew it, and that it was a sad place—and I found myself crying. I wanted to come to you, but I couldn't; I had to go back. I was unhappy for a while, and then I forgot it."

She put her hand in mine; it was trembling a little. "I'm sorry that you asked me," she said. "I didn't want to remember it."

I turned her hand over, and patted it. "It's a funny little river, Jennie," I said, "and not sad at all. It comes in from the bay, and it's not very deep. The children play there, and the bitterns croak in the reeds at night. And at low tide, everybody goes out and digs for clams."

She smiled uncertainly. "I know," she said. "I'm being silly. Don't let's talk about it any more. Tell me about Paris, instead—you were there, weren't you? Is it very lovely? My school is in Passy—is that near where you were? Tell me what to see, and what to do—so that some day we'll have done it all together. . . ."

We sat on the edge of the bed, and talked for a long time. I told her about Arne, about the Atelier Dufoix, about the Clos des Lilas, where we used to go sometimes when we had money, and the little bistro on the Rue du Bac where we went when we didn't. She listened to me hungrily, seeing it all ahead of her. "Oh Eben," she said; "it's going to be such fun."

We even planned what we'd do together. I remembered a room on the Ile St. Louis, where a friend of mine had lived—a room like the prow of a ship, butting its way up the Seine, and the river pouring by on both sides, under the windows. I promised to take her to the Luxembourg, to the Quai des Marinières, and to the Fair at Neuilly—I promised to dance with her in the Place Pigalle on Bastille Day—and to take her out into the Forest of St. Cloud in the spring, to drink new wine under the trees. "It's going to be such fun," she said.

It was late when Mrs. Jekes knocked on the door. I think I shall remember the sound of it all my life. When death comes at last, I expect he'll sound like that, too.

Even before the door opened, I think I had an idea of what was coming. She stood in the doorway, a still, wintry figure, her hands folded, as always, across her stomach. "Oh no," she said; "oh no. Not in my house, not at night, you won't. There's a limit to everything, my friends. I've run a decent place all my life, and I mean to keep it so."

And pointing a white, shaking finger at Jennie, she cried suddenly, "Get out."

I was too startled even to speak. I seemed to freeze up inside; perhaps it was just as well, for otherwise there's no telling what I might have done. Jennie got up from the bed, slowly, as though in a dream; she turned her frightened face away from me, so that I shouldn't see how ashamed she was. She went quietly over to the chair where she had laid her hat and coat.

"I'm sorry, Eben," she faltered. "I didn't think . . ."

"Get out," said Mrs. Jekes.

I found my voice then. "Be still," I cried to her; and to Jennie: "Don't listen . . . don't listen to her."

But Jennie shook her head. "No," she said; "no—it's too late now: it's been said. It couldn't ever not be said again."

She took up her hat and coat, and stooped to pick up the little suitcase which lay by the door where she had dropped it that morning. Mrs. Jekes moved aside to let her pass. She went by her without a glance, but she turned in the doorway, and looked back at me—a look so full of longing, of love, and of trust, that it was like a hand laid for a moment against my cheek. It was that look, more than anything else, which kept me from rushing after her.

"Goodbye, Eben," she said clearly. "I'll be back again some day—

But not like this. Not ever again like this. Not until we can be together always."

Mrs. Jekes watched her go. She followed her down the stairs; I heard her footsteps grow fainter and fainter down the stairs.

Chapter 15

I MOVED OUT OF MRS. JEKES' HOUSE after that; and since summer was not far off, I decided to join Arne on the Cape at once. Mr. Mathews and Miss Spinney said goodbye to me like old friends; Mr. Mathews gave me a little folding easel which had belonged to Fromkes, and Miss Spinney gave me a bottle of brandy—to keep, as she put it, the fog out of my fingers. "I want another flower-piece," she declared; "a two-and-a-half by four; and a church. I'm sort of fond of churches, the little white ones, with the big steeples. Goodbye, and God bless you. Don't drown yourself in the sea."

"What would I want to drown myself in the sea for?" I asked.

"I don't know," she answered. "Men are fools enough to do anything. Personally, I don't trust the sea. I wouldn't go within fifty miles of it."

"You're tough," I said. "The sea would never get you."

She looked at me with a strange expression; I saw the red start to creep up over her chin. "It's the tough ones drown easy," she said, and turned away.

Mr. Mathews walked to the door with me; he kept reaching up every now and then to pat me on the back. "Goodbye, my boy," he said, "goodbye. I'm glad you came to me; we'll do big things together. You've earned a rest; now enjoy it. But remember—no landscapes. Leave the dunes to Eastwood."

"I want to do the fishermen," I said.

"Fishermen," he echoed doubtfully; "well . . ."

"In the traps," I said, "in the early morning, with the fish churning in the nets."

Mr. Mathews looked at me gloomily. "Listen," he said. "There are enough fish in the world."

He sighed heavily. "But not enough women," he added.

Gus took me to my train. "Take care of yourself, Mack," he said. "Don't do anything I wouldn't do." I had Jennie's violets in a paper bag in my pocket; they were withered by now, but they still retained a little of their fragrance. My paints and canvases and my easel were in one

bundle, and my clothes were in another. The train went at midnight, the great office buildings were dark as we drove down to the station. I kept thinking of how Jennie had been there in the cab with me only the day before.

I knew that I'd see her again, and I told Gus so. "Sure," he said; "sure. Why not? You don't want to be too wise in this world, Mack, because there's always something happens you don't expect. You take my own people, now—they thought they weren't going to get out of Egypt. But they got out all right. And why? So they could write the Bible.

"They couldn't have guessed that."

"They didn't have to guess it," I said.

"I know," said Gus; "you mean Somebody told them. Well—what did He tell them? That's what I want to know."

"I thought He made it clear," I said.

"Not to me," said Gus. "I'm still trying to figure it out. And the way I figure it, is like this: whatever it was, it was good news, on account of the only bad news would be that what we knew was all there was."

I started to pull out some money to pay him for the ride, but he waved it away. "Forget it," he said. "The flag wasn't down. You've done plenty for me."

"Goodbye, Gus," I said. "I'll see you in the fall."

"Sure," he agreed. "Drop me a postal."

I hesitated a moment before picking up my bags. "You think God is trying to tell me something?" I asked, half in earnest.

"I wouldn't put it past Him," said Gus.

"But what?" I cried.

He shook his head. "I wouldn't know," he said.

I came down into Provincetown the next afternoon. The moment we crossed the bridge at Bourne, and I breathed the warm, sunny fragrance of scrub pine and broom, I felt the old peace of summer flow into me. Lilac was out in the Yarmouth yards and doorways, and in Brewster the juice-pear and the wild plum had opened their blossoms, white as snow. The marshes at Wellfleet were all a silvery green; and beyond Truro, there was the bay, still and shining, bluer than a bluebird's wing, with Plymouth clear, dark, and distant on the horizon.

Arne was waiting for me; he had a room in the west end of town, down near Furtado's boat yard, and he took me there to wash up and get settled. I went to the window, and drew in a deep breath of the past. How well I remembered it. The old weedy, fishy smell rose from the tide; the gulls were circling and crying, out in the harbor; and on the sand below, Manuel was hammering at the white hull of a lobsterman. The schooner *Mary P. Goulart* was in harbor, along with most of the fisheries' fleet; and I saw John Worthington's tunaman, the *Bocage*, come chugging in across the blue water from the North Truro nets,

kicking up a little foam at her bows. Slowly and peacefully sky and water deepened; the sun went down over Peaked Hill Bars, and the ruby light came on at Wood End, and the white light at the Point.

We walked down to the fish wharf, past Dyer's hardware store and Page's Garage, past the post office, and the little square with its great elms. The summer visitors hadn't begun to arrive yet, and the town was quiet, with only its own people in the streets. Dark faced fishermen lounged in the doorways, talking together in their own language, half argot and half Portuguese; and the girls went by, two by two in the dusk, hatless and laughing. We stopped in at Taylor's for supper, and I ordered a chowder, the way they make it down there. I wanted to hear the Provincetown news:—who was teaching that year, and how the classes were shaping up, whether Jerry Farnsworth had his old studio, and whether Tom Blakeman was going to take a class in etching again. And then, of course, Arne had to hear about the portrait. When I told him that Mr. Mathews hoped to sell it to a museum some day, he flung out his hands in horror.

"Don't have it, Eben," he thundered. "Never allow it. A museum? The death of the soul."

"Sure," I said. "Like Innes, or Chase."

"They're dead," he answered. "That's all past and done with."

"Is it?" I asked. "I'm not so sure."

"Good God," he bellowed earnestly; "the past is behind us. What?"

"There's still Rembrandt," I said, "and Van Gogh. We're not quite done with them yet. . . . The past isn't behind us, Arne—it's all around us. And down here, on the Cape, is where one ought to feel it most—where the years follow each other like tides in the Pamet, and the boats come in each day with the same fish they had before."

I smiled at him across the table. "I'm only beginning to think about things like that," I said.

"Well," he said unhappily, "I wish you wouldn't. The artist ought not to think so much, it's bad for his color sense."

And with that, we plunged into the old debate, and for the rest of the meal the talk was all of color and line, symbol, form, and mass. "I tell you," cried Arne, pulling at his beard, "we must be like little children again. We must bring back color into the world. That is what color is for, to look at. Do not think: paint. Like children."

He pounded the table, clutched his beard, and roared like a bull. He was perfectly happy. I asked him whether he expected the children to understand his paintings, and he gave me a look of scorn. "Only an artist," he declared, "can hope to understand what another artist is trying to do. That is why there is so little understanding of art among the masses.

"Just the same," he added inconsequentially, "the museums are always full of children."

It was always like that with Arne.

As we went out into the street again after supper, on our way home, he said to me in a hopeful way,

"Is this model of yours coming to the Cape this summer, Eben?" I answered almost without thinking. "Yes," I said. "Some day." He nodded his great head thoughtfully. "Good," he said. "I shall do a portrait of her, myself."

It amused me, as I laughed quietly in the darkness. That would be something to see, that picture.

But it made me feel lonely all of a sudden. I wondered where Jennie was, and what she was doing—in what far off place over which this velvet blue and soft spring evening of ours had long since passed like a wind. Was she still at sea? Night was on the sea, the dark sweep of earth's shadow; but tomorrow's sun was already rising above the eastern slopes of the Urals. And yesterday's sun? did it still shine on the low stone wall at the meadow's edge, near the little wood? It was still today, still noon on the Pacific, on the long, blue swells which washed Hawaii. Yesterday . . . tomorrow . . . where were they?

It would be a long time until Jennie came back to me. Not until we could be together always, she had said. A long summer . . . Hurry, I said to her, in my heart.

I knew that I could never explain it to Arne. I didn't try.

The damp sea air, salty and fresh from the flats, or suddenly pierced with spice from the flowering gardens of Provincetown, flowed around us as we wandered home under the white street lamps. In the harbor the riding lights of the *Mary P. Goulart* rocked gently in the gloom; the beams of the lighthouses at Long Point and Wood End, blinked at the bay; and the great white cross of High Land Light at North Truro swept like the spokes of a wheel through the heavens. The stars burned calmly overhead . . . how many years ago had those metallic rays first leaped out across the empty spaces between their home and ours? Long, long ago; from beyond our furthest yesterday.

The gulls were sleeping out on the water, in the blue dark, silent and forgetful, ranged in rows along the decks of the empty fishing boats. The streets were quiet and deserted; we heard our footsteps following us home.

Chapter 16

BUT I DIDN'T WANT TO STAY in Provincetown for the summer. I still had more than two hundred dollars left of the money I had received for the portrait, and I decided to take a small house in Truro, on the Pamet. It was little more than a shack, really, up on the bluff above the water; the pines stood close, making a brown carpet of needles all around the house, and you looked down at the river through their branches. I could hear the waters of the bay endlessly sounding, and the wind in the pines, not unlike the sound of the sea. The air was warm and sweet with the odor of earth and sun, and there was shelter from the easterly rains, and from the northwest wind, which soared up strong and cold over Cornhill behind me. I was right in the path of a southeast blow, or a smoky sou'wester, but that was an advantage; the winds from the south were fair weather winds, and came in warm and soft.

At low tide the Pamet is no more than a trickle of water among the reeds; but at full moon, and with a full course tide, it overflows the marshes, and one can imagine it as it once was, before the sand piled up at the harbor mouth—a wide, deep river on which as many as thirty whalers could ride to their moorings. But that was long ago. Today the little river pours in and out of a narrow channel to the bay, and wanders crookedly across the Cape between the bay and the ocean. Perhaps a hundred yards from where the Pamet rises among its springs, the low dunes begin; and just across them is the beach and the sea. It's not a long trip from ocean to bay; the Cape is narrow at that end, less than three miles wide.

The little houses nestle in the hollows, safe from the northwest winds which blow so hard in winter. There is pine, and scrub oak, locust, aspen, and elm, bearberry, gorse, wintergreen, beach plum, and cherry. Everything is on a small scale; the tiny hills and hollows, seen in perspective, have the appearance of mountains and valleys. The spires of the two old churches and the meeting house dominate everything; they rise on the highest ridge, and brood serene and lovely over the valleys.

Families still live in Truro from the old days: the Snows, the Dyers, the Atwoods, Atkinses, Cobbs, Paines, Riches. Old names, old families of Cape Cod. . . . It is their country, their home, it belongs to them. They are quiet and kind, hard-working people.

I settled down to work, too. But for a week or so, the colors of the Cape made all my senses drowsy—the pale sand-yellow, the light green, and the faded blue of water and sky deepening off to violet in the dis-

tance. Birds on their way north were stopping off to visit; robins searched the lawns, finches darted like minnows in and out of the trees, a pair of orioles had built a nest in the elm tree back of my house.

By June the gorse was yellow, and the bearberries pink and white on the downs; bob-whites called to each other in the grass. I went down to swim in the river; it was swift and fresh, and the little green crabs fled away from me in the shallows. Some children were there already, playing in an old hulk drawn up on the shore. One, with hair the color of hay, was playing that he was a pirate. He had his crew ready for battle; they consisted of a cap pistol, and his sister. He could not find an enemy.

All summer the children play on the beaches. They are happy and friendly; as each wave sweeps in across the sand, the smaller ones turn their backs to the sea, and run sensibly away. When the water, edged with foam, draws back again, they go running after it, with an air of driving the ocean before them. But at the next wave, they flee as before, with shrill alarm, and fresh surprise. The sun warms their small brown legs, and they collect with enthusiasm bits of clam shell, sand dollars, and colored stones worn by the tide. The larger children plunge into the waves like little dolphins. The water is clear and cold.

Time stands still in Truro; the weeks slip by, one after another. In June there was a nor'easter, the wind came whistling in from the sea, driving the rain almost level before it; it blew for three days, doors swelled and stuck, bureau drawers wouldn't open, and a green mold appeared on some of my canvases. Even the pine logs which burned all day in the fireplace couldn't keep my little house warm or dry. Then the wind swung around to the west, the sun came out, and there was the summer again, the pale sand-yellow, the light green, and the faded blue.

I did a good deal of painting: I did a canvas of the South Truro church for Miss Spinney, the old building, lonely and empty on the downs above the bay; and a watercolor of the sea from the end of Long Nook valley. It was a breezy day, with the wind northeast, the sea was dark, the wine-dark of the Greeks, with bands of green in it, darkening out to the horizon; and the sky was like the inside of a blue porcelain bowl with the light shining through it. I sent them both to Mr. Mathews. But the best thing I did was a painting of the men out in the traps in the early morning. I had to do it mostly from memory: the boats go out to the nets before it's light.

Everything is quiet and dark, the water comes in in long swells out of the darkness. The boats head out into the swells . . . in the east the sky turns grey, and then pink, the dawn comes up slowly. The stars pale out, tones of blue begin to show in the sky. Far out from shore, one boat slips into the traps, drawing the nets up as it goes. The fish are down there, they pass backwards and forwards under the boat like shadows. The nets come higher; suddenly they break water in a rush of silver, and

the fishermen begin scooping them in over the sides. The sun rises, the bay sparkles in the light, the fish are silver underfoot. Slowly and heavily one of the boats crosses the bay to Provincetown, while the other heads back again to the shore.

I wanted Arne to go with me, but he said there wasn't enough color in it for him. He was painting the Provincetown Electric Light and Power Plant; he said that it represented industry, and that industry represented the real world of today, and that it was this real world in which an artist should look for a subject worthy of him.

"Let us not fool ourselves, Eben," he exclaimed. "Beauty is only noble when it is useful. The symbol of the world today is a power plant; and if it appears ugly to us, that is only because we do not look at it in the right way."

But he came to Truro for the beach picnics in July. We lay on the sand at Cornhill, while the sun set, and the moon rose over the hill behind us, and men in corduroys and women with kerchiefs around their hair tended the fire of driftwood gathered on the beach. The sunset paled away into rose and green; the old blue night came down dim and hazy over the shore, and across the bay the lanterns of Provincetown twinkled in the dusk. Within the leaping yellow light of our fire the figures of our friends moved about; more wood was gathered, baskets unpacked, rugs laid down. As the flames burned lower toward the coals, steaks and sausages were broiled; a great bean pot was set beside the fire, a pail of mussels, a kettle of coffee. Afterwards we sang, sitting around the fire, while the moon sailed gently overhead, and the tide sent little ripples to break against the sand . . . *"I dream of Jeannie with the light brown hair . . ."*

Or in the still, warm afternoons of August, we swam together in the sea, as the long rollers came lifting in, green and clear, to break in a bounce of foam, and slide hissing and dying up the beach. Far out, beyond the line of the horizon, beyond sight, over the world's rim, lay Europe, torn with her wars; but here all was peace, the empty shore curved away endlessly to the south under the summer sun, the light breeze stirred the grasses on the dunes, and only the shouts of children rose against the rolling thunder of the sea.

It was then that I longed for Jennie, at such times as these, when the world's beauty fell most upon my heart. And yet, in a way which I found hard to explain, I was not lonely; for I had a sense—as I have had ever since—of not being alone—a feeling that the world and Jennie and I were one, joined together in a unity for which there was no name, an inexpressible one-ness. Her very absence, not only from my sight, but from the slow-wheeling days around me, made them seem less real and solid to me; she was nowhere in the weather, the rains which fell across the Cape were not the rains which fell upon her little figure hurrying along somewhere—in what city, in what year?—yet for that reason all weathers seemed one weather to me, and the seasons of the past mingled in my

dreams with the summer all around me. For she was somewhere in the world; and wherever she was, there, too, was something of me.

She had said: "How beautiful the world is, Eben. It was never made for anything but beauty—whether we lived now, or long ago."

We had that beauty together. We never lost it.

Chapter 17

SUMMER DRAINED AWAY INTO FALL, but Jennie did not return. By September the bearberries were red, and people were picking beach plums in the fields along the roads, to make into jelly. The reeds in the river were silver-brown; and in the afternoons the sun slanted lower through the pines around my house. The birds which had been gone most of the summer, began to appear again, on their way south: red-headed woodpeckers, bluebirds, warblers, and grackles. Swallows swept nervously through the air, and sometimes at evening I saw a wedge of wild duck wavering southward against the sky.

I had received a good-sized check from Mr. Mathews, and decided to use some of it to rent a little sailboat from John Worthington's brother, Bill, who lived near the railroad bridge, close to where the Pamet emptied into the bay. I knew something about sailing, though not a great deal; but I didn't think I could get into much trouble. The boat, an eighteen-foot center-board knock-about, was kept moored near the mouth of the river, in a small backwater to one side of the swiftly moving stream. It took a good bit of navigating to get out into the bay, through the narrow channel; tide and wind both had to be right, but the wind seemed almost always easterly that month, streaming back from the Bermuda high which stood like a formidable but invisible cloud somewhere out at sea; and with a stiff breeze behind me, I could usually manage to make out, even against the tide. Coming back, I had to wait for the current, and then come in close-hauled. Arne constituted himself my crew; he sat forward, ducked the boom when we came about, and handled the jib sheets with a sort of wild solemnity. It was exciting to lean against the wind, and feel the boat fight back against it; to watch the green water slide by, and hear the current chuckle against the planking. It was good exercise, too; it made my arms ache, and put blisters on my hands.

We used to sail out into the bay, sometimes as far as the traps, once or twice as far as Provincetown. It was a world by itself, out there on the water, in the shine and sun-dazzle, a world of never-ending blue,

of steady wind, of clear and arrowy distance; and I was happy there.

Late in September a hurricane was reported in the Caribbean. We thought little about it, it was the time of year for hurricanes, they either hit the Florida Keys, or blew themselves out in the Atlantic. This one apparently was headed for Florida.

On the Cape we had a period of unusually clear weather—a weather-breeder, Arne said. We made the most of it, for the season was drawing to an end, the line storm would be along soon, and after that it would be too cold and rough for sailing. We went out every day. The weather was warm—unnaturally so for that time of year—and the wind southeast. We waited for it to swing around into the north.

On Monday the report was that the storm had missed Florida, and was heading for the Carolinas. That meant rain and a southwest blow; but on Tuesday we heard that it had turned east again, and would lose itself out at sea. So we figured we still had a few days' good sailing weather left to us, and decided to make a long trip up the coast, camp over night on Great Island off Wellfleet, and come home the next day. We left a little before noon on Tuesday; there was a steady breeze from the southeast, and we made a fair reach of it all the way.

We camped that night on the island, and built a fire at the sand's edge. We talked for a long time in the firelight; the shadows danced in the scrub behind us, the pale sky, sown with its stars, lay like a great lake above us, and the little boat rocked quietly at its anchor, on the tide. I tried to tell Arne something of what was in my mind, about myself, and about the world. "We know so little," I said, "and there's so much to know. We live by taste and touch; we see only what is under our noses. There are solar systems up there above us, greater than our own; and whole universes in a drop of water. And time stretches out endlessly on every side. This earth, this ocean, this little moment of living, has no meaning by itself . . . Yesterday is just as true as today; only we forget."

Arne yawned. "Yes," he said. "So it is. Go to sleep."

"And love," I said, "is endless, too; and today's little happiness is only part of it."

"Go to sleep," said Arne. "Tomorrow is another day."

That night, for the first time in my life, I dreamed of Jennie: I dreamed of our meeting, long ago, I dreamed it over again as it had happened; I saw her as the child, walking down the long empty row of benches in the Mall, and I heard her say as she had said then, "I wish you'd wait for me to grow up, but you won't, I guess." And in my dream, I remembered the words of her little tuneless song—

"The wind blows, the sea flows . . ."

I woke with a sense of alarm, with a feeling that something was wrong. The wind was still blowing, warm and steadily southeast, but I thought a little stronger. There was a faint haze in the air, and a few

strange looking clouds passed by overhead. They seemed to be travelling fast. I leaned over and shook Arne by the shoulder. "Get up, Arne," I said. "We've got to get home."

We put the sail up and headed north for Truro. We didn't waste any time. Out on the water, the wind seemed even stronger; it was a little aft of us, and I let the sail take all it would. It was something of a job to hold the tiller, for a fair sea was running, and the boat yawed a good deal. Arne said nothing; he kept watching the sky.

The haze deepened very slowly, but the clouds increased; they were at different levels, moving rapidly, and of a shape I'd never seen before— long cylinders, fog-like tentacles, smoky fingers. They were a different tone of white, too, like cotton gone a little dusty. I had made the main sheet fast, but I wondered if the sail would hold. "Arne," I called to him, "hadn't we better reef?"

He nodded without speaking, and I managed to bring the boat up into the wind. I noticed that my fingers were trembling, and I thought that Arne looked a little pale. There was a curious urgency in the wind. "We'd better get out of here," I said.

The boat went off with a rush under a single reef, and I tried to head up a little to windward, to get some shelter from the shore. The waves were running a good deal higher now, and breaking at the crests; I had to put all my weight on the tiller to hold her steady. I was feeling decidedly uneasy, and I wondered whether I oughtn't to try to make for shore directly, but there was nowhere except the Pamet at Truro where I could have found shelter for the boat. I had no idea how hard the wind was blowing, but I knew it was blowing hard. And there was a strange sound to it, from somewhere far away.

A little before noon I saw Arne point behind us, and followed his glance back over the stern. The horizon to the south had disappeared behind a grey haze. It wasn't altogether grey, but grey-yellow, like mud. I thought perhaps it was rain, but it didn't look like it. We've got to get out of this, I thought.

My arms and hands were aching from holding the tiller, and my legs were tired from bracing myself against the sides. I beckoned Arne to come aft and take over, while I went forward to bail some of the water that had come in, mostly over the stern. Down in the cockpit, the waves seemed higher than ever; we would tilt up at the stern, hang for a moment on a crest, and then rush down the slope after it, and slew around in the hollow till Arne straightened us out. Each time the tip of the boom hit the water, I thought we'd go over. My throat was dry, but I didn't feel frightened, I didn't have time. I kept listening to the wind; it wasn't like anything I'd ever heard before.

A little after that we started to work in toward the Pamet. I went back to the tiller, and told Arne to take the sheet, and let it out whenever

we got over too far. He snubbed it around a cleat as well as he could, but it took all his great strength to hold it. We lay out to windward on the deck, with our legs braced against the centerboard scabbard; the huge seas broke behind us, and then foamed up over the counter, and the dark green water poured along the leeward deck up to the coaming. It seemed to me that we looked right down at the sea under our feet; it rose sometimes in a slice of wave and curled up over the cockpit; then I kicked the tiller, and we came up. We seemed half in and half out of the water most of the time, I couldn't tell which. "I think we'll make it, though," I said. Arne shook his head. "Maybe," he answered.

About two hundred yards from shore, the mainsail went out, torn loose near the peak; and a moment later, the jib. I thought we were done for then; but both sails caught in the rigging and snagged, and the boat eased. I saw that as long as they held, we had a sort of double reef; and we hadn't much further to go. "I think we'll make it, Arne," I said.

I could barely see the river mouth for the waves, which gave me an idea of how high the tide was running; but I set a course for the railroad bridge, and trusted to luck. We hit it right, and went in through a white fury of foam, on a roaring breaker which picked us up and ran us up the channel like a chip of wood, and flung us out on the sand a hundred yards from the bay. Arne was out first, but before he could get the mainsail down, the wind tore it out of his hands, and sent it ballooning across the river, with half the rigging attached to it. We got the anchor out, but I knew it wouldn't hold. The waves were booming in through the river mouth, six feet high, and coming up the channel like wild horses. "It's no good, Arne," I said. "The tide's coming in; she'll drag right down to the bridge, and lose her mast." There was nothing we could do. I hadn't figured on such a high tide.

Bill Worthington had seen us come in. He was waiting for us as we climbed up onto the road from what was left of the beach. "Well, by God," he said, "you boys were out in something."

I grinned back at him, but I felt pretty shaky. My legs were trembling, and I couldn't keep my teeth together. "I'm sorry about the boat, Bill," I said. "I didn't figure the storm would be so bad."

Bill looked at me, and shook his head. "Storm, hell," he said. "This one's a hurricane."

Chapter 18

BILL TOLD US THAT HURRICANE SIGNALS were flying at High Land Light; he said it made him feel queer in the pit of his stomach. But it was still only the beginning; we all knew that.

We made the boat fast as well as we could, and then Bill drove us home to the north side of the river. We could hear the sand pit against the car whenever we crossed an exposed place in the road, and once or twice the car swerved sharply in a sudden gust. Bill left us at the house, and went back to watch the tide. His own house wasn't any too far above high water.

It was only then, as we started down the path to the shack, that I began to have an idea of what the wind was really like. Out there, on the water, I'd been too busy; and besides, in a sort of way, we had been part of it, moving with it, running before it. But here, facing the open sweep from the southeast, I caught it full and fair, and it hit me like a blow.

The wind was coming across the Pamet in a steady flow, almost like a river of air in flood. There was no let up to it, it came flowing over heavy and solid and fast; it had pushed the marsh grass down flat, and bent the pines over in a quarter circle. There was something unnatural about it; it seemed to be coming from far away, but all the time it was coming nearer, and I had a feeling that it was darkness itself coming, and a force that didn't belong on this earth. My heart was beating fast; I felt cold and excited. I could hear that strange sound I had heard out on the bay, a sort of roaring hum, high up and far off; and the yellow-grey wall was still down there to the south. Or had it come closer? I couldn't tell. I looked down the slope at the river; it was up over the marsh, and the water was brown, and streaked with yellow foam. "I'm glad we're here," I said to Arne, shouting against the wind. He smiled then, for the first time. "If the house holds," he said.

A branch from a locust down at the water's edge suddenly snapped, and sailed a few yards up the slope toward us. "Come on," I said; "let's go in."

We went around the back way, to get out of the direct force of the wind. While we'd been gone the grocer had left a box of eggs on the little back porch; they were all over the floor. I thought, that'll be a mess to clean up tomorrow, but I didn't stop. The wind picked us up, and swept us in through the door, and we had to lean back against it to close it. It was cold and still in the house, but I could hear the roaring in my ears,

554

from those hours out on the bay. After a while the noise in my ears went away, and then I could hear the storm itself, and that high, far off, humming sound.

Arne made a fire, and I got out the whiskey. I took a big drink; I could feel it warm me all the way down. We stood in front of the fire, and looked at each other. I could feel the house shake every now and then, and I heard the windows rattle; I wondered if I ought to try to put up the shutters, I tried to remember what I'd read about hurricanes. But then I remembered that the house had no shutters. There didn't seem to be anything to do.

"I wonder if the boat will hold," I said.

"I wouldn't think so," said Arne.

"We were lucky, at that," I said.

I took another drink. "I wonder how they're making out in Provincetown," I said.

Arne shook his head gloomily. "It'll be bad, all right," he remarked.

The rain began about then. It wasn't much of a downpour, but it came in almost level. In ten minutes there was a fair-sized puddle just inside the door. I laid a towel along the lintel, to keep the water out.

The wind seemed to be getting stronger all the time; once or twice it shook the house so hard I thought the walls would go. There was nothing to do but just sit there and wait for something to happen; and after a while, Arne said he thought we ought to go out and have a look around. He said he wanted to see what a hurricane looked like. We went out the back way, and it took all our strength to get the door closed after us. But when we got around to the front of the house, we couldn't breathe; the wind tore the air right out of our mouths. "Boy," said Arne, holding his hands in front of his face, "I'm glad I'm not out on the bay now."

I tried to see the bay, but it was lost in weather, a grey smother of rain and spray and blowing sand. I saw that the telegraph poles beyond Cat Island were down, and I pointed at them. And then the big elm behind the house went.

It went over slowly, with a sort of sigh, taking a lot of ground with it. Arne didn't say anything, but his eyes had a wild look in them. He grabbed my arm, and pointed across the river. A moment later we saw Bill Worthington's old barn sag over on its side, and watched the wind worry it along toward the river. "Maybe we ought to go over and help him," I shouted, with my mouth close to Arne's ear. He made a gesture of helplessness. "How are we going to get there?" he shouted back.

We were still watching Bill's house, crouched together with our arms wrapped around one of the straining pines, when the coastguard truck came by. It stopped on the road behind us, and a guardsman came clumping over in boots and oilskins. "Jeez," he said, "what do you guys think you're doing?" We told him that we were watching Bill's barn being blown into the river. "Well," he said, "there'll be more than that in the

river soon. The ocean's breaking through at Dune Hollow." He walked back to the truck, and they went on, toward Cat Island, and John Rule's house out at the edge of the marsh.

We were pretty high above the water where we were, and I didn't think even the ocean would reach that far. At any rate, we didn't have long to wait; in about ten minutes we saw the wave coming down the valley toward us, from the sea. It didn't look very high—just a line of brown foam, with branches and sand in it, but it was scary. It passed under us, and then there wasn't any marsh left, just water, moving fast.

And a moment later, I saw her.

She was below me, and a little to the east, near the town landing, trying to get up the slope from the river. She seemed tired; and the wind was worrying her like a dog. While I watched, she lost her balance, and half fell; and then she began to slip backward toward the water again. Another wave was coming down the valley from the east; I could see it coming.

I don't know how I got down the hill to her, against the wind, but I did. I got my arm around her just in time, and pulled her up out of the way; the crest went by almost a foot below us. She lay back against me, white and spent, with closed eyes. "I was afraid I wouldn't get here, darling," she said.

I held her close. Even then, with that mad flood below us, I thought we'd make it all right. I put my face down against hers; her cheeks were deathly cold. She lifted her hands slowly, as though they were a great weight, and put her arms around my neck. "I had to get back to you, Eben," she said.

"We'll have to hurry, Jennie," I told her. I tried to pull her along, up the slope, but she was like a dead weight, she seemed to have no strength left at all. She smiled at me piteously, and shook her head. "You go, Eben," she said; "I can't make it."

I tried to lift her, then, but she was too heavy for me; I couldn't find a foothold on the slippery ground. The water was higher, now, almost at our feet; a dark ripple washed in over my ankles. "Jennie," I cried, "for God's sake . . ."

"Let me look at you," she whispered. I couldn't hear her, but I knew what she was saying. She held my face in her hands, and looked at me for a moment with wide, dark eyes. "It's been a long time, darling," she said.

I didn't want to talk, I wanted to get out of there, I wanted to get her up the slope away from the water. "Look," I said, "if I could lift you up on my back . . ."

But she didn't seem to hear me. "Yes," she said, almost to herself; "I wasn't wrong."

"Jennie," I cried; "please . . ."

Her arms tightened around me for a moment. "Hold me close, Eben," she said. "We're together, now."

I held her close, but my mind was in a panic. I couldn't lift her, I couldn't get her away, and the ground where we were standing was beginning to give. "Arne," I shouted as loudly as I could; "Arne."

It was then I saw it coming.

It came in from the bay, a great brown wave, sweeping back up the valley toward the sea. There was no escape from it; we could never have climbed above it; it came in steady and very fast, with a strange sucking noise. Well, I thought, we'll go together, anyhow.

Bending over, I kissed her full on the lips. "Yes, Jennie," I said; "we're together now."

She knew what was coming. "Eben," she whispered, pressed against my cheek, "there's only one love . . . nothing can change it. It's still all right, darling, whatever happens, because we'll always be together . . . somewhere . . ."

"I know," I said.

And then the wave hit us. I tried to hold on to her, to go out with her, but it tore us apart. I felt her whirled out of my arms; the water drew me under, and rolled me over and over; I felt myself flung upwards, sucked down, and then flung upwards again. Then something crashed into me, and that was all I knew.

Arne found me sprawled in a tree half in and half out of the water, and dragged me back to safety. How he managed to carry me up the slope and back to the house in that wind, I don't know. He put me to bed, and made me drink almost a pint of whiskey; and he sat beside me all that night. He told me later that he had to hold me down in bed, that I kept trying to get back to the river. I don't remember much about it, it was all dark for me, all I remember is the dark.

It was a week before I could travel, but it made no difference, because the roads were out, and we couldn't have gotten through, anyway. I lay in bed, and ate what Arne gave me, and tried not to think about what had happened. Arne brought back the news from outside; he told me that there hadn't been as much damage in Truro as we'd thought; a lot of trees had gone over in Provincetown, and a fishing boat had been flung up on the rocks; John Worthington's nets were gone at North Truro, but except for the ocean breaking through into the Pamet, it hadn't been so bad. Even Bill's home had escaped, though the water had come up as high as the windows. The beach at Dune Hollow had started to build up again; pretty soon everything would be the same as before.

I came back to the city on a bright autumn day, deep blue and sun-yellow in the streets, and the great buildings rising clear and sharp in the keen, high air. Mr. Mathews was waiting for me at the gallery. "We

worried about you, Eben," he said. "Miss Spinney and I . . . we couldn't get any news for a long while."

He patted me awkwardly on the shoulder. "I'm glad to see you, my boy," he said. "I—I'm very glad . . ."

Miss Spinney didn't say anything. She looked to me as though she had been crying.

It was Gus who gave me the little clipping from the newspaper. "I thought maybe you hadn't seen it, Mack," he said.

It was from the Times, of September 22nd. "The steamship Latania," it read, "has reported by wireless today the loss of one of its passengers in the storm, a hundred miles off the Nantucket Lightship. Miss Jennie Appleton, who was returning to America after a stay of eight years abroad, was swept overboard by a wave which smashed a part of the bridge, and injured several of the passengers. Officials of the line are endeavoring to discover the whereabouts of Miss Appleton's relatives in this country."

Gus hesitated; he looked at me, and then he looked away. "I thought maybe you didn't know," he said. "I'm sorry, Mack."

I gave the clipping back to him. "No," I said, "I knew.

"It's still all right," I said. "It's all right."

Truro,
1949

X

THE LOST SEA

by Jan de Hartog

A Story of the Zuider Zee

Much of the land on which Holland stands was reclaimed from the sea, and the aggressive people of the Low Countries are building huge dams to close off more of the ocean and make rich provinces where the Zuider Zee flowed. The ports which ringed the shores are turning into inland towns, and on the fertile soil great crops will be raised.

Jan de Hartog was born in Haarlem in 1914. Haarlem looked eastward to Amsterdam, and Amsterdam looked on the Zee; and it was not strange that as a boy he felt the urge to become a sailor. He ran away at the age of ten and served for some time on a fishing smack. It was a rough life, but it carried its own reward for a boy with a discerning eye and an imaginative mind. Out of those days came the material for what he has always regarded as his best book, a short novel called *The Lost Sea*.

There are countless stories of boys who ran away to become sailors, but *The Lost Sea* is different from all of them. It is a story of strange customs and strange talk. The boys were drudges on board the fishing ships, but an aura of almost piratical glory surrounded them when they went strutting on shore.

The sea is still in the blood of this fine Dutch novelist. He and his family live on a windjammer which has been fitted out as a houseboat. Their home port is Amsterdam, but most of the time they live on the Seine or on the French Riviera.

THE TRUE CHARACTER OF A NATION comes out in its children's songs. As a ten-year-old, at school in Holland, I sang with the class in triple descant about a little horseman who fell in love with a little maiden and betrayed her. The little maiden went into a nunnery, the little horseman came to take her out with three of his friends; after they had found the nunnery locked and the little maiden had addressed them through a peephole, they dragged up a blunderbuss and razed the nunnery to the ground. When the little maiden came, blackened, out of the ruins and still did not want to marry the little horseman, he shot himself, and his three friends became monks.

We sang this song beautifully, without wondering at its contents. One fell in love, one betrayed, one blew up nunneries and one was overcome by remorse; that seemed to be the way of the world we were about to enter.

A windy world of narrow streets lined with nets drying, leading to the harbor with its forest of masts and its quay silver with the scales of fish. To us ten-year-olds this world was peopled with giants who never seemed to notice us at all. When we were playing on the quay our game was constantly interrupted by huge barrels crashing down from the ships onto the cobbles, scattering us as if we were sparrows. When we were playing at marbles on the sidewalk, and so absorbed in our game that we had momentarily lost our sparrow's alertness, we would suddenly duck with terror as one of the giants stepped right over us on his way to his ship. When we took off our clogs to go into a house or a shop and we looked at them in the row of giants' clogs outside, we felt painfully small.

We would play at being big. We'd strut along the streets with the giants' swagger, and call at each other: "Oi-oi, Dirk!" or "Wind's changing, Karel!" But we could never keep that up for long, for then the mist-gun would boom, or a burst of hammering from the yard would rattle the silence, or a true giant would round the corner like a jammer turning in the wind; and we would scatter, sparrows again, the clatter of our clogs streaking down to the harbor like a gust of hail.

We had many games, but we always played at being grownups. We picked up wooden shoes, thrown away by the giants, and rigged them as ships, numbered with the famous numbers of the fastest botters from our village, for Huizen was famous for the speed of its ships. We would send

561

the clogs fishing in the dead end of the harbor, where the driftwood and the pink corpses of cats were gently rocked by the tide that swirled outside. We would split into two groups, one of Huizers, and the other of Volendammers. The Huizers would lie peacefully fishing among the Brasso tins and the cats, and suddenly the Volendammers would swoop down on them, get caught in their nets, and cause havoc, and tear sails, and we would dance on the quay screaming like sea gulls, and yet there was nothing to see but half a dozen waterlogged old clogs dumbly rocking among the refuse.

Any stranger from beyond the harbor or the tramway station wouldn't have understood at all what we were playing at. To the strangers the Zuider Zee was a picturesque little inland sea which was born in 1302, when the great Elizabeth Flood swept half of Holland, and which would die in 1931 when the big dam thrown across its entrance would be completed, after which the sea would be reclaimed and turn into land again. Occasionally strangers from even further away would pass through the village in big buses, or enter the harbor in motorboats painted white and gold. They would crowd the streets for a while, men with spectacles and women with painted mouths, speaking a funny language and wearing outlandish clothes, pointing cameras at old Henk on his way from the smokery with his arms full of eels, or at mad Barbara who had lost three sons at sea and who was called "Crabby" because her madness made her walk sideways. They would also point their cameras at the giants' ships lying in the harbor; but then a yell would burst from the forest of masts and clogs and stones would be thrown at them, and the voices of the giants would holler: "Get out of here, dirty red lips! Away, ye whores of Babylon!" Then the strangers would be rounded up quickly by their shepherds and herded back on board their motorboat, or to the market where the bus was, pursued by us, crying shrilly: "Get out of here," and "Whores of Babylon," until they were gone.

The tourists came to marvel at the quaint old costumes, the little streets, the baggy trousers and mad Crabby, who after her last son died began showing her bed to strangers for a penny, saying that the Black Skipper had slept in it. The tourists didn't know about the Black Skipper. Like the strangers from nearer home they knew what they were going to see before they got there, and so they never saw the truth. The Zuider Zee was pretty to look at; anyone sailing along its coast in a white motorboat and looking at the little red and green towns in the flamingo-colored haze of the dawn thought it a pity that this wonderful world of sunlight and water should be doomed to turn back into land.

To the people in the villages it was more than a pity, for they were doomed themselves. The Zuider Zee, still the richest fishing ground of northern Europe, where the herring were so thick that sometimes the shoals made the shallow sea boil, would turn brackish with the growing of the dam. The two thousand botters of the little towns along the coast,

which had hardly been able to cope with the harvest for six centuries, would find less and less to catch. The result would be poverty, and an even bitterer competition between the local fleets.

Now the most ferocious competition was between the Volendammers and the Huizers. They owned the biggest ships and had been enemies since the great flood, for the Volendammers were Catholics and the Huizers Protestants, and the Volendammers fished before the wind, dragging a single net, whereas the Huizers fished in pairs, drifting cross-seas, dragging their net between them. The two always got in each other's way.

The tourists, photographing a bunch of little boys in quaint costumes, playing with ships made of wooden shoes in the dead end of the harbor, heard our shrill cries and the clatter of our clogs when we danced with excitement, and thought we were just children at play. They had never heard of pairs of Huizer botters quietly fishing at sunrise, their long shallow nets stretched between them, their crews asleep; and then the sudden red cloud of the Volendammers' sails descending upon them out of the dawn. The Volendammers, groaning with sail, would pass between the pairs of sleeping Huizers, dragging their sharp triangular net at great speed, and try to cut the nets of the enemy with the sharp cables of their draggers. But the Huizers' nets were strong; the Volendammers who tried to cut them would be braked by the impact, their topsails would come crashing down, bollards would splinter, burning stoves in the fo'c'sles would topple over, filling the pokey cabins with screams and smoke. Then the crews of the two Huizers and the crew of the Volendammer would scramble aft and start hauling in their nets frantically, trying to be the first to reach the center of the tangle. Whoever reached that first would cut the other man's net; but usually all three would arrive there at the same moment. Then a battle would begin, the ferocity of which was echoed by the sea gull screeches of dancing children on the quays for months to come. The crews would lash out at each other with handspikes and poles, and when they got nearer with hatchets and knives. They would board each other's ships, fighting; the Volendammers would throw burning wads of cotton waste drenched in paraffin on board the Huizers' ships; the Huizers would crowd in on them brandishing the pole with the sharp hook they used for hauling in their nets. They would try to slam that hook in the top of the Volendammer's mainsail just underneath the leech, for if they managed to do that and hung at the pole with their full three men's weight, the sail would be torn down to the bottom, the wind would burst it and blow it right out of the leeches.

If that happened the Volendammer was lost. The mainsail was his heart; once that was cut out, the big evil bird would lie fluttering in the wind, turning aimlessly. Once a Volendammer saw his mainsail go he wept and gave in; then the Huizers would tear the baggy trousers off the vanquished and beat their bare behinds until they howled with pain and humiliation. They would tear all the sails, smash up the cabin, set fire to

the beds, cut the net at its roots and leave the smoking wreck to be picked up by its countrymen. The Volendammers' trousers would be stored away until the Huizer fleet sailed home; then, when the ships swung into the harbor one by one, the crowd lining the quay would cheer and wave when they saw on the flag line of the victor the trousers of the slain enemy flapping bulkily in the breeze.

We children of Huizen had seen this several times, and those were the moments in which to be grownup seemed a state of glory. Oh, for the day that we ourselves would sail into the harbor with our ship, and see the quay thick with the white bonnets and the multicolored shawls of the women and the girls, and hear that big sickening roar of glory roll toward us like sunlight driven by a sailing cloud. That was what we played, when we danced at the dead end of the harbor and the tourists pointed their cameras at us and we screamed: "Get out of here, whores of Babylon." That was life, the world that lay ahead of us: the red clouds of the Volendammer sails, the terrible fight among banging beams and billowing smoke, the screams of the wounded, the home-coming in the sunset with all the world shouting: "Hurray! Down with the Catholics! Glory to the Black Skipper! Hurray!" We all wanted to grow up to be the Black Skipper, for the Black Skipper was the only one who always won.

The Black Skipper was the King of Huizen; a blue-eyed giant of incredible age with gold rings in his ears, and a black astrakhan cap on the back of his white-haired head. His ship was the HZ 69, one of the two largest among the hundred that homed at Huizen. The other big one was the HZ 55, sailed by Arie Kos, the Black Skipper's fishing partner. Everybody around the Zuider Zee knew the Black Skipper's name, and the children of Volendam were in terror of him without ever having set eyes on him. When the children of Volendam were naughty, their mothers said: "Go to sleep, or I'll sell you to the Black Skipper!" and there wouldn't be another squeak out of them until dawn.

We children of Huizen knew the Black Skipper well. Wherever he went on the rare occasions that he was home he drew a wake of silence through the streets full of playing kids. We would follow him, a silent body at a distance, to see which bed he would sleep in that night. He would turn around after a while, hearing the rumbling of a hundred tiny clogs behind him, and say: "Go home." The clogs would splatter, with the sound of a barrel thrown into the harbor; and then we would peer round corners and below the hedges of the drying nets, and see him knocking, and hear his voice: "Hello, love," when a woman opened her door. He never said a name, he only said: "Love," and the wise ones among us whispered that this was because he couldn't remember any names. Mad Crabby showed her bed to strangers for a penny, saying that the Black Skipper had slept there as if it was something special. That was because she was mad.

The legend was that there wasn't a spinster or a widow, young or

old, sad or gay, in whose bed the Black Skipper had not slept. None but one: the widow of the lighthouse keeper of the Island of Schokland, who had taken over her dead man's job.

One day long ago the Black Skipper had sailed into her lonely port, rattled the door of the lighthouse to ask for water, and she had thrown the water on his head from the top window of her tower. The Black Skipper had been as angry as the little horseman; he had gone back to the HZ 69, taken out an ice bomb used to burst the pack ice in the winter, and blown her door out of its hinges. Out of the blackened hole, after the white smoke had lifted, the woman came with an oar in her hands and pushed him into the harbor. Ever since that day, whenever the HZ 69 passed Schokland's lighthouse, the Black Skipper was said to shake his fist at the white tower and shout: "I'll have you yet one day!"

This was the legend, and there were many legends about the Black Skipper. So many that he moved among us like an aging god, turning the grownups into sparrows like us, because he never noticed them. And that was why the children loved him: in the light of his setting sun even the smallest objects threw long shadows.

WHILE I WAS STILL A LITTLE BOY among the hundreds, I dreamed like all of us only of growing up. In school we were told that we were growing up all the time, every day a little bit, and that if we waited long enough, one day we would be giants ourselves. We didn't believe this; we believed in a magic moment somewhere ahead of us, when we would suddenly be admitted into the real world, the world beyond the harbor. To us to be grown up meant to sail.

For the real life of the giants was not lived ashore. They came home every two months or so to sleep, all three hundred of them, and they seemed to be sleeping even when they walked the streets. Every time the woman said that the fleet would stay home for a week, and when the giants arrived they contradicted this and said they would stay for a fortnight; but they never stayed longer than three days. One morning, soon after their arrival, we would be woken up by a great sound of anchor chains, and when we shot out of bed and clattered to the harbor, hundreds of breathless little kids, capless, buttoning their coats as they ran, we would find the quay full of angry women and weeping girls. The black birds of the botters would spread their wings and sail out into the pink haze of the sunrise, the sky vast and green above them. They would sail out with hoarse cries and hollered shouts of: "Go home!"; the women would shout back with high, angry voices until the last of the botters had rounded the pier. Then a great chill of loneliness would come out of the empty harbor, there would be a silence which lasted until one woman

began to cry: "Good-by," and then the multicolored shawls would start waving at the sunrise, as if all the women on the quay had suddenly become twice their size, and the good-bys would mount in volume and in ardor until they sounded like a chord on a big organ. We children, who didn't know what it was all about, would always catch the sadness and the love of that last chorus, and we would weep with the women because it was beautiful.

The months that the village was a women's village only were dreary and slow. We would play our games and go to school and sing in triple descant behind the steamed windows, but behind our games and behind our songs was always the great longing for that magic moment. We were children waiting to be born.

The law said that no child could sail or work until he was fourteen, but this was not true. The magic moment could come any time between the ages of ten and twelve, for every botter from every port around the Zuider Zee carried, apart from its crew of three or six, two secret people: a cat and a little boy. The cats were occasionally seen when the fleet was home: big ugly monsters the size of dogs, with cauliflower ears and broken tails, covered with patches of tar. The children were never seen; because they were illegal they were kept out of sight, and that was why they were called "sea mice."

Every boy was waiting for the moment when he would be turned from a sparrow into a sea mouse, but nobody could say when that moment would come; it depended on whether there was a vacancy. Sea mice grew up into sea boys or drowned. One day the mother of Kris Muis, who had sung with our class and vanished, was seen weeping in the streets without her bonnet, running with her hair losing its pins; people said that was because her son had been killed by a sea lion. We weren't sad at all that Kris Muis was dead; we weren't even frightened by the sea lion; we were jealous of the one who would take his place and who didn't yet know it himself.

Nobody knew how sea mice were chosen. Some said you had to go and hide on board a ship that had lost its sea mouse; others that if you waited at the dead end of the harbor until the dusk became night, the skipper would come and pick one. We tried to hide as soon as a ship came in that had lost its sea mouse; but there were too many of us, and we were always chased away. When the fleet was in we loitered at the dead end of the harbor and got frightened and cold in the gathering darkness; some of us would go home, the others were rounded up by the women. It was a mystery how the botters got their sea mice, what miracle had happened to the boy whose name would be called in vain at the beginning of school the morning after the fleet left.

I was ten years old when the miracle happened to me. It was a miracle so vast and unbelievable that thinking of it still fills me with pride and wonder, for I became the sea mouse of the Black Skipper.

HUIZEN HAD NO ORPHANAGE. Whenever there were children whose parents had died, they were taken into the families of relatives.

As everybody in the village was related in some way or other, there was never much difficulty in finding a home for waifs. But through the years it had become the custom to concentrate the waifs around widows.

There were widows who, when their husbands drowned, were left behind with one child, and who within a couple of years found themselves mothering a family of sixteen. Sometimes these families got too large for one woman; it depended on what she could take. Annie Snoek, for instance, had never less than a dozen and yet she was always cheerful, singing all day and laughing, and whenever you passed her house there was a smell of something delicious from the kitchen. Her children were noisy but nice to have as friends; although she hadn't brought them into the world she somehow gave them a bit of her light.

Mother Bout, however, who never had more than three, couldn't cope with them at all, perhaps because she was too thin. She ran her house like a prison. There were times for everything and she stuck to them as if the universe depended upon it. If we were five minutes late for dinner she would breathe through her teeth; if we played on the quay too late at night she'd bring the time home to us with a shiver as we heard her running through the streets screeching like an owl. Originally she must have been a nice woman, otherwise she would never have taken us in; but after we had gone to bed, all three of us in one cupboard bed, and she vanished with her candle through the hatch in the attic floor, hissing: "Say your prayers or I'll smack you!" we prayed to God that he might make Mother Bout break a leg.

She had no favorites among us, but she had scapegoats. The scapegoats changed about every month; one month Bulle Groot would be the cause of anything that went wrong, the next it would be me, the one after that Jaap Bros. The last time it was me was because of an arrow.

We had made a bow of a broken fishing rod, and two arrows of bull-rushes with fishing hooks for heads and plumes at their tails. In the courtyard behind the house was an open washing place: a corner screened off by a thin wall of dry rushes. Inside a watering can was suspended from a little gallows, a rope attached to its spout; if you pulled the rope you had a shower. We had painted a bull's eye on the screen around the washing place; the morning it happened two of us pulled the bow taut, Bulle Groot held the arrow and I shouted: "Fire!" The arrow swished off with a zing, pierced the screen, and from behind it came such a bloodcurdling yell of agony that we nearly died on our feet. Before Mother Bout had

appeared around the corner of the screen, we were already halfway to the harbor, carrying our clogs to run faster.

When we finally piled up in the dank straw in the hidden corner behind the smokery, three panting bodies shivering with fright, I asked: "Where do you think we hit her?" Jaap Bros said: "In her behind." Bulle said: "She hasn't got one." We were very brave, joking about her and giggling, huddled close together in the straw; but we came home very late. She sat waiting for us in the lamplight, her spectacles on the tip of her nose which gave her a second set of eyes. She looked straight at me and said: "I know who did this." I was sent to bed without dinner; Bulle hid some bread for me under his shirt, and I munched it in the darkness after she had gone down with her candle. Bulle said: "From now on it's you," and I knew he was right.

Two days later the fleet came home. I wasn't allowed to go out, but Bulle and Jaap helped me climb through the attic window. I went to the harbor with a feverish feeling, shouting and running as soon as I was out of her earshot. I did all sorts of crazy things that night; I threw stones at cats, made faces at mad Crabby, chased Jaap along the quay, snatched off his cap and threw it in the harbor.

The moment I had done that I was sorry and frightened; we tried to fish it out but the tide carried it away. We followed it along the pier, throwing stones at it, trying to force it inland; when at last it had got within reach it was nearly sunk. Bulle and Jaap both held my left hand while I bent over as far as possible to grab it; then Bulle slipped, Jaap let go of me, and I fell headlong into the harbor.

I couldn't have been in the water for longer than a few seconds, but it seemed very long. My eyes were wide open and I saw a swaying trunk of air go up from my mouth to the surface of the green glassy water. I don't remember choking or being afraid; I just felt as a man must feel the second after he is beheaded: very surprised, seeing a last vision. I remember seeing a wonderful black botter sailing out, its wings covering the sun, and a man in a red cloak standing at the helm, his arms crossed, steering with the small of his back. The man was me, but not really me; he was the promise inside me which would have been fulfilled one glorious day if I hadn't been drowned in the harbor.

Bulle and Jaap pulled me ashore. The world reeled around me: water turned into sky, the botters in the harbor seemed to stand swaying upside down on their thin masts like toadstools. I felt a choking pressure on my chest, and that was the first moment I struggled; the pressure was Bulle who had sat down on top of me because we had been taught at school that was the thing to do with a drowned man, to get the water out of his lungs. No water came out of me, only a shrill cry of pain and fear, and the odd thing about that cry was that I called "Mem!" the name by which Mother Bout insisted we should call her.

As soon as Bulle had got off me I got up and saw the water and the sky drop back into their places. The botters lay upright in the harbor again, their masts pointing at the green evening sky, and from the sea the night came creeping in with the blue haze of the dusk. It was a wonderful world to look at; I felt a rush of happiness and gratitude that I had returned to it.

But reality oozed back into that void of happiness with a feeling of fear that soon grew into panic: the reality of Mem's anger on finding out that I had escaped from my confinement, of the wet clothes and Jaap's lost cap, which could still be seen, a small black dot bobbing peacefully toward the night. If only my clothes hadn't been wet, I might have climbed back through the attic window the way I had come; Jaap could say about the loss of his cap that the wind had blown it away.

We decided, all three of us, that we must dry my clothes quickly; whatever happened, no matter how late we got home, we must dry my clothes. While I started to undress on the seaward side of the pier, where we couldn't be seen from the shore, Bulle and Jaap gathered some driftwood which the high tide had left in the cracks between the huge pieces of basalt which the pier was made of. The wood had lain there for weeks bleaching in the sun, and was quite dry.

We made a fire with Jaap's three matches, put up a stick on either side of it and strung my belt between them. We hung my clothes over the belt, but the wind blew the flames from underneath them; occasionally there was a faint hissing sound like a kettle starting to boil. The waves lapped lazily against the pier, and withdrew with a soft gurgling sound in the cracks. From the harbor came distant shouts and laughter, and the hollow crunch of wood as the tide made the botters rub shoulders. A late sea gull circled gackering overhead, an unnerving gossipy sound, as if after having had a good look at us it would sail in one sweep to Mother Bout's house and tell her what it had seen.

We sat there until it was dark and the sounds from the harbor grew faint. The tide reached its turning point, the waves grew still and gurgled no more in the cracks. The hissing of my wet clothes when touched by the flames grew louder, until it sounded like a steam winch waiting. I grew colder and colder, sitting stark naked on the basalt, my knees drawn up under my chin, my arms around my legs. The numbness of the earth seemed to creep up inside me until I had become part of it: of the water, the stones, the dead seaweed glistening in the night.

In the end it felt as if I was living only with my eyes. The wind stirred my hair that was no longer part of me. I felt it like the pier must have felt the stirring of the frayed bits of old rope hanging from its rusty rings. I was beyond fear and hope, as if I would sit there forever: cast-iron child, with the world playing around it, like the mermaid on the village pump.

In the end Bulle and Jaap decided that they would go home; they

would imitate my body in the cupboard bed with a pillow and a mop, and tell Mem I was asleep. I would wait where I was until my clothes were dry; Jaap and Bulle would take turns at keeping awake, and when they heard the soft screech of a sea gull outside they would open the attic window and let me in.

After they had left time came to a stop. Night had descended forever; I would never grow up any more but sit there, motionless, waiting for the dawn of Judgment Day. My eyes went on living, for I remember the warm softness of tears in them, but I never felt them going down my face. A pale half-moon arose on its back from the haze, until it floated in the night like a ship emerged. And then, as I sat there listening in my grave, the miracle happened.

I heard wooden steps approaching, but couldn't look around. The steps didn't bring back any fear or hope; I just listened and waited. The steps paused on the crown of the pier, and I felt someone looking at me. Then they came down, slithering on the seaweed, cracking the twigs of dead reed in the cracks as they crushed them. I saw two gigantic wooden shoes appear in the faint red glow of the dying fire. I saw striped stockings, blue and white, and the bottom of black breeches dissolving into night. Above those there seemed to be a gap, but after looking long and intently I saw, somewhere high up, two gleams. They frightened me, because if they were eyes they were set very far apart.

When in the end I made out what they were it took me a long time to believe it; for this was the miracle. They weren't eyes: what reflected the glow of the fire was two little gold earrings. The giant who looked down on me was the Black Skipper.

I don't know how long it took him to speak, for I had lost all sense of time. When in the end he asked: "What are you doing here?" I couldn't answer. If he had come a few hours earlier, just after Jaap and Bulle had left, I would still have had the strength to flee, as we had done all our lives whenever he addressed us. Now I sat there, motionless, living only with my eyes, a sparrow with a broken wing.

He didn't say any more. After looking at me for a while, his face slowly taking shape in the moonlight, he bent over me and picked me up.

I squeaked for the last time: "Mem!" then I died in his arms. When I woke up I had turned into a sea mouse.

I WAS WOKEN UP, by a very rough feeling, and the strong smell of coffee. It felt as if I was a coffee bean among many being turned and shaken, being slowly sucked down to be crushed in a mill which was turned with a loud grinding noise. I couldn't get out of this nightmare of being a coffee bean; when I finally opened my eyes and squealed in

terror, I saw two enormous sweaty faces bent over me, glistening in the oil light as if they had been blown with gold dust.

I recognized the Black Skipper and Krelis, his deckhand; both had black astrakhan caps on the backs of their heads and squatted underneath a wooden ceiling that was very low. They were rubbing me with large horny hands and I screamed in pain. The Black Skipper said: "All right, that'll do," and the words were heavy with the smell of tobacco and fish. They turned away and I followed them with my eyes, and then I saw where the smell of coffee came from.

I was lying in the big bunk in a botter's fo'c'sle. A little stove stood against the mast; on it a black coffee kettle was steaming. Krelis said: "What are we going to do with him?" and the Black Skipper answered: "Keep him." Then he poured coffee into a white mug and said: "It's such a devil of a job to find a mouse that I'm not going to let this one get away now I've got him." Krelis said: "Aye, let's hope he'll last longer than the others." The Black Skipper grunted as he sipped his coffee. "Have you found out yet how the others got away?" he asked. "No," said Krelis. "Somebody must have sneaked on board and let them out."

I hardly listened to the last things they said; it was the first that had made my mouth fall open: "It's such a devil of a job to find a mouse."

I couldn't believe my ears. All the boys of Huizen had wondered how to become a sea mouse, but one thought had never entered their heads: that the skippers should wonder as much how to get one. The secret must have been that we never offered ourselves alone; there were always scores of us trying to sneak on board or offering ourselves in the dusk at the dead end of the harbor. The skippers never got hold of one of us alone, and they daren't choose one from a crowd for fear of being given away.

That realization was so complicated and so enormous, that I was about to fall asleep again from exhaustion, when I felt something heavy on four legs walk across my chest. I was too terrified to sit up. I just opened my eyes wide and saw it was an animal. I couldn't make out at first whether it was a dog or a cat; I saw it stand up on its hind legs, put up one paw toward a ring hanging from the ceiling, and suddenly with a loud bang a trap door fell open just beside me. The animal vanished through the square hole into the darkness beyond, from which came a seaweedy stench of wet ropes and bilge water.

It was a cat.

When I woke up again we were at sea. A dented square of sunlight slid to and fro on the cabin floor. There was a regular rattling, shoving and sloshing sound of the kettle moving on its stove, the lamp swinging, oil skins rubbing against the wall, and the bilge water in the gutter outside the door to the cockpit flowing from starboard to port. I felt as if all

my insides had turned into water and were sloshing from port to starboard too. I had never been at sea before, and somehow the thought of being sick had never been connected in my mind with the magic moment.

As I lay there clenching my teeth, trying to keep my insides inside, the sliding patch of sunlight was darkened by a body stooping into the cabin. He was the third member of the crew of the HZ 69: a boy of about fifteen years of age whom I knew well enough by sight to know that he was called Bonk. In my eyes he was a man; he had big red hands and big red ears and very blue eyes wide apart in a freckled face underneath invisible eyebrows. He eyed me as cruelly as a fish, and said: "What are you doing in my bed, you little stinker? Scram where you belong!" He had a high piping voice like Mother Bout's, and I remembered having heard him singing a solo in the church choir last Christmas: "Where sheep may safely graze."

I didn't know where I belonged, and so I asked him. One of his big red hands flew up as if it had an independent life of its own, and he smacked me in the face. "Rat!" he cried as the smack rang out. "Whenever you address me you'll have to call me sir!" I said: "Yes, sir," and I bit my lip to keep it from trembling. He said: "Get your skeleton out of my bunk and go forrard!" I saw no forrard, so I asked: "Where, sir?" "Forrard!" he screamed. "Through that hatch! And hurry or I'll kick you through!" I crawled hastily into the square black hole, that had opened beside me when the cat had pulled the catch of the trap door the night before; as I did so the voice that once so soothingly had assured the sheep that they might safely graze screamed, "Hurry up!" and a big knobby stockinged foot hit me on the tailbone and shoved me down the hole. There was a sharp click of a lock snapping shut and darkness closed over me.

I lay trembling in that darkness for quite a while. It was full of creakings and crunchings and the sound of waves breaking against the bow. Every time the ship hit a wave there would be a hard resounding blow, setting everything aquiver—a sound so hard and loud that every time my heart nearly stopped as I thought we had hit a rock. The blows were accompanied by a metallic clank, as if a hammer hit an anvil. After a quarter of an hour of motionless, terrified listening I realized it was the ring of the anchor, clanking every time the ship reared.

It took me quite a while before I began to discern any shapes in the darkness. The first I saw were two faintly luminous disks very near, occasionally obscured as if something hid them. Then I realized it was the cat, sleepily blinking. When I began to see him more clearly I saw the most horrifying cat I had ever set eyes on.

His size was enormous, the pattern on his forehead so irregular that it made him look as if he squinted. He was, like all botter cats, covered so solidly with patches of tar that it coated him almost completely. Round the small of his back there was a distinct gap and this made him look as

if he was wearing an ill-fitting suit. The suggestion of his wearing a suit was enhanced by the fact that he had no tail left at all; it looked as if he was wearing it tucked away inside his trousers. His claws were so dirty and broken and swollen with salt that he couldn't retract them any more; they looked like horrible little black fingers and clicked when he walked on something hard.

The very sight of him squinting at me with that bleary drunken gaze terrified me. When he yawned, opening his jaws wide enough for me to put my fist in, the smell of rotting fish he sent across to me was so overpowering that the seasickness lurched up inside me with a wave of nausea, and I vomited on the floor. The cat got up, arched its back, at which the gap between its coat and its trousers widened to a belt of bare pale skin, knelt down on its elbows and began lapping it up.

I rolled on my back, sicker than before, wishing to be dead. I saw that I was lying in what was called the cable hole: a triangular coffin of about a yard high, crammed with piles of curled-up ropes, disused nets, broken lamps, and frayed rope cushions. The ceiling was thick with glass floats in nets, bunches of hooks strung together, blocks, holed pieces of cork on strings, all of them swaying jerkily with the sickening rise and fall of the bow of the ship. In the center of the biggest pile of rope was a sort of nest: a dog's basket of old clothes and cotton waste.

I dragged myself toward it; and the moment I curled up inside, the cat joined me. I was too sick to defend myself; I let the monster snuggle up against me with his horrible scratchy suit. It took him some time to find a comfortable position and then he began to purr. Never had I heard a cat purring louder. It was a deep roaring noise, like an engine. I tried to sleep again, but every time the ship rose it seemed to rear on its hind legs, to hover for a breath-taking second suspended in the air, after which it crashed headlong into a wave that seemed to consist of gravel. Every time we hit a wave the purring of the cat was interrupted by a hiccup; every time I thought we would never rise again.

It was a sad, despairing hour. In the end I lost all hope of ever seeing the sun again. I lay there gasping in the darkness, in the embrace of a monster, relentlessly being hammered to pulp. But after that hour, a hatch was opened among the rubble swinging at the ceiling, and I saw Krelis' enormous head silhouetted against the most beautiful background I ever saw.

It was the vast hollow expanse of a black triangular sail, reaching up to the sky: the jib of the HZ 69, the fastest botter of the fleet. The jib I had so often seen from afar, sailing into the harbor like a thunderous cloud.

And now the jib was mine. I was a man.

IT TOOK ME FOUR DAYS to get over my seasickness, and they were days on the rack. I was dressed in clothes that were too big for me; but Krelis cut off the legs of the breeches and the arms of the coat with a knife, and so they fitted me. I was put to work regardless of my condition, and the work was not helpful to one who constantly felt on the brink of vomiting.

When at night the nets were hauled in, and the silver of the catch poured into the cockpit until I was standing up to the hips in a boiling mass of squiggling, slithering herrings, I was given a little net of my own and told to pick the dinner. We fished for herring, but among the thousands of slender, silver green fish were occasionally found ugly flat flappers, sole or plaice. I was to pick those from the jumping silver while the men poured the herrings by the basketful into the "bun"—a large reservoir inside the ship in which the water was constantly refreshed from outside.

Usually there were about two dozen flappers among the herrings, but while the cockpit was still full it was difficult to catch them as I was immobilized by the squirming mass in which I stood half submerged. Every time I saw one but missed it, Bonk the boy saw it too, and he would never fail to throw a herring at my head. He seldom missed, and so in the end I stood there, shivering, numbed with the cold of the sea, covered with scales, my face dripping with slime and tears, heaving with dry choking sobs as there was nothing left inside me to vomit. Then I would be given a knife and told to prepare the dinner.

It was the most sickening job of all. I was told to get hold of the strong, struggling flappers one by one, press them down on the deck, cut their crunching heads off, slit open their bellies, and take the guts out. Murk, the cat, would sit waiting for me, his pink tongue slightly protruded, panting with anticipation; and the horrible crunching would go on as he chewed their heads with the side of his mouth, squinting up at me with the falseness of the jungle. After I had beheaded and gutted the flappers I had to scrape them, and that was the sound that invariably made me get up and stagger to the rail, which was half as high as I. I would pull myself up with a frantic effort, lift my chin on the gunwale and wretch. At those moments the sea would seem to swirl around me until I felt like being sucked down by the whirl of dirty water emptying from a bath. The second time he saw me do this the Black Skipper said to me: "Don't kill yourself, child; be sick in the gutter," the first words he had spoken to me since the moment he took me in his arms.

Once the fish was ready to cook, I took it into the cabin, which would seem pitch-dark after the brilliance of the silver fish reflecting the sun; I would grope my way to the shelf on starboard, finger along the Bible, the candle, the skipper's spectacles, the broken alarm clock until I

574

got to the jam jar in which the sail needles were kept. The needles should on no account get rusty, so they were kept in oil; this oil was used to fry the fish in. I would pour some of it into the frying pan, light the stove and put the pan on the fire. I had to hold on to it with both hands, for the catch was hauled in while we were lying cross-seas, and the ship would roll with colossal swayings. It was quite a job to keep the pan horizontal and prevent the oil from spilling on the stove; before I mastered it the cabin used to get so thick with evil-smelling blue smoke, that I had to dash out several times before the oil was hot enough to put the fish into.

The terrifying thing about frying flappers was that they seemed to come to life again. They would curl up and arch their backs as if in a horrible dream of life, but after a minute or so they would give up, stretch themselves quiveringly in the attitude of death and turn into food. Each of the men would have nearly half a dozen fish for his dinner, the rest of the meal consisted of potatoes. I had brought those to the boil before in a big iron pot, and after the water had boiled for a couple of minutes I put the pot in the hay chest and covered it with a pillow; when I took it out an hour later, the potatoes would be cooked to a turn. The pot was put in the center of the floor and I would pile up three stacks of half a dozen fish each on the bare board; then I'd stick my head out and call: "Skipper! Dinner!" and they would let everything drop and file into the cabin, leaving their clogs outside.

They squatted on the floor, each behind his own pile of fish; I'd hand the skipper the Bible and his spectacles. He'd open the book at random and read exactly ten lines, never mind where they began or where they ended, because it was all God's word. After that he would say: "God, thank you for the catch, guide the winds and keep the rain, and typhus to the Catholic pirates, Amen." After that they would eat silently and with great speed, picking potatoes from the pot with one hand and holding their fish with the other.

They would stack the bones neatly in front of them, while I poured the cooled-off oil back into the jam jar with the needles, put on the coffee kettle and took out the mugs and the tin of babblers. Babblers were square lumps of hard brown sugar; after they had finished their meal and the coffee had been poured into their mugs, they would pass the tin, put a babbler in their mouths, take a sip of coffee and rinse their mouths with it, the babblers clattering against their teeth. One babbler would do for two mugs; after those, they would lie down on their backs and suck the rest of it until it was gone.

Perhaps the lumps of sugar were called babblers because as they sucked them they would begin to talk. The quarter of an hour after dinner, while the three of them were lying on their backs, their hands behind their heads, blinking sleepily at the ceiling, was the time of the stories. They would discuss the catch, the weather, and women; during

that quarter of an hour Murk the cat and I were supposed to clean the floor and to remove all traces of the meal. But Murk worked hardest at it, because he couldn't understand the human language; the stories meant nothing to him but the purrings of the big animals in whose nest he lived. I took a very long time wiping the mugs, cleaning and piling up the bones for Murk to take outside, for never in my life had I heard more fascinating stories.

It was a pity that the Black Skipper used to fall asleep so soon after the meal was ended, for his stories were the best of all. They were glimpses of the true giants' world, flashing visions of ferocious battles, of fights with sea lions the size of a man caught in the net on a cold October morning, of sunken villages whose churchbells still could be heard ringing when a gale turned the sea into a raging caldron; of women unlike Mother Bout or even Annie Snoek: so large and gay and pink and generous that a man felt like dying in their arms and understood the gospel in their kisses because they made him love all mankind. When Krelis began to talk about women it was different, but whenever the Black Skipper mumbled about them, the rest of his babbler clattering against his teeth, they seemed to be large pink angels, beyond fear and jealousy and anger, holding in their hands the keys to some promised land, which had to be taken away from them in a big struggle full of laughter and kisses and resounding smacks.

The Black Skipper's stories of women gave me my first wish to love. Somehow the fights with the Catholic pirates and the romps with the pink angels became one: an initiation, a glorious trial of ferocity and tenderness from which one would emerge as a giant at last. When at night the nets were out and we were drifting sideways along with the wind and I had finally curled up in my dog's basket in the cable hole, exhausted like Murk from a heavy day, I dreamed for a while, half awake half asleep, of what life would be like once I had reached the size and the power of the Black Skipper. It seemed a life glowing with memories, and one thing he said I never forgot until this day: "Only memories make for happiness." He said that to go through a thing for the first time was agony, the second time: boredom, but the third time: happiness. I began counting the experiences I went through: waking up in the morning, scrubbing the cabin floor, straightening the bed in which the three men slept like herrings in a cask—Bonk with his head between the feet of the skipper and Krelis; I tried to taste the happiness when I did these things for the third time, but it was very faint; perhaps the experiences were not big enough.

I waited impatiently for the big experiences to come, but they took a long time. Every day seemed to be exactly the same as the one before; the nets were hauled in at dawn, put out again at noon; I peeled the potatoes, boiled them and put them in the haychest; I got the flappers, killed them, and watched them writhing in the boiling fat; then after the

meal was over and the sleepy stories had been told, the nets would be hauled in again and a second day seemed to start before the sun had gone under: the stream of squiggling silver, the coldness of the sea mounting, squirming up to my hips, the herrings thrown in my face by Bonk, the desperate dashes of the jumping flappers in the slithering mass of herrings, slowly sliding from starboard to port with the rolling of the ship.

I never saw the sea for I was not allowed on the foredeck, and the rail was too high for me to look over. All I saw was the sky with the mast, the rigging, and the sails swaying in it. At nightfall when the sky turned green, another mast and another rigging would loom up beside us: the "buyer," the fastest ship of the fleet, carrying three times as much sail as the other botters and manned by six people. They would take over the living fish from all the botters of Huizen, count them by basketsful and store them in their vast hold. Then, when they were full, they would hoist every sail they had and race to the west, to Amsterdam, trying to be there ahead of the buyers of the other fleets, to be the first at the market in the morning and get the highest price.

I was longing to see the buyers racing; in my imagination it became a magnificent sight: more than a dozen ships, their hulks and their rigging hidden by a colored cloud of sail, foaming away toward the sunset, trying to beat each other by putting on more than their masts could carry. I had seen our buyer in the harbor: a colossal ship, its mast sheathed with iron, its stays as thick as my arm; but I never saw it at sea, for I was too small. Never was the agony of my smallness brought home to me more acutely than during those days; just over the edge, just beyond the black wall of the rail lay a wonderful glittering world of sea and ships and clouds and horizon; but whenever I tried to pull myself up to have a look at that promised land, Bonk kicked me or Krelis shouted or the Black Skipper said: "Don't kill yourself, child; be sick in the gutter."

I was jealous of Murk who was allowed to climb the foredeck and sit there, high up, licking himself in a hopeless effort to clean some of the tar away before he curled up and fell asleep, blind to the marvel of the world around him. I grew so jealous of him that I threw things at him when he fell asleep up there, on the very spot where I longed to go more than anywhere else; but then Bonk would smack me and shout: "Rat! What do you mean by pestering dumb animals? I'll teach you!" and he would go on punching me and kicking me in the side with his knee until Krelis smacked him and kicked his behind with a wooden shoe as big as a boat and then the Black Skipper would say: "Stop it."

The Black Skipper standing at the helm, steering with his back, his light blue eyes looking at the things I couldn't see, was a sight I could look at for minutes on end. He was a promise, a goal, a vision of a wonderful future; he seemed to sail with a host of angels behind him,

fat angels blowing trumpets, like the gold dolls on top of the organ in church.

I didn't understand at the time why the mere looking at him made me feel as if I was hearing music; only much later did I realize why. He was the first human being I loved.

THE FIRST TIME I SAW THE SEA was on Saturday night toward sunset. After the noon catch had been hauled in, the buyer came much earlier than usual. I didn't dare ask, but I understood from the snatches of conversation I overheard that we would be putting into port that night and that was how I realized that it was Saturday.

I knew that every Sunday every botter on the Zuider Zee put into port to go to church. This was seldom their home port; as the fish was bought at sea while they followed the shoals on their circular way along the coast they often found themselves far from home at the end of the week. But as to go to church twice on Sunday was necessary for the soul, two or three ports below the wind got all the botters there were, depending on where the shoals were on Saturday.

Like all the children of Huizen I had heard stories about these fishermen's Sundays, and we had hoped feverishly that one Sunday the whole fleet would sail into our port. But this never happened; not only was Huizen a difficult port to get into, lying right in the prevailing wind, it also was too small.

But the main reason why Huizen was never chosen for a fisherman's Sunday was the size of its church. Our church could hold one thousand people at the utmost, if extra stools were put up in the aisles, and a fishermen's Sunday meant an invasion of anything from four to five thousand fishermen at a time.

Hoorn and Enkhuizen were the favorite Sunday ports. Both had a big harbor and enormous churches that rose from the little towns like ancient battleships; both had a wide-open anchorage, sheltered from the winds and with an easily accessible shore. The reason why we children of Huizen had hoped so fervently for the miracle of our village being chosen for a fishermen's Sunday was the stories we were told about them. It was said that the fishermen went to church twice each Sunday in order to make good the damage to the towns and to their souls they had done on finding themselves together in such a happy number. The stories told about incredible orgies: screaming women chased through the streets, customs shacks set on fire, shops pillaged; one legend said that on a Monday morning long ago Bokke Bas, a famous fisherman from the Island of Urk, had sailed out of Enkhuizen with the head of a statue

of Jan Pieterzoon Coen, the hero who discovered the Dutch Indies, covered with the burgomaster's wig.

After that Saturday evening the buyer had left and the net was not put out again. I knew it was one of the golden towns we were sailing to at such great speed. They were called "the golden towns" and in my imagination that was because the steeples of their churches and the roofs of their houses were inlaid with gold.

I had given up trying to look over the rail several days before; but when I realized where we were bound for I couldn't resist the temptation and tried it again. Hardly had I pulled myself halfway up when Bonk kicked me again, Krelis kicked Bonk, and the Black Skipper said: "Stop it." My face must have been very miserable for suddenly I heard him say: "Come here, child."

I approached him fearfully; I thought he was going to punish me for he looked very severe.

"Are you still sick?" he asked.

I whispered: "No, sir."

"Then what were you scrambling up that rail for?"

"I wanted to look, sir," I said.

He looked at me so grimly that I felt the tears welling up in my eyes. "Look at what?" he asked.

I swallowed and whispered: "The sea."

"The sea?" he replied incredulously, knitting his brows in what to me seemed to be divine wrath. Then his face slowly relaxed as the realization of my smallness dawned on him. He didn't smile; I never saw him smile during the months I sailed with him; but the expression on his face at that moment was the nearest I ever saw him get to it.

"Come here," he said, and stretched out his hand. I approached hesitantly, overcoming the resistance of ten years' sparrow's experience; then suddenly he grabbed me by the collar of my coat, flung me in the air like a sack, and caught me in his elbow.

This was so unexpected that during the first half minute or so I saw nothing. I felt a sudden wave of nausea as if I was going to be sick again. Then I heard him say: "All right, look!" and I did.

The sight I saw took my breath away. The sea was a sheet of silver under a tremendous dome of a cloudless evening sky, green like weathered brass. On that sea, in line with us and behind us, sailed the biggest fleet I had ever seen. Hundreds and hundreds of botters sailing in formation, town by town. The most impressive thing about that fleet was the colors of the sails. I knew that all the fishing ports around the Zuider Zee had slightly different colored sails; fishermen's sails were never white—they were cured immediately after manufacture to withstand the weather and the salt. The curing was done locally, each town had its own secret process; that was why our sails were black and the Volendammers' red. But only that night, looking around me openmouthed from the arm of

the Black Skipper, did I realize how many ports there were around the Zuider Zee. There were blue sails, green sails, orange sails, black sails; they had been mended by patches of other colors and over them fluttered the town pennants: thin ribbons twelve yards long, stretched taut in the breeze, blue for the west coast, red for the east. Some of the pennants were almost as long as the masts, and I felt a pang of jealousy at the thought that we hadn't got one, but at the same moment I saw Bonk hoisting it. Our pennant was the longest of all: a bright blue ribbon jumping out toward the shore, fluttering nervously in the green sky, reaching for the promised land.

I looked ahead and saw the coast. An orange sunset flamed behind the silhouette of what seemed a miracle city seen from afar. It had at least a dozen steeples and what looked like gold domes glistening in the sun. The haze of the night had begun to rise: a thin white streak on the horizon colored pink by the setting sun, and it made the city look as if it floated on a cloud. I must have thought aloud: "What is that?" for the Black Skipper said with a voice that was curiously proud: "Hoorn the Golden," as if he had created it himself.

I looked away from the city because I heard a rush of water and the singing wind in rigging overtaking us. It was the HZ 55, Arie Kos's botter, our fishing partner whom I hadn't seen all week. I had only heard the shouts passing from ship to ship and known it was there; now I saw it. It was the first botter under full sail I saw from close quarters; at first she seemed nothing but a cloud of black sails riding a white wave. Her pennant was stretched so taut in the wind that it seemed to crackle; the number HZ 55 in her black mainsail was so dazzling white that it seemed to dance in the sunlight. She overtook us and I saw a deckhand waving; Krelis and Bonk waved back and shouted, but at that moment a flash of lightning struck in that dream of color and sails and sea. It was a moment of such unreality that I felt a shiver of fear, like realizing that I was about to wake up from a wonderful miracle world, for at the helm of the HZ 55 stood Skipper Arie Kos, also with a child in his arms. They came so close that I couldn't be mistaken any longer; the child looked at me gravely and I stared back openmouthed. Then it waved and I waved back; a newly dead arriving on a distant shore.

For the child on Skipper Kos's arm was Kris Muis, our playmate from school who had been killed by a sea lion.

IT SEEMED SO UNBELIEVABLE that I could think of nothing else any more. I remembered his mother running through the streets weeping. I remembered the whispered gossip among us as to who would be the successor to our drowned friend. I remembered lying awake at

night, with Bulle and Jaap breathing in sleep beside me, imagining what it had been like: the struggle in the water, the sea lion's ferocious teeth, the terrible pain, the blood. The story said that a sea lion, when it caught a boy, ate only his head; I had seen Kris Muis's headless body bobbing lonely in an endless sea, limp like the dead cats in the harbor. And now, for one long hollow minute, I gazed at him, alive, sitting on Skipper Kos's arm, and he waved at me and smiled.

It was such a dark and menacing mystery that I simply had to talk to somebody about it and find out that it was true. After the Black Skipper had put me down, I sidled over to Bonk squatting on the deck, his back against the mast, whitewashing the clogs for the Sunday. It took me a long time before I had worked up enough courage to address him, a thing I had never dared do before. I was still wondering whether I should when I heard myself say: "Sir . . ."

Bonk looked up and stared at me with his fish eyes and grunted.

"Was that Kris Muis?" I asked.

His face changed as if only then he had caught sight of me, an unpleasant sight indeed. "Kris who?" he said, flabbergasted, as if he had been addressed by a cat that could suddenly speak.

I felt a trembling creep up my spine but I went on recklessly: "The mouse on board the 55," I said. "Is that Kris Muis?"

Bonk's mouth sagged open in blank amazement. Then he suddenly snarled, as if at last the realization of the outrage began to ooze into his consciousness. "Jesus Christ!" he said. "Do you think I know the names of mice?! Holy Mother! The cheek of it! Actually sitting there, one thumb high, and asking me the name of a mouse! ME!" Then he pushed a brushful of whitewash in my face, so that I toppled over backward with a stinging pain in my eyes. "Rat!" he screamed. "Scram to your nest in the forehole and write a thousand lines: mice have no names, mice are . . ."

Then a clog as big as a boat nearly skinned my nose as it swung past my face, and Bonk yelped. I heard the Black Skipper's voice say: "Stop it," and I scurried away to the cable hole where I wiped the whitewash off my face with one of the rags on which I slept. Murk was there, asleep; he got up when I pulled the rag from underneath him, arched his back showing the white belt of his tummy, and yawned. Then he sniffed at the white stuff dripping on the ropes, and jumped up toward the square of sky, disgusted.

I didn't actually see us entering the harbor, I heard it. At first there was a great noise of water as the botters of our line converged toward the narrow entrance between the piers. I heard shouts all around and the rattle and rush of jibs swishing down; then the Black Skipper's voice hollered and our own jib dropped from the sky with a terrific sound of heavy sail furling and iron rings screeching down the forestay; the heavy top block hit the deck overhead with a colossal bang and the roar of the

water against the bow shrunk to a soft splashing. There was a noise of clogs on decks all around us, the banging of beams, and the flapping of huge sails in the wind like cannon shots. Then all of a sudden the whole cable hole seemed to explode to dust in a terrific collision. There was a noise of iron so loud that it made my throat ache, and I was flung back among the lamps and the glass floats, screaming with terror.

For a minute I seemed to suffocate in a dense red cloud; my lungs stung as if I was breathing pepper. I sat trembling in that corner until the red cloud lifted, then I saw that my bed had been thrown aside and some of the rags sucked into the hawsehole. All that had happened was that the HZ 69 had dropped anchor in the bay of Hoorn the Golden; I had slept on the chain for a week without knowing it.

When, exhausted, I had hoisted myself onto the foredeck through the manhole and stood blinking in the sunset, I heard laughter all around me. The Black Skipper's voice called: "Child, come here," and I was picked up by Krelis and carried to the cockpit. "Wash him," said the skipper. "What on earth has happened to the brat?"

I never saw myself; but when Krelis washed my face with a wad of cotton waste in a pail, I saw the water turn orange and realized that the whitewash and the rust must have got mixed on my face. When I finally stood, clean, in front of the Black Skipper, with the cold drops of water that had run into my collar squiggling down my back, he said to Krelis: "Take him ashore and buy him a suit."

"Aye aye," said Krelis, and he picked me up. "And have his head shaved!" shouted the skipper after us; then I was lowered into a boat.

In the boat I got the proof that the incredible vision was true. Looking up at me with very blue eyes, in a wonderful suit of black baggy breeches and a black vest separated by a red sash, blue and white striped stockings and dazzling white new clogs, sat Kris Muis, an astrakhan cap with an orange top on the back of his shaven head. He lifted his hand lazily, in a very grown-up greeting, and when I had overcome my awe, my first feeling was an intense, deep jealousy. For on the back of his left hand was tattooed a big blue anchor.

THAT FIRST EVENING IN HOORN was crammed so full of wondrous things that in the end I accepted everything happening to me in a sort of daze.

I was taken through streets teeming with men in at least a dozen different costumes, past brilliantly lit shop windows piled high with treasures I didn't even begin to know the uses of, until at last we ended up at the tailor: a hunchback in shirt sleeves in an alley of shelves stacked with bundles of clothes. He asked Krelis where we came from and when

Krelis said: "Huizen," the hunchback wheeled a ladder to a corner, climbed to the top layer, looked at me with one eye shut and pulled out a bundle. Kris Muis, who had left his clogs outside, sat on the corner of the counter, yawning and chewing, a bored man.

I didn't get a chance to speak to him until we were on our way home, for after the tailor I was taken to the clog-maker, after the clog-maker to the cap-seller, after the cap-seller to the barber and after that my cap didn't fit any more but rested on my ears. The barber tore a strip off a newspaper and tucked it in the band. I decided secretly that every day I would take out one layer of paper to keep the cap fitting.

When we got out of the barber's it was night and my head felt very cold. I wasn't sleepy at all although I had been used to going to bed at sunset, but I had a headache and my feet hurt in the new clogs as I stumbled along, dragged by Krelis who got maddened by the little steps I made. The lights in the streets were on but I couldn't see the shops any more, because by then there were too many men about. I seemed to be dragged through a furrow Krelis plowed in a solid mass of fishermen: Urkers, Elburgers, Stavoreners, Enkhuizers and Bunschoters. Every port around the Zuider Zee had its men there, except Volendam.

Nobody knew where the Catholics went to church and nobody cared. It was wise of them not to show their noses, because there were so many Protestants about that liked to do something together and didn't know what. If a Volendammer had appeared among them, they would have known what; now they were looking for policemen, as the women of Hoorn had got wise long ago and stayed indoors with bread for two days and all their pails full of water, so as not to be forced by thirst to break through the siege.

Kris Muis, who sauntered along beside me as if he was twice my size and could see everything, told me about the policemen on our way back to the bay. I didn't hear half of what he said, because of the noise the thousands of clogs made on the pavement, the bellowing wisps of song, the terrifying gusts of laughter, the murderous back-slapping and the oi-oi-ing going on all around me. I gathered that the only times sea mice could show themselves in the open was on Saturday nights and Sundays in the golden towns, when all the fleet was in. Then there were so many fishermen about in the streets looking for trouble that the policemen packed their bags as soon as the sails of the armada were sighted and went to stay with their aunts in the country. Kris Muis said this was a pity, for that if the fishermen found a constable who had decided to stick it they disarmed him, took off his trousers, slammed his cap so deep over his eyes that it turned into a collar and carried him, singing, to the burgomaster's house, where they threw him through the window into the parlor. The burgomaster, Kris said, had tried shutters of steel, but they hadn't worked for the fishermen had uprooted the iron statue of Her Majesty and used it as a battering ram, after which the

policeman had been chucked through the hole, screaming as he sailed.

We passed a large crowd in the market place on our way; they were shouting and singing: "What happened on Baldhead's nuptial night," which Kris Muis said was in honor of the burgomaster. Krelis took me on his shoulder as we crossed the crowd, because the legs stood so thick that I nearly suffocated. I saw the burgomaster's house: a gabled façade with huge windows in gaslight, but not a candle showed inside, and the handles of the big double doors were tied together with a chain and padlock. The crowd went on singing and calling for Baldhead, asking to see his daughter, and shouting questions about the weight of his wife, but nobody showed behind the vast windows; it looked like a deserted palace.

I wasn't feeling happy, swaying on Krelis' shoulders over the shouting heads. I was afraid of losing my new clogs which were too big for me and the wind was very cold on the back of my shaven head. Kris Muis vanished in the crowd on the market place; I shouted in Krelis' ear that he had gone, but Krelis said: "Don't you worry, he'll find his way back all right. And so will you, if you have been around this town once." We passed a tumble of arms and legs of men joyfully fighting; a monster with a flat Urker cap and only two yellow teeth left in his lower jaw leered up at me and shrieked: "There goes my breakfast!" but I held tight on to Krelis' shoulder and we lost him safely in the milling crowd.

We passed another palace with a lion and a unicorn on top of its façade, so big that it looked as if the house itself was peeping between their legs. Krelis said that it was the governor's house, but that he hadn't been in town for centuries because the noise on Saturday nights made it impossible for him to govern. He said that it was going to be turned into a museum, showing the riches of the past and the ruins of tomorrow.

I heard a lot about the ruins of tomorrow, once we got back on board. I was ordered to go to sleep instantly, after the skipper had made me turn around twice in front of him to show what Krelis had got me. The cabin was full of people: Huizers and Elburgers squatting in a thick ring around the coffeepot that sat in a multitude of mugs, like a chicken too small for its eggs. Three tins of babblers stood open on the floor between them, and the tobacco smoke hung so thick under the ceiling that the shadows of the rings around the lamp cut it in slices. I vanished through my hole in the bunk and shut the trap door behind me; but I didn't go to sleep at once. I sat there listening, with Murk purring and yawning in the darkness behind me and finally smacking his lips in his sleep.

All the voices on the other side of the partition talked about was the ruins of tomorrow; the ruins that would be left of their towns and their fleet once the big dam was laid across the mouth of the Zuider Zee. I had never thought much about the big dam, although I had often heard of it. It lay so far ahead in the future that it seemed as unreal as death.

That night I heard that the first step had been made; the dam between the mainland and the Island of Wieringen had been completed a week ago. It didn't make much difference yet; the botters had seldom crossed the narrow straits as they were too shallow and the herring never went there. But even so, it was the first step, one-eighth of the total distance across. If the fishermen on the Zuider Zee let that onslaught on their livelihood pass unpunished, the Negroes from below Amsterdam would take courage and go on with their devilish plan. Something had to be done, the voices said; whatever happened, that dam had to be blown so high that the sods of it would hail down on their damned cities, Babylons of sin, homes of the painted mouths, the steam trawlers and the electric frying pans.

Never before had I heard such grim emotion in men's voices, as when I sat listening motionlessly behind that trap door in the darkness. For the first time in my life I overheard the giants talking among themselves and all they talked about was the day the dam would be blown up. I felt very frightened, and yet curiously elated; for now I was a member of a big conspiracy no children or women knew of. I felt the same grim emotion rise inside me; I saw in that darkness a fleet of empty botters under full sail soaring down toward the wicked dam, their fo'c'sles crammed with dynamite. I saw the bursting volcano of the explosion, heard the mounting thunder of the colossal bangs piling on top of each other, until the sky trembled with noise. It seemed like the victory of a fleet of Saint Jorises: a large sluggish dragon made of mud, stretched out in the sea. Teeming with Negroes from below Amsterdam, with wide painted mouths, brandishing electric frying pans.

I felt a slight sadness at the same time, because to me the worst enemies in the world had been the Catholic pirates of Volendam, for so long that I had almost begun to like them. It felt like a good-by to a trusted homeland, like entering a new vast space full of frightening emptiness and strange shadows and a new enemy.

I fell asleep where I sat, before the voices stopped, dazed and exhausted, and very much alone.

THE NEXT MORNING WE WENT TO CHURCH, and that was the first time I realized how many sea mice there were hidden in the botters of the Zuider Zee.

There seemed to be thousands of us, silently trooping down the streets toward the sound of the big bell tolling. It was like a funereal procession of dwarfs, for we were separated from the giants the moment we set out for church. I followed the crowd of boys without knowing which way we were taking; it was a different way from the giants, for all

the way to church there wasn't a full-sized fisherman in sight. All of us were carrying a psalm book; Krelis had given me one when I set out.

We met our skippers again at the doors, but they behaved as if they didn't see us; this caused the curious sensation of being invisible again, that I had known so well when I was still a child in Huizen. It gave us an anticipation of the authority of God, as if, even though we were now being shown in the open, we were still illegal, with God frowning on us from the skies with a big policeman's cap on.

In church itself we were separated from our skippers also; the giants sat below with the sea boys, the mice crowded the gallery. We sat down in the long high benches, leaving our clogs in the alley.

The first few minutes were not boring, because there was slow solemn organ music and from the ceiling hung scores of little ships, complete with sails and life boats, turning slowly in the slanting beams of sunlight. The ships and the tops of the arches were all we could see of the church, for the benches were so high that we had to look upward all the time. The church was cold, but there was a warmth of many boys around me and the thick rich smell of soft soap and baize.

Only when the service started did we become intolerably bored. The preacher howled in such an unnatural voice that it would have been difficult to understand him anyhow. But apart from that there were so many echoes in the church, that it sounded as if five invisible preachers were hollering at the same time. The deserts of meaningless bawling between the hymns seemed endless; and when the hymns came, only the beginning and the end of them were beautiful, for then the organ played by itself. As soon as the men began to sing it sounded like an angry crowd clamoring for blood. Nobody could keep the tune, because nobody knew what it was; and the song was sung in such a slow tempo that the organ sounded as if it were dragging a thousand wailing voices along, grinding its way mercilessly.

We children sang a song entirely our own; and it wasn't one song, it was a dozen. We had been sitting still, silently, for so long that the chance to make a noise went straight to our heads. Some of us sang about Jesus, others about Baldhead's nuptial night. Toward the end of the hymn it sounded like a screaming battle of music between God and the Devil. The mice of Urk, in the bench next to us, sang a very filthy song very fast, beating time with their fists on the high ledges of their benches; they ended by shooting peas at the little ships with slingshots and dancing on the seats. But punishment swished down on us, with angry shouts and the biting pain of a fishing rod. It was the "dog beater," a man appointed to keep animals out of the church during the services who also made the collection. He spent most of his time prowling behind the benches, looking for mischief among us, at which he would lash out with his fishing rod and hit the instigator on the head. When collection time came he turned the fishing rod around it; it had a little black sack

attached to it in which we were supposed to put the cents given to us by
our skippers before we set out to church. Nobody put a cent in; when
the black bag came back to the dog beater it seemed like a garbage sack.
Buttons, bits of paper, wet sweets and chewed cigar butts had all got
together into a sticky lump which he emptied in the alley, his eyes
bloodshot with rage. He shook his fist at us, turned around his rod and
slammed it down on the row, regardless. At first I was frightened and
tried to hide myself from the blows, but Kris Muis, sitting beside me,
nudged me and said: "Scream!" I soon found out that if we screamed
loud enough the blows would stop; so we resumed our mischief with a
feeling of victory, while the invisible parson resumed his fivefold hollering
and the dog beater stood choking in the alley between us, forming words
with his lips.

The service lasted three hours, from nine to twelve, and the last
hour was the longest. We groaned and writhed with boredom. We made
rabbits with our handkerchiefs, put on our caps square-ways, the Urker
boys began to undress and put on their clothes inside out. In the end
there was nothing left to do to make life last, but to pull faces in unison
or to stick out one hundred tongues at the same moment at the dog beater,
dying with helpless rage. The dog beater became our only hope of sur-
vival; the Urker boys took off their trousers and turned their bare be-
hinds toward him, at which he grabbed his fishing rod like a harpoonist
going berserk and lashed out at them with such ferocity that the smacks
resounded underneath the arches like pistol shots multiplied a dozenfold.
The Urker boys began to scream so sharply that I felt it in my teeth.
We all began to scream, and out of that rising spiral of pointless scream-
ing came a chorus: "A-men, a-men, a-men!" and then suddenly we shut
up, almost at the same moment, and sat very still and stared piously in
front of us.

Five huge skippers had appeared behind the benches; five Urkers
of such enormous size and with such terrifying faces that I felt my legs
tingle with fear at the mere sight of them. One of the Urkers advanced
slowly in the alley, between our benches, noiseless in his stockinged
feet. By then the Urker mice were silently praying, but their prayers
were of no avail. The giant looked at the benchful of motionless children
with a long motionless stare, then his big hand rose in the air, descended
in the middle of the second row and grabbed an ear. It pulled out one of
the praying boys, who didn't even struggle. The boy was led toward the
back, half walking half squatting; we didn't dare look around, the eerie
silence hung over us menacingly for minutes on end. Kris Muis whispered:
"He's taking off his breeches." Then there was one colossal smack, a yelp
as of a rabbit at the moment its neck was wrung, and then silence again,
with the shapeless howling of the preacher lapping against the ceiling,
multitudinous and monotonous like the surf. The boy came back to his
seat with stooped shoulders, whimpering, and he seemed much smaller.

The silent guard of Urkers stood glowering at the back of our heads until our limbs went asleep; then there was a last hopeless, murderous song of the men down below, a last blast from the organ, a last wail from the five invisible parsons, and never had I muttered "Amen" with more sincerity.

When we were out of the church at last and started on our way home we ran, danced, shouted and sang like school children setting out for the year's big holiday. I felt, like all of us, an irresistible urge to do mischief, to break things, and I started shouting filthy words, throwing my clogs at windows, rattling doorknobs and ringing bells like all of us. We were swept to the harbor by a wave of communal emotion, and the emotion was relief, so profound, so inexpressible that I came home with a brass bell knob in my hand. Kris Muis had a black eye and everywhere were boys who limped on one clog or tried to pin up tears in their jackets. Many of us were wet, for when the wave of our relief had washed down the empty streets of Hoorn the Golden, windows had been opened and pails of water had been emptied on our heads: futile protests against the fruits of Christianity.

THE HOUR AFTER SUNDAY LUNCH was the only time off the sea mice had during the week.

After the bones had been thrown overboard, the potato pot washed, the coffee mugs wiped and the floor cleaned by the cat and the men sank down on their backs, sleepily sucking the remains of their babblers, then we mice slunk out of the cabins, manned the boats and rowed ashore.

The boats had to be back at half-past two, to ferry the fishermen ashore for a second church service that began at three. Between half-past one and half-past two on Sunday the golden towns were handed over to the children.

When Kris Muis, who had told me about this, had hissed and whistled from the boat until all the mice of the two dozen botters lying side by side in the bay piled up in it, we set out for the shore. There was not much room in the boat to row, as we were too many. Kris and a boy called Freek of the HZ 11 took hold of one oar together and paddled from the stern.

When we arrived at the quay it was already full of kids. The harbor itself was jam-packed with botters; they were lying in solid rows, side by side and stem to bow; you could walk right across the harbor by jumping from ship to ship. We, anchored in the bay, were the overflow; if the weather had been rough we would have had to go on and put into Enkhuizen. But it was a cloudless week end, with bright sunlight and a gentle breeze, and so the whole fleet had descended on Hoorn. I had no

idea of the number of ships, but, according to the number of mice that sprung forth from them during that one hour when the giants lay sleeping, there must have been hundreds for the big quay was teeming with us.

I had thought that we went ashore to play, but I was mistaken. We went ashore to be men. During one glorious hour each week we were giants ourselves; we smoked pipes, put our caps as far on the back of our heads as possible, and waddled with our legs wide apart, our fists in our pockets, grunting: "Oi-oi" and discussing the dam in little groups, loitering around the bollards. We talked about our ships, our nets, our catch, and when we were tired of grumbling about the price of the herring and the quality of the sails coming from that new factory in Friesland, we waddled along the water's edge and made a tour of the punished.

The punished were the big attraction of the week's hour of manliness. As even mice occasionally did something which made their skippers angry, and as they couldn't be spared to be punished during the week or the hours of the church services, retribution for the week's big sins befell them between half-past one and half-past two on Sundays.

The way of punishment was the same on all botters. Before the giants went to sleep after lunch, they took the mouse who had sinned to the foredeck, tied his hands behind his back, passed the loose end of the rope with which the jib was hoisted under his arms and hauled him halfway up the mast. Then he was left during the hour of rest.

It was a painful punishment, but mainly a humiliating one, for all the mice of the fleet would file past during that hour, and laugh at the wretches, who vainly tried to throw their hanging bodies round so as to hide their faces from the crowd. We would shout and jeer at them, and occasionally pull out a slingshot to have a potshot at them. They looked ludicrous, dangling there at half staff height; some of them were weeping, others were angry and shouted back at us. They were the ones that were shot at.

That afternoon I saw about two dozen hanged, and the preventive effect of that spectacle was very strong. I made up my mind never to do anything that would result in my exposing myself to such utter humiliation, or at least never to get caught at anything. Kris Muis said that he had hung there himself one Sunday and enjoyed it; you had a lovely view of the town from there, but he didn't manage to make the idea attractive.

I told him, in our bored grown-up way, that everybody in our village thought he was dead. He snorted and said: "Pah! Children." I asked him whether his mother knew he was still alive; he shrugged his shoulders and said he had sent her a postcard from Enkhuizen some time ago, telling her to stop worrying. He would not go back ashore, he said, until he had been promoted to sea boy; then he would marry Annie Sluiters and beat the hell out of her, because she had screamed out when she saw him peeping through the hawsehole last time the fleet was in, and he was sure that she had given him away.

589

I deduced from his conversation that his skipper had the same idea about women as Krelis; he talked about "beating" a lot, and said that he didn't care what his mother thought as she was only married into the family. I tried to talk about women the way the Black Skipper did, but Kris never realized what I discussed. When I began to talk about a green eye opening in a kiss, very close and large, looking as if you saw the Zuider Zee through a porthole on an early autumn morning, he shrugged his shoulders and spat. I was hurt, because I had repeated the phrase word for word as I heard it from the mouth of the Black Skipper, but I was too impressed by the way he spat to go on about it. He said his sea boy was the best spitter of the fleet; when the nets were out and the breeches folded and skipper and deckhand in their bunk, the seaboy would sit up on his elbows between their legs, take aim, and spit out the candle on the shelf four yards away. He, himself, was not a bad spitter, he said; he tried to demonstrate it on one of the punished, a very small Urker boy hanging very low, but he got no further than a yard or two—his spittle never even reached the ship. I heard it dropping in the water, although he said: "Bullseye," shoved his cap on the back of his head and waddled on.

I began to think that Kris Muis was a bit of a bragger, but as he was my friend I didn't want to believe this until I saw it proved. The spittle was no proof; it might have been the wind. But when we rowed back on board he dropped the oar, snatched it out of the water in the nick of time, and although he did this very deftly he got his arm wet up to the elbow. When we finally reached our ships and the mice scrambled up the gunwales, I saw a sight that filled me with anger and sadness.

The beautiful anchor, tattooed on Kris's left hand, of which I had been so jealous, had turned into a shapeless blot. He had painted it on with ink.

AT A QUARTER TO THREE the double procession of men and boys again set out toward the sound of the solemn bell calling the faithful.

The second service lasted as long as the first, but somehow it seemed to be over more quickly for we spent most of it asleep. Most of the mice had been listening the night before to the conversation of the giants behind the partition, and so they were sleepy now. Furthermore Kris Muis had warned me that Sunday night was the best night of all, for then stories were told in the cabins by the Liars; so if I wanted to listen I had better take this chance to snatch some sleep.

I had heard about the Liars before, but I had never been very interested in them for they never did anything real; they just sat down in a circle of people and told lies. I had never seen one because for

some reason all Liars were Urkers. Kris told me more about them; he said they were very funny because they told impossible stories about mermen ringing at midwives' doors at night to get help for their mermaid-wives who were having a child, about turtles in China so big that whole gardens grew on their backs, about sea monsters with seven heads, and the skinning of Eskimo women. The funny thing about these stories was that the Liars told them as if all this had happened to them personally; they never told a story in the third person, but always began: "One day when I was in Tasmania," although everybody knew that they had never been out of the Zuider Zee. There was only one Liar who was really good, and he was called Bokke Prins. When he told a story you forgot where you were, and he could go on until the dawn without one of his listeners falling asleep. Kris had heard him only once, because he was very expensive; first he had to be given half a bottle of Geneva to drink before he even started, then he drank another half a bottle during his story, and if he wasn't given a second whole bottle to take away with him, he would never come back again, for he liked to hit that second bottle as soon as he got into the cold morning air. They said he was such a clumsy sailor that his skipper would have fired him long ago, if it hadn't been for the half bottles he arrived with and which were taken away from him the moment he sank into his bunk.

When that night, while I was cleaning away the supper, Skipper Arie Kos and his crew stooped into the cabin and the Black Skipper said: "Let's get a Liar," I hurried, for I wanted to be snug, wrapped up in my rags behind the partition before he arrived. Kos said: "Let's get Bokke Prins—I'm sick of the children's babble of the others," and the Black Skipper ordered Bonk to go ashore and get three bottles of Geneva.

It was so long before he came back, that I was nearly asleep, cold and disappointed. I was sure that Bokke had been snatched up by some other botter in the harbor as we were lying so far out. But after what seemed at least an hour I heard the splashing and crunching of oars drawing near, a thud when the boat hit the ship, and Bonk's voice saying: "Steady, sir, let me give you a hand." I heard another voice mumble something shapeless, a high-pitched voice like a woman's, and I sagged back in disappointment because I was sure this couldn't be Bokke. Bonk must have caught some second-rate Liar, loitering on the quay, who hadn't been able to find a drink yet.

But whoever it might be that was ushered into the cabin, he had certainly been able to find a drink. The high-pitched voice was so drunk that it strung words together like a child of two stringing colored beads. There was a lot of stumbling, scraping and hiccuping and I understood that the drunk had entered the cabin with his clogs on. I was about to turn away and go to sleep when I heard the Black Skipper say: "Oi-oi, Bokke; how are you, my boy?" The high-pitched voice chirped and giggled and slurred a string of words of which I understood only one:

"Thirsty." There was a plop of a bottle being uncorked and the glugglug of gin in glasses; I felt angry with Kris Muis, because he obviously had pulled my leg. Bokke Prins must be the worst of all the Liars. The only thing I couldn't understand was why the Black Skipper should have spent so much money to have a speechless drunk hauled all the way from the harbor. Three bottles of gin were worth a fortune.

They sat drinking in there for the better part of an hour. The noises the drunk made got less and less human. He played a lopsided little tune on a mouth organ which ended in a slobber of spittle. He giggled, cooed, gave feminine little shrieks; his voice got higher and higher until he sounded like a baby chortling to itself in its cradle. If I hadn't been so cold and so tired I would have dragged myself to my basket where Murk lay already snoring, but the idea of having to unwrap myself and crawl all the way through the icy cold was so unpleasant that I just sat there uncomfortably and dozed.

I must have been asleep at one time because when I woke up something had changed and I couldn't remember when this had happened. A soft man's voice was talking behind the partition, a voice so melodious and fascinating that I thought someone else had come in, but it was unmistakably Bokke's. It spoke with the soft, slurring Urker accent, and was so beautiful, that I listened to it for a while, without realizing what it was saying.

The cabin was so silent that I could hear the water lapping against the side of the ship, the sleepy shuffling of our leeboard against Arie Kos's botter, the faraway squeak of the rudder stirring in its hinges, the soft tapping of ropes against the mast. The voice seemed to be alone in a world of wind and water.

It was telling the story of a girl, who had lived on the Island of Schokland before the village of Emmeloord had been submerged. I knew of the village of Emmeloord; it was the one whose bells could be heard ringing when the ground seas of a gale stirred them in the depth. I had often wondered what Emmeloord had been like, and the voice told me.

A wind-swept village of small red houses huddled close together, peeping over the dike at the Zuider Zee with their attic windows, barred against the gales. The girl was called Mensje and she had a lover called Jan Viool who was a sailor for the East India Company. They were to marry after his next voyage, and Mensje had started fitting out her hope chest when one night she had a curious dream.

She saw Jan standing at the bottom of a broken red tower. She couldn't make out whether it was night or day for the light was very strange: a curious blue that sometimes changed to green. The tower was covered with a sort of creeper the like of which she had never seen before. Jan stood there, clad only in his trousers, a blood-soaked kerchief knotted around his head, and he was calling her. The curious thing was that although she saw him calling she didn't hear a sound. She saw his

mouth move in a deep heavy silence, as if he was trying to make himself heard through a thick glass plate. She tried to understand what he was calling and he tried to make himself understood, but the heavy silence was impenetrable, and she woke up with a feeling of great urgency. She was sure he was in danger and that he wanted her to do something for him but she had no idea what it could be.

The next night she had the same dream again. Again she saw him standing at the bottom of that curious tower in that green light changing to blue; again he tried to make her understand what he was saying, but the heavy glass silence remained impenetrable. Before she woke up, however, it seemed as if his message had been brought back to two words: two words he kept on repeating time after time, forming them slowly, pleadingly with his lips. He was still repeating them when she woke up, without any idea of what he was trying to say.

During the month that followed she had the dream several times. It was always the same: the tower, the creeper, the green light, the silence, and Jan, weary and wounded, trying to make her understand two words, two words only. And every time she woke up in tears, because she had no idea what they were.

The fortnight after she had dreamed the dream for the last time the news came that Jan's ship was missing. People came to comfort her, but although she let them say what they wanted in order not to hurt their feelings, she didn't for a second believe that Jan was dead. He was standing somewhere at the bottom of a red tower in green sunlight calling her, and she would help him, if it would cost her everything she had.

But there was nothing she could do. She thought of boarding a ship to the East Indies but nobody knew exactly where the ship had got lost. She decided to remain where she was and to wait until, somehow, they would be able to reach each other through the thick glass plate that separated them. She dreamed the dream many times after that and she began slowly to realize that the first word was "your" and that the second word had an "o" in it; but she never found that second word.

Her waking life became less and less important to her. She would have wanted to sleep and dream forever, if there hadn't been the hope that someday someone would come who would bring her news about Jan or his ship.

Every night she sat listening in the lamplight, knitting socks for him, alone in her little house; and whenever she heard the distant splash and rattle of an anchor dropping in the bay, she would put on her shawl and go out in the night and climb the dike to wait for the first boat coming ashore. Whatever the ship, she would invariably ask the same question: "Have you met the *Rising Hope,* the flagship of the East India Company?" The men in the boat would always be nice to her, for she was a pretty girl with the innocence of the faithful in her eyes. They would say: "Not that we know of, but we have passed so many ships in the

distance which we didn't recognize that it's quite possible." Then she would ask: "Have you heard any news about Jan Viool, a sailor? He may have changed ships abroad." Then the men would get uncomfortable with pity and self-consciousness and say: "No."

This happened many times during the months that followed. She must have asked those questions on dozens of nights; misty, moonlit, stormy or rainy nights. She asked it in snow and hail, shouting against the gale or whispering in the summer breeze; but every time she got the same answer. She would always say: "Thank you, gentlemen," politely, and walk back along the dike: very pretty, very brave, and resume her knitting in the lamplight, alone.

One night, almost a year after Jan had got lost, a night when there was no moon and no breeze and fog enclosed the Island of Schokland, she looked up in the lamplight, amazed, for she heard distinctly the splash and the rattle of an anchor dropping in the bay. That was very strange, for there was no wind and no visibility; the ships in the harbor were lying dead, the ropes silent against the masts, and everybody in the village was asleep in the comfortable certainty that no ship could reach the island that night.

She got up, put her shawl around her shoulders, went out and climbed the dike. She had been used to walking along it to the jetty, for that was where all boats moored; but the night was so thick with fog that she couldn't see one step in front of her, and so she stood still, listening.

She heard distinctly the creaking of oars approaching in the fog, the murmur of water against the bow of a boat, she even heard the oarsmen sighing and the soft clanking of the rudder chain, but she saw nothing. The sounds seemed to come straight at her, and for the first time since Jan had left she became conscious of being alone.

Then there was the scraping of an iron keel on the basalt of the dike, the rumbling of oars being pulled in, the splashing of people getting out and wading through the shallow water; then, suddenly, there came a faint light climbing toward her, with the scraping of hobnailed boots on the rocks.

The light came nearer and nearer, until she saw that it was a very old-fashioned lantern. Then it stood still, and the steps fell silent. She saw only that lantern, and nothing else; but she knew there must be men around it hidden in the fog, and she asked her question without seeing whom she was addressing.

"Have you met the *Rising Hope,* the flagship of the East India Company?" she asked, and for the first time she realized how often she had asked it before. The lantern shone motionlessly in the fog, and she was about to turn away when a voice said: "We have."

She took a long time asking her second question, for she had suddenly become afraid. This was the answer she had been waiting for, for almost a year; but now that she finally heard it a cold fear started creep-

ing up her legs. "Have you heard any news about Jan Viool, a sailor?" she asked. "He may have changed ships abroad."

Again the lantern shone motionlessly in the fog for minutes on end, before the voice answered: "We have."

The fear had crept up so high now, that it nearly numbed her lips. "Do you know where he is?" she whispered.

Again the voice answered: "We do."

Then she asked her last question, and even before she had spoken she realized that it was going to decide her life. Asking that question was the bravest thing she had ever done; but as she had decided that she would help Jan even if it would cost her everything she had, she looked at the motionless lantern bravely and said: "Could you take me to him?"

The silence that met her question lasted so long that she repeated it. Then the voice said: "We can. But it will cost you a lot."

"It doesn't matter," she said. "You can have anything I possess; tell me your price."

The voice answered: "It will cost you your soul."

And that was the moment she knew what had been the second word of the two Jan had tried to make her understand in all those dreams. It was "soul."

The Liar's voice behind the partition fell silent. I heard the plop of a bottle, the small sound of Geneva poured into a glass, and they were the only sounds. Nobody stirred in the cabin; they were more silent than if they had been asleep, for there wasn't even a sound of breathing. Then I heard the Liar smack his lips, and the sharp click of the glass as it was put down on the platter.

Mensje, said the Liar, was the girl we have all been dreaming of all our lives. Her love was so unselfish that she said to the lantern: "All right, take me," giving up Heaven for that one vision: the weary, wounded Jan of her dreams, talking to her, as silent as a fish. If the voice had told her to go through fire to save him she would have done it; she was so generous and gentle that she understood that her love was worth more than her soul. She didn't want to live another sixty arid years, turn into a bedridden mummy in a nightshirt before she died, and then to lie rigid in her grave, her skeleton hands crossed on her barren chest, to get up in that nightshirt at the sound of the Last Trump and face God alone. She would rather sink to the bottom of the ocean, a swollen sack of shark's food, if that meant sinking into the arms of her lover.

Ah, said the Liar, she was the woman we all saw once, for one fleeting second: shaking a mop out of an attic window, or smiling at us as she passed carrying a basket of fish, and when we turned round to look again she had gone forever. He sighed, and there was another sound of Geneva, again the smacking of lips, and another sigh.

When he spoke again his voice was more beautiful than ever It

sounded like the mellow flutelike pipes of the church organ that always made me feel like weeping. It sounded as if the love of Mensje throbbed in his voice, and I wished there was a hole in the partition for I wanted to see him. But there was no hole; the picture I made of him in the darkness was of a wonderful man in robes with a beard, somebody like Jesus, whom I had never really liked before.

Well, said the Liar, she went. She didn't go back to her house to pack a bag or put on clogs; she went as she was: in her slippers, her shawl around her shoulders; the knitting needle, which she had stuck in her hair when she heard the splash and the rattle of the anchor dropping, went with her. The lantern guided her down the dike toward the sea, and she heard the splashing of boots in the water as the invisible men waded toward their invisible boat. Nobody offered to help her, so she put her slippers in her apron, gathered up her skirts, and waded after the lantern through the icy water. She saw the flank of a boat glistening in the fog, and had to climb into it unaided. The moment she sat down, dripping, on the middle bench, the oars rumbled out, the keel scraped free of the rocks, and the boat swung around in the darkness.

The lantern light had gone and she sat there quite alone, shivering in the fog with the sound of oars plowing the water all around her. She sat there for almost half an hour; then the lantern light flashed on again and she saw the dark, glistening wall of a big ship's side rising up beside her. A rope ladder was thrown down to her and she climbed it. The little swinging moon of the lantern followed her and made her climb into her own shadow.

She reached the rail, and climbed it, and stood on a vast deserted deck. The lantern appeared beside her and the voice said: "Follow."

She was taken to a small cabin, that at first looked quite ordinary. The lantern was left with her, the voice said: "Go to sleep," and then there was the sound of a door shutting and of a key turning in the lock.

When she began to undress and put her shawl on the little stool in the cabin, she realized that it was not an ordinary cabin at all. When she tried to lift the stool, to put it nearer to the bunk, she couldn't move it because it was too heavy. It was made of stone. She looked around her at the small objects that had seemed so normal at first glance; they were all made either of lead or stone. When she had undressed and climbed into the bunk and tried to lift the blanket, she had to use both hands for it was a rug of closely knitted iron rings. She wriggled her way underneath it, and when she put her head on the pillow it felt hard and unyielding. It was filled with sand.

She lay there on her back, gazing at the ceiling, getting colder and colder under the iron blanket and on the pillow of sand. She folded her hands to pray; but before her fingers had met she stopped and lay still, for there was no use any longer to pray for her soul. She shut her eyes and thought: good-by life, good-by sound of the wind in the drying nets,

good-by smell of freshly ironed aprons, good-by Schokland, my home, good-by.

She felt very sorry for herself when she thought that, but then an image dawned in the darkness of her closed eyes: a red tower, covered with unknown creeper, and a boy with a blood-soaked kerchief around his head calling her name. She smiled, because she realized that there was no point in saying good-by to anything; her life was him. With that smile on her lips she fell asleep.

When she woke up again the lantern shone no more. The cabin was light: the curious blue-green light she knew so well from her dream. The first thing she saw gave her a shiver of terror: her hair seemed to be standing on end, it rose right to the ceiling and moved softly, waving about. She was so cold that it felt as if her body wasn't there any longer; when she swung the blanket aside it was much lighter than it had been the night before.

But she didn't notice this, for when she swung the blanket aside she saw a sight that nearly made her heart stop: the lower part of her body had changed into a glistening fishtail.

While she lay staring, aghast, at her scales and the forked fin that had once been her feet, a swift shadow passed above her. When she looked up she saw it was a little fish, that had swum in through the open porthole and now floated in the middle of the cabin. The little fish stared at her curiously out of the side of its head with one gold eye, then it turned, swam around the lantern, dived, and nibbled at her cloths. When she slowly stretched out her hand toward it, it flashed away, a streak of silver, and shot out of the porthole into the green light. She rose on her elbows and was amazed how light she was; then she looked out of the porthole and saw where she was.

The ship was lying in the deserted market place of a village of ruins. On the other side of the market place was a roofless church of red bricks, its tower broken; and the tower was covered with the curious creeper that she had never been able to recognize until this moment. It was seaweed.

She got out of the bunk, but never touched the floor, for she floated. Her tail was very strong; when she made a movement of walking she shot ahead and bumped her head against the wall, but her cry of pain was soundless. She understood that she was now in a world of gentle movements and silence.

She tried to open the door but found it was still locked; then she swung around and a quiver of her tail sent her soaring toward the porthole. She stretched her arms through it and tried to make her body follow, but the porthole was too narrow. Then she gave one strong sweep with her tail, and with a tearing pain she shot out into the green light, rose high up in the sky, turned, circled over the roofs of the ruins, and

descended gently at the bottom of the broken tower, the very spot where Jan had stood.

While she hovered there sadly, looking around for her lost lover, an old man crossed the market place with slow long steps, rising into the air at each step as if he danced. She stirred her tail and flashed toward him so fast that she had to rise over his head and circle around before she cautiously descended beside him. He was a very old man with one eye and old-fashioned clothes; on the top of his bald head was a brand-mark of a skull and crossbones, and she understood that he was a pirate. She had a moment of fear, but the thought that she could flash out of his reach with one sweep of her tail gave her a feeling of security. The old man didn't look a bit amazed on seeing her; his one eye gazed at her sadly, as if the sight of her filled him with pity.

She wondered how to communicate with him in this soundless world, but he took her head between his hands, pressed his cold lips against her ear and she heard a whisper: "Jan Viool has just left." Then the old man pointed at the green dusk behind the town, and moved his lips as if to say good-by. She hesitated, for the dusk seemed to be filled with fear: slowly rising in blue circles, waving with the limp dead trees of seaweed, floating with the fleeting shadows of unseen fish. But she thought of Jan and his despair, swung her tail and shot away into the terror of that un-known world, her long hair streaming behind her, spurred by the one hope left to her: that one day, one night, she would find him.

When the Liar filled his glass again, he did it slowly. When I stirred in my rags I did it slowly. It seemed as if the world was entirely silent now; as if we had all sunk to the bottom of the ocean, unnoticed. He didn't sigh any more or smack his lips, and the click of his glass being put back on the platter was a soft thud. When he spoke again his voice was much slower, as if he was the only one who could speak under water and as if every word he said was precious to us, mute fish, gathered around him to hear the news he brought from the land we had lost.

She went, he said, from town to town. She had never known that the bottom of the sea was dotted with submerged villages and cities in which the drowned sailors waited for Judgment Day. She passed through scores of them and found that in every city there lived different people: Dutch, Norwegians, Greeks, Turks. There were cities entirely peopled by women, and villages in which only children lived. Everywhere along her way between the towns she found the silent wrecks of sunken ships, with weeds growing up their rigging and little fish playing around the mouths of their guns. It was the crews and the passengers of those sunken ships that peopled the ruins of the sunken towns.

But everywhere she arrived she got the same message whispered into her ear: "Jan Viool has just left," and every time the one who gave her

that message, man, woman or child, pointed at the green dusk ahead of her.

She swam through the North Sea, the Gulf of Biscay, along the coast of Africa, until she arrived at a little village at the edge of a forest as dark as ink. The village was peopled with Portuguese fishermen, with rings in their ears, blue breeches, and long red caps on their heads with tassels which stretched out behind them when they walked with the long, dancing steps of the drowned. After one of these fishermen had taken her head between his hands again and whispered: "Jan Viool has just left," his hand rose slowly and pointed at the forest.

She wavered, for the darkness ahead of her looked so threatening that she couldn't find the courage to swing her tail and shoot into it. The fisherman saw her fear, took her head in his hands again and whispered: "Wait here." She nodded, saw him dance away into the dark inside of a roofless building, the windows of which were barred with rusty iron bars. After a while she saw the red cap emerge again from the darkness, the fisherman danced out into the green light, and behind him came a row of five people: black, naked people, their left legs linked by a chain. She understood that they must be Negro slaves, drowned while crossing from Africa to America, and wondered what the fisherman had brought them out for.

The fisherman took the head of the first Negro in his hands and pressed his lips against his ear. He whispered for a long time; the Negro nodded and his dark, dead eyes glanced at her. A silent crowd had gathered around them: Arabs in red cloaks, naked Negro girls, Turks with turbans on which still flashed the glitter of diamonds that had once been worth so much. Then the fisherman shook the Negro by the hand, and the five chained men bobbed slowly toward her until they had reached her. The first Negro put out his arms and took her head between the pale palms of his hands. She felt the brush of his thick dead lips against her ear, and heard him whisper: "Follow me."

Before she vanished into the inky darkness of the forest, following the slow procession of the five chained Negroes bobbing along, she looked around once more and saw the crowd staring after her. The fisherman stood alone in the circle; when he saw her glancing back at him he took off his red cap and waved slowly, a last good-by.

The voyage through the forest lasted for weeks. It was so full of creeping fear and sudden streaks of terror that she got exhausted by darting aside all the time, away from the shadows that swooped down on her from the tangle of the high dead trees. The trees were peopled by monsters: sharks, inkfish, horrible crabs. They all attacked her: the sharks like streaks of white lightning, turning around on their backs as they swooped down, their white bellies flashing past her as she darted away from their terrible fangs in the nick of time; the inkfish spurting darkness,

slowly slithering down the trees, their slimy tentacles groping for her in swirling clouds of ink; the crabs swinging out arms as long as derricks, with wide-open claws, snapping shut just behind her glistening, flickering tail. Every time she managed to escape from the attacks of the monsters, and to rejoin the faint shimmer of the five chained men below her, whose path was lit by tiny luminous sea horses, dancing ahead like glowworms, playful sparks in the utter darkness of the sunken jungle between the continents.

When at last, exhausted, she reached the other side of the forest, she emerged into a desert overhung by solid green clouds. She had no idea where she was, but when she saw sticking out of the clouds the keels of ships, and hanging anchors slowly stirring in the circular tide, she understood that the Negroes were moving toward the center of a sea of weeds called the Sargasso Sea.

She had often heard about this sea. Sailors said that all the wrecks of the ocean that did not sink were slowly dragged toward it, to end up in the weeds and join the ghostly fleet of barnacled hulks with broken masts covered with seaweed, slowly spinning around the center of the Sargasso Sea which no human being had ever set eyes on. She remembered that when she was still a child at school an old fisherman had once told them the story of how the Sargasso Sea came into being. Jesus, the old man had said, on finding out that the land was peopled with sinners, got so disgusted that He and His apostles boarded a ship called the *Aldebaran.* In it they sailed the seven seas for centuries, and whenever a ship was being drowned by a gale and battered by waves, there would at the ultimate moment appear a blue light on the horizon, and a cross would shine in the stormy darkness: the *Aldebaran,* coming to save them. But, so the old man had said, Jesus discovered in due course that the sailors were just as disgusting a crowd of sinners as the landlubbers had been. Hopeless and tired, He had ordered His apostles to drop anchor in the loneliest spot of the Atlantic Ocean and wait there for Judgment Day. Like all ships lying still, the *Aldebaran* had started to grow weeds and barnacles. The weeds grew and grew, until they had completely overgrown the ship and covered the sea for miles around.

So when, on a dark green morning, she reached a rusty chain going straight up into the clouds, and the five Negroes sat down on the blade of an enormous anchor sticking out of the desert sand, she knew where she was. The old Negro who was the first of the gang crossed himself and then pointed upward with a pale hand to where the chain vanished in the clouds of the weeds. She hesitated for a while; but then she thought of Jan's desperate face, rose slowly along the chain and vanished in the clouds.

She seemed to rise through that swirling green mass of weeds for a very long time; then she saw a light overhead, a soft white glow like that

of the sun hidden by the thin mist of a winter morning. She saw, as she got nearer, the bottom of an enormous ship, so overgrown with barnacles and mussels that it looked like the ceiling of a grotto that had been born when the world was very young. Somewhere among the rocks was a crack of light, and she swam toward it.

Amid the mussels and the barnacles she found, after searching for a long time, a huge rusty iron ring, like a door knocker, and using all her strength she swung it to and fro until at last it knocked. There was a sound of heavy bolts, a creaking of huge hinges, and the crack got wider until a flat beam of golden light shone into the green darkness of the weeds like sunlight falling into a wood.

In that light she saw the face of a very old man with a white beard appear, and his blue innocent eyes gazed at her in amazement. He must be one of the apostles, and somehow she knew instantly that he was Peter. When she spoke she discovered that she had suddenly got her voice back; it sounded faint and distant, but it was unmistakably hers.

"Could you tell me," she asked, "where I can find Jan Viool, a sailor?"

"Who are you?" the old man asked gently.

"I am his girl," she said.

Old Peter looked at her intently, and then his face changed; as if only at that moment he realized that she was a mermaid. "You are just a few days too late," he said. "He went back to the Island of Schokland the day before yesterday, alive again."

She felt a terrible sadness and at the same time a great joy overcome her, and when she repeated: "Alive!" she felt something warm go down her cheeks, the first warmth she had felt since she had woken up in that cabin of stone, long ago.

"Yes," said Peter, while shutting the door. "He has been lucky: some fool ashore has given up his soul for him."

She didn't know what to say any more. She saw, through her tears, the sunlight shrink to a vanishing crack; then it was dark again around her, and she sank slowly down along the chain until she was back in the desert, where the huge rusty blade of the anchor lay waiting to be lifted from the sand at Judgment Day.

She sat down on the anchor, and wept. The Negroes had gone, and she was quite alone. The thought of wandering among the drowned forever without even the hope of ever reaching the man she loved made her very sad, and for a while it seemed to her as if now there was nothing left to live for. But then she thought of his despair when he would arrive in the Island of Schokland and find her gone, and it was that thought that made her sweep her tail and shoot back into the horror of the black forest, across the nightmarish miles of sunken jungle, across ocean and seas, until at last she reached the dike over which she saw the timid roofs of Emmeloord peeping at the horizon.

On the dike stood a lonely man, staring sadly at the sea. She rose from the waves and waved, but he didn't see her. She called his name, but he didn't hear her. She pleaded, shouted, jumped out of the water with a burst of silver spray, lashing the waves with her tail; but he saw and he heard nothing. He sighed, and he turned slowly around, and vanished behind the dike to go into the little house, in which she knew he would lie down to sleep and dream of a girl, standing at the foot of a broken red tower covered with seaweed, smiling at him through a green glass plate, and forming three small words with her lips which he would, one night, perhaps understand.

The Liar sighed, and uncorked the bottle. He took a long, long drink, after which he smacked his lips sadly, but then he said: "This is not the end of the story."

Jan Viool became the lighthouse keeper of Schokland and remained a brooder until the end of his life; but the mermaid, who was immortal, realized in the end that all men were brothers, and her love became like a fountain: it shot up toward one sailor, but it rained down on all of them. She remained in the sea around the Island of Schokland until this day, and every time a storm is brewing the fishermen hear a soft girl's voice, singing above the murmur of the waves. When they hear it they furl their sails, lock their cabins and go home to wait in bed with their wives until the gale is over, which they know will come before the dawn.

There she swims, said the Liar's voice with a hiccup, the only woman we have all looked for all our lives, and whom we will go on looking for until the Last Trump will make us one.

There was a long silence; then a voice said: "Where's my extra bottle?" and it was the high-pitched drunkard's voice again that I had first heard when the clogs entered the cabin.

I did not hear him leave; I woke up the next morning in my dog's nest on the ropes with the furry warmth of Murk close to my face. Overhead clogs were banging, and I heard the rattle of blocks as the mainsail was hoisted by Krelis and Bonk. The trap door in the partition was open, and I scrambled out before the wet anchor chain would pile up on my bed. I climbed out of the men's bunk, and when I emerged in the open I saw the Black Skipper standing at the helm and he saw me.

He beckoned to me and asked: "Like to look again, child?" and I nodded and said: "Please, sir."

He took me on his arm again, and I saw the fleet leave: hundreds of sails streaming out toward the rising sun. At one moment an Urker botter foamed past us very close and I saw, peeping over its side, a fat piggy face with a tiny Urker cap on and blue watery eyes, that blinked at the flashing silver of the sun on the sea. I thought it was a stupid fat man about to go sick, and then I heard the skipper say: "Look, there's the Liar. Boy, he must have a hangover after all the Geneva he got out of me!"

I didn't believe it until Krelis described him. The man who had sounded like Jesus was a drunk with the face of a pig, gazing sickly at the big wet sea. It took a long time before I got over the damage his face did to his story.

I SAILED ON BOARD THE HZ 69 for three months, before the dawn of terror befell me.

I got to like my work; I became Krelis' friend and Bonk's mortal enemy, but I had an ally in Murk, who was also Bonk's mortal enemy because he would open the trap door in the partition and, on his way there, would walk over Bonk's face as he had once done over mine. I fell overboard in Enkhuizen harbor; was hung during punishment hour on Sunday in the bay of Monnickendam, after I had smashed up one of Krelis' clogs to make a boat out of the other; and every time we sighted the white tower of Schokland lighthouse in the distance I thought of the mermaid, and listened secretly for her song. The story that the Black Skipper raised his fist and shouted: "I'll have you yet one day!" whenever Schokland lighthouse came in sight was not true; the only thing I ever overheard him saying in reference to the lonely widow was: "There lives one hell of a female," that was all. We were struck by a gale near Urk which made me seasick again; we lay becalmed for two whole days south of Wieringen, and I had plenty of time to look at the wicked dam. It looked innocent and feeble, only a couple of yards of mud sticking out of the water at high tide. While we lay becalmed there, I overheard much talk of the blowing up, and somehow it seemed that the Black Skipper had much to do with this; I even thought for a breathless hour that we might be going to do it ourselves; but nothing happened at all.

I found a sea mouse's life was a happy one; I could think of no brighter future than to grow up into a sea boy, then into a deckhand and then into a skipper with a botter of my own, without ever going ashore again except on Sundays in the golden towns. Whenever I heard the giants talking about going home I felt miserable; but luckily the Black Skipper always said: "Why should we?" and Krelis always answered: "Why indeed."

But then came the half hour of dawn during which all this was changed. After that half hour I had but one timorous longing: to go home.

The night before we had put out our nets in the moonlight as usual. It was a soft misty night, with little wind and wisps of laughter and harmonica music floating in the rising haze. I went to bed snuggled up with Murk on my lap and fell asleep instantly.

I half woke during the night because of a growing noise of whistling

wind and thumping water, and the loud banging of the main beam, but I went to sleep again when I heard clogs overhead and realized that Krelis and Bonk were shortening sail. The waves rocked me to sleep as they had done so often before.

I was woken up by an earthquake, a shock so tremendous that it seemed to split the ship. With one jerk the world which had become my home crumbled to ruins. While I heard the men screaming in the bunk behind the partition, everything that had hung gently rocking overhead during all those months hailed down on me in a nightmarish bombardment: blocks, glass floats, lamps, bunches of iron hooks came crashing down with a shower of glass. The ropes, piled up beside me, which had sat there solidly without shifting even during the Urker gale, were flung sideways and piled up on top of me. Murk shrieked, and tried to crawl away across me, scratching my face.

While all this happened within one second below, overhead the ship seemed to go berserk. The jib slammed its sheet-block up and down its iron rail like a horse in a stable stung by a hornet. The mainsail rattled and banged its beam from one side to the other with explosions of flapping sails: the leeboard battered the side of the ship like a ram; the whole world seemed to swing around and hurl itself into perdition, as if the moon had crashed onto the earth.

Then there was a loud tearing noise, so terrifying that I couldn't regain my breath under the pile of ropes. The leeboard, after a last reverberating bang which seemed to fill the ship with its sound until it split its sides, was torn right off with the noise of a tree falling, and I understood that we were being dragged backward at great speed.

How I managed to free myself from the pile of rubble on top of me I do not know. I heard Bonk's voice far away screaming, screaming. I heard Krelis' voice barking senseless curses, and, while biting smoke and the stench of smoldering blankets began to ooze through the cracks in the partition, I heard the Black Skipper's voice in the pandemonium, shouting: "Haul in the net!" I crawled on top of the rubble, scrambled frantically toward the manhole, and tried to lift the hatch covering it. But however much I pushed I couldn't open it more than a crack, for the fallen jib pressed it down. I stumbled toward the trap door in the partition and tried to open that, although I knew that I couldn't do so from the inside. As I banged and kicked it senselessly, the smoke pouring in through the cracks choked me and I scurried back to the hatch and attempted to lift it again, gasping for air. Then I saw, my eyes on the level of the deck, a sight which froze me.

Through the clouds of smoke, billowing from the cabin underneath the slamming beam of the mainsail, I saw the streak of a yellow dawn. And silhouetted against it, so terrifying that the sight became forever imprinted in my memory, I saw the red wings of a Volendammer's sails. Never before had I seen a Volendammer so near; it seemed huge, evil

and of boundless strength. It was racing down before the wind with a mainsail on the port side of its mast and its jib stretched on a beam on starboard; in the mainsail was painted in large white letters: VD 10. But apart from these two sails it seemed to carry a dozen others: topsails, leesails, staysails and ahead of it all the huge bulging cloud of the largest balloon jib I had ever seen.

I heard a splintering crash, and beams and woodwork came tumbling down on the foredeck; it was Arie Kos's botter, slammed against us as the Volendammer with incredible strength pulled both of us backward toward the yellow dawn, dragging us by the top cable of our net folded double. I saw Skipper Kos and his deckhand, frantic black shadows against the light, hauling in their net as Krelis and the Black Skipper were doing; I saw in the cockpit of the Volendammer ahead a crowd of men in red jackets with wide baggy trousers flapping in the wind doing the same. There seemed to be dozens of them, although I had always been told that the crew of a Volendammer numbered six. They seemed to haul in their cable much faster than Arie Kos and the Black Skipper did our net; I saw the murky silver of fish pouring in over our sterns, and heard among the banging, crackling and creaking noises around me the splatter of thousands of herrings jumping on the floor of the cockpit, until they piled up so thick that I heard the men's clogs crunching them.

Perhaps it was that sound that brought me the final realization of the disaster that had befallen us: whenever I had trodden on a single fish, Krelis had called out: "It's gold!" The herrings were more precious than money, women, sleep; our lives were lived to get the herrings safe and sound on board the buyers who would race them to Amsterdam. Now the herrings, the very reason of our existence, were being crushed, in hundreds.

The Volendammers stooped and pulled while hauling in the cable of their dragnet with quick rhythmic movements, as if they were pumping; and every pull brought them nearer to the tangle that had slowly risen from the sea between us and them: a tangle of floats and ropes and net and fish. The precision and the speed of their movements filled me with despair when I looked at the slow, clumsy dragging of our and Kos's crew, who were being buried by their own catch.

And yet, somehow, the tangle in the sea between us seemed to get no nearer to the Volendammers than it did to us. This was the moment I had been innocently dreaming of as a child: the battle approaching, the initiation to manhood by blood and fire; but my terror at seeing the three ships draw closer relentlessly, slowly, was indescribable. I wept and choked and scratched away at the trap door and the hatch of the manhole like a frantic caged rat; if the jib hadn't rested on it like a rock and had I been able to scramble on deck it would have meant the end of me, for I would have thrown myself overboard in panic.

When the sterns of our three ships finally touched and the slaughter began, deciding who would cut the other's net first, I could hardly see what happened, so thick was the smoke by then that poured from the cabin. I heard the animal roar of angry men, when the first pole lashed out at the enemy and its sharpened hook bit into living flesh. I didn't recognize the voices any more; it seemed as if even my world of people was now tumbling down in ruins. All human silhouettes I saw staggering in the smoke, red with the dark glow of fire, bellowed with the same bestial roar; I saw the flicker and the blow of hatchets; I saw the balls of fire of burning wads of cotton waste fall all around me. I heard a stampede of splintering clogs; the gnashing of wood crushing wood as the three ships smashed into each other, and above it all the high-pitched screech of the wind, screaming in the Volendammer's rigging.

At first the nightmare raged and swirled around me; then it sprang up from the trampled nest of my cable hole itself. I felt a double lash of pain streaking down my legs and turned around with a scream. A demon seemed to be attacking me, trying to jump up at my throat, burying its claws in my flesh; it was Murk, trying in a frenzy of animal fear to force his way out of the cracking cave we were buried in together. I didn't realize that all he did was try to jump on my shoulder to get out through the gap of the lifted hatch. I thought he was attacking me, struck by the wave of madness that had washed my world away. Time after time he sprung up at me, his claws tearing my shirt and scratching my chest as he slithered down my body. The fishy stench of his snarl as he jumped at my throat set me howling with terror. I lashed out at him with flailing arms, took off my clogs and flung them aimlessly into the darkness, then I groped around for something to defend myself with. I don't know what I grabbed, but when he jumped up at me again in a last, desperate effort to escape, I smashed the thing I had in my hands at him, heard a sickening thud, and the impact flung me backward onto the rubble.

The silence that followed was so thick with disgust that I pulled myself up at the edge of the manhole as though I was trying to drag myself out of a hole in the ice. I gazed at the hell outside with wide stinging eyes. There was a loud tearing noise, followed by a howl of wounded animals; then an explosion that racked the ship, and I saw two huge red wings soar birdless into the sea. The wail of pain clamoring from afar was drowned by a beastly shriek of victory of many voices; for a second I saw a huge shadow with a spear stagger victoriously against the smoke, the yellow sky and the red rags of the Volendammer's torn mainsail; then the spear was thrust down. The silhouette fell headlong out of my view, and there was a piercing scream of pain.

I realized, in a senseless way, that we had won and that what I had seen flying through the dawn was the Volendammer's heart, but it made no difference. I hung clinging to the edge of the ice, when I saw, distorted as in a weathered mirror, a foredeck and a lifted hatch. Out of

the gap peered a child's face, weeping, so contorted with unspeakable terror that it seemed to express everything I felt. It was the beaten Volendammer's sea mouse; and never as long as I live will I forget that face. After seeing that face, for a few seconds only of one yellow dawn on the Zuider Zee, war has never contained any glory for me.

THAT DAY I CAME TO UNDERSTAND why the Huizer fleet always returned home without notice.

After a fight the two damaged botters had to return home for repairs; and the rest of the fleet returned with them to give them protection. For once the Volendammers had picked up their countrymen's wreck, they would line up on the course to Huizen and wait for us. If the two damaged botters went home alone, they would doubtlessly be rammed and sunk by the Volendammers swooping down on them, all their sails hoisted, traveling at great speed before the wind. Even if the whole Huizer fleet protected the victors the Volendammers might still attack, try to cross the line of the enemy and do as much damage as possible in a single thrust.

I had never heard of a full sea battle between the two fleets in the recent past, but there were various waifs in Huizen with whom I had played in the street about whom it was said that their fathers had drowned when the two fleets clashed. For while the object of a three-man scuffle was only to cut the enemy's net, once the fleets met in battle the object was to sink ships. It depended how the Volendammers took their defeat, whether it made them mad or just angry.

When, hours after we had set out for home, Krelis opened the hatch of the cable hole and found me hidden in a corner, he picked me up and carried me to the cockpit. Both he and the Black Skipper were wounded; he had his arm in a sling and the Black Skipper wore a handkerchief around his head as if he had a toothache; one of the rings in his ears had been torn out during the fight. The cockpit was covered with the bloody pulp of crushed herrings; the cabin looked terrible. The floor was scarred with burns, the bunk a blackened hole from which the wet rags of burned blankets were hanging. Everything on the shelves had come down and lay scattered on the floor. The stove itself lay dead and upturned in a corner, and sunlight shone in through the chimney hole in the deck.

I remained silent for most of the day, but normal life seemed to come back slowly with the warmth of the sun. Yet something had been destroyed in that half hour of terror that I couldn't find again. I did not know what it was: a state of mind, a feeling, a faith; but whatever it was it didn't come back, even when I saw Murk limp to his favorite spot at

the foot of the mast again, groggy and dazed, attempting to lick the tar out of his fur, as if he had already forgotten what had happened.

What I lost in that half hour was my childhood, but of course I couldn't realize that. I only realized in a vague, hopeless way that I no longer wanted to be a fisherman with a botter of my own. I didn't know what to want instead because there was no other life I knew of.

I overheard the men talking about the possibility of a battle between our fleet and the Volendammers. Other botters of our village came very close to us, and I heard the skippers shout: "Will you give battle?" But every time the Black Skipper waved his hand and shook his head. Krelis argued with him; he said that we might as well stamp out the menace of the Catholic pirates now as any other time. There was half a gale blowing and if the Volendammers came down on us before the wind and we let them through they would soon be forced to turn back from the shore and start tacking into the wind. That was the time to tackle them; sailing by the wind they were much slower and clumsier than we because they had to take in all their fancy linen.

But the Black Skipper just shook his head, he didn't even bother to speak. He looked very grim with that handkerchief round his head and the blood trickling down his neck, and somehow much older. I suddenly suspected that he didn't want to give battle because he was so old, and this notion ought to have made him lose much of his glory in my eyes. But the glory of war had been frightened out of me.

We didn't give battle; the Volendammers attacked us all right but we let them through. It was a moment which caused an echo of the fear I had felt that morning: Bonk at the jib, Krelis at the sheet of the mainsail, the Black Skipper at the helm, all staring tense and rigid at starboard. The roaring gush of the bow waves of a fleet of botters approaching, a sharp command from the skipper at the helm; then the jib swished down, the ship swung into the wind, and on each side of us the towering red sails of a Volendammer soared past. There were a few shouts and a stone crashed into our cockpit, but that was all; Krelis screamed: "Let's get them now! Let's get them now!" but the Black Skipper said: "Shut up," and brought the ship back on its course.

I knew we were approaching our village when I saw Krelis and Bonk that night hoist six baggy trousers on the flag line. I heard the echo of our bow waves as we sailed into the piers. Then there came what had once been the most glorious sound of my dreams: the cheering of the women and the children on the quay, but it was nothing like what I had imagined it to be; for one thing it sounded much fainter to us on board than it did to the cheering crowd itself. But the main reason why it didn't elate me the way I had always thought it would, was that I now knew what they were cheering about: the face of a Volendammer sea mouse, contorted with fear.

It suddenly seemed that of all the hours I had spent on board the

Black Skipper's ship only one remained untainted by that face: the hour I had sat behind the partition listening to the voice with the soft Urker accent telling the story of the mermaid.

I felt very tired and dispirited and wanted to go home, never mind what Mem would do to me; but when we were about to make fast Krelis locked me up in the cable hole. I said: "I want to go home," but he answered: "No," no, you are a big boy now; tomorrow we will sail again." Before he shut the hatch he said: "And don't whistle or call through the hawsehole or I'll hang you." Then the light went out and I heard the sounds of a chain being padlocked.

I sat there for a while, and slowly the realization dawned on me that whatever I might dream and whatever I wanted, my life was being decided for me. I would never get off this ship again, but be forced to grow up into a sea boy and then into a deckhand and then into a skipper with a ship of my own. I got up, scrambled to the hawsehole and shouted: "Help! Help!" and "Mem! Mother Bout!" and "Let me out! Let me out!" but nobody answered. At first I thought that surely Mother Bout and Jaap and Bulle would be looking for me on board all the ships of the fleet and end up by finding me; but then I realized that nobody had seen the Black Skipper pick me up that night after I fell into the harbor. They must have found my clothes on the pier, hanging over the dead remains of a fire, and thought I was drowned.

The knowledge that in all the cable holes of all the botters in the harbor a sea mouse sat in the darkness, locked up like me, didn't give me any comfort. I didn't want to be a sea mouse any longer like Kris Muis and the others; I wanted to go home—I was a coward. I shouted, whistled, banged on the hatch and the partition, rattled the anchor chain until it grew dark; but all I heard was the sound of the water lapping against the sides of the ship, the creaking of wood of the botters rubbing sides, and distant steps of clogs on the quay. The wind rose, the tapping of the ropes against the masts grew to a rattle; nobody would ever hear me in that world full of wind and noise. I fell asleep miserably, cold and lonely without the warmth of Murk on my lap; he was promenading the quay with the other cats—nobody would ever dream of caging him.

I was woken up in the middle of the night by a sound of heavy rain. It drowned all other noises in the harbor, a monotonous relentless sound of utter melancholy. I came back to the surface of reality feeling as if the rest of my life would be like this: lying on my back in the dark, alone, listening to an endless rain. Then suddenly there was a sharp scratching overhead and a dotted line of tiny ticking noises crossed the deck. I understood it was Murk who had jumped back on board, sheltering from the rain; and the moment I realized that I heard the sharp click of a lock and a bang in the darkness, and a gust of cold air came toward me. I heard a soft meow, and then I was sprayed with drops as Murk shook the rain out of his suit.

It had happened so suddenly and unexpectedly, that I didn't realize that Murk, by opening the trap door, had set me free until I heard in my memory the voices of the Black Skipper and Krelis, that first night long ago: "Have you found out yet how the others got away?" and: "No, someone must have sneaked on board and let them out."

When Murk's wet fur touched my face, as he curled up to go to sleep the way he had been used to for all these months, I jumped and flashed out of the open trap door, the way the other mice had escaped before me.

WHEN I HAD LOWERED MYSELF cautiously along the hawser onto the quay I peered along it for minutes, hidden behind a bollard before I dared venture into the open. The rain was so heavy that it soaked me instantly, but I didn't notice it. The rain had emptied the quay of giants; it had made them hurry for shelter like Murk had done.

I left my clogs behind and scurried across the quay to the smokery. As I sidled my way along it, toward the first houses of the village, it was like coming home to a sunken world. The sound of water was tremendous, the rain fell in straight silver wires through the gaslight. I crept along walls and through the narrow wet alleys of dripping nets, until I had reached home. I had no idea what the time was, but it must have been very late for I had passed no lighted windows on my way, and the windows of our house were also dark. I climbed over the gate, ran through puddles and past gurgling gutters to the back of the house. There I looked up at the attic window, put my cold hands around my mouth and gave the soft screech of a sea gull.

The rain clattered on the tiles of the courtyard, gushed down from the roof, rustled in the dead rushes of the screen around the washing place. I screeched again, louder, but no one answered. The rain drowned everything.

I stood there screeching for a long time; then suddenly a wavering light appeared behind the flyscreen of the kitchen window. A huge shadow shrunk on the steamed glass, a hand wiped an opening in the moisture and I saw two anxious eyes peep out in candlelight: it was Mem.

I heard her voice from very far away calling: "Who's there?" and I answered, still the sea gull: "Me!"

The next instant the kitchen door was torn open and she appeared like a ghost in the doorway. Her head was covered with bits of newspaper and she wore a long white nightshirt, her hand on her throat. I went slowly toward her through the rain. She lifted the candle, and the scream she gave made me dart past her like a wet cat into the safety of the

kitchen, for I was sure that it had made all the fisherman of Huizen sit bolt upright in their beds.

She turned around, aghast, her mouth wide open, and she suddenly looked very human and nice, perhaps because she was without her spectacles and her teeth. "Darling!" she cried, put the candle down on the kitchen table and soaked herself to the skin by picking me up and pressing me against her and kissing me all over my face with a thin hard mouth. Then she let go of me, staggered toward the door to the attic with the arid front of her body clearly imprinted in her wet gown, opened the door and shrieked: "Jaap! Bulle! Come downstairs, he's back!"

There was no sound from upstairs. She had to climb halfway up and beat the attic floor with her bare hands, screaming: "Get downstairs or I'll smack you!" before I heard the thumping of feet on the ceiling. When she came back she looked at me with tears in her eyes, shivering. "Darling," she said, "look at you, I must make you something hot!" And then she scuttled toward the stove and began banging and clattering with pans, while Jaap and Bulle came creeping down the stairs, yawning, with tousled hair and very light eyes.

At first they weren't at all excited to see me. They said: "Hello" and "Oi-oi," rubbed their eyes and yawned again; then they climbed onto the chairs around the table and sat down with their faces in their fists, blinking at the candle and yawning.

Mem screamed: "Undress!" and lit the lamp. I took off my wet clothes until I stood naked in the kitchen. Then the sight of me seemed to make some memory stir in Bulle's head. He looked at me vaguely and said: "Coo; we thought you were dead." I said: "No, I was stolen by the Black Skipper."

Then their eyes woke up. "The Black Skipper?" said Jaap; he blinked, sat up and asked eagerly: "Then were you in the fight?" I said: "Yes," and then Mother Bout came tumbling down the attic steps with a blanket and a pair of bed slippers. She wrapped me up in the blanket, put me on a chair, said: "Put his slippers on, can't you see he is freezing?" Jaap and Bulle got off their chairs and put on my slippers for me, while she was rubbing my hair with a towel. It was a pity that she did it so roughly, for I felt that this was a moment that should have been beautiful: Jaap and Bulle kneeling at my feet, and a pan of milk steaming on the stove at dawn.

When I had my slippers on and Mother Bout had finished rubbing my head she sat down, her eyes wide and innocent in the lamplight, and said: "Now tell us everything! Where on earth have you been?" And I began to tell my story.

I had never told a story before in my life, but I didn't realize this at first. All I had done so far was to listen and to talk, but I had never talked alone, there had always been others talking with me. I only realized that I was telling a story to three silent listening people, when I

came to the moment that the Black Skipper had picked me up. I suddenly became conscious of the fact that if I told the truth it would do him harm, and I halted for a moment, at a loss. Then I heard myself saying: "When I found that my clothes didn't dry I set out for home, but at the harbor when I saw men in the distance I remembered that I was naked and I thought how angry you would be, and perhaps beat me, and so I stowed away on board the Black Skipper's botter."

It was a lie, so stupendous, that after finishing it breathlessly, I sat for a second waiting for Jesus to swoop down on me in hot revenge. But nothing happened but that Mother Bout's eyes filled with tears. "Poor darling," she sniffed, "I knew it was all my fault."

The stupendousness of my lie was topped by the stupendousness of the truth it had evoked, and I felt during that long moment as if my whole world of laws and conscience was sagging. How could it be that instead of slapping me, Jesus had come so justly down on Mother Bout who had indeed been the cause of it all?

But my voice went on without betraying the chaos in my conscience. I told about Murk and Bonk and the silver of the fish in the sunrise, of the triangular black expanse of the jib when Krelis opened the hatch that morning, of the needles in the frying oil, the smell of the coffee, the Black Skipper's spectacles and the glittering promise of the golden towns floating in the evening haze. Then Mother Bout uttered a sharp cry, as there was a hissing sound; the milk had boiled over.

We were given steaming hot mugs of chocolate and crunchy biscuits with more butter on them than we used to get in a whole day; she even sprinkled sugar on top of them. And when we had finished with the biscuits she brought out the tin with the colored portrait of the Queen on top, in which the Sunday sweets were hidden that we had never even seen, because she handed them out only to the gossiping women who used to come to visit her between the church services, in the stuffy parlor smelling of wax and mothballs that we were not allowed to enter.

The sweets should have been the biggest treat we ever had, but neither Jaap nor Bulle nor I took more than five, munching them without really noticing what we were doing; and the reason was that I had gone on telling my story.

It was a story that amazed me as much as the others, gazing at me motionlessly in the lamplight, wide awake without hearing the wheels of the first milk cart rattling past on the cobbles. For although I told the truth, yet it was one big bunch of lies; for I got mixed up with what I had been told and what I had experienced. I found myself telling about a singing crowd carrying a helpless policeman in torchlight and flinging him through the window into the burgomaster's parlor. I told about the big conspiracy to blow up the dike as if I had sat in on all the secret meetings instead of only having guessed what the whispers behind the partition were about. I told, the saddest lie of all, how brave I had been

during the terrific battle with the Catholic pirates; how I had seen the baggy trousers torn off the behinds of the cringing Volendammers, wailing for mercy; how the enormous hands of the Black Skipper had beaten howls of pain and humiliation out of them while Krelis held their arms and Bonk and I each sat on a squirming leg. I couldn't understand why I told this, for the face of the Volendammer sea mouse seemed to look at me in despair as if I was betraying something, a secret pledge that was worth more than all the flags and the cheers and the glory. But yet somehow the story I told was the truth. This was the way I would have told it if I had floated overhead like a sea gull and seen it all happen below me, instead of having been trapped in the cable hole full of smoke with Murk going mad in the darkness.

It was not until I began telling the story of the mermaid that the great truth came to me, like a sunrise in the chaos. The lamp remained lit, although the dawn had long since bleached its light. The three listening people gazed at me in wonder and didn't notice the growing sounds of the morning. When the mermaid sank slowly down the anchor chain through the waving green clouds of the seaweed, and sobbed on the rusty blade sticking out of the desert sand at the thought that she now had nothing left to live for, Mother Bout shook her head in pity and sighed.

Then I knew for the first time what I have known ever since, and I still have not decided whether to be glad or sorry.

I was a born Liar.

TWENTY-FIVE YEARS AFTER I had become a Liar, I passed once more the place where I had seen the face that I betrayed. I passed it in a car.

The Zuider Zee was no more. The big dam across its mouth had been completed long ago without anybody ever trying to blow it up; most of the land submerged by the great flood of 1302 had been reclaimed.

I had passed through the villages of my youth and found them unrecognizably changed. The harbors were dead, the smokeries, net-knitteries and shipyards had vanished and been replaced by bicycle works, radio stations and factories of anti-indigestion pills. The old costumes were seen no longer in the streets, except on very old people who had sunken below the general social level. Louts in plus fours and zoot suits chewed gum and smoked drooling cigarettes under the old elm trees, where once the fishermen had cursed the price of the herring and whispered about blowing up the dam. The clogs had been replaced by high-heeled shoes, and the "oi-oi" of yore by "hiya."

After this sad voyage through the land of my childhood I arrived at the border of the new polder that had once been the sea. I was in a dark

mood, haunted by the wolf calls of a loud-speaker in the market place, where once old Henk's croaking voice had sung the praise of his smoked eels with an Arabian melody. But after I had driven through the gap in the dike which was the entrance to the northeast polder, the newest part of our planet, I forgot what had happened to my past.

Where once the silver sheet of the sea had stretched out to the blue haze of the horizon, underneath that green sky the like of which I have never seen again, lay now a plain so breath-taking in its geometric vastness, with the straight lines of its canals and its roads all converging on the distant horizon, that it seemed for a moment as if I heard again that sickening roar of the cheering crowd on the quay after a great victory.

I hazarded into this strange forbidding land with a curious shyness. It was unbelievable that so small a country as Holland could suddenly take on the vastness of a continent. The new land wasn't ready yet to be plowed and sown; it was still only a colossal flat expanse of water, roads and mud, under a sky with lonely sailing clouds.

The strangest thing about this plain was its utter loneliness. It seemed as if suddenly—with my car, my memories and my tweed cap—I found myself on the moon. I crawled along a muddy road, stretching straight into infinity, and passed close to a narrow hill with a house and a cluster of old trees rising from the desert of mud. Only when I saw a sort of quarry surrounded by a jetty with football goals in its center, did I realize that this had been the Island of Schokland. I looked for the lighthouse, but it was no longer there; it must have been demolished for its bricks, and used to harden the roads.

As I sat staring at the hill, which seemed to be a relic from Roman times in the emptiness of this new geometric world, I experienced a wintry feeling that must be known to very old people only. A world had vanished which was the source of my life; I sat there lonely, tired, helpless with the memories I seemed no longer to share with anybody.

I penetrated deeper into the new land, and as I did so I saw at long intervals the scaffoldings of new farms being built, sticking pointlessly in the mud. Next to them were little wooden shacks looking like hen-coops, in which families seemed to live waiting until their houses would be finished, for I saw lonely laundry fluttering on lines but I saw no human being, not even an animal about.

In the heart of this boundless emptiness I hit upon a village of prefabricated wooden houses, and it was there that I heard the first sound since I had entered the northeast polder, except for the humming of my car's engine. I heard a choir of high-pitched children's voices singing in triple descant about a little horseman who fell in love with a little maiden and betrayed her.

I stopped the car and looked around for where the sound came from. It came from one of the prefabricated houses, slightly larger than the others, with steamed windows and a brand-new bell on top. When the

little horseman had blown up the nunnery and shot himself, and his three friends had become monks, there was a confused noise of chirping voices and the stumbling of clogs on wooden floors; then the bright new doors of the shack burst open and from it poured a swarm of children, whose shrill little voices seemed to fill only a handful of sky with their tiny sparrow's sound.

Three little girls with white plaits flying came running toward me, swinging their school bags. "Are you going to Emmeloord?" they called. "Are you going to Emmeloord?"

I looked at them stupidly, for to me Emmeloord was a sunken village whose bells still rung when the ground seas of a gale stirred them; the village from which the mermaid of Schokland had set out for her pilgrimage of love. I said: "Yes, but you will have to tell me where it is."

"Road 65-B!" the girls chanted, thinly as high sea gulls, and they clambered into the car.

We set out to cross the moon again, and when I took one of the dead-straight mud tracks, leading to nowhere, at random, they cried: "That's 80-C! That one goes to Rutten!"

I asked where Rutten was; and they said it didn't exist yet, but they could point it out on the map. I took another road, which they pointed out to me, and then I asked whether Emmeloord existed. They laughed at the joke and said: "Of course! Emmeloord is Mom and Dad and Kees and us. It's a very big town, the biggest in the polder. One day the governor will live there in a stone house and there will be a cinema."

I asked whether anybody else lived there yet but Mom and Dad and Kees and they. They said no, Dad was still making it.

At first, as I drove into nothing with the three tiny voices of a new race of man chippering behind me, I felt older than when I had looked at the football goals in Schokland harbor. But when I asked whether there was anything growing in the new polder yet, they said: "Oh yes, the forest of Urk."

They said it with a curious conspiratory softness in their voices, that I seemed to remember from long ago. I asked them whether they had ever been there; and then they told me a curious story.

Around a little village on a hill called Urk there was a wood which had not been sown, but that had just grown up when the water receded. It was a very thin wood, and always misty, and the strangest things grew there: giant ferns, silver willows, toadstools as big as tables, and one night not long ago one of them, walking home from school along the edge of this wood, had seen something move among the waving reeds. At first she had not known what it was, and she was frightened for it looked like a dead tree following her silently, peering at her over the reeds. Then there had been a sudden rustle, a brown shadow had flashed from one shrub to the other. Dad and Mom did not believe her, but she knew what she had seen. It was a deer. Did I know how it had got there? It must

have got there somehow, although Dad and the master said it was impossible as there were no deer in Holland for hundreds of miles around.

When I said that what she saw must have been the mermaid, they looked at me blankly and I realized that her story had died with the sea. When one of them asked: "Mermaid, what is that?" I didn't know the answer, for "a woman with a fishtail" would have sounded preposterous in this merciless new land.

When I put them down at a muddy crossroads, about a mile from a little wooden shack with a smoking chimney hidden in the gathering dusk, one of them said to the other: "Careful, careful," and I saw her stoop to pick up a piece of bread that had fallen in the mud. She noticed that I had seen it, looked around at the shack a mile away as if afraid of being overheard, and then she whispered: "We always take that with us for when we shall see the deer again."

Then they rushed off, very small on that road under that sky, and I set out for home.

When I drove through the gap in the dike I no longer felt old and alone, nor did I feel that anything real had been lost. All that had happened was that a children's sea had turned into a children's land.

XI

FATHER OF
THE BRIDE

by Edward Streeter

Suburban Americana

Edward Streeter is one of the mysterious characters in the book field. At the close of the First World War, in which he served in the artillery, he produced a volume of humor, *Dere Mable,* which convulsed the nation. After that he published several more books in rapid succession, all of which were well liked although not as spectacularly received as the first. Then a silence closed down and for a matter of thirty years nothing more was heard from him. The only information available was that he had become a banker and, presumably, was too busy for any more ventures into the world of the printed page.

Then his antic spirits broke out again. In 1949 he published *Father of the Bride,* which was selected by the book-of-the-Month Club and went spinning dizzily up to the top of the best-seller lists. Later it was made into a motion picture, for which *Variety* had to invent new adjectives of praise.

The banking business is, no doubt, a highly pleasant and profitable one, but can it have compensated for that long stretch of years when his pencil was idle and the cover remained on his typewriter? Certainly a wide circle of readers missed him.

Father of the Bride is an authentic piece of Americana of the suburban variety, a lighthearted description of the troubles of a middle-aged couple whose daughter is being married and who feel it must be done "right." It is pure comedy, securing its effects without slapstick or recourse to shady dialogue, a rare achievement indeed.

Chapter I

THE GREAT DECISION

No matter what Kay might have done about marriage it would not have been looked upon with any great favor by Mr. Stanley Banks, merely because he happened to be fonder of his first-born than he realized.

During her teens he had dismissed all aspirants with a contemptuous snort. From the time that Kay had first revealed herself to the social world, minus a mouthful of braces and plus a permanent, leggy adolescents with porcupine hair had begun to beat a path to 24 Maple Drive. Mr. Banks had regarded these inarticulate sufferers with a jaundiced eye.

If they caused him any uneasiness it had been wasted. Not that Kay spurned male attention, but, during those exciting days, she preferred it to be universal rather than specific. Nature had endowed her with what amounted to a season pass to every dance, sporting event and week-end party that her strength permitted—and she had the stamina of a six-day bicycle rider.

She was also restrained by an early infatuation for her English teacher, a brilliant young man with large front teeth and a tendency to stomach ulcers, who had once told her that she had an intellect. This otherwise unconfirmed diagnosis gave her secret ambitions. The result was that the youths who fluttered around her with such unco-ordinated eagerness seemed callow to her beautiful blue eyes. Lord Byron and Leonardo da Vinci being dead, the field had struck her as limited.

And so the tender years had slipped by. With their passing Mr. Banks' emotional pendulum had swung the other way. He found himself wondering what was wrong with the child. What was it that caused men to bob into her life for a few brief weeks or months—and then disappear forever? She couldn't go on being a bridesmaid until she was an old lady!

It worried him and unconsciously his attitude changed, even toward Kay's most casual acquaintances. Unlike the old days, when he had been curt, suspicious and, on occasions, frankly hostile, he now began to receive them with an open-armed cordiality that would have driven any alert young male out into a snowstorm.

Then suddenly—without warning—it was obvious that something was happening to Kay. Some alchemy was at work within her. There was a light in her eyes that none of Dr. Barnes' vitamins had ever kindled. The fashionable, dead-pan expression that she usually wore for home use

was replaced with a radiance that made her, at times, almost a stranger to Mr. Banks.

"What's gotten into Kay, Ellie? She acts queer to me."

"I don't know," said Mrs. Banks. "Maybe she's in love."

Mr. Banks made noises of contempt. "In love! Who would she be in love with?"

"I haven't the wildest idea."

"Nonsense," said Mr. Banks. "You must have some idea."

"Well, do you remember that about two weeks ago Kay said she'd met a boy named Buckley Something-or-other at a cocktail party?"

"Never heard of him," said Mr. Banks.

"Of course you have, dear. Don't *try* to be stupid. And do you remember that a few nights later he came here to take her to some cocktail party?"

"You don't mean that big overgrown ham with the shoulders? Listen, Ellie, you women jump at the damnedest conclusions. Just because a man—"

"All right. I'm wrong. You just wait and see."

They waited, and as the days passed it became apparent that Buckley was coming more sharply into focus. His name crept into Kay's chatter with increasing frequency, though always casually. It had never been very clear to Mr. Banks just where Kay spent her time, but wherever it was Buckley evidently spent his there also. Furthermore, he was apparently a young man with decided views on everything from football to God—views which, for Kay's money, had not been equaled since the Delphic oracles went out of business.

Mr. Banks felt a resurgence of his old attitude. This new moth, which was beginning to fly so close to the flame, became definitely distasteful to him.

"I don't think much of that fellow," he said to Mrs. Banks after Buckley had spent a painful ten minutes in the living room waiting for Kay.

"I don't know, dear," said Mrs. Banks. "Why don't you just leave Kay alone and let her work things out for herself?"

"I'm not interfering with her," said Mr. Banks crossly. "You're the one that's always worrying."

A hush of anticipation had fallen over the Banks family as in a theater just before the curtain rises—but nothing happened. Kay continued to look dreamy. Buckley, during his brief appearances, maintained his air of uneasy aloofness. After a few stiff moments they would both rush, unleashed, into the night.

Then, unexpectedly, the storm broke.

They were gathered round the dinner table on one of the increasingly rare occasions when Kay ate at home.

"Where are the boys?" asked Mr. Banks.

"They've gone to a night game with Joe Stanley," said Mrs. Banks. "They couldn't wait for dinner. Ben said they'd pick up something to eat in town."

"Don't those two boys ever stay at home for a meal?" grumbled Mr. Banks.

Kay sighed. "Ben's not a *boy,* Pops. He's a man. He's old enough to have a family."

"Well, Tommy isn't," said Mr. Banks. "He's in high school and he's supposed to stay home nights and do some work."

"Oh, by the way, Mom, that reminds me. I won't be home this week end," said Kay.

"Where are you going, dear?" asked Mrs. Banks.

"I'm going to spend it with Buckley's family."

Mr. Banks dropped an unbroken cracker into his soup. "Look here," he asked, "are you going to marry this character?"

"I guess so," replied Kay. She continued to work on her soup. Her tone had been so even and casual that the import of her words did not immediately register, and the conversation threatened to end on this simple note. As a matter of fact it did for quite a while. Nothing could be heard but the thoughtful intake of cream of tomato.

Mrs. Banks broke the silence. "And when," she asked with timid sarcasm, "are you thinking of getting married?"

"I really don't know, Mother. It all depends on Buckley's *plans.*" Kay's voice was that of a tired kindergarten teacher. "It might be months or it might be in a few weeks—or it might be just any time at *all.* We can't *tell* yet. And there's one thing—we *won't* be pinned down. Buckley's *very* decided about that sort of thing. He just *won't* be pinned down."

Mr. Banks felt his neck begin to push against his collar. He took a long drink of water. "I hope," he said in a strained voice, "that Buckley won't think I'm nosy or trying to pin him down if I ask a few simple questions."

Kay looked bored. "O.K., Pops. I suppose we have to go *through* this. It does seem to me, though—"

"Well, to begin with, who the hell is this Buckley anyway?"

"Now, Pops, please. If we're going—"

"—and what's his last name? I hope it's better than his first one."

"Pops, I'm not going to sit here—"

"—and where the hell does he come from—and who does he think is going to support him? If it's me he's got another guess coming. And who in God's name—"

Mrs. Banks interrupted. "Stanley, nobody's deaf and you don't have to swear every other word. It's just plain mortifying with Delilah in the kitchen listening. You don't give Kay a chance. Let her—"

At that moment Kay, the darling of his heart, turned on him for the first time in her life. "Listen, Pops, I'm twenty-four years old and Buckley's twenty-six and we're grown *people*—and as far as your supporting *Buckley*, I'll tell you right now he's the kind that wouldn't let *anybody* support him. He'd rather *die* first.

"*That's* the kind of person he *is*. He's a *wonderful* person. He's the kind of a person that's absolutely—I mean *absolutely*—independent. The kind that will always take care of his own. You don't need to worry about *that,* Pops—*ever.* Buckley wouldn't come to you for help not even if we were starving in the *gutter.*

"And his name is *Dunstan. That's* what it is—Buckley Dunstan. And he's a *wonderful* businessman—I mean a *really* wonderful businessman—and—and he has a wonderful *job."*

"Doing what?" asked Mr. Banks, seizing the first factual straw.

"Oh, I don't *know,* Pops. He makes something. Does it *really* make any difference what it is? He's the kind of a person that can do *anything* —anything at *all.*

"As for his *parents*—well, I'll tell you this, Pops—they're just as good as you and *Mom."* There was a suggestion in her voice that this was an understatement. "They're *swell* people and they live in East Smithfield and I guess you'll agree that East Smithfield is just as good a place as Fairview *Manor*—although I don't see what that's got to do with it *anyway."*

Mr. Banks agreed silently.

His blood pressure had gone down as quickly as it had risen. He scarcely heard what Kay was saying and he had forgotten all about Buckley. He was looking at his daughter's flushed face and remembering a small girl with brown pigtails and dirty overalls who used to fly at her two younger brothers when they goaded her too far.

It seemed like such an incredibly short time ago. That was all. He had a panicky feeling that tears were coming into his eyes. Rising from his chair, he kissed the top of her head.

"O.K., Kitten," he said. "I love him already. What did you say his last name was?"

At this point Mr. Banks began to come down with some strange kind of psychic rash. From the night of that conversation at the dinner table he could feel it creeping through his system. With a detachment which was anything but calm, he watched himself change from a logical, well-balanced lawyer into an unreasoning, anxiety-ridden psychopathic. It disturbed him so that he did not even mention it to Mrs. Banks.

Each night he lay on his back in the darkness, his hands folded across his chest like a figure on a sarcophagus in Westminster Abbey. A street lamp threw a milky patch of light on a corner of the bedroom ceiling. The intervening foliage of a tree caused it to shimmer like water. He stared at it rigidly, struggling to make his mind a blank.

Father of the Bride

Who was this bounder who had invaded the sanctity of his home and snatched his child from under his nose? Child—that's what she was— a child. What did she know about the qualities in a man which are so necessary to a successful marriage? She was only a child who, a few months ago, was running around in pigtails—was it a few months or a few years?

He mustn't let himself go on like this or he would be a gibbering idiot in the office tomorrow.

Snatched. That was the word for it. She was sleeping in her own room, but only in body. Her spirit had moved out. She would always love them of course, but never in the old way—never again with her whole trusting, needing self. From here in her love would be doled out like a farmer's wife tossing scraps to the family rooster.

What mawkish bunk! He *must* cut it out. Wasn't this what he'd always been building up to? He flopped over on his side and tried burying his face in the crook of his arm. He had sometimes found self-smothering helpful.

He knew that, under similar circumstances, he wouldn't feel this way about Ben and Tommy. Somehow or other Kay was more identified with those early years of married life than either of the boys. He had been used to the idea of parenthood by the time they arrived. Kay had been born in the uncertain days when his relationship to the firm of Barthlum, Henderson and Peck had been as nebulous as his salary—years before he had been made a junior partner and they had bought the white shingled house in Fairview Manor. It had been a happy period in spite of the struggle— a period unmarred by the adolescent features of any questing male.

Well, the beans were spilt now! Casually! Over a cup of tomato soup! Not asking by your leave, but giving him the devil for trying to find out what the goon's last name was! Outside of his name, what else did Kay know about him? Oh, yes. He was wonderful. That was going to be a great help when he started to raise a family.

Could he support a family? That was the point. How could he know that this guy had what it took? Up to date he'd sounded vaguer than dishwater every time he'd opened his mouth. An impractical dreamer—that's what he was. Kay was an idealist and she'd fallen for this fellow because he agreed with all her ideas and didn't make any sense.

He flopped onto his other side and looked over at Mrs. Banks. She seemed to be sleeping peacefully. Women were inconsistent creatures. If the kids were out at some little dance she couldn't sleep until she heard them come in. But when it was a question of how (or if) her only daughter was going to eat for the rest of her life, she fell asleep like a baby.

Wise men never discuss topics of a potentially up-setting nature until they have finished their breakfast. The wisest refuse to talk at all until they have been spiritually fortified by a couple of fried eggs.

For many years this had been one of Mr. Banks' ground rules. It was a sound, functional rule, for by the time he had gulped his breakfast he was invariably late for the eight-fifteen. One could not get into much of a controversy while trotting from the breakfast table to the garage. Thus the day was automatically started right and morning problems, like morning mists, had a tendency to disperse as the sun rose higher.

But Mr. Banks was no longer a wise man. During these last few days (and nights) he had become aware that his sense of balance was being dragged from under him like sand under the impact of surf.

To his surprise Mrs. Banks did not seem to share his apprehensions although she was usually the timid one when faced with change. On the contrary, she seemed to float through her days in a state of ecstasy. This was an added annoyance to Mr. Banks.

From her casual remarks it became gradually clear to him that her mind was not on Buckley at all, but rather on the ceremony which he promised to bring into being and on the material things connected with it—on dresses and hats and shoes—on underwear and sheets and towels —on all the thousand things which, to a woman, truly legalize a marriage.

He had always known that, at heart, Mrs. Banks was a natural-born purchasing agent, although her talents had been somewhat restricted by circumstances. Now at last she was presented with a buyers' field day, fully authorized and aboveboard, and she was merely letting her imagination take a trial run around the track to get the stiffness out of its joints.

Mr. Banks was standing before the medicine cabinet mirror, thoughtfully lathering his face. It rather pleased him to think that he could detect lines in it that had not been there a week before.

"Kay's going to make a beautiful bride," murmured Mrs. Banks dreamily, half to herself, half to Mr. Banks' pajamaed back. "She's got just the figure and the coloring. I know exactly the kind of a dress she should have—the sleeves long and tight-fitting—and the skirt—"

Mr. Banks' hand trembled and a drop of blood discolored the soap on his chin. The stout, dependable dam which had heretofore restrained his morning thoughts gave way without warning. Over Mrs. Banks' unprepared head poured the swollen torrent of his accumulated apprehensions.

He was possessed of a doomsday eloquence. As he warmed up to his theme it began to sound like a description of Hiroshima. She listened in dismay to the recital of possibilities that she had not even considered. By the time her husband's emotional reservoir was emptied he had missed three trains to the city. Shaken to the roots, she did not attempt to follow him downstairs.

When she heard him slam up the patent garage door she watched anxiously from the bedroom window as he backed the sedan into the drive and disappeared around the corner in a spray of gravel.

Mr. Banks found himself a seat on the eight-forty-two and opened

his morning paper. Theoretically his day was ruined. Actually, and to his surprise, he was conscious of a pleasant feeling of lightness. The sun shone impartially on the alternating garbage dumps and suburban developments that flashed past the window. The air was dry and bracing. The world was suddenly beginning to snap back into place.

His pleasure at this discovery was dimmed at the edges, however, by a small gnawing sense of guilt lest he might have upset Ellie unduly. Women were so emotional about these matters and inclined to take them overseriously. He toyed with the idea of calling her up when he got to town. Then he became interested in the paper and forgot about it.

But not so Mrs. Banks. All day long the Seidlitz powder of anxiety which her husband had dumped into her tranquil soul seethed and boiled within her. As she made her rounds from the A.&P. Supermarket to Kohoe's Fish Store to Sammy Lee's Hand Laundry, the uneasiness within her mounted to a bubbling panic.

She was not a complex person. Although she had strong instinctive convictions, years of battering by the massed forces of male reasoning caused moments when her self-confidence wavered.

Of course she never let Mr. Banks know about these weaknesses. Under attack she would defend her position as if it were the Alamo. But in this particular case she had had no chance to fight. The onslaught had been so unexpected and violent that it had left her stunned. Until this moment her world had seemed so beautiful. Now it lay in pieces about her.

When Mr. Banks re-entered the house that evening he still retained the pleasant sensation of being at once relaxed and gathered and he hummed a little tune as he threw his hat on the shelf of the coat closet. Mrs. Banks came out of the living room and put her hands on his shoulders. As he kissed her he was surprised by the worried look in her eyes. One might have thought she had been crying.

"Stan, I'm so upset about Kay."

"Kay? What's the matter with Kay? What's she done now?" he asked absent-mindedly, removing his overcoat.

"Oh, Stan, suppose Buckley *shouldn't* be the man for her. How can *we* tell? We know so little about him. And she's *so* young. Suppose he *didn't* have business judgment and *couldn't* earn a decent living. Suppose he made Kay *unhappy*. Suppose—"

Mr. Banks stopped fumbling for the coathook. He stared at her in amazement. "For heaven's sake, Ellie, what in the world's getting into you? For years you've been worried about Kay's not getting married. Now she finds herself a perfectly nice guy and you get the jitters. I'll bet he'll do a better job than that poopadoop you were so crazy about that hung around here all last winter."

He took her chin in his cupped hand and gazed down at her thought-

fully. "You know what, darling? I think you're tired. You've been going it too hard lately. You've got to take care of yourself. Tell you what I'll do. I'll knock together a couple of old-fashioneds. It'll do you good. And we'll drink a little toast to the bride and groom."

Chapter 2

GETTING ACQUAINTED

Buckley, Kay informed her parents with her best Old School irony, *also* had a father and mother. It seemed to her that the situation called for a minimum display of interest from the Banks family unless, of course, they preferred to make it look like a shotgun wedding and introduce themselves at the altar rail.

Mr. Banks agreed moodily. The obvious fact that he must do something about meeting Buckley's family had been weighing on him for some time. Although he had never considered himself a shy man, the idea gave him as much pleasure as a summons to appear before a congressional committee. He had been postponing action from day to day in the same way that he put off wearing a pair of new shoes to the office.

"I suppose Kay's right," he admitted gloomily to Mrs. Banks. "We've got to face it."

"I don't understand why you get in such a lather about it," she said. "What's so awful about meeting Buckley's father and mother?"

"Who said I was in a lather?" he retorted sharply. "All I mean is you'd think Kay might have picked out somebody we knew instead of a family we never laid eyes on and that are probably God-awful. I just know the kind of people they are. It's going to be terrible."

"Stanley Banks, for a grown man you sometimes don't make any sense. In the first place I don't see why you assume the Dunstans are terrible and in the second you're not marrying Buckley's family."

"I might just as well be," groaned Mr. Banks. "I'll probably have to support them."

The Dunstans eventually took matters into their own hands and invited Mr. and Mrs. Banks to East Smithfield for Sunday dinner; just the four of them—without Kay and Buckley—so they could get acquainted.

"That's the pay-off," said Mr. Banks. "They're the cozy type."

He made no further comment, but during the intervening days he showed all the symptoms of a debutante about to be introduced at Buckingham Palace. On Sunday morning he dressed carefully in a sport coat

and slacks, then went upstairs after breakfast and changed into a business suit. He insisted on starting half an hour earlier than was necessary—just to allow for a blowout or something. The result was that they arrived in East Smithfield shortly after twelve.

Mr. Banks said he'd be damned if he was going to sit and moon at the Dunstans' for an hour. He preferred to slum around the town and get a line on the natives.

"I'll bet they won't even have a drink before dinner," he said gloomily.

"How do you know they won't?"

"Because I know. That's the kind of people they are."

"Well, suppose they don't. You're not an alcoholic, are you?"

Mr. Banks sighed but didn't pursue the argument.

"I think it might be more intelligent to find out where the Dunstans live instead of driving around aimlessly," said Mrs. Banks. "At least we won't end up by being late."

"I'll bet it's a shack," said Mr. Banks.

When they finally located it, the Dunstan shack turned out to be a large, whitewashed brick house about a mile out of town. It sat well back from the road surrounded by old elm trees. The discovery that it was at least twice the size of his own seemed to add fuel to Mr. Banks' agitation. He looked at his watch.

"I'm going back to that hotel we passed and wash up," he announced.

"Nonsense," said Mrs. Banks. "You can wash at the Dunstans'. They probably have running water."

"I prefer to wash at the hotel," said Mr. Banks with dignity. She sensed that this was not the time to cross him.

When they drew up in front of the hotel he did not suggest that she get out, but hurried through the revolving doors. On his return, ten minutes later, it was obvious that he was more composed. The interior of the sedan immediately took on the Saturday night odor of a bar-and-grill.

"Stanley Banks, you've been drinking."

Mr. Banks did not take his eyes off the road ahead. "Why is it," he asked, "that a person can't take a casual drink without being accused of 'drinking'? It does seem to me that a man over fifty—"

"I think it's perfectly outrageous for you to meet the Dunstans smelling like an old whiskey bottle. It's humiliating, that's what it is. What in the world's gotten into you? And Sunday morning, too."

"What's Sunday morning got to do with it?" asked Mr. Banks, hoping to divert the argument. But Mrs. Banks was still being difficult when they turned in at the Dunstans' entrance.

The first meeting of in-laws is comparable to the original hookup of the Lewis and Clark Expedition with the Rocky Mountain Indians.

In the latter instance it is recorded that for a brief moment after the

encounter both sides glared at one another with mingled hostility and curiosity. At this point a false move would have been fatal. If anyone had so much as reached for his tobacco pouch the famous Journals would never have seen the light of day.

Then, each side finding the other apparently unarmed, the tension eased. The leaders stepped forward, embraced, rubbed noses and muttered "How." Skins were spread and refreshments laid on them by squaws. The party was in the bag.

The Banks-Dunstan meeting followed similar lines. For a split second the two families stared at one another in the Dunstan entrance hall. During that instant Mrs. Banks took inventory of Mrs. Dunstan from hair-do to shoes. Mrs. Dunstan did the same for Mrs. Banks. Then, finding everything mutually satisfactory, they approached one another with outstretched arms, embraced and said, "My dear."

The two males merely shook hands awkwardly and said in unison, "It certainly is nice to meet you."

Mrs. Dunstan started to lead the way into the living room. "Would you like to wash your hands?" asked Mr. Dunstan.

"I've washed them," said Mr. Banks, glancing at him suspiciously.

"I can't tell you how crazy we are about your Kay," said Mrs. Dunstan.

"Well, that's just the way we feel about Buckley," said Mrs. Banks.

"Yes indeed," said Mr. Banks. Obviously something was called for. As far as he was concerned that seemed about all there was to be said. He would have been quite ready to second a motion to adjourn.

The situation was saved by the appearance of a maid with a shaker full of martinis and a tray of hot hors d'oeuvres. Mr. Banks looked at this arrangement with pleased incredulity.

He took a martini and found it excellent. "I think we should drink to the bride and groom," said Mr. Dunstan. Mr. Banks drank deeply and relaxed like a deflating balloon. Mr. Dunstan refilled the glasses.

Warmed by this unexpected hospitality and his previous wash-up at the hotel, Mr. Banks felt impelled to words. "This is an important occasion," he said. "My wife and I have been looking forward to it for a long time. Personally I thought your son was a great fellow the moment I set eyes on him. Now that I've met his father and mother I like him even better. From here in I foresee that the Dunstan-Banks families will beat as one."

"I am sure we're going to be most congenial," said Mrs. Dunstan apprehensively, "and do call us Doris and Herbert, not Mr. and Mrs. Dunstan."

"And Stanley and Ellie," said Mrs. Banks somewhat overeagerly. There was an embarrassed silence.

"Have you ever been in Fairview Manor, Herbert?" asked Mr. Banks.

"No, we haven't, Stanley. We've heard a lot about it, of course."

"I love your house, Doris," said Mrs. Banks, who had by this time sized up and appraised critically every article of furniture in the living room.

"Thank you, Ellie. We like it. I'm crazy to see yours. Buckley's always talking about it."

"Another, Stan?" asked Mr. Dunstan.

"Well, just to help you out, Herb," said Mr. Banks.

His wife moved over beside him. "You'd better watch your step," she muttered.

It was too late. The release from supertension was more than he could combat. He graciously helped his friend Herb finish up the shaker.

"I think dinner is ready," said Mrs. Dunstan, who had known it for a long time.

She led the way toward the dining room. "You've got a wonderful place here, Edith," said Mr. Banks, falling in beside her.

"Doris," she said. "Won't you sit there, Ellie. And now we want to hear all about our new daughter."

"I'm afraid there isn't much to tell," said Mrs. Banks.

"Nonsense," said Mr. Banks. "Would you like to hear the story about how Ellie left Kay in her baby carriage outside the A.&P. and then forgot about her and went home?"

He told them in hilarious detail. A flood of memories and anecdotes poured from him like a mountain brook. He took them through Kay's childhood and school days step by step. Then, as a kind of appendix, he gave them a detailed account of his own boyhood, early manhood and married life. Occasionally one of the Dunstans broke in with a comment. Toward the end of the meal they ceased to compete.

After dinner Mr. Banks picked out a comfortable-looking chair in the darkest corner of the living room. He felt suddenly drowsy. "Now," he said, "you must tell us all about Buckley." The desire to take just forty winks became overpowering. As Buckley entered his first year in high school Mr. Banks' eyes closed and he was instantly asleep.

They drove back to Fairview Manor late in the afternoon, Mrs. Banks at the controls. Mr. Banks felt relaxed and happy. It was hard for him to understand why he had dreaded this meeting so much. He sought in vain among his acquaintances for a finer family than the Dunstans. Certainly no one could have been easier to talk to. He hummed a contented little song. Mrs. Banks said nothing.

Chapter 3

FINANCIAL MATTERS

It was quite clear to Mr. Banks that things couldn't drift along like this forever. When two people decided to get married they announced their engagement and then there was a wedding. The only question was when.

As his mind focused on the actual ceremony he began to have secret qualms about it. Weddings had never meant much to him one way or the other. They were pleasant parties where he was apt to run into a lot of people whom he had not seen lately. Now, when he considered his role as father of the bride, it became alarmingly apparent that he was slated to play a lead part in what looked more and more to him like a public spectacle. Unconsciously he was experiencing the first symptoms of aisle-shyness.

When it came to discussing the date, therefore, he was like a man who has rashly committed himself to go swimming in a glacial stream. His idea was either to get the affair over as quickly as possible or else postpone it to a point so far distant in time that, like death, he wouldn't have to worry about it for the present at least.

Mrs. Banks, on the other hand, looked at the matter more from the point of view of a stage manager. How long would it take to prepare the costumes, build the scenery and collect the props? She concluded that, working day and night, the production might be staged in three months —not a minute earlier.

During the discussions that followed Buckley remained unusually silent. He was obviously a young man who was not used to getting married and these unfolding and complex plans seemed to bewilder him. As he listened to his future mother-in-law he became gradually panic-stricken. He explained to her with desperate finality that he was a simple fellow who wanted no trappings or lugs. His idea of a wedding was a little ivy-covered chapel in some lovely country spot where he and Kay could walk down the aisle hand in hand.

Mr. Banks decided to switch the conversation into lighter vein. Buckley was inclined to have a heavy touch at moments. He said that was a fine idea. He liked it. The trouble was that the only kind of ivy that grew around Fairview Manor was poisonous and the only place that approximated a lovely country spot was the golf course.

Kay interrupted. This was scarcely the time for cheap comedy. And besides, everyone seemed to have forgotten an important point. This was

630

her wedding. *She* was the one who was getting married—not Pops or Mom. Buckley of course—but it was *her* wedding nonetheless and she didn't propose to be pushed around by *anybody*. She would marry *when* and *where* the spirit moved her. Perhaps it would be in two weeks, perhaps in six *months*.

What was more, there was no need for all this fussing. Her mother didn't need to raise a *hand*—not a finger. When she (Kay) gave the word everything would fall into place. That was the way she and Buckley were going to live. Simply and without all this *effort*. She had seen *nothing* but fuss and feathers all her life. Now she wanted no more of it. That might as well be understood.

From this point on the conversation began to resemble the Chicago wheat pit on the day of a big break. It was Buckley's first family free-for-all. Quite obviously it upset him. From where he sat, in a corner of the living room, it seemed like the breakup of basic relationships. He watched with dismay as the storm raged. Then, like a tropical hurricane, it was unexpectedly over. Instead of the tangled and broken wreckage which he had anticipated, he was astonished to learn that it had been harmoniously agreed that the wedding would take place on Friday, June 10, at four-thirty P.M. at St. George's Church.

"Are you awake?" asked Mr. Banks. "Hey, Ellie."

Mrs. Banks stirred uneasily.

"Are you awake?"

"What's the matter?" she asked, noncommitally, regarding him with one unfriendly eye.

"I've been thinking," said Mr. Banks. "I've been thinking all night. I haven't slept."

"You were snoring when I woke up," she said, without sympathy.

Mr. Banks ignored the remark. It was merely part of Mrs. Banks' morning routine.

"I've been thinking about Buckley," he said. "I'm worried. Good and worried. Do you realize, Ellie, that we know next to nothing about this boy? Just because his family has a big house and a couple of maids doesn't mean anything. What do we know about *him?*"

He raised himself on his elbow. "Think it over a minute. One day Kay comes home and says, 'This is Buckley. Isn't he cute? I'm going to marry him.' And we all make faces at him and dance around. But what do we *know* about him?"

Mr. Banks began to check off his points on his fingers. "Has he got any money? You don't know. What's he making? Nobody knows. Can he support her? We just don't know a darn thing about the guy. He walks in the door and we hand him Kay and—"

"Darling," interrupted Mrs. Banks, "we've been through all this before. Ask Buckley. Don't ask me."

"Don't try to laugh it off." Mr. Banks was working himself into one of his pre-breakfast frenzies. *"I'm* not going to support him. Not by a damn sight. I'm—"

Mrs. Banks interrupted again. "Listen, dear. I think you're absolutely right. I've told you so every time you've brought this up. We should have found out about these things long ago. I don't know why you haven't. You've been going to have a talk with Buckley ever since Kay first told us. Sometimes I think you're a little afraid of him."

Mr. Banks snorted. "That's a fine remark, I must say. I intend to have a talk with him, all right. We might just as well have it out."

He sat on the edge of his bed radiating aggressiveness. Mrs. Banks thought he looked rather gray and tired.

By the time he reached home that evening he had decided not to make a direct approach. No use scaring the boy to death. Instead he told Kay that he wanted to have a little talk with Buckley about finances. You know—what he was earning and all that sort of thing. As a sop to liberalism he indicated that he thought Buckley was entitled to know something about *his* affairs.

Kay accepted this with irritating patience. She said O.K. if that was what he wanted. Buckley was big enough to take it. *She* knew what he was making and that should be all that was necessary, *but* if Pops wanted to go into all that old-fashioned rigamarole—O.K. She'd give Buckley the message.

Several nights later Buckley arrived for dinner carrying a bulging briefcase. Mr. Banks eyed it dubiously. What did the fellow think he was—a C.P.A.? On the other hand, if he had enough papers to fill that thing, the picture might not be as grim as he had feared. Rather decent of the boy to take it so seriously.

Mr. Banks had visualized a quiet, dignified conversation during which he would be seated in a large armchair and Buckley in a straight chair facing him. Instead he found himself sitting beside Buckley on the living-room sofa making old-fashioneds.

He finished his quickly. Somehow he felt the need of fortification. After a while Ben and Tommy drifted off on their own affairs and a few minutes later Mrs. Banks and Kay disappeared in the direction of the kitchen. It was Delilah's night out. Mr. Banks was glad of this. Buckley would see that they were a quiet, simple family, well able to take care of itself, but not equipped to assume extra burdens.

They were alone. The time had come. Mixing himself another old-fashioned, he plunged.

"I guess Kay has told you," he said, "that I wanted to have a little financial chat with you." He thought this rather a footless opening in view of the briefcase resting at Buckley's feet.

"Yes, sir," said Buckley, reaching for the briefcase.

Mr. Banks raised a delaying hand. "In the old days," he continued,

"fathers used to say to prospective sons-in-law, 'Are you going to be able to support my daughter in the manner to which she's accustomed?'" Unintentionally he gave a throaty laugh. Buckley did not even smile.

"I know what you kids are up against, though, and I've got modern ideas about these things." He stopped himself from adding, "although I may not look it."

Buckley nodded understandingly. He reminded Mr. Banks more and more of a family doctor paying a professional visit.

"What I mean is I know what you young people are up against. You all need help and I believe parents should give it as far as they are able."

"Yes, sir," agreed Buckley.

"What I was going on to say," continued Mr. Banks hurriedly, "is that parents are also up against it these days."

"They certainly are," said Buckley.

"You know what I mean—with high taxes and high prices and one thing and another."

Buckley nodded sympathetically.

"The long and the short of it is I think you're just as entitled to know where I stand as I am to know about you."

"Yes, sir," said Buckley, reaching for his briefcase.

Mr. Banks hurried on. "So here's what I propose. I'll start out and tell you a little about my own setup. You and Kay ought to know just how much you can count on us for help in the pinches—and just how much you can't. Then you can go into your financial picture. How about it, eh?"

Buckley continued to regard him gravely.

"What I mean is, we ought to know about each other," added Mr. Banks.

"Yes, sir," said Buckley.

Mr. Banks took a thoughtful drink. "I've often wished my father-in-law had sat down with me before Kay's mother and I were married and told me more about himself. Young people are so apt to take things for granted and expect things that aren't possible."

"That's right," said Buckley.

Mr. Banks glanced at him quickly, but Buckley was fumbling with the catch on his briefcase.

"Well, to begin with—" said Mr. Banks nervously.

At the end of fifteen minutes Buckley knew more about Mr. Banks' affairs than Mrs. Banks had been able to dig out in a lifetime. He listened with grave attention and nodded understandingly from time to time. Mr. Banks' feeling that he was consulting his doctor became stronger as he went on. When he had finished if Buckley had pulled a stethoscope out of his briefcase and asked him to strip to the waist he

would have complied without question. Instead Buckley removed a large sheaf of papers from the briefcase.

"I've brought some papers," he said, somewhat unnecessarily.

"Soup's on," cried Mrs. Banks from the living-room door, in her gayest company manner. "My, you two look solemn. Come now or it will get cold."

"That's all right, my boy. We'll do your side later."

Kay jumped up from the table before they had finished dessert. "Come on, Buckley, we're late. Sorry, Mom, we promised to meet the Bakers and go to the movies. Pops kept Buckley talking too long. You don't mind if we skip the dishes do you?"

"Of course not, dear. Run along."

"Did you have a good talk with Buckley?" she asked as they cleared the dining-room table.

"Very satisfactory," said Mr. Banks moodily.

Chapter 4

THE NEWS IS BROKEN

It had been agreed that only a few intimate friends and members of the family were to be told before the engagement was formally announced in the papers. Kay said this involved a cocktail party for everyone but the relatives. She would write them when she had a chance.

The news was too big, however. It was more than she could cope with. She told everyone she met—in absolute confidence, of course—with the result that in twenty-four hours the only ones who did not know were those who would be mortally hurt if not told first.

Mr. Banks said that, under the circumstances, the cocktail party was about as necessary as a G.I.'s pajamas. Kay said that was ridiculous. She had only told a few people and they had *promised* to say nothing about it and *everybody* announced their engagement to their close friends at a cocktail party whether they knew about it already or *not*.

And so it was that, a few days later, Mr. Banks came out from town on the three-fifty-seven, composing an informal and, he hoped, dryly humorous little speech. It was to be about Kay as a little girl, Kay growing up and finally, in a big surprise climax, Kay announcing her engagement.

634

She had estimated that there would be between twenty-five and thirty people at the party. Experience had taught him that on this basis he could expect between thirty-five and fifty. In the pantry he stared with a sinking heart at the neatly arranged phalanxes of glasses that Mrs. Banks had borrowed during the day from unwilling friends. Clearly he hadn't thought this thing through. How was any one man to make drinks for a crowd like that? It would take a trained octopus.

However, this was no time for panic. Decisive action was called for. Martinis for everybody. That would be simplest. With perhaps just a few old-fashioneds ready for those allergic to gin. He pulled two large pitchers from a cupboard and went to work.

Mr. Banks was a hospitable man and in many ways a generous one. There were limits, however. He groaned with pain as he listened to one bottle after another of his best gurgle its lifeblood into the pitchers. But when it was all done and he stood back to inspect the result, he realized that it had been a labor of love. He cherished a special fondness for these kids who had been running through his house for twenty years and whose names he could no longer remember now that they had suddenly grown up.

The early ones were arriving. He could hear the high-pitched entrance screams of the females. He wiped his hands on a dishcloth and was about to go out and greet them when the pantry door was blocked by a rosy-cheeked young man with a disarming smile.

"How are you, sir?"

"I'm fine, how are you?" said Mr. Banks, trying to remember where he had seen him before. "Are they starting in already?"

"That's it, sir. I was wondering if I could have four old-fashioneds."

"No martinis?" suggested Mr. Banks.

"Oh, no indeed, sir. That's very kind of you. Just old-fashioneds."

Mr. Banks filled four of his emergency glasses with ice cubes and pushed them down the pantry shelf. "Thank you, sir. That's service," said the young man. His place was immediately taken by a stout youth with horn-rimmed glasses.

"Sir, four old-fashioneds and one scotch and soda."

"I haven't any scotch," said Mr. Banks. He hoped that his voice did not betray the fact that he had just hidden three bottles in the end cupboard behind Mrs. Banks' flower vases.

The stout young man looked nonplused. He was silent for a moment as he considered this unexpected situation from every angle.

"I don't know, sir. I guess bourbon and soda will do."

Mr. Banks, irritated by a sense of guilt, poured a highball from a bottle labeled "Whiskey—A Blend." "Wouldn't those people like martinis?" he asked.

"Oh no, sir. This is plenty."

The doorway was now filled with young men who observed him

gravely. "Sir, four old-fashioneds, no garbage in two, if you know what I mean. One on the rocks and one with a dash of sugar and no bitters."

"Good God," said Mr. Banks, "do they think I'm filling out prescriptions in here?"

A tall young man with a long neck peered around the frame of the door. "Good evening, sir," he said cordially. "Looks as if it was going to be a nice party."

"I haven't seen it," said Mr. Banks testily. "What would you like? Half a dozen frozen daiquiris?"

"Oh no, sir. Just a couple of martinis."

Mr. Banks stared at him delightedly. "You mean martinis?"

"Yes, sir. Can I help you, sir? It'll speed things up a bit."

"No thank you," said Mr. Banks grimly. "I enjoy doing this. It's my hobby."

For half an hour he sloshed around frantically, trying to keep up with the demand. Then there was a sudden lull in business. "To hell with it," he muttered. Mopping his suit off as best he could, he took a martini and made for the living room, from which there now came a steady roar, like the beating of surf on rocks.

He shouldered his way into the room. Except for a few absent-minded smiles, no one paid the least attention to him. He found himself a bit of standing room in the corner by the bookcases. An intellectual type with black bangs and lovely eyes appeared before him.

"You look like a nice sort of person," she said. "Do you mind if I talk to you? I'm visiting and I don't know anyone."

"Neither do I," said Mr. Banks.

"These things can be pretty grim rat races if you don't know anybody," she said sympathetically. "I like to study types, though. Don't you?"

"It's a passion with me," said Mr. Banks. "Have you located any?"

"Oh, sure," she said. "At a party like this it's a cinch. Now, for instance, there are just two female types here—those who are married and the still unasked. You can spot them a mile off."

"How?" asked Mr. Banks.

"Oh, it's the way they're enthusiastic about the news," she said. "You see, with the married ones it's more relief than enthusiasm. You know. Like the way you feel when somebody you're fond of, that's sort of backward, passes an exam."

"Exactly," said Mr. Banks.

"And those who are still among the unasked are full of beans in that fine old Playing-Fields-of-Eaton sort of way. You know. You're a better man than I am Gunga Din and pip pip."

"I think you've got something there," said Mr. Banks.

At this moment they were caught in an eddy that swept the black-banged girl out of sight. Mr. Banks found himself in a group which was

being addressed with gestures by the stout young man with bone glasses.

"Oh, Mr. Banks. Joe's telling us a story. It's a scream. Start it again for Mr. Banks, Joe."

"Well, it's a very old story, sir. I'm sure you've heard it. It's about a caliph's daughter." This struck the girl beside Mr. Banks as excruciating. She began to giggle hysterically. "It seems that many years ago in Persia there was a caliph who had a beautiful daughter. Have you heard this, sir? Well, one day a traveling salesman—"

"Stanley, where have you been? Doris and Herbert are here." It was Mrs. Banks.

"Doris and Herbert who?" he asked.

"Well, well, well. Glad to see you, Stanley," boomed Mr. Dunstan. "Sorry to be so late. We got lost. Doris always insists—"

"Now go and get Doris and Herb something to drink," said Mrs. Banks.

"Would you like a martini?" asked Mr. Banks hopefully.

"If it's all the same to you, Stan, we'll take old-fashioneds. Can't I help you?"

"No, no," said Mr. Banks. "It won't take a second."

He didn't get back to the pantry a minute too soon. A group of thirst-crazed young men were just about to take the matter of service into their own hands. He sent the drinks out to the Dunstans and for the next hour he worked like a dike mender. The only compensation was that the guests now seemed less fussy about what they got. The roar from the living room sounded like a mob scene in a Cecil B. de Mille superspectacle.

Then the crowd began to thin. The roar subsided. He could hear the die-hards gathering in the front hall for a final stand. Mr. Banks closed down his dispensary and rejoined the remnants, outwardly a genial host, but at heart a professional bouncer.

"*You're* a help," said Mrs. Banks. "Good-by, dear. You were sweet to come."

"What do you think I've been doing? Playing pool?"

"I know. But why must you always leave the whole thing on *my* shoulders? Good-by, Helen dear. You look sweet in that hat."

He considered the first part of her remark as unjust as the last was untrue. "Where are the Dunstans?"

"They're all right. They're talking to Uncle Charlie or vice versa. Good-by, Sam. Glad you could come."

He found himself facing a blond young woman with big deer-like eyes. To his dismay she suddenly burst into tears. She was sorry, she sniffled, but this sort of thing did something to her. The thought occurred to Mr. Banks that it usually did if you took enough of it. He turned to help a highly pregnant young woman into her coat.

She was joined immediately by the young man with horn-rimmed

glasses who appeared to be her husband. "Hi, hi," he said. "What's going on here? What's the idea? Who's leaving? Party's just warming up." He raised his glass to Mr. Banks, who noted with dismay that it was a fresh one. "Sir, the best party ever. And that reminds me, you never heard the end of that story. It was about the caliph's daughter. Remember? Well it seems a traveling salesman came to the palace. O.K., June, we'll be on our way in a minute. I just want to tell Mr. Banks something. Well, as I say, this salesman came to the palace and he fell in love with the caliph's daughter. Have you heard this one, sir?"

A carefully manicured hand plucked his sleeve. "Mr. Banks. Please. I've lost an earring and Grace can't find her gold compact and we're absolutely *sick* about it. We've looked *everywhere*. It's very peculiar."

Something in her voice gave Mr. Banks the feeling that he was under suspicion. Then he saw Mrs. Banks cornered underneath the curve of the stairs by a blond giant. She had her distress signals flying.

"Don't give it a thought," he said, patting the manicured hand. "We'll find everything later—after you've gone," he added hastily. The blond giant was explaining to Mrs. Banks how lucky any man would be to have her for a mother-in-law. Mrs. Banks was obviously lapping it up like a kitten. Yet she had called for help. Queer things, women, mused Mr. Banks, as he moved in.

Like an old cattleman cutting calves from the herd, he disentangled his guests one by one and propelled them through the front door with such light-handed skill that they were unaware of his treachery until they found themselves in the open air.

The young man with the bone glasses was still working on the story about the caliph's daughter. His audience had shrunk to his pregnant wife and Mrs. Banks, both of whom seemed to have an allergy for Oriental folklore. Placing a fatherly arm about his shoulder, Mr. Banks removed the glass from his cramped fingers.

"Good night," he purred. "Good night, my boy. You were both swell to come." As the door closed after them he instinctively placed his back against it. With a sick heart he surveyed the wreckage of what had once been his home. It occurred to him that he had forgotten to announce the engagement.

Somehow it didn't seem to matter.

Chapter 5

THE FAT IS IN THE FIRE

The only step remaining to make the whole thing irretrievable was the announcement of the engagement in the papers.

Mrs. Banks considered the wording of the notice of vital importance. Her brother, Uncle Charlie, had worked on a Chicago newspaper for several weeks when he was a boy. Since then he had been regarded as an authority on all matters concerning the press. He was now called in as a consultant.

Uncle Charlie said it didn't make a damn bit of difference how you wrote the notice. The Society Editor would hand your copy to the office boy, who would bitch the whole thing up anyhow.

Mrs. Banks pooh-poohed this. She declared that, in spite of such journalistic cynicism, this notice was going to be letter-perfect. It was written, read, rewritten, reread, submitted to the Dunstan family, revised and resubmitted. There were eventually so many drafts lying around that Mr. Banks couldn't remember which was the one that had been finally approved.

Kay was the only person who showed no interest. As long as they spelled her name with a "K" and not with a "C" she was satisfied.

Mr. Banks finally took what he hoped was the right draft down to the office to have Miss Bellamy make six copies.

Miss Bellamy was more excited about the wedding than any of the principals. She had been his secretary for fifteen years, during which she had devoted so much time to his personal as well as his business affairs that she had found no opportunity to get married herself. As a compensation she had gradually assumed remote, but nonetheless complete, control of the Banks family.

In a crisis such as this, therefore, Miss Bellamy naturally felt the weight of her responsibility. She had a real affection for Mr. Banks, but it was that of a mother for a backward son. Mrs. Banks she secretly regarded as a cultured incompetent. She had no illusions, therefore, that anything about this whole affair would be handled properly or efficiently, but she was out to do her best to pick up the pieces.

Miss Bellamy made several editorial changes in the copy without even referring the matter to Mr. Banks. Then she typed it with unerring speed. "We must read this back," she said. "There mustn't be any mis-

takes at this point." She read while Mr. Banks stared unseeingly at the original with fierce concentration.

"There," he said. "That's one job done as it should be." Miss Bellamy nodded understandingly. She was a great comfort to Mr. Banks. Although much too tactful to make any direct comment, she always made it quite clear to him that she knew what he was up against.

The following morning he was out of bed before the alarm went off. The morning paper lay on the door mat. He glanced up and down the shaded length of Maple Drive. Not a soul was in sight. His neighbors slumbered, unconscious of the bombshell about to explode among them.

Sitting on the bottom steps of the front stairs, he turned to the Society Section. There was Kay's face, smiling at him, and in the news column next to the picture the headline "Catherine Banks to Wed Ex-Marine Officer."

He looked again. Unfortunately he had not been mistaken. It was spelled with a "C" instead of a "K." That damn fool editor. He'd go around and give him (or was it her?) a piece of his mind. In the meanwhile he had the home team to cope with.

He padded in his bare feet to the little room behind the stairs known as "The Office." Two of Miss Bellamy's copies of the release were lying on the desk. He had to force himself to look. "Mr. and Mrs. Stanley Banks of Fairview Manor announce the engagement of their daughter Catherine." How *could* Miss Bellamy! Then he remembered that he had read it back with her.

"Is it in?" Mrs. Bank was standing in the doorway.

"Yes, but they've garbled it up just as Uncle Charlie said they would. They've spelled Kay's name wrong."

"Oh, Stanley! The one thing the child—"

"I know. I know. But what can you do? That's labor for you. They don't care any more. It's the reason the country's in such a mess."

He climbed the stairs noiselessly, hoping that Kay might sleep until he was safely on the train to town.

A modern wedding is somewhat like a new theatrical production. Once the cast has been decided upon, the next thing is to determine whether it is to be Big Theater or Little Theater and then fill the house.

Kay opened the argument at dinner. "I'll tell you one thing," she said. "This is going to be a *small* wedding and a small *reception.*"

In theory this should have been music to Mr. Banks, but his trained ear sensed a discord. "I was talking to Jack Gibbons the other day," he said. "Jack's married off four daughters and he says weddings are either confined to the bosom of the family or held in Madison Square Garden."

"Well, mine is neither," said Kay. "I'm going to have my own friends and it's *not* going to be a business convention."

"I suppose I can't ask any of *my* friends," said Ben indignantly. "I suppose Tommy and I can't have—"

"Who said anything about a business convention?" interrupted Mr. Banks. "All I'm saying is you'll end up with either thirty or three hundred."

"Three *hundred!*" There was a suggestion of hysteria in Kay's voice. "Pops, if you mean that you're *crazy.* I know what you and Mom want. You want every old fogy in town so that you can hear them say, 'Yes, she really was *too* lovely. And the *most* beautiful dress, my dear.' Well I just won't *have* it. This is *my* wedding and it's going to be *my* friends."

"Listen, dear," said Mr. Banks with guarded gentleness, "this may be your wedding, but that doesn't mean it's going to be a kids' party. What do you think *we're* going to do? Leave out all our friends? Do you think we can leave out the Gibbons and the Roes and the Harts and all that crowd you've grown up with? Nonsense."

"All right, Pops. Who said you couldn't have the Roes? Molly Roe is one of my *best* friends. Of course they'd be there. But that isn't three hundred, is it?"

The argument grew more violent. Mrs. Banks was for a very small wedding to which everyone should be asked. Tommy and Ben shouted unheeded opinions. Mr. Banks pounded the table and skirted apoplexy. Kay's voice was teary. Delilah, hardened though she was to such scenes, retired to the kitchen in terror.

Mr. Banks finally had an inspiration. He fetched a yellow pad of paper from "The Office" and placed it beside his plate. On it he wrote three names.

"There," he said, "that's the smallest wedding you can have under the law—you and Buckley and the Reverend Cyrus Galsworthy. Now. Anybody else?"

Kay threw up her hands. "Really, this is so *childish,* Pops. You always get so *technical.*"

"Sometimes your father has good ideas, Kay. Go on, Stanley. Just put down the Dunstans and ourselves and Ben and Tommy."

"And Aunt Harriet, naturally, and Uncle Charlie," said Kay.

"Of course," said Mr. Banks. "But I'd go slow from there in." He wrote rapidly, keeping a tally on the side of the paper. After three quarters of an hour he ran out of sheets.

"Do you know how many you have on the list now?"

"About fifty," said Kay sulkily.

"Two hundred and six. And that doesn't include most of our friends, and perhaps Buckley's family might have one or two people they'd like to squeeze in."

"Oh, all *right,* Pops, if you're going to be so disagreeable about it. But I tell you it's *my* wedding and it's going to be *small.* I don't *care.*"

She suddenly left the table and rushed up the stairs. Mr. Banks stared after her in amazement. "Good God, Ellie. What's the matter with Kay? We're just sitting here quietly putting down a few names and she goes all to pieces."

"She's nervous," said Tommy, through a mouthful of cake. "All women are nervous."

Late that night, when the hush of sleep had fallen over Fairview Manor, Mr. Banks lay on his back gazing at the watery reflection of the street light on the ceiling.

Three hundred people drinking his champagne. Three hundred people eating his food. Three hundred—

He was ruined. Clearly and utterly ruined. All his life he had been a prudent and thrifty man. Now he was caught in the nutcracker of the conventions and was about to squeeze out his economic life with his own hands.

"I won't do it," he groaned, rolling onto his side. But he knew he would.

Kay was alone at the breakfast table when he came down the next morning, feeling as if he had just returned from a three-day college reunion. Looking like a May morning, she slipped a piece of bread into the toaster for him.

"Hi, Pops."

"Hi," he said gloomily. He wondered how it was that women could go through these shattering emotional scenes and bounce up a few hours later as carefree as a sea gull behind the *Queen Mary*. He watched her butter the toast and a thought began to formulate in his jaded mind.

"Listen, Kitten. I've got an idea."

"Good," she said, putting his toast on the Lazy Susan and twirling it toward him.

"I don't know whether it's good or not—and for God's sake don't tell your mother."

"Of course not. What is it, Pops?"

"I'll give you and Buckley fifteen hundred dollars to elope."

She looked at him incredulously. "Are you kidding?"

"No, honest."

"Why, Pops, you must be out of your *mind*. Elope? Not have a *wedding*? Why, I wouldn't *dream* of it! Why, you *know* Mom would *die* if I didn't have a wedding with all the trimmings. I guess I would too. Not have any *friends* to see me get married—and all the people I've grown *up* with. Why, it wouldn't be getting married, Pops. But you're just pulling my leg."

"O.K.," he said. "I just thought—O.K."

She came around the table and kissed him on the ear. "You're sweet, Pops. Only don't *stew* so much."

Chapter 6

THESE SHALL BE THE WEDDING GUESTS

You people are looking at this whole thing upside down," said Mr. Banks. "It's not a question of how many people you *want*. You must start with the *house*. How many can stand in it at one time? The extras get jammed into the church."

After tense debate it was decided that one hundred and fifty was the absolute maximum that could be packed into 24 Maple Drive without physical injury. An additional one hundred might receive invitations to the church, but certainly not to the reception.

This did not mean, of course, that the invitations must be limited to these numbers. People living at great distances wouldn't show up if they were in their right minds, so the Bankses might as well get the credit for having asked them. Then, with any luck at all, it was safe to count on a certain number of local people being sick, or out of town, on the day of the wedding.

Mr. Banks estimated that they could rely on refusals from a third of the local invitations. On that basis, and excluding the out-of-towners, they could ask two hundred and twenty-five to both the church and the reception and one hundred and fifty additional just to the church.

To Mrs. Banks, who was used to entertaining on a retail level, this seemed like a staggering number. She proposed that each one make a separate list—just the people they *really* wanted. Then these could be combined, the duplicates eliminated—and there you were. If there were more than two hundred and twenty-five, which was unlikely, the excess could be asked to the church only.

This task occupied an harmonious evening.

Mrs. Banks jotted down the names of all living relatives (and her memory was encyclopedic), plus her special cronies in the Garden and Bridge Clubs; also all the people who had invited Mr. Banks and herself to dinner in the last few years—and whom she had neglected to ask back.

Kay put down the classmates who had written fatuous messages across her photograph in her copy of the Heathwood Hall class album, all the young men who had ever asked her to major football games, and people whom she had visited for more than two days. In a burst of gratitude she threw in the fathers and mothers of those who had put her up (or vice versa) for more than a week. To these were added her

former cronies at the Fiarview Manor Country Day School and sundry strays.

Mr. Banks thought in terms of old friends. As his memory limbered up, their dim forms passed before him almost faster than he could write them down. By the time he had finished with World War I his heart was overflowing with good-fellowship. Unfortunately, he couldn't remember the last names of many of them and was obliged to let them go their way. Then he could not remember where most of the balance lived (or if they did). As a result his list was a small one.

He spent the following evening combining the lists. There were alarmingly few duplications. Apparently the members of the Banks family had no friends in common. Finally he turned to his wife and daughter with a sadistic leer. "Guess how many."

Mrs. Banks squirmed uneasily. "Two hundred?" she ventured, without conviction.

"Five hundred and seventy-two," shouted Mr. Banks triumphantly. *"Five! Seven! Two!* What did I tell you? It's either the immediate family or Madison Square Garden."

Mrs. Banks grabbed the lists. "Nonsense. Let me see. You've done something wrong. I'll bet I can cut this down. Now look here, we certainly don't need to have the Sparkmans. We never see them and as for that dyed-haired woman I don't care if I ever have her in my house again."

Mr. Banks wondered why it was that, every time he discovered an attractive woman, Mrs. Banks said her hair was dyed. And anyway what if it was? "Listen," he said. He was dignified now; cool, austere—and on guard. "Do you realize that Harry Sparkman is one of my most intimate friends, to say nothing of being a very good client? Why, I'd go to the ends of the earth for that fellow and he would for me."

"How ridiculous. You hardly ever see him."

"There you are," said Kay. "I *told* you these were just customers. I *knew* it."

Mr. Banks bit his lip and said nothing. He realized that he was licked for the moment. "And who in the world are the DeLancey Crawfords?" continued Mrs. Banks smoothly. "I never even heard of them."

It was Kay's inning. "Listen, Mom. How can you be so *stupid?* Don't you remember that I spent half the *summer* with them at Western Point two years ago? And Twinkey Crawford is one of my *closest, closest* friends. Why, Mother, they've been right here in this *house*. Now if we're going on like *this*, Mother—"

"Maybe they won't come," suggested Mr. Banks. "Don't they live in Pittsburgh or someplace?"

"We can ask those families to the church and not the reception," said Mrs. Banks, disposing of the matter.

"The *church!*" cried Mr. Banks. "You mean to say you want to ask

644

Harry and Jane Sparkman to the *church* and not to the *house?* Harry *Sparkman?* My intimate friend? Did *they* ask *us* just to the church when *their* daughter got married? No. And you were delighted to go to the reception. The *church!*"

The following evening Mr. Banks returned with a card file and large quantities of three-by-five cards.

"The pink are for 'Church Only,'" he explained. "The white ones are 'Church and Reception.' Now here's a rubber stamp. Whenever you're sure someone can't come because they live out of town or something, stamp that card 'P.N.C.' That means 'Probably Not Coming.'"

Three nights later everyone's name had been written on a pink or a white card. The out-of-towners and the local 4Fs had been happily stamped "P.N.C." Then Mr. Banks took the second census.

Mrs. Banks watched him nervously. "Maybe they'll come out about right now," she said.

Kay looked bored. "The whole thing is just *too* sordid. I had always thought a wedding was a *joyous* occasion. The way *you're* going at it you might as well hire a couple of *bookkeepers* to put it on for you."

Mr. Banks' only reply was to count audibly to help his concentration. "Here's the box score," he announced at last. "Ten people have been asked to the church and not the reception. Five hundred and sixty-two have been asked to both. There are one hundred and fifty-two cards stamped 'P.N.C.' That leaves four hundred and ten people who might show up. Figuring that a third of them won't, you'll have two hundred and seventy-three people at the reception."

"I don't follow you very well," said Mrs. Banks in a dazed voice, "but it looks as if we'd have to cut out a few."

"All you've got to do is to throw a hundred and twenty-three people out on their necks," said Mr. Banks grimly.

Kay yawned. "I'm going to bed. *My* list is right down to the *bone,* so I can't be of much help."

Mr. Banks opened his mouth, but Mrs. Banks motioned it shut again. Kay stalked out of the room, swinging her hips with dignity.

"We can work it out," said Mrs. Banks. "Kay's upset. All we have to do is to shift these superfluous people over to the church and not invite them to the reception. Now the Harry Sparkmans—"

Mr. Banks refused the gage. The timing didn't seem right. "All right," he said. "Let's go. We'll start by putting the Garden Club in the church—and leaving 'em there."

Each white card was removed from the box, debated at length, and returned to its original place with a sigh. At the end of each round, when they came to Carlton B. Zachery, they had succeeded in eliminating or relegating to the church only a handful of names. Quite obviously

645

they were getting nowhere. They had too many dear, close, loyal, lifelong friends, to all of whom they seemed to be indebted.

After three fruitless evenings of this sort of thing Mr. Banks had lunch with a client who was head of a large accounting firm. He had just run the gauntlet himself and, after the manner of all survivors, he liked to strut his scars. As a form of wound-licking he had reduced everything to neat figures.

Wedding guests, he explained, should be broken down into church units and reception units. That was the only way to get at the per-unit cost. At his wedding each reception unit cost $3.72, including champagne, caterers, tips, breakage, flowers, furniture-moving and extra insurance. He had not included wear and tear, feeling that, considering the occasion, it would be on the mercenary side.

Mr. Banks made some calculations on the tablecloth, and the spirit of hospitality fled from him. That evening he had a business dinner in town, but the following morning he faced the shaving mirror with the set jaw of leadership.

Someone had to take the helm. Someone had to tie up this disintegrating situation before it fell apart completely. For three seventy-two a unit he would undertake to tie up a wounded lion.

"I'll tell you one thing, Ellie," he announced as he rubbed in the shaving soap vigorously. "Only a hundred and fifty people are coming to this reception. You've got to cut down the list. I don't care who you leave out. I don't care how many just get asked to the church. Pack 'em in. Build a grandstand in the chancel if you want. All I say is that the hundred and fifty-first person to enter this house gets thrown out on his ear even if it's your own mother."

Mrs. Banks looked at him with an astonishment that experience never seemed to dim. "Why, Stanley, that's what I said at the very beginning. And you said it was an insult to ask anybody to the church and not the reception. I'm willing enough to cut and have been right along. Now people like the Sparkmans can just as well—"

Mr. Banks winced. "It's not a question now of insulting people. It's a matter of survival. What's the world going to say when we land in the gutter just because we insisted on giving a wedding reception like a Roman emperor? No sir. It's no use arguing with me now, Ellie. I've made up my mind. One fifty is the limit."

Things looked better after he had had his breakfast, but he didn't weaken. "Now, Ellie," he said, as he left the house, "I want you to take that list today and slash it down to a realistic basis. I leave it all to you."

He felt masterful and composed that evening as he entered 24 Maple Drive. Next to achieving sudden riches, acquiring financial equilibrium is almost equally gratifying.

"Got everything fixed up, Ellie?" he called into the living room.

646

"Yes, only—"

"Pops." Kay came out and threw a slim arm around his neck. "Pops, you big stupid. Do you know what you did? You forgot Buckley's list. It just came today."

Mr. Banks' psyche collapsed like an abandoned bathrobe. He walked slowly to the big wing chair and sat down heavily. "How many?" he asked. His voice sounded choked.

Mrs. Banks came boiling into action beside her daughter. "He couldn't have been cuter," she declared. "He only wants a hundred and twenty-five including *everybody*. And I mean that's *everybody*. And he's marked those that he doesn't think will come—like the officers in his squadron and so on."

"Oh, they've *got* to come." Kay clasped her hands ecstatically.

Mrs. Banks hurried on. "There are about fifty 'P.N.C.s' on the list. So that really cuts it down to seventy-five. And if you figure only two thirds of those will show up—"

"O.K.," interrupted Mr. Banks firmly. "That just means cutting seventy-five more from our list. If I haven't got a friend left when this thing is over—why, I haven't got a friend left—and that's that."

All evening the list was slashed. Everyone finally got into the spirit of the thing until bosom friends were thrown out with a whoop of joy. By eleven-thirty it was reduced to two hundred and four. If a third of those didn't come there would be one hundred and fifty-three at the house. Beyond that point they could not go.

Two nights later Kay came into the living room and sat on the arm of her father's chair. She ran her fingers through his thinning hair.

"Pops darling, are you going to miss me?"

He swallowed quickly and patted her knee. "Don't let's talk about it, Kitten. If you're happy, I'm happy. That's straight."

"You're so sweet, Pops." She kissed him lightly on the forehead. "Do you know something? I hate to tell you—but I've done the stupidest thing."

"Now what have you done? Mislaid Buckley?"

"No, Pops, but for the last few days I've been thinking of people I forgot. I mean *important* people. People that I'd have simply *died* if they hadn't been at the reception."

Mr. Banks sat up suddenly, his warm mood evaporated. "How many people?"

"Oh, I *knew* you'd be cross, Pops. I know it was very dumb. I'm afraid there are quite a *lot*."

"How many is that?"

"Well, maybe forty."

From this point on morale tended to disintegrate. So did the list.

Each evening Mr. Banks thumbed through the "Church Only" cards with sad eyes.

"Bob and Liz!" he murmured. "If anybody'd told me Bob and Liz wouldn't be at my daughter's wedding reception I'd have said they were crazy. Remember the week ends we used to spend at their camp. Those were—"

"Why don't you ask them, Stan? I agree with you. It just isn't right not to have Bob and Liz. Why not make an exception?"

"Guess we should." Mr. Banks tore up the pink card venomously and carefully made out a white one. "Maybe a third of them won't come."

Or again: "Len and Louise Warner! Imagine what they're going to say. Our best friends. Three seventy-two a head. What price lifelong friends?"

"I know, dear. It's so cold and calculating when you put it that way. I should think lifelong friends were very cheap at three seventy-two a pair."

"A head," corrected Mr. Banks, transferring the Warners to a white card.

The pink cards gradually shrank. The white ones increased daily. Mrs. Banks' apprehensive look returned.

"I just don't see what's going to happen if all these people come," she said.

"They can go out on the back lawn," said Mr. Banks.

"Suppose it rains."

"It won't," said Mr. Banks.

The day came when the list must be sent to the lady who spent her life addressing wedding invitations in a copperplate handwriting. There was a last futile attempt to get it under control.

"Who are all these clucks?" fumed Mr. Banks, pawing through the cards. "I've never heard of half of them. Here I am throwing an Irish picnic for a lot of fuddyduds I never heard of."

"Well, they certainly aren't *my* friends," wailed Kay. "You all know I wanted a small wedding with just *my* friends. Now we seem to be putting on a *convention* or something."

"I know, dear," Mrs. Banks soothed. "It's a shame we don't have a bigger house. There are a lot of people I'd like to ask, I'll admit. For instance, it seems to me we've left out all of Mother's friends."

"Whoever these people may be," announced Mr. Banks quickly, "they are the Wedding Guests. The books are closed."

Chapter 7

YOU CAN'T WIN

It was Mr. Banks' last decisive act for many days. He and Ben and Tommy continued to live at home, outwardly just as usual, but actually more like three harmless family ghosts than active participants.

The clothes carnival was on.

Although Mrs. Banks had always contended that she never had a minute to spare from morning until night, she and Kay now rushed to town each day immediately after breakfast. Mr. Banks' socks lay undarned in the sewing bag. His buttonless shirts were stacked in neat piles in his dresser.

Each evening he and the two boys ate their dinner in glum silence while they listened to discussions of the dresses which were not there, the dresses which would have been becoming if they had been different and the dresses which would have been ravishing if Kay and her mother had been consulted about their design.

Mr. Banks gathered that the nation's dress manufacturers had suddenly gone haywire and that nothing which they had produced during the last few months would be used by a self-respecting charwoman for work clothes. He had supposed that the principal worries connected with weddings revolved around things like champagne and caterers. Now he discovered that these were small beer.

Although Kay's closest was bulging with clothes, he learned to his surprise that, for her money (or perhaps for his), it was as bare as Mother Hubbard's cupboard. Had she been Venus rising from the sea her outfitting problem could not have been more basic.

Because no one would pay any attention to him he was forced to resort to indirect methods. He would open the door of the closest and make playful remarks about the rows of dresses and shoes. He drew subtle comparisons with the children of Europe. He told anecdotes about his grandmother's frugal girlhood in a parsonage. The only recognition he received was when Kay occasionally pushed him aside with *"Please,* Pops. Can't you see you're right in the *way?* Why don't you go downstairs and *read?* You just don't *understand."*

At those moments he would be in full agreement with his daughter for the first time in days.

Mrs. Banks' own costume seemed to be giving her a perplexing amount of trouble. She had interminable and costly telephone conversations with Mrs. Dunstan on the subject.

"What in the world has her dress got to do with yours?" asked Mr. Banks. "Are you two going as Tweedledum and Tweedledee?"

Buckley never lost confidence during these trying times. He appeared each evening like a faithful sheep dog, to spend it staring at Mr. Banks. Neither of them could think of much to say to one another so they usually listened moodily to the radio and to the undertone of women's voices from the floor above—a never-ending dialogue occasionally punctuated by screams of pleasure. At each scream Mr. Banks winced, for he knew from experience that such female ecstasy is purchased at a high price.

As time went on, however, Buckley began to show signs of alarm. He would revert occasionally to his old theme of simple weddings in little country churches. Mr. Banks said that given his choice he would pick a desert island. Once Buckley asked how much a girl—say a girl like Kay for instance—spent on clothes in the course of a year. Mr. Banks muttered something about millions. The bond of sympathy between them grew stronger daily.

Ignoring the fact that Kay and Buckley were going to live in a tiny house where Kay, at least, would spend a large part of her time with her head in the oven, she was finally outfitted for every social and sporting event that could conceivably take place between Sun Valley and Hobe Sound.

Mysterious boxes began to arrive. They appeared to be from women who did not have any last names— "Annette," "Estelle," "Helene," "Babette."

"They sound like a bunch of madams," said Mr. Banks to no one in particular.

The force of example, however, is like a mighty glacier. Mr. Banks suddenly became clothes-conscious himself. Fortunately, and unlike so many of his friends, he did not have to depend on his wedding cutaway. During those fine, flush days of the twenties he had bought a new one in order to act as best man for some backsliding old bachelor. The twenties were a long way off, however, and although Mr. Banks was proud of his figure, even he was conscious that subtle changes had taken place.

When he had last seen the suit it had been a splendid thing—a badge of old-world aristocracy. Now it lay in an attic trunk under a hailstorm of moth balls. When Mrs. Banks finally dug it out it reminded him of something out of a sailor's slop chest.

For a long time it lay dejectedly across the chair beside Mr. Banks' bed. Each day he could think of good reasons for postponing the try-on. In the morning he was too rushed. At night he was too tired. Finally, choosing a moment when no one was around, he slipped out of his business suit and stuck a foot gingerly into a trouser leg like a bather testing the water.

Well, his legs were through at least. A bit snug, perhaps, but it might not be noticeable if he sat on the edge of things. Inhaling deeply, he sucked in his stomach as far as possible and buttoned the trousers. The effect was like squeezing the lower half of a sausage balloon.

"If any of these buttons give way they'll put somebody's eye out," he muttered, walking stiffly to the long mirror on the back of the bathroom door. Not bad for fifty, though. It was going to be a strain, of course, to keep his chest blown out like a pouter pigeon and his stomach wrapped around his back bone, but the general effect was good—like a well-preserved old oarsman.

He put on the vest carefully. The cloth around the buttons had the strained look of a sail in a heavy blow, but if it held there was nothing to worry about.

Now for the coat. This was the crucial garment—the one which must withstand the hostile eye of the general public. Nobody looked at a man's pants. He wished the sleeves didn't fit like a freshly laundered union suit and that the back didn't make him feel as if he had been taped up by a surgeon. But these were minor inconveniences. The coat was on and holding at every seam.

Lifting his diaphragm as high as possible, he buttoned it quickly under his ribs. Mrs. Banks came in and surveyed him admiringly. "It's really wonderful, Stan. I'm proud of you."

Mr. Banks made a deprecating grimace and undid the single button of the coat. The edges parted as if they were on springs. "I think I like these coats better unbuttoned," he said thoughtfully. "You really think it fits, then?"

"Perfectly," said Mrs. Banks. "It might be a trifle snug, but that's all."

Mr. Banks continued to study himself appraisingly. "Perhaps I might manage to lose a pound or two before the wedding." He turned on her sternly. "Remember, now. From here in no more butter or potatoes or dessert."

"All right, dear. All right. But you don't need to be so cross about it."

"Well, people insist on offering them to me," said Mr. Banks.

For some time Mr. Banks had been keeping a notebook handy for ideas about the wedding. During the day he would stop in unlikely places and jot down new items. When he went to bed he placed it on the table beside him. In the middle of the night he would suddenly switch on the light and write "confetti" or "bride's bouquet—who pays?"

The book was getting filled up now. Many of the notations were illegible. There were also numerous unexplained names and addresses which had been pressed on him by experienced friends. They were the

651

names of people who were indispensable to weddings in one way or another, but who they were or what they were supposed to do, Mr. Banks did not know.

One of the first notations in the book was the word "Champagne." It seemed a long time ago since he had written it. Life had seemed so simple and straightforward in those days. During the ensuing weeks he had received so much conflicting advice on this subject alone that he had become thoroughly confused and done nothing at all about it.

He finally stopped on his way up from the station to discuss the matter with that *bon vivant* and connoisseur of good living, Sam Locuzos, owner of the Fairview Manor Wines and Liquor Company, whom he had been patronizing, illegally and legally, for many years.

Champagne, to Mr. Banks, was a commodity which was kept on the top shelf of the hall closet in two-bottle lots and used only on very special occasions. Sam, however, didn't have the same reverence for the stuff.

"Sure," he said. "Got plenty champagne. What kind you want? All the same. No good. Here's some. Good enough. Make it forty-five dollars a case."

Mr. Banks turned pale. "How many cases do I need?"

"How many come?"

"Oh, let's say a hundred and fifty."

"Six cases, eh?"

"Six cases! Good God, Sam, that's almost three hundred dollars."

"Sure. Got something cheaper. Forty-two dollars. No good," said Sam impassively. He was used to scenes like this. There had been other weddings in Fairview Manor.

"Tell you what," he said, and his voice was full of sympathy. "You been a good customer. I give you three bottles. Three different kinds, see. Present. You take home an' try. Then you tell me which one."

Mr. Banks watched Sam's skillful fingers as they wrapped the bottles. "There," he said. "Don't drop. An' don't forget to freeze cold. Then nobody don't taste."

"Thank you," said Mr. Banks.

On Sunday afternoon he invited two carefully selected couples to help him make the test. None of them knew anything about champagne, but Mr. Banks did not know anyone who did. He had chosen them on the theory that people who drank as enthusiastically as this group must have judgment on anything alcoholic.

They consumed the three bottles with the casual dispatch of people at a public drinking fountain. Each couple had a favorite brand of their own which they considered necessary to the success of any wedding—and it was not one of the three Mr. Locuzos had selected. They became

so heated about it that everyone forgot the three empty bottles and Mr. Banks went out and made old-fashioneds. When they had gone Mr. and Mrs. Banks selected the bottle with the most impressive-looking label and let it go at that.

"Got the champagne this afternoon," remarked Mr. Banks casually to his wife that evening.

"How much did you get?"

He immediately went on the defensive. "Well, I wanted to be sure there was enough. Nothing's worse than running out the way George Evans did. Then if there's a little left over we can always—"

"But how much did you get?"

"Ten cases. But when you think—"

"Ten *cases!* How much did you have to pay?"

"Sam made me a special price. Forty-five dollars. Very reasonable."

"Forty-five dollars? For what?"

"For a case, of course. Now—"

"Stanley Banks, do you mean to tell me that you laid out four hundred and fifty dollars on champagne when you've been complaining about every cent I spend on poor little Kay for things the child absolutely *has* to have? I think it's just wicked. Don't ever speak to me again about expenses. That's all I say."

Chapter 8

BIG BUSINESS

The telephone, which had never been an inarticulate instrument in the Banks home, now started ringing the moment the receiver was replaced in its cradle.

"Who was it, Ellie?"

"Oh, just a woman who wants to take Kay's bridal pictures."

"Some orchestra that wants to play at the reception."

"A candid camera man, dear."

"It was the little man that puts up the awning."

"Just another caterer."

"A man who wants to do the flowers."

"Only the dressmaker, darling."

What an innocent he had been! His original wedding budget had included a case or two of champagne, a couple of hundred water cress

sandwiches, a wedding dress (if he was unfortunate enough to have reared a daughter who couldn't slip into her mother's), a handsome present to the bride, some miscellaneous tips and that was about all (although bad enough). The church was free. What else was there?

Now he suddenly appeared to be the sole customer of an immense and highly organized industry. He reminded himself of the Government during the war. "Keep those production lines moving for Banks. Get the finished goods to him. He's committed now. He's in this mess up to his ears. There's no drawing back. We're all behind you, Banks; behind you with caterers, photographers, policemen, dressmakers, tent pitchers —behind you with champagne and salads and clothes and candid cameras and potted palms and orchestras and everything it takes to win a wedding."

He sat in the big wing chair, shoulders slumped, staring unseeingly at the rows of books on either side of the fireplace.

"I do wish," said Mrs. Banks, "that you could arrange to meet me in town someday soon, Stanley. We've just *got* to get together with Kay and pick out the flat silver if we want to get it marked in time." Mr. Banks regarded her with dull eyes. "The what?"

"Kay's flat silver. Her *table* silver. You know perfectly well that we give Kay her flat silver and her linen."

"Her linen?" repeated Mr. Banks. His voice sounded as if he had been drugged.

"Yes, dear. Of course. Her sheets and towels and napkins and all that sort of thing."

"My God!" It wasn't an oath. It was a prayer. "Doesn't Buckley's family give anything but Buckley?"

"For an intelligent man, Stanley, you are very stupid," said Mrs. Banks.

Tommy and Ben came in. Perhaps it was just as well to let the matter drop. He looked at them closely for the first time in weeks—Ben, six feet of good looks—Tommy, a bean pole which seemed to add an inch a week. They were no longer boys but men—men ready to rear families of their own.

A warm comforting thought burst upon him and filled him with sudden peace. Soon they, also, would be getting married. Then it would be his turn to hand them over to some bride's father as *his* contribution —his sole contribution.

The only ones who seemed thoroughly immune to the situation were Kay and Buckley. As it grew more complex they grew more serene, until they seemed to Mr. Banks to be floating away like disembodied spirits, leaving the entire mess in his lap. It was a kind of spiritual sit-down strike.

"Look here," he announced sternly, "there are a lot of details we've

got to talk over and I never can get you two kids together. Now I want a few minutes of your undivided attention."

But before the words were out of his mouth Kay and Buckley had drifted back into an interminable half-whispered conversation. Judging by the almost continuous giggling which rippled through it, each appeared to regard the other as a combination of Joe E. Brown and Jack Benny. Mr. Banks hated whispered conversations and detested giggling. There were moments when it seemed to him that Buckley had the most vapid expression he had ever seen on a young man's face.

"Silly ass," he muttered under his breath—and then aloud to nobody in particular, "I'm damned if I can run this circus single-handed and try to run my business too."

"*You* run it single-handed!" said Mrs. Banks indignantly. "All *you* have to do is to hand everything over to Miss Bellamy. I wish you'd stay around *here* all day. You might find out what's going on."

Basically it should have been so simple. Boy and girl meet, fall in love, marry, have babies—who eventually grow up, meet other babies, fall in love, marry. Looked at from this angle, it was not only simple, it was positively monotonous. Why then must Kay's wedding assume the organizational complexity of a major political campaign?

Take the question of bridesmaids, for example. Kay, who had almost become a professional brides-maid during the last five years, was now repaying her obligations with a reckless disregard for numbers.

"It's going to look more like a daisy-chain parade than a wedding," grumbled Mr. Banks as the list grew.

Fortunately, a large number were obliged to decline on the grounds of pregnancy. This reduced the length of the procession, but it did not simplify the dress problem. These must be the most beautiful bridesmaids' dresses ever worn outside of a technicolor film. They must look as if they had been snatched from Bergdorf Goodman's window, but under no circumstances must they cost a penny more than $24.50.

"They should suggest the spirit of spring," said Mrs. Banks dreamily. "Like wood nymphs in glades."

"Sort of on the idea of the White Rock girl," suggested Mr. Banks.

"*Light* green pastel with three-quarter sleeves—and a *tight* bodice and a bouffant skirt," said Kay.

"That's it," said Mrs. Banks. "And wreaths of natural flowers."

"You girls ought to work for Billy Rose," offered Mr. Banks.

Kay's face fell. "*Mom,* can you *picture* Jane Bloomer in that dress! Why, she'll look like an elephant in a *ballet* skirt. Oh, dear. This is a *mess*. Wouldn't you *know* she'd accept."

And so it went while Mr. Banks browsed absent-mindedly through the evening paper and wondered what would happen if he suddenly began to make queer noises and froth at the mouth. The incident of the

champagne was still too recent, however, to make free speech advisable.

"Oh, Kay," exclaimed Mrs. Banks, "there's one thing we've forgotten. Mrs. Pulitzski. Remind me to phone her. She's simply got to be at the church to straighten you out before you go down the aisle."

Mr. Banks lowered his paper. "What's the child going to do—have the bends?"

"Oh, men never understand. Don't you see, dear, somebody's got to be there to arrange Kay's train and veil before she starts down the aisle with you?"

"I think I'll go to bed," said Mr. Banks.

It has been said that a man's home is his castle. Mr. Banks began to realize that his should have been nothing less in order to take care of the traffic that now began to flow daily through 24 Maple Drive. Joe Marvin, the architect, had certainly not designed it for a public institution.

In the pre-engagement days it had been Mr. Banks' pleasant custom to give out a cheerful "Hi" each evening as he entered his front door. And from somewhere in the house there was sure to come an answering "Hi." It was comforting and warming after an embattled day in the city.

Now, as he entered the house, he was more apt to be greeted by a din of youthful voices from the living room. There was no use calling "Hi." No one would have heard him.

It was not intentional. In fact, they were all so polite they embarrassed him. As he entered the room the young males rose in a body and mumbled something ending in "sir." Then Kay would embrace him dramatically, one foot raised slightly behind her, and say *"Pops! We were waiting for you to make us a cocktail."*

It was no time to protest. Mr. Banks would take a hasty inventory and retire to the pantry. It seemed to him that each night another empty went into the garbage pail, where Delilah observed it glumly, brooding obviously on her rather meager salary.

Sam, of the Fairview Manor Wines and Liquor Company, became steadily more enthusiastic. "Nice wedding you have," he would remark cheerily, his deft fingers wrapping up another three bottles. "Sure I charge. Against law. You bet. Come again."

In the front hall someone was always sitting at the telephone table making a long-distance call. As far as Mr. Banks could observe none of Kay's friends had any local acquaintances. They would nod pleasantly to him as he passed.

Occasionally he would find a dime and several odd pennies beside the phone. At other times there would be a note scribbled on the memorandum pad—

656

Each day there were several frantic messages from Buckley's family about V.I.P.s who had been overlooked and must be invited immediately. It was Mr. Banks' job to get these belated invitations into the mailbox on the corner before going to bed. As he remembered it in after years, it seemed to him that, like a figure from a Brontë novel, he was always struggling through violent rain and sleet storms on these profitless errands.

He scuffed doggedly through unseen rain puddles. Wet branches sprang out of the darkness to slap at his eyeglasses. It would have been so easy to drop the pocketful of envelopes behind a bush and go home.

When he returned to the house he could usually hear the sound of strange bodies being disposed of for the night in various parts of the house. He used to wonder what it was about weddings that made youth so peripatetic—and where these characters would have slept on that particular night if Kay had not happened to meet Buckley.

Chapter 9

PANIC

For many years a light truck, modeled along the lines of a dog-catcher's wagon and labeled "U. S. Mail," had skidded into the Banks drive each morning and delivered a stack of assorted envelopes.

During the course of breakfast Mrs. Banks had ripped hers open with an impatient forefinger, glanced at the contents and tossed them into the wastebasket. Mr. Banks, who resented anything that interfered with his morning paper, tossed most of his in without opening.

Since the invitations had gone out, however, his attitude had changed. The arrival of the morning mail was now a matter of top priority, although there didn't seem to be much family agreement on the information it contained.

"Oh, what a shame! The Lindley Davises can't come," exclaimed Mrs. Banks.

Mr. Banks' face beamed with pleasure.

"Mr. and Mrs. Throckum Nesbitt accept with pleasure. Who in the world are Mr. and Mrs. Throckum Nesbitt? And they say if we don't mind they're bringing their daughter."

"Never heard of them. They've got the wrong wedding." Mr. Banks was fumbling with the card file. "My God, they're some people from *Pittsburgh!* We had them down as "P.N.C." Haven't they ever been asked to a wedding before? We don't even know who they are. That's

some crust, I'll say. Coming all the way from *Pittsburgh!* And bringing their daughter. I'd—"

"The Cramptons are coming—oh, and the Lewises—and the Quincy Browns—and the Gaylords and—oh, how nice—"

"What's the matter? Somebody refuse?"

"No. The Whiteheads were asked to another wedding and they're giving it up because they didn't want to miss ours. How sweet of them."

Mr. Banks buried himself in the morning paper. The news from Europe was more cheering.

Each day an increasing number of people, known and unknown, accepted with pleasure. Apparently Kay had selected a day for her wedding when no one within a range of four hundred miles had anything to do. The Banks-Dunstan marriage was evidently an oasis in a desert of boredom.

Mr. Banks became increasingly impressed with the stupendousness of the spectacle which he was about to produce, and with the importance of the role which he was slated to play. It wasn't a wedding. It was a pageant. There should be an electric sign on the awning into the church:

MARRIAGE BELLS.
A SUPERCOLOSSAL SCENIC DISPLAY.
PRODUCED, DIRECTED AND ACTED
BY STANLEY BANKS.

As a form of self-torture the idea pleased him. He developed it leisurely as he composed himself to sleep that night. No one had thought of loud-speakers outside the church to take care of the overflow, or of putting the show on the air, or of billboards.

Sometime during the night he woke up filled with vague apprehension. For a few minutes he couldn't figure out what was bothering him. Then, gradually, the interior of a great cathedral took shape in his half-conscious brain. Its monolithic columns towered up and up, disappearing finally into the darkness above. The place was jammed to the doors with flashily dressed people. Somewhere an organ was thundering like a summer storm.

Suddenly the organ stopped and there was a dead silence broken only by the creaking of stiff collars and the rattle of pearls as a thousand heads turned as if on swivels to the point where he, Stanley Banks, found himself standing, quite alone, at the head of the aisle.

He tried to slip into one of the rear pews, but his feet were rooted to the floor. Then there was a series of terrific boomps from the organ and the peals of the wedding march resounded through the vaulted shadows. A shaft of white light sprang from the gloom above him and placed him in the center of a glaring pool of brilliance.

Father of the Bride

Alone, pacing slowly to the measured rhythm of the organ, he started down the aisle. It was several hundred yards long and at the end of it he could distinguish the figure of the minister which kept growing larger and larger until it towered over the whole scene and reached into the shadows—huge, sinister, forbidding, daring him to run the gauntlet.

Now he could hear titters from either side. "It's Banks. How grotesque! Why, his clothes don't fit him. Look at his figure! Why, he can't even get his coat buttoned! What a clown of a man!"

The tittering was giving way to shrieks of laughter. People were standing on the seats of the pews and pointing at him. "Look at his knees shake! He'll never make it. He'll go down in a minute. How could a man like that have such a beautiful daughter? They say she isn't his. It's a joke. He's a joke. Banks is nothing but a big fat joke—a big fat joke—a big fat joke. My God, his pants are undone!"

He was sitting up in bed. His forehead was clammy.

"Why don't you take a sleeping pill, dear?" said Mrs. Banks. "It'll quiet you down."

Of course Mr. Banks realized that this sort of nocturnal shenanigans was immature and silly. For a successful lawyer it indicated an alarming lack of self-control. However, in spite of his efforts to reason the matter through logically, he felt queasy all day. When he arrived in Fairview Manor late in the afternoon it occurred to him that it might be a good idea to go up and look at the church. Not that he wasn't thoroughly familiar with it. He merely wished to look it over in its new role as a Wedding Church.

The side door was open. The leveling rays of the late afternoon sun sifted through the stained-glass windows and filled the interior with a rich tapestry of subdued color. The place was deserted. He felt like an intruder bursting in on its introspective silence.

Standing at the head of the aisle, he studied the terrain like a hunter. Why had he thought of this intimate place as a cathedral? The pillars on either side, as he studied them critically for the first time, looked rather short and dumpy. As for the aisle, from where he stood a hop, skip and a jump would land him in the minister's arms.

"Anything I can do for you, sir?" It was Mr. Tringle, the sexton of St. George's. "Oh, it's you, Mr. Banks. I didn't recognize you. Come to look things over for the wedding? Well, don't get nervous, Mr. Banks. We'll handle everything the way you want it."

"I'm *not* nervous," said Mr. Banks irritably.

"Of course not. No sir. Some fathers get nervous, though. Good Lord, you wouldn't believe it unless you saw it with your own eyes. Fine upstanding men falling to pieces like that. Why, I've had 'em out in the vestry shakin' so's their hair was in their eyes. Shockin', some of 'em. Didn't think I'd ever get 'em down the aisle. Somethin' about the sight of a church seems to set 'em off. Seems like men's more high-strung than

women that way. Everything'll be all right. Don't give it a thought, sir. Worryin' won't make it any better anyways. I can remember— Oh, have you got to go? Will you go out this door please. Good night, Mr. Banks."

A short time later he found himself sitting on the living-room sofa with Kay, sipping his evening old-fashioned. Delilah was out. Mrs. Banks was in the kitchen. Kay suddenly slipped her arm through his. He patted her hand absently, his mind on Mr. Tringle.

"I know I'm a *fool,* Pops, but I want to talk to you about something. You won't think I'm *silly,* will you?"

"Of course not, Kitten. What's bothering?"

"I'm scared, Pops. Scared to *death."*

Mr. Banks started and took a substantial swallow. "Scared? What are you scared of? Getting married isn't anything to be scared of. Marriage is the most normal—"

"Oh, Pops, I'm not scared of *marriage.* It's much sillier than *that.* You see—" He always had a particular yen for Kay when she said "You see" and snuggled.

"It's this way, Pops. You know how I wanted a *simple* wedding—out in the country somewhere. Well, that's *out.* We don't *live* in the country. Period. But this thing is getting bigger an' bigger an' *bigger.* Oh, I know it's ungrateful, Pops. You're wonderful. But sometimes it scares the living daylights out of me."

Mr. Banks glanced toward the kitchen and dropped his voice. "You mean like going down the aisle?"

"Every time I *think* of it, Pops, I turn into a cold sweat. Suppose my *knees* got shaking just as I started. And suppose they shook so finally that they let me down *entirely* and you had to *drag* me to the altar like a sack of *meal."*

Mr. Banks regarded her for some moments with despair in his eyes. "We might both have a short snort just before the show starts," he suggested finally, but without conviction.

"No sir. That won't do, Pops. I'm not going to blow gin in the minister's face at my own wedding."

"I was thinking of a whiskey and soda," said Mr. Banks. Then he pulled himself together with an almost visible effort. "Listen, Kitten. Get this into your head. There's nothing to worry about. See? *Nothing* to worry about. All your life when you've been bothered *I've* been there, haven't I? Well, I'll be there when that wedding march starts. All you've got to do is to take my arm, lean on me and think about how you're the most beautiful bride in the world and how proud I am of you. That's all. Just relax. I'll do the rest."

"Oh, Pops!" Kay was looking at him with loving reverence. "You *are* wonderful. *Nobody* could be scared with you. Nothing *ever* fazes you, *does* it, Pops?"

Chapter 10

IT IS EASIER TO GIVE THAN TO RECEIVE

Anyone faced with the necessity of giving a wedding present should remember that only the first few to arrive will receive the admiration they deserve. Shop early and avoid oblivion.

The first present came two days after the engagement had been announced in the papers. It was a hand-painted tray. Mrs. Banks had cleared out the spare room and set up, against the wall, a card table covered with her best tablecloth. Kay placed the tray on it like an acolyte arranging an altarpiece, while the family gathered reverently around. The boys became a bit shy and treated Kay with a new respect.

For a few days it looked as if the first present might achieve the double honor of being the last as well. Then they began to move in; a thin trickle at first, growing steadily to a mighty stream. Mrs. Banks borrowed more card tables. Kay fluttered over them like a maternal barn swallow.

The Banks family had not yet become accustomed to endless bounty. That someone should take the trouble to go out and purchase with hard money a gift of any sort, still filled them with tender gratitude. Regardless of merit, utility or beauty, these first presents were snatched from their wrappings with cries of wonder and delight.

What puzzled Mr. Banks was that neither Mrs. Banks nor Kay ever forgot a detail in connection with any gift. For twenty-three years he had been impressed by the fact that neither of them seemed capable of grasping or retaining the most elementary details. Mrs. Banks could never remember, for example, whether the mortgage company owed Mr. Banks money or vice versa, and Kay still thought that the Rubaiyat was a toothpaste, but when it came to the matter of wedding presents, their donors and their sources, they both had memories like rogue elephants.

In an attempt to show paternal interest Mr. Banks tried to compete during the early days. By occasionally visiting the spare room for a private refresher course he was in control of the situation up to the thirty-sixth present. Then, while he was at the office one day, Mrs. Banks borrowed three more card tables and shifted everything around.

After that he struggled for a short while, then gave up. He never forgot the first thirty-five presents, however. Occasionally he tried to establish himself by picking up some object from this restricted group and remarking, "This bowl from the Appleblossoms is a nice thing." No one

paid any attention to him, but it made him feel that he still had a stake in the situation.

At first he had taken special pleasure in the drinking merchandise. This department led off with a dozen old-fashioned glasses. Then came ditto highball glasses. A cocktail shaker from Steuben, he was chagrined to note, was better than anything of the sort he had ever owned or probably ever would. A gleaming copper bar-table with red leather side rails filled him with envy.

Time passed and in its course Kay accumulated three dozen old-fashioned glasses, two dozen glass muddlers, four dozen highball glasses, three large cocktail shakers, two martini stirrers, two bride and groom midget cocktail sets, two whiskey decanters, five silver bottle openers, a half acre of wineglasses, a portable bar and sundry jiggers and corkscrews. The place began to look like a setup for *The Lost Weekend*. Mr. Banks' connoisseur's enthusiasm was displaced by misgivings.

He was no teetotaler. On the other hand he now began to wonder whether he possibly had not overdone things a bit and conveyed to the world the impression that he was rearing a brood of alcoholics.

Given enough ointment there is always a fly. Given enough presents there is always One-of-Them. They are as inevitable as death. The only thing that is unpredictable is the direction from which they come. Kay's arrived one Saturday in a large wooden box, buried deep in Its nest of excelsior as if trying to hide Its shame.

It was a china lad in a china pink coat and a china maid in a Harlem pink skirt, crossing a china bridge which did not bridge anything, on Harlem blue china feet. As It rose from Its hiding place the family looked at It in stunned silence as the crew of a South Seas whaler might have watched a sea serpent emerge from the waters beside the ship. They knew, without the necessity of words, that this was IT.

Mr. Banks was the first to recover himself. "Who?" he demanded through clenched teeth. They pawed through the excelsior and fished out a card. "With love and affection from Aunt Marne."

A composite sound came from the Banks family. It was the cumulative cry of man's frustration through the ages. It might have been made by a Neanderthal father who, returning to his cave, finds a saber-toothed tiger licking his whiskers at the entrance.

Aunt Marne, of all people! The one member of the family who had been counted on to come across handsomely—preferably with a substantial check! She was rich, she was unmarried and she spent a week with the Bankses each fall. When Mr. Banks thought of all the evenings he had spent listening to Aunt Marne's non-stop chatter he was sorry he had not given way to his instincts while the opportunity was at hand and regardless of the consequences.

This was the Great Betrayal. From now on the name of Aunt Marne would be coupled with those of Judas Iscariot, Brutus, Benedict Arnold and Tojo.

"What are we going to *do* with it?" wailed Kay.

"Do you want me to tell you?" asked Mr. Banks.

Mrs. Banks examined it at arm's length. "I suppose we'll have to put it with the other presents. She's apt to come popping in any time."

"Perhaps we could change it"—hopefully.

"I've been looking. It doesn't say where it came from."

"It would be a pity to drop it," said Mr. Banks.

They put It on a card table in a far corner. They tried It on top of a chest of drawers. They hid It on a window sill behind an electric clock. No matter where they placed It, It was the first object which struck the eye when one entered the room.

The visitors' opening gambit was unvaried. "My *dear,* I never saw so many lovely presents." Then they would walk straight to the Thing and stand before It, picking up little objects in the neighborhood and laying them down. It was only a matter of minutes before they would have their hands on It. Operating on the theory that offense is the best defense, Mrs. Banks stepped in at this moment and explained that it was all a huge practical joke. Once they knew how excruciating it was everyone laughed heartily, but there was a malicious note in their mirth that Mr. Banks did not like.

Life was never quite the same after the arrival of Aunt Marne's present. Gone now the simple note. Gone the spirit of guileless appreciation for a gift as such. Gone the impartial screams of pleasure as the wrappings fell away. He who deceives a trusting dog does harm. From this point on the contents of each incoming package were appraised with the cold commercialism of an Oriental bazaar.

"What is it?"

"Another tray."

Deep groan from Kay. "It's a stinker, too."

"We can take it back. Where's it from?"

"The Tucker Gift Shop."

"We have almost enough junk from there, darling, to get something you really want."

"The trouble is there's nothing in the Tucker Gift Shop that *anybody* wants."

Mr. Banks, the erstwhile cynic of the family, found himself cringing in the face of this cold brutality. His heart went out in sympathy to the army of breadwinners who would soon be tearing out what little hair was left over the bills from the Tucker Gift Shop.

"That's a *nice* tray," he would remark fatuously. "What's the matter with it? There are lots of girls would give their eyeteeth—"

"Oh, Pops, you don't know anything *about* it. Let them *keep* their teeth. They can have it for nothing."

Mr. Banks hated to see Kay get hard.

Someone had given Kay a Bride's Book for an engagement present. A Bride's Book is, to a prospective bride, what a score card is to a baseball fan. The statistics are as important as the game itself. Kay's book was bound with white satin, already autographed with her thumb prints. It contained a quotation from Longfellow on the title page.

> *O fortunate, O happy day*
> *When a new household finds its place*
> *Among the myriad homes of earth.*

Mr. Banks read this several times with interest. To him it put Longfellow in the running with the prophet Isaiah. Anybody who found a place for a new household in this cockeyed world would not only be fortunate and happy, but also shot in the pants with luck. Nevertheless, he thought it struck rather a gloomy note for a book of this kind.

But Kay wasn't interested in housing. Her competitive sense was aroused by the blank pages for listing each present and the name of the donor. A number was printed before each entry space, and in the back of the book were perforated sheets of corresponding gummed numbers to be pasted on the presents.

Kay had examined these sheets immediately to be sure there were enough numbers to meet her estimates. Although her memory for figures was notoriously bad, she knew exactly how many presents each of her friends had received since Sally Gross had led off the bridal procession five years ago.

Booboo Batchelder had held the record for the last two years at 234. Her friends had always regarded it as unfair competition inasmuch as Booboo's father had once been a Senator. But statistics were statistics nevertheless.

Kay made no predictions. She was an ambitious young woman, however, accustomed to setting her sights high. Her motto was "235 or bust." She had no Senator father to fall back on, but she had built up a clientele of her own over the years. From her point of view at the moment quality or desirability did not matter. It was quantity that counted.

True to the American tradition, the receiving of gifts, which had been started so simply and spontaneously, soon developed into an organized industry in which each person became a specialist.

Mr. Banks' field was the disposal of empty cartons, wrapping paper

and excelsior. No one appointed him to this important work. It merely seemed to fall to his lot by a process of natural selection.

Being a thrifty man, when left to his own devices, he foresaw a vague future use for all this material. He cleaned out a corner of the cellar by consolidating other objects for which he also had a vague future use.

Each day the debris was piled waist-high in the back hall. One by one he bumped the cartons down the cellar stairs, sorted out the wrapping paper, jammed the excelsior into a special box and nested the empties neatly.

The corner filled rapidly and, as the boxes began to cover the entire cellar floor, his system broke down. Now he merely stuffed the loose debris into the cartons, carried them to the foot of the stairs and kicked them toward the nearest available space. The restoration of order was clearly something to be deferred for a rainy Saturday afternoon. Ultimately his chief problem was to keep a passageway open to the oil burner.

His task would have been dull, but relatively simple, had it not been for gross inefficiency in the higher echelons.

"Mother, what in the *world* did you do with that box from Rose Wood?"

"You mean the one with the tumblers?"

"Yes."

"Why, I don't know, dear. I suppose I put it in the back hall."

"But, *Mother,* I hadn't finished *unpacking* it. I was called away. I *do* wish, Mother—"

"Your father will know, dear," said Mrs. Banks soothingly, going to the head of the stairs.

"Stanley."

"Yes?"

"Did you notice that one of those boxes you took down to the cellar wasn't quite unpacked?"

Mr. Banks put down his newspaper. "Now listen, Ellie—"

"Well, won't you just run down in the cellar and have a look, dear. It's a box from Scranton. Just bring it up and we'll go through it up here."

Or again: "Darling, I'm afraid we've left a card somewhere in one of the boxes. A set of beautiful salad plates came and we don't know who sent them. Are you sure there wasn't a card in one of those cartons you brought down?"

Mr. Banks admitted that it was barely possible that he had carried a card down to the cellar without noticing it.

"Well, won't you try and find that box, dear, and just run through it. It was from the Tucker Gift Shop, so it ought to be easy."

Mr. Banks returned to the cellar. The place began to remind him of the hold of a badly packed cargo ship. Which boxes had come today,

which yesterday or which a week ago was any man's guess. And half of them were from the Tucker Gift Shop.

He plunged his hands into the nearest carton, came up with an armful of paper shavings and tossed them moodily onto the concrete floor. Half an hour later he reappeared dragging streamers of packing from either ankle.

Mrs. Banks called to him from the living room. "Oh, Stanley. Thanks, dear. Kay found the card. It was stuck between two plates. Mrs. Morley sent them. Wasn't that sweet of her?"

"I'm going to take a bath," said Mr. Banks.

The present-gazers began to arrive now in substantial numbers. Although their words were floated on milk and honey, they were obviously there for one, or all, of four purposes:

1. to see how their present stacked up with those of their competitors;
2. to find out if it was being given a favorable display position;
3. to judge if Kay was faring better in either quality or quantity than their recently married daughter;
4. to pick up ideas for cheap presents that look expensive.

Mrs. Banks, having been a present-gazer for years, knew only too well the importance of position. She became an expert at juggling the arrangement of the objects on the card tables. While she engaged her guests in animated chatter her eyes were on the door and her fingers were moving ceaselessly about the tables. As a result, by the time a donor moved across the room he would find his gift enshrined between Kay's flat silver and the super-de-luxe china from Aunt Emily.

It was a woman's world. Accompanying male present-gazers appeared only between five-thirty and seven. They would totter around the room behind their female convoys, staring over their shoulders with codlike eyes, until Mr. Banks took pity on them and put drinks into their hands. As their vicelike fingers closed over the cool, moist surface of the glass they would look at him gratefully murmuring, "Oh, I really don't want this. Thanks."

At this point male gazers abandoned all further attempts to examine presents. Mr. Banks talked to them at the other end of the room until their knees began to sag. Then he converted the living room into a kind of crèche and spread them around in vacant chairs until they were called for.

Chapter 11

GENTLEMEN'S CATERERS ALL ARE WE

We must do something about the caterer," said Mrs. Banks.

"The what?" Mr. Banks understood perfectly.

"Darling, did you think Delilah was going to handle the wedding reception all by herself?"

Mr. Banks couldn't truthfully say that he had thought about the matter at all—or that he wanted to think about it now.

"I've been finding out about caterers," continued Mrs. Banks in the bland tone of one conscious of having done her work while others fiddled. "The only thing to do is to have one come out from town. Sally Harrison had one for little Sally's wedding. She was crazy about him. His men were efficient and courteous and he's done a lot of weddings for people we know so he understands the sort of thing we want and she said he was very reasonable. Let's see. She gave me a card. I put it somewhere. Now let me think—"

Mr. Banks picked up his book, knowing that he wouldn't be troubled by the subject again for at least half an hour.

On the following Saturday morning Mr. and Mrs. Banks drove to town and visited the offices of Buckingham Caterers, specialists in luncheons, dinners, buffet suppers, cocktail parties, wedding receptions, christenings, lodge meetings and general social functions.

Mr. Massoula, who appeared to be in charge, was obviously a young man who knew his way about. He had a long upper lip decorated on its lower edge with a tiny mustache, reminiscent of a fringe on a lamp shade. His double-breasted, blue suit was sharply creased and his thin, black hair was plastered down so tightly that it might have been painted on his skull.

Wedding reception? Yes indeed. Buckingham Caterers were fully equipped to take the whole affair over. Mr. and Mrs. Banks didn't need to give the matter another thought. Just specify the date and they could romp off to the Arizona Biltmore or Palm Beach or Palm Springs or wherever it was that people like Mr. and Mrs. Banks spent their time. The point was they *did not need to worry*.

Buckingham Caterers had handled some of the biggest and most expensive weddings in the country. Mr. Massoula let it be understood clearly that they were not in the habit of putting their shoulder to weddings which were not in the upper brackets of the social scale.

"But first," said Mr. Massoula, reaching under the table and producing several large photograph albums, "I'd like to get your ideas about a wedding cake. Once the wedding cake has been established Buckingham Caterers take over. Now here is a very popular cake. That's Brenda Santanya. You know. Daughter of Princess Fraschisi by her second husband."

Mr. Banks looked at his wife. They hadn't even thought about a wedding cake. To Buckingham Caterers it was obviously not a matter for discussion. Mr. Massoula turned over dozens of photographs showing brides and grooms about to destroy hideous cakes of every size and shape. One could see that the cakes were different, but the brides and grooms all looked alike.

Mr. Massoula had an encyclopedic memory for names and social connections. The First Families of the nation passed in review before Mr. and Mrs. Banks. They had never heard of most of them, but they were pleased by the way that Mr. Massoula assumed that all these people were their buddies.

"That's one of Tommy Manville's weddings," he said. "We've done almost all of them. Good old Tommy. Delightful person, isn't he?"

Mr. Banks was about to say "Yes" but checked himself. He began to wish he had chosen a less socially prominent caterer.

"Ours isn't going to be a big reception," he ventured.

"Small and select. I understand perfectly. Buckingham Caterers can handle them any size."

Mr. Banks' fingers tightened on the edge of the table. "We don't want a cake," he said with dignity. Mrs. Banks' admiring glance fortified his courage.

"What! You don't want a cake! Why—"

Mr. Banks shot the works. "I think cakes are cheap," he said. "Every Tom, Dick and Harry has cakes. We don't want one."

Mr. Massoula looked at him with new respect. "I understand," he murmured. "It is true that the *very* select weddings no longer have them. We must show them, though. Most people wouldn't understand if we didn't."

"Of course not," said Mr. Banks. He dreaded the moment when he had to tell Mr. Massoula that this particular reception was to be held in a place called Fairview Manor.

Mr. Massoula brought up another large album from under the table. "While you're here I'd like to have you look at a few shots of some of our receptions."

As he looked Mr. Banks' dismay turned to panic. Buckingham Caterers not only dealt exclusively with the uncrowned heads of American Industrial Aristocracy, but apparently they catered only on huge estates and in palaces. He wondered how he could get out of the whole thing gracefully. Maple Drive had suddenly become a kind of suburban back

alley. Quite obviously his home would look like somebody's gatehouse to Mr. Massoula.

But it was too late. Mr. Massoula had pulled out a pad of forms. "Now we should get some idea of what you would like to serve. We will supply the champagne of course."

Much to his chagrin Mr. Banks turned slightly red. "I'm sorry. What I mean is I didn't know. That is to say I've bought the champagne already."

Mr. Massoula's face clouded with politely restrained annoyance. "Then we will have to charge corkage, of course."

"Corkage?"

"A dollar a bottle for drawing and pouring."

"Oh, Delilah can take care of all that."

"If you are referring to one of your house staff," said Mr. Massoula firmly, "you must understand that in an affair of this kind the caterer takes over completely. Any other arrangement would cause friction in the servants' quarters. I am sure *you* understand, madam." He smiled at Mrs. Banks as mothers smile at one another over the heads of their wayward young.

Mrs. Banks returned the smile. "Indeed I do."

"By the way," said Mr. Massoula, "are you serving French champagne?" Had he said, "You are serving French champagne, of course?" the meaning would have been the same.

"As a matter of fact I'm not," said Mr. Banks in a tone that acknowledged the eccentricity of his decision. "I just think it's a shame to waste good vintage champagne on these kids. So I'm giving them American," he finished lamely.

Mr. Massoula nodded understandingly. "That will be all right with us," he said graciously. "Now, about the food. Let's see. The wedding is in early June. How about a large cold salmon at either end of the table with the various salads in great bowls in the center? Another dramatic arrangement is a cold sturgeon in the middle of the table. Now for the ices, we pride ourselves on a very special effect with colored electric lights embedded in a huge cake of ice, capped—"

"But," interrupted Mrs. Banks timidly, "we hadn't intended to have that kind of a reception."

Mr. Massoula gave her a puzzled look and laid down his pencil. "What did you have in mind, madam?"

Mrs. Banks fingered her handbag nervously. "Well, we thought that maybe some small assorted sandwiches—different kinds, you know— and ice cream and little cakes—"

"Of course you can have what you wish, madam, but that is usually what we serve at children's parties."

"Well, it's what we *want*," said Mrs. Banks with a sudden harshness that in turn surprised her husband.

"Of course. Of course," said Mr. Massoula, making notes. "And I can assure you that you will be pleased when you see the results. Now where will the reception take place?"

"Twenty-four Maple Drive, Fairview Manor," said Mr. Banks belligerently.

"Is that a club or a country estate?" asked Mr. Massoula.

"It's my *home*," replied Mr. Banks with dignity.

Mr. Massoula bowed slightly in deference to the generic sacredness of all homes. "What attendance do you anticipate?"

"About a hundred and fifty."

"Is it a large house?"

"No," said Mr. Banks defiantly. "It's a small house."

"Then of course you are planning for a marquee on the terrace."

"I have no terrace. If they overflow the house they can tramp around in the yard."

"And what if it rains?" asked Mr. Massoula with a rising inflection, glancing at Mrs. Banks. "What if it pours that day?"

"That's just what *I* said," put in Mrs. Banks. "Stanley, what *would* we do if it poured?"

"A marquee is very inexpensive," reassured Mr. Massoula soothingly, "and even if it doesn't rain you really *should* have it. I'll tell you what we'll do. I'll have one of our field engineers go over the property. We always have to do that anyway to study circulation problems and that sort of thing."

"Listen," said Mr. Banks desperately. "We've talked about everything but how much this is going to cost."

"The cost," said Mr. Massoula, "will be relatively small for a party such as you describe." His tone indicated that the kind of party which Mr. Banks had described wasn't much of a party. "For the *minimum* refreshments which you have specified the cost will be a dollar and a half a head, plus corkage, plus the cost of the marquee and sundry small expenses. For that Buckingham Caterers take *complete* charge, including experienced and courteous men who have been with us for years. Don't consider the cost, Mr. Banks. It will be trifling compared to the service which you will receive."

Apparently the social season was dragging a bit, for a few days later Mr. Massoula arrived in person at 24 Maple Drive. He was accompanied by a sheepish-looking character with handlebar mustaches, whom he referred to as Joe. Mrs. Banks assumed that he was one of the field engineers whom Mr. Massoula had spoken about, although he looked more like a horsecar conductor.

Mrs. Banks was a meticulous housekeeper and she had always been proud of her home. Now, as Mr. Massoula and Joe wandered from room to room with cold appraising eyes and occasional mumbled com-

ments, she realized that neither of them had ever before catered in such a hovel.

"Small," said Mr. Massoula.

"I'll say," agreed Joe. "How many head did you say?"

"Hundred fifty."

"Jesus," said Joe. Mrs. Banks was afraid he was going to expectorate, but he refrained with an obvious effort.

"Circulation's bad," said Mr. Massoula.

"I'll say," agreed Joe.

"We'll have all the windows open on that day," assured Mrs. Banks.

"What *we* mean by circulation," said Mr. Massoula kindly, "is the *guest* flow from room to room. A room with two interior doors has minimum circulation. A room like this with only one is—is—well, it's a death trap. Where does this go?"

Mr. Massoula pulled the knob of a door. It came off in his hands.

"I'm so sorry," said Mrs. Banks miserably. "It does that unless you push it in first. That just goes into a closet anyway."

Mr. Massoula placed the knob on the dining-room table. "Is this the pantry?" The two men seemed to fill the little room.

"Small," said Mr. Massoula.

"Dark," said Joe.

Mrs. Banks snapped the electric switch. Nothing happened.

"Bulb's busted," said Joe. "I seen enough."

Mrs. Banks followed them gloomily back to the living room.

"Circulation in this room's O.K.," said Mr. Massoula.

"Only one that is," said Joe.

"But you couldn't get more than a hundred and twenty-five in the house."

"Squash 'em like bugs if you did," said Joe.

"I'm planning to take a lot of these things up to the attic, you know," explained Mrs. Banks. "All those straight chairs go up, and the small tables and standing lamps, and we're thinking of taking up the rug."

"Takin' th' rug up ain't goin' to give any more room," said Joe. Mr. Massoula maintained a displeased silence.

"Have you any suggestions?" asked Mrs. Banks nervously.

"Yes, madam, I have," said Mr. Massoula. "Even with a marquee you're going to be cramped. By the way, Joe, go out in the back and measure for the marquee. Now you see, madam, circulation's your big problem. The first thing you've got to do is clear this room of *all* furniture."

There was a suggestion of tears in Mrs. Banks' voice. "You don't mean the big davenport and the armchairs and—"

"Of course. *And* the piano. *Everything* must come out of this room. Now in the dining room—"

"Does the dining-room table have to go too?" she wailed, but Mr. Massoula was not listening.

"That chandelier over the dining-room table—could that be looped up or something?"

In view of the fact that the chandelier was not made of rubber tubing Mrs. Banks did not see how it could.

"Then you better have the electrician take it out an' cap it temporarily," said Mr. Massoula. "It's in the way. Now about these doors between the rooms. They've got to be taken off. You'd be surprised to see how much circulation you lose on account of doors. Especially doors like these."

Mrs. Banks might have forgiven him if he had not added that last sentence. As it was she lost her temper as an alternative to tears. "What in the world do you think I've got upstairs—a cold-storage warehouse? And who do you think is going to lug all this stuff up there—if there was room? And who do you think is going to get it down again?"

But Mr. Massoula was a creative artist. Details were not in his line. "We'll connect the marquee to this French door from the living room," he said. He tried to open the door but it merely slammed violently back and forth at the top. The bottom was apparently glued to the sill.

"It's stuck," explained Mrs. Banks. "I've been meaning to have that door fixed."

Mr. Massoula opened a window and leaned out. "Hi, Joe," he bawled. "Figure on a connecting angle through the French door here. Measure from the outside. The thing's stuck."

"I'll say," came an angry voice from the lilacs. "Too many God-damn bushes out here. Ought to get rid of 'em."

Chapter 12

TOMORROW'S MY DAUGHTER'S WEDDING DAY

The day before the wedding came at last.

When one concentrates fiercely and at length on an event in the distant future it eventually becomes fixed in the mind as something forever remote. As a result it is a shock to awake some morning and find that the distant future has suddenly become the immediate present. It is like a foolish rumor about a lion in the district, which no one takes seriously until the beast springs at you from behind a lilac bush.

Father of the Bride

The wedding rehearsal was scheduled for five-thirty. Mr. Banks set out for the office exhibiting a nonchalance that he did not feel. Yes, of course, he would take the three-ten from town. There was nothing to get so excited about. Beneath the surface, however, he was distinctly nervous. He felt like a man moving beneath powerful floodlights.

The floodlight operator must have been off duty during his trip to town, however. The same apathetic faces greeted him at the station with the same apathetic comments about the weather, their health, or their lack of it. As the train pulled out of Fairview Manor, Reggie Fry lurched into the seat beside him and spent three stations describing an intricate real-estate deal in the course of which he had outwitted and discomfited the best brains in the business. Mr. Banks could stand it no longer.

"My daughter's getting married tomorrow," he said simply.

"Really?" said Mr. Fry. "Didn't know you had a daughter. Time flies, eh? I hope she's got a place to live after she's married. It's a bad situation. Getting worse. The Real-Estate Board put out some interesting figures about it in their last bulletin. I've got it here somewhere. Here it is. Now just let me read you these few paragraphs. This is on the volume of building of one-family homes in the mid-continent states during the first quarter."

Mr. Banks shuddered and gave himself up to his thoughts.

He would have found it hard to describe just what he expected when he arrived at the office. Obviously he had not anticipated organized cheering as he came in the door, yet it depressed him to have Miss Rooney nod to him from the switchboard and say, "MorningMrBanksnicemorning," just as she did on the other three hundred working days of the year.

Even his partners failed to grasp the significance of current events. As each one drifted into Mr. Banks' office during the morning he offered some fatuous remark about not falling down in the aisle or trying to bend over in his cutaway. Then, having made their concessions to the trivia of life, they concentrated on the task of dumping on his desk every unanswerable and boring problem they could dig out of their pending files. They reminded Mr. Banks of executives cleaning out their desks before leaving for their summer vacations.

During the moments when his partners were not bedeviling him the outside world took up the torch. The cream of the dullest and most long-winded of Mr. Banks' clients flocked into his office for no other apparent reason than to make sheep eyes at him and fill up an idle hour with the sound of their own voices.

The only positive note was the telephone. Whenever Mr. Banks thought about that morning during later years it was his telephone buzzer which sounded the motif of the nightmare cacophony.

"Darling, the worst thing. Old Mr. McQuade is down at the station. —McQuade, dear. I don't know. He's some relative of *yours*.—Well, it's

673

no use arguing about that *now*. He's down at the station and he wants to know where he's supposed to *go*. Where in the world am I going to put him?"

Only the presence of a customer mooning beside his desk restrained Mr. Banks from detailed instructions.

"Hello. Is this you, Stanley?—This is Ella. *Ella*.—Is this Stanley Banks?—This is *Ella*. Yes. How *are* you? We came down in the last minute as a surprise. Now we don't want you to bother your *head* about us. Just tell us how the trains run to Fairview Manor and how to get from the station to your house. If you haven't room to put us up we can go *anywhere* at all. The last thing we want to do is put you to any trouble. I guess you've got troubles enough just now." (Hysterical laughter.)

The sheep-eyed gentleman beside Mr. Banks' desk looked at him anxiously. "I hope that wasn't bad news," he said.

"No, no," said Mr. Banks. "I've got a daughter getting married tomorrow."

"Oh, of course. Quite," said the sheep-eyed gentleman and resumed his narrative.

"Darling, I'm so sorry to bother you again but I'm almost crazy. You can't imagine what's happened. The Bennett boy has come down with measles and they can't take in Cousin Laura and Bob. What in the *world* are we—I know, dear, but I thought you might have some *ideas*."

By twelve-thirty he could stand it no longer. Shoving a pile of papers into a desk drawer, he rang for Miss Bellamy. "I'm getting the hell out of here," he said defiantly. The phone rang. "I'm gone."

"So sorry," murmured Miss Bellamy into the mouthpiece. "He was called away very hurriedly. He just this moment left the office. No, I don't think I could catch him. I know how sorry he'll be. He wanted to talk to you. Yes, I'll certainly tell him." She hung up the receiver. "It's that Mr. Wadley you've been trying to get for three days."

"That fellow has no judgment," said Mr. Banks.

"Yes indeed," said Miss Bellamy soothingly. "Now I have everything ready in this envelope. Here's a list of all the ushers and bridesmaids and where they're staying and their telephone numbers. And then here's a full set of church seating lists. There's one for each usher with his name typed on it and special instructions for those who have special jobs. I've put in some extra copies just in case. Oh, yes, and I've phoned all the papers just to make sure they remember and—well—I guess that's all till I see you in church."

Miss Bellamy looked suddenly deflated and wistful. Mr. Banks had never seen her like that before. For one terrible moment he thought she was going to cry.

"You've been wonderful," he said awkwardly. "Wonderful. I'll never forget it." He left quickly as the phone started to ring.

Several days earlier Miss Bellamy had sent crisp little notes to all the ushers and bridesmaids, attempting to impress upon their scattered minds that the rehearsal would be at five-thirty at St. George's Church and the importance of being prompt.

Mr. Banks had insisted on being there fifteen minutes ahead of time. He wanted this wedding well rehearsed—no sloppy business—and he felt somehow that if he and Mrs. Banks were early it would expedite things. To his dismay he found the church in complete darkness. The Reverend Mr. Galsworthy and the organist were nowhere about. The smoothly functioning machinery of St. George's was at dead center and the self-starter was missing.

Mr. Banks had pictured the organist busily warming up his instrument with a burst of arpeggios and Mr. Galsworthy nervously pacing the aisle, measuring distances, putting markers in his book and making a few final notes. Not even Mr. Tringle, the sexton, was puttering around.

He finally located Mr. Tringle in the cellar of the rectory gluing the back of a broken chair. "Good gracious," he exclaimed. "That late a'ready? Maybe we best go up an' put on the lights."

The first bridesmaid turned up at a quarter to six. She was a wispy little number who seemed to have been left out of everything to date and was obviously terrified at the thought of what lay ahead. The organist strolled in several minutes later.

"Are you sure," asked Mrs. Banks anxiously, "that you know what you are going to play at the wedding?"

"Oh, yes," said the organist. He was an earnest-looking young man with heavy horn spectacles. "Oh, quite. This is the Broadhurst wedding, isn't it?"

The knuckles of Mr. Banks' hand grew white as he clutched the end of the pew. "No," he said gently. "This is the *Banks* wedding—and it's *tomorrow*," he added with subtle sarcasm.

"Surely," agreed the organist and disappeared through the gloom of the side aisle.

By six-thirty Kay and all but four of the bridal party had appeared. The minister was still absent. The groom was still absent. The ushers and bridesmaids who had made the great sacrifice stood in small groups glaring at Mr. Banks with unconcealed hostility. It was evident that each and all had torn themselves away from agreeable situations for what they clearly considered to be an old-fashioned whim of Mr. Banks'. By their attitude they said, "You got us here. You ruined our fun. Now what are you going to do about it?"

It made Mr. Banks nervous. He distributed the seating lists to the ushers and made a little talk about over-all strategy. Somehow it didn't go very well. They listened to him with the detached boredom of tourists harangued by a Grand Canyon guide. Their aspirations were obviously elsewhere.

675

"I wonder where Mr. Galsworthy is?" asked Mr. Banks for the tenth time.

"Oh, he's somewhere. He's always late," said Mr. Tringle amiably. "I run the rehearsal."

"But some of the bridal party aren't here yet," protested Mr. Banks. "The groom isn't here. Nobody's here."

"Some of the bridal party is never here," said Mr. Tringle. "The groom don't do nothing in weddings. Everything goes all right. You see. Don't worry. Now if you young ladies will line up in pairs outside that there door—"

They lined up, tittering and unwilling, as people line up for a group photograph which nobody wants taken. Once in place they unlined immediately. Mr. Tringle pushed them back like errant cattle. "O.K., Fritz," he yelled irreligiously. The organ suddenly gave a series of bumps and broke into the wedding march. Mrs. Banks watched nervously from a pew.

"It's too fast," she cried hopelessly as the skeleton procession dashed past her. "You're running. It's awful."

"You want to do it again?" asked Mr. Tringle, rubbing his hands with the air of one who has staged a great dramatic spectacle. "It comes O.K. next time. Take it easy. Line up now. Hey, you. Big girl. You get in back row this time so's they can see the other bridesmaids. O.K., Fritz, shoot," he bawled.

They were off again. It wasn't the way Mr. Banks had pictured it. In fact, it reminded him more of the mob scene in the *Vagabond King* than a wedding rehearsal. He gave a sigh of relief as he saw the Reverend Galsworthy enter the church, trotting like a pony and exuding geniality. Now they would get the situation in hand.

"Well, well, well," said Mr. Galsworthy. "All over, I see. That means I'm just in time. So sorry. Had a meeting. Mr. Tringle's an old hand, though." He put his arm around Mr. Tringle's shoulder and squeezed him with impersonal affection. "Do they know their stuff, Mr. Tringle? Good. Well, I'm sure it will all go off very smoothly and that it will be a beautiful wedding."

Mr. Banks could hardly believe what he heard. "But they haven't really begun to rehearse. Four of the bridal party aren't even here yet and the groom isn't here either. They tried it a couple of times and it was awful."

Mr. Galsworthy looked at his watch and clucked.

"They do all right," said Mr. Tringle. "O.K. tomorrow."

"Good," said Mr. Galsworthy. "Good. I have a meeting now. As for the groom—well, the groom is not very important at weddings, is he, my dear?" He smiled benignly at the wispy bridesmaid under the impression that she was the bride-to-be.

"You're not nervous, are you, dear?" he continued, taking the wispy

676

girl's hand in his. "No, of course not. Have your young man call me in the morning. I'll put him through his paces. I hate to rush, but I must. Don't worry. Everything will be fine."

Mr. Banks opened his mouth. "But—" A secretarial-looking person bustled down the aisle. "Mrs. Banks? There's a phone call for you in the Rector's office. I believe it's the groom's father and mother. They're at your house and they want to know if the rehearsal's over. I think the groom is with them."

"Sure," said Mr. Tringle cheerily. "Rehearsal's all over. Tell 'em to take it easy. Everybody'll be right home."

"Don't forget to have the groom call me in the morning," said Mr. Galsworthy. "Now don't worry. It will go beautifully tomorrow. I know. You see I've done this before."

"But—" began Mr. Banks. Then he looked around. The bridal party had disappeared, bearing Kay and the wispy girl with them. Mr. and Mrs. Banks shook hands cordially with Mr. Galsworthy and followed them.

On the way out Mr. Banks noted that most of Miss Bellamy's beautifully typed seating lists had been laid on the seats of pews and abandoned. He gathered them up. With the extras there might be enough for a redistribution.

"I do hope—" said Mrs. Banks.

"So do I," agreed her husband.

They went home to dress for the party at the Club.

Chapter 13

THEY'RE COMING INTO THE STRETCH

Mr. Banks awoke early the following morning, conscious that many things were wrong. The first to register positively was his body, which felt as if it had been run over. He moved his head on the pillow. For a moment he was convinced that his skull had been fractured.

Gradually he became aware that there was something particularly unusual about this day that was beginning so inauspiciously. Then his slowly awakening mind grasped the fact that he had come home rather late from the Country Club and that in a few hours his oldest child was going to be married.

Instinctively he turned to look out the window. The sun was shining. A cool breeze stirred the leaves of the maple tree outside. His eyes

traveled lower and encountered those of the mother of the bride. They were appraising him with an expression that struck him as being on the cold side.

"Nice day," he said.

"Yes," she said, "thank God. And now we're getting up. There's work to be done."

Mr. Banks would have given a year of life to lie quite still, indefinitely, but he felt the moment was a poor one for advancing whimsical ideas. As unostentatiously as possible he went to the bathroom cabinet and poured a large spoonful of Bromo Seltzer into a glass of water. It fizzed delightfully against his dry palate. The world looked better, although his sensations were still those of a sleeping leg. Perhaps this was a day when a bit of numbness might be helpful.

Downstairs the house was unrecognizable. The furniture had disappeared. The whole place smelled, not too faintly, of floor wax and soap suds. Delilah met him at the foot of the stairs.

"Mis' Banks, yo's goin' t'have yo' breakfas' in th' kitchen this mo'-nin'," she announced. The idea seemed to strike her as high comedy. She disappeared into the pantry doubled up with laughter.

Mr. Banks ate his eggs self-consciously at Delilah's white-enameled table. It seemed to him that women used poor judgment about such matters. Why couldn't he have had his breakfast in the usual way and in the usual place? There was plenty of time to get things ready. No need for all this jitter.

After a second cup of black coffee he wandered aimlessly through the bare rooms. A truck pulled into the driveway followed by a black sedan from which a bald-headed man alighted. The front door was open. The bald-headed man walked in without ceremony. "I'm Tim's man," he said.

"Oh," said Mr. Banks, pleasantly, but with reserve.

"I guess we'll be settin' up th' flowers an' stuff," said Tim's man.

"Yes indeed," said Mr. Banks.

Mr. Tim's man stuck his head out the front door. "Lug 'em in, boys."

A few minutes later the floor of the living room was covered with potted plants, ferns and lumps of damp earth. Mr. Banks strolled restlessly through the debris and out the French door into the back garden. There he found three strangers unrolling a huge bundle of canvas.

"Is that the marquee?" he asked.

"It's the tent for the Banks weddin'," corrected one of the men.

Mr. Banks squinted at the cloudless sky. A brilliant idea flashed across his thrifty mind. "You know," he said casually, "on a day like this I don't think we'll need a tent. I think it would be pleasanter to walk through that door right onto the open lawn. Don't you think so yourselves?"

678

The men stopped unrolling the tent and stared at him in silent amazement. One of them finally recovered his voice. "Don't need a tent!" he exclaimed. "Listen, Jack, this here tent is *con*tracted for three weeks ago. There's people yellin' for it all over th' place. You're just lucky, that's all."

"Yes, of course," said Mr. Banks. "I only thought—Yes, of course."

He stepped around the bulky pile and walked down the driveway. Maple Drive was quiet. Several houses away his new neighbor, Mr. Hoggson, was cutting his front lawn. It seemed incredible to Mr. Banks that anyone could be engaged in such trivial work at a time like this. He strolled aimlessly toward him.

"Hi," said Mr. Hoggson, pausing. "Going to be a nice week end."

"I certainly hope so," said Mr. Banks. "My daughter's getting married this afternoon."

"Well, you don't say so!" Mr. Hoggson relinquished his moist grip on the handles of the lawn mower and shook Mr. Banks' hand warmly. "That's your first child to go, isn't it? Quite a wrench, all right. You bring 'em up to the best you got and spend a lot of money educatin' 'em an' then they run off with some football player an' that's the last you hear of 'em till you get a post card from Reno. Well, I certainly wish her all the happiness in the world. You won't come in and have a spot, perhaps? You got a hard day ahead of you."

"Sorry," said Mr. Banks. "We're kind of busy at the house this morning. I'm just doing an errand for my wife."

He walked briskly away without the slightest notion where he was going. It was the same everywhere. The world was proceeding quietly about its week-end tasks, heedless of what was happening at 24 Maple Drive. After about a mile he cut through a patch of woods and came back through the village in order to avoid Mr. Hoggson.

By the time he returned to the house the artisans had given way to relatives. The place was swarming with them. They had all made a great effort to be present. Now that they were here they wanted attention.

The phone was ringing continuously. He took charge of it. Anything was better than making conversation. The phone at least demanded concrete answers. Uncle Joe was in town and wanted detailed instructions on how to get out to Fairview Manor. Cousin Bertha was at the station. Would someone come down and get her? Aunt Harriet had lost her suitcase with her best dress in it. Would someone look around the house and see if she had left it there by any chance?

Mr. Banks said he would find it for her and tiptoed up the back stairs. But he was not looking for Aunt Harriet's suitcase. He was looking for Kay. He had suddenly noticed that she was not around.

Her door was closed. When there was no answer to his knock he opened it and looked in. Kay was lying on her bed, her face buried in the pillow, her shoulders shaking.

"Kitten," he said, "what's the trouble?"

She motioned him away violently, but he came over and sat on the side of her bed, running his fingers up and down her spine as he used to do when she was going to sleep.

"Tell me about it. What's hurt you? You shouldn't cry today, Kitten. This is your wedding day."

"Oh, I know it, Pops. That's just the *trouble*. It's my wedding day, but it *isn't*. It's everybody *else's* wedding day but it just isn't *mine*." She let her face down into the pillow again, but now she was quieter.

Mr. Banks rubbed her back for a few minutes without answering. "I know," he said finally. "I know. Mine either."

The Bill Harcourts gave a luncheon before the wedding. It was to have been a small affair: just the bride and groom, the bridal party and the immediate family. Nothing about this wedding, however, seemed capable of remaining small.

The house was crowded with people when Mr. and Mrs. Banks arrived. The bridesmaids, made confident by the conspicuous newness of their clothes, exuded vitality and youth. The ushers, on the other hand, had the drawn, haggard look of men who have just completed a dangerous bombing mission. They grabbed the cocktails from the passing trays as the occupants of a life raft would seize a wounded albatross as it floated by.

The place was alive with relatives whose names Mr. Banks could not remember. It was obvious that they were all out for a field day and expected him to meet their mood.

As he entered the room a barge of a woman, wearing pince-nez, bore down on him like a tugboat, backed him neatly between some bookcases and the piano and began a detailed account of Buckley's early childhood. She was up to his fifth year with nineteen years to go, and no sign of faltering, when someone spilled a plate of lobster salad on one of her ample hips. In the confusion Mr. Banks managed to escape, only to be recaptured by a man with a walrus mustache.

This character appeared to regard the gathering as a kind of public forum. He drew Mr. Banks to a window seat. This was the first opportunity he had had for a quiet chat, owing to the unaccountable confusion which seemed to pervade this whole affair. His primary interest was in world politics and his mind would not be at rest until he had Mr. Banks' opinion of the international situation. When Mr. Banks disclosed the fact that he had no opinions on the international or any other situation, the floor passed to the stranger, who obviously had a direct wire to God.

Athletic young men kept coming up with plates heaped to the gunwales with lobster and chicken salad, to which buttered rolls clung precariously. Mr. Banks felt slightly bilious and compromised on a cup of soup and a highball.

Kay approached them. "Mother's looking for you. She thinks we'd better be getting home." He gazed at her with awe. An hour ago she had been sobbing on her bed. Now she looked radiant—like a goddess of spring—serene and beautiful.

Mrs. Pulitzski, who had made over Mrs. Banks' wedding dress for Kay, had insisted on coming to the house that afternoon to be sure that all was in order.

"Good God," said Mr. Banks to the world at large, "this is a swell time to find out if it fits her. What's the woman going to do? Start making alterations now? Do you people realize it's a quarter to three and that there's a wedding in an hour and forty-five minutes?"

Any allusion to the passage of time always called forth a protest from Ben and Tommy.

"Gee, Pops, you might think it took us an hour to dress."

"Why, I can be dressed in ten minutes." Tommy stretched out languidly on his bed. "It won't take me ten minutes to get into that old fool suit."

Mr. Banks pushed down his temper with an effort. This was no time for a test of strength. "You two boys have a big responsibility this afternoon," he said with feigned calm. "You're the only two ushers who know our family. You're taking our car and you're to get there by four o'clock."

"We'll be there, Pops. Don't worry. Just relax."

Mr. Banks gave up and went to his room to dress. Somehow he felt alone and out of the picture. Mrs. Banks was dressing in the guest room which adjoined Kay's. He made his preparations moodily.

He was not nervous, as he had feared he might be, only confused and ill at ease. While he regarded himself gloomily in the mirror Tommy burst into the room.

"Hey, Pops, I haven't anything but soft shirts. These stiff collars won't fit on soft shirts. What am I going to do?"

If Mr. Banks had had a blunt instrument in his hands he would undoubtedly have used it. As it was he merely stared at Tommy without affection.

"What size do you wear?"

"Fourteen and a half."

"Well, I wear fifteen and a half, so that's that. Hasn't Ben got a shirt without a collar?"

"Yeah, but he's got it on."

"Didn't you have an evening shirt?"

"Yeah. Mom put it in the wash. *Can't* I wear a soft shirt, Pops?"

"No," shouted Mr. Banks.

"Well, what'll I *do?*"

"Take the car and *get* one," yelled Mr. Banks. "Good God, it's

quarter after three. You and Ben are due at the church in forty-five minutes. Have I got to think for—"

But Tommy was gone. Mr. Banks resumed dressing, musing on the sordid eugenic tricks that Nature plays on men. When he had finished he surveyed himself in the long mirror and found the sight rather pleasing. Not many of his friends could wear their old cutaways at their daughters' weddings. If he didn't move impulsively it was perfect.

He started downstairs. As he passed Kay's door he heard voices. He was about to stop. Then the feeling of strangeness came over him once more and he continued on his way.

Without premeditation he found himself in the pantry. There he poured himself a highball which he regarded contemplatively for some time before drinking. When he had finished it he could think of nothing else to do so he started back upstairs.

Tommy almost knocked him down as he came leaping up the steps three at a time, a package under his arm. "I got it," he panted from the door of his bedroom. "I had to move some. A cop stopped me, but I talked him out of it. Gee, what a ride." His door slammed. Mr. Banks shuddered. He stood uncertainly at the head of the stairs, not knowing just where to go. A low murmur of voices came from behind Kay's closed door.

"Hi, Pops, this kind of a shirt has to have studs. Got any?" He felt himself going rigid again.

"You *must* have some. Your mother gave you a set for your evening shirt."

"I know, Pops. I can't find 'em. Must have gone to the wash."

In his bedroom Mr. Banks pawed vainly through the jewel case which had stood on his bureau for decades. It contained a miscellaneous collection of old fraternity pins, unidentified skeleton keys, a patent nail-clipper and his World War I identification tag. No collar buttons.

His voice sounded strained and unreal. "Listen, you've had two months to think of this. You take Ben to the church. Then go and get your damn collar buttons—and swallow them."

Tommy opened his mouth to protest at this injustice, but he saw an expression on his father's face that made him think better of it. He went out, closing the door quietly behind him.

A moment later Mrs. Banks entered the room and Mr. Banks forgot everything else. He knew that he would never be able to remember what she was wearing. He knew also that, to his dying day, he would never forget her as she stood, framed in the doorway, waiting for his approval—slim, graceful and lovely. All the beauty of her own wedding day lay upon her, tempered by a serenity and dignity that made Mr. Banks feel suddenly shy.

She saw the startled admiration in his face. "Don't say any more,

darling," she said. "You like it. I saw that. You'll spoil it if you try to tell me why. And for heaven's sake don't muss my hair."

"Kay is ready," announced Mrs. Pulitzski. They filed down the hall after her. She paused before Kay's door and threw it open dramatically. Kay was standing in the middle of the room, her train and veil carefully arranged behind her, no longer a brown-haired girl of five feet four, but a princess from some medieval court. Her head was thrown back slightly and she watched the effect upon her courtiers with the calm assurance of one born to the cloth of gold.

Mr. Banks would not have been surprised if she had extended her hand for him to kiss. His eyes became suddenly blurred. Good God, this would be a hell of a time for him to start crying. What was the matter with everybody today?

"You're wonderful, Kitten. Wonderful."

She squeezed his hand. "Thanks, Pops." For an instant her eyes met his—not as a daughter but as a woman. "Now, on to the slaughter," she said.

He looked at his watch. "Good God, it's five after four."

"The cars *must* be here," said Mrs. Banks. "I ordered both of them to be here at four sharp." She looked out Kay's window into the empty street.

"I'll call the garage," said Mr. Banks. "I'll give them a piece of my mind." Before he was halfway downstairs the telephone rang.

"Hello.—Yes. Speaking.—WHAT? WHO? Wait a minute." He covered the receiver with his hand. "It's those two cousins of yours from Baltimore. They came as a surprise. They're down at the station and there aren't any taxis. They want to know how they're going to get to the church."

Mrs. Banks stared blankly down at him over the stair rail.

"Well, what'll I tell them?" asked her husband. "They're *your* relatives."

"Tell them—Tell them—Oh, tell them I don't give a damn how they get there. Tell them to jump in the lake and swim."

If Mrs. Banks had done a hand stand on the banisters she could not have startled her husband more. "Ellie can't be disturbed at the moment," he said apologetically to the telephone. "I'm sure there'll be a taxi along in a minute, though. There always is.—Yes indeed. It was good of you to come.—I certainly hope so."

The two black limousines drove up at quarter after four, their drivers immaculate in whipcord uniforms and visored caps.

"Where the hell—" began Mr. Banks.

The driver of the rear car got out and stood before Mr. Banks, cap in hand. He had white, wavy hair and a pontifical face that radiated gentle loving-kindness.

"I'm sorry, sir," he said. His voice sounded like a benediction. "They gave us the wrong address. I'm truly sorry, sir. I know the importance of punctuality at a time like this. I hope it hasn't upset the young lady."

Mr. Banks deflated visibly. "Not at all," he said. "Not at all." He helped Mrs. Banks and her mother into the front car, which dashed off immediately. Mrs. Pulitzski already had Kay carefully folded into the rear one. He climbed in beside his daughter, knocking his high hat over his nose. The white-haired chauffeur closed the door tenderly.

It was immediately opened again by a small man in a brown suit. "I'm Weisgold," he said. "Weisgold of Weisgold and Weisgold. The candid men." Mr. Banks' eyes shut as a blinding flash went off in his face. "Thanks," said Mr. Weisgold. "See you in church."

"Drive," said Mr. Banks to the saintly wheelsman, "as if the seven hounds of hell were on your tail."

Chapter 14

WHO GIVETH THIS WOMAN?

Mr. Banks sat uneasily in the rear of the black limousine. Beside this lovely, calm stranger he felt small and a bit ridiculous. Their ages had somehow been mysteriously reversed. Instead of being the father of the bride he was a small boy being taken to dancing school in an asinine costume.

A neatly framed card on the back of the chauffeur's partition caught his eye. "The driver of this car is Mr. Pomus. He is Careful—Courteous—Co-operative." He read it over several times.

The shiny high hat cut his forehead. It had fitted him once. Why should it be too small for him now? He wondered if the forehead grew fat with the rest of the body. There was no reason why it should not, when you came to think of it. Or one's ears either, for that matter. That was a quaint thought. "How stout your ears have grown, Mr. Banks."

Ruminating along these philosophical lines, he half observed their progress through the elm-shaded and self-consciously meandering streets of Fairview Manor. It should have created at least a ripple of disturbance. Someone should have stopped trimming a hedge long enough to step to the curb and wave them on their way. Someone should have cried, "There goes the bride and her father."

But no one did.

684

Solid citizens continued their ceaseless, neurotic fight to civilize nature with a pair of clippers and a lawn mower. Little boys continued their suicidal ball games under the very fenders of the car. In the front seat Mr. Pomus gazed benignly over his wheel. If he had raised two fingers in blessing to the urchins that he so nearly ran over, it would have been in character.

They rounded a corner into Red Brook Road. Far down its leafy vista Mr. Banks caught a glimpse of the striped awning in front of St. George's. Considerably nearer, however, was the father of all moving vans. A veritable freight car of a vehicle. It was backed against the curb and completely blocked the street. As they came to a stop the driver of this behemoth looked down on them from his cab with lackluster eyes.

Mr. Pomus thrust his white locks through the window. "We want to get by," he said gently.

The driver eyed him impersonally as one observes passers-by in a station waiting room. "Hold yer glasses on, gran'pa. Don't let yerself get sweated up."

Mr. Pomus' face took on the ethereal look of a saint about to be martyred. "I'm telling you to pull that God-damn crate out of the way an' lemme get the hell by," he said with unexpected firmness.

The truck driver spat through the cab window as if to rid himself of an unpleasant taste. "Yeah? You an' who?"

Mr. Pomus opened the door quietly and half stood on the running board. From his lips there poured, without warning, a torrent of electric invective. It contained many words which Mr. Banks had not heard since World War I with adaptations of old ideas. For a few moments he stared at Mr. Pomus in dismay. Then something long dormant within him was touched into life.

Lowering the rear window and carefully removing his high hat, he stuck his head out and joined Mr. Pomus, adding a number of words that the latter seemed to have forgotten. For the first time that day he felt like himself. He also felt Kay tugging at his coattails.

The driver descended from his cab and approached them, his shoulders swaying like those of a boxer moving into the ring. When he reached the car he noticed Kay and stopped. "Whyn't you tell me you was on yer way to a weddin'? Jesus, what's bitin' people these days?"

He climbed back into his cab and stepped on the starter. Mr. Banks looked at his watch. It was twenty-three minutes past four. As they drew up to the curb in front of St. George's he noted the usual crowd grouped around the sidewalk openings of the striped awning. He alighted and, his hat once more knocked over his left eye, helped his daughter from the car.

She smiled up at him and took his arm. "You were wonderful, Pops." Mr. Weisgold of Weisgold and Weisgold danced before them like a leprechaun, his ever-candid camera at his eye. Preceded by flashing bulbs, they walked together toward the dim entrance of the church.

Mr. Tringle, radiating efficiency, was waiting for them at the top of the stone steps. "This way," he said, and dove into a small passage. Through an open door Mr. Banks had a momentary glimpse of the interior of the church. He was conscious of heads and color and lights. It looked more like a stage backdrop than a real scene. The organ was booming complacently.

They were in some sort of vestibule that opened into the church through double doors that were now closed. The bridesmaids were there and a few of the ushers. Mr. Banks noted with surprise that everyone seemed dressed according to instructions.

Tommy appeared from somewhere, looking as if he were in the habit of wearing a cutaway and a wing collar every afternoon. "Sorry I messed things up, Pops," he said. "But I made it. Ben's going to take Mom down now."

Everyone seemed to know just what was going on except Mr. Banks. It was incredible that such complex details should be falling into place without his supervision. He almost resented it. With a dramatic flourish Mr. Tringle threw open the double doors that led into the church.

He saw Ben swing into the center aisle with his mother on his arm. A feeling of elation spread through Mr. Banks as he watched his wife's straight, slender back. For years she had been the focus of attention at all social events. Now she was being led humbly to her place in a front pew. For once he had stolen the show.

The remaining ushers fell into line. Mr. Tringle stood beside the leaders. "Ready?" he asked. No one gave the slightest indication as to whether he was or not. Mr. Tringle pushed a small button on the wall.

The organ made a few ad lib sounds intended to convey the idea that the organist had come to the end of whatever it was he was playing. A hush fell over St. George's, broken only by the rustle of several hundred people trying to face in two directions at once.

This was the supreme moment—the moment Mr. Banks had dreaded and anticipated for so many weeks. It had all come with such a rush at the end that he scarcely had time to grasp its significance. Now that it was here, he was serenely calm. It was not an ordinary, workday calm, however, but rather one of detached unreality.

Although he had been in St. George's many times before it was as strange to him at this instant as a Byzantine mosque. The sea of faces that shot suddenly upward from the pews as the organ paused were unreal. They reminded him of a high-speed movie he had once seen of a growing poppy field. Even the girl beside him was a stranger. She was no longer his little daughter, but a beautiful, serene woman into whom all wisdom had suddenly and mysteriously flowed. She stood, poised on the threshold of her greatest adventure, her face lit with understanding and confidence.

It was difficult to conceive how an earthly chap like Buckley could

686

have produced this miracle. Having produced it, his responsibility to maintain it was great. It would be a terrible thing to betray that expression in Kay's eyes. They were fixed far beyond Buckley, on an ideal which perhaps no mortal could hope to achieve, but which was all the more precious because of its unattainability. A thousand generations of women were standing behind Kay now. For a mystic instant she was a generic part of that selfless, intuitive race which since the days of the mastodons has been quietly guiding awkward, bumbling Man to an unknown destiny of greatness.

At this particular instant he was horrified to note that two of the bridesmaids had begun to sniffle. In the unscrupulous way of all women in little things they had snatched carefully folded handkerchiefs from ushers' pockets and were dabbing their eyes and blowing their noses.

"Good God," said Mr. Banks, but he had no time to develop the idea. The organ sounded off with its warning thumps. Kay patted his arm. "Well, Pops, we're off."

"O.K. with the right foot," hissed Mr. Tringle. *"Right* foot, I said." Mr. Banks shifted quickly. Everyone else changed step at the same moment and he had to shift back again. Good God, was this a wedding march or a minuet? The procession passed through the oak doorway into the church.

Mr. Banks and Kay reached the rear pews. He would have continued, but she held him back. "Hold it, Pops," she murmured. With the calmness of a general watching his forces deploy into battle, she stood poised, awaiting the proper moment.

The maid of honor was twenty feet ahead when he felt the gentle pressure of her arm. The stage was set as she wished it. She was ready for her entrance.

Out of the corners of his eyes Mr. Banks caught glimpses of familiar faces. Their expression paid tribute to the girl at his side. Pride dispelled all other emotions.

He saw Buckley and the best man waiting for them at the end of the aisle. Mr. Galsworthy stood on the chancel steps smiling ever so slightly. Mr. Banks was struck by his resemblance to Mr. Pomus.

Now they were lined up before the steps and the minister was reading from a white satin book with a purple marker hanging from it. As he stood on the top step he towered above them in his robes like a genie emerging from a bottle.

It gave Mr. Banks an entirely new view of Mr. Galsworthy's face—a kind of worm's-eye view. He became vividly aware of the minister's nostrils, which were unusually long and worked in and out like bellows as he spoke. He wrenched his eyes away with an effort, conscious that this was not the memory he wished to treasure in later years. At a moment like this it did seem as if he might be doing something more worth while than studying Mr. Galsworthy's nostrils.

Besides which he had a cue coming. When Mr. Galsworthy reached the place where he asked, "Who giveth this woman—?" Mr. Banks was to say, "I do." It was his only line in the show. He wanted to acquit himself creditably and began to consider his delivery.

Should he say, "*I* do" or "I *do?*" "*I* do" sounded silly. It implied that any number of people might do it and that he was pushing himself forward for the job.

On the other hand "I *do*" didn't make much sense either. It certainly wasn't the proper way to answer a general question. The whole passage struck him as fatuous. It put the minister in a ridiculous position, forcing him to overlook the fact that the father of the bride was standing right under his nose—no!—not that!—not his nose again!—keep off that. But he was obliged to put the question in such a way that it carried the implication that perhaps *no one* would wish to undertake the job.

It all struck Mr. Banks as lacking in forthrightness. Obviously, however, this was an inappropriate time to suggest revision of the marriage service, so he decided on "*I* do." His next problem was the tone of voice to be used.

He didn't want to mumble it in a shamefaced kind of way. On the other hand if he boomed it out it would have an eager-beaver quality suggesting that he was delighted to get Kay off his hands. He compromised on a well-modulated, dignified delivery; about the tone a man would use if someone asked who would volunteer for a dangerous mission.

He was mindful of the fact that, when his one line had been spoken, his final part played, he was supposed to drop back a step, turn on his heel, and join his wife in the front pew. He wished that he had noticed just what lay in his immediate rear. He had an unpleasant vision of stepping back and tripping over something unexpected like an upturned corner of carpet or the end of the pew. He began to reach behind him stealthily with his right foot, using it like the antenna of an insect. He hoped that no one would notice it. People were always so quick to attribute such fumblings to alcohol.

"Who giveth this woman—?" intoned the rich baritone of the Reverend Mr. Galsworthy from far above him.

It caught him off guard in spite of all precautions. Kay nudged him and placed her hand in his. "*I* do," he murmured almost inaudibly, and passed her hand to Buckley. As he performed the simple act he was conscious that something deep within him ripped slightly.

He did not see the rest. Turning slowly, he stared defiantly at the rows of faces, then entered the first pew and stood beside Mrs. Banks. He tried in vain to listen to the words of the service—and then suddenly it was all over.

It seemed impossible, but it was definitely over. Kay and Buckley were kissing. The organ had broken into the joyous notes of the Mendelssohn Wedding March, like a little boy released from Sunday

school into spring sunshine. The maid of honor was struggling with Kay's train. The wedding guests were searching under the pews for lost gear and poking out hats that wives had sat on.

Kay beamed at them happily as she went by, her arm through Buckley's, and again Mr. Banks felt that queer little rending in the center of his being. The flashing of bulbs indicated that Weisgold and Weisgold were still their old candid selves. Tommy appeared, to take his mother out.

It was over. The wedding dress, the bridesmaids' dresses, the struggles with cutaways, the invitations, the flowers, the lists, the rehearsal, the arguments, apprehensions, doubts and bewilderments had all suddenly become memories.

A wedding was like the experimental explosion of an atom bomb, thought Mr. Banks as he walked out behind his wife, smirking to right and left. You made the most careful preparations for months, then someone like Mr. Tringle pressed a button—and it was all over. There was scarcely any present tense in connection with weddings. They existed either in the future or in the past.

"Stanley, your hat looks like a cat in a thunderstorm," said Mrs. Banks as they descended the entrance steps of the church. "But it was lovely, darling, wasn't it?"

Chapter 15

RECEPTION

It is traditional that, between the church and the house, wedding guests are free agents. This is the one period in the schedule where they can express their own individuality.

The majority appreciate this unsupervised interlude and are apt to turn it into a kind of hare-and-hound race in which the bride, groom and immediate progenitors are the hares, the guests assuming the role of hounds.

The latter are held in check briefly by a few yards of satin ribbon and a rear guard of ushers whose hearts are no longer in their work. Scarcely have the hares disappeared down the striped tunnel of awning than the pack is after them with lolling tongues.

Gone the little pre-wedding courtesies when one car waited politely for another to pull in to the curb and friends exchanged genial words of greeting while trying to crawl out of underslung sedans. Now it is

every man for himself, *sauve qui peut,* and devil take the hindmost, for the last man to arrive at the house knows that he must spend the balance of the afternoon standing in the reception line watching his more active neighbors guzzling free champagne.

Mr. and Mrs. Banks arrived at 24 Maple Drive a few minutes behind the bridal party. During their absence Mr. Massoula had taken over completely in accordance with his promises. His Buckingham Caterers were darting about like Walt Disney gnomes.

Mr. Massoula met them at the front door. "Everything is in hand," he said. "Don't worry about anything. Go right into the living room. They're taking pictures of the bridal party."

In the living room Mr. Weisgold of Weisgold and Weisgold was perspiring freely and photographing the bridal party in various combinations. Those not engaged in being self-consciously photogenic stood about making wisecracks about those who were, between deep draughts of Mr. Banks' champagne, which had already begun to flow. A Buckingham representative approached with a tray full of glasses.

Mr. Banks took one. He felt like those men in the whiskey ads who go through nerve-shattering experiences in jungles or on mountain precipices, then, their job well done, settle down calmly with friends in the last picture to a glass of their favorite grog. He had also gone through his own private ordeal and, he thought complacently, not without distinction. Now it was all over but the shouting. "Don't go away," he hissed to the waiter.

The bridesmaids were being photographed. Finally the Bankses and the Dunstans took their places before the flash bulbs. Mr. Weisgold's ability to produce an endless supply of bulbs fascinated Mr. Banks. The man must have been a hand grenade thrower in the war.

Over Mr. Weisgold's shoulder he suddenly noticed a cluster of faces in the doorway of the living room. Behind them were other faces. Faces jammed the front doorway. Through the window he could see them stretching in close formation halfway down the walk. Mr. Massoula blocked the entrance to the living room with firm urbanity, like the headwaiter of the Persian Room on a busy night.

The faces that peered at him were not of the happy, laughing type traditionally associated with wedding feasts. They were, rather, the glum, frustrated faces of those who had broken their fenders to get there early and were now denied the fruits of their sacrifices. They were the faces of citizens who definitely wanted to get this runkydunk over with and proceed with the main business of the afternoon.

Mr. Weisgold stopped flashing. The receiving line suddenly snapped to attention as if at the bark of a phantom drill sergeant. Mr. Massoula stepped aside nimbly to avoid being trampled. Mr. Banks never had a connected memory of the next forty-five minutes.

Father of the Bride

No one had told him whether or not he was to be part of the receiving line. For a moment he decided against it. Then it occurred to him that if he just stood in the middle of the living room he might be mistaken for the caterer. He slid quietly into place between his wife and Mrs. Dunstan as the first guest began to pump Mrs. Banks' arm.

It became immediately apparent that one of his duties was to introduce the guests to Mrs. Dunstan. Introducing one old friend to another had always been enough to give him complete aphasia. On ordinary occasions when guests arrived he disappeared into the pantry and busied himself with the refreshment department, leaving to Mrs. Banks the task of making people known to one another.

Those who were now so eagerly pushing forward to shake his hand were, for the most part, lifelong friends. In spite of this he fell immediately into his accustomed groove and could not remember anyone's name. Occasionally he would recollect their first names, but he couldn't very well say to Mrs. Dunstan, "This is Joe and Booboo." For once his retreat to the pantry was blocked.

Mrs. Banks felt herself jabbed from the rear with a thumb. She jumped slightly and turned toward her husband with the injured look common to all people when jabbed unexpectedly from the rear. "Sing out the last names," he whispered desperately.

Mrs. Banks glanced at him anxiously. She knew he had been going through a considerable strain, but she had hoped with all her being that he would hold together for another couple of hours. "Why, Jack and Nancy *Hilliard*," she cried gaily. "My dear, you look adorable. Yes. Wasn't it. I am so glad you thought so. And Grace *Lippincott*, I am so glad you could get here."

"Mr. and Mrs. Lippincott," mumbled Mr. Banks uncertainly in the general direction of Mrs. Dunstan. "I mean—that is to say—Mr. and Mrs. Hilliard."

He gave it up. He found that, by turning to the next pair of guests before they left Mrs. Banks, it was possible to pass up the whole business and let Mrs. Dunstan rock along as best she could. After all, she would probably never see any of these people again. Maybe she had something there.

Mr. Weisgold struggled through the line. "Lookit," he complained. "You told me you was goin' to have somebody with me to tell me who to shoot. I can't shoot no specials if I dunno who they are."

Mr. Banks looked despairingly around for Ben and Tommy. He had covered this point with the greatest care. Both had assured him that they would not leave Mr. Weisgold's side come hell or high water. Now they had disappeared. "Good God," he said. "Find one of the boys. Find one of the ushers. I've got my hands full here and besides I don't know who these people are any more than you do. Shoot anybody for

all I care. Shoot them all. How do you do. So nice to see you. Wasn't it? Yes, she *is* a grand girl."

"O.K.," said Mr. Weisgold. "You'll get what you get. I ain't no mind reader."

A battle-ax of a woman was wringing his hand. "Buckley is my sweetheart," she was saying. "I have known him since he was a little boy." She released his hand to indicate how very tiny Buckley was. "He used to visit us at North Deering, you know. I expect he's told you all about me. I am Mrs. Butterton. Mrs. *Matilda* Butterton. Buckley was a darling little—" Mr. Banks took her great hand in both of his and transferred it to Mrs. Dunstan.

If only people wouldn't stop and talk. There should be a law requiring them to pass silently in front of receiving lines the way they did before the biers of statesmen. They were still pouring in the front door. Glancing through the window, he could see the line extending beyond his field of vision. God knew where it ended. Had someone issued a general invitation by radio?

"Well, well, well." It was Joe Bludsoe and his diminutive wife. Joe was exuding good-fellowship and looking as if he might have apoplexy at any moment. "So you're on your way to joining the grandfather's club, eh? Well, well, well, I'm glad you lived through the wedding. God, you certainly looked awful when you came down that aisle. I said to Martha, 'Let me go out and drag him off the course. He's never going to make it.' You don't look so good now either. Still look green. When Mary was married—"

He continued to pump Mr. Banks' arm rhythmically. Mr. Banks transferred him to Mrs. Dunstan without causing him to miss a beat. "How do you do, Mrs. Karp," he said. "It was good of you to come. Oh, excuse me. Of course. Mrs. Park. Why, of course I knew it. Yes, we couldn't be happier about the whole thing."

It was over at last and not a minute too soon. If another person had injected himself into the living room the receiving line would have been squeezed into the fireplace.

Something was wrong, very wrong, with Mr. Massoula's "circulation." Theoretically the guests were supposed to slither off the end of the reception line, through a French door, and into the marquee where Mr. Massoula had set up his bar and buffet tables. It was all laid out like a pinball game.

The first few couples to come off the line, however, had chosen the French door in which to hold a long, eager conversation. Those who followed had merely rebounded from this obstacle back into the living room. The pinball idea still held, but it was not working according to plan.

Mr. Massoula's gnomes were so efficient that no one needed to go to the bar anyway. They slid like eels through the melee, mysteriously

carrying trays full of champagne glasses where no amateur could have transported an uncorked bottle.

It seemed to Mr. Banks that these busy little figures must be paid on a piece basis—so much per glass dispensed. Never had he seen men more devoted to their work. The moment a person tilted his glass they were at his elbow waiting eagerly with a fresh supply. It was true that he had told Mr. Massoula to keep things moving. He had merely been thinking of other weddings where he had stood around for hours with an empty glass talking to someone whose name he did not know. It was one thing to avoid that and another to hurl the stuff down people's throats every time they opened their mouths.

The sickening idea occurred to him that at this rate it would be all gone in half an hour. For the third time that day he felt damp and clammy. His emotions were beginning to set up a distasteful system of hot and cold running perspiration.

He decided to go to the marquee and investigate. As he started for the door he tripped over a dog which, he noted, was being followed by another dog. To the best of his knowledge he had never seen either animal before. However, even if they had been his two favorite canines this did not seem a proper place for dogs.

A lovely young creature approached.

"*Mr.* Banks," she cried. "What a darling, *darling* wedding. Kay looked too, *too* beautiful. You should be so *proud,* Mr. Banks. And Buckley's just *divine.* We are all crazy for him. And Mrs. Banks looked too, too—"

"Where the hell are all the dogs coming from?" interrupted Mr. Banks. He had just noted a brown and tan number entering the room through the legs grouped in the French door. It was apparently in search of some friend. "Is this a Bide-a-Wee Home or a wedding?" He wondered if the Buckingham Caterers were beginning to pour his champagne into the neighborhood crossbreeds.

His unknown companion gave a silvery laugh. "Oh, Mr. Banks, that's *cute.* The place does seem to be getting filled up with pooches, doesn't it."

"Listen," said Mr. Banks. "Do me a favor. Get hold of Tommy or Ben, if they haven't left town, and tell them that part of an usher's job is to throw out livestock."

"Oh, I will, Mr. Banks. I will. That's darling." She gave him a look that might have meant anything—but didn't—and disappeared into the crowd. He made another start for the marquee, but the impromptu reunion in the French door had grown to such proportions that he gave it up for the moment and pushed his way about the room at random.

Later he could remember a roar of voices—and people making faces at him—and making faces back at people—but it was a scene which would remain forever out of focus in his memory. Eventually he

felt a tug at his sleeve. Kay and Buckley were standing behind him, Kay holding her crumpled train over her arm and grinning.

"Hi, Pops. We're going to get ready now. Don't you want to see me hurl my bridal bouquet?"

He followed them to the front hall while the wedding guests whooped noisily after. Kay and Buckley were already looking down from the landing.

Mr. Banks was astonished to discover an entirely new expression on Kay's face. Vanished the ethereal look she had worn as they started down the aisle. Now her ordinarily placid features radiated a self-confident, roguish gaiety that he had never seen before.

For twenty-four years Kay had been as satisfactory a daughter as any man could desire. His only complaint, if one could use so strong a word, was that she was too repressed, too shy—not a scared rabbit exactly, but lacking that bold grasp of the realities which he admired in women.

He had thought of her thus handicapped, leaving the cloisters and facing the world, in all the intimacy of married life and with a man whom she scarcely knew. Until this moment it had seemed to Mr. Banks that convention forced a transition that was brutal in its suddenness and completeness—a transition floodlighted by a glare of publicity which convention also demanded. From Mr. Banks' point of view it was enough to make the boldest maiden hesitate.

Yet here was Kay, who only a few days before had been telling him that she didn't have the nerve to go through with it, standing beside Buckley on the landing, looking over the faces below her with all the happy, relaxed assurance of a hunting dog which has just retrieved a bird.

His eye rested balefully for a moment on Buckley. Ordinarily a shy fellow in crowds, he now had a look of smug possessiveness that sent an unexpected wave of irritation down Mr. Banks' spine.

The maid of honor was jockeying for position under the landing. Kay was waiting for her with the bridal bouquet poised. Small chance for the eager virgins clamoring with outstretched arms, their faces expressing in half-light what glowed so brightly and unashamed in Kay's. It struck Mr. Banks that the accepted belief that men married women was a colossal hoax—they were merely married *by* women.

There was a shrill yelping as the bridal bouquet came sailing over the rail and fell, with its usual precision, into the outstretched arms of the maid of honor. Then Kay and Buckley disappeared around the corner of the stairs followed by the bridal party.

The crowd began to spread out again and Mr. Massoula's walking dispensaries, apparently refreshed by the pause, went into action with renewed enthusiasm. Again Mr. Banks was struck by the need for taking inventory and he turned once more toward the marquee. Ralph Dixon

collared him at the French door. He was a lawyer who took two things in life seriously. One was Ralph Dixon, the other the law.

"Hello, Banks," he said.

Mr. Banks wished Ralph Dixon wouldn't call him "Banks." He considered himself equally successful as a lawyer and they were the same age. He realized that the English all addressed one another this way, but he wasn't English and when addressed as "Banks" he always felt like a stage butler.

He should, of course, have said, "Hello, Dixon." Instead he said, "Hi, Ralph."

"Nice wedding," said Mr. Dixon and apparently considered that he had thereby paid his tribute to the amenities. "Got a minute?"

"Well, the fact is—" began Mr. Banks with a sinking heart.

"It's about that Shatton matter," said Mr. Dixon. "I don't like to be on the other side of the fence from you, Banks, and I think in this case you're all wet. Now just take the facts."

Mr. Dixon then took the facts and laid them out in orderly rows for Mr. Banks' appraisal. A waiter appeared with champagne and as Mr. Banks drank it he suddenly realized that he did not have the slightest idea what Ralph Dixon was talking about. Perhaps this stuff was getting him. He decided to hold his glass quietly and not touch it for a few minutes.

It was all the same to Mr. Dixon, however, whether Mr. Banks understood him or not. He was marshaling his facts and he would have marshaled them with equal gusto if Mr. Banks had been stretched out insensible on a window seat.

"Heidee-ho, heidee-ho. This *is* a party." A pasty-faced gentleman with jowls like a bloodhound injected himself into the summation. It was Uncle Peter, who had come all the way from Sioux City and was obviously not going back empty. Although Mr. Banks had always privately considered Uncle Peter an old bum, at the moment he was delighted to see him.

"Peter," he said. "I want you to meet a friend of mine, Mr. Dixon. Ralph, this is Peter Quackenbush—he's related to my wife," he explained parenthetically.

Mr. Dixon glared silently at Uncle Peter and gave evidence of being about to move away. This would have been merely a transference of evils for Mr. Banks. Danger made him alert. Within the bat of an eye he had disappeared through the French door.

Judging by the crowd in the living room he had expected to find the marquee half empty. On the contrary, it was also jammed with people. The temperature was midway between that of a Turkish bath and a greenhouse.

Mrs. Banks had hired a push-and-pull man to circulate among the guests. Mr. Banks discovered him standing unnoted by one of the tent

poles, dressed in his interpretation of a Neapolitan costume, obviously bursting his lungs and his instrument in the public weal. The din in the tent was so great, however, that he might have been squeezing a black-smith's bellows and gargling his throat. Mr. Banks wondered why, from an economic viewpoint if no other, his wife had considered it necessary to pay someone to add to a confusion which was contributed gratis.

In spite of the Buckingham boys, who were getting rid of Mr. Banks' champagne just as eagerly here as in the house, there was a crowd of eager customers in front of the bar table. He shouldered his way in and tried to get the attention of one of the sweating men behind it. They were engrossed in snatching bottles from huge tubs of icewater, uncorking them and dividing their contents between massed glasses and the tablecloth.

A strange man next to Mr. Banks watched them with the tense concentration of a bird dog. "Lousy service," he said finally to Mr. Banks in what was obviously meant as a friendly opening.

"Terrible," agreed Mr. Banks.

"About on a par with the champagne," said the stranger.

"I thought the champagne was pretty good," said Mr. Banks defensively. "For American champagne, of course."

"Bilge," said the genial stranger. "Sparkling bilge. I regard all champagne as bilge, but some comes from a lower part of the hold than others. This comes from just over the keel." The young man took two dripping glasses and backed away.

Mr. Banks beckoned to one of the barmen.

"How is the champagne holding out?" he asked.

The barman looked at him coldly. "O.K., O.K.," he said. "Don't worry, mister. You'll get plenty." Mr. Banks found himself blushing, then he remembered the old Chinese proverb and decided to relax and have a look at the garden. It would be interesting to find out if it were also filled with people.

His progress through the tent was slow. Near the entrance he spotted Miss Bellamy talking to a group from the office. She detached herself and came toward him balancing a glass of champagne without too great success. He had never seen Miss Bellamy dressed like this before and it rather startled him. He didn't know just what to say, but she was obviously quite at ease.

"Boss, we certainly put on a wonderful wedding. Yes, sir. If I do say so, it was beautiful. I want to drink a toast. I want to drink a couple of toasts. First, to the bride. Say, you were swell coming down the aisle. No one would ever have known you were scared."

"Thank you," said Mr. Banks. Somehow or other this was not the self-effacing Miss Bellamy he had left at the office yesterday afternoon. They drank solemnly.

"And now I want to drink to the best boss in the world. Yes, sir, the

696

finest boss in the world." She had certainly never looked at him quite like that before.

"And I'll drink to the finest secretary," said Mr. Banks, embarrassed.

"Oh, you're just saying that," said Miss Bellamy, her large brown eyes searching his face intently. "You're just making that up, I know you are. Got a cigarette?" As he lit her cigarette he wondered if the world could ever again be forced back into its comfortable old normalcy.

"You got to watch this stuff," said Miss Bellamy, gazing thoughtfully into her glass. "You got to watch it every minute. If you don't—it'll get you. No question about it. Want to know something?" She leaned toward Mr. Banks' ear. "That Miss Didrickson's plastered. She's the new one with the dyed hair. Come on over. The bunch will want to see you. She's a silly ass, though. I didn't like her from the start. She was saying—"

A young man in a cutaway approached. "Mrs. Banks is looking for you, sir. She sounds as if she wants to see you right away."

Relieved to have some objective, Mr. Banks began to fight his way back to the house. He had almost made the exit from the marquee when an enormous woman blocked his way. She was accompanied by a gangling young girl with a mouthful of braces.

"Oh, Mr. Banks, it was such a heavenly wedding. I want you to meet my daughter Betsy. This is Kay's father, dear." Betsy tittered as if she found the idea grotesque. "Humphrey couldn't come." Mr. Banks cast vainly about in his mind for anyone by the name of Humphrey. "He wanted me to tell you how sorry he was. You were *so* nice to ask us. I said to Humphrey, 'That was *so* nice of the Bankses to include us. And to the reception too.' I brought Betsy. I didn't think you'd mind. She adores Kay so and she's been so excited about the wedding. Haven't you, dear?"

Betsy's excitement seemed to have died down since the ceremony. At the moment she looked like a captured German prisoner brought to headquarters for questioning. "Kay looked perfectly beautiful," continued the large woman. "Simply ravishing. And the bridesmaids' dresses — Well, my dear, they were out of another world. I think the whole thing—"

A second young man in a cutaway approached. "Mrs. Banks is sort of tearing her hair out, sir. She said for me to tell you that Kay and Buckley are getting ready to go and where are you."

Mr. Banks made a mumbling noise and forced a passage between the stout woman and Betsy. Mrs. Banks pushed toward him through the crowded room. "Stanley Banks, where have you been? I'm almost crazy. I suppose you've been in that tent telling stories. Now come. Kay and Buckley will be coming down any minute."

Again there was a dense crowd in the front of the house. Mr. Massoula's henchmen moved through it bearing salad bowls filled with

confetti. At least they were distributing something inexpensive for the moment. People were self-consciously grabbing handfuls, most of which they immediately let slip through their fingers to the floor. Everyone was watching the stairs tensely as if they expected a couple of whippets to come streaking down and out the door before they could get rid of the balls of damp paper in their clenched fists.

This was the scene that Mr. Banks had visualized so often during the last twenty-five years; the moment when his first-born would come running down a broad staircase on the arm of a muscle-bound stranger, to disappear from his life forever—at least in the role of his little daughter.

When he had stood at the foot of other people's staircases waiting to throw damp paper at their daughters, his heart had been warm with sympathy for the fathers of the brides, who strolled with such brave nonchalance among their guests. He had hoped that he would have equal courage when his time came.

Now that it was here he only felt numbness. He had rehearsed it all so often in his mind—he had hugged his private sadness to his bosom so many times—that its fulfillment was less real than its anticipation.

A bridesmaid peered around the corner of the stair landing, grinned sheepishly and disappeared. Someone cried, "Here they come," as if it were a horse race. Then Kay and Buckley, conspicuously new in every detail, were tearing across the landing and down the final flight of stairs with that hunched, headlong look of charging moose that Mr. Banks had observed in all brides and grooms coming downstairs.

They were on the front walk now, their shoulders covered with confetti, their heads still lowered between their shoulders. Mr. Banks was right behind them, running in form, the ushers and bridesmaids bringing up the rear in full cry. Buckley's car stood at the end of the walk. It was amazing how these details fell into place against all odds. They were in. Kay leaned through the open window while Buckley fought off ushers on the other side.

"Good-by, Pops. You've been wonderful. I love you."

The car lurched forward. Mr. Banks revolved off the rear mudguard into the arms of a bridesmaid. "Good-by, good luck." They were already half a block away. A few ushers, who had gone through the usual routine of almost being run over in the getaway, were brushing the dirt from their trousers.

When Mr. Banks returned to the house he realized that the reception had entered a new and final phase. Its connection with the bride and groom had already been forgotten. For all practical purposes the bride and groom themselves had been forgotten. The Reception had become a Party and only a few cutaways and bridesmaids' dresses recalled the event that had brought it into being.

The more conservative element began to leave. A few said good-by.

698

The majority took advantage of the confusion and merely walked away. Officer Mullins, who had undertaken to act as parking attendant, had long since left his post and retired to the kitchen, where one or two other members of the force were already at work on material furnished by the ever-thoughtful Mr. Massoula.

Officer Mullins had packed the parking field efficiently and solidly before he left. This had been quite satisfactory during the parking, but unfortunately the guests were not departing on the modern accounting basis of last in first out. If there were any order to their leaving, it appeared to be just the opposite.

And so it came about that, while Officer Mullins exchanged views on wine and women with his fellow craftsmen, the more prominent citizens of Fairview Manor locked bumpers and cursed in the scarred field behind the house.

Mr. Banks felt restless. A sudden desire seized him to speed his parting guests. He wandered out of the house and across the lawn in the direction of the parking field, carefully balancing a glass of champagne as he walked. The scene which burst upon him as he rounded the lilac hedge reminded him of a picture in an old geography of sampans milling on a Chinese river front.

For the next half hour, disregarding the dangerous snugness of his cutaway, he leaped up and down on entwined bumpers, directed backing cars into other backing cars and helped angry citizens to pull their bashed mudguards free from their tires.

Then, retrieving his glass, which he had left on a fence post, he returned to the house, dirty but satisfied, feeling that for the first time in many hours he had been of some practical use in the world.

The bitter-enders were in full swing. The Neapolitan push-and-pull artist was hard and soundlessly at work in the living room, which was jammed with people, all of them obviously prepared to see the thing through to the final bottle.

Chapter 16

ALL OVER

The last guest had gone. The last damp hand had been wrung. The bridal party had disappeared noisily to seek bigger and newer adventure. The Dunstans had left. The relatives had returned to the oblivion from which they had emerged. Mr. and Mrs. Banks were alone with the wreckage.

They sat limply in two armchairs which Mr. Banks had dragged

down from upstairs. The rug was covered with confetti. The few casual tables which Mr. Massoula had left in the living room were garnished with gray rings. Here and there on the white paint of the sills were the dark signatures of cigarettes. The floral background of the reception line obliterated the fireplace. They stared at it in silence.

"She did look lovely in that going-away suit," said Mrs. Banks dreamily. "Didn't you think it was good-looking?"

Mr. Banks couldn't remember it very well. He knew she had had on something tan. There his detail stopped. But her face was etched forever on his memory as she stood on the landing waiting to throw the bride's bouquet.

"She's a darling," he said.

"Queer the Griswolds didn't come," mused Mrs. Banks. "They accepted and Jane told me they were coming."

"I don't see how you know whether they came or not."

"I know everybody that was here and everybody that wasn't," said Mrs. Banks complacently.

Mr. Banks did not question it. This woman who couldn't remember the details of the most elementary problem for five minutes would remember now and forever everyone who came, everyone who didn't— and also those who crashed the gate.

"My God," exclaimed Mrs. Banks, pressing her hand over her face. "We forgot to ask the Storers."

"We couldn't have," said Mr. Banks.

"We did, though."

"That's terrible. Couldn't we pretend we sent them an invitation? You could call Esther tomorrow and ask her why she didn't come."

"I might at that," said Mrs. Banks.

There was a brief silence. "What are we going to do with all those presents?" asked Mr. Banks.

"I don't know. Somebody's got to pack them, I suppose. I think I'll just leave them as they are for a while."

"I guess that's the best thing," said Mr. Banks.

They lapsed into exhausted silence. In the brain of each a projector was unreeling the film of the day's events. It would have amazed them if they could have known how different the films were.

In another compartment of Mr. Banks' brain an adding machine was relentlessly at work. The figures came pouring out and each time they were greater than before.

"Didn't the decorations in the church look too lovely?" asked Mrs. Banks.

Mr. Banks was startled to discover that he had not even noticed if there were any decorations in the church. It was a relief to know that someone had checked on that dog-robber Tim.

"They were beautiful," he said simply.

"Mr. Tim did a wonderful job considering how little money we gave him to work with," said Mrs. Banks. Her husband started, then pressed his lips together and made no comment.

"I suppose," said Mrs. Banks, "we ought to get out the vacuum cleaner and not leave this whole mess for Delilah tomorrow. I'll go up and change my dress."

Mr. Banks followed her upstairs glumly. Like a fog blowing in from the sea, he could feel the first wisps of depression fingering into his soul.

Here was the place where she had stood. He paused and looked over the rail at the confetti-strewn hall. Queer about places and houses. They remained the same yet they were never the same. By no stretch of the imagination was this the spot from which Kay had tossed her flowers to the waving arms below.

He continued up the stairs, thinking of all the money and energy that was wasted each year visiting the scenes of great events under the impression that they were still the same places.

At the door of the spare room where the presents were on display, he paused, then lit the light and went in. This morning it had been a gay, exciting place, full of anticipation and promise of things to come. The animating spirit was gone. Now it was just a bare room with card tables along the walls covered with china and glassware. It was as impersonal as a store.

He tried to shake off the cloud that was settling over him. In the bathroom a single bottle of champagne rested quietly in the washbasin. It had been put there by someone just before Mr. Massoula ran out. Heaven knew what for. It was still cold. For a moment he debated whether to open it. Then he turned, went downstairs and got out the vacuum cleaner.

An hour later the last particle of confetti had been transferred to the bulging bag of the machine. They sat once more in their chairs in the living room gazing with exhausted faces at the banked greens in front of the fireplace.

On the floor near the edge of the rug Mr. Banks spied a few bits of confetti that the cleaner had overlooked. He rose to pick them up. There seemed to be more just under the edge. He turned back the corner and disclosed a solid mat of multicolored paper.

Without comment he dropped the rug back into place. Mrs. Banks was watching, but said nothing. He went quietly up to the bathroom and drew the cork in the last remaining bottle. From the spare room he selected two of Kay's new champagne glasses and returned to his wife.

Carefully he filled the two glasses and handed one to Mrs. Banks. Behind the floral background the clock on the mantel struck twelve. The whistle of a train from the city hooted in the distance as it rounded the curve into the Fairview Manor station. A dog was barking somewhere.

"How," said Mr. Banks raising his glass.

"How," said Mrs. Banks.

XII

THE SHORT
REIGN
OF PIPPIN IV

by John Steinbeck

A Story of What Might Have Happened

Supposing a descendant of two almost legendary figures in history, Charles Martel and Pippin the Short, were to come forward today and elevate himself to a throne in France? Utterly, fantastically, absurdly impossible! And yet de Gaulle became head of the state without anything much more than raising a hand. And certainly it does not seem impossible the way John Steinbeck tells it.

This is satire, of course, with a firm foundation of common sense and truth underlying it, particularly in regard to economic and political conditions in America; and told with great deftness and wit. Perhaps never before has an author, strongly established in certain well-understood areas, proven his versatility in a more spectacular way or with more success. *The Short Reign of Pippin IV* shows us a new Steinbeck, a keenly observant and urbane fellow who can turn a phrase with all the neatness and lightness of touch ascribed to writers of the country he has selected for his parable. It is, necessarily, a short novel, for the satiric approach cannot be sustained too long. The re-establishment of the monarchial form of government is terminated before the full enjoyment of the paradox has been exhausted.

We feel that the story of Pippin's brief moment of glory (he, poor fellow, did not enjoy it at all), his practical wife, his heavy-footed daughter, and his official mistress (on whom he never sets an eye), add an inimitable variety to our list.

NUMBER ONE AVENUE DE MARIGNY in Paris is a large, square house of dark and venerable appearance. The mansion is on the corner where de Marigny crosses the Avenue Gabriel, a short block from the Champs Elysées and across the street from the Elysée Palace, which is the home of the President of France. Number One abuts on a glass-roofed courtyard, on the other side of which is a tall and narrow building, once the stables and coachmen's quarters. On the ground level are still the stables, very elegant with carved marble mangers and water troughs, but upstairs there are three pleasant floors, a small but pleasant house in the center of Paris. On the second floor large glass doors open on the unglassed portion of the courtyard which connects the two buildings.

It is said that Number One, together with its coach house, was built as the Paris headquarters of the Knights of St. John, but it is presently owned and occupied by a noble French family who for a number of years have leased the converted coach house, the use of the courtyard, and half of the flat connecting roof to M. Pippin Arnulf Héristal and his family, consisting of his wife, Marie, and his daughter, Clotilde. Soon after leasing the stable house, M. Héristal called on his noble landlord and requested permission to set up the base and mount for an eight-inch refracting telescope on the portion of the flat roof to which he had access. This request was granted, and thereafter, since M. Héristal was prompt with the rent, intercourse between the two families was limited to formal greetings when they happened to meet in the courtyard, which was of course guarded by heavy iron bars on the street side. Héristal and landlord shared a concierge, a brooding provincial, who after years of living in Paris still refused to believe in it. And there were never any complaints from the noble landlord, since M. Héristal's celestial hobby was carried on at night and silently. The passions of astronomy, however, are no less profound because they are not noisy.

The Héristal income was almost perfect of its kind for a Frenchman. It derived from certain eastward-facing slopes near Auxerre, on the Loire, on which the vines sucked the benevolence from the early sun and avoided the poisons of the afternoon, and this, together with a fortunate soil and a cave of perfect temperature, produced a white wine tasting like the odor of spring wildflowers—a wine which, while it

did not travel well, had no need, for its devotees made pilgrimage to it. This estate, while small, was perhaps the very best of a holding once very great. Furthermore, it was cultivated and nurtured by tenants expert to the point of magic, who moreover paid their rent regularly and had, generation by generation. M. Héristal's income was far from great, but it was constant and it permitted him to live comfortably in the coach house of Number One Avenue de Marigny; to attend carefully selected plays, concerts, and ballet; to belong to a good social club and three learned societies; to purchase books as he needed them; and to peer as a respected amateur at the incredible heavens over the Eighth Arrondissement of Paris.

Indeed, if Pippin Héristal could have chosen the life he would most like to live, he would have spoken, with very few changes, for the life he was living in February of 19—. He was fifty-four, lean, handsome, and healthy in so far as he knew. By that I mean his health was so good that he was not aware he had it.

His wife, Marie, was a good wife and a good manager who knew her province and stayed in it. She was buxom and pleasant and under other circumstances might have taken her place at the bar of a very good small restaurant. Like most Frenchwomen of her class, she hated waste and heretics, considering the latter a waste of good heavenly material. She admired her husband without trying to understand him and had a degree of friendship with him which is not found in those marriages where passionate love sets torch to peace of mind. Her duty as she saw it was to keep a good, clean, economical house for her husband and her daughter, to do what she could about her liver, and to maintain the spiritual payments on her escrowed property in Heaven. These activities took up all her time. Her emotional overflow was absorbed by an occasional fight with the cook, Rose, and her steady warfare with wine-merchant and grocer, who were cheats and pigs, and, at certain times of the year, ancient camels. Madame's closest friend and perhaps only confidante was Sister Hyacinthe, of whom there will be more later.

M. Héristal was French of the French and yet French plus. For instance, he did not believe it was a sin not to speak French and an affectation for a Frenchman to learn other languages. He knew German, Italian, and English. He had a scholarly interest in progressive jazz, and he loved the cartoons in *Punch*. He admired the English for their intensity and their passion for roses, horses, and some kinds of conduct.

"An Englishman is a bomb," he would say, "but a bomb with a hidden fuse." He also observed, "Almost any generality one makes about the English turns out at some time to be untrue." And he would continue, "How different from the Americans they are!"

He knew and liked Cole Porter, Ludwig Bemelmans, and, until a few years before, had known sixty per cent of the Harmonica Rascals.

He had once shaken hands with Louis Armstrong and addressed him as Cher Maître Satchmo, to which the master replied, "You frogs ape me."

The Héristal household was comfortable without being extravagant, and carefully keyed to the family income, which was sufficient for the pleasant but frugal life which, as good French, Pippin and Madame preferred to live. Monsieur's main extravagance lay in the instruments of astronomy. His telescope of more than amateur power was equipped with mounting of sufficient weight and stability to overcome oscillation, and mechanism to compensate for the earth's turning. Some of Pippin's celestial photographs have appeared in the magazine *Match,* and properly so, for he is given credit for discovering the comet of 1951, designated the Elysée Comet. A Japanese amateur in California, Walter Haschi, made a simultaneous report and shared credit for the discovery. Haschi and Héristal still corresponded regularly and compared photographs and techniques.

Under ordinary circumstances Pippin read four daily papers like any good and alert citizen. He was not political except in so far as he distrusted all governments, particularly the one in power, but this too might be said to be more French than individual.

The family Héristal was blessed with only one child—Clotilde, twenty years old, intense, violent, pretty, and overweight. Her background was interesting. At an early age she had revolted against everything she could think of. At fourteen, Clotilde determined to be a doctor of medicine; at fifteen she wrote a novel entitled *Adieu Ma Vie,* which sold widely and was made into a motion picture. As a result of her literary and cinemagraphic success she toured America and returned to France wearing blue jeans, saddle oxfords, and a man's shirt, a style which instantly caught on with millions of gamines who for several years were known as "Les Jeannes Bleues" and caused untold pain to their parents. It was said that Les Jeannes Bleues were, if anything, sloppier than the Existentialists, while their stern-faced gyrations in le jitterbug caused many a French father to clench agonized fists over his head.

From the arts, Clotilde went directly into politics. At sixteen and a half she joined the Communists and held the all-time record of sixty-two hours of picketing the Citroën plant. It was during this association with the lower classes that Clotilde met Père Méchant, the little Pastor of the Pediment, who so impressed her that she seriously considered taking the veil in an order of nuns dedicated to silence, black bread, and pedicures for the poor. St. Hannah, patron saint of feet, founded the order.

On February 14, a celestial accident occurred which had a sharp effect on the Héristal household. A pre-equinoctial meteor shower put in an untimely and unpredicted appearance. Pippin worked frantically with the blazing heavens, exposing film after film, but even before he retired

to his darkroom in the wine cellar off the stable he knew that his camera was not adequate to stop the fiery missiles in their flight. The developed film verified his fear. Cursing gently, he walked to a great optical supply house, conferred with the management, telephoned several learned friends. Then he strolled reluctantly back to Number One Avenue de Marigny, and so preoccupied was he that he did not notice the Gardes Républicains in shining cuirasses and red-plumed helmets, milling their horses around the gates of the Elysée Palace.

Madame was concluding an argument with Rose, the cook, as Pippin climbed the stairs. She emerged from the kitchen, victorious and a little red in the face, while the sullen muttering of the defeated Rose followed her down the hall.

In the salon she told her husband, "Closed the window over the cheese—a full kilogram of cheese suffocating all night with the window closed. And do you know what her excuse was? She was cold. For her own comfort the cheese must strangle. You can't trust servants any more."

Monsieur said, "One finds oneself in a difficult situation."

"Difficult—of course it's difficult with the kind of trash who call themselves cooks—"

"Madame—the meteor shower continues. This is verified. I find that I must procure a new camera."

The outgo of money was definitely in Madame's province. She remained silent, but Monsieur sensed danger in her narrowing eyes and in her hands, which rose slowly and saddled her hips.

He said uneasily, "It is a decision one must make. No one is to blame. One might say the order comes from Heaven itself."

Madame's voice was steel. "The cost of this—this camera, Monsieur?"

He named a price which shook her sturdy frame as though an internal explosion had occurred. But almost immediately she marshaled herself with iron discipline for the attack.

"Last month, M'sieur, it was a new—what do you call it? The expenditure for film is already ruinous. May I remind you, M'sieur, of the letter recently arrived from Auxerre, of the need for new cooperage, of the insistence that we stand half of the cost?"

"Madame," he cried, "I did not call down the meteor shower."

"Nor did I decay the casks at Auxerre."

"I have no choice, Madame."

She seemed to grow to a tower with castellations, and darkness hung about her like a personal thunderstorm.

"M'sieur is master of the house," she said. "If M'sieur wishes to allow the meteors to bring bankruptcy down on the heads of his family —who am I to complain? I must go to apologize to Rose. A kilo of strangulated cheese is a laughable nothing compared to the blobs of light on film. Can one eat meteors, M'sieur? Can one wear them to keep

out the night damp? Can one make wine barrels of these precious meteors? M'sieur, I leave you to make your choice." And she moved on quiet, deadly feet out of the room.

Anger fought with panic in Pippin Héristal. Through the double glass doors he could see his telescope in its garment of waterproof silk. And anger won. He walked sternly down the stairs, crushed his hat on his head, took his stick from the rack and Clotilde's briefcase from the table. With furious dignity he crossed the courtyard and waited while the concierge opened the iron gate. In a moment of weakness he looked back and saw Madame watching him from the kitchen window and Rose scowling happily beside her.

"I am going to see Uncle Charlie," said Pippin Héristal, and he slammed the iron gate behind him.

Charles Martel was proprietor of a small but prosperous art gallery and antique store in the Rue de Seine, a dark and pleasant place with pictures properly ill-lighted and provocative. He sold unsigned paintings which he would not guarantee as early Renoirs, and also bits of crystal, gilt, and chinoiserie which he could and did attest as coming from the great and ancient houses of France.

At the rear of the gallery a red velvet curtain concealed one of the most comfortable and discreet bachelor's quarters in all Paris. The chairs, softened by velvet cushions stuffed with down, were a joy to sit in. His bed, a triumph of Napoleonic work in gilded wood, had high curved head and foot like the prow and stern of a Viking dragon ship. During the day a cover and pillows made from softly faded altar cloths converted his sleeping arrangements into a charming nook, inviting and subtly sinful. Green-shaded lamps spread just enough light in the room to bring out beauties and to conceal defects. His cooking arrangements, a sink and a gas ring, were hidden behind a Chinese screen mellowed by the years to pearly black and melted butter. His bookcase was filled with leather and gold volumes, inviting to the eye without demanding that they be read.

Charles had always been a worldly man, gentle but inflexible, of impeccable carriage and dress. Now in his late sixties, he still adored ladies and his manner made ladies of all women until they insisted otherwise. Even now, when his impulse aimed more toward sleep than gallantry, he nevertheless kept his standard so high that selected young ladies felt a pleasant thrill on being invited past the red velvet curtain for an apéritif. And to the best of Charles's ability, they were not disappointed. A little door opened on an alleyway behind the shop—a small thing, but one to give his companions confidence.

When the custodian of an ancient name and a bat-ridden château required a relaxing day at Auteuil or a new lining for a fur-collared topcoat, where was there a better place to take the crystal chandelier

from the ballroom or the inlaid piquet table once the property of a king's mistress than to the gallery of Uncle Charlie? And a chosen group of customers understood that, if pressed, Charles Martel could come up with a rarity. Willie Chitling, the movie producer, built the entire bar in his ranch house at Palm Springs with the furniture, paneling, and thirteenth-century altar from the chapel of the Château Vieilleculotte. Charles also made reasonable loans. He was said to hold the personal IOUs of nine out of the Twelve Peers of France.

Charles Martel was the uncle and friend of Pippin Arnulf Héristal. He went out of his field of art and bric-a-brac to trace the Bix Beiderbecke records for Pippin's almost perfect collection. Also he was his nephew's adviser in matters spiritual and temporal.

When M. Héristal stormed into the gallery in the Rue de Seine, Charles noted that he had come in a taxi. The mission was therefore serious.

Charles gestured his nephew past the velvet curtain and quickly concluded the sale of a Louis-Quinze make-up box to an elderly lady tourist for whom it had no practical value. He closed the negotiation not by lowering the price but by suddenly raising it, which convinced the lady that she should buy it at once or she wouldn't get it at all. Charles bowed her out of the gallery, shut the front door, and hung a battered card which read "Closed for Renovation." Then he himself went past the velvet curtain and greeted his pacing nephew.

"You are troubled, my child," he said. "Sit down, sit down. Let me give you a drop of cognac for your nerves."

"I am in a fury," Pippin said, but he did sit down and he did accept the cognac.

"It is Marie?" said Uncle Charlie. "Or perhaps Clotilde?"

"It is Marie."

"It is about money?"

"It is about money," said Pippin.

"How much?"

"I did not come to borrow."

"You come, then, to complain?"

"Exactly, to complain."

"A good idea. It removes pressures. You will return to your home in a more agreeable humor, in a word a better husband. Do you wish to be specific in your complaint?"

Pippin said, "An unpredicted meteor shower has blundered into earth's atmosphere. My camera is not adequate to—well, I need a new camera."

"Expensive, and Marie does not find it necessary?"

"You understand the situation very well. She wears her hurt look, that damnable injured expression. She is planning revenge."

"You have bought the camera?"

"Not yet."

"But you have decided."

"Understand, my uncle, it is unusual to find showers of meteors at this season. Who knows what is going on up there? Do not forget that it was I who first reported the Elysée Comet. I was commended by the Academy. It is whispered that in the not too distant future I may be elected."

"Congratulations, my child. What an honor! While I myself do not view the heavens with passion, I support passion, whatever its source. Begin your complaint, my dear nephew. Now—I am Marie and you are you. Shall we start with the undeniable fact that your income springs from your property, rather than from *dot?*"

"Exactly."

"This land has belonged to your family since the dawn of history."

"Since the Salic Franks invaded from the east."

"In very truth your vineyard hills are the remains of a kingdom."

"An empire."

"You stem from a family so ancient, so noble, that you do not condescend to remind the upstart nobility of your origin by the use of titles clearly yours."

"You put it very well, Uncle Charlie. And all I want is a new camera."

"There," said Charles. "You feel better now?"

"I really do."

"Let me lend you the money for the camera, my child. You can pay it back little by little. Marie does not shy at little things—it is large expenditures which frighten and confuse her."

"I did not come to borrow."

"You have not asked. I have offered. You will purchase the camera. You will inform Marie that you have decided not to buy it. Does Marie know one camera from another?"

"Of course not. But will I not have surrendered my position in the house?"

"Quite the contrary, my child. You will have put her in a position of guilt. She will urge you to buy many little things. Thus you will repay the loan."

"I wonder you have never married."

"I prefer to see other people happy. Now—for what amount shall I make the check?"

When M. Héristal had slammed the iron gate and stormed to the taxi rank on Avenue Gabriel, Madame, for all her cold and deadly triumph, was shaken and uncertain—and at such times it was her habit to visit her old friend Sister Hyacinthe in her convent not far from the Porte

711

de Vincennes—a large, low, orderly building within sight of the Bois. Madame changed her dress, took purse and black shopping bag, and took the métro.

Sister Hyacinthe had been her childhood friend and moreover they had gone to school together. Suzanne Lescault was a pretty child, with a thin, true singing voice and a natural ability as a dancer so that she dominated the pageants and little plays of the school. Inevitably Suzanne rose from wood sprite to fairy queen to Pierrette, and later, for three successive years, she acted *Joan the Maid* to the complete satisfaction of its authoress, the Sister Superior. And Marie, who could neither sing nor dance, far from being jealous, adored her gifted friend and felt that she somehow participated in her triumphs.

In the normal course of events Suzanne would have married and retired her talents and her blossoming figure. However, a distant manipulation of the Crédit Lyonnais and the subsequent suicide of her father, an officer in that organization, left Suzanne with a sickly mother, a dwarflike schoolboy brother in a black smock, and the necessity for making her way in the world. Only then did the often heard comment that she should be on the stage make some sense to Suzanne and more to her mother.

The Comédie Française had no immediate openings but took her name, and while she waited Suzanne was employed by the Folies Bergère, where her voice, her grace, and her high and perfect bosom were instantly appreciated and utilized. Her mother's professional illness, and her brother's interminable education, followed by his death by misadventure with a motorcycle, made it economically unsound for Suzanne to jeopardize a permanent and well-paid position for the uncertainty of higher art.

For many years she graced the stage of the Folies, not only in the line of lovely undressed girls, but also with speaking, singing, and dancing parts. After twenty years of complicated and complaining illness, her mother died without a single symptom. By this time Suzanne had become not only a performer but ballet mistress.

She was very tired. Her bosom had remained high; her arches had fallen. She had lived a life of comparative virtue, as do most Frenchwomen. Indeed it is a matter of disillusion to young male Americans otherwise informed, to discover that the French are a moral people— judged, that is, by American country-club standards.

Suzanne wanted to rest her feet. She left a world about which she knew perhaps too much and after a proper novitiate took the veil as Sister Hyacinthe in an order of contemplation which demanded a great deal of sitting down.

As a nun Sister Hyacinthe radiated such peace and piety that she became an ornament to her order, while her knowledge and background made her both tolerant and helpful to younger sisters with troubles.

During all the years of both her lives she had maintained contact

with her old school friend Marie. Even between visits they kept up a detailed and dull correspondence, exchanging complaints and recipes. Marie still adored her talented and now saintly friend. It was perfectly natural that she called upon her in the matter of the camera.

In the tidy and comfortable little visiting room of the convent near Vincennes, Marie said, "I am at my wit's end. In most things M'sieur is as considerate as one could wish, but where his ill-named stars are concerned he pours out money like water."

Sister Hyacinthe smiled at her. "Why don't you beat him?" she asked pleasantly.

"Pardon? Oh! I see you make a jollity. I assure you it is a serious matter. The cooperage at Auxerre—"

"Is there food on the table, Marie? Is the rent paid? Have they cut off the electricity?"

"It is a matter of principle and of precedent," said Marie a little stiffly.

"My dear friend," said the nun, "did you come to me for advice or to complain?"

"Why, for advice of course. I never complain."

"Of course not," said Sister Hyacinthe, and she continued softly, "I have known many people to ask for advice but very few who wanted it and none who followed it. However, I will advise you."

"Please do," said Marie distantly.

"In my profession, Marie, I have had contacts with many men. I think I am in a position to make some generalities about them. First, they are like children, sometimes spoiled children."

"Now there I agree with you."

"The ones who really truly grow up, Marie, are no good because men are either children or old—there is nothing in between. But in their childlike unreason and irresponsibility there is sometimes greatness. Please understand that I know most women are more intelligent, but women grow up, women face realities—and women are very rarely great. One of the few regrets I have in my present profession is the lack of male nonsense. It at least makes for contrast," said Sister Hyacinthe.

"He discovered a comet," said Marie. "The Academy commended him. But this new camera business—that goes too far."

"Again I ask—do you want my advice?"

"Of course."

"Then advise him to buy the camera—insist on it."

"But I have already taken my stand. I would lose his respect."

"On the contrary," said Sister Hyacinthe, "if you should advise the expenditure, even suggest a greater one, you might find a reluctance on his part to spend the money. He might then have to inspect realities instead of simply opposing you. They are very curious creatures, men."

"I've brought you some handkerchiefs," said Marie.

"Oh, how beautiful! Marie, there is genius in your fingers. How do your eyes permit this tiny embroidery?"

"My eyes have always been good," said Marie.

When Madame returned to Number One Avenue de Marigny she found the double doors of the salon open and her husband busy with small shining tools at his telescope.

"I have been thinking," she said. "It occurs to me that you should buy the camera."

"Eh?" he said.

"Why, it might mean your election to the Academy."

"You are kind," said her husband. "But I too have been thinking. First things must come first. No, I will get along with what I have."

"I implore you."

"No," he said.

"I command it."

"My dear, let us not be confused about who is the head of this house. Do not let us, like the Americans, hear the hens crowing."

"Forgive me," said Marie.

"It is nothing, Madame. And now I must prepare for the night. The meteor shower continues, my dear. The stars have no interest in our problems."

From the floor above came a metallic crash. M. Héristal looked up apprehensively. "I didn't know Clotilde was in."

"The copper table in the hallway," said Madame. "It leaps out at her. I must put it somewhere else."

"Please don't allow her on the terrace, Marie," he said. "My telescope might leap at her."

Clotilde sauntered down the stairs, her dress a little tight over her growing inches. A sullen-looking little fur, savagely biting its own tail, hung limply from her shoulders.

"You are going out, my dear?" Madame asked.

"Oh, yes, Maman. I am having a screen test."

"Not another one!"

"One does as one's director suggests," said Clotilde.

M'sieur moved protectively in front of his telescope as his daughter glided through the double doors and tripped slightly on the doorstep.

"You have then a director?" he asked.

"They are casting for the novel *The Ragamuffin Princess*. You see, there's an orphan girl and—"

"And she finds out she is a princess. It is an American novel."

"You have read it?"

"No, my dear, but I know it."

"How do you know it is American?"

"For one thing because the Americans have perhaps an exaggerated

interest in princesses, and for another thing they have a strong feeling for the Cinderella story."

"Cinderella?"

"You should read it, my dear," he said.

"Gregory Peck is going to play the prince."

"Of course he is," said M'sieur. "Now if it were a French novel the princess would find out that— Careful, my dear—please don't come near the telescope. It is arranged for tonight's show."

When their daughter had oozed away down the stairs and the gate to the courtyard had clanged behind her, Madame said, "I liked it almost better when she was writing novels. She was at home more often. In a way I will be glad when she finds a nice boy of good family."

"She must be a princess first," said her husband. "Everyone must."

"You should not make fun of her."

"Perhaps I was not. I can remember such dreams. They were very real."

"You are amiable, M'sieur."

"I am curiously excited and content, Marie. For a whole week I shall be entertained"—he raised his fingers lightly—"by my friends up there."

"And you will be up all night and sleep all day."

"Of a certainty," said M. Héristal.

The events of 19— in France should be studied not for their uniqueness but rather for their inevitability. The study of history, while it does not endow with prophecy, may indicate lines of probability.

It was and is no new thing for a French government to fall for lack of a vote of confidence. What has been called in other countries "instability" is in France a kind of stability. Lord Cotten has said that "In France anarchy has been refined to the point of reaction," and later, "Stability to a Frenchman is intolerable tyranny." Alas, too few are emotionally capable of understanding Lord Cotten.

Many millions of words partisan and passionate have been written about the recent French crisis and re-crisis. It remains to trace the process with the cool and appraising eye of the historian.

On February 12, 19—, when M. Rumorgue was finally placed in the position of asking for a vote on the issue of Monaco, it is conceded that he knew the result in advance. Indeed, there were many around him who felt he welcomed the termination of his premiership. M. Rumorgue, in addition to his titular leadership of the Proto-Communist party, which is traditionally two degrees right of center, is an authority in psycho-botany. To accept the premiership at all, he had reluctantly abandoned for the time being the experiments concerning pain in plants which he had been carrying on for many years at his nursery at Juan les Pins. Few people outside this field are even aware of Professor Ru-

morgue's Separate entitled *Tendencies and Symptoms of Hysteria in Red Clover*, reprinted from his address to the Academy of Horticulture. His academic triumph over his critics, some of whom went to the extreme of denouncing him as being crazier than his clover, must have made him doubly reluctant to assume not only the leadership of his party but also the premiership of France. The newspaper *Peace Thru War,* although in opposition to the Proto-Communists, very likely quoted M. Rumorgue correctly in remarking that white clover with all its faults was easier to deal with emotionally than the elected representatives of the people of France.

The question on which M. Rumorgue's government failed, while interesting, was not nationally important. It is widely believed that if the Monaco question had not arisen, some other difficulty would have taken its place. M. Rumorgue himself emerged with honor and was able to work quietly on his forthcoming book on "Inherited Schizophrenia in Legumes" —a group of Mendelian by-laws.

At any rate, France found herself without a government. It will be remembered that when President Sonnet called on the Christian Atheists to form a government they could not agree even within their own ranks. Likewise the Socialists failed to draw support. The Christian Communists, with the support of the Non-Tax-Payers' League, failed to qualify. Only then did M. Sonnet call the historic conference of leaders of all parties at the Elysée Palace.

The parties involved at this time should be listed, since some of them have since disappeared and been replaced by others. Those groups attending the president's call are here listed, not by their power but simply geographically in relation to the center. Gathered in the Elysée Palace were:

The Conservative Radicals
The Radical Conservatives
The Royalists
The Right Centrists
The Left Centrists
The Christian Atheists
The Christian Christians
The Christian Communists
The Proto-Communists
The Neo-Communists
The Socialists
 and
The Communists

The Communists were broken up into:
Stalinists
Trotskyists
Khrushchevniks
Bulganinians

For three days the struggle raged. The leaders slept on the brocade couches of the Grand Ballroom and subsisted on the bread and cheese and Algerian wine furnished by M. le Président. It was a scene of activity and turmoil. The Elysée Ballroom is not only wainscoted with mirrors but also has mirrors on its ceiling, which created the impression that instead of forty-two party chiefs there were literally thousands. Every raised fist became fifty fists, while the echo from the hard mirror surfaces threw back the sounds of a multitude.

M. Rumorgue, the fallen minister and leader of the Proto-Communists, left the meeting and went back to Juan les Pins on receipt of a telegram from Madame Rumorgue saying that the Poland China sow, named Anxious, had farrowed.

At the end of seven days the conference had accomplished nothing. President Sonnet put the Elysée bathroom at the disposal of the delegates, at the same time refusing to be responsible for their linen.

The seriousness of the impasse at last began to be reflected in the Paris press. The humorous periodical *Alligator* suggested that the situation should be made permanent, since no national crisis had arisen since the party leaders were taken out of circulation.

Great historic decisions often result from small and even flippant causes. Well into the second week, the leaders of the larger political parties found that their voices, which had gone from loud to harsh to hoarse, were finally disappearing completely.

It was at this time that the compact group of the leaders of the Royalist party took the floor. Having had no hope of being included in any new government, they had abstained from making speeches, and thus had kept their voices. After the confusion of eight days of meetings, the calm of the Royalists was by contrast explosive.

The Comte de Terrefranque advanced to the rostrum and took the floor in spite of an impassioned but whispered address by M. Triflet, the Radical Conservative.

M. le Comte in a clear, loud voice announced that the Royalist group had joined forces. He himself, he said, in spite of his basic and unchanging loyalty to the Merovingian line, from which his title derived, had agreed to join the Bourbons, not from lack of respect and love for his own great tradition, but simply because the Merovingians were not able to produce a prince of clear and direct descent. He therefore introduced the Duc des Troisfronts, whose proposal would have the backing not only of the other Royalist parties but also of the noble and intelligent people of France.

The Duc des Troisfronts, who under ordinary circumstances was shielded from public appearances, because of the split palate which has been his family's chief characteristic for many generations, now took the stand and was able to make himself not only heard but even understood.

France, he said, stood at the crossroads. Under the tattered flag of

the unwashed, the greedy, and the inept, France had seen herself reduced from the glorious leadership of the world to a bitter, bickering, third-rate power, a craven province trying unsuccessfully to lick the boots of England and the United States on the one hand—or rather foot—and of the Commissars on the other.

M. le Duc was so surprised that he had been able to say all of this that he sat down and had to be reminded that he had not arrived at the point. Once reminded, however, he graciously arose again. He suggested, even commanded, that the monarchy be restored so that France might rise again like the phoenix out of the ashes of the Republic to cast her light over the world. He ended his address in tears and immediately left the room, crying to the Gardes Républicains at the gates of the palace, "I have failed! I have failed!" But, indeed, as everyone knows, he had not failed.

The announcement by the Duc des Troisfronts had the effect of shocking the party leaders to silence. Every man seemed frozen within himself. Only very gradually did a series of whispered conferences begin. Party leaders collected in knots and spoke together in low tones, glancing occasionally over their shoulders.

M. Deuxcloches, actual leader of the Communist bloc, although he himself holds only the humble party position of Cultural Custodian, seems to have been the first to realize the implications of the proposal of des Troisfronts.

At M. Deuxcloches' behest, the Communist group left the ballroom and reassembled in the president's bathroom. But here a protocolic impasse arose. Two officials were involved, and two seats. M. Douxpied was indeed party Secretary, but Cultural Custodian Deuxcloches was conceded to hold the actual power. This being so, the question arose as to which took precedence, toilet or bidet? Such a consideration might have engaged the meeting indefinitely had not M. Gustave Harmonie flung himself passionately into the breach. It was true, he argued, that the Communist party was the Communist party, but, he continued—France was France.

M. Deuxcloches stroked his chin nervously and made his historic choice by taking his position on the bidet. However, in view of possible review, he held that the apparent deviation was only local. The German party, he maintained, might feel called upon to take an opposite course. The burst of applause at his decision gave him courage to go on.

M. Deuxcloches argued as follows. The Communist party's natural function was revolution, he said. Any change which made revolution more feasible was undeniably to the party's advantage. French politics were in a state of anarchy. It is very difficult to revolt against anarchy, since in the popular mind, undialectically informed, revolution *is* anarchy. There is no point, to the uninstructed, in substituting anarchy for anarchy. On the other hand, he continued, monarchy is the natural magnet for revolu-

tion, as can be historically verified. Therefore, it would be to the Communists' advantage if the French monarchy were restored. That would be a position to kick off from and, indeed, would speed up the revolution.

M. Douxpied broke in at this juncture to point out that world opinion might be startled to find the French Communist party advocating the return of a king.

M. Deuxcloches assured the party Secretary that no such report would go out. The French party would not vote at all. Once the king was crowned, it would be time to announce that France had been misled by unkept promises and imperialist pressures. Meanwhile, definite work toward the revolution could proceed.

After a few moments of thought, M. Douxpied arose and warmly clasped the hand of M. Deuxcloches, a simple and symbolic gesture of agreement. The other members instantly followed suit. However, one delegate did suggest that perhaps, with the Communists abstaining, the Socialists might join the Christian Atheists and the Proto-Communists to defeat the measure.

"Then we must make sure they do not," M. Deuxcloches replied. "If the Socialists do not think of it themselves it might be suggested to them that a king would keep the Communists in check."

His statement drew applause and the meeting adjourned back to the Ballroom.

Meanwhile, there had been other conferences among other partisans. The Socialists, for example, did not need any suggestion. It was obvious to them that a king would indeed keep the Communists in check. With that stumbling block out of the way, the Socialists could look forward to the gradual change which was their advocation.

The Christian Atheists agreed together that under the present scattering of parties, with resulting confusion, the unconfused Church was making inroads. Monarchy, on the other hand, was the natural enemy of the Church Militant; England was the perfect example of popular monarchy's successful stand against inroads of Rome.

The Christian Christians took the position that the royal family had always been unequivocally Catholic, while the aristocracy, particularly those members stemming from the Ancien Régime, if they had not deviated in adversity would not be likely to do so once their dream had come true.

The Left Centrists are a powerful force, particularly when they are able to find a common ground with the Right Centrists. Together these parties represent what have been called the Hundred Families, although since the Second World War and American economic aid, they might be better designated as the Two Hundred Families. These two parties represent not only mining and manufacturing, but also banking and insurance and real estate, the only difference between them being that the Left Centrists favor retirement and medical provisions common to American

corporations, while the Right Centrists do not. These two parties were able to agree almost immediately on restoration of the monarchy, because a king would undoubtedly curb both Socialists and Communists and in so doing would put an end to demands for pay increases and shorter hours.

The Non-Tax-Payers' League concluded that a Royalist regime would collect taxes from Right and Left Centrists, and this was their main reason for being. They were quite aware that the projected monarchy would not collect taxes from the aristocracy, but they argued that this was a very small group and moreover bankrupt so that it was not important if Royalists were exempt.

There grew up a unanimity of direction among the political parties unique in recent history. Each group favored the restoration of the monarchy for different reasons and for reasons beneficial to itself. The Communists, true to their position, maintained a sullen silence.

The debate caught fire in the French press, which found, in increased circulation, its own reasons for keeping the matter in the public eye. *Le Figaro*, in a front-page editorial, argued that French dignity and integrity would be better served if its symbol were a king rather than a dressmaker. The Parisians in general favored a proposal which promised variety, while the Association of Restaurateurs, the Couture, and the Hotel Association, felt that, since Americans loved royalty, the increase in tourism and spending alone would justify the change. As for the farmers, provincial and peasant, they are traditionally opposed to any government in power and so are automatically in favor of change, good or bad. In the National Assembly the enthusiasts demanded an immediate vote.

The Royalists of France, or for that matter of any country where royalty has been eliminated as a governing principle, have never given up. Indeed, it is a part of the nature, even of the triumphant gallantry of an aristocracy, that it does not, it cannot, abandon the certainty of its return, bringing with it the golden days, the prosperous and courteous days. Then again will come honor and truthfulness, devotion to duty and reverence for the king; then will servants and peasants be protected and sheltered, not turned out into a rapacious world; then will a man be properly known for his illustrious past rather than for his aggressive and greedy present; then will Gracious Majesty preside like a benevolent umpire over the refined and well-born. The king will tenderly direct and correct proper families and sternly reproach and punish any who attempt to force themselves in or to change the rules. Then will gentlemen be gallant to ladies and ladies lovely and gracious to gentlemen. Anyone who does not hold these things to be true has no place in the ranks of the noblesse.

The Royalists were a clot in the bloodstream of the Republic. The Royalist party, while not numerous, rich, nor vocal, was close-knit and passionately devoted. Any difficulties among its members were social or

had to do with ancient prestige and the maintenance of a permanently fragile honor.

While the National Assembly debated the return of the monarchy with increasing fervor and approval, the Royalists met in a hall which had once housed the Czech Social Gymnastic and Oratory Club and been abandoned after the *Anschluss* with the Soviet Union.

No one could have foreseen any difficulty. The Bourbon Pretender was available, legitimate, and trained for his position. Fortunately, he had not been asked to the meeting. There were present:

Vercingetorians
Merovingians
Carolingians
Capetians
Burgundians
Orleanists
Bourbons
Bonapartists

And two very small groups—

Angevins, who were rumored to have British support, and
Caesarians, who claimed their descent from Julius and bore the
bend sinister proudly.

The Bourbons walked like emperors and smiled little Bourbon smiles when the king's health was drunk. But when they named their Pretender, the Comte de Paris—all hell broke loose.

Bonapartists leaped up, their eyes wild. Comte de Jour, whose great-grandfather had carried his marshal's baton in his knapsack, cried, "Bourbon! Why Bourbon? Has the sacred blood of Napoleon run out? And aligned with Orleans? Gentlemen, are we to live under the shadow of Bourbon and Orleans, the two lines which contributed most to the fall of the French monarchy? Are we—?"

"No," screamed the Angevins, with what some thought was an English accent.

"Better the Merovingians, better the Rois Fainéants," shrieked the Capetians.

For a day and a night the battle raged while noble voices grew hoarse and noble hearts pounded. Of all the aristocratic partisans, only the Merovingians sat back, quiet, listless, content, and faint.

It was mid-morning of the second day when exhaustion proclaimed to all the undeniable fact that the Royalists could no more settle on a king than the Republicans could form a government. In the night they had sent for a sheaf of swords and altered the Code by acclamation. Hardly a gentleman there was who did not wear scratches and cuts which proclaimed that his honor was intact. Only the lazy Merovingians were unruffled and unscarred.

At 10:37 A.M., February 21, 19—, the elderly Childéric de Saône

stood gradually up and spoke softly in his dusty Merovingian voice, which nevertheless was one of the few voices left.

"My noble friends," he began, "as you know, I adhere to a dynasty which does not admit that you exist."

A Bourbon lunged tiredly toward the umbrella stand of swords, but Childéric stopped him with an upraised hand.

"Desist, dear Marquis," he said. "My kings, it is recorded, disappeared through lassitude. We Merovingians do not want the crown. Consequently, perhaps we are in a position to arbitrate—to advise." He smiled wanly. "It appears to us that the Republican years have left their mark on this gathering. You, sirs, have conducted yourselves with all the foolishness of the elected representatives of an even less endowed populace but without their endurance. I am glad that this has been a closed meeting so that no one could see us."

A guilty silence fell on the gathering. The nobles hung their heads in shame while Childéric continued.

"In the days of my ancestors," he said, "these matters of succession were handled in a nobler manner—with poison, poniard, or the quick and merciful hands of the strangler. Now we have surrendered to the ballot. Very well, let us use it like noblemen. Let him who can vote most often, win."

Childéric paused, unscrewed the handle of his walking stick, and took a sip of the cognac which replaced the blade the stick had once concealed.

"Is anyone ready to interrupt me now?" he asked courteously. "Very well, I will continue. It seems apparent that Bourbon, Orleans, Burgundy, even cadet Capet, can only reign by the old method of decimation. I suggest, therefore, that we go farther back. As for Anjou—" He spread his first and second fingers in the Churchill victory sign but pointed them forward, which alters the meaning of the gesture.

Burgundy leaped up, intending to shout, "Who? You?" but the bleat his tortured throat emitted sounded more like, "Whee? Yee?"

"No," said Childéric, "I am content to live as my latter kings lived and to solve the problem as they did. I suggest for the throne of France the holy blood of Charlemagne."

Bourbon exploded in a thunderous whisper. "Are you insane? The line has disappeared."

"Not so," said Childéric quietly. "You will recall, noble sirs, although at the time your ancestors were herding sheep, that Pippin II of Héristal, ignoring the Salic custom of partition, gave all his realm to his son Charles —later called the Hammer."

"What of it?" Bourbon demanded. "There is no issue now."

"Not from Charles Martel, no. But I ask you also to remember that Charles was illegitimate. Perhaps this has blinded you to the fact

that Pippin II had two legitimate sons and these he passed over *de jure,* but could he, did he have the power *in esse* or *de facto?*

"In Paris today lives Pippin Arnulf Héristal, a pleasant man, an amateur astronomer, while his uncle Charles Martel is proprietor of a small gallery in the Rue de Seine. Being descended from the legitimate branch, perhaps he uses the name Martel improperly."

"But can they prove it?"

"They can prove it," Childéric assured the nobles pleasantly. "Pippin is an old friend of mine. He is clever. He balances my checkbook. I call him the Mayor of the Palace—a poor joke, but we laugh. Pippin lives on the proceeds of two vineyards, the last remnant of the monster estates of Héristal and Arnulf. Noble sirs, I have the honor to propose that we unite under His Gracious Majesty Pippin of Héristal and Arnulf, of the line of Charlemagne."

The die was cast, although the whispering went on until weary evening proved that no other agreement was possible.

Finally the nobility concurred. They even tried to cheer—to cheer the king. They succeeded in drinking his health and they carried the name and origin of Pippin to the floor of the National Assembly, where it was received with relieved enthusiasm, for it had already occurred to the more astute representatives of the French people that 1789 was not so long ago. But who could hate Héristal—or Charlemagne?

Under ordinary circumstances M. Héristal kept himself informed of the activities and processes of government. However, the double excitement of the meteor shower and the triumphant intricacy of the new camera kept him on the roof terrace at night and in the wine-cellar darkroom in the morning, wherefrom he retired, exhausted but happy, to recuperate for the next evening.

M. Héristal was one of very few in France, perhaps in the world, who were not aware that the Republic had been voted out of existence and the French Monarchy proclaimed. It follows that he was also ignorant that he himself had been elected by acclamation King of France with the name Pippin IV. Pippin the Short, son of Charles Martel, who died in 768 A.D., was considered to have been Pippin III.

When the triumphant committee bore the official will of the people of France to the house at Number One Avenue de Marigny at nine o'clock in the morning, M. Héristal, in wine-colored dressing gown, was sitting in his study, drinking a cup of hot Sanka imported from America and preparing to go to bed.

He listened courteously, removing his pince-nez and rubbing his reddened eyes. At first he was wearily amused. But when he realized that the suggestion was serious he was deeply shocked. He placed his pince-nez astraddle his right forefinger, where it rode like a saddle.

"Gentlemen," he said, "you are making a joke, and, if you will excuse my observation, a joke not in good taste."

His unbelief increased the vehemence of the committee. They shouted with renewed voices. They demanded his instant acceptance of the throne for the safety and the future of France.

In the midst of the tumult, Pippin leaned back in his chair and put his blue-veined hand to his forehead as though to shut the unreal scene away.

"Sometimes," he said, "a man imagines things, particularly when he is fatigued. I do hope, gentlemen, that when I open my eyes you will not be here. I will then take something for my liver."

"But Your Majesty—"

Pippin's eyes popped open. "Oh, well," he said. "There was just a chance. That term 'Your Majesty' makes me uneasy. I must believe, I suppose, that you gentlemen are not playing some complicated practical joke—no, you do not appear to be joking types—but if you are not insane, what is your authority for this ridiculous proposal?"

M. Flosse of the Right Centrists put an oratorical edge to his voice. "France has found it impossible to form a government, Sire. For a number of years governments have fallen as soon as they have agreed on a policy."

"I know," said Pippin. "Perhaps policy is what we are afraid of."

M. Flosse went on. "France needs a continuity to ride secure above party and above faction. Look at England! Parties may change in England but there is a direction inherent in the monarchy. This France once had. This France has lost. We believe, Your Majesty, that it can be restored."

Pippin said softly, "England's monarchs lay cornerstones and take unequivocal positions on the kind of hat to wear to a race track. But have you thought, my friends, that Englishmen love their government and spend most of their time celebrating it, while Frenchmen on the contrary automatically detest any government in power? I am of the same persuasion. It is the French way of regarding government. Until I am better informed, I would like to go to sleep. But have you thought of the difficulties involved in your—plan? France has been a republic for some time now. Her institutions are republican, her thinking is republican. I think I had better go to bed. You still haven't told me who sent this deputation."

M. Flosse cried, "The Senate and the Assembly of France only await Your Majesty's gracious acceptance. We are sent by the representatives of the people of France."

"Will the Communists vote for the monarchy?" Héristal asked gently.

"They will not oppose, Sire. They guarantee that."

"And how about the people of France? I seem to remember that

724

they swarmed into Paris with pitchforks and that some royalty—fortunately no relatives of mine—did not survive."

Senator Veauvache, the Socialist, rose to his feet. This is the same Veauvache who aroused national attention in 1948 by refusing a bribe. At that time he was given the honorary title Honnête Jean, which he has carried with humility to this day. M. Veauvache said solemnly, "A sampling of opinion indicates that the French people will unite behind you as one man."

"Whom did you sample?" Pippin asked.

"That is beside the point," Honnête Jean said. "In America, the home of the opinion poll, does anyone ask that insulting question?"

"I'm sorry," Pippin apologized. "I guess it is because I am sleepy and confused and tired. I am not as young as I was—"

"Poof!" said M. Flosse flatteringly.

"And, too, I have been busy with—" He gestured upward. "Madame doesn't bother me with news when I am preoccupied. You see, gentlemen, I am taken off guard."

"You must be crowned at Reims," cried M. Flosse, and his eyes brimmed with emotion. "We must follow the old customs. France needs you, Sire. Will you deny your country the security of your great bloodline?"

"My bloodline?"

"Are you not directly descended from Pippin the Second?"

"Oh! Is that what it's all about? But there have been so many other royal houses since—"

"But you do not deny your descent?"

"How could I? I believe it is a matter of record."

"Do you forbid us, Sire?"

"That's silly," said Pippin. "How can I forbid anything a republic might take it into its head to do, even destroy itself? I am the broken tip of a long dog's long tail. Can I wag that dog?"

"France needs—"

"And I need sleep, gentlemen. Please leave me now and I will awaken some hours hence, hoping that you have been a dream."

And while he slept what has been called in the press the "Historic Nap," students from the Sorbonne marched up the Champs Elysées, shouting "Vive le roi!" and "Saint Denis pour la France." Four of them climbed the girders of the Eiffel Tower and raised an antique royal standard on the very top, where it fluttered triumphantly among the wind gauges.

The citizens boiled into the streets, dancing and singing with excitement.

Barrels of wine from the cooperative warehouses up-Seine were rolled through the streets and broached on the street corners.

The Lords of the Couture rushed to their drawing boards.

Schiaparelli, within the hour, announced a new perfume called "Rêve Royale."

Special editions of *L'Espèce, Cormoran, Paris Minuit, L'Era,* and *Monde Dieu* rolled from the presses and were snatched up.

The royal standard of Charlemagne appeared like magic in shop windows.

The American Ambassador, with instructions from his government, sought in vain for someone to congratulate.

The wave overflowed Paris, and concentric circles spread into the provinces, lighting bonfires and raising flags.

And through it all, the king slept. But Madame made hourly visits to the kiosk for the new editions and piled them neatly on his desk for his perusal.

Pippin might well have slept through the night and into the next day had not the anti-aircraft batteries disposed about Paris fired a royal salute at two-thirty in the morning. Five citizens were killed and thirty-two were wounded by the fallback. The thirty-two wounded made loyal and enthusiastic statements from their hospital beds.

The firing of the anti-aircraft guns awakened Pippin. His first thought was, It must be Clotilde coming in. What has she stumbled over now?

A second salvo of anti-aircraft guns brought him up on his elbow, his left hand thrashing about, seeking the bed reading light. "Marie!" he called. "Marie! What is that?"

Madame opened the door. Her arms were loaded with newspapers. "It is the Royal Salute," she said. "*L'Espèce* says there will be one hundred and one guns."

"My God!" said Pippin. "I thought it was Clotilde." He looked at his watch, then raised his voice to be heard over the guns. "It is three, less fifteen minutes. Where is Clotilde?"

Madame said coldly, "La Princesse, on a motor scooter, is leading her loyal subjects to Versailles. She is going to start the fountains."

Pippin said, "Then it was no dream! When the Minister of Public Works hears of this, I smell the guillotine. Marie, these people seem to mean this nonsense. I want to talk to Uncle Charlie."

In the early dawn the king and his uncle faced each other in the rear of the gallery in the Rue de Seine.

Pippin had battered on the shutters of Charles Martel's establishment until that gentleman, clad in a long nightgown and a tarboosh, ill-tempered with sleep, peered out at him. After a time of grumbling, of making his morning chocolate, and of pulling on his trousers, Uncle Charlie settled back on his dusty Morocco armchair, adjusted the green-shaded reading light, polished his glasses, and prepared for business.

"You must study calmness, Pippin," he said. "For years I have recommended calmness. When you burst in here with your——comet, I

suggested that the stars would wait on a cup of chocolate. When Clotilde had her small difficulty with the gendarmes about the improper use of firearms at the shooting gallery, did I not recommend calm? And it came out all right, you remember. You paid for a few light globes she shot from a carousel, and Clotilde sold her life story to an American magazine. Calm! Pippin. Calm! I recommend calm."

"But they have gone insane, Uncle Charlie."

"No, my boy, abandon that theory. The French do not go insane unless there is some advantage in it. Now you say that the delegation was composed of all parties, and you further say that they mentioned the future well-being of France."

"They say France must have a stable government."

"Hmmm," said Uncle Charlie. "It has always seemed to me that this is the last thing they want. It is possible, Pippin, that the parties have chosen a direction, but for different reasons. Yes, that must be it, and you, my poor boy, have been chosen for the role of what the Americans call a 'patsy.'"

"What can I do, Uncle Charlie? How can I avoid this—this patsy?"

Uncle Charlie tapped his glasses on his knee, sneezed, poured himself a fresh cup of chocolate from the saucepan on the gas ring at his elbow, and slowly shook his head.

"With time and calm," he said, "I could possibly work out the political background. But right at the moment I cannot see any escape for you unless you wish to retire with dignity to a warm bath and cut your wrists."

"I don't want to be king!"

"If suicide does not appeal to you, dear boy, you may relax in the certainty that in the near future there will be attempts at assassination and, who knows, one of them may succeed."

"Can't I say no, Uncle Charlie? No, no, no, no! Why not?"

Uncle Charlie sighed. "I can think of two reasons now. Later, several more will come to me. In the first place, you will be told that France needs you. No one has ever been able to resist such a suggestion, here or elsewhere. Let a man, old, sick, stupid, tired, cynical, wise, even dangerous to the future of his country, be told that his country needs him and him alone, and he will respond even though he must be carried to the rostrum on a stretcher and take the oath and Extreme Unction simultaneously. No, I can see no escape for you. If they tell you that France needs you, you are lost. You can only pray that France is not also lost."

"But maybe—"

"You see," said Uncle Charlie, "you are already caught. The second force is more subtle but no less powerful. It is the overwhelming numerical strength of the aristocracy. Let me develop this.

"Aristocracy thrives and breeds most luxuriantly under democratic or republican regimes. Whereas in a kingdom the aristocrats are screened and

controlled, even eliminated for one reason or another, in republican climates the noblesse breed like rabbits. At the same time, the lower orders seem to become sterile. You will find the best proof of this in America, where there is no single individual who is not descended from an aristocrat, where there is not even an Indian who is not a tribal chief. In republican France, to only a slightly lesser degree, the aristocracy has shown a fecundity beyond belief.

"They will be down on you like sparrows on a— No, I won't complete that simile. They will demand privileges unremembered since Louis the Ugly, but more than that, my dear child, they will want money."

Pippin said miserably, "What am I to do, Uncle Charlie? Why couldn't it have waited a generation or two? Isn't there a collateral branch of the family who might—"

"No," said Charles, "there isn't. And if there were, the combination of reason number one, plus Madame, plus Clotilde, would pull you under. And there's another thing. If every Frenchman should oppose your accession to the monarchy, every Frenchwoman would force you to reign. Too long have they looked with craving eyes across the channel, sneered at the frumpiness of British royalty, and envied it.

"Pippin, my child, you are sunk," said Charles. "You are the royal patsy. I suggest that you search deeply in the situation for something to enjoy. And now I know you will excuse me. A client is coming in with three unsigned Renoirs."

Pippin said, "Well, anyway, I don't feel so alone, knowing that you will have to assume your titles."

"Name of a thrice-soiled name!" cried Uncle Charlie. "I had forgotten that!"

In a daze, Pippin left the gallery. He wandered blindly up-Seine on the Left Bank, past Notre-Dame, past warehouses, past wine storage, over bridges, past factories, and he did not look around until he came to Bercy.

During his long and slow peramble it is more than possible that his mind, like a rat in a laboratory maze, sought every possible avenue of escape, explored runways and aisles and holes, only to run against the wire netting of fact. Again and again he butted his mental nose against the screen at the end of a promising passage, and there was the fact. He was king and there was no escaping it.

In Bercy he stumbled wearily into a café, sat at a small marble table, observed, without seeing it, a passionate domino game, and, although it was not yet noon, he ordered a Pernod. He drank so rapidly and ordered another so promptly that the domino-players thought him a tourist and guarded their language.

With his third Pernod, Pippin was heard to say, "All right, then. All right, then." He swallowed his drink and waved for another and, when it came, he addressed his glass.

728

"So you want a king, my friends? But have you considered the danger? Do you know what you might have conjured up?" He turned to the domino-players. "Will you do me the honor of drinking a toast with me?" he demanded.

Sullenly they accepted. For an American, they thought, he spoke excellent French.

When they were served, Pippin raised his glass. "They want a king! I drink to the King! Long live the King!" He drained his glass. "Very well, my friends," he said. "It is just possible that they will *get* a king—and that's the last thing in the world they want. Yes, they may find they have a king on their hands." He got up from his table and moved to the door. It was noted that he had a slow and regal step.

IT IS NOT SO EASY as might appear on the surface to reactivate a monarchy. There is the matter of what kind of monarchy you are going to have. Pippin leaned strongly toward the constitutional form, not only because he was a liberal man at heart, but also because the responsibility of absolutism is very great. He owned himself too lazy to make all the effort for success and too cowardly to take all the blame for mistakes.

The meeting of all parties called to determine procedure constituted itself, at Pippin's request, a deliberative body. A troubling question was introduced by the king very early in the discussion. What would the American government think of the change, and would the American State Department be likely to continue to recommend the same financial aid to the Kingdom as it had to the Republic of France?

M. Flosse, representing both Right and Left Centrists, was able to put any such doubts at rest. "It is the nature of American foreign policy to distrust liberal governments and strongly to favor the more authoritarian, which it considers the more responsible."

M. Flosse named Venezuela, Portugal, Saudi Arabia, Trans-Jordan, Egypt, Spain, and Monaco as examples of this American peculiarity. He went even further, proving that the People's Republics of the USSR, plus Poland, Czechoslovakia, Bulgaria, China, and North Korea, also had in the past shown a strong preference for dictatorships and absolute monarchies over democratically elected governments.

It was not necessary to inquire into the reasons for these preferences, said M. Flosse. Indeed, it might even be embarrassing. The fact that such preference was a historical fact was sufficient. In the case of America, he went on, there was, in addition, a sentimental attachment for the throne of France.

"When the American colonies were alone in their war for independence, who came to their aid with men, money, and material? A re-

public? No, the Kingdom of France. Who crossed the ocean to serve in the armies of America? Common people? No, aristocrats."

M. Flosse suggested that the king's first official act should be to request a subsidy for his government from America for the purpose of making France strong against Communism, and an equal subsidy from the Communist nations in the interests of world peace.

The enthusiastic response from both the United States and the Union of Soviet Socialist Republics is proof enough that M. Flosse had properly assessed the situation. It is history by now that not only did the American Congress advance more money than was requested, but also that the Lafayette Fund, collected from school children, made possible the beginning of the refurbishing of the royal quarters at Versailles.

After the first explosion of enthusiasm there was some worry among government functionaries: the postmen, the inspectors, the myriads of little officials, public toilet keepers, national monument guardians, custom inspectors, inspectors of inspectors; all of whom feared on second consideration that their livings might be curtailed. A general proclamation from the king, freezing the status quo, however, put all minds at rest and created a passionate loyalty among the concessionaires.

At this time the Minister of National Monuments presented a bill to the king for three hundred thousand francs, an expense incurred when the Princess Clotilde not only turned on the fountains at Versailles but also made use of the floodlights during two whole nights. The princess herself had waved the bill aside regally.

Pippin was able to prove that his total balance in the Chase Bank in the Rue Cambon was one hundred and twenty thousand francs. The first loan from America, however, solved the matter to everyone's satisfaction.

Complex as it was to establish the monarchy, the actual crowning of the king at Reims proved even more difficult. Charles had been correct in his estimate of the increase in the numbers of the aristocracy under the Republic. Not only had the noblesse multiplied beyond all belief, but they could not agree on the actual form of the crowning. That it should take an ancient and traditional form was conceded, but which ancient form?

Vitally interested groups demanded that the crowning be put off until the summer. The Couture was swamped with orders for court dresses. The ceramics industries needed time to make the millions of cups and plates and ashtrays and plaques bearing not only the royal arms, but the profile of the king and queen. The summer would bring a tidal wave of tourists, which alone would make the whole venture profitable.

Matters not previously contemplated became of vital importance. Newly appointed lords of protocol, kings-at-arms, nobles of the bedcham-

ber, ladies in waiting, ran in circles, while the offices of the Royal Historians were lighted all night.

The museums were ransacked for coaches, for costumes, for flags. The libraries were turned inside out. The coinage had to be changed. There was no artist whose brush and palette could not find employment in repainting coats of arms and armorial bearings. Such had been the progenitive activity of the nobility that every shield required new quarterings. By general agreement the bend sinister was abandoned, since its inclusion would have given a tiresome sameness to the bearings of the living and a lack of dignity to the hatchments of the deceased.

Carriage-makers, unemployed for half a lifetime, were dragged out of senile retirement to swell the spokes and felloes of state coaches and to direct the replacement of leather springs.

Armorers relearned the burnishing and lubrication of gauntlets, of greaves, of visors, of basinets, for many of the younger peers insisted on attending the coronation armed cap-a-pie, regardless of the weather.

The nylon industry put on an extra shift in all plants to fill the demand for velvets and artificial mothproof ermine.

The actual crown presented a problem, since it did not exist. However, Van Cleef and Arpels, Harry Winston, and Tiffany's pooled their resources, their craftsmen, and their precious stones to create a diadem three feet high and so thickly jeweled that a support had to be built on the back of the throne, else its weight would have broken the neck of the monarch. This crown was carried by four priests and when, after the coronation, it was broken up and its individual stones properly attested, it sold for a profit of twelve million dollars and the firms which had created it were granted the right to display the royal arms and to use the title "Crown Makers to the King of France."

Apart from affairs of state, of finance, of international relations, and of protocol, a change from republic to monarchy involved a thousand details which might escape the ordinary citizen.

In Paris schools sprang up to revivify lost arts and graces—Schools of the Walk (with or without staff), Schools of the Bow, of the Curtsy, the Hand Kiss; Schools of the Fan, Schools of the Insult, Schools of Honor. Fencing masters found their classes crowded. Old General Victor Gonzel, who is the world's final authority on the proper use of the muzzle-loading pistol, gave daily instructions to half a hundred budding courtiers.

On all of this preparation Pippin looked with consternation. A delegation proposing to establish a company of Life Guards armed with halberds made him miss an eclipse of the moon. The clamors of the Hereditary Royal Order of Dwarfs drove him to seclusion in the rear of Uncle Charles's gallery.

"The Folies Bergère is holding a competition," he complained. "They are choosing a King's Mistress. Uncle Charlie, in my young days when it

731

was expected of me, I went along with our national practice even though it was expensive and, after a while, boring. But now—do you know they have entries from every nation in the world? I won't do it, Uncle Charlie. Even Marie has been after me about it. Damn it, Uncle Charlie, have you ever heard those girls talk?"

"I have by various methods sought to avoid that," said Uncle Charlie. "My child, in some things you may be able to assert your royal authority, but if you think you can be King of France without a mistress to enlighten your people with her extravagance and her charming unreliability, you are very much mistaken."

"But kings' mistresses have kept the nation in hot water almost invariably."

"Of course, my boy. Of course, that is part of it. Has your astronomy robbed you of any sense of proportion or knowledge of history?"

"I'll get myself a minister," said Pippin violently. "That's what I'll do! Somewhere I'll find myself a Mazarin or a Richelieu and let him do the work."

"You'll find that a minister worth his salt will be very firm about a mistress," said Uncle Charles. "Figure it to yourself—it would be like going without your clothes. The French nation would not tolerate it."

"I don't have any privacy," said Pippin. "I am not even crowned yet and already I haven't a moment of peace. And I must say you are not taking your hereditary duties very seriously. The report has come to me that you have uncovered a whole atticful of unsigned Bouchers."

"A man must live," said his uncle. "But you must not imagine that I have deserted you. I have been thinking in your behalf. Pippin, I want your complete attention. In America a chief executive who has found the duties and requirements of his office in conflict with his interests has discovered an interesting and practical expedient. He has turned over details of his office or of his party to one of the great advertising agencies.

"Now these companies, with their huge staffs and—how do you say it?—their 'know-how,' are able to manage public relations, organization, correspondence, news releases, and appointments. If such a company can merchandise a president and a political party, why not a king? Consider their intelligence! In foreign relations their policy derives not from some disinterested public servant, but from doing the most profitable business with the principality in question. And who would be more tender and wise than an agency whose profits depend on its tenderness and its wisdom? If such a connection could be made, Pippin, you could go back to your telescope. The advertising agency would handle everything and would also see that proper reports were furnished to the press. Why, they would even take care of the career of your mistress."

"It sounds ideal," said Pippin.

"Oh! There is more than that, my boy. Consider the simple matter

of a speech on television. I can foresee that you will have to appear on television as King of France."

"What do they do?"

"Let us say the president must make a speech. Nothing is left to accident. He is rehearsed by an authority in speech, in pronunciation, and in emotion; coached by a man who has proved beyond doubt his—what they call 'draw.'"

"Like Marilyn Monroe—"

"Well, something like. But that is not all. He then is made up by the Westmore Brothers, the best. He does not just talk. Not at all. He has a stage manager, the scene is set. It is rehearsed. It rises to a glorious climax. If the man were simply speaking, he might *be* sincere, but he would not *sound* sincere, and this is important because the speaker did not write the speech, you see. The agency did. The duties of the office sometimes make it impossible for the president even to read the speech before he goes into rehearsal. I wonder—"

"What?"

"Do you have a dog?"

"Marie has a cat."

"Never mind. Maybe it is not so important in France."

"Do you think one of those agencies would take the account, Uncle Charlie?" Pippin demanded eagerly. "Would it be worth their while?"

"I shall make discreet inquiries, my child. At least it will do no harm to ask. Even if it were not as profitable as other accounts, a reputable agency might feel that the prestige of representing the King of France would be worth their while. It is called 'institutional prestige,' I believe. I shall inquire, Pippin. We can only hope."

"I do sincerely hope," said the king.

The spring in Paris was traditionally beautiful. Production of all things royal and all things French caused factories to put on night shifts. An era of good feeling and security justified a reduction in wages.

As might have been expected, Madame took the change in her status with realism and vigor. To her it was like moving from one apartment to another—on a larger scale, of course, but having the same problems. Madame made lists. She complained that her husband did not take his duties as seriously as he should.

"You loll about the house," she said to him, "when anyone can see that there are a thousand things to be done."

"I know," said Pippin in the tone she knew meant he had not listened.

"You just sit around reading."

"I know, my dear."

"What are you reading that is so important at a time like this?"

"I beg your pardon?"

"I said, what are you reading?"

"History."

"History? At a time like this?"

"I have been going over the history of my family and also the records of some of the families which followed us."

Madame said tartly, "It has always seemed to me that the Kings of France, with singularly few gifts, have done very well for themselves. There are some exceptions, of course."

"It is the exceptions I am thinking of, my dear. I have been thinking of the Sixteenth Louis. He was a good man. His intentions and his impulses were good."

"Perhaps he was a fool," said Marie.

"Perhaps he was," said Pippin. "But I understand him, even though we are not of the same family. To a certain extent I think I am like him. I am trying to see where he made his errors. I should hate to fall into the same trap."

"While you have been daydreaming, have you given a single thought to your daughter?"

"What has she done now?" Pippin demanded.

It cannot be denied that Clotilde had led a rather unusual existence. When, at fifteen, she wrote the best-selling novel *Adieu Ma Vie,* she was sought out and courted by the most celebrated and complex minds of our times. She was acclaimed by the Reductionists, the Resurrectionists, the Protonists, the Non-Existentialists, and the Quantumists, while the very nature of her book set hundreds of psychoanalysts clamoring to sift her unconscious. She had her table at the Café des Trois Puces, where she held court and freely answered questions on religion, philosophy, politics, and aesthetics. It was at this very table that she started her second novel, which, while never finished, was to be titled "Le Printemps des Mortes." Her devotees formed the school called Clotildisme, which was denounced by the clergy and caused sixty-eight adolescents to commit ecstatic suicide by leaping from the top of the Arc de Triomphe.

Clotilde's subsequent involvement in politics and religion was followed by her symbolic marriage to a white bull in the Bois de Boulogne. Her celebrated affairs of honor, in which she wounded three elderly Academicians and herself received a rapier thrust in the right buttock, caused some comment—and all this before she was twenty. In an article in *Souffrance,* she wrote that her career had left her no time for childhood.

She then reached the phase when she spent her afternoons at the movies and her evenings arguing the merits of Gregory Peck, Tab Hunter, Marlon Brando, and Frank Sinatra. Marilyn Monroe she found overbloomed and Lollobrigida bovine. She went to Rome, where she acted in three versions of *War and Peace* and two of *Quo Vadis,* but her notices

threw her into such despair that her elevation to Princesse Royale came just in time. In this field the competition was less fierce.

Clotilde began to think of herself, at least pronominally, in the plural. She referred to "our people," "our position," "our duty." Her first royal act, that of turning on the fountains at Versailles, was followed by a detailed plan very dear to her heart and not without its parallel in history. She set apart an area quite near to Versailles, to be called "Le Petit Round-Up." Here there would be small ranch houses, corrals, barns, bunkhouses. Here branding irons would be constantly in bonfires and cayuses would leap wild-eyed against the barriers. To Le Petit Round-Up would come Roy Rogers, Alan Ladd, Hoot Gibson, Gary Cooper, the taciturn and the strong. They would feel at home at Le Petit Round-Up. Clotilde, in leather skirt and black shirt, would move about, serving red-eye in shot-glasses. If there were gun-play—and how can this be avoided where passionate and inarticulate men gather?—then the princess would be ready to stanch wounds and cool with her royal hand the pain-racked but silent sufferer. This was only one of Clotilde's plans for the future.

It was at this time that she began to take her old Teddy bear to bed. It was at this time that she fell madly in love with Tod Johnson.

Clotilde met him at Les Ambassadeurs, where she had gone with young Georges de Marine—the Comte de Marine, that is, who was seventeen and listless. Georges knew perfectly well that Clotilde knew Tab Hunter was in Paris. He knew also, because he belonged to the same fan club, that Tab Hunter would put in an appearance at Les Ambassadeurs sometime during the evening.

Tod Johnson sat next to Clotilde in the banquette seats which faced the dance floor. She noticed him with a quickened breath, watched him with blood-pounding interest, and finally, under the roaring of violins, she leaned toward him and asked, "You are American?"

"Sure."

"Then you must be careful. They will keep opening champagne if you do not tell them to stop."

"Thank you," said Tod. "They already have. You are French?"

"Of course."

"I didn't think any French people came here," said Tod.

Georges kicked Clotilde viciously on the ankle, and her face reddened with pain.

Tod said, "I hope you don't mind. May I introduce myself? I am Tod Johnson."

"I know how you do these things in America," Clotilde said. "I have been to America. May I introduce the Comte de Marine? Now," she said to Georges, "you must introduce me. That is how they do it."

George squinted his eyes craftily. "Mademoiselle Clotilde Héristal," he said evenly.

Tod said, "That name rings a bell. Are you an actress?"

Clotilde dropped her eyelashes. "No, Monsieur, except in so far as everyone is an actress."

"That's good," said Tod. "Your English is wonderful."

Georges spoke without inflection in the tone he considered insulting. "Does Monsieur perhaps speak French?"

"Princeton French," said Tod. "I can ask questions but I can't understand the answers. But I'm learning. It isn't all running together the way it did a few week ago."

"You stay a while in Paris?"

"I don't have any plans. Would you permit me to order champagne?"

"If you will tell them to stop. You must not let them cheat you as though you were some Argentine."

That is how it started.

Tod Johnson was the ideal American young man—tall, stiff-haired, blue-eyed, well dressed, well educated by going standards, well mannered, and soft-spoken. He was equally fortunate in his background. His father, H. W. Johnson, the Egg King, of Petaluma, California, was reputed to have two hundred and thirty million white leghorn chickens. Even more fortunate was the fact that H.W. was a poor man who had built his chicken kingdom by his own efforts.

It will be seen that, although Tod Johnson was very rich, he did not suffer from lineage. At the end of his six months' shakedown in Europe he was expected to go home to Petaluma and begin at the bottom of the chicken business, eventually to rise to the top and take it over.

It was only after several meetings with Clotilde that he told her about his father and the egg empire. By then she was so warm and gooey with love that she forgot to tell him her own family news. Clotilde the novelist, the worldly, the Communist, the princess, had for the moment ceased to exist. At twenty she slopped into a fifteen-year-old love affair, all sighs and a full gassy feeling in the stomach. She was so vague and listless that Madame gave her an old country remedy that put her to bed in earnest and removed the necessity for a psychiatrist. Her body was so hard put to survive the remedy that her mind was left to take care of itself. When this happens the mind does very well. Her love remained, but she found she could breathe again.

19— was a monster year for American advertising. BBD & O was up to its ears rewriting the Constitution of the United States and at the same time marketing a new golfmobile with pontoons.

Riker, Dunlap, Hodgson, and Fellows would have taken the French job in the fall, but could not pull its key people off promotion of Nudent, the dentifrice which grows teeth.

Merchison Associates was busy with a trans-Atlantic pipeline, called

in the public press "Tapal," a twenty-four-inch main which ran under the sea from Saudi Arabia to New Jersey with floating pumping stations every fifty miles. The matter would not have been so difficult but for the constant meddling of Senator Banger, Democrat, New Mexico, with his nuisance questioning as to why Army and Navy personnel and material were being used by a privately owned corporation. Merchison Associates were in Washington most of the spring and summer. If any of these agencies had been free to function, the coronation of the King of France might have been run more smoothly.

Who could set down all the drama, the pageantry and glories, and, yes, the confusion of the coronation at Reims on July 15? Newspaper coverage ran to many millions of words. Color photographs filled the split-page of every newspaper with a circulation of over twenty thousand.

The New York *Daily News* front page carried a headline, of which each letter was four inches high, that read: FROGS CROWN PIP.

Every by-line writer and commentator in America was in attendance.

Conrad Hilton took this occasion to open the Versailles-Hilton.

The life story of every aristocrat in France was bought in advance.

Louella Parsons had a front-page box headed: WILL CLOTILDE COME TO HOLLYWOOD?

The reader should consult back issues of newspapers for accounts of the great day at Reims and Paris—the cathedral crowded to the doors, the cries of the scalpers, the stands of ceramics, the miniatures of royal coaches, the crush of people in the square, the traffic jam on the road to Reims, unparalleled even at the finish of the Tour de France. One company made a small fortune selling miniature guillotines.

The coronation itself was a triumph of disorder. It was discovered at the last moment that horses had not been provided to draw the state coaches, but this lack was filled by the abattoirs of Paris, even though their gesture made certain sections of Paris meatless for three days. Miss France, representing Joan of Arc, stood beside the throne, banner in one hand and drawn sword in the other, until she fainted from heat and the weight of her armor. She crashed with the sound of falling kitchenware during the royal oath. However, six altarboys quickly propped her against a Gothic column, where she remained forgotten until late in the evening.

The Communists, acting purely from habit, painted "Go Home Napoleon" on the walls of the cathedral, but this slip both in history and in manners was taken by all with good humor.

The coronation was completed by eleven in the morning. Then the wave of spectators rushed back to Paris for the parade which was to move from the Place de la Concorde to the Arc de Triomphe. This state procession was scheduled for two o'clock. It started at five.

The windows along the Champs Elysées were sold out. A place at the curb brought as much as five thousand francs. The owners of step-

ladders were able to extend their vacations in the country by a week or more.

The procession was artfully arranged to represent past and present. First came the state carriages of the Great Peers, decorated with gold leaf and tumbling angels; then a battery of heavy artillery drawn by tractors; then a company of crossbowmen in slashed doublets and plumed hats; then a regiment of dragoons with burnished breastplates; then a group of heavy tanks and weapon-carriers, followed by the Noble Youth in full armor. A battalion of paratroopers followed, armed with submachine guns, leading the king's ministers in their robes of office, and behind them a platoon of musketeers in lace, knee-breeches, silk stockings, and high-heeled shoes with great buckles. These last moved along regally, using their musket crutches as staffs.

At last the royal coach creaked by. Pippin IV, an uncomfortable bundle of purple velvet and ermine, with the queen, equally befurred, sitting beside him, acknowledged the cheers of the loyal bystanders and responded with equal courtesy to hisses.

Where the Avenue de Marigny crosses the Champs Elysées, a crazed critic fired a pistol at the king, using a periscope to aim over the heads of the crowd. He killed a royal horse. A musketeer of the Rear Guard gallantly cut it free and took its place in harness. The coach moved on.

For this loyal service the musketeer, Raoul de Potoir by name, demanded and received a pension for life.

The procession moved on: bands, ambassadors, professions, veterans, peasants in nylon country dress, leaders of parties, and loyal factions.

When at last the royal coach reached the Arc de Triomphe, the streets about the Place de la Concorde were still blocked with marchers waiting to get into the parade. But all of this is a matter of public record and of unparalleled newspaper coverage.

As the royal coach paused at the Arc de Triomphe, Queen Marie turned to speak to the king and found him gone. He had propped up his royal robes and crept away unnoticed in the crowd.

It was an angry queen who found him later, sitting on his balcony, polishing the eyepiece of his telescope.

"This is a fine thing," she said. "I have never been so embarrassed in my life. What will the papers say? You will be the laughingstock of the world. What will the English say? Oh, I know. They won't say anything, but they'll look, and you'll see in their eyes that they remember how *their* queen stood and sat, stood and sat for thirteen hours without even going to the— Pippin, will you stop polishing that silly glass?"

"Be silent," Pippin said softly.

"I beg your pardon?"

"You have it, my dear, but be silent."

"I don't understand you," cried Marie. "Where in the world do

you find the right to tell me to be silent? Who do you think you are?"

"*I am the King,*" said Pippin, and this had not occurred to Marie. "That's funny," he said. "I am, you know." And it was so obviously true that Marie looked at him with startled eyes.

"Yes, Sire," she said, and was silent.

"Starting to be a king is difficult, my dear," he said apologetically.

The king paced back and forth in Charles Martel's room.

"You don't answer the telephone," he complained. "You pay no attention to the pneumatique. I see there on that bust of Napoleon three letters delivered by hand, unopened. What is your explanation, sir?"

"Don't be so damn royal with me," said Uncle Charlie irritably. "I don't even dare go out on the street. I haven't taken my shutters down since the coronation."

"Which you did not attend," said the king.

"Which I did not dare attend. I am driven to despair. Descendants of the old nobility think I have your private ear. I am glad to be able to tell the truth—that I have not seen you. There is a line in front of my shop every day. Were you followed here?"

"Followed? I was escorted!" said the king. "I haven't been alone for a week. They watch me awaken. They help me dress. They are in my bedroom. They practically come into my bathroom. When I crack my eggs their lips tighten. When I raise my spoon their eyes follow it to my mouth. And you think you are driven—"

"But you are their property," said Uncle Charlie. "You, my dear nephew, are an extension of your people, and they have inalienable rights over your person."

"I can't imagine how I let myself in for this," and Pippin. "I didn't want to move to Versailles. I wasn't asked. I was moved. It's drafty there, Uncle Charlie. The beds are horrible. The floors creak. What are you mixing there?"

"A martini," said Uncle Charlie. "I've learned it from a young friend of Clotilde's, an American. The first taste is dreadful, but it becomes progressively more delicious. It has some of the hypnotic qualities of morphine. Try it! Don't let the ice frighten you."

"That's horrible," said the king and he drained the little glass. "Pour me another one, will you?" He licked his lips. "I had forgotten that the king has guests, built-in guests. Two hundred aristocrats are living with me at Versailles."

"Well, you have room for them."

"Room, yes, but nothing else. They sleep on the floor, in the halls. They've broken up the furniture to burn in the fireplaces to keep warm."

"In August?"

"Versailles would be cold in hell," said the king. "Say, what is in this? Gin I can taste, but what else?"

"Vermouth. Just a breath of vermouth. When they become delicious you've had too many. Try sipping this one, Sire. You are nervous, my child."

"Nervous? Why wouldn't I be nervous? Uncle Charlie, I am sure that somewhere in France there must be aristocrats who are solvent, but not among my guests. The word has gone out, under the bridges and under the barrows and to the subway gratings. I am surrounded by what, if they were not so high-born, would be called bums, but stately bums. They stroll majestically in the gardens. They touch their lips with bits of lace. They speak in words directly out of Corneille. And they aren't honest, Uncle Charlie. They steal."

"What do you mean, 'they steal?'"

"My uncle, there isn't a hen coop nor a rabbit hutch within ten miles that is safe from them. When the farmers complain, my guests smile and lash out the lace handkerchiefs they have shoplifted from Printemps. I have had complaints about that too. Every department store in Paris has set up a Nobility Detail to protect its counters. I'm afraid, Uncle Charlie; I am told the peasants are beginning to sharpen their scythes."

"Maybe you'll have to modernize the throne, my dear nephew; you may have to take a stand. You understand, of course, that what to ordinary people is simple theft, to the nobility is their ancient right. Do you think you ought to have another? Your color is a little high."

"What do you call them?"

"Martinis."

"Italian?"

"It isn't," said Uncle Charlie. "Pippin, I don't want you to leave me, but I think it only fair to warn you that Clotilde is bringing her new friend. I've opened the little rear door for my own convenience. If you would care to leave without being seen—"

"What friend is this?"

"An American friend. I thought he might be interested in some sketches."

"Uncle Charlie!"

"A man must live, my nephew. No royal revenues have been assigned to me. Are there any royal revenues, by the way?"

"Not that I know of," said the king. "There's the new American loan, but the Privy Council won't release any of it. You know the Privy Council is not unlike the recent republican government."

"Why shouldn't it be?" said Uncle Charlie. "It's the same people. As I said, the little rear door opens into the alley."

"Are you going to use your position to cheat this American? Uncle Charlie, is that the noble thing to do?"

"As a matter of fact, it is," said Charles Martel. "We invented it. I make no representations. If he likes a picture, he buys it. I simply say Boucher *might* have painted it. So he might. Anything is possible."

"But you are the king's uncle! To cheat a commoner, and an American commoner, at that, is—is like shooting sitting birds. The British would take a dim view of it."

"The British have developed their own methods of combining aristocracy with profit. They have more recent experience than we. But we will learn—and meanwhile, what is wrong with practicing on a rich American?"

"He is rich?"

"He is what the Americans call 'loaded.' His father is the Egg King of a province called Petaluma."

"Well, at least you're not stealing from the—the lower orders."

"Indeed I am not, my child. In America one only becomes a member of the lower orders when one is insolvent."

"Uncle Charlie, if you're making another one of those what-do-you-call-thems, I think I will stay and meet this Egg Prince. Is Clotilde serious in this—friendship?"

"I should hope so," said Uncle Charlie. "His father, H. W. Johnson, the king, has two hundred and thirty million chickens."

"Gracious!" said Pippin. "Well, thank Heaven Clotilde is not falling into the error of a certain English princess, giving her heart to a commoner. Thank you, Uncle Charlie. You know, you're getting the knack. This is far superior to the first one."

Tod Johnson was no more born to the purple than was the original Charles Martel. In 1932 the Johnson Grocery in Petaluma, California, nudged on by what was called "The Great Depression," slipped quietly out of existence. In 1933 H. W. Johnson, Tod's father, was enrolled on federal relief and assigned to road work.

H. W. Johnson never blamed President Hoover for the loss of his grocery store, but he could never forgive President Roosevelt for having fed him.

When, lacking refrigeration, the relief organization distributed live chickens, Mr. Johnson kept them a while before he ate them. He was fascinated by birds so unintelligent, which nevertheless could find subsistence in the weed patch behind his house.

During his two years on the road gang, Hank Johnson thought about chickens. When his grandmother died, leaving him three thousand dollars, he promptly bought ten thousand baby chicks. Most of this first venture died of a disease which darkened their combs and withered their feathers, but Johnson was not one to cry failure. It was hard enough to engage his interest in the first place, but once engaged, it was

even more difficult to budge it. He wrote to the Department of Agriculture for its chicken booklet and from it he learned chicken economy. Apart from diseases, he read, chickens are a luxury until you have fifty thousand of them. With that number, you may break even. With one hundred thousand you can show a small profit. Over half a million, you begin to get some place.

One need not go into Mr. Johnson's organizational plans. They involved small investments by some of his neighbors and all of his relatives, who were persuaded to put up the capital for the initial two hundred thousand baby chicks. When half a million birds guaranteed a profit, this money was returned with thanks and a small bonus. From then on, H. W. Johnson was on his own.

Tod was three when the first million chicks marched in their little wire-floored cells. H.W. by that time was getting government surplus for feed and was selling eggs and fryers to the Army and Navy.

Tod went to the Petaluma public schools. In high school he joined the 4-H Club, where he learned a good deal about chickens: their habits, their diseases, and their propensities. He learned also to detest them for their stupidity, their odor, and their mess.

By the time he had graduated from high school there was no need for his further interest in the birds that were building the family fortune. H. W. Johnson was a factory by then. Dressed pullets and millions of eggs rolled off an assembly line. The Johnson offices were far from the smell and sight of chickens. The Johnson estate was on a lovely hill beyond the country club, while the Johnson energy and genius now concerned itself with figures rather than white leghorns. The unit was no longer a hen, but fifty thousand hens. The company had become a corporation with stock held by H. W. Johnson, Mrs. H. W. Johnson, Tod Johnson, and young Miss Hazel Johnson, a beautiful girl who on three separate occasions was named Egg Queen at the Petaluma Poultry Pageant.

It was now time for the family to expand to a dynasty, in the American pattern.

When Tod went to Princeton there were one hundred million chickens represented by stock certificates. But it must not be thought that only chickens were represented. Johnson, Inc., also sold feed, wire, brooders, incubators, refrigeration plants, and all the equipment which must be purchased by a small operator before he can proceed toward bankruptcy.

H. W. Johnson wore his title of Egg King gracefully and, true tycoon that he was, bought back his old grocery store and set it up as a museum. His only violence lay in his hatred for the Democratic party, for which he had every reason. Otherwise he was a kindly, generous man, a man of vision. He had peacocks on his lawn at Johnson Vista and an artificial pond for white ducks.

Tod, meanwhile, dipped into four universities—Princeton for clothes, Harvard for accent, Yale for attitude, and the University of Virginia for manners. He emerged equipped for life with everything except the arts and foreign travel. The first he acquired in New York, where his taste for progressive jazz was developed, and his Grand Tour during the restoration of the French monarchy took care of the second.

His friendship with Clotilde grew like a mushroom in the caves of Paris; flourished like the pelargoniums in the flower boxes of the sidewalk cafés. Clotilde nurtured the pale plant with care, never letting it stray beyond Fouquet's on one side and the Hotel George V on the other, in which district Tod's Brooks-Brothers look did not cause comment. Neither would the princess be embarrassed by meeting any French people.

The affair reached its crescendo of passion, however, at the Select, when Tod leaned over the table, tore his eyes upward from her bosom, and said hoarsely, "Baby, you're a dish. A real dish."

Clotilde felt it to be a declaration. Afterward, inspecting her well-filled body in a full-length mirror, she growled, "I am a deesh."

Clotilde introduced her new friend to Uncle Charlie as a prospective husband, and Charlie accepted him as a prospective customer.

"You might be interested," he said to Tod, "in a group of paintings I have heard about. They have just come to light. Buried during the Occupation—"

"Uncle—please!" said Clotilde.

"I don't know much about painting, sir," said Tod.

"Perhaps you will learn," said Charles Martel happily, and later, after he had telephoned the Chase Bank, Paris Branch, he said to Clotilde, "I like that young man. He has an air. You must bring him again to call on me."

"Promise me you will not sell him pictures," the princess pleaded.

"My dear," said her great-uncle, "I have made certain discreet inquiries. Should I rob this young man of beauty and art simply because he is rich? Figure to yourself how many are two hundred and thirty million chickens. If one took twenty centimeters as the approximate length of one chicken, they would be—let me see—forty-six million meters, which is forty-six thousand kilometers, which is a procession of chickens extending nearly twice around the world at the equator—imagine!"

"What would they be going around the world for?" Clotilde asked.

"I beg your pardon?" said Uncle Charlie. "Oh! Please ask your friend to show me again how to make those—those martinis. There is something I do not accomplish."

Clotilde was surprised to find her father in the back room of the

Galerie Martel, but she said, "Sire, I wish to present Mr. Tod Johnson. Mr. Tod Johnson, this is my father"—she blushed—"the king."

"Glad to know you, Mr. King," said Tod.

Uncle Charlie said delicately. "Not Mister—*the.*"

"Come again?" said Tod.

"Il n'est pas Monsieur King. Il est *Le Roi.*"

"No kidding!" said Tod.

"He is very democratic," said Uncle Charlie.

"I voted the Democratic ticket," said Tod. "My old—my father would kill me if he knew. He's a Taft man."

Pippin spoke for the first time. "Correct me if I am wrong. Have I not heard that Monsieur Taft is dead?"

"That doesn't mean a thing to my father," said Tod. "Let's get this straight in my mind. What kind of a king?"

Pippin said, "I do not understand."

"I mean like—well, they call my father the Egg King, and Benny Goodman is the King of Swing, and like that."

Pippin cried, "You know Benny Goodman?"

"Well, not really, but I've sat close enough to his clarinet to get my ear splashed."

"What joy," said the king. "I have the recording from Carnegie Hall."

"I'm more on the progressive kick myself," said Tod.

"And you are right in a way," said Pippin. "This is creative and good, but you must allow, Monsieur Egg, that Goodman, he is classic—at least when he inserts himself in the groove."

"Say," said Tod, "you talk good for a—"

Pippin chuckled. "Were you about to say 'king' or 'Frog?'"

"How about that?" said Tod. "You aren't kidding me, sir?"

"I am King of France," said the king. "It was not my choice of profession."

"The hell you are!"

"The hell I'm not."

"How'd you learn talk like that, sir?"

"For a number of years I have subscribed to *Downbeat,*" said Pippin.

"Well, that explains it." Tod turned to Clotilde. "Baby, I'm ape about him. He's a Georgier George."

Uncle Charlie cleared his throat. "Perhaps Monsieur Tod would care to see some of the paintings I spoke about. Apparently they were hidden during the Occupation of France. Two of them are attributed to Boucher."

"What do you mean, attributed?" Tod asked. "Aren't they signed?"

"Well, no. But there are many indications—the colors, the brush technique—"

744

"I'll lay it on the line, sir," Tod said. "I thought of buying a present for my father. You see, I want to stay away from the business a little longer and I'll have to put the bite on him. I thought a real nice present might grease the slide—not that it will fool him. He'll know what I'm up to, but he may go along with it. He doesn't mind being fooled if he knows about it."

"These paintings—" Uncle Charlie began.

"You say Boucher. I halfway remember him from Art Appreciation. Suppose I buy a Boucher with no signature. Know what will happen? Father will get an expert—he's hell on experts. And suppose this Boucher is a phony. You see the position I'd be in—hustling my own father."

"But a signature would save you that difficulty?"

"It would help. Understand, it wouldn't be certain. My father is no dope."

"Perhaps we had better look at something else," said Uncle Charlie. "I know where I can put my hand on a very nice Matisse *with* a signature. There is a 'Tete de Femme' of Rouault, very fine—or maybe you would like to see a veritable swarm of Pasquins. These will have a great future value."

"I'd like to look at everything," said Tod. "Bugsy said you were doing something wrong with the martinis."

"They do not taste the same."

"Are you getting them cold enough? Mac Kriendler once told me that the only good martini is a cold martini. Here, let me mix you one. Will you have one too, sir?"

"Thank you. I should like to discuss with you your father, the king."

"Egg King."

"Exactly. Has he been this for a long time?"

"Since the depression. He hit bottom then. That was before I was born."

"Then he invented his kingdom as he went along?"

"You might say that, sir. And in his line there is nobody who can touch him."

"He has a principality, your father?"

"Well, it's a corporation—kind of the same thing if you control the stock."

"My young friend, I hope you will come to see me very soon. I wish to discuss the king business with you."

"Where do you live, sir? Bugsy wouldn't ever tell me. I thought she was ashamed."

"Perhaps she was," said the king. "I live at the Palace at Versailles."

"Holy mackerel!" said Tod. "Wait till my old man hears this—"

AS THOUGH IN CELEBRATION of the king's return, the summer slipped benignly over France—warm, but not hot; cool, but not cold.

The rains waited until the flowers of the vines exchanged their pollen and set their clusters densely, and then gentle moisture stirred the growth. The earth gave sugar and the warm air breed. Before a single grape ripened, it was felt that, barring some ugly trick by nature, this would be a vintage year, the kind remembered from the time when an old man was young.

And the wheat headed full and yellow. The butter took an unearthly sweetness from the vintage grass. The truffles crowded one another under the ground. The geese happily stuffed themselves until their livers nearly burst. The farmers complained, as their duty demanded, but even their complaints had a cheerful tone.

From overseas the tourists boiled in and every one of them was rich and appreciative so that the porters were seen to smile—whether you believe it or not. Taxi drivers scowled in a good-humored way, and one or two were heard to say that perhaps ruin would not come this year, an admission they will not care to have repeated.

And what of the political groups now firmly rooted in the Privy Council? Even they had an era of good feeling. Christian Christians saw the churches full. Christian Atheists saw them empty.

The Socialists went happily about writing their own constitution for France.

The Communists were very busy explaining to one another a shift in the party line which seemed to place leadership in the hands of the people, a subtlety later to be explained and exploited. Besides this, the collective leadership in the Kremlin not only had congratulated the French Crown but had offered a tremendous loan.

Alexis Kroupoff, writing in *Pravda,* proved beyond question that Lenin had foreseen this move on the part of the French and had approved of it as a step in the direction of eventual socialization. This explanation put the French Communists under an obligation not only to tolerate but actually to support the monarchy.

The Non-Tax-Payers' League was lulled to a state of bliss, since American and Russian loans made it unnecessary to collect any taxes at all. A few pessimists argued that there would come a day of reckoning, but these were laughed to scorn as prophets of gloom and pilloried by caricatures in nearly all the French press.

The French Rotary Club grew to such proportions that it achieved the strength and influence of a party itself.

The landlords prepared their plan for government subsidy in addition to a rise in rent ceilings.

746

Right and Left Centrists were so confident of the future that they freely suggested a rise in prices together with a lowering of wages, and no riots ensued, which proved to most people that the Communists had indeed been defanged.

To such a stable government there was no end to the loans America was happy to advance. The outpouring of American money had the effect of strengthening the Royalist parties of Portugal, Spain, and Italy. England looked dourly on.

At Versailles the nobility happily quarreled over an honors list of four thousand names while a secret committee went forward with plans for restoring the land of France to its ancient and obviously its proper owners.

As Marie was one of the first to point out, it was the king this and the king that . . . No one will ever know what the queen went through. Being a queen takes some doing, but you are never going to make a man understand this. Marie had ladies in waiting, certainly, but just ask a lady in waiting to do something and see where you get. And it wasn't as though there were nearly enough servants and what there were were public servants who would argue for an hour rather than turn a dust cloth and then complain to the privy councilor who had procured the appointment.

Consider, for a moment, that gigantic old dustbox Versailles. How could any human being keep it clean? The halls and staircases and chandeliers and corners and wainscoting seemed to draw dust. There had never been any plumbing worth mentioning inside the place, although there were millions of pipes to the fountains and the fish ponds outside.

The kitchens were miles away from the apartments, and just try to get a modern servant to carry a covered tray from the kitchens to the royal apartments. The king could not eat his meals in the state dining rooms. If he did he would have two hundred dinner guests, and the royal family were just managing to scrape by as it was. In dividing the royal monies nobody gave a thought to the queen. She ran from morning until night, and still the housekeeping kept ahead of her. The extravagance was enough to drive a good Frenchwoman insane.

Besides all this, there were the nobles in residence. Their bowings and scrapings and grand manners disgusted Marie. They were always deferring to her opinion and then not listening, particularly when she asked them— asked them nicely, mind you—please to turn out the lights when they left a room, please to pick up their dirty clothes, please to clean the bathtub after themselves. But it was worse than that. They ignored her requests that they stop breaking up the furniture to burn in the fireplaces, stop emptying their chamber pots in the garden. It was impossible for Marie to figure to herself how such people could live with themselves.

And would the king listen? King indeed! He had his head in the clouds even more than he had had when he played at being an astronomer.

Clotilde was no help to her. Clotilde was in love, not in love like a well-brought-up French girl, but in slob-love like an American student at the Sorbonne. And Clotilde had got so grand or so forgetful that she no longer made her bed or even washed out her underthings.

Worst of all, Marie had no one to talk to, to complain to, to gossip with.

There is no doubt that every woman needs another woman now and then as an escape valve for the pressures of being a woman. For her the man's releases are not available, the killing of small or large animals, vicarious murder from a seat at the prize ring. Flight into the hidden kingdom of the abstract is denied her. The Church and the confessor can let out some of the tensions, but even that is sometimes not enough.

Marie needed the sanctuary of another woman. Her good sense revolted against the ladies in waiting and the intolerable corps of nobles. Being queen, she was fearful of old friends of her Marigny days, because they could not fail to use their fancied influence in the interest of their husbands.

Queen Marie, casting in her mind, thought of her old friend and schoolmate Suzanne Lescault.

Sister Hyacinthe was perfect as a companion to the queen. Her order was able to change a rule and to uncloister the nun upon recognition of certain advantages which might accrue to itself as well as the natural satisfaction of knowing that the dear queen was in good hands. Sister Hyacinthe was removed to Versailles and encelled in a lovely little room overlooking box hedges and a carp pool—a few steps, indeed, from the royal apartments.

It may never be known exactly how much Sister Hyacinthe contributed to the peace and security of France. For example:

The queen closed the door firmly, put her fists on her hips, and breathed so tightly that her nostrils whitened. "Suzanne, I'm not going to put up with that dirty Duchess of P—— another minute—the insulting, insufferable slut. Do you know what she said to me?"

"Gently, Marie," said Sister Hyacinthe. "Gently, my dear."

"What do you mean gently? I don't have to suffer—"

"Of course not, dear. Hand me a cigarette, will you?"

"What am I going to do?" the queen cried.

Sister Hyacinthe slipped a hairpin around the cigarette to keep stain from her fingers, and she blew the smoke from lips pursed to whistle. "Ask the duchess if she ever hears from Gogi!"

"Who?"

"Gogi," said Sister Hyacinthe. "He was a high-wire man, very handsome, but nervous. So many artists are."

"Ha!" said Marie, "I understand. I'll do it! Then we'll see what she does with her lifted face."

"You mean those scars, dear? No. Her face was not lifted. It was, you might say, dropped. Gogi was very nervous."

Marie charged for the door, her eyes shining. Under her breath, as she searched the long painted halls, she muttered, "My dear Duchess —have you heard from Gogi lately?"

Or again:

"Suzanne, the king is being a bore about this mistress business. The Privy Council have appealed to me. Do you think you could talk to the king about it?"

"I have just the mistress for him," said Sister Hyacinthe. "Grand-niece of our Superior—quiet, well bred, a little stocky, but, Marie, she does beautiful needlework. She could be valuable to you."

"He won't consider her. He won't even discuss it."

"He won't have to see her," said Sister Hyacinthe. "In fact, it might be better if he didn't."

Or again:

"I don't know what I'm going to do with Clotilde. She's sloppy and listless. She won't pick up her clothes. She's selfish and inattentive."

"We have this problem in the order sometimes, dear, particularly with young girls who confuse other impulses with the religious."

"And what do you do?"

"Walk calmly up to her and punch her in the nose."

"What good will that do?"

"It will get her attention," said Sister Hyacinthe.

The queen never regretted calling in her old friend. And in the palace the wayward nobility began to be nervously aware of a force, of an iron influence which could be neither ignored nor sneered out of existence.

For her birthday, Marie presented Sister Hyacinthe with a daily foot massage by the best man in Paris. She ordered a tall screen with two holes near the bottom, through which Suzanne's feet and ankles could protrude.

"I don't know what I would do without her," said the queen.

"What?" the king asked.

Pippin was in a state of shock for a long time. He said to himself in wonder and in fear, "I am the king and I don't even know what a king is." He read the stories of his ancestors. "But they wanted to be kings," he told himself. "At least most of them did. And some of them wanted to be more. There I have it. If I could only find some sense of mission, of divinity of purpose."

He visited his uncle again. "Am I right in thinking that you would be glad if you were not related to me?" he asked.

Uncle Charlie said, "You take it too hard."

"That's easy to say."

"I know. And I'm sorry I said it. I am your loyal subject."

"Well, suppose there were a revolt?"

"Do you want truth or loyalty?"

"I don't know—both, I guess."

Uncle Charlie said, "I will not hide from you that my position as your uncle has increased my business. I am doing very well, particularly with the tourists."

"Then your loyalty is tied to profit. Would you be disloyal if you suffered a loss?"

Uncle Charlie went behind a screen and brought out a bottle of cognac. "With water?" he asked.

"How good is the cognac?"

"I suggest water. . . . Now. You want to turn over stones and find the insects underneath. One always hopes for virtue—right up to the point of exercising it. I hope I would stick with you to the death. But I also hope that I would have the judgment to join the opposition a few moments before it is generally apparent that it will succeed."

"You are very honest, my uncle."

"Can you tell me what is really troubling you?"

Pippin sipped his fine à l'eau. He said uncertainly, "The function of a king is to rule. To rule, one must have power. To have power one must take power . . ."

"Go on, child."

"The men who forced the crown on me were not intent on giving anything away."

"Ah! You learn, I see. You are becoming what is called cynical by those who fear reality. And you feel that you are a wheel unturning, a plant without a flower."

"Something like that. A king without power is a contradiction in terms, and a king with power is an abomination."

"Excuse me," said Uncle Charlie. "Mice are moving on the cheese." He went to the front of his shop. "Yes?" Pippin heard him say. "It is lovely. If I told you who I suspect painted it— No. I must say I do not know. Notice the brushwork here, see how the composition soars— and the subject, the costume— Oh! That? A nothing. Came in with a pile of trash from the cellar of a château. I haven't inspected it. I suppose you *could* buy it, but would it be wise? I would have to ask two hundred thousand francs because it would cost me that to have it cleaned and inspected. Consider again! Here, for example, is a Rouault about which there is no doubt . . ." There was a time of soft muttering, and then Uncle Charlie's voice. "Won't you let me dust it? I tell you I have not even inspected it."

In a few moments he came back, rubbing his hands.

"I'm ashamed of you," said the king.

Charles Martel went to a pile of dirty unframed canvases in a

corner. "I must replace it," he said. "I do my best to discourage them. Perhaps I would feel worse if I did not know they thought they were cheating me." He carried the dusty painting to the front. "Ah, come in, Clotilde," he said. "Your father is here." He called, "It's Clotilde and the Egg Prince."

The three of them came past the red velvet drapery which hung over the doorway, and their passage left a thin cloud of dust in the air.

"Good evening, sir," said Tod. "He's teaching me the business. We're going to open galleries in Dallas and Cincinnati and one in Beverly Hills."

"Shame on him!" said the king.

"I try to discourage them but they demand—" Uncle Charlie began.

"Very clever," said the king. "But who tricks them into demanding?"

"I don't think that's quite fair, sir," said Tod. "The first function of business is to create the demand and the second to fulfill it. Think of all the things that wouldn't be made at all if people hadn't been told they needed them—medicines and cosmetics and deodorants. Can you say, sir, that the automobile is wasteful and unnecessary—that it keeps people in debt for transportation they don't need? You can't say that to people who want automobiles even if they and you know it is true."

"The line must be drawn somewhere," Pippin said. "Has my fine uncle told you why the Mona Lisa was stolen?"

"Now wait, dear nephew!"

Pippin cried, "He usually starts it—'I can't mention any names but I have heard—' Heard indeed!"

"It never made any sense to me," Tod said. "The Mona Lisa was stolen from the Louvre. Right? And then, after a year, it was returned. Do you mean they returned a fake?"

"Not at all," said the king. "The picture in the Louvre is genuine."

Clotilde pouted. "Must we talk business?"

"Wait, Bugsy, I want to hear."

"Go on, my uncle," said the king. "It's your story. It's your—"

"I can't say I approved of it," said Charles Martel, "and yet no honest person was injured."

Clotilde said, "Oh, tell him and get it over with."

"Well, I can't mention any names but I have heard that during the time the Mona Lisa was—away, eight Mona Lisas were bought by very rich men."

"Where?"

"Well, wherever very rich men were—Brazil, Argentina, Texas, New York, Hollywood . . ."

"But why was the original returned?"

"Well you see, once the picture was returned, there was no further search for the—ah—thief."

"Ah!" said Tod. "But how about the people who bought the fakes?"

Uncle Charlie said piously, "When you buy a stolen masterpiece, you are committing a crime. But even though they must hide the treasure, there do seem to be men capable of this. If, after they have bought, they discover the treasure to be a, shall we say, replica, these men are still not likely to discuss it. There are, I am told, rich men who are willing to be dishonest. I believe I am safe in saying there are none who are willing to admit they are fools."

Tod laughed. "So if they had been honest—"

"Exactly," said Uncle Charlie.

"Then why is the king against it?"

"He is sensitive."

Tod turned toward the king.

Pippin said slowly, 'I believe that all men are honest where they are disinterested. I believe that most people are vulnerable where they are interested. I believe that some men are honest in spite of interest. It seems to me reprehensible to search out areas of weakness and to exploit them."

"Aren't you going to have some difficulty being king, sir?" Tod asked.

"He is already," Clotilde said bitterly. "He not only wants to be above everything, every human weakness, he wants his family to be too. He wants everybody to be good—and people just aren't good."

Pippin said, "Stop there, miss! I will not have you say that. People are good—just as long as they can be. Everybody wants to be good. That is why I resent it when goodness is made difficult or impossible for them."

Uncle Charlie said vindictively, "Before they came in, you were talking about power. You were saying, I believe, that a king without power is emasculate. If that is so, my dear nephew, what do you think of the proposition that power corrupts and absolute power corrupts absolutely?"

The king said, "Power does not corrupt. Fear corrupts, perhaps fear of a loss of power."

"But does not power create in other men the impulse which must cause fear in the holder of power? Can power exist without the ultimate fear that makes corruption? Can you have one without the other?"

"Oh, dear!" said Pippin. "I wish I knew."

Uncle Charlie bored in. "If you took power, don't you think the very people who made you king would turn against you?"

The king threw up his hands, "And you told me to relax! To you these things are only ideas. To me—I eat them and dress in them, breathe them and dream of them. Uncle Charlie, this is no intellectual game to me. It is anguish."

"My poor child," said Uncle Charlie. "I did not mean to hurt you. Wait! I will get another bottle. This time you shall have it without water."

Tod watched the king sip his brandy and ruddy relaxation come over him. The tremble went out of his hands and lips and he loosened his muscles to the embrace of the velvet chairs.

"Thank you," he said to Uncle Charlie. "This is exquisite cognac."

"It should be. It has been waiting around since the Treaty of Ghent. Will you have a little more? You will notice I have not offered it to these commoners."

Tod Johnson picked Clotilde's hand from her lap and held it between both of his.

"I've been worried, sir," he began uneasily. "You know I've been dating your daughter. I like her. Under ordinary circumstances, I wouldn't give a—I mean I'd just go ahead—but, you see, sir, I like you too, and, well—I want to ask you—"

Pippin smiled at him. "Thank you," he said. "I guess one of the hard things about being king is that no one can afford to like the king, nor can the king dare to like anyone. You are worried because Clotilde is a royal princess, is that not so?"

"Well, yes, and you know all the trouble they have had in England. I don't want to hurt her and, well—I'm—I don't want to get hurt myself."

Clotilde broke in angrily. "Toddy, is it that you place yourself to absorb a powder?"

"I don't think I understand," said Pippin. "What is this powder?"

Tod laughed. "Clotilde is taking a Berlitz course in American slang. I think her instructors are a little confused about it too. She means am I winding up for a run-out."

"Preparing to say adieu," Uncle Charlie filled in.

"The king asked kindly, "And are you?"

"That's what I don't know. Now what I want to ask you in this: I've been reading a little. The French kings have always observed the Salic Law, is that not so? And this law says that women cannot succeed. Isn't that true also? And therefore it is not so important to the state who noblewomen marry? Is that so?"

Pippin nodded approvingly. "You have read properly. That is true up to a point. But in one place you are in error, and this has nothing to do with the Salic Law. Women of great houses have always been used as magnets for other great houses, along with their lands and their holdings and their titles."

"Kind of catalysts for mergers," Tod suggested.

Uncle Charlie broke in. "The Salic Law is not a law. It is only a custom brought to us by Germans. Don't give it a thought."

Pippin said, "My uncle, by your definition our ancestors were Ger-

mans too—Héristal, Arnulf." He turned back to Tod. "My young friend, I don't know what the decision will be about succession. Clotilde is my only child. I am not prepared to divorce my wife for the sake of an heir, and my wife has passed— But you understand. It is quite possible that public pressure may force Clotilde to be a breeding ground for kings. Custom, particularly meaningless custom, is generally more powerful than law. Would you be content to leave the—the powder untaken until we see? By the way, does this refer to gunpowder or to medicinal powder?"

"Darned if I know," said Tod. "The only people who try to find out what slang means are the ones who can't use it. You mean, sir, that I should stick around a while?"

"Exactly," said the king. "You see, a second function of nice-looking noblewomen was to bring money into the family."

"If you're thinking of Petaluma, forget it," said Tod. "If I know my father, he'll have it tied up in trust funds and things."

"But you see," said Uncle Charlie, "his reputation for having it will make you not an undesirable suitor. The French resent more than anything else being fools. Marrying a rich man, no matter what the drawbacks, has never been considered foolish in France."

"I see. You're covering for me. Thanks. Make me kind of like part of the family—for a while, at least. That's why I asked in the first place. I know you're the king and you're older than I am but you haven't had much practice kinging. You've got a great little thing here, great, but it can blow up in your face if you don't play your cards right."

"This has happened in the past," said Pippin. "And not so very long ago either."

"I'd like to talk to you about that, sir, now that I'm a—you might say apprentice—member of the family."

Clotilde cried, "Nots! Politics. You are a droopys. I am a bore."

Tod laughed shortly. "Maybe she's right," he said. "They say that Americans talk sex in the office and business in the bedroom. I'll take her out violin-dodging, but I would like to talk to you."

"I should be glad," said Pippin. "Will you come to Versailles?"

"I've been out there," said Tod. "It's crawling with freeloaders. Tell you what, sir. Why don't you come to my suite at the George Cinq?"

The king said, "One of the drawbacks of my office is that I can't go where I wish. The management would have to be told, the secret police, the newspapers privately informed. Your suite would be searched and men placed on the roofs across the way. It's not very much fun to be royalty."

Tod said, "Not at the George Cinq. There hasn't been a French-man there in years. Besides, Ava Gardner and H. S. H. Kelly are in residence. You couldn't raise an eyebrow. It might be the most private place in France for a French king."

"Perhaps so," said Pippin. "I have even thought of disguises."

"My God," Uncle Charlie said, "you'd be so bad at it. You have absolutely no talent as an actor."

The queen drew her chair close to the chaise longue where Sister Hyacinthe sat in pious contemplation.

"I've always told you Pippin was vague," she said. "He was bad enough with his telescope, but he's worse now. He paces—with his hands behind his back—and he mutters. When I speak to him, he doesn't hear. And he is miserably unhappy. There's something on his mind. I wish you'd talk to him, Suzanne. You were always good with men—they say."

"They say," Sister Hyacinthe observed. "But maybe not good enough. What would I say to him?"

"Find out what's bothering him—"

"Maybe just being king is bothering him."

"Nonsense," said Marie. "Anybody would want to be king."

Marie steered her husband to Sister Hyacinthe's cell. "This is my old friend," she said, and then cleverly, "Oh! There's something I forgot. Excuse me for a moment." And she went out.

The king looked casually at the nun.

"Sit down, Sire."

"I haven't been very dutiful toward the Church. Since I was a child," he said.

"You might say I haven't either. I was twenty years on the musical stage."

"I thought you were familiar."

"In this costume? I am complimented, M'sieur. Very few ever looked at my face."

He tried for gallantry. "Then there must be incredible beauties . . ."

"Under this habit? Thank you. I went to school with Madame. You may have heard her speak of me as Mademoiselle Lescault. I don't think she will have mentioned my profession. Marie is one of those fortunate people who forbid existence to matters they do not approve of. I envy her this gift."

"My wife is remarkable in many ways, but not for subtlety. It is true that quite often I do not know what she is up to but I have never any doubt when she is up to something."

Suzanne put her head back and closed her eyes. "You wonder why she brought you here and left you here?"

"I imagine that is what I wonder."

"She feels that you are uneasy, restless."

"I have often been uneasy and nearly always restless. This has not troubled her before. She attacked it with sauces and small delicious sweets."

"That is the housewife's remedy. I hope it cured you, or at least that you said it did."

"I hope I tried, Sister."

"You are amiable, M'sieur. Could you tell me why you are uneasy now? Something I can twist around for Marie? She worries about you."

The king said, "I would help you if I could. Many of the causes I do not know myself. I did not ask to be king. I was picked like a berry from a bush and placed in a position where there are many precedents, nearly all of them bad and all of them unsuccessful."

"You cannot, like a berry, let happen what will happen?"

"No," said the king, "it is the misfortune of men to want to do a thing well, even a thing they do not want to do at all. You will not believe this, Sister, but once I wanted to dance well. It was ridiculous."

"You are afraid you will make mistakes?"

"My dear Sister, the path is solid with mistakes. Even the best of kings failed."

"I am sorry for you."

"No, you must not be sorry. My uncle told me I had the choice of cutting my wrists. I did not take advantage of it."

Sister Hyacinthe said, "There have been kings who put the whole business in others' hands—the ministry, the council, the team—and went about enjoying themselves."

"I think, Sister, that was only after they had given up. There is a strong pressure on a king to be a king. The purpose of a king is to rule and the purpose of rule is to increase the well-being of the kingdom."

"It is a trap," said Sister Hyacinthe, "like all other virtue—it is a trap. Where virtue is involved it is very difficult to tell oneself the truth, M'sieur. There are two kinds of virtue. One is passionate ambition and the other simply a desire for the peace which comes from not giving anyone any trouble."

"You are thoughtful, Sister," said the king, and she knew from the brightness of his eyes that she had captured his attention.

"I have not been without this problem," she said. "When after twenty years of standing nude on a stage, inspiring dreams, I hope, in lonely men, I took the veil, it would have been very easy to assume a holy impulse—I could recite you all the ways of saying it. But I knew that I was simply tired."

"You are honest."

"I don't know. Having admitted that my impulse was less than pure, I found in myself kindnesses, understandings, that even I can find no fault with—by-products of the initial laziness—I didn't even have to worry about virtue once I took the weight off my feet."

"How about the ritual—the rising, kneeling, reciting of magic religious formulae?"

"It is no more than breathing after a little while. Easier to do than not to do."

The king got up and scratched his elbows, walked around his chair, sat down.

"It seems a big jump," he said, "from sinner to—saint."

Sister Hyacinthe laughed. "Sin is difficult to isolate in oneself," she observed. "In others it is easy to discern, but in ourselves it has a way of being based on necessity or good intentions. Please don't repeat this to Marie—"

"Pardon? Oh! I don't think it would occur to me."

"Marie is a wife—that's different."

"She is very kind to me," said the king.

Sister Hyacinthe regarded him with amazement. "I hope that was said only in courtesy," she said, "not as a truth."

"I don't know what you mean."

"There is no kindness in women," said the nun. "There is love, but that is a subjective thing. If I had ever married I might have convinced myself otherwise." She regarded him narrowly. "What is the best thing that ever happened to you, Sire?"

"Why—"

"If you can tell me, perhaps I can tell you what it is you are missing and mourning for."

"Why, I guess—I guess it was when the comet appeared in my reflector and I knew I was the first human ever to see it. I was—I was filled with wonder."

"They had no right to make you king," she said. "A king only repeats old mistakes, and if he knows this in advance—I understand now, Sire—but I can't help you. You didn't cut your wrists and now it is too late. A comet. Yes, I can see . . ."

"I like you, Sister," said the king. "Will you permit me to call on you now and then?"

"If I were sure your feeling was purely intellectual . . ."

"But Sister—"

"I should forbid it," said Sister Hyacinthe, and her laughter was reminiscent of the ladies' dressing room backstage. "You are a good man, Sire, and a good man draws women as cheese draws mice."

One of the great burdens on the king was his lack of privacy. He was followed, fawned on, protected, stared at. He had considered the use of disguises in the manner of Haroun-al-Raschid. At times he locked himself in his room simply to get away from the eyes and voices of the people who surrounded him.

At about this time he made a happy accidental discovery. The queen, finding it necessary to clean his office, sent him out until she could get it swept and dusted. He was wearing his corduroy jacket, a little frayed at

the elbows, flannel trousers in need of a press, and espadrilles. He slipped some papers in a briefcase and went to the gardens to finish his work. As he sat on the coping of a fish pond, a gardener approached him.

"It is not permitted to sit here, M'sieur," said the gardener.

The king moved to a place in the shade on a great stairway. Immediately a gendarme touched his elbow.

"The visiting hours are from two to five, M'sieur. Please go to the entrance and await a guide."

Pippin gaped at him. He gathered up his papers and sauntered to the entrance. He paid his fee for the guided tour. He bought postcards and peered with the crowd into rooms guarded by velvet ropes.

All through the palace he saw servants and nobility and ministers of state and not one of them looked at the man in the corduroy jacket and espadrilles. Even the queen bustled by and did not notice him as the tour stared after her.

In delight he followed the tourists back to the entrance and boarded the chartered bus for Paris. His heart was light. To test himself thoroughly he strolled up the Champs Elysées and no one saw him.

He took a table at the Select and ordered a Pernod and water and he watched the passing throng. He listened to tourist talk, and his freedom grew on him like wings.

He indulged himself in a mildly anti-monarchist argument with a correspondent from *Life* magazine, who retorted, "I suppose the king hasn't yet been able to clean out all the Communists."

Pippin sneered, borrowed a cigarette, and strolled across the Champs Elysées, past Fouquet's, and into the Avenue George V, past the Hotel Prince de Galles, and to the entrance of the Hotel George V itself. As he entered the lobby, he was stopped by an official.

"You wish something?"

"I wish to see Mr. Tod Johnson."

"You are delivering something? Leave it at the—"

"I have his briefcase," said Pippin. "He has asked me to hand it to him personally."

"The hall porter—" began the official, his eyes fastened on the espadrilles.

"Please call Mr. Tod Johnson's suite, M'sieur. Tell him that Mr. King has brought his briefcase from Uncle Charlie's Gallery."

Tod welcomed Pippin at the door to his apartment, tipped the suspicious guide, and clapped the king on the back.

"Well, I'll be damned," he said.

"Isn't it wonderful? I had a hard time getting in," said the king.

Tod said, "I have a friend who claims that, if you want to hide, get a job as a waiter in a good restaurant. No one ever looks at a waiter. Sit down, sir. Can I get you a drink?"

"A—how do you call it?—mar— mart—?"

"Martini?"

"Exactly, a martini," said the king happily. "Do you know, a tourist nearly had me arrested for lèse majesté."

"Won't they be looking for you, sir?"

"I hope so," said the king. "But they won't look here. You said yourself that the French do not come here. . . . Now that, my friend, is a better one than my uncle makes."

"He can't bring himself to use enough ice," said Tod.

"One of my own guards ejected me from my own garden," said the king happily.

"I guess people see what they expect to see. They don't expect a bareheaded king with a bald spot. Did you think of it yourself, sir?"

"Oh, no! It was an accident. You see, Marie wanted to clean my little office. And then a gardener wouldn't let me sit down on a coping."

"You aren't insulted?"

"How do you mean, insulted? I've never been happier."

"Well, I know some great stars of Hollywood who disguise themselves with dark glasses and pulled-down hats. They're pretty upset if no one recognizes them. Then there's the owner of three of our biggest magazines. He has a real hatred for publicity but he just happens to get photographed all the time. Take my father, now—"

Pippin broke in. "I wanted to talk to you about your father."

"Had a long letter from him this morning. He doesn't approve of me going around with Bugsy, with the princess."

"He doesn't?"

"No. He's a snob. You see, he's a self-made man and there's no snob like a self-made man. They say he only looks up to his maker. The second generation can relax a little—even be democratic.

"My father's letter is funny. He's interested in what is going on here. He says for me to tell you that you've got a real chance here, if you play your cards right. But he doesn't believe you will."

"Do you think he would come here to advise me?"

"Oh, no!" said Tod. "He's a snob. He might come over later and criticize. There's a dividend here." And Tod filled the king's glass.

"I came to see you because I want to ask you some questions. It is true that at first your father actually raised chickens?"

"Sure he did, and he hates chickens."

"Is it not also true that many of the heads of your greatest corporations worked up from the bottom? I seem to remember . . ."

"Sure. Knudsen was an iron puddler; Ben Fairless worked on an open hearth, I think. I could name you lots—Charlie Wilson—oh, lots!"

"Then they know their business on all levels—"

"True," said Tod. "But don't think that makes them democratic. It's just the opposite."

"I've never understood America," said the king.

"Neither do we, sir. You might say we have two governments, kind of overlapping. First we have the elected government. It's Democratic or Republican, doesn't make much difference, and then there's corporation government."

"They get along together, these governments?"

"Sometimes," said Tod. "I don't understand it myself. You see, the elected government pretends to be democratic, and actually it is autocratic. The corporation governments pretend to be autocratic and they're all the time accusing the others of socialism. They hate socialism."

"So I have heard," said Pippin.

"Well, here's the funny thing, sir. You take a big corporation in America, say like General Motors or Du Pont or US Steel. The thing they're most afraid of is socialism, and at the same time they themselves are socialist states."

The king sat bolt upright. "Please?" he said.

"Well, just look at it, sir. They've got medical care for employees and their families and accident insurance and retirement pensions, paid vacations—even vacation places—and they're beginning to get guaranteed pay over the year. The employees have representation in pretty nearly everything, even the color they paint the factories. As a matter of fact, they've got socialism that makes the USSR look silly. Our corporations make the US government seem like an absolute monarchy. Why, if the US government tried to do one-tenth of what General Motors does, General Motors would go into armed revolt. It's what you might call a paradox, sir."

Pippin shook his head. He got up and went to the window and looked down on the tree-shaded Avenue George V. "Can you explain why they do these things?" he asked.

Tod Johnson poured gin by eye into the tall mixer, dashed a few drops of vermouth in, and stirred ice cubes round and round in the mixture.

"That is the oddest thing of all and the most reasonable," he said. "Do you like a squeeze of lemon peel, sir?"

"Yes, please. But why?"

"They don't do it out of kindness, sir. It's just that some of them have found out they can produce and sell more goods that way. They used to fight the employees. That's expensive. And sick workers are expensive. Do you think my father likes to feed his chickens vitamins and cod-liver oil and minerals and keep them warm and dry and happy? Hell, no! They lay more eggs that way. Oh, it wasn't quick and it's far from finished, but isn't it strange, sir, that out of the most autocratic system in the world the only really workable socialism seems to be growing? If my father heard me say that he'd string me up by the thumbs. He thinks *he* makes the decisions."

760

"And who does, Tod?"

"Circumstances and pressures," said Tod. "If he hadn't gone along with the pressures he wouldn't be in business." He drained the new martini gently into the glasses. "I'm going to send for a sandwich, sir. These things are murder if you don't eat."

The king sipped at his drink. "These changes didn't come easily?"

"Hell, no. It took about a hundred years and a lot of fighting, and some of it is still going on." Tod laughed gently. "You know, sir, I think my old man's itching to get his fingers on this operation. He wrote me nine pages in his letter, mostly questions to ask you. When my old man asks a question, he's telling you."

The king said dreamily, "Perhaps I had better wait for the sandwich before I hear the questions. How do you get along with—what do you call her, Bugsy?"

"It's kind of off and on, sir. I'm fond of her, but every once in a while when she goes royal on me I want to kick her in the pants."

"She matured early," said Pippin. "By the time she was eighteen she had lived several lives."

"That's just it. She didn't have a decent adolescence when she was fourteen and fifteen, and now it's snapping back at her. She jumps from little kid to Mrs. Astor, back and forth."

Pippin said a little thickly, "I am basically a scientist and a scientist is or should be an observer. Now, young sir, the artistic, the creative side of a scientist indulges in hypothesis. Watching Clotilde and her friends, I have formulated a maturity hypothesis." His speech had the slow precision of mild intoxication. "Those drinks are very strong," he said.

"It's not their strength, it's their inherent meanness," said Tod. "Look, King, you've got me talking that way too. What's your maturity business?"

Pippin's eyes had closed, but they opened a slit and he shook his head as though his ears were full of water. "The human fetus is born upside down," he said solemnly. "But it is not true that a child becomes upright after birth. Observe the feet of children and young people when they are at rest. The feet are nearly always higher than the head. No matter how hard he may try, the growing boy, and particularly girl, cannot keep the feet down. The fetal position is very strong. It takes eighteen to twenty years for the feet finally to accept the ground as their normal home. It is my hypothesis that you can judge maturity exactly by the relationship of the feet to the ground."

Tod laughed. "I have a sister—" he began.

The king suddenly arose. "Please—" he said, "please direct me to the—"

Tod leaped up and took his arm. "This way, sir," he said. "Here— let me help you. Mind the little step here."

The dawn was breaking when the king awakened in one of Tod's twin beds. He looked in wonder about the room. "Où suis-je?" he asked plaintively.

"You're all right, King," said Tod from the other bed. "How do you feel?"

"Feel?" said the king. "Why—all—I feel all right."

"I loaded you with aspirin and B₁ tablets," said Tod. "Sometimes that will head off a hangover."

The king sat up. "My God!—Marie! She'll have the police out."

"Take it easy," said Tod. "I telephoned Bugsy."

"What did you tell her?"

"I told her you were drunk," said Tod.

"But Marie?"

"Don't worry, sir. The princess has informed Her Majesty that you are in a top-secret conference with Your Majesty's ministers—a matter of international importance."

"You're a good boy," said the king. "I ought to make you a minister."

"I've got enough trouble," said Tod. "Did you ever have a Bloody Mary?"

"What is that?"

"Had to change the name in France. You had no Queen Mary in France, so the name seemed a little sacrilegious. Here it is called Marie Blessée."

"Wounded Mary," said the king. "What is it?"

"Leave it in my hands, sir. It is elixir, it is pretty close to a transfusion." He reached for the telephone. "Louis? Tod Johnson, ici. Quatre Maries Blessées, s'il vous plaît. Vite. Oui—quatre. Très bien. Merci bien."

"You speak abominable French," said the king.

"I know," said Tod. "I won't be surprised if Louis sends four wounded girls." And then he said irritably, "You might have a little trouble with language in New York, King."

"But I speak English."

"They don't," said Tod, and he went to the door to receive the tray of Bloody Marys.

By nine o'clock the king had recovered, and a little more.

"I should go back," he said.

"Make the most of it, sir. You may never get out again."

"You must beware of my Uncle Charles," said Pippin. "There are times when I feel he is not quite—"

"He certainly isn't—but do you know, sir, he hasn't sold me a single picture. He is charmed with my resistance. He admires me. Do you feel well enough now to hear some of my father's questions?"

The king sighed. "I suppose so. I wish I could forget the throne

for a little while. I would rather be a corporation. Are all of your pajamas silk, my friend?"

"No, the ones you have on are my social pajamas. I sleep in a T-shirt. It doesn't bind.

"My father says you've got to break it down. He always says you've got to break everything down. What have you got to sell and who is going to buy it and have they got the money?"

"Sell?"

"Sure—now we sell eggs and pullets and supplies."

"What has a government to sell? It is a government."

"Sure, I know, but it has to sell something or you wouldn't need a government."

The king frowned. "I hadn't thought of it that way. Well, perhaps peace, order—perhaps progress, happiness."

"That's quite a business," said Tod. "Now my father wants to know have you the capital and organization to do it?"

"I have the throne."

Tod said, "Seems to me the throne has some assets but it has some liabilities too. Take that bunch of freeloaders out at your place. You ought to get rid of them. They'll eat up the profit."

"But they are the nobility, the foundation of the throne."

"More like termites in the foundation. Maybe if you had a sinking fund you could pension them off. One thing is sure, you can't put them to work."

"Heavens, no!"

"How did they get to be nobles in the first place?"

"By service to the throne," said the king. "Spiritual, military, financial."

"There—you see? Those old boys weren't stupid. Now spiritual is taken care of, military is out of your hands, but financial—you could use."

"Most of the nobility through misfortune—"

"Are broke," said Tod. "So let's put them out to pasture and get in a new crop."

"I don't understand."

"Look, king, I could sell titles in Texas and Beverly Hills for anything I want to ask. Why, I know people who would give the bottom dollar of a big stack for a patent of nobility."

"That isn't right."

"What do you mean, right? That's how these boys got it. The British still do it. You don't have to own a distillery to sit in the House of Lords, but it helps."

"My friend, you are speaking of tradition."

Tod said, "The Dukedom of Dallas?—why, ten billionaires would

be after it. I could do it by sealed bid. Only trouble is the Earl of Fort Worth might declare war on the Duke of Dallas. Say, this is wonderful! I can see those dames snooting each other. All they've got to throw at each other now is oil wells and air conditioning."

"You make jokes, my friend."

"Don't you believe it! Drink up, King, and I'll order another round. These things don't trick you like martinis."

"Don't—shouldn't we have some breakfast?"

"Breakfast is right in them—good healthy tomato juice, and then there's liver in Worcestershire."

"Well, in that case—" said the king.

"How about it? We can put out the word privately like a stock issue—dignified."

"I believe," said the king, "that you have laws forbidding your citizens to hold titles."

"Forget it," said Tod. "If those oil and cattle boys can rig the tax laws and the utilities laws, they aren't going to have any trouble with a little old law against titles. We could guarantee a knighthood for every congressman who voted in favor—but the big titles, that's where the money is."

The king said, "I have met some Texans. They seemed very democratic. In fact, they usually announce themselves as 'little old country boys.'"

"Yes, King, and those little old country boys usually have half a million acres, three airplanes, a yacht, and a house in Cannes. But we don't have to limit it to Texas. Think of Los Angeles, and when we've worked that over there's Brazil, Argentina—the field is unlimited."

"The whole thing smacks of my uncle," said the king.

"Well, I did discuss it with him. There's pots in it, King. I can arrange the whole thing."

The king was silent so long that Tod looked at him in alarm. "You feel bad again, sir?"

Pippin was staring straight ahead and, although his eyes crossed slightly, his chin was firm and his bearing regal.

"You have forgotten, my friend, that the purpose of a king is the well-being of his people—all of his people."

"I know," said Tod. "But it's like my father says. You've got to have capital and organization. The people who put you in didn't do it for nothing. Sooner or later you're going to have to fight them or join them."

"How about simple honesty—simple logic?"

"That has never worked," said Tod. "I hate to remind you of your own history. Louis the Fourteenth was a spendthrift. He busted the nation. He was at war all the time. He drained the treasury and wiped

764

out a generation of young men. But he was the Sun King and he was adored, while France was flat on its pants.

"Then along came Louis the Sixteenth and he was simple and honest. He brought in efficiency experts. He called assemblies, he tried to listen, to understand. He tried everything and—" Tod drew his hand across his throat.

Pippin's head sank on his chest. He said sadly, "Why did they have to make me king?"

"I'm sorry," said Tod. "I guess I haven't helped much. But you get a thing like a throne in your hands and pretty soon you want to use it."

"I want peace—and my telescope."

"You'll want to use it," said Tod. "Everyone does. Look, I've been lousy to you. Let's you and me go out on the town and see how the other half lives."

"I must go back."

"But you may never break loose again. Besides, you owe it to your people to associate with them."

"Well, if you put it that way."

"I'll lend you some clothes," said Tod. "Nobody will ever recognize you."

"Do you want to call Clotilde?"

"No," said Tod. "Let's you and me stag it."

At three-thirty in the morning, the Life Guard, Lieutenant Emile de Samothrace, on duty at the gate of Versailles, was alerted by a disturbance in front of the palace. In the half-darkness he was able to discern two men who clung solicitously together while they marched to the gate, singing:

"*Allons, enfants de la Patrie*
All the livelong day.
Le jour de gloire est arrivé
And the monkey wrapped his tail
around the flagpole.
Baa! Baa! Baa!"

Lieutenant de Samothrace intercepted the two while he shouted for the guard, whereupon they charged him with umbrellas, shrieking, "To the Bastille!"

The lieutenant's report read: "One of these men claimed to be Crown Prince of Petaluma while the other continued to mutter 'Baa! Baa! Baa!' I turned them over to the commandant of the palace for questioning."

The next evening, coming on duty, the lieutenant found that his report had been removed from the book and in its place was the

notation: "Three hours and thirty minutes and all is well." And it was initialed by the commandant.

Lieutenant de Samothrace found that the words of the song kept running through his head. "Baa! Baa! Baa!"

AND MEANWHILE FRANCE ENJOYED such peace and prosperity and profit that the newspapers began to refer to the time as the Platinum Age. The New York *Daily News* called Pippin "The Atomic King." The *Reader's Digest* reprinted three articles it had commissioned: one in the *Saturday Evening Post,* called, "Royalty Re-examined"; one in the *Ladies' Home Journal,* "The Glorious Present," and one in the *American Legion Monthly,* "A King against Communism."

Citroën announced a new model.

Christian Dior introduced the R line with the highest waistline and the most bursting bodice since Montesquieu.

The Italian Couture out of jealousy maintained that the R line made breasts look like goiters. Gina Lollobrigida, always loyal to Italy, said, on arriving at Idlewild en route to Hollywood, that she refused to look out between herself. But criticism of France was largely grounded in envy of the Platinum Age.

England smoldered and waited.

The Soviet Purchasing Agency ordered four tank cars of French perfume.

In America the excitement rose to fever pitch. Bonwit Teller named one whole floor L'Etage Royal.

A benevolent autumn slipped warmly over France, moved up-Seine and then up-Loire, spread over the Dordogne, climbed the Jura, and lapped against the Alps. A great wheat crop had been harvested, and the grapes were warm and fat and happy. Even the truffles were benevolent—black and full, almost leaping out of the limestone earth. In the north the cows staggered cream-heavy in the pasturage, while the apple crop for once was ready and sufficient for the champagne the English love.

At no time in history had the tourists been so openhanded and humble nor their French hosts so happily sullen.

International relations reached fraternal heights. The most conservative peasants bought new corduroy pants. The red rivers of Bordeaux flowed from the wine presses. The sheep gave milk of a milkness for the cheese.

Vacations being over, parties and sub-parties met in Paris to complete their contributions to the Code Pippin to be adopted in November.

The Christian Atheists achieved a clause imposing an amusement

tax on church services. The Christian Christians were ready with a law for compulsory attendance of mass.

Right and Left Centrists walked arm in arm.

Communists and Socialists took to raising their hats to one another.

M. Deuxcloches, Cultural Custodian, but actual leader of the Communist party of France, put into words what every party was thinking. Speaking in secret caucus, he outlined a series of traps and deadfalls so artfully conceived that no possible move by the king could avoid being disastrous.

France was on a peak of good fortune. Everyone admitted it. Tourists were sleeping in the flowerbeds of the better hotels.

This being so, how does one explain the little cloud that peered over the horizon in mid-September, blackened and spread during the first weeks of October, towered like a thunderhead as November approached?

It is common to explain historic events after the fact in terms of the preoccupation of the historian. Thus the economist finds his pattern in economics, the politician in politics, the medical man in pollens or parasites. Very few if any historians have looked for causes simply in how people feel about things. Is it not true that in the United States the eras of greatest peace and prosperity have been also the periods of greatest uneasiness and discontent? Is it not also true that in these weeks of France's fruition there began to develop and grow among all classes a restlessness, a nervousness, a rustle of fear?

If this should seem unreasonable, even unbelievable, consider to yourself how on a lovely sunny day a man will say to his neighbor, "Probably rain tomorrow." How in a cold, damp winter the general opinion is that it will be a hot, dry summer. Who has not heard a farmer, looking at his abundant crop, complain, "There won't be any market?"

I do not think the historian need look any further in this. It is the tendency of human beings to distrust good fortune. In evil times we are too busy protecting ourselves. We are equipped for this. The one thing our species is helpless against is good fortune. It first puzzles, then frightens, then angers, and finally destroys us. Our basic conviction was put into words by a great and illiterate third baseman.

"Everything in life," he said, "is seven to five against."

The peasant, counting his profits, found time to wonder how much he had lost to the wholesaler. The retail merchant could be heard to curse under his breath when the wholesaler turned his back.

This climate of suspicion on an individual level did not remain there. For example, the Foreign Policy Committee of the United States Senate, hearing of the Russian purchase of four tank cars of French perfume, requested samples from the Secret Service and put them in the hands of qualified scientists to find what offensive qualities—

explosive, poisonous, or hypnotic—might lurk in "Quatre-Vingt Fleurs" or the newest product, "L'Eau d'Eau."

On the other hand, Russian operatives secretly inspected a shipment of plastic helicopters designed for the toy shops of Paris.

A troop of French Boy Scouts, drilling with quarterstaffs, was photographed by the silent services of four nations and the pictures sent home for evaluation.

Worst badgered of all were the speleologists, who found that they could not be alone and unobserved even in the deepest caves.

Suspicion of France was on the rise throughout the world. And in France there were gusts of nervousness. Luxembourg's addition of eight soldiers to its standing army caused a hurried meeting in the Quai d'Orsay.

In the provinces, people glanced nervously in the direction of Paris. In Paris it was whispered that the provinces were growing increasingly restless.

Armed robbery increased. Juvenile delinquency sky-rocketed.

When on September 17 the police discovered in a cellar on the Ile Saint-Louis a cache of buried Communist arms, a ripple of terror spread through France. The police perhaps were not sufficiently explicit. They did not make public that the arms had been hidden by the Commune of 1871, that the cap-and-ball rifles and ancient bayonets were not only obsolete but heavily rusted.

And while this cloud was rising and darkening—what of the king?

It is generally agreed that within a short time of his coronation the king began to change. Such a thing was to be expected, or at least to be anticipated.

Let us draw a parallel. Consider a strain of bird dogs, say pointers, developed, selected, and trained for a thousand generations for the trait of hunting. Then imagine a morganatic marriage and a resulting intermixture of blood until finally we have a puppy of this mingling in a pet-shop window. He is taken to live in a city apartment, walked twice a day on leash, sniffing his way from automobile tire to trash basket to fire hydrant. His nose is accustomed to perfume, gasoline, and mothballs. His toenails are clipped; his skin scented with pine soap; his food taken from a tin can.

This dog, growing up, is trained perhaps to carry the morning paper from the apartment door, to sit, to lie down, to shake hands, to beg, to bring his master's slippers. He is disciplined to stay clear of the hors-d'oeuvre tray, to control his bladder. The only birds he has ever known are fat waddling pigeons, or frantic sparrows in the street; the only love a sneer from a passing pekinese.

Let us then suppose that in his prime of life this dog—the descendant of greatness—is taken on a picnic in the country, to a pleasant place

beside a little stream. In the war against sand and ants and the winds which whip up the corners of the tablecloth, our dog is forgotten for a moment.

He smells the lusciousness of running water and strolls to the stream-side and drinks deeply of a fluid uninfused with germicides. An ancient feeling fills his breast. He moves along a little path, sniffing at leaves and brown treetrunks and at grass. He pauses at a track where a rabbit has crossed. The fresh wind teases his skin.

Suddenly an emotion falls upon him: an ecstasy, a fullness, like a memory. To his nose comes a scent unknown but remembered. He shivers and makes a little whining sound, then moves uncertainly toward the magic.

Then hypnosis falls upon him. His shoulders hunch a little. His thin tail straightens. One foot creeps after its fellow. His neck stretches forward until nose and head and spine and tail become one line. His right front paw rises. He freezes. He does not breathe. His body is like a compass needle, or like a gun pointing at a covey of quail hidden in the under-brush.

In February 19— a gentle, inquisitive man lived in a small house in Avenue de Marigny, together with his daughter and his pleasant wife, his balcony and his telescope, his rubbers and umbrella, and his briefcase always. He had dentists, and insurance, and a little stock in the Crédit Lyonnais. A vineyard in Auxerre . . .

Then without warning this little man was made king. Who of us who do not have the blood can know what happened at Reims when the royal crown descended? Did Paris look the same to the king as it had to the amateur astronomer? How did the word "France" sound in the ears of the king?—and the word "People" in the ears of the king?

It would be strange if ancient mechanisms failed to operate. Perhaps the king did not know what was happening. Perhaps he, like the pointer, responded to forgotten stimuli. It seems undeniable that the kingdom created a king.

Once he became the king he was alone, set apart and alone, and this is a part of being a king. Monarchy created a king.

Uncle Charlie had been to Versailles once in his life when as a child in black smock and white collar he marched in a ragged line of smocked school children through halls and bedchambers, ballrooms and cellars of that national monument, on order of the Minister of Public Instruction.

At that time Charles conceived a hatred and horror for the royal palace from which he never recovered. He remembered the cracked and painted paneling, the squeaking parquetry, the velvet ropes, the drafty halls, as a kind of nightmare.

It was, therefore, a surprise to the king when Uncle Charlie called

on him in the royal apartments, and even a greater surprise that he was accompanied by Tod Johnson.

Charles gazed about the painted room. The floors screamed with shrunken pain when he moved. A blanket was tacked over the windows to keep the chill autumn winds out, and a log fire burned in the great fireplace. The gilt clocks sat on their marble tables and the stiff chairs stood against the wall as Charles remembered them.

Uncle Charlie said, "I must speak to you, my child."

Tod broke in. "I read in the Paris *Herald Tribune* that you had a mistress, sir. Art Buchwald said it."

The king raised his eyebrows.

Uncle Charlie said quickly, "I am teaching Tod my business. He's opening a branch in Beverly Hills."

"You can sell them anything as long as the price is high," said Tod. "Where do you keep your mistress, sir?"

"I have made some changes," the king said, "but in the matter of a mistress I had to compromise. The feeling was too strong. She is a nice little woman, I am told. Does her job well."

"You were told, sir? Haven't you seen her?"

"No," said the king, "I haven't. The queen insists that I ask her for an apéritif one day soon. Everyone says she is very nice; dresses well— neat, pleasant. It's just a form, but in this business forms are very important, particularly if one has plans."

"Aha," said Uncle Charlie. "Plans. That's just what I was afraid of. That's why I came."

"What do you mean?" the king asked mildly.

"Listen, my child. Do you think your secret is a secret? All Paris, all France knows."

"Knows what?"

"My dear nephew, did you think a mechanic's jumper and a false mustache was a disguise? Do you think, when you applied for a job at Citroën and stood all day at the gates talking to the workmen, that you were actually incognito? And when you went through the old buildings on the Left Bank, pretending to be an inspector, tapping on walls, looking down drains—did you imagine that anyone thought you were an inspector?"

"I am amazed," said the king. "I had the cap, the badge."

"And it's not only that," cried Uncle Charlie. "You've been out in the vineyards, pretending to be a vine-dresser. You have driven the concessionaires at Les Halles insane with your questioning." He mimicked, "'What do you pay for carrots? What do you sell them for? What does the wholesaler pay the farmer for them?' And the working man: 'What rent do you pay? What are your wages? How much do you pay to the union? What benefits do you get? What is your average cost for food

and rent for the week?' I think there you pretended to be a reporter from *L'Humanité*."

"I had a press card," said the king.

"Pippin," demanded Uncle Charlie, "what are you up to? I warn you! People are growing nervous."

The king tried to pace the floor until the squealing of the inlaid wood stopped him. He removed his pince-nez and straddled it on the forefinger of his left hand.

"I was trying to learn. There are so many things to be done. Did you know, Uncle Charlie, that twenty per cent of the rented buildings of Paris are a danger to health as well as a threat to safety? Only last week a family in Montmartre was nearly smothered with falling plaster. Do you know that the wholesaler takes thirty per cent of the selling price of those same carrots and the retailer takes forty per cent? And do you know what that leaves for the farmer who raises a bunch of carrots?"

"Stop!" cried Uncle Charlie. "Stop right there! You are playing with fire. Do you want barricades in the streets again? Do you wish Paris in flames? What makes you think you can reduce the numbers of the captains of police?"

"Nine out of ten of them do nothing," said the king.

"Oh, my child," said Uncle Charlie. "My poor bewildered child. You are not going to fall into the old trap, are you? Study the British. When the present Duke of Windsor was king he went down into a coal mine just once and the resulting shock not only caused questions in Parliament but nearly lost the prime minister a vote of confidence. Pippin, my dear, dear child, I order you to desist!"

The king sat down in a little chair and it became a throne.

"I did not ask to be king," he said, "but I am king and I find this dear, rich, productive France torn by selfish factions, fleeced by greedy promoters, deceived by parties. I find that there are six hundred ways of avoiding taxes if you are rich enough—sixty-five methods of raising rent in controlled rental areas. The riches of France, which should have some kind of distribution, are gobbled up. Everyone robs everyone, until a level is reached where there is nothing left to steal. No new houses are built and the old ones are falling to pieces. And on this favored land the maggots are feeding."

"Pippin, stop it!"

"I am a king, Uncle Charlie. Please do not forget that. I know now why confusion in government is not only tolerated but encouraged. I have learned. A confused people can make no clear demands.

"Do you know what a French workman or peasant says when he refers to the government? He calls it 'them.' *They* are doing this. *They, they, they.* Something set apart, nameless, unidentifiable, and so unattackable. Anger dwindles down to grumbling. How can you force redress from something which does not exist?

771

"And consider the intellectuals, the dried-up minds. The writers in the past burned the name 'France' on the world. Do you know what they are doing now? They're sitting in huddled misery, building a philosophy of despair, while the painters, with few exceptions, paint apathy and jealous anarchy."

Uncle Charlie sat on the edge of one of the brocaded chairs and he rested his head in his cupped hands and he swayed from side to side like a mourner at a funeral.

Tod Johnson stood at the fireplace, warming his back. He asked quietly, "Have you got the capital and organization to change it?"

"He's got nothing," Uncle Charlie moaned. "Not one person. Not one sou."

"I have the Crown," said Pippin.

"They'll have you in the tumbril. Don't think the guillotine is beyond recall. You'll fail before you start. They'll destroy you."

"You use the word yourself," said Pippin. *"They, they,* the nameless *they.* It seems to me that even though the king may know he will fail, the king must try."

"Not so, my child. Not so. There have been many kings who simply sat back and—"

"I don't believe it," said the king. "I believe they tried, whatever was said of them. They must have tried; every one of them must have tried."

"How about a war?" Charlie suggested.

The king chuckled. "I know you have my welfare at heart, dear Uncle."

"Come on, Tod," said Charles Martel. "Let's get the hell out of here."

"I want to talk to Tod," said Pippin. "Good night, dear Uncle. You can go down that staircase in the corner and avoid the aristocrats. Creep out through the garden. Give the Royal Guard a cigarette!"

After Charles had gone, Pippin raised a corner of the blanket and peered out. The chill night was full of frog sounds and the carp were burping and spluttering in the ponds. He saw his unfortunate uncle moving along the path, his arm clutched by an elderly nobleman who spoke earnestly and loudly in Gothic type into Charles's ear.

The king sighed and dropped the blanket and turned back to Tod. "Such a pessimist," said Pippin. "He never married, you know. He always said that by the time he knew the woman well enough to marry her, he knew better."

"He's an operator," said Tod. "But you know he didn't really want to enlarge his business. I had to guarantee it wouldn't be any work or trouble to him."

The king pressed the edge of the blanket against the chill from the window. "The frames are shrunk," he said. "Marie hates to have me put the blanket up—but I get cold."

"How about plastic wood?" said Tod. "It's a kind of putty."

Pippin observed, "Modern repairs for an old structure. Now that's one of the reasons I asked you to wait. Perhaps my memory is a little cloudy about our last meeting."

"But sir—"

"It was very pleasant and it did help me. I believe you lectured me about American corporations—"

"I don't know much about them, sir, but, you see, our family *is* a corporation and so naturally—"

"I understand. Now your government is a democracy—a system of checks and balances. Is that not right?"

"Right, sir," said Tod.

"And within that structure you have great corporations which themselves have somewhat the nature of governments. Is that not also right?"

"You're ahead of me, sir, but I guess that's right. You've been burning brain juice."

"Thank you. I guess I have. Is it not so that there is in a corporation a, shall we say, flexibility, one does not find in your government? I mean, could not a change of policy be carried out quickly and effectively in a corporation, let us say by an order from the chairman of the board, without consulting all the stockholders, an order which is presumed to be for the good and profit of the shareholders?"

Tod regarded the sovereign with speculative eyes. "I see what you're getting at, sir."

"What would be the procedure?"

"You think you might get farther as chairman of the board than as king?"

"I am asking, perhaps, a leading question."

"Well, let me think, sir. If it was a big change the chairman would put the question up to the board members, and if they agreed the order would go out. If they split, they'd have to call on the stockholders."

"I guess that's out of the question, then," said the king. "I can't get even two of our people to agree."

"You see, sir," said Tod, "each member of the board represents a certain amount of stock. If there's a rhubarb, the members vote proxies from the stockholders. The one with the most proxies gets control. Then the unions must be consulted if they have a beef."

"Oh, dear! Even for a program obviously good and desirable?"

"Yes, sir. You might say particularly then."

The king sighed. "Apparently a corporation isn't much different from a government."

"Well, it's a little different. It depends on how the stock is held. All the stock in our corporation is held by our family. Remember when we talked about selling titles in America?"

"Through a haze I remember it."

"There's a fortune in it," cried Tod. "Why, sir, it might solve this proxy business. Why don't you just put it in my hands? I can get a hundred thousand dollars for a little old knighthood. I'll bet I can sell a dukedom for anything I want to ask."

The king held up his hand.

"Now wait," said Tod, "listen to this. I can put it in the patent that you keep the proxy. Why, it's better than a stock division. I can get Neiman-Marcus in back of it. It will be bigger than Miss Rheingold and the Academy Awards and the Aquacade put together."

The king said, "Don't you call that watering the stock?"

"Oh, no!" cried Tod. "It's better than that. More like a reissue—kind of refinancing. Maybe Billy Rose would produce it. He's looking around for something big."

The king had sunk his head deep between his shoulders. He shivered. And then he chuckled. "I, Pippin the Fourth, King of France, find that I can only talk to a rich young tourist and an old nun who used to be a chorus girl."

Tod asked, "Is it true what Uncle Charlie said, sir? Have you been going around in disguises?"

"It was a mistake," said the king. "When I visited you no one saw me. The caps and mustaches and badges were a mistake."

"Why did you do it, sir?"

"I thought it might be a good idea to know something about France. Have you noticed a chill in the air?"

"Well, in a way. There's a lot of talk."

"I know," said the king. "I've heard it."

"There's one thing that makes me feel bad," said Tod. "My father—"

"He is ill?"

"You might call it that. He's got duke fever—of all the people in the world."

"Maybe there's a little of it in all of us, Tod."

"But you don't understand—my father—"

"Perhaps I do—a little," said the king.

As the autumnal days grew shorter, more and more private audiences were asked or even demanded of the king. Then he would sit behind his audience desk in a room that had been built and embellished for another king, while two or three representatives of faction or interest spoke to him privately. Each deputation was confident that the king was their partisan. They never came alone. The thought drifted through Pippin's mind that they did not trust one another. Every one of the representatives had the good of France at heart, but it was also true that the ultimate good of France rested on the primary good of faction—or even individual.

In this manner the king learned what was in store for France, what plans were being made. He sat silently and listened while Socialists

proved that Communists must be outlawed, while Centrists showed beyond doubt that only if the financial backbone of France were bolstered and defended could prosperity trickle down to the lower orders.

Religionists and anti-Religionists each made their irrefutable points.

The king listened silently. And he emerged depressed.

Pippin's mind often sought shelter in the memory of his little balcony in the Avenue de Marigny. He could see and feel the dark and silent sky and the slow-flailing nebulae.

Outwardly he was calm and friendly. Now and then he nodded his head, which the audience took to mean the king's agreement and which was actually only the king's growing knowledge of government and of kingship.

He accepted loneliness, but he could not control a scurrying search for either solution or escape, and he did not find them anywhere.

Where the partisans left off the ambassadors continued. Sitting in his painted room, Pippin politely heard the neat and statesmanlike ambitions of other nations to use France, each for its own purpose—and again he nodded and gray depression fogged his soul.

On November 15 the various parties to be represented in the Constitutional Convention petitioned the crown to set the date for convening ahead to December 5. The king graciously agreed, and it was so ordered.

In the evenings Pippin took to making notes in the small lined copybooks which in other days he had used to log the heavens.

Madame Marie was worried about him. "He is so listless—so detached," she told Sister Hyacinthe. "It's not like his old detachment. He asked me yesterday if I liked being queen—*liked!*"

"What did you say?" the nun asked.

"I told what is true, that I had never thought of it one way or another. I just do what each day demands."

"Well, did you like *not* being queen?"

"It was perhaps easier," said the queen, "but not much different. A clean, well-run house is the same everywhere, and husbands are husbands—kings or astronomers. But I think M'sieur is sad."

Chill mornings came, with heartening sunshine in the midday. The leaves fell from chestnuts and plane trees, and the street-sweepers' brooms were busy.

The king went back to his original disguise, which was himself. Dressed in his corduroy jacket and espadrilles, he took to riding a motor scooter about the country. After two falls he added a crash helmet to his costume.

One day he scooted to the little town of Gambais, famous for its perfect if partly ruined Château de Neuville. Pippin ate his lunch beside the overgrown moat of the château. He watched an elderly man feeling about in the reedy water of the moat with a long-tined rake.

The old man made contact with a hard and heavy object, and dragged it up the bank. It was a mossy bust of Pan, horned and garlanded. Only when the ancient struggled to lift Pan to a granite pedestal on the moat's edge did the king get up and move to help him. The two of them heaved the heavy statue up on its base, and then they stood back and regarded it, wiping their green and slippery fingers on their trousers.

"I like it facing a little more east," the old man said. The two of them edged it around. Pippin with his handkerchief wiped the crusted Panic face until the feral lips and the sly, lecherous eyes were visible.

"How did he get in the moat?" the king asked.

"Oh, someone pushed him in. They always do, sometimes two or three times a year."

"But why?"

The old man raised his shoulders and spread his hands. "Who knows?" he said. "There's people that push things in the moat. Pretty hard work too. There's just people that push things in the moat. See those other stands along there? There's a marble vase and a baby with a shell and a Leda in the water down there."

"I wonder why they do it—angry, do you think?"

"Who knows? It's what they do—creep in at night."

"And you always pull them out?"

"I'm late this year. I've had too much to do, and rheumatism."

"Why don't you anchor the statues to the bases?"

"Why, don't you see," the old man explained patiently, "then they'd push the base in too. I don't know if I could manage to get them out then."

The king asked gently, "Are you the owner here?"

"No, I'm not. I live hereabouts."

"Then why do you pull them out?"

The old man looked puzzled—searched for an answer. "Why—I don't know. I guess there's people that pull things out—that's what they do. I guess I'm one of that kind."

The king stared at the green, slimy Pan.

The old man said helplessly, "I guess there's people that do different things, and," he added as though he had just discovered it, "I guess that's how things get done."

"Good or bad?" the king asked.

"I don't understand," said the old man helplessly. "There's just people—just what people do."

The king often called on Sister Hyacinthe, sometimes to speak quietly of the day's happenings and at other times to sit silently. And she, who had had more—if different—experience than Marie, knew when to chatter and when to join him in a healing quietness.

Once she told him, "I wonder what the Superior would think if she

knew that, with one exception, I am fulfilling the functions of the king's mistress. You really should see your mistress, Sire. She feels left out. She had to struggle with her soul to become your mistress, and now she finds the struggle in vain. You haven't even spoken to her, let alone seduce her."

"Later," said the king. "Perhaps later I'll ask her to tea—what is her name again?"

After returning from Gambais, the king went without announcement to call on Sister Hyacinthe, and he found her in the midst of her massage. All he could see of her were two pink feet and ankles protruding through the holes in the screen.

"He's almost finished, Sire," her voice said from behind the partition.

The master bowed and went back to his work, making little mewing sounds of affection and respect over the pink toes, giving pats and squeezes of encouragement to her flattened arches.

"I see an improvement," he said professionally. And to the king, "Regard, Sire—a month ago one could not slip a sheet of thinnest paper under the metatarsal, and now, Sire, even the unpracticed eye is aware of a concavity."

Sister Hyacinthe boomed, "Don't dare to cure them to the point where I will be encouraged to use them."

"She considers only her feet," he said stiffly. "I have my profession and my reputation to think of."

When he was gone and the screen folded and put away, she said, "You know, that pompous little stinker really is curing them, and I dread to think of it."

"One may keep this a secret, Sister," said the king.

"Your color is high, Sire. You have been taking the sun?"

"I've been riding my scooter through the countryside, Sister."

She laughed. "I should like to see the Sun King doing it," she said. "Times are changed, I guess—a motor scooter, and I imagine your ministers are quarreling over the horsepower of their limousines."

"How did you know?" he asked.

"There are things one knows, Sire. For example, I know that you have a problem, that it is a grave problem, and that you have come to me for help in its solution."

"You are very wise," said the king.

"Not wise enough to get out of the chorus before my arches fell."

"But once out, Sister, you took a very long step toward Heaven."

"You are amiable, M'sieur. It may well be that my closeness to Heaven is a by-product. Stumble would be a better word than step. Are you ready to state your problem?"

"I have first to isolate it, Sister. In general it might be stated with the question, 'What is a man to do?'"

"It is not precisely a new problem," she said musingly. "And it usually resolves itself that one does what one is. The first move should be to determine what the man is; that being established, there is very little latitude in what he does."

"One learns so much more easily about other people," said Pippin.

Sister Hyacinthe said, "On leaving the excellent school where Madame was my friend and on taking my place in the Folies, I was troubled about—loss of innocence. Then I discovered that not its loss but the timing of its loss was the problem. My timing was ill-advised, with the result that I had to lose my innocence on several occasions, and after that it was of no importance. But then I was one of many naked girls on a stage—not a king."

"At this moment I feel very naked," said the king.

"Of course you do. It takes time and a certain blunting. But do you know, after a few years I felt much more naked in clothes than without them?"

Pippin said abruptly, "Sister, I am not allowed the time."

"I know," she said. "I'm sorry."

"What shall I do?"

"I don't know what you should do, Sire, but I think I know what you will do."

"You know my dilemma?"

"Only the self-blinded could fail to see it. You will do what you do."

"That's what the old man said. But he was only pulling statues out of the mud. If I am in error, people will suffer—Marie, Clotilde, even France. What would you say, Sister, if a good deed set off an explosion?"

The nun said, "I should say that a good deed may be unwise, but it cannot be evil. It seems to me that the forward history of humans is based on good deeds that exploded—oh! and many were hurt or killed or impoverished, but some of the good remained. I wish—" She paused. "Why not say it? I wish that for the moment I did not wear this—habit."

"Why, Sister?"

"So that I might give you one of the few solaces one human can offer another."

"Thank you, Sister."

"Thank Suzanne, not Hyacinthe. I will ask you to believe, Sire, that at one time Suzanne was not afraid either for her feet or for her soul. Suzanne would have had the courage—and the love."

In the early morning Pippin rode his motor scooter toward Gambais. In his pocket he had a bottle of wine.

He parked his scooter near the road and strolled through the overgrown park, smelling the hint of frost, picking the orange pips from the winter-ready wild-rose vines. A gust of wind dropped curling, darkened leaves from the restless trees on his head and shoulders.

Then he heard a weak shouting ahead of him near the moat and hurried forward until he cleared the edge of the forest and saw three burly youths laughing and wrestling playfully with the ancient. They had the bust of Pan in their arms and they moved toward the moat while the old man tugged helplessly at their jackets and shouted curses at them.

Pippin broke into a run, and then he was in the midst of it. The strong young men turned on the furious king, and then they were rolling and fighting and scratching on the ground, and then the squirming clot went over the edge and down into the dark water of the moat. And still the fight continued until the young men held the bleeding king under water. He ceased to struggle. Then in fear they clambered, dripping, up the slippery bank and ran, ran in panic and disappeared into the autumn forest.

Pippin gradually came back to consciousness. The ancient had pulled his head and chest out of the water.

"I'm all right, I guess," said the king.

"Don't look it! Them young thugs. I know 'em. I'll go to their people. I'll bring a charge."

"As long as I'm wet already, I might as well dig around in the water for the vase and the Leda and the baby with a shell."

"You'll do no such of a thing. I got the vase yesterday. You'll come to my place and get dry and warmed up. I got a half-bottle of cognac."

Pippin crawled up the slippery bank. He was covered with green scum like the bust of Pan, one eye was black, and a line of blood ran from his split lips.

In a little shack hidden within the fringe of the forest his friend built up the fire and helped him to remove his clothes and bathed him with a sponge and a bucket of warm water, and dried him with frayed clean rags.

"You look like you been in a cat fight," he said. "Here, take a nip of this. Put this blanket around you. I'll hang your clothes over the stove."

Pippin dug in the pocket of his spongy corduroy jacket for the bottle of wine.

"I brought you this as a present," he said.

The old man held the bottle away from him as far as his arms would reach and squinted at the label.

"Why this—this is—is christening wine—this is wine for a wedding. I don't know if I'll ever have a day again would justify pulling this cork."

"Nonsense," said Pippin. "Open it. I'll help you drink it."

"It not yet the hour of nine?"

"Open it," said the king, and he gathered the blanket about his shoulders.

The ancient drew the cork tenderly. "Now why would you think to bring a wine like this to me?"

"Maybe in celebration of the ones who pull things out."

"Oh! You mean like the statues—"

"Or like me. Drink up! drink up!"

The old man tasted and smacked his lips. "A wine like this—" he said helplessly. He wiped his lips with his sleeve for fear some extraneous flavor might creep in.

Pippin said, "Last night I thought of something I wanted to ask you. What do you think of the king?"

"Which king?"

"The king—Pippin the Fourth, by the Grace of God Monarch of France."

"Oh! him." And then suspiciously: "What you getting at? I don't want trouble, wine or no wine. Why'd you come to think of it at night?"

"I just wondered. It's only a question—no trouble. Who could give you trouble?"

"You never can tell," the old man said.

"Fill up your glass and tell me. What do you think of him?"

"I've got no politics outside of right here in Gambais. What do I know about the king? He's just the king, I guess. There's kings and then there's not kings, only—"

"Only what?"

"Well, there isn't rightly any kings any more. Kings? They're like those blasted big lizards, big as a house. They run out. They disappeared, they're ex—ex—"

"Extinct?"

"That's it, extinct. Seems like there wasn't room for them."

"But there is a King of France."

"He's like a play game for children," the old man said. "He's like Father Christmas. He's there, but when you get old enough you don't believe in him any more. He—well—he's just a dream, like."

"Do you think there will ever be any kings any more?"

"How should I know? What do you keep picking at me for? You'd think you was related to him." He surveyed the clothes hanging over the stove. "But you ain't."

"Would you know if there was a real king, not just a dream?"

"I guess so."

"How would you know?"

"Well, he'd come riding down the crops on his horses—or there'd be trouble and he'd hang a lot of folks—or he'd say, maybe, 'There's a raft of bad things going on and I'm going to fix them—'" His voice dwindled away. "No, I guess none of them would answer. I know plenty of rich men that do like that, but they ain't kings. I guess there's only one way you'd know for sure."

"What?"

"Well—if they'd take him out and guillotine him I guess you'd be pretty sure he was a king. I guess you would."

Pippin got up and went to the stove and lifted down his damp and steaming clothes from the drying cords.

"They're not dry yet."

"I know—but I must go."

"You going to report me to somebody for something?"

"No," said the king. "You've answered my question. And—by God, I'll do it. A man can't stand being extinct. Perhaps I'll do it badly, but I'll do it."

"What are you talking about? You haven't had that much wine."

Pippin pulled on his clammy clothes. "I'll send you some wine," he said. "I owe it to you."

"For what?"

"You have told me. To be guillotined a man must have done something to make him worthy of the guillotine. The guillotine or—or the Cross requires either a thief or— Thank you, my puller-out-of-things."

The king strode out of the shack and walked rapidly through the forest to the thicket by the roadside where his scooter was hidden.

In the royal apartment the queen rubbed lemon oil on a polished tabletop.

"How many times must I say that a glass should not be set down without something under it?"

The king put his arms around her and drew her close.

"What are you doing? Pippin, you're wet! Pippin, look at your face—your eye! What have you done?"

"Tripped over the coping and fell in the carp pond."

"You'll never learn to look where you're going. Pippin! Someone might come in— M'sieur—they don't knock."

ON ONE POINT all ministers, delegates, nobles, and academicians were agreed. The opening of the convention must be regal. Too many of the recently honored had not yet been able to display publicly their robes and feathers, hats, medals, rosettes, and braid. The king was requested to attend the opening and deliver a short and tasteful address from the throne. A number of sample speeches were sent to him, based on the cautious sentiments of British royalty.

The King of France should accept the love and support of his

subjects, should mention his own love both for his subjects and for the Kingdom of France, should recognize the glorious past and anticipate a glorious future. He should then retire and leave the making of the constitution, or rather of the Code Pippin, to the delegates.

Pippin agreed to this, but then the argument about costumes raged for two hours. The committee was large, and its members insisted on standing, although the sovereign suggested that they sit. Furthermore, two elderly noblemen uncomfortably wore their hats, a right their forebears had been granted by Francis I—to remain covered in the presence of the king.

Pippin IV said acidly, "It was my impression and my hope, gentlemen, that this coming deliberation was for the purpose of devising a constitution, a body of laws dealing with ordinary things in the lives of ordinary people. Why is it necessary that we turn it into a costume party reminiscent of those given by South American millionaires in Venice? Why may we all not wear sober clothing of our own time?"

A Socialist and a nobleman fought for the floor and the Socialist won, no less a Socialist than Honnête Jean Veauvache, now Comte des Quatre Chats. M. le Comte replied for the whole committee, as the nodding of heads indicated.

"Your Majesty," he said, "there is nothing ordinary about law. On the contrary, it is a mystical matter, in most minds closely related to religion. And, as the dispensers of holy law find vestments necessary, so do the servants of civil law. Remark, Sire, that our judges preside in gowns and caps. Think of English judges, who require themselves not only to sit in robes and wigs, regardless of the heat of the weather, but even to carry nosegays of flowers, once designed to cover the smell of the people, but not abandoned in a less odoriferous period. And in America, Sire, the most irascibly democratic of nations, where panoply in government is forbidden and where the chief of state is required to be the worst dressed of all—even there, I am told, the ordinary people, feeling robbed, join secret organizations, where regularly they wear crowns and robes and ermine, and speak in rituals of antiquity which give them solemn solace even though they do not understand the words.

"No, Majesty, the common people not only do not want commonness; they will not permit it.

"I ask you to remember Louis Philippe, the so-called Bourgeois King, who dared to walk the streets in ordinary clothing and moreover to carry an umbrella. He was banished from France by an outraged people.

"Finally, Sire, the flower of France will be sitting and their ladies will be in the galleries. They have purchased new robes—even coronets. They are not to be denied the right to wear them. These may seem small things, but actually they are very large and very important. And if to this assembly should come the king, dressed in a two-button suit

and a Sulka tie, carrying his papers in a briefcase, I shudder to think of the reaction. Indeed I feel that such a king would be laughed out of office."

The committee was nodding as one man, and when Honnête Jean finished, the members were constrained to applaud.

He was followed by a venerable Academician, a man whose name and whose wisdom are bywords in the world.

"I wish to second the words of Monsieur le Comte," said the master, "but I wish to go one step further. Majesty may do almost anything it wishes save one. The king may not permit himself to be ridiculous. It is the one thing which will inevitably destroy him. In my youth, Sire, it was my good fortune to study under a very learned man, but also a man of huge understanding. At one time he told me the following: 'If,' he said, 'the greatest intellect in the world should be called before the fifty next greatest minds in the world to discuss a problem of such importance that the earth's existence depended on it, and if that greatest man in his preoccupation had neglected to button his fly, the meeting not only would not hear a word he said—its members would be unable to control their giggles.'"

The king had his pince-nez riding on his forefinger.

"My lords," he said, "I do not wish to be obstructive. Neither have I any desire to inhibit you in your new wardrobes and those of your wives, but at the coronation, in all that stuff, I felt a fool; moreover, I must have looked a fool."

"Not so, Your Majesty," they chorused.

"Well, anyway, I was so hot I couldn't breathe."

Le Comte des Quatre Chats held up his hand again to be recognized.

"It would be sufficient, Sire, if you would appear in the uniform, say, of a Grand Marshal of France."

"But I am not a Grand Marshal."

"The king, Sire, is whatever he wishes to appoint himself."

"But I have no such uniform."

"There are the museums, Sire. Surely Les Invalides can furnish a Grand Marshal's uniform."

The king was silent for a moment, and then he said, "If I agree to this, gentlemen, will you permit that I arrive from Versailles by automobile rather than by the state coach? You don't know how uncomfortable that coach can be."

After a whispered conference it was so agreed, but Honnête Jean said finally, "We, your loyal servants, Sire, would be pleased if during your address—only during—you would permit the purple robe of royalty to be dropped over your shoulders."

"Oh, Lord!" said Pippin. "All right, I'll agree, but only during the speech."

And it was so concluded.

On the afternoon of December 4, while the palace of Versailles was a madhouse of scurrying noblemen, trying on, shortening, lengthening, mending, and walking before mirrors in the robes of their station, the king in his corduroy jacket and crash helmet walked to the guard post at the gate, winked at the captain of the guard, with whom he had struck up a friendship, and passed into his hands a package of Lucky Strikes.

Pippin knew that the captain was in the service of the Minister of Secret Police—but then, he was also in the service of the Socialist party, the British Embassy, and the Peruvian Purchasing Agency, and half-owner of a pâtisserie in Charonne, just off the Boulevard Voltaire. Capitaine Pasmouches reported to each of his clients about all the others, but he genuinely liked the king and he genuinely liked Lucky Strikes.

"This way, M'sieur," he said, and escorted the helmeted and goggled Pippin to the guards' house, where the motor scooter reposed under a tarpaulin. "Will you be going near Charonne, M'sieur?" he asked.

"I can, I suppose," said the king.

"Could you carry a note to my wife at the Pâtisserie Pasmouches?"

"Gladly," said the king. "It's a little out of my way, of course." And as he pocketed the folded paper he said, "Of course if there should be inquiries—"

"I have seen nothing, M'sieur," said the captain. "Even to M'sieur the Minister, I have seen nothing."

The king kicked the starter and mounted the scooter. "It is plain to see that you carry a marshal's baton in your boot, my Captain," he said.

"You are amiable, M'sieur," said Capitaine Pasmouches.

It was very considerably out of his way, but the afternoon was pleasant and sunny, a good day for riding and a relief from the towering nonsense of Versailles. The king presented the note to Madame Pasmouches, who treated him to a cup of coffee and an assortment of petits fours.

After compliments given and taken, the king scooted in the howling traffic of the Place de la Bastille, gunned along the Rue de Rivoli, crossed at the Pont Neuf, and turned into the Rue de Seine.

The shutters of Charles Martel were closed and so was the door. Pippin banged on the door with his fist, and no response came from within. He moved aside and waited patiently until the door opened a crack, then placed his toe firmly in the opening.

Uncle Charlie complained, "Can't a man have privacy even of a gallant nature?"

"I don't believe it," said the king.

"Oh! Come on in. What is it that you want?"

The king slipped into the darkened gallery and saw that the walls

were bare and that large wooden boxes stood about, packed and ready to be nailed shut.

"You are going on a trip, my Uncle?"

"Yes."

"Won't you invite me to sit down? Why are you angry with me?"

"Come in, then. The chairs are covered. You will have to sit on a box."

"You are running away?"

"I don't trust you," said Charlie. "I can put two and two together. You're up to something. And you will lose, my child. I don't see any reason why I also should lose because of your foolishness."

"I came for advice."

"Then I'll give it to you. Go and be a king in a proper way and stop sticking your nose into business and—and government, where it isn't wanted. That's my advice to you. If you would take it, I could unpack."

"You told me once that I was a patsy—a royal patsy. A patsy is a kind of pawn, is it not, something to be used as long as possible and then lost without grieving?"

"I suppose so. But when a pawn tries to do the work of government —then the pawn is a fool."

Pippin seated himself on a crate. "Will you give me a glass of brandy?"

"I don't have any."

"What is that bottle I see back there?"

"That is marc."

"Perhaps, then, a thimbleful of marc. You must be terrified, my Uncle, to have lost your courtesy."

"I am terrified. And I'm afraid for you."

The king said, "A king can move one square forward, backward, sideways, aslant, but a patsy—or a pawn—only ahead. Thank you, Uncle Charlie, won't you have one with me? Won't you drink my health? Must your sense of guilty disloyalty make you hate me?"

Uncle Charlie sighed very deeply. "I *am* ashamed," he said at last. "However, my shame will not change my course. I am going to America for a while, until—until it blows over. I don't know exactly what you intend to do, but I know it is disaster. And you are right about one thing. There is no excuse for discourtesy. Forgive me!"

"I know how you must feel, but I have thought deeply about this, my Uncle. A king is an anachronism—a king doesn't really exist."

"What do you propose?"

"Simply to make a few suggestions, based on my observations."

"They will guillotine you. They don't want suggestions."

"That is one thing I have learned. A king must be worthy of the

guillotine. And maybe one or two of my suggestions might take root."

"I've always hated martyrs."

Pippin drank his marc and shuddered. "I'm not a martyr, Uncle Charlie. A martyr trades something he has for something he wants. I am not ambitious."

"What are you then—mischievous?"

"Perhaps. Or maybe only curious. And surely not brave."

"I used to think I knew you. How about Marie? How about Clotilde? Have you no feeling for them?"

"That is what I came to see you about, to ask you to look after them—that is, if an occasion should arise."

"How about yourself?"

"I am being dramatic. I think the time and my office require it. I can take care of myself."

"You plan to do this thing tomorrow?"

"Yes. And I would be glad if you invited Madame and Clotilde to visit you tomorrow—perhaps you could take them on a little trip into the country. Perhaps the young Mr. Johnson might assist you. He has an automobile. A weekend on the Loire. There is a beautiful little inn at Sancerre. But I imagine you know it."

"I know it."

"Will you do it?"

Uncle Charlie cursed filthily for several seconds.

"Then you will do it!" said the king.

"It's a trick! You think you have the right to maneuver me because we are related. It is a detestable piece of blackmail."

"Then that is settled!" said Pippin. "Thank you, Uncle Charlie. I don't anticipate trouble and so I anticipate trouble." He arose from the crate.

"Oh, have another drink," said Uncle Charlie. "I think I have just a few drops of brandy."

"You make me very happy," said the king. "I knew I could depend on you."

"Merde!" said Uncle Charlie.

Half a mile from the Palace of Versailles, Pippin turned his scooter off the road and into the forest. He pushed it over the deep carpet of fallen leaves far back from the highway. In the lee of an outcropping of stone he dogpaddled the fallen autumn leaves away, then put his scooter in the hollow, and covered it with leaves. He piled a few wind-fallen branches on top to hold the leaves in place. Then he walked out of the forest and continued on foot.

At the gate he told the captain, "I delivered your letter. Madame says to tell you she will take care of it. She would like you to telephone

to Ars et Fils and tell them, so they may tell her when you can come in.
I must say her cakes are delicious."

"Thank you, M'sieur. Where is your machine?"

The king shrugged. "I had a small accident. It is being repaired.
A kind tourist brought me nearly here. Naturally I did not want him
to—"

"I understand, M'sieur. There has been no inquiry."

"I guess they're all too busy with themselves," said the king.

At dinner the queen said, "Your Uncle Charles has asked Clotilde
and me to drive to Sancerre. I don't think this is a time—"

"On the contrary, my dear. I shall be busy at the convention. And
you need a holiday. You have worked hard and long."

"But I have a million things—"

"Quite between us, my dear, I think it would be well to take
Clotilde away from Paris for a few days. Just as a matter of policy, you
know—she is talking too much to the newspapers. Sancerre, eh? I
remember it as a lovely little town with a great wine if you can get any of
it."

"I'll think about it," said the queen. "I have so much on my
mind. I wonder, Pippin, whether I should tell you now—the agents
absolutely refuse to terminate the lease at Number One Avenue de
Marigny. They insist that a lease is a lease, no matter what the govern-
ment."

"Perhaps we can sublet it later."

"Just one more thing to worry about," said the queen. "You know
how tenants are. And most of my mother's furniture is still there."

"You need a little holiday, my dear. You've had too many re-
sponsibilities."

"I wonder what I should take."

"Just simple things for motoring and a warm coat. It may be quite
chilly on the river this time of year. I wish I could go with you."

The queen looked at him speculatively. "I don't like to leave you
just at this time."

He took her hand and turned it palm upward and kissed it. "It's
the perfect time," he said. "I'll be so busy with the convention, you would
not even see me."

"Perhaps you're right," she said. "So much talk and politics buzzing
around. I'm tired of the nobility, my dear. I'm bored with politics.
Sometimes I wish we still lived in our little stable-house. That is a very
pleasant neighborhood. But the concierge is impossible."

"I know," said the king, "but what can you expect of Alsatians?"

"There you have it," said the queen. "Alsatians—provincials, I say.
Only interested in their tight little lives. Provincials! Do you think I
should take my fur coat?"

"I strongly advise it," said the king.

Everyone has seen photographs of the historic opening of the convention to deliberate the Code Pippin. Every newspaper and magazine in the world printed at least one version of it. The half-circle of rows of seats, filled with robed delegates, the speakers' rostrum and the high, thronelike chair of the Chief Minister, whose duty it was to control and govern the proceedings.

The photographs show the eager faces of the delegates in every manner of ceremonial costume; the galleries filled to overflowing with ladies, also costumed and coroneted; the guards at the doorways in slashed doublets and carrying halberds. Not visible in the pictures are the bales of papers, the mountains of books of precedent, the ledgers, briefcases, even small filing cabinets which rested on the floor among the delegates' feet, containing the weapons wherewith each party planned to save France by aggrandizing itself.

The meeting convened at three P.M. December 5, and it was agreed that after the address from the throne it should recess until the next day. The king was neither invited to nor wanted at the subsequent meetings. At the end he was expected to place his royal signature on the Code, preferably without reading it.

It will be remembered that the Duc des Troisfronts had made the first demand for the return of the monarchy. It was therefore considered only proper that he should announce the king, in spite of his cleft palate.

At 3:15 the Chief Minister raised the royal gavel, actually a wooden replica of the hammer from which Charles Martel took his name.

The hammer crashed nobly down three times. From the entrance to the right of the rostrum the halberdiers wheeled inward, opened the double doors, and presented their arms.

The Duc des Troisfronts entered. He was scaled like a lizard with orders and decorations, while a toupee which was an integral part of his coronet gave him an alert look—a little like the March Hare. He advanced to the rostrum and glanced about in panic. Academician Poitin of the Royal Academy of Music rapped three times with his baton, and six trumpeters in tabards raised six-foot straight trumpets from which hung the royal arms. M. Poitin gave them a downbeat, and they blew a fanfare which seemed to rock the great room.

The Duc des Troisfronts struggled for breath. "Hentulmeh. I hive you the Hing of Fhance!"

From the gallery the Duchesse was heard to break into applause.

Again the fanfare.

Again the halberdiers swung open the double doors—and Pippin entered.

By no stretch of imagination could he have been thought to have either a military figure or carriage. The marshal's uniform was a mistake. Moreover, the uniform—rented from a theatrical costumer—had at the last moment been discovered to be far too large. The tunic had been made

to fit by a row of safety pins up the back. Nothing could be done about the crotch of the trousers, which, even though the waistband was high on his chest, still dangled halfway to his knees. The purple velvet cape with edging of ermine hung from his shoulders and was followed by two pages delegated to control it. They did their best, and when the king reached the rostrum and turned they brought the trailing ends of the train inward to try to conceal his pants, so that he arose out of its folds like the stamen of a lily.

The king placed the manuscript of his address on the rostrum. His hands wandered to his breast, searched frantically amongst the great stars and orders. His glasses were not there. He remembered putting his pince-nez and the ribbon down while his tunic was being pinned up the back. He spoke to one of the boys, who dashed out through the side entrance, knocking a halberd from a guard's hand.

Meanwhile Le Maître Poitin, who after all had been fifty years in the theater, signaled the trumpeters to break into the traditional hunting call whose triumphant theme, "There goes the fox," puts a strain on the versatility of the straight trumpet.

While this brilliant improvisation continued, the page returned and handed the king his pince-nez. Pippin bent over his pages, written in the precise but minute hand of the mathematician.

Pippin read his speech exactly as though he was reading a speech. His voice had no rise and fall. His points were made with no underlining and no declamation.

No one could find any fault with the opening statement:

"My Lords, and my People—

"We, Pippin, King of France by right of blood and by further authority of election, do hold that this land has been singularly favored by God with richness of soil and geniality of climate, while its people are endowed with intelligence and talent above many others—"

At this point applause broke out, which caused him to look up, remove his pince-nez, and lose his place.

When the noise had subsided he replaced his pince-nez and bent over the tiny handwriting.

"Let's see. M-mmm—here it is—talent above many others. When we assumed the crown, we made a careful study of the nation, its riches, its failures, and its potentials. Not only did we study available statistics but also we went out among the people, not in our royal character but on the level of the people themselves—"

He paused and looked up and remarked conversationally, "If that seems romantic to some of you, I ask you how else I could have found out."

He went back to his manuscript.

A slight uneasiness crept into the great gathering.

"We found," he said pedantically—"we found that the power, the

products, the comforts, the profits, and the opportunities of our nation deserve a wider distribution than they now have."

Right and Left Centrists looked at one another in consternation.

"We believe that changes, programs, and some restrictions are necessary to the end that our people may live in comfort and peace and that the genius of the French, which once lighted the world, may be rekindled."

During the time it took him to turn a page there was a little pattering of scattered handclapping. The delegates restlessly moved their feet among their books and briefcases.

Pippin continued.

"The People of France have created a king. It is not only the nature but the duty of a king to rule. Where a president may suggest, a king must order—otherwise his office is meaningless and his kingdom does not exist.

"We therefore order and decree that the Code you are creating shall contain the following. . . ."

And then the bomb exploded.

The first section dealt with taxes—to be kept as low as possible and to be collected from all.

The second, wages—to be keyed to profits and to move up and down with the cost of living.

Prices—to be strictly controlled against manipulation.

Housing—existing housing to be improved and new construction to be undertaken with supervision as to quality and rents.

The fifth section called for a reorganization of government to the end that it perform its functions with the least expenditure of money and personnel.

The sixth considered public health insurance and retirement pensions.

The seventh ordered the break-up of great land holdings to restore the wasted earth to productivity.

"To the great three words I want to add a fourth," he said, "so that henceforth the motto of the French shall be 'Liberty, Equality, Fraternity, *and* Opportunity.' "

The king, his head still down, waited for applause, and when none came he looked out over the thunder-struck gathering. The delegates were hypnotized with horror. They stared glassily back at the king. They seemed scarcely to breathe.

Pippin IV had planned to bow at this point and to leave with dignity on the heels of his applause, but there was only aching silence. Uproar he could have understood. He had even prepared himself for denunciation, but the silence held him and confused him. He took off his pince-nez and mounted it on his forefinger.

"I meant every word I said," he began uneasily. "I have really seen France, France which has survived three invasions, two occupations

in three generations, and emerged whole and strong and free. I tell you what an enemy could not do to us we are doing to ourselves, like greedy, destructive children throwing cake at a birthday party."

And suddenly he was angry—coldly angry.

"I didn't ask to be king," he said hoarsely. "I begged not to be king. And you didn't want a king. You wanted a patsy."

Then he shouted, "But you elected a king, and by God you've got a king—or a gigantic joke."

Delegates cleared their throats, took off their glasses and polished them.

"I know as well as you do that the time for kings is past," he said quietly. "Royalty is extinct and its place is taken by boards of directors. What I have tried to do is to help you make the leap, for you are not one thing or the other. I am going to leave you now to your deliberations. You have my orders—but, whether you obey them or not, try to be worthy of our beautiful nation."

The king bowed slightly and turned to walk toward the door, but an open-mouthed page was standing on the edge of his purple and ermine-collared cape. It ripped from his shoulders and fell to the floor, exposing the row of safety pins up the back of his tunic, and the baggy crotch of the trousers flopping between his knees.

Strain in children and adults opens two avenues of relief—laughter or tears—and either is equally accessible. The safety pins did it.

Beginning with a snigger in the front benches, it spread to giggles, and then to hysteric laughter. Delegates pounded the backs of the delegates in front of them and honked and roared and wiped their eyes. Thus they channeled the shock the king's message had given them, the shock and the terror and their own deep sense of guilt.

Pippin could hear the laughter through the closed doors. He removed the baggy pants and hung them on a chair. He put on his dark blue suit with its pin stripe and tied his black silk knitted tie.

Quietly he went out a rear entrance and walked around the building and stood in the crowd gathered at the noble marble entrance. People said, "What's all the noise? What's going on in there?"

The king moved slowly away from the excited people. He walked in the streets a while, looked in windows. At a music store he bought a small cheap harmonica, and, concealing it in his hand, he blew a chord on it now and then. He walked down to the Seine embankment and watched the eternal fishermen with their filament lines and bread-crumb bait.

And then, because the days were growing short, he bought a ticket on the Versailles bus and went home. He wandered about in the empty royal apartments.

He turned out the lights and pulled a chair to the leaded window overlooking the gardens. He took the harmonica from his pocket and

tried it timidly. In an hour he had worked out the scale. In two hours he produced a slow and labored "Auprès de ma blonde, qu'il fait bon, fait bon, fait bon."

Pippin smiled, sitting in the dark. The palace was quiet. He played "Frère Jacques" slowly but accurately from beginning to end. The carp burped loudly in the fish ponds.

Meanwhile, telegraph and radio and transoceanic telephones staggered under the weight of traffic.

Dark-suited men sped to chancelleries. Private and secret wires went into action. The State Department in Washington froze French assets in the United States.

Luxembourg mobilized.

Monaco closed its borders and its soldiers tore the flowers from their rifle barrels.

A Soviet submarine was sighted in San Francisco Bay.

A squadron of Soviet destroyers gave chase to an American submarine in the Gulf of Finland.

Sweden and Switzerland declared their neutrality while putting themselves in a position of defense.

England growled and grumbled with delight and suggested that the royal family could find traditional sanctuary in London.

Paris was shuttered. Students from the Sorbonne swarmed up the Eiffel Tower and ripped down the royal standard and raised the Tricolor among the wind gauges.

At Suze-sous-Cure, the populace, led by the chief of police, burned the town hall, whereupon the police station was burned by the same populace under leadership of the mayor.

Falaise in Normandy rounded up all strangers and guarded them.

At Le Puy bonfires burned on the pinnacles.

Marseille rioted courteously and looted with discrimination.

The Pope offered arbitration.

In Paris the gendarmes helped the rioters build barricades, using police hurdles.

The warehouses up-Seine were broken open, and wine barrels rumbled over the cobbles.

Partisans howled with enthusiasm and revolt. Right Centrists posted ink-wet bills saying TO THE BASTILLE.

The American Ambassador denounced revolution.

The Kremlin, China, the satellites, and Egypt telegraphed congratulations to the heroic People's Republic of France.

In the dark and quiet room at Versailles, Pippin tried to play the "Memphis Blues" and found he had no sharps and flats on his instrument. He moved on to "Home on the Range," which requires none, and was so intent on his work that he did not hear the soft knocking on the door.

Sister Hyacinthe opened the door, looked in, and saw the king silhouetted against the window. Her low laughter made him stop his playing and peer around at her. She looked like a great black bird against the painted wall.

"It is well to have a second trade," she said.

The king stood up awkwardly and knocked the moisture from the harmonica against the palm of his hand. "I didn't hear you, Sister."

"No. You were too busy, Sire."

He said a little stiffly, "One finds oneself doing silly things."

"Perhaps not silly, Sire. The mind seeks curious retreats. I did not know you were here. Nearly everyone else has gone."

"Where have they gone, Sister?"

"Some went to save themselves, but most have simply gone to Paris to see the fireworks. They are drawn to activity as insects are drawn to light. I myself am leaving, Sire. My Superior has ordered me to return. I am afraid, Sire, that your short reign is over. I am told that all France is in revolt."

"I was not ready to think about it," said Pippin. "I suppose I have failed."

"I don't know," said the nun. "I have read your remarks to the convention. They were bold remarks, Sire. Yes, I imagine that you have failed, you personally, but I wonder whether your words have failed. I remember another who failed—whose words we live by." She placed a small bundle on the table beside him. "A present for you, Sire, the time-honored disguise."

"What is it?"

"One of my habits, a nun's dress, the traditional means of escape. I see no reason for either hemlock or cross."

Pippin said, "Is it that bad? Are they really so furious?"

"I don't know," said Sister Hyacinthe. "You have caught them in error. It will be very difficult for them to forgive you. Your words will be thorns in every future government. You will haunt them. Perhaps they sense that."

"I want to find Marie," he said. "I thought perhaps she would come here."

"Maybe she will—or maybe she is not able to get back. I understand there is an uproar in Paris. When they have exhausted the fun in Paris the rioters may come here. If you intend to go, I suggest that you go tonight."

"Without Marie—without Clotilde?"

"I don't think they are in as much danger as you, Sire. If you will put on this habit, you can go with me. My convent will conceal you until it is safe to cross the frontier."

"I don't want to cross the frontier, Sister. I really don't think I am so important that they will want my life."

"Your Majesty," the nun said, "they may well be afraid of each other. Every group may feel that the others might join you."

"I can't believe it," said the king. "The kingdom was a myth—it didn't exist. And the king? What is he but a kind of national joke? I don't believe they will dignify the kingship with murder."

"I don't know," she said uncertainly. "I really don't know."

He said, "If I escape or try to, I will be making myself important enough to kill. I've often wondered what would have happened if Louis the Sixteenth had not tried to escape—if he had walked alone and unguarded to the Jeu de Paume."

"You are brave, Sire."

"No, Sister, I am not brave. Perhaps I am stupid, but I am not brave. I do not want to be a sacrifice. I want my little house, my wife, and my telescope—nothing more. If they had not forced me to be king I would not have been forced to be kingly. It was a series of psychological accidents."

"I wish I could be sure that you were safe. But I must go, M'sieur. Do you know that so-and-so has cured my feet? I may not forgive him for that. You will not come with me?"

"No, Sister."

"Give me your hand!"

Sister Hyacinthe bowed over his hand and kissed it. "Good-by— Your Majesty."

When he looked up she had gone, so silently that not even the parquetry had protested.

Pippin put the still warm harmonica against his lips and played very slowly, *do-re-mi-fa-sol-la*— He missed on the *si*, went back and corrected it, and completed with *do*.

He went down the circular staircase to the garden. His footsteps sounded loud on the gravel. He strolled around to the great entrance and for a time he could not see that any guard was posted. Then a match was lighted and he saw a single guardsman seated on the ground, his back against the kiosk, his rifle leaning against the wall. The king approached.

"Are you all alone?"

"They all went to Paris," the guard complained. "It isn't fair. Why should I be picked to stay—and told—and ordered to stay? My service record will show that I have been a good soldier."

"Would you like a Lucky Strike?"

"Do you have one?"

"You may have the whole package."

The guard stood up suspiciously. "Who are you?"

"I am the king."

"Pardon, Sire. I didn't recognize you. I beg pardon."

"What is going on in Paris?"

"That's just it. I don't know. Great doings. They say riots and all such like—maybe even looting—and here I have to sit and miss it all."

"It doesn't seem fair," said Pippin. "Why don't you go?"

"Oh, I couldn't do that. I would be court-martialed, and I have a family. I have to think of them. The captain ordered—"

Pippin said, "Do you believe that I outrank the captain?"

"Certainly, Sire."

"Then I relieve you of your duty."

"It can't be just word of mouth. What proof do I have?"

"Do you have a flashlight?"

"Of course, Sire."

"Lend it to me." Pippin went into the kiosk to the little shelf with its pad and pencil. "What is your name?" he asked.

"Vautin, Sergeant Vautin, Sire."

Pippin wrote on the pad, "Sergeant Vautin is hereby relieved of duty and authorized to begin furlough of two weeks beginning at—" "What time is it?"

"Twelve and twenty minutes, Sire."

Pippin continued: "at 12:20 A.M." He filled in the date and signed it "Pippin IV, King of France, Commander-in-Chief of All Armed Forces." He handed the order and the flashlight to the soldier.

Sergeant Vautin put the light on the paper and read it carefully.

"I can't see who could find fault with that, Sire. But who is to guard the gate?"

"I'll keep an eye on it."

"Don't you want to go to the riots, Sire?"

"Not particularly," said Pippin.

He watched the soldier ride happily away on his bicycle and then he sat down with his back against the kiosk.

The night was chilly but brilliant with stars, and it was very quiet. No automobiles moved on the highways. Far away the lights of Paris were reflected in a glow against the sky. The great palace was dark behind him. He thought to himself that no night had been so still here for fifty years at least.

And then he heard the distant hum of a motor, then saw the lights of a speeding car. It screeched to a stop at the gates—a Buick convertible. The headlights blinded Pippin sitting against the kiosk.

Tod Johnson leaped out of the car and left the motor running. "Hurry up, sir. Get in."

Clotilde called from the car, "Hurry, Father!"

Tod said, "You can put on some of my clothes in the car. We'll get to the Channel by daylight."

Pippin got slowly to his feet. "What is it you intend to do?"

"We're going to try to get across the Channel."

"Is it so bad, then?"

"You don't know, sir. Paris is a mess. You've been deposed, sir. They're yelling for the Republic. If I didn't have an American car we wouldn't have got through."

Pippin asked, "Where is Madame?"

"I don't know, sir. She was supposed to go with Uncle Charlie, but she disappeared."

"And where is Uncle Charlie?"

"He went south. He's going to try to cross into Portugal. Come on, sir! Hurry!!"

"You aren't in any danger," Pippin said. "What happened?"

"You didn't listen to what I told you," said Tod. "You didn't have the money and the proxies. You didn't even have the stockholders."

Pippin walked to the car. "Are you all right, Clotilde?"

"I guess so."

"Where will you go?"

"To Hollywood," she said. "Don't forget, I'm an artiste."

"I had forgotten," he said. And to Tod, "You will take care of her?"

"Sure, but come on—get in! Don't worry about anything. Maybe you'd like to learn the chicken business. And you can write articles. They all do. You've got to get away, now, sir. Here, I've got a bottle of brandy. Have a drink."

Pippin took a swallow from the bottle. And suddenly he laughed.

"Don't be upset," said Tod. "We'll get you through."

"I'm not upset," said Pippin Héristal. "I was just thinking about Julius Caesar. He did it once. With five legions he surrounded Vercingetorix at Alesia and he pacified Gaul."

"Maybe Gaul doesn't want to be pacified," said Tod.

The king was silent for a moment and then he said, "That seems to be the truth. And so perhaps even Caesar didn't do it. Maybe Gaul can only be pacified by Gaul."

"Do hurry, Father," said the subdued Clotilde. "You don't know what it's like."

The king said, "Take care of her—as much as anyone can take care of anyone."

"Come along, sir."

"No," said Pippin. "I am not going. I think in a very little while they will forget me."

"They'll kill you, sir."

"I don't think so," said the king. "I really don't think so. And besides, I can't leave Marie. I wonder where she could have gone? You're sure she isn't with Uncle Charlie?"

"No. The last we saw her was in Sancerre. She went shopping with a basket on her arm. Won't you get in?"

Pippin said, "This is probably my last act as king. These are my orders. You will proceed to a Channel port. You will do your best to

find a boat to take you and Clotilde to England. These are your orders, Tod. See that you carry them out."

"But—"

"You have your orders," said the king. "Grant me the final courtesy of obeying them."

He watched the Buick move away and then he strolled back to the palace to find his corduroy jacket and his crash helmet.

It was during that night that the delegates constituted themselves a National Assembly. They proclaimed the Republic. The Tricolor rose on public buildings.

The gendarmerie moved out to put a stop to looting. The banks were declared closed for the time being.

M. Sonnet, to great applause, asked M. Magot to form a coalition government. The king was declared deposed and outlawed.

M. Magot was able to form a government in a few hours. It will be remembered that the Coalition Government lasted until February third of the following year.

The motor scooter ran out of gasoline in the Bois de Boulogne, and Pippin left it leaning against a tree and continued on foot. It was dawn when he turned off the Champs Elysées into the Avenue de Marigny.

From out of the shadows a gendarme moved to intercept him. "You have your card of identity, M'sieur?"

Pippin brought out his wallet and handed over his card. The gendarme studied it and said, "Pippin Héristal. Why, I remember you, M'sieur. You live at Number One."

"That is correct," said Pippin.

"There's been looting," the gendarme observed. "I didn't recognize you in the helmet. Have you been on a trip, M'sieur?"

"Yes," said Pippin, "quite a long trip."

The gendarme saluted. "Everything seems quiet now," he said.

"Will you have a cigarette?"

"Thank you. Ah! a Lucky Strike."

"Keep the package," said Pippin. He winked. "I've been out of the country."

The gendarme smiled. "I understand, M'sieur." And he put the package in his pocket under his cape.

Pippin had to ring the bell endlessly before the concierge shuffled bleary-eyed and ill-tempered to open the iron gate for him.

"A strange time to be coming in," he muttered.

Pippin placed a bill in his hand. "It's a long trip from Strasbourg."

"You have come from Strasbourg?"

"Well, in one jump from Nancy."

"I myself am from Lunéville. How does the country look?"

"They had a great harvest. The geese looked fine and fat. And they say the wine—"

"I've heard—I've heard. But did you hear how the elections in Lunéville came out? That is a very important thing. You see, the mayoralty has been held—" He closed his fist in front of him. "It is time for change—everyone feels that. Everyone, that is, but—" He tightened his fist again.

Pippin said, "I will have to trouble you to open my door—my keys—"

"But Madame is in. You have only to ring. And what a turning out she's given it. Carry this, carry that. What a fury! Now the party in Lunéville that has held it in a grip—"

Pippin said, "Good night, M'sieur. I will want to hear another time. It's a long ride from Nancy."

He crossed the courtyard to the entrance of the stablehouse. He took off his crash helmet and brushed back his hair with his fingers—and finally he laid his finger on the ivory button of the bell.